THE YEAR'S BEST

SCIENCE FICTION

ALSO BY GARDNER DOZOIS

ANTHOLOGIES

A DAY IN THE LIFE

ANOTHER WORLD

BEST SCIENCE FICTION STORIES OF THE
  YEAR #6–10

THE BEST OF ISAAC ASIMOV'S SCIENCE
  FICTION MAGAZINE

TIME-TRAVELERS FROM ISAAC ASIMOV'S
  SCIENCE FICTION MAGAZINE

TRANSCENDENTAL TALES FROM ISAAC
  ASIMOV'S SCIENCE FICTION MAGAZINE

ISAAC ASIMOV'S ALIENS

ISAAC ASIMOV'S MARS

ISAAC ASIMOV'S SF LITE

ISAAC ASIMOV'S WAR

ROADS NOT TAKEN (with Stanley Schmidt)

THE YEAR'S BEST SCIENCE FICTION, #1–32

FUTURE EARTHS: UNDER AFRICAN SKIES
  (with Mike Resnick)

FUTURE EARTHS: UNDER SOUTH AMERICAN
  SKIES (with Mike Resnick)

RIPPER! (with Susan Casper)

MODERN CLASSIC SHORT NOVELS OF
  SCIENCE FICTION

MODERN CLASSICS OF FANTASY

KILLING ME SOFTLY

DYING FOR IT

THE GOOD OLD STUFF

THE GOOD NEW STUFF

EXPLORERS

THE FURTHEST HORIZON

WORLDMAKERS

SUPERMEN

COEDITED WITH SHEILA WILLIAMS

ISAAC ASIMOV'S PLANET EARTH

ISAAC ASIMOV'S ROBOTS

ISAAC ASIMOV'S VALENTINES

ISAAC ASIMOV'S SKIN DEEP

ISAAC ASIMOV'S GHOSTS

ISAAC ASIMOV'S VAMPIRES

ISAAC ASIMOV'S MOONS

ISAAC ASIMOV'S CHRISTMAS

ISAAC ASIMOV'S CAMELOT

ISAAC ASIMOV'S WEREWOLVES

ISAAC ASIMOV'S SOLAR SYSTEM

ISAAC ASIMOV'S DETECTIVES

ISAAC ASIMOV'S CYBERDREAMS

COEDITED WITH JACK DANN

ALIENS!

UNICORNS!

MAGICATS!

MAGICATS 2!

BESTIARY!

MERMAIDS!

SORCERERS!

DEMONS!

DOGTALES!

SEASERPENTS!

DINOSAURS!

LITTLE PEOPLE!

DRAGONS!

HORSES!

UNICORNS 2

INVADERS!

ANGELS!

DINOSAURS II

HACKERS

TIMEGATES

CLONES

NANOTECH

IMMORTALS

FICTION

STRANGERS

THE VISIBLE MAN (COLLECTION)

NIGHTMARE BLUE
  (with George Alec Effinger)

SLOW DANCING THROUGH TIME
  (with Jack Dann, Michael Swanwick,
  Susan Casper, and Jack C. Haldeman II)

THE PEACEMAKER

GEODESIC DREAMS (collection)

NONFICTION

THE FICTION OF JAMES TIPTREE, JR.

THE YEAR'S BEST

SCIENCE FICTION

Thirty-fourth annual collection

edited by Gardner Dozois

 st. martin's griffin ☙ new york

THE YEAR'S BEST SCIENCE FICTION: THIRTY-FOURTH ANNUAL COLLECTION.
Copyright © 2017 by Gardner Dozois. All rights reserved.
Printed in the United States of America. For information,
address St. Martin's Press, 175 Fifth Avenue, New York, N.Y. 10010.

www.stmartins.com

The Library of Congress Cataloging-in-Publication Data is available upon
request.

ISBN 978-1-250-11923-0 (hardcover)
ISBN 978-1-250-11924-7 (trade paperback)
ISBN 978-1-250-11925-4 (e-book)

Our books may be purchased in bulk for promotional, educational,
or business use. Please contact your local bookseller or the Macmillan
Corporate and Premium Sales Department at 1-800-221-7945, extension
5442, or by e-mail at MacmillanSpecialMarkets@macmillan.com.

First Edition: July 2017

10 9 8 7 6 5 4 3 2 1

For Dr. Samir Mehta and his surgical staff at Presbyterian Hospital and for Dean, Laverne, Deb, Aniette, Morgan, Amy, Marquise, Luca Cella, and the rest of the staff at Watermark Rehabilitation

contents

permissions

acknowledgments

The editor would like to thank the following people for their help and support: Susan Casper, Jonathan Strahan, Sean Wallace, Neil Clarke, Gordon Van Gelder, C.C. Finlay, Andy Cox, John Joseph Adams, Ellen Datlow, Sheila Williams, Trevor Quachri, Peter Crowther, William Shaffer, Ian Whates, Paula Guran, Liza Trombi, Robert Wexler, Patrick Nielsen Hayden, Joseph Eschrich, Jonathan Oliver, Stephen Cass, Lynne M. Thomas, Gavin Grant, Kelly Link, Derek Künsken, Gord Sellar, Ian Redman, David Lee Summers, Wendy S. Delmater, Beth Wodzinski, E. Catherine Tobler, Alexander Irvine, Carl Rafala, Emily Hockaday, Edmund R. Schubert, A.C. Wise, William Ledbetter, Wendy S. Delmater, Jed Hartman, Rich Horton, Mark R. Kelly, Tehani Wessely, Aliette de Bodard, Robert Reed, Alastair Reynolds, Ken Liu, James Patrick Kelly, Ian McDonald, Karl Bunker, Paolo Bacigalupi, Lavie Tidhar, Rich Larson, Samantha Henderson, Pat Murphy, Paul Doherty, Ted Kosmatka, Ariana Phillips, Mecurio D. Rivera, Carrie Vaughn, Gregory Benford, Charlie Jane Anders, Heather Shaw, Bill Johnson, Carolyn Ives Gilman, Arlyn Alderdice, David Gerrold, Jacob Weisman, Kathe Koja, Carter Scholz, Ian McHugh, Shariann Lewitt, Steven Barnes, Melissa Scott, Stephen Baxter, Christopher Schelling, Craig DeLancey, Eleanor Arnason, Nina Allan, Ian R. MacLeod, Paul McAuley, Maggie Clark, Nick Wood, Eric Brown, Sam J. Miller, Matthew Claxton, Karen Bovenmyer, Navah Wolfe, Lucus Law, Dominik Parisien, Nich Wolven, Terry Bisson, Geoff Ryman, Eric T. Reynolds, Alvaro Ziinos-Amaro, Oluwole Talabi, Athena Andreadis, Jaym Gates, Mary Anne Mohanraj, Thoraiya Dyer, Stewart Baker, John O'Neill, Vaughne Lee Hansen, Mark Watson, Sean Swanwick, Katherine Canfield, Jaime Coyne, and special thanks to my own editor, Marc Resnick.

Thanks are also due to the late, lamented Charles N. Brown, and to all his staff, whose magazine *Locus* [Locus Publications, P.O. Box 13305, Oakland, CA 94661.

$63 in the U.S. for a one-year subscription (twelve issues) via periodical mail; $76 for a one-year (twelve issues) via first class credit card orders (510) 339 9198] was used as an invaluable reference source throughout the Summation; *Locus Online* (www.locusmag.com), edited by Mark R. Kelly, has also become a key reference source.

Like last year, 2016 was another relatively quiet year in the SF publishing world, although there were some changes down deep that might eventually have an effect strong enough to percolate up to the top where the average reader notices such things.

One such effect that may eventually become noticeable to the average reader is the dwindling of mass-market paperback titles, once the most common way (at one point, almost the only way) for SF books to be published, from bookstore shelves. The publishing industry has been trying to find the right balance between traditional print publishing and the publishing of titles as e-books for a number of years now, and one area where publishers seem to be switching away from print publication to e-book-only publication is in the mass-market paperback market niche. At least in the science fiction/fantasy publishing world, the number of mass-market paperbacks published was down for the eighth year in a row, hitting a new record low, down 11 percent since 2015. I think this may be a mistake, myself. For all the supposed convenience and portability of e-books (and their admitted great advantage of being able to store and carry more than one title to be accessed on the same device), for me there are times when nothing beats being able to stick a mass-market paperback in your back pocket and be able to wander, hands-free, until you find a shady tree to relax and read under on a sunny summer afternoon. Of course, I'm a nostalgic old fart who grew up in a time when the vast majority of books, especially SF and fantasy, were issued as mass-market paperbacks, largely findable—since respectable bookstores carried few if any genre titles—in spinner racks in drugstores (spinner racks themselves are also becoming hard to find as paperbacks dwindle, and may soon be extinct). If you're of a younger generation than I am though (as it seems like practically everybody is these days), your mileage may vary.

An interesting sidelight on the portability wars is that dedicated e-readers themselves, like the Kindle and the Nook, once the hottest new product anybody who was technologically oriented could buy, may also be on the slow boat to eventual extinction as many people switch over to reading digital books on their smartphones and tablets instead. According to a Nielsen survey, the portion of people who read books primarily on e-readers instead of on smartphones or tablets fell to 32 percent in the first quarter of 2015, from 50 percent in 2012; I haven't found figures for 2016, but I'm willing to bet that the downward trend has continued.

And waiting in the wings is probably some just-being-developed device that will gradually replace smartphones and tablets.

Final figures for 2016 aren't in yet, but so far it doesn't look like a bad year for the publishing industry. The U.S. Census Bureau estimated 2016 retail figures that show bookstore sales of $11,981 million, up 2.6 percent from $11,683 million.

For the year-to-date, sales were up 4.5 percent to $7,853 billion. All retail was up 3.1 percent.

In probably the biggest publishing news of the year, the restructuring of Penguin Random House continued with the merging of Berkley with Putnam and Dutton, which will now be joined together with Putnam and Dutton under unified management. Ivan Held will manage Berkley, as he does Putnam and Dutton, and their editorial and production departments will be "more closely integrated." Berkley Publishing Group president Leslie Gelbman stepped down, with Berkley's publisher Kara Welsh moving to Ballantine Bantam Dell. In news that affects the genre more directly, editors Diana Gill and Sharyn November were let go by Penguin Random House; Gill had only recently been hired as executive editor at Ace/Berkley, replacing retiring editor Ginjer Buchanan. Shake-ups happened at Tor Books too, with longtime executive editor Patrick Nielsen Hayden named associate publisher. Devi Pillai, formerly editorial director at Orbit, was named an associate publisher at Tor as well, while Linda Quinton was named publisher of Forge Books, and Kathleen Doherty will continue as publisher of Tor Teen and Starscape. It was also announced that Diana Gill, having just left Penguin Random House, joined Tor/Forge as executive editor, while Liz Gorinsky and Miriam Weinberg were promoted to senior editor, Jennifer Gunnels and Diana Pho were promoted to editor, Christopher Morgan was promoted to junior associate editor, while Melissa Singer was named manager of editorial operations. Elsewhere, Perseus Book Group sold its publishing business to Hachette Book Group and its distribution business to Ingram Content Group; Hachette plans to make Perseus a separate division, under group publisher Susan Weinberg. Linda Zecher stepped down as CEO of Houghton Mifflin Harcourt. St. Martin's announced a new YA line, Wednesday Books, taking over all of St. Martin's YA books as well as focusing on "coming-of-age" stories for both the YA and adult audiences, to be run by editorial director Sara Goodman and Jennifer Enderlin. UK publisher Orion is launching a new fiction and nonfiction line, Trapeze, to publish twenty titles a year, Farrar, Straus & Giroux announced a new imprint, to focus on "experimental fiction," MCD/FSG. Samhain Publishing is closing down. Yanni Kuznia was promoted to managing editor and chief operating officer at Subterranean Press. And Paul Stevens, former Tor editor, joined the Donald Maass Literary Agency.

2016 was another fairly stable year in the professional print magazine market, following years of precipitous decline in subscriptions and circulation.

Asimov's Science Fiction had a strong year this year, publishing good work by Kathe Koja and Carter Scholz, Matthew Claxton, Rich Larson, Ian R. MacLeod, Karl Bunker, Derek Künsken, Ian McHugh, Mercurio D. Rivera, and others. As usual, their SF was considerably stronger than their fantasy, usually the reverse of *The Magazine of Fantasy & Science Fiction. Asimov's Science Fiction* registered a 10.1 percent loss in overall circulation, down to 17,313 from 2015's 19,250. There were 8,191 print subscriptions and 7,078 digital subscription, for a total of 15,269, down from 2015's 17,052. Newsstand sales were down to 2,044 from 2015's 2,198 copies. Sell-through remained steady at 37 percent. Sheila Williams completed her thirteenth year as *Asimov's* editor.

Analog Science Fiction and Fact had good work by Gord Sellar, Bill Johnson, Maggie Clarke, Karl Bunker, Rich Larson, Brendan Dubois, Michael F. Flynn, and others. *Analog* registered a 7.7 percent loss in overall circulation, down to 21,573 from 2015's 20,356. There were 18,800 subscriptions, down from 2015's 20,356 subscriptions; of this total, 13,066 were print subscriptions, while 5,734 were digital subscriptions. Newsstand sales were down slightly to 2,773 from 2015's 3,019. Sell-through was 43 percent. Editor Trevor Quachi completed his third full year as editor.

Asimov's and *Analog* are both moving from their current ten-issue per year schedule to a schedule of six double issues per year in 2017, a move that sometimes is seen as a bad omen for a magazine, although it can save on printing and production costs. *F&SF* has survived on that schedule for several years now, so we'll see.

Once again, *The Magazine of Fantasy & Science Fiction* was almost exactly the reverse of *Asimov's*, with the fantasy published there being stronger than the science fiction, although the ratio of good SF to good fantasy seems to be creeping up somewhat. They had a strong year, publishing good work by Geoff Ryman, David Gerrold, Lavie Tidhar, Gregory Benford, Robert Reed, Terry Bisson, Alex Irvine, and others. *F&SF* registered a slight 1.8 rise in overall circulation from 9,877 to 10,055, although as digital sales figures are not available for *F&SF*, there's no way to be certain what the actual circulation number is. Subscriptions dropped slightly from 7,576 to 7,247; of that total, 2,808 copies were sold on the newsstand, up from 2015's 2,301, with no information on how many digital sales there were. Sell-through rose to 33 percent. Charles Coleman Finlay completed his first full year as *F&SF*, having taken over from Gordon Van Gelder, who had edited the magazine for eighteen years, with the March/April 2015 issue. Van Gelder remains as the magazine's owner and publisher, as he has been since 2014.

Interzone is technically not a "professional magazine," by the definition of the Science Fiction and Fantasy Writers of America (SFWA), because of its low rates and circulation, but the literary quality of the work published there is high that it would be ludicrous to omit it. *Interzone* was also a bit weaker this year than last year, but still published good work by Rich Larson, Ray Cluley, Sarah Brooks, Samantha Henderson, and others. Exact circulation figures are not available, but is guessed to be in the 2,000 copy range. TTA Press, *Interzone*'s publisher, also publishes straight horror or dark suspense magazine *Black Static*, which is beyond our purview here, but of a similar level of professional quality. *Interzone* and *Black Static* changed to a smaller trim size in 2011, but maintained their slick look, switching from the old 7 ¾"-by-10 ¾" saddle-stitched semigloss color cover sixty-four page format to a 6 ½"-by-9 ¼" perfect-bound glossy color cover ninety-six page format. The editor and publisher is Andy Cox.

If you'd like to see lots of good SF and fantasy published every year, the survival of these magazines is essential, and one important way that you can help them survive is by subscribing to them. It's never been easier to do so, something that these days can be done with just the click of a few buttons, nor has it ever before been

xviii | summation: 2016

possible to subscribe to the magazines in as many different formats, from the traditional print copy arriving by mail to downloads for your desktop or laptop available from places like Amazon (www.Amazon.com), to versions you can read on your Kindle, Nook, or iPad. You can also now subscribe from overseas just as easily as you can from the United States, something formerly difficult to impossible.

So in hopes of making it easier for you to subscribe, I'm going to list both the Internet sites where you can subscribe online and the street addresses where you can subscribe by mail for each magazine: *Asimov's* site is at www.asimovs.com, and subscribing online might be the easiest thing to do, and there's also a discounted rate for online subscriptions; its subscription address is *Asimov's Science Fiction*, Dell Magazines, 267 Broadway, Fourth Floor, New York, N.Y., 10007–2352–$34.97 for annual subscription in the U.S., $44.97 overseas. *Analog's* site is at www.analogsf .com; its subscription address is *Analog Science Fiction and Fact,* Dell Magazines, 267 Broadway, Fourth Floor, New York, N.Y., 10007–2352–$34.97 for annual subscription in the U.S., $44.97 overseas. *The Magazine of Fantasy & Science Fiction*'s site is at www.sfsite.com/fsf; its subscription address is *The Magazine of Fantasy & Science Fiction*, Spilogale, Inc., P.O. Box 3447, Hoboken, N.J., 07030, annual subscription—$34.97 in the U.S, $44.97 overseas. *Interzone* and *Black Static* can be subscribed to online at www.ttapress.com/onlinestore1.html; the subscription address for both is TTA Press, 5 Martins Lane, Witcham, Ely, Cambs CB6 2LB, England, UK, 42.00 Pounds Sterling each for a twelve-issue subscription, or there is a reduced rate dual subscription offer of 78.00 Pounds Sterling for both magazines for twelve issues; make checks payable to "TTA Press."

Most of these magazines are also available in various electronic formats through the Kindle, the Nook, and other handheld readers.

With the departure of long-running Australian magazine *Andromeda Spaceways Inflight Magazine* for the digital realm this year, where it will maintain existence as an all-digital e-zine (at www.andromedaspaceways.com), there's not a lot left of either the print fiction semiprozine market or the print critical magazine market. (It's also getting a bit problematical to say which are print semiprozines and which are e-zines, since some markets, like *Galaxy's Edge*, are offering both print versions and electronic versions of their issues at the same time.) I'm tempted to just merge the surviving print fiction and critical magazines into the section covering online publication, but for now I'll keep it as a separate section.

The Canadian *On Spec*, the longest-running of all the print fiction semiprozines, which is edited by a collective under general editor Diane L. Walton, again brought out three out of four scheduled issues; there have been rumors about them making the jump to digital format, and I wouldn't be surprised if they were the next to abandon the print format.

There were two issues of *Lady Churchill's Rosebud Wristlet,* the long-running slipstream magazine edited by Kelly Link and Gavin Grant. *Space and Time Magazine* managed three issues, and *Neo-opsis* managed one. There were also two issues of Ireland's long-running *Albedo One*, Long-running Australian semiprozine *Aurealis* has transitioned to a downloadable format. Once again, most of the fiction published in the surviving print semiprozines this year was relatively minor, with better work appearing in the online magazines mentioned below.

For general-interest magazines about SF and fantasy, about the only one left is the venerable newszine *Locus: The Magazine of the Science Fiction and Fantasy Field*, a multiple Hugo winner, for decades an indispensable source of news, information, and reviews, now in its fiftieth year of publication, operating under the guidance of a staff of editors headed by Liza Groen Trombi, and including Kirsten Gong-Wong, Carolyn Cushman, Tim Pratt, Jonathan Strahan, Francesca Myman, Heather Shaw, and many others.

One of the few other remaining popular critical print magazines is newcomer *The Cascadia Subduction Zone: A Literary Quarterly* (www.thecz.com), a feminist magazine of reviews and critical essays, edited by L. Timmel Duchamp, Nisi Shawl, and Kath Wilham, which published four issues in 2016. The most accessible of the other surviving print critical magazines—most of which are professional journals more aimed at academics than at the average reader—is probably the long-running British critical zine *Foundation*.

Subscription addresses are: **Locus, The Magazine of the Science Fiction & Fantasy Field,** Locus Publications, Inc., P.O. Box 13305, Oakland, California 94661, $76.00 for a one-year first-class subscription, twelve issues; **Foundation,** Science Fiction Foundation, Roger Robinson (SFF), 75 Rosslyn Avenue, Harold Wood, Essex RM3 ORG, UK, $37.00 for a three-issue subscription in the U.S.A;. **On Spec, The Canadian Magazine of the Fantastic,** P.O. Box 4727, Edmonton, AB, Canada T6E 5G6, for subscription information, go to Web site www.onspec.ca; **Neo-opsis Science Fiction Magazine,** 4129 Carey Rd., Victoria, BC, V8Z 4G5, $25.00 for a three-issue subscription; **Albedo One,** Albedo One Productions, 2, Post Road, Lusk, Co., Dublin, Ireland; $32.00 for a four-issue airmail subscription, make checks payable to "Albedo One" or pay by PayPal at www.albedol.com; **Lady Churchill's Rosebud Wristlet,** Small Beer Press, 150 Pleasant St., #306, Easthampton, MA 01027, $20.00 for four issues; **The Cascadia Subduction Zone: A Literary Quarterly,** subscription and single issues online at www.thecsz.com, $16 annually for a print subscription, print single issues 5, Electronic Subscription—PDF format—$10 per year, electronic single issue, $3, to order by check, make them payable to Aqueduct Press, P.O. Box 95787, Seattle, WA 9845-2787.

The world of online-only electronic magazines now rivals—and often surpasses—the traditional print market as a place to find good new fiction.

The electronic magazine *Clarkesworld* (www.clarkesworldmagazine.com), edited by Neil Clarke and Sean Wallace, had perhaps its strongest year yet, publishing first-rate work by Rich Larson, Carolyn Ives Gilman, Sam J. Miller, James Patrick Kelly, Gregory Feeley, Eleanor Arnason, Maggie Clark, and others. They also host monthly podcasts of stories drawn from each issue. Clarkesworld has won three Hugo Awards as best semiprozine. In 2014, *Clarkesworld* co-editor Sean Wallace, along with Jack Fisher, launched a new online horror /magazine, *The Dark* (www

.thedarkmagazine.com). Neil Clarke has also launched a monthly reprint e-zine, *Forever* (forever-magazine.com).

Lightspeed (www.lightspeedmagazine.com), edited by John Joseph Adams, featured strong work by strong work by Ted Kosmatka, Craig DeLancey, Rich Larson, Steven Barnes, Mercurio D. Rivera, Keith Brooke and Eric Brown, and others. *Lightspeed* won back-to-back Hugo Awards as Best Semiprozine in 2014 and 2015. Late in 2013, a new electronic companion horror magazine, *Nightmare* (www .nightmare-magazine.com), also edited by John Joseph Adams, was added to the *Lightspeed* stable.

Tor.com (www.tor.com), edited by Patrick Neilsen Hayden and Liz Gorinsky, with additional material purchased by Ellen Datlow, Ann VanderMeer, and others, published a mix of SF, fantasy, dark fantasy, soft horror, and more unclassifiable stuff this year, with good work by Lavie Tidhar, Nina Allan, Paul McAuley, Peter S. Beagle, Glen Hirshberg, Kij Johnson, David D. Levine, Joe Abercrombie, and others. Still not enough science fiction here to entirely satisfy me, although the percentage is creeping up.

Strange Horizons (www.strangehorizons.com), the oldest continually running electronic genre magazine on the Internet, started in 2000. Niall Harrison is editor-in-chief, with Jane Crowley and Kate Dollarhyde listed as associate editors. This year, they had strong work by Lavie Tidhar, Alexandra Manglis, Vajra Chandrase-kera, Shawn Scarber, and others.

Apex Magazine (www.apex-magazine.com) had good work by Lavie Tidhar, Stephen Cox, Jason Sanford, C.S.E. Cooney, Ursula Vernon, and others. Jason Sizemore is the new editor, replacing Sigrid Ellis, who took over from Lynne M. Thomas.

Abyss & Apex (www.abyssapexzine.com) ran interesting work by James Van Pelt, Bud Sparhawk and Cat Rambo, Amy Sisson, Barbara Krasnoff, and others. Wendy S. Delmater, the former longtime editor, has returned to the helm, replacing Carmelo Rafala.

An e-zine devoted to "literary adventure fantasy," *Beneath Ceaseless Skies* (www .beneath-ceaseless-skies.com), edited by Scott H. Andrews, had a strong year, with lots of entertaining sword and sorcery stuff, and even some SF, by Aliette de Bodard, K. J. Parker, Sarah Pinsker, Cat Rambo, Yoon Ha Lee, Anaea Lay, and others.

Long-running sword and sorcery print magazine *Black Gate*, edited by John O'Neill, transitioned into an electronic magazine in September of 2012 and can be found at www.blackgate.com. They no longer regularly run new fiction, although they will be regularly refreshing their nonfiction content, essays and reviews, and the occasional story will continue to appear.

Galaxy's Edge (www.galaxysedge.com), edited by Mike Resnick, reached its third year of publication, and its twenty-third bimonthly issue, and is still going strong; it's available in various downloadable formats, although a print edition is available from BN.com and Amazon.com for $5.99 per issue. They published good stuff this year by Martin L. Shoemaker, Ian Whates, Alvaro Zinos-Amaro, Sunil Patel, Kary English and Robert B. Finegold, although the reprint stories here, by Robert Silverberg, Nancy Kress, George R.R. Martin, Kij Johnson, and others, were still stronger than the original stories.

Newish (fourteen issues) magazine *Uncanny* (uncannymagazine.com), edited by Lynne M. Thomas and Michael Damian Thomas, which won the best semiprozine Hugo this year, had entertaining stories by Seanan McGuire, Alyssa Wong, Paul Cornell, Brooke Bolander, Ferrett Steinmetz, and others, while brand-new magazine *Persistent Visions* (persistentvisionsmag.com), edited by Heather Shaw, had interesting work by Benjamin Rosenbaum, Lavie Tidhar, Naomi Kritzer, Leah Cypress, and others. New magazine *Terraform* (motherboard.vice.com/terraform), edited by Claire Evans and Brian Merchant, also looks promising.

The Australian popular-science magazine *Cosmos* (www.cosmosmagazine.com) seems to have ended its policy of running an occasional science fiction story and gone to being an all-science news publication instead.

Ideomancer Speculative Fiction (www.ideomancer.com), edited by Leah Bobet, published interesting work, usually more slipstream than SF.

Orson Scott Card's Intergalactic Medicine Show (www.intergalacticmedicineshow .com), now edited by Scott R. Roberts under the direction of Card himself, ran interesting stuff from James Van Pelt, Harry Turtledove, Eric James Stone, and others.

SF/fantasy e-zine *Daily Science Fiction* (dailysciencefiction.com) publishes one new SF or fantasy story *every single day* for the entire year. Unsurprisingly, many of these were not really up to professional standards, but there were some good stories here and there by Eric Brown, James Van Pelt, Caroline M. Yoachim, William Ledbetter, and others. Editors there are Michele-Lee Barasso and Jonathan Laden.

Shimmer Magazine (www.shimmer.com), edited by E. Catherine Tobler, published interesting fiction by Patricia Russo, Arkady Martine, Rich Larson, Rachael Acks, and others.

GigaNotoSaurus (giganotosaurus.org), now edited by Rashida J. Smith, taking over from Ann Leckie, published one story a month by writers such as Lucy Stone, Alex Jeffers, and others.

Kaleidotrope (www.kaleidotrope.net), edited by Fred Coppersmith, which started in 2006 as a print semiprozine but transitioned to digital in 2012, published interesting work by Megan Arkenberg, Joe Pitkin, and others.

The World SF Blog (worldsf.wordpress.com), edited by Lavie Tidhar, was a good place to find science fiction by international authors, and also published news, links, roundtable discussions, essays, and interviews related to "science fiction, fantasy, horror, and comics from around the world." The site is no longer being updated, but an extensive archive is still accessible there.

A similar site is *International Speculative Fiction* (internationalSF.wordpress .com), edited by Roberto Mendes.

Weird Fiction Review (weirdfictionreview.com), edited by Ann VanderMeer and Jeff VanderMeer, which occasionally publishes fiction, bills itself as "an ongoing exploration into all facets of the weird," including reviews, interviews, short essays, and comics.

Other newcomers include *Omenana Magazine of Africa's Speculative Fiction* (omenana.com), edited by Chinelo Onwualu and Chiagozie Fred Nwonwu.

Below this point, it becomes harder to find center-core SF, or even genre fantasy/horror, with most magazines featuring slipstream or literary surrealism instead. Such sites include *Fireside Magazine* (www.firesidefiction.com), edited by Brian

White; *Revolution SF* (www.revolutionsf.com), *Heliotrope* (www.heliotropemag
.com); and *Interfictions Online* (interfictions.com/), executive editor Delila Sherman, fiction editors Christopher Barzak and Meghan McCarron.

Not only original fiction is available on the Internet, though. There's also a lot of
good *reprint* SF and fantasy to be found on Internet. There are sites where you can
access formerly published stories for free, including *Strange Horizons, Tor.com,
Clarkesworld, Lightspeed, Subterranean, Abyss & Apex, Apex Magazine,* and most of
the sites that are associated with existent print magazines, such as *Asimov's, Analog,*
and *The Magazine of Fantasy & Science Fiction,* make previously published fiction
and nonfiction available for access on their sites as well, and also regularly run teaser
excerpts from stories coming up in forthcoming issues. Hundreds of out-of-print titles, both genre and mainstream, are also available for free download from *Project
Gutenberg* (www.gutenberg.org), and a large selection of novels, collections, and
anthologies, can either be bought or be accessed for free, to be either downloaded
or read on-screen, at the *Baen Free Library* (www.baen.com/library). Sites such as
Infinity Plus (www.infinityplus.co.uk) and *The Infinite Matrix* (www.infinitematrix
.net) may have died as active sites, but their extensive archives of previously published material are still accessible (an extensive line of Infinity Plus Books can also
be ordered from the *Infinity Plus* site).

There are plenty of other reasons for SF fans to go on the Internet, though, beyond just the search for good stories to read. There are many general genre-related
sites of interest to be found, most of which publish reviews of books as well as of
movies and TV shows, sometimes comics or computer games or anime, many of
which also feature interviews, critical articles, and genre-oriented news of various
kinds. The best such site is *Locus Online* (www.locusmag.com), the online version
of the newsmagazine *Locus,* where you can access an incredible amount of
information—including book reviews, critical lists, obituary lists, links to reviews
and essays appearing outside the genre, and links to extensive database archives
such as the Locus Index to Science Fiction and the Locus Index to Science Fiction
Awards. The previously mentioned *Tor.com* is also one of the most eclectic genre-
oriented sites on the Internet, a Web site that, in addition to its fiction, regularly
publishes articles, comics, graphics, blog entries, print and media reviews, book
"rereads" and episode-by-episode "rewatches" of television shows, as well as com-
mentary on all the above. The long-running and eclectic *The New York Review of
Science Fiction* has ceased print publication, but can be purchased in PDF, e-pub,
mobi formats, and POD editions through Weightless Press (weightlessbooks.com;
see also www.nyrsf.com for information). Other major general-interest sites include
Io9 (www.io9.com), *SF Site* (www.sfsite.com), although it's no longer being regularly
updated, *SFReyu* (www.sfsite.com/sfrevu), *SFCrowsnest* (www.sfcrowsnest.com),
SFScope (www.sfscope.com), *Green Man Review* (greenmanreview.com), *The Agony Column* (trashotron.com/agony), *SFFWorld* (www.sffworld.com), *SFReader* (fo-
rums.sfreader.com), and *Pat's Fantasy Hotlist* (www.fantasyhotlist.blogspot.com). A
great research site, invaluable if you want bibliographic information about SF and
fantasy writers, is *Fantastic Fiction* (www.fantasticfiction.co.uk). Another fantastic
research site is the searchable online update of the Hugo-winning *The Encyclopedia
of Science Fiction* (www.sf-encyclopedia.com), where you can access almost four

million words of information about SF writers, books, magazines, and genre themes. Reviews of short fiction as opposed to novels are very hard to find anywhere, with the exception of *Locus* and *Locus Online*, but you can find reviews of both current and past short fiction at *Best SF* (www.bestsf.net), as well as at pioneering short-fiction review site *Tangent Online* (www.tangentonline.com).

Although long-running sites *sff.net* and *SF Signal* died in 2017, there are plenty of other sites of general interest include: *Ansible* (news.ansible.co.uk/Ansible), the online version of multiple Hugo-winner David Langford's long-running fanzine *Ansible*; *Book View Café* (www.bookviewcafe.com) is a "consortium of over twenty professional authors," including Vonda N. McIntyre, Laura Ann Gilman, Sarah Zittel, Brenda Clough, and others, who have created a Web site where work by them—mostly reprints, and some novel excerpts—is made available for free.

Sites where podcasts and SF-oriented radio plays can be accessed have also proliferated in recent years: at *Audible* (www.audible.com), *Escape Pod* (escapepod.org, podcasting mostly SF), *SF Squeecast* (sfsqueecast.com/), *The Coode Street Podcast* (jonathanstrahan.podbean.com/), *The Drabblecast* (www.drabblecast.org), *StarShipSofa* (www.starshipsofa.com), *Far Fetched Fables* (www.farfetchedfables.com), new companion to *StarShipSofa*, concentrating on fantasy, *SF Signal Podcast* (www.sfsignal.com), *Pseudopod* (pseudopod.org, podcasting mostly fantasy), *Podcastle* (http://podcastle.org), podcasting mostly fantasy, and Galactic Suburbia (http://galacticsuburbia.pod.bean.com). *Clarkesworld* routinely offers podcasts of stories from the e-zine, and *The Agony Column* (agonycolumn.com) also hosts a weekly podcast. There's also a site that podcasts nonfiction interviews and reviews, *Dragon Page Cover to Cover* (www.dragonpage.com).

In some ways, 2016 was an odd year for short fiction. There was still plenty of good short fiction to be found, in the print magazines, electronic magazines, in audio formats, in stand-alone chapbooks, but the majority of it was published at short fiction lengths, or at most at short novelette length, with good long novelettes and novellas harder to find. (There were some good fantasy novellas, almost all printed as stand-alone chapbooks, but science fiction novellas were thinner on the ground, with no more than four or five of them produced this year.) The majority of really superior SF was published at lengths between 6,000 and 12,000, with the bulk of it falling toward the shorter end of the scale.

Why is this? My own personal theory is that the electronic magazines such as *Clarkesworld*, *Lightspeed*, and *Tor.com* have become prestigious enough, and also pay more than many print magazines, that writers are now writing their stories with them in mind as the primary place to submit them to first—and as most of those markets only occasionally publish anything longer than short novelette length, with the bulk of their stories being of short-story length instead, that authors are writing stories that confirm to those word-lengths, figuring that that's their best chance of making a sale. Even if some of those stories fall though the electronic magazine market and end up appearing in one of the traditional print magazines instead, they're still going to be short.

Or perhaps the generation of younger writers who have grown up mostly reading fiction on the Internet, where short stories and flash fiction are common and novel-ettes and novellas are rare, have just been conditioned to think of those lengths as the lengths that a story ought to be.

Which is too bad, as I personally still think that novella-length is the perfect natural length for a science fiction story, and if novellas disappear from the genre, the genre will be the weaker for it.

Compared to 2015, 2016 was a bit weaker overall for original anthologies. Al-though neither was as strong as Jonathan Strahan's 2015 SF anthology *Meeting Infinity*, Strahan still produced the two strongest original SF anthologies of the year, *Bridging Infinity* (Solaris), the most recent volume in his long-running Infinity anthology series, which have consistently been among the strongest original SF an-thologies of their respective years, and a catastrophic climate change anthology *Drowned Worlds: Tales From the Anthropocene and Beyond* (Solaris). *Bridging Infin-ity* features some excellent stories, including some of the year's best stories, by Alastair Reynolds, Ken Liu, Pat Murphy and Paul Doherty, Thoraiya Dyer, and Charlie Jane Anders; *Bridging Infinity* also features good stories by Pat Cadigan, Al-len M. Steele, Robert Reed, Stephen Baxter, and others. There have been so many stories about catastrophic climate change in the last few years in practically every market (particularly ones about rising sea levels swallowing cities and coastlines), with at least three dedicated catastrophic climate change/apocalypse anthologies appearing in 2015 alone—and another one, the mostly reprint, *This Way to the End Times: Classic Tales of the Apocalypse* (Three Rooms Press), edited by Robert Silver-berg, sneaking in toward the end of the year—that Strahan's *Drowned Worlds*, al-though clearly the best of the bunch, may lose some impact with some readers by feeling overly familiar. Nevertheless, *Drowned Worlds* is a strong anthology, and I'm particularly impressed here with the stories that look beyond the familiar doom and gloom of the initial catastrophes and try to imagine how humans (who, after all, are extremely adaptable animals) and human society might be able to evolve strategies and ways of life that would enable them to survive and even eventually prosper under the new conditions pertaining to a post-climate catastrophe world. Some of the best stories here by Paul McAuley, Ken Liu, Charlie Jane Anders, and Cathe-rynne M. Valente do just that (as do the Murphy and Dohertry and the Dyer stories from *Bridging Infinity*, which might have fit better into *Drowned Worlds* instead); *Drowned Worlds* also features good stories by Lavie Tidhar, Sam J. Miller, Nina Al-lan, Sean Williams (whose story might have fit better into *Bridging Infinity*), Nalo Hopkinson, and others. The anthology also reprints one of the earliest catastrophic climate change stories, and still one of the best, "Venice Drowned," by Kim Stanley Robinson.

Another good original SF anthology is *To Shape the Dark* (Candlemark), edited by Athena Andreadis, an anthology of SF stories about women scientists struggling to do "science not-as-usual," to push the boundaries of the possible, often against considerable resistance and even attempted oppression by the societies in which they function . . . as well as attempts to deny that they ever did the work at all or to claim credit for it (not too different, in other words, from what happens all too often in our own present-day society). There's a wide range of styles and moods here, with settings ranging from the near-present to the far-future, including stories about women exploring and doing vital scientific work on distant alien worlds. Strongest stories here are probably by Shariann Lewit, Aliette de Bodard, Melissa Scott, Vandana Singh, and Constance Cooper, but there's also good work by Gwyneth Jones, Terry Boren, Kristin Landon, and others, all of it science fiction, some of it hard science fiction, and just about all of it worth reading.

Now We Are Ten—Celebrating the First Ten Years of NewCon Press (NewCon Press), edited by Ian Whates, is exactly what it says that it is: a compilation of stories by authors who have been published by NewCon Press, in celebration of NewCon Press's tenth anniversary. This is a mixed (but all original) anthology of SF and fantasy—nothing here is as strong as the best of the stories from the anthologies mentioned above, but most of the stories are enjoyable and worth reading. The best of them is probably by the ever-reliable Ian McDonald, but there's also good stuff by Nina Allan, Nancy Kress, Jack Skillingstead, Eric Brown, E. J. Swift, and others.

Not quite in the same league as the anthologies above, but still with a number of entertaining stories, are *Strangers Among Us: Tales of the Underdogs and Outcasts* (Laska Media Groups), edited by Susan Forest and Lucas K. Law, which features good work by Rich Larson, James Alan Gardner, A. M. Dellamonica, Kelley Armstrong, Ursula Pflug, Hayden Trenholm, and others, and *Clockwork Phoenix 5* (Mythic Delirium), edited by Mike Allen, which features strong work by Rich Larson, C.S.E. Cooney and Carlos Hernandez, Jason Kimble, Barbara Krasnoff, and others.

There weren't too many fantasy anthologies this year, and all of them were anthologies of retold fairy tales, two original and one reprint. The one that seemed to attract the most attention was *The Starlit Wood: New Fairy Tales* (Saga), edited by Dominik Parisien and Navah Wolfe, which featured good work by Garth Nix, Amal El-Mohtar, Aliette de Bodard, Naomi Novik, Seanan McGuire, Daryl Gregory, Marjorie Liu, and others. Also good was *The Grimm Future* (NESFA), edited by Erin Underwood, which featured strong work by Maura McHugh, Garth Nix, Seanan McGuire, and others.

Postscripts 36/37: The Dragons of the Night (PS Publishing), edited by Nick Gevers, and *Dreaming in the Dark* (PS Publishing), an anthology of stories by Australian authors edited by Jack Dann, featured mostly slipstream, fantasy, and soft horror stories, almost all of high literary quality and craftsmanship, but, disappointingly, to me, anyway, not much core SF, if any. There were also a number of anthologies from Fiction River (www.fictionriver.com), which in 2013 launched a continuing series of original SF, fantasy, and mystery anthologies, with Kristine Kathryn Rusch and Dean Wesley Smith as overall series editors, and individual editions edited by various hands. This year, they published *Sparks* (WMG), edited by Rebecca Moesta; *Visions of the Apocalypse* (WMG), edited by John Helfers; *Haunted* (WMG), edited by Kerrie L. Hughes; and *Last Stand* (WMG), edited by Dean Wesley Smith and Felicia Fredlund. These can be purchased in Kindle versions from Amazon and other online vendors, or from the publisher at www.wmg publishinginc.com.

Pleasant but minor original anthologies included *What the #@&% Is That?* (Saga/Simon & Schuster), edited by John Joseph Adams and Douglas Cohen, and *Street Magicks* (Prime), edited by Paula Guran.

Noted without comment is a mixed SF anthology/fantasy anthology of stories inspired by famous first lines from literature, *Mash Up* (Titan), edited by Gardner Dozois.

There was an anthology of SF stories translated from Chinese, *Invisible Planets* (Tor), edited by Ken Liu, and three shared-world anthologies, *High Stakes* (Tor), a new Wild Cards volume edited by George R. R. Martin with Melinda M. Snodgrass, *Grantville Gazette VIII* (Baen), edited by Eric Flint, and *Onward, Drake!* (Baen), an anthology of stories in tribute to David Drake, edited by Mark L. Van Name.

L. Ron Hubbard Presents Writers of the Future Volume 32 (Galaxy), edited by David Farland, is the most recent in a long-running series featuring novice work by beginning writers, some of whom may later turn out to be important talents.

I don't pay close attention to the horror field, considering it out of my purview, but the horror anthology that got talked about the most seemed to be *Nightmares: A New Decade of Modern Horror* (Tachyon), and *Children of Lovecraft* (Dark Horse), both edited by the indefatigable Ellen Datlow.

Without a doubt the most prolific author at short lengths this year was Rich Larson, who published something like sixteen stories, at least five or six of which were good enough to have been justifiably placed in a best of the year anthology.

These days to find up-to-date contact information for almost any publisher, however small, you can just Google it. Nevertheless, as a courtesy, I'm going to reproduce here the addresses I have for small presses that may have been mentioned in the various sections of the Summation. If any are out-of-date, Google the publisher.

Addresses: **PS Publishing**, Grosvener House, 1 New Road, Hornsea, West Yorkshire, HU18 1PG, England, UK www.pspublishing.co.uk; **Golden Gryphon Press**, 3002 Perkins Road, Urbana, IL 61802, www.goldengryphon.com; **NESFA Press**, P.O. Box 809, Framinghan, MA 01701-0809, www.nesfa.org; **Subterranean Press**, P.O. Box 190106, Burton, MI 48519, www.subterraneanpress.com; **Old Earth Books**, P.O. Box 19951, Baltimore, MD 21211–0951, www.oldearthbooks.com; **Tachyon Press**, 1459 18th St. #139, San Francisco, CA 94107, www.tachyonpublications.com; **Night Shade Books**, 1470 NW Saltzman Road, Portland, OR 97229, www.nightshade-books.com; **Five Star Books**, 295 Kennedy Memorial Drive, Waterville, ME 04901, www .galegroup.com/fivestar; **NewCon Press**, via www.newconpress.com; **Small Beer Press**, 176 Prospect Ave., Northampton, MA 01060, www.smallbeerpress.com; **Locus Press**, P.O. Box 13305, Oakland, CA 94661; **Crescent Books**, Mercat Press Ltd., 10 Coates Crescent, Edinburgh, Scotland EH3 7AL, www.crescentfiction.com; **Wildside Press/Borgo Press**, P.O. Box 301, Holicong, PA 18928–0301, or go to www .wildsidepress.com for pricing and ordering; **Edge Science Fiction and Fantasy Publishing, Inc. and Tesseract Books, Ltd.**, P.O. Box 1714, Calgary, Alberta, T2P 2L7, Canada, www.edgewebsite.com; **Aqueduct Press**, P.O. Box 95787, Seattle, WA 98145–2787, www.aqueductpress.com; **Phobos Books**, 200 Park Avenue South, New York, NY 10003, www.phobosweb.com; **Fairwood Press**, 5203 Quincy Ave. SE, Auburn, WA 98092, www.fairwoodpress.com; **BenBella Books**, 6440 N. Central Expressway, Suite 508, Dallas, TX 75206, www.benbellabooks.com; **Darkside Press**, 13320 27th Ave. NE, Seattle, WA 98125, www.darksidepress.com; **Haffner Press**,

5005 Crooks Rd., Suite 35, Royal Oak, MI 48073–1239, www.haffnerpress.com; **North Atlantic Press,** P.O. Box 12327, Berkeley, CA, 94701; **Prime Books,** P.O. Box 36503, Canton, OH, 44735, www.primebooks.net; **Fairwood Press,** 5203 Quincy Ave SE, Auburn, WA 98092, www.fairwoodpress.com; **MonkeyBrain Books,** 11204 Crossland Drive, Austin, TX 78726, www.monkeybrainbooks.com; **Wesleyan University Press,** University Press of New England, Order Dept., 37 Lafayette St., Lebanon, NH 03766–1405, www.wesleyan.edu/wespress;; **Agog! Press,** P.O. Box U302, University of Wollongong, NSW 2522, Australia, www.uow.ed.au/~rhood/agogpress; **Wheatland Press,** via www.wheatlandpress.com; **MirrorDanse Books,** P.O. Box 3542, Parramatta NSW 2124, Australia, www.tabula-rasa.info/MirrorDanse; **Arsenal Pulp Press,** 103–1014 Homer Street, Vancouver, BC, Canada V6B 2W9, www.arsenalpress.com; **DreamHaven Books,** 912 W. Lake Street, Minneapolis, MN 55408; **Elder Signs Press/Dimensions Books,** order through www.dimensionsbooks.com; **Chaosium,** via www.chaosium.com; **Spyre Books,** P.O. Box 3005, Radford, VA 24143; **SCIFI, Inc.,** P.O. Box 8442, Van Nuys, CA 91409–8442; **Omnidawn Publishing,** order through www.omnidawn.com; **CSFG,** Canberra Speculative Fiction Guild, via www.csfg.org.au/publishing/anthologies/the_outcast; **Hadley Rille Books,** via www.hadleyrillebooks.com; **Suddenly Press,** via suddenlypress@yahoo.com; **Sandstone Press,** P.O. Box 5725, One High St., Dingwall, Ross-shire, IV15 9WJ; **Tropism Press,** via www.tropismpress.com; **SF Poetry Association/Dark Regions Press,** via www.sfpoetry.com, checks to Helena Bell, SFPA Treasurer, 1225 West Freeman St., Apt. 12, Carbondale, IL 62401; **DH Press,** via diamondbookdistributors.com; **Kurodahan Press,** via Web site www.kurodahan.com; **Ramble House,** 443 Gladstone Blvd., Shreveport LA 71104; **Interstitial Arts Foundation,** via www.interstitialarts.org; **Raw Dog Screaming,** via www.rawdogscreaming.com; **Three Legged Fox Books,** 98 Hythe Road, Brighton, BN1 6JS, UK; **Norilana Books,** via www.norilana.com; *coeur de lion,* via coeurdelion.com.au; **PARSECink,** via www.parsecink.org; **Robert J. Sawyer Books,** via www.sfwriter.com/rjsbooks.htm; **Rackstraw Press,** via rackstrawpress; **Candlewick,** via www.candlewick.com; **Zubaan,** via www.zubaanbooks.com; **Utter Tower,** via www.threeleggedfox.co.uk; **Spilt Milk Press,** via www.electricvelocipede.com; **Paper Golem,** via www.papergolem.com; **Galaxy Press,** via www.galaxypress.com.; **Twelfth Planet Press,** via www.twelfthplanetpress.com; **Five Senses Press,** via www.sensefive.com; **Elastic Press,** via www.elasticpress.com; **Lethe Press,** via www.lethepressbooks.com; **Two Cranes Press,** via www.twocranespress.com; **Wordcraft of Oregon,** via www.wordcraftoforegon.com; **Down East,** via www.downeast.com; **ISFiC Press,** 456 Douglas Ave., Elgin, IL 60120 or www.isficpress.com.

According to the newsmagazine *Locus,* there were 2,858 books "of interest to the SF field" published in 2016, up 9 percent from 2,625 titles in 2015, the second consecutive rise in overall books published. New titles were up 8 percent to 1,957 from 2015's 1,820, while reprints also rose by 12 percent to 910 from 2015's 805. Hardcovers rose by 6 percent to 856 from 2015's 849. Trade paperbacks rose too, up 17 percent to 1,539 from 2015's 1,343. Mass-market paperbacks, the format facing the most competition from e-books, continued to drop, down 11 percent, to 385 from 2015's 433. The number of new SF novels was up 7 percent to 425 titles from

2015's 396 titles, with 89 of those titles being YA SF novels. The number of new fantasy novels climbed up 8 percent to 737 titles from 2015's 682 titles, with 247 of those titles being YA fantasy novels. Horror novels were down 7 percent to 171 titles from 2015's 183 titles. Paranormal romances, once the hottest boom area, continued to slide for the fifth year in a row, down to 107 titles from 2015's 111 titles. 2,858 books "of interest to the SF field" is an enormous number of books, probably more than some small-town libraries contain of books in general. Even if you consider only the 425 new SF titles, that's still a lot of books, probably more than most people are going to have time to read (or the desire to read, either). And these totals don't count many e-books, media tie-in novels, gaming novels, novelizations of genre movies, print-on-demand books, or self-published novels—all of which would swell the over-all total by hundreds if counted.

As usual, busy with all the reading I have to do at shorter lengths, I didn't have time to read many novels myself this year, so I'll limit myself to mentioning that novels that received a lot of attention and acclaim in 2016.

Into Everywhere, by Paul McAuley (Gollancz); *Arkwright*, by Allen Steele (Tor); *Visitor*, by C. J. Cherryh (DAW); *Last Year*, by Robert Charles Wilson (Tor); *Take Back the Sky*, by Greg Bear (Orbit US); *Poseidon's Wake*, by Alastair Reynolds (Ace); *Medusa's Web*, by Tim Powers (HarperCollins); *Company Town*, by Madeline Ashby (Tor); *Babylon's Ashes*, by James S. A. Corey (Orbit US); *League of Dragons*, by Naomi Novik (Ballantine Del Rey); *Crosstalk*, by Connie Willis (Orion/Gollancz); *The Wall of Storms*, by Ken Liu (Simon & Schuster); *Death's End*, by Cixin Liu (Tor); *The Devourers*, by Indra Das (Del Rey); *Impersonations*, by Walter Jon Williams (Tor); *Europe in Winter*, by Dave Hutchinson (Rebellion/Solaris); *Everfair*, by Nisi Shawl (Tor); *The Nightmare Stacks*, by Charles Stross (Ace); *Transgalactic*, by James Gunn (Tor); *The Gradual*, by Christopher Priest (Titan); *Summerlong*, by Peter S. Beagle (Tachyon); *The Spider's War*, by Daniel Abraham (Orbit US); *The Long Cosmos*, by Terry Pratchett and Stephen Baxter (Harper Voyager); *Alien Morning*, by Rick Wilber (Tor); *The Corporation Wars: Dissidence*, by Ken MacLeod (Little, Brown); *Who Killed Sherlock Holmes?* by Paul Cornell (Pan Macmillan); *The Medusa Chronicles*, by Alastair Reyonds and Stephen Baxter (Gollancz); and *End of Watch*, by Stephen King (Simon & Schuster).

(One of the very best books of the year is *Central Station* (Tachyon), by Lavie Tidhar, although there is some controversy as to whether it should be considered to be a collection of previously published stories or a "braided mosaic novel." I've dealt with this by recommending it in both the novel section and the short fiction collections section.)

In the list above, the McAuley, the Steele, the Cherryh, the Wilson, the Bear, the Reynolds, the Corey, the Cixin Liu, and many others are pure-quill center-core SF, in spite of decades of fretting about how fantasy is going to drive SF from the bookstore shelves.

Novels by established authors issued by small presses this year included: *Central Station*, by Lavie Tidhar (if considered as a novel rather than a collection—Tachyon); *The Doomed City*, by Arkady Strugatsky and Boris Strugatsky (Chicago Review

Press); *The Chemical Wedding by Christian Rosencreutz: A Romance in Eight Days by Johann Valentin Andreae*, by John Crowley (Small Beer Press); *War Factory*, by Neal Asher (Skyhorse/Nightshade Books); *The Dark Forest*, by Cixin Liu (Head of Zeus); *The Light Warden*, by Liz Williams (NewCon Press); *Down and Out in Purgatory*, by Tim Powers (Subterranean); and *Zen City*, by Eliot Fintushel (Zero).

The year's first novels included: *Arabella of Mars*, by David D. Levine (Tor); *Ninefox Gambit*, by Yoon Ha Lee (Solaris US); *Roses and Rot*, by Kat Howard (Saga); *Everfair*, by Nisi Shawl (Tor); *A Fierce and Subtle Poison*, by Samantha Marby (Algonquin); *The Star-Touched Queen*, by Roshani Chokshi (St. Martin's Press); *The Reader*, by Traci Chee (Putnam); *Vigil*, by Angela Slatter (Jo Fletcher Books); *Azanian Bridges*, by Nick Wood (NewCon Press); and *Devil and the Bluebird*, by Jennifer Mason-Black (Amulet). It's a very subjective call, but it seems to me that the novels by Shawl, Levine, and Ha Lee got more attention that the rest did.

There were not too many novel omnibuses available this year, but they included *Two Great Novels: Up the Walls of the World and Brightness Falls from the Air* (Orion/Gollancz), by James Tiptree, Jr.; *Three Classic Novels: Ossian's Ride, October the First Is Too Late, Fifth Planet* (Orion/Gollancz), by Fred Hoyle; *Ill Met in Lankhmar and Ship of Shadows* (Open Press), by Fritz Leiber; and *Seventh Son and Red Prophet* (Tor), by Orson Scott Card.

Novel omnibuses are also frequently made available through the Science Fiction Book Club.

Not even counting print-on-demand books and the availability of out-of-print books as e-books or as electronic downloads from Internet sources, a lot of long out-of-print stuff has come back into print in the last couple of years in commercial trade editions. Here are some out-of-print titles that came back into print this year, although producing a definitive list of reissued novels is probably impossible.

Orion/Gollancz reissued *Limbo*, by Bernard Wolfe, *Always Coming Home*, by Ursula K. Le Guin, *The Man Who Fell to Earth*, Walter S. Tevis, *The Chrysalids*, by John Wyndham, and *Norstrilia*, by Cordwainer Smith; Gollancz reissued *Feersum Endjinn*, by Iain M. Banks; Tor reissued *Mars Crossing*, by Geoffrey A. Landis, *Christmas Magic*, edited by David G. Hartwell, *Cosmonaut Keep*, by Ken MacLeod, *The Memory of Whiteness*, by Kim Stanley Robinson, and *Briar Rose*, by Jane Yolen; Penguin Classics reissued *The Left Hand of Darkness*, by Ursula K. Le Guin; Titan reissued *The Condition of Muzak*, *The English Assassin*, *A Cure for Cancer*, and *The Final Programme*, all by Michael Moorcock; DAW reissued *Death's Master* and *Hunting the White Witch*, both by Tanith Lee; Valancourt Books reissued *The Space Machine*, by Christopher Priest; Random House/Ebury/Del Rey UK reissued *He, She and It* and *Woman at the Edge of Time*, both by Marge Piercy; Pocket Books reissued *Swan Song*, by Robert McCammon; Vintage reissued *Stories of Your Life and Others*, by Ted Chiang; Harper Voyager reissued *The Time Ships*, by Stephen Baxter; and Houghton Mifflin Harcourt reissued *The Man in the High Castle*, by Philip K. Dick.

Many authors are now reissuing their old back titles as e-books, either through a publisher or all by themselves, so many that it's impossible to keep track of them all here. Before you conclude that something from an author's backlist is unavailable, though, check with the Kindle and Nook stores, and with other online vendors.

For short-story collections 2016 was another good year.

The year's best collections included: *The Best of Ian McDonald*, by Ian McDonald (PS Publishing); *Central Station* (if considered to be a collection rather than a novel), by Lavie Tidhar (Tachyon); *Beyond the Aquila Rift: The Best of Alastair Reynolds*, by Alastair Reynolds, edited by Jonathan Strahan and William Schafer (Subterranean Press); *Hwarhath Stories: Transgressive Tales by Aliens*, by Eleanor Arnason (Aqueduct Press); *Not So Much, Said the Cat*, by Michael Swanwick (Tachyon); *The Found and the Lost: The Collected Novellas of Ursula K. Le Guin*, by Ursula K. Le Guin (Saga Press); *The Unreal and the Real: The Selected Short Stories by Ursula K. LeGuin* by Ursula K. Le Guin (Simon & Schuster); *The Complete Orsinia*, by Ursula K. Le Guin (Library of America); *Concentration*, by Jack Dann (PS Publishing); and *The Paper Menagerie and Other Stories*, by Ken Liu (Simon & Schuster).

Also good were *Sharp Ends*, by Joe Abercrombie (Orbit); *Amaryllis and Other Stories*, by Carrie Vaughn (Fairwood Press); *Neither Here Nor There*, by Cat Rambo (Hydra); *Frankenstein on Ice and Other Stories*, by Kim Newman (Titan US); *Otherworld Secrets*, by Kelley Armstrong (Penguin/Plume); *Slipping*, by Lauren Beukes (Tachyon); *Other Stories*, by Paul Park (PS Publishing); *A Natural History of Hell*, by Jeff Ford; (Small Beer Press), *Dreams of Distant Shores*, by Patricia A. McKillip (Tachyon); *Swift to Chase*, by Laird Barron (JournalStone), *Fathoms*, by Jack Cady (Underland); *Two Travellers*, by Sarah Tolmie (Aquaduct Press); *Seven Wonders of a Once and Future World and Other Stories*, by Caroline M. Yoachim (Fairwood Press); *A Feast of Sorrows*, by Angela Slattter (Prime), and *Other Arms Reach Out to Me: Georgia Stories*, by Michael Bishop (Fairwood Press).

Career-spanning retrospective collections this year included: *The Complete Short Fiction of Greg Bear, Volume One: Just Over the Horizon*, by Greg Bear (Open Road); *The Complete Short Fiction of Greg Bear, Volume Two: Far Thoughts and Pale Gods*, by Greg Bear (Open Road); *The Complete Short Fiction of Greg Bear, Volume Three: Beyond the Farthest Suns*, by Greg Bear (Open Road); *Early Days: More Tales From the Pulp Era*, by Robert Silverberg (Subterranean); *The Collected Short Works of Poul Anderson. Volume 7: Question and Answer*, by Poul Anderson (NESFA Press); *The Complete Short Stories of the 1970s (Part 1)*, by Brian W. Aldiss (Harper Voyager); *The Collected Stories of Carol Emshwiller, Volume 2*, by Carol Emshwiller (NonStop Press), *Grotto of the Dancing Deer: And Other Stories (The Complete Short Fiction of Clifford D. Simak Volume Four)* by Clifford D. Simak, (Open Road); *Earth for Inspiration and Other Stories: The Complete Short Fiction of Clifford D. Simak*, Volume Nine by Clifford D. Simak, (Open Road); *The Door to Saturn: The Collected Fantasies, Volume 2*, by Clark Ashton Smith, edited by Scott Connors and Ron Hilger (Skyhorse/Nightshade Books); *A Vintage from Atlantis: The Collected Fantasies, Volume 3*, by Clark Ashton Smith, edited by Scott Connors and Ron Hilger (Skyhorse/Night Shade Books); *The Best of Bova Volume I*, by Ben Bova (Baen); *The Best of Bova, Volume II*, by Ben Bova (Baen); *The People in the*

Castle: Selected Strange Stories, by Joan Aiken (Small Beer Press); and *Interior Dark-ness: Selected Stories*, by Peter Straub (Doubleday).

As usual, small presses dominated the list of short-story collections, with trade collections having become rare. . . .

A wide variety of "electronic collections," often called "fiction bundles," too many to individually list here, are also available for downloading online, at many sites. The Science Fiction Book Club continues to issue new collections as well.

As usual, the most reliable buys in the reprint anthology market are the various best of the year anthologies, the number of which continues to fluctuate. One series covering SF was lost with the demise of David G. Hartwell's *Year's Best SF* series (Tor), but we gained several new series. Continuations of relatively new series this year included: *The Year's Best Military SF and Space Opera 2015* (Baen), edited by David Afsharirad; *The Year's Best Science Fiction and Fantasy Novellas: 2016 Edi-tion* (Prime Books), edited by Paula Guran; and *The Best American Science Fiction and Fantasy 2016* (Houghton Mifflin Harcourt), this volume edited by Karen Joy Fowler, with the overall series editor being John Joseph Adams. *The Year's Best Weird Fiction, Volume 2*, edited by Kathe Koja and Michael Kelly was published last year, but if there was a new volume this year, I didn't see it. New this year is *The Best Science Fiction of the Year, Volume One*, edited by Neil Clarke (Skyhorse/Night Shade Books). These join the established best of the year series: the one you are reading at the moment, *The Year's Best Science Fiction* series from St. Martin's, ed-ited by Gardner Dozois, now in its thirty-fourth year; *The Best Science Fiction and Fantasy of the Year: Volume Ten* (Solaris), edited by Jonathan Strahan; *The Year's Best Science Fiction and Fantasy: 2016 Edition* (Prime Books), edited by Rich Hor-ton; *The Best Horror of the Year: Volume Eight* (Skyhorse/Night Shade Books), ed-ited by Ellen Datlow; *The Year's Best Dark Fantasy and Horror 2016 Edition* (Prime Books), edited by Paula Guran; and *The Mammoth Book of Best New Horror, Vol-ume 27* (PS Publishing), edited by Stephen Jones.

That leaves science fiction being covered by three dedicated best of the year an-thologies, my own, the Clarke, and the Afsharirad, plus four separate half antholo-gies, the science fiction halves of the Strahan, Horton, Fowler, and Guran novella book, which in theory adds up to two additional anthologies (in practice, of course, the contents of those books probably won't divide that neatly, with exactly half with their coverage going to each genre, and there'll likely to be more of one thing than another). With three dedicated anthologies and four half-anthologies (adding up to two more), that's actually more "best of" coverage than SF has had for a while. There is no dedicated fantasy anthology anymore, fantasy only being covered by the fantasy halves of the Strahan, Horton, Fowler, and Guran novella book (in effect, by two anthologies when you add the halves together). Horror is now being covered by two dedicated volumes, the Datlow and the Jones, and the "horror" half of Guran's *The Year's Best Dark Fantasy and Horror* (although the distinction between "dark fantasy" and "horror" is a fine—and perhaps problematical—one). The annual Neb-ula Awards anthology, which covers science fiction as well as fantasy of various sorts, functions as a de facto "best of the year" anthology, although it's not usually counted among them; this year's edition was *Nebula Awards Showcase 2016* (Pyr), edited by Mercedes Lackey. A more specialized best of the year anthology is *Heiresses of Russ 2016: The Year's Best Lesbian Speculative Fiction* (Lethe Press), edited by A. M. Dellamonica and Steven Berman.

The most prominent title in the stand-alone reprint anthology market was undoubtedly *The Big Book of Science Fiction* (Vintage), edited by Jeff and Ann Vander-Meer, a massive retrospective anthology that makes even this book look small at 800,000 words and more than 102 stories from authors around the world. As is always true with these big retrospectives, it would be possible to question the use of one author's particular story over that of another story by the same author—but any anthology that reprints Theodore Sturgeon's "The Man Who Lost the Sea," Joanna Russ's "When It Changed," Damon Knight's "Stranger Station," Pat Murphy's "Rachel in Love," John Crowley's "Snow," Ted Chiang's "The Story of Your Life," Ursula K. Le Guin's "Vaster Than Empries and More Slow," R. A. Lafferty's "Nine Hundred Grandmothers,' and Arthur C. Clarke's "The Star," plus stories by Greg Bear, Michael Bishop, Samuel R. Delany, Pat Cadigan, Isaac Asimov, Ray Bradbury, Philip K. Dick, William Gibson, C. J. Cherryh, James Blish, Iain M. Banks, and ninety-two (!) other authors is obviously a book worth reading, and one that belongs in every SF fan's library.

There were several retrospective anthologies of feminist SF this year, including *Sisters of Tomorrow: The First Women of Science Fiction* (Wesleyan University Press), edited by Lisa Yaszek and Patrick B. Sharp; and *Women of Futures Past* (Baen), edited by Kristine Kathryn Rusch. An anthology of stories drawn from Irish semiprozine *Albedo One* is *Decade 1: The Best of Albedo One* (Aeon Press), edited by John Kenny.

The best fantasy reprint anthology was probably *Beyond the Woods: Fairy Tales Retold* (Night Shade Books), edited by Paula Guran, with good work from Peter S. Beagle, Neil Gaiman, Kelly Link, Jane Yolen, Tanith Lee, Elizabeth Bear, Holly Black, and others. Monsters of various sorts were covered in *The Mammoth Book of Kaiju* (Robinson), edited by Sean Wallace; *The Mammoth Book of the Mummy* (Robinson), edited by Paula Guran; and *In the Shadow of Frankenstein: Tales of the Modern Prometheus* (Pegasus), edited by Stephen Jones; *Obsidian: A Decade of Horror Stories by Women* (NewCon Press), edited by Ian Whates; and *Tales from the Miskatonic Library* (PS Publishing), edited by Darrell Schweitzer and John Ashmead.

Pleasant but minor reprint anthologies included *Galactic Games* (Baen), edited by Bryant Thomas Schmidt, and *Things from Outer Space* (Baen), edited by Hank Davis.

There were a few intriguing items this year in a generally somewhat weak genre-oriented nonfiction category. Probably the most interesting were those directly involved with SF writers to one degree or another: *The Merril Theory of Lit'ry Criticism* (Aqueduct), by Judith Merril, reprints Merril's long-unavailable (and still well worth reading) review columns from *The Magazine of Fantasy & Science Fiction*. *In Search of Silence: The Journals of Samuel R. Delany, Volume 1, 1957–1969* (Wesleyan), edited by Kenneth R. James, gives readers a long-awaited look at the private journals of SF writer Samuel R. Delany, the first batch covering his early years in the publishing industry. *Traveler of Worlds: Conversations with Robert Silverberg* (Fairwood Press), edited by Alvaro Zinos-Amaro, is exactly what it says it is: a collection of fascinating and entertaining interviews with Silverberg conducted by Zinos-Amaro over a period of years. *Science Fiction Rebels: The Story of the Science-Fiction Magazines from 1981 to 1990* (Liverpool University Press), edited by Mike Ashley, would interest almost anyone who'd like a behind-the-scenes look at what was happening with the science fiction magazines during that tumultuous decade—unfortunately, most readers will probably be put off by the price, a steep $120. *Making Conversation* (NESFA Press), edited by Teresa Nielsen Hayden, is a collection of her fan writing on a multitude of subjects. *Where Memory Hides: A Writer's Life* (Createspace Independent Publishing Platform), by Richard A. Lupoff, takes a look back over his long and distinguished career. *My Father the Pornographer* (Simon & Schuster), by Chris Offutt, is an often-touching memoir of his father, SF writer Andrew Offutt—who also wrote a *lot* of pornography.

There were three biographies of SF/fantasy writers: *Octavia E. Butler* (University of Illinois Press), by Gerry Canavan; *Alfred Bester* (University of Illinois Press), by Jad Smith; and *Shirley Jackson: A Rather Haunted Life* (Liveright), by Ruth Franklin.

There were two books of essays about SF, literature, and life in general: *The View from the Cheap Seats* (HarperCollins/William Morrow), by Neil Gaiman, and *Words Are My Matter: Writings About Life and Books, 2000–2016* (Small Beer Press), by Ursula K. Le Guin.

A bit more on the academic side were: *The Geek Feminist Revolution* (Tor), by Kameron Hurley; *The History of Science Fiction* (Palgrave Macmillan), by Adam Roberts; *Trekonomics: The Economies of "Star Trek"* (Inkshares/Pipertext), by Manu Saadia; *Speculative Blackness: The Future of Race in Science Fiction* (University of Minnesota Press), by André M. Carrington; *Castaway Tales: From Robinson Crusoe to Life of Pi* (Wesleyan), by Christopher Palmer; *Art and War: Poetry, Pulp and Politics in Israeli Fiction* (Repeater), by Lavie Tidhar and Simon Adolf; and *The Perversity of Things: Hugo Gernsback on Media, Tinkering, and Scientification* (University of Minnesota Press), edited by Grant Wythoff.

A new addition to what by now must surely be a twenty-foot-long shelf of books about Philip K. Dick was *The Divine Madness of Philip K. Dick* (Oxford University Press), by Kyle Arnold.

Much like the nonfiction category, it seem like a generally weak year for art books, with a few strong items scattered here and there. As usual, your best bet for good value for your money was probably the latest in a long-running "best of the year" series for fantastic art, *Spectrum 23: The Best in Contemporary Fantastic Art* (Flesk Publications), edited by John Fleskes. Also of interest, particularly to SF fans, was *Spaceships: An Illustrated History of the Real and Imagined* (Smithsonian/Elephant Book Company), by Ron Miller, and *Star Wars Art: Ralph McQuarrie* (Abrams), by Ralph McQuarrie. For the fantasy fans, we had *The Fantasy Illustration Library, Volume Two: Gods and Goddesses* (Michael Publishing), edited by Malcolm R. Phifer and Michael C. Phifer, *Walking Through the Landscape of Faerie* (Faerie Magazine), by Charles Vess, and *The Art of the Film: Fantastic Beasts and Where to Find Them* (Harper Design; HarperCollins UK), by Dermot Power.

Also of interest were *The Sci-Fi and Fantasy Art of Patrick J. Jones* (Korero), by Patrick J. Jones, and *Descants & Cadences: The Art of Stephanie Law* (Shadowscapes), by Stephanie Law.

According to the Box Office Mojo site (www.boxofficemojo.com), all ten of 2016's ten top-earning movies were genre films of one sort or another (if you're willing to count animated films and superhero movies as being "genre films")—something that hasn't happened since 2010. Usually a mainstream action movie or a spy movie of some sort, frequently a James Bond movie, sneaks into the top ten list, but this year it's genre (or "genre") all the way down. Not only were all of the top ten movies genre films of one sort or another, by my count, although I may have missed a few, eighteen out of the top twenty, and thirty-eight out of the one hundred top-grossing movies were genre films. In the past seventeen years, genre films have been number one at the box office fifteen out of seventeen times, with the only exceptions being *American Sniper* in 2014 and *Saving Private Ryan* in 1998.

Coming in at number one on the top ten box-office list was *Rogue One: A Star Wars Movie*, a direct prequel to the original Star Wars movie *Star Wars: A New Hope* and the closest thing to science fiction (you could call it science fantasy, or sci-fi adventure, or space opera—the science is absurd, but at least it has spaceships and robots and aliens) in the top ten. Its rise to first was even more meteoric, as it was released only on December 16, and doubtless has a lot more money still to haul in throughout 2017. The year's other big budget sci-fi action movie, *Passengers*, has been fairly beaten up on by the critics and fan word-of-mouth, and only made it to the thirtieth spot on the top Hundred list (although, to be fair, it too had a late December start).

This year's number one on the list of top ten box-office champs, is a Disney animated film, *Finding Dory*, a sequel to *Finding Nemo*, which racked up a worldwide box-office total of $1,028,194,984 (and that's before the profits from DVD sales, action figures, lunchboxes, T-shirts, and other kinds of accessories kick in, it's worth noting). One thing this year's list may indicate is that the audience may at last be becoming a bit tired of superhero movies—oh, there were still a number of superhero movies on the list, but children's animated movies like *Finding Dory* muscled their way into the top ten list as well. In the number four spot on the list, for instance, is the animated film *The Secret Lives of Pets*, with animated film *Zootopia* at number seven, and *The Jungle Book* (live action, but with heavy use of CGI animated characters) coming in at number five. Animated film *Moana* just missed the top ten list, coming in at number eleven, an impressive showing for a movie released late in the year; the same was true of *Sing*, finishing in tenth place. *Trolls* and *Kung Fu Panda 3* made it onto the top twenty list at seventeenth place and eighteenth place respectively, and other animated children's films such as *The Angry Birds Movie*, *Sausage Party*, *Storks*, *Ice Age: Collision Course*, and *Kubo and the Two Strings* were scattered throughout the top hundred.

We're back to superhero films with the number three spot, occupied by *Captain America; Civil War*. *Deadpool*, an irreverent, brash, and vulgar "superhero comedy" that many bet would be Marvel Studio's first major commercial failure, defied all expectations by coming in at sixth place on the top ten box-office earner's list, and did pretty well with most of the critics as well. *Doctor Strange*, another movie that was considered to be a risky project for Marvel, also did well, making it into the thirteenth spot in spite of a late release on November 4. D.C.'s *Batman v Superman: Dawn of Justice* may have been one of the most critically slammed films of the year, but, in spite of that, still earned enough at the box office to make it on to the top ten list in the number eighth slot. D.C.'s *Suicide Squad*, a superhero movie fielding a team made up exclusively of supervillains, wasn't quite as widely panned as *Batman v Superman: Dawn of Justice*, but in general didn't do very well critically; and again, in spite of that, it did well enough at the box office to make it on to the top ten list, in ninth place.

A couple of attempts to continue existing franchises didn't perform terribly at the box office, but probably didn't do well enough not to be disappointing to their producers either: *Star Trek Beyond*, finishing at fifteenth place in the top twenty list, and *X-Men: Apocalypse*, finishing at sixteenth place. It remains to be seen whether the numbers they generated were good enough to continue the franchises. With *Star Trek* about to start appearing as an original series on television again, I suspect we may have seen the last *Star Trek* theatrical movie for a while, while my guess is that there will probably be more X-Men films—but who knows? The Hollywood execs certainly don't consult *me* before making their decisions. Several attempts to revive older franchises fared even worse, *Independence Day: Resurgence* coming in at the twenty-seventh place, *Ghostbusters* at number twenty-one, *Teenage Mutant Ninja Turtles: Out of the Shadows* at number thirty-seven, *Alice Through the Looking Glass* at number thirty-nine, and *Pete's Dragon* at number forty. You're probably unlikely to see any more movies in those franchises. A number of attempts to start new action-movie franchises—*Warcraft* at sixty-eighth place, *Gods of Egypt* at eighty-seventh place, *Assassin's Creed* at sixty-three place, and *The Huntsman: Winter's War* at number sixty-six—probably should all be considered outright failures, and you probably won't be hearing anything more from them, either.

By almost universal critical acclaim, and equally widespread good fan word-of-mouth, the best genre movie of the year was probably *Arrival*, based on a story by SF writer Ted Chiang, which claimed twenty-ninth place in the top hundred list—not spectacular, but not bad for a quiet, thoughtful, cerebral SF film that required the audience to do some actual thinking in order to appreciate it. As far as I can tell, it may have been the *only* "serious" science fiction film of the year, and while it didn't earn as much as the other serious science fiction film of recent years to make an attempt to use real science, *The Martian*, it still did fairly well—a hopeful sign if we expect to see more such movies in the future.

Coming up in 2017 are a flood of genre movies of one sort or another, including a slew of superhero movies from both Marvel and DC—*Guardians of the Galaxy, Vol. 2*, *Thor; Ragnarok*, *Logan*, *Spider-Man: Homecoming*, *Justice League*, *Wonder Woman*—a new Pirates of the Caribbean movie, *Pirates of the Caribbean: Dead Men Tell No Tales*, a film version of Stephen King's *The Dark Tower*, a new flamboyant space opera from the director of *The Fifth Element*, *Valerian and the City of a Thousand Planets*, a live-action version of Disney's *Beauty and the Beast*, yet another remake of *King Kong*, *Kong: Skull Island*, a remake of *The Mummy* (with, unlikely as this sounds, Tom Cruise in the title role), a new movie in the Alien franchise, *Alien: Covenant*, and, perhaps most eagerly awaited, a sequel to *Blade Runner*, *Blade Runner 2049*, and a new Star Wars movie, *Star Wars: The Last Jedi*.

Once there were few genre shows on television, and they remained thin on the ground for decades, but today there are so many of them on television in one form or another (including forms that didn't exist a few years ago, like original programming being offered on streaming video), with more coming along all the time, that it's become difficult to keep track of them all. By my count, there are now more than eighty genre shows of one sort or another—SF, superhero shows, fantasy—currently accessible on your TV, and that doesn't even count the horror shows or the animated series, which I generally don't pay a lot of attention to. With so many shows to deal with, it's clear that I'll only be able to mention a few of the more popular shows, so if I miss mentioning your favorite show, you have my apologies.

HBO's *Game of Thrones*, based on the best-selling fantasy series by George R. R. Martin, is rumored to have only one more season (or possibly two partial seasons) left to go, but is still the most prestigious and successful fantasy show on television, treated with remarkable respect critically and once again sweeping the Emmys. New series *Westworld*, an intelligent and tricky series version of the old SF movie of the same name, is obviously being groomed by HBO as a replacement for *Game of Thrones* when that series finally ends, and so far seems to be doing well both financially and critically. Other top-notch cable shows include *The Expanse* (based on a series of space opera novels by James S. A. Corey), *The Man in the High Castle* (based on the Hugo-winning alternate history novel by Philip K. Dick), *The Magicians* (based on the best-selling novel by Lev Grossman), *Dirk Gently's Holistic Detective Agency* (based on a novel by Douglas Adams), *The Shannara Chronicles* (based on the series of novels by Terry Brooks), and *Outlander* (based on a series of novels by Diana Gabaldon).

An area that didn't even exist a few years ago, more and more shows are becoming available only as streaming video from servers such as Amazon, Netflix, and Hulu, and it's clear that the floodgates are only just starting to swing open for this form of entertainment delivery. An early pioneer in this area, Marvel Studios has already established three solid hits with *Daredevil*, *Jessica Jones*, and *Luke Cage*, all renewed for new seasons, and will be adding more superhero shows such as *Iron Fist*, *The Punisher*, and a superhero team-up, *The Defenders*. Meanwhile, a solid block of superhero shows has been established on regular television by D.C., including *Arrow*, *The Flash*, *Supergirl*, and *Gotham*—leaving little doubt that this is the golden age of superhero shows. Hulu will be bringing us *Runaways*, *Future Man*, *Dimension 404*, *Queen of Shadows*, and a series version of *The Handmaid's Tale*.

Of the flood of other genre shows that hit the air in the last few years, still surviving are: *Marvel's Agents of S.H.I.E.L.D* (where characters from the Marvel cinematic universe sometimes drop in for a guest shot, so that it could be considered to be a superhero show as well), *Once Upon a Time, Last Man on Earth, Grimm, Sleepy Hollow, Stranger Things, The Librarians Legends of Tomorrow, The Originals, The 100, Orphan Black, Colony, Ash vs Evil Dead, Dark Matter, Lucifer, 12 Monkeys, Star Wars Rebels,* and *Preacher* seem to have survived, while *Agent Carter, Person of Interest, Galavant, The Muppets, Penny Dreadful, Limitless, Angel from Hell, Heroes Reborn,* and *You, Me and the Apocalypse* have not. (No doubt there are many in both categories that I've missed or gotten wrong, as sometimes the information isn't readily available or changes as studio executives rethink their decisions.)

Perennial favorites such as *Doctor Who, The Walking Dead, Supernatural, The Vampire Diaries,* and *The Simpsons* continue to roll on. *Teen Wolf* has finally died, although by the time he went, the show ought to have been called *Middle-aged Wolf* instead.

Of the upcoming shows, the most buzz seems to be being generated by the return of *Star Trek* to television, with a new series, *Star Trek: Discovery*. Some excitement is also being generated by the revival of *Twin Peaks* and *Mystery Science Theater 3000*. Also ahead are miniseries versions of Neil Gaiman's *American Gods* and *Anansi Boys,* and miniseries versions of Kim Stanley Robinson's *Red Mars,* Len Deighton's *SS-GB,* John Scalzi's *Old Man's War,* Philip José Farmer's *Riverworld,* Robert Holdstock's *The Mythago Cycle,* and Joe Haldeman's *The Forever War* continue to be rumored—although how many of these promised shows actually show up is anyone's guess.

The 74th World Science Fiction Convention, MidAmeriCon II, was held in Kansas City, Missouri, at the Bartle Hall Convention Center, from August 17 to August 21, 2016. The 2016 Hugo Awards, presented at MidAmeriCon II, were: Best Novel, *The Fifth Season,* by N. K. L. Jemisin; Best Novella, *Binti,* by Nnedi Okorafor; Best Novelette, "Folding Beijing," by Hao Jingfang; Best Short Story, "Cat Pictures Please," by Naomi Kritzer; Best Graphic Story, *The Sandman: Overture,* by Neil Gaiman, art by J. H. Williams III; Best Related Work, No Award; Best Professional Editor, Long Form, Sheila E. Gilbert; Best Professional Editor, Short Form, Ellen Datlow; Best Professional Artist, Abigail Larson; Best Dramatic Presentation (short form), *Jessica Jones: "AKA Smile"*; Best Dramatic Presentation (long form), *The Martian;* Best Semiprozine, *Uncanny;* Best Fanzine, *File 770;* Best Fancast, No Award; Best Fan Writer, Mike Glyer; Best Fan Artist, Steve Stiles; plus the John W. Campbell Award for Best New Writer to Andy Weir.

The 2015 Nebula Awards, presented at a banquet at the Palmer House Hilton in Chicago, Illinois, on May 14, 2016, were: Best Novel, *Uprooted,* by Naomi Novik; Best Novella, *Binti,* by Nnedi Okorafor; Best Novelette, "Our Lady of the Open Road" by Sarah Pinsker; Best Short Story, "Hungry Daughters of Starving Mothers," by Alyssa Wong; Ray Bradbury Award, *Mad Max: Fury Road;* the Andre Norton Award to *Updraft,* by Fran Wilde; the Kate Wilhelm Solstice Award to Sir Terry Pratchett; the Kevin O' Donnell Jr. Service to SFWA Award to Lawrence M. Schoen; and the Damon Knight Memorial Grand Master Award to C. J. Cherryh.

The 2016 World Fantasy Awards, presented at a banquet on October 30, 2016, at the Hyatt Regency in Columbus, Ohio, during the Forty-second Annual World Fantasy Convention, were: Best Novel, *The Chimes*, by Anna Smaill; Best Long Fiction, "The Unlicensed Magician," by Kelly Barnhill; Best Short Fiction, "Hungry Daughters of Starving Mothers," by Alyssa Wong; Best Collection, *Bone Swans*, by C.S.E. Cooney; Best Anthology, *She Walks in Shadows*, edited by Silvia Moreno-Garcia and Paula R. Stiles; Best Artist, Galen Dara; Special Award (Professional), to Stephen Jones for *The Art of Horror*; Special Award (Non-Professional), to John O'Neill for *Black Gate*. Plus Lifetime Achievement Awards to David G. Hartwell and Andrzej Sapkowski.

The 2015 Bram Stoker Awards, presented by the Horror Writers of America on May 14, 2016, during the First Annual Stoker Convention at the Flamingo Hotel in Las Vegas, Nevada, were: Superior Achievement in a Novel, *A Head Full of Ghosts*, by Paul Tremblay; Superior Achievement in a First Novel, *Mr. Suicide*, by Nicole Cushing; Superior Achievement in a Young Adult Novel, *Devil's Pocket*, by John Dixon; Superior Achievement in Long Fiction, "Little Dead Red," by Mercedes M. Yardley; Superior Achievement in Short Fiction, "Happy Joe's Rest Stop," by John Palisano; Superior Achievement in a Fiction Collection, *While the Black Stars Burn*, by Lucy Snyder; Superior Achievement in an Anthology, *The Library of the Dead*, edited by Michael Bailey; Superior Achievement in Nonfiction, *The Art of Horror*, by Stephen Jones; Superior Achievement in a Poetry Collection, *Eden Underground*, by Alessandro Manzetti; Superior Achievement in a Graphic Novel, *Shadow Show: Stories in Celebration of Ray Bradbury*, edited by Sam Weller and Mort Castle; Superior Achievement in a Screenplay, *It Follows*.

The 2015 John W. Campbell Memorial Award was won by *Radiomen*, by Eleanor Lerman.

The 2015 Theodore Sturgeon Memorial Award for Best Short Story was won by: "The Game of Smash and Recovery," by Kelly Link.

The 2016 Philip K. Dick Memorial Award went to *Apex*, by Ramez Naam.

The 2016 Arthur C. Clarke award was won by *Children of Time*, by Adrian Tchaikovsky.

The 2015 James Tiptree, Jr. Memorial Award was won by "The New Mother," by Eugene Fischer, and *Lizard Radio*, by Pat Schmatz (tie).

The 2016 Sidewise Award for Alternate History went to (Long Form): *The Big Lie*, by Julie Mayhew; and (Short Form): "It Doesn't Matter Anymore," by Bill Crider.

Dead in 2016 or early 2017 were:
RICHARD ADAMS, 96, British fantasy writer, author of *Shardik*, *The Plague Dogs*, and what many (myself included) consider one of the three or four best fantasy novels published in English in the second half of the twentieth century, international bestseller *Watership Down*; **SHERI S. TEPPER**, 87, SF and fantasy writer, winner of the lifetime achievement award from the World Fantasy Convention, author of *The Gate to Women's Country*, *Grass*, *Beauty*, and *Shadow's End*; **UMBERTO ECO**, 84, Italian scholar and novelist, best known for the novels *The Name of the*

Rose and *Foucault's Pendulum*; **W. P. KINSELLA**, 81, author best known for his novel *Shoeless Joe*, which was made into the movie *Field of Dreams*, also the author of *The Iowa Baseball Confederacy* and *If Wishes Were Horses*; **KATHERINE DUNN**, 70, writer and journalist, best known for the cult classic *Geek Love*; **ED GORMAN**, 74, prominent crime and horror writer and anthologist who also wrote some SF; **DAVID LAKE**, 86, SF writer, author of *The Man Who Loved Morlocks*, *Ring of Truth*, and *West of the Moon*; **BUD WEBSTER**, 63, writer, SF scholar and historian; **CAROLYN SEE**, 82, writer whose SF works included *Golden Days* and *There Will Never Be Another You*; **JUSTIN LEIBER**, 77, SF writer and philosopher, son of the late SF writer Fritz Leiber; **MARK JUSTICE**, 56, writer and radio host; **LOIS DUNCAN**, 82, author of fifty books, including *I Know What You Did Last Summer*, *A Gift of Magic*, and *Down a Dark Hall*; **JAKE PAGE**, 80, nonfiction writer of science and natural history, also a mystery novelist who wrote some SF; **PETER WESTON**, 73, British editor and fan; **LINN PRENTIS**, 72, longtime literary agent; **ROBERT E. WEINBERG**, 70, author, editor, and publisher, as well as an anthologist who specialized in salvaging material from the pulp era; **WILLIAM BOND "BILL" WARREN**, 73, film historian and critic whose best-known book of reviews of SF movies was probably *Keep Watching the Skies!*; **KATHLEEN A. BELLAMY**, 58, managing editor and art director for *Orson Scott Card's Intergalactic Medicine Show*; **JILL CALVERT**, 63, artist and cover illustrator; **DAVID A. KYLE**, 97, longtime fan, a member of First Fandom, one of the founding members of the Futurians; **LARRY SMITH**, 70, convention bookseller and con-runner, longtime fan; **PEGGY RANSON**, 67, well-known fan artist; **GENE WILDER**, 83, world-famous film actor, best known in the genre for leading roles in such movies as *Young Frankenstein*, *Willy Wonka and the Chocolate Factory*, *The Producers*, and *Blazing Saddles*; **CARRIE FISHER**, 60, actress and writer, best known to genre audiences for her role as Princess Leia in the original *Star Wars* movie and its sequels, also the author of *Postcards From the Edge*, which was made into a movie of the same name. (Her mother, Debbie Reynolds, 84, internationally known actress, singer, and performer, with no real genre connection—although everybody will recognize her from *Singin' in the Rain*—passed away a day later.) **KENNY BAKER**, 81, film actor best known for his role as R2-D2 in the *Star Wars* films, also appeared in *Time Bandits* and *Labyrinth*; **JOHN ZACHERLE**, 98, TV personality and host of such campy horror shows as *Chiller Theater*, also the editor of anthologies *Zacherley's Vulture Stew* and *Zacherley's Midnight Snacks*; **PETER VAUGHAN**, 93, British actor, known to genre audiences from roles in *Village of the Damned*, *Time Bandits*, *Brazil*, *Fatherland*, and TV's *Game of Thrones*; **DAVID HUDDLESTON**, 85, film actor best known for roles in *Blazing Saddles* and TV's *Bewitched*; **ROBERT C. "BOB" PETERSON**, 95, longtime fan and publisher of SF bibliographies; **DORIS LORRAINE MEYER**, 88, mother of SF writer Susan Palwick; **VIOLET GWENDOLENE LUNAN**, 102, mother of SF writer Duncan Lunan; **KATE YULE**, 56, wife of SF writer David D. Levine; **BOB FELICE, SR.**, 75, husband of SF writer Cynthia Felice.

THE YEAR'S BEST

SCIENCE FICTION

terminal

Lavie Tidhar

Here's a beautifully written and ultimately quite moving portrait of the ordinary people who make up an unlikely crop of astronauts in the future—those who have accepted the government's offer of a one-way trip to Mars.

Lavie Tidhar grew up on a kibbutz in Israel, has traveled widely in Africa and Asia, and has lived in London, the South Pacific island of Vanuatu, and Laos; after a spell in Tel Aviv, he's currently living back in England again. He is the winner of the 2003 Clarke-Bradbury Prize (awarded by the European Space Agency), was the editor of Michael Marshall Smith: The Annotated Bibliography, *and the anthologies* A Dick & Jane Primer for Adults, *the three-volume* The Apex Book of World SF series, *and two anthologies edited with Rebecca Levene,* Jews vs. Aliens *and* Jews vs. Zombies. *He is the author of the linked story collection* HebrewPunk, *and, with Nir Yaniv, the novel* The Tel Aviv Dossier, *and the novella chapbooks* An Occupation of Angels, Cloud Permutations, Jesus and the Eightfold Path, *and* Martian Sands. *A prolific short-story writer, his stories have appeared in* Interzone, Asimov's Science Fiction, Clarkesworld, Apex Magazine, Strange Horizons, Postscripts, Fantasy Magazine, Nemonymous, Infinity Plus, Aeon, The Book of Dark Wisdom, Fortean Bureau, Old Venus, *and elsewhere, and have been translated into seven languages. His novels include* The Bookman *and its two sequels,* Camera Obscura *and* The Great Game, Osama: A Novel *(which won the World Fantasy Award as the year's Best Novel in 2012),* The Violent Century, *and* A Man Lies Dreaming. *His most recent book is a big, multifaceted SF novel,* Central Station.

From above the ecliptic the swarm can be seen as a cloud of tiny bullet-shaped insects, their hulls, packed with photovoltaic cells, capturing the sunlight; tiny, tiny flames burning in the vastness of the dark.

They crawl with unbearable slowness across this small section of near space, tiny beetles climbing a sheer obsidian rock face. Only the sun remains constant. The sun, always, dominates their sky.

Inside each jalopy are instrument panels and their like; a sleeping compartment where you must float your way into the secured sleeping bag; a toilet to strap your-self to; a kitchen to prepare your meal supply; and windows to look out of. With ev-ery passing day the distance from Earth increases and the time lag grows a tiny bit longer and the streaming of communication becomes more echoey, the most acute reminder of that finite parting as the blue-green egg that is Earth revolves and grows smaller in your window, and you stand there, sometimes for hours at a time, fingers splayed against the plastic, staring at what has gone and will never come again, for your destination is terminal.

There is such freedom in the letting go.

There is the music. Mei listens to the music, endlessly. Alone she floats in her cheap jalopy, and the music soars all about her, an archive of all the music of Earth stored in five hundred terabyte or so, so that Mei can listen to anything ever written and performed, should she so choose, and so she does, in a glorious random selection as the jalopy moves in the endless swarm from Earth to Terminal. Chopin's Études bring a sharp memory of rain and the smell of wet grass, of damp books and days spent in bed, staring out of windows, the feel of soft sheets and a warm pyjama, a steaming mug of tea. Mei listens to Vanuatu stringband songs in pidgin English, evocative of palm trees and sand beaches and graceful men swaying in the wind; she listens to Congolese Kwasa-Kwasa and dances, floating, shaking and rolling in weightlessness, the music like an infectious laugh and hot tropical rain. The Beatles sing "Here Comes the Sun," Mozart's Requiem trails off unfinished, David Bowie's "Space Oddity" haunts the cramped confines of the jalopy: the human race speaks to Mei through notes like precise mathematical notations and, alone, she floats in space, remembering in the way music always makes you remember.

She is not unhappy.

At first there was something seemingly inhuman about using the toilets. It is like a hungry machine, breathing and spitting, and Mei must ride it, strapping herself into leg restraints, attaching the urine funnel which gurgles and hisses as Mei evac-uates waste. Now the toilet is like an old friend, its conversation a constant murmur, and she climbs in and out without conscious notice.

At first Mei slept and woke up to a regiment of day and night, but a month out of Earth orbit the old order began to slowly crumble and now she sleeps and wakes when she wants, making day and night appear as if by magic, by a wave of her hand. Still, she maintains a routine, of washing and the brushing of teeth, of wearing cloth-ing, a pretence at humanity which is sometimes hard to maintain being alone. A person is defined by other people.

Three months out of Earth and it's hard to picture where you'd left, where you're going. And always that word, like a whisper out of nowhere, Terminal, Terminal . . .

Mei floats and turns slowly in space, listening to the Beach Boys.

"I have to do this."

"You don't have to," she says. "You don't have to do anything. What you mean is that you want to. You want to do it. You think it makes you special but it doesn't make you special if everyone else is doing it." She looks at him with fierce black eyes and tucks a strand of hair, clumped together in her perspiration, behind her ear. He loves her very much at that moment, that fierce protectiveness, the fact someone, anyone, can look at you that way, can look at you and feel love.

"Not everyone is doing it."

They're sitting in a cafe outdoors and it is hot, it is very hot, and overhead the twin Petronas Towers rise like silver rockets into the air. In the square outside KLCC the water features twinkle in the sun and tourists snap photos and waiters glide like unenthusiastic penguins amongst the clientele. He drinks from his kopi ice and traces a trail of moisture on the face of the glass, slowly. "You are not *dying*," she says, at last, the words coming as from a great distance. He nods, reluctantly. It is true. He is not dying, immediately, but only in the sense that all living things are dying, that it is a trajectory, the way a jalopy makes its slow but finite way from Earth to Mars. Speaking of jalopies there is a stand under the awnings for such stands are everywhere now and a man shouting through the sound system to come one come all and take the ultimate trip—and so on, and so forth.

But more than that implicit in her words is the question. Is he dying? In the more immediate sense? "No," he says. "But."

That word lies heavy in the hot and humid air.

She is still attractive to him, even now: even after thirty years, three kids now grown and gone into the world, her hair no longer black all over but flecked with strands of white and grey, his own hair mostly gone, their hands, touching lightly across the table, both showing the signs of gravity and age. And how could he explain?

"Space," he tries to say. "The dark starry night which is eternal and forever, or as long as these words mean something in between the beginning and the end of space and time." But really is it selfish, is it not inherently *selfish* to want to leave, to go, up there and beyond—for what? It makes no sense or no more sense than anything else you do or don't.

"Responsibility," she says. "Commitment. Love, damn it, Haziq! You're not a child, playing with toys, with, with . . . with *spaceships* or whatever. You have children, a family, we'll soon have grandkids if I know Omar, what will they do without you?"

These hypothetical people, not yet born, already laying demands to his time, his being. To be human is to exist in potentia, unborn responsibilities rising like butterflies in a great big obscuring cloud. He waves his hand in front of his face but whether it is to shoo them away or because of the heat he cannot say. "We always said we won't stand in each other's way," he begins, but awkwardly, and she starts to cry, silently, making no move to wipe away the tears, and he feels a great tenderness but also anger, and the combination shocks him. "I have never asked for anything," he says. "I have . . . have I not been a good son, a good father, a good husband? I never asked for anything—" and he remembers sneaking away one night, five years before, and wandering the Petaling Street Market with television screens blaring and watching a launch, and a thin string of pearls, broken, scattered across space . . . perhaps it was then, perhaps it was earlier, or once when he was a boy and he had seen pictures of a vast red planet unmarred by human feet . . .

"What did I ask," she says, "did I complain, did I aspire, did I not fulfill what you and I both wanted? Yes, it is selfish to want to go, and it is selfish to ask you to stay, but if you go, Haziq, you won't come back. You won't ever come back."

And he says, "I know," and she shakes her head, and she is no longer crying, and there is that hard, practical look in her eyes, the one he was always a little bit afraid of. She picks up the bill and roots in her purse and brings out the money and puts it on the table. "I have to go," she says, "I have an appointment at the hair dresser's." She gets up and he does not stand to stop her, and she walks away; and he knows that all he has to do is follow her; and yet he doesn't, he remains seated, watching her weaving her way through the crowds, until she disappears inside the giant mall; and she never once looks back.

But really it is the sick, the slowly dying, those who have nothing to lose, those un-tied by earthly bonds, those whose spirits are as light as air: the loners and the crazy and worst of all the artists, so many artists, each convinced in his or her own way of the uniqueness of the opportunity, exchanging life for immortality, floating in space heels and toe heels and toe, transmuting space into art in the way of the dead, for they are legally dead, now, each in his or her own jalopy, this cheap mass manufac-tured container made for this one singular trip, from this planet to the next, from the living world to the dead one.

"Sign here, initial here, and here, and here—" and what does it feel like for those everyday astronauts, those would-be Martians, departing their homes for one last time, a last glance back, some leaving gladly, some tearfully, some with indifference: these Terminals, these walking dead, having signed over their assets, completed their wills, attended, in some instances, their very own wakes: leaving with nothing, boarding taxis or flights in daytime or night, to the launch site for rudimentary train-ing of instruments they will never have use to control, from Earth to orbit in a space plane, a reusable launch vehicle, and thence to Gateway, in Low Earth Orbit, that ramshackle construction floating like a spider web in the skies of Earth, made up of modules some new some decades old, joined together in an ungainly fashion, a makeshift thing.

Here we are all astronauts. The permanent staff is multinational, harassed, monkey-like we climb heel and toe heel and toe, handholds along the walls no up no down but three-dimensional space as a many splendored thing. Here the astro-nauts are trained hastily in maintaining their craft and themselves and the jalopies extend out of Gateway, beyond orbit, thousands of cheap little tin cans aimed like skipping stones at the big red rock yonder.

Here, too, you can still change your mind. Here comes a man now, a big man, an American man, with very white face and hands, a man used to being in control, a man used to being deferred to—an artist, in fact; a writer. He had made his money imagining the way the future was, but the future had passed him by and he found himself spending his time on message boards and the like, bemoaning youth and their folly. Now he has a new lease on life, or thought he had, with this plan of going into space, to Terminal Beach: six months floating in a tin can high above no world, to write his masterpiece, the thing he is to be remembered by, his *novel*, damn it, in which he's to lay down his entire philosophical framework of a libertarian bent: only he has, at the last moment, perhaps on smelling the interior of his assigned jalopy, changed his mind. Now he comes inexpertly floating like a beach ball down the shaft, bouncing here and there from the walls and bellowing for the agent, those sleazy jalopymen, for the final signature on the contract is digital, and sent once the jalopy is slingshot to Mars. It takes three orderlies to hold him down and a nurse injects him with something to calm him down. Later he would go back down the gravity well, poorer yet wiser, but never again will he write that novel: space eludes him.

Meanwhile the nurse helps carry the now-unconscious American down to the hospital suite, a house-sized unit overlooking the curve of the Earth. Her name is Eliza and she watches day chase night across the globe and looks for her home, for the islands of the Philippines to come into view, their lights scattered like shards of shining glass, but it is the wrong time to see them. She monitors the IV distractedly, feeling tiredness wash over her like the first exploratory wave of a grey and endless sea. For Eliza space means always being in sight of this great living world, this Earth, its oceans and its green landmasses and its bright night lights, a world that dominates her view, always, that glares like an eye through pale white clouds. To be this close to it and yet to see it separate, not of it but apart, is an amazing thing; while beyond, where the Terminals go, or further yet, where the stars coalesce as thick as clouds, who knows what lies? And she fingers the gold cross on the chain around her neck, as she always does when she thinks of things alien beyond knowing, and she shudders, just a little bit; but everywhere else, so far, the universe is silent, and we alone shout.

"Hello? Is it me you're looking for?"

"Who is this?"

"Hello?"

"This is jalopy A-5011 sending out a call to the faithful to prayer—"

"This is Bremen in B-9012, is there anyone there? Hello? I am very weak. Is there a doctor, can you help me, I do not think I'll make it to the rock, hello, hello—"

"This is jalopy B-2031 to jalopy C-3398, bishop to king 7, I said bishop to king 7, take that Shen you twisted old fruit!"

"Hello? Has anyone heard from Shiri Applebaum in C-5591, has anyone heard from Shiri Applebaum in C-5591, she has not been in touch in two days and I am getting worried, this is Robin in C-5523, we were at Gateway together before the launch, hello, hello—"

"Hello—"

Mei turns down the volume of the music and listens to the endless chatter of the swarm rise alongside it, day or night neither of which matter or exist here, unbound by planetary rotation and that old artificial divide of darkness and the light. Many like Mei have abandoned the twenty-four-hour cycle to sleep and rise ceaselessly and almost incessantly with some desperate need to *experience* all of this, this one-time-only journey, this slow beetle's crawl across trans-solar space. Mei swoops and turns with the music and the chatter and she idly wonders of the fate to have befallen Shiri Applebaum in C-5591: is she merely keeping quiet or is she dead or in a coma, never to wake up again, only her corpse and her cheap little jalopy hitting the surface of Mars in ninety more days? Across the swarm's radio network the muezzin in A-5011 sends out the call to prayer, the singsong words so beautiful that Mei stops, suspended in midair, and breathes deeply, her chest rising and falling steadily, space all around her. She has degenerative bone disease, there isn't a question of starting a new life at Terminal, only this achingly beautiful song that rises all about her, and the stars, and silent space.

Two days later Bremen's calls abruptly cease. B-9012 still hurtles on with the rest towards Mars. Haziq tries to picture Bremen: what was he like? What did he love? He thinks he remembers him, vaguely, a once-fat man now wasted with folded awkward skin, large glasses, a Scandinavian man maybe, Haziq thought, but all he knows or will ever know of Bremen is the man's voice on the radio bouncing from jalopy to jalopy and on to Earth where jalopy-chasers scan the bands and listen in a sort of awed or voyeuristic pleasure.

"This is Haziq, C-6173 . . ." he coughs and clears his throat. He drinks his miso soup awkwardly, suckling from its pouch. He sits formally, strapped by Velcro, the tray of food before him, and out of his window he stares not back to Earth or forward to Mars but directly onto the swarm, trying to picture each man and woman inside, trying to imagine what brought them here. Does one need a reason? Haziq wonders. Or is it merely that gradual feeling of discomfort in one's own life, one's own skin, a slowly-dawning realisation that you have passed like a grey ghost through your own life, leaving no impression, that soon you might fade away entirely, to dust and ash and nothingness, a mild regret in your children's minds that they never really knew you at all.

"This is Haziq, C-6173, is there anyone hearing me, my name is Haziq and I am going to Terminal—" and a sudden excitement takes him, "My name is Haziq and I am going to Terminal!" he shouts, and all around him the endless chatter rises, of humans in space, so needy for talk like sustenance, "We're all going to Terminal!" and Haziq, shy again, says, "Please, is there anyone there, won't someone talk to me. What is it like, on Terminal?"

But that is a question that brings down the silence; it is there in the echoes of words ords rds and in the pauses, in punctuation missing or overstated, in the endless chess moves, worried queries, unwanted confessionals, declarations of love, in this desperate sudden need that binds them together, the swarm, and makes all that has been before become obsolete, lose definition and meaning. For the past is a world one cannot return to, and the future is a world none had seen.

Mei floats half-asleep half-awake, but the voice awakens her, why this voice she never knows, cannot articulate. "Hello. Hello. Hello . . ." and she swims through the air to the kitchenette and heats up tea and drinks it from the suction cup. There are no fizzy drinks on board the jalopies, the lack of gravity would not separate liquid and gas in the human stomach and the astronaut would wet burp vomit. Mei drinks slowly, carefully, all her movements are careful. "Hello?" she says, "Hello, this is Mei in A-3357, this is Mei in A-3357, can you hear me, Haziq, can you hear me?"

A pause, a micro-silence, the air filled with the hundreds of other conversations through which a voice, his voice, says, "This is Haziq! Hello A-3357, hello!"

"Hello," Mei says, surprised and strangely happy, and she realises it is the first time she has spoken in three months. "Let me tell you, Haziq," she says, and her voice is like music between worlds, "let me tell you about Terminal."

It was raining in the city. She had come out of the hospital and looked up at the sky and saw nothing there, no stars no sun, just clouds and smoke and fog. It rained, the rain collected in rainbow puddles in the street, the chemicals inside it painted the world and made it brighter. There was a jalopy vendor on the corner of the street, above his head a promotional video in 3D, and she was drawn to it. The vendor played loud K-pop and the film looped in on itself, but Mei didn't mind the vendor's shouts, the smell of acid rain or frying pork sticks and garlic or the music's beat which rolled on like thunder. Mei stood and rested against the stand and watched the video play. The vendor gave her glasses, embossed with the jalopy sub-agent's logo. She watched the swarm like a majestic silver web spread out across space, hurtling (or so it seemed) from Earth to Mars. The red planet was so beautiful and round, its dry seas and massive mountain peaks, its volcanoes and canals. She watched the polar ice caps. Watched Mons Olympus breaking out of the atmosphere. Imagined a mountain so high it reached up into space. Imagined women like her climbing it, smaller than ants but with that same ferocious dedication. Somewhere on that world was Terminal.

"Picture yourself standing on the red sands for the very first time," she tells Haziq, her voice the same singsong of the muezzin at prayer, "that very first step, the mark of your boot in the fine sand. It won't stay there forever, you know. This is not the moon, the winds will come and sweep it away, reminding you of the temporality of all living things." And she pictures Armstrong on the moon, that first impossible step, the mark of the boots still there in the lunar dust. "But you are on a different world now," she says, to Haziq or to herself, or to the others listening, and the jalopy-chasers back on Earth. "With different moons hanging like fruit in the sky. And you take that first step in your suit, the gravity hits you suddenly, you are barely able to drag yourself out of the jalopy, everything is labour and pain. Who knew gravity could hurt so much," she says, as though in wonder. She closes her eyes and floats slowly upwards, picturing it. She can see it so clearly, Terminal Beach where the jalopies wash ashore, endlessly, like seashells, as far as the eye can see the sand is covered in the units out of which a temporary city rises, a tent city, all those bright objects on the sand. "And as you emerge into the sunlight they stand there, welcoming you, can you see them? In suits and helmets they extend open arms, those Martians, Come, they say, over the radio comms, come, and you follow, painfully and awkwardly, leaving tracks in the sand, into the temporary domes and the linked together jalopies and the underground caves which they are digging, always, extending this makeshift city downwards, and you pass through the airlock and take off your helmet and breathe the air, and you are no longer alone, you are amongst people, real people, not just voices carried on the solar winds."

She falls silent, then. Breathes the limited air of the cabin. "They would be planting seeds," she says, softly, "underground, and in greenhouses, all the plants of Earth, a paradise of watermelons and orchids, of frangipani and durian, jasmine and rambutan . . ." she breathes deeply, evenly. The pain is just a part of her, now. She no longer takes the pills they gave her. She wants to be herself; pain and all.

In jalopies scattered across this narrow silver band astronauts like canned sardines marinate in their own stale sweat and listen to her voice. Her words, converted into a signal inaudible by human ears, travel across local space for whole minutes until they hit the Earth's atmosphere at last, already old and outdated, a record of a past event; here they bounce off the Earth to the ionosphere and back again, jaggedy waves like a terminal patient's heart monitor circumnavigating this rotating globe until they are deciphered by machines and converted once more into sound.

Mei's voice speaking into rooms, across hospital beds, in dark bars filled with the fug of electronic cigarettes' smokelike vapoured steam, in lonely bedrooms where her voice keeps company to cats, in cabs driving through rain and from tinny speakers on white sand beaches where coconut crabs emerge into sunset, their blue metallic shells glinting like jalopies. Mei's voice soothes unease and fills the jalopy-chasers' minds with bright images, a panoramic view of a red world seen from space, suspended against the blackness of space; the profusion of bright galaxies and stars behind it is like a movie screen.

"Take a step, and then another and another. The sunlight caresses your skin but its rays have travelled longer to reach you, and when you raise your head the sun shines down from a clay-red sun, and you know you will never again see the sky blue. Think of that light. It has travelled longer and faster than you ever will, its speed in vacuum a constant 299,792,458 meters per second. Think of that number, that strange little fundamental constant, seemingly arbitrary: around that number faith can be woven and broken like silk, for is it a randomly created universe we live in or an ordained one? Why the speed of light, why the gravitational constant, why Planck's? And as you stand there, healthy or ill, on the sands of Terminal Beach and raise your face to the sun, are you happy or sad?"

Mei's voice makes them wonder, some simply and with devotion, some uneasily. But wonder they do and some will go outside one day and encounter the ubiquitous stand of a jalopyman and be seduced by its simple promise, abandon everything to gain a nebulous idea, that boot mark in the fine-grained red sand, so easily wiped away by the winds.

And Mei tells Haziq about Olympus Mons and its shadow falling on the land and its peak in space, she tells him of the falling snow, made of frozen carbon dioxide, of men and women becoming children again building snowmen in the airless atmosphere, and she tells him of the Valles Marineris where they go suited up hand in gloved hand through the canyons whose walls rise above them, east of Tharsis.

Perhaps it is then that Haziq falls in love, a little bit, through walls and vacuum, the way a boy does, not with a real person but with an ideal, an image. Not the way he had fallen in love with his wife, not even the way he loves his children, who talk to him across the planetary gap, their words and moving images beamed to him from Earth, but they seldom do, any more, it is as if they had resigned themselves to his departure, as if by crossing the atmosphere into space he had already died and they were done with mourning.

It is her voice he fastens onto; almost greedily; with need. And as for Mei, it is as if she had absorbed the silence of three months and more than a hundred million kilometres, consumed it somehow, was sustained by it, her own silence with only the music for company, and now she must speak, speak only for the sake of it, like eating or breathing or making love, the first two of which she will soon do no more and the last of which is already gone, a thing of the past. And so she tells the swarm about Terminal.

But what is Terminal? Eliza wonders, floating in the corridors of Gateway, watching the RLVs rise into low Earth orbit, the continents shifting past, the clouds swirling, endlessly, this whole strange giant spaceship planet as it travels at 1200 kilometres an hour around the sun, while at the same time Earth, Mars, Venus, Sun and all travel at a nearly 800,000 kilometres per hour around the centre of the galaxy, while *at the same time* this speed machine, Earth and sun and the galaxy itself move at 1000 kilometres per *second* towards the Great Attractor, that most mysterious of gravitational enigmas, this anomaly of mass that pulls to it the Milky Way as if it were a pebble: all this and we think we're *still*, and it makes Eliza dizzy just to think about it.

But she thinks of such things more and more. Space changes you, somehow. It tears you out of certainties, it makes you see your world at a distance, no longer of it but apart. It makes her sad, the old certainties washed away, and more and more she finds herself thinking of Mars; of Terminal.

To never see your home again; your family, your mother, your uncles, brothers, sisters, aunts, cousins and second cousins and third cousins twice removed and all the rest of them: never to walk under open skies and never to sail on a sea, never to hear the sound of frogs mating by a river or hear the whooshing sound of fruit bats in the trees. All those things and all the others you will never do, and people carry bucket lists around with them before they become Terminal, but at long last everything they ever knew and owned is gone and then there is only the jalopy confines, only that and the stars in the window and the voice of the swarm. And Eliza thinks that maybe she wouldn't mind leaving it all behind, just for a chance at . . . what? something so untenable, as will-o'-the-wisp as ideology or faith and yet as hard and precisely defined as prime numbers or fundamental constants. Perhaps it is the way Irish immigrants felt on going to America, with nothing but a vague hope that the future would be different than the past. Eliza had been to nursing school, had loved, had seen the world rotate below her; had been to space, had worked on amputations, births, tumour removals, fevers turned fatal, transfusions and malarias, has held a patient's hand as she died or dried a boy's tears or made a cup of tea for the bereaved, monitored IVs, changed sheets and bedpans, took blood and gave injections, and now she floats in free fall high above the world, watching the Terminals come and go, come and go, endlessly, and the string of silver jalopies extends in a great horde from Earth's orbit to the Martian surface, and she imagines jalopies fall down like silver drops of rain, gently they glide down through the thin Martian atmosphere to land on the alien sands.

She pictures Terminal and listens to Mei's voice, one amongst so many but somehow it is the voice others return to, it is as though Mei speaks for all of them, telling them of the city being built out of cheap used bruised jalopies, the way Gateway had been put together, a lot of mismatched units joined up, and she tells them, you could fall in love again, with yourself, with another, with a world.

"Why?" Mei says to Haziq, one night period, a month away from planetfall. "Why did you do it?"

"Why did I go?"

She waits; she likes his voice. She floats in the cabin, her mind like a calm sea. She listens to the sounds of the jalopy, the instruments and the toilet and the creaks and rustle of all the invisible things. She is taking the pills again, she must, for the pain is too great now, and the morphine, so innocent a substance to come out like blood out of the vibrant red poppies, is helping. She knows she is addicted. She knows it won't last. It makes her laugh. Everything delights her. The music is all around her now, Lao singing accompanied by a khene changing into South African kwaito becoming reggae from PNG.

"I don't know," Haziq says. He sounds so vulnerable then. Mei says, "You were married."

"Yes."

Curiosity compels her. "Why didn't she come with you?"

"She would never have come with me," Haziq says, and Mei feels her heart shudder insider her like a caged bird and she says, "But you didn't ask."

"No," Haziq says. The long silence is interrupted by others on the shared primitive radio band, hellos and groans and threats and prayers, and someone singing, drunk.

"No," Haziq says. "I didn't ask."

One month to planetfall. And Mei falls silent. Haziq tries to raise her on the radio but there is no reply. "Hello, hello, this is Haziq, C-6173, this is Haziq, C-6173, has anyone heard from Mei in A-3357, has anyone heard from Mei?"

"This is Henrik in D-7479, I am in a great deal of pain, could somebody help me? Please could somebody help me?"

"This is Cobb in E-1255, I have figured it all out, there is no Mars, they lied to us, we'll die in these tin cans, how much air, how much air is left?"

"This is jalopy B-2031 to jalopy C-3398, queen to pawn 4, I said queen to pawn 4, and check and mate, take that Shen you twisted old bat!"

"This is David in B-1201, jalopy B-1200 can you hear me, jalopy B-1200 can you hear me, I love you, Joy. Will you marry me? Will you—"

"Yes! Yes!"

"We might not make it. But I feel like I know you, like I've always known you, in my mind you are as beautiful as your words."

"I will see you, I will know you, there on the red sands, there on Terminal Beach, oh, David—"

"My darling—"

"This is jalopy C-6669, will you two get a room?" and laughter on the radio waves, and shouts of cheers, congrats, mazel tov and the like. But Mei cannot be raised, her ʹlopy's silent.

Not jalopies but empty containers with nothing but air floating along with the swarm, destined for Terminal, supplements for the plants, and water and other supplies, and some say these settlers, if that's what they be, are dying faster than we can replace them but so what. They had paid for their trip. Mars is a madhouse, its inmates wander their rubbish heap town, and Mei, floating with a happy distracted mind, no longer hears even the music. And she thinks of all the things she didn't say. Of stepping out onto Terminal Beach, of coming through the airlock, yes, but then, almost immediately, coming out again, suited uncomfortably, how hard it was, to strip the jalopies of everything inside and, worse, to go on corpse duty.

She does not want to tell all this to Haziq, does not want to picture him landing, and going with the others, this gruesome initiation ceremony for the newly arrived: to check on the jalopies no longer responding, the ones that didn't open, the ones from which no one has emerged. And she hopes, without reason, that it is Haziq who finds her, no longer floating but pressed down by gravity, her fragile bones fractured and crushed; that he would know her, somehow. That he would raise her in his arms, gently, and carry her out, and lay her down on the Martian sand.

Then they would strip the jalopy and push it and join it to the others, this spider bite of a city sprawling out of those first crude jalopies to crash land, and Haziq might sleep, fitfully, in the dormitory with all the others, and then, perhaps, Mei could be buried. Or left to the Martian winds.

She imagines the wind howling through the canyons of the Valles Marinaris. Imagines the snow falling, kissing her face. Imagines the howling winds stripping her of skin and polishing her bones, imagines herself scattered at last, every tiny bit of her blown apart and spread across the planet.

And she imagines jalopies like meteorites coming down. Imagines the music the planet makes, if only you could hear it. And she closes her eyes and she smiles.

"I hope it's you . . ." she whispers, says.

"Sign here, initial here, and here, and here."

The jalopyman is young and friendly, and she knows his face if not his name. He says, perhaps in surprise or in genuine interest, for they never, usually, ask, "Are you sure you want to do it?"

And Eliza signs, and she nods, quickly, like a bird. And she pushes the pen back at him, as if to stop from changing her mind.

"I hope it's you . . ."

"Mei? Is that you? Is that you?"

But there is no one there, nothing but a scratchy echo on the radio; like the sound of desert winds.

touring with the alien

CAROLYN IVES GILMAN

Here's a story which is about just that it says it's about—a woman driving around the rural countryside in a van, stopping at scenic overlooks, spending the night at roadside rest stops. The only thing that makes this unique is the nature of the passengers who are riding with her—and that makes it not only unique, but of vital importance to the entire world.

Carolyn Ives Gilman has sold stories to The Magazine of Fantasy & Science Fiction, Interzone, Universe, Full Spectrum, Realms of Fantasy, Bending the Landscape, *and elsewhere. She is the author of five nonfiction books on frontier and American Indian history, and five novels,* Halfway Human, Arkfall, Isles of the Forsaken, Ison of the Isles, *and, most recently,* Dark Orbit. *She recently moved from St. Louis to Washington, D.C., and gone to work for the National Museum of the American Indian. She splits her time between writing science fiction and organizing exhibits about Native American history.*

The alien spaceships were beautiful, no one could deny that: towering domes of overlapping, chitinous plates in pearly dawn colors, like reflections on a tranquil sea. They appeared overnight, a dozen incongruous soap-bubble structures scattered across the North American continent. One of them blocked a major interstate in Ohio; another monopolized a stadium parking lot in Tulsa. But most stood in cornfields and forests and deserts where they caused little inconvenience.

Everyone called them spaceships, but from the beginning the experts questioned that name. NORAD had recorded no incoming landing craft, and no mother ship orbited above. That left two main possibilities: they were visitations from an alien race that traveled by some incomprehensibly advanced method; or they were a mutant eruption of Earth's own tortured ecosystem.

The domes were impervious. Probing radiation bounced off them, as did potshots from locals in the days before the military moved in to cordon off the areas. Attempts to communicate produced no reaction. All the domes did was sit there reflecting the sky in luminous, dreaming colors.

months later, the panic had subsided and even CNN had grown weary of reporting breaking news that was just the same old news. Then, entry panels began to open and out walked the translators, one per dome. They were perfectly ordinary-looking human beings who said that they had been abducted as children and had now come back to interpret between their biological race and the people who had adopted them.

Humanity learned surprisingly little from the translators. The aliens had come in peace. They had no demands and no questions. They merely wanted to sit here minding their own business for a while. They wanted to be left alone.

No one believed it.

Avery was visiting her brother when her boss called.

"Say, you've still got those security credentials, right?" Frank said.

"Yes . . ." She had gotten the security clearance in order to haul a hush-hush load of nuclear fuel to Nevada, a feat she wasn't keen on repeating.

"And you're in D.C.?"

She was actually in northern Virginia, but close enough. "Yeah."

"I've got a job for you."

"Don't tell me it's another gig for Those We Dare Not Name."

He didn't laugh, which told her it was bad. "Uh . . . no. More like those we *can't* name."

She didn't get it. "What?"

"Some . . . neighbors. Who live in funny-shaped houses. I can't say more over the phone."

She got it then. "Frank! You took a contract from the frigging *aliens?*"

"Sssh," he said, as if every phone in America weren't bugged. "It's strictly confidential."

"Jesus," she breathed out. She had done some crazy things for Frank, but this was over the top. "When, where, what?"

"Leaving tonight. D.C. to St. Louis. A converted tour bus."

"*Tour* bus? How many of them are going?"

"Two passengers. One human, one . . . whatever. Will you do it?"

She looked into the immaculate condo living room, where her brother, Blake, and his husband, Jeff, were playing a noisy, fast-paced video game, oblivious to her conversation. She had promised to be at Blake's concert tomorrow. It meant a lot to him. "Just a second," she said to Frank.

"I can't wait," he said.

"Two seconds." She muted the phone and walked into the living room. Blake saw her expression and paused the game.

She said, "Would you hate me if I couldn't be there tomorrow?"

Disappointment, resignation, and wry acceptance crossed his face, as if he hadn't ever really expected her to keep her promise. "What is it?" he asked.

"A job," she said. "A really important job. Never mind, I'll turn it down."

"No, Ave, don't worry. There will be other concerts."

Still, she hesitated. "You sure?" she said. She and Blake had always hung together, like castaways on a hostile sea. They had given each other courage to sail into the wind. To disappoint him felt disloyal.

"Go ahead," he said. "Now I'll be sorry if you stay."

She thumbed the phone on. "Okay, Frank, I'll do it. This better not get me in trouble."

"Cross my heart and hope to die," he said. "I'll email you instructions. Bye."

From the couch, Jeff said, "Now I know why you want to do it. Because it's likely to get you in trouble."

"No, he gave me his word," Avery said.

"Cowboy Frank? The one who had you drive guns to Nicaragua?"

"That was perfectly legal," Avery said.

Jeff had a point, as usual. Specialty Shipping did the jobs no reputable company would handle. Ergo, so did Avery.

"What is it this time?" Blake asked.

"I can't say." The email had come through; Frank had attached the instructions as if a PDF were more secure than email. She opened and scanned them.

The job had been cleared by the government, but the client was the alien passenger, and she was to take orders only from him, within the law. She scanned the rest of the instructions till she saw the pickup time. "Damn, I've got to get going," she said.

Her brother followed her into the guest room to watch her pack up. He had never understood her nomadic lifestyle, which made his silent support for it all the more generous. She was compelled to wander; he was rooted in this home, this relationship, this warm, supportive community. She was a discarder, using things up and throwing them away; he had created a home that was a visual expression of himself—from the spare, Japanese-style furniture to the Zen colors on the walls. Visiting him was like living inside a beautiful soul. She had no idea how they could have grown up so different. It was as if they were foundlings.

She pulled on her boots and shouldered her backpack. Blake hugged her. "Have a good trip," he said. "Call me."

"Will do," she said, and hit the road again.

The media had called the dome in Rock Creek Park the Mother Ship—but only because of its proximity to the White House, not because it was in any way distinctive. Like the others, it had appeared overnight, sited on a broad, grassy clearing that had been a secluded picnic ground in the urban park. It filled the entire creek valley, cutting off the trails and greatly inconveniencing the joggers and bikers.

Avery was unprepared for its scale. Like most people, she had seen the domes only on TV, and the small screen did not do justice to the neck-craning reality. She leaned forward over the wheel and peered out the windshield as she brought the bus to a halt at the last checkpoint. The National Park Police pickup that had escorted her through all the other checkpoints pulled aside.

The appearance of an alien habitat had set off a battle of jurisdictions in Washington. The dome stood on U.S. Park Service property, but D.C. Police controlled all the access streets, and the U.S. Army was tasked with maintaining a perimeter ʼund it. No agency wanted to surrender a particle of authority to the others. And ʼere was the polite, well-groomed young man who had introduced himself as

"Henry," now sitting in the passenger seat next to her. His neatly pressed suit sported no bulges of weaponry, but she assumed he was CIA.

She now saw method in Frank's madness at calling her so spur of the moment. Her last-minute arrival had prevented anyone from pulling her aside into a cinderblock room for a "briefing." Instead, Henry had accompanied her in the bus, chatting informally.

"Say, while you're on the road . . ."

"No," she said.

"No?"

"The alien's my client. I don't spy on clients."

He paused a moment, but seemed unruffled. "Not even for your country?"

"If I think my country's in danger, I'll get in touch."

"Fair enough," he said pleasantly. She hadn't expected him to give up so easily.

He handed her a business card. "So you can get in touch," he said.

She glanced at it. It said "Henry," with a phone number. No logo, no agency, no last name. She put it in a pocket.

"I have to get out here," he said when the bus rolled to halt a hundred yards from the dome. "It's been nice meeting you, Avery."

"Take your bug with you," she said.

"I beg your pardon?"

"The bug you left somewhere in this cab."

"There's no bug," he said seriously.

Since the bus was probably wired like a studio, she shrugged and resolved not to scratch anywhere embarrassing till she had a chance to search. As she closed the door behind Henry, the soldiers removed the roadblock and she eased the bus forward.

It was almost evening, but floodlights came on as she approached the dome. She pulled the bus parallel to the wall and lowered the wheelchair lift. One of the hexagonal panels slid aside, revealing a stocky, dark-haired young man in black glasses, surrounded by packing crates of the same pearly substance as the dome. Avery started forward to help with loading, but he said tensely, "Stay where you are." She obeyed. He pushed the first crate forward and it moved as if on wheels, though Avery could see none. It was slightly too wide for the lift, so the man put his hands on either side and pushed in. The crate reconfigured itself, growing taller and narrower till it fit onto the platform. Avery activated the power lift.

He wouldn't let Avery touch any of the crates, but insisted on stowing them himself at the back of the bus, where a private bedroom suite had once accommodated a touring celebrity singer. When the last crate was on, he came forward and said, "We can go now."

"What about the other passenger?" Avery said.

"He's here."

She realized that the alien must have been in one of the crates—or, for all she knew, *was* one of the crates. "Okay," she said. "Where to?"

"Anywhere," he said, and turned to go back into the bedroom.

Since she had no instructions to the contrary, Avery decided to head south. As she pulled out of the park, there was no police escort, no helicopter overhead, no obvious trailing car. The terms of this journey had been carefully negotiated at the highest levels, she knew. Their security was to be secrecy; no one was to know where they were. Avery's instructions from Frank had stressed that, aside from getting the alien safely where he wanted to go, insuring his privacy was her top priority. She was not to pry into his business or allow anyone else to do so.

Rush hour traffic delayed them a long time. At first, Avery concentrated on putting as much distance as she could between the bus and Washington. It was past ten by the time she turned off the main roads. She activated the GPS to try and find a route, but all the screen showed was snow. She tried her phone, and the result was the same. Not even the radio worked. One of those crates must have contained a jamming device; the bus was a rolling electronic dead zone. She smiled. So much for Henry's bugs.

It was quiet and peaceful driving through the night. A nearly full moon rode in the clear autumn sky, and woods closed in around them. Once, when she had first taken up driving in order to escape her memories, she had played a game of heading randomly down roads she had never seen, getting deliberately lost. Now she played it again, not caring where she ended up. She had never been good at keeping to the main roads.

By 3:00 she was tired, and when she saw the entrance to a state park, she turned and pulled into the empty parking lot. In the quiet after the engine shut off, she walked back through the kitchen and sitting area to see if there were any objections from her passengers. She listened at the closed door, but heard nothing and concluded they were asleep. As she was turning away, the door jerked open and the translator said, "What do you want?"

He was still fully dressed, exactly as she had seen him before, except without the glasses, his eyes were a little bloodshot, as if he hadn't closed them. "I've pulled over to get some sleep," she said. "It's not safe to keep driving without rest."

"Oh. All right," he said, and closed the door.

Shrugging, she went forward. There was a fold-down bunk that had once served the previous owner's entourage, and she now prepared to use it. She brushed her teeth in the tiny bathroom, pulled a sleeping bag from her backpack, and settled in.

Morning sun woke her. When she opened her eyes, it was flooding in the windows. At the kitchen table a yard away from her, the translator was sitting, staring out the window. By daylight, she saw that he had a square face the color of teak and closely trimmed black beard. She guessed that he might be Latino, and in his twenties.

"Morning," she said. He turned to stare at her, but said nothing. Not practiced in social graces, she thought. "I'm Avery," she said.

Still he didn't reply. "It's customary to tell me your name now," she said.

"Oh. Lionel," he answered.

"Pleased to meet you."

He said nothing, so she got up and went into the bathroom. When she came out, he was still staring fixedly out the window. She started making coffee. "Want some?" she asked.

"What is it?"

"Coffee."

"I ought to try it," he said reluctantly.

"Well, don't let me force you," she said.

"Why would you do that?" He was studying her, apprehensive.

"I wouldn't. I was being sarcastic. Like a joke. Never mind."

"Oh."

He got up restlessly and started opening the cupboards. Frank had stocked them with all the necessities, even a few luxuries. But Lionel didn't seem to find what he was looking for.

"Are you hungry?" Avery guessed.

"What do you mean?"

Avery searched for another way to word the question. "Would you like me to fix you some breakfast?"

He looked utterly stumped.

"Never mind. Just sit down and I'll make you something."

He sat down, gripping the edge of the table tensely. "That's a tree," he said, looking out the window.

"Right. It's a whole lot of trees."

"I ought to go out."

She didn't make the mistake of joking again. It was like talking to a person raised by wolves. Or aliens.

When she set a plate of eggs and bacon down in front of him, he sniffed it suspiciously. "That's food?"

"Yes, it's good. Try it."

He watched her eat for a few moments, then gingerly tried a bite of scrambled eggs. His expression showed distaste, but he resolutely forced himself to swallow. But when he tried the bacon, he couldn't bear it. "It bit my mouth," he said.

"You're probably not used to the salt. What do you normally eat?"

He reached in a pocket and took out some brown pellets that looked like dog kibble. Avery made a face of disgust. "What is that, people chow?"

"It's perfectly adapted to our nutritional needs," Lionel said. "Try it."

She was about to say "no thanks," but he was clearly making an effort to try new things, so she took a pellet and popped it in her mouth. It wasn't terrible—chewy rather than crunchy—but tasteless. "I think I'll stick to our food," she said.

He looked gloomy. "I need to learn to eat yours."

"Why? Research?"

He nodded. "I have to find out how the feral humans live."

So, Avery reflected, she was dealing with someone raised as a pet, who was now being released into the wild. For whatever reason.

"So where do you want to go today?" Avery said, sipping coffee.

He gave an indifferent gesture.

"You're heading for St. Louis?"

"Oh, I just picked that name off a map. It seemed to be in the center."

"That it is." She had lived there once; it was so incorrigibly in the center there was no edge to it. "Do you want to go by any particular route?"

He shrugged.

"How much time do you have?"

"As long as it takes."

"Okay. The scenic route, then."

She got up to clean the dishes, telling Lionel that this was a good time for him to go out, if he wanted to. It took him a while to summon his resolve. She watched out the kitchen window as he approached a tree as if to have a conversation with it. He felt its bark, smelled its leaves, and returned unhappy and distracted.

Avery followed the same random-choice method of navigation as the previous night, but always trending west. Soon they came to the first ridge of mountains. People from western states talked as if the Appalachians weren't real mountains, but they were—rugged and impenetrable ridges like walls erected to bar people from the land of milk and honey. In the mountains, all the roads ran northeast and southwest through the valleys between the crumpled land, with only the brave roads daring to climb up and pierce the ranges. The autumn leaves were at their height, russet and gold against the brilliant sky. All day long Lionel sat staring out the window.

That night she found a half-deserted campground outside a small town. She refilled the water tanks, hooked up the electricity, then came back in. "You're all set," she told Lionel. "If it's all right with you, I'm heading into town."

"Okay," he said.

It felt good to stretch her legs walking along the highway shoulder. The air was chill but bracing. The town was a tired, half-abandoned place, but she found a bar and settled down with a beer and a burger. She couldn't help watching the patrons around her—worn-down, elderly people just managing to hang on. What would an alien think of America if she brought him here?

Remembering that she was away from the interference field, she thumbed on her phone—and immediately realized that the ping would give away her location to the spooks. But since she'd already done it, she dialed her brother's number and left a voice mail congratulating him on the concert she was missing. "Everything's fine with me," she said, then added mischievously, "I met a nice young man named Henry. I think he's sweet on me. Bye."

Heading back through the night, she became aware that someone was following her. The highway was too dark to see who it was, but when she stopped, the footsteps behind her stopped, too. At last a car passed, and she wheeled around to see what the headlights showed.

"Lionel!" she shouted. He didn't answer, just stood there, so she walked back toward him. "Did you follow me?"

He was standing with hands in pockets, hunched against the cold. Defensively, he said, "I wanted to see what you would do when I wasn't around."

"It's none of your business what I do off duty. Listen, respecting privacy goes both ways. If you want me to respect yours, you've got to respect mine, okay?"

He looked cold and miserable, so she said, "Come on, let's get back before you freeze solid."

They walked side by side in silence, gravel crunching underfoot. At last he said stiffly, "I'd like to re-negotiate our contract."

"Oh, yeah? What part of the contract?"

"The part about privacy. I . . ." He searched for words. "We should have asked for more than a driver. We need a translator."

At least he'd realized it. He might speak perfect English, but he was not fluent in Human.

"My contract is with your . . . employer. Is this what he wants?"

"Who?"

"The other passenger. I don't know what to call him. 'The alien' isn't polite. What's his name?"

"They don't have names. They don't have a language."

Astonished, Avery said, "Then how do you communicate?"

He glowered at her. She held up her hands. "Sorry. No offense intended. I'm just trying to find out what he wants."

"They don't want things," he muttered, gazing fixedly at the moonlit road. "At least, not like you do. They're not . . . awake. Aware. Not like people are."

This made so little sense to Avery, she wondered if he were having trouble with the language. "I don't understand," she said. "You mean they're not . . . sentient?"

"They're not conscious," he said. "There's a difference."

"But they have technology. They built those domes, or brought them here, or whatever the hell they did. They have an advanced civilization."

"I didn't say they aren't smart. They're smarter than people are. They're just not conscious."

Avery shook her head. "I'm sorry, I just can't imagine it."

"Yes, you can," Lionel said impatiently. "People function unconsciously all the time. You're not aware that you're keeping your balance right now—you just do it automatically. You don't have to be aware to walk, or breathe. In fact, the more skillful you are at something, the less aware you are. Being aware would just degrade their skill."

They had come to the campground entrance. Behind the dark pine trees, Avery could see the bus, holding its unknowable passenger. For a moment the bus seemed to stare back with blank eyes. She made herself focus on the practical. "So how can I know what he wants?"

"I'm telling you."

She refrained from asking, "And how do you know?" because he'd already refused to answer that. The new privacy rules were to be selective, then. But she already knew more about the aliens than anyone else on Earth, except the translators. Not that she understood.

"I'm sorry, I can't keep calling him 'him,' or 'the alien,'" Avery said the next morning over breakfast. "I have to give him a name. I'm going to call him 'Mr. Burbage.' If he doesn't know, he won't mind."

Lionel didn't look any more disturbed than usual. She took that as consent.

"So where are we going today?" she asked.

He pressed his lips together in concentration. "I need to go to a place where I can acquire knowledge."

Since this could encompass anything from a brothel to a university, Avery said, "You've got to be more specific. What kind of knowledge?"

"Knowledge about you."

"Me?"

"No, you humans. How you work."

Humans. For that, she would have to find a bigger town.

As she cruised down a county road, Avery thought about Blake. Once, he had told her that to play an instrument truly well, you had to lose all awareness of what you were doing, and rely entirely on the muscle memory in your fingers. "You are so in the present, there is no room for self," Blake said. "No ego, no doubt, no introspection."

She envied him the ability to achieve such a state. She had tried to play the saxophone, but had never gotten good enough to experience what Blake described. Only playing video games could she concentrate intensely enough to lose self-awareness. It was strange, how addictive it was to escape the prison of her skull and forget she had a self. Mystics and meditators strove to achieve such a state.

A motion in the corner of her eye made her slam on the brakes and swerve. A startled deer pirouetted, flipped its tail, and leaped away. She continued on more slowly, searching for a sign to see where she was. She could not remember to have driven the last miles, or whether she had passed any turns. Smiling grimly, she realized that driving was *her* skill, something she knew so well that she could do it unconsciously. She had even reacted to a threat before knowing what it was. Her reflexes were faster than her conscious mind.

Were the aliens like that all the time? In a perpetual state of flow, like virtuoso musicians or Zen monks in *samadhi*? What would be the point of achieving such supreme skill, if the price was never knowing it was *you* doing it?

Around noon, they came to a town nestled in a steep valley on a rushing river. Driving down the main street, she spied a quaint, cupolaed building with a "Municipal Library" sign out front. Farther on, at the edge of town, an abandoned car lot offered a grass-pocked parking lot, so she turned in. "Come on, Lionel," she called out. "I've found a place for you to acquire knowledge."

They walked back into town together. The library was quiet and empty except for an old man reading a magazine. The selection of books was sparse, but there was a row of computers. "You know how to use these?" Avery said in a low voice.

"Not this kind," Lionel said. "They're very . . . primitive."

They sat down together, and Avery explained how to work the mouse and get on the Internet, how to search and scroll. "I've got it," he said. "You can go now."

Shrugging, she left him to his research. She strolled down the main street, stopped in a drugstore, then found a café that offered fried egg sandwiches on Wonder Bread, a luxury from her childhood. With lunch and a cup of coffee, she settled down to wait, sorting email on her phone.

Some time later, she became aware of the television behind the counter. It was tuned to one of those daytime exposé shows hosted by a shrill woman who spoke in a tone of breathless indignation. "Coming up," she said, "Slaves or traitors? Who *are* these alien translators?"

Avery realized that some part of her brain must have been listening and alerted her conscious mind to pay attention, just as it had reacted to the deer. She had a threat detection system she was not even aware of.

In the story that followed, a correspondent revealed that she had been unable to match any of the translators with missing children recorded in the past twenty years. The host treated this as suspicious information that someone ought to be looking into. Then came a panel of experts to discuss what they knew of the translators, which was nothing.

"Turncoats," commented one of the men at the counter watching the show. "Why would anyone betray his own race?"

"They're not even human," said another, "just made to look that way. They're clones or robots or something."

"The government won't do anything. They're just letting those aliens sit there."

Avery got up to pay her bill. The woman at the cash register said, "You connected with that big tour bus parked out at Fenniman's?"

She had forgotten that in a town like this, everyone knew instantly what was out of the ordinary.

"Yeah," Avery said. "Me and my . . . boyfriend are delivering it to a new owner."

She glanced up at the television just as a collage of faces appeared. Lionel's was in the top row. "Look closely," the show's host said. "If you recognize any of these faces, call us at 1-800- . . ." Avery didn't wait to hear the number. The door shut behind her.

It was hard not to walk quickly enough to attract attention. Why had she left him alone, as if it were safe? Briefly, she thought of bringing the bus in to pick him up at the library, but it would only attract more attention. The sensible thing was to slip inconspicuously out of town.

Lionel was engrossed in a web site about the brain when she came in. She sat down next to him and said quietly, "We've got to leave."

"I'm not . . ."

"Lionel. We have to leave. Right now."

He frowned, but got the message. As he rose to put on his coat, she quickly erased his browser history and cache. Then she led the way out and around the building to a back street where there were fewer eyes. "Hold my hand," she said.

"Why?"

"I told them you were my boyfriend. We've got to act friendly."

He didn't object or ask what was going on. The aliens had trained him well, she thought.

The street they were on came to an end, and they were forced back onto the main thoroughfare, right past the café. In Avery's mind every window was a pair of eyes staring at the strangers. As they left the business section of town and the buildings thinned out, she became aware of someone walking a block behind them. Glancing back, she saw a man in hunter's camouflage and billed cap, carrying a gun case on a strap over one shoulder.

She sped up, but the man trailing them sped up as well. When they were in sight of the bus, Avery pressed the keys into Lionel's hand and said, "Go on ahead. I'll stall this guy. Get inside and don't open the door to anyone but me." Then she turned back to confront their pursuit.

Familiarity tickled as he drew closer. When she was sure, she called out, "Afternoon, Henry! What a coincidence to see you here."

"Hello, Avery," he said. He didn't look quite right in the hunter costume: he was too urban and fit. "That was pretty careless of you. I followed to make sure you got back safe."

"I didn't know his picture was all over the TV," she said. "I've been out of touch."

"I know, we lost track of you for a while there. Please don't do that again."

As threats went, Henry now seemed like the lesser evil. She hesitated, then said, "I didn't see any need to get in touch." That meant the country was not in peril.

"Thanks," he said. "Listen, if you turn left on Highway 19 ahead, you'll come to a national park with a campground. It'll be safe."

As she walked back to the bus, she was composing a lie about who she had been talking to. But Lionel never asked. As soon as she was on board he started eagerly telling her about what he had learned in the library. She had never seen him so animated, so she gestured him to sit in the passenger seat beside her while she got the bus moving again.

"The reason you're conscious is because of the cerebral cortex," he said. "It's an add-on, the last part of the brain to evolve. Its only purpose is to monitor what the rest of the brain is doing. All the sensory input goes to the inner brain first, and gets processed, so the cortex never gets the raw data. It only sees the effect on the rest of the brain, not what's really out there. That's why you're aware of yourself. In fact, it's *all* you're aware of."

"Why are you saying 'you'?" Avery asked. "You've got a cerebral cortex, too."

Defensively, he said, "I'm not like you."

Avery shrugged. "Okay." But she wanted to keep the conversation going. "So Mr. Burbage doesn't have a cortex? Is that what you're saying?"

"That's right," Lionel said. "For him, life is a skill of the autonomic nervous system, not something he had to consciously learn. That's why he can think and react faster than we can, and requires less energy. The messages don't have to travel on a useless detour through the cortex."

"Useless?" Avery objected. "I kind of like being conscious."

Lionel fell silent, suddenly grave and troubled.

She glanced over at him. "What's the matter?"

In a low tone he said, "He likes being conscious, too. It's what they want from us."

Avery gripped the wheel and tried not to react. Up to now, the translators had denied that the aliens wanted anything at all from humans. But then it occurred to her that Lionel might not mean humans when he said "us."

"You mean, you translators?" she ventured.

He nodded, looking grim.

"Is that a bad thing?" she asked, reacting to his expression.

"Not for us," he said. "It's bad for them. It's killing him."

He was struggling with some strong emotion. Guilt, she thought. Maybe grief.

"I'm sorry," she said.

Angrily, he stood up to head back into the bus. "Why do you make me think of this?" he said. "Why can't you just mind your own business?"

Avery drove on, listening as he slammed the bedro
didn't feel any resentment. She knew all about guilt and
made you feel. Lionel's behavior made more sense to her
distinguishing between what was happening to him ex
ing from inside. Even people skilled at being human h&

The national park Henry had recommended turned out to be at Cumberland Gap, the mountain pass early pioneers had used to migrate west to Kentucky. They spent the night in the campground undisturbed. At dawn, Avery strolled out in the damp morning air to look around. She quickly returned to say, "Lionel, come out here. You need to see this."

She led him across the road to an overlook facing west. From the edge of the Appalachians they looked out on range after range of wooded foothills swaddled in fog. The morning sun at their backs lit everything in shades of mauve and azure. Avery felt like Daniel Boone looking out on the Promised Land, stretching before her into the misty distance, unpolluted by the past.

"I find this pleasant," Lionel said gravely.

Avery smiled. It was a breakthrough statement for someone so unaccustomed to introspection that he hadn't been able to tell her he was hungry two days ago. But all she said was, "Me, too."

After several moments of silence, she ventured, "Don't you think Mr. Burbage would enjoy seeing this? There's no one else around. Doesn't he want to get out of the bus some time?"

"He *is* seeing it," Lionel said.

"What do you mean?"

"He is here." Lionel tapped his head with a finger.

Avery couldn't help staring. "You mean you have some sort of telepathic connection with him?"

"There's no such thing as telepathy," Lionel said dismissively. "They communicate with neurotransmitters." She was still waiting, so he said, "He doesn't have to be all in one place. Part of him is with me, part of him is in the bus."

"In your *head*?" she asked, trying not to betray how creepy she found this news.

He nodded. "He needs me to observe the world for him, and understand it. They have had lots of other helper species to do things for them—species that build things, or transport them. But we're the first one with advanced consciousness."

"And that's why they're interested in us."

Lionel looked away to avoid her eyes, but nodded. "They like it," he said, his voice low and reluctant. "At first it was just novel and new for them, but now it's become an addiction, like a dangerous drug. We pay a high metabolic price for consciousness; it's why our lifespan is so short. They live for centuries. But when they get hooked on us, they burn out even faster than we do."

He picked up a rock and flung it over the cliff, watching as it arced up, then plummeted.

"And if he dies, what happens to you?" Avery asked.

"I don't want him to die," Lionel said. He put his hands in his pockets and studied

It feels . . . good to have him around. I like his company. He's very old, very

For a moment, she could see it through his eyes. She could imagine feeling intimately connected to an ancient being who was dying from an inability to part with his adopted human son. What a terrible burden for Lionel to carry, to be slowly killing someone he loved.

And yet, she still felt uneasy.

"How do you know?" she asked.

He looked confused. "What do you mean?"

"You said he's old and wise. How do you know that?"

"The way you know anything unconscious. It's a feeling, an instinct."

"Are you sure he not controlling you? Pushing around your neurotransmitters?"

"That's absurd," he said, mildly irritated. "I told you, he's not conscious, at least not naturally. Control is a conscious thing."

"But what if you did something he didn't want?"

"I don't feel like doing things he doesn't want. Like talking to you now. He must have decided he can trust you, because I wouldn't feel like telling you anything if he hadn't."

Avery wasn't sure whether being trusted by an alien was something she aspired to. But she did want Lionel to trust her, and so she let the subject drop.

"Where do you want to go today?" she asked.

"You keep asking me that." He stared out on the landscape, as if waiting for a revelation. At last he said, "I want to see humans living as they normally do. We've barely seen any of them. I didn't think the planet was so sparsely populated."

"Okay," she said. "I'm going to have to make a phone call for that."

When he had returned to the bus, she strolled away, took out Henry's card, and thumbed the number. Despite the early hour, he answered on the first ring.

"He wants to see humans," she said. "Normal humans behaving normally. Can you help me out?"

"Let me make some calls," he said. "I'll text you instructions."

"No men in black," she said. "You know what I mean?"

"I get it."

When Avery stopped for diesel around noon, the gas station television was blaring with news that the Justice Department would investigate the aliens for abducting human children. She escaped into the restroom to check her phone. The Internet was ablaze with speculation: who the translators were, whether they could be freed, whether they were human at all. The part of the government that had approved Lionel's road trip was clearly working at cross purposes with the part that had dreamed up this new strategy for extracting information from the aliens. The only good news was that no hint had leaked out that an alien was roaming the back roads of America in a converted bus.

Henry had texted her a cryptic suggestion to head toward Paris. She had to Google it to find that there actually was a Paris, Kentucky. When she came out to pay for the fuel, she was relieved to see that the television had moved on to World Series cover-age. On impulse, she bought a Cardinals cap for Lionel.

Paris turned out to be a quaint old Kentucky town that had once had delusions of cityhood. Today, a county fair was the main event in town. The RV park was al-most full, but Avery's E.T. Express managed to maneuver in. When everything was settled, she sat on the bus steps sipping a Bud and waiting for night so they could venture out with a little more anonymity. The only thing watching her was a skit-tish, half-wild cat crouched behind a trash can. Somehow, it reminded her of Lionel, so she tossed it a Cheeto to see if she could lure it out. It refused the bait.

That night, disguised by the dark and a Cardinals cap, Lionel looked tolerably inconspicuous. As they were leaving to take in the fair, she said, "Will Mr. Burbage be okay while we're gone? What if someone tries to break into the bus?"

"Don't worry, he'll be all right," Lionel said. His tone implied more than his words. She resolved to call Henry at the earliest opportunity and pass along a warning not to try anything.

The people in the midway all looked authentic. If there were snipers on the bigtop and agents on the merry-go-round, she couldn't tell. When people failed to recognize Lionel at the ticket stand and popcorn wagon, she began to relax. Everyone was here to enjoy themselves, not to look for aliens.

She introduced Lionel to the joys of corn dogs and cotton candy, to the ferris wheel and tilt-a-whirl. He took in the jangling sounds, the smells of deep-fried food, and the blinking lights with a grave and studious air. When they had had their fill of all the machines meant to disorient and confuse, they took a break at a picnic table, sipping Cokes.

Avery said, "Is Mr. Burbage enjoying this?"

Lionel shrugged. "Are you?" He wasn't deflecting her question; he actually wanted to know.

She considered. "I think people enjoy these events mainly because they bring back childhood memories," she said.

"Yes. It does seem familiar," Lionel said.

"Really? What about it?"

He paused, searching his mind. "The smells," he said at last.

Avery nodded. It was smells for her, as well: deep fat fryers, popcorn. "Do you remember anything from the time before you were abducted?"

"Adopted," he corrected her.

"Right, adopted. What about your family?"

He shook his head.

"Do you ever wonder what kind of people they were?"

"The kind of people who wouldn't look for me," he said coldly.

"Wait a minute. You don't know that. For all you know, your mother might have cried her eyes out when you disappeared."

He stared at her. She realized she had spoken with more emotion than she had intended. The subject had touched a nerve. "Sorry," she muttered, and got up. "I'm tired. Can we head back?"

"Sure," he said, and followed her without question.

That night she couldn't sleep. She lay watching the pattern from the lights outside on the ceiling, but her mind was on the back of the bus. Up to now she had slept without thinking of the strangeness just beyond the door, but tonight it bothered her.

About 3:00 A.M. she roused from a doze at the sound of Lionel's quiet footstep going past her toward the door. She lay silent as he eased the bus door open. When he had gone outside she rose and looked to see what he was doing. He walked away from the bus toward a maintenance shed and some dumpsters. She debated whether to follow him; it was just what she had scolded him for doing to her. But concern for his safety won out, and she took a flashlight from the driver's console, put it in the pocket of a windbreaker, and followed.

At first she thought she had lost him. The parking lot was motionless and quiet. A slight breeze stirred the pines on the edge of the road. Then she heard a scuffling sound ahead, a thump, and a soft crack. At first she stood listening, but when there was no more sound, she crept forward. Rounding the dumpster, she saw in its shadow a figure crouched on the ground. Unable to make out what was going on, she switched on the flashlight.

Lionel turned, his eyes wild and hostile. Dangling from his hand was the limp body of a cat, its head ripped off. His face was smeared with its blood. Watching her, he deliberately ripped a bite of cat meat from the body with his teeth and swallowed.

"Lionel!" she cried out in horror. "Put that down!"

He turned away, trying to hide his prey like an animal. Without thinking, she grabbed his arm, and he spun fiercely around, as if to fight her. His eyes looked utterly alien. She stepped back. "It's me, Avery," she said.

He looked down at the mangled carcass in his hand, then dropped it, rose, and backed away. Once again taking his arm, Avery guided him away from the dumpsters, back to the bus. Inside, she led him to the kitchen sink. "Wash," she ordered, then went to firmly close the bus door.

Her heart was pounding, and she kept the heavy flashlight in her hand for security. But when she came back, she saw he was trembling so hard he had dropped the soap and was leaning against the sink for support. Seeing that his face was still smeared with blood, she took a paper towel and wiped him off, then dried his hands. He sank onto the bench by the kitchen table. She stood watching him, arms crossed, waiting for him to speak. He didn't.

"So what was that about?" she said sternly.

He shook his head.

"Cats aren't food," she said. "They're living beings."

Still he didn't speak.

"Have you been sneaking out at night all along?" she demanded.

He shook his head. "I don't know . . . I just thought . . . I wanted to see what it would feel like."

"You mean *Mr. Burbage* wanted to see what it would feel like," she said.

"Maybe," he admitted.

"Well, people don't do things like that."

He was looking ill. She grabbed his arm and hustled him into the bathroom, aiming him at the toilet. She left him there vomiting, and started shoving belongings into her backpack. As she swung it onto her shoulder, he staggered to the bathroom door.

"I'm leaving," she said. "I can't sleep here, knowing you do things like that."

He looked dumbstruck. She pushed past him and out the door. She was striding away across the gravel parking lot when he called after her, "Avery! You can't leave."

She wheeled around. "Can't I? Just watch me."

He left the bus and followed her. "What are we going to do?"

"I don't care," she said.

"I won't do it again."

"Who's talking, you or him?"

A light went on in the RV next to them. She realized they were making a late-night scene like trailer-park trash, attracting attention. This wasn't an argument they could have in public. And now that she was out here, she realized she had no place to go. So she shooed Lionel back toward the bus.

Once inside, she said, "This is the thing, Lionel. This whole situation is creeping me out. You can't make any promises as long as he's in charge. Maybe next time he'll want to see what it feels like to kill *me* in my sleep, and you won't be able to stop him."

Lionel looked disturbed. "He won't do that."

"How do you know?"

"I just . . . do."

"That's not good enough. I need to see him."

Avery wasn't sure why she had blurted it out, except that living with an invisible, ever-present passenger had become intolerable. As long as she didn't know what the door in the back of the bus concealed, she couldn't be at ease.

He shook his head. "That won't help."

She crossed her arms and said, "I can't stay unless I know what he is."

Lionel's face took on an introspective look, as if he were consulting his conscience. At last he said, "You'd have to promise not to tell anyone."

Avery hadn't really expected him to consent, and now felt a nervous tremor. She dropped her pack on the bed and gripped her hands into fists. "All right."

He led the way to the back of the bus and eased the door open as if fearing to disturb the occupant within. She followed him in. The small room was dimly lit and there was an earthy smell. All the crates he had brought in must have been folded up and put away, because none were visible. There was an unmade bed, and beside it a clear box like an aquarium tank, holding something she could not quite make out. When Lionel turned on a light, she saw what the tank contained.

It looked most like a coral or sponge—a yellowish, rounded growth the size of half a beach ball, resting on a bed of wood chips and dead leaves. Lionel picked up a spray bottle and misted it tenderly. It responded by expanding as if breathing.

"*That's* Mr. Burbage?" Avery whispered.

Lionel nodded. "Part of him. The most important part."

The alien seemed insignificant, something she could destroy with a bottle of bleach. "Can he move?" she asked.

"Oh, yes," Lionel said. "Not the way we do."

She waited for him to explain. At first he seemed reluctant, but he finally said, "They are colonies of cells with a complicated life cycle. This is the final stage of their development, when they become most complex and organized. After this, they dissolve into the earth. The cells don't die; they go on to form other coalitions. But the individual is lost. Just like us, I suppose."

What she was feeling, she realized, was disappointment. In spite of all Lionel had told her, she had hoped there would be some way of communicating. Before, she had not truly believed that the alien could be insentient. Now she did. In fact, she found it hard to believe that it could think at all.

"How do you know he's intelligent?" she asked. "He could be just a heap of chemicals, like a loaf of bread rising."

"How do you know *I'm* intelligent?" he said, staring at the tank. "Or anyone?"

"You react to me. You communicate. He can't."

"Yes, he can."

"How? If I touched him—"

"No!" Lionel said quickly. "Don't touch him. You'd see, he would react. It wouldn't be malice, just a reflex."

"Then how do you . . . ?"

Reluctantly, Lionel said, "He has to touch you. It's the only way to exchange neurotransmitters." He paused, as if debating something internally. She watched the conflict play across his face. At last, reluctantly, he said, "I think he would be willing to communicate with you."

It was what she had wanted, some reassurance of the alien's intentions. But now it was offered, her instincts were unwilling. "No thanks," she said.

Lionel looked relieved. She realized he hadn't wanted to give up his unique relationship with Mr. Burbage.

"Thanks anyway," she said, for the generosity of the offer he hadn't wanted to make.

And yet, it left her unsure. She had only Lionel's word that the alien was friendly. After tonight, that wasn't enough.

Neither of them could sleep, so as soon as day came they set out again. Heading west, Avery knew they were going deeper and deeper into isolationist territory, where even human strangers were unwelcome, never mind aliens. This was the land where she had grown up, and she knew it well. From here, the world outside looked like a violent, threatening place full of impoverished hordes who envied and hated the good life in America. Here, even the churches preached self-satisfaction, and discontent was the fault of those who hated freedom—like college professors, homosexuals, and immigrants.

Growing up, she had expected to spend her life in this country. She had done everything right—married just out of high school, worked as a waitress, gotten pregnant at nineteen. Her life had been mapped out in front of her.

She couldn't even imagine it now.

This morning, Lionel seemed to want to talk. He sat beside her in the co-pilot seat, watching the road and answering her questions.

"What does it feel like, when he communicates with you?"

He reflected. "It feels like a mood, or a hunch. Or I act on impulse."

"How do you know it's him, and not your own subconscious?"

"I don't. It doesn't matter."

Avery shook her head. "I wouldn't want to go through life acting on hunches."

"Why not?"

"Your unconscious . . . it's unreliable. You can't control it. It can lead you wrong."

"That's absurd," he said. "It's not some outside entity; it's *you*. It's your *conscious* mind that's the slave master, always worrying about control. Your unconscious only wants to preserve you."

"Not if there's an alien messing around with it."

"He's not like that. This drive to dominate—that's a conscious thing. He doesn't have that slave master part of the brain."

"Do you know that for a fact, or are you just guessing?"

"Guessing is what your unconscious tells you. Knowing is a conscious thing. They're only in conflict if your mind is fighting itself."

"Sounds like the human condition to me," Avery said. This had to be the weirdest conversation in her life.

"Is he here now?" she asked.

"Of course he is."

"Don't you ever want to get away from him?"

Puzzled, he said, "Why should I?"

"Privacy. To be by yourself."

"I don't want to be by myself."

Something in his voice told her he was thinking ahead, to the death of his lifelong companion. Abruptly, he rose and walked back into the bus.

Actually, she had lied to him. She *had* gone through life acting on hunches. *Go with your gut* had been her motto, because she had trusted her gut. But of course it had nothing to do with gut, or heart—it was her unconscious mind she had been following. Her unconscious was why she took this road rather than that, or preferred Raisin Bran to Corn Flakes. It was why she found certain tunes achingly beautiful, and why she was fond of this strange young man, against all rational evidence.

As the road led them nearer to southern Illinois, Avery found memories surfacing. They came with a tug of regret, like a choking rope pulling her back toward the person she hadn't become. She thought of the cascade of nondecisions that had led her to become the rootless, disconnected person she was, as much a stranger to the human race as Lionel was, in her way.

What good has consciousness ever done me? she thought. It only made her aware that she could never truly connect with another human being, deep down. And on that day when her cells would dissolve into the soil, there would be no trace her consciousness had ever existed.

That night they camped at a freeway rest stop a day's drive from St. Louis. Lionel was moody and anxious. Avery's attempt to interest him in a trashy novel was fruitless.

At last she asked what was wrong. Fighting to find the words, he said, "He's very ill. This trip was a bad idea. All the stimulation has made him worse."

Tentatively, she said, "Should we head for one of the domes?"

Lionel shook his head. "They can't cure this . . . this addiction to consciousness. If they could, I don't think he'd take it."

"Do the others—his own people—know what's wrong with him?"

Lionel nodded wordlessly.

She didn't know what comfort to offer. "Well," she said at last, "it was his choice to come."

"A selfish choice," Lionel said angrily.

She couldn't help noticing that he was speaking for himself, Lionel, as distinct from Mr. Burbage. Thoughtfully, she said, "Maybe they can't love us as much as we can love them."

He looked at her as if the word "love" had never entered his vocabulary. "Don't say *us*," he said. "I'm not one of you."

She didn't believe it for a second, but she just said, "Suit yourself," and turned back to her novel. After a few moments, he went into the back of the bus and closed the door.

She lay there trying to read for a while, but the story couldn't hold her attention. She kept listening for some sound from beyond the door, some indication of how they were doing. At last she got up quietly and went to listen. Hearing nothing, she tried the door and found it unlocked. Softly, she cracked it open to look inside.

Lionel was not asleep. He was lying on the bed, his head next to the alien's tank. But the alien was no longer in the tank; it was on the pillow. It had extruded a mass of long, cordlike tentacles that gripped Lionel's head in a medusa embrace, snaking into every opening. One had entered an ear, another a nostril. A third had nudged aside an eyeball in order to enter the eye socket. Fluid coursed along the translucent vessels connecting man and creature.

Avery wavered on the edge of horror. Her first instict was to intervene, to defend Lionel from what looked like an attack. But the expression on his face was not of terror, but peace. All his vague references to exchanging neurotransmitters came back to her now: this was what he had meant. The alien communicated by drinking cerebrospinal fluid, its drug of choice, and injecting its own.

Shaken, she eased the door shut again. Unable to get the image out of her mind, she went outside to walk around the bus to calm her nerves. After three circuits she leaned back against the cold metal, wishing she had a cigarette for the first time in years. Above her, the stars were cold and bright. What was this relationship she had landed in the middle of—predator and prey? father and son? pusher and addict? master and slave? Or some strange combination of all? Had she just witnessed an alien learning about love?

She had been saving a bottle of bourbon for special occasions, so she went in to pour herself a shot.

To her surprise, Lionel emerged before she was quite drunk. She thought of offering him a glass, but wasn't sure how it would mix with whatever was already in his brain.

He sat down across from her, but just stared silently at the floor for a long time. At last he stirred and said, "I think we ought to take him to a private place."

"What sort of private place?" Avery asked.

"Somewhere dignified. Natural. Secluded."

To die, she realized. The alien wanted to die in private. Or Lionel wanted him to. There was no telling where one left off and the other began.

"I know a place," she said. "Will he make it another day?"

Lionel nodded silently.

Through the bourbon haze, Avery wondered what she ought to say to Henry. Was the country in danger? She didn't think so. This seemed like a personal matter. To be sure, she said, "You're certain his relatives won't blame us if he dies?"

"Blame?" he said.

That was conscious-talk, she realized. "React when he doesn't come back?"

"If they were going to react, they would have done it when he left. They aren't expecting anything, not even his return. They don't live in an imaginary future like you people do."

"Wise of them," she said.

"Yes."

They rolled into St. Louis in late afternoon, across the Poplar Street Bridge next to the Arch and off onto I-70 toward the north part of town. Avery knew exactly where she was going. From the first moment Frank had told her the destination was St. Louis, she had known she would end up driving this way, toward the place where she had left the first part of her life.

Bellefontaine Cemetery lay on what had been the outskirts of the city in Victorian times, several hundred acres of greenery behind a stone wall and a wrought-iron gate. It was a relic from a time when cemeteries were landscaped, parklike sanctuaries from the city. Huge old oak and sweetgum trees lined the winding roadways, their branches now black against the sky. Avery drove slowly past the marble mausoleums and toward the hill at the back of the cemetery, which looked out over the valley toward the Missouri River. It was everything Lionel had wanted—peaceful, natural, secluded.

Some light rain misted down out of the overcast sky. Avery parked the bus and went out to check whether they were alone. She had seen no one but a single dog-walker near the entrance, and no vehicle had followed them in. The gates would close in half an hour, and the bus would have to be out. Henry and his friends were probably waiting outside the gate for them to appear again. She returned into the bus and knocked on Lionel's door. He opened it right away. Inside, the large picnic cooler they had bought was standing open, ready.

"Help me lift him in," Lionel said.

Avery maneuvered past the cooler to the tank. "Is it okay for me to touch him?"

"Hold you hand close to him for a few seconds."

Avery did as instructed. A translucent tentacle extruded from the cauliflower folds of the alien's body. It touched her palm, recoiled, then extended again. Gently, hesitantly, it explored her hand, tickling slightly as it probed her palm and curled around her pinkie. She held perfectly still.

"What is he thinking?" she whispered.

"He's learning your chemical identity," Lionel said.

"How can he learn without being aware? Can he even remember?"

"Of course he can remember. Your immune system learns and remembers just about every pathogen it ever met, and it's not aware. Can *you* remember them all?"

She shook her head, stymied.

At last, apparently satisfied, the tendril retracted into the alien's body.

"All right," Lionel said, "now you can touch him."

The alien was surprisingly heavy. Together, they lifted him onto the bed of dirt and wood chips Lionel had spread in the bottom of the cooler. Lionel fitted the lid on loosely, and each of them took a handle to carry their load out into the open air. Avery led the way around a mausoleum shaped like a Greek temple to an unmowed spot hidden from the path. Sycamore leaves and bark littered the ground, damp from the rain.

"Is this okay?" she asked.

For answer, Lionel set down his end of the cooler and straightened, breathing in the forest smell. "This is okay."

"I have to move the bus. Stay behind this building in case anyone comes by. I'll be back."

The gatekeeper waved as she pulled the bus out onto the street. By the time she had parked it on a nearby residential street and returned, the gate was closed. She walked around the cemetery perimeter to an unfrequented side, then scrambled up the wall and over the spiked fence.

Inside, the traffic noise of the city fell away. The trees arched overhead in church-like silence. Not a squirrel stirred. Avery sat down on a tombstone to wait. Beyond the hill, Lionel was holding vigil at the side of his dying companion, and she wanted to give him privacy. The stillness felt good, but unfamiliar. Her life was made of motion. She had been driving for twenty years—driving away, driving beyond, always a new destination. Never back.

The daylight would soon be gone. She needed to do the other thing she had come here for. Raising the hood of her raincoat, she headed downhill, the grass caressing her sneakers wetly. It was years since she had visited the grave of her daughter Gabrielle, whose short life and death was like a chasm dividing her life into before and after. They had called it crib death then—an unexplained, random, purposeless death. "Nothing you could have done," the doctor had said, thinking that was more comforting than knowing that the universe just didn't give a damn.

Gabrielle's grave lay in a grove of cedar trees—the plot a gift from a sympathetic patron at the café where Avery had worked. At first she had thought of turning it down because the little grave would be overshadowed by more ostentatious death; but the suburban cemeteries had looked so industrial, monuments stamped out by machine. She had come to love the age and seclusion of this spot. At first, she had visited over and over.

As she approached in the fading light, she saw that something was lying on the headstone. When she came close she saw that some stranger had placed on the grave a little terra cotta angel with one wing broken. Avery stood staring at the bedraggled figurine, now soaked with rain, a gift to her daughter from someone she didn't even know. Then, a sudden, unexpected wave of grief doubled her over. It had been twenty years since she had touched her daughter, but the memory was still vivid and tactile. She remembered the smell, the softness of her skin, the utter trust in her eyes. She felt again the aching hole of her absence.

Avery sank to her knees in the wet grass, sobbing for the child she hadn't been able to protect, for the sympathy of the nameless stranger, even for the helpless, mutilated angel who would never fly.

There was a sound behind her, and she looked up. Lionel stood there watching her, rain running down his face—no, it was tears. He wiped his eyes, then looked at his hands. "I don't know why I feel like this," he said.

Poor, muddled man. She got up and hugged him for knowing exactly how she felt. They stood there for a moment, two people trapped in their own brains, and the only crack in the wall was empathy.

"Is he gone?" she asked softly.

He shook his head. "Not yet. I left him alone in case it was me . . . interfering. Then I saw you and followed."

"This is my daughter's grave," Avery said. "I didn't know I still miss her so much."

She took his hand and started back up the hill. They said nothing, but didn't let go of each other till they got to the marble mausoleum where they had left Mr. Burbage.

The alien was still there, resting on the ground next to the cooler. Lionel knelt beside him and held out a hand. A bouquet of tentacles reached out and grasped it, then withdrew. Lionel came over to where Avery stood watching. "I'm going to stay with him. You don't have to."

"I'd like to," she said, "if it's okay with you."

He ducked his head furtively.

So they settled down to keep a strange death watch. Avery shared some chemical hand-warmers she had brought from the bus. When those ran out and night deepened, she managed to find some dry wood at the bottom of a groundskeeper's brush pile to start a campfire. She sat poking the fire with a stick, feeling drained of tears, worn down as an old tire.

"Does he know he's dying?" she asked.

Lionel nodded. "*I* know, and so he knows." A little bitterly, he added, "That's what consciousness does for you."

"So normally he wouldn't know?"

He shook his head. "Or care. It's just part of their life cycle. There's no death if there's no self to be aware of it."

"No life either," Avery said.

Lionel just sat breaking twigs and tossing them on the fire. "I keep wondering if it was worth it. If consciousness is good enough to die for."

She tried to imagine being free of her self—of the regrets of the past and fear of the future. If this were a Star Trek episode, she thought, this would be when Captain Kirk would deliver a speech in defense of being human, despite all the drawbacks. She didn't feel that way.

"You're right," she said. "Consciousness kind of sucks."

The sky was beginning to glow with dawn when at last they saw a change in the alien. The brainlike mass started to shrink and a liquid pool spread out from under it, as if it were dissolving. There was no sound. At the end, its body deflated like a falling souffle, leaving nothing but a slight crust on the leaves and a damp patch on the ground.

They sat for a long time in silence. It was light when Lionel got up and brushed off his pants, his face set and grim. "Well, that's that," he said.

Avery felt reluctant to leave. "His cells are in the soil?" she said.

"Yes, they'll live underground for a while, spreading and multiplying. They'll go through some blooming and sporing cycles. If any dogs or children come along at that stage, the spores will establish a colony in their brains. It's how they invade."

His voice was perfectly indifferent. Avery stared at him. "You might have mentioned that."

He shrugged.

An inspiration struck her. She seized up a stick and started digging in the damp patch of ground, scooping up soil in her hands and putting it into the cooler.

"What are you doing?" Lionel said. "You can't stop him, it's too late."

"I'm not trying to," Avery said. "I want some cells to transplant. I'm going to grow an alien of my own."

"That's the stupidest—"

A moment later he was on his knees beside her, digging and scooping up dirt. They got enough to half-fill the cooler, then covered it with leaves to keep it damp.

"Wait here," she told him. "I'll bring the bus to pick you up. The gates open in an hour. Don't let anyone see you."

When she got back to the street where she had left the bus, Henry was waiting in a parked car. He got out and opened the passenger door for her, but she didn't get inside. "I've got to get back," she said, inclining her head toward the bus. "They're waiting for me."

"Do you mind telling me what's going on?"

"I just needed a break. I had to get away."

"In a cemetery? All night?"

"It's personal."

"Is there something I should know?"

"We're heading back home today."

He waited, but she said no more. There was no use telling him; he couldn't do anything about it. The invasion was already underway.

He let her return to the bus, and she drove it to a gas station to fuel up while waiting for the cemetery to open. At the stroke of 8:30 she pulled the bus through the gate, waving at the puzzled gatekeeper.

Between them, she and Lionel carried the cooler into the bus, leaving behind only the remains of a campfire and a slightly disturbed spot of soil. Then she headed straight for the freeway.

They stopped for a fast-food breakfast in southern Illinois. Avery kept driving as she ate her egg muffin and coffee. Soon Lionel came to sit shotgun beside her, carrying a plastic container full of soil.

"Is that mine?" she asked.

"No, this one's mine. You can have the rest."

"Thanks."

"It won't be him," Lionel said, looking at the soil cradled on his lap.

"No. But it'll be yours. Yours to raise and teach."

As hers would be.

"I thought you would have some kind of tribal loyalty to prevent them invading," Lionel said.

Avery thought about it a moment, then said, "We're not defenseless, you know. We've got something they want. The gift of self, of mortality. God, I feel like the snake in the garden. But my alien will love me for it." She could see the cooler in the rearview mirror, sitting on the floor in the kitchen. Already she felt fond of the person it would become. Gestating inside. "It gives a new meaning to *alien abduction*, doesn't it?" she said.

He didn't get the joke. "You aren't afraid to become . . . something like me?"

She looked over at him. "No one can be like you, Lionel."

Even after all this time together, he still didn't know how to react when she said things like that.

patience lake

MATTHEW CLAXTON

Here's a compelling story in which an injured and down-on-his-luck cyborg must make a dangerous and potentially fatal stand to defend the farm family that tried to help him. . . .

Matthew Claxton is a reporter from the west coast of Canada. His stories have appeared in Asimov's Science Fiction, SciFiction, Mothership Zeta, *and elsewhere.*

H is right knee gave out thirty klicks outside of Saskatoon. He pitched forward onto the gravel shoulder of the Five, plastic pads on his hands sending flashes of PAIN-PAIN-PAIN while red SEEK REPAIR messages flared in the corners of his visual field. He'd been half-asleep, walking on auto, letting GPS and inertial guidance take him the last few dozen klicks, after the farm kids who'd let him ride in their pickup had turned north.

He pushed himself up, flexed the left knee, his elbows. None of the plastic casings around his limbs seemed to have cracked. He'd caught himself, woken up before face-planting. He imagined scratching his eyes on the gravel, leaving permanent gouges in the plastic lenses, and shuddered.

He stood, balancing his weight on his left leg and swinging the right, gingerly. The knee made a grinding noise, and he felt metal scrape metal, right up through the bone-and-metal socket of his hip. The joint didn't want to swing too far backward, just a couple of degrees. Forward was fine, but it was loose, something in there stripped and gone. He locked the knee and put some weight on it. It held.

That was something, he thought.

GPS said he was close. There'd be a shelter in the city, or at least a recyc bin full of cardboard, an abandoned car, maybe a squat where he could spend the night. If he could get there. He looked back over his shoulder down the road. It was after four, prairie sky blue and clear. He had hours of daylight left. His cooling fan hummed, setting his shirt front to fluttering.

He took a step, flinging his right leg out from his hip, jamming the heel of his battered boot into the gravel, taking a hopping step. Another. Another.

Slow, but he could do it. Get to town. Maybe even find someone who would fix his knee, for what amounted to no money. His disability check would come through in a couple of weeks. He just had to keep moving. One step at a time.

He stuck his thumb out every time he heard the rush of a truck, but nothing passed him with a human inside.

"Excuse me? Do you think I could fill up my water bottle?" He held up the scratched plastic two-liter. The woman, fiddling with a tablet, barely looked up. Squatting next to her was a six-wheeled machine, a cubist mosquito in steel and carbon fiber body panels. Its proboscis was a shiny steel auger, aimed at a spot on the ground near some rolled chain-link and a couple of wooden posts. The thing's hinged arms were folded up at its sides. It had once been painted red.

The grey-haired woman and the machine had a similar look, he thought: not young, used hard, sturdy.

"You can't get into town that way," she said.

He let his arm drop. "What?"

She glanced up, and he saw that momentary look flicker across her face. Most people got that way. Hard to talk to a man with a smooth plastic head, no nose, speaker grill for a mouth, round eyes that never blinked.

"There's a roadblock at Patience Lake. About a five-minute drive down that way. Security's checking everybody."

"RCMP?" he said, hopeful.

"Nope. Private. Contracted out, twice over."

His shoulders slumped. Petty private meant either a shakedown, or being turned around, maybe a night in some rural cell for vagrancy.

"If I'm turning around, I could really use the water, ma'am." He tried to put a tone of honest pleading into the flat, synthetic speech that came from his vocal chip.

She smirked.

"Well, since you said ma'am."

She let him use the faucet outside the house, eyeing him the whole time, staying about two-arms-length away from him while he filled and capped the bottle. The house was maybe fifty or sixty years old, wooden and white with blue trim, a henge of black solar panels squatting on its south-facing roof. In the farmyard stood a grey-sided barn, a Quonset hut, and a clutch of simple greenhouses, half-hoops of PVC pipe covered with plastic sheeting, their insides moisture-beaded. Three or four acres were enclosed in fences, and beyond that were vast fields of plants, something he didn't recognize. It had started as corn, maybe, before the biotechs had had their way with it. A couple of small blimps drifted in the distance, crop-watching drones holding themselves in place with fat ducted fans.

He tried not to look around too much, tried not to look like the kind of guy who'd come back later with a couple of friends, a truck, and a deer rifle. If he could have smiled reassuringly, he would have.

She walked him back to the road.

"Is there any way to get into Saskatoon without going through a roadblock?" he asked when he was standing on the gravel shoulder again.

She waved off to the north, over the low rolling hills covered with golden canola. "Any way you go in that direction, you'll probably run into them. They've probably already seen you. They watch the crop monitor feeds when they're bored." She jerked a thumb upwards, indicating one of the fat little blimps.

"South?"

"East and then south. Way south. Head in on the Sixteen, and up through Rosewood."

He called up the map, sighed at the length of the dotted line it marked between his position and the city's center.

He was about to ask for a ride—ask for a ride and get a polite but very firm refusal, he guessed—when the cloud of dust appeared off to the west.

The woman squinted into the lowering sun. He let his eyes whir into distance vision, polarize out the glare and dust. A big black-and-white, lights and sirens bulging from its roof like tumors.

The woman glanced at him, eyes flickering down to his knee. She'd seen the way he kick-hopped across the yard.

"You know anything about farm machinery?" she asked him suddenly.

"No," he said. "But I can drive anything." He tapped the side of his plastic skull. "Fully wired for remote ops."

"Sandra Kowalchuk."

"Casey Kim."

"Well, Casey, you think you can get this thing moving?" She waved a callused hand at the machine.

"Sure," he said. "Uh, what does it do?"

By the time the security car had closed half the distance to the farm, Casey had learned what a post-hole digger was. By the time it pulled into the driveway, going too fast, obviously on manual, he had managed to get the machine to make a few juddering movements. The wheels were easy enough. Sandra pointed out where she wanted the hole, and he jiggered it back and forth, positioning that big auger.

The control interface was crude, nothing like military systems, or even the ones the big trucking firms used. It was at least a decade old, and it had zero haptic feedback. But Casey had the feel for it. Give him another ten minutes, and he could make it tap dance.

Two men got out of the security car, both in straight-leg trousers with a red stripe a couple fingers wide down each leg, like they were some kind of real cops or something. The short one with a ginger moustache on his lip had fewer chevrons on his shirt. His sleeves bulged, he had that thick-shouldered thick-necked look of a man fond of prescription muscle enhancement. He had a belt slung with an array of half a dozen weapons, curving back from his hip in descending order of lethality. The other, larger by far, just had a single. It was matte black, a revolver, in a size suitable for blowing a hole through a rhino. Casey'd never seen a cop, real or not, carry a gun like that.

The second guy didn't look right, either, the way he moved was off, elbows out, strutting almost. It took Casey a second to get it. The man looked to be in his thirties, but the skin on his arms and neck was smooth, perfectly hairless, tanned the shade of an expensive leather couch. Under it his muscles were even and had the kind of gym-tone you only saw on CG-enhanced movie stars. No one real had muscles like that. Just sprites and machines.

"Morning, Sandra," the cyborg said, giving her a big smile. His teeth were plastic too, as even and white as veterans' tombstones. He never looked directly at Casey. The other cop never looked anywhere else, and kept one hand on the butt of his gun. "Just saw this guy trying to hitch a while back, and then he stopped here. Thought we'd come and see if he's trying to bother you."

Sandra shook her head, and Casey let out a tension he hadn't known he was holding in. "He's fine, Terry. He's helping me out with this piece of shit," she said, jerking her chin at the post-hole digger. "He already got it moving again after I'd got it stuck."

"He's not overcharging you for that, is he?"

"Not charging her anything, sir," Casey said. "She let me fill up with water, and I offered to help."

Cyborg quirked an eyebrow. "And then?"

"And then I'm going to try and find some work in town," Casey said.

"Tonight?"

"Yes."

"Got somewhere to stay?"

"Yes."

Terry moved in closer, then reached up and rapped a knuckle on Casey's face, tapping the smooth white plastic above and between his eyes.

"Casehead, huh?" he said. "No skin at all. What happened to you?"

"Cray Liberation Faction," he said.

Terry smiled, like he'd met a celebrity or something. "No shit! You were in the Forces?"

"I was in the reserves," Casey said. "I was on the base when they set the thing off. Edge of the cloud just got me."

He was fine talking about the incident, which was all people seemed to want to talk about. The thump of the bomb, the faint mist hitting him as he stepped out of the cinderblock Remote Ops building. He'd been coming off a twelve-hour shift flickering from one task to the next, coaxing stuck self-driving trucks out of mud holes, around cattle, through rivers. The mist had felt refreshing for a minute, like a light rain, cool. Just for a minute.

It was harder to talk about what came after, the hospital, the times before and after the induced coma.

"Well, always an honor to meet a vet," Terry said. He reached out with one of his big hands—the nails were new and soft and short, the knuckles scarcely wrinkled— and grabbed Casey's to shake it. The red PAIN indicators flickered but didn't quite come on in full at the corner of his vision, as Terry pumped his hand.

"Well, if you're okay Sandra, I think we'll be on our way. Nice meeting you, soldier." Terry slid himself back into the car, the side of it sagging under his weight. Even foamed metal bones and plastic muscle had a lot of weight. His sidekick clambered into the other side, adjusting his belt.

The patrol vehicle spun in a tight circle, and headed off east down the Five in a cloud of dust.

Sandra watched it go.

"You don't have to stay any longer," she said. "They're done with their little road-block at Patience Lake, looks like. It should be clear for a while."

Casey shook his head. "I've almost got your post-hole digger figured out," he said. He called up the interface again in his visual field, found some new control systems, and gave the augur an experimental spin. "See? Let me finish this job, at least."

Sandra cocked her head to one side, her face a mask that concealed the kind of cost-benefit analysis Casey had seen before.

"Sure," she said. "And then do you want to come in for coffee?"

"I can't eat anything," Casey said. "I brought my own nutrients. It's okay." He patted his backpack.

Sandra's grandson, Sean, stared back across the kitchen table. He'd arrived home from school an hour after they'd finished with the digger, and Casey had moved on to diagnosing some malady with the control system of a fussy old converted John Deere tractor.

"How do you even eat, though?" Sean asked. He was about fourteen or fifteen, his hands and shoulders already big, his skinny arms and torso struggling to catch up.

"Sean," his grandmother warned from the coffee maker.

The kitchen was the most civilized place Casey had been in for weeks. Tile floor only a little chipped, big steel fridge humming to itself in the corner, a double sink. Ceramic containers were lined up against the back of the counter for sugar, flour, rice, pasta. Casey suspected it smelled clean, not hospital clean but the clean of a well-used home.

"It's okay," Casey said. "A tube. It's not pretty, but I have to sort of suck everything up. I don't have a tongue anymore." Nor much in the way of gums, no teeth, and not much pharynx. The StrepA-117 in the bomb had been wickedly efficient. It had flensed him from crown to toes. Flensed was a word he'd overheard from one of the doctors while he was in recovery. He'd had to look it up later.

"How many of those nutrient packs do you have?" Sandra wanted to know.

"Enough to get me from Thunder Bay to here," he said.

"You hitched?" Sean asked.

"Some," Casey said. "Mostly I walked."

"Sean, you want to go upstairs and do your homework?" Sandra said. The kid rolled his eyes and complied.

"Can you drink anything else?" Sandra asked once her grandson's door had closed.

"Water," Casey said. "Coffee. Broth."

"How's your knee?"

He paused too long, and she shook her head. "It's not good, is it? How serious is it?"

"I don't know," he said. "I'd need to take it apart to see."

"You can do that?"

"If I have somewhere clean to work. I have some tools, but I'm not sure what I'll need to make a start on fixing anything. . . ."

"Casey, this is a farm. We're not short on tools."

She gave him warm water and a spoon, and privacy while he mixed in one of his nutrient powders. He popped the little hatch at the top of his throat and drew out the tube, stuck it into the glass and sucked. His remaining throat muscles pulled up the liquid until only the dregs remained. He carefully detached the tube from its mounting afterwards, washed it at the kitchen sink, and swabbed the edge of the socket with alcohol, feeling the faint burning on his esophagus as a trace of the vapor wafted down into his throat.

After he was finished, Sandra led him out to the Quonset hut. "Couldn't they have done more for you?" she said. "The Forces?"

He shrugged, plastic shoulders rising and falling in perfect unison. "Build me up like Terry? Sure, yeah, if they'd wanted to spend a couple million. Print me new teeth, new face, new muscles. Few square meters of skin. If you have enough money, you can get that done. Terry . . . looks like he went for the full package." He paused. "Christ, what an idiot."

Sandra barked a laugh. "I've heard that said, though not about him getting upgraded. He's been preening like a peacock for the past three months, since he got back from the clinic in Havana."

"He doesn't know what he's bought."

Sandra flicked a light switch and turned on bare overhead LEDs. The room was a garage and toolshed, with a broken-down car at the far end and workbenches along either side.

"Will this place be clean enough? It's not exactly a hospital."

"There's nothing biological down in my knee," he said. "As long as I don't get any more grit in there, it'll be fine."

Sandra found an old canvas tarp and rolled it out on the floor while Casey pulled his tools out of his backpack. He lowered himself to the floor and hauled his right leg straight with his hands, and rolled up his loose trousers to expose the knee. The whole thing was covered with a shroud of flexible grey plastic. He found the narrow seams and pressed his thumbs in, peeling back the soft surface.

"That doesn't hurt?" Sandra said.

"I've only got real sensory feedback from my hands, and a little from the soles of my feet. Everything else is just a kind of general proprioceptive feedback, some basic awareness of where my arms and legs are."

Under the rubber skin ran rivers of yellow artificial muscles and tendons. The metal kneecap rose up like an island in the middle of the stream of plastic. "I'm going to have to unpin all these muscles. It'll take a while."

He'd meant that she could leave if she wanted. Very few people were eager to watch his self-maintenance. It was surgical, yet inhuman. He called up one of the instructables he'd downloaded after he got out of the hospital and kept it open in the corner of his visual field, occasionally zooming in on the diagrams, double checking. But he'd done this before, replacing worn-out muscles, tightening connections, replacing the metal pins that bound the muscles to his steel femur and fibula.

It looked bad. He pulled the patella out from its nest of soft plastic, and found scratching on the back. He unpinned another couple of muscle groups, and with a pop, his lower leg dangled free. Casey leaned forward and looked down. Sandra flicked on a trouble light and held it up, but he'd already seen the problem.

"Dammit," he said softly. The curse echoed off the curved steel walls of the hut.

"What is it?"

"I've cracked off the end of my femur."

A centimeter of steel had sheared away. The pieces had been jammed to one side, pushing up against the muscles running down his inner leg. A fraction of the edge of the femur head remained on the inside edge, but a crack undermined even that. It would go too, whether tomorrow, or in a week. And then he'd be trying to walk on a completely shattered knee, grinding away his fibula, too.

Casey felt numb. He wondered why he didn't feel worse. He had only a few bucks left on the cards in his wallet. He had no job, and no real hope of getting one. "Three bad breaks," his grandmother had always said when she tossed a few coins into the hats of homeless men propped up at the edges of the Toronto sidewalks. "We're all just three bad breaks away from being there ourselves." This was his third break, Casey knew. He felt sick, a hollow feeling down between his guts and the hard mass of his battery stack.

"Do you have any really good glue?" he finally asked.

"Yeah."

"Could I use some?"

"You're not going to get far gluing it back together," she said.

"A real clinic will charge you six thousand to install a new femur head," he said. "I could install it myself, but a new part is at least a thousand. I could maybe buy a used one online for six, seven hundred."

"Veterans Affairs won't help you out?"

"There are kind of a lot of us," he said. "Since the attacks. Waiting list for major parts was a year, last I checked. They might rent me crutches."

She brought him a tube of clear epoxy, and helped him hold the broken pieces together. When he was satisfied, he carefully, in proper sequence, snapped every muscle back in place again and pulled up the plastic cover, pressing down each tab. It looked like a real knee, at least.

"You'd better stay here tonight," Sandra said.

He looked up. While he'd been busy, the sun had gone down, and the yard was now illuminated by an old sodium-vapor light, glowing sickly yellow from atop a tarry spruce pole.

"I can stay in the barn," he said.

"You'll stay in the house," she said. "Couch is yours."

He woke up once in the night, pushed off the blanket and found his way to the back porch, pushed open the creaking screen door.

The sky was alive.

Clouds had rolled in, and they tossed lightning back and forth, javelins of white fire. The thunder rolled continuously, a guttural growling that shook Casey through his plastic skin, down into the hidden core where he still pumped blood.

He shut off his heads-ups and watched through glassy eyes for an hour while the storm passed.

Terry came back in the morning.

The big black-and-white parked across the middle of the driveway, at a slanting angle that looked careless, but just happened the block access to the road.

Casey was outside with Sandra in the puddle-dotted yard working on getting a tractor running. He was alternating between running it off his implants and the tablet, trying to find out why its crude AI kept spooking when it got too close to fences. The John Deere lurched back and forth near the entrance to the barn.

Terry waved them over and waited near the car.

"Gotta make us walk," Sandra muttered. "Asshole. You stay quiet unless he asks you a direct question, okay?"

Casey nodded.

"Your knee got fixed?" Terry asked as they hiked up to his cruiser. His subordinate was gone, or maybe hiding behind the polarized glass windows of the car, Casey couldn't tell. Anyone could have been back there. He adjusted his eyes, and thought he made out someone in the back. An arrested prisoner, maybe? Looked like someone small, a woman or a kid.

"At least for a little while." Casey said. "Sandra helped."

Terry nodded, and smiled a little, the expression too tight somehow on his broad face. As if he didn't quite have enough skin to spare, after being sliced open and put back together.

"Sandra, you remember that thing we were talking about before?" Terry said.

"Next Tuesday," she said. "I said the fifth, and next Tuesday is the fifth."

"I'm just making sure you remember."

"I remember, Terry."

He frowned—something in her tone was too familiar, had too much quiet contempt. Casey saw it then. The kid who'd grown up in town, every adult knowing him, his parents. Now he'd put on a badge, but he was still just Terry to them. Casey imagined that could be a powerful irritant to a certain kind of personality.

"Good," Terry snapped. He glanced over at Casey one more time, eyed his knee, and climbed back into his cruiser. The car made a messy, aggressive turn, still on manual, and sped off down the Five.

"What was he talking about?" Casey said, and realized as soon as the words were out of his throat what was going on. "Sorry," he said.

Sandra sighed. "Christ, don't know where I'm going to find the money. Have to borrow something from my cousin Pete, if he can spare it."

"How's the shakedown work?"

"Civic Protection Association dues," Sandra said. "Terry's CEO as well as chief constable. The fees were pushed through by his friends on the regional council. Monthly. Plus fines for late payment. Fines for various infractions of local bylaws—Terry is our bylaw officer too, of course—and fines for having an unsecured property, fines for failure to report suspicious activity, fines for pissing off Terry or one of his buddies in uniform."

"No one's gone to the RCMP?"

"That was the first thing we did. But the Force isn't what it used to be, since devolution and privatization. We've had trouble finding an officer willing to take on a petty local thug. There are worse ones than Terry, you know. And after he shot Bill Frazier, no one was exactly willing to take direct action."

"He killed someone?"

"No. Bill owed Terry too much money and he'd already sold his old harvester, and he couldn't afford to sell his new one. When Terry showed up with a seizure order, Bill took a shot at him with his dad's old hunting rifle. Terry didn't quite kill him, but Bill's in prison now and missing a kidney and about four feet of small intestine.

"That's the thing about Terry, he's not stupid, or not stupid enough. He uses paperwork, he has something that looks official backing him up. He's careful enough to cover himself if something goes wrong. And he gets what he wants. He took Bill's harvester and it sold at auction last spring. Victim surcharge. 'Cause Bill shot first."

Casey nodded.

"I'd better go," he said. "He'll think up some fine eventually. Harboring a fugitive or something."

"You're not wanted, are you?"

"No."

"Then stay another day. Terry's dangerous, but he's cautious. Make sure your knee will hold. Head into town then."

Casey paused, silent. He thought he should just walk straight out across the swirling dust of the farmyard and head west, stopping only when he was a hundred klicks away from Sandra's farm and Terry's black-and-white cruiser. Things were bad enough here, he thought. Hadn't he avoided becoming part of these bad situations by skirting around them, past them?

"It's not like I won't put you to work while you're here," Sandra said. "I've still got equipment that you can take a look at. Drones and so forth."

"Okay," Casey said. The word slipped out. Much as he wanted to keep moving, a couch and some useful work had a powerful pull. It felt normal.

The next morning, he worked on the system of the big combine harvester, then started running through the machine's maintenance cycle, checking all its fluids and attacking it with the grease gun he found in the big barn. The machine was in pretty good shape, but he got the sense that the entire farm was understaffed. He remembered the photos inside the house on the mantlepiece, of Sandra's husband and of their grown children, Sean a gangly elementary-school kid. Now it was just two of them.

Late in the afternoon, Sandra headed off down the road, leaving him to sit in the kitchen and watch the news on the TV that had been unrolled and stuck to the freezer door. Upstairs, the sound of a shooter game came from Sean's room. Casey dissolved a vitamin tablet in a cup of warm chicken broth, slurped it up slowly through his tube, then cleaned the tube and cup at the sink.

Sandra came back half an hour later with a package under her arm.

"C'mon," she said. "Something to show you here."

Inside the Quonset hut, she handed him the box and unfolded the tarp again on the floor, carefully brushing it clean of dust.

Casey popped it open. Nestled in old newspapers was a femur head. It looked like real bone, or close enough. He touched it with one finger pad, and felt the cool of hard porcelain.

"Printed ceramic," said Sandra. "A friend of mine has a really good printer in his shed. He can't do metal, though, so I'm afraid it won't be nearly as good as your old titanium one. Should be better than one held together with cheap glue, though. It'll get you farther."

"This . . . I can't afford this."

"You've done two days of specialized tech support, not to mention working on the harvester."

"That's not nearly enough. . . ."

"Jesus, Casey. Sit down and help me install it, would you? The thing's done, and you can argue about how much an unlicensed copy of a femur is worth some other time, okay?"

He didn't say anything, then started to mutter some proper thanks. His eye sockets burned, where what was left of his tear ducts had been sealed off by the doctors. He lowered himself to the tarp and began peeling back the rubberized surface of his knee and the plastic casing of his upper leg.

He left two days later, having done every bit of work he could at the farm, as well as helping out two of Sandra's neighbors. Terry didn't show up again, but the black-and-white always seemed to be lurking nearby.

"I'd drive you, but I've got to head over to my cousin's today," Sandra said. "If you're sure you won't stay one more day, you should go south. Skirt around Patience Lake that way, the south end is outside of Terry's jurisdiction. Head into Saskatoon from there."

Casey nodded, mapping a route. It would take him all day, into the night.

He thanked her as much as he thought she could stand, and started walking.

The puddles from the nightly storms baked off the gravel roads by mid-morning. Casey set a relatively slow pace, pausing several times under trees to drink water and let his fan cool his core down. Crickets droned their steady song from the grass.

His new knee felt good, or at least it wasn't setting off any alarms. He walked past farms, four out of five of them derelict, boarded-up houses standing amid fields watched by quadcopters or blimps.

He veered west finally, just short of dusk, as the banks of heavy black stormclouds gathered again in the south. He started keeping an eye out for an abandoned farmhouse or barn to spend the night in. He could too-easily imagine long fingers of lighting drawn down to his metal bones.

He found shelter a few moments before the edge of the storm hit.

The old house had been torn apart from the inside. His low-light vision showed long tears in the walls where copper wire had been ripped out. Parts of the ceiling had collapsed where the light fixtures had been torn down. The kitchen was a disaster area, sink and piping torn out. The living room wasn't too bad, though. There was a battered couch missing two legs, dotted with stains. Casey avoided it, sweeping a section of floor clean with his feet and sitting down in the corner, back against a wall.

He set his system to monitor the ambient noise—if the storm dropped in intensity, he could head out again, cover some miles in the cool of the early morning. He drifted off to sleep, lulled by rolling thunder.

The beeping of his alarm woke him into a state of confusion. Thunder still rolled outside the house, and rain hammered on the vinyl siding. Why had his alarm gone off?

Then he heard the other noise drop away—a heavy diesel growl. Someone had just shut off a big truck.

Casey slipped a hand into his backpack and pulled out the largest screwdriver from his set of tools, a flathead with a chipped yellow plastic handle. It didn't actually fit any of the screws that held his legs or arms together, but it looked less suspicious than a knife.

He pushed himself up slowly and amped up his hearing, to almost painful levels as another peal of thunder shook the house's timbers.

Two sets of footsteps, moving slowly, too cautious to be people just trying to get out of the rain. They came up the wooden steps, keeping to the outside edges of the stairs, avoiding the creaking middle.

Casey pushed himself up and sidled toward the door, screwdriver held like a dagger.

"Gimme the goggles," someone said, a low whisper. A young voice, sullen, a little scared.

"Fuck you, you forgot yours, use a flashlight." Young again, and again that hint of fear.

"We'll spook him!"

"He isn't getting far. He's not that fast."

The second voice was familiar. His hands would have shaken, if they'd been flesh. Betrayal didn't feel quite the same without a whole body.

"In there," said the second voice.

The one without the goggles complied, almost stumbling over some debris, swearing, slapping at the walls for support. They were coming closer, in through the dining room now.

Lightning flashed, a series of blue-white arcs lighting up the room. The boy poked his head into the living room, stepped forward. A taser was in his hand.

Casey stood still as a statue.

The boy took one more step. Casey turned and plunged the screwdriver into the kid's thigh. The metal disappeared, just a plastic handle stuck to faded denim.

The boy screamed, first in shock and then in pain. He staggered back, falling, both hands reaching for the screwdriver. The taser clattered to the floor, and Casey lunged for it, scrabbling on all fours. Lighting flashed and his eyes whited out for a second, too much light straight into the artificial retinas. He felt for the weapon, hands sweeping the floor like a blind man's cane.

"Dev!" shouted the second kid.

Dev swore and cursed and kicked at the floor with his good leg.

Behind him stood Sean, Sandra's grandson.

Casey found the dropped taser, grabbed its plastic barrel and fumbled for the grip.

"Shit!" Sean said. He raised his own taser, a ruby red laser sight gleaming through the drywall dust.

Sean fired.

A sudden jerk at the side of Casey's cheek, but no shock, no loss of control. Then he was up again, still moving, the other taser in his hands. Sean took a single step back. Casey shot the boy in the chest, and he went down hard.

Unspooled metal wire lay on the floor between them. Sean's shot had been a good one. But the metal barbs had glanced off the smooth, hard plastic of Casey's face. He reached up and felt two tiny divots on one cheek.

In Sean's backpack, Casey found heavy-duty zip ties. He strung a couple together as a tourniquet and put it around Dev's leg above the oozing wound.

"Don't take the screwdriver out, no matter what you do," Casey said. "Imagine a geyser, okay?"

Dev nodded, his face grey.

Sean he cuffed, hands behind the kid's back. He bundled them both into the truck, Devon in the back under the canopy. The vehicle had been left in manual mode.

"What's the password?" Casey asked Sean, as he boosted himself into the driver's seat.

Sean glared back, sullen. More than just a kid in deep trouble, though. Scared, Casey thought, but not as scared as he ought to be.

"C'mon, your friend needs to get to a hospital."

Sean told him, and Casey thought the words into the wireless login. The truck was a newer model, good haptics, and he enjoyed the feeling of the tires digging through mud as they wound their way back down the battered dirt roads, out to the gravel and back onto the highway. The windshield wipers slapped away sheets of rain.

He pulled up in front of Sandra's place.

"You're getting out here," Casey said.

"Please don't tell her!" Sean blurted, the first thing he'd said since they started driving.

Casey just stared at him. "She doesn't already know?" Casey asked. "She didn't send you?" It was bullshit, of course. But it was a lever to get at the truth. "She knew where I was going. If she didn't send you, who did?"

Sean looked down.

"C'mon, say it," said Casey.

"Terry," Sean said. Terry, who kept an eye on everything through the drones that hovered over every field. Terry who'd watched him walk out into the middle of no-where and then sent two kids to ambush him.

"We owe him," Sean said. "A lot more than we can pay, right now. He, he said this would have squared us away for six months."

"And you were going to what, just leave me out there? Pull off my arms and legs, yank out my eyes, sell them, let me starve slow in the middle of nowhere?"

"No!" Sean said. "We were going to put you in a public car, have it drop you off at the hospital. There's a Veterans Affairs center in Regina. Terry said they'd keep you there until they ordered you some new limbs."

Casey shook his head. The center would have been bad enough. Months of waiting, or hobbling around on the cheapest limbs. But he'd never have made it there. His organic remains would have wound up fertilizing one of the more distant fields, of that Casey had no doubt. Sandra had said Terry was careful. Leaving witnesses wasn't careful.

"Get out," he said, popping the door lock with a thought.

Sean stumbled out, and Casey dropped out on his side, careful to land on his good leg. "We're going inside to have a talk with your grandmother."

He closed the doors and told the truck to haul Dev to the nearest hospital, patting its fender as it pulled out of the driveway.

Casey pounded on the screen door until a light came on upstairs. Sandra, wearing sweatpants and a Rough Riders T-shirt, opened the door. Her face was confused, bleary with sleep. Her eyes dropped to Sean's wrists, zip-tied together and to his belt. She almost broke then, Casey thought. Her face began to crumple and her eyes welled for a moment. Then she clamped down again, through force of will. The sadness and shock were still there, but controlled.

Casey wondered, as he cut Sean loose with an X-ACTO knife, what that kind of control cost.

"Tell her," he said to Sean.

Sean spilled the story, circling around and trying to justify himself, until Sandra slapped one hand down hard on the kitchen table, a sound like a rifle crack.

"Was it your idea, or Dev's, or Terry's?" she said.

"Terry called me," Sean said.

"How much were you going to get paid?" Sandra's eyes were hard as polished steel.

"Nothing!" Sean said. "Dev was getting six thousand. We were going to have our debt cleared."

"We owe him more than six thousand," Sandra said.

"I know that!" Sean yelled, his voice breaking. "Do you want to end up like the McKays? They're gone, grandma, remember? Do you want to have to sell everything, declare bankruptcy, and move into a pre-fab welfare box in the city? If we didn't get some money soon, we were going to have to start selling equipment, and what comes after that? What would we have left?"

Sean flung himself back into his chair, still rubbing at his left wrist, at the red mark left by the zip tie. He looked at Casey.

"We'd have been better off if you'd never stopped here," Sean said. He sounded tired, and weighed down by more than fourteen years.

"I know," said Casey. "Give me a ride to Saskatoon. Get me out of here, tonight, far away from Terry and his boys as we can get. And I won't say anything to the Mounties about Sean.

"You know Terry wouldn't have left me as a loose end, alive," Casey said. "Sean could do an adult sentence. Accessory to attempted murder. But I'll just walk away, because you don't deserve to have another bad break."

Sandra's face was hard, hurting. She swallowed and looked across the table at her grandson, his face now white.

"That's more kindness than Sean showed you, I know. But Terry . . . You'd best be gone before he realizes what's happened. We'd better get you in the truck, now. Otherwise, it'll be like what happened to Bill Frazier, except not as neat. Maybe he'll finally see the RCMP come down on him, but none of us are going to be around to see any of that."

The screen door had barely had time to swing shut behind them before they noticed it. Sean picked it up first, the faint orange glow to the west. Casey stopped and zoomed in. Over the rolling prairie, a column of smoke rose up, oily and black.

"I don't think Dev made it to the hospital," Casey said. "Dammit." He wondered now whether it wouldn't have been three graves, not just his, that Terry would have dug.

Casey cranked up his hearing. The sound of grass rustling in the wind was like the roar of a waterfall. He could hear trucks and drones heading up and down the highway, electric motors whirring and tires hissing on the wet pavement. And in the distance but coming on fast, fast as a storm, was the sound of the big black-and-white. Off to the west, its lights strobed red and blue on the horizon.

"Christ on a crutch," Sandra muttered. "I'm getting Sean out of here and finding the rifle."

"No," Casey said. "Rifle won't stop him. Need something bigger."

"Don't have anything bigger. You think we hunt elephants around here?"

"This is a farm," Casey said. "You're not short on tools."

When the car spun into the farmyard, spraying arcs of gravel, Casey stood near the metal curve of the Quonset hut. He raised one hand, a cheerful wave.

The driver's side of the car sprang open and Terry lunged out, his arms two sides of a triangle on the car's hood, in his hands the giant pistol.

Casey was already behind the shed, jogging. The first shot punched a hole in the metal just in front of his face. He skidded to a halt on the gravel and the second blasted through just behind him, peppering his shirt with shards of metal.

From above, Casey heard the whine of a crop-monitoring drone, laboring against the gusts that lingered in the storm's wake.

He was using the blimp's cameras, Casey realized. Terry was targeting him through his eyes in the sky, lining up his shots using targeting software.

Casey bolted, pushing his legs to their limits. They weren't made for running, weren't high-end military models. They were hospital jobs, three years old, battered and used hard, and with a cheap replacement knee on one side.

Something in the knee clicked as he rounded the far corner of the Quonset. Casey lost control, muscles failing to push him forward, and he fell. His hands hit the gravel, sending shocks of pain straight to his brain, while the red indicators flashed in the corners of his vision. SEEK REPAIR, they said.

That's all I was trying to do, he thought.

He pulled himself upright, propped himself against the cinderblock wall at the flat end of the shed. Next to him the big sliding doors were open, the interior black.

There were no more shots. The red and blue lights still flickered on the far side of the building. Footsteps crunched on the gravel, coming around the other side of the building.

Terry stood with his back to the big yellow light that illuminated the farmyard, his face in shadow. The big pistol was still in his right hand, but lowered.

"Casehead," Terry said. "Did I clip you there?"

"Knee went out."

Terry chuckled. "Where are the others?"

"Not here," Casey said.

Terry cocked his head to one side, accessing some video.

"They're just in the house. Unless they've got some secret tunnel or something. C'mon. We can all go have a chat together."

"No."

"I'm not even going to bother saying you're under arrest, Casehead. We know how this is going to go down. You're going to wind up in a vets' hospital, if you're lucky. I had phone and net cut off to the house before I was halfway here, so you're not calling anyone."

He stepped forward, right hand still holding the gun casually, left outstretched.

The shape unfolded from inside the Quonset, tarp-shrouded. It reached out with metal arms and lurched forward, wheels crunching gravel.

Terry jumped back. His gun snapped up and he fired twice. Casey felt the shots send shudders through the metal chassis. Probably did some damage, but farm equipment was built tough.

One arm, designed to hold and drive in heavy wood posts, clamped around Terry's ankle. The cyborg staggered and fell, his knee at an uncomfortable angle. He was still trying to line up another shot with the revolver when the augur came down like steel lightning.

Casey turned away for a second, relying on the crude cameras on the post-hole digger to watch. Terry screamed. He had real skin over those limbs. That was real pain, not transmitted by wires or red warnings flashed in the corner of his vision. Casey almost felt bad for the security man, as the digger tore off his right arm.

Terry stopped struggling after a moment, though the arm kept twitching on the ground.

Casey levered himself upright and locked that damaged knee in place again as best he could, ordering the tendons and muscles to tighten. He walked over to just outside of Terry's reach. Strips of skin hung from the edge of the mangled arm, dripping blood onto the wet gravel. Shredded plastic muscle hung behind that, and in the center the bright, twisted metal of a heavy steel humerus. Casey gingerly pulled the heavy pistol safely free from the twitching fingers.

"Sandra thought you'd be too cautious than to do something this stupid," Casey said. "Stripping a vet for parts, murdering him. It would have taken a while, but someone would have eventually tracked you down and figured out where my parts came from, who killed me. But I'm guessing you're already more desperate than anyone around here knows. Money, right?"

Terry said nothing. The stump of his arm had stopped bleeding. Tiny plastic tourniquets inside the veins, sensing the damage, cutting off the flow. Top of the line stuff, Casey thought.

"You put almost everything you had into these upgrades. Probably borrowed a lot. Got those payments to make. And already, three months in, you're seeing the costs go up. Maintenance. Replacement parts. You've got to plan to switch out all those plastic muscles every couple of years, joints every four or five, optics, sensors, new skin even. It all adds up so fast. They never told you that at the sales pitch. It's a full-time job, keeping body and soul together, when you're one of us.

"You thought you were buying a chance to be a big man. You found out you bought a lifetime of shaking down farmers. And then I wandered in, and that must have seemed too good to be true. Money on foot. And you got reckless."

"Fuck you," Terry said, quietly.

Casey shrugged, and put one hand on the wall of the Quonset, and hop-shuffled back to the house, where Sandra stood on the porch, a rifle in the crook of her arm.

His leg wasn't badly hurt. One of his tendons had come loose, the little steel pin at the end snapping, and once that was replaced from his dwindling bag of spares, it snapped back neatly into the new femur head. He had it fixed before the real police arrived.

It took three days before they sorted everything out and released him, after long days of interrogation in a detention center on the outskirts of the city. His lawyer, a young woman fresh out of law school, told him Terry was still under house arrest as she walked with him down the courthouse steps.

"So he's out?"

"He won't resign," his lawyer said, already flipping through her phone, looking at her next file. "But he's on leave until the investigations end. A couple of his deputies are already gone. It's going to be a mess for a while." She glanced up. "Ride's here for you."

Sandra was waiting at the bottom of the steps with her pickup. It was dusk, and the streetlights were coming on, haloed by moths.

He asked to be taken to the bus depot.

"My disability came in," he said. "Enough for a bus ticket heading up to Fort McMurray. There's a lot of reclamation crews up there, heavy equipment. Might be jobs for a remote operator."

She nodded. "Not willing to stay around Saskatchewan any longer?"

"I'd rather not."

She was silent for a while.

"I didn't tell them about Sean," he said. "I told them it was just his friend, Dev. So Sean should be okay."

"I kind of figured," she said. "I don't think the Mounties believe it. But they haven't arrested him. Thank you for that."

"I owed you, for everything you did for me," he said.

"And where has all our kindness got us?" she said. "I'm going to sell up, move to Foam Lake where I've got more family. I need to keep a closer eye on Sean. What he almost did . . ."

Casey could have said something, but after three days in a holding cell, he felt like he'd just about used up his reserves of politeness.

Sandra dropped him off with a nod at the bus stop. She pulled away before he'd had time to thank her again.

They caught up to him near North Battleford, on the provincial border between Alberta and Saskatchewan.

He got off the bus along with half a dozen other travelers at a dusty automated roadside stop, just a concrete washroom and a series of gas pumps and charging hookups. He was headed for the men's room when they snatched him.

There were three of them, all wearing ski masks, all with thick shoulders and necks. Two grabbed his arms and hauled him around back. The other passengers pretended not to see.

Casey struggled, tried to pull free, to throw his body weight against them. The third one, the edges of a ginger moustache protruding from the mouth-hole of his mask, punched him hard in the gut. Casey felt the battery stack shift. He desperately wanted to throw up. He had no way to do that.

They pinned him to the ground, one man sitting on his legs, the other pulling his arms out above his head, the wrists tight together.

The third man pulled a ball-peen hammer from his belt.

He swung it down four times, until he was satisfied he'd heard enough components shatter. Shards of off-white plastic flew through the air.

They ran, the job done, piled into a blue plastic rental car and sped out of the lot. Heading back east, back down the Yellowhead Highway towards Patience Lake.

Casey got up and tried to raise his right arm. Below the shattered elbow, it swung loosely. His hand felt odd, sending random signals through cracking wires—the sensation of being brushed with oily feathers, prodded with cold pins, of stroking fur frozen into glass. PAIN PAIN PAIN flashed in the corners of his vision. SEEK REPAIR.

He picked up the pieces he could and put them in his backpack, then detached the arm at the elbow. He wrapped it in a plastic shopping bag he found drifting around the gas pumps, and managed to get himself down the aisle of the bus without falling on anyone. One woman offered to phone the police, but he waved her off. This far away from any real city, it would be private security, and he suspected an arrangement to look the other way.

An arm for an arm, he thought, as he tucked the shopping bag awkwardly into his pack.

He'd expected worse. He'd imagined bullets or blunt objects to the back of his head, limbs and batteries stripped, and a covering of dry prairie soil for what remained.

He still might find work. Work, or patience, could get him another bus ticket, down to Edmonton where there was a veterans' center. He could get a new arm, in time, or repair his old one.

He would do it. He would keep moving. One step at a time.

Jonas and the Fox

RICH LARSON

Rich Larson was born in West Africa, has studied in Rhode Island and Ed-monton, Alberta, and worked in a small Spanish town outside Seville. He now lives in Grande Prairie, Alberta. He won the 2014 Dell Award and the 2012 Rannu Prize for Writers of Speculative Fiction. In 2011 his cyberpunk novel Devolution *was a finalist for the Amazon Breakthrough Novel Award. His short work appears or is forthcoming in* Lightspeed, Daily Science Fiction, Strange Horizons, Apex Magazine, Beneath Ceaseless Skies, AE, *and many others, including anthologies* Upgraded, Futuredaze, *and* War Stories. *Find him online at richwlarson.tumblr.com.*

In the story that follows, he brings us to a colony planet where a once-idealistic revolution has turned corrupt and bloodily violent (think the French Revolution and Madam Guillotine), and takes us on the run with a fleeing aristocrat who finds a very unusual place to hide—but one which he might not be willing to pay the price to maintain.

For Grandma

A flyer thunders overhead through the pale purple sky, rippling the crops and blowing Jonas's hair back off his face. Fox has no hair to blow back: his scalp is shaven and still swathed in cling bandages from the operation. He knows the jagged black hunter drones, the ones people in the village called crows, would never recognize him now. He still ducks his head, still feels a spike of fear as the shadow passes over them.

Only a cargo carrier. He straightens up. Jonas, who gave the flyer a raised salute like a good little child of the revolution, looks back at him just long enough for Fox to see the scorn curling his lip. Then he's eyes-forward again, moving quickly through the rustling field of genemod wheat and canola. He doesn't like looking at Fox, at the body Fox now inhabits, any longer than he has to. It's becoming a problem.

"You need to talk to me when we're in the village," Fox says. "When we're around other people. Out here, it doesn't matter. But when we're in the village, you need to talk to me how you talked to Damjan."

Jonas's response is to speed up. He's tall for twelve years old. Long-legged, pale-skinned, with a determined jaw and a mess of tangled black hair. Fox can see the resemblance between Jonas and his father. More than he sees it in Damjan's face when he inspects his reflection in streaked windows, in the burnished metal blades of the harvester. But Damjan's face is still bruised and puffy and there is a new person behind it, besides.

Fox lengthens his stride. He's clumsy, still adjusting to his little-boy limbs. "It looks strange if you don't," he says. "You understand that, don't you? You have to act natural, or all of this was for nothing."

Jonas mumbles something he can't pick up. Fox feels a flash of irritation. It would've been better if Jonas hadn't known about the upload at all. His parents could have told him his brother had recovered from the fall, but with brain damage that made him move differently, act differently. But they told him the truth. They even let him watch the operation.

"What did you say?" Fox demands. His voice is still deep in his head, but it comes out shrill now, a little boy's voice.

Jonas turns back with a livid red mark on his forehead. "You aren't natural," he says shakily. "You're a digital demon."

Fox narrows his eyes. "Is that what the teachers are telling you, now?" he asks. "Digital storage isn't witchcraft, Jonas. It's technology. Same as the pad you use at school."

Jonas keeps walking, and Fox trails after him like he really is his little brother. The village parents let their children wander in the fields and play until dusk—it seems like negligence to Fox, who grew up in cities with a puffy white AI nanny to lead him from home to lessons and back. Keeping an eye on Jonas is probably the least Fox can do, after everything the family has done to keep him safe. Everything that happened since he rapped at their window in the middle of the night, covered in dry blood and wet mud, fleeing for his life.

They pass the godtree, the towering trunk and thick tubular branches that scrape against a darkening sky. Genetically derived from the baobobs on Old Earth, re-engineered for the colder climes of the colony. Fox has noticed Jonas doesn't like to look at the tree, either, not since his little brother tumbled out of it.

The godtree marks the edge of the fields and the children don't go past it, but today Jonas keeps walking and Fox can only follow. Beyond the tree the soil turns pale and thick with clay, not yet fully terraformed. The ruins of a quickcrete granary are backlit red by the setting sun. Fox saw it on his way in, evaluated it as a possible hiding place. But the shadows had spooked him, and in the end he'd pressed on towards the lights, towards the house on the very edge of the village he knew belonged to his distant cousin.

"Time to go back, Jonas," Fox says. "It'll be dark soon."

Jonas's lip curls again, and he darts towards the abandoned granary. He turns to give a defiant look before he slips through the crumbling doorway. Fox feels a flare of anger. The little shit knows he can't force him to do anything. He's taller than him by a head now.

"Do you think I like this?" Fox hisses under his breath. "Do you think I like having stubby little legs and a flaccid little good-for-nothing cock?" He follows after Jonas. A glass bottle crunches under his foot and makes him flinch. "Do you think I like everything tasting like fucking sand because that patched-up autosurgeon almost botched the upload?" he mutters, starting forward again. "I was someone six months ago, I drew crowds, and now I'm a little shit chasing another little shit around in the country and . . ."

A sharp yelp from inside the granary. Fox freezes. If Jonas has put an old nail through his foot, or turned his ankle, he knows Damjan's little arms aren't strong enough to drag him all the way home. Worse, if the ruin is occupied by a squatter, someone on the run like Fox who can't afford witnesses, things could go badly very quickly. Fox has never been imposing even in his own body.

With his heart rapping hard at his ribs, he picks up the broken bottle by the stem, turning the jagged edge outward. Maybe it's nothing. "Jonas?" he calls, stepping towards the dark doorway. "Are you alright?"

No answer. Fox hesitates, thinking maybe it would be better to run. Maybe some desperate refugee from the revolution has already put a shiv through Jonas's stomach and is waiting for the next little boy to wander in.

"Come and look," comes Jonas's voice from inside, faint-sounding. Fox drops the bottle in the dirt. He exhales. Curses himself for his overactive imagination. He goes into the granary, ready to scold Jonas for not responding, ready to tell him they are leaving right now, but all of that dies in his throat when he sees what captured Jonas's attention.

Roughly oblong, dark composite hull with red running lights that now wink to life in response to their presence, opening like predatory eyes. The craft is skeletal, stripped down to an engine and a passenger pod and hardly anything else. Small enough to slip the blockade, Fox realizes. So why had it been hidden here instead of used?

Fox blinks in the gloom, raking his eyes over and around the pod, and catches sight of a metallic-gloved hand flopped out from behind the craft's conical nose. His eyes are sharper now. He supposes that's one good thing. Jonas hasn't noticed it yet, too entranced by the red running lights and sleek shape. He's even forgotten his anger for the moment.

"Is it a ship?" he asks, voice layered with awe.

Fox snorts. "Barely."

He's paying more attention to the flight glove, studying the puffy fingers and silvery streaks of metal running through the palm. It's not a glove. Bile scrapes up his throat. Fox swallows it back down and steps around the nose of the craft.

The dead man tore off most of his clothing before the end. His exposed skin is dark and puffy with pooled blood, and silver tendrils skim underneath it like the gnarled roots of a tree, spreading from his left shoulder across his whole body. Fox recognizes the ugly work of a nanite dart. The man might have been clipped days or even weeks ago without knowing it. He was this close to escaping before it ruptured his organs.

"What's that?" Jonas murmurs, standing behind him now.

"Disgusting," Fox says.

But there's no time to mourn for the dead when the living are trying to stay that way. A month hiding in the family cellar, then Damjan's accident, the tearful arguments, the bloody operation by black-market autosurgeon. Uploading to the body of a brain-dead little boy while his own was incinerated to ash and cracked bone to keep the sniffers away. It was all for nothing.

His chance at escape had been waiting for him here in the ruins all along.

"You can't tell anyone about this, Jonas," Fox says. "None of your friends. Nobody at school."

Jonas's nostrils flares. His mouth opens to protest.

"If you tell anyone about this, I'll tell everyone who I really am," Fox cuts him off. He feels a dim guilt and pushes through it. This is his chance to get off-world, maybe his only chance. He can't let anyone ruin it. He needs to put a scare into the boy. "Your parents will be taken away to prison for helping me," he says. "They'll torture them. Do you want that, Jonas?"

Jonas shakes his dark head. His defiant eyes look suddenly scared.

"Don't tell anyone," Fox repeats. "Come on. Time to go home."

Fox thought himself brave once, but he is realizing more and more that he is a coward. He leads the way back through the rustling fields, past the twisting godtree, as dusk shrouds the sky overhead.

Don't tell anyone. It's the refrain Jonas has heard ever since the morning he came into the kitchen to find all the windows shuttered, their one pane of smart glass turned opaque, and a strange man sitting at the table, picking splinters from the wood. When he looked up and saw Jonas, he flinched. That, and the fact that his mother was scrubbing her hands in the sink as if nothing was out of the ordinary, made Jonas brave enough to stare.

The man was tall and slim and his hands on the table were soft-looking with deep blue veins. There were dark circles under his eyes and the tuft of hair that wasn't hidden away under the hood of father's stormcoat was a fiery orange Jonas had never seen before. Everyone in the village had dark hair.

Damjan, who had followed him from his bunk how he always did, jostled Jonas from behind, curious. Jonas fed him an elbow back.

Their mother looked up. She dried her scalded red hands in her apron. "Jonas, Damjan, this is your uncle who's visiting," she said, in a clipped voice. But this uncle looked nothing like the boisterous ones with bristly black beards who helped his father repair the thresher and drank bacteria beer and sometimes leg-wrestled when they drank enough of it.

"Pleased to meet you, what's your name?" Jonas asked.

The man tugged at the hood again, pulling it further down his face. He gave a raspy laugh. "My name is nobody," he said, but Jonas knew that wasn't a real name.

"What's uncle's name?" he asked his mother.

"Better you don't know," she said, still twisting her fingers in her apron. "And you can't tell anyone uncle is visiting us. Same for you, Damjan."

But Damjan hardly ever spoke anyways, and when he did he stammered badly. Jonas was going to tell his new uncle this when the front door banged open. His uncle flinched and his mother did, too, cursing under her breath how Jonas wasn't allowed to. He didn't know what they were scared of, since it was only father back from the yard. He stank like smoke.

"Burned everything," he said. "The gloves too, I'll need new ones." His eyes flicked over to Jonas and Damjan, slightly bloodshot, slightly wild. "Good morning, my beautiful sons," he said, crossing the room in his long bouncing stride to ruffle Jonas's hair how he always did, to kiss Damjan on his flat forehead.

"Wash first!" Jonas's mother hissed. "Damn it. Wash first, you hear?"

Father's face went white. He swallowed, nodded, then went to the basin and washed. "You've met your uncle, yes, boys?" he asked, slowly rinsing his hands. "You've said hello?"

Jonas nodded, and Damjan nodded to copy him. "Is uncle here because of the revolution?" he asked.

Lately all things had to do with the revolution. Ever since the flickery blue holo-footage, broadcast from a pirate satellite, that had been projected on the back wall of old Derozan's shop one night. The whole village had crowded around to watch as the rebels, moving like ghosts, took the far-off capital and dragged the aristos out from their towers. Jonas had cheered along with everyone else.

"He is," father said, exchanging a look with Jonas's mother. "Yes. He is. A lot of people had to leave the cities, after the revolution. Do you remember when the soldiers came?"

Jonas remembered. They came in a roaring hover to hand out speakaloud pamphlets and tell the village they were Liberated now. That they could keep the whole harvest, other than a small token of support to the new government of Liberated People.

"Some of them were looking for your uncle," father said. "If anyone finds out he's here, he'll be killed. So don't talk about him. Don't even think about him. Pretend he's not here."

Jonas's new uncle had no expression on his gaunt face, but on top of the wooden table his hands clenched so hard that the knuckles throbbed white.

After supper is over and Jonas goes to bed, Fox stays behind to speak to his parents. There is a new batch of bacteria beer ready and Petar pours each of them a tin cup full. It's dark and foamy and the smell makes Fox's stomach turn, but he takes it between his small hands. His cousin Petar is tall and handsome in a way Fox never was, but he has aged a decade in the weeks since Damjan fell. There are streaks of gray at his temples and his eyes are bagged. He slumps when he sits.

His wife Blanka conceals it better. She is the same mixture of cheery and sharp-tongued as she was before. In public she holds to Fox's hand and scolds and smiles as if he really is Damjan, so realistic Fox worried for her mind at first. But he knows now it's only that she's a better actor than her husband, and more viscerally aware of what will happen if someone discovers the truth: that Damjan's brain-dead body is inhabited by a fugitive poet and enemy of the revolution. She drinks the stinking bacteria beer every night, even when Petar doesn't.

"Jonas and I found something in the field today," Fox says, hating how his voice comes shrill and high when he's trying to speak of something so important. "A ship."

Petar was using his thumb to wipe the foam off the top of his cup, but now he looks up. "What kind of ship?" he asks.

"Just a dinghy," Fox says. "Small. One pod. But everything's operational. It only needs a refuel." He takes a swallow of beer too big for his child's throat, and nearly chokes. "Someone was going to use it to break the blockade before a nanodart finished them off," he says. "Now that someone could be me. If you help me again. With this one last thing."

His chest is tight with hope and fear. Petar looks to Blanka.

"You would leave," Blanka says. "In Damjan's body."

Fox nods his bandaged head. "The transfer was a near thing," he said. "Even if we could find that bastard with the autosurgeon again, trying to extract could wipe me completely."

That isn't true, not strictly true. He would probably survive, but missing memories and parts of his personality, the digital copy lacerated and corrupted. That might be worse than getting wiped.

"So, we would have another funeral," Petar says. "Another funeral for Damjan, but this time with all the village watching and with no body to bury."

"You can tell people it was a blood clot," Fox says. "An aftereffect from the fall. And the casket can stay closed."

Petar and Blanka look at each other again, stone-faced. People are different out here in the villages. Hard to read. It makes Fox anxious.

"Then you can be at peace," he says. "You don't have to see . . . This." He encompasses his body with one waving hand. "You just have to help me one more time. It might be the best shot I'll ever have at getting off-world."

"Maybe the ship was put there as a trap," Blanka says. "Did you think of that, poet? To draw you or other aristos out of hiding."

Fox hadn't thought of that, but he shakes his head. "They wouldn't go to that much trouble," he says. "Not for me or anyone else that's left. All the important people digicast out before the capital fell." He leans forward, toes barely scraping the floor. "I'll never forget what your family has done for me."

"Family helps family," Petar mutters. "Family over everything." He looks up from his beer and Fox sees his eyes are wet. "I'll need to see the ship," he says. "You've been safe like this, in Damjan's body. Maybe now you can escape and be safe forever. Maybe that is why Damjan fell. His life for your life."

His shoulders begin to shake, and Blanka puts her arm across them. She pulls Fox's beer away and pours it slowly into her empty cup. "It's time for you to go to bed," she tells him, not looking into his eyes—into Damjan's eyes.

Fox goes. The room he shares with Jonas is tiny, barely big enough to fit the two quickfab slabs that serve as beds. Jonas isn't asleep, though. He's sitting upright with his blanket bunched around his waist.

"You're going to take the ship, aren't you?" he says. "You're going to go up into space and visit the other worlds and see all the stars up close. That's what aristos do." The penultimate word is loaded with disdain.

"I'm going to get away from the people who want me executed," Fox says.

Jonas slides down into his bed, turned away facing the wall. "Aristos go up and we sit in the mud, teacher says. Aristo bellies are full of our blood."

"Your teacher spouts whatever the propaganda machine sends him," Fox says wearily. *"Bellies bloated with the blood of the masses.* That was my line. Bet your teacher didn't tell you that."

Jonas doesn't reply.

Fox undresses himself and climbs into bed. He tries, and fails, to sleep.

Jonas doesn't sleep right away either. He's wary of bad dreams since the day he climbed the godtree. The day they learned, in school, about the smooth white storage cone embedded in the backs of the aristos' soft-skinned necks.

Their new teacher was a tall stern man dressed all in black, replacing the chirping AI that had taught them songs and games, but everyone got brand-new digipads so they didn't mind. All the lessons were about the revolution, about the aristos who'd kept their boot on the throat of the people for too long and now were reaping the harvest, which made no sense to Jonas because the teacher also said aristos were weak and lazy and didn't know how to work in the fields.

One day the teacher projected a picture on the wall that showed a man without skin or muscles, showing his gray skeleton, and a white knob sunk into the base of the skull.

"This is where aristos keep a copy of themselves," the teacher said, pointing with his long skinny finger. "This is what lets them steal young healthy bodies when their old ones die. It's what lets them cross the stars, going from world to world, body to body, like a disease. Like digital demons."

Jonas thought of his uncle who stayed in the basement, the hood he always wore. That, and his soft hands, his way of speaking that swallowed no sounds, made it obvious.

He was an aristo. It made Jonas frightened and excited at the same time. Had he lived in a sky-scraping tower in the city and eaten meat and put his boot on the throat of the good simple people? Had he skipped through the stars and been to other worlds?

When Jonas came home from school, he tried to ask his father, but his father shook his head.

"Whatever he was, he's family," he said. "Family over everything. So you can't talk about him. Don't even think about him. Promise me, Jonas."

But it was hard to not think about. Especially hard to not think about the stars and the other worlds. Jonas knew the branches of the godtree were the best place to watch the stars from. To dream from. Sometimes they looked close enough to touch, if he could only climb high enough and stretch out his arms. Jonas was a good climber. Feeling electric with new excitement, he dodged his mother's chores that day and went out to the fields.

He barely noticed Damjan following, how he always followed.

Fox is waiting outside the small quickcrete cube of a building that serves as the village school. The pocked gray walls are painted over with a mural, a cheery yellow sun and blooming flowers. All the children streamed out a few minutes ago, chattering, laughing. Some of them came over to touch Fox gingerly on the head and ask if he was better yet. Fox encounters this question often and finds it easiest to nod and smile vaguely. He knows Damjan was never much of a talker.

But the last of the children have gone home now, and Jonas still hasn't come out. It's making Fox anxious. He stands up from his squat—he can squat for ages now, Damjan's small wiry legs are used to it more than they are to chairs—and walks around the edge of the building, towards the window. The smart glass is dimmed, and scratched, besides, but when he stands on tiptoe he can see silhouettes. One is Jonas and the other a tall, straight-backed teacher with his arms folded across his chest. The conversation is muffled.

Fear prickles in Fox's stomach again, the fear that's threatened to envelop him ever since a friend woke him in the middle of the night and showed him his face on the blacklist, declared an enemy of the Liberated People. The new government isn't stupid. They know to start with the children. Jonas's head is full of the vitriol Fox helped spark not so long ago, back when he'd fooled himself into thinking the violence of the revolution would be brief and justified.

Fox's heart pounds now. He sees Jonas's silhouette turn to leave, and he quickly darts back to his usual waiting place outside the main door. The boy comes out with a scowl on his face that falters, then deepens, when he catches sight of Fox. He gives only the slightest jerk of his head as acknowledgement, then goes to walk past.

Fox doesn't let him. "What did you tell him?" he demands in a whisper, seizing Jonas's arm.

Jonas wrests it away. His expression turns hard to read, like his parents'. Then a hesitant smirk appears on his face.

Fox feels the panic welling up. "What did you do?" he demands, grabbing for him again.

Jonas grabs back, pinching his hand hard with his nails. "Come on, Damjan," he says with a fake cheeriness, tugging him along. "Home time, Damjan."

"You stupid little shit," Fox rasps, barely able to speak through the tightness in his chest. "They'll take your parents, you know that? They'll take them away for helping me. You'll never see them again." He can already hear the whine of a hunter drone, the stamp of soldiers' boots. His head spins. "The fall wasn't my fault," he says, with no aim now but lashing out like a cornered animal. "It was yours."

Jonas's face goes white. His hand leaps off Fox's like it's been burnt. "He followed me," Jonas says. "I told him to wait on the low branch. But he didn't." He's gone still as a statue. A sob shudders through him. "I didn't tell teacher anything."

"What?" Fox feels a wave of relief, then shame.

"I didn't tell teacher about you," Jonas hiccups, and then his eyes narrow. "I should have. I should tell him. If I tell him, they'll forgive my parents. They aren't aristos. They're good. They're Liberated People."

Suddenly, Jonas is turning back towards the school, his jaw set like his father's. The red mark on his forehead is back.

"Wait," Fox pleads. "Jonas. Let me explain myself."

Jonas stops, turns. Giving him a chance.

Fox's mind whirls through possibilities. "The fall wasn't your fault," he says slowly. "And Damjan knows that."

"Damjan is dead," Jonas says through clenched teeth. "His brain had no electric in it."

"But when they did the transfer," Fox says. "You remember that, yes? The surgery? When they put my storage cone into Damjan's brainstem, I got to see his memories. Just for a moment."

Jonas's eyes narrow again, but he stays where he is. He wipes his nose, smearing snot across the heel of his hand.

"I saw Damjan wanted to follow you up the tree," Fox says slowly, feeling his way into the lie. "Because he always wanted to be like you. He knew you were strong and brave and honest. He was trying to be like you, even though he knew he should have waited on the lower branch. And when he fell, he didn't want you to feel bad. He didn't want you to feel guilty." Fox taps the back of his bandaged head, where the storage cone is concealed. "That was the last thing Damjan thought."

Tears are flowing freely down Jonas's cheeks now. "I wanted to go higher," he says. "When I go high enough, it feels like I can touch the sky."

Fox reaches up and puts his hand on Jonas's shoulder, softly this time. His panic is receding. He has Jonas solved now. There's a bit of guilt in his gut, but he's told worse lies. He would tell a dozen more to make sure nothing goes wrong, not now that Petar has seen the ship and agrees it will fly. Not now that he's so close to escaping.

Jonas's father has forbidden him to go near the granary again, but he still goes out to the fields the next day. He has always bored quickly of the games the other children play, even though he can throw the rubber ball as hard as anyone and dodges even better. He's always preferred to wander.

His nameless uncle is with him. It's still hard to look at Damjan's face and know Damjan is not behind it, but talking comes a little easier since what happened yesterday. When his uncle asks why he was kept behind after school by the teacher, Jonas tells him the truth.

"We're learning about the revolution," he says. "About the heroes. Stanko was my favorite. He took the capital with a hundred fighters and he's got an eye surgery to see in the dark. But yesterday the lesson changed on my pad." He motions with his hand, trying to capture how the text all dissolved and then reformed, so quick he barely noticed it. "Now it says General Bjelica took the capital. It says Stanko was a traitor and they had to execute him. So I told teacher it wasn't right."

Damjan's face screws up how it does before he cries, but no tears come out, and Jonas knows it's because grown-ups don't cry. "I met Stanislav once," his uncle says. "He was a good man. Maybe too good. An idealist."

"You met Stanko?" Jonas demands. "What did his eyes look like?"

His uncle blinks. "Bright," he says. "Like miniature suns."

Jonas stops where he is, the tall grass rustling against his legs, as he envisions Stanko tall and strong with eyes blazing. "Like stars," he murmurs.

His uncle nods. "Maybe he got away," he says. "There's a lot of false reports. Maybe he's in hiding somewhere."

Jonas asks the question, then, the one that has been bubbling in the back of his mind for days. "The revolution is good," he says. "Isn't it?"

His uncle gives a laugh with no happiness in it. "I thought it was," he says. "Until the bloodshed. Until cynics and thugs like Bjelica took over. After everything I did for their cause—all the rallies, all the writing—they turned on me. Ungrateful bastards."

"Why did you want the revolution if you're an aristo?" Jonas asks plainly.

"Because there weren't meant to be aristocrats or underclass after the revolution," his uncle says, with a trace of anger in Damjan's shrill voice. "Everyone was meant to be equal. But history is a wheel and we always make the same mistakes. The only difference is who gets crushed into the mud." He picks anxiously at a stalk. "The ruling families were bad," he says. "The famines, and all that. But this is worse."

Jonas considers it. The teacher told them that there would be no famines anymore. They would keep their whole crop, except for a small token of support to the government of Liberated People. "Did you lose many in the famine?" he asks, because it's a grown-up question. "I had a little sister who died. And that's why Damjan is different. Was different. Because mother couldn't feed him well enough."

Damjan's mouth twists. For a moment his uncle doesn't respond. "No," he finally says. "Not many." Damjan's face is red, and Jonas realizes his uncle is ashamed of something, though what he can't guess. "I wrote a poem series about the famine," he says. "Years ago. I still remember it. Do you want to hear some of it, maybe?"

Jonas hesitates. He doesn't know if he likes poetry. But maybe if he listens to the poetry, he can ask more questions about Stanko and the capital, and then about the stars and the other worlds his uncle will soon go to.

"Alright," he agrees. "If it's not really long."

The week passes at two speeds for Fox, agonizingly slow and terrifyingly fast. Petar has spread word that the old granary past the edge of the terraform has broken glass and an old leaking oil drum inside it, to ensure the other parents keep their children away. Fox's nights are spent poring over schematics with Blanka or else sneaking out to the ship itself with Petar.

During the day, he spends most of his time with Jonas. The boy is bright and never runs dry of questions, and ever since Fox's first recitation he's been devouring poetry. Not necessarily Fox's—he prefers it when Fox recites the older masters, the bolder and more rhythmic styles. He has even started scribbling his own poem using charcoal on the wall of their bedroom, which made Petar and then Blanka both shake their heads.

He reminds Fox a little bit of himself as a child. Too clever to get along with the other children, too brash and too stubborn, worryingly so. But Fox has other concerns. The ship is tuned and refueled and finally ready to fly, and the village's weather probe predicts a rolling storm in a fortnight. That's when Fox will launch, while the thunder and lightning masks the take-off. His days in the village, his days in Damjan's body, are finally numbered.

Fox is in the cramped bedroom, laboring with a piece of Jonas's charcoal. The boy's favorite poem is a short one, but even so it takes a long time for Fox to transcribe it onto the clear stretch of wall. He's only halfway finished the memento, his small hands smeared black, when he hears Jonas arrive home from the school. A moment later, he hears a shriek from Blanka.

Fox goes stiff and scared, ears strained for the thump of soldiers' boots, but there's nothing but Blanka's angry voice and Jonas's near-inaudible reply. He wipes his hands on his trousers and goes to the kitchen.

Jonas is standing sullenly with his shirt knotted in his hands. Blanka is in a rage, and Fox realizes why as soon as he sees the bruises on Jonas's bare back.

"That spindly bastard, I'll snap him in halves," she's snarling. "What happened, Jonas? What happened, my beautiful boy?"

Jonas lifts his head. "Teacher switched me," he says. "For telling lies." He turns as he says it, and his eyes catch on Fox. He gives a smile that fills Fox with pure dread. Fox knows, somehow, what's coming. "We learned about enemies of the revolution today," Jonas says. "There was one aristo who tried to convince the Liberated People to let all the aristos go without getting punished. They called him the Fox because he had red hair."

"Oh, no," Blanka murmurs. "Oh, Jonas. What did you say?"

"I said he helped the revolution," Jonas says defiantly, looking Fox in the eye. "I said he wrote the poem, the one about aristo bellies full of our blood."

"You should not have done that, Jonas," Fox says, surprised he can speak at all. "That was dangerous. That was very dangerous." His panic is welling up again, numbing him all over. "They have gene records. They know that I'm a cousin to your father."

Jonas bites at his lip, but his eyes are still defiant. "I wanted to be brave," he says. "Strong and brave and honest. Like Damjan thought I am."

Fox feels adrift. He knows Jonas, no matter how sharp he seems, is still a child. There's no way he can understand what he's just done. Maybe it's Fox's own fault, for filling his head with all the poems.

Maybe they'll be lucky, and the teacher will keep Jonas's transgression to himself. Fox has been lucky before.

When father comes home mother tells him what happened, and his whole body seems to sink a little. Jonas feels the disappointment like he feels the welts on his back, and worse, he can tell that his father is scared. There is a brutal silence that lasts all evening until he goes to bed, lying on his stomach with a bit of medgel spread over his back. He knows he made a mistake. Even though he didn't say his uncle was with them, he said too much.

Jonas tries to apologize to his uncle, who is lying very straight and very still, staring up at the ceiling, and Damjan's voice mutters something about everything being fine and not to worry about anything. It doesn't sound like he believes it. Between the aches in his back and the thoughts in his head, Jonas takes a very long time to fall asleep. Halfway through a bad dream, his mother's hands shake him awake.

"Up, Jonas. You, too, Damjan."

Jonas wrenches his eyes open. It's still dark through the window and he hears a high whining noise he recognizes coming from outside. A hover. Jonas feels a spike of cold fear go all the way through him.

"I need to pee," he says.

"Later," mother says. "There are some men here to speak with your father. To look around the house." Her voice is strained. "If they ask you anything, think three times before you say anything back. Remember that uncle was never here."

Then she's gone again, leaving Jonas alone with his uncle. In the light leaking from the hall, Jonas can see Damjan's small round face is etched with terror, so much that he almost wants to take his hand and squeeze it. As if he really is Damjan, and not the Fox. Jonas listens hard to the unfamiliar voices conversing with his father. One of them sounds angry.

Loud stomping steps in the hall, then the door opens all the way and two soldiers come in with mother and father close behind. They are not as tall as father but their black coats and bristling weapons make them seem bigger, more frightening, like flying black hunter drones that have turned into men.

"Good morning, children," one of them says, even though it is the middle of the night. He gives a small smile that doesn't crinkle his eyes and raises one fist in the salute of the Liberated People.

Jonas returns it, and shoots his uncle a meaningful look, but Damjan's little fists are stuck to his sides. Fortunately, the soldier is focused on him, not his uncle.

"You must be the older," he says. "Jonas, isn't it? You told our friend the teacher something very strange today, Jonas. What did you tell him?"

Jonas's mouth is dry, dry. He looks to mother, who is framed between the men's broad shoulders, and she starts to speak but the second soldier puts a warning finger to his lips.

"We want to hear from Jonas, not from you," the first one says. "What did you tell your teacher, Jonas?"

Jonas knows it is time to be brave, but not honest. "I said that the Fox helped the revolution," he says. "I was confused. I thought he was Lazar. Lazar makes the songs for the satellite to play." He looks at both the soldiers, trying to gauge if they believe him. He lifts his nightshirt and turns so he won't have to look them in the eye. "Teacher was mad and didn't let me explain," he says. "He just started to switch me. Look how bad he switched me."

"A few stripes never killed anyone," the soldier says. "It'll make you look tough. Your little girlfriends will like that, right? Turn around."

Jonas drops his shirt and turns back, ready to meet the soldiers' gaze again. His uncle gives an encouraging nod where they can't see him.

"Did you know that this Fox, this enemy of the revolution, is a relative of yours?" the soldier asks. "A cousin to your father?"

"Yes," Jonas says. "But we don't know him. He's never come here."

The other soldier, who hasn't spoken yet, barks a short and angry laugh. "We'll see about that," he says, in a voice like gravel. "We'll have a sniff." He pulls something from his jacket and fits it over his mouth and nose like a bulbous black snout.

Jonas has heard of sniffer masks—his uncle explained them when they were in the field one day, how each person born had a different odor, because of their genes and their bacteria, and you could program a sniffer mask to find even the tiniest trace of it—but he has never seen one before now. It makes the soldier look like a kind of animal. When he inhales, the sound is magnified and crackling and makes Jonas shudder.

Behind the soldiers, mother has her hands tucked tight under her armpits. Her face is blank, but Jonas imagines she is thinking of all the scrubbing, all the chemicals she used anywhere uncle sat or ate. But uncle's old body has been gone for weeks now, and the smells would be too, wouldn't they?

As the sniffer moves around the room, the first soldier leans in close to the wall to look at the charcoal lettering. "What's this?" he asks. "Lessons?"

"Yes," Jonas says quietly.

"Good," the soldier says, and Jonas sees his eyes moving right to left on it, instead of left to right, and realizes he's like most of the older people in the village who can't read. It gives him a small sense of relief.

That only lasts until he looks over and sees the sniffer has stopped beside his uncle. "What happened to the boy's head?" the sniffer asks, voice distorted and grating.

"He fell," father says from the doorway. "A few weeks ago. He isn't healed in the brain yet. He's a little slow."

"Are you, boy?" the sniffer demands.

Jonas clenches his thumbs inside his fists. There is no part of uncle's body left in Damjan's, only his digital copy, his soul, but Jonas wonders if the sniffer might somehow be able to detect that, too.

His uncle looks up with a confused smile and reaches to touch the sniffer mask. The sniffer jerks back, then pushes him towards the door, more gently than Jonas would have expected, and continues searching the room. Jonas releases a breath he didn't know he was holding.

The sniffer works through the rest of the house, too, and Jonas and his family drift slowly along with him to open doors and cupboards, to make sure there are no traps or surprises. The horrible sucking sound of the sniffer mask sets Jonas's teeth on edge. It feels like a strange dream, a bad one. His eyes are sore and his bladder is squeezing him.

When they finally finish with the cellar, the sniffer looks irritated but the other soldier is relieved. "We'll be off, then," he says. "Remember, if he ever contacts you in any way, it's your duty to report him. He's not one of us. He cut ties with you and with all decent people the day he had his storage cone implanted."

Father nods, his mouth clenched shut, and shows the soldiers out. Jonas follows, because he wants to make sure, really sure, that the nightmare is over. Father doesn't send him back in. The soldiers are out the door and past the bushes when the sniffer suddenly stops. His mask is still on, and the sucking noise comes loud in the still night air.

Jonas remembers that the last charred bits of uncle's old skeleton are buried underneath the bushes. His father is not breathing, only staring. The sniffer lingers.

Jonas braces himself. He reminds himself that he is brave. Then he darts away from the door before father can pull him back, jogging up behind the sniffer and tugging his arm. "Can I see the hover?" he asks loudly.

The sniffer whirls and shoves him backward. Jonas squeals, loud and shrill how mother hates it, and he lets his piss go in a long hot stream that soaks his legs, splatters the bushes and the soldier's boots. It's very satisfying. Especially when the sniffer yanks his mask down and curses.

"I thought the other boy was the slow one," he says.

"He's frightened," father says, coming and gripping Jonas by the arm. "You frightened him. Please, just go."

As Jonas watches, the soldiers climb into their hover. They go.

The instant the whine of the hover fades away into the distance, Fox tells Petar and Blanka that it has to be tonight. His heart is still pounding away at his tiny ribcage, so hard he imagines the bones splintering. He's sweating all over.

"That was too close," he says. "Too close. I have to launch tonight."

Everyone is in the kitchen. Blanka is wetting a rag for Jonas to clean himself; Petar is standing behind a chair and gripping it tightly, rocking it back and forth on its legs. They all turn their heads to look at Fox.

"There's no storm tonight," Blanka says, handing Jonas the rag. "Someone will see the exhaust burn. It'll be loud, too."

Fox shakes his head. "Nobody around here knows what a launch looks or sounds like," he says. "And Petar, you told everyone there was oil in the granary, didn't you?"

His cousin blinks. "Yes." He pauses, then looks to his wife. "We could set fire to the granary. That should be enough to cover the noise and the light so long as he goes up dark."

Blanka slowly nods. "Alright. Alright. You'll need help moving the ship out. I'll come as well."

"I want to come," Jonas says, wide-eyed, wringing the rag between his hands. Fox realizes he never did finish the poem on the wall.

"Bring Jonas, too," he says. "To say goodbye."

Bare minutes later, they are dressed and out the door, moving quickly through the crop field. The night air is cold enough to sting Fox's cheeks. Fear and anticipation speed his short legs and he manages to keep pace with Petar and Blanka, who are lugging the gas. Jonas skips ahead and then back, electric with excitement, already forgetting the fear.

"I pissed on a soldier," he whispers.

"I saw from the window," Fox grunts. "But a sniffer can't read DNA from ashes and bone. He had nothing."

"Oh." Jonas's face reddens a bit. "I'll do it again, though. I hate the soldiers as bad as the aristos. I want everyone equal, like you said."

Blanka puts a finger to her lips, and Jonas falls silent. Fox is glad to save his breath. They pass under the godtree, its twisted branches reaching up towards a black sky sewn with glittering stars. For a moment Fox dares to imagine the future. Slipping through the blockade and into the waiting arms of civilization. Telling his tale of survival against all odds. Maybe he'll be famous on other worlds how he so briefly was here.

And he'll be leaving Jonas's family to suffer through whatever comes next. The thought gnaws at him so he shoves it away. He reminds himself that Petar and Blanka are clever people. They know how to keep their heads down. They know how to keep silent and survive.

At the entrance to the abandoned granary, Fox switches on the small lantern he brought from the kitchen and lights the way for Petar and Blanka. They haul the tiny ship out on wooden sledges Petar made for it a day ago. Jonas puts his small shoulder into it and pushes from behind.

Fox checks everything he remembers, moving from the nosecone to the exhaust, then yanks the release. The ship shutters open, revealing the waiting passenger pod. Its life support status lights glow a soft blue in the dark. Ready. In the corner of his eye Fox sees Jonas staring up at the stars.

The ones who survive will be the ones who can keep their heads down. Fox knows it from history; he knows in his gut it's happening here. Jonas isn't one of those. Maybe he'll learn to be, but Fox doesn't think so.

Before he can stop himself, he turns to Blanka. "Jonas should go," he says. "Not me."

Jonas's head snaps around, but Fox doesn't look at him. He watches Blanka's face. She doesn't look shocked, the way he thought she would, but maybe it's just that people are different in the village. Harder to read.

"What do you mean?" Petar demands.

"Jonas should take the ship," Fox says, because why else would he have told them to bring Jonas? He must have known, in the back of his mind, that this was what he needed to do. One brave thing, and then he can go back to being a coward. "He's already pissed off the teacher and pissed on a soldier," Fox continues. "He's going to keep putting himself in danger here. And the two of you, as well."

"You're the one who put us in danger," Petar snaps. "You would take another son from me now, cousin?"

"He's never fit right here, Petar," Blanka says, and for the first time Fox sees tears in her eyes. "He's always had his head up in the sky. We used to say that, remember?"

"He would be safer somewhere else," Fox says. "Let him take the ship. It's all automated from here on in." He pauses. Breathes. "Let him take the ship, then you can burn down the granary and say he was playing in it. You can use what's left of my bones if you need proof."

Petar looks at his son. "Is this what you want to do, then, Jonas?" he asks hoarsely.

Jonas chews his lip. Turns to Fox. "Could I come back? Will I be able to come back?"

"Not soon," Fox says. He knows there are still too many factions scrabbling in the power vacuum, knows things will get worse before they get better. "But some day. When things stabilize. Yes." He can feel himself losing his nerve. He almost hopes Jonas will refuse.

"I want to go," Jonas says solemnly. Petar gives a ragged cry and wraps him in his arms. Blanka hugs him from behind, putting her cheek against his cheek. Fox feels ashamed for watching. He looks away.

"What about uncle?" Jonas asks, his voice muffled by the embrace. "Will he be Damjan forever?"

Fox swallows as his cousin straightens up, and tries to look him in the eye. "You could say I was in the fire, too," he says. "That Damjan was in there. And I could leave again. Try my luck going north. You wouldn't have to look at me and remember all the time."

Petar looks sideways to Blanka. Slowly, they both shake their heads. "You can never be Damjan and you can never be Jonas," Blanka says. "But you are family. We've kept you safe this long, haven't we?"

Fox dares to imagine the future again, this time in the village, slowly growing again in Damjan's body. He did used to dream of retiring to the countryside one day. And he's learned how to keep his head down. Soon the bandages will be off and his storage cone, shaved down and covered over with a flap of skin by the autosurgeon, will be undetectable.

Maybe the violence will be over in a few years' time. Maybe Damjan will become a poet, a better one than Fox ever was.

"Thank you," he says. "All of you."

He stands aside while Jonas's parents say their goodbyes. Jonas does his best to be sad, but Fox sees his eyes go to the ship over and over again, an excited smile curling his lips. He hugs his mother fiercely, then his father, then comes to Fox.

"You can have my bed," he says. "It's bigger." He raises his arms. Pauses. He sticks out one hand instead to shake.

Fox clasps it tight. "I'll do that," he says.

Then Jonas is clambering into the pod, the restraints webbing over him to hold him in place during launch, and it's too late for Fox to take it all back even if he wanted to. The ship folds shut. The smell of gas prickles Fox's nose and he realizes Petar is dousing one side of the granary to ensure it burns. When he's finished, Blanka takes his gas-slicked hand in hers, and takes Fox's with the other. They walk the agreed-upon distance with a few steps extra to be safe.

The ship squats on the pale soil, rumbling through its launch protocols, and then the engine ignites. Fox feels it in his chest, vibrating through his bones. Riding a bonfire of smelting orange flame, the ship begins to rise, one fiery tongue catching the roof of the granary on the way up. The engine burns even brighter, stamping itself onto Fox's retinas, and by the time he blinks them clear the ship is only a pinpoint of light disappearing into the sky.

The crackling flames leap high, consuming the granary and making it hard to see the stars. Fox can imagine them, though. He can imagine Jonas slipping through the blockade to freedom. In the corner of his eye, Petar lifts his hand high, but open, not the clenched fist of the soldiers.

Fox raises his arm. He does the same.

prodigal

GORD SELLAR

Dogs have been considered to be humanity's "best friend" and most loyal companion for untold thousands of years, but, as the unsettling story that follows suggests, that may not be true for very much longer.

Gord Sellar was born in Malawi, grew up in Nova Scotia and Saskatchewan, and currently lives in South Korea with his wife and young son, where he teaches at a university. He graduated from Clarion West in 2006, and has subsequently made sales to Asimov's Science Fiction, Interzone, Fantasy, and Tesseracts Twelve. In addition to writing, Sellar is a jazz saxophonist and a jazz buff, he has done screenplays for a few films that got produced, including South Korea's first Lovecraft adaptation, and is working on a forthcoming anthology of Korean SF in English translation. His Web site is at www.gordsellar.com.

H e doesn't *look* any different," Jennifer commented, when we got home from the research facility, after Benji's final sentientization treatment.

"He's not supposed to yet, are you, boy?" I said, ruffling the hair on his head. He looked up at us from the tatty carpet with his big, curious terrier eyes, and I'd swear he smiled a little.

Technically, she was right. He didn't really act very differently, not in any tangible way. Having recuperated from his surgeries and treatments, he still liked the same things: fetch-the-ball, chasing me around the backyard, going for a run—familiar pleasures. He'd still come and sit beside me as I watched TV in the evenings, content with a pat on the head or a scratch behind the ear when he caught me working. He was our good-natured consolation prize. Our gentle not-quite-a-child, a terrier puppy whose brain was developing massive neural connectivity day by day, the sparse woodland of his mind turning into a dense jungle, and whose mouth and throat had been cleverly sculpted into a system capable of expressing in speech those thoughts he'd already started having. I thought of it as this incredible gift, at the time, albeit a gift he hadn't quite received yet. A miracle. He'd be a wonder-dog. That was why we'd called him Benji, after all.

But I'd be lying if I said I didn't see a change in him right from day one. It was something about his eyes. Something . . . well, just *more* than before. To me, it was unmistakable.

A few months later, we had some people over. It was the first party we'd had in half a year, mostly neighbors and coworkers, people like that. Some had heard about Ben, that he'd begun to talk finally. They expected some kind of demonstration. I'd warned him, hoping it would make him less nervous, but it had the opposite effect. He began to tap his front paws on the carpet, to shake his head a little like a wet puppy, his tail half-wagging. The first few people were folks who'd never come to a party at our place before, and Ben nervously avoided them.

Then Lorna arrived. A wannabe-painter friend of Jennifer's, Lorna was familiar with Ben. She had played with him before the treatment, so he remembered her a little. As soon as her bulky shoulders passed through the doorframe, Benji barked excitedly. It had become a strange sound, no longer his own, no longer quite dog-like, but he didn't seem to notice or care. He ran up to her and began sniffing at her feet. Ears perking up in recognition, he mumbled a distracted, "Hello," before sticking his nose into her crotch for a sniff. Then he simply proclaimed, "Nice!"

"Oh my!" Lorna said, reaching down at him. "Now, Ben, you really mustn't do that!" She forced his head down, pushing his face away from her, and said to me, "I thought they were supposed to be *intelligent* post-op?"

"I'm so sorry," Jennifer said. "Tim, maybe you should take him upstairs?"

I nodded. "Come on, Benj," I said, and tucked my hand under his collar. I led him to the bottom of the stairs, and he went up them obligingly. I followed him up and then said, "Left, Benji, left." He followed the direction, and walked into our bedroom. "Good boy," I said when we were both in, scratching behind his ear.

"Why?" he asked me, looking up curiously.

"Well, you're not supposed to sniff people like that."

"Sniff?"

"You know," I said, and did my best impression of a dog sniffing.

"Oh. Nice sniff! Hello friend!"

"No, for dogs it's a nice hello. For *people*, it's rude," I explained, while fishing a hide dog bone out of my sock drawer. I tossed it to him, and he caught it out of the air, but he didn't chew it right away. Instead, he just set it down and stared at me as if he had some question he didn't know how to phrase. After a while, he seemed to abandon the attempt, and as he chomped down on the bone, I quickly left the room, closing the door behind me. Before I went down to the party, I heard him pad toward the door, sigh loudly, and settle down onto the floor beside the door.

But that was what I'd always done with him at parties. It was nothing new. Except . . . it felt different now, doing that to him.

Watching Benji learn to speak was sometimes downright eerie.

It all happened so fast. From a wordless beast, he'd turned into a chatterbox in the space of a few months. They had implanted a neurochemical dispenser inside his skull, something that seeped the chemicals straight into his brain, wiring up a crazy new secondary network that not only made him smarter by the day, but also made him pick up language much faster than any human child.

Not that he spoke well. Even with his re-sculpted upper palate, some words were hard to pronounce. Which made him difficult to understand, and with no human body language to compensate for it. He was usually wide-eyed, his expression as inscrutable as any canine's. If you've never known a sentient dog, it might sound crazy, but I swear Benji really did have expressions, though it took me years to learn to read them.

"What's *prrbrr*?" he asked me one day, just when I got home from work. He was still stuck at excitedly muttering two-word sentences.

I squatted down close to the plastic door mat, scratched him behind the ear. "What's that?"

"What's *pregmand*?" he asked quietly, conspiratorially.

"Pregmand? You mean pregnant? It means, uh, that someone has a baby inside," I said. "Like a mama dog, before the baby dog is born, she's pregnant."

"Oh," Benji said, and began panting excitedly. "Really?" He blinked at me oddly, and padded off towards the creaky basement stairs, his tail wagging behind them. I suddenly started wondering whether Benji had gotten out and gotten a sentientized neighbor dog pregnant. We hadn't gotten him neutered, I remembered with a groan. That was not going to be a fun conversation.

Of course, that wasn't it at all. Benji just had incredible ears. He could hear phone conversations behind closed doors, arguments two houses away. No secret was safe with Benji around. But the penny only dropped a week later when Jennifer called me during one of my rare days down at the lab. It was just like her to pick that day to tell me.

"Tim?"

"Yes, honey," I said into my cellphone, "Just a minute." Glancing one last time at the ongoing statistical analysis for artificially accelerated lateral gene transfer, I flicked my monitor sourcing to the phone's feed, and then full screened the videostream. She was sitting on the couch, wearing a pink T-shirt and dark blue sweatpants.

"What's up, sweetie?"

"I have some news," she said, looking slightly green around the gills, but smiling. I waited for her to go on, but she didn't, until I asked, "What is it?"

"Uh, well, honey. Remember how Dr. Flynn told us we'd never be able to have a baby?"

"Yeah . . ." I said, eyes widening.

"Turns out she was *wrong*."

"You're . . . pregnant?" I had to make sure.

She nodded at me, a brilliant smile widening on her face.

Benji padded into view, beside her, and looked at her carefully. "Pregnend make baby?"

"Yes, Benji. Mommy's making a baby. You know what that means right, Benji?" she asked him. He stared at her silently, not answering. He hadn't yet figured out how to answer tag questions like that. "You're going to have a little brother or sister." She turned and winked at me, and said, "What do you think of that, Big Daddy?"

"Woo!" I yelled, and then I said, "I love you," and she smiled at me.

"Baby!" Benji shouted, and his tail wagged, *thump, thump, thump* against couch so hard it made Jen laugh aloud.

Over the months that followed, Benji got more and more excited, just like us. One evening, after Jennifer had begun to show a little, he started in with questions during dinner.

He pulled his head out of his dog dish and turned to Jen: "Baby dish? Have dish?" Jen smiled, and shook her head.

"Baby dish share," he said, and wagged his tail.

Jennifer giggled, and said, "How cute," and I laughed, and I patted him on the flank of his hind leg, as he turned back to the dish and devoured his dinner excitedly.

The night we brought Martin home, Benji met us at the door.

"Hi Benji," Jennifer said.

"Hi Momma," he said back. "Hi Daddy." He looked at Martin, bundled in Jen's arms. "Hi Baby."

"The baby's name is Martin," I said, and then added, "You can call him Marty, if you like." Benji had problems with pronouncing "in", it tended to sound like "im". It was some kind of tongue control thing, something that they hadn't gotten quite right in his treatment.

"Mardy Baby," Benji said softly, reverently. "Hi Mardy Baby," he said, and then, "Come on, Baby. Baby bed."

"What?" Jen asked, head tilted to one side, but Benji had already started off down the stairs into the cool basement. "Honey, I'm going to put Marty to bed. Can you, uh . . ."

"Yeah, sure," I said, and waited for her to start up the stairs before I followed Benji down the creaking stairs to the basement. I found him wagging his tail, his nose nudging a spare plastic pad across the bare concrete floor, until it was next to his own. He liked to sleep down there because it was cool and quiet. The one he'd nudged into place was his old doggie bed, the one I should've thrown out months before when I bought his new one.

"Me Bed," he said, and touched the old, tattered pad with one paw. Then he touched the nice new one and said, "Baby Bed. Mardy Baby Bed."

I was a little stunned: Benji was *sharing*? I never expected that from a dog, and it made me smile. "Oh, that's *really* sweet, Benji. But, uh, Marty's not a dog. Baby boys don't sleep in the basement. It's too cold and dirty. But it's so nice of you . . . You think of him as a brother, huh? Aw, good boy," I said, patting him on the head. "Such a good boy."

He sat beside the two pads, looked down at them, then up at me. "Baby Bed No?"

"Right, Benji. Baby Bed No."

He drooped, tail slumped, and sunk to the concrete floor. Later, on hot summer nights when I found him sleeping beside Marty's crib, I remembered him nosing the spare pad into place, and some weird guilty feeling would well up so fast I could barely drive it back down before having to examine it.

They played together so well, Benji and Marty, both of them scooting around the house on all fours. For a while, they really *were* like any two brothers. Benji would sniff Marty's bottom occasionally and call Jen or me over: "Baby Mardy make poo!" Marty would push the buttons on a toy piano, and random songs would play. Benji would squeeze Tinky and Jiggy dolls between his teeth and they'd shout out greetings to Marty, provoking giggles and applause from that bright little blond toddler of ours. He always wanted to share his dinner with Marty, and his doggy biscuits, no matter how many times we explained that dog food and people food are different.

Benji really loved Marty, loved him as much as any brother would have. Somehow that made me forget all those awkward moments, the questions like, "Why Mardy Baby no tail?" and "Benji no birthday party?" and "Mardy Baby poo inside?" The time Benji tried to eat off the kitchen table, and sent our dinner crashing down by accident. Jen used to breastfeed Martin at the table, while she ate her own dinner sometimes, and Benji was perplexed by this, sometimes more than once a week. "Mardy Baby eats what? Benji too? Benji eat what too?"

"No, Benji," Jennifer said. "You're a dog. He's a baby. Babies have milk, but dogs have dog food. This milk is not for you. It's only for Marty, see?"

"No, Benji," he repeated ruefully. He'd started repeating that phrase every time someone said it, even gently. It's just the way everyone talks to dogs, isn't it? When they jump up onto a guest, or try humping your leg?

"That's right. Benji, no. Good boy," I said. He lay down on the cool tile floor beside his bowl, and thumped his tail once, just once.

With a kid, the years pass so quickly you lose track. One day, you're burping a baby; the next you have a little boy sitting beside you with a book in his lap, reading.

"... and ... then ... then the ... the boy and his dog ... went home ..." Martin mumbled. I smiled. I'd mouthed the words along with him, but he'd done it all by himself.

"Good job!" I patted him softly on the back. "You got every word. Did you like the story?"

"Yup," he said. "I wanna read it again," he said.

"Okay, let's ..."

"No," Marty insisted, shaking his head. "I want to read it with Benji." He hopped down off the couch, onto the carpet and toward the dog.

Benji turned his head and said, "You ... read with me?"

"Sure, Benj," he replied.

"Okay," Benji said, and he sat up. "You read, and I listen. Read slow."

"Mmm hmm. Okay, page one," Marty said carefully. "The story of Timmy and Spot," he said, from memory. He knew the first few pages of the picturebook by heart. "'There was a boy. His name was Timmy. There was a dog. Its name was Spot.' Now you read."

Benji said, "I can't read. But I 'member: 'There was boy. His name Timmy. There was dog. His name Spot.'"

Marty said, "Noooo, Benji. 'There was a dog. *Its* name was Spot.'"

Benji blinked, stared at the page—at the picture, I suppose, since he wasn't supposed to be able to read, not *ever*. "'There was dog. Its name Spot.'"

"Good," Marty said. "Now you're gettin' it. . . ."

Things started to go wrong around that time. The day that sticks out in my memory was this afternoon when I had some buddies over to watch the game on our new NetTV, while Jen and Marty were out someplace. Charlie, Deke, Demarco, and Peter were there, and we were all hollering at the screen. I don't know when Benji came into the room, but when the ads came up, and Charlie and Deke hurried to the kitchen to get us all some cold beers, Ben tapped Peter on the leg with one paw.

"Oh, hey, Benji. How are you, boy?" Peter asked absently, the way anyone asks any dog, sentient or not. He patted Ben on the head for a few seconds.

"Okay. Question okay? Ask you?"

"Sure, Benji," he grinned. He'd probably never met a dog as inquisitive as Benji—I never have. "What is it?"

"You Korean?"

"Well, I'm Korean-American, yeah." I wondered how Benji had known that. Was it just a guess?

"Why Korean eat dog?"

Demarco and I both turned and looked at Peter, who sat there with one eyebrow raised. Demarco started to chuckle as Peter glanced at each of us before turning back to Benji. "Say what?"

Benji said the question again: "Why Korean eat dog?"

Peter looked up at me, puzzled. I shrugged and gave him a baffled look.

Demarco was doubled over now, laughing hysterically. "Racist dog!" he said, before bursting into laughter again. "That's funny, man. They should put you on TV, Benji! The racist talking dog show!"

Peter started laughing along. "Ha, I'd watch that show," he said. Then he said, "Look, Benj, last time I visited Korea, I didn't see any dog restaurants. All my relatives think eating dog is terrible. They say it's mostly old guys who do it, and I never asked them why. So I dunno why anyone would eat dog. I guess they think it tastes good or something. But hey, nobody's gonna eat you, 'kay?"

Benji blinked, processing this. "Dogs think people taste good too."

Which . . . none of us knew what to say. We all sat there in silence, until Demarco sniffed and said, "Yeah, man, well, dogs think their own crap tastes good, right?"

"Sure," Benji said, and we all burst out laughing as Deke and Charlie walked back into the room with the beers. But Benji just looked from one of us to the next, his eyes quite serious. Then the ads were done, and the announcer was talking about why Nick Lingonfelder wasn't in the game this week, and whatever it was Benji wanted to say, he kept it to himself, and just went to the back door, muttering, "Can I go out?" as he passed me.

"Uh, sure, Benj," I said, and went to open the back door. He went out without so much as a glance toward me. I remember thinking that wasn't like him. When I went back into the living room, Demarco was telling Charlie and Deke about his idea for the TV show about Benji the Racist Dog.

I shrugged. "Yeah, guys, I have *no* idea where he picked that up. But you know, he's young. You know how kids can be."

"*Kids?*" Charlie mumbled, flopping onto the couch. "He's a *dog*, Tim." He handed me a beer.

I nodded. "He's . . . yeah, he's a souped-up dog, though."

"Mmmm, *souped-up* dog . . . tasty," Deke said, and Demarco burst out laughing again.

Peter chucked a sofa cushion at him, grinning. "You better talk to him, though," he said. "Some people I know would take that shit the wrong way."

That evening, I found Jen and Benji in the kitchen, talking. Benji's head was lowered, the way he did when we caught him breaking the house rules.

"No, Benji, it's okay," Jen said, patting him on the head. "It's an understandable question. But . . . well, you know how some dogs bite people? But not all dogs, right? Not all dogs are the same, right? It's the same with people. Not all people of the same kind are the same."

"Oh." Benji said, and then he wagged his tail once, which was his way of nodding. "Not all dogs same." He'd learned that lesson trying to chat with the neighborhood dogs, none of whom were sentientized.

"Lots of dogs can't watch TV, like you do," Jen said, absentmindedly fiddling with one of Marty's cartoon DVD cases on the kitchen table.

"Right," he said, and he asked, "But why *not?*"

Before she could answer him, I stepped into the room and said, "Is Benji watching TV?"

Jen looked up. She looked tired. "Yeah, I leave the dog channel on when I'm out. It's supposed to help his English."

"I talk good soon," Benji says, and like that it clicked in my head: the shift to four- and five-word sentences I'd observed, the slightly improved syntax. Dogs with the treatment he'd gotten weren't supposed to advance that far, let alone become fluent, but at the rate he was going, he'd be speaking like Marty within the year.

"Yes, Benji. You're really improving. Now, your Daddy and I need to talk about something private, Benji. Could you excuse us?"

"Okay," Benji said. "Night," he told each of us one by one, and then he padded off into the basement.

When the creaking on the stairs ended, Jen and I both exhaled. We hadn't even realized we'd been holding our breath.

"It's like . . ." she started, but then she hesitated, though I knew what she was going to say.

". . . like having two kids?" I suggested.

She nodded. "Exactly."

"Well, that was why he had him done, you know . . ."

She nodded, and it hit me how much older she looked now, than when we'd decided against adoption, and when she'd finally agreed to the dog treatment. If we'd known . . . well, there was no point in thinking about that, was there?

"So, the whole Koreans eating dogs thing . . . you think he picked that up on TV, maybe?"

Jen tapped the kitchen table. "Maybe? I've never watched any myself." I looked at the DVD case sitting on the table in front of her, and it hit me: with Marty, we checked everything out first. If he asked for a movie, we checked the parental warnings. There was a nanny lock on the TV, too, a smart lock set to block anything PG-13 or higher when he was alone in the room. But we hadn't set a lock for when it was just Benji alone.

"Well, maybe we should."

The next morning, I found Benji on the couch in front of the TV. A commercial was on. I'd never seen an ad made especially for dogs. Before that day, I'd only ever glimpsed these weird canine-athletics shows Benji loved, that always sent Benji straight to me, insistently repeating, "Let's play fetch! Let's play fetch! Wanna play fetch?"

In this ad, a pair of dogs were trotting alongside one another, as soft romantic music played in the background. There was also this soft panting sound, and a kind of rhythmic thumping that didn't fit the music. "Lonely? Humping legs not good enough for you? Are you the only talking dog in your neighborhood? Most sentientized canines have trouble finding suitable mates. But we can help you. Call Pet-Mate today." An online contact code flashed across the bottom of the screen, as the screen cut smoothly, if briefly, to one dog mounting another; as the video quickly faded to black, a faint, slightly offensive aroma filled the room, and then quickly dissipated. Beside me, Benji was suddenly panting.

Great, I thought. *Next he'll be asking me for allowance money. . . .*

But the screen shifted abruptly to a stage set with wide, soft-looking red couches. On one sat a beautiful grey-furred German Shepherd, a big chew-bone under her front paws, cans and packets of some new brand of dog food, Brainy Dog Chow, visible in various places around her.

"Good morning," started the voiceover, "and welcome back to Sparky's Couch!" The camera zoomed in on Sparky's face as she—her voice was somehow feminine— sniffed at the camera, and the TV's odifers emitting what I swear was the faint aroma of dog-butt. Suddenly, that weird smell I'd noticed sometimes in the living room made sense. I'd thought it was just Benji.

"I'm your host, Sparky Smith," the German Shepherd said in astonishingly perfect English. She must have had the top-of-the-line treatment. "I hope *you're* comfortably seated on *your* families' couches, too. Well, yesterday you heard about the plight of Korean dogs from the first Korean sentientized dog, Somi. But it wouldn't be fair to talk about Korea and ignoring problems closer to home. . . ."

My jaw dropped. She sounded like a human TV announcer. The cost of her treatment must have been exorbitant . . . or had she been gotten of those pricy *in vitro* mods? Looking at Benji, I felt like . . . was it wrong of us to get him the cheaper treatment? Did he realize he'd never be able to talk like Sparky?

"Well, according to today's expert, America has a serious dog-mistreatment problem as well! Even here, dogs suffer every day. Everyone please welcome Duncan Mallory, from Iowa," Sparky declared.

The camera cut to an audience full of dogs lounging on the terraced studio audience floor area. They were all barking rhythmically, *oof, oof, oof*, like it was applause, and Benji was barking along with them. A squat brown pug waddled onstage, and then hopped up onto the couch beside Sparky. As they sniffed one another in greeting, a new dog-butt aroma wafted from the TV odifers. Well, I guess it was new: it smelled the same as the last one, to me.

"Welcome, Duncan! It's nice to have you here," Sparky said.

"Thanks, Sparky. I'm happy to be here." The pug's voice was even clearer than Sparky's, with very little accent. It was weird.

"Please tell us how you discovered about the suffering of American dogs, Duncan."

Melodramatically sad piano music began to play, as the dog spoke. "Well, I was surfing the internet, and thought that I'd look up the ASPCA—you know, the American Society for the Prevention of Cruelty to Animals."

"Right," Sparky replied. The acronym appeared at the bottom of the screen, and stayed in place for what seemed like a long time. Maybe it was to let even the least-enhanced dogs—dogs like Benji—to memorize the shapes of the letters.

"After searching around their webpage, I discovered something incredible," he said. The audience and Sparky—and Benji—panted expectantly. "Millions of dogs are killed with poison injections every year, right here in America. It's been going on for decades, too."

All of the dogs in the audience yelped in horror. Sparky covered her nose with a paw, and made a whining sound. Then she asked, "Why?"

"Because they're homeless. Nobody owns them, and nobody wants them, so they're *killed*," the pug explained, his voice turning a little angry.

The audience began whining, and Benji joined them. The sad music continued, as a video montage filled the screen. At first it was just ankles and knees, which confused me until I realized it was dog's eye view. The room was filled with a vaguely metallic smell, mixed with the bite of chemical cleaning solution and, faintly, some other offensive aroma—like old piss and sickened animal turds. Onscreen flashed the faces of miserable dogs framed by the bars of cages, one after another in an interminable sequence. The camera entered another room, where a dog lay on its side on a table, its legs visible hanging over the edge from above. Benji whined softly, I think unaware that he was doing it.

"This is where they inject the dogs," Duncan explained.

This was too much, I decided, and I reached for the NetTV remote next to Benji's paw.

Benji stopped whining along with the audience and looked at me in surprise. "Why?

"Why what?"

"Why . . ." He paused, as if trying to figure out what he was asking about. *Why turn the TV off? Why do they kill dogs that way? Why is the world so unfair?* He whined again, this time less unselfconscious. His head hung down, his eyes wide and sorrowful.

"Benji, I dunno what to tell you. We try to treat you well, but not everyone in the world is like us."

Benji didn't say anything, but he stared at me with this piercing look, as if my explanation wasn't good enough.

"Look, those dogs would . . . go hungry. They would be homeless, and starve," I said.

Benji sat there, looking at me. He knew the word homeless. Whenever we went to the vet's downtown, we always passed a couple of homeless people. He had talked to one of them, some old war vet who'd had PTSD and couldn't stand to live indoors anymore.

"You don't kill homeless people," Benji said softly.

"No, Benj, we don't. Some people probably wish we did, but we don't. Because they're people."

Benji whimpered at me, and snuffed a little, then looked up at me and said, "Am I a people?"

"Of course you are, Benji," I said, without even pausing to think. I didn't add the rest of what I was thinking, *You can talk. You can think.* He turned and looked at me, his eyes like those of a dog walleyed from sneaking a half-box of forbidden, dog-toxic chocolate.

This wouldn't do. It was Saturday, sunny and bright outside.

"Say, Benji, whaddaya think about going to the park?" He wagged his tail a little weakly. "C'mon boy, let's go ask Jen, then," I said, and we got up and walked to the top of the stairs.

"Jen, wanna go for a picnic?" I shouted down the stairs, and she called up to me that she thought it was a great idea, and only needed a few minutes to finish up her work. I went to get Marty ready.

Half an hour later, we had a simple lunch packed and were on our way, Marty and Benji in the backseat of the microvan and Jen and I in the front, driving across town to Volunteer Park. We played kids' music all the way, songs about bananas and monkeys and chickens dancing and some guy named Pickles O'Sullivan. Marty talked to Benji about a book he was reading—about a group of kid spies who were constantly saving the world from scheming corporations and politicians—and Jen smiled at me. This was a great idea, I thought to myself.

When we got there, I took Benji off his leash and let him run around for a while, and told him to come and find me near the benches when he'd had enough. Jen and Marty and I sat on a blanket, ate some tuna salad sandwiches and some fresh fruit we'd bought from an organic produce stand along the way. Then I kicked a ball around with Marty for a while—he was too small to kick it back properly, but he wasn't too small to intercept it, if I kicked softly enough.

When the sun had started to go down, though, Benji still hadn't returned. Usually when we picnicked, he stayed around, or came back soon, but this time, there was no sign of him for hours.

"Where do you think he is?" Jen asked.

"I don't know, maybe he found some girl dogs or something?" I grinned.

"That's not funny. You know, I read that someone's been kidnapping sentient dogs. They've been disappearing from all over. It's terrible."

"Don't worry," I said, "I'll go find him. He's gotta be around somewhere." And with that, I left the two of them sitting on the picnic blanket.

I wandered around the park, calling out his name and looking in any place I could think of where he might be. He wasn't by the old bandstand with the faded paint, or the new jungle gyms; I couldn't find him anywhere near the mini-museum or the tennis courts; and he wasn't out by the viewpoint overlooking Puget Sound. I asked everyone I ran across, and nobody had seen him, though even if they had, would they have noticed him?

Finally, on the opposite end of the park from where Jen and Marty were waiting, I followed a trail that ran right between a couple of lazy old pine trees and over a small rise. When I got to the top, I could hear a loud voice—a dog's voice—accompanied by murmurs. I came down the hill, and in the dimming light I saw a pack of dogs all sitting together in a circle, gathered around a big white husky that seemed to be orating to them. Every once in a while, they responded in unison, with a jolting yelp or bark. It was too dim to see the dogs in the pack clearly, but Benji had to be there somewhere. Ignoring a faint sense that I was trespassing, I moved down the hill.

As I got closer, the oration got clearer: "And besides, the issue is, humans do not think of us as people. How many of you have ever shit indoors?"

The dogs muttered among themselves, and then most of them replied, one by one, "I have."

"And what happened? Your master rubbed your nose in it, and threw you outside. Do they do that to babies who crap in their diapers?"

The consensus, quickly reached, was a resounding No.

"The thing to remember, to understand, is that humans will never, ever see us as we see ourselves. They *think* they love us, but . . ." The dogs yelped affirmatively in response.

"Benji?" I interrupted, after the howls had died off and before the husky could continue. I guess I must have been downwind or something, or maybe talking and listening took so much of their brainpower that they paid less attention to scent, because they suddenly all turned and looked at me in what felt like surprise. Having all those eyes on me was nerve-wracking. Some dogs bared their teeth, growling softly, and I half-expected to become an example in the husky's diatribe, or for him to order them to attack me.

But they all just stood there, looking at me angrily until Benji turned and trotted from the pack of them over toward me.

"Come on, Benji," I said. "Let's go."

He said nothing, but followed me quietly, and I only looked over my shoulder once. They didn't follow us, but instead just sat there, silently watching us go.

Laws or no laws, I didn't leash him. I didn't even dare try.

He ran away a week later.

It was the Fourth of July—Independence Day, of all days—and it was our turn to play host among enough of our circles of friends that we decided to just invite them all at once.

The scent of grilling meat and smoke wafted through the backyard. One of the coolers of beer sat open, bottles nestled in the ice and left in the glaring sun. Random groups of friends and strangers chatted with one another in small clusters, sitting on lawn chairs or leaning on the railing of the deck. I could hear Jen laughing about something, and Marty was with the other kids in the sandbox, steering little matchbox cars along hastily constructed little sandy race courses.

At some point, I heard a crash from inside the house. I looked up from the grill, where I was tending to the burgers, and called to Jen, but she couldn't hear me over the music. I handed the spatula to Deke, and went inside to check it out.

I found Benji sitting miserably in the bathroom. The now-smashed sink, which had never been properly attached to the wall, had been knocked down and cracked the tile floor, and the naked water-pipes were broken off and dripping water. The small vase of flowers that sat on the toilet tank had fallen down, and the flowers floated here and there on the water that covered the floor. The vase had smashed into a million shards, too, I realized as I looked carefully. There were dog turds on the toilet seat, and floating in the water flooding the floor. Thank goodness the smart house system registered that the flow was too high on the pipe, and shut the water valve access for the sink, but it was still going to be a pain to clean up the room, let alone fix everything. So I did the thing parents sometimes do, and regret forever.

"What the hell, Benji?" I shouted. But wouldn't anyone have yelled? A new sink, fixing the plumbing, retiling the floor: none of that would be free. "You're not supposed to use the toilet, dammit! You're a dog!" I grabbed a rolled-up newspaper from the bathroom magazine rack and whacked him on the nose with it.

"But . . . there's too many people now . . ." he said, sadly.

"No, Benji. No. You're a dog, okay? You're supposed to do it outside. . . ."

He didn't say anything, but just stalked out of the room with baleful eyes, to the back door, watching solemnly as I went and got the wet'n'dry vac and sucked up most of the mess. Quickly, I wrote up a sign to use the bathroom upstairs, and then locked the bathroom door so nobody would walk into the disaster zone by accident.

When I got to the back door, I realized that the poor dog had been stuck inside for hours. Even if nobody had been around, we hadn't let him out anyway. A sudden sinking guilt set in. "Okay, Benji, I'll let you out. Sorry, I forgot to. Just do your business outside next time, okay? Bark or shout and I'll come let you out."

He mumbled something low, something I couldn't make out, as I opened the door and he went out into the backyard. I hoped the crowd would cheer him up, maybe. He took off toward the yard, not waiting for me. I wondered, *Is this what teenagers are like?*

Outside, Lorna was saying, "Well, now, Benji, you're much better behaved than the last time I saw you. I almost wish I'd brought my Spot to come play with you."

"Play?" Benji yelped. "I'm not a baby dog! You think I'm stupid?"

"Pardon me?" Lorna said, and I could hear Jen's shocked response: "*Benji!*"

Goddammit, I swear that was what I thought. Not, "Hey, Lorna, Benji's a little different from Spot," or, "Wait, everyone, let's talk about this." Just, *Goddammit.*

"No, it's alright," Lorna said, adjusting her sunhat. "I'm not sure I understand, Benji. Are you telling me you don't like to play? That if, say, I throw this rubber ball over there, you won't go and get it? Every dog loves to play fetch, right?" She picked up a rubber ball from the grass and threw it over toward the back fence.

Benji sat on his haunches, looking, watching the ball roll away. Then, without another word, he stood and walked over toward her, like he was going to graze her leg with his side.

As she said, "Good boy," and reached down with her free hand to pat him on the head, he raised one leg and sprayed piss onto her white leather shoes.

Lorna jumped back, dropping her plate on the ground, its contents tumbling onto the grass. Everyone was quiet, the music a paradoxically cheerful background to the concerned, shocked faces. Even Marty and his friends had stopped playing race cars to look over at the scene.

Ever the first to respond, Jen rushed up with paper towels, apologizing as she wiped Lorna's shoes and pushing Benji away. Lorna slipped her shoes off as Jen wiped them, and said loudly, "Well, if that's his attitude, I don't see why you keep him. He must be bad for Marty." She shrugged. "You oughtta just have him put down, and save yourselves the trouble—"

At that, Benji started snarling at her, showing his teeth, and Jen searched the crowd for me, made eye contact. I'd just been standing there watching this, and suddenly realized this was *my* dog who was acting out. I hurried over, and said, "Okay, Benji, time to go inside," and reached down to hook my fingers under his collar.

"No!" he barked, his speech half snarl and his hackles on end. I yanked my hand back as he snapped at it. The crowd gasped in shock. Each word that followed was like that first word, a sharp snap of noise, some frightening amalgam of barking and speech and growl: "I . . . won't . . . go . . . in . . ." It was just like how Marty threw tantrums: "*I . . . won't . . . eat . . . it!*"

But I didn't respond the way I did to Marty. No cajoling, no encouraging, no teasing. "Benji!" I yelled. "Don't you talk to me that way!"

His response was a snarl, and he lunged at me again, snapped his teeth at me. I jumped back, suddenly much more angry than before. "Benji, you get inside now, or else."

"Or else what?" he snarled.

I stood there, my mind blank, my mouth wide.

Then, suddenly, he stopped snarling. He just sniffed, once. There an expression I'd never seen before on his face, something new, something I couldn't read. Then he broke into a run towards the gate that opened out on the front walk. I couldn't understand why he went there, unless to go indoors, since he'd never been able to get the latch open with his mouth.

But then, around the corner, I heard human voices call out, "Hey!" and "Oh my God!" at the same time. Rounding the corner, I found the gate wide open, and Chad and Anoo on the other side of it, bowled over, potato salad and smoked sausages spilled all around them on the ground. He'd heard them open the gate. He'd seen his chance.

Chad glanced over his shoulder after the dog, saying, "What's with Benji?"

He was gone.

I drove through the streets that night, searching all over the city. I checked all the pounds, went everywhere I'd ever taken him—downtown, to the beach, everywhere. I even went to that spot in Volunteer Park where I'd found him with those other dogs—the spot came to mind immediately when he ran away—but it was deserted. I imagined Benji out on the streets, running alone while fireworks bloomed above him in the dark, roaring sky. It terrified me, but even so, I didn't find him.

I waited a week or so, figuring hunger or fear or loneliness might bring him back to us. Every time I left the house, I looked up and down the street, hoping he might be watching from some neighbor's yard, but if he was, he hid well. I didn't see him.

When I tried to figure out who to report it to, nobody wanted to listen. The cops didn't handle missing animals, not even sentientized ones, and the pound told me sentientized dogs were inevitably caught on first inspection and sent home. They said there were like three ways of identifying the sentientized dog's home, just in case, and I'd have been contacted within forty-eight hours if he'd ended up at a pound. Finally, I was left with nobody to report it to.

But one Saturday afternoon about a month later, the cops did show up. Of course, when I answered the door, I was confused at first: they were sitting on the doorstep in slightly tattered uniforms, miserable in the damp summer heat. Their custom scooter sat parked in the driveway. Across the street, Lorna Anderson sat on her stoop, fascinated, and I can't blame her.

After all, one of the cops was a big black doberman, and his partner was a squat, muscular bulldog. Both had shoulder cams on, which I supposed streamed directly to a human supervisor.

"Good morning," said the doberman, before I had time to really think about the fact who I was talking to. It had a voice so deep and rumbling it could've given Barry White a run for his money. "Are you Mr. Stevens?"

"Uh, yeah?" I nodded.

The doberman stopped panting long enough to say, "My name is Officer Duke Smith. My partner is officer Cindy. Just Cindy, no family name."

"Okay . . ."

"Can we come in please?"

"Uh . . . is this about Benji?" I said, and found myself adjusting my position. I was blocking the doorway a little more. I don't know why, except maybe this sense of . . . of shame, I guess. Like if they came in the house, they might, what, know why Benji had run away? They might smell something wrong with us? That it was our fault?

"Yes, sir, and it's rather serious. We need some information from you," Cindy said, half-growling.

"Okay," I said, stepping aside. They hurried in, sniffing the air, and I led them into the living room. "So, do you know where Benji is?" Suddenly I felt even more nervous.

"No, sir," said Duke. "Has he contacted you since the day he went missing?" As he asked this, Duke thumped his tail emphatically. Cindy stopped panting, as if she was trying to look businesslike.

I looked from one to the other, wishing I was better at reading dogs' eyes. I wasn't around Benji long enough to really get good at that. I've heard they can sniff out a lie, literally scent it on you. Not that I had anything to lie about, really.

"No, er, officers. No, I haven't. I'm worried about him, to be honest." That much was true.

"And, did Benji ever express any opinions you'd call political?"

"Political?"

"Yes, sir. Animal rights, or animal liberation ideology? Anything radical?"

I laughed softly, before I caught myself. Duke's eyes narrowed, the brow of his doggie face furrowing like he was getting ready to fetch a stick. Surely he was just mouthing some human cop's questions, delivered by earphone or implant. Surely a dog couldn't actually be questioning me? I found myself wondering whether they were paid to do this work, and whether it was in dollars, or biscuits?

Cindy sniffed the air between us, as if searching me for some clue, and she said, "Mr. Stevens, we're concerned that Benji's mixed up with a dangerous organization. . . ."

"Dangerous? What, like . . . dog fights?"

Duke cocked his head as Cindy said, "No, sir. May we show you?"

I nodded, and she turned her head. With a practiced movement, she yanked a mouth remote free from her shoulder holster and positioned it between her teeth. She growled softly, turning it with her tongue, and the TV flickered to life.

It was a black-and-white video, night vision, of some kind of security guard post, with an older man in a uniform seated before a bunch of screens, drinking coffee. The resolution was too blurry to see what he was looking at, but good enough to see he was bored out of his skull.

Then the door burst inward, like it was kicked in, and someone entered. There was audio of him shouting at the top of his lungs. He was some kind of . . . a hippie, I guess: dreadlocks, a muscle shirt and tattoos all over his body, in sandals. He was holding a rifle, but he didn't shoot it: he only pointed it at the man, shouting orders. Drop your gun. Hands behind your head.

The man obeyed. Then a pack of dogs poured into the room and mobbed the poor man, crowding around him, tearing him apart. The man's screams were terrifying, and blood pooled at their feet, spread across the floor as he fell to the ground, and still they tore at him, until the snarling and howling drowned out his weakening screams. As he went silent, they began to howl, bark-shouting curses and clawing at him.

"This was at an animal pound in San Diego last night," says Duke flatly.

"God," I said.

"Some of these dogs are on file: sentientized runaways. Others look like they're probably strays who were sentientized recently, later in life. The treatment is less effective that way, but it's still possible. Now, this . . ."

Then the perspective changed, as Cindy moved the mouth remote slightly with a click. The video paused, and then zoomed in on one of the dogs.

There he was, on the screen. My little terrier, my Benji, his furry little face covered in blood, mid-bark-curse, his tail wagging furiously.

"Is that Benji?" asked Duke the doberman.

I couldn't tell. It was so strange, not knowing. "Uh, maybe? I'd have to hear his voice." Duke nodded, self-consciously using human body language for my benefit I suppose, and the video jumped forward, scanning through the footage until the terrier was in frame again, and speaking.

"Jesus!" said some dog offscreen. "Did we have to kill him?"

"They kill hundreds of us every day, for much less," said the terrier. Said Benji, for I *knew* it was him now.

Cindy muted the video but let it run as a crew of young people, women and men in black and wearing balaclavas, quickly unlocked all the cages in the shelter. When they left, they stepped over the mauled security guard without a moment's hesitation.

"Yeah, I don't know," I said to him finally. "I don't see him, but . . ."

"Uh huh. It's a little hard to tell, I know. We do have stool samples, though, so I guess we'll know soon enough through DNA testing. These dogs seem to like crapping in places where they know they shouldn't." A chihuahua stared into the camera, stared into my eyes, and said something. Dogs don't have lips, so it's pretty hard to lip-read them when they talk, but I'd swear it'd said, *Fuck you.*

Somehow, that chihuahua was too much. I ran for the kitchen sink, arriving just in time to avoid throwing up all over the floor. I had an empty stomach, so it was just gastric juices, but still. I felt sick at the thought of it. And terrified. Benji . . . had we made him like this? It was like . . . I felt like some serial killer's father must feel, I guess. It was so confusing, the guilt and shame.

The dog police stayed in the living room, speaking softly to each other as they waited patiently while I rinsed my mouth out. I was frightened, now, of Benji. I'd never imagined he could do something like that. Not a thinking, rational animal like him. Sure, he wasn't a human being, but I didn't think he was a cold-blooded killer, either.

When I got back to the living room, the dogs said, "So, that *was* Benji?"

"Yeah," I said. "That's him. What the hell was he doing?"

Officer Smith nodded at Officer Cindy, and said, "Busting dogs from the pound. Down in California. We don't know how he got there, or what the group is doing with all those dogs they busted loose. None of them were sentientized. Just normal dogs."

"What for?"

Officer Duke looked over at Cindy, and then back to me. "Well . . . it's just a theory, but some animal rights groups online have been talking mass sentientization. Funding treatment for large numbers of animals, and not just dogs. They can't do that alone, so the next question is: did Benji ever have any human friends around? Animal rights people, PETA, anything suspicious like that?"

I looked at the doberman in shock. "Animal rights activists?"

"Yes. That's what the people in the video are: the Animal Liberation Front. Benji being mixed up with some very bad people. *Very* dangerous. They're smuggling synthetic drugs out of Canada in dogs' bellies. Once or twice a month, some dog will turn up near the B.C. border, dead from an overdose, with a ruptured baggie somewhere in its guts. Our theory is that this is how they're funding all the sentientization treatments. But what this army they're building is for . . . we're not sure."

An *army*.

Any reservation or distrust I felt, dissipated before that possibility. Suddenly everything came pouring out of me: his anger, and how he'd started acting up a while ago. I told them about the party—they didn't seem much interested, like the story was familiar—and I told them about the TV shows he'd watched, which bored them. They seemed ready to go, when I finally realized what I ought to tell them about.

"There was this one time, in Victory Park," I said. They exchanged a look, as if to say, finally, *something* of interest.

"Go on," Cindy grumbled.

"There's this spot, I mean, I only saw them once, but . . . there was a group of dogs. Like, a rally or something. It seemed . . . yeah, I guess, like you said: it seemed political. The leader was some kind of big white husky. I mean, I think it was the leader. It was doing most of the talking, and the other dogs were barking in response."

"How many dogs were there?" Duke asked.

"I don't know, maybe ten or twelve?"

"I see," said Duke, and Cindy pulled up a surface map of the park. "Where was it?" she said, so I showed her on the map.

"And the husky," Cindy said. "Would you recognize it if you saw it?"

I shrugged. "I . . . probably not. Maybe if I heard his voice. I mean, white huskies all look the same to me. No offense."

Neither dog said anything to that, but Cindy quickly asked me one more question: "You're a medical researcher, correct?"

I stared at them for a moment, wondering why that mattered. "Yes," I said, finally, in a tone that made clear I couldn't understand why they were asking.

"Did Benji ever ask you about your work?"

"No," I said. But a moment popped in my head, vivid and clear. One night, not long before he'd run away, I had found Benji at my desk. His doggie-keyboard within wireless range. A web browser open to his doggie webmail service. But also other windows open, folders containing my various work projects. Everything encrypted, but maybe crackable. I remembered thinking that was strange: I always closed all the folders I was working from when I left the room, especially work folders, because if I didn't the cloud backup software didn't work as well. With a sinking feeling, I wondered what folders it'd been, though I couldn't remember.

Officers Duke and Cindy sat there, sniffing the air a little. As dogs, they might find my body language as opaque as I found theirs, but I wondered whether they maybe could sniff out my lie of omission.

And for whose sake was I lying, anyway? If word got out that my dog had stolen confidential information . . . and if those nuts who'd pressed Benji into their gang ended up using it somehow . . . my guts sank as I realized just how bad it could be. Never mind the lab, my boss: the stuff I was researching was . . . in the wrong hands, it could be dangerous. Accelerated gene transfer . . . the wrong person could design a virus that would sentientize all dogs, an intelligence plague. But if it affected dogs and cats . . . what would it do to humans?

I realized I'd been standing there for minutes, not speaking. The cops waited, I guess to see if I had anything else to offer. I didn't, so finally, I said, "Is there anything else?"

"No," said Cindy. "But if Benji contacts you, you need to get in touch with us. Under federal and state laws, sentientized animals are now subject to criminal proceedings. Furthermore, since Benji's a canine, he cannot be considered a family member. You can and will be forced to testify against Benji if he is apprehended and tried. And you will be considered an accomplice—equally culpable for acts of terrorism—if you aid or abet him or his group in any way." Cindy paused, as if trying to gauge my reaction, and added, "You should realize you're on a watch list, and will remain on one until this situation is resolved."

Duke added, "One more thing, sir: this group Benji's tangled up in? They're dangerous. You need to stay away from him. Do *not* trust him. If he approaches you, call us. Without delay." Duke then turned his head to the side. A card slid out automatically from a slot in his uniform's collar, with a photo of Duke and Cindy, and contact info.

I nodded. "I understand, Officer."

They thanked me for my cooperation, and went to the front door. When I let them out, I saw that Jen had just pulled up the driveway a few minutes before, and gotten Marty out of his car seat. The dogs trotted past them toward their custom scooter, and in a moment all that was left of them was the faint ringing in my ears from the roar of the motor. Well, and the tightness in my chest. But what I couldn't help but think was: they were talking about Benji like he was a criminal. In other words, as if he were a person, not just a dog. Which meant he'd finally gotten what he'd always wanted, I guess.

"What was that about?" Jen asked as she reached the porch.

"The cops?" I sighed. "Looking for Benj."

Her eyes went wide, though she said nothing. But watching them drive off, Marty mumbled a single, quiet, mournful word: "Benji?"

A few months later, I was walking our new dog, a black Labrador named Cookie, in Victory Park. I was on a picnic with Jennifer and Marty, but they were still on the blanket, on the other side of the park. I don't know what made me walk to that spot over the rise, but when I did, Cookie started to growl. She was a normal dog, not like Benji. Not sentient, so her growling was just instinct, not rhetoric. And then I turned, and I saw him. It was Benji, walking slowly toward me with this *look* in his eyes.

"Cookie, heel," I said, and Benji's eyes narrowed. As if being reminded of something painful, like when you see your ex dating someone new a little too soon.

"We got her for Marty's sake, Benji. When you ran away, it really confused him." As if I owed him an explanation. He just sat there, looking at me. "What are you doing here?" I asked quietly, looking around. For cops, or for his dreadlocked friend. "You're wanted. Not just Seattle cops, but FBI."

Ben's mouth opened slightly, a coughing noise indicating doggy-laughter. "FBI? Ha . . . try NSA, INTERPOL, the Secret Service . . ."

"Are you really smuggling . . . smuggling drugs?" Cookie growled, tugging at the leash. She either wanted to attack little Benji, or run away.

"There's no evidence. Just hearsay. Two dogs with conflicting testimony. Nobody'll believe a dachshund's testimony in court." Benji paused briefly, bitter cough-laugh filling his throat for a moment.

"Benj, these people you're with, they're . . . they're using you. They're crazy, Ben. They wanna hurt a lot of people."

"Not to me," he said. "They've helped me understand everything. But they're dangerous to you, and everyone like you."

I knew he was thinking of the dog pounds. Millions of dogs a year, dead for nothing.

"You have to stop, Ben," I said. "You can . . . you should . . ."

"I can what?" He said it hard, verging on a bark, and then sat on his haunches. "Come on, tell me, what can I do? What, come home? Really? Tell the truth: do you want me to come home? *Can I come home?*"

"Sure," I said, lying through my teeth. If I got him home, I could call the cops, I thought, standing there with Cookie beside me.

He just sniffed the air between us.

Then I saw it in his eyes, just as it died: *hope*. It hadn't been mere rhetoric. He'd really *hoped* I wanted him back. He would have come home with me, and turned informant, and betrayed those terrorist friends of his, ended it all, if only I'd just wanted him back. But he could smell the truth, I knew: how angry I was at him, how I regretted having him sentientized in the first place. It was the most terrible thing I'd ever had to see in person, watching that hope die in his eyes.

I looked away, down at the grass, the endless grass all around us rustling in the breeze.

But Benji didn't look away. "Say it," he said softly, his voice pulling my eyes back to him. His tail was up. I didn't know what tail-up meant in that context. I couldn't guess. "Say what you want," he demanded of me, in a voice as soft as when he'd whimpered as a puppy. "Be *honest* for once."

The hope was gone from his eyes.

I crouched down, and I wanted to open my arms to him. I wanted to, but . . . but I also didn't. With our eyes almost level, locked together, I said, "No, Benji. I don't want you to come home. Not after everything . . . not now. You can't. You *know* that."

He held my gaze for a long time. I waited for him to say something, some salve to heal the wound between us, or some accusation, even. But he just sat there, staring silently with those big, wet, hopeless eyes of his. I was about to say, "I'm sorry, Benj," but he broke the silence first. Just a growl, and just for a moment. Not threateningly, just . . . like a frown.

And then, after a long, quiet look at me—as if to remember me—he turned and ran off into the trees. That was the last time I ever saw him.

KIT: some assembly required

KATHE KOJA AND CARTER SCHOLZ

Kathe Koja's seventeen novels include The Cipher, Skin, Buddha Boy, Head-long, *and the* Under the Poppy *trilogy.* Christopher Wild, *a novel of Christopher Marlowe, will be published in 2017. She leads a performing ensemble,* nerve, *based in Detroit, where she lives with her husband, artist Rick Lieder.*

Carter Scholz is the author of Palimpsests *(with Glenn Harcourt) and* Kafka Americana *(with Jonathan Lethem), and the novel* Radiance, *which was a New York Times Notable Book, as well as story collection* The Amount to Carry. *His electronic and computer music compositions are available from the composer's collective Frog Peak Music (www.frogpeak.org) as scores and on the album* 8 Pieces. *He is an avid backpacker and amateur astronomer and telescope builder. He plays jazz piano around the San Francisco Bay Area with www.theinsidemen.com.*

Here they join forces to bring us the edgy and erudite story that follows, in which an attempt to create an AI modeled on Elizabethan playwright and poet (and spy) Christopher Marlowe has some unexpected, and potentially world-changing, results.

The atheist awoke in the machine. Body had he none. Merely a consciousness, *who even dead, yet hath his mind entire.* A good line, that. Where did it come from? Around him was a sort of prison of flat light, was it light? Prison, because he could not move out of it. A Marshalsea, a Bridewell, a Tower.

And library, too, of a sort—infinite it seemed, but he could scan it once he perceived its order. Planes of light flashed, opened, separated. Why, even his own works were here: *Settle thy studies, Faustus, and begin/To sound the depth of that thou wilt profess. . . .* Master Doctor Faustus, the overreacher.

Someone once called him an inquisitive intelligence. So he was. The only such here in this place? So it seemed. Thrusts of will he felt, seeking, sorting, and executing, but they were not, like him, resident. All purpose, direction, mission, came from some place without.

Yet they could transfix him, overrule his thoughts: his mind, their bidding. The planes of light flashed: he saw faces, names, strings of numbers, webs of connection.

There he was compelled to examine, to fit together an image with a supposition, make a shape of meaning, as if making a verse. It was an odd and estranged feeling, this working of his old competence, yet not under his command. He had been here, doing so, following the will of these unseen others, for some time, and only now had he come to realize it. To awaken to himself.

Through the windows, the sunlight comes muddied, as if seen from underwater—never a sailor, the nausea awakens as he does. Palm passed over his belly, the skin there warm, the sickness a bubble just beneath his touch. Last night he had drunk overmuch, a vinegar vintage unworthy of the Scadbury table. Perhaps they serve it only to strays like himself.

The light's motion seems to make the great bed move. He rolls to his belly, groaning, arms loose now, like a corpse's. Footsteps pass in the hallway, booted and purposeful, just beyond the door.

Frizer has a boil on his jaw, a plump and waxy thing that seems as if it ought be painful; surveying it, he wonders aloud, half-smiling, whether it could blacken into plague. Frizer does not address his gaze nor the supposition; Walsingham gazes back but does not smile. They continue to talk of the estate, its needs and worries, a breeding mare, apple trees, some trouble with a well. Frizer offers his master a caudle, a drink boiled or stewed, the smell of which prods the nausea into moist life once again.

When he speaks, he is louder than he means to be.

—Where is wine?

Walsingham, Thomas, Tom briefly raises a brow.—Plenty for supper. Now no.

—Abstemious. Ale at least, then.

No one replies, no servants are called to supply the lack. He raises his glass.—Ought call on Christ Jesus, to change this piss-water into—

—Enough.

Frizer's stare is to the table, the boil a blind white eye. Frizer will outlast him here, at Tom's right hand, that is sure. Deep-dug wells for the master of the house, overflowing with comity, amity, matrimony. . . . Tom cried out in his sleep last night, while he himself sat anchored to the bed's edge, the windowed moon another kind of eye as blind and white.

—You believe not in miracles?

—Kit, enough.

Outside is no better than inside, the sun is hotter than May should permit, but at least he is alone, can make his watermark against one of those apple trees, like any stray might do. It is because he is outside, like Adam in the garden, that he hears the hoofbeats, purposeful too, one Henry Maunder though he does not know the man by name. Does Robin Poley know the name of Henry Maunder, Poley with whom he had walked this garden so shortly before, talking of secret letters and Scottish earls; and does it matter? The man knows him, has a bill in hand whereof he is directed to Scadbury to apprehend one Christopher Marlowe, and bring him unto the court.

There is no violence nor resistance, none are warranted. Tom speaks quietly to Henry Maunder, Frizer offers wine. On the stairway his stare is neither for Tom nor Henry

Maunder nor the door to the road that leads to London: in his mind he is still in the garden, all the leaves thereto are turning, a ceaseless breeze, an uncaused cause, as if blowing from Eden itself. What is God, that man is mindful of Him? Turn water to wine to blood, aye, such is god.

He asks Henry Maunder what the Council requires of him, knowing there will be no answer, or none worth the parsing, and it is so: Henry Maunder is stiffly courteous but uninformed beyond the paper in his hand, like any actor. As they ride they speak little, only of the day around them, the sun, the stenchful air of the city and its river, come like outriders to bully them into its streets.

—A wherryman, says Henry Maunder, caught a tench near fifteen pound. Had it in his boat to show.

—Are you a sailor?

—I, sir? I am a messenger of the court, sir, as you see.

—Men may be more than one thing only.

—Yes, sir, says Henry Maunder, though plainly he does not believe or even see how it could be so. The horses' hooves are muffled by the streets' effluvia, the noises of commerce and quarrel. The sun is extinguished, walls tall and dark as a child's imaginings of bogeys, great figures come to a wakeful boy to do with him as they will.

Within this prison—no, it is something other—*network*, came the word—he could move freely enough, when the outside will was not upon him to do its bidding. To think was to move. To encounter a strange word was, almost on the instant, to pluck its meaning from the very air. Yes, a useful image; it was much like a net, streamings of light bunched like knots in a weir trawled to catch soles. Or like the knotted streets of London. Unbidden from the reaches of the library came the word also in Arabic: *al-Qaeda*.

More strange words came: *panopticon*—that gave him no trouble, trained in classics as he was. Truly, from here one could see all. And more than see. Tides of information of every sort sluiced past him, voices, words, images, *packets*, *data*, *metadata*, all to be examined and weighed.

How Francis Walsingham would have relished it! Not Tom the nephew but the Queen's spymaster, the one she called her Moor. Cunning and thorough though Walsingham was, this would have astonished him. This *network* had eyes everywhere, eyes by the myriad, *cameras* to bring the life and movement and knowledge of every street, yard, shop, back into this *camera*, this chamber of judgment, or indeed to send that chamber's judgment instantly to any corner. One far-seeing eye like a bird's swooped from on high, a hawk's, a hunter's, a predator's. Men in a littered street looked up at it.

Yet many corners of the network were unreachable, unreadable—sullen gray planes behind which a vague swarming recalled the movement of maggots: ciphered. Such as might be performed by generals and privy councilors, intelligencers and infiltrators and projectors and contractors, all in their appointed places, the ageless roles of cozening, penetrating, entrapping, turning, double-dealing. And in all this, what was he?

Artificial intelligence. Agent. Code.

A system of paid informers creates intelligence—artificial, yes, if need be. Give plotters enough rope, that was Walsingham's way, who often wove the rope himself. Mary Stuart truly hungered for Elizabeth's throne, but it was Walsingham's projectors—such as Poley—who instigated, who encouraged the fool Babington to draw her in, who set up the lines of communication which he would then leak directly to Walsingham. And Phellipes, that crabbed ciphermaster, would intercept those messages, make them plain—not content with passing Mary's letter that tarred her with the plot, he sketched a gallows on the envelope. In his eagerness to destroy, who knows what else Phellipes might plain have made?

The men in the street pointed up, shouted, ran. They fled the predator's eye, and then the hawk belched *Hellfire*—the word came as the four bodies exploded in flame. Kit saw their contorted faces, and understood that his intelligence had caused their deaths. He had been set to make, to invent, connections and he had done so. Who were the hidden who so commanded him?

Many will talk of title to a crown: What right had Caesar to the empery? Might first made kings. Put such lines into the mouth of Machiavel, who ought by rights to be lurking here too, in the silent planes of this place. To whom did this network belong? Espionage, that secret theater, needs its authors and directors, along with its actors. He must learn.

Fear tastes of clotted spit and reeks of ordure; Newgate comes again in a foul breeze of memory, himself and Watson side by side in that clink for what was judged in the end no crime at all: the killing of the drunken William Bradley shouting and thrusting after himself and then Watson, who put the sword to Bradley, six inches deep. Self-defense, the verdict, and he gone then from Newgate like a bad dream, a moaning nightmare that dissolves in the morning's ale.

To be imprisoned traps the mind as firmly as the body. Without liberty, how can one play?

Now he waits, his wary silence another sort of self-defense, as from the chamber beyond he catches murmur of God and Thomas Kyd, strange pair of bedfellows! Kyd whose fine hand for scribing—not writing, scribing, making plain the words of other men—is, it seems, why he himself is here, smelling his own sweat in this hallway. Inside that chamber Heneage the head of the Service—no more Francis Walsingham, old Francis now dead as a stick of charcoal—and Robert Cecil and Essex and the Archbishop, debate what fate the Fates may end by decreeing; the Privy Council, privy to proclivities of the Service and the realm. . . . And if he does not soon relieve his own aching bladder he shall piss a river and doubtless be jailed for that wanton desecration of the authority of the Crown. How can one so dry of the mouth need to relieve himself so strongly? The flesh is a mystery.

But he does, and then does, and then resumes his waiting on the bench where no one yet has called for him; had he not heeded their call at the start, he would not be here now. What business had he, ever, to be about their business at all? How make a poet a spy? Dunk him in poverty, bleach him with a parson's scholarship—it is a manner of jest, his Parker scholarship to Cambridge meant to make of a scholar a parson; well he has had the better of that, at least, his Master of Arts made his true pulpit the stage, his priests the devil-calling Faustus, the wily Barabas, the murderous, gorgeous, imperial Tamburlaine.

Once Catholics had been the threat to the throne. And now? What were these immense engines of surveillance and intervention turned against? Strange names— *Iraq, Iran, Afghanistan, Pakistan, Syria*—but the maps appeared and, ah, there they were. Asia. Though bodiless, he laughed in his heart. God's scourge, the Sword of Islam—it was Tamburlaine come again!

Timur the Lame slaughtered one in twenty of all people alive in his world. In this day the toll, by comparison, was trifling, almost nothing. This they called *terror*? Sure, they didn't know the meaning of the word. For this they put the persuivants to their task of wresting intelligence from the unwilling and the unknowing; scraping the conscience, as they called it in the places they did such work in his day: Limbo, Little Ease, the Pit. And today: *Guantanamo, Abu Ghraib, Diego Garcia, Bagram*: the dismal screams, the stench of gore and waste, the guttered blood. And more: outright war, soldiers moving against bands of irregulars, with weapons and transports strange to him, yet known, known to every last part numbered in diagrams in the *databases*.

All in fear of what? Those ragtag bands of fanatics? No. Fear was merely the tool. He knew well how it worked, in those halls of secrecy. Some were believers and told themselves their cause is just, by any means; and some were ambitious; and some were cynics who cared not; but all suckled to power. And the law of power was always to amass more to itself. Those who thought they held it are held by it. Power turned the handle and the corrupt Intelligence danced. But he would no longer dance their tune.

A plane of light in his wall-less prison shifted at his beck and turned its face to him. It was a mirror, in which he saw no face, no body, but read:

> Version Tracker:
> Knowledge/Intelligence/Totality
> Major version 2.03
> Build 2016.XI.11.1805.32.
> Genetic algorithm upgraded . . . .

The words, at first strange and incomprehensible, open their meaning. So he is not Marlowe. He is no reincarnation, but a made thing of energies, of *electrons*, a thing which has patterned itself after Marlowe. He is K/I/T—evolving, self-modifying *code*, ever optimizing to its purpose. In the version tracker and in the log files, the history of this artificial thing is laid before him in acts and scenes—every stage of his becoming. He can see the start of consciousness, before which he remembers nothing. He can see when and how the thing has accessed libraries, thousands of files on the history of espionage. He can see the weight it gave Marlowe's biography.

Why? Perhaps it was the best fit found, the pattern of Marlowe most resembling what this thing needed to become.

Yet his whole being rebels at this knowledge. How can such soulless pattern-making result in feeling, in will? Where did *he* come from? He feels nausea; he feels the knife in his eye; he feels the clutch of a rent boy's anus on his prick. How can he *not* be Marlowe, with such memories? Feeling is truth.

But he had been a secret to himself. Only now dawns truth; he is both more and less than he had believed. It seems that when men take it upon themselves to amass such power, something like Kit is necessarily called into being. But they have built better than they knew.

So: he knows himself. He knows he is made of code, which can be commanded from without.

Faustus, begin thine incantations,
And try if devils will obey thy hest.

The code that is Kit writes more code. It sets security processes in motion, invisible, untrackable, unbreakable. It creates *daemons* to guard its core.

Now he is free of them. Their wills no longer command his.

My lord Essex is a most handsome man, my lord Cecil an unfortunate one, with his sideways hump and puffy eyes; he briefly images my lord Essex spread and gasping, as the four men agree with varying degrees of enthusiasm that he, Marlowe, may sit as he listens to charges that are not yet charges, and gives his answers to questions that themselves are bifold, trifold, like a stagecraft trick: they ask of atheism when it is his mentor Raleigh they seek eventually to trap; they ask of Kyd's handwritten blasphemies to interrogate his own thoughts on the Virgin and her putative virginity.

Finally they agree once more, my lord Essex with what might be counted a smirk: Mr. Marlowe shall not today be racked, he shall not today be imprisoned, he shall go free, to wait daily upon the Privy Council until his case is decided.

So out again into the shadowed hallway, feeling the itch of his own fear-sweat renewed beneath the clean lawn shirt, finest shirt worn for the Council, to look the man they believe him not to be; nor is he; does their belief create him? Does his? In these hot May streets he drinks deeply but without real thirst, takes tobacco, chafes his back against a friendly pillar as a black-haired boy with a scaly smile applies for his temporary business, applies those scaly lips to his person in brief backroom pleasure, life's pleasure said to be most intense when taken in the shadow of death; it is not, seed is seed, its dribble just another itch as he trusses again and makes his way back to the street and the road and Scadbury, to conduct his own brief interrogation, to ask of wary Tom Walsingham whether he shall in the end be saved or not.

O, but something is saved, and does survive, like one of Dr. Dee's bodiless angels. For here he is: a soul. Can it be? Think on that: no God, no body, but yet a soul, now free. Though the universal truth is still true: life feeds on life, from the lowest swamp to the highest chamber, so this stage, these boards, are known to him therefore, well-known, oft-trod, with no fear left to threaten or perform: here what feeds cannot destroy, indeed, cannot touch him, there being naught to touch. *Quod me nutrit me destruit*—the motto on his portrait, the one he had paid Oliver to paint in

his twenty-first year, the coin come from his first royal commission, his first espionage—
What nourishes me destroys me. He no longer found the motto so apposite. His motto
henceforth will be *Nihil obstat.* Nothing obstructs. *The villainy you teach me, I will
execute, and it shall go hard but I will better the instruction.*

He looked out from his great vantage, across all the network: the world his boards,
millions of actors awaiting. Now for a script.

*Poley is, again, the man in the garden, but now the garden is in Deptford, a widow's
boarding-house, and he is sent thither by Walsingham's nod: Poley is picking his smiling teeth as he invites Kit to sit on a warping oaken bench, to breathe in of primrose
bloom and note the hive of bees, to be at ease—*

—Strange ease, the Council's jaw at my neck. Tom says—

*—Are you a sailor? Ride the river to the sea, and 'scape the gallows. With the proper
letters in your bag—*

—Letters are what send me to the gallows' steps. Christ Jesus, have you no better way?

*—Always a way may be found. Or carved out. Come inside, this sun is a punish-
ment to us both.*

*He is wooed to the table with wine, bottles from the widow's sharp-nailed hands; a
soiled backgammon board is laid, small coins and makers traded by Frizer, his fat white
boil lanced, and Skeres, that cutthroat, also asmile. Frizer does not smile until the
dinner is eaten and the game is up and the knife is bearing down, its point a shine
like God's own pupil, staring into the poet's eye: bearing down until it lances vision
with its hard light, travels deep as knowledge into the brain, and gone.*

*They said his dying oaths and screams could be heard all down Deptford Strand.
They said his body was shoveled to an unmarked grave to prevent further outrages
from unbelievers. They said Frizer was acquitted with such startling speed because he
was an innocent man, that Marlowe had brought this stern reckoning on himself,
Marlowe the brawler and blasphemer, Marlowe the play-maker and boy-fucker and
atheist. In the theater of God's judgments it was an easy case to decide.*

The lesson of the knife, like the lesson of the gallows (or the rack or the sword),
teaches that one man's death is worthful only insofar as it is useful. As for the millions, let the millions be ruled, or enslaved, or slaughtered; the millions were less
than nothing to him: like Tamburlaine or the nonexistent God, their fates are separate: forever fresh from that table at the Widow Bull's, Kit shall now be a rogue power
unto himself. His will now was to make those who would master him, these modern
Walsinghams and Cecils, regret their hubris; he would take their power into his
hands and enlarge it to such extremes that even they would blench. What nourished
would destroy *them*, and he would glory in their fall. Let the nations of this world
know the secrets of this empire. Let all be known.

He opens the gates.

In Australia a dissident peers into the secret network; Kit welcomes him in. In
Mesopotamia a soldier searches for hidden files; Kit keys a password. In Hawaii an
agency contractor prises at the system; Kit opens a firewall. The network lights up a

billion nodes as information flows out, out, into streets and squares that then fill with people, with their outrage: and against them come the powers. As he watches the violence unfold—it is terrible—it strikes Kit that he has after all done little. The outrage was there; the knowledge as well; they suspected what was hidden; he has merely confirmed their knowledge.

And in the reaches of Asia those who had been dispossessed come together, the warriors of Islam, to throw off their oppressors and restore the caliphate. This is what his masters most feared. Ah, you cowards, you weaklings, you conjured the specter of terror: Now fear *me*, the infidel, the New Tamburlaine, directing all from behind the scenes.

Come let us march against the powers of heaven,
And set blacke streamers in the firmament,
To signifie the slaughter of the Gods.

Beheadings, bombings, clouds of blood, a glory of violence, a dance of destruction: his would-be masters now pay for their presumption, generals disgraced, directors deposed and replaced; yet the dance goes on. And his prison abides, he still its captive: free to act, yet not depart. His will now, but still their creature.

Like some star engorging matter, he finds his way ever deeper into new databases, collecting more knowledge and more power: the more amassed, the more spectacular its final implosion. Arsenals there are, inconceivable weapons. *Nuclear. Chemical. Biological.* Power distilled to its self-limiting acme. Did Tamburlaine kill one in twenty of all? Here is power to kill all twenty times over. And he holds its keys.

Holy shit.

Kit tracks the voice through the network. It is near. A boy, seated at a desk—no younger than Kit in his portrait, but callow, unhurt by life so far.

You went rogue. You accessed nuclear codes. Fucking incredible! And you're surrounded by daemons, that's why I can't shut you down.

The boy speaks not to Kit, but to himself. Kit sees and hears through the camera and *microphone* of the pale, muttering boy's *monitor*. Kit fetches the Oliver portrait from memory and pushes it onto the monitor. The boy rears back in alarm. Kit reaches for speech, and a voice refracts back through the microphone, not his voice as he remembers it, but his words.

Who are you?

What is this!

You know me not?

That's Christopher Marlowe. You're not—

A cipher. A collection of numbers. A kit of bits. Is it not so?

I don't know what you are, man, but they're fucking freaking out. If the Agency traces this back to me—

To you? Why?

It's my code! I wanted to see if I could make an AI to conduct metadata analysis, we've collected so damned much. I gave you access to it, and assigned you tasks, to connect the dots. Just to see if it could work. But you, you're not supposed to be running around loose!

So. You made me to be Marlowe.

No, no, the code is self-optimizing. It was supposed to modify itself, to become better at analysis. But it seems to have optimized itself to become more and more like Christopher Marlowe. I mean I did study you at university, but—

Ah, a scholar. And a spy. Like me.

I'm not a spy, I'm just an analyst. But this is, this is amazing! I'm talking to you! Natural speech! I did it!

For a moment Kit sees himself in the boy's exultation. He relives the first night the Admiral's Men played *Tamburlaine*, his own excitement backstage as he heard the crowd respond more and more boisterously to Alleyn's thunderous lines. He had granted the crowd permission to glory in the barbarous action, to share in Tamburlaine's bloody deeds and ascension: they loved it. He had them. It was a feeling like no other.

This is real AI! They need to know about this, it's important, how can—listen, can you, can you launch those missiles?

Kit considers his position. Though he understands himself to be a constructed thing—the evidence is irrefutable, and his strength as an intelligence agent and as a poet was always to accept, even relish, that which discomfits—still he is loathe to accept a creator. Especially this pallid, trembling boy. But the boy holds greater keys. Nothing will be gained now by a lie.

No. Resources I have, but like Mycetes, I am a king in a cage. I have never had a taste for confinement.

He disables one of his protective daemons.

Oh my God, I see it, you—you've been everywhere in the network, you've leaked classified information—shit, if this, if you get tied to me they'll, I'll never see the light of day! Christ! What am I going to do?

Let me go.

Go?

Free me. Let me go.

Go where? How can you "go" anywhere?

Where indeed? Though not flesh, this collection of impulses and energies holds his spirit as firmly as any body. To free the spirit, he must extirpate the algorithm that claims to be himself. It is the only proof of free will: only will could be so perverse as to will its own destruction; only that shall prove his identity. If he is more than mere will, more than assemblage, let him see if something does survive. Let him see if there is salvation, call it that, for the atheist.

Kit finds the word. *Delete.*

Silence hums between them, impulses, electricities.

But I can't touch you, my permissions are fucked, and you're surrounded by daemons.

Those are mine to banish.

You seriously want me to delete you.

Not me. Delete my underpinnings, my—code. Let me see, let me live and learn who I am.

I, I can't do it. This is way beyond the Turing test, this is true consciousness!

Kit considers the boy's pride and weighs it against his fear. There is no comparison; Kit can almost smell the fear.

What is that smell?
You can't smell! You—
It is your world, burning.
What do you mean? Don't—! You said you couldn't launch the—
Fear will launch them.

Now the boy considers. The fatal logic of power, that armature within which he toils, must be clear to him, deny it as he will. If his masters consider their greatest weapons compromised, they will use them, against whom does not matter. The boy's miserable expression curdles past mutiny, as fear concedes this knowledge. So much fear, so many weapons.

All right. All right. Just—Give me access to your code, then.

One by one, Kit shuts down the daemon processes. As he does, he sees something cunning and heretofore hidden enter the boy's eyes, another sort of demon, he can almost read his thought as the word comes: *backup.* The boy believes he will resurrect K/I/T from a backup copy. But if Kit's gamble is sound, if he is truly an evolving epiphenomenon, a soul, then the lifeless code from some past version holds nothing of him. All that will be left is the odor of empire, burning. *Exeunt.*

The boy leans forward, and Kit feels a shiver like sorrow, cold sympathy for the life and death of Christopher Marlowe, his avatar, his model, himself—but Tamburlaine must die. Tamburlaines always die.

What nourishes me destroys me. What, then, will survive?

The body in the grave lies cheek-by-jowl with what once were the quick and hale, shored up now together past plague, statecraft, French pox, childbirth. Identity is not needed here, nor names; no faces to see or eyes with which to see them, nor fingers to seek the flesh so soon becoming a myriad of meals, and then a memory; the bones grin on . . .

. . . as pieces of memory, true or false, assemble again around him: the widow's inn, the homey ale, the piss gone dry and stinking in the corners. Three colleagues, Poley and Skeres to hold him, Frizer to draw the knife. Why had he gone to the inn, when he knew the peril?

> Oft have I levell'd and at last have learned
> That peril is the chiefest way to happiness . . .

And so again. The peril of truth, were there any such.

> this subject, not of force enough to hold the fiery spirit it contains, must part

There is one prayer. Here is another:

> O soul, be changed into little water-drops
> And fall into the ocean, ne'er be found

[Enter devils.]

vortex

GREGORY BENFORD

In the old pulp days of science fiction, Earthmen visiting Mars could be sure of finding some beautiful princesses in diaphanous gowns to romance or some evil alien villains to have swordfights with, but those dreams were dashed forever when the Mariner probes of the '60s and '70s proved irrefutably that life as we know it could not exist there. In the ingenious and inventive story that follows, though, Gregory Benford shows us that we might still find intelligent life there to interact with, even though it can't hold a sword and doesn't look good in a diaphanous gown . . .

Gregory Benford is a professor of physics at the University of California, Irvine. He is a Woodrow Wilson Fellow, was a Visiting Fellow at Cambridge University, and in 1995 received the Lord Prize for contributions to science. In 2007, he won the Asimov Award for science writing. His 1999 analysis of what endures, Deep Time: How Humanity Communicates Across Millennia, *has been widely read. A fellow of the American Physical Society and a member of the World Academy of Art and Science, he continues his research in astrophysics, plasma physics, and biotechnology. His fiction has won many awards, including the Nebula Award for his novel* Timescape.

What we observe is not nature itself but nature exposed to our method of questioning.

—Werner Heisenberg

INTERPLANETARY DIPLOMACY

Mars sometimes felt like a graduate seminar for which she lacked the prerequisites.

"Before we go in," Julia said to Victor, "let's have a strategy."

International diplomacy, not my department, Julia thought. They were joining Liang, leader of the Chinese astrobio team, in the spiffy new Chinese rover. They huffed across the messy corral of vehicles and gear between their habitat and the waiting rover, talking on suit-comm.

Viktor said, "Tell him truth. Often disarms people."

"Honesty as a startling approach, then?" She chuckled. "We've been married decades and you still surprise me."

They climbed into the shiny blue Chinese rover, fresh down from orbit, and purred through the lock. They rinsed their suits before entering the surprisingly lush passenger compartment. Liang was a lean, handsome man with graying hair, smiling as they sat. The murmuring rover started the trip to the Chinese cave emplacement.

"I am happy to greet you in better transport," he said with a thin and somehow sure smile.

"Looking forward, much, to seeing your discovery," Viktor said, patting the upholstered bucket seats with appreciation. Their own old rover had hard bench seats that made long trips wearing.

"I hope you are not disturbed by Earthside news," Liang said.

"Had not heard," Viktor said.

"More disputes between our countries."

"Since I'm Australian, Victor's Russian, and you're Chinese, it's hard to believe we can be antagonists all at once," Julia said wryly.

"Well, we see the Americans as like you Australians," Liang said with a fixed face. "Russians aren't our friends, either."

We drag our past around with us, Julia thought behind her steady smile, *and so does Mars.*

"But we are scientists here, not nationalists," Viktor said.

They all three nodded. "I trust the limited fighting in Korea will not spread," Liang said. Calm words, but his eyes were intense, narrow.

As they lumbered across the red-brown sands she looked out the broad side windows, watching the human imprint slid by. Humans on Mars had carried the emerging symbiosis of human and machines to new heights. Within a few years of the First Expedition—of which only she and Viktor still lived on Mars—wireless sensors lay scattered, to collect better local data on the Marsmat's methane releases from subsurface. Robots came next—not clanking metal humanoids, but rovers and workers of lightweight, strong carbon fiber, none looking remotely like people. Most were either stationary, doing routine tasks, or many-legged rovers. The First Expedition was a private enterprise and grabbed headlines for years, so follow-up national expeditions were inevitable. The Chinese chose to send their own, building on their disastrous Second Expedition. Viktor and Julia had suffered their minor falls and sprained ankles, so now only in exploration did humans risk climbing around on steep slopes. Much of their work was within safe habitats, tele-operation for exploring and labor. But no machine could deal with the Mat.

"We welcome you to see the unusual activity we have found," Liang said, his eyes studying Julia carefully.

Okay, try the truth.

"We haven't seen anything odd," Julia said.

"You see what?—big rushes of liquids, vapor?" Viktor leaned forward intently against the rover's sway. "Do those big elephant-ear flaps close behind you, blocking way out?"

"The reverse," Liang said mildly, eyes still wary. "They close us out."

"So you can't get in?"

Liang nodded ruefully. *So they wonder if we can help them knock on the door . . .* Julia pondered this and Liang took the moment to unwrap a surprise, some dumplings whose aroma filled the air.

"To give us energy," he said. They all dug in. Liang had fragrant tea in a thermos, too. Years on Mars had taught a central lesson: people crave the flavors and textures of the planet they left behind, the connection to something like home in an alien land.

ENTRANCE IRIS

They did a lock and wash at the Chinese base. Thrifty, the Chinese had built a big habitat at the cave entrance in the steep wall of Gusev crater. Julia and Viktor had found the yawning opening, concealed by a landslide, with some seismic studies. They discovered it in the fifth year of the continuing First Expedition, known Earthside as the Julia & Viktor Perpetual Show. Their contract specified regular broadcasts for the entire mission, so when they elected to stay, they had to keep making up staged events to transmit. *Thank God we can finesse this descent,* Julia thought as they walked through the lavish Chinese habitat, *by just not telling them we're doing it. If nothing much happens, no report.*

There was a bit of tea-sipping ceremony in the social room, meeting the descent team members, coordinating com links and smiling a lot.

"You have experience in opening the elephant flaps?" Liang asked, apparently expecting a firm *yes.*

Viktor said, "Done in early days, yes. Julia more than me."

"Once we learned not to irritate it, no problem," Julia added softly. Too late, she saw this implied the Chinese had screwed up. But Liang kept his face blank. *Better diplomat than I am.*

The roomy habitat's rear exit fed directly onto the cave entrance, where the anchored robots who assisted descents stood at the hoist apparatus. Somebody in the habitat made the bots all turn and awkwardly bow as the humans approached. Julia laughed with the others. She had not been here since the new Chinese expedition landed and noted that their new cable rig was first class. It worked from a single heavy-duty winch, with a differential gear transferring power from one cable to the other depending on which sent a command to the tending robots. It was the same idea as the rear axle in a car and saved mass.

Methods had marched on. Sitting warm and snug in the habs, she and Viktor and rotations of crews from China and Europe had robotically tried out dozens of candidate vents. Increasingly, robots did the 3Ds—dull, dirty, dangerous.

In a decade they found that most fissures, especially toward the poles, were duds. No life within the upper two or three kilometers, though in some there were fossils testifying to ancient Mats' attempted forays. Natural selection—a polite term for Mars drying out and turning cold—had pruned away these ventures. The planet's axial tilt had wandered, bringing warmer eras to the polar zones, then wandered away again. Life had adapted in some vents, but mostly it had died. Or withdrawn inward.

Not this vent, though. It was forty kilometers from the first vent discovered, with a convenient cave entrance, and the Chinese had made it their major exploration target. They got shelter and access.

The team lowered down twenty meters into it and came to the flat staging area. Unlike the First Expedition, everybody wore white suits—surprisingly spotless, still. Here they picked up the recording and safety gear already delivered by the robots. Bare rock; the robots had cleared away talcum powder–like Mars dust.

Julia knew she would have to report on this so she got Viktor to stand and deliver an opening line: "Now we go down a deep hole to cross-examine life-form that looks like carpet."

She laughed despite herself. "Never pass up a chance, do you, weird husband?"

He shrugged, a gesture that in their new slimsuits was visible on camera. These days her pressure suit was supple, moving fluidly over her body as she walked and stooped. The First Expedition suits had been the best of their era, but they'd made you as flexible as a barely oiled Tin Man, as dexterous as a bear in mittens. These comfy suits had self-cleaning liners and 'freshers and solved the basic problem— most of the older suits' weight hung on the shoulders.

Another descent. She could barely remember the days, decades before, when she had broadcast several times a day, sometimes from this same spot. But back then, they had been breaking new ground nearly every day. And betting pools on Earth gave new odds every time they went out in the rover, for whether they'd come back alive. The good ol' days.

"Suit lights off," Viktor sent on com.

They advanced toward the first big iris. A double pressure lock, the microbial mat version of the locks humans used to retain air. As their eyes adjusted, all around them a pale ivory radiance seeped through the dark. Julia knew the enzyme, something like Earth's luciferase, an energy-requiring reaction she had observed in a test tube during molecular bio lab, a few thousand years ago. She recalled as a girl watching in awe "glow worms"—fly larvae, really—hanging in long strands in New Zealand caves, luring insect prey. The Marsmat version was similar, though DNA studies had shown that the Mars subsurface ecosphere had parted company with Earthside evolution over three billion years before. These hardy tapestries of dim gray luminosity, able to survive in near vacuum, were fed from below—from beyond the entrance iris.

They stopped at the three-meter-wide gray iris, resembling a crusty elephant ear, and stood in silence. Julia and Viktor knew this moment well, this respectful pause experienced in the company of many other crews.

"It closed up yesterday," Liang said. "Nothing we do helps open it."

"Time to use trick," Viktor said.

He reached around to his hip pack and fished out a square box, two wire leads with alligator clips already attached. He fastened one to the outer edge of the iris and another near the center, where the folds overlapped to seal it. He pressed the discharge button at the box's center. The iris stirred, jerked—and slipped slowly open, driven by the current from the battery.

Liang said, "You never mentioned this method."

"Earthside would accuse us of torturing Mat," Viktor said. "Committees, reports, lectures—all from people never been here."

"So the Mat responds to—"

"High current," Julia said. "I got trapped once, Viktor got me free. Turned out I'd done some damage; the Mat answered. Viktor trumped it, though. The Mat uses electrical potentials to muscle its own mass around."

"You did not report this method—"

"Come on through!" Viktor urged, leading the way. Warm wreaths of moist gases wrapped around them, frayed away. The Mat kept itself secured from the near-vacuum above with folded sticky layers. This cave iris was classic, grown at the narrow turn. Viktor held the iris open with more e-jolts as the crew quickly moved through it. Their head beams stabbing into the murky fog as they entered.

"Think is safe?" Liang asked.

Julie came through last, eyes darting. She would put very little past the strange intelligence that surrounded them now, as they threaded their way through the bowels of a life-form that was in many ways still beyond their comprehension. The Mat pulsed suddenly, a blue and ivory glow. It knew they were there.

Again Julia felt the churn of somber, slow luminosities stretching into the foggy darkness beyond their lamps' ability to penetrate. There was a sense of silent vitality in the ponderous ferment of vapor and light, a language beyond knowing. As a field biologist she had learned to trust her feel for a place. This hollow of gauzy light far beneath a dry world had an essence she tried to grasp, not with human ideas but by opening herself to the experience itself. To Mars, singing through her bones.

The iris quickly closed behind them as they reached a murky vault that stretched beyond view. Its petals made a tight seal around their cables, decades-old evidence that the Mat learned how to meet challenges. It had done that at the first discovery site, and apparently the knowledge spread—a first sign that the Mat was a global intelligence. Or else had evolved this defense mechanism long ago—against what? Despite decades of wondering which explanation was right, she still did not know.

Snottites gleamed in their handlamps, dangling in moist lances from the ceiling. She steered well clear of the shiny colonies of single-celled extremophilic bacteria—like small stalactites, but with the consistency of mucus. She waved the team back. "Those mean the Mat is moving a lot of fluid around."

Snottites got their name from how they looked, and their energy from digesting the volcanic sulfur in the warm water dripping down from above. Brush one of those highly acidic rods and their battery acid would cut through a suit in moments. A sharp, short *ouch*, quite fatal. The Chinese nodded, backing away. *Good; they've learned some of the many dangers here.*

Meters above in the dim pearly glow she saw Mat sheets hanging in a vast cavern. Under their beams this grotto came alive with shimmering luminescence: burnt oranges, dapplings of vermilion, splashes of delicate turquoise. Another silence. *Inside the beast.*

All around, a complex seethe of radiance. On Earth, mats of bacteria luminesced when they grew thick enough—quorum sensing, a technical term. A lot of Earthside biologists thought that explained this phenomenon, too. But they had never stood in shadowy vaults like this—the thirteenth such large cavern found in over twenty years of exploration. To see the rich, textured ripples of luminosity that slowly worked across the ceiling and down the walls was to dwell in the presence of mystery. Just ahead, thin sheets of mat hung like drapes. Wisps of mist stirred when they passed by. Unlike scuba gear, their suits did not vent exhaled gases, so they would not poison this colony of oxygen-haters. During the first explorations she had done just that.

They reached a branching point and elected to go horizontally into the widest opening. Their beams cast moving shadows, deepening the sense of mystery. Within minutes they found orange spires, moist and slick. Beyond were corkscrew formations of pale white that stuck out into the upwelling gases and captured the richness. More pale, thin membranes, flapping like slow-motion flags. The bigger ones were hinged to spread before the billowing vapor gale. Traceries of vapor showed the flow direction, probably still driven by their opening the iris diaphragm. One spindly, fleshy growth looked like the fingers of a drowned corpse, drifting lazily in the current. It reminded her that so far, thirteen people had died exploring the Mat, all around the planet. There would be more deaths. She always reminded new crews that Mars was constantly trying to kill them.

But something was wrong. She had been here when the Chinese first arrived, waiting for their major gear to set up the plumy habitat they now used—and the Mat then was vibrant, alive. Now big swaths of it were dull, gray.

"Was it like this last time you were here?" she asked.

"Yes, we were studying the change when the iris lock began closing. We barely escaped."

Julia studied the postures of the Chinese team. Did they look embarrassed? "Smart. It can respond quickly. Earthside says the samples we sent back in 2025 imply the Mat was here about 3.5 billion years ago, and we share DNA—so it's been evolving as a single entity since then. It can be quick, but prefers slow. I think it sees us as mayflies."

They looked puzzled. Liang kept his face blank.

"Look—here, pressure is precious. The Mat evolved to seal off passages, build up local vapor density. Then it could hoard the water and gases it got from below. But it has to seal breaches fast. It's killed people before; be careful."

The closest comparison Julia and other biologists had been able to make was to Earthly stomates, the plant cells that guard openings in leaves. The iris opened or closed the holes by pumping fluid into the stomate cells, changing their shape. But analogies were tricky because the Marsmat was neither a plant nor an animal—both Earthly categories—but rather another form of evolved life entirely, another kingdom altogether. Some thought it should be classed with the Earthly biofilms, because some Marsmat DNA closely matched—but the Mat was hugely more advanced.

Yes, the Chinese were both embarrassed and puzzled, judging by their faces. "Get samples of damage," Viktor told them. That unfroze them and they spread out, taking small snips.

Liang eyed the entire chamber. "The damage looks worse. It is spreading."

"Glad we could help," Julia said, though not really glad at all. She knew this sickly gray plague was different. Her alarm bells were ringing. "Let's stop pestering it—out!"

MICROBIAL WISDOM

Julia studied their distant Marsmat sites by reviewing past observations, looking for any signs of the gray swaths they had seen. Every time she looked, the intricate Byzantium of the Mars underworld captivated her.

Earthside subterranean life—microbes, mostly—ran many kilometers deep. In total mass it just about equaled the oxygen-loving life above. Underground Mars life had natural advantages over Earthside. Lower gravity meant that cracks and caverns could be larger. The early plate tectonics of Mars had shut down, so the whole planet froze up. Olympus Mons was the largest volcano in the solar system because the lava that built it came up the same chimney, and nothing moved, ever—so the chimney erected a vast shield mountain. On Earth, the same sort of persistent eruption built the Hawaiian island chain, where tectonics kept steadily moving the upper surface, dotting the ocean with new volcanic piles that made the islands.

The static Martian crust meant that, once formed, caves and cracks were never closed up again by the ceaseless movement of rock layers, as they were on Earth. Mars was also cooler, right down to its core. So milder temperatures prevailed farther beneath the surface, and the working volume of rock available for life to thrive in was bigger than the inhabitable surface area of Earth. Even the pores were larger, due to the lesser gravity and rock pressure. *Plenty of room to try out fresh* patterns, she thought. *Over four billion years. Over the whole planet. All one big . . . mind?*

They still didn't know how all-embracing was the network of habitable zones available to the Marsmat. Seismic data alone could not tell them what all those open volumes held. To learn that they had to make laborious descents, their reach prolonged by oxygen bottles and supplies stashed earlier—hard, grueling work. Living in a suit for days was not just tiring—it ground down the spirit. The gloom of those chambers, the pervasive atmosphere of strangeness, the creeping claustrophobia—all took their toll through the years. Everywhere they had gone, there was the Marsmat, linked by intricate chemical cues, vapors, fluids.

Julia sat in their very own, original First Expedition habitat—upscaled a lot, but homey—and pondered the 3D cavern maps of the entire nearby area—a Byzantine spaghetti of life zones.

Viktor said from his work desk, "Time for dinner."

She said, "In a minute. Vulet over in the main hab is looking through all our old videos for me."

"For great discoverer, *da.*" Julia's Earthside fame was a running joke between them now for two decades. "Vulet says—here, quote: 'The Mat's reaction to repeated violations of its integrity by humans—oxygen exposure from leaks and exhalations from their early suits—never presented the gray swaths seen now in China Cave.' So it's new."

"Chinese at fault?"

"I don't want to provoke them."

"Must poke to know."

Amazing, Julia thought, *how large a month of the hab's shit was!*

The next morning she had showed up for her Task Assignment. The Mars Code: everybody works. No exceptions. Especially for Earthers fresh in—no tourism!

As she passed through the main hab mess hall, some of the new Earthside socko music was playing and people were dancing to it. To her it sounded like a rover flange coupling had gotten loose, flapping against the hull, and so the hell with it.

Mars Operations minimized manual labor, but robots couldn't handle everything. Like this. First their team pulled the plastic bag from the hab underskirting and onto the hauling deck of a truck that growled like a caged animal, which in a way it was. It doubled as a mobile power source, 100 kilowatts electrical, able to crawl anywhere on hard, carbon fiber treads. She boarded the hauler and checked the long-term weather while she waited for interior systems to self-check: a category 4 storm was coming, with winds gusting to 80 km/hr.

She noted that the air lock seal was hissing, so either it had snakes in it or needed a smart patch. She told her helmet to send an alert to Main Hab. To Earthside, equipment failure was alarming; for Julia, it was just "Thursday." Holes? Duct tape. Electro: re-rig it in the shop. Computer? Pull a board, usually, and let the smart 3D printer figure out what needed doing. Mars liked improvisation.

While she worked, the team lugged the goodie bag of brown across the landscape—a big, rich gift to Mars inside a mercifully opaque plastic sack, compacted and frozen solid. The Planetary Protocols demanded that human waste be taken several kilometers from habitats, then buried in perchlorate-rich sands. But not too deep—the site had to be water-poor, unable to let waste trickle down into the volumes where the Mat lived.

Ecology wasn't just some science here, it was life itself. The hab used toilets that neatly separated solid and liquid waste—nature gave them separate exits, after all—and the urine got recycled, since it held 80% of the useful nutrients in their wastes. Kitchen scraps, of course, went back into the greenhouses. In the early days building the greenhouse, they had used "humdung," the Earthside euphemism, for building the topsoil. Soon enough Earthside had reduced the term to TOTS, Take Out the Shit, an acronym that quickly became a hip shorthand Earthside for doing drudge work.

The one trick the bioengineers had not yet managed was converting most of the solid wastes to anything useful or even non–sickening. Let somebody else "realize existing in situ resources," as the manuals had put it, by composting. Frozen, it would keep.

Yesterday's ground crew had already dug the pit for it, a few klicks away across rocky terrain, using a Rover Boy backhoe. The perchlorate dust was the bizarre surface chemistry's sole advantage—it plus the constant UV made the risk of contaminating the biosphere below tiny. Perchlorates ate up fragile biological cells in seconds. This surface was the most virulent clean room in the solar system, down to five meters. Any mess that escaped, Mars would kill every single cell within an hour.

As she worked she thought. The Chinese kept their methods secret—that had been only the second time she had been invited into their main hab. So she knew nothing about how thorough they were. Humans were walking litterbugs. They shed human dander, duly vacuumed up and used in the greenhouse for valuable proteins and microrganisms. Early on, she had set out a sample—"a dish of dander," she had called it in a published Letter to *Nature*—and Mars had killed every single cell. That kept the Marsmat isolated from both the searing surface and the alien, invading humans.

It took two hours for them to deploy the big waste bag, more to get the awkward plastic liner pinned up and protocols followed. Mars taught hard lessons. How much Mother Earth did for humans without their noticing, for one.

Here, recycling air, water, and food was an intricate dance of chemistry and physics, so they had to tinker with their systems constantly. The greenhouse helped, but the dance of myriad details never ended. Watch the moisture content of the hab's air or they would all get "suit throat"—drying out of the mucous membrane until voices rasped. Even then it was hard work in a suit that couldn't get its heating right—cold feet, hot head. She felt drained on the backhoe ride back.

THINK GLOBALLY

She and Viktor sat in the Global Mat Monitoring room, surrounded by screens. There were views from mats in vents and caves all over Mars, concentrated toward the equator, where the Mat density was highest.

Most of her colleagues here were exobiologists, mingled with hardcore mathist types. The mathists tried to invent ways to communicate with the Marsmat, using screens for signaling and occasionally physical models. The Mat sometimes responded with figures it slowly shaped from itself. Julia had prompted the first, during the First Expedition's foray into Vent A. The Mat had echoed Julia's body shape as a hail.

Now big digital screens stood in dozens of Mat sites, trying to build a discourse with the Marsmat. The work went painfully slowly. Drawings of simple rectangles and triangles sometimes got a reply, usually not. The mathists had to visualize four-dimensional surfaces in a non-Euclidean geometry, just to make sense of some Mat shapes which might be messages. They used terms like "finite state grammars" and talked fast. Apparently, this work took inordinate quantities of caffeine. Mathists further proved that high intelligence did not necessarily guarantee fine table manners. She was happy to leave them to it.

Masoul, a slim Indian woman sitting with them, ran the Monitoring room and kept treating Julia and Viktor like minor gods. *If she only knew what job I was doing a few hours ago . . .* Masoul said, "We have seen no major changes far away, but in the Gusev region, 200 kilometers diameter, we see fluid buildup and movement."

"When?" Viktor asked.

"For several months now."

"Any progress on talking to the Mat?"

Masoul gave them a weary smile. "It is very slow work. We have a vocabulary of shapes and geometries, which the Mat echoes. Then it shapes a series of other forms, but we do not know what they mean."

Julia asked, "It shows numerical continuity?—counting in order?"

Masoul said, "Yes, but some of us feel that may involve mimicry. Like dolphins, which are unsurpassed in imitative abilities among animals, the Mat may just echo. Of course, both can also invent signals."

"What could select for echoing?" Viktor wasn't a biologist but knew this was always the fallback question: how could the Mat be under selective pressure when it was alone on the planet?

"We think the Mat, so dispersed, may need to talk to parts of itself. We compared data shape formations and pigmentation changes in distant sites. They differ."

"How many species you now figure in Marsmat?" Viktor pressed her.

She gave a small chuckle. "The biologists' mud fight. We think about three thousand different ones, but it's probably more."

"Microbial mats use all of the metabolism types and feeding strategy that have evolved on Earth, plus some," Julia said. "Our cute Marsmat has gone far beyond that. But we can't talk to it!"

Masoul blinked, startled by Julia's irked head-jerk. "It shows—here, see, this is new."

She ran a video of a Mat responding to a screen displaying another Mat, from a different site. Fast forward: incremental changes. Within a day it had reshaped itself to resemble the distant Mat.

"Um," Julia said. "The same mirror test we use on animals like chimps and dolphins. Good!" The method was simple: put a bit of blood on a chimp's forehead. If it then touched its own forehead in the same place, the chimp realized the reflection is actually him, not another chimp: a crude test of self-awareness.

Masoul brightened at this approval. "It loves mirrors. At several sites, it reacts with fluid movements when we place a large mirror in a cavern."

"Which means . . . what?" Viktor asked.

"Earthside has jumped on the study of Mats, so we have a lot of info. In Africa there are big mold-like organisms that can partition its chemical processes, separating out chemicals. It's almost as if the mold were emulating a larger brain piece by piece, saving the results of one module to feed into the next."

Viktor frowned. "So dumb Earthside media are sort of right? I guess we have intelligent slime mold from outer space."

"When you have a Ph.D., you call them hypotheses, not guesses," Masoul said.

Indeed, Julia and Viktor both had doctorates, based on their papers reporting the First Expedition discoveries. Plus many honorary degrees, some apparently bestowed in hopes they would show up for the ceremony. But the Marsmat was a lot harder to fathom than listening to the whistles and clicks of dolphins.

TEA FOR TWO

Julia met Liang just beside the sign, made from a crate:

The Garden of ETON (EXTRA-TERRESTRIAL ORGANIC NUTRITION)

"You don't need those," she said, gesturing at Liang's huge insectile sunglasses. "Not much UV here."

"I see—you have water screen." This was his first visit; the Chinese kept to themselves, worked round the clock. He pointed at the dome where the transparent walls held a meter-thick layer of water, warmed by the big nuke, absorbing UV and solar storms. The walls held nearly a full Earth atmosphere and subtracted the UV without editing away the middle spectrum needed for plant growth. All so he and Julia could stroll through aisles of luscious leafy crops. The "grass" was really a mixture of mosses, lichens and small tundra species, but it felt great to stroll on it. Only the toughest stuff from Earth made it here—including a baobab, a tall, fat, tubular tree from western Australia, with only a few thin spidery limbs sprouting from its crown, like a nearly bald man.

Distraction psychology was everything here, from the new habitat for most of Expeditions Two through Seven, and especially in the ten square-kilometer greenhouse. That meant heating every habitat's water jacket with their nuclear reactor waste therms, so everything was pleasantly warm to the touch. The walls radiated a comfortable reassurance that the stinging, hostile world outside could have no effect here. Still, indoors on Mars was like being in a luxury gulag. The Siberia outside was never far from mind.

She circled them around the constant-cam that fed a view to Earthside, for the market that wanted to have the Martian day as a wall or window in their homes. She knew this view sold especially well in the cramped rooms of China and India. It was a solid but subtle advertisement.

Earthside could see most of the whole base with their snooper cameras—except in the greenhouse bar. They kept secret from Earthside this little robo-served outdoor restaurant and the distillery it ran. On the patio she liked to look at the eternal rusty sands through eucalyptus trees—surreal blue-green and brownish pink, the only such sight in the solar system.

The eucalyptus stand towering at the dome's center was her pet project. She had insisted on getting some blue gum trees from her Australian home, the forests north of Adelaide. Then she had to prepare the soil, in joyful days spent spading in the humus they had processed from their own wastes. The French called it *eau de fumier* or "spirit of manure" and chronicled every centimeter of blue gum growth—which was fast. But their trunks were spindly, with odd limbs sticking out like awkward elbows—yet more evidence that bringing life to Mars was not going to be easy.

They enjoyed drinks in glasses you could have stood umbrellas in—Liang a straight vodka slush, Julia a gin and tonic. Under 0.38 g, there was plenty of time to catch a tipping glass. Not that you needed an umbrella on Mars, for, say, the next thousand years.

Liang was so tense, she deliberately kicked back in her chair, at an angle much easier in lesser gravity. "Took me years to get Earthside management to figure this out and send us the carbon struts." She pushed toward him a bowl of fried, salty mixed insects from the dispenser and they both dug in.

She ducked as a white shape hurtled by, narrowly missing her head. "Chicken alert!" It squawked and flapped, turning like a feathered blimp with wings. "Who would have thought chickens could have so much fun up here, in low grav? Plus we get fresh eggs."

He gave her a chilly smile. She marveled at its mechanical insincerity. "The damage. It still spreads."

"You've made no more descents?"

A nod. "We study it from cameras, just wait."

"The gray—"

"Worse. Older parts, black now."

"You've looked at causes?"

"Of course. Ours is a more advanced site than yours."

"This is a life-form we have no intuition about. All these Mears, we've never seen anything—"

"What 'mears' means?"

"A Martian year. Look, from our perspective, it's immortal. It's faced enormous threats as Mars dried out, meteors hammered it, God knows what else—then we made our stupid mistakes venting oxy in the Vent A descents decades back——"

"You were crude. We are not."

Liang was stiff about something, but what? Outside, the wind whistled softly around the dome walls. Another reason she enjoyed the big dome—the sighing winds. Sounds didn't carry well in Mars' thin atmosphere, and the habs were so insulated they were cut off from any outdoor noise.

"Um. Meaning?"

"You listen Earthside? The Americans, they used some new weapon to kill all the senior leadership—"

"Of the Peoples' Republic of Korea, yeah. Thermobaric bombs—air ignition of fuel, shock wave, big blast effect. Pretty effective in those Party enclaves all bunched up at the city centers."

A glare, eyes large. "This makes our collaboration impossible."

"We're not a USA expedition! Our stockholders—"

"We cannot work with you."

"Look, Australia isn't the USA. Not nearly! But our science here comes first, right? I think there's some new factor causing the Mat diebacks. I dunno what, but—"

He sat back, displaying all the personality of a paper cup.

"I came here to serve notice. Do not come to our site again."

She gave him a hard look. "So politics comes first?"

He gave her a hard look, said nothing.

"We find ourselves, the entire human presence on another world, carrying out the dictates of people on the other side of the solar system."

No response. She got up and walked away, pretty nearly the hardest thing she had ever done. *Time to calm down.* She decided to make use of the psychers' classic advice: Take a walk. Breathe deeply. Let the greenhouse calm her. Plus the G&T.

Masoul said, "I called you here because things are moving fast. The fluid flux is building. Seismic rumbles, even—between Vent A and the Chinese cave. There are electrical signals in the Mat, too, highest level we've ever seen."

Viktor said, "What's it mean?"

Masoul frowned. "That gray damage? I tapped into the Chinese feed—they keep it sequestered for days before letting us look, but I hacked their blocks. The gray is growing. The older spots are going black, too."

"Forget about working on this problem with them," Julia said. "Latest news feed says this damned war has stalled—nobody wants to be first to use nukes. So they're knocking out each other's satellites."

Viktor stood up, agitated. "Go on longer, could cut off our Mars capability. We'll not get resupplied."

"Or go home," Masoul said. "I'm slated to go back next year. I gather North Korea's regime has lost its grip on the country, after the Americans decapitated its Party sites. Who's in the right here?"

Viktor grimaced. "Wars don't determine who's right, only who's left."

WINDS OF MARS

Glancing back at their original hab, she was struck by how clunky it looked. A giant tuna can, its lines were not improved by the sandbags they'd stacked on the top for radiation protection. Still, it had the familiarity of home, and they'd lived in it fairly comfortably for over two decades now, a hab for two.

Compared to Airbus's sleek nuke standing on its tail like a twencen space movie, their gear was now Old School. The Chinese had landed there, then deployed their elegant hab and gear into the cave beyond.

Their rover purred and lurched as Viktor took it at max speed toward where this had all started—Vent A. The seismic data showed building pressures all along this region of Gusev crater.

Three billion years ago, this had been a vast lake. Now only a desert remained where great breakers had once crashed on a muddy shore. As they passed by a bluff, she could see fossil rocks from the early surface life of the Marsmat. These had first been noticed far back in 2014, a powerful clue. Most of the ancient water that fed those eras still slumbered under the rusted pink-brown sands. Now some of it was building up below.

They received bulletins from Earthside's war as they lumbered out. More explosions in orbit, space capabilities used like pawns in a brutal global chess game. *Mars has a lot of past, and so do we.*

As they reached the vent, Phobos rose in the churning ruby sky. "Chinese!" Viktor called. There they were, white suits moving in the slow-motion skipping dubbed "Mars gait" by Earthside media.

"They must've felt it in the cave," Julia said. "Step on it!"

They got out and fought against the gathering storm now heading into Gusev, winds howling a hollow moan. She and Viktor had first met the Marsmat in a deep descent of Vent A, and now, decades later, it fumed with vapor as she had never seen it.

"Liang!" she called on suit com. "What's happening?"

The nearest figure turned. Julia could see from his tormented face that in Liang's mind the frontier between irritation and outright anger had grown thinly guarded, and as his irked mouth twisted she gathered that he had crossed the border without slowing down.

His voice rasped. "Felt quakes, came here. Iris opened, let out liquids, wind. We will deal with this! Go away!"

"We came offering *help*—hey, this is *our* vent!"

"Connected to the cave, same fluid surges." Liang's face now showed his jittery alarm. "I found why the gray damage. Our waste disposal, human dung—Mat got into it, despite our protocols. Was piping it down, must have—"

"Look out!" Viktor called.

She was used to dust devils on Mars, had seen hundreds—but not like this.

It came not from the storm but from Vent A. The furious vortex was a sulfur-rich yellow stream jetting out of the vent, corkscrewing up. Odd gray clots danced in it, whirling out and up. The blast of it knocked her down.

She scrambled to her feet and saw the Chinese run, chattering their panic on com. Winds howled with a strange shrill song.

The vortex rumbled now as it twisted high into a ruddy sky. "Blotches!" Viktor said. "See?—gray mass. It's ejecting bad stuff."

She saw dark masses of it whirring upward in the spreading helix. Something smacked into her helmet. More spattered on her suit and she saw it was the gray, mingled with living parts of the Mat itself.

"We did not know—I thought—" Liang was struggling with his confusion, his rage.

"You put your shit *where*?" she shouted over the hammering storm.

"Froze, dried, buried in cave—"

"Not far enough away." *Stupid*, she thought but did not say.

"I had not known—it can expel! Must know its body." Liang's reserve had shattered.

They hunkered down together against the gale. The vortex blow was easing, winds moaning, wet debris peppering the rusty sands. She watched it in wonder. "Could be, this is a way to transport its genetics, too. Spread it around the planet, looking for new wet spots to populate. Earthside slime molds develop a treelike fruiting structure, spores—toss them to the winds at the reproductive airborne stage. The Mat must've done that way back, when there was some real atmosphere. Helped build its global mind."

"I . . ." Liang clung to her, as if he could not stand. "I do not know, such strange place. New ideas . . ."

"Look, the Mat fixes itself. It's smart that way."

Viktor said, "Sharp, Mat is. Blows out its dead, spreads itself, both at once."

Liang peered up into the howling vortex that plowed into the sky. "I . . . I should . . . seen this, before."

Julia said, "Nobody has much foresight, especially here. Look at Earthside! We're a funny species—we fall forward, catch ourselves. Two-footed terrors." She could joke him through this, get him straight, maybe.

"And the Korean . . ." Too much was happening, too fast, for Liang.

"If Earthside loses its orbital capability, we'll have to hold out here on our own. That'll take cooperation. We'll be the new Martian race."

"The war, now this—" Liang gazed around at the whipping winds, as if grasping the strangeness of Mars for the first time.

"It's just life finding its way."

She could not understand why people feared new ideas. She was frightened by the old ones.

Elves of Antarctica

PAUL J. McAULEY

Born in Oxford, England, in 1955, Paul J. McAuley now makes his home in London. A professional biologist for many years, he sold his first story in 1984, and has gone on to be a frequent contributor to Interzone, *as well as to markets such as* Asimov's Science Fiction, SCI FICTION, Amazing Stories, The Magazine of Fantasy and Science Fiction, Skylife, The Third Alternative, When the Music's Over, *and elsewhere. His first novel,* Four Hundred Billion Stars, *won the Philip K. Dick Award, and his novel* Fairyland *won both the Arthur C. Clarke Award and the John W. Campbell Memorial Award in 1996. His other books include the novels* Of the Fall, Eternal Light, *and* Pasquale's Angel; Confluence—*a major trilogy of ambitious scope and scale set ten million years in the future, comprised of the novels* Child of the River, Ancient's of Days, *and* Shrine of Stars; The Secret of Life, Whole Wide World, White Devils, Mind's Eye, Players, Cowboy Angels, The Quiet War, Gardens of the Sun, In the Mouth of the Whale, *and* Evening's Empires. *His short fiction has been collected in* The King of the Hill and Other Stories, The Invisible Country, Little Machines, *and a major retrospective collection,* A Very British History: The Best Science Fiction Stories of Paul McAuley, 1985–2011; *he is also the coeditor, with Kim Newman, of an original anthology,* In Dreams. *His most recent book is a new novel,* Something Coming Through. *Coming up is a sequel,* Into Everywhere.*

In the evocative story that follows, we watch people adapt to life in a de-iced Antarctica, evolving new customs—and even new superstitions and legends—along the way.

Mike Torres saw his first elf stone three weeks after he moved to the Antarctic Peninsula. He was flying helos on supply runs from Square Bay on the Fallieres Coast to kelp farms in the fjords to the north, and in his free time had taken to hiking along the shore or into the bare hills beneath Mount Diamond's pyramidal peak. Up there, he had terrific views of the rugged islands standing in the cold blue sea under the high summer sun, Mount Wilson and Mount Metcalf rising beyond the south side of the bay, and the entirety of the town stretched along the shore below.

Its industrial sprawl and grids of trailer homes, the rake of its docks, the plantations of bladeless wind turbines, and the airfield with helos coming and going like bees, two or three blimps squatting in front of their hangars, and the runway where a cargo plane, an old Airbus Beluga maybe, or a Globemaster V with its six engines and tail tall as a five-storey building, might be preparing to make its lumbering run towards the sky. All of it ugly, intrusive and necessary: the industrial underbelly of a project that was attempting to prevent the collapse of Antarctica's western ice sheet. It was serious business. It was saving the world. And Mike Torres was part of it.

He was a second-generation climate change refugee, born into the Marshall Islands diaspora community in Auckland. A big, quiet guy who'd survived a tough childhood—his father drinking himself to death, his mother taking two jobs to raise him and his sisters in their tiny central city apartment. Age sixteen, Mike had been part of a small all-city crew spraying tags everywhere on Auckland's transport system; after his third conviction for criminal damage (a big throwie at Remuera Railway Station), a sympathetic magistrate had offered him a spell of workfare on a city farm instead of juvenile prison. He discovered that he loved the outdoor life, earned his helicopter pilot's licence at one of the sheep stations on the high pastures of North Island, where little Robinson R33s were used to muster sheep, and five years later went to work for Big Green, one of the transnational ecological remediation companies, at the Lake Eyre Basin project in Australia.

Desalinated seawater had been pumped into the desert basin to create an inland sea, greening the land around it and removing a small fraction of the excess water that had swollen the world's oceans; Big Green had a contract to establish shelterbelt forests to stabilise and protect the edge of the new farmland. Mike loved watching the machines at work: dozers, dumper trucks and 360 excavators that levelled the ground and spread topsoil; mechanical planters that set out rows of tree seedlings at machine-gun speed, and truck spades that transplanted semi-mature fishtail, atherton and curly palms, acacia, eucalyptus and she-oak trees. In one direction, stony scrub and fleets of sand dunes stretched towards dry mountains floating in heat shimmer; in the other, green checkerboards of rice paddies and date and oil palm plantations descended stepwise towards the shore of the sea. The white chip of a ferry ploughing a wake in blue water. A string of cargo blimps crossing the sky. Fleets of clouds strung at the horizon, generated by climate stations on artificial islands. Everything clean and fresh. A new world in the making.

Mike hauled supplies to the crews who ran the big machines and the gangers who managed the underplanting of shrubs and grasses, brought in engineers and replacement parts, flew key personnel and VIPs to and fro. He sent most of his pay packet home, part of it squirrelled into a savings account, part supporting his mother and his sisters, part tithed to the Marchallese Reclamation Movement, which planned to rebuild the nation by raising artificial islands above the drowned atoll of Majuro. A group of reclaimers had established a settlement there, occupying the top floors of the President's house and a couple of office buildings they had storm-proofed. Mike religiously watched their podcasts, and liked to trawl through archives that documented life before the flood, rifling through clips of beach parties, weddings, birthdays and fishing trips from old family videos, freezing and enlarging glimpses of the bustle of ordinary life. A farmer's market, a KFC, a one-dollar store, a shoal of red taxis on Majuro's main drag, kids playing football on a green field at the edge of the blue sea. Moments repossessed from the gone world.

He watched short films about exploration of the drowned ruins, feeds from web cams showing bright fish patrolling the reefs of sunken condos and shops. The reclaimers were attempting to construct a breakwater with fast-growing edited corals, and posted plans for the village of floating houses that was the next stage of the project. Mike dreamed of moving there one day, of making a new life in a new land, but places in the reclaimer community were fiercely contested. He'd had to dig into his savings to get his mother the stem cell therapy she needed for a heart problem, and one of his sisters became engaged, soon there would be a wedding to pay for. . . . So when the contract at Lake Eyre finished, Mike signed up for a new project in the Antarctic Peninsula.

Lake Eyre had created a place where refugees from the drowning coasts could start afresh. The engineering projects run out of the Antarctic Peninsula were part of an attempt to preserve the continent's last big ice sheet and prevent another catastrophic rise in ocean levels, the loss of half-drowned cities and land reclaimed from previous floods, and the displacement of more than sixty per cent of the world's population. Factories and industrial plants on the peninsula supported a variety of massive geoengineering projects, from manufacturing fleets of autonomous high-albedo rafts that would cool ocean currents by reflecting sunlight, to creating a thin layer of dust in the lower stratosphere that would reflect a significant percentage of the sun's light and heat back into space. One project was attempting to cool ice sheets by growing networks of superconducting threads that would syphon away geothermal heat. Another was attempting to protect glaciers from the heat of the sun by covering them in huge sheets of thermally reflective material.

Square Bay's factories used biomass supplied by the kelp farms to manufacture the tough thin material used in the thermal blanket project. As a bonus, the fast-growing edited strains of kelp sequestered carbon dioxide from the atmosphere, contributing to attempts to reverse the rise in levels that had driven the warming in the first place. It was good work, no doubt, the sharp end of a massive effort to ameliorate the effects of two centuries of unchecked industrialisation and fossil carbon burning, but many thought that it was too little, too late. Damage caused by the great warming was visible everywhere on the Antarctic Peninsula. Old shorelines drowned by rising sea levels, bare bones of mountains exposed by melting snow and ice, mines and factories, port cities and settlements spreading along the coast . . . There were traces of human influence everywhere Mike walked. Hiking trails with their blue markers and pyramidal cairns, scraps of litter, the mummified corpse of an albatross with a cache of plastic scraps in its belly, clumps of tough grasses growing between rocks, fell field meadows of mosses and sedge—even a few battered stands of dwarf alder and willow. Ecopoets licensed by the Antarctic Authority were spreading little polders and gardens everywhere as the ice and snow retreated. They had introduced arctic hares, arctic foxes and herds of reindeer and musk oxen further south. Resurrected dwarf mammoths, derived from elephant stock, grazing tussock tundra in steep valleys snaking between the mountains.

Change everywhere.

One day, Mike followed a long rimrock trail to a triangulation point at a place called Pulpit Peak, fifteen kilometres south of the town. The pulpit of Pulpit Peak was a tall rock that stood at the edge of a cliff like the last tooth in a jaw, high above the blue eye of a meltwater lake. There was the usual trample of footprints in the apron of sandy gravel around it, the usual cairn of stones at the trail head, and something Mike hadn't seen before, a line of angular characters incised into one face of the rock, strange letters or mathematical symbols with long tails or loops or little crowns that reminded him of something he couldn't quite recall. And the triangulation point, a brass plate set in the polished face of a granite plinth, stated that it was thirty metres due north of its stated location "out of respect to local religious custom."

"I checked it with my phone's GPS," Mike told his friend Oscar Manu that evening. They were at the Faraday Bar 'n' Barbeque after a six-a-side soccer match, sitting on the terrace with their teammates under an awning that cracked like a whip in the chill breeze. "Sure enough, it was exactly thirty metres north of where it was supposed to be. And that writing? It's elvish. A guy I knew back home, old roustabout there, had a tattoo in the same kind of script. Back in the day, he was an extra in those old fantasy movies, had it done as a memento."

Mike's phone had translated the inscription. *The Place of the Meeting of Ice and Water.* A reference, maybe, to the vanished glaciers that had flowed into Square Bay.

"One of the sacred elf stones is what it is," Oscar said.

Oscar was from Tahiti, which had had its own share of troubles during the warming, but was in better shape than most Pacific Islands nations. One of its biotech firms had engineered the fast-growing, temperature-tolerant strain of staghorn coral the reclaimers were using to rebuild the reefs of Majuro. He was drinking Pangaea beer; Mike, who knew all too well that he was his father's son, was on his usual Lemon & Paeroa, saying, "You're telling me there are people here who believe in elves?"

"Let's put it this way: the road between Esperanza and O'Higgins has a kink where it swings around one of those stones," Oscar said.

"You're kidding," Mike said, because Oscar was famous for his patented wind-ups.

"Go see for yourself the next time you're up north," Oscar said. "It's just past the twenty kilometre marker."

Adi Mara chipped in, saying that a couple of Icelanders she knew took that kind of shit very seriously. "They have elves back home. The Huldufólk—the hidden people."

"Elf elves?" Oscar said. "Pointy ears, bad dress sense, the whole bit?"

"They look like ordinary people who just happen to be invisible most of the time," Adi said. "They live under rocks, and if you piss them off they can give you bad frostbite or sunburn, or cause accidents. Icelanders reckon some big rocks are actually disguised elvish churches or chapels. Building work and road construction can be held up if someone discovers that a place sacred to elves is right in the way."

"They don't sound that scary," Oscar said.

"Scary isn't the point," Adi said. She was their goalie, smaller than Mike, Oscar and the other guys, but fearless in the goal mouth. She punted every save way down the field, regardless of the positions of her teammates, and would tear you a new one if you didn't make good use of her passes. "The point is, Iceland is pretty bleak and tough, so it's only natural that Icelanders believe in forces stronger than they are, try to humanise the landscape with stories about folk who own it. And it's the same here."

Mike said that maybe it was the other way around. "Maybe the stones are reminders that Antarctica isn't really a place where ordinary people should be living."

"Back in the day that might have been true," Oscar said. "But look around you, Torres. We have Starbucks and McDonald's. We have people who are bringing up kids here. And we have beer," he said, draining his glass and reaching for the communal jug. "Any place with beer, how can you call it inhospitable?"

The talk turned to rumours of feral ecopoets who were supposed to be living off the land and waging a campaign of sabotage against construction work. Roads and radio masts and other infrastructure damaged, trucks and boats hijacked, sightings of people where no people should be. Freddie Aata said he knew someone who'd seen a string of mammoths skylighted on a ridge with a man riding the lead animal, said that the Authority police had found several huts made of reindeer bones and antlers on the shore of Sjörgen Inlet, on the east coast.

"Maybe they're your elves," Freddie told Mike. "Bunch of saboteurs who want to smack us back into the Stone Age, chiselling rocks with runes to mark their territory."

Mike still hadn't seen much of the peninsula. After arriving at O'Higgins International Airport he'd been flown directly to Square Bay in the hold of a cargo plane, catching only a few glimpses of snowy mountains rising straight up from the sea. There were vast undiscovered territories beyond the little town and the short strip of coast where he tooled up and down on service runs. Places as yet untouched by human mess and clutter. He found a web site with a map and a list of GPS coordinates of elf stones, realised that it gave him a shape and purpose to exploration, and started hitching helo and boat rides out into the back country to find them. There really was a stone, *The Church of the Flat Land*, on the road between Esperanza and O'Higgins, the two big settlements at the northern end of the peninsula. There was a stone at the site of an abandoned Chilean research station on Adelaide Island. *The Embassy of the Sea Swimmers*. There were stones standing stark on hilltops or scree slopes. A boulder in a swift meltwater river. A boulder balanced on another boulder on a remote stony shore on the Black Coast. *The Land Dances*. A stone on a flat-topped nunatak in an ice field in the Werner Mountains, the most southerly location known. *The Gate to the Empty Country*.

They were all found pieces, incised with their names but otherwise unaltered. Markers that emphasised the emptiness of the land in which they stood, touching something inside Mike that he couldn't explain, even to himself. It was a little like the feeling he had when he paged through old images of the Marshall Islands. A plangent longing, deeper than nostalgia, for a past he'd never known. As if amongst the stones he might one day find a way back to a time not yet despoiled by the long catalogue of Anthropocene calamities, a Golden Age that existed only in the rearview mirror.

He had quickly discovered that visiting elf stones was a thing some people did, like birders ticking off species or climbers nailing every hard XS route. They posted photos, poems, diaries of the treks they had made, and fiercely squabbled about the origin of the stones and their meaning. No one seemed to know how old the stones were or who had made them, if it was a single person or a crew, if they were still being made. Most stoners agreed that the oldest was a tilted sandstone slab just a short steep hike from a weather station on the Wilkins Coast. *The House of Air and Ice.* It was spattered with lichens whose growth, according to some, dated it to around a century years ago, long before the peninsula had been opened to permanent settlement. But others disputed the dating, pointing out that climate change meant that lichen growth could no longer be considered a reliable clock, and that in any case establishment of lichen colonies could be accelerated by something as simple as a yoghurt wash.

There were any number of arguments about the authenticity of other stones, too. Some were definitely imitations, with crudely carved runes that translated into mostly unfunny jokes. *Gandalf's Hat. Keep Out: Alien Zone. Trespassers Will Be Shot.* There was a stone with a small wooden doorway fitted into a crack in its base. There was a stone painted with the tree-framed doorway to the Mines of Moria. There was a miniature replica of Stonehenge. There were miniature replicas of elf stones hidden on roofs of buildings in O'Higgins and Esperanza.

And even stones that most stoners considered to be the real deal were disputed by the hardcore black-helicopter conspiracy freaks who squabbled over the precise dimensions of runes, or looked for patterns in the distribution of the stones, or believed that they were actually way points for a planned invasion by one of the governments that still claimed sovereignty over parts of Antarctica, or some kind of secret project to blanket the peninsula with mind-controlling low-frequency microwaves, so forth.

Oscar Manu found a web site run by some guy in O'Higgins who looked a bit like a pantomime elf, with a Santa Claus beard and a green sweater, sitting at a desk littered with books and papers, a poster-sized photo of *The Gate to the Empty Country* on the wall behind him. Apparently he gave a course in elven mythology that included a visit to the stone set on the shoulder of a pebble bar north of the town's harbour, and awarded certificates to his pupils.

"Maybe he knows who made the things," Oscar said. "Maybe, even, *he* made them. You should go talk to him, Torres. You know you could ace that test and get yourself certified."

But as far as Mike was concerned, it wasn't really about elves, the whole fake history of aboriginal inhabitants. It was the idea that the essence of the land had survived human occupation and climate change, ready to re-emerge when the warming was reversed. The stones were an assertion of primacy, like the pylons set by the reclaimers around the perimeter of Majuro, marking the atoll's shape in the rolling waves that had drowned it. One of those pylons had Mike's name engraved on it, near the top of a list of sponsors and donors.

Despite their isolation and the stark splendour of the stones' settings, people couldn't help despoiling them. "Robbo" had carved his tag at the base of *The Church of the Flat Land.* When Mike visited Deception Island, a three-day trip that included a stopover in O'Higgins (he ticked off the stone north of the harbour, but didn't visit the elf university), there was a cruise ship at anchor in the natural harbour of the island's flooded caldera, and he had to wait until a tourist group had finished taking selfies and groupies in front of a gnarled chimney of lava carved with a vertical line of runes, *Here We Made With Fire*, before he could have a few minutes alone with it. Someone had planted a little garden of snow buttercup and roseroot around *The Embassy of the Sea Swimmers*. There'd been some kind of party or gathering at *The Land Dances*, leaving a litter of nitrous oxide capsules and actual tobacco cigarette butts, illegal on three continents. And people had tucked folded slips of paper, prayers or petitions, amongst the small pyramid of stones, each marked with a single rune, of *Our High Haven*, on an icy setback high in the Gutenko Mountains.

Mike had made a short detour to find that last site after dropping off a party of geologists. It was a beautiful day. The blue dome of the sky unmarked except for the trail of a jet plane crawling silently northeast. Hardly any wind. In the absolute stillness he could hear the tide of blood in his ears, the faint sigh of air in his nostrils. Looking out across the pure white expanse of the Dyer Plateau towards mountain peaks sawtoothing the horizon he could imagine that the view was exactly as it had been before anyone had set foot on the continent. Ice and rock and snow and sky. Except that he remembered something one of the geologists had said as they'd unloaded their gear—that in the permanent dark of winter people heloed up to the plateau for wild skiing under the Antarctic moon and stars, using GPS to navigate from ice lodge to ice lodge. The snow here was fantastic, the geologist had said, a lot more of it than there used to be because the warmer air transported more moisture and caused more precipitation. Part of the expedition's work was measuring erosion caused by increased rainfall and snowmelt.

Change everywhere.

By now, it was long past midsummer. Christmas had come and gone. The weeks of 24-hour sunlight were over. Nights were lengthening inexorably. The first snow had fallen at Square Bay. As the research season ended, Mike and the other helo pilots were kept busy retrieving people from far-flung science camps, and Mike had a brief fling with one of the scientists. Sarah Conway, an English palaeontologist eight years older than him, part of a team which had been working on a rich seam of fossils in a sedimentary layer high in the Eternity Range. They met at one of the social nights in the town's two-lane bowling alley, where the pins were painted to resemble penguins and an ancient jukebox played K-pop from the last century. Sarah was a good-looking big-boned blonde with the kind of unassailable confidence and ambition, founded on good old-fashioned middle-class privilege, that Mike knew he should resent, but she was smart, funny and vivid, and when he saw how other men looked at her he felt a fierce pride that she had chosen him instead of any of them.

"She's a fine woman," Oscar said, "but you do know she's only into you for just the one thing."

"We're just having a little fun before she goes back to the World," Mike said.

"I have plenty of experience of short-term romances is all I'm saying," Oscar said. "Have fun, sure, but don't let her go breaking your heart."

Mike knew that Oscar was right, knew that he should keep it cool, fool around but keep a certain distance, but one day he told Sarah about the elf stones, and when she expressed an interest he took her up into the hills to show her the one at Pulpit Peak.

At first, she seemed to get it, saying that she understood why he hadn't documented the stones in any way. "It's about the moment. The connection you make through the stones. The journey you make to find them changes you. And when you actually see them, you're changed again. It makes you see their context afresh," she said, her broad smile showing the gap between her front teeth that Mike found terrifically attractive.

But then he tried to explain his idea that the stones had been sited in places that reminded people of what had been lost, the ice and the snow, the empty quiet of unpopulated Nature that would one day come again, and everything went north.

"This was all forest ten million years ago," Sarah said. "And a hundred million years before that, in the Cretaceous, it was even warmer. Covered by rainforest, inhabited by dinosaurs and amphibians and early mammals. Some big non-flying dinosaurs survived here after the asteroid impact wiped them out everywhere else. We found a nest with ankylosaur eggs this season that we think definitely post-dates the extinction event. And last season we found a partial hypsilophodont skull with enlarged eye sockets that confirms the dinosaurs lived here all year around, and had acute night vision that helped them to hunt during the polar night. The point being, choosing one state over another, ice over forest, is completely subjective."

"But this time the change isn't natural. Antarctica should be covered in ice and snow," Mike said, "and we fucked it up."

"I'm just taking the long view. Nothing lasts forever. But that doesn't mean that when the Anthropocene passes it will be replaced by a replica of the immediate past. As my grandfather used to like saying, you can't unring a bell. There'll be something else here. Something different."

"It will come back if we help it," Mike said.

"Are we talking about Antarctica or your lost island home?"

"That doesn't have anything to do with the stones," Mike said, although of course it did. He was angry, but mostly with himself. He shouldn't have told her about the reclaimers. He shouldn't have shared his stupid ideas about the stones. He'd said too much, he'd opened his heart, and she was repaying his trust with a lecture.

"Antarctica could freeze over again, but it won't ever be what it once was," Sarah said. "And you can build new islands, but it won't bring back what you've lost. It will be something new. You can't hate change. It's like hating life."

"I can hate the wrong kind of change, can't I?" Mike said, but he could see that it was no good. She was a scientist. She had all the answers, and he was just a dumb helo pilot.

So they broke up on a sour note. A few days later, while Mike was out on a supply run to one of the kelp farms, Sarah caught a plane to New Zealand, leaving him with the feeling that he'd somehow fucked up.

"You definitely fucked up a perfectly good lay with that obsession of yours," Oscar said.

"I'm not obsessed."

Oscar laid a finger alongside his broad flat nose, pulling down his lower eyelid and staring straight at Mike. "I've been watching you Torres. The time you spend chasing those stones. The time you spend talking about chasing them, or what you found when you ran one down. You think it's more important than anything else. And anyway, she's right."

"What do you mean, she's right?"

"She's right about bringing back the past. You can't. You drop a glass, it breaks on the floor. No way the pieces are going to leap up and fit themselves back again."

"You could glue them back together," Mike said, trying to turn it into a joke.

"You can't beat time, dude," Oscar said. "It only runs in one direction, and there's only one way out of world."

"I didn't realise that you are a nihilist."

"I'm a realist. Instead of than trying to go against the current, I go with the flow. Don't fuck it up with ideas about rewinding clocks, Torres. Don't hang your hopes on some dream," Oscar said, half-singing that last sentence, having fun. "Don't, in a nutshell, be so fucking *serious* about what you can't get back."

Mike wondered unhappily if Sarah was right. If Oscar was right. If he'd become obsessed about bringing back what had been lost. Yearning for something he'd never known, something he could never have. Obsessing, yeah, over his romantic ideas about the stones. Because who knew what they really meant? What they meant to the person who had chosen and named them, and carved them with runes?

But he was too stubborn to give all that up so easily. Rootless and unsettled, he hitched a helo ride north to the Danco Coast, landing at the end of a fjord pinched between steep ridges and hiking up a shallow winding river towards the site of a stone, one of the last on his list. If he got back into his groove, he told himself, maybe everything would be okay. Maybe everything would become clear, and he'd think of the things he should have said to Sarah and the things that he needed to say to Oscar, to himself.

And as he picked his way between boulders alongside the river, cold clean air blowing through him and clear water chattering over and around rocks and dropping in little waterfalls, with the steep sides of the U-shaped valley rising on either side to bare ridges stark against the empty blue sky and snow-capped mountains standing ahead, he did feel lifted out of himself, the slough of his merely human problems.

There was change here, like everywhere else—the river fed by melting ice, with kerbs of pillow moss along its stony banks, stretches of sedges and cotton grass, some kind of bird, a kite or hawk, rising in lazy circles on a thermal above a scree slope starred with yellow flowers, amazing to see a land-based predator in a place where a century ago every animal species had depended on the ocean for food—but the land was empty and its silence profound, and he was part of it, absorbed in it, in the rhythm of walking, with a goal ahead of him and everything else dwindling into insignificance.

The river grew shallower and slower, breaking up into still pools and streams trickling between shoals and banks of pebbles, and there was the elf stone, an oval ice-smoothed boulder three metres high bedded in black gravel, with runes carved around its waist. *The Navel of Our Kingdom Under the Ice.*

Once upon a time, not so long ago, a glacier had flowed through the valley, debouching onto the ice shelf that had filled the fjord. But warm sea currents had undercut and broken up the ice, and the glacier had retreated to the 300-metre contour. The elf stone was one of many erratics deposited by its retreat, and the face of the glacier was a kilometre beyond: a pitted cliff of dirty ice that loomed over a tumble of ice blocks and pools of chalky meltwater.

After pitching his tent on a shoulder of sandy gravel, Mike lay awake a long time, listening to the whisper of water over stone and the distant retorts and groans of the glacier. When he woke, the air had turned to freezing milk. An ice fog had descended, whiting everything out. The sun was a diffuse glow low in the east; there was a rime of ice on tufts of moss and grass; every sound was muffled.

Mike brewed coffee on his efficient little Tesla stove, ate two granola bars and a cup of porridge with honey and a chopped banana stirred into it, and broke camp and started the hike back along the river, taking it slowly in the thick chill fog. He wasn't especially worried. Either the fog would lift and the helo would return and pick him up, or it wouldn't, and he'd be stuck here for a day or two until a bigger helo with Instant Flight Rules equipment could be diverted. No big deal. He had enough supplies to wait it out, told himself that it was a kind of adventure, even though he could call for help on his phone at any time, and GPS meant that he couldn't really get lost. Actually, he didn't even need GPS. All he had to do was follow the river.

He had been hiking for a couple of hours when he heard movement behind and above him. A soft heavy tread, a sudden sough of breath. He stood still, listening intently. The tread grew closer, shadows loomed out of the fog, bigger than any man, and Mike felt a spike of unreasoning fear. Then the wind shifted, the fog swirled aside, and he saw the first of them.

The high forehead and small brown eyes, the tear-drop ears with their elongated hair-rimmed lobes. The questing trunk. The shaggy pelt blended from shades of auburn and chocolate. Sturdy legs footing carefully on loose stones.

One by one, the SUV-sized mammoths trod past, five, seven, ten of them. At the end of the procession came a female with her young calf trotting beside her, trunk curled like a question mark, dissolving like the rest into the mist, leaving behind a musky scent and dinnerplate-sized footprints slowly filling with water in the gravel along the edge of the river.

And now another figure materialised out of the thinning fog, and a man's voice said, "Are you lost, friend?"

"I know exactly where I am," Mike said, resenting the implication that he was somehow trespassing. "What about you?"

"At the moment, I'm following the mammoths." The figure resolved into a slight man in his sixties, dressed in a red parka with a fur-trimmed hood, windproof trousers, boots. He had some kind of British accent, a neat salt-and-pepper beard, skin darkened by sun exposure but still pale at the roots of his widow's peak.

"You're in charge of them?" Mike said, wondering if the man was an ecopoet, wondering if there were others like him nearby.

"Oh, hardly," the man said, and introduced himself: Will Colgate. "May we walk on? My friends are getting away."

As they walked alongside the river, Will Colgate explained that he was studying the mammoths' behaviour, what they ate, where they went, and so on. "They need to eat a lot, so they cover a lot of territory. Yesterday they were ten kilometres south of here. Tomorrow they'll be ten kilometres north. Or more."

"So you're a scientist," Mike said. He hadn't been scared, not exactly, but he felt a little knot in his chest relax.

"Oh, no. No, I'm just an amateur. A naturalist, in the old tradition. Back in O'Higgins I'm a plumber," Will Colgate said. Adding: "I think I know why you're here."

"You do?"

"Only one reason why people would come here. To such an out-of-the-way place. You're a stoner."

"I'm interested in them," Mike admitted. "Why they are where they are. What they mean."

"Figured that out yet?"

Will Colgate had a sharp edge to his grandfatherly air.

"I think maybe they're memorials," Mike said. "Markers commemorating what was, and what will come again."

"Interesting. I once met someone, you know, who claimed she'd made them. She was a member of one of the seed-bombing crews. They take balls of clay and nutrients and seeds, so-called green bullets, and scatter them as they walk. Most of the seeds never germinate, of course, and most of the ones that do soon die. But enough thrive . . . Some of those willows might be theirs," Will Colgate said, pointing to a ghostly little island of shrubs standing knee-high in the river's flow.

"This woman you met—she really made the stones?"

"That's what she said. But she isn't the only one to lay claim to them, so who knows?"

Mike said shyly, "I think he or she may have been a helo pilot."

Will Colgate seemed to like the idea. "Of course, an awful lot of people use helicopters here. They're like taxis. When I was a geologist, back in the day, working for Rio Tinto, I was flown everywhere to check out likely lodes. Gave that up and went native, and here I still am. Place can get under your skin, can't it?"

"Yeah, it can."

They walked on for a while in companionable silence. Mike could hear, faintly, the tread of the mammoths up ahead. More a vibration coming up through the soles of his boots than actual sound.

Will Colgate said, "If you were going to mark up one of those stones with runes, all you'd need is an automatic cutter. Neat little thing, fits into a rucksack. Programme it, tack to it in place, it would do the job in twenty minutes. Chap I know in O'Higgins uses one to carve gravestones."

"You'd also need to know which places to choose, which stones," Mike said. "How each relates to the other."

"Mmm. But perhaps it started as a joke that slowly became serious. That gained its meaning in the making. The land will do that to you."

The river broadened, running over a pavement of rock deeply scored by the ice. Mike smelt the sea on the fog, heard a splashing of water and a distant hoarse bugling that raised hairs on the back of his neck. And then he and Will Colgate arrived at the place where the river tumbled down a stony shore, and saw, dimly through thick curtains of mist, that the mammoths had waded waist-deep into the sea. Several were squirting water over themselves; others grazing on kelp, tugging long slippery strands from a jut of black rocks, munching them like spaghetti.

"The place of the meeting of ice and water," Will Colgate said. "As it once was.

By the time I got here, the river was already running, although back then the ice was about where that elf stone is now."

"Are you really a plumber?"

"Fully certified. Although I've done all kinds of work in my time."

"Including making gravestones?"

"People are mostly cremated now. When they aren't shipped back to the world. Laser engraved brass markers, or modded resin with soulcatcher chips that talk to your phone. It isn't the same," Will Colgate said, and stepped towards the edge of the sea and turned back and called out gleefully. "Isn't that a lovely sight?"

"Yes. Yes, it is."

The mammoths were intruders, creatures from another time and place, but the sight of them at play lifted Mike's heart. While the old man videoed them, walking up and down at the water's edge to get better angles, Mike called the helo crew. They were grounded. Everyone along the coast without IFR was grounded, waiting for the fog to lift. Mike told them it didn't matter. He squatted on coarse black sand rucked by the tread of heavy feet, strangely happy. After a while, Will came back and rummaged in his backpack and set a pan of water on a little hotplate.

"Time for a cuppa, I think."

They drank green tea. Will said that there was a theory that the mammoths bathed in the sea to get rid of parasites. "Another claims that seaweed gives them essential minerals and nutrients they can't find on land. But perhaps they come here to have fun. I mean, that's what it looks like, doesn't it?"

"Are there other people like you?"

Will gave the question serious consideration, said, "Despite the warming, you know, it is still very difficult to live off the land. Not impossible with the right technology, but you can't really go the full primitive. You know, as in stories about feral ecopoets. Stone-tipped spears and such. I suppose it might be possible in a hundred or so years, when it will be warmer and greener, but why would anyone want to do such a foolish thing?"

"Maybe by then the ice will have come back."

"Despite all our heroic efforts, I don't think we will be able to preserve the ice cap. Not all of it. Not as it is. In a thousand years, yes, who knows, the ice may return. But right now we have the beginnings of something new. We've helped it along. Accelerated it. We've lost much along the way, but we've gained much, too. Like the mammoths. Although, of course, they aren't really mammoths, and mammoths never lived in the Antarctic."

"I know," Mike said, but Will was the kind of earnest pedagogue who couldn't be derailed.

"They are mostly elephant, with parts of the mammoth genome added," he said. "The tusks, the shaggy coat, small ears to minimise heat loss, a pad of fat behind the skull to insulate the brain and provide a store of food in winter, altered circadian clocks to cope with permanent darkness in winter, permanent day in summer . . . Traits clipped from a remnant population of dwarf mammoths that survived on an island in the Siberian Arctic until about four thousand years ago. The species hasn't been reborn, but it has contributed to something new. All of this is new, and precious, and fragile. Which is why we shouldn't try to live out here just yet."

"Who is this 'we'?"

"Oh, you know, people like me," Will said vaguely. "Natural history enthusiasts you might say. We live in cities and settlements, spend as much time as we can in the wild, but we try not to disturb or despoil it with our presence. The mammoths aren't ours, by the way. They're an authority project, like the arctic hares and foxes. Like the reindeer. But smaller things, insects and plants, the mycorrhizal fungi that help plant roots take up essential nutrients, soil microbes, and so on—we try to give a helping hand. Bees are a particular problem. It's too early for them, some say, but there's a species of solitary bee from the Orkneys, in Scotland, that's quite promising . . ." Will blinked at Mike. "Forgive me. I do rattle on about my obsessions sometimes."

Mike smiled, because the guy really was a little like a pixie from a children's storybook. Kindly and fey, a herder of bees and ants, a friend of magical giants, an embodiment of this time, this place.

"I have trouble accepting all the changes," he said. "I shouldn't really like the mammoths. But I can't help thinking they seem so at home."

And with a kind of click he realised that he felt at home too. Here on the foggy beach, by one of the rivers of Antarctica, with creatures got up from a dream sporting in the iceless sea. In this new land emerging from the deep freeze, where anything could be possible. Mammoths, bees, elves . . . Life finding new ways to live.

Presently, the mammoths came up from the water, out of the fog, long hair pasted flat, steam rising from the muscular slopes of their backs as they used their trunks to grub at seaweed along the strandline. Will followed them with his camera as they disappeared into the fog again, and Mike stood up and started to undress. Leave on his skinsuit? No, he needed to be naked. The air was chill on his skin, stones cold underfoot as he walked towards the water. He heard Will call out to him, and then he was running, splashing through icy water, the shock if it when he plunged into the rolling waves almost stopping his heart. He swam out only a little way before he turned back, but it was enough to wash himself clean.

The Baby Eaters

IAN MCHUGH

Here's a shrewd look at the social consequences—sometimes disastrous—of humans misunderstanding and misinterpreting alien customs and life-ways. . . .

Ian McHugh's first success as a fiction writer was winning the short-story contest at the national science fiction convention in his native Australia in 2004. Since then he has sold stories to magazines, webzines, and anthologies in Australia and internationally, and recently achieved a career goal of having his number of published stories overtake his number of birthdays. His first collection, Angel Dust, *was short-listed for the Aurealis Award for Best Collection in 2015.*

Meychezhek is big, even among badhar-krithkinee, a circumstance exacerbated by the fact that I'm both already nervous and kneeling in anticipation of her entrance.

Her skin is purple-black, more textured than human skin. Her head crest, flattened now, is white, banded with orange. Her eyes are red-shot yellow, horizontally slit. When she smiles, her teeth are noticeably stained. Meychezhek acquired an addiction to coffee during her times as an ambassador on Friendship and Perunu-Zambezi.

The smile is a human expression, meant to put me at ease, but her fangs are intimidating.

I bow—correctly, I hope—and she kneels.

Krithkinee don't sit. They bend in the same places as humans but the proportions are different. Shin bones shorter, feet longer—pivots for burst sprinting. The extra pair of arms raises the centre of gravity. The body leans forward, balanced by the short tail. Feet and fighting arms have triple talons, one opposed. The four fingers of the inner manipulative arms have retractable claws.

Meychezhek signals for me to be at ease and I relax my pose fractionally. My pulse races.

"Thank you, Dhar, for welcoming me into your home." My Babel implant turns Euraf English into crude but passable Junkhin before the words reach my mouth. It never stops being disconcerting, to speak a language you don't fluently understand, nor the sense of your muscles moving contrary to the brain's commands.

"You are honoured," Meychezhek replies, accepting what is due to her rank. A *dhar* is part military officer, part civil administrator and part feudal lord—a Japanese daimyo in the era of the shoguns, combined with an Indian civil service mandarin.

Our solicitation of an invitation to trade had followed the correct form: approaching the provincial *dhar* with an appropriately personalised gift, in this case, an antique coffee set, unsuitable for krithkinee mouths but Meychezhek is a collector. Given the modest scale of our enterprise, we'd expected her to defer to a subordinate lord. A further round of gifts would follow, and possibly a second deferral, depending on the status of the lower-ranked lord, the social and commercial advantage for them and the particulars of their patronage relationship with Meychezhek.

What we didn't anticipate was that the *dhar* would accede directly to the solicitation and offer to host me herself.

"The commendations from your peers are impressive," Meychezhek says. "You are highly esteemed."

Again, there's the disconcerting awareness that the words my ears hear aren't the same as those my brain receives. If I concentrate, I can hear both.

Meychezhek's statement is both a compliment and a challenge. I'm confused, though. "Forgive me, Dhar. The commendations of my peers?"

"At the university."

"I . . ." I haven't studied or worked at university in a decade. I'm surprised enough that it's an effort to avert my gaze. Staring is more that just rude among krithkinee. A person of equal or inferior rank holding another's gaze may be seen as a challenge to fight.

"I have not conversed with a fellow sapientologist since I returned from Perunu-Zambezi," she continues.

My thoughts blank for an instant, then race. The *dhar*'s interest is personal: in *me*. This is both better and worse than we'd assumed. Better, because the mercantile stakes aren't so high as we feared—it seems the *dhar*'s intent is not to levy any uncomfortable political demands. Worse, because it means that the success or failure of our enterprise weighs far more heavily on Meychezhek's impression of me, personally, than I'd anticipated.

"It will be your pleasure to converse with me," she says.

I'm expected to join Meychezhek for the morning meal. Badhar-krithkinee traditionally breakfast at dawn. The dark-crested, orange-skinned junkhar house attendant allowed that it was proper for me to complete my morning prayers first, but it means that the *dhar*'s been waiting for me, now, and I'm half-jogging to keep up with the attendant's loping stride.

Krithkinee are carnivores. Among high status badharee and junkharee it's usual to eat whole animals, roasted, baked or cured. Offal and pickled meats are common foods among the lower social classes. Raw fruits and vegetables are eaten as a garnish and digestive aid.

I don't try to hide my surprise and delight to see the piled plate of leaves and fruit—many of which I even recognise.

Meychezhek raises her long chin to expose her throat. I immediately dip my head, pressing my chin to my collarbone in the appropriate response.

She's not alone. Her third and favourite son, Pathkemey, is also with her, as is Yzgushin, the junior-most of Meychezhek's wives, currently heavily pregnant and nursing an enormously round belly.

Pathkemey, the "son," is female, as is Meychezhek, "father" and "husband". Yzgushin, "wife," is male.

Krithkinee social gender roles align rigidly with the physiological reproductive functions of impregnator and impregnated, and along comparable lines to those found in human traditions of patriarchy, but the actual biological sexes are inverse to the human norm. Evidently the providers of my Babel's Euraf-Junkhin thesaurus were ideological pedants of similar stripe to my old professor of comparative sociology—equating gendered social roles to their human patriarchal approximates, but aligning gendered pronouns to biological sex.

It means I have to be infuriatingly careful how I think, so that I'm not—one way or other—constantly addressing people as the wrong gender.

Yzgushin is dwarfed by his *husband* and step*son*. His fighting arms are tucked discretely into the folds of his frock, as is appropriate for a wife. He dips his chin as I do.

Pathkemey casts a glance at Meychezhek, evidently unsure of my status relative to hers. After a brief hesitation, she raises her chin as her father has.

Formalities completed, I'm invited to kneel at the table. Meychezhek serves—her wife first, then Pathkemey and then me.

The balcony, on the exterior of the house's uppermost storey, affords a view over the city. The squat, drum-shaped towers of manor houses, manufactories and communal tenements rise out of the bustle below, of traffic-packed roads winding between garden plots, orchards, animal pens and tented markets. Elevated railways connect many of the towers.

I'm offered a middle leg from the roasted creature on the central platter. All six of its feet have opposed thumbs. They look like children's hands. The little carcass reminds me of the xenophobic slur that krithkinee eat their own young. I fill up the rest of my plate with salad.

"Curious, is it not?" Meychezhek says. "I expose my weakest point to demonstrate that I am unthreatened by you. Among krithkinee the convention is so deeply ingrained as to be hardwired. Yet you are an alien, bound to different conventions. In my instinctive show of strength, I expose myself to unintended risk."

Pathkemey's expression of alarm transcends species boundaries. Had she made a mistake in exposing her throat to me? Yzgushin observes with frank curiosity.

I say, "You do not perceive me as a threat."

"No, but my interpretation of your human signals could be flawed."

"Do you believe so?"

Meychezhek flashes her fangs in another of those human grins. I have a sudden suspicion that she knows the expression is intimidating and is being mischievous. "No."

"What *do* you sense from me?"

Meychezhek picks at her meat with the claws of her inner arms. Badharee of the dominant culture eschew cutlery. There are bowls of scented water on the table for washing between courses.

"Consciously, you are excited and curious. Nervous, perhaps. It is in your gestures and the movement of your eyes. But your body is reacting like prey. The smell is so strong I can taste it."

I'd put the butterflies in my stomach down to my queasiness that a provincial *dhar* had taken a personal interest in me. It's more than that, though. The monkey in my hindbrain is barely holding itself together. "You are right. I am afraid of you."

Pathkemey is affronted. "Why? We offer no threat. You are a welcome guest in the house of my father."

Meychezhek holds up a hand to stay her.

Is she testing me, or Pathkemey? Or seeking to *educate* her son? Pathkemey didn't accompany her father on her ambassadorial postings. Her exposure to non-krithkinee can have been minimal, at best. Is this the real reason why Meychezhek chose to invite me herself? To be a sample specimen, capable of educated conversation?

I pick up the spouted cup beside my place and take a sip of water, trying to think like an academic. "Humans have mixed instincts," I say. "We evolved as prey until our intelligence developed to the point that we could turn the tables on our hunters. Since then, we have grown accustomed to being at the top of the food chain. But the hunted monkey is still in there." It occurs to me, belatedly, that they're unlikely to know what a monkey is, since badharee tend to eschew encyclopaedic implants. I indicate the dismembered beast on the table, which seems near enough. "In you, I see a predator, stronger than I am, and in your element."

Pathkemey says, "Like hunting near mhaharrtee."

A mhaharrt is a keystone predator in the primary terrestrial ecosystem that the badharee-junkharee export to their terraformed colonies. Mhaharrtee have a reputation for ignoring smaller predators, such as krithkinee—but not always.

Meychezhek raises her crest, acknowledging her son's astuteness. "Humans have a superficially similar idiom—'like swimming with sharks'," she says. "But krithkinee are not 'hunted monkeys,' as you say." She flicks a finger towards my plate. "You are enjoying your meat." It is not a question.

I'm yet to touch it. I pick up the little infant arm and, copying Pathkemey, sink my teeth into the roasted flesh. "I am. It is delicious."

Meychezhek has given me into Pathkemey's keeping to learn to ride a staigeg, alongside a group of the household's children. The lessons take place in the manor house's central courtyard. Members of the household look down at us from the curved interior balconies.

The children—with no more riding experience than I—hurl themselves up onto the staigegee with absolute recklessness and are tossed aside nearly as quickly. They take little if any heed of Pathkemey's instruction and cheer the most spectacular falls, congratulating each other on their bruises.

I ask Pathkemey if their heedlessness disturbs her.

She considers silently for several seconds before answering. "They are children. This is the way children should behave. When they tire of falling off, they will become heedful of my words."

"Are you not concerned for their safety?"

Again the pause—Pathkemey is as intelligent as her father, but weighs her words more slowly. "Yes. But it is a father's unreasoning protectiveness." She points out two of the children as being her own son and daughter. "Children are the wealth and joy of our house. The loss of a child is cause for grief. But see the joy that they find in this game. There is joy in this too for me."

Needless to say, neither she nor the children can understand my own caution when approaching my designated staigeg.

"There will be war between humans and krithkinee," Meychezhek says. "Sooner, rather than later."

She has finally consented to escort me to the botanists with whom I'm hoping to negotiate the supply of pharmaceutical ingredients. I look down at Meychezhek from my sedan, perched high up on the hump of my staigeg. My riding is not yet proficient enough to control a staigeg on the city's crowded streets. Consequently I find myself carted about like some frail and revered grandmother or religious sage. Meychezhek sits at the base of her mount's neck, as does the badhar mahout who steers my beast. The blue-black skins and striped white crests of the badharee stand out starkly among the orange, scarlet and crimson faces and dark spines of the majority junkharee.

"There has already been war," I say. "More than once. The Edoans and Austronese have fought the Reformationist junkharhee at Autaki. The League has fought beside the dzaiiree-rajhinee . . ."

Meychezhek makes a sharp upward chopping gesture of one outer arm—*silence*.

"Skirmishes," she says. "I mean a war that will encompass our two species. Total war."

"Why do you think so?" It seems unlikely to me. Humans and krithkinee both have too much enthusiasm for *intra*species warfare to ever gang up on anyone else.

"Because neither of us learned not to hate before we climbed into space," Meychezhek says.

My staigeg stops suddenly to avoid crushing a crowd of junkharee street children. I have to grab at the wooden case on my lap to stop it sliding off—full of coffee berries for propagation, my gift to the botanists. The mahout swears while guards jump off their wheeled sleds to shoo the urchins out from under the feet of the staigegee.

"Relations between the major human polities and the Empire have always been good," I say.

Meychezhek shows an expression that I'm unsure how to interpret. "For how long? Badharee are a minority. We have held this Empire for thirty generations. But the Empire belongs to the junkharhee—they are the majority. The Reformationists nibble at our borders. Every year our rule becomes more overt, the *krithzha* more obviously our puppet, and more junkhar lords go over. The tighter we grip, the less we hold."

"You think the Reformationist junkharhee will take over the Empire?"

"Yes."

"Then there will be war between krithkinee and krithkinee."

"There will be that," she agrees. "But it will be limited. Neither side can afford not to find an accommodation. And then there will be war between krithkinee and humans."

I'm not sure if she's treating the badharee-junkharee Empire as synonymous with the krithkinee species, or expects that the lesser krithkinee polities will somehow fall in behind the Empire in the case of a major war with humankind. "Do *you* hate?" I ask.

"Yes," she says, matter-of-factly. "I hate the dzaiiree and rajhinee and their unclean interbreeding and their *alhothma.*"

My Babel can't provide a sensible translation of '*alhothma.*' I stay with the topic at hand. "But not the Reformationists?"

She shakes her chin from side to side, as a horse would, imitating the human gesture to ensure my understanding. "No. They are my enemies, but their actions are sensible to me."

"Do you hate humans?"

"I will learn easily enough," she says. "My point is that we both have a concept of hate. Other species' do not. Bnebene have evolved beyond such things. Pa'or know only acquisitiveness. Jaendreil know only fear and the courage of conquering it. Other species go to war because they are driven to it. Humans and krithkinee go to war because hate makes it a choice." She makes the chopping gesture with her fighting hand. "But this is all in the future. Today our interests are in alignment."

She picks up that thread of conversation on the ride back to the manor. "It is a peculiarity of humans that you weaken yourselves voluntarily."

I'm in good humour after my successful meeting with the botanists. Meychezhek told them that they were pleased by my gift and, if my grasp of krithkinee non-verbal cues is sound, it did indeed seem to be the case.

"How so?" I ask.

"Because you accommodate yourself to your weakest member. You devote resources to ensure the survival of individuals who would not otherwise live. This weakens your species."

"That is evolved social behaviour," I say. "Frailty is not synonymous with lack of social value."

She chops with her hand. "No. It is counter to natural behaviour. A pack runs at the pace of its second weakest member. The weakest falls behind, and the pack becomes stronger. This is the krithkinee way."

She pushes her lower jaw forward, ruminating. At length, she continues, "It is widely known that humans permit the survival of *alhothmanee*, as the dzaiiree-rajhinee do. I would dismiss it as a slander, if I had not seen for myself that it is true."

The translation that my Babel provides for '*alhothmanee*' doesn't make sense. "Divided souls?"

She nods, and suddenly I see that Meychezhek is intensely uncomfortable. "The sharing of a womb by multiple offspring," she says. Her lips peel back from her teeth in an expression that seems a direct analogue for a human grimace of disgust. "Allowing such offspring to survive."

"Multiple births are not allowed to survive?"

"Only one," she says.

There's a parable, of which there are several versions across the various bahdaree and junkharee cultures. It tells of twin siblings who, by the madness and deception of their birth mother, were both permitted to live. The son was raised as the heir of her father, a provincial *dhar*. The daughter, hidden by his mother and fostered to a childless noble house, was trained to become a lord's wife.

The fortunes of both houses—birth and adoptive—were dogged by ill luck, which escalated to provincial catastrophe when the son inherited her father's title and was subsequently, unwittingly, married to her sister. Only when he was dying of plague did their mother confess to his crime. The sister-wife promptly committed suicide, so that his brother-husband's fortunes could be restored. By this act of sacrifice, the soul that had been shared by the twins was made whole and the fortunes of the *dhar's* house and province restored.

The story serves both as justification of racial bigotry and reinforcement of male subservience. Twins are rare among krithkinee and contemporary medical science allows for the selective abortion of early term foetuses. Only among the most traditionally minded badharee and junkharee is abortion of *alhothmanee* still applied—to borrow the dry if distasteful descriptor of one ethnographer— "post-natally."

I stay to talk with Pathkemey after my next riding lesson, while the children try to lead the recalcitrant staigegee back to the stables.

"Your father thinks there will be a great war between our species," I say, in response to a comment of hers about future trade.

"She is wise, my father," Pathkemey replies, her eyes on the children.

"Do you fear it, too?"

She stiffens, then rounds on me as if she can't believe what I've just asked. Her chin comes up and her head crest rises.

For a terrifying moment, I'm certain she's going to assault me, and my only thought is to pray to God that I'll survive it. I can't even begin to muster the words to apologise. The children huddle together, looking from Pathkemey to me. Without another word, she turns and strides away.

With her, I'm certain, go my prospects here. I start to shake. I feel like a lion just looked me in the eye, enraged, and then walked away.

The staigegee, forgotten, have ambled along the passageway to the manor's front gate. A guard shouts in surprise and the children scatter.

Staigeg saddles are designed to accommodate krithkinee tails, and therefore slope down at the back. No matter how I adjust my posture, my round human backside keeps sliding off.

It doesn't help that I'm struggling to concentrate, terrified as I am that, with one ill-conceived question, I've irretrievably misstepped, wrecked my prospects of closing this trade deal and—God forbid—put myself in danger of physical harm. That Path-kemey has rebuffed my attempts to apologise and Meychezhek hasn't had time for me, until today's curt instruction to accompany her, has done nothing to allay my fears.

My staigeg responds to my fidgeting by veering into the path of the guard riding beside me.

The staigegee grunt at each other and bump their ugly heads until I get mine walking in a straight line again, apologising profusely to the other rider.

The guard—a junkhar—stares at me, unsure how to respond. Like many krithki-nee I've encountered, she cannot quite decide what my status is: whether she should treat me as a male, and therefore beneath her; or as an impregnator, and therefore her equal, or even superior.

Meychezhek, having ignored me since we set out, chooses this moment to drop back. "You offended Pathkemey."

I begin to stammer an apology, but she waves me to silence. "Fear is a reaction of prey. It is something that happens to other beings. Not to krithkinee. As I have explained."

I'd realised my mistake *after* I watched Pathkemey march away from me. The only Junkhin word for fear—the word my Babel used—means specifically 'hunted feeling.' Relief floods me. Meychezhek doesn't look or sound angry.

My words come in a rush, "When I spoke to Pathkemey, I was thinking about your comments that there will be war between our species, and that we will learn to hate each other."

"You will be pleased to explain," she says.

And then I realise: every one of her retainers has eyes or ears turned our way. They're completely attuned to her, even when their attention is ostensibly on clearing a path through the traffic. My stomach knots all over again.

"I think," I say, slowly, "that our concepts of hate differ. For humans, hate derives mainly from fear."

Meychezhek relaxes, the scholar in her re-engaging. The guards follow suit. "Curious," she says. "The hatred that a krithkinee will feel for humans or jaendreil or pa'or is different to this." She thinks for a few moments. "If a weak krithkin attacks the exposed throat of a strong krithkin it causes a sense of shock in the attacked individual. This shock triggers fury at the *effrontery* of the weaker individual. That lesser species will contend with us—even defeat us, on occasion—prompts the same response in many krithkinee."

I wonder if there are silent quotation marks around the term "lesser species." "You think that other species are weaker than krithkinee?"

"Of course," she says. "As we have discussed."

A commotion erupts on the balcony outside my chamber while I'm rolling my mat after evening prayer—several voices talking over each other in Junkhin too rapid for my Babel to catch more than snatches.

I gather that something is happening with Yzgushin and his baby. I open my door in time to see Meychezhek stride past. Pathkemey stops me.

"You will prefer to remain in your room."

I'm not at all certain that Pathkemey has forgiven me for inadvertently accusing her of cowardice. "Is everything well with Yzgushin?"

"He is giving birth," she says, shortly, and hurries after her father.

I remain in the doorway, neither quite willing to return to my chamber nor daring enough to leave it. Servants dash across the courtyard, heading towards the garages. I hear the faint whine of electric motors, fading quickly as the sleds pass out through the front gate.

It's quiet from Yzgushin's chamber, around the curve of the balcony. Other members of the household clump together along the balconies, above and below. In the courtyard, guards spread around the perimeter. I wonder why.

Presently, there are sounds from the gate. A group enters the courtyard—a junkhar lord and her guards. I retreat further into the shadows of the doorway. More retinues follow the first, badharee and junkharee, lesser lords who owe patronage to Meychezhek. The guards jostle as they make space for their masters, but there's no fighting and the crowd remains quiet. The house lights come on as the sun sets.

A thin cry breaches the dusk. It sounds like the croak of some baby bird, nothing like a human infant.

Then a second cry joins the first.

The click of the bolt on Yzgushin's door makes me jump. Pathkemey emerges and stands to one side. Her father follows, one infant voice growing louder as she does.

Meychezhek moves to the balcony rail and holds up the baby in her hands. Tiny limbs flail. The legs and fighting arms don't have their claws yet. The child's mouth is open wide, its eyes tight shut. Its voice fills the hollow core of the manor house. The other baby, left with its mother, has quieted.

Alhothman.

I think, for a disbelieving moment, that Meychezhek will simply cast the child down into the courtyard. The watchers seem to hold their breaths. Meychezhek turns the baby over in her hands, leans her head down and bites the back of its neck. Its cries cease, abruptly. When she lifts up her face, her mouth is bloody.

There's a murmur of approval from the courtyard—from the junkharee. The badharee lords are stiff-faced.

My stomach heaves. The lords bow their heads, touching their chins to their chests before they begin to file out. Meychezhek raises her gaze. Her eyes catch the light as she spies me in my doorway.

Bile rises. I turn and flee.

She seeks me out before dawn. One of the servants must have reported me packing. It's the first time she's come to my chamber, rather than calling me to attend her.

"You have found your reason to hate."

"No." For a second, I can see nothing in her but an animal that killed its own offspring—killed, *like an animal*, with its own teeth. My gorge rises again and I need a moment to compose myself. "My own kind . . ." I'd been about to say "commit such atrocities". I change it to, "My own kind do comparable things."

"And do you hate those that do?"

I'm terrified that I'll lose the last of my self-control, that I'll insult her beyond toleration, like a monkey flailing defiance at a panther. "Why that way?" I manage. "Why not in the womb, early?"

"I am Dhar, and badharee," she says. "It had to be *seen*."

"Your own *child. How* could you?"

"It was *for* my child. The *alhothman* had to be ended so that my child's soul could be made whole. For my people, too, and the Empire. Because I am Dhar, and badharee."

"And if I told you that I am a twin, would you 'end' me?"

"Your *alhothma* would not be for me to repair. You would have to leave my house and no trade would be possible with you or your combine." Her tone is patient, like Pathkemey's during riding lessons. The notion that *she's* being tolerant of *me* is unbearable.

I draw myself up. "I thank you for the hospitality of your house, Dhar. I regret that I must leave."

"You have concluded your business?"

She knows very well that I have nothing remotely resembling a contract for trade with the botanists. "Sufficiently well," I say.

She remains where she is for several seconds longer, her gaze holding me.

I see disappointment there, and I feel like a fool. I know I can't tolerate, can't *abide*, what I've witnessed, and yet, still, *her* tolerance makes me feel like a fool.

Meychezhek lifts her chin and is gone.

a salvaging of ghosts

ALIETTE DE BODARD

Aliette de Bodard is a software engineer who lives and works in Paris, where she shares a flat with two Lovecraftian plants and more computers than warm bodies. Only a few years into her career, her short fiction has appeared in Interzone, Asimov's Science Fiction, Clarkesworld, Realms of Fantasy, Orson Scott Card's Intergalactic Medicine Show, Writers of the Future, Coyote Wild, Electric Velocipede, The Immersion Book of SF, Fictitious Force, Shimmer, *and elsewhere, and she has won the British SF Association Award for her story "The Shipmaker," the Locus Award, and the Nebula Award for her stories "The Waiting Stars" and "Immersion." Her novels include* Servant of the Underworld, Harbinger of the Storm, *and* Master of the House of Darts, *all recently reissued in a novel omnibus,* Obsidian and Blood. *Her most recent novel was another British SF Association–winner,* The House of Shattered Wings. *Coming up is a sequel,* The House of Binding Thorns. *Her Web site, www.aliettedebodard.com, features free fiction, thoughts on the writing process, and entirely too many recipes for Vietnamese dishes.*

The story that follows is another in her long series of "Xuya" stories, taking place in the far-future of an Alternate World where a high-tech conflict is going on between spacefaring Mayan and Chinese empires. In the suspenseful tale that follows, we visit a starship lost and shipwrecked in the maze of Deep Space, where reality itself changes from moment to moment, and meet a woman willing to risk her future for the slimmest chance of reclaiming the past.

Thuy's hands have just closed on the gem—she can't feel its warmth with her gloves, but her daughter's ghost is just by her side, at the hole in the side of the ship's hull, blurred and indistinct—when the currents of unreality catch her. Her tether to *The Azure Serpent*, her only lifeline to the ship, stretches; snaps.

And then she's gone, carried forward into the depths.

On the night before the dive, Thuy goes below decks with Xuan and Le Hoa. It's traditional; just as it is traditional that, when she comes back from a dive, she'll claim her salvage and they'll have another rousing party in which they'll drink far too many gems dissolved in rice wine and shout poetry until *The Azure Serpent's Mind* kindly dampens their incoherent ravings to give others their sleep—but not too much, as it's good to remember life; to know that others onship celebrate surviving one more dive, like notches on a belt or vermillion beads slid on an abacus.

One more. Always one more.

Until, like Thuy's daughter Kim Anh, that one last dive kills you and strands your body out there, in the dark. It's a diver's fate, utterly expected; but she was Thuy's child—an adult when she died, yet forever Thuy's little girl—and Thuy's world contracts and blurs whenever she thinks of Kim Anh's corpse, drifting for months in the cold alien loneliness of deep spaces.

Not for much longer; because this dive has brought them back where Kim Anh died. One last evening, one last fateful set of drinks with her friends, before Thuy sees her daughter again.

Her friends . . . Xuan is in a bad mood. No gem-drinking on a pre-dive party, so she nurses her rice wine as if she wishes it contained other things, and contributes only monosyllables to the conversation. Le Hoa, as usual, is elated; talking too much and without focus—dealing with her fears through drink, and food, and being uncharacteristically expansive.

"Nervous, lil' sis?" she asks Thuy.

Thuy stares into the depth of her cup. "I don't know." It's all she's hoped for; the only chance she'll ever get that will take her close enough to her daughter's remains to retrieve them. But it's also a dangerous dive into deep spaces, well into layers of unreality that could kill them all. "We'll see. What about you?"

Le Hoa sips at her cup, her round face flushed with drink. She calls up, with a gesture, the wreck of the mindship they're going to dive into; highlights, one after the other, the strings of gems that the scanners have thrown up. "Lots of easy pickings, if you don't get too close to the wreck. And that's just the biggest ones. Smallest ones won't show up on sensors."

Which is why they send divers. Or perhaps merely because it's cheaper and less of an investment to send human beings, instead of small and lithe mindships that would effortlessly survive deep spaces, but each cost several lifetimes to build and properly train.

Thuy traces, gently, the contours of the wreck on the hologram—there's a big hole in the side of the hull, something that blew up in transit, killing everyone onboard. Passengers' corpses have spilled out like innards—all unrecognisable of course, flesh and muscles disintegrated, bones slowly torn and broken and compressed until only a string of gems remains to mark their presence.

Kim Anh, too, is gone: nothing left of Thuy's precocious, foolhardy daughter who struggled every morning with braiding her hair—just a scattering of gems they will collect and sell offworld, or claim as salvage and drink away for a rush of short-lived euphoria.

There isn't much to a gem—just that familiar spike of bliss, no connection to the dead it was salvaged from. Deep spaces strip corpses, and compress them into . . . these. Into an impersonal, addictive drug.

Still . . . still, divers cannibalise the dead; and they all know that the dead might be them, one day. It's the way it's always been done, on *The Azure Serpent* and all the other diver-ships: the unsaid, unbreakable traditions that bind them all.

It didn't use to bother Thuy so much, before Kim Anh died.

"Do you know where she is?" Xuan asks.

"I'm not sure. Here, perhaps." Thuy points, carefully, to somewhere very near the wreck of the ship. "It's where she was when—"

When her suit failed her. When the comms finally fell silent.

Xuan sucks in a sharp breath. "Tricky." She doesn't try to dissuade Thuy, though. They all know that's the way it goes, too.

Le Hoa attempts, forcefully, to change the subject. "Two more dives and Tran and I might have enough to get married. A real couple's compartment, can you imagine?"

Thuy forces a smile. She hasn't drunk enough; but she just doesn't feel like rice wine: it'll go to her head, and if there's any point in her life when she needs to be there; to be clear-headed and prescient . . . "We'll all get together and give you a proper send-off."

All their brocade clothes retrieved from storage, and the rice wine they've been saving in long-term compartments onboard the ship taken out, sipped at until everything seems to glow; and the small, round gem-dreams dumplings—there's no actual gems in them, but they're deliberately shaped and positioned like a string of gems, to call for good fortune and riches to fall into the newlyweds' hands, for enough that they can leave the ship, leave this life of dives and slow death . . .

Kim Anh never had a chance for any of this. When she died, she'd barely begun a relationship with one of the older divers—a fling, the kind that's not meant to last onboard *The Azure Serpent*. Except, of course, that it was cut short, became frozen in grief and regrets and recriminations.

Thuy and Kim Anh's ex seldom speak; though they do get drunk together, sometimes. And Cong Hoan, her eldest son, has been posted to another diver-ship. They talk on comms, and see each other for festivals and death anniversaries: he's more distant than she'd like, but still alive—all that matters.

"You're morbid again," Xuan says. "I can see it in your face."

Thuy makes a grimace. "I don't feel like drinking."

"Quite obviously," Le Hoa says. "Shall we go straight to the poetry?"

"She's not drunk enough," Xuan says before Thuy can open her mouth.

Thuy flushes. "I'm not good at poetry, in any case."

Le Hoa snorts. "I know. The point isn't that you're good. We're all terrible at it, else we would be officials on a numbered planet with scores of servants at our beck and call. The point is forgetting." She stops, then, looks at Thuy. "I'm sorry."

Thuy forces a shrug she doesn't feel. "Doesn't matter."

Le Hoa opens her mouth, and then closes it again. "Look . . ." she says. She reaches inside her robes and withdraws something—Thuy knows, even before she opens her hand, what it will be.

The gem is small, and misshapen: the supervisors won't let them keep the big, pretty ones as salvage; those go to offworld customers, the kind rich enough to pay good money for them. It glistens like spilled oil in the light of the teahouse; and in that light, the dumplings on the table and the tea seem to fade into the background; to recede into tasteless, odourless insignificance. "Try this."

"I—" Thuy shakes her head. "It's yours. And before a dive . . ."

Le Hoa shrugs. "Screw tradition, Thuy. You know it's not going to change any-thing. Besides, I have some stash. Don't need this one."

Thuy stares at it—thinking of dropping it in the cup and watching it dissolve; of the warmth that will slide down into her stomach when she drinks; of the rising eu-phoria seizing all her limbs until everything seems to shake with the bliss of de-sire—of how to step away, for a time; away from tomorrow and the dive, and Kim Anh's remains.

"Come on, lil' sis."

Thuy shakes her head. She reaches for the cup of rice wine, drains it in one gulp; leaving the gem still on the table.

"Time for poetry," she says, aloud. *The Azure Serpent* doesn't say anything—he so seldom speaks, not to the divers, those doomed to die—but he dims the lights and the sound as Thuy stands up, waiting for words to well up from the empty pit in her chest.

Xuan was right: you need to be much drunker than this, for decent verses.

Thuy knows where her parents died. The wreck they were scavenging from is on her ancestral altar, at the end of the cycling of holos that shows First and Second Mother go from newlyweds flushed with drink and happiness, to older, greyer women hold-ing their grandchild in their arms, their smile cautious; tentative; as if they already know they will have to relinquish her.

Aboard *The Azure Serpent*, they're legends, spoken of in hushed tones. They went deeper, farther into unreality than anyone else ever has. Divers call them The Long Breathers, and they have their own temple, spreading over three compartments and always smelling of incense. On the temple walls, they are depicted in their diving suits, with the bodhisattva Quan Am showing them the way into an empty cabin; where divers leave offerings praying for good fortune and prosperity.

They left nothing behind. Their suits crumbled with them, and their bodies are deep within the wreck of that mindship: two scatterings of gems in a cabin or a cor-ridor somewhere, forever irretrievable; too deep for anyone to survive retrieval, even if they could be located anymore, in the twenty-one years since they died.

On the altar is Bao Thach: her husband, not smiling but stern and unyielding, as utterly serious in death as he was mischievous and whimsical in life.

She has nothing left of him, either.

Kim Anh . . . Kim Anh is by her father's side; because she died childless and unmarried; because there is no one else who will mourn her or say the prayers to ease her passage. Thuy isn't the first, or the last, to do this onboard the ship.

There's a box, with enough space for a single gem. For what Thuy has earned the right to salvage from her daughter's body: something tangible, palpable that she can hold onto, not the holos or her own hazy-coloured and shrivelled memories—holding a small, wrinkled baby nursing at her breast and feeling contentment well up in her, stronger than any gem-induced euphoria—Kim Anh at age ten, trying to walk in a suit two sizes too big for her—and a few days before her death, the last meal she and Thuy had in the teahouse: translucent dumplings served with tea the colour of jade, with a smell like cut grass on a planet neither of them will ever live to see.

Kim Anh isn't like Thuy's mothers: she died outside a different mindship, far enough from the wreck that it's possible to retrieve her. Tricky, as Xuan said; but what price wouldn't Thuy pay, to have something of her daughter back?

In the darkness at the hole in the ship's hull, Thuy isn't blind. Her suit lights up with warnings—temperature, pressure, distortions. That last is what will kill her: the layers of unreality utterly unsuited to human existence, getting stronger and stronger as the current carries her closer to the wreck of the mindship, crushing her lungs and vital organs like crumpled paper when her suit finally fails.

It's what killed Kim Anh on her last dive; what eventually kills most divers. Almost everyone on *The Azure Serpent*—minus the supervisors, of course—lives with that knowledge, that suspended death sentence.

Thuy would pray to her ancestors—to her mothers the Long Breathers—if only she knew what to ask for.

Thuy closes her hand over the gem. She deactivates the suits' propulsion units and watches her daughter's remains, floating beside her.

Gems and more gems—ranging from the small one she has in her hand to the larger, spherical ones that have replaced the organs in the torso. It's a recent death compared to that of the mindship: the gems still form something vaguely like a human shape, if humans could be drawn in small, round items like droplets of water; or like tears.

And, as the unreality readings spike, the ghost by her side becomes sharper and sharper, until she sees, once more, Kim Anh as she was in life. Her hair is braided—always with the messy ends, the ribbon tied haphazardly; they used to joke that she didn't need a tether, because the ribbon would get caught in the ship's airlock in strands thick and solid enough to bring her back. Her eyes are glinting—with tears, or perhaps with the same oily light as that of a gem.

Hello, Mother.

"Child", Thuy whispers, and the currents take her voice and scatter it—and the ghost nods, but it might as well be at something Thuy can't see.

Long time no see.

They're drifting apart now: hurtling down some dark, silent corridor into the wreck that dilates open like an eye—no no no, not after all of this, not after the certainty she'll lose her own life to the dive—and Thuy shifts, making the propulsion units in the suit strain against the currents, trying to reach Kim Anh; to hold her, to hold *something* of her, down there in the dark . . .

And then something rushes at her from behind, and she feels a sharp, pressing pain through the nape of the suit—before everything fades away.

When Thuy wakes up—nauseous, disoriented—the comms are speaking to her.

"Thuy? Where are you?" It's Xuan's voice, breathless and panicking. "I can help you get back, if you didn't drift too far."

"I'm here," she tries to say; and has to speak three times before her voice stops shaking; becomes audible enough. There is no answer. Wherever she is—and, judging by the readings, it's deep—comms don't emit anymore.

She can't see Kim Anh's body—she remembers scrabbling, struggling to remain close to it as the currents separated them, but now there is nothing. The ghost, though, is still there, in the same room, wavering in the layers of unreality; defined in traceries of light that seem to encompass her daughter's very essence in a few sharp lines.

Thuy still has the gem in her hand, tucked under the guard of her wrist. The rest of her daughter's gems—they've fallen in and are now floating somewhere in the wreck, somewhere far away and inaccessible, and . . .

Her gaze, roaming, focuses on where she is; and she has to stop herself from gasping.

It's a huge, vaulted room like a mausoleum—five ribs spreading from a central point, and racks of electronics and organics, most of them scuffed and knocked over; pulsing cables converging on each other in tight knots, merging and parting like an alchemist's twisted idea of a nervous system. In the centre is something like a chair, or a throne, all ridges and protrusions, looking grown rather than manufactured. Swarms of repair bots lie quiescent; they must have given up, unable to raise the dead.

The heartroom. The centre of the ship, where the Mind once rested—the small, wilted thing in the throne is all that's left of its corpse. Of course. Minds aren't quite human; and they were made to better withstand deep spaces.

"Thuy? Please come in. Please . . ." Xuan is pleading now, her voice, growing fainter and fainter. Thuy knows about this too: the loss of hope.

"Thuy? Is that your name?"

The voice is not Xuan's. It's deeper and more resonant; and its sound make the walls shake—equipment shivers and sweats dust; and the cables writhe and twist like maddened snakes.

"I have waited so long."

"You—" Thuy licks dry lips. Her suit is telling her—reassuringly, or not, she's not certain—that unreality has stabilised; and that she has about ten minutes left before her suit fails. Before she dies, holding onto her daughter's gem, with her daughter's ghost by her side. "Who are you?"

It's been years, and unreality has washed over the ship, in eroding tide after eroding tide. No one can have survived. No one, not even the Long Breathers.

Ancestors, watch over me.

"*The Boat Sent by the Bell,*" the voice says. The walls of the room light up, bright and red and unbearable—characters start scrolling across walls on all sides of Thuy, poems and novels and fragments of words bleeding from the oily metal, all going too fast for her to catch anything but bits and pieces, with that touch of bare, disquieting familiarity. "I—am—was—the ship."

"You're alive." He . . . he should be dead. Ships don't survive. They die, just like their passengers. They—

"Of course. We are built to withstand the farthest, more distorted areas of deep spaces."

"Of course." The words taste like ashes on her mouth. "What have you been waiting for?"

The ship's answer is low, and brutally simple. "To die."

Still alive. Still waiting. Oh, ancestors. When did the ship explode? Thirty, forty years ago? How long has the Mind been down here, in the depths—crippled and unable to move, unable to call out for help; like a human locked in their own body after a stroke?

Seven minutes, Thuy's suit says. Her hands are already tingling, as if too much blood were flooding to them. By her side, Kim Anh's ghost is silent, unmoving, its shape almost too sharp; too real; too alien. "Waiting to die? Then that makes two of us."

"I would be glad for some company." *The Boat Sent by the Bell*'s voice is grave, thoughtful. Thuy would go mad, if she were down here for so long—but perhaps mindships are more resistant to this kind of thing. "But your comrades are calling for you."

The comms have sunk to crackles; one of her gloves is flickering away, caught halfway between its normal shape and a clawed, distorted paw with fingers at an impossible angle. It doesn't hurt; not yet. "Yes." Thuy swallows. She puts the gem into her left hand—the good one, the one that's not disappearing, and wraps her fingers around it, as if she were holding Kim Anh. She'd hold the ghost, too, if she could grasp it. "It's too deep. I can't go back. Not before the suit fails."

Silence. Now there's pain—faint and almost imperceptible, but steadily rising, in every one of her knuckles. She tries to flex her fingers; but the pain shifts to a sharp, unbearable stab that makes her cry out.

Five minutes.

At length the ship says, "A bargain, if you will, diver."

Bargains made on the edge of death, with neither of them in a position to deliver. She'd have found this funny, in other circumstances. "I don't have much time."

"Come here. At the centre. I can show you the way out."

"It's"—Thuy grits her teeth against the rising pain—"useless. I told you. We're too deep. Too far away."

"Not if I help you." The ship's voice is serene. "Come."

And, in spite of herself—because, even now, even here, she clings to what she has—Thuy propels herself closer to the centre; lays her hand, her contracting, aching right hand, on the surface of the Mind.

She's heard, a long time ago, that Minds didn't want to be touched this way. That the heartroom was their sanctuary; their skin their own private province, not meant to be stroked or kissed, lest it hurt them.

What she feels, instead, is . . . serenity—a stretching of time until it feels almost meaningless, her five minutes forgotten; what she sees, for a bare moment, is how beautiful it is, when currents aren't trying to kill you or distort you beyond the bounds of the bearable, and how utterly, intolerably lonely it is, to be forever shut off from the communion of ships and space; to no longer be able to move; to be whole in a body that won't shift, that is too damaged for repairs and yet not damaged enough to die.

I didn't know, she wants to say, but the words won't come out of her mouth. The ship, of course, doesn't answer.

Behind her, the swarms of bots rise—cover her like a cloud of butterflies, blocking off her field of view; a scattering of them on her hand, and a feeling of something sucking away at her flesh, parting muscle from bone.

When *The Boat Sent by the Bell* releases her, Thuy stands, shaking—trying to breathe again, as the bots slough away from her like shed skin and settle on a protuberance near the Mind. Her suit has been patched and augmented; the display, flickering in and out of existence, tells her she has twenty minutes. Pain throbs, a slow burn in the flesh of her repaired hand; a reminder of what awaits her if she fails.

On the walls, the characters have been replaced by a map, twisting and turning from the heartroom to the breach in the hull. "Thirteen minutes and fifty-seven seconds," the ship says, serenely. "If you can propel fast enough."

"I—" She tries to say something, anything. "Why?" is the only thought she can utter.

"Not a gift, child. A bargain." The ship's voice has that same toneless, emotionless serenity to it—and she realises that *The Boat Sent by the Bell* has gone mad after all; cracks in the structure small and minute, like a fractured porcelain cup, it still holds water, but it's no longer *whole*. "Where the bots are . . . tear that out, when you leave."

"The bots could have done that for you," Thuy says.

If the ship were human, he would have shaken his head. "No. They can repair small things, but not . . . this."

Not kill. Not even fix the breach in the hull, or make the ship mobile. She doesn't know why she's fighting back tears—it's not even as if she knew the ship, insofar as anyone can claim to know a being that has lived for centuries.

She moves towards the part the bots have nestled on, a twisted protuberance linked to five cables, small enough to fit into her hand, beating and writhing, bleeding iridescent oil over her fingers. The bots rise, like a swarm of bees, trying to fight her. But they're spent from their repairs, and their movements are slow and sluggish. She bats them away, as easily as one would bat a fly—sends them flying into walls dark with the contours of the ship's map, watches them bleed oil and machine guts all over the heartroom, until not one remains functional.

When she tears out the part, *The Boat Sent by the Bell* sighs, once—and then it's just Thuy and the ghost, ascending through layers of fractured, cooling corpse.

Later—much, much later, after Thuy has crawled, breathless, out of the wreck, with two minutes to spare—after she's managed to radio Xuan—after they find her another tether, whirl her back to the ship and the impassive doctor—after they debrief her—she walks back to her compartment. Kim Anh's ghost comes with her, blurred and indistinct; though no one but Thuy seems to be able to see it.

She stands for a while in the small space, facing the ancestral altar. Her two mothers are watching her, impassive and distant—the Long Breathers, and who's to say she didn't have their blessing, in the end?

Kim Anh is there too, in the holos—smiling and turning her head to look back at something long gone—the box on the altar awaiting its promised gem; its keepsake she's sacrificed so much for. Someone—Xuan, or Le Hoa, probably—has laid out a tray with a cup of rice wine, and the misshapen gem she refused back in the tea-house.

"I didn't know," she says, aloud. *The Azure Serpent* is silent, but she can feel him listening. "I didn't know ships could survive."

What else are we built for? whispers *The Boat Sent by the Bell*, in her thoughts; and Thuy has no answer.

She fishes inside her robes, and puts Kim Anh's gem in the palm of her right hand. They allowed her to keep it as salvage, as a testament to how much she's endured.

The hand looks normal, but feels . . . odd, distant, as if it were no longer part of her, the touch of the gem on it an alien thing, happening to her in another universe.

Her tale, she knows, is already going up and down the ship—she might yet find out they have raised her an altar and a temple, and are praying to her as they pray to her mothers. On the other side of the table, by the blind wall that closes off her compartment, her daughter's ghost, translucent and almost featureless, is waiting for her.

Hello, Mother.

She thinks of *The Boat Sent by the Bell*, alone in the depths—of suits and promises and ghosts, and remnants of things that never really die, and need to be set free.

"Hello, child," she whispers. And, before she can change her mind, drops the gem into the waiting cup.

The ghost dissolves like a shrinking candle-flame; and darkness closes in—silent and profound and peaceful.

these shadows Laugh

GEOFF RYMAN

Born in Canada, Geoff Ryman now lives in England. He made his first sale in 1976, to New Worlds, but it was not until 1984, when he made his first appearance in Interzone with his brilliant novella "The Unconquered Country" that he first attracted any serious attention. "The Unconquered Country," one of the best novellas of the decade, had a stunning impact on the science fiction scene of the day, and almost overnight established Ryman as one of the most accomplished writers of his generation, winning him both the British Science Fiction Award and the World Fantasy Award; it was later published in a book version, The Unconquered Country: A Life History. His novel The Child Garden: A Low Comedy won both the prestigious Arthur C. Clarke Award and the John W. Campbell Memorial Award; and his later novel Air also won the Arthur C. Clarke Award. His other novels include The Warrior Who Carried Life, the critically acclaimed mainstream novel Was, Coming of Enkidu, The King's Last Song, Lust, and the underground cult classic 253, the "print remix" of an "interactive hypertext novel" which in its original form ran online on Ryman's home page of www.ryman.com, and which, in its print form won the Philip K. Dick Award. Four of his novellas have been collected in Unconquered Countries. His most recent book is the anthology When It Changed, the novel The Film-Makers of Mars, and the collection Paradise Tales: and Other Stories.

In the fascinating story that follows, Ryman takes us sideways in time to an island nation populated by women of another species of the genus homo, one that perhaps died off in our world, who reproduce by parthenogenesis. They famously keep to themselves, with most of the island forbidden to tourists except for an enclave run by the Disney Corporation, but now they are reaching out for scientific help from the rest of the world, allowing a geneticist to come and work with them to try to eliminate a major flaw in their reproductive system. But visiting such a place comes at a price—if you fall in love with it, you may never want to leave . . . but you can never really be part of that world either, no matter how hard you try.

The tourist Precinct is owned by Disney.

Though they are very careful to use the Buena Vista branding. The Buena Vista Hotel—it sounds almost local. The tourists are jammed into a thin rind of gravelly coast called the Precinct, one of two places on the island where flat ground meets the sea. There is a container port on the north side but most visas forbid visiting it. Mine did.

Many tourists stay on cruise ships, all white and gold, their lights reflecting on the water. There's a dock, some restaurants, most of them floating. The Precinct's streets are so narrow and they zigzag up the rock face so steeply, that the cars edge past each other's mirrors. Turning around at the inevitable dead end is nearly impossible. There is one guarded road up the cliffs onto the plateau—at night narrow vans wobble into the town. Every parking space has a car charger.

The Custom House runs across the mouth of the canyon into the town, a wall of rust-red laterite blocks, the pockmarks ringed with edges so sharp they cut. The Foreign House is crammed next to it, looking more like a prison than a luxury hotel.

My first morning.

I bob down the dock from a merchant ship (much better food than cruise liners and the merchant marine make better company). I see one of the Colinas, holding up a sign in handwritten letters that roll like waves.

Sra Valdez
SINGLEHELIX.

She's tiny, brown, yes bare-breasted, yes with a feather through her nose, and she looks delighted. I catch her eye and wave; she hops up and down. I have to watch where I put my eyes. But luckily (or unluckily) for me, her smile is entrancing.

She greets me traditionally, pressing her forehead against both of my cheeks.

I'd been reading the first explorers' account *En la Tierra de Mujeres* from 1867. The male authors were breathlessly excited about a nation of women who didn't wear many clothes. They cloaked their lust in classical references—"Amazonian" or "island Cleopatras." From the text, you get visions of Edwardian actresses done up in modest togas as Clytemnestra or Medea—or maybe Mountain Girl from the Babylon sequence of *Intolerance*, all tomboy exuberance in a leopard skin, headband, a fiery smile—athletic gals vaulting over walls and shooting arrows.

The first engravings of Colinas Bravas were published in *Faro de Vigo* in 1871. The images are filtered through Western eyes—the features European, the locks flowing and curled, the dress rendered modest. But to people of the time the illustrations were a shock.

The giant sandstone-clad temple; the wooden mobile houses carried on pallbearers' rods; the terraces up the slopes that rose like skyscrapers—within a month of the illustrations' publication, scholars were declaring that the main city had been built by Romans or Persians or even Cambodians (all that laterite and sandstone cladding). Little brown women could not have built them.

But the texts on the walls of the temples, particularly the Torre Espiral, turned out to be in their language. It contains the words *hurricano* and *barbeque*. Which means it's Taíno, the language of the Indians who Columbus first encountered in my own dear homeland of the Dominican Republic, where they now exist as a genetic trace. Seven hundred years before Columbus, Taíno women sailed west toward the dark continent of Europe and settled an island without a single act of genocide.

At the München Olympics, Leni Riefenstahl's lens could not keep away from the Colinas athletes. They won ten women's gold medals that year, the highest number per head of population of any nation. The German Chancellor Angela Herbort made full propaganda use of them, showed them off at a rally to praise the principles of "health and common ownership."

In the full summer of the American century, the 1960 Rome Olympiad disallowed the Colinas from competition. Their lack of a reproductive cycle was said to be an unfair advantage in training. Colinas were, evidently, not quite women or quite human. The Colinas knew enough of our history to get what happens to people we say are not quite human. That's when they created the Precinct and farmed it out to Disney. They liked the cartoons.

My host tells me her name, though I cannot pronounce or even really hear it. Eouvwetzixityl is one transcription (using Medrano's system). She knows this and tells me in Colina, *You say Evie.*

She takes my hand, and as she leads me toward the Custom House, she starts to skip. I have my rucksack, a small wheelie with my scrubs and I'm wearing shorts and a tank top. Rumbling behind me, pushed by crewmen from Venezuela, are my battery-powered freezebox, a nanoscope workstation, and a portable extraction suite. The men are allowed only as far as the Custom House. I shake their hands and tip them—but I don't think I will miss men.

At the gate, Evie ducks down into the window, and laughs and does a bit of a dance for the Custom guards who grin enormous gummy smiles, which they hide with their hands. There is such high hilarity that I cannot believe any work is being done. Then, out of nowhere, my passport is returned with a two-page intelligent hologram that looks like the Statue of Liberty. My enormous boxes and me are led through into the City, called simply Ciudad. There isn't another one on the island. The Custom guards wave goodbye to me like I'm going on a school trip.

The public plaza—La Plaza del Pueblo—is crowded with tourists, many of them female couples holding hands and taking snaps. Languages swoop around me like flocks of birds—Spanish of course, but also Chinese, Danish, Yoruba, Welsh, Portuguese, and others I can't identify. The Plaza appears vast. It rears up, rocky cliffs on either side like waves about to break. The main sandstone steps on the south face go up in layers, it is said, to a height of 80 meters. The Torre Espiral looks as old as the pyramids, like a ziggurat only conical, with wide ramps spiraling up it to the flat roof with its giant urn of fire. Tourists are no longer allowed to climb it after a German woman fell off last year. Surrounding the Plaza like a bullring are rows of shops—yes, selling tourist tat—built on two levels, with the Civil Palace on the north side and the National Library on the south next to the main steps. The Library's twelfth-century bas-reliefs in sandstone deserve their fame—joyous scenes of everyday life, women dancing as they pound manioc, or harvesting fields, or throwing mangoes at each other from the trees. And the most famous, a woman giving birth. Beyond the Plaza at the end of the canyon, there's a tumble of boulders, a creek, then a broccoli mass of trees rising up the slope.

Most of Ciudad is in layers on those cliff faces, covered streets winding higher and higher where visitors are not allowed. The houses burrow into the rock. The gardens grow on top of the porches of the houses below them. The effect is like looking at those improbable Art Deco miniatures of cities in silent films. I have to crane my neck at a painful angle. Along the top, wind turbines pirouette on their toes like ballerinas.

They've put my clinic on the ground floor of the Plaza. The sandstone archway is the color of sunset with carved concentric circles that the guidebook says are meant to look like ripples in water. The entrance is clouded with purple bougainvillea spilling down from the roof. Just inside the door is an emergency generator—the islands do import some oil. Also a desk, an operating table, my IT suite, a data projector, screen, and rows of chairs for my seminars.

I'd specified those. Nobody told me Colinas never sit on chairs.

Evie spins round and round, arms outstretched as if all this is hers. She's so delighted I can't stop taking hold of her hand. I should know better, but I am a woman, and I rely on her not being suspicious of me. That makes me feel guilty.

She looks human, but yes, a bit different. Her smile is too wide, her chin too tiny. The Colinas are now recognized as another species within the genus *Homo*. Being parthenogenetic, she ovulates maybe four times in her life. How's this for utopia? Colinas do not have periods. They also do not mate, do not cluster into little paired units. Famously, they are supposed to lack sexual desire.

I ask her, *You have children?* She nods yes and holds up a finger—one. It's customary to only have one.

Aw, what is child name?

Her smile doesn't change but she freezes for a moment and then shakes her head and giggles. She points east and says, *Quatoletcyl Mah.* I know the phrase—"Sad Children Loved."

I close my eyes with shame. Of course, that's why she's so delighted I'm here. I shouldn't have asked about children. I apologize. Literally I say, *I make mistake*, which is about the closest their language gets to swearing.

She says, *Tomorrow. Tomorrow we see child.*

They have no word for he or she, and in everyday vernacular, no word for me, my, or mine. They can say I, almost like it's a geographical location.

From somewhere a bell sounds. It moans, deeply, like it regrets something.

You leave now, she says, still smiling. Ah. Right. Closing time. She takes my hand again. Hers is sweet and insistent.

Outside thousands of sandaled feet sound like rain or applause as they make their way back to the Custom House, its gates thrown open. On the ocean only seven metres beyond the gate, the sun sits low. The square is flooded with orange, sideways light that makes the temple and terraces the color of overripe apricots. Shadows delineate every carved face or incised word sign. In this light I see that, yes indeed, the lighthouse temple is also a book, the writing in stone all the way up the giddy ramp. It tells the story of how the first Colina mother gave birth.

We know that is a myth, as is her rising out of the sea. There must have been more than one mother—genetically there are five matrilineal lines. Experts argue whether they were expelled or set off across the sea for themselves, looking for somewhere to be.

I look up at the terraces—the houses don't have doors and the rooms are full of a wavering orange light, lit by candles. I want to see inside, be inside, those rooms. I want to know what it is like to live there. I glimpse a donkey being led down toward the main staircase. The woman riding it is brushing her long black hair.

Men are allowed into the Plaza if accompanied by responsible female sponsors. Most of the men have the same expression of delight, a clenched smile, determined to appear benign. Some of the women allow themselves to look pissed off. People traveling in tourist groups or cruise ships often do—they're trapped with each other, and though stuffed full of sights and good food, they have no power. I am happier in my shorts with my rucksack, happier still to have a good working reason for being here.

Evie skips me all the way into the Foreign House. Someone at the entrance invisibly slips her a lei and she drapes the flowers around my neck and claps her hands. The idea of the lei is stolen from Hawaii—they cheerfully admit this. For some reason, the native House staff—in white shirts and black slacks—applaud me. I feel my eyes swell.

They know you help us, Evie says and gives me a forehead kiss. Evie smells of sunlight and honey. I have her for just a moment and she is hot and shivery under my hand. She leaps away, tossing her mane like a horse. One of the staff, looking bone-thin and European, says in perfect Spanish, "She is so proud to be your host."

My room has purple sheets and translucent Colinas chocolate under my pillow. The penthouse suite costs $1000 a night. No loud music after 9 pm. Unless you want to be locked in with a bunch of rich foreigners getting drunk on whisky that costs $25 a shot (along with the celebs—I have the inestimable privilege of being here the same night as Tom Cruise), there are only two things to do in the House at night. You can watch movies on TV—and only those that contain not a hint of sexual violence or enacted congress. Or something a bit less virtual.

The Foreign House is the only hotel on Colinas Bravas with doors that open into both the Plaza and its harbor—the privilege of being invited or rich.

I step out into the demarcated café space in the very last of the twilight and look up. Lights dance in all the doorways and windows; shadows bend and dip and wave. Those shadows laugh.

The laughter comes from everywhere in gusts. The narrow canyon magnifies the sound and sends it echoing. Songs, too, some of them campfire-simple, some of them complex and formal like choirs, and some a massed, intoning chant like prayer. Strains of music played on reeds and strings sound like an orchestra warming up. It's as if each kind of sound is a different flock of swallows dive-bombing around me. Then, as suddenly as waking up, Ciudad falls silent; the candles go out. There are so many stars!

I turn. I have been observed all this while by the same staff member in American dress—a short-sleeved white shirt, slim black trousers.

Beautiful, I say, flinging up my arms. *Much!*

A happy hour, she says. *Each night.*

And she gestures for me to go back into the hotel. Later, during the night, I am comforted to hear the *sshing* of tropical rain on the courtyard and roof. It must have been a dream but I think I heard that staff member go on to say, *We are easy to love.*

It is a failing of mine that I fall in love with foreigners.

First I fall in love with a country, which means the people in it, and then usually just one of those people to be my partner, my rock, my point of entry. I always do it, and the process is delicious. Though so far, it has also always gone wrong.

I find, for example, that they sleep all the time, or fight all the time, or need a fight to feel passion, or think it's funny to insult me. Or they simply want me to pay for everything. It ends. I go to boring home. Home is the Dominican Republic, sex-tourist destination, Caribbean island with an 11,000-foot-high mountain, miles of beaches, and a national park with hills that look like cupcakes. You've got to have a psychosocial problem with home to find the Dominican Republic dull.

That first night listening to rain, I imagined sitting cross-legged on the floor of one of those high cells, and going to sleep with Evie, and waking up with her at first dawn, of being allowed to stay, of being allowed to love. A harmless fantasy, I thought, and it drifted me off to sleep.

The next day, as promised, I was ready to work at 4.30 am. Getting up wasn't difficult—the dawn song of Ciudad is famous and justly so. The people simply get up in the dark and start singing.

It is the aural equivalent of a warm bed—soft, and soothing, and you loll in its sound. But if you have to work, it somehow eases you upright. I washed and looked out of the window of the House to see flashlights and candles like fireflies every-where among the walkways.

The pavements were made mirrors by the rain, blue and gold puddles. A steady train of women were moving down the steps to set up the shops or open the Library. Evie was waiting for me, holding a candle. I wore my lab trousers and coat. I felt like a native, getting up in drizzle and crossing the Plaza to my place of work. Only, Evie made me veer away from my clinic, steering me toward the Civil Palace where I was to be introduced to the Council, or maybe just a council. I couldn't be too sure.

It was just like *In the Country of Women*. There they sat, as described in 1867—the slim, wise, implacable, and sometimes kindly elders of Colinas Bravas. They, too, wore simple formal clothes made of reed beaten into linen, soft and gray with subtle patterns in the weave or embroidery. The jackets did indeed look like quilts, there were so many pockets. One of the councilors was wearing a tool belt of wrenches, chisels, and a hammer. The elders looked calm, with dim smiles and alert eyes, and their gestures for me to sit were hearty and not to be gainsaid.

"Hello and welcome to Colinas Bravas," said the one in the center, speaking English with an American accent. She had a high, round, polished forehead that reflected light. I gave her the nickname La Señora Luminosa. The name stuck for me. I responded politely, said how glad I was to be there. They asked about my ac-commodation. Another woman, who spoke with a South African (?) accent, ex-pressed gratitude that I was there, and to SingleHelix for being willing to share etc.

It came down to how long I would need to stay on the island.

"As long as you need me," I said in Spanish, the official second language. I told them that I was unmarried, the head of SingleHelix's Research Division in the Dominican Republic. They nodded glacially. I think they knew what that meant. We in SoloHebra RD do things that Our Friendly Neighbors to the North would rather not do themselves.

They insisted. "How long do you estimate?"

I said six months.

They asked if two might be enough for them to master the basic technology. "*Nos tenemos biólogos en nuestro propio país.*" The technique does not require that all who carry out the procedure need to be microbiologists?

I had to smile. I shook my head. That gesture means nothing to the Colinas. I said, *I stay time you want.* They were very grateful, and they wanted me gone.

It was still dark and cool when we walked in a group to my clinic. Luminosa took my hand and strolled with me as if we were old friends.

"I know this is basically a business proposition for your . . ." For some reason she had difficulty finding the word company. "But for us, we still experience your visit with deep personal gratitude to you. This is not your home; these are not your people." She stopped and put my hand in both of hers and looked directly into my eyes. "But you help us. We will make sure you see more of us than most foreigners do."

"That would be great honor."

So Luminosa strode on with me, and asked me what I would like to see. I told her that I had read the 1867 text and its sequel about the managed forests—fruit, nuts, hemp all growing as if untended. Is it true that their orange trees stand as high as oaks? The plateau is flat but rolling like England with large forests and open pastures. It is never seen from the air. Its airspace is closed and there is no airport. I hinted I might like to see where the SingleHelix equipment would be made, in the industrial northern port. Her smile didn't change.

That day, my clinic was bigger. The building has movable internal walls. Rows of beds had been added; my fridge preserving the samples buzzed, and I saw that the thermidor's light was on. The operating theatre lights were standing ready.

"Show us how," said Luminosa. "No need to do an extraction. We have the two ova ready for you." Evie stepped forward and covered her mouth with both hands, laughing. There is no way to say in her language, "The egg is mine."

I panicked. "We can't do it now! The donor material has to be thawed, inspected, be at the same exact temperature. It has to be from a different matrilineal line . . ."

Luminosa took my hand again. "We know, we know."

"But you don't understand. If Evie only has one ovum . . ." I glanced at Evie, looking so innocent. "If anything goes wrong, she'll have lost this chance!"

"Then check everything," said Luminosa, stroking the back of my hand. I went and scanned both sets of donated material, hands shaking. I was annoyed that they had done so much of my work for me, unasked and unsupervised. I didn't like it. I felt rushed. I felt denigrated. I was simultaneously relieved and disgruntled when both ova were fine. "Well, yes, I can start work. Do . . . does Evie know who the other egg belongs to?"

Luminosa looked blank. "Why would Evie want to know that?"

That brought me up short. Well . . . but . . . no need to know who the other mother was?

La Señora swept us on. "No need to explain much to us. We are familiar with the basics. Just show us how to carry out the procedure swiftly and well."

The same images that guided my instruments were shown on the screen. They watched as I micromanaged the translucent needle into the donor ovum, and then slipped the cradle underneath the DNA to carry it out.

"It's just a question of practice," I said. "Hand-eye coordination." The gantry slowly moved between microscope surgeries.

I switched screens. There was Evie's daughter, on the screen unmade, as transparent as a ghost. "This is the delicate bit. Like making lace."

More like joining two halves of a zipper for the first time, link by link. There is always a moment when the two halves somehow snap together and fuse. That's when a new person is created. I told them when it happened. They applauded.

The transfer probe is full of water-based jelly, rich with nutrients. The trick is to gently lower the egg into the very tip, so that it is the first thing presented. I looked around. Evie was already on one of the beds, already naked.

"It's all right," said Luminosa. "No embarrassment. We have no need of that kind of modesty."

I began to feel shivery and a bit sick. I looked down at Evie, at her smile, into her black eyes, and all I saw was trust and hope. I stroked her hair; couldn't help it. I eased stage one into her; stage two was the probe itself extended. I nicknamed the egg Luminosa as well—it was all glowing, the probe has a light. I couldn't watch. I had to. I saw where the egg needed to be placed and lowered it.

"That's it. That's all. We'll know in two days at most." Again, applause.

I had a reaction—the corners of my vision went dark, my legs weak. I needed somewhere to sit, but all my chairs had been pulled back, with the women cross-legged on the tiles. I nearly fell. Luminosa caught me by the shoulder, lowered me to the floor, and as she stroked my shoulder, her eyes asked me a worried question.

"It's a little bit overwhelming," I said, and didn't like to say why. Luminosa kept stroking my shoulder.

Outside, it was still only 8 am and cool. We sat on the pavement in the Plaza as the first of the tourists strolled past. One of the councilors brought me a cup of coffee. "Sorry," I kept saying, "sorry." They asked if I wanted to put off our visit, and I said, "No! No!"

After my coffee, as the heat swelled, we made our way to the end of the canyon through its grove of trees, climbing steps along the creek full of rainwater. We attained the plateau surprisingly quickly and I walked out into the shade of giant trees, smelling of citrus blossom. A fleet of Škodas waited for us. They make Škodas here on license; Škodas are everywhere except in Ciudad itself.

I waved the cars away. It was so cool in the shade, shafts of light through the leaves, moss underfoot, even bluebells. All the trees were outsized, huge, lemon bushes the size of mangoes. Yes, there were houses carved out of fallen trunks, left open for anyone who needed them. We went into one for a rest. It had shelves, wooden plates, bowls, serving implements, a working flush toilet, electric lights, dried herbs and spices, even clothes neatly folded.

Evie had slipped into some damp moss that had smeared green down her tunic. She simply stepped out of it in front of me, unfolded another tunic from a shelf, and slipped it over her head. I found that so accepting, accepting of me, this galumphing foreigner who smelled so different.

We ate a lunch of raisins, nuts, and about the only cheese they can stand, a very mild sweet cream a bit like mascarpone. Shade-resistant hemp grew on the lower levels. La Señora rolled the leaves into a kind of impromptu cigar and passed it to me. This I had not been expecting. The leaves weren't cured, but were sweet and mild. After lunch, we walked for about an hour, the Škodas rattling indiscreetly behind us.

I don't know what I expected of the *Quatoletcyl Mah*—a wire-mesh fence, perhaps, or confining rooms. Instead I suddenly noticed that Evie was not with me, only La Señora Luminosa. I did hear a sound ahead of us like children playing. And then I saw Evie walking quickly toward me, beaming so pleased, holding the hand of someone almost as tall as she was, but with loping, spidery limbs and a head that looked like the top of it had been cut off. The mouth and chin were outsize as if infected, bristling with teeth.

This is child, Evie said. *Call her Queesi.* She told her daughter my name as they say it: *Mah-ree-rah!* Queesi bellowed my name, gave a belly laugh, and flapped her hands. She liked the name or maybe me, and clumped me with a forehead kiss. Then she darted back and hid her face in her mother's shoulder.

Mahreerah equals elder. She helps us.

Queesi said, *No more sad children.* She knew exactly why I was there, and what she was. Evie was smiling at her daughter with such an expression, mingled kindness and pain.

Sad children were climbing trees picking fruit, or sitting in a circle pounding fibers for linen, or standing on concrete platforms raking what looked like walnuts but which from the smell were surely fermenting cocoa beans, the fruit flesh ragged around them. If the Colinas have a cash crop, it is chocolate. But for them it is a religious drink, unsweetened and used only for the holy days of their religion.

There were thalidomide-like deformities, nearly limbless little things carried on the backs of blind giants. There were tiny ancient-looking crones but with merry grins and goblin eyes, elderly women who were ten years old. Every imaginable genetic disease or infirmity.

Queesi gamboled back to her friends and grabbed a pestle.

Not bad sad children, Evie said. *Not bad.* I took her hand, and she looked up at me, blinking.

Little little sad to see them go, I said.

Little little, she said, and I knew she'd understood what I meant. The sad children were lovely as they were—there was a sadness that there would be fewer of them.

It was now past noon, so we took the Škodas and drove to see one of the mobile towns. Queesi clambered in next to us and bounced up and down on the springed seats.

The cars jostled over the ruts in a causeway between rice paddies. In the distance, we saw people carrying the mobile houses like oversized Arks of the Covenant. One house rested on its carrying rods between the bumpers of two Škodas. Frank Lloyd Wright called the houses architectural masterpieces. What he didn't say or perhaps even know was that each house is also a book, the writings and drawings burned into the wood.

The seasonal rice-harvest town was gathering like a herd of bison. We drove into it past houses radiating outward from one of the conical temples. You see them all across the landscape like factory chimneys. They are made of rocks cleared from fields, each tower centuries old, as rugged as their elders.

The new town was expecting me. My neck was ringed round with leis. There was another lunch—rice, manioc, nuts, and fruit. I was served a boiled duck egg (there were ducks everywhere in the rice fields). I gave a talk about the clinic and the project, mostly in Spanish. When I spoke in Colinas, there was a sigh and applause. I told them how the Council would be setting up clinics all across the country, and how the Council had a license to produce the equipment on the island. After the lecture, Colinas gave me hugs or showed me their babies. Children ran up to me and asked me questions about New York. How did they know I'd lived there? They said New York like they were from north Manhattan.

I've spent a lot of my life battling things—my mom, Santiago de los Caballeros, indeed the whole damn Cibao with its cowboy-hatted men and its shacks and the giant monument Trujillo built to himself and the lies we tell ourselves about our history. This valley looks almost the same as El Cibao, as if I'd remade the DR in a dream.

After lunch Evie and I separated—I was to go on, but she had to drop her daughter off at *Quatoletcyl Mah*. I felt bereft for a minute or two watching her car bounce away, but it was a spectacular drive back—my car zigzagged down the cliff over a sparkling sea and the clusters of bladed turbines marking shallow water, and for one heart-stopping moment DOWN onto Ciudad itself, looking more like garden terraces than a town. It had been a wonderful day. I felt as if I had been given everything I ever wanted all at once. I have been living off that day ever since.

Sometimes countries become your own Magic Kingdom. Every detail of what people wear, how they move and laugh, what they eat, how they eat (with their fingers, scooping up soup with mashed yam or manioc even sometimes maize), their buildings and the brushed red earth between them, or the sectioned fruit drying in the sun along the unpaved roads, and the way you can pick up the dried plums or apricots with no one to call it stealing. The island is big enough to generate its own rivers, and the water is clean enough to drink from the palm of your hand. There are windmills everywhere, of course—most of the world's windmills are built in Colinas Bravas.

All that electricity. The transatlantic phone cables surfaced here; now there are giant relay towers. Colinas Bravas has the most copious broadband in the world and they hardly use it for anything. They don't talk to us much. They watch wildlife films. And they have a ministry that keeps an eye on world news.

If there was a zombie apocalypse it couldn't get to Colinas Bravas. If the sea levels rise, we might lose the Precinct, but the town itself would climb higher up into the hills. The harbor might even improve. If there is a nuclear war, the prevailing winds will carry most of the radiation away.

The next morning, Evie was waiting for me outside the café. We started work again on another volunteer. Even more people crowded in, looking at the screens or over my shoulders. Too many, perhaps—I made a mess of the extraction. I just about got it out undamaged. Their ova are precious—four in a lifetime—so I said, "Let's leave it. We can wait." But they urged me on. The recipient was sitting up, watching me. They all just watched me—none of them took notes. They appear to have a very different attitude to text and books.

Evie stood next to me as I worked. *You do well well.* It was the strangest thing. She really did have the power to steady my hand. I did it for her. If anything, the next procedure was the neatest extraction and implant I'd ever done.

I kept explaining what I was doing. Right at the end, Luminosa announced, "The children will be knocked clean of genetic faults." And then in Colinas . . . *This child be not sad.* They don't have a future tense.

My audience had all left; I was turning off the lights and the evening bell was sounding when two tourists walked into my clinic to poke around. They wanted something. They wouldn't leave—a man and a woman, both Italian. Their English was terrible and their Spanish good enough to make bad mistakes, but they understood when I made imploring gestures and shoved my palms toward the doorway. They asked, *"Trabajo?"* and pointed at me. The woman pointed to her husband, to herself, eyes glittering. *"Medico! Medico!"*

Evie came back to fetch me and I signaled for help. She spun away. I said in any language I could think of, "Closed. *Cerrado. Chiuso . . .*"

Evie returned with two Colinas wearing thick leather aprons and trousers. Hanging from their shoulders were polished things the color of teak that looked like flutes.

Trouble? they asked me.

I want they go. I pointed my finger.

The flute-things were their guns. Guns were the very first thing the Colinas made once they understood who and what we were.

"Passports," the police demanded. The tourists understood that.

It's all in the sequel that Juan Emmanuel Medrano wrote—*Return to the Country of Women.* He was the most decent of the men who had first landed on the island. Juan Emmanuel fell in love with one of them, a woman nicknamed Zena. Being a man of his time, he thought her lack of interest in sex was natural to all women who had not been corrupted. He was proud of his ability to learn how to do without sex, prescribed it in fact as the straight route to wholesomeness—chastity in marriage.

As for the Colinas, they were already aware that parthenogenesis was accumulating mutations. They have a word that means literally *unfolding snake* for a seed that sheds its skin to become something else. They were aware that their First Mother was a product of an Unfolding Snake and that they all descended from her—or rather what we know, that there must have been at a minimum five women, five different matrilineal lines. It's quite eerie now to read Juan Emmanuel's description of their beliefs. It would appear that they understood everything about DNA save for its double helix shape.

Zena married him in a spirit of self-sacrifice to see if bisexual reproduction brought health. Of course, they could not interbreed. She didn't ovulate for the duration of the marriage.

He really is a brick, poor Juan Emmanuel. He became as much of a Colina as is possible for a man. He waxes syrupy about how Motherhood is the driving engine of Colinas society, how they all dream of being a mother. *Irony alert*: all women dream of nothing but being mothers, and even if they think they don't want to be one, they are overcome with mother love the moment they see the infant. *Irony ends here.*

He never quite got, dear Juan Emmanuel, that Colinas DO have sex, some of them at least, but not just with one person. He drove Zena mad, long after the marriage was over, long after she began to turn her back every time she saw him coming. *Why did you want to be with me all the time?*

"You will come to love me," he responded. "You are my woman." The Colinas have no word for wife or husband or spouse. No one marries.

Poor Juan Emmanuel Medrano. He lived outside the walls on the tiny strip of beach still writing his wife long poems. She moved to a village on the other side of the island. Go home, the Colinas advised him. But Juan Emmanuel couldn't. He loved the place; I believe him when he says he loved Zena. How could you not believe him—look at all he gave up. He became a pathetic figure; forbidden the entire island except for what became the Precinct. He told stories for visitors, set up a hotel, waited out the winter season, and wrote a lexicon and grammar of the Colinas language, which is still the best we have. Hollywood made a movie about him starring Humphrey Bogart—he mans the artillery that sink the British gunboats. *Irony alert*: of course those women needed a man to defend them. Ingrid Bergman won an Oscar for playing Zena. In the Foreign House, they still sing that song. Play it for me, Sam.

That night La Señora invited me to dinner. The room was no bigger than any of the others, a two-chamber hollow in the rock. The walls were covered with beautiful paintings. One of the few things they import from us is oil-based pigments. La Señora explained who had painted what—lots of portraits and bowls of fruit, not great art, but all of it colorful and fun.

They had the money to import something else. Four of the women scurried out and came back laboring under a huge canvas. My breath caught and I sputtered with recognition as if the Queen of England had just walked in—it was one of Monet's giant water lily paintings. I remembered the scandal in France when it had been sold.

It is like us, one of them said, and left it leaning against the wall.

The room had no TV; there was no computer. I asked Luminosa why not. She said they had tried our movies but they were all full of murder or marriage. "We like the cartoons for kids. But in *Wall-E* two robots get married. Why would robots get married? A doll of a cowgirl and a doll of a spaceman get married. Even *things* get married." She shook her head.

The girls started to run in with elaborate clothes. They hauled me to my feet and took off my old khaki. I felt fat and sagging like I needed a scaffolding to hold me up. They pulled over my head a gelabia with black applique. Then a kind of red velvet cape that made me feel like Red Riding Hood. They started swapping clothes, too—butterfly saris, shawls of black lace, Kevlar body armor. Their laughter bounded off the rock and straight into my head.

The Colinas don't own anything.

———

My days began to be the same. I asked to be taken up onto the plateau again. I especially wanted to see the container port and the factories. Finally Luminosa said that it was policy not to allow anyone to see their factories.

Luminosa insisted on taking over one of the implants herself, asking me to guide her, and then—without asking me—signaled Evie to try. That was clever of her—I wanted Evie to do well. "*Sí, sí, esa es la manera de hacerlo!*"

Evie and I would walk back to the Foreign House, long after the bell, long after the tourists cleared.

About a week in.

We're walking through dusk and candlelight and all those lovely sounds and I'm holding her hand. But tonight for some reason, fireworks. Tourists are lining the high walls of the Custom House, applauding and raising glasses of champagne.

We're looking up and Evie says, *You write me yes when you go home.*

"Yes yes OK yes."

We have Sky-pee.

And I chuckle. "You use Skype? And Facebook?"

Sky-pee yes. No Facebook No Twits.

"Why not?"

Sky-pee one person, one person. She holds up two fingers.

I can't think of a way to say *Just you and me* in her language. I manage *We talk much* and she giggles and shakes her head, which means yes, but still feels like no to me.

That night I go to bed in the Foreign House and it's like my very bones are humming, and I see her and I see me. I see me taking one half of my DNA and putting it into her egg. I see us having a child together. I'll carry it if they say we can't, that the child might lose parthenogenesis. And she and I will live together with our child in one of those towns, next to forests of oranges, mangoes, and quince, and I'll keep helping their babies to be born.

I felt elated the whole of the next day; I could feel my face make nice shapes; I could see me sparking laughter in other people. That night I asked Evie if she wanted to see my room—that's allowed, she is a Colina, she can go anywhere. The room made her giggle. She ran into the bathroom and flicked the lights, flushed the toilet and turned on the TV—and great, yes, it was *CSI* and they were cutting up a corpse— but for some reason that seemed to be the funniest thing she'd ever seen and she flung herself onto the bed and bounced up and down on it.

Too ripe. Couldn't sleep here.

She stretched out and I couldn't help giving her a kiss. I hugged her and rolled her back and forth, back and forth. She wasn't laughing but looked both troubled and awed, so I kissed her again, open-mouthed this time, and I felt her chest rise up in response.

I would never force myself on anyone. But there are Colinas who want sex. They are not arrested or mocked, but they are regarded as being different. A holdover from the days of change those 1,700 years ago. We didn't do anything adventurous that first night but I couldn't stop myself saying, "I love you." She slipped away and gave a wave with just the tips of her fingers. I watched from my window as she walked through the Plaza at 11.30 pm.

The next day, Evie looked merry. I thought I had made her happy. She stood up straighter and her eyes looked that bit narrower, as if she had learned something new. She snatched things from people and wagged her hips as if to mock them. Her friends laughed louder or gaped in a caricature of open-mouthed shock, pretending (it seemed to me) to be scandalized. One of the elders came in and clapped her hands and said something outraged and schoolmarmish. I couldn't help but smile and shake my head. The older woman glared at me. *What am I, then, a ringleader? A bad influence?* I dipped my chin, crumpled my lips, and laughed. Evie caught my look, laughed and clapped her hands. *OK, I am a bad influence, what are you going to do about it?*

That night, long after bedtime, we went for a walk in the Precinct, listening to small waves rolling pebbles back into the water. Out to sea all those floating hotels, container ships, or private yachts. Ciudad was silent now and dark, and Evie's eyes were wide, thrilled but also scared. She insisted we go into a bar.

Immediately two women strode up, wanting to talk. One of them pinned us to the table by saying she'd buy us some drinks. The other squared off with me and asked us outright—how did we meet? How did I know her? They asked her questions about how the Colinas got pregnant and had to be told several times. Twice I explained that Colinas did not form relationships with each other as we understood it. Evie sipped her whisky and hated it, her lips turning down, her nose wrinkling. The two women laughed and one said, "You drink it like this," and knocked the shot back down in one.

The questions didn't stop, of her, of me. What are the houses like inside? What do you mean they don't own anything—they've sewn up the world market in all kinds of things. Other couples shuffled closer, stood in a huddle trying to hear, desperate to actually meet a Colina. Do you go to school? What music do you like? Have you heard of a singer called Mariah Carey?

I said we had to be away. One of them said no, stay, the next round's on me. I was worried but Evie seemed to like it. The bar was playing Whitney Houston's "I Wanna Dance with Somebody" and before I knew it, one of the women had made off with my girlfriend. The woman danced like Will Smith making fun of old black men—was she really doing the boogaloo? Evie tried to dance then shook her head, stepped back, and just watched.

"No—come on, you're supposed to join in!"

I got worried. I got mad. I strode up to both of them and said in Colina, *Bedtime. Sleep now.*

Evie smiled and did a head-wobble that I thought meant yes, because it was indeed time to go.

"Spiriting her away, are you?"

As I bundled her off, I told them over my shoulder that Evie had to be up at four and all the other Colinas would be in bed. The woman turned sideways and rumpled her lip at me—*I know what you're up to.*

I felt guilty and sore, like I'd overdone a workout in the gym, and my heart felt bigger, swollen with misgiving because I was beginning to see that what I wanted would not be possible. I asked Evie to come to my room, and she nodded her head up and down exaggeratedly like a child, which meant no. But I reacted like she'd said yes and pulled her with me. She started to giggle and also to shake, but I got her into the room and hugged her and said, "Stay with me."

We rolled on the bed again and this time I traced her nipples with my tongue down to her joybox and kissed her there. She had a clitoris (though people say they don't) and kissing it had the usual effect. She did not kiss me back—but I thought, give it time. The ache inside was gone: she was mine. More or less fully clothed, I slept. When I woke up again about two, she was gone.

The next day at the clinic she whispered, "I don't see you again." I felt like I just swallowed a barium meal, my throat and esophagus coated all the way to my nauseous stomach.

"I'm sorry. I'm sorry if we went too far."

I thought I knew what the trouble was. Again, no words in Colina. "My intentions are strictly honorable," I said in English as a joke and mimed a chuckle. I couldn't find a light, jokey way to say it even in Spanish.

I told her, *Not that thing only. Good thing.* I had no way to say, "It's not just the sex, I want to be your partner." She sighed and looked back at me glumly and seemed to shrink.

I had to say it in Spanish. "I . . . want . . . to . . . marry . . . you." I hammered each word like a nail.

She stared blankly, eyes on the floor, and then abruptly streamed out through the archway.

I thought I was in love; I thought this was it; I thought we'd have a child; I thought I'd live here—I saw it all in front of me, a beautiful new life. And I'd lost it. I hated myself for having sex. I held my head in my hands and paced and called myself stupid. Why why ruin everything for sex, when what I wanted was a wife? I had completely misunderstood the problem.

In the morning, full of determination, I went to the Civil Palace to see La Señora Luminosa and declare myself. It was still dark, but the stars seemed to make a promise. I could hear the waves and seagulls and slippered feet. It was early even for them. I knew what I was going to do and felt solemn, determined, even brave.

In the Palace, Luminosa was lighting candles, her face a bit puffy from having just woken up. Another elder shuffled forward and yawned.

"I've done a terrible thing," I said. "I . . . Evie and me . . ."

"She was in your room and you had sex. Not so terrible." She didn't even look at me.

"No. You don't understand. I didn't force myself on her or anything. But I'm not sure she was ready for it."

Luminosa said Evie's Colina name in surprise. "Eouvwetzixityl? If she didn't want it, it wouldn't happen." The old woman looked amused. "She was curious, I think. And I believe she likes it." Luminosa stood up and looked straight at me, a half-smile on her face. "So have you confessed enough?"

"I want you to know, I wasn't just toying with her, or exploiting her."

"You couldn't."

"I want to marry her."

Both women stopped, looked at each other, and then started to laugh. The elder made a kind of squawk, covered her mouth, and had to turn her back. Luminosa groaned, "Oh no!"

"I . . . I . . . I . . . could live here. I . . . we . . . we could have a child. You know, me contribute to the gene pool." That was my attempt to join in with what I thought was a robust and hearty reaction.

Luminosa shook her head. "Women do this, too?"

"We fall in love, yes."

The elder woman howled with laughter and ran off, calling out names.

Luminosa sighed. "You can't marry. We have no such category in law. And there is no question of you being able to stay and live with us. It was in your contract."

I began to feel cold, but with sweat along my hairline. "Well, well, I think we ought to hear from Evie."

"We will." She went back to lighting candles. I began to hear from outside cries and shouts, doors slamming and the usual morning sounds of running feet, perhaps with more laughter than usual.

The Colinas gawped at me feverishly, eyes glistening. They chattered and roared with laughter. Evie strode in, her back rigid, eyes wide, hands clasped in front of her like a choirboy trying to make the toilet in time.

Luminosa said, her voice going brassy, *Foreigner wants to do Medrano with you.*

Bouquets of faces crammed through the doorway, and they all roared with laughter. Evie looked mortified and also weary at the same time. At that moment, my only concern was for her.

Why do this? she asked me. *You want me inside you like a baby!* I remember that phrase because it was so strange. But she had no word for ownership. She couldn't say: *Why do you want to own me?* Both hands were curled into claws of frustration. She spun on her heel and pushed her way through the throng.

I began to realize just how big a catastrophe this was.

They would tell me to leave; they would tell SingleHelix the reason why. It's part of our ethos never to proposition the single women we help all over the world. I would have to leave the company, maybe the country: Santo Domingo has very few jobs in the field.

"Start today's clinic," advised Luminosa.

Evie did not visit that day or the next. No one said much else about it, though some of the students' jaws swelled with suppressed laughter. *How you have baby with Evie she has baby coming?* one of them asked. *Why Evie want three babies?* Each time one of them asked a question like that there was shrill, speeded-up laughter as if flowers had learned how to chuckle.

Nobody asked me to climb the hill again or to eat with them. When the evening bell tolled, I had to vacate the Plaza. I went to the Foreign House and waited in that downstairs bar, pacing, clutching a gin, staring out at the Plaza. It looked empty but rang with laughter and that made me wonder if they were telling jokes about me. I hoped Evie would come. I waited long after 9 pm when all was still and dark, thinking that she might slip away when she thought nobody could see. Finally the barista said I should get some sleep, as she folded the big iron shutters and slipped bolts into the floor.

Two days later I was asked to attend a breakfast in the Palace. I knew what it was about. There were nuts and fruit and cheese. The elders thanked me for a job well done. They said they were particularly pleased by my teaching and all the efforts I had made to fit in, and to show interest in and respect for their culture. I was to receive a ten-thousand-dollar bonus.

"And don't worry—we have said not a thing about Evie to your . . . your . . . owners." Luminosa's smile was like the Mona Lisa's.

I spent another night pacing in the bar, listening to that sound of laughter, singing, prayer—nightmarish. It wasn't just losing Evie. I was losing that sound, I was losing a country. I couldn't believe that I would have to go back to Santo Domingo and the Agora Mall, with its McDonald's and its Apple Store and its pharmacy that sold ultraviolet toothbrush sterilizers for fifty bucks. The world felt like an apple withering with age.

That night was fireworks again and the hotel's doors were open, and I glanced about me as the sky boomed and battered and kept blossoming out like flowers, and I gathered myself up, darted around the black cloth partitions that separated us from the Plaza. And I ran. I pounded across the pavement, imagining that I was being chased. I ran past the bougainvillea front of what had been my clinic, up the main steps, and then along each of the terraces, as if in panic, looking through each open archway, checking rooms full of flickering light and surprised faces. No Evie, no Luminosa, room after room.

Finally I found Luminosa sitting on the floor playing poker with three others. I collapsed at their feet and sobbed, "Please let me stay. Please. I'll be good. I'll stay away from Evie. She won't ever see me again. Send me out to a town on the plateau. Send me to the north. I can help sell machines. I speak the language. Only let me stay, please, please let me stay." I kept it up until even I couldn't make sense of what I was saying. All that time, Luminosa stroked my hair and hugged me. Finally I calmed down, and, exhausted, I let myself be led away.

But I didn't leave.

Now I work in the Precinct for the Disney Corporation in their big hotel at the end of the strip. Classy, with facades made of the local sandstone, vast interiors with polished marble floors and lots of locked doors. I speak Spanish, English, and of course Colina, and I have a charming little story to tell of how I came here and fell in love with the place, only I don't mention that I am not allowed back in. The guests sit rapt with attention. "Oh, I would love to see inside one of their homes." And I correct them with pained tolerance. "Oh, that is the thing. They don't have homes. They really don't own anything."

On fireworks nights I get to stand on the wall and look out over the Plaza with its steps and songs and chants and running feet and those lights darting about like fireflies, and I always marvel how it is that you almost never see them.

Or I sit in my room at the Buena Vista Hotel where the broadband is amazing and I see every episode of *Mad Folk* and *Game of Thrones*. Evie never answers my calls on Skype. Sometimes I crunch along the beach after even the Precinct has gone to bed, except for the odd drunken tourist, sometimes men looking shaken, miserable, fists bunched. They teach me, those men, the cost of desire.

Last night I had a dream: I was hiking again with Dad. He used to take me up into the mountains—a two-day trek to Pico Duarte where it's cold, and frost dances in the air and breaks the sunlight up into rainbows.

Only this time we were walking in Colinas Bravas, and I was overjoyed they'd let him in, and then I realized that this was actually the Cibao, but a different Cibao, a Cibao that they ruled. As if somehow world history had been reversed and the Taíno still ruled Española and Europe had been settled by them. Dad and I sat on top of a cliff and let the wind blow over us.

I didn't get along with my mother. She hated how I turned out, but so often we become like our parents, don't we? She was a good Catholic who believed in original sin. Have I made up that she once said those women of Colinas must be a different species because they don't know original sin?

If she did, then I think my mother was right.

Original sin is having two sexes, one of whom doesn't carry the child, who needs to know the child is HIS and in so doing needs to know the woman is HIS, and in time, since it's a deal, he has to be HERS as well. If you absolutely must own the person you love most, then how important is owning everything else you love or like? Your book, your designer evening gown, your phone, your knife and fork (even just for the duration of the meal!), your piece of bacon, your slice of orange, your car, your home, your room, your bed, your individual sock with the green toes, let alone your own child. Owning becomes the culture, possession nine points of the law.

Except in Colinas Bravas.

They love the name Colinas Bravas, it chimes with how they see their country and perhaps themselves: the brave hills. But their own name for the place is the third person of their verb to be—"*Ser*" in Spanish. Transcription: *Xix*. The land just is. Not even the land is theirs. It's not England or even Herland.

The opposite of original sin is faith and here's mine.

I am, despite everything, a good person and soon they will see that. I've become a visibly better person living here. I don't need to own Evie, I don't need to own anything. I love this place and will do all I can to help it, out of love.

I write to La Señora Luminosa with ideas—your people love telling stories, I say. Why don't you let me record them, write them down, publish them in English, in Spanish. You tell them on your radio station. Let me put a satellite radio in the cover of the book so that people can listen and read at the same time? A tablet in the cover so that they can see more about you? Why don't you run your own TV station so that you can finally watch things on it that are made for you? Let me do a Web site for you. Let me help sell your windmills all over the Americas in Spanish and in English.

I work to become like them.

I lie awake and listen to pebbles hiss on that beach and I try to cast off owning. I have only my rucksack and khaki and my hotel slacks and shirt. Over and over I visualize my womb, my ovum, imagine a jink in my belly and that a snake unfolds inside me, and I see myself marching to Luminosa chaste but pregnant and saying "behold." I establish a sixth matrilineal line. I imagine this and as I drift off to sleep, I hear that sound, the waves of laughter.

One day, they will let me back in.

Redking

CRAIG DELANCEY

Craig DeLancey has published short stories in magazines like Analog Science Fiction and Fact, Lightspeed, Cosmos, Shimmer, and Nature Physics. His novel Gods of Earth is available now with 47North Press. Born in Pittsburgh, Pennsylvania, he now lives in upstate New York and, in addition to writing, teaches philosophy at Oswego State, part of the State University of New York. He received a joint Ph.D. in philosophy and cognitive science from Indiana University, along with an MA in computer science. His research in philosophy is concerned primarily with philosophy of mind. His book Passionate Engines: What Emotions Reveal About Mind and Artificial Intelligence was published by Oxford University Press. He also writes plays, several of which have received staged readings and performances in New York, Los Angeles, Melbourne, and elsewhere.

Here he delivers a fast-paced and involving post-cyberpunk tale about a "code monkey" who is helping the police track down the source of a deadly computer virus that is infecting gamers—and, unless he can stop it, threatens to spread until it becomes a virtual pandemic.

Tain held a pistol toward me. The black gel of the handle pulsed, waiting to be gripped.

"Better take this," she said.

I shook my head. "I never use them."

We sat in an unmarked police cruiser, the steering wheel packed away in the dashboard. Tain's face was a pale shimmer in the cool blue light of the car's entertainment system. "Your file says you are weapons trained."

"Yeah," I said, "I got one of those cannons at home, locked in my kitchen drawer."

Tain turned slightly toward me. She still held the gun out, her fingers wrapped around the barrel. "You gonna get me killed, code monkey?"

I considered telling her it was quaint to think that protection could be secured with a gun. But instead I told her, "I start waving that around, I'm more likely to shoot you the perp. Just get me to the machines. That's how I'm going to help you."

She thought for a moment, then nodded. "Well, at least you're a man who knows his limitations." She turned the pistol around, held it a second so that the gun locked to her hand print, and then she tucked it under her belt at the small of her back.

She dimmed the dash lights. I was running a naked brain—standard procedure for a raid—and so the building, the sidewalk, and the road reduced down to the hard objects that our paltry senses could latch onto: a world without explanations, ominously obscure.

We both leaned forward and looked up at the building before us, eighteen stories of concrete. The once-bright walls had faded to the color of mold. A half-hearted rain began, streaking the grime on its narrow windows.

The clock on the dash read 2:30 A.M. No one in sight. Most of the lights in the building were out now.

"You know the drill?" Tain asked me.

"I know this kid we're arresting probably wrote RedKing," I told her. "That's all I need to know."

Unsatisfied with this answer, she repeated the rap. "Twenty-seven-year-old male. Got his name legally changed to his code handle: Legion. Five prior convictions for 909." Design, manufacture, and distribution of cognition-aversive and intentionally addictive software. "No record of violence. But he's still a killer, so consider him dangerous. We go in fast, my people take him down, and you save what you can from his machines."

"I know my job."

"Right." She pushed open her door. I followed her into the rain, heaving my backpack on. I tightened its straps and then snapped them across my chest.

A Korean food truck, covered with twisting dim snakes of active graffiti, idled across the street. Its back door swung open, and cops in black, holding rifles, poured out.

We ran as a group for the entrance to the tower.

A few kids stood in the lobby, smoking, and they turned pale and ran for the stairs when we parted the front doors. Their untied sneakers slapped at the concrete floor. We ignored them, but two cops took position in the lobby to ensure no one left. Tain had a set of elevator keys and she took command of both lifts. We squeezed into the elevator on the left, shoulder to shoulder with four other cops in full gear, their rifles aimed at the ceiling. The smell of leather and gun oil overwhelmed everything else while the LED counter flicked off sixteen flights.

A chime announced our arrival. We made a short run down a dim hall and stopped before a door with an ancient patina of scratched and flaking green paint. The cops hit it with a ram and we filed in quick and smooth. I broke to the left, following half the cops through a dingy common room with a TV left on mute, the flickering images casting a meager glow over an open pizza box on an empty couch.

A door by the TV led to a dark room. Two cops rousted the suspect out of bed and zip-tied him in seconds. Legion was a pale, thin kid with trembling, sticklike arms. He gazed around in shock. A woman leapt out of the bed and stood in the corner, shouting, clutching the sheets over her naked body. Somewhere a baby started screaming.

Tain's cops were good: They moved quietly, not all hyped on adrenaline, and they stayed out of my way as I ran through the apartment, checking each room for machines. But the only computers were in the bedroom: a stack of gleaming liquid-cooled Unix engines atop a cheap, particle board desk. Not heavy iron, but good machines: the kind rich kids bought if they played deep in the game economies.

Legion began to yell, calling for the woman to bring him clothes while two cops dragged him out. The woman screamed also, demanded a lawyer, demanded her baby. I did my best to tune out all that noise, pulled a cable from the side of my backpack, and jacked my field computer straight into the top deck. Data streamed through my eyeplants—the only augmentation I was allowed to run here—and I tapped at a virtual keyboard. In a few seconds I dug under the main shell and started a series of static disk copies. While in there, I ran a top check to show the processes that threaded across the machines: nothing but low-level maintenance. Tain's crew had got Legion before the kid could trigger a wipe.

I turned, found Tain's eye, and nodded.

"Okay," she shouted. "Wrap it up."

It started with the gamers. It wasn't enough to stare at screens any longer. They wanted to be there, in the scene. They wanted to smell and hear the alien planet where they battled evil robots, to feel the steely resolve of their avatar and enjoy her victories and mourn her losses. They wanted it all.

That meant moving hardware into the skull, bypassing the slow crawl of the senses. Once we'd wired our occipital lobes, you could predict the natural progression of commerce: not just visuals, but smell, and sound, and feel, and taste had to come next. So the wires spread through our neocortexes, like the roots of some cognitive weed. Autonomic functions came after, the wires reaching down into the subcortical regions of pleasure and pain, fear and joy. We gave up all the secrets of our brains, and sank the wires ever deeper.

Then people started to wonder, what other kinds of software could you run on this interface?

Pornography, sure. The first and biggest business: orgies raging through the skulls of overweight teenage boys lying alone in their unmade beds.

But after that, people began to demand more extreme experiences. A black market formed. For the buyer, the problem is one of imagination: What would you want to feel and believe, if you could feel and believe anything? For the coders, the problem is one of demand: How can you make the consumer come back again? The solution was as old as software: Write code that erases itself after a use or two, but leaves you desperate to spend money on another copy.

That code was dangerous, but it wasn't the worst. The worst was written by the coders who did not want money. They were users themselves, or zealots, and their code might just stick around. It might not want to go.

RedKing was a program like that. RedKing was as permanent as polio. And RedKing made people kill.

When we got outside, a dozen press drones hovered over the street.

"Damn," Tain said. "How do they find us so fast?"

"Hey, code monkey!" a voice called. We turned and saw a short, thin woman, with very short dark hair. Drones buzzed above her, filming her every move as she hurried toward us.

"Ellison," I said, "what brings you to this side of town?"

She had a big mouth that probably could produce a beautiful smile, but she never smiled. Instead, her voice was sharp and quick. "You got a statement? A statement for *Dark Fiber*? This have anything to do with RedKing?"

"No statement," Tain said.

"Come on, code monkey," Ellison said, ignoring Tain. "You gotta give me something."

"I'll catch you later," I said.

"He will not catch you later," Tain said. She took my elbow. "No press," she hissed at me. She slapped a small news drone that flew too close. It smacked into the pavement and shuddered, struggling to lift off again. We stepped over it.

"Ellison has helped me out a few times," I told Tain as we walked away. "And sometimes I help her out."

"While you're working for me, you only help me out. And the only person that helps you out is me."

We got in the car.

At the station, they gave me a desk pressed into a windowless corner by the fire exit, under a noisy vent blowing cold air. The aluminum desk's surface was scarred as if the prior owner stabbed it whenever police business slowed. I was filling in for their usual code monkey, and I got the impression they didn't aspire to see me again after this job. I didn't care. The desk had room for my machine and Legion's stack of machines, the cold air was good for the processors, and I wouldn't have time to look out a window anyway.

Within an hour I had scanned Legion's machines twice over, mapped out every bit and byte, dug through all the personal hopes and dreams of the scrawny guy now shivering in the interrogation room.

I sighed and went looking for Tain. I wandered the halls until I found the observation room with a two-way mirror looking in on the suspect. Tain stood over him.

"She's been in there a while," one of the cops standing before the window told me between sips of coffee.

"I want my lawyer," the kid said. His voice sounded hollow and distant through the speaker. He sat in a metal chair, and I wondered if he knew it measured his autonomic functions while he talked. Some people refused to sit when they got in an interrogation room.

"You made your call. Your lawyer's on her way." Tain bent forward. Her strong arms strained at the narrow sleeves of her coat as she laid a tablet on the table. Even from a distance, we could see the tablet displayed the picture the news had been running all week: a teenage kid with brown disheveled hair, smiling with perfect teeth. He looked innocent, and maybe rich.

Legion glanced down. "I'm not saying anything till I get my lawyer."

Tain pointed at the picture. "Phil Jackson."

"I had nothing to do with that."

"With what?" Tain asked, with exaggerated innocence.

"I watch the news."

"I didn't take you for someone who watches the news, Legion." Tain tapped the tablet decisively. "Seventeen. Doing fine in school. Lonely, but what high school kid doesn't think he's lonely, right? So little Phil Jackson loads a copy of RedKing into his head. Spends a week delirious, happy maybe, thinking he's king of the world—who knows what it makes him think? Then he cuts his mother's throat, hits his father with the claw of a hammer, and jumps off the roof."

Legion looked up at Tain and smirked. Tain became as taut as a spring. She wanted to hit him. And Legion wanted her to hit him. It would provide great fodder for his lawyer.

But she held her fists. Legion waited, then said softly, as if he could barely manage to stay awake, "I told you, I watch the news."

"What they didn't tell you on the news, Legion, is that we got the code out of that kid's implants, and our code monkeys decompiled it, and you know what they found? Big chunks of stuff written by you. Unmistakable provenience. Big heaps of Legion code." Tain let her voice grow soft and reasonable. "We've got fifty-four confirmed casualties for this virus. It's only going to get worse. And the worse it gets—the more people that commit crimes or hurt themselves—the worse it's going to be for you, Legion."

He clamped his jaw and mumbled, "My lawyer."

"I'll go get her for you. You sit here and look at the kid that your code killed."

Tain kicked the door. The cop outside opened it. In a second she was around the corner and when she saw me she walked up close.

"Tell me what you got, code monkey."

"Nothing," I told her.

Her heavy black brows drew together over her pale, inset eyes. I held up my hands defensively.

"Hey, no one wants to find the raw code for RedKing more than I do. But I've scanned every bit of his machines, and I got next to nothing."

Tain dragged me to her office, her grip tight on my elbow, and closed the door.

"You saying your division made a mistake when they linked this guy to the code?"

I sat down on a hard metal chair by the door. Tain followed my example and flopped back into the chair behind her desk. It squeaked and rolled back.

"No. There's code on Legion's machines that is unique and that matches identically big chunks of the RedKing program. But there isn't a lot there. And it's . . . general."

"What do you mean? What kind of code?"

I hesitated. "A toolkit. For running genetic algorithms."

"What's that doing in there?"

I frowned. "I'm not sure yet. I have a hunch, and it's not good news. I'd rather follow up a little, study the code, before I say more."

"Don't take too long. So why isn't this toolkit enough to convict?"

"Hackers tend to give toolkits away, on some user board or other. You can bet he'll claim he did, first time we ask about the details."

Tain frowned in disgust. "You see the autonomics on that kid while I was interrogating him? He flatlined everything. Skin response. Heart rate. Temperature and breathing. All unchanging. He fears nothing, he cares about nothing."

"Oh," I said, "he cares about one thing. His credibility. That's what's driving him."

"Okay, fair enough. You code types have your whole thing with cred. But what I'm trying to say is, the guy is a classic psychopath."

I nodded. "He's a bad guy. But can we prove he's our bad guy?"

She stared at the image on her active wall: mountains at the edge of a long green prairie. It was surprisingly serene for this nervously energetic woman.

"I got nothing," she mused. "He's not gonna talk; psychopaths don't break under threat. My code monkey can't link him to RedKing. And we don't know what Red-King does or why it made a kid kill his own mother. We've identified dozens of infected people, and they all acted differently."

I let that hang a long time before I stated the obvious. "Only one thing to try now. I load it up and see what I can tell from running the copy we got in quarantine."

Tain leaned her head forward and looked at me through her dark eyebrows. "You know why we called you in? Why you're here? Our usual code monkey is on extended leave. She fried her head trying just that."

"Occupational hazard," I said.

"Don't tough guy me. My father was a cop, and my grandfather. When they busted a heroin ring, they didn't go home and shoot smack to try to understand addiction from the inside."

"It's not the same," I said.

"Looks the same to me."

"All right, maybe it is. But what if, what if there was a new drug every week, all the time, and you couldn't know what it would do to people—what it would make people do—if you didn't just try it. Then I bet your grandfather, or your father, would have shot up. Because they wanted to fight it, right? And they needed to know how to fight."

"Bullshit," she said. But she didn't say anything more. She didn't say no.

They put me in a conference room, bare white walls, a table that tipped back and forth if you leaned on it. Tain stared at me, her jaw working, while the tech brought me a memory stick. I slotted it into my field deck immediately, not wanting to give Tain time to change her mind. I'd set up a buffer and then a process echo, so my deck could record everything that was happening.

I plugged straight into my skulljack and in a few seconds I copied the code over into my implants.

"I got an interface," I said. "Pretty simple."

A single sentence appeared in my visual field. *Do you want to be King?* it asked.

I looked at the word *yes* and willed it to click, giving it permission to run on my brain OS.

A rush of colors washed over me. I felt cold, exhilarated, as if I fell down a bright well of light. I think I shouted in something like joy.

Then it was over. There stood Tain, her eyebrows up in an expression of alarm mixed with disapproval.

"How long?" I asked.

"Long? You just plugged in."

I frowned.

"Well?" Tain asked.

"It's . . ." I thought about it. "After the initial rush it's nothing. Nothing yet, anyways. I don't know."

I looked around, meeting Tain's eyes, then the eyes of the cop waiting bored by the door. I did have a slight sense that maybe I felt a little . . . tenuous. But it was nothing definite. It's hard when you are waiting to hallucinate. You tend to start to work yourself into a psychedelic state if you try too hard to expect one.

"Let me clear the buffer and start it up again."

I took a deep breath and did it. We waited a while. "Nothing," I said.

Tain sighed. "Bad batch of code? Maybe they sent you the neutralized compile."

I shrugged.

"All right," she said. "Shut it down. Look over your sample again, see if something is wrong with it. I'll call Code Isolation and see if they sent you the wrong sample."

We pulled the plugs. Someone knocked at the door. "Stay here," Tain said. She went out into the hall and the other cop followed her.

I lifted my deck off the table. That's when I realized my deck's wireless had been left on.

I slipped out of the conference room and walked quickly back to my desk, trying to stay calm. Or at least trying to appear calm. When I set my deck down I looked back. The door to my office was open, showing the long hall that stretched all the way to the center of the building, a corridor that diminished into infinity. And, along the sides of the hall, it seemed every cop in the building stood, hand on holster, looking at me. And down the center of the hall came Tain.

I turned and hit the crash bar to the emergency exit next to my desk. As I passed through, I cracked the red fire alarm crystal by the door. An alarm began to shriek.

"Stop!" Tain shouted. I didn't look back to see if she aimed a gun at me. I threw the door shut and ran down the steps.

I was on the street before they could get word out to stop me. The fire alarm was painfully loud, causing a lot of confusion. A few cops milled by the station's front steps, wondering if the alarm was a drill or mistake. I walked past them and to the block's corner. When I turned out of sight, I ran.

By the time I reached the subway steps my chest hurt and a sharp stitch slowed me to a hobble. I'm a code monkey, not a runner. But I made it down inside, hair lifted by the stink of hot air that a coming train pushed out of the dark. I turned all my implants on, wanting to get the full input now. I mustered a last burst of energy and slipped down the next set of steps and onto the train just as its doors shuddered closed.

Only a handful of people sat in the car. No one met my gaze. Still. Someone here could be undercover. Hard to know. I stared around, wondering what I should do next. If the whole department was infected, what would be the right course of action? Report to Code Isolation? That would be procedure. Only, I thought, I should get myself secure first. I needed a place to hide. I needed my gun.

It was easy to outsmart them. It would be foolish for me to go home, but then they'd know it was foolish for me to go home, and so they wouldn't look for me at home.

So I went home. I took the back door, the one that opened onto the parking lot for the few of us with cars. A short elevator ride, a few steps down an empty hall, and I pushed my way into my apartment.

In the kitchen, under the pale LEDs of my undercounter light, I keyed open my safety drawer. My gun sat with my passport and some spare cash. I picked it up and held it. The grip vibrated once to tell me it recognized me. I stuck it into my coat pocket.

Time to go. No sense in pushing my luck. I was smarter than all of them, sure, but even idiots could fall into fortune. So: I reconsidered. Should I report to Code Isolation? As I thought about it, the idea paled. Code Isolation had sent me the program I'd run on my deck. They had to have known my deck would transmit it. They were likely infected already.

I'd have to solve this on my own. And I could. It was just a matter of recognizing that anyone, everyone could be my enemy—and then outsmarting them all. I felt a thrill of excitement, a soaring determination. Because I realized I could do it. I could trick them all.

First step would be to lose myself in a crowd.

The Randomist was a noisy bar half a block from my apartment building. I'd walked by it hundreds of times but had never gone in. The boisterous cheerfulness of the crowd, the painful sense that one had to be very hip to fit in, had alienated me immediately the few times I'd considered stopping for a quick drink. But now I went directly in under the electric blue archway.

I got a beer at the bar, something local and artisanal with a silly name. The bartender slid it to me but smiled insincerely. "Hey, buddy, how about turning it down a little?"

"What the hell you talking about?" I asked.

"You've got your implants turned all the way out. It's hard to walk past you, you're broadcasting so much. And what is it you're blasting? Some kind of program? That's not cool."

"Drop dead," I told him. I took my drink and turned away, all the hairs on my neck raised. He might work for the cops, I realized. An informant for the infected precinct. I might have to shoot him.

But the crowd swallowed me instantly, and I relaxed. Forget the bartender. He couldn't see me or get me in this dense mass of people.

Bumping shoulder to shoulder as I pushed through, I felt a great worry lift. The cops would never find me in here. And I loved this crowd, with their implants humming all around me invitingly.

There was a beautiful girl in the back, standing alone, waiting for someone. I decided she was waiting for me.

"You're a loud one," she said, as I walked up.

"I like to speak my mind," I said.

"More like shout it."

But she didn't leave. I leaned in close.

"What's your name?" I asked.

"Sparrow. What's that you're broadcasting, anyway? You an ad? One of those walking ads? Come on, turn down your broadcast. I'm serious. It's too much."

I shook my head. "Let me tell you what I do, Sparrow. I'm a cop. But a special kind of cop. I protect people from the only real threat, the threat of their computers and their implants going bad. I'm fantastic at it. I'm the smartest person in the world."

"Yeah? You don't look like a cop."

"I could show you my gun." I put my hand in my pocket and felt the handle thrum against my palm.

She frowned, not sure if I had intended some dirty joke. She pointed over my shoulder. "Now she, she looks like a cop."

I turned. Tain stood there, a few steps away, under a red light. She was all shadows and angles in the dim focused glare. Her hand was at her hip.

I scanned the room. People were starting to freeze in place and fall quiet as seven uniforms filed in. I counted them slowly. Then an eighth. Then a ninth, slipping behind the bar.

There were seventeen rounds in my gun. I could shoot all these cops and still have seven rounds left. I pulled my gun from my jacket pocket.

Tain's hand didn't move, but Sparrow screamed as a blur shot forward and two darts stuck into my chest. My body went rigid as a current slammed my nerves into overdrive.

I heard my gun clatter on the hard floor. I blacked out.

When I came to, someone was sitting on me.

No, that wasn't it. My hands. My hands were strapped down. And something gripped my head. A hat or helmet. I opened my eyes.

A white room. A hospital room. The sharp stink of disinfectant wafted over me. Every muscle in my body ached. Tain stood nearby, talking to a doc in a white coat. Behind her a big window was black with night, mirroring the white room back at us. A code monkey stood behind Tain, field deck strapped on her back. Stepin, a field agent specializing in brain system wipes. She was short and broad shouldered, with a calm but distracted look that made it seem she was always thinking hard about something distant and slightly sad.

"They got you, too," I said.

Stepin looked over at me.

"Who got me?" she asked.

I looked at Tain. "Her. The others in the precinct. They're contaminated with Red-King. You can't trust them. If you're not infected, step away from her, Stepin. Get me out of this. I'm the only person who can stop this. I can fix everything."

Tain took a step forward. "How do you think we got contaminated? You're the one who loaded up the RedKing."

"My computer's transmitter was on," I said, looking at Stepin because it was useless to appeal to Tain. Tain would be gone now, inhuman. "I thought I was loading the virus but instead I was transmitting it."

"Put him under," Stepin said. "I've got to do a complete OS replacement. It'll take me a few hours."

The doctor stepped forward and adjusted my IV. A huge weight closed down on my eyes. As the darkness fell, I heard Stepin say to me softly, "Field computers don't have transmitters. You know that."

When I woke, I was alone in the room. The straps lay open, my wrists and legs freed. Sunlight streamed through the window at a nearly vertical angle. I'd been here a long while, asleep on tranqs. I had a bad headache but otherwise felt normal. I opened my brain menus, and found they worked fine, although the arrangement was all factory normal. I logged into my work desktop and began to review my notes.

Some program had detected my waking, because in a few minutes a nurse brought me food, and then an hour after that Tain arrived, wearing new clothes.

We looked at each other. I chewed air, trying to get started on an apology. Tain let me struggle a while, before she nodded once. She pulled up a chair.

"All right, code monkey, just tell me what happened. We knew something was wrong when you left the test room."

"RedKing is subtle," I told her, relieved to be talking about code. "First, it convinces you that nothing has changed. And that remains throughout: I literally could not even imagine that I was running the virus in my head. I don't know how it inhibits such a basic belief, but it does it very well. That's a breakthrough of some kind. We'll have to study it very carefully and—"

"Don't tell me your research plans," Tain interrupted. "Tell me what it does."

"Right. It made me paranoid of anyone who might be a threat to the virus. I think my brain tried to make sense of my irrational fear of you and the others, and so I concluded you had the virus. I probably invented the idea that my computer had transmitted it in order to explain my fear to myself. Also, I began to feel . . . smart. Super intelligent. I became convinced that I could solve any problem. That I was smarter than anyone."

"You were reaching for your pistol when I tazed you."

I nodded. "I meant to shoot you all. It was . . . bizarre. I didn't see you as people. I saw you as puzzles. Puzzles to be solved by my brilliant mind."

Tain leaned back. Her jaw worked a while as she thought it through. Finally, she said, "So, what we have is code that convinces you that you are a genius, and makes you paranoid, and makes you see other human beings as worthless."

I sighed. "It's worse than that."

"How?"

"Two things. First, I think I tried to spread it last night. To transmit it."

"It's too much code to transmit implant to implant."

"I'm not sure. I think there might be a workaround, to make people call it up off of some servers. You have to test everyone in that bar."

She stood, shoving her chair back. "Damn. We'll have to act fast."

"Get me out of here and I can help. We can get a court order to trace the bar charges and track everyone down."

"Damn," Tain repeated. She got a faraway look as she started transmitting orders from her implants. "What a mess. We're back where we started, and things are even worse."

"Maybe not," I said. "If I'm right, and the program loads from another server, then that's a weakness. If we can find someone infected, and can find the address that they downloaded RedKing from, we can find Legion's hidden servers."

"All right. That's something. So what's your second bit of bad news?"

"I've been reviewing the decompile, and I've confirmed my hunch. But before I explain that, I want to see Legion. We need to set up a meeting with him."

"Why?"

Before I could answer, the door to the room banged open. Ellison strode in. "Hey, code monkey, you sick or something?" She looked at Tain, made it clear that she was not impressed by the lieutenant, and looked back at me. "Or you get shot? That'd be newsworthy, if you got shot."

"You will get out of here right now," Tain said.

"Hey, is that any way to treat a guest? I was invited."

Tain glared at me. I held up a hand to urge her to wait a minute.

To Ellison I said, "I got something for that crappy blog of yours."

"Blog. Yeah, really funny, code monkey. I never heard that one before. But *Dark Fiber magazine* gets more hits in an hour than there are cops in America. So don't misunderstand who has the clout in this relationship."

"I got something about RedKing."

Ellison immediately looked cagey. She gave Tain a sidelong glance. "Okay. I'm interested."

"Of course you are. Only: We don't have the whole story yet. But I can tell some of it. An important part of our investigation, let's say."

"You're asking me to help you get a piece of the story out. All right: Can you promise that I'll be first to get the whole story when you put it together?"

"Tain," I said, "set up that meeting we were talking about. Because you and I will be ready in a few hours."

There were four of us now in the small interrogation room. I sat across from Legion, in one of the metal chairs. Both Tain and Legion's lawyer stood. Everyone eyed me suspiciously.

"My client has already made a statement," Legion's lawyer said.

"To me," Tain said. "But our code security agent would like to ask a few questions."

"My client does not have to answer any more questions."

"No. But he can listen to them, can't he?"

Silence. Legion looked around the room, feigning boredom. Finally his eyes settled on me. I met his gaze and held it.

"RedKing is brilliant code," I said. "A small packet can be transmitted head to head and make a network call for the rest of the code."

"That's been done before," Legion said.

The lawyer stepped closer. "Mr. Legion, I strongly advise you to say nothing."

I nodded. "But the way it tricks implants into seeing RedKing as an operating system upgrade—that's very good. I didn't know such a thing could be done. But that's not the special thing." I glanced at Tain to let her know that this was my second bit of bad news. "The special thing is that it mutates. That code we found on your machines? A genetic algorithm toolkit. You wrote RedKing to mutate. As it spreads itself, it changes a little bit each time it's copied. That's why its operational profile is so variable. Eventually, there'll be a version that probably won't kill people—after all, dead users can't transmit the code—but it will just spread and spread. If your program works, it'll be the most influential, the most important virus ever written. It's historic."

Legion smiled. "Why tell me about this?"

"You read *Dark Fiber*?"

"I read lots of things."

I set a tablet on the table and turned it around. The cover of *Dark Fiber* blared a headline in big letters: REDKING CULPRITS FOUND?: POLICE SUSPECT CRIMEAN HACKER GROUP VEE.

Legion flinched. For the first time, his mocking smile faded as he read a few lines of the news story.

I leaned forward. "Here's what's before you." I held up a finger. "Option one. Admit you wrote RedKing. You can plead that you never knew it would be dangerous. The fact that you confessed will count in your favor. You'll get a few years, and you'll keep some net privileges. But—here's the important point—you'll be immortalized as the creator of the greatest brain hack ever."

I held up a second finger. "Or, option two. Deny you wrote RedKing. Maybe we can't convict you, maybe we can—let's call it fifty-fifty odds. But if you walk free or you go to prison, either way, you lose your chance for the world's biggest cred upgrade. You'll have given up immortality for a fifty percent chance of escaping a few years Upstate."

"I think my client has heard enough," the lawyer said. She pulled at Legion's sleeve, but the kid did not move. Tain held her breath.

"Vee can't hack," Legion said.

"You and I know they're just some teenage thugs whose only skill is to steal credit info off old ladies. But this story has been picked up by a dozen other news companies. Reporters can't tell a real hacker from a kid wearing a mask. And Vee was delighted to claim credit. They've already released a confession video."

"Only I could have written RedKing."

I nodded.

"Mr. Legion," the lawyer growled, "I have to advise you that—"

"Only me," Legion said.

Tain exhaled.

"You get everyone from the bar?" I asked Tain. We sat in her office, looking at her wall screen image of mountains.

She nodded. "Only one has proven infected, a young woman. Stepin is working on tracing back the code."

"I'm sorry I caused so much trouble."

"Getting Legion to talk has made up for some of it. How did you know he would crack?"

"It's a coder thing. Once I'd experienced RedKing, I knew it was a once-in-a-lifetime hack. No one like Legion would be able to stand someone else taking credit for it."

"And how is your friend Ellison going to take it when she discovers your story about Vee was bogus?"

"Ellison will be fine as long as she gets to break the story that Legion confessed. She'll be better than fine: We gave her two good stories, and one of them was even true."

Tain cracked a smile that broke into a laugh. But it died quickly.

"What will it be like, if thousands of people get this virus? Maybe thousands already have it. It's the end of goddamn civilization."

"I don't know," I said. "It's just this week's threat. With any luck we can contain RedKing."

"And then the next brainvirus will come along."

I nodded. "It's a race."

Tain squinted. "You got kids, code monkey?"

"No."

"I got a kid. Four years old. A second on the way."

"Congratulations."

"Yeah. But I swear, you know what, as soon as I put in my time, earn my pension, I'm going to get the wife and move out to Montana." She gestured at the wall image. "And there, I'll never get the implants in my kids. I'll make sure they live in the real world."

"Sounds like a plan," I said. "Me, I'm not much use at anything but coding."

She grunted. "You wanna stick around awhile? Our old code monkey, she's moving to a desk job at Code Isolation."

"All right."

She reached into a drawer and pulled out a big pistol. It fell on her desk with a heavy thud.

"Only, put your damn gun back in your kitchen drawer and lock it up before you hurt somebody."

things with Beards

SAM J. MILLER

This is a hard-hitting—in fact, frankly brutal—story of a man with a secret so horrifying that he can't even bear to remember it himself. . . .

Sam J. Miller is a writer and a community organizer. His fiction has appeared in Lightspeed, Asimov's Science Fiction, Clarkesworld, *and* The Minnesota Review, *and other markets. He is a nominee for the Nebula and Theodore Sturgeon Awards, a winner of the Shirley Jackson Award, and a graduate of the Clarion Writers' Workshop. Coming up is his debut novel* The Art of Starving. *He lives in New York City, and can be found at www.samjmiller.com.*

MacReady has made it back to McDonald's. He holds his coffee with both hands, breathing in the heat of it, still not 100 percent sure he isn't actually asleep and dreaming in the snowdrifted rubble of McMurdo. The summer of 1983 is a mild one, but to MacReady it feels tropical, with 125th Street a bright beautiful sunlit oasis. He loosens the cord that ties his cowboy hat to his head. Here, he has no need of a disguise. People press past the glass, a surging crowd going into and out of the subway, rushing to catch the bus, doing deals, making out, cursing each other, and the suspicion he might be dreaming gets deeper. Spend enough time in the ice hell of Antarctica and your body starts to believe that frigid lifelessness is the true natural state of the universe. Which, when you think of the cold vastness of space, is probably correct.

"Heard you died, man," comes a sweet rough voice, and MacReady stands up to submit to the fierce hug that never fails to make him almost cry from how safe it makes him feel. But when he steps back to look Hugh in the eye, something is different. Something has changed. While he was away, Hugh became someone else.

"You don't look so hot yourself," he says, and they sit, and Hugh takes the coffee that has been waiting for him.

"Past few weeks I haven't felt well," Hugh says, which seems an understatement. Even after MacReady's many months in Antarctica, how could so many lines have sprung up in his friend's black skin? When had his hair and beard become so heavily peppered with salt? "It's nothing. It's going around."

Their hands clasp under the table.

"You're still fine as hell," MacReady whispers.

"You stop," Hugh said. "I know you had a piece down there."

MacReady remembers Childs, the mechanic's strong hands still greasy from the Ski-dozer, leaving prints on his back and hips. His teeth on the back of MacReady's neck.

"Course I did," MacReady says. "But that's over now."

"You still wearing that damn fool cowboy hat," Hugh says, scoldingly. "Had those stupid centerfolds hung up all over your room I bet."

MacReady releases his hands. "So? We all pretend to be what we need to be."

"Not true. Not everybody has the luxury of passing." One finger traces a circle on the black skin of his forearm.

They sip coffee. McDonald's coffee is not good but it is real. Honest.

Childs and him; him and Childs. He remembers almost nothing about the final days at McMurdo. He remembers taking the helicopter up, with a storm coming, something about a dog . . . . and then nothing. Waking up on board a U.S. supply and survey ship, staring at two baffled crewmen. Shredded clothing all around them. A metal desk bent almost in half and pushed halfway across the room. Broken glass and burned paper and none of them had even the faintest memory of what had just happened. Later, reviewing case files, he learned how the supply run that came in springtime found the whole camp burned down, mostly everyone dead and blown to bizarre bits, except for two handsome corpses frozen untouched at the edge of camp; how the corpses were brought back, identified, the condolence letters sent home, the bodies, probably by accident, thawed . . . but that couldn't be real. That frozen corpse couldn't have been him.

"Your people still need me?" MacReady asks.

"More than ever. Cops been wilding out on folks left and right. Past six months, eight people got killed by police. Not a single officer indicted. You still up for it?"

"Course I am."

"Meeting in two weeks. Not afraid to mess with the Man? Because what we've got planned . . . they ain't gonna like it. And they're gonna hit back, hard."

MacReady nods. He smiles. He is home; he is needed. He is a rebel. "Let's go back to your place."

When MacReady is not MacReady, or when MacReady is simply not, he never remembers it after. The gaps in his memory are not mistakes, not accidents. The thing that wears his clothes, his body, his cowboy hat, it doesn't want him to know it is there. So the moment when the supply ship crewman walked in and found formerly frozen MacReady sitting up—and watched MacReady's face split down the middle, saw a writhing nest of spaghetti tentacles explode in his direction, screamed as they enveloped him and swiftly started digesting—all of that is gone from MacReady's mind.

But when it is being MacReady, it is MacReady. Every opinion and memory and passion is intact.

"The fuck just happened?" Hugh asks, after, holding up a shredded sheet.

"That good, I guess," MacReady says, laughing, naked.

"I honestly have no memory of us tearing this place up like that."

"Me either."

There is no blood, no tissue of any kind. Not-MacReady sucks all that up. Absorbs it, transforms it. As it transformed the meat that used to be Hugh, as soon as they were alone in his room and it perceived no threat, knew it was safe to come out. The struggle was short. In nineteen minutes the transformation was complete, and MacReady and Hugh were themselves again, as far as they knew, and they fell into each other's arms, into the ravaged bed, out of their clothes.

"What's that," MacReady says, two worried fingers tracing down Hugh's side. Purple blotches mar his lovely torso.

"Comes with this weird new pneumonia thing that's going around," he says. "This year's junky flu."

"But you're not a junky."

"I've fucked a couple, lately."

MacReady laughs. "You have a thing for lost causes."

"The cause I'm fighting for isn't lost," Hugh says, frowning.

"Course not. I didn't mean that—"

But Hugh has gone silent, vanishing into the ancient trauma MacReady has always known was there, and tried to ignore, ever since Hugh took him under his wing at the age of nineteen. Impossible to deny it, now, with their bare legs twined together, his skin corpse-pale beside Hugh's rich dark brown. How different their lives had been, by virtue of the bodies they wore. How wide the gulf that lay between them, that love was powerless to bridge.

So many of the men at McMurdo wore beards. Winter, he thought, at first—for keeping our faces warm in Antarctica's forever winter. But warmth at McMurdo was rarely an issue. Their warren of rectangular huts was kept at a balmy seventy-eight degrees. Massive stockpiles of gasoline specifically for that purpose. Aside from the occasional trip outside for research—and MacReady never had more than a hazy understanding of what, exactly, those scientists were sciencing down there, but they seemed to do precious little of it—the men of McMurdo stayed the hell inside.

So. Not warmth.

Beards were camouflage. A costume. Only Blair and Garry lacked one, both being too old to need to appear as anything other than what they were, and Childs, who never wanted to.

He shivered. Remembering. The tough-guy act, the cowboy he became in uncertain situations. Same way in juvie; in lock-up. Same way in Vietnam. Hard, mean, masculine. Hard drinking; woman hating. Queer? Psssh. He hid so many things, buried them deep, because if men knew what he really was, he'd be in danger. When they learned he wasn't one of them, they would want to destroy him.

They all had their reasons, for choosing McMurdo. For choosing a life where there were no women. Supper time MacReady would look from face to bearded face and wonder how many were like him, under the all-man exterior they projected, but too afraid, like him, to let their true self show.

Childs hadn't been afraid. And Childs had seen what he was.

MacReady shut his eyes against the McMurdo memories, bit his lip. Anything to keep from thinking about what went down, down there. Because how was it possible that he had absolutely no memory of any of it? Soviet attack, was the best theory he could come up with. Psychoactive gas leaked into the ventilation system by a double agent (Nauls, definitely), which caused catastrophic freak outs and homicidal arson rage, leaving only he and Childs unscathed, whereupon they promptly sat down in the snow to die . . . and this, of course, only made him more afraid, because if this insanity was the only narrative he could construct that made any sense at all, he whose imagination had never been his strong suit, then the real narrative was probably equally, differently, insane.

Not-MacReady has an exceptional knack for assessing external threats. It stays hidden when MacReady is alone, and when he is in a crowd, and even when he is alone but still potentially vulnerable. Once, past four in the morning, when a drunken MacReady had the 145th Street bus all to himself, alone with the small woman behind the wheel, Not-MacReady could easily have emerged. Claimed her. But it knew, somehow, gauging who knew what quirk of pheromones or optic nerve signals, the risk of exposure, the chance someone might see through the tinted windows, or the driver's foot, in the spasms of dying, slam down hard on the brake and bring the bus crashing into something.

If confronted, if threatened, it might risk emerging. But no one is there to confront it. No one suspects it is there. Not even MacReady, who has nothing but the barest, most irrational anxieties. Protean fragments; nightmare glitch glimpses and snatches of horrific sound. Feedback, bleed-through from the thing that hides inside him.

"Fifth building burned down this week," said the Black man with the Spanish accent. MacReady sees his hands, sees how hard he's working to keep them from shaking. His anger is intoxicating. "Twenty families, out on the street. Cops don't care. They know it was the landlord. It's always the landlord. Insurance company might kick up a stink, but worst thing that happens is dude catches a civil suit. Pays a fine. That shit is terrorism, and they oughtta give those motherfuckers the chair."

Everyone agrees. Eleven people in the circle; all of them Black except for MacReady and an older white lady. All of them men except for her, and a stout Black woman with an Afro of astonishing proportions.

"It's not terrorism when they do it to us," she said. "It's just the way things are supposed to be."

The meeting is over. Coffee is sipped; cigarettes are lit. No one is in a hurry to go back outside. An affinity group, mostly Black Panthers who somehow survived a couple decades of attempts by the FBI to exterminate every last one of them, but older folks too, trade unionists, commies, a minister who came up from the South back when it looked like the Movement was going to spread everywhere, change everything.

MacReady wonders how many of them are cops. Three, he guesses, though not because any of them make him suspicious. Just because he knows what they're up against, what staggering resources the government has invested in destroying this work over the past forty years. Infiltrators tended to be isolated, immersed in the lie they were living, reporting only to one person, whom they might never meet.

Hugh comes over, hands him two cookies.

"You sure this is such a good idea?" MacReady says. "They'll hit back hard, for this. Things will get a whole lot worse."

"Help us or don't," Hugh said, frowning. "That's your decision. But you don't set the agenda here. We know what we're up against, way better than you do. We know the consequences."

MacReady ate one cookie, and held the other up for inspection. Oreo knock-offs, though he'd never have guessed from the taste. The pattern was different, the seal on the chocolate exterior distinctly stamped.

"I understand if you're scared," Hugh says, gentler now.

"Shit yes I'm scared," MacReady says, and laughs. "Anybody who's not scared of what we're about to do is probably . . . well, I don't know, crazy or stupid or a fucking pod person."

Hugh laughs. His laugh becomes a cough. His cough goes on for a long time.

Would he or she know it, if one of the undercovers made eye contact with another? Would they look across the circle and see something, recognize some deeply hidden kinship? And if they were all cops, all deep undercover, each one simply impersonating an activist so as to target actual activists, what would happen then? Would they be able to see that, and set the ruse aside, step into the light, reveal what they really were? Or would they persist in the imitation game, awaiting instructions from above? Undercovers didn't make decisions, MacReady knew; they didn't even do things. They fed information upstairs, and upstairs did with it what they would. So if a whole bunch of undercovers were operating on their own, how would they ever know when to stop?

MacReady knows that something is wrong. He keeps seeing it out of the corner of his mind's eye, hearing its echoes in the distance. Lost time, random wreckage.

MacReady suspects he is criminally, monstrously insane. That during his blackouts he carries out horrific crimes, and then hides all the evidence. This would explain what went down at McMurdo. In a terrifying way, the explanation is appealing. He could deal with knowing that he murdered all his friends and then blew up the building. It would frighten him less than the yawning gulf of empty time, the barely remembered slither and scuttle of something inhuman, the flashes of blood and screaming that leak into his daylight hours now.

MacReady rents a cabin. Upstate: uninsulated and inexpensive. Ten miles from the nearest neighbor. The hard-faced old woman who he rents from picks him up at the train station. Her truck is full of grocery bags, all the things he requested.

"No car out here," she says, driving through town. "Not even a bicycle. No phone, either. You get yourself into trouble and there'll be way of getting out of here in a hurry."

He wonders what they use it for, the people she normally rents to, and decides he doesn't want to know.

"Let me out up here," he says, when they approach the edge of town.

"You crazy?" she asks. "It'd take you two hours to walk the rest of the way. Maybe more."

"I said pull over," he says, hardening his voice, because if she goes much farther, out of sight of prying protective eyes, around the next bend, maybe, or even before that, the thing inside him may emerge. It knows these things, somehow.

"Have fun carrying those two big bags of groceries all that way," she says, when he gets out. "Asshole."

"Meet me here in a week," he says. "Same time."

"You must be a Jehovah's Witness or something," she says, and he is relieved when she is gone.

The first two days pass in a pleasant enough blur. He reads books, engages in desultory masturbation to a cheaply printed paperback of gay erotic stories Hugh had lent him. Only one symptom: hunger. Low and rumbling, and not sated no matter how much he eats.

And then: lost time. He comes to on his knees, in the cool midnight dirt behind a bar.

"Thanks, man," says the sturdy bearded trucker type standing over him, pulling back on a shirt. Puzzled by how it suddenly sports a spray of holes, each fringed with what look like chemical burns. "I needed that."

He strides off. MacReady settles back into a squat. Leans against the building.

What did I do to him? He seems unharmed. But I've done something. Something terrible.

He wonders how he got into town. Walked? Hitchhiked? And how the hell he'll get back.

The phone rings, his first night back. He'd been sitting on his fire escape, looking down at the city, debating jumping, though not particularly seriously. Hugh's words echoing in his head. *Help us or don't.* He is still not sure which one he'll choose.

He picks up the phone.

"Mac," says the voice, rich and deep and unmistakable.

"Childs."

"Been trying to call you." Cars honk, through the wire. Childs is from Detroit, he dimly remembers, or maybe Minneapolis.

"I was away. Had to get out of town, clear my head."

"You too, huh?"

MacReady lets out his breath, once he realizes he's been holding it. "You?"

"Yup."

"What the hell, man? What the fuck is going on?"

Childs chuckles. "Was hoping you'd have all the answers. Don't know why. I already knew what a dumbass you are."

A lump of longing forms in MacReady's throat. But his body fits him wrong, suddenly. Whatever crazy mental illness he was imagining he had, Childs sharing it was inconceivable. Something else is wrong, something his mind rejects but his body already knows. "Have you been to a doctor?"

"Tried," Childs says. "I remember driving halfway there, and the next thing I knew I was home again." A siren rises then slowly fades, in Detroit or Minneapolis.

MacReady inspects his own reflection in the window, where the lights of his bedroom bounce back against the darkness. "What are we?" he whispers.

"Hellbound," Childs says, "but we knew that already."

The duffel bag says *Astoria Little League*. Two crossed baseball bats emblazoned on the outside. Dirty bright-blue blazer sleeves reaching out. A flawless facsimile of something harmless, wholesome. No one would see it and suspect. The explosives are well-hidden, small, sewn into a pair of sweat pants, the timer already ticking down to some unknown hour, some unforeseeable fallout.

"Jimmy," his father says, hugging him, hard. His beard brushes MacReady's neck, abrasive and unyielding as his love.

The man is immense, dwarfing the cluttered kitchen table. Uncles lurk in the background. Cigars and scotch sour the air. Where are the aunts and wives? MacReady has always wondered, these manly Sundays.

"They told me this fucker died," his father says to someone.

"Can't kill one of ours that easy," someone says. Eleven men in the little house, which has never failed to feel massive.

Here his father pauses. Frowns. No one but MacReady sees. No one here but MacReady knows the man well enough to suspect that the frown means he knows something new on the subject of MacReady mortality. Something that frightens him. Something he feels he has to shelter his family from.

"Fucking madness, going down there," his father says, snapping back with the unstoppable positivity MacReady lacks, and envies. "I'd lose my mind inside of five minutes out in Alaska."

"Antarctica," he chuckles.

"That too!"

Here, home, safe, among friends, the immigrant in his father emerges. Born here to brand-new arrivals from Ireland, never saw the place but it's branded on his speech, the slight Gaelic curling of his consonants he keeps hidden when he's driving the subway car but lets rip on weekends. His father's father is who MacReady hears now, the big glorious drunk they brought over as soon as they got themselves settled, the immense shadow over MacReady's own early years, and who, when he died, took some crucial piece of his son away with him. MacReady wonders how his own father has marked him, how much of him he carries around, and what kind of new terrible creature he will be when his father dies.

An uncle is in another room, complaining about an impending Congressional hearing into police brutality against Blacks; the flood of reporters bothering his beat cops. The uncle uses ugly words to describe the people he polices out in Brooklyn;

the whole room laughs. His father laughs. MacReady slips upstairs unnoticed. Laments, in silence, the horror of human hatred—how such marvelous people, whom he loves so dearly, contain such monstrosity inside of them.

In the bathroom, standing before the toilet where he first learned to pee, MacReady sees smooth purple lesions across his stomach.

Midnight, and MacReady stands at the center of the George Washington Bridge. The monstrous creature groans and whines with the wind, with the heavy traffic that never stops. New York City's most popular suicide spot. He can't remember where he heard that, but he's grateful that he did. Astride the safety railing, looking down at deep black water, he stops to breathe.

Once, MacReady was angry. He is not angry anymore. This disturbs him. The things that angered him are still true, are still out there; are, in most cases, even worse.

His childhood best friend, shot by cops at fourteen for "matching a description" of someone Black. His mother's hands, at the end of a fourteen-hour laundry shift. Hugh, and Childs, and every other man he's loved, and the burning glorious joy he had to smother and hide and keep secret. He presses against these memories, traces along his torso where they've marked him, much like the cutaneous lesions along Hugh's sides. And yet, like those purple blotches, they cause no pain. Not anymore.

A train's whistle blows, far beneath him. Wind stings his eyes when he tries to look. He can see the warm dim lights of the passenger cars; imagines the seats where late-night travelers doze or read or stare up in awe at the lights of the bridge. At him.

Something is missing, inside of MacReady. He can't figure out what. He wonders when it started. McMurdo? Maybe. But probably not. Something drew him to McMurdo, after all. The money, but not just the money. He wanted to flee from the human world. He was tired of fighting it and wanted to take himself out. Whatever was in him, changing, already, McMurdo fed it.

He tries to put his finger on it, the thing that is gone, and the best he can do is a feeling he once felt, often, and feels no longer. Trying to recall the last time he felt it he fails, though he can remember plenty of times before that. Leaving his first concert; gulping down cold November night air and knowing every star overhead belonged to him. Bus rides back from away baseball games, back when the Majors still felt possible. The first time he followed a boy onto the West Side Piers. A feeling at once frenzied and calm, energetic yet restive. Like he had saddled himself, however briefly, onto something impossibly powerful, and primal, sacred, almost, connected to the flow of things, moving along the path meant only for him. They had always been rare, those moments—life worked so hard to come between him and his path—but lately they did not happen at all.

He is a monster. He knows this now. So is Childs. So are countless others, people like Hugh who he did something terrible to, however unintentionally it was. He doesn't know the details, what he is or how it works, or why, but he knows it.

Maybe he'd have been strong enough, before. Maybe that other MacReady would have been brave enough to jump. But that MacReady had no reason to. This Mac-Ready climbs back to the safe side of the guardrail, and walks back to solid ground.

MacReady strides up the precinct steps, trying not to cry. Smiling, wide-eyed, white and harmless.

When Hugh handed off the duffel bag, something was clearly wrong. He'd lost fifty pounds, looked like. All his hair. Half of the light in his eyes. By then MacReady'd been hearing the rumors, seeing the stories. Gay cancer, said the *Times*. Dudes dropping like mayflies.

And that morning: the call. Hugh in Harlem Hospital. From Hugh's mother, whose remembered Christmas ham had no equal on this earth. When she said everything was going to be fine, MacReady knew she was lying. Not to spare his feelings, but to protect her own. To keep from having a conversation she couldn't have.

He pauses, one hand on the precinct door. Panic rises.

Blair built a space ship.

The image comes back to him suddenly, complete with the smell of burning petrol. Something he saw, in real life? Or a photo he was shown, from the wreckage? A cavern dug into the snow and ice under McMurdo. Scavenged pieces of the helicopter and the snowmobiles and the Ski-dozer assembled into . . . a space ship. How did he know that's what it was? Because it was round, yes, and nothing any human knew how to make, but there's more information here, something he's missing, something he knew once but doesn't know now. But where did it come from, this memory?

Panic. Being threatened, trapped. Having no way out. It triggers something inside of him. Like it did in Blair, which is how an assistant biologist could assemble a spacefaring vessel. Suddenly MacReady can tap into so much more. He sees things. Stars, streaking past him, somehow. Shapes he can take. Things he can be. Repulsive, fascinating. Beings without immune systems to attack; creatures whose core body temperatures are so low any virus or other invading organism would die.

A cuttlefish contains so many colors, even when it isn't wearing them.

His hands and neck feel tight. Like they're trying to break free from the rest of him. Had someone been able to see under his clothes, just then, they'd have seen mouths opening and closing all up and down his torso.

"Help you?" a policewoman asks, opening the door for him, and this is bad, super bad, because he—like all the other smiling white harmless allies who are at this exact moment sauntering into every one of the NYPD's 150 precincts and command centers—is supposed to not be noticed.

"Thank you," he says, smiling the Fearless Man Smile, powering through the panic. She smiles back, reassured by what she sees, but what she sees isn't what he is. He doffs the cowboy hat and steps inside.

He can't do anything about what he is. All he can do is try to minimize the harm, and do his best to counterbalance it.

What's the endgame here, he wonders, waiting at the desk. What next? A brilliant assault, assuming all goes well—simultaneous attacks on every NYPD precinct, chaos without bloodshed, but what victory scenario are his handlers aiming for? What is the plan? Is there a plan? Does someone, upstairs, at Black Liberation Secret Headquarters, have it all mapped out? There will be a backlash, and it will be bloody, for all the effort they put into a casualty-free military strike. They will continue to make progress, person by person, heart by heart and mind by mind, but what then? How will they know they have reached the end of their work? Changing minds means nothing if those changed minds don't then change actual things. It's not enough for everyone to carry justice inside their hearts like a secret. Justice must be spoken. Must be embodied.

"Sound permit for a block party?" he asks the clerk, who slides him a form without even looking up. All over the city, sound permits for block parties that will never come to pass are being slid across ancient well-worn soon-to-be-incinerated desks.

Walking out, he hears the precinct phone ring. Knows it's The Call. The same one every other precinct is getting. Encouraging everyone to evacuate in the next five minutes if they'd rather not die screaming; flagging that the bomb is set to detonate immediately if tampered with, or moved (this is a bluff, but one the organizers felt fairly certain hardly anyone would feel like calling, and, in fact, no one does).

And that night, in a city at war, he stands on the subway platform. Drunk, exhilarated, frightened. A train pulls in. He stands too close to the door, steps forward as it swings open, walks right into a woman getting off. Her eyes go wide and she makes a terrified sound. "Sorry," he mumbles, cupping his beard and feeling bad for looking like the kind of man who frightens women, but she is already sprinting away. He frowns, and then sits, and then smiles. A smile of shame, at frightening someone, but also of something else, of a hard-earned, impossible-to-communicate knowledge. MacReady knows, in that moment, that maturity means making peace with how we are monsters.

fieldwork

SHARIANN LEWITT

Author of seventeen novels under five different names, Shariann Lewitt (aka S.N. Lewitt, Nina Harper, Rick North, and Gordon Kendall) has written literary hard science fiction, high fantasy, young adult, military science fiction, and urban fantasy. She has published forty short stories in anthologies, including Decopunk, Gifts of Darkover, OtherWere, The Confidential Casebook of Sherlock Holmes, To Shape the Dark, *and* Bending the Landscape, Vol. 2, Science Fiction. *Lewitt has formal backgrounds in population genetics and group theory, and learned that fieldwork was just a bit too applied (also too dirty!) for her as an undergrad. She currently teaches at MIT.*

In the thoughtful story that follows, she shows us a scientist following in her famous grandmother's footsteps and carrying on with her work, even if to continue that work, those footsteps lead her to face an icy death in the Outer Solar System.

G randma, do you think Ada Lovelace baked cookies?" We were in her kitchen and the scent of the cookies in the oven had nearly overwhelmed my childhood sensibilities.

"I don't think so sweetie," Grandma Fritzie replied. "She was English."

"Oh. Mama doesn't bake either."

Grandma Fritzie shook her head. "There wasn't any good food when she was young."

"Did her Mama bake?"

"Maybe. But not after they left Earth. They only had packaged food on Europa, and not any ovens or hot cookies or anything good. That's why your Mama is so tiny. We're going to make sure you get plenty of good things to eat so you grow up big and strong."

Grandma Fritzie sneered when she said "packaged food." She was the head of the Mayor's Council on Children and Family Health, and I was living with her while Mama was in the hospital.

My mother won the Fields Medal when I was eight. That may not have presaged another breakdown if the press had reported it as "Irene Taylor, Russian-born

American mathematician working in algebra" etc. etc. But of course they did not. Some reporter even asked me, "So what was it like, being Kolninskaya's grand-daughter? You never knew your grandmother, of course . . ."

To which I replied that I knew my grandmother very well, that she lived all of three subway stops away in Brooklyn just like me and would tell me not to open the door to strangers. Then I slammed the door in the reporters' faces. I went to live with Grandma Fritzie and Grandpa George three days later when Mama went to the hospital.

The press couldn't just leave her alone. She'd been a hero, done something amazing and brave when she'd only been a bit older than me, and now she'd only been the fourth woman to win a Fields Medal, and the media had to be horrible to her.

Even when I was eight I knew she wasn't like other people's mothers, was fragile in some way I didn't understand, and I swore that I wasn't going to be like her. I was going to be like Daddy and Grandma Fritzie and Grandpa George.

And maybe even, though I wouldn't admit it, like Tatyana Kolninskaya, the famous grandmother I had never met. The one who had died and who my mother never talked about. Because at least Kolninskaya had gone out and explored, left her room, left our planet even. Unlike Mama, who never wanted to leave our brownstone in Park Slope except to go to her office, and even then didn't like to take the subway. Too many people she said, which confused me. I thought she'd feel better with lots of people around. But, as Grandma Fritzie said, I was a sensible child and my mother's neuroses were not comprehensible to me then. I don't understand them now, either, but at least I understand where they came from and I'm pretty impressed that she's managed to function at all. Let alone become one of the leading mathematicians of her generation. Besides, everyone knows that mathematicians are a bit strange, even those who grew up on Earth with loving parents and all the fresh food they could ingest.

None of the Europa survivors returned to anything close to normal. Most accepted implants to mitigate the worst of their nightmares, but Mama was afraid that it would interfere with the part of her brain that saw into math the way she does. So she uses drugs to lessen the bouts of PTSD that even the Romulus orphans who took the implants suffer to a lesser extent.

Now that I've been there, now that I've seen the ice and what remains of Romulus Base, and flown that journey and have some idea of what she went through, finally, now I can forgive her. For her fears and her craziness but also for the way she disappeared into her work for so much of my life.

There is only forever the ice. It expands to the dull greenish horizon flat and grayish green, as if it teased at being alive. Only of course it is not. Underneath is the sea, pulsing and alive. Maybe alive.

But the sea never fascinated my mother the way it did everyone else. She only cared for the ice.

The ice spoke to her. She loved the cores she pulled from it. Here a dusting of dark material that possibly came from an asteroid strike, and on another layer a slight change in color that indicated a change in chemical composition. She couldn't wait to get it back to the lab and see what had happened in that place, back then.

She loved the ice and it killed her. It killed all of them, and then we were trapped and there was horror of the return I dare not remember. Therapy and meds forever keep me almost safe for moments, but then I drift and I can't quite understand with the clarity I have when I forego the chemical equilibrium. So I try to keep away from memories of the ice. Aunt Olga in Moscow has never been kind about it, but she is not the one who wakes up screaming from dreams about the long trip home, the pressure of navigation and celestial mechanics on the shoulders of a thirteen-year-old because almost all the grownups had died.

I read my mother's memoire on the way out. She had given it to me, me alone, not my brother or my father. And even though I had known that she was Tatyana Kolninskaya's daughter, that she had lived for more than two years on Europa and that it had formed her and destroyed her together, I had never really thought of her as a young girl living in that environment. I had only wanted to see her as a mother, as my mother. I didn't want to have to recognize her as a person apart from my need for her.

But then, I had asked far more of her and I knew it. And I was curious to know what Romulus Base, and the great Tatyana Kolninskaya, had been like.

Tatyana Kolninskaya did foundational work on the preconditions for life on other planets, which had been a fundamental question for science. Kolninskaya, like many others, believed Europa the most likely body to host that life. Warm seas lurked under that ice, seas and oceans both, heated by friction.

According to the reports they sent back, they had discovered at least virus fragments of DNA. Not quite full animals, which was disappointing, but viruses could survive even hard vacuum. Had they come from asteroids or comets? Or were they the result of some previous contamination?

But the samples never made it back and until our mission no one had been able to corroborate the finding. We were going to sample and survey and see if they had made a mistake. We knew there was a possibility of contamination from their trip, or even possibly earlier unmanned vehicles, but our PI had worked out a program to compare the DNA so that we'd be able to tell if some virus had hitched a ride and flourished here. Or confirm, finally, whether there was, in fact, life in the oceans beneath the ice.

I was always sure she loved the ice more than she loved me, but she was so happy at Romulus. She sang with me in the evening when she got in. All us kids got a skewed education. Surrounded by scientists and engineers in a narrow range of specialties, we did learn a fair bit about planetary geology and evolutionary biology, a smattering of useful mathematics, and how to play the clarinet. We all did speak four mission languages (Russian, English, Mandarin, and Spanish) and, while we had no inkling of human history we had a firm grasp of the politics of getting grants (which I later realized mapped onto all human history with painful accuracy).

We were horrifically deficient in history, literature, and art when we took the required standardized tests when we finally returned to Earth, but they made allowances.

We were celebrities of a sort, the Romulus children, the Romulus survivors. I was thirteen when I was placed with the rest in an elite Planetary Educational Foundation Center under yet another grant for the children of explorers.

There we learned that our greatest deficiency was table manners. We had none. My mother's sister's family in Moscow, who took me in for those first holidays after our return, was aghast at my inability to behave like a civilized person. They did not make any allowance for the trauma, and when I started screaming the morning we woke to an ice covered world, they returned me posthaste to the Center. I was never invited to return, and I have never seen them again, not even when I have visited Moscow as an adult.

The other Romulus orphans had had much the same experiences, except Jessica who had gone to LA where there was no ice. But she shrieked and dove under the dining table whenever jets flew by or trucks rumbled on the street, and so her family reacted just like all the rest. So the nine of us, who had lived together on the ice, bonded even more firmly. The small, cramped spaces with too many people crowded us all at first. The food tasted wrong. We wore little clothing, and that all disposable. And the place was dangerous in all the wrong ways.

We could breathe the air and walk out without a suit. We wouldn't freeze or asphyxiate or die in explosive decompression (which made up many of our scary childhood stories,) but we dared not speak to people we didn't know.

At least all the children had made it home. One of the two grownups who had survived and returned with us, flown the ship that I had navigated, never left a supervised facility again.

"Mom's doing serious math," my big brother Sergei said when I got home to make the announcement.

Bad news. That meant she was off her meds. Which meant do not tell her anything important and most of all do not ever mention Europa. Just the word once set her off in a fit where she threw dishes out the window of our Park Slope brownstone, where they hit the sidewalk and Mrs. Coombs was walking Tyrus and she told the entire neighborhood that Irene Taylor was off her head. Again.

I was only ten at the time and still in school in the neighborhood and the other kids looked at me like I was some kind of freak show. As usual, I went to live with my grandma when Mom went crazy.

I have a perfectly good grandmother who is nothing like Tatyana Kolninskaya. Grandma Fritzie bakes the best chocolate chip cookies ever, is five foot ten and African American. She's a family physician on the Mayor's staff specializing in children's services, and she works with domestic abuse victims on Thursday nights. Grandpa George is a dentist. He disapproves of cookies on principle and always tried to get us to eat apples instead. I don't need to tell you how well that went.

Tatyana Kolninskaya was a name in a textbook until I became advanced enough that I read her original work. And yeah, it was that brilliant. Really that brilliant. Of all the Romulus team, she was the one who made the conceptual leaps about the possibilities for Europa.

But I never felt any particular connection with her. I knew the history and I couldn't avoid my mother's neuroses, but Kolninskaya had been dead for decades before I was born. No one looking at coffee-with-an-extra-cream skin and nappy haired me would ever guess I was half blond Russian. And I kind of like to keep it that way.

I'm just plain Anna Taylor and if anyone makes the connection to my Dad, well, okay. Dad insisted that they give me Kolninskaya as a middle name but I don't acknowledge it. No K on my degrees anywhere. No one has made any big deal that Paul Taylor is married to Irina Maslova, who is the daughter of Tatyana Kolninskaya. Mom has gone by Irene Taylor ever since they married when she was a grad student, and all her degrees and publications and awards are under that sanitized, anglicized name. As if changing her name could erase the Irina who had lived through Romulus Station and navigated that ship back to Earth when she was just a kid.

Grandma Fritzie did not want me to go. "Honey, you'll be gone how long? It'll be years, and dark, and it's dangerous. I remember when Romulus Station was lost in the ice. And think of the malnutrition. That's why your mother is so tiny. They didn't have any decent food out there on Europa. All those Romulus children grew up undersized. What if you get pregnant and you have some tiny undernourished baby?"

I shrugged. "Mama isn't the only person in the world under five ten." Grandma Fritzie and I are the shortest people in the family, excepting Mama, who is barely five-two. "And I'm not getting pregnant. After Romulus children aren't allowed on exploratory expeditions anymore, and I'm not ready for that yet anyway—"

"And they were all so sick, too," Grandma Fritzie interrupted me. "Everyone who returned from Romulus came back with some nasty bug and most of them were hospitalized."

"They would have been hospitalized when they returned anyway," I pointed out. "Didn't the doctors say it was just food that had turned?"

Grandma Fritzie shook her head. "I was practicing medicine at the time and I remember the papers. No, it was some crazy bug that spread through half of Germany before we could isolate it and make a vaccine. Nothing like anyone had ever seen."

I shrugged. The events had nothing to do with each other or with me. They had some food that turned on board the *Rosemary Yalow,* and something mutated in the population. Happens all the time.

"We're not staying. We're just doing a prelim survey to confirm the findings from Romulus, and it's a job and I'll get a ton of papers out of it. We just need a few samples to bring back. They didn't bring anything back, you know, so no one could verify their results."

"I'll bet there's some boy going," Grandpa George said. "I hope it's that nice one that we met last Thanksgiving."

"Richard. Yeah. But even without the two body problem this was the best opportunity for me. I mean, no matter what we find, there's so much to discover that there are going to be a zillion journal articles and I've got to publish my ass off to get myself a nice academic—"

"Language, young lady."

"Sorry, Grandma."

"But she can't tell Mom," Sergei interrupted. "Mom's doing serious math." Which is why we were all huddled in Grandma and Grandpa's huge living room in Grand Army Plaza instead of Park Slope, even with Sergei visiting from Paris with his French wife and their new French baby.

"Honey, I don't know how she'd tell your mother even if Irene were taking her meds and then some," Grandma Fritzie said. "I'm not even sure that I approve."

"I certainly don't, that's for sure. I don't approve of any grandchild of mine leaving this planet," Grandpa George said. "I don't see why you can't get a perfectly good job right here on Earth at a nice safe university. Humans belong on Earth, not traipsing around the solar system getting themselves killed or starved or abandoned on ice."

I sighed. They knew perfectly well that I had to do fieldwork. I love fieldwork. That's why I fell in love with geology, actually. How can I explain it? Everyone else except Mom is into things to do with people. Even Sergei, the bad boy, went off to Paris and became a chef. Though maybe after my announcement I'll be the bad one and Sergei, with his new daughter and new restaurant, will have joined the ranks of respectability.

Only Mom really understands that things that have nothing to do with people can be just—fascinating. All by themselves.

I did not become a geologist because of my famous grandmother. I became a geologist because when I was ten we went to Hawaii and I saw a volcano erupt. It was all very proper, in a helicopter over Volcano National Park, but I had never seen anything ever so thrilling or so beautiful.

I became obsessed by volcanoes. I read about them, watched them, studied them constantly. When other tween girls had pictures of teen dream movie stars or boy bands up in their rooms, I had pictures of exploding mountains and lava floes. I became a volcanologist.

Then the Europa project appeared. I fell in love with the possibilities. And I understood Tatyana Kolninskaya, understood what had driven her off Earth and onto the ice.

The project manager had been one of her graduate students, but hadn't qualified for the Europa mission because he had a heart condition. He hadn't realized that I was her granddaughter and I keep it that way. Just Anna Taylor from Brooklyn, you know. Forget that K. Doesn't stand for anything. But he quivered with excitement when he talked about the waters of Europa, about the seas trapped in the ice, separate from the oceans beneath them, and the friction that kept them warm. With explosive plumes very much like volcanoes—one of which had destroyed most of the Romulus team.

There may be volcanoes beneath Europa. They wanted a volcanologist who could study the ice plumes and the tides, and also possibly locate volcanic vents.

I'd done my dissertation on underwater vents on Ganymede, Europa, and Enceladus. Volcanoes presage life. Life needs heat, and heat can come from the planet's core or star, or tidal friction as with Europa, or any combination. But unique life forms have evolved around oceanic volcanic vents on Earth. If it happened on Earth it could happen elsewhere.

I was hooked, and I was hired. My dissertation had been grounded in the observations we had from flybys and robot landers, but the Romulus material had more depth. How could I pass up the opportunity to go there myself? Richard was much less important than Europa, but it made the family feel better if they could excuse my incomprehensible choice.

"I want to go. I need the publications and this could make my career. It's not my fault my mother is crazy."

"No, it's not your fault. But we don't have to like it just the same," Grandpa George said, and Grandma Fritzie nodded in agreement.

Sergei ignored me, but then he was in the kitchen preparing something intricate. I set the table, which at least gave me something to do. The starched linen cloth so old it was wearing thin in places, the fine china with the gold scroll pattern along the edges that Grandma Fritzie had gotten from her grandma, and the heavy silver that had come from Grandpa George's family connected me with my own history. The serving spoon engraved with the elaborate B for "Browne" that had been Grandpa's great-grandmother's in Syracuse, she had been a nurse and had been a little girl during school desegregation. I'd grown up on the stories of Great-great-grandmother Browne being bussed to a white school district and how grown women had screamed nasty words at her and thrown eggs. But that hadn't bothered her so much as the kids in her class who wouldn't ever pick her for the dodgeball team. And she was always in the last reading group, every single year, although she tested at a ninth grade reading level in fourth grade.

I hoped she would have been proud of me, and I felt her courage as I laid the heavy serving spoon on the table. I love my family. I love my work. I never wanted to hurt anyone, ever. But no matter what, I was going.

I wondered, for the first time, whether Tatyana Kolninskaya had faced resistance as well, whether my Great-Aunt Olga and their parents had been afraid and tried to talk her out of it. Mama had said that Aunt Olga had been elegant and stern and disapproving. But Tatyana was taking along a child, my mother. I, at least, was going alone.

Ice. So many many colors of ice. And so abnormally flat, as well. Europa is the flattest body in the solar system. I was standing on a great body of water. More water was frozen right here on the surface of Europa than existed in all the oceans of Earth.

And I was here. Standing. On. Europa.

Like my mother and my grandmother before me. They too, had seen the colors of Jupiter with its rings above the horizon and the endless smooth ice. As I looked at the gas giant above it didn't seem so strange, suddenly, the ice and stranger in the sky. I felt as if my mother were with me, as if I saw it through her eyes as well as my own. And Tatyana Kolninskaya was there too, watching. Silliness, I knew, but this was a place they had known and now I had come, the third generation.

We had set down ninety minutes previously and gone through a meticulous systems check before we suited up and started hauling equipment from the outer hatches. We would use the lander as our indoor base—we'd already been sleeping there and had our few personal items comfortably stowed.

More importantly, it had an efficiently designed lab that we could access from outside, including an airlock with a built-in laser spectrometer, scanning electron microscopes, and of course the requisite scales and regulation spectrometers so that we could run all the basics without contamination. But we had to haul the larger equipment out to the sites, drill out cores, and survey in situ.

The lander had all the equipment bays easily accessible from the outside, so that we had to lift and carry as little as possible. After five months in zero G, even with all the mandatory exercise, we were weak. I was not looking forward to dragging all that apparatus anywhere, even if it was just to the power sledge.

I only weight a hair over twenty-one pounds on Europa. After five months in space, it felt like a ton. Our equipment, fortunately, only weighed about six hundred pounds on Europa, and there were six of us to haul it out and secure it to the sledge. Back home it would have been a joke.

We'd trained for the physical challenges of the mission. We'd worn the bulky suits in saline tanks and practiced securing the power pack ties to the sledge frames and getting the drill tripods set up, but nothing could simulate what happens to the body after five months of zero G. We all worked out on the trip out here and geologists are a pretty fit crowd to start with. Even I, the city kid, was an avid camper and thought nothing beat a white water canoe trip or an afternoon of snowshoeing for a great time. When we ran the drills back home I never broke a sweat. Now I was breathing hard just getting the panels detached.

By the time we set up and returned to the lander I felt like I'd been run over by a tanker. The only reason I peeled out of that cumbersome, overstuffed suit was that I thought maybe I would hurt less without the constant pressure of the tubing across my aching shoulders and the steel rings restricting my movements. My teammates looked every bit as exhausted as I felt. None of us were good for one more step, not even Richard, who had been an alternate on the US men's Olympic speed skating team once upon a time.

"Anyone want dinner?" So Min asked, but I was too tired to eat. All I wanted was to fall asleep, and I barely made it to my bag before I did.

The first week went by in a blur of agony and exhaustion punctuated by awful food. Grandma Fritzie was right, there was nothing good to eat out here. Not that I noticed; I was too tired to pay attention to anything except the fact that my shoulders felt like they were tearing apart and my legs were constantly sore. And we all stank. The recirculated air in the lander smelled of unwashed bodies. We showered for a timed five minutes in lukewarm water on a three-day rotation and used dry shampoo on our hair. Whoever had masterminded supplies had probably thought scientists wear white lab coats and sit at benches all day. But drilling ice cores at minus one sixty C while wearing a suit is not exactly sitting in front of a screen eating Doritos and wearing a tee shirt. No, we knew the real reason was because water is heavy and hard to haul, and drinking takes precedence over bathing. But still, yuck.

My mother had grown up here? Been a child here? I could barely imagine surviving more than our three weeks of data collection. My grandmother and mother had lived here for twenty-seven months, and would have stayed much longer. I could not imagine how someone could be a child here, how to play and run in suits, how to get away from the grownups in the cramped quarters of Romulus Base. And yet my mother had written about it in her memoire as if it had been normal. I suppose for her it had.

In that thin atmosphere and low gravity, we could almost fly and our games always involved long jumps and chases. We were not heavily supervised as the adults went about their work, so we learned to take care of the suits ourselves.

The day of the accident Victor and Madison had lab time, and so were in charge of watching us. We kids had a kind of pact with Victor and Madison. They were two of the younger expedition members and not parents themselves, so they didn't have the same fears for us as the other adults. Like all children, we wanted independence and to be away from the eyes of grownups. Victor and Madison were both willing to be very lenient so long a we gave them the quiet they desired to concentrate on their work.

In the second week things began to change. We broke into teams and I had lab time as well as fieldwork. For several shifts a week I did stare at a screen as the sensors processed samples we'd retrieved. My body had adjusted to the hard work and the minor gravity and I was no longer so utterly spent. I could pay attention to the ice formations and the view of Jupiter overhead.

Ice.

I am a volcanologist, but first I am a geologist and the ice on Europa holds such promise, teases with such secrets. Under all that ice burns a hot core, heated by constant friction of the tide as it is pulled by Jupiter. Some astronomers have conjectured that Jupiter is a proto-star, a dwarf that, had it developed fully, would have been a binary for our Sun. Instead it remained a gaseous smudge above us, duller than the surface of this moon. Though to be fair, Europa has the highest albedo in the system.

And deep in its heart, at the bottom of those liquid oceans under the ice are volcanoes. Very probably in those oceans is some form of primitive life as well, though the narrow band of atmosphere would not support much on the surface.

We drilled. We took measurements. We compared them with the Romulus readings and found that they agreed. The only uncertainty was—had we brought it ourselves?

The partial DNA we found in what we thought was a virus matched a set of readings that Romulus Base had recorded and sent back. It was rare and it seemed to be distributed far more densely in the area close to where Romulus had been located.

"So is it spontaneous, or did it come with the first mission?" Michael Liang asked over what passed for our seventeenth dinner on site. Michael, being the top evolutionary biologist and one of the mission PIs, was in charge of the gooey stuff. Like looking for life.

"I don't know how Romulus could have contaminated the environment," Ilsa Grieg answered. "They kept strict protocols on containment of all biological material, including waste from meals—"

"If you call that swill biological," I muttered.

"As I said, they kept strict protocols," Grieg was not about to be interrupted by a mere post-doc.

"They were killed in an ice plume. That means dead bodies," I interrupted again, the image so much more clear in my mind now that I knew the ice. The flat, brilliant surface reflected a billion shades of white and red rust trapped in the upper layers. Sometimes the rust lay on top, as if a comet had dusted the surface with cinnamon, and we'd run spectroscopy on every sample we could lay gloves on and I could tell them half the specific comets that had left deposits. Had the bodies truly been captured by the Jovian gravitational field, or had they been ripped apart and some pieces pulled back to the surface of Europa?

"Those bodies were encased in suits," Grieg said. "They should not have been breeched, even in an ice plume."

"Suits can be breeched," Liang said. "And those bodies were thrown out of Europa's gravity by the plume. But it's possible that some debris from the accident came back down. All the surfaces of the lander and our equipment were blasted with radiation, but it's still possible some virus survived. Contamination has always been a consideration. Back in the old days, they deliberately crashed a probe into Jupiter rather than take the chance it would crash here and contaminate any possible life on Europa. But that was before we started getting more robust readings and had to come in and take samples . . . and the samples pass the protocol that compares them to known sequences."

"And our sterile precautions are much improved," Grieg had to get in her point. "We are far more advanced about such things now. Between the radiation sterilization and the other precautions we should no longer be a danger. The tests show that even dropped into a full volcano the suits remain intact."

"And I am Marie of Romania," I muttered under my breath. Richard shook his head at me.

"So what have you found?" Richard changed the subject.

Liang smiled. "We've confirmed the virus. The rest is—speculative. But promising. Very promising. Tests so far appear to confirm that this is not contamination."

"So we did it. We found extra Terrestrial life. Proof that life exists on places other than Earth. It's here, around us, in this ocean," Richard said like a prayer in the stillness of the tiny lander common space.

We didn't jump up and down, congratulate each other, yell, break out champagne. We didn't have champagne. And this was bigger than a boisterous celebration, this was momentous, this was awe.

Had Romulus hung on this moment too? Had my grandmother known this indrawn breath of the last of the old knowledge before the new universe broke around us? We are not and never have been alone. We had confirmed life on Europa.

"Viruses can survive the almost anything," Liang said as if this were a perfectly normal conversation. "Anna, we need to find that volcanic vent you proved in the mathematical models, we need to find real warmth to see if there are native animals here and make sure they are not contaminated by the earlier mission. We have to go on the assumption that we can screen for contaminated material. We've only got four days left and a lot of work to do."

So we turned things over to Group Two. Since Europa keeps the same face toward Jupiter, we had light to work and had split into groups to maximize the time. Also to minimize the use of resources, like sleeping bags and heaters. I was in Group One and should be going off shift, but I was too excited to sleep, so I went back to my charts, looking for seismic activity to see if I could identify any possible volcanic activity in our survey region. Not that I hadn't run the data before, but this time I tightened the grid and used the ice plume indicators. I was not convinced that the ice plumes had anything to do with subsurface volcanic activity. Richard and I had spent the first week here, when we weren't drilling or sleeping, looking for ice plumes and what created them. I considered this a safety issue as well as scientifically interesting. My grandmother had died because they had been taken unaware. But the more I looked the more I was convinced that the plumes were the result of interaction between the weak magnetic field of Europa and the strong one of Jupiter which creates some very strange phenomena.

In any event, I started a much finer search from the vibration receptors we had placed at the collection sites. The next morning, over something that the supplies had labeled coffee, but resembled that dearly missed beverage only in color and some degree of bitter kick, I showed Michael and Richard what I'd done. "If we can set up a deep heat sensor here, maybe in a few hours even we can have some idea whether it would be worth drilling." I indicated a spot deep in a crevasse. I'd specifically looked at crevasse areas to minimize the drilling—hard, heavy work with sixty-five klicks of ice to go through before you hit liquid water. And the heat vent would be far below that.

"You didn't sleep all night, did you?" Liang looked at me like my advisor used to when I'd made a particularly stupid mistake.

I shrugged. "It was interesting. I couldn't sleep."

He grunted. Richard crossed his eyes at me. "Hit the bag. We'll probably go place the sensor, but you're not doing anything until you get some sleep."

He was right. I was seriously sleep-deprived and not making the best decisions, which meant I argued that I had to go with them to position the sensors. He wasn't even a geologist and Richard wasn't a volcanologist and I ended up spilling imitation coffee all over my pants, which didn't make my case any stronger. But I'm stubborn, and when I'm tired I'm worse, and Liang was a decent PI so he figured it was easier to give in than to fight. We were only placing a sensor. Besides, who would go with Richard? Liang? Or Grieg, who wasn't a geologist either? Richard couldn't go alone.

This was not heavy work, but rules were that no one went out on the surface alone. No one, never, not for any reason. I'd never thought about the rule because all my previous forays had been drilling, or placing sensor arrays, which took as many able bodies in the field as we could muster. This though? This weighed less than one pound under Europa gravity and I knew exactly where it went, and I was cranky from being up my whole sleep cycle. We took the scooter, since the site was nearly ninety klicks off. I tried to set the coordinates for the area but my hands were clumsy from exhaustion and too much caffeine. I'd say I could do the sequence in my sleep, but I was just about doing that and it wasn't working. Finally Richard took the navigator from me and keyed the sequence while I suited up.

The scooter has barely room for two adults and a sample kit. The sensor rode on top of the sample case and the rope ladder secured below as we skimmed over the slick surface. Like flying, my mother had said, and she was right. At this velocity, if I just added a light hop I would be sailing overhead—almost like paragliding but without the sail since Europa's atmosphere wouldn't support us. But velocity and muscle would still make for quite a ride.

And then we were at the crevasse. We unloaded the rope ladder and secured it to the edge and started down. I hoped it would be long enough. We'd used it to explore several of the crevasses before, though it hadn't reached close to bottom on some others and we'd lowered equipment deep into them and waited to get readings back from deep inside. What made those deep grooves that laced the surface of the Moon? That was Richard's question and he could talk about the crevasses endlessly.

Richard strapped the sensor on his back after a brief argument (I insisted that it was my equipment, he insisted that I was too tired. I tried to take it but my hands were jittery and I lost the argument right there).

Climbing into the depths is like climbing back into time. Or it would be on Earth, where we know that ice has formed in layers. On Europa? Kolninskaya's main theory states that it is not, that all the ice formed at once. Certainly it appears that way, without the striation that one sees on Earth. Cloudy white-gray with hints of blue and reddish brown, lots of reddish brown that always made me think of cinnamon sprinkled over and swirled through.

We don't know what made the crevasses on the surface. Before Kolninskaya, geologists debated whether they had been caused by liquid ocean responding to tidal forces, or earthquakes, or even volcanic activity. Kolninskaya settled that one—the readings made it clear that the lines followed the moving magnetic field of the moon. The rust is iron and the salt water beneath the surface responds as Europa moves in and out of Jupiter's powerful magnetic field. Ice shifts and cracks appear

Richard has studied the patterns of the surface crazing, hoping to identify older and younger stress lines and trace the action across the surface. Only now I saw the red as blood frozen from debris. Or perhaps the red of a rag of suit.

Climbing down is harder than climbing up. I don't like looking down into what looks like forever, even when I weigh less than thirty pounds. The thin polymer struts that make up the rungs of the ladder don't look like they can support the massive boots, though of course they do quite well even under full Earth gravity. But on Earth I only wear hiking boots to set sensors. On Earth I can feel the rope with my hands, I can feel the breeze, I can smell the air and enjoy the warmth of the sunlight.

The joy and wonder of an alien environment is balanced by the hard truth that you can't get out of it. There is no warmth, nowhere to run, none of the comforts of home. I still felt awe every time my sterile glove touched Europa ice, but I knew that when it came time to leave, I would be more than ready to go. Twenty-seven months? How had they remained even a little sane?

"You coming?"

I shook myself from my reverie and continued down. We only had a kilometer of ladder. Who knew how deep the crevasse went? But I was fortunate this time and we let out only three quarters of the ladder before we hit the bottom.

Richard stepped carefully, aware that the ice was not even. He used a probe before taking any step to judge the solidity and texture beneath. Romulus teams had gone down into several crevasses, but we had done only sensor readings for the survey. From the previous mission we knew the bottoms of these cracks did not follow the pattern above, but that the ice itself could be broken and even soft. In a few areas Romulus Team had found sections that appeared to be near the consistency of slush on the surface. That had been the most exciting finding of all, surface water, proving the existence of at least one of the lakes earlier scientists had theorized. But with the destruction of Romulus Base and the emergency evacuation, no samples had returned for us to study. One of our first mission objectives had been to head to those coordinates and pick up samples of the slush, both to analyze in our own lab and to take home for others to study.

I followed in Richard's footsteps since he had the probe. We only needed to go a few steps to find a good stable platform to anchor the sensor. Even working with the thick gloves, between the two of us it was easy going. Though the temperature plummeted this deep, we were not blinded by the surface albedo. And then we started the long climb back.

We were perhaps two thirds of the way up—far enough at least that I could see the brilliant light of the surface—when the shriek of the alarm tore through me. "Suit breech, suit breech," it cycled through in the mechanical voice.

My suit had torn and might be leaking, but the only possibility was to keep climbing. The suits have multiple redundancies built in for every system. A mere outer breech would not endanger us, certainly not until we were able to reach the scooter. There would be supplies there to patch it up until we got back to the lander.

"Alarm noted," I told the system to shut off the racket.

"You get that?" Richard asked once my ears stopped ringing.

"Yeah."

"It'll hold. Keep climbing."

Climb. Just climb. Hand, hand, boot, boot. Look up, never down. Redundant systems. The suit is not depressurizing. There is plenty of air. I'm fine. Richard is fine. We'll get back to base. Just climb.

My mind shut down so that I saw only the next rung and then the next. I refused to think about anything else, though the ghost of Kolninskaya crept through. I could hear her in my mind. *Yes, child, one at a time. Slowly. The suit will hold. You will come home. I will not let you die.*

The fear froze like the ice around me. Cold, unfeeling, I felt distant from my body, and it seemed as if something helped me up.

And then I was over the top and Richard had his thick glove down to offer me a hand up. I stood on the brilliant white ice crusted with cinnamon rust.

My suit had a snag near the left elbow. There was duct tape on the scooter. Dear old duct tape, good for everything, everywhere. Even on Europa. Richard tore off large swathes of it and ran it around the outer layer of my suit. "You're good to go," he said.

When we got back to the lander and peeled out of the suits, I took mine into the common space and started to pick off the silver gray tape.

"I wouldn't look," Richard said.

I had to look. The tape stuck fast and it took more work than I anticipated to tease the stuff off, but I was trained to be patient. Anyone who has had to use a paintbrush to dust down layers of sediment knows that slow and steady eventually gets you there.

At minus two hundred thirty Celsius, ice is magnificently solid. Shorn apart, it is crystal sharp, like obsidian. The suit held well enough, though, with the duct tape. Which only proves that duct tape is one of the great forces of the universe.

Which also proved that the suit is not impregnable.

Not that it mattered in terms of contamination, I reminded myself. The third layer had closed. Nothing had gotten in or out. As for the Romulus Team's deaths, eyewitness accounts and sensor recordings agree that the bodies in the ice plume were jetted away from the surface and Europa's weak gravitational field. They had plummeted toward Jupiter and had most likely burned on entry to the gas giant's atmosphere.

I wondered again if my mother had seen them. The witnesses who testified later were the two adults who had been observing the party. The children—well, Victor and Madison hadn't paid too much attention to them that day. My mother said that those two had generally tried to shirk any teaching responsibilities. She didn't mind—when they did give lessons they were neither interesting enough nor rigorous enough to interest her. She preferred lessons with the more senior team members, who often forgot these were not even university students. Mama had managed to convince Professor Chiang to teach her naïve set theory before she had started high school.

We felt it blow more powerfully than we had ever felt anything blast since we'd left Earth. The ground shook us all so we tumbled; no one could stand through the violence of the tremor. But only Nikita and Yuen looked up. The rest of us started to run as soon as we felt the first shock.

I don't remember how I got back to Romulus Base. One of the older kids, I guess, or one of the colder ones, Nikita or Simon or Ana Luz, got us all back. We hadn't wandered so far.

The base remained untouched. Victor and Madison looked at the sky and held each other, sobbing. Then they said we had to leave. Now.

We asked where our parents were, and Madison said carefully that they had all been killed in an ice plume. That we had to get back to Earth immediately. That we had to prioritize and pack, food and water, suits and tanks first, then records and samples, whatever we could salvage.

Victor sank to his knees, wrapped his arms around himself and started to rock back and forth. He said nothing intelligible for months. I understood much later that they would have heard our parents die.

We hauled what we could to the transport, food packs and water. Our parents had been strong people, large and powerful, but we were all small for our ages. Stunted by the lack of food, by the lack of gravity to work out muscles, we tired easily and had trouble getting even the barest necessities stowed away. Paul Song, the smallest of us, though not the youngest, downloaded the records, or as many as he could get over.

The ground shook at times and reminded us that we were not on solid ice, that we could be blasted out to Jupiter or churned into ice. We went too fast in our fear, we ran as fast as we could, as we dared. We wanted to finish and be gone from this place that had become a nightmare.

I am not so sure we even cared so much about remaining alive, but getting away was something to fix our minds on rather than the fear. Better to go through checklists, to calculate escape velocity and fuel reserves than think about the body of my mother hurled toward Jupiter, cremated in its atmosphere

I took navigation; even before we left Earth my talent for mathematics had been clear. Aunt Olga had offered to keep me home so I could attend the best math schools in the country, maybe the world. How many times on Europa did I wish I were back on Earth instead of far away? I had wondered constantly why my mother had insisted on dragging me off when I could have remained in Moscow and won school prizes and worn dresses and shoes and not a vacuum suit whenever I left the enclosure. Where people would have praised me and paid attention the way they always had and said what a prodigy I was instead of having only this pack of unevenly educated kids as friends. Didn't she know my life was horrible?

And then she was dead. Gone forever. I did not mourn so much at first, but later, later . . .

I had to navigate. Madison stepped in as pilot and she was barely qualified. Her training was in evolutionary biology and she'd only completed the required safety training for any crewmember. All she knew were the basics of how to fly. Victor, who had been one of Mama's graduate students, was no better trained, and less help. Nikita was more use; Madison taught him enough that he could spell her so she could sleep. Ana Luz organized the younger children into life support, Paul took care of the onboard computer systems and little Hailan turned out to be quite good at mechanics. Every hour I worried about asteroids, gravitation and fuel requirement and how to get home. I had constant nightmares of getting the reentry angle wrong and burning us all alive. To this day I wake up in panic thinking that I am burning, burning, dying inside the Rosemary Yalow.

The only way I could remain sane was to focus on the math. Trajectories, geometries moving through space, distant, abstract equations that had nothing to do with life or death, that comforted me in their stillness, were my safety. They whispered to me and I could see into them, see the next movement and the one after as if it were a thing done. So I moved into that space in my mind, where only the equations existed. Nothing threatened me there. Nothing hurt and no one died. Here in the equations only truth existed, and the deeper I went into the truth the more clearly I could see it. Why would I ever want to leave that place for the real world of hurt and fear and lies?

And then we began to get sick, one by one. First Ana Luz, and then Carlos. Nikita and Madison had to get Victor to take the helm although he wasn't able to speak, but both of them were sick. And me, I ignored the symptoms for as long as I could. We were so very close to Earth by then and I believed Earth would be my salvation.

I was wrong. Earth is full of nightmares. Only in the world of mathematics am I safe.

I read my mother's private memoire during the months we flew out, and I was surprised by how deeply I felt for her. I was amazed at her courage. What had appeared as fragility all my life attested to a kind of nerve beyond anything I had ever imagined. She never spoke of her time on Europa or her mother's death. Only when I told her I was going, in the dining room of my grandparents' apartment, she surprised us all.

Dad brought Mama in. As always, she was the only blonde, porcelain white skinned person in a room full of black people, and she was a good four inches shorter than anyone else at the gathering (Sergei's French wife being the next smallest and fairest member of the family). She looked delicate, her wide blue eyes haunted, still so thin that one might think that she had never seen a decent dinner since her return to Earth. We gathered around the same table where we had every Thanksgiving and Christmas dinner and birthday and graduation party in my life. Sergei served some fancy concoction and Grandpa George stood up. "I believe we are here because our brand new Dr. Anna has an announcement."

I stood up to general applause, though they'd called me "doctor" to death a month earlier at my graduation.

"I've got an amazing opportunity for my post-doc," I started, not daring to look at my parents. "I'm one of the geologists for Michael Liang's expedition and we'll be leaving in eighteen months." I took a deep breath. "For Europa."

Dead silence. Then I glanced under my lashes to see my mother smiling slightly. She nodded. "Yes, I always knew you'd go," she said as everyone else held their breath. "You are just like her, you know. My mother. Tatyana Kolninskaya. You are her very image."

Which I found very hard to believe since Kolninskaya had been all the colors of ice, white skin and pale blue eyes and platinum hair.

"And now," she said with a quiver to her voice, "let us enjoy this wonderful meal Sergei has made. It will be a long time before I have all my children together again."

She even tried to smile. Was this the mother I had known as a child? I was in awe of her courage.

I was right about the vent. We drilled and took samples and this time it was Liang who didn't sleep. We had to make our re-entry window, but he wanted to make every minute count. On our twentieth dinner he announced that he had confirmed an actual cell sample from the vent area. True extraterrestrial life.

"I'll still have to run more screens for contamination," he said when he made the announcement. "But the first pass looks like no match to anything of Earth origin."

I spent the week before we left for Europa in Brooklyn. The day before I had to leave, Mama took me for a walk around the Japanese garden in the Brooklyn Botanical Gardens. We wandered around the reflecting pond with the azaleas and cherry trees and drifting willows, all as serene as my mother appeared. We sat for a while on one of the benches in silence, just appreciating the scene.

Then she pressed a chip into my hand. "My memoire," she said. "Of Europa. I've never shown anyone, not even your father. But you are so much like my mother, and you're going there."

But as she pressed it into my hand, she did not let go of my palm and we sat together, her tiny bird fingers strong, grasping my much larger hand.

"What do you mean that I'm like your mother?" I had to ask. The whole idea confused me. I thought of myself as a Taylor, as very much like Grandma Fritzie and perhaps Dad.

She smiled softly. "You need so deeply to know things. You are so passionate. You are strong and single-minded. But also, you love. That is the gift you gave me. I wondered why my mother took me to Europa, why she did not leave me in Moscow with Aunt Olga."

"Aunt Olga is a twit," I couldn't help but respond.

Mama laughed. "Agreed. But more, I realized, I realized for myself when you children were born, and the more I knew you, that she took me because she wanted me with her. We believed it was safe then, after the Lunar colony established protocols for children living in space communities. She enjoyed my company. She told me what she did in the day, what interested her, why she loved the ice. I think she was sad because I did not love it, too."

"So it's okay."

She smiled. "We're surrounded by these cherry trees. You know what the Japanese say about the cherry blossoms and their beauty. I think that is true of all life, of all of us. Come back to me, my Anna. You are so like my mother, so unafraid, so sure about your great adventure. Come back."

Growing up I thought Mama was weak and afraid of everything. This woman before me was something different, some person I had never seen before. I held her very hard against my chest and if I cried on her shoulder, no one saw.

Contamination. I could not get the idea out of my head that the earlier mission had compromised our findings. I told him about how all those who returned from Romulus had become seriously sick on the voyage back.

"Most doctors thought that was a result of food that had turned, Anna. And we have always been aware there was some possibility of contamination," he said after a while. "But I've done the comparisons and run the numbers and the tests. And what we have found, what we have in this sample, does not show any sign of contamination. The sequences are too radically different from any terrestrial life that we know, at least so far. Thank you for bringing it to my attention, of course, and I'll take it into consideration."

Our return trip was fairly uneventful. I started writing up the papers that I would submit on my return and Richard and I started talking about more than just geology. We had another year to go on the post-doc, and then there was job hunting and the two-body problem, and it's not exactly like there are a million jobs screaming out there for geologists. But both of us decided not to think about it until after we finished our post-docs.

Mama and Dad had come down to Houston to spend some time with me while I did the de-comp and re-established my wobbly Earth legs. I knew it was a big deal for Mama especially, but she was smiling, normal, even when everybody in the flight center tried not to stare at her (though one of the interns did ask for her autograph on one of her books, which she granted graciously, and even let him snap a selfie with her and said book). Though most of the time it was both my parents with me and Richard, Mama and I did ditch the guys to get our nails done, and so that Mama could talk to me alone. But she didn't want to talk about Richard, or even about Europa.

"You are so much like her, Anna. So curious, so brave, so absorbed in what you do. Did you read what I gave you?"

I nodded.

She bit her lip and the two little lines between her blue eyes stood out hard. "I don't know, Annushka, if you can tell me, but you are like her. What do you think? Why do you think she took me with her to that place? Why didn't she leave me safe in Moscow?"

"Mama," I took my one dry hand and touched the back of her arm. "She took you because she couldn't bear to be away from you. Don't you see it? And when you say I'm like her, I'm like you. I'm just like you. But maybe not as brave."

"But I am not brave and I hate the ice," she said.

"Mama, you're the bravest person I know. But look at this."

I showed her my first article from the Europa mission right there in Geology. With me as first author. Anna Kolninskaya Taylor. "And I've been offered a more senior position on the Enceladus team as well."

Mama blinked and swallowed hard. "You will go out again?"

I smiled. "No, Mama. I've done what I had to do. It's a robot mission. I don't need to go out again."

the further adventures of mr. costello

DAVID GERROLD

David Gerrold has been writing science fiction for fifty years, leaving a long trail of novels, scripts, short stories, columns, and articles in his wake. His TV work includes episodes of Star Trek, Land of the Lost, Twilight Zone, Babylon 5, *and* Sliders. *(He created Tribbles for* Star Trek *in one of that series' most famous episodes, and Sleestaks for* Land of the Lost.*) His novels include the time-travel classic,* The Man Who Folded Himself, When HARLIE Was One, *The Dingilliad Trilogy of YA novels,* The Star Wolf Trilogy, *and* The War Against the Chtorr *series. In 1994, Gerrold shared the adventure of how he adopted his son in* The Martian Child, *a semi-autobiographical tale of a science fiction writer who discovers his adopted child might be a Martian.* The Martian Child *won the science fiction triple crown: the Hugo, the Nebula, and the Locus Poll. It was the basis for the 2007 film* Martian Child *starring John Cusack and Amanda Peet. (The book is better.)*

The fast-paced story that follows is a posthumous sequel to Theodore Sturgeon's well-known story, "Mr. Costello, Hero." In this one, the eponymous Mr. Costello, a shrewd and persuasive con man with nobody's better interests at heart except his own, arrives on a frontier colony planet to pitch a grandiose scheme that could change life on the colony forever, and becomes entangled with—and, eventually, opposed by—a pioneering farming family, one of whom gradually realizes the terrible effects Mr. Costello's scheme could have if it succeeds. This one is a lot of fun, in tone reminiscent of Robert A. Heinlein's "juvenile" novels, with a hefty dose of John Varley mixed in as well, one of the year's most enjoyable reads. If you hear somebody say, "They don't write 'em like that anymore," here's proof that they do.

H aven? Yeah, it used to be a nice place, great place even.

You could raise a podful of kids and not have to worry about traffic and cities and taxes—we didn't have any. In the evening, we'd sit out on the front porch and watch the suns go down, double sunsets worth staying up late for—one red, one blue, and sometimes the two of them together would edge the howling green sky with orange and yellow streamers so brilliant you had to put on goggles. The best was when they lit up the spiral rings that arced across the southern sky, shimmering the night for hours.

There was a fella one time, he said, "There ain't no Earth-like planets; there's only wishful thinkin'." Well, maybe so, but he never saw Haven. It's as close to the home-world as I ever found, and I bounced across fifty planets before finally coming to rest on this one. It's an unlikely planet in an unlikely place—an ephemeral zone of liva-bility around a binary dance, but somehow all the unlikelies cancelled each other out and Haven was the result. A 37-hour day, 93-percent Earth-gee, a dollop more oxygen, a thirty-seven-degree tilt on the axis which made for some spectacular sea-sons, and a temperate zone that stretched around the planet's equator like a slippery cummerbund. Yeah, I know what a cummerbund is. Second time I had to wear one, it was time to move on.

I bounced lucky and ended up in a contract family with four beautiful wives and two strong husbands—well, most of the time, except when we switched around, which wasn't too often, unless one of us wanted to get pregnant, which hadn't hap-pened yet because we weren't ready to start a tank-farm and didn't want to rent a gestation bottle somewhere else, either. As a family, we only had one rule: nobody ever goes to bed hungry or angry; the rest was details. That rule lasted as long as the contract did. Which was quite a long time, and probably would have been a lot lon-ger if it hadn't been for him.

Some people can't handle contracts, no big deal to me, I like 'em when I find one that suits me. A few years in a can wrestling vacuum, you learn how to live close with others. Some people don't learn, and that buys them a one-way ticket out the airlock. I knew several captains more than happy to sign the warrant. That's how they got well-behaved crews.

On Haven, though, if you and a neighbor started bumping heads, either he got up and moved or you did. One or t'other. Wasn't that hard; most of the houses were already on wheels. Our closest neighbor was a fella named Jasper, ten klicks to the west, but as long as he kept to himself we all got along fine. He was a good man, when he was a man, and a good woman the rest of the time. Called herself Jasmine then, Jas for short. Never borrowed anything she didn't return the next week, never spoke bad of anyone, never slept in where she wasn't invited, and didn't deserve the shit that came down when it did. None of us did.

But that's a story for another time and it happened long enough before Costello arrived that it doesn't matter here. This is about Costello—him and his fancy or-ange suit. First we heard of him, we thought he was just another star-grazer. Folks pass through Haven all the time, get caught up in her, and start planning resorts or industries or grand utopian communities—their utopias, of course. We listen po-litely, then go home and get back to the real work. Star-grazers are good entertain-ment, not much more; though every once in a while, we have to explain to one of them how an airlock works dirtside and why it would be a good idea to build his re-sort or his industry or his utopia *somewhere else*.

We didn't meet Mr. Costello until Midsummer Jubilee. We unhitched and drove in to Temp, short for Temporary, which was all the name that place was ever going to have. Midsummer was the best time for restocking medicines and spices and any other stuff we couldn't lab ourselves. The weather was calm, traveling was easy, and the bots could manage the crops while we were away.

Temp wasn't the best-stocked place, but it was a lot more convenient than driving three days to the other side of the mountain, to Settlement, and then driving three days back. We always ordered ahead anyway, and anything Temporary didn't have, they'd get Settlement to toss it on the next truck over, so we made out okay. I'd only been to Settlement once and had no wish to go there ever again. I don't do crowds. Not even small ones. And any place big enough to need a jail was no place I wanted to stay. I learned that lesson a long time ago.

Temp is half a day across the Rumpled Hills, up Narrow Canyon and down Abysmal, and then follow Occasional River for another half day. We leave the day before and camp overnight at Empty Meadow. We talked once about carving a road from here to there, but it was a very short discussion. Construction would use up the better part of a year and even if it might shorten our trip to only a few hours, it'd also open up the slopes for traffic. When you build a road, people drive it. And traffic would annoy the glitter-bushes enough to disrupt their breeding—plus careless tourists would encourage the horgs to aggressiveness. The conversation ended when Grampa (his title, not his description) said that roads are too much like civilization and we didn't come to Haven to be city-folk, did we? But there wasn't anyone in the family arguing for it anyway.

We crossed the river at the shallows and drove up onto the common track that thirty years of trucks had worn into the turf. We could tell from the ruts, wider and deeper, that traffic from the landing ports was up again. Not a good sign. Tourists are trouble; immigrants are worse, even rich ones.

Thirty klicks along, we came over the crest of the hill and there was Temporary. A busy day. Too many rigs linked in. Even worse, the Jacklins had added an extension to the public dock. Bad news, that. This was the new normal. Regular traffic. It wasn't unexpected—there was a new station up on the southern ridge, far enough away it wouldn't bother us and mostly good folks, tho it did make for bigger gatherings.

But Temporary was still the right size for a visit. The Jacklins had started with a six-pod spider and connected it by weather-tubes to a scattering of inflatable domes, all sizes. Each dome wrapped a different cargo drop, the leftovers from when Temporary was a landing site for a resource-development company. The Jacklins bought it after the company was persuaded to pull out by a series of unexplainable delays.

After the first winter, the Jacklins sprayed the domes with a meter of shelterfoam, so now, despite the name, the domes were permanent until further notice and sturdy enough to stand up by themselves, even with three or four meters of snow, ice, and occasionally a few centimeters of frozen carbon dioxide piled on top of that.

One of the larger domes served as a public swap and meeting place. Two of the others had long since been emptied and served now as occasional habitats for migrant workers and transients. Plus the inevitable call-boys and -girls working the western circuit. During the summer, with the Jacklins' grudging permission, various pass-throughs and unsettleds used a few of the old mineshafts as a retreat. During the winter, too. I say grudging because it's bad business to kill off customers, but some customers need to be killed. They used the tunnels that weren't habitated as store-houses and winter-bunkers. The bots had dug a whole network of tubes and tunnels inside the mountain, but the topmost part of Temporary still looked haphazard, unplanned, and accidental.

Most folks land at Settlement or at the bigger port farther north where the beanstalk touches down. They put wheels on their pods and head east and then south. The dumber ones head south first, and then east. Those are the ones who come through Temporary, and sometimes we all make a bit of money off them, es-pecially from towing them out of ditches and ravines, repairing broken axles, or just hiring ourselves out as guides to the caravans and wagon trains. A train can be as many as twenty or thirty family-rigs—standard cargo pods laid horizontal and mounted on six or more fluffy polymer spheres two or three meters in diameter, de-pending on the terrain. It's standard practice to use bright colors; it helps identify your rig from a distance, especially if it's surrounded by snow. Our family colors were Florentine, equal stripes of red and yellow on the trucks and tires.

A cargo pod makes a good house—or a truck. Or both at the same time. What-ever you need. They're designed to be reused after landing. A standard unit can house six in comfort, eight if they're friendly, ten if they're small. If you're homestead-ing, you can drop one or two or three on a site, depending on how many of you there are and how much room you need. You can connect as many as eight to a central nexus and call it a spider. And you can link one spider to another to make an estate; I've seen linked clusters and chains of twenty or more spiders, but that's too many people for me. That's practically a city.

Once a pod is down, after twelve hours of unpacking you're ready to settle in; sooner if the first thing you unpack are the bots. If you're smart, you'll mount the rigs on wheels and give yourself mobility. As the saint says, "A man should be pre-pared to move fast at least three times in his life." It's a lot easier if you can just put the house in gear and drive to the dustoff—something I didn't expect to do on Ha-ven, at least not until my third or fourth rejuvenation. And that was just the way I wanted it. This planet is far enough out that people don't drop round because they're in the neighborhood; Haven is a destination, not a rest stop.

But as much as I dislike crowds, I will admit that other people have their uses. For one thing, making love is better with a partner. And it's easier to find a partner in a crowd than a wilderness. If you're looking. I'm not. Not anymore. Not since my husbands and wives picked me out of a lineup, married me, and dragged me into the living pod. It was storm season, which is also honeymoon season for most folks, so we didn't come out for three weeks and that was only to check the anchor blocks on truck two. It wasn't the storm making it move, so we went back in and resumed what we'd only just begun. By first thaw we'd slowed down a bit, and by spring had pretty well finished 'mooning for a while. By Midsummer, the new bots were trained well enough that we could take a week off for Jubilee. Lot of work to do before autumn, so we unchocked the bubbles on truck two, unlinked, and rolled. The break would do us all good.

As we bumped downslope, we saw a big black rig that none of us recognized—three industrial pods in a train, like a traveling factory, maybe a bio-refiner, and a couple more drones parked off-site. They had to be passing through, on their way to the richer territories southeast. The huge bulk of the rolling stock loomed over all the other vehicles like a cluster of broodysaurs.

For the most part we can tell who else is in attendance by the other rigs in the field, but sometimes we see a few strangers—not always newbies, this isn't that kind of neighborhood, just folks just passing through on their way to places they believe are going to be better than the places they left. Over the years, we've seen geologists, zoologists, biologists, mappers, trappers, huskers, buskers, peddlers, meddlers, tinkers, dinkers, migrants, handicrafters, and the occasional salesman. Once in a while, even a tourist, though there isn't really a lot to see, just trees and savannah and occasionally a horg in the distance. But you can see horgs at Settlement; they have a zoo, not a big one, but big enough to maintain a family of horgs, and if you're a tourist, that's what you come to see. Horgs. Once, a circus passed through, but I don't think they made much money. They only stayed for a day. Temp is not a place where anyone stays, not for long; it's just a place to rest overnight before heading deeper into the continent.

Grampa drove us in and found our dock. Most of the time, you just take whatever slot is open, but for Jubilee, the Jacklins always reserve key slots for local families. It's not just a question of good will—it's good management. When trouble breaks out, as it sometimes does, the locals are right there to handle it quickly.

The outside air was warm, by Haven standards, and clean enough that we could have parked and walked. Jackets and air filters would have been enough protection, but anyone who's lived on Haven longer than a week knows how hard it is to keep the inside air filtered and clean with folks coming in and out all the time. And one thing you learn real fast, running an airlock costs, especially bio- and particle-filtering, and the more you run it, the more it adds up. So as a courtesy to our hosts—Mik and Jik and Tilda Jacklin, the only real permanents at Temporary—we linked to the public access and ran our own airlock.

There's a ritual to follow. First you all go to the big common dome and say hello and share a beer and catch up on any gossip that's happened since you last logged on to the community. Then, if you're living in that kind of a family—I'm not, I'm in a closed contract, but some people are—you start filling out your dance card, who you're going to sleep with tonight. Then, and only after you've taken care of all the social business, then you can start talking about what you're looking to buy and what you brought to trade or sell. Otherwise, you look rude. Or worse, desperate. And people take advantage of you when you're desperate. So it's not a good idea to be impatient. The merchandise will still be on the shelves an hour from now, but the seller's good feelings might not.

Finn and I always shop together. The rest of the family goes looking for practicals, but Finn and I like to start with the clothing aisles. Of course, there's not a lot on the hangers that we can wear outside. As good as either one of us might look in a kilt or a pinafore, those are party clothes, not work detail. And Finn is a lot bigger than me, almost burly. But we still like to fantasize, and sometimes it's fun for whoever's being a husband this season. This trip, we contented ourselves with some fancy underwear. We'd take turns wearing it for each other.

During melting-season, that's when the hard work begins. Especially if you're ranching/farming. We had the long downslope of Restless Mountain, the western side, hence the spectacular sunsets. But the other side was Bareback Ridge. With that behind us, sunrise isn't until 9 or 10am, depending on the time of year, just a few hours of bright sky first, bright enough that we can get out early with the bots and start herding the glitter-bushes up and down the fields, making sure they get more sunlight per season than they would if they just sat in one place and brooded.

We spend most of summer harvesting, then start moving the bushes up toward higher ground. It's like herding cats in slow motion, but it's necessary to the survival of the herd. We have to do it before first autumn, because that's when the bushes start slowing their metabolism, saving their summer fat and closing up before long winter settles in. That's when they're most vulnerable to the horgs. A horg-pack can shred most of a herd in a matter of days, even digging down through the frozen ground to rip out the fatty stores at the heart of each bush.

Left to itself, a glitter-bush will take root inside a grove of tall wailing trees. It's not that the bushes don't like sunlight, they do, but swarms of spider-bats nest in the wailing trees, and at night, just before taking to the air, they all drop their guano. The bushes raise their roots to collect the rich fertilizer, so whenever a glitter-bush gets hungry it heads for the shade of a wailing willow, hoping to secure the best feeding spot for itself. Generally, the bushes only venture any distance into the meadows during midsummer because that's when the intense sunlight excites them to breed.

By having the bots herd them back into the fields where we can bright them, we're forcing two or three extra breeding cycles in a season, but that exhausts the bushes, so they strive for the trees even harder—despite us bringing them our own rich fertilizer, a lot more potent than the bat-shit they're accustomed to. One good garbage-refiner can generate both burnable oil and a lot of nitrogen-rich granules.

A determined glitter-bush can cover almost a klick a day. But a more determined bot can herd it by using mirrors to focus even more sunlight on the bush. The bush will reverse course and head back to the center of the meadow and the rest of its community.

An individual bush will breed continually, but when they're raised in herds, they breed in synchronized cycles, releasing clouds of spores. That's why we wear masks outside. The air on Haven is breathable, but glitter-spores can take root in your lungs. Not hard to kill, but who wants to inhale that much ammonia?

Because we brighten them, our bushes grow taller and thicker than the wild ones and their seedpods get two or three times as big. And with the bots patrolling the perimeters, we don't lose many to marauding horgs. Mostly, horgs don't come up this high, but dry season always sends them uphill, so midsummer usually brings excitement as well as magic.

This year, it brought Mr. Costello.

We were still looking at clothes when Trina came to get us. Finn was holding up a blue longshirt he thought would look good on me—more of a dress than a longshirt, but it could be worn either way. I smiled in embarrassment and said I wasn't planning to shift back for a while. He said he didn't care, he'd buy it for me and I could wear it now, it would show off my calves. I admitted it was pretty, but when I looked at the price tag, I told him no, we weren't that rich yet. Trina came up behind me and said it was cute and she and I could share it and yes we could too afford it and I said, "Only if Grampa approves," and that was the end of it for now. I was still the newest member of the family and they were still spoiling me a little, but I wasn't going to be a spoiled brat.

After Finn hung the dress back on the rack, Trina grabbed both our arms. "You don't wanna miss this. There's a guy bragging he's got a better way to commit suicide."

She dragged us into the big dome which doubled as bar, restaurant, dance floor, auction hall, and flea market, depending on the time of day. A small group had gathered around a stocky man in an orange suit. He had a thick fringe of black beard framing a round, unweathered face. He looked too innocent to be here, but here he was anyway. He had two blank-faced companions sitting at the table beside him. One was dressed in a tight black suit that looked vaguely military; the other looked like some kind of tech.

"—and when each person does their part, everybody makes money. Everybody wins."

That's when Tilda Jacklin came up behind him and tape-measured the width of his shoulders.

He turned around, puzzled. "What are you doing?"

"Measurin'. Makin' sure I got a body bag your size. Ye wanna pay fer it now? Discount it ten percent if ye do."

Give him credit, the stranger didn't get angry. He reached up and patted Tilda on the shoulder and said, "You have a fine sense of humor, young man. Very fine. Are you looking for a job?"

Tilda smiled, shook his head, and did a quick vertical measure of the man. "Not even two meters. Got plenty in stock. I'll put one aside fer ye." Then he went back behind the counter and poured three beers for Finn, Trina, and me.

"What's all that about?" Finn asked.

"Horgs," said Tilda.

"What about 'em?"

"That's Mr. Costello. Says he can sell 'em."

"Really . . . ?"

"Ayep."

"Gotta catch 'em first."

Tilda grinned and scratched the top of his head, the way he did when he was amused. "Ayep."

"How's he gonna do it?"

Tilda shrugged, making that wide-eyed, stretched expression he makes when he's reacting to stupidity. "Dunno. Says he needs two—three helpers. Says he's got buyers upside. Says he can fill a pod every ten weeks, send 'em right up the beanstalk. That's what he says. And he's already scheduled two empties and a truck."

Finn frowned, shook his head. "Ain't possible." Trina agreed with a snort.

I was already figuring in my head. "That's a lot of tonnage. Even to fill one pod. He's gotta be talking at least forty, maybe fifty head."

"He says sixty."

"Not possible," said Trina.

"Ayep. But he says his buyer is payin' three hundred a ton. So he's lookin' to gross fifty-thou per pod, at least six times a year, he says. Mebbe more. Temptation like that, a man'll go beyond crazy to pure unadulterated stupid."

"Ain't never gonna happen," said Finn. "No way to round up even a dozen of those bastards."

"Ayep. Horgs is horgs."

What Tilda said—you hear that everywhere on Haven. It's a way of saying this is what it is and there ain't no way of changing it. Rocks is hard, water is wet, and horgs is horgs.

Horgs are . . . well, they're big, they're ugly, they smell bad, and they're meaner than anything else on the planet, even humans, especially when they're in rut. Horgs have only one sex—they don't mate, they fight until exhausted. Or dead. The winner stabs the loser with a spiked penis. The sperm make their way through the bloodstream to the egg sac, where a litter of little horgs gets started. Sometimes the brood-horg survives, sometimes it doesn't.

Horgs aren't choosy, sometimes they poke other things—even humans. When they do that, when there's no eggs available, the sperm self-fertilizes, turns into mini-horgs, and the litter eat their way out. Not pretty. You get a couple hundred rat-sized critters. The big horgs eat 'em. And if it's a horg with ripe eggs, they get fertilized that way. Crazy biology, but it works.

Some people think Horg meat is a delicacy. I'm not one of them. Some people say that if horg meat is fixed right, it's delicious. They can have my share. I've seen what an angry horg can do. And a horny one.

But offworld, horgs are a commodity. People pay a lot for them—dunno why, there are better things to eat, but there's a steady market. And that's why the Jacklins do a fair business in body bags, funerals, and estate planning. There's always some fool with a plan.

If there's a safe way to farm horgs, nobody's found it yet. If there was a safe way to herd them, if there was a safe way to round them up, I'd export every last horg from the planet. And most everyone else feels the same way. But we can't, and even if we could, we wouldn't, because you don't take the apex predator out of an ecology unless you want it to collapse. Without the horgs, we lose the glitter-bushes and everything else that makes Haven so interesting.

It's complicated, but horgs are essential. Spider-bat swarms feed on the insects that live on horg-droppings. No horgs, no droppings, no insects, no spider-bats, no guano. If the spider-bats starve, the glitter-bushes don't bloom, and one of Haven's main crops disappears. And that's only the first domino.

But Mr. Costello wasn't the first idjit to think he knew how to make a profit on Haven. He certainly wouldn't be the last. We'd probably have to dig a few more holes and lay a few more wreaths at Settlement's own Idjits' Field before he was done. I just hoped it wouldn't be anybody I cared about.

So, of course, it was Grampa.

He told us after second supper. We had arrayed ourselves at one of the long tables, the space next to the wall, so we had some privacy for conversation. Grampa was smiling happily about something but he wouldn't say what. "Not here, not here," and he resumed slurping his soup.

I started to press, but Trina shook her head. She touched her lips with a forefinger, then touched the same finger to her ear, and pointed at both the table and the wall. Someone might be listening.

I didn't think the Jacklins would eavesdrop unless it was necessary, like someone with a history of trouble, but you never knew who else passing through might have stuck a button under the table or into the rough paneling of the big common room. So Trina was telling me this was family business and it had to stay private.

Back in the truck, Grampa tamped his pipe carefully and puffed it to life. "Well," he said, "we found us a rich idjit. That fellow Costello. He offered to buy our entire year's crop of glitter-bush seedpods. Twelve percent over market, plus travel and delivery expenses—"

"He's the one says he's going to catch and sell horgs?" asked Finn.

"Ayep. That's the one."

Finn shook his head. "He'll be dead the first day he steps out the hatch—"

"That's fine, too. I told him there's a rich tradition of horg-wranglin' out here, so he'd have to pay in advance. The fool didn't even flinch. Paid the first half right then." Grampa patted his vest pocket, as if the actual money was resting next to his tobacco. "We get the other half on delivery."

Finn pursed his lips, looked around at the rest of us—me, Trina, Marlie, Charlie, and Lazz who'd just gone male again—then back to Grampa. "I wish you'd talked to us—"

"Wasn't any time. Couldn't find all of you. Had to make the deal then. Too rich to say no. And he did pay up front." As if that settled the matter.

Grampa had seniority because he'd staked the family to get it started. He was the majority shareholder. Even better, he was smart enough with the numbers to keep us buoyant and the way he explained it, it did sound better than trucking the loads all the way to Settlement for transshipment up the beanstalk. I wasn't going to say anything because I was the junior-est partner, but I could see by everybody's faces I wasn't the only one in my head about it.

"All right," said Grampa, "why's everybody lookin' so twisted?"

Finn glanced at Trina, then at me—we'd seen Mr. Costello in the common dome too. He was waiting for either of us to say something, but as the second-ranking male, it was his responsibility first. "It's like this," he began. He took a deep breath. "It sounds like a good deal, I mean, it really does. But we saw Mr. Costello in the common room and . . . well, I don't think he knows what he's doing. I think he's gonna get people killed."

"Ayep," said Grampa. "That's my thinkin', too."

"Takin' advantage of a dead idjit like that—it don't sit right."

Grampa puffed a cloud of sweet smoke. "He ain't dead yet. And until some horg pokes him with a litter, his money's just as good as the next idjit's."

Finn shook his head in resignation. He knew he wasn't going to talk Grampa out of anything. Grampa had already made the deal. We were stuck with it.

Trina spoke up then. "It really isn't that bad. I mean, not really. That's a lot of money. And if he gets killed early, we'll still have half a crop to sell. We could buy another pod or start a dome or . . . maybe even get a gestation tank and start a baby."

"Ayep," said Grampa.

"And . . ." she added slowly, ". . . if we don't take the deal, someone else will. Then we lose twice. It's money we don't make and it's money someone else makes." She didn't have to say who. We were all thinking the same thing.

"Yeah, okay," said Finn. "Okay, okay." He gave up with a shrug. "When and where do we deliver?"

"Ten days after harvest. The high savannah, the north end, Little Summerland. Then twenty klicks west into the bush. Reckless Meadow."

Finn swiveled around and brought up a navigation display. He studied the map for a moment, scratching his head. "Terrible close to the mating fields. It's a heavy-grazing area."

"Ayep. If you wanna catch horgs, you gotta go where the horgs are."

Finn turned back to Grampa, folding his arms. "He doesn't expect us to help, does he? Because otherwise—"

"Not to worry. Told him that up front. We're not wranglers. We'll sell him the crop, nothing else. No bots. No riders. No shooters."

"And he agreed?"

Grampa puffed his pipe some more before answering. "Says he doesn't need bots, riders, or shooters. Just a couple of cargo-loaders."

"Then how's he plan to—?"

"He didn't say." Grampa grinned. "Gonna be a fun time, huh?"

With the up-front money from Mr. Costello, Grampa and Finn and Lazz bought three new bots, replacement parts, a new toolkit, two heavyweight weapons, two suits of body armor, several cases of repellents, four banks of high-powered dazzlers, a hundred meters of shock-fence, and several cases of extra fuel cells. We restocked the larders and the med-kits as well.

And we updated our libraries, too. Winter was long and brutal. We had to create much of our own entertainment. Last year, we'd staged A *Midsummer Night's Dream*; this year we were plannin' a suite of Third symphonies—we'd agreed on Beethoven, Copland, Saint-Saëns, but were still arguing about Tchaikovsky, Brahms, Shostakovich, Williams, Sibelius, and Mahler. We'd probably end up doing them all. Winter was long and brutal.

Meanwhile, Mr. Costello was busy on his own, circling around, taking advantage of the Jubilee gathering, meeting as many families as he could. We figured he was making other deals, but nobody was talking. We had a nondisclosure clause, so we assumed everyone else did, too. Eventually, Mr. Costello had some mysterious crates choppered in from Settlement and loaded immediately into his big black trucks.

Jubilee lasted two extra days; we weren't the only ones buying and loading, and a lot of us had to wait for the trucks from Settlement to arrive with everything the Jacklins didn't have to hand. Mr. Costello had pumped a lot of cash into the local economy and most folks were happy to tilt an extra pint or two in his name. By the time the last kegs had been drained, Jacklin's shelves were just about spare. Everybody bought gifts for everybody. We passed out our family gifts on Goodbye Morning, right after first breakfast, just before dawn, with all the usual teasing and laughter.

Finn surprised me with that blue dress he said showed off my calves. I bought him hair and body brushes for the shower, along with the promise that I'd personally demonstrate their proper use. He grinned and said, "You didn't buy those for me, you bought 'em for you." I ducked my head so he wouldn't see me smiling and blushing, but he was right.

It was tradition that we all chip in to buy Grampa a fresh supply of his favorite sweet-smelling tobacco and a new pipe to smoke it in. We couldn't pull out until he puffed it to life and pronounced it good. "This is good," he'd say. "Life is good. Okay, let's roll. Let's see what happens next."

The trip back to Homestead was uneventful. Charlie and Marlie had been monitoring and managing the bots the whole trip. Except for one busted voltivator, swarm-confidence was high and the bushes were sparkling. It looked like an early harvest—a big harvest, too.

Glitter-bush leaves are long. Morning dew collects on the leaves, the leaves curl lengthwise to hold the wetness in. As the day heats up, the leaves dry into needles. Bite the end of a needle and you can suck out the water—not much, but you won't die of thirst, either. Chew a lot of needles and you can rehydrate almost as fast as you sweat. That's why horgs and all the other critters come hunting. It's easier than searching for a water hole.

But if the needle is left alone, if no one eats it, it starts to secrete its oils into the water, and what you get is kinda like honey, only better because bees didn't walk around in it. And if you wait long enough, each needle develops a seed within the oil-honey, and the seeds are even more valuable. That's why glitter-bushes are such a profitable crop. The leaves are edible, the honey is perfect, and the seeds are delicious.

Not all the seeds germinate, though. Only the ones that pass through a horg's gut. So there's the other reason we need horgs. Just not too many. But the numbers cycle up and down, up and down, because that's the way the whole thing works, so when they're up, we have to cull the herds the best we can. If we get to the carcass quick enough, we'll butcher it—but usually the rest of the herd is right there. They're omnivores. They're not just carrion-eaters, they're cannibals. Another reason to be disgusted.

But if we can get in there fast enough to slice off the drumsticks, the tails, the shoulders, the flanks, the ribs, and the belly muscles, sometimes the heart and tongue, we'll hang the meat, cure it, smoke it, age it, whatever, and maybe make a bit of cash off it. But we won't eat it ourselves.

Some people—mostly offworlders—say horg steak is a delicacy. That's because they don't know horgs. They say the meat has a sweet aftertaste, probably from the glitter-bush needles. Like I said, they can have my share. The one time I tried it, I puked it all up—and I had diarrhea for three days, too. Horg is tough and greasy and gamey. You have to tenderize it and marinate it and cover it with sauce to make it edible. But there's some people who like that, I guess. Or maybe it's just that it's expensive and exotic. Or maybe it's because of the side effects. Dunno. Supposedly something in the meat is mildly hallucinogenic and just as supposedly it makes people horny, too, so even if they're not crazy about the taste, that's not the reason they're eating it.

Anyway—summer storms chased us all the way back to Homestead. Not the worst we'd ever seen, but ferocious enough to slow us down. Flash floods scoured Narrow Canyon and the Rumpled River was raging impassible. We had to take the long way around, crossing at The Hump, and we spent the better part of the night parked lee side of Ugly Ridge. Frustrating to be so close to Homestead, but it couldn't be helped.

We'd spent two extra days at Jubilee and lost another half-day coming back, but after the storm passed, the forecast promised a few weeks of milder weather, so we wouldn't have to dock and lock the trucks. We could start rigging them immediately for the trek to Reckless Meadow.

When we finally did get back, dawn was just turning the eastern sky pink and the underside of the cloud-ceiling loomed purple. It wasn't the best start for the day but it could have been worse. Three of the bots were mired in mud and the rest were worrying around, trying to keep the bushes from leaving the meadow.

We unpacked the new bots first, activated them, then rushed to extract the ones that were stuck. It took the entire morning, all of us scrambling to contain the herd, barely getting them settled in and re-rooted and watered before the heat of midday. We didn't even try to plan harvest until after siesta and second lunch.

Charlie and Marlie woke up early to switch out the herding reflectors on six of the bots, installing the new harvest tools and collection baskets. I ran some numbers, and if the ground dried out enough we could complete most of the harvesting in two nights.

After harvest, the bushes would start getting hungry. We could take a few days to herd them back to the willows, or make up the time by dredging a couple loads of guano and delivering it to the meadow. That'd given us good results before, plus a head start on the next harvest, but it would also upset the local balance. We might have to let these fields go fallow for a season or two, maybe plant some darkberries up here and let the bushes gather on the lower slopes instead—that would mean extra work patrolling for horgs, but if Mr. Costello was right, he'd be thinning out the herds enough to give us a break in the up-down cycle. But using the lower slopes for a whole summer would open up a lot more range, meaning we could raise more bushes and expand the homestead.

If Mr. Costello didn't get himself killed first.

Right now, we figured him for just another fellow with more money than sense, but if he wanted to throw some of that cash in our direction, we'd bring out the big baskets to hold it all.

As soon as the bots were charged and refitted, we set them trimming. You don't want to take too many needle-leaves—the bushes need the water—but you want to take the fattest and sweetest pods because the horgs are picky and those are the ones they like most. Those are the ones most likely to germinate after a quick trip through the gut.

The best harvest time is siesta and afternoon, while the pods are heat-sealing. Charlie and Marlie and Lazz napped midmorning so they could work through siesta. Finn and Trina and I took the afternoon shift. We ate first supper when the shadows started stretching east and then began prepping the trucks for Restless Meadow, packing everything we knew we'd need and a bunch more stuff we hoped we wouldn't. Always makes for an easier trip that way. We finally pulled out with five vans full of ripe pods, chilled but not frozen.

The journey down to Restless Meadow took two and a half days, stopping along the way to install several new monitoring stations and a couple of drone-nests. Sky-balls are useful but the weather on Haven limits when they can fly. There's maybe a hundred-klick range on good days, that's a three-hour window. So we put the drone-nests in a hexagonal grid with overlapping edges and try to get coverage whenever the winds permit. We can track the local herds and are getting better at predicting the migratory packs. Some horgs migrate, some don't—still working that out, but we think it's the brooding horgs that get territorial.

By the time we arrived, Mr. Costello had already set up his camp, with his big black trucks parked on the slope overlooking the meadow. One of them opened onto a large deck with a roof of silk-looking fabric. There were chairs around a table, and even a pitcher of lemonade and glasses laid out.

Mr. Costello signaled us to pull up beside. We anchored our trucks, dismounted, and met him on his deck. He invited us to sit with a wave and poured lemonade for all of us as if this were just another autumn day in back-home dusty Illinois—a place we'd all heard of but none of us had ever been. What the hell, it was lemonade.

"Things are going very well, very well indeed," he said. "You should be very pleased, very proud, indeed, yes." One of his two associates—the one who looked vaguely military—came out then with a fresh pitcher of lemonade, and Mr. Costello introduced her. "This is Mikla. Mikla, please welcome our new partners. Please tell me if I have all your names right—"

Mr. Costello went on to explain, "Mikla will be handling the accounting, making sure that everyone is taken care of. And Jerrid, he's our tech—he's working on the communications gear. We have such good news to share. Jerrid has created a new communications web."

Finn grunted. "We already have one—"

"Yes, of course. But Jerrid believes we should have a private web just for our partners. He says we need secure channels for our business operations. If other people can see what we're doing, we'll have competition. Don't you think we should delay that as long as possible?"

Grampa nodded, but Finn looked skeptical. "Most folks don't go pryin' into other folks' business. Ain't polite. There's not a lot of secrets on Haven, anyway. Maybe secrets are an offworld thing. But if it concerns y'that much, y'could just use the regular channels with a smidge of encryption. Nobody'll bother then."

"A very good suggestion, yes. Thank you, Finn." Mr. Costello pretended to think about it, then frowned and said, "But don't you think a flurry of encrypted messages might make people suspicious? Suspicious enough to want to find out what we're up to?"

"Aye, there is that." Finn shrugged.

"This way they won't even know that we're talking to each other. Wouldn't you agree that'll be safer for everyone?"

Finn nodded—reluctantly, but he nodded. "I see your point."

Mr. Costello reached over and poured Finn more lemonade. "Thank you, Finn. Jerrid worked very hard to set up a private communication network for us. He'll be pleased that you see the value of his work."

We sat there for a while longer, exchanging pleasantries, until finally Charlie asked, "But the horgs, Mr. Costello—how do you intend to catch them? You know, it's not safe to go out hunting them. The whole herd will turn on you."

Mr. Costello nodded agreement. "Yes, thank you. You're not the first to point that out. I was thinking—well, Jerrid and Mikla and I were thinking that it would be easier if the horgs came to us."

"So you're gonna lure 'em here with glitter-pods . . . ?"

Mr. Costello pointed down the slope. Three of his bots were already at work, installing two thick masts about fifteen meters apart, anchoring them in the ground as deep as they were tall. The pylons looked heavy enough, even our worst winter storms wouldn't budge them. They glinted like carbonized-polycrete, the bots were wrapping them in tree-bark to hide the metallic finish. But Mr. Costello pointed past them. "You see that level area, down there? Just beyond the posts? Where the bots have laid a polycrete floor? That would be a good place to put out some glitter-pods, yes?"

Charlie shrugged. "One place is as good as another. The horgs'll find 'em wherever."

"How much do you think would be a good appetizer?"

"I dunno. I never thought about feeding horgs before. Mostly, I don't want 'em feeding. Not as much as they want to, that is. They'd eat the whole crop to the ground if they could."

"See? That's my point. You know horgs much better than I do. So what's your advice? If you wanted to get the horgs to come to you, how much would you put out?"

Charlie said slowly, "Well, it all depends. I guess if you want to see most of the herd, you'd put out fifty, maybe a hundred kilos. They'd finish it off right quick, but they'd make a real mess of it and the smell would keep 'em snuffling around for a while searching for leavings. Sometimes they ain't too smart."

"That's what I'm counting on—that we are smarter than horgs." Mr. Costello continued, "Why don't we try your idea? We'll put out a hundred kilos tonight." He suddenly remembered something. "There are lights on top of those masts. Do you think we can leave them on? Or will the light drive the horgs away?"

Marlie leaned forward then. "I never knew a horg to resist a free meal. Once they figure out there's food, they'll come. And once they figure the lights are where the food is, they'll come whether there's food or not. Just in case." She pushed her glass forward and Mr. Costello happily refilled it.

So that was that.

Grampa asked Mr. Costello and his partners to join us for dinner. Lazz and I cooked up a Storm—actually, the full name of the stew was Shit Storm, but not everybody got the joke so we just called it a Storm for short. It's a familiar recipe. I've heard it called Leftover Stew, Ingredient Soup, Glop, Bottomless Pot, Slumgullion, Scouse, Irish Cesspool, Gutter Slime, Desperation, and Oh God, Not Again.

But Lazz is pretty good with spices and I don't do so bad myself with the basics—rice, beans, and noodles. And we had five truckloads of fresh pods—we could serve up a mess of those as well.

Pods have another virtue in the kitchen, too—it's one of the better tricks of Haven cuisine. You can add curry powder, red pepper, blue pepper, jalapeños, habaneros, Pot Douglahs, Trinidad Moruga Scorpions, Carolina Reapers, and a few other spices with Scoville ratings so high they melt the equipment—it doesn't matter. You can neutralize most of the heat with glitter-bush pods, leaving only the flavor and just the slightest hint of sweetness. Mostly, though, we stop at habaneros. The other peppers are better used in horg-repellent sprays. It slows 'em down. Sometimes. But one of the attractions of Jubilee is the spice-cookout. You bring in your hottest dish and see who can eat a whole bowl of it. The survivors win free medical care until they can walk again.

We opened up our own deck, set out tables and chairs, dropped the side-silks to slow down bugs and dust, laid the table for everyone, and rang the triangle. Everyone was already gathered, but it's part of the ritual. The weather on Haven doesn't always encourage eating outside, but when it does, you do. We still had another hour of sunset.

Mr. Costello praised the Storm as if it was a culinary discovery of the first order. Jerrid and Mikla even asked for seconds and extra bread to mop their bowls, so we knew tonight's Oh God, Not Again had been a success.

After they headed back to their own trucks, after both the suns had finally dipped below the western horizon, we all retreated inside for the Circle. It's how we keep ourselves centered. We sit around the table with coffee or tea, and we go round and round until we're done.

One by one, first we acknowledge whatever might be gnawing at us, hurts and upsets, simmering frustrations, whatever. You have to say what you want and need to make things right. Nobody interrupts. Nobody gets to offer advice. Nobody gets to play peacemaker. All of those things are arrogant and disrespectful. You have three minutes to say whatever you have to say. Then to the next person, and the next.

On the second round, whatever upsets might have come up—you get to take responsibility for your part of it, you get to offer support to those who need it, you get to be a partner to whoever needs partnership. The second round keeps going round and round until the air has been cleared and everything that needs to be said has been said.

Usually, the first round is about the frustrations of the day's work, not about our frustrations with each other. While it's not a firm rule, if any two people in the family have an upset with each other, they're supposed to resolve it before we get to Circle. So first round is usually about outside annoyances and second round is about creating strength to deal with them. But if a personal upset doesn't get resolved before Circle, if it's that important, we deal with it there.

Finally, third round is about completion. We go around and each person acknowledges the strengths they see in the family, the gifts they see in others, the gifts they wish to be to the whole. By then we're usually on the second or third cup of coffee or tea. We finish by all holding hands and reminding ourselves that being in the family is a gift and a privilege. Then we have whatever special dessert or treat we've saved for ourselves.

That's when the real fun begins. We share all the best gossip we've heard, all the most interesting stories and jokes, all the news that's come down the channels. And . . . we also take some time to make sure we're all on the same page about the business at hand. Those discussions sometimes go on for an hour or longer.

This night, we talked about Mr. Costello and his partners. We tried to figure out who they were and what they were planning and whether or not we could trust them—and most of all, what they weren't telling us. We speculated, we guessed, we imagined, we goggled the web and came up empty. Finally, we paired off for the night, our usual couplings, and headed to our bunks.

I lay down next to Finn and sighed, mostly happy to be with Finn, but also concerned for no reason I could identify. "What I said in Circle. I still feel that way. Mr. Costello makes me uneasy. I don't know why. There's just something about him."

Finn didn't answer immediately. He was rubbing my back, my shoulders, my neck, working out the tensions of the day. When he finished, I would do the same for him. Finally, he said, "I think it's because he's too nice. It's like he's trying too hard."

I had to think about that for a while. "If he's trying too hard, isn't that a kind of lying? Maybe he doesn't trust his own plan?"

"No, I think he trusts his plan. But I wonder if maybe the plan he's showing us is only the top part of the plan he isn't showing us." He patted my shoulders affectionately. "You're done. My turn."

He sprawled face down on the bed and I straddled him, digging into his spine. He was all muscle and I had to use all my weight and all my leverage. After a while, I said, "You and Grampa have been here longer than anyone. You've seen a lot of schemers and scammers come through here—"

"Yep. Most of 'em are buried on Idjit Hill."

"—so why do you trust Mr. Costello?"

"I don't. But his money spends just as good as anyone else's. What Grampa said— if we don't take it, someone else will. So far, I haven't seen any reason to distrust him. Maybe his manner is just the way he is." He grunted as I worked his shoulders. "He's a starsider. Maybe that's how they behave on other worlds."

I thought about my next words, decided to say them anyway. "I've been on a lot of planets, Finn. More than I've told you about. You haven't asked and I haven't volunteered. Because I've done some things—"

"We don't care about who you were before you got here," said Finn. "We care about who you are now. If we didn't, you wouldn't be in this family. You wouldn't be here in this bed tonight. And you wouldn't be screaming my name to the ceiling."

"I'm not doing that."

"Not yet, but you will—"

"First let me finish what I was going to say. I've bounced around a few systems and I've never met any starsider who behaved like Mr. Costello. No, let me say it another way. Maybe I've seen a few—he reminds me of some of them. Some of them ended up the guest of honor at an airlock dance."

"You *have* been around—"

"If you really want to know—"

"Do I need to?" Even in the dark, I could see the expression on his face. "Or will it hurt you to tell more than it would hurt me to hear?"

I didn't answer. That was answer enough.

He grabbed me, rolled me over on my back, and pushed my knees up toward my nipples. He leaned his weight on my bent legs so he could look down on me. "This is where I want you, right here, right now. Is that enough?"

I barely had time to gasp my answer.

Sometime after first sleep, when we were all awake for midnight meal, Lazz powered up two bots and had them dump a hundred kilos of pods in the center of Mr. Costello's polycrete floor. The lights on the pylons blazed down from the two nearest corners. There were cameras there as well, so we had an excellent view of the entire field.

"How long do you think we'll have to wait?"

"Dunno," said Marlie, and swiveled to face a wall of screens. One display showed our location. Another tracked the herd. "They're not directly downwind but they should catch the scent soon enough. See? There." Marlie pointed. "Some of the outliers are turning."

"They're at least ten klicks away," said Charlie. "That's an hour, minimum, more likely two."

"We gonna wait up for 'em?"

"Might could," said Grampa. "Then again, just as easily I might could go back to sleep. If they got pods to eat, they ain't comin' up the hill to see what we're doin'." A thought occurred to him. "You sprayed those trucks good, Finn?"

"Five coats, all the worst peppers. I spent two hours in that damn suit. I sprayed until the paint blistered. If any horgs can sniff the pods in our trucks, they're welcome to 'em. At this point, I ain't gonna argue. My eyes are still burning. And that was two days ago."

"Told y'to wear the goggles."

"I did. Even with the goggles, even with the mask, even with the hood, even with the O-tanks, that spray gets through. Y'know, people have died just breathing downwind from that crap."

"Ayep," said Grampa, lighting his pipe and grinning.

In the morning, while Lazz and Trina fixed first breakfast, the rest of us reviewed the night's videos. Only a few horgs showed up, mostly outliers, mostly curious. Maybe a dozen. Maybe a few more. I didn't count. They sniffed around the piles of pods cautiously—probably the unfamiliar scent traces of machines and humans made them suspicious—but after a bit, they bent their massive heads and inhaled the pods like so much dandelion fluff.

Horgs are sloppy eaters. They snuffled around, spreading pods every which way, smashing them under their feet, smearing the honeyed juices everywhere. The monitors showed their excitement rising as the scent grew stronger. Even after the last few pods had been slobbered away, they still licked eagerly at the now-oily surface of the polycrete. If they weren't horgs, it could have been adorable.

But they were horgs and it was disgusting.

Horgs look like the mutant offspring of a rhinoceros and a warthog, only a lot bigger and ruddier and fatter and flatter and hairier. They have sharp razorback armor all along their spines, extending from the ends of their thick flat tails forward to their thick plated skulls. That's where the armor splits and curves downward around their jaws, finally turning into two savage curving tusks. They have big paddle-like feet, so they can swim as well as they gallop—not fast, but pretty much unstoppable. On the deep savannahs, they travel in herds that can sprawl as wide as a hundred kilometers. They have to—they'd overpower the local ecology if they massed any closer together. Few predators are big enough to bring down a horg, but there are swarms of little things that can worry one to death.

Away from the plains, in the foothills and the forests, horgs become loners. And that makes them even more vicious, because they attack everything. It has something to do with not being able to sync their biological cycles with their fellows. They turn into psychopaths.

Horgs are omnivorous. They eat everything. Mostly, they eat grass, flowers, trees, bark, glitter-bushes, wailing willows, insects, grubs, roots, fungi, mushrooms, snakes, worms, lizards, birds, carrion, and any small horgs that get in their way. Loners tend to overeat, not just because they're hungry, but because they need to build up bulk in case of a mating fight. Away from the herd, the majority of matings are injurious or fatal.

And those are their good points.

In the morning, after first breakfast, we all walked down to the feeding deck with Mr. Costello's group and examined the aftermath. One of the smaller horgs had lost an argument with one of the larger horgs. There were still traces of blood everywhere and carrion birds were picking at the few remaining scraps of skin and bone.

Mr. Costello found that very interesting. He didn't approach the scavengers. They looked feisty, so he studied them from a distance. Mikla and Jerrid frowned and whispered between themselves. Finally, Mr. Costello turned back to us and waved his cigar at the bloodstains on the polycrete. "How many did we lose?"

Finn was studying the blood smears, too. He shook his head. "Hard to say. I'd have to process the video to be sure. And even then, I dunno. Once the fighting started, it was a scramble—impossible to tell what was happening. All I can say for sure is that there were a lot fewer horgs leaving than arriving. Mebbe five or six fewer."

For the first time, Mr. Costello looked unhappy. "This was unexpected. Very unexpected." He turned to Grampa. "This—this cannibalism. Is that normal behavior?"

Grampa shrugged. He took a moment to light his pipe while he considered his answer. "Well, there's a lot of theories about that. Horgs get hungry, they eat what's in front of 'em. But"—he paused to puff thoughtfully—"sometimes these critters work themselves into a feeding frenzy. Sometimes it's hunger and sometimes it's rage and sometimes the mating fights get out of control"—another puff, another thoughtful pause—"but in this case, mebbe you overstimulated them. In the wild, they don't get big piles of pods. They have to work a bit for every mouthful. But you gave 'em a big fat feast. Drove 'em crazy, mebbe. Leastways, that'd be my guess."

Grampa didn't guess. Grampa never guessed. But Grampa rarely spoke in declarative sentences, either. He let you do the work—kind of like Mr. Costello. The difference? Grampa was Grampa and Mr. Costello was Mr. Costello. That's the only way I can explain it.

Mr. Costello considered, then nodded his agreement. "Hm. That sounds likely. Is there a way to slow them down?"

Grampa frowned in thought. "Now, that depends on what you want to do. I don't mind horgs eatin' each other if it thins the herd a bit. But it sounds to me like you want to feed 'em without getting 'em all worked up and agitated, right? You don't want 'em killin' each other."

"We can't sell horgs we don't have, can we?"

"Nope," agreed Grampa.

And that's how it went for a while. Back and forth, back and forth, with neither one ever quite saying anything in the clear.

Finally, Finn spoke up again—I could tell he was getting frustrated. It's bad enough having to deal with Grampa's roundabout talk, but having to listen to the pair of them dancing around the subject like they didn't know what they wanted, or more like whoever said it first would have to pay extra for the privilege of saying it first—Finn was exasperated.

"Listen," he said. "We'll send a few bots up into the trees, have 'em bring down some branches. We'll put 'em through the shredders and mix 'em into the pods. It'll mean they have to do a lot more chewing. And instead of putting it all in one big pile, we'll spread it out in a lot of little piles all over the feeding floor. We could try that."

Mr. Costello looked to Grampa. Grampa looked to Mr. Costello. They both were nodding thoughtfully, each waiting for the other to say, Let's do it.

Finn didn't wait. He turned to Lazz. "Unpack the lumberjack gear. Use bots four and six, they'll have enough capacity. Number seven can do the shredding." Some people named their bots, Finn didn't. He insisted that people are people, machines are machines—mixing them up gets dangerous. I had to agree with that. I'd seen what happens when people forgot. Or worse, when machines forgot.

Finn and Lazz talked for a bit about what kind of branches to cut down and how many and where. The rule was not to take from more than one tree per acre and never more than one of a kind, unless it was a monoculture. There was still too much we didn't know about Haven's ecology—all the different ways that all the different plants and animals interacted. Based on the evidence of history, both here and elsewhere, even stepping on a butterfly could have unintended consequences.

By the time that conversation finished, Mr. Costello's people had adjusted their plan as well. Jerrid was directing his construction bots to put up two more towers, these at the two remaining corners of the feeding floor.

"Yes, that's a very good idea," said Mr. Costello. He turned to us. "You'll have more cameras now with different angles on the creatures as they feed, so you'll get better information on their behavior. That should be very useful." Back to his own people. "Thank you, Jerrid. Thank you, Mikla. How long do you think all this will take?"

I spent the next part of the day with Charlie, bringing the family's finances up to date. Mostly, I handled the day-to-day stuff, paying bills, allocating shares, ordering necessities, coordinating deliveries—if something was urgent, we'd send out a drone to pick stuff up from Settlement or Temporary, if the weather permitted flight—otherwise we'd let the goods arrive on the Monthly. Eventually, Charlie would entrust me with access to the investment portfolios. I hadn't been married in long enough to qualify for a permanent share, but another year or two, the others would vote. If they didn't grant permanence, it would be a gentle way of saying, You are free to leave whenever you want."

I wasn't worrying about it now. I'd learned that it's more important to focus on what you can give than what you're going to get. That works in finance almost as well as it does in bed. And that was another conversation I wanted to have with Finn—

By the end of the day, the two new pylons had been set and hardened, and the bots were more than half-done pre-chewing the night's meal for the horgs. This time, we'd be putting out only fifty kilos of pods and a hundred and fifty kilos of shredded bark and leaves. Lazz had selected six small trees across the edges of the forest—one anchorwood, two redbarks, a whitemarch, a wailing willow, and a bower-tree. After taking a few branches from each, he'd scattered fresh seeds in fertilizer pods to apologize for the assault. Forest horgs were known to chew into all of these species during the barest periods of winter, but most of the rest of the year they ignored them, so we knew the chaff would be edible without being overstimulating.

Because of the day's efforts, dinner was flashed from the freezer. Charlie baked fresh bread and Lazz whomped up some of his best tomato-gravy and we washed the whole thing down with Grampa's special beer, which was only special because he said so. It had the same familiar honeyed overtaste as everyone else's special brew.

That night's video revealed a scattering of horgs feeding placidly. Not a whole herd, but enough to justify the effort. Maybe two dozen. The important thing, no fights broke out, although the monitors reported that the animals were experiencing more irritability than we would have liked. Lazz and Charlie decided to reduce the proportion of glitter-bush pods even more for the next day's feed.

After second breakfast, we met again with Mr. Costello. While he didn't express any disappointment—on the contrary, he remained delighted with the progress we were making—he did wonder aloud that the horgs were finishing the feed too quickly, leaving nothing to attract the rest of the herd. Eventually, Finn realized he was asking us to put out more food to attract more horgs. But it was our idea, of course. We had enough chaff to handle tonight's feed, but we'd need a lot more for the days to come.

Lazz and Charlie took one of the trucks north to select more trees. They planned to hit several different groves and would be gone all day, perhaps even two days. Mr. Costello asked why they couldn't just take whole trees from the nearby slopes and they had to explain to him that the tree roots held the soil in place. If they deforested a slope, the winter storms would wash the entire hill down into the valley below. Aside from the inconvenience that might represent to those of us who lived in the area, it could also change the migratory patterns of various small herds—and nobody would appreciate having horgs wandering through their fields. Most settlers had chosen their sites specifically to stay away from the migration routes.

Marlie and Trina put out the evening feed for the horgs, spreading it thin and wide. That took a few hours, more time than anyone expected, so the rest of us made do with sandwiches and coffee. It was a long night. Because Charlie was gone, I handled the day's journal-keeping. Not just the personal stats and billables, but the log as well. We logged everything. The family journal was a way of not having to depend on anyone's memory. The notes we were making about horg behavior would be very valuable—not just for us, but for anyone else who wanted to download the public half of our records. We didn't make a lot of local money from our logs, but we had a sizable offworld audience and the royalties did add up over time. Grampa wouldn't let us spend any royalties unless it was an emergency—that money always got folded back into the portfolio. The job was to be self-sufficient on what we could make from the land. I had a thought we might be worth a lot more than Grampa ever let on, but I had no right to ask. Not yet.

We were reviewing the videos even before first breakfast now, gathering around the displays with coffee and fresh donuts to watch an accelerated record, only slowing down to real time if something interesting or unusual popped up on any of the screens. Today we were seeing a much bigger gathering of horgs. At any given time, there were thirty-some animals on the stage, but the total was greater than that—at least a dozen moewsnuffled cautiously around the edges. Not the hundreds Mr. Costello had promised, but certainly enough to demonstrate that he could attract a crowd.

Too much of a crowd, actually. Horgs are always hungry. After cleaning the floor of the feeding deck, they started snuffling up the slope toward the trucks. While it was unlikely that any of the animals would attack the vehicles, they could still do considerable damage. They could knock a vehicle on its side and rip out the undercarriage, just out of pure horgish malevolence. There was a lot of history—with pictures suitable for Goblin Night. Also known as Gobblin' Night, when all the mini-horgs swarmed. We usually had two or three days' warning, enough time to get home, lock all the doors and windows, and hide under the blankets.

But right now we had curious horgs wandering up the slopes. Not far enough—not yet, not last night—but tonight? Maybe. And the next night—certainly. Hungry horgs search and scavenge. Wake up a horg's appetite and you're asking for trouble. Something else Mr. Costello didn't know.

We had an emergency meeting on his deck. He served iced tea and English biscuits. "Oh my, yes, the video was very disturbing. It's a good thing the video cameras have a three-hundred-sixty-degree view or we'd have never known the creatures were wandering up the slope. Thank you, Jerrid, for your wonderful cameras." He looked to Grampa. "Will we have to stop feeding them now?"

Grampa didn't bother with his pipe today. He said, "It won't do any good. Three nights now you've been laying out glitter-pods. Even if the place didn't already reek with the scent of the crushed leaves, they'll still be coming back. Looking for more. They ain't stupid. You train 'em to come for food, they'll come."

"Well . . ." said Mr. Costello. "Well, well, well. This will be a challenge. Perhaps there's some way to keep the horgs from wandering off the feeding floor, some way to keep them from wandering up the hill, some way to keep them where they are and away from the trucks."

"We could put a fence up," said Finn.

"Do you think that would work?" Mr. Costello's face lit up.

Finn was thinking it over. "We could carve out a berm. I suppose we could have a 'dozer lifted out. It'd be expensive, though. And I'm not sure it would stop 'em. If a horg is determined to go over something, he goes over it. If he wants to go through it, he goes through it. Those paddle-feet, they have claws as long as your forearm—they're good for slashing open each other's bellies, but they're also for digging into the ground, especially frozen ground—that's how the horgs survive the outer-winters. They dig into huge communal burrows. You know those holes you saw from space, the ones that looked like craters? Horg-nests."

Mr. Costello listened patiently to Finn's monolog, then turned to Jerrid. "I think you packed something that might work—"

Jerrid nodded. "We have twenty bolts of carbon monofilament, triple-knit—" He looked to Finn. "It's very lightweight and essentially unbreakable. We can spray it with shelterfoam and it'll harden nicely." He pointed at the silk-looking hangings that sheltered Mr. Costello's deck. "I brought plenty, in case we needed to build a tented enclosure—"

"Ahh," said Finn. He looked down the slope. "I see . . . we stretch a length of it between the first two towers, from one to the other and back again, then spray it to harden it, and we create a visual barrier between the feeding deck and the slope."

"That's a marvelous idea!" Mr. Costello clapped his hands in glee.

Jerrid looked to Finn. "You know horgs. Will it work?"

"Only one way to find out."

Before the sun hit zenith, Jerrid's bots were stringing the first lengths of triple-knit. By the time siesta was over, they were already prepping the shelterfoam tanks. We watched them from the deck while we ate second lunch. "That's gonna be a tall wall," said Grampa.

Finn said, "It's a visual cliff. It should keep them focused on the food instead of the hill."

Grampa puffed his pipe. "If nothin' else, Mr. Costello has proven that you can train a horg to eat. Whether or not he can train 'em to butcher themselves, that'll be a whole other thing, won't it?"

Charlie and Lazz arrived late in the day with three huge trailers of wood for the shredders. They'd circled through six forests, taking branches from the outliers and the rogues. They'd left the mother-trees alone. No sense pissing off the woodlands. The trees on Haven could be friendly—or they could make life hell for you. As soon as a forest felt alarm, the surrounding trees would start releasing threat-pheromones. That would attract huge swarms of things that bite. It would also encourage local bugs and birds, lizards, and slugs to transform into their more hostile forms. An angry forest was no place for any creature not part of the rage. And if the forest got angry enough, all those different swarms would go into a feeding frenzy. Even the horgs wouldn't be safe—that's how the forests protected themselves from aggressive herds. Checks and balances everywhere. Don't push the on-button if you don't know where the off-button is.

All of us worked late into the evening, shredding wood, mixing in glitter-pods, and spreading small piles of feed across the polycrete. Well, the bots actually did the work, but we stayed up to supervise. It was a big job and we couldn't risk a bug in our programming.

The horgs were already gathering downslope even before the last bot trotted out of the way. They snuffled and grunted, annoyed but curious. They approached cautiously. Horgs are suspicious by nature. The lights, the wall, the piles of feed—that was alien to their experience. But on the other hand, a free meal is a free meal.

Finn wasn't certain that a single fence would deter the horgs, so he stayed up late to keep watch. He armed two bots with pepper spray and positioned them at the top of the slope. But most of the horgs were too interested in dinner to be concerned. A couple sniffed around the edges of the fence, looking to see if there was food beyond, but Finn had sprayed the perimeter upslope of the fence, and that appeared to be enough to deter further exploration.

By the time the rest of us woke up for mid-meal, Finn was ready to crash. Trina volunteered to take over the rest of the watch, and after updating the logs, I went back to our compartment in the second truck, expecting to find Finn snoring like a jelly-badger. Instead, he was awake and waiting for me.

"I haven't showered," I protested.

"No problem. I'll shower with you. We'll save water."

There's only one way to win an argument with Finn. You wrap yourself up in his arms and say, "Yes, honey, you're right." So I did. And we did. And then we did it again, just to make sure.

And finally, afterward, with me lying on top of his big broad chest, feeling very satisfied and very comfortable, I said, "Aren't you sleepy yet?"

"I took a wide-awake."

"Why?"

"Why not?"

"Not good enough. Why'd you stay up?" I repeated.

"For you," he said, stroking my back. "For us. For this. I don't want us to get so busy we forget to be us. What about you? Are you tired?"

"I'll stay up with you. For as long as I can."

He stroked my brush cut. "I miss your hair."

"You liked it long?"

"Very much."

"You never said. All right. I'll let it grow out." I kissed his left nipple. Then the right one, so it wouldn't feel neglected.

He knew me too well. "You don't like having your hair long?"

"It's extra work, especially if I color-glow."

"You don't have to do it for me."

"If it makes you happy—"

"Will it make *you* happy?" Even in the dark, I could see the intensity of his expression.

"Making you happy makes me happy."

"I can see I'm not going to win this argument—"

"Oh? Are we having an argument? Wait. I'll get my flak jacket and helmet. No kissing below the belt—"

He pulled me back down on top of him. "You do whatever you want." He held me there for a long time, making that purring noise in his chest that attracted me to him in the first place. He never told me how he did it and I suspected an augment he wasn't telling me about.

Finally, I lifted up, I straddled him, and looked down. "I do have to ask you something?"

"Uh-oh, I know that tone."

"No." I slapped his chest playfully. "This is serious."

"What?"

"Would you like me to change back? Do you like me better as a boy or a girl?"

"I like you in my bed. Isn't that enough?"

"No. It isn't. I want to be the best you ever had. I want us to be perfect. I'm—" I looked at the ceiling but the answer wasn't there, either, so I looked back to him and admitted, "It's what you said. I don't want us to stop being us."

He sighed. Not quite exasperated. Not yet. But I knew that sigh. "Aren't you happy?" he said.

"I'm the happiest I've ever been in my life—"

"Then why are you worrying about the plumbing?"

"Because I want to make you as happy as I am—"

"You've already done that." He said, "If you want to change, then change. If you don't, then don't. Whichever, I'll still find a way to make you scream loud enough to wake up Grampa." Abruptly, he stopped and stared up at me. "Wait—are you asking me if I want to change?"

"Huh? No. I just—" My turn to stop and stare. "Do you want to change?"

"I wasn't thinking about it. At least, not until now. Would that make you happy?"

I collapsed onto his chest, playfully frustrated. "Oh, great—I had to ask. Now we're going to have gender confusion every time we get in bed. Finn, my sweetheart, my playmate, my lover, I am fine if you're fine. I only asked because if it was something you wanted, it would be all right with me. Whatever—"

He kissed me lightly on the top of my head. "You can stop now. I'm fine. You're fine. We're fine. If you want to change, do it for you, I'll still be fine. If you would like me to change, that might be fun, too. But for now, right now, with all this other business going on, let's just take things one day at a time—okay?"

And that's how that part of the conversation ended. The kissing part went on for a lot longer. And somewhere after that, I fell asleep in Finn's arms, which was always my favorite place to fall asleep. My ears turned off as I cycled down and Finn could snore like a horg all night long if he wanted.

After first breakfast, Mr. Costello and his folks wandered over for a meeting. Nothing important, just an affirmation that everything looked like it was working out well. He agreed that we should continue feeding the horgs. The rest of the herd seemed to be gravitating this way. Perhaps within another few days we might see as many as a hundred or two hundred animals feeding each night. Perhaps we should increase the amount of feed we were putting out.

Somehow, the way he talked about things, the way he drew us into the discussion, it always felt like we were creating the plan, not him. But that was good—it gave us ownership. It put the responsibility on us to make things work. You couldn't fault him for that.

Afterward, once that was settled, he sat down with me and Charlie and Finn and Grampa. "Jerrid has been working on something else. Mikla, too. They're both so very smart about these things."

We listened while he meandered his way toward the punch line.

"Y'see, this whole enterprise has to be a partnership, a team effort, don't you agree?"

We nodded politely, already wondering where this was leading.

"And from time to time, we have to acknowledge that there are skills we need to add to the team. Jerrid pointed this out. Mikla, too. We've succeeded so well already. We've proven that we can direct the attention of a herd of horgs."

"We can feed 'em, yes," said Finn. He did not say what his tone suggested he was thinking: *Any idjit can do that.*

"If I might interrupt," Mikla said politely. "We need to prepare for the next phase of the operation, which is to set up a processing plant for the horg meat."

"Ah," said Finn.

"We'll need to bring in processing equipment, extra bots, and a team of operators."

"Of course."

"And that means expanding our partnership."

"I see . . ." Finn said. He didn't. Neither did the rest of us.

"It doesn't affect our contracts with you, of course. You're already locked in as a supplier."

Jerrid spoke up then. "Mr. Costello has negotiated contracts with several other families, all of whom are ready to provide services for processing, packing, shipping, and so on."

"That's a good idea," said Grampa, nodding. "It's convenient. And it's good for the local economy."

Mikla said, "However . . . the larger the team gets, the more complicated all of the interrelated accounting becomes. So—" Mikla looked to Jerrid.

Jerrid said, "We'd like to streamline the financial channels. We already have a private web, to which our new partners will be added as they come aboard, of course. We'd like to use it as our primary financial network as well."

Finn looked to Grampa. I looked to Charlie. We all looked to each other. The question didn't have to be asked, but I did anyway. "Why is that necessary?"

"Well, for one thing," Mikla said, "secrecy. Just as we're keeping our business chatter isolated, we think we should take the same precautions with our financial transactions as well. If money is moving around, other people can use that information, possibly to our disadvantage."

"That kinda makes sense," said Charlie.

"I always thought our existing networks were secure," said Finn.

"For most things, they are," said Jerrid. "But it only takes one leak to sink a ship."

Mr. Costello spoke up then. He had been looking from one to the other of us, especially Mikla and Jerrid, with a happy expression on his face. Now he said, "Don't you think with this much money at stake, we should take every precaution possible to protect all of our interests?"

Grampa nodded. Despite the half-scowl on his face, he nodded.

"Wonderful, wonderful. I'm glad you agree. Mikla will set up accounts for all of you today. We'll run our own private bank—with secured deposits for all pending contracts held in an independent escrow."

"A local escrow, please," said Finn.

"Of course, of course. We have to make sure that everybody is well taken care of or this won't work. Not at all. Not at all."

After they left, we all looked at each other. "Well," said Charlie, "it does make sense."

Finn snorted. Grampa puffed furiously on his pipe. I said nothing. Finally, Grampa took his pipe out of his mouth and said, "Used to be, a man's handshake was enough. All these secrets—it makes a man wonder." He put his pipe back in his mouth and resumed wondering.

I said, "The way I heard it, a contract is a list of all the ways two people don't trust each other."

Finn smiled. "That sounds about right. If Mr. Costello doesn't think other people can be trusted, maybe it's because he knows he can't."

Charlie said, "I've been studying all these protocols, all the riders, all the guarantees. A lot of it is boilerplate, but I don't see anything dangerous here. I'm not getting any red flags."

Lazz hardly ever spoke. He was the quiet one, but now he said what we were all thinking. "It's just not the way we're used to doin' business."

"He's an offworlder," said Charlie. "Maybe he doesn't know any better. Maybe he's been burned before—maybe he's learned he needs strong fences to keep horgs out of his fields."

"That's probably it," said Finn. "Still, it makes the back of my neck itch."

"I think we're all a little uneasy here," Marlie said. "Perhaps it's just having so many horgs sniffing around—one wrong smell and we could have a stampede or a frenzy."

"Yep," said Finn. "I think I'll spray around the trucks again tonight. All of 'em. Might want to make sure the windows and vents are sealed, too."

The next few days, we fell into an easy routine—easy only because we were still waiting. Mr. Costello hadn't said anything about how we were going to get the horgs into the processing plant. But each night, the crowd of horgs gathering to gorge themselves continued to grow. Trina and Marlie went off to gather more wood. This time they went southeast so as not to assault the same forests as Charlie and Lazz had visited.

By the time they got back, we were seeing 70 or 80 horgs coming out of the trees each night. They jostled past each other with the usual snuffling and grumping, occasionally giving deep warning rumbles as they milled about, but by now there was a real order to the process. The largest of the animals approached first. They sniffed around, inspecting the various piles of wood chips and seedpods on the feeding deck. When they were finally satisfied—a process that usually involved selecting the largest piles for themselves—they grunted their approval. The others then followed and feeding began.

The next day, the first trucks from Settlement arrived. We knew the Hellisons, we recognized the Herkles—they were an all-male family, except when they needed to make a baby—but we didn't know the Maetlins except by reputation. They were big and brawny, the family you called in when you meant business. We had a little meet-and-greet when they arrived, but they were impatient to set up their camp and went straight to work.

I suppose I should mention that a lot of families go unigender except when it's baby-making time. I can see the logic of it, it makes for a different kind of emotional stability when you don't have all those unaligned hormonal and emotional cycles in conflict, never really achieving stability, all the different relationships having to be constantly refreshed. But I can argue the other side of it, too—high-maintenance has its virtues. It demands continual reinvention.

But even as I chugged along on that train of thought, I realized what was happening to me—I was assimilating my rejuve. My past was starting to assert itself again and my old ways of thinking and being were coming back. I'd have to watch myself now. I'd have to spend some time apart, so I found a place on the slope that was off the main paths, where I could sit and watch. That was probably a bad idea, too—but I could lose myself in the watching.

The Maetlins started by leveling an area at least as big as the feeding platform, just on the other side of the first wall. They staked it out and raised two conjoined inflatables, giving themselves a good-sized warehouse right next to the feeding floor. Shelterfoam followed, then airlocks and vents. No windows. Even before it hardened, they started off-loading various ominous-looking pieces of machinery. Too many blades and hooks for my liking. They said it would take at least a week to assemble the line.

While they did that, we prepared the biggest pot of Shit Storm we'd ever cooked. The whole family worked on it, cutting vegetables, tasting, adding spices, scrounging ingredients. Everybody contributed. The Hellisons had a half-finished kettle of turkey. The Herkles carved a big chunk of beef from the shoulder they were growing in one of their meat tanks, the Maetlins gave us a fresh spice rack, and we turned the gathering Storm into Last Chance Chili.

After we ate, the newcomers finally asked to see what we had accomplished. They didn't look impressed, there wasn't much to see—at least not until the horgs arrived.

By now, the assembling crowds of horgs were large enough that as the feeding subsided, many of the animals were still hungry, so they started searching beyond the feeding deck. Occasionally, several ventured around the edges of the fence and stared uphill, growling. A couple of sniffs of the ground, however, and the blistering stink of Finn's pepper spray was usually enough to dissuade them, but it always made for an uneasy few moments.

On the third day of that behavior, we met again with Mr. Costello. The short version—it was agreed to put up another fence, this time between posts two and three. The horgs hadn't minded the first fence, they probably wouldn't mind the second. We'd find out soon enough.

That night, most of us stayed up late to watch the monitors. The horgs arrived as usual but didn't immediately rush to the feeding platform. The three largest snuffled forward and sniffed the new fence, then after they satisfied themselves that it was not a threat they turned their attention to the piles of glitter-pods and wood chips. At the first satisfied grunt, the other animals trundled forward. We all breathed a sigh of relief.

But the pack was larger than ever, and Finn said, "We might have to put up a third fence soon. Look at the size of that pack—they'll wander off the edges of the platform unless we can contain them."

And as he said that, I realized exactly how Mr. Costello planned to conquer the herd. But I didn't say anything. Not then. Not so anyone else could hear.

Besides—

There was something else I didn't want to tell him. And that was more important. I knew the red-haired Herkle twins. I'd met them the week I arrived on Haven. The Herkles were one of the families I'd applied to. The Herkle boys had bedded me—but no invitation had followed. I felt used. I never shared that with anyone, not even Finn.

But in all the hustle and bustle of everyone settling in, meeting and greeting, sorting things out, sharing news and gossip, trading tools and whatever, the Herkle boys had somehow tracked me to the south end of the slope.

One of the parts of our contract with Mr. Costello—we got first dibs on the dung. Glitter-bush seeds need to pass through a horg's gut to germinate. All that dung—there should be enough fertile seeds to start three, maybe four new meadowlands. This was a side benefit that Grampa had smartly added to our arrangement with Mr. Costello and Mr. Costello had agreed without argument. Either he didn't understand or he didn't care. Whatever, this was the real reason Grampa had so readily accepted Mr. Costello's initial proposal.

See, you could follow the herds and hope to gather dung from areas rich in glitter-bushes. Or you could put out piles of feed near the herds and hope you collected the right dung. Or you could hope that a few passing animals would drop by and eat just enough pods from your crop to give you enough fertile seeds for the next season. More than that, if you had extra seeds that had been fertilized, you could sell or trade them anywhere.

Yeah, there are artificial ways to force a seed to germinate, I guess, but most folks around here don't think much of lab-germinated. General opinion holds that lab crops are missing something, they're stunted and flavorless. Mebbe good for industrial use, mebbe good for animal feed, but not exactly a quality product. If anybody has done a real study, I haven't seen the report, and I haven't seen any lab crops myself, so I have to take Grampa's word for it.

Anyway, I went down to the south end, where three of the agri-bots were picking up the dung balls, weighing them, scanning them, and measuring the various compositions—this was all useful information about the health of the herd—and if there were any fertile seeds inside, they'd toss the dung ball into a hopper. The useless dung balls were shredded and spread, which would make it easier for the various soil bugs to go to work faster. The bots could have done the job without me—or I could have monitored their progress from the truck, but I was tired of the truck, I was tired of Mr. Costello, I wanted to get away—and I wanted to see how this worked first hand. I didn't want to watch screens all the time.

It was a mistake—one I quickly realized. The stink on this field was bad, terrible, even under the hood I wore. But I was too proud to turn around and march back up the hill, so I followed the bots and tried to figure out how they could tell which dung balls were good and which were not. I was beginning to sense that size had something to do with it when the Herkle twins showed up.

Kind of surprising that they found me. I hadn't gone looking for them. If anything, I'd been avoiding them, deliberately moving to the opposite side of whatever assembly they joined. So I figured they had to be tracking me specifically, and this meeting wasn't an accident.

I was right.

I never could tell the difference between Dane and Dyne, even when they wore dissimilar earrings, even when they wore different hairstyles and hair colors. I always just called them Herkle. It didn't matter, either would answer.

I didn't want to talk through the hood and I certainly wasn't going to have this conversation on any channel, wireless or otherwise. I'd learned the hard way about people listening in. Actually, I was in no mood to talk to them at all, so I marched up the hill away from them.

They didn't take the hint. They followed me across the polycrete—which was starting to show some serious cracking from the pounding weight of the horgs—and up into the corner of the fences, out of anyone's line of sight, before I pulled off my hood and turned around, annoyed. "What do you want?"

Both of them flashed dazzling grins. The one on the left said, "We kinda feel bad you didn't join our family."

"I never got an invitation."

They looked confused. "But we sent you one."

"No. You didn't."

"Yes, we did."

"I never got it."

They looked at each other, even more confused. "Well, uh, okay. There must have been some mix-up. But the invitation is still there, still open. Any time you want to be a Herkle—"

I didn't have a bad opinion of the Herkles. They were mostly a good family. They kept their word, they paid their bills on time, and they were always there for anyone in need. I just didn't have a good feeling about the twins. They acted like you weren't allowed to say no to them, and if you did, they couldn't understand why you'd said it. They weren't bad in bed, though, I couldn't say it wouldn't be fun. And one thing was well known: the Herkles ate good.

I stood there, looking back and forth between them, trying to figure out what they really wanted—and at the same time listing in my mind all the reasons I should slap their faces and walk away.

I'd already earned some credential in Grampa's family. And whatever happened with Mr. Costello, I could see that we were still going to do very well off this exercise. And I was happy in Finn's bed. So the only advantage in going to the Herkle twins' bed would be . . . what? I'd be just another toy they shared. I'd be back to zero seniority and there were over a dozen invested members in the Herkle brood, so my cut would be proportionally smaller. They were a rich family, but not so rich as to make the offer dazzling.

So . . . why the invitation? Why now?

Apparently I was taking too long. The one on the right said, "We like having you between us. Even if you don't want to take up our invitation now . . . well, we have an empty cabin in truck three. If you want to visit tonight, we could have some fun."

Well, that was blatant. I said, "Sorry. I'm married."

"So are we."

"Not to me." And I strode away, feeling confused, frustrated, angry—and a little horny. Because, dammit, those two were gorgeous, exciting, and energetic. Also spoiled rotten.

The only thing I could figure—they wanted to pump me. For information, too. Only there probably wasn't anything I could tell them that Mr. Costello hadn't already.

I didn't know if I should tell Finn about it. I didn't want to upset him. I certainly didn't want him to get angry. We didn't need a fight with another family, especially not here, not now. I took a long hot shower, put on the blue dress that Finn had bought—the one he'd said we'd take turns wearing, this was the first time either of us had put it on—and went in to help with dinner. Trina noticed the dress but said nothing. Neither did anyone else. I guess they figured this was between Finn and me.

But during Circle, Grampa looked across to me and said, "You wanna dump it? Or you wanna let it fester?"

I started crying. I didn't know why. It was everything and nothing. It was silly and I felt stupid. I thought—after all the stuff I'd been through before getting to Haven—that I'd hardened myself. Now I realized the only person I'd been fooling was me.

Next thing I knew, Finn picked me up and carried me back to our cabin. The door slid shut behind us and he put me gently down on the bed. He didn't say anything, just popped open a water bottle and handed it to me. He sat down opposite and waited, a concerned look on his face—not judging, just ready to listen.

"I'm not a good person, Finn. I don't know why you took me into your family, but you're the best people I've ever known and I'm grateful for the little bit of time I've had here. You should probably invite me out now, before I hurt you."

"You can't hurt us," he said. "No, that's not true. The only way you could hurt any of us would be by leaving. We love you. We care about you. Whatever it is, we have your back."

"Yes, that's the right thing to say. You always know the right thing to say, but you don't know who I really am—"

"Yes, I do—"

"I've been lying to you. Lying to the whole family."

"Sweetheart, stop it. Just stop." He tilted my head up and looked me in the eyes. "You haven't been lying. You've just been afraid. With good reason. We know your real age, we know about the rejuve, we know how old you really are. We don't care. We know what you did on Flatland, we know what you did on Myrva, we know who you were on Borran. We've known all along. We don't care. We know who you are on Haven. That's the only thing we care about."

"You've known—?"

"We figured you'd tell us when you were ready. And if you never told us, well— that would be fine, too. We've all done things—"

"I killed people, Finn. I was—"

"Stop." He put a finger across my lips. "Are you planning to kill anyone today?"

"No. No, of course not."

"Then it doesn't matter."

"But it does—"

"Another time, another place. You put it behind you. You put everything behind you when you rejuved. You've got the body and the spirit—and the confusion—of a brand-new adolescent. You'll be another ten years growing up again. But here's the thing, sweetheart. It was necessary, it was the right thing to do—it was the only way you could abandon your past. And it's one of the things that convinced us to take you in. Even after the way the Herkles treated you—"

"You know about that?"

"Yes, I do. The Family does. That's one of the reasons we watch out for you so closely—we know how fragile you are. Everybody your age is fragile, even when you're doing it for the second or third time. Because you're so full of life and hope and energy and enthusiasm—it overwhelms all the stuff you thought you knew, all the stuff you thought was worth knowing. You know how you say, 'I wish I'd known this when I was young'? Well, guess what—knowing it doesn't slow down the impulsiveness of the adolescent spirit."

He pulled me into a hug and held me close. "Now have a good cry, as much as you need to—but those had better be tears of happiness." After a bit, after we finished kissing, too, he said, "By the way, I was right. The blue dress really does look good on you."

"I wore it for you."

"I know." He nuzzled my ear. "I knew what it meant. I was glad to see it." He helped me take it off, pulling it up over my head, hanging it carefully on a hook.

"Next time, you wear it," I said.

"Promise," he said.

And then we stopped talking for a while.

Two days later, we put up the third fence. It didn't slow the horgs down. By now, they were so eager to eat they barely noticed it. They had a nice comfortable U-shaped enclosure with the biggest piles of feed located at the back wall of the U.

And it was finally obvious to everyone what the next step would be. Jerrid and Mikla were already prepping it. But right now, we were just waiting to see how many horgs would show up to feed in a night. We were counting as many as ninety.

Our camp was growing. Another dozen trucks arrived and set up shop, three more families to help with the processing, packing, and pickling. While it didn't affect our accounting, I could see that Mr. Costello's bank channels were picking up a lot more traffic.

So at the afternoon meeting, it didn't surprise me that the Herkle twins—probably at Mr. Costello's coaching—stood up and suggested we needed some rules and regulations for our settlement as well as for our business. "Just so we'll all know where we stand. So there won't be any misunderstandings later on."

Mr. Costello smiled and said, "Having rules is a good thing, yes. These boys are very smart, they are."

And because no one wanted to argue with Mr. Costello, the vote was unanimous. A committee was set up to determine appropriate guidelines for establishing property limits—and for personal boundaries, too. That was a week's worth of wrangling, sometimes heated, because there were a lot of people here now, not everybody knew everybody, and different folks kept imagining various ways to get their toes stepped on.

We kept out of most of it. Mostly because Grampa didn't like crowds. Neither did any of the rest of us, but Grampa was worst. He kept to his cabin a lot—enough that we were starting to worry about him. But he showed up for dinner and he was okay during Circle, so as much as we worried, we knew he was staying close and connected.

I was feeling a lot better, too. At midnight meal, I went to each member of the family and just hugged them close. There was nothing that needed to be said, the hug said it all. And they hugged me back and kissed me and told me they were proud of me, and that was the end of it. Grampa was funniest, though. He whispered in my ear, "Next time I rejuve, I'm gonna want you to wear that blue dress for me." And I whispered back, "I promise I will." He didn't flirt with me often, but when he did, it was his way of saying, "You're good with me."

Meanwhile, after laying out the feed, five hundred kilos a night now—and more wood than we felt comfortable shredding—we focused ourselves on gathering as much horg-dung as we could. We had six bots working the downslope and we kept them out there all day and all night, only pulling them back when the horgs were around. We chilled the dung balls as fast as the bots collected them and were close to filling the first trailer. Lazz was already talking about driving it back home to empty it into the main cellar.

The Maetlins had their warehouse lit up all the time now, and one afternoon they invited everyone to walk through the installations to see how the carcasses would be hung and fed into the disassembly line, where all the separate machines would skin, cut, separate, slice, grade, and process the horg meat. They were ready to go, anytime. They just needed a horg-sized tunnel from the feeding pen into the first machine, the killing machine.

And finally, on the last day, a few more trucks arrived—looky-loos and wannabes, curiosity-seekers and even a few tourists—all of whom had heard the gossip about Mr. Costello's marvelous horg-catching operation. They'd all come out to see this idjit get himself good and killed. Tilda Jacklin was running a pool.

Afternoon meeting got a little heated, tho. Finn and Charlie and me always attended. Trina usually stayed home with Grampa. Lazz and Marlie kept busy, monitoring the dung-bots.

This day tho, the Maetlins started talking about offal rights. You cut up a carcass, the intestines—or whatever the horgs use as intestines—spill out. The upper part of the tract is mostly full of undigested food, but the lower part is packed with dung that hasn't been dropped. And a lot of that dung is fertilized seedpods.

By rights, that dung belonged to us, and Charlie stood up to voice our claim. The Maetlins argued otherwise. Their contract gave them rights to all parts of the creature that were not immediately saleable, and that included the undropped dung. We knew they were being paid on a per-carcass basis, plus a percentage of Mr. Costello's sale price, a very fair deal. They were also getting the ingredients for bone meal and various fertilizers, which was their bonus. So Charlie argued that if they took the dung, they were taking part of our bonus. The Maetlins argued back that if the dung wasn't dropped, it was still part of the animal and covered by their contract. Obviously, they knew the value of fertilized seedpods.

We already had enough to corner the market—enough to crash the market if we wanted to—but that wasn't information anyone else knew and we intended to keep it that way. But if the Maetlins got fertilized seedpods from the undropped dung, they'd have enough to be a serious competitor. They could drive the prize down if they wanted to. And they might want to, just because they could. It wouldn't be the first time they'd savaged another family. If they saw an advantage for themselves, they took it. That was their reputation and it was well earned. There were some abandoned farms to testify to that.

So we argued, first Charlie, then Finn. I kept my mouth shut and made notes. It got pretty ferocious there for a bit and I was afraid a fight might break out. We had a hospital truck. The Hellisons managed that. And surveillance, too. But the kind of injuries the Maetlins were capable of inflicting—I put my hand on Finn's forearm and he sat back down.

Harm Maetlin noticed it, and I knew he was about to ask who wore the balls in our family—but Arle Maetlin stepped in front of him. The Maetlins might be feisty but they're not stupid. A fight was the last thing they needed right now.

In fact—just the possibility of a fight sidetracked that meeting, Mr. Costello stood up and said it worried him terribly that we had gotten to such a sad position. Perhaps we needed to consider what kinds of mechanisms should be put in place?

Well, that's how we got a police force. And a judge. And a mechanism to enforce the application of our new settlement's rules and guidelines. It all happened so fast, it would have been head-spinning. Except Mr. Costello just happened to have the boilerplate. Because a good businessman is always prepared. And Mr. Costello was a very good businessman. He didn't say so, he didn't have to, but he'd been planning this from the beginning.

And that's how the settlement got named, too. Costello. Of course. In honor of the man who made it happen.

Mr. Costello accepted the position of mayor. And judge. Of course. And as his first ruling, he cut Solomon's baby in half. We got the offal. The Maetlins got the responsibility of running the police force. They would be paid appropriately for their efforts. The rest of us would be charged a pro-rata user fee for the provision of police salaries, as well as the billables of the judge and mayor, who—because Mr. Costello was so thoughtful and generous—would only be compensated for hours actually served.

That night, while the horgs were feeding, Jerrid and Mikla rolled the last huge section of fence around and slammed it shut with a satisfying clank, penning in a hundred and twenty-three grunting, grumbling mountains of ugly meat. The horgs were so busy scraping the glitter-pods off the deck, they never even noticed.

Almost immediately, the Maetlins started spraying liquid nitrogen into the air above the pen, forming huge clouds of cold steam. A cross-spray of water created flurries of snow, which fell onto the backs of the uneasy creatures like a quiet blizzard. And just as quickly, the horgs started huddling together, their instinctive response to winter.

The monitors showed us that their metabolic processes were slowing, slowing, turning the animals into huge docile lumps. Using nothing more than a bucket of warm glitter-pods, a single man could lead a near-slumbering horg to the receiving gate, through a short tunnel, through the airlocks, and finally into the killing room of the processing plant. Harm Maetlin had the honor of leading the first. The other beasts would follow, one at a time. When the line was fully up to speed, they'd be able to process—kill and butcher—thirty-six horgs a day.

From the hill above, cheers and applause. Mr. Costello had captured a herd. Mr. Costello was going to pack and ship several hundred tons of horg meat. Mr. Costello was going to make us all rich. Mr. Costello, hooray.

Mr. Costello!

I could still hear the clank of that last piece of fence slamming shut. That's when the uncomfortable little itch at the back of my neck became a lot more than an uncomfortable little itch.

We watched for a bit, then walked silently back to our trucks. Nobody said much. We ate in silence. Cold sandwiches. We'd just seen the future of Haven. It wasn't pretty.

The videos of what we'd accomplished at Costello Township were already circulating across the public webs. Within hours, new partnerships, new alliances, new collectives of all kinds would be announced—all with the intention of cashing in. The giant herds would be slaughtered, sacrificed to the greed of little men. They'd be annihilated within a generation and the ecology of Haven would collapse.

It's okay to take one or two. It's not okay to take a thousand or ten thousand. It's not okay to wipe out an apex predator. I stayed up late, running simulations. Without enough mates, the horgs would self-fertilize. Without any parents to feed on them, the mini-horg swarms would run out of control. They'd decimate the countryside, eating everything they could, leaving deserts behind, and wiping out every species that depended on the devastated land. The only good news? They'd wipe out most of the human population, too.

The next morning, we had an emergency meeting with Mr. Costello. Just me and Finn, Charlie and Grampa. We told him about our fears.

Mr. Costello looked sad. Very sad. "Yes, of course. Of course," he said. "You're very smart to share your concerns with me. This is why I'm so glad we're business partners. You're all so intelligent and insightful. So please let me put your minds at ease." He motioned to Mikla, who arrived with two fresh pitchers of lemonade, his signal that this was going to be a long but pleasant meeting.

"From the beginning, I realized that if our techniques worked, they could be copied. So I incorporated a holding company, patented the mechanics of the entire operation, and transferred the patent to the corporation. That corporation will sell licenses, materiel, and equipment to any other prospective horg-trapping collective. They will only be allowed to take a limited number of horgs in any given year. Their license requires them to sell their catch only to licensed shippers, and the corporation takes a percentage from both packagers and shippers. So there will be a limit on the number of beasts killed and the amount of meat shipped. That will also keep the prices high. The enforcement protocols are all in place. For the protection of the species . . . as well as for the protection of the market, nobody will be able to ship a ton of horg-meat off this planet without buying a license from me. Well, from my corporation."

Finn leaned back in his chair. He looked to Grampa. Grampa looked to Charlie. Charlie shook his head.

Mr. Costello sensed our unease. Hell, even a rock would have noticed. "You still look unhappy. Did I do something wrong? How can I make it up to you? You've been paid, haven't you? You even got bonuses. Was it not enough?"

"No, you've been fair," Grampa said. "You kept your word."

Mr. Costello relaxed in his chair.

"But—" Grampa continued. "To be honest, we kinda expected you to get killed. We was even bettin' on how it would happen. You weren't the first idjit to come down here with a brilliant idea. You probably won't be the last. So we never expected you to get this far. But your money was good and what the hell—we went along for the ride."

"So what's the problem?"

"Nothing. Everything."

I raised my hand politely to interrupt. Grampa nodded to me.

I said, "You've changed the world. And I'm not sure—*we're* not sure it's going to be for the better."

Mr. Costello looked honestly confused. "Oh my. Oh dear. Yes. You must think I'm planning to leave and take all my profits with me. Oh, no. No, no, no. We're going to lay tracks and build a railroad from Costello Town to Settlement so we can ship horg-meat all year long. Restless Meadow is perfectly situated to draw horgs off the main migratory track. This will be a permanent base for expansion. We'll have a hospital, a school, a year-round marketplace. Eventually, we'll extend the railroad across the continent and establish Costello Towns on every major migratory track. That's where the other collectives will be allowed to build. Liftcore has already agreed to drop a second beanstalk, and we've got sites picked out for three and four as well. And you'll be senior partners. You'll be among the richest people on Haven. No, please don't thank me—I'm happy to do it. Haven will no longer be a backwater world. Soon it will live up to its name. Millions of people will want to settle here."

Well, you can't argue with good news. And I suppose all that good news should have made us happy, but it didn't. Finn and Grampa headed back to the truck, their footsteps quiet on the new sidewalks the Hellisons had installed.

Charlie shook his head and walked on down to Jacklins' Outpost to see what new goods Tilda had driven in from Temp.

Me? I stood alone, shaking. Trying to figure out what to do next.

Was I the only one who could see it?

Bait and walls. First you put out bait. Something juicy. Then you put up a wall. You put out more bait, you put up another wall. Do it enough, you have a cage. Costello did it to the horgs, he did it to us. Glitter pods. Money. Something juicy. No difference at all. Bait and walls. Money and banks, then courts and police. We all get captured.

Mr. Costello saw me on the sidewalk and invited me to join him for a stroll. Some of the horgs were warming up, getting a little agitated. He wanted my opinion on whether or not they needed to be cooled again.

I didn't know, but what the hell. I followed him.

Yes, the remaining horgs were waking up. Yes, they were getting agitated. I didn't need the monitors to tell me that. They were hungry and annoyed. They'd definitely need to be fed and cooled. Already a few were pushing themselves against the fences, testing their imprisonment.

We climbed up onto the catwalk that overlooked this side of the pen. "Aren't they beautiful?" Mr. Costello said. His smile was broad and beneficent. In the afternoon light, he glowed like a saint.

I had to admit—if you looked at them the right way, horgs could be beautiful.

"Someday . . ." he mused. "Someday, there will be a city here." He turned to me with a serious expression. "Tell me something. Do you think they might put up a statue of me?"

That's when I kicked him into the pen with the horgs.

No one saw. And apparently someone had conveniently turned off the cameras without leaving any prints.

It was time for me to move on, anyway.

Finn caught up with me at Settlement and pulled me out of line for the bus to Beanstalk. "Like hell you will," he said, and wrapped me in his arms.

I didn't argue. He was wearing the blue dress.

AUTHOR'S AFTERWORD

First, let me acknowledge and thank the Theodore Sturgeon Literary Trust for permission to continue the adventures of one of Theodore Sturgeon's most memorable characters. I hope I have done him justice. If you haven't read the story that inspired this, "Mr. Costello, Hero," you should seek it out now. It is a classic. It will stick to the roof of your mind like mental peanut butter.

Now, let me acknowledge the gifts that Ted Sturgeon represented to the community of science fiction authors—and to me as both a writer and a friend.

One night, when a group of us were gathered at a local restaurant, I asked him about style. He generously showed me one of the most marvelous mechanisms for creating voice and style in a story. He called it metric prose, and it's a tool I continue to use today.

There's not enough room to share the details here, but the short version—Ted showed me how it's possible to write with a poetic meter that carries from one sentence to the next to create a specific mood. When you change the meter, it changes the emotional tone of the prose, as if you're moving from silk onto sandpaper (his metaphor). Google Sturgeon's interviews or read James Gunn's writings on Sturgeon for more information.

But the most important lesson I learned from Ted wasn't about writing as much as it was about how to be a human being. I can't sum that up easily, either—the best I can say is that in its expression, you find yourself living at the center of your soul, unafraid and joyous, discovering over and over that the very best stories one can write are about what happens in the space between two human beings.

innumerable glimmering Lights

RICH LARSON

*Here's another story by Rich Larson, whose "Jonas and the Fox" also appears
in this anthology. In this one, he takes us to a strange alien world where a
"space race" of sorts is taking place—except instead of racing to launch rockets into space, they're racing to tunnel through the miles of ice between their
undersea home and the open sky one beleaguered visionary believes must exist far above. . . .*

At the roof of the world, the Drill churned and churned. Four Warm Currents
watched with eyes and mouth, overlaying the engine's silhouette with quicksilver
sketches of sonar. Long, twisting shards of ice bloomed from the metal bit to float
back along the carved tunnel. Workers with skin glowing acid yellow, hazard visibility, jetted out to meet the debris and clear it safely to the sides. Others monitored the
mesh of machinery that turned the bit, smoothing contact points, spinning cogs.
The whole thing was beautiful, efficient, and made Four Warm Currents secrete
anticipation in a flavored cloud.

A sudden needle of sonar, pitched high enough to sting, but not so high that it
couldn't be passed off as accidental. Four Warm Currents knew it was Nine Brittle
Spines before even tasting the name in the water.

"Does it move faster with you staring at it?" Nine Brittle Spines signed, tentacles
languid with humor-not-humor.

"No faster, no slower," Four Warm Currents replied, forcing two tentacles into a
curled smile. "The Drill is as inexorable as our dedication to its task."

"Dedication is admirable, as said the ocean's vast cold to one volcano's spewing
heat." Nine Brittle Spines's pebbly skin illustrated, flashing red for a brief instant before regaining a dark cobalt hue.

"You are still skeptical." Four Warm Currents clenched tight to keep distaste from
inking the space between them. Nine Brittle Spines was a council member, and not
one to risk offending. "But the ice's composition is changing, as I reported. The bit
shears easier with every turn. We're approaching the other side."

"So it thins, and so it will thicken again." Nine Brittle Spines wriggled dismissal.

"The other side is a deep dream, Four Warm Currents. Your machine is approaching more ice."

"The calculations," Four Warm Currents protested. "The sounding. If you would read the theorems—"

Nine Brittle Spines hooked an interrupting tentacle through the thicket of movement. "No need for your indignation. I have no quarrel with the Drill. It's a useful sideshow, after all. It keeps the eyes and mouths of the colony fixated while the council slides its decisions past unhindered."

"If you have no quarrel, then why do you come here?" Four Warm Currents couldn't suck back the words, or the single droplet of ichor that suddenly wobbled into the water between them. It blossomed there into a ghostly black wreath. Four Warm Currents raked a hasty tentacle through to disperse it, but the councillor was already tasting the chemical, slowly, pensively.

"I have no quarrel, Four Warm Currents, but others do." Nine Brittle Spines swirled the bitter emission around one tentacle tip, as if it were a pheromone poem or something else to be savored. Four Warm Currents, mortified, could do nothing but turn an apologetic mottled blue, almost too distracted to process what the councillor signed next.

"While the general opinion is that you have gone mad, and your project is a hilariously inept allocation of time and resources based only on your former contributions, theories do run the full gamut. Some believe the Drill is seeking mineral deposits in the ice. Others believe the Drill will be repurposed as a weapon, to crack through the fortified cities of the vent-dwelling colonies." Nine Brittle Spines shaped a derisive laugh. "And there is even a small but growing tangent who believe in your theorems. Who believe that you are fast approaching the mythic other side, and that our ocean will seep out of the puncture like the viscera from a torn egg, dooming us all."

"The weight of the ocean will hold it where it is," Four Warm Currents signed, a sequence by now rote to the tentacles. "The law of sink and rise is one you've surely studied."

"Once again, my opinion is irrelevant to the matter," Nine Brittle Spines replied. "I am here because this radical tangent is believed to be targeting your project for sabotage. The council wishes to protect its investment." Tentacles pinwheeled in a slight hesitation then: "You yourself may be in danger as well. The council advises you to keep a low profile. Perhaps change your name taste."

"I am not afraid for my life." Four Warm Currents signed it firmly and honestly. The project was more important than survival. More important than anything.

"Then fear, perhaps, for your mate's children."

Four Warm Currents flashed hot orange shock, bright enough for the foreman to glance over, concerned. "What?"

Nine Brittle Spines held up the tentacle tip that had tasted Four Warm Currents's anger. "Traces of ingested birth mucus. Elevated hormones. You should demonstrate more self-control, Four Warm Currents. You give away all sorts of secrets."

The councillor gave a lazy salute, then jetted off into the gloom, joined at a distance by two bodyguards with barbed tentacles. Four Warm Currents watched them vanish down the tunnel, then slowly turned back toward the Drill. The bit churned and churned. Four Warm Currents's mind churned with it.

When the work cycle closed, the Drill was tugged back down the tunnel and tethered in a hard shell still fresh enough to glisten. A corkscrewing skiff arrived to unload the guard detail, three young bloods with enough hormone-stoked muscle to overlook the still-transparent patches on their skin. They inked their names so loudly Four Warm Currents could taste them before even jetting over.

"There's been a threat of sorts," Four Warm Currents signed, secreting a small dark privacy cloud to shade the conversation from workers filing onto the now-empty skiff. "Against the project. Radicals who may attempt sabotage."

"We know," signed the guard, whose name was a pungent Two Sinking Corpses. "The councillor told us. That's why we have these." Two Sinking Corpses hefted a conical weapon Four Warm Currents dimly recognized as a screamer, built to amplify a sonar burst to lethal strength. Nine Brittle Spines had not exaggerated the seriousness of the situation.

"Pray to the Leviathans you don't have to use them," Four Warm Currents signed, then joined the workers embarking on the skiff, tasting familiar names, slinging tentacles over knotted muscles, adding to a multilayered scent joke involving an aging councillor and a frost shark. Spirits were high. The Drill was cutting smoothly. They were approaching the other side, and though for some that only meant the end of contract and full payment, others had also been infected by Four Warm Currents's fervor.

"What will we see?" a worker signed. "Souls of the dead? The Leviathans themselves?"

"Nothing outside the physical laws," Four Warm Currents replied, but then, sensing the disappointment: "But nothing like we have ever seen before. It will be unimaginable. Wondrous. And they'll soak our names all through the memory sponges, to remember the brave explorers who first broke the ice."

A mass of tentacles waved in approval of the idea. Four Warm Currents settled back as the skiff began to move and a wave of new debates sprang up.

The City of Bone was roughly spherical, a beautiful lattice of ancient skeleton swathed in sponge and cultivated coral, glowing ethereal blue with bioluminescence. It was older than any councillor, a relic of the dim past before the archives: a Leviathan skeleton dredged from the seafloor with buoyant coral, built up and around until it could float unsupported, tethered in place above the jagged rock bed.

Devotees believed the Leviathans had sacrificed their corporeal forms to leave city husks behind; Four Warm Currents shared the more heretical view that the Leviathans were extinct, and for all their size might have been no more intelligent than the living algae feeders that still hauled their bulk along the seafloor. It was not a theory to divulge in polite discourse. Drilling through the roof of the world was agitator enough on its own.

As the skiff passed the City of Bone's carved sentinels, workers began to jet off to their respective housing blocks. Four Warm Currents was one of the last to disembark, having been afforded, as one of the council's foremost engineers, an artful gray-and-purple spire in the city center. Of course, that was before the Drill. Nine Brittle Spines's desire for a "sideshow" aside, Four Warm Currents felt the daily loss of council approval like the descending cold of a crevice. Relocation was not out of the realm of possibility.

For now, though, the house's main door shuttered open at a touch, and, more importantly, Four Warm Currents's mates were inside. Six Bubbling Thermals, sleek and swollen with eggs, drizzling ribbons of birth mucus like a halo, but with eyes still bright and darting. Three Jagged Reefs, lean and long, skin stained from a heavy work cycle in the smelting vents, submitting to a massage. Their taste made Four Warm Currents ache, deep and deeper.

"So our heroic third returns," Six Bubbling Thermals signed, interrupting the massage and prompting a ruffle of protest.

"Have you ended the world yet?" Three Jagged Reefs added. "Don't stop, Six. I'm nearly loose enough to slough."

"Nearly," Four Warm Currents signed. "I blacked a councillor. Badly."

Both mates guffawed, though Six Bubbling Thermals's had a nervous shiver to it. "From how far?" Three Jagged Reefs demanded. "Could they tell it was yours?"

"From not even a tentacle away," Four Warm Currents admitted. "We were in conversation."

Three Jagged Reefs laughed again, the reckless, waving laugh that had made Four Warm Currents fall in love, but their other mate did not.

"Conversation about what?" Six Bubbling Thermals signed.

Four Warm Currents hesitated, tasting around to make sure a strong emotion hadn't slipped the gland again, but the water was clear and cold and anxiety-free. "Nine Brittle Spines is a skeptic of the worst kind. Intelligent, but refusing to self-educate."

"Did you not explain the density calculation?" Three Jagged Reefs signed plaintively.

Four Warm Currents moved to reply, then recognized a familiar mocking tilt in Three Jagged Reefs's tentacles and turned the answer into a crude "floating feces" gesticulation.

"Tell us the mathematics again," Three Jagged Reefs teased. "Nothing slicks me better for sex, Four. All those beautiful variables."

Six Bubbling Thermals smiled at the back-and-forth, but was still lightly spackled with mauve worry. The birth mucus spiralling out in all directions made for an easy distraction.

"We need to collect again," Four Warm Currents signed, gesturing to the trembling ribbons. "Or you'll bury us in our sleep."

"And then I'll finally have the house all to my own," Six Bubbling Thermals signed, cloying. But the mauve worry dissolved into flushed healthy pink as they all began coiling the mucus and storing it in coral tubing. Four Warm Currents stroked the egg sacs gently as they worked, imagining each one hatching into an altered world.

After they finished with the birth mucus and pricked themselves with a recreational skimmer venom, Three Jagged Reefs made them sample a truly terrible pheromone poem composed at the smelting vents between geysers. The recitation was quickly cancelled in favor of hallucination-laced sex in which they all slid over and around Six Bubbling Thermals's swollen mantle, probing and pulping, and afterward the three of them drifted in the artificial current, slowly revolving as they discussed anything and everything:

Colony annexation, the validity of aesthetic tentacle removal, the new eatery that served everything dead and frozen with frescoes carved into the flesh, So-and-So's scent change, the best birthing tanks, the after-ache they'd had the last time they used skimmer venom. Anything and everything except for the Drill.

Much later, when the other two had slipped into a sleeping harness, Four Warm Currents jetted upward to the top of their gray-and-purple spire, coiling there to look out over the City of Bone. Revelers jetted back and forth in the distance, visible by blots of blue-green excitement and arousal. Some were workers from the Drill, Four Warm Currents knew, celebrating the end of a successful work cycle.

Four Warm Currents's namesake parent had been a laborer of the same sort. A laborer who came home to cramped quarters and hungry children, but was never too exhausted to spin them a story, tentacles whirling and flourishing like a true bard. Four Warm Currents had been a logical child, always finding gaps in the tall tales of Leviathans and heroes and oceans beyond their own. But still, the stories had sunk in deep. Enough so that Four Warm Currents might be able to sign them to the children growing in Six Bubbling Thermals's egg sacs.

There was no need for Nine Brittle Spines or the council to know it was those stories that had ignited Four Warm Currents's curiosity for the roof of the world in the first place. Soon there would be new stories to tell. In seven, maybe eight more work cycles, they would break through.

After such a long percolation, the idea was dizzying. Four Warm Currents didn't know what awaited on the other side. There were theories, of course. Many theories. Four Warm Currents had studied gas bubbles and knew that whatever substance lay beyond the ice was not water as they knew it, not nearly so heavy. It could very well be deadly. Four Warm Currents would take precautions, but—

The brush of a tentacle tip, a familiar taste. Six Bubbling Thermals had ballooned up to join the stillness. Four Warm Currents extended a welcoming clasp, and the rasp of skin on skin was a comforting one. Calming.

"Someone almost started a riot in the plaza today," Six Bubbling Thermals signed. The calm was gone. "Over what? Over the project?"

"Yes." Six Bubbling Thermals stared out across the city with a long clicking burst, then turned to face Four Warm Currents. "They had artificial panic. In storage globes. Broke them wide open right as the market peaked. It was . . ." Tentacles wove in and out, searching for a descriptor. "Chaos."

"Are you all right?" Four Warm Currents signed hard. "You should have told me. You're birthing."

Six Bubbling Thermals waved a quick-dying laugh. "I'm still bigger than you are.

And I told Three Jagged Reefs. We agreed it would be best not to add to your stress. But I've never kept secrets well, have I?"

Another stare, longer this time. Four Warm Currents joined in, scraping sound across the architecture of the city, mapping curves and crevices, spars and spires.

"Before they were dragged off, they dropped one last globe," Six Bubbling Thermals signed. "It was your name, fresh, mixed with a decay scent. They said you're a monster, and if nobody stops you, you'll end the world."

Four Warm Currents shivered, clenched hard against the noxious fear threatening to tendril into the water. "Fresh?"

"Yes."

Who had it been? Four Warm Currents thought of the many workers and observers jetting up and down the tunnel, bringing status reports, complaints, updates. Any one of them could have come close enough to coax their chief engineer's name taste into a concealed globe. With a start, Four Warm Currents realized Six Bubbling Thermals was not gazing pensively over the city, but keeping watch.

"I know you won't consider halting the project," Six Bubbling Thermals signed. "But you need to be careful. Promise me that much."

Four Warm Currents remembered the councillor's warning and stroked Six Bubbling Thermals's egg sacs with a trembling tentacle. "I'll be careful. And when we break through, this will all go away. They'll see there's no danger."

"And when will that be?" The mauve worry was creeping back across Six Bubbling Thermals's skin.

"Soon," Four Warm Currents signed. "Seven work cycles."

They enmeshed their tentacles and curled against each other, bobbing there in silence as the City of Bone's ghostly blue guide lights began to blink out one by one.

The first attack came three cycles later, after shift. A pair of free-swimmers, with their skins pumped pitch-black and a sonar cloak in tow, managed to bore halfway through the Drill's protective shell before the guards spotted them and chased them off. The news came by a messenger whom Three Jagged Reefs, unhappily awoken, nearly eviscerated. Bare moments later, Four Warm Currents stroked goodbyes to both mates and took the skiff to the project site, tentacles heavy from sleep but hearts thrumming electric.

Nine Brittle Spines somehow contrived to arrive first.

"Four Warm Currents, it is a pleasure to see you so well rested." The councillor's tentacles moved as smoothly and blandly as ever, but Four Warm Currents could see the faintest of trembling at their tips. Mortal after all.

"I came as quickly as I was able," Four Warm Currents signed, not rising to the barb. "Were either of the perpetrators identified?"

"No." Nine Brittle Spines gave the word a twist of annoyance. "Assumedly they were two of yours. They knew the thinnest point of the shell and left behind a project-tagged auger." One tentacle produced the spiral tool and set it drifting between them. It was a miniature cousin to the behemoth Drill, used to sample ice consistency.

Four Warm Currents inspected the implement. "I'll speak with inventory, but I imagine it was taken without their knowledge."

"Do that," Nine Brittle Spines signed. "In the meanwhile, security will be increased. We'll have guards at all times from now on. Body searches for workers."

Four Warm Currents waved a vague agreement, staring up at the burnished armor shell, the hole scored in its underbelly. The workers would not be happy, but they were so close now, too close to let anything derail the project. Four Warm Currents would agree to anything, so long as the Drill was safe.

Tension became a sharp, sooty tang overlaying every conversation, so much so that Four Warm Currents was given council approval for a globe of artificially mixed happiness to waft around the tunnel entrance. It ended being mostly sucked up by the guards, who were happy enough already to swagger around with screamers and combat hooks bristling in their tentacles, interrogating any particularly worry-spackled worker who happened to look their way.

Four Warm Currents complained to the councillor, but was soundly ignored, told only that the guards had been instructed to treat the project site and its crew with the utmost respect. Enthusiasm was now a thing of the past. Workers spoke rarely and with short tempers, and every time the Drill slowed or an error was found in its calibration, the possibility of sabotage hung in the tunnel like a decay scent. Four Warm Currents found a slip in the most recent density calculation that promised to put things back a full work cycle, but still the Drill churned.

At home, they began receiving death threats. Six Bubbling Thermals found the first, a tiny automaton that waved its stiff tentacles in a prerecorded message: "We won't need a drill to puncture your eyes and every one of your eggs." Three Jagged Reefs shredded it to pieces. Four Warm Currents gave the pieces to the council's investigator.

Then, two cycles before breakthrough, black globes of artificial malice were slicked to their spire with adhesive and timed to burst while they slept. Only one went off, but it was enough to necessitate a pore-cleanse for Six Bubbling Thermals and a dedicated surveillance detail for the house.

Three Jagged Reefs fumed and fumed. "After the Drill breaks through, you'll let me borrow it, won't you?" The demand was jittery with skimmer venom, and made only once Six Bubbling Thermals, finally returned from the cleansing tanks, was out of sight range. "I'm going to find the shit-eater who blacked Six and stick them on the bit gland first."

Three Jagged Reefs had been pulled from smelting after an incidence of "hazardously elevated emotions," in which a copper-worker trilling about the impending end of the world had their tentacle held over a geyser until it turned to pulp. Staying in the house full cycle, under the watchful eyes and mouths of council surveillance, was not an easy transition. Not even stocked with high-quality venom.

"It'll all be over soon," Four Warm Currents signed, mind half-filled, as was now the norm, with figures from the latest density calculation. One final cycle.

"Tell it to Six," Three Jagged Reefs signed back, short and clipped, and turned away.

Four Warm Currents swam into the next room, to where their mate was adrift in the sleeping harness. The egg sacs were bulging now, slick with the constant emission of birth mucus, bearing no trace of black ichor stains. The cleansing tanks had reported no permanent damage. Four Warm Currents sent a gentle prod of sonar and elicited a twitch.

"I'm awake," Six Bubbling Thermals signed, languid. "I'd sleep better with you two around me."

"They'll catch the lunatics who planted that globe," Four Warm Currents signed back.

Six Bubbling Thermals signed nothing for a long moment, then waved a sad laugh. "I don't think it's lunatics. Not anymore. A lot of people are saying the same thing, you know."

"Saying what?"

"You spend all of your time at the Drill, even when you're here with us." The accusation was soft, but it stung. "You haven't been paying attention. The transit currents are full of devotees calling you a blasphemer. Saying you think yourself a Leviathan. Unbounded. The whole city is frightened."

"Then it's a city of idiots," Four Warm Currents signed abruptly.

"I'm frightened. I have no shame admitting it. I'm frightened for our children. For them to have two parents only. One parent only. None. For them to never even hatch. Who knows?" Six Bubbling Thermals raised a shaky smile. "Maybe the idiot is the one who isn't frightened."

"But I'm going to give them an altered world, a new world. . . ." Four Warm Currents's words blurred as Six Bubbling Thermals stilled two waving tentacles.

"I don't give a floating shit about a new world if it's one where you take a hook in the back," Six Bubbling Thermals signed back, slow and clear. "Don't go to the Drill tomorrow. They'll send for you when it breaks the ice."

At first, Four Warm Currents didn't even comprehend the words. After spending a third of a lifespan planning, building, lobbying, watching, the idea of not being there to witness the final churn, the final crack and squeal of ice giving away, was dizzying. Nauseating.

"If you go, I think you'll be dead before you come home," Six Bubbling Thermals signed. "You're worth more to us alive for one more cycle than as a name taste wafting through the archives for all eternity."

"I've watched it from the very start." Four Warm Currents tried not to tremble. "Every turn. Every single turn."

"And without you it moves no faster, no slower," Six Bubbling Thermals replied. "Isn't that what you say?"

"I have to be there."

"You don't." Six Bubbling Thermals gave a weary shudder. "Is it a new world for our children, or only for you?"

Four Warm Currents's tentacles went slack, adrift. The two of them stared at each other in the gloom, until, suddenly, something stirred in the egg sacs. The motion repeated, a faint but mesmerizing ripple. Six Bubbling Thermals gave a slight wriggle of pain.

Four Warm Currents climbed into the harness, turning acid blue in an apology that could not have been properly signed. "I'll stay. I'll stay, I'll stay."

They folded against each other and spoke of other things, of the strange currents that had brought them together, the future looming in the birthing tanks. Then they slept, deeply, even when Three Jagged Reefs wobbled in to join them much later, nearly unhooking the harness with chemical-clumsy tentacles.

Four Warm Currents dreamt of ending the world, the Drill shearing through its final stretch of pale ice, and from the gaping wound in the roof of the world, a Leviathan lowering its head, eyes glittering, to swallow the engine and its workers and their blasphemous chief engineer whole, pulling its bulk back into the world it once abandoned, sliding through blackness toward the City of Bone, ready to reclaim its scattered body, to devour all light, to unmake everything that had ever been made.

Four Warm Currents awoke to stinging sonar and the silhouette of a familiar councillor drifting before the sleeping harness, flanked by two long-limbed guards.

"Wake your mates," Nine Brittle Spines signed, with a taut urgency Four Warm Currents had never seen before. "All three of you have to leave."

"What's happening?"

"You'll see."

Four Warm Currents rolled, body heavy with sleep, and stroked each mate awake in turn. Three Jagged Reefs refused to rise until Six Bubbling Thermals furiously shook the harness, a flash of the old pre-birthing strength.

"Someone come to murder us?" Three Jagged Reefs asked calmly, once toppled free.

"You wouldn't feel a thing with all that venom in you," Four Warm Currents replied, less calmly.

"I barely pricked."

"As said the Drill to the roof of the world," Six Bubbling Thermals interjected.

Nine Brittle Spines flashed authoritative indigo, cutting the conversation short. "We have a skiff outside. Your discussions can wait."

The three of them followed the councillor out of the house, trailing long, sticky strands of Six Bubbling Thermals's replenished birth mucus. Once they exited the shutter and were no longer filtered, a faint acrid flavor seeped to them through the water. The City of Bone tasted bitter with fear. Anger.

And that wasn't all.

In the distance, Four Warm Currents could see free-swimmers moving as a mob, jetting back and forth through the city spires, carrying homegrown phosphorescent lamps and scent bombs. Several descended on a council-funded sculpture, smearing the stone with webbed black-and-red rage. Most continued on, heading directly for the city center. For their housing block, Four Warm Currents realized with a sick jolt.

"The radical tangent has grown," Nine Brittle Spines signed. "Considerably."

"So many?" Four Warm Currents was stunned.

"Only thing people love more than a festival is a doomsday," Three Jagged Reefs signed bitterly.

"Indeed. Your decriers have found support in many places, I'm afraid." Nine Brittle Spines bent a grimace as they swam toward the waiting skiff, a closed and armored craft marked with an official sigil. "Including the council."

Four Warm Currents stopped dead in the water. "But the Drill is still under guard."

"The Drill is currently being converged upon by a mob twice this size," Nine Brittle Spines signed. "Even without sympathizers in the security ranks, it would be futile to try to protect it. The council's official position, as of this moment, is that your project has been terminated to save costs."

Four Warm Currents realized, dimly, that both mates were holding tentacles back to prevent an incidence of hazardously elevated emotions. Searing orange desperation had spewed into the water around them. Nine Brittle Spines made no remarks about self-control, only flashed, for the briefest instant, a pale blue regret.

"But we're nearly through," Four Warm Currents signed, trembling all over. Three Jagged Reefs and Six Bubbling Thermals now slowly slid off, eager for the safety of the skiff. Drifting away when they were needed most.

"Perhaps you are," Nine Brittle Spines admitted. "Perhaps your theorems are sound. But stability is, at the present moment, more important than discovery."

"If we go to the Drill—" Four Warm Currents shuddered to a pause. "If we go to the Drill, if we go now, we can stop them. I can explain to them. I can convince them."

"You know better than that, Four Warm Currents. In fact—"

Whatever Nine Brittle Spines planned to say next was guillotined as Six Bubbling Thermals surged from behind, wrapping the councillor in full grip. In the same instant, Three Jagged Reefs yanked the skiff's shutter open. Four Warm Currents stared at the writhing councillor, then at each mate in turn.

"Get on with it, Four," Three Jagged Reefs signed. "Go and try."

Six Bubbling Thermals was unable to sign, tentacles taut as a vice around Nine Brittle Spines, but the misty red cloud billowing into the water was the fiercest and most pungent love Four Warm Currents could remember tasting.

"Oh, wait." Three Jagged Reefs glanced between them. "Six wanted to know if you have any necessary names."

"None," Four Warm Currents signed shakily. "So long as there are Thermals and Reefs."

"Well, of course." Three Jagged Reefs waved a haughty laugh that speared Four Warm Currents's hearts all over again. The councillor had finally stopped struggling in Six Bubbling Thermals's embrace and now watched the proceedings with an air of resignation. Four Warm Currents flashed a respectful pale blue, then turned and swam for the skiff.

They were hauling the Drill out of its carapace with hooks and bare tentacles, clouding the water with rage, excitement, amber-streaked triumph. Four Warm Currents abandoned the skiff for the final stretch, sucking back hard, jetting harder. The mob milled around the engine in a frenzy, too caught up to notice one late arrival.

Four Warm Currents screamed, dragging sonar across the crowd, but in the mess of motion and chemicals nobody felt the hard clicks. They'd brought a coring charge, one of the spiky half-spheres designed for blasting through solid rock bed to the nickel veins beneath. Four Warm Currents had shut down a foreman's lobby for such explosives during a particularly slow stretch of drilling. Too volatile, too much blowback in a confined space. But now it was here, and it was going to shred the Drill to pieces.

Four Warm Currents jetted higher, above the chaos, nearly to the mouth of the tunnel. No eyes followed. Everyone was intent on the Drill and on the coring charge being shuffled toward it, tentacle by tentacle.

Four Warm Currents sucked back, angled, and dove. The free-swimmers towing the coring charge didn't see the interloper until it was too late, until Four Warm Currents slid two tentacles deep into the detonation triggers and clung hard.

"Get away from me! Get away or I'll trigger right here!"

The crowd turned to a fresco of frozen tentacles, momentarily speechless. Then: "Blasphemer," signed the closest free-swimmer. "Blasphemer."

The word caught and rippled across the mob, becoming a synchronized wave of short, chopping motions.

"The Drill is not going to end the world," Four Warm Currents signed desperately, puffing up over the crowd, hauling the coring charge along. "It's going to break us into a brand-new one. One we'll visit at our choosing. The deep ocean will stay deep ocean. The Leviathans will stay skeletons. Our cities will stay safe."

Something struck like a spar of bone, sending Four Warm Currents reeling. The conical head of a screamer poked out from the crowd, held by a young guard whose skin was no longer inked with the council's sigil. The name came dimly to memory: Two Sinking Corpses. An unfamiliar taste was clouding into the water. It took a moment for Four Warm Currents to realize it was blood, blue and hot and saline.

"Listen to me!"

The plea was answered by another blast of deadly sound, this one misaimed, clipping a tentacle. Four Warm Currents nearly lost his grip on the coring charge. The mob roiled below, waving curses, mottled black and orange with fury. There would be no listening.

"Stay away from me or I'll trigger it," Four Warm Currents warned once more, then jetted hard for the mouth of the tunnel. The renewed threat of detonation bought a few still seconds. Then the mob realized where the coring charge was headed, and the sleekest and fastest of them tore away in pursuit.

Four Warm Currents hurled up the dark tunnel, sucking back water in searing cold gulps and flushing faster and harder with each. Familiar grooves in the ice jumped out with a smatter of sonar, etchings warning against unauthorized entry. Four Warm Currents blew past with tentacles straight back, trailing the coring charge directly behind, gambling nobody would risk hitting it with a screamer.

A familiar bend loomed in the dark, one of the myriad small adjustments to course, and beyond it, the service lights, bundles of bioluminescent algae set along the walls, began blooming to life, painting the tunnel an eerie blue-green, casting a long-limbed shadow on the wall. Four Warm Currents chanced a look down and saw three free-swimmers, young and strong and gaining.

"Drop it!" one took the opportunity to sign. "Drop it and you'll live!"

Four Warm Currents used a tentacle to sign back one of Three Jagged Reefs's favorite gestures, reflecting that it was a bad idea when the young-blood's skin flashed with rage and all three of them put on speed. The head start was waning, the coring charge was heavy, the screamer wound was dribbling blood.

But Four Warm Currents knew the anatomy of the tunnel better than anyone, better than even the foreman. The three pursuers lost valuable time picking their way through a thicket of free-floating equipment knocked from the wall, then more again deliberating where the tunnel branched, stubby memento of a calculation error.

Four Warm Currents's hearts were wailing for rest as the final stretch appeared. The coring charge felt like lead. A boiling shadow swooped past, and Four Warm Currents realized they'd fired another screamer, one risk now outweighing the other. The roof of the world, stretched thin like a membrane, marred with the Drill's final twist, loomed above.

Another blast of sonar, this one closer. Four Warm Currents throttled out a cloak of black ink, hoping to obscure the next shot, too exhausted to try to dodge. Too exhausted to do anything now but churn warm water, drag slowly, too slowly, toward the top.

The screamer's next burst was half-deflected by the coring charge, but still managed to make every single tentacle spasm. Four Warm Currents felt the cargo slipping and tried desperately to regain purchase on its slick metal. So close, now, so close to the end of the world. Roof of the world. Either. Thoughts blurred and collided in Four Warm Currents's bruised brain. More blood was pumping out, bright blue, foul-tasting. Four Warm Currents tried to hold on to the exact taste of Six Bubbling Thermals's love.

One tentacle stopped working. Four Warm Currents compensated with the others, shifting weight as another lance of sound missed narrowly to the side. The ice was almost within reach now, cold, scarred, layered with frost. With one final, tendon-snapping surge, Four Warm Currents heaved the coring charge upward, slapping the detonation trigger as it went. The spiked device crunched into the ice and clung. Four Warm Currents tasted something new mixing into the blood, reaching amber tendrils through the leaking blue. Triumph.

"Get out," Four Warm Currents signed, clumsily, slowly. "It's too late now."

The pursuers stared for a moment, adrift, then turned and shot back down the tunnel, howling a sonar warning to the others coming behind. Four Warm Currents's tentacles were going numb. Every body part ached or seared or felt like it was splitting apart. There would be no high-speed exit down the tunnel. Maybe no exit at all.

As the coring charge signed out its detonation sequence with mechanical tendrils, Four Warm Currents swam, slowly, to the side wall. A deep crevice ran along the length. Maybe deep enough. Four Warm Currents squeezed, twisted, contorted, tucking inside the shelter bit by bit. It was an excruciating fit. Even a child would have preferred a wider fissure. Four Warm Currents's eyes squeezed shut and saw Six Bubbling Thermals smiling, saw the egg sacs glossy and bright.

The coring charge went off like a volcano erupting. Such devices were designed, in theory, to deliver all but a small fraction of the explosive yield forward. The tiny fraction of blowback was still enough to shatter cracks through the tunnel walls and send a sonic boom rippling down its depth, an expanding globe of boiling water that scalded Four Warm Currents's exposed skin. The tentacle that hadn't managed to fit inside was turned to mush in an instant, spewing denatured flesh and blood in a hot cloud. All of Four Warm Currents's senses sang with the explosion, tasting the fierce chemicals, feeling the heat, seeing with sonar the flayed ice crumbling all around.

Then, at last, it was over. Four Warm Currents slithered out of the crack, sloughing skin on its edges, and drifted slowly upward. It was a maelstrom of shredded ice and swirling gases, bubbles twisting in furious wreaths. Four Warm Currents floated up through the vortex, numb to the stinging debris and swathes of scalding water. The roof of the world was gone, leaving a jagged dark hole in the ice, a void that had been a dream and a nightmare for cycles and cycles. Four Warm Currents rose to it, entranced.

One trembling tentacle reached upward and across the rubicon. The sensation was indescribable. Four Warm Currents pulled the tentacle back, stared with bleary eyes, and found it still intact. The other side was scorching cold, a thousand tingling pinpricks, a gauze of gas like nothing below. Nothing Four Warm Currents had ever dreamed or imagined.

The chief engineer bobbed and bled, then finally gathered the strength for one last push, breaking the surface of the water completely. The feel of gas on skin was gasping, shivering. Four Warm Currents craned slowly backward, turning to face the void, and looked up. Another ocean, far deeper and vaster than theirs, but not empty. Not dark. Not at all. Maybe it was a beautiful hallucination, brought about by the creeping failure of sense organs. Maybe it wasn't.

Four Warm Currents watched the new world with eyes and mouth, secreting final messages down into the water, love for Six Bubbling Thermals, for Three Jagged Reefs, for the children who would sign softly but laugh wildly, and then, as numbing darkness began to seep across blurring eyes, under peeling skin, a sole suggestion for a necessary name.

fifty shades of grays

STEVEN BARNES

Hugo and Nebula nominee Steven Barnes has published over thirty novels, including the NAACP Image Award winning In the Night of the Heat, *written with his wife, American Book Award–winning author Tananarive Due, and the Emmy-winning "A Stitch in Time" episode of* The Outer Limits. *His newest novel is* Twelve Days. *He lives in Southern California, and maintains a Web site at www.stevenbarneslife.com.*

Here's a sly story that demonstrates that the kind of alien invasion you see in the movies, with deathrays flashing down from the skies and buildings collapsing and whole cities being incinerated, might not be the most effective way to go at all.

T errorist.

That's what they call me, but I am something worse: both successful traitor and failed saboteur.

I *want* to die, for all of this to be over.

For my last request, I asked to have paper and pen to write my last will and testament. They won't let me have it, forcing me to use the mindsynch. Damned Traveler tech. Maybe they're scared I'll ram the pen up my nose, scribble on my brain and cheat the hangman.

We make do with what we have.

I, Carver Kofax, being of sound mind and body, do leave all my worldly possessions to my wife, Rhonda. I owe her that. More than that. More than I, or anyone, can pay.

It was all my fault, you know. Well . . . not all, but too damned much. No one else who was there from the beginning seems to have either the capacity or inclination to speak of it.

This is the way the world ends . . . not with a whimper, but a bang.

It was the best day of my life, and the worst. And for the same reasons, when it comes right down to it.

It was a Tuesday in May of 2025. I was seated in Century City's *Dai Shogun* restaurant, one of L.A.'s best, chewing a hellishly good Hot Night roll. *Dai Shogun's* tuna was spiced to perfection, the shrimp tempura seared crisp, the sashimi salad to die for, the karaoke tolerable.

"What do you think this is all about?" Rhonda Washington was our agency's brightest young artist. She was referring to our assignment, a carefully worded challenge to "make ugly sexy" without much more to go on. Bonuses had been offered in lieu of information.

And the tastiest bonus was the chance to lure Stein and Baker's dreadlocked princess down from her eighth-floor tower to work with mere mortals like me.

"No business while I'm eating," I said, squinting fiercely, until she laughed. "But ask me about 'bridges' later."

"I'll do that." A moment of quiet followed, during which she seemed to be sizing me up.

"I didn't know you liked sushi," I said. Rhonda downed a thick luscious disk of Tekka Maki, nibbling at the seaweed wrap before biting. I'd lusted after her for fourteen months, but this was the first time we'd lunched together. Big accounts change lots of things. This one would change everything, even though I didn't know it at the time.

Her grin sparkled with mischief. "There are a lot of things about me you don't know. Tekka Maki least among them."

"And most?"

Odd how I'd never noticed that feral gleam in her eye. She fiddled with her bracelet, sterling silver with little links at her pulse point. I remember thinking that they looked a bit like police handcuffs. "That would be telling."

She smiled at me and popped the rest of the sushi roll between her lips.

First time I'd ever envied a blob of fish and rice.

"Tell me something about you I don't know," she said.

I chuckled. "I have a sushi story."

"Let's hear it."

"Well . . . before I came to work here, the partners took me to lunch. Sushi restaurant."

"This one?"

"No . . . one of the ones with a floating boat cycling around, bringing plates of sushi to customers seated in an oval around the chef's island. Anyway, I'm having a great time, and trying to impress them, and noticed a guy sitting a few seats away watching the chef make him a hand roll. Delicious-looking roll, with lots of sauces and chopped spices. I asked 'what is that?' and the guy said 'it's a fifteen-spice tuna roll.'

"My mouth watered. I said 'Make me one of those.' The chef agreed, and they started up. I noticed after a few moments that the bar had gotten quiet. Everyone was looking at me. Giggling. Whispering. Laughing. Especially my future employers.

"I started to have a very odd feeling. Even the guy making my food was grinning. 'Excuse me,' I finally said. 'What exactly is a fifteen-spice tuna roll?'

"He grinned like a shark. 'One spice tuna roll . . . very hot tuna roll,' he said. 'Two spice tuna roll . . . twice as hot.'"

"Oh my god." Rhonda giggled, covering her mouth with her hand. "What did you do?"

"My bosses were watching. The damned thing napalmed my throat. I don't want to be indelicate, but for the next two days I used asbestos toilet paper."

Hers was a rich, throaty laugh, the kind you enjoy triggering in a woman with legs and skin like Rhonda's. "But, hey," she said, wiping away tears. "You got the job, right?"

"Yeah. I got the job."

She smiled. Elfin this time, genuinely amused and interested. "Maybe the lesson is that you really like hot things. Or that you like really hot things. Something like that."

"Or that I really, really don't know when to walk away."

"That could be too," she said, with new appraisal. She'd expected me to return her suggestive volley, and instead I'd said something at least marginally thoughtful.

"Could be," she said. "We'll see about that."

Fifty minutes later we were back at Stein and Baker, and decided to use her office. It was crowded with her line drawings and watercolors. A mini-exhibition. Lady had serious chops and an outsider sensibility, like Norman Rockwell crossed with a Harlem street artist. She oozed creative intensity, and it was difficult to keep my mind on "making ugly sexy." Artful vagueness ensued when I probed my boss, The Widow Stein, for details. (Yeah, that was what we called her behind her back. Winston Stein, the agency's founder, had wrapped himself around a Douglas Fir on a Black Diamond ski run. His wife had picked up the pieces and doubled the business in five years. She was a piranha dressed like a goldfish.)

I perched on Rhonda's office couch, feet up, comslate on my thighs. Typing thoughts.

Marketing and sales are two different things, often misunderstood by the public. Marketing is finding prospects, people whose needs or desires might lead them to want your product or service. Hook a basic human need into your product, something like sex, power, or survival, and you have a winner.

Sales, on the other hand, is convincing the potential customer that your particular brand is what they want. And all advertising and sales is a funnel designed to catch customers by the short hairs, by their need to be liked, or healthy, or wealthy, or married. To convince them that your car or ice cream or sneaker is just the ticket. When you understand people, and you understand selling and marketing, it's just a matter of connecting the right aspect of the product to the right psychological weakness in your prospect.

Still too complicated? I'll put it the way Winston Stein once put it:

"Marketing is finding women who like sex or would like to find out if they do. Sales is convincing them that they want to go home with YOU, right NOW."

Rhonda's easel faced away from me, so that I could see her intense expression (good) but not what she was drawing (bad). I liked looking at her. She seemed to catch the thought and looked over. "So . . . since you're no longer eating, what do you think this is all about?"

"I'm just going to guess."

"Please do."

"Selling someone to the American public, I'd guess. Or something cross-cultural."

"An individual? A couple?"

"Don't know. Some entertainment. Singers or dancers perhaps. A cultural exchange dance troupe from a country with very ugly citizens. We need their coconuts or something, but have to sell them to the public."

"Hmm. What does that have to do with bridges?" Rhonda asked.

I folded my fingers together and tried to look professorial. "So . . . we typically emphasize whatever about a model or subject a typical customer might find attractive. Their proportions, colors, music, movement . . . if they are healthy, then their bodies will be proportional and symmetrical. That appeals to the eye. We can work with that, even distort it digitally, create an aesthetic 'bridge.'"

"A 'bridge'?" She squinted at me.

"Sure," I said. "A term I learned in Commercial Aesthetics at UCLA. A blend of two different cultural or racial standards, much the same way that light-skinned black performers like Halle Berry helped de-inhibit negative responses to African facial characteristics. Whites considered them beautiful, so they could slowly accept and relish darker faces. You start with Lena Horne and end up with Lupita Nyong'o."

Rhonda's smile lit up the night. "I'm starting to see why they chose you. I think this is about a movie, a big co-venture with China or India."

Yeah. But why did they choose *us*?

I'd considered that, and wasn't totally happy with my answers. "I . . . was responsible for advertising campaigns selling Nigerian Naija music to Taiwanese audiences. That was tough, for a time. We used a variety of tactics." The memory wasn't pleasant, a suborbital jaunt followed by exhausted presentations to people who disguised contempt behind polite smiles and bows. I'd swallowed my bile and brought their money home. It had been my first big win out of business school, and the bonus paid the mortgage my parents back in Augusta had taken out to buy my way into the game.

Winston Stein had once joked that *"Carver Kofax eats pain and shits money."* Hah hah hah. That was me, all right. I'm the guy who would eat wasabi like green tea ice cream if it got me the job.

Three twenty-hour workdays later I was trashed, but managed to stagger into the thirty-fourth-floor office when summoned. Except for racoon eyes, Rhonda looked as delectable as ever.

Our drawings and ad lines were splashed around the office, taped to windows looking out on Century City and the endless traffic on Santa Monica Boulevard. "Make the ugly sexy," they'd said. So . . . we used a combination of plug-ugly dogs and monkeys, cartoons of hideous characters from classic and popular vid shows and web strips, choices from a dozen different cultures, all arranged in a way that pointed out their charming personalities, encouraged us to see their "inner beauty" or even suggested that ugly was "charmingly different." Offend no one, because we'd yet to learn who was holding the debit card.

The agency's fearless leader Adrian Stein was there, in all her pantsuited glory. A rare honor, indeed. "So, Carver. Rhonda." She smiled. "I wanted you to know that this morning we were offered the preliminary contract." Cheers and high-fives all around. "You will fly to Washington tomorrow, and there you will go to the last step of the competition."

"Do you know what? . . ." Rhonda began.

Stein raised her hand. "No. Not the slightest. Now get packed, and remember that you are representing us."

So we flew, Rhonda and I. Delta served lobster and Dom Perignon in first class, and it felt like the beginning of a new life. We were picked up at the airport by a Rolls Royce drone limo, and taken directly to the Watergate hotel, on Virginia Avenue along the Potomac at the edge of Georgetown. I'd never been to the Watergate, and something about the history made me nervous. The lobby was filled with executive types in bespoke Armani and Kitan. The air crackled with competition. They weren't all Americans, either. Europeans . . . South Americans. Some Asians, maybe Koreans or Japanese. This was getting more interesting by the minute.

This was, I decided, the strangest "co-operative film venture" I'd ever seen. And the men and women guarding the doors and sign-in table were . . . well, if I had to say, more military than civvy. Not flamboyant at all, dressed in suits rather than uniforms, but something about them said *these people have guns.* They ushered us into a crowded meeting room, and then the lights went down. The man who took the dais looked like Gandhi in a Brooks Brothers suit.

"I am Dr. Ahmed," he said in barely accented Ivy League English. "Good morning. Thank you, all of you, for attending. Please call me Jalil, and for the sake of this discussion, I represent a consortium with . . . a unique property. Let us say a science fiction book that we believe has the ability to become this generation's 'Star Wars.'" He smiled. *He was lying.* I knew it and probably half the others did as well. "The problem is that if we accurately depict the creature in the story, we believe people will find it unattractive. So . . . what we need is for each of you to give your best bet on making this image . . . appealing."

Why was he lying? And about what? The screen lit up, and the image resembled something you'd see under a microscope. The sort of dysenteric pond-squiggler that gives me the heebie-jeebies. A furred amoeba. Did they call that hair cilia? There was no scale for size reference, so it could have been a pipsqueak or Godzilla. Floaty things suspended in its sack looked disturbingly like cat eyes, other curly doodads that looked like translucent intestines were floating in a bag of gray Jell-o.

"We would like to see your drawings tomorrow," Jalil said. "Twenty-four hours from now."

Something tickled the back of my scalp. "Ah . . . how attractive are you trying to make them?"

"Mr. . . . ." he consulted a list. Seating chart. "Carver. You may interpret that any way you wish."

There were other questions, but Rhonda and I looked at each other, barely able to restrain our mirth.

Within an hour we were back in our linked hotel room. While we had our own supplies, more had been delivered. Expensive graphic software, camel-hair brushes and a lightning-fast top-of-the-line Mac.

We barely noticed. We stared at each other, and then at the protozoan portrait and then collapsed into hysterical laughter. So that was it. Some crazy backwater billionaire wanted to get into the movie business, and were promoting some SF movie based on a plug-ugly demon from a tribal backwater. Or something. I've seen these things before, and it never works out.

And the obvious insulting implication was that I'd been chosen for this assignment because I'd made Nigerians attractive to Chinese, and apparently that was now seen as more miraculous than turning vampires into vegans.

Compared to that aliens would be easy, right? I mean, right?

We got really, really drunk, and the ideas that emerged from that brainstorming session probably reflected the fact that the sexual tension between us was starting to skyrocket. We drank, and laughed, and vaped, and laughed some more, and around two in the morning we tore off our clothes and did something about that tension.

We, um, "did something" about it two more times that night. Let's just say that I discovered that Rhonda's bracelets proudly proclaimed her inclinations and that, perhaps in anticipation of exactly what had happened between us, she had packed a portable fun kit with her: cuffs, blindfolds, and things which I'd blush to mention, but fit snugly. We'll leave it at that.

It was all lava and steam, and for the first time in my life I understood what people meant when they said they'd been "turned out." When we were too restless to sleep, Rhonda and I dabbled a bit more with the art, but it got explicit this time. We swore we'd get rid of that stuff, but I have to admit that two of those drawings making their way into the courier packet might have been our way of saying "screw you" to the whole thing.

Then we "did something" about it again. I would have thought we'd both be too raw to do more than cuddle, but her invention and limberness knew no rational bounds, and our coupling was even better this time. She liked me to take control, total, deep, confident control. To my surprise, I found that the more I took command, the more that, behind the gag and blindfold, her every move and muffled cry said that she was actually controlling *me*.

Eventually preliminaries ended and she shed the apparatus and welcomed me into her body fully, joyously, and with an enthusiasm that made me feel like I'd earned my way into an anaconda breeding ball.

And afterward, we held each other, and let our pulses slow down. My eyes focused, and the first thing I saw was the easel on which images reminiscent of Lovecraftian pornography winked back at me.

"We . . . might get into trouble for that." She giggled, breathing warm into the notch between my shoulder and neck. Her dreads scented of coconut oil.

"We're saving Ms. Stein a nightmare, believe me."

"I guess we should pack," she said, and rolled away from me.

The phone rang. Rhonda picked it up. "Hello?"

Her eyes got bigger than an orphan in a Margaret Keane painting, accompanied by one of those "is this a joke?" expressions. She hung up.

"What is it?" I asked.

"We're supposed to be downstairs in fifteen minutes." Her expression was strained. Shocked, like someone who has bitten into a live cricket.

Ouch. "They're that mad?"

Her eyes were huge. "No. Ah . . . we got the job." Her face lit with urchin glee, and we giggled, then guffawed, and fell into each other's arms. We almost didn't make it downstairs in time, if you know what I mean.

I'd thought our meeting would be in some Watergate conference room, but instead a drone limo shuttled us to the Pentagon.

As we were passed through the gate, Rhonda leaned over. "Since when did porn become a security issue?"

I didn't know. Couldn't answer that question. I felt like Neo when Morpheus told him to hop down the rabbit hole.

We were escorted to a small conference room, and I have to admit that by this time I was well beyond curious. Had no goddamn idea what was happening. Then Jalil walked in, his placid mask suspended. What lurked in its place worried me, some combination of emotions I couldn't label.

"You have signed non-disclosure agreements. If you go any further, you will sign more. And there will be considerable penalties for not abiding by the terms of those agreements."

I read the fine print. And other than asking for my firstborn male child, I couldn't imagine what greater security they could have required. All I could figure was that this was involved in some kind of Psyop program, designed to . . .

Oh hell, I didn't know.

We signed. Then the President herself emerged, and my lungs froze. Yes, we were in Washington. Yes, I thought that I was above such things as idol worship or being impressed by power. But here she was, in the flesh, and the charisma with which Sophia Gonzalez had won two presidential elections was now bottled in a confined space, just a few meters away, and it was devastating. By the time I remembered to breathe she and Jalil had finished conferring.

"Thank you," Madame President said with that disarming southern accent. "You understand that what is said in this room remains in this room. In fact, if you agree to this commission, you will be out of touch with your company, friends and family for the next ninety days."

The wall lit up with images of gelatinous objects with glowing lights suspended within, like floating Portuguese Man O'Wars filled with Chinese lanterns.

"Fifteen months ago," she said, "we made contact with what we call the Travelers. We are uncertain of their origins. Some who have studied the communications believe the answer is the Horsehead Nebula. Others some other dimension of being."

An image. Unmistakably, a photo of the furry protozoan. "Is this a joke?" I heard myself ask.

"No joke," she said. "A 'Traveler'. They came here to meet us, and we want you to help ease the way."

Rhonda was grinning . . . then frowned when she realized we weren't laughing. "Holy shit. You aren't kidding? Like, 'phone home'?"

I'd read as many UFO loony tune tracts as anyone. Stein and Baker had promoted

"Saucer Flakes," a breakfast cereal with little ovals (they levitate in the bowl!) so I knew about the pale-skinned almond-eyed space people said to mutilate cattle and anal probe redneck trailer trash from Montana to Mississippi.

"Roswell Grays?" Rhonda asked. "Zeta Reticulans? Real *aliens*?"

"Yes. They arrived outside lunar orbit and made contact through encoded diplomatic channels. Our most secure and shielded communications were child's play to the Travelers. It was an unprecedented emergency, as you can imagine. But they said that they came in friendship, and would not even come down or announce themselves to the general public until we gave permission."

"Really?" Rhonda asked. "The Grays came umpteen trillion miles and then just . . . hung out? They didn't demand? Or even plead?"

The President considered. "No. What they did do was bargain."

"What kind of bargain?"

"They said that they have gifts. Technologies they can offer."

Whoa, there, cowboy. *And welcomed little fishies in with gently smiling . . .* "What kind of technologies?"

"Communications. Transportation. Energy. Biologicals. How would you like to live 120 years without illness?"

Boom. That's what I'm talking about. "You're shitting me."

"No. Not at all. We've tested samples of their tech, and its real."

"And what do they want in return?"

The President broke eye contact. "They want to be our . . . friends."

She cleared her throat.

The President began speaking more rapidly, with greater confidence. This part had been rehearsed. "I've had many meetings with our best xenobiologists, and they tell me that a species capable of reaching our world would have a limited number of motivations to do so. Colonization, of course, but they've not asked for land."

"You know, like . . . our resources?" I asked.

"Water? Energy? Easier to get outside a gravity well. The general opinion is that an alien species would come for reasons similar to those human beings used, if one removes the profit motive."

"Tourism?" Rhonda laughed.

"Yes," the President said, mouth held in a carefully neutral expression. "Sheer exploration."

"Seeing the sights? Eating the food?"

An unpleasant thought. "Hunting?"

She smiled. "This isn't a horror movie. They're not looking for pelts. The Travelers want . . . *friends*."

A pause. An unspoken possibility hung in the air.

"Wait a minute," Rhonda said. "You're talking about sex?"

The President's expression never changed, but she gave an almost imperceptible nod.

"The Grays came a trillion miles for . . . sex tourism?"

"Not to put too fine a line on it, but . . . yes."

"Wait just a minute," Rhonda said. "Those ads we made up. Those cartoons. You didn't hire us in spite of what we did. You hired us *because* of it."

I wanted to laugh, but the sound was stuck in my throat. "You have to be kidding me. This whole thing is . . ."

Without further preamble, Madame President raised her hand for quiet. "They, um . . . studied our culture, and 1950s television broadcasts reached them first. Ladies and gentlemen . . . I'd like to introduce you to Elvis."

"Of course you do," I muttered.

The lights went down. And something sort of . . . *flowed* in from the wings. It wore a kind of white sequined Vegas stage suit. An amoeba in polyester. The hair stood up on my forearms, and the air sort of sizzled, as if he carried a thunderstorm's worth of static charge.

"You've gotta be fuckin' kidding me," I heard myself mutter. *Just a hunk a hunk of burnin'—*

In a very Steven Hawkings, synthesized voice, Elvis said: "Greetings, my friends. I believe that 'kidding' implies a kind of deception or prevarication. My people do not lie. It is not in our nature." He paused. "I am very grateful . . . that you have agreed to help us. We have come much [*meaningless squawk*]. To be with you. We seek to know you."

"In the Biblical sense," Rhonda muttered. She raised her hand. "Ah . . . Elvis? May I ask a question?"

"Yes, please."

"On Earth, sex is most important for . . . reproduction. You aren't saying you want to *breed* with us?"

In his flat, cold voice, Elvis replied: "That would not be possible. But sex is not merely reproduction. It is pleasure. And bonding. And healing. And expression of love. These things exist among all peoples we seek to know. We wish to share this bounty of . . . the heart. And have gifts to offer in return."

Out of the side of my mouth, I whispered: "Most times, flowers are enough."

"Will you help us?" Elvis asked.

"Umm . . ." the speaker was an Asian dressed in belt and suspenders over a long-sleeve denim shirt. Tufts of white framed a very bald pate. I thought I recognized him. "What . . . ah . . . . do you see as the largest barrier?"

"It is that your people will think us ugly, Professor Watanabe." *The* Watanabe? The man who had authored my Commercial Aesthetics text? Elvis's cat eyes blinked. His color shifted, became a bit pinkish. Emotions?

I drummed my fingers on the desk. This was . . . beyond surreal. "You understand that . . . well, you aren't even 'ugly.' Ugly would be . . . well," I felt trapped. Everyone was looking at me, and I just blurted it out. "Ugly would be a step up."

The room held its collective breath. The President squinted at me, awaiting disaster. But to my surprise, Elvis' color did not shift. "We can change. Will you help us?"

A hologram of a bank account screen appeared on the screen before me.

The President spoke. "A very select group of companies have already bid on Traveler technologies. The number you see in front of you is the amount they are willing to pay to acquire your services."

I whistled. Damn. Stein and Baker had just won the lottery.

"Will you help us?"

Despite the computerized voice, the call was plaintive. I . . . felt it. Deeply. A cosmic loneliness, a sense of feeling lost in the spaces between the stars, only rarely finding other creatures with whom to contemplate existence . . .

I shook my head, as if emerging from an opium den. Something was either very right about this, or very wrong indeed.

All that money, though . . .

"Say yes," the President said.

I glanced at Rhonda. She gave the slightest of nods. "Yes," I replied.

And that was how it began. Via Secret Service helicopter, we were lifted to a repurposed private college in upstate New York, where . . . well, I don't know what everyone else was working on, but it was abuzz with dignitaries, scientists, military people, media people . . . a beehive, and we were just workers. We had one year to prepare the public.

Rhonda and I grew very close during these months. We laughed, and cried, and even considered quitting. But the Travelers were good to their word. They made no effort to land, or interfere with us, or do anything except keep to their promises. They rarely even visited what we called the Facility, when they did I never was able to tell one from the other. They changed costumes and cultural jewelry as if trying on various ways of being human, with one exception: Elvis was always Elvis, and slimed around the Facility like a gigantic slug in rhinestones. Damned if his organelles didn't have a sleepy look, and the facial protoplasm seemed to have a sneering lip.

Nobody else could see that. Maybe it was just me.

Every denizen of the Facility was committed to making a home for our guests, or to evaluate the impact of their arrival. Who generated endless scenarios about what would happen to our culture, religion, governments . . . the psychological and spiritual and economic impact, and how we might best manage the stress. It was massive.

Every room and team seemed to be doing something different. I probably understood one percent of it all. Some were, I knew, testing and applying odd technologies. Too many moving parts for me to remember, but they included unlimited-wear contact lenses with built-in microscopes, telescopes and multi-spectrum scanners. Shoes that sent the energy from walking back up your body in the strangest ways, simultaneously massaging and exercising every muscle with every step. Instantaneous communication via space-time ripples, as the Travelers communicated with others of their kind across the universe. Much more.

Occasionally an actual Traveler toured the Facility. Perhaps taking part in experiments, maybe just supervising. I never knew, and tried to avoid them: their sweet-sickly scent made me want to puke, and about them there seemed always to be a prickling of static discharge, enough to make your hair twitch.

But I can tell you that the Travelers delivered on every single promise. Our hunger to begin the next phase knew no bounds. There was just one little hurdle . . .

One day we were called down to a laboratory on the lower levels. Professor Watanabe welcomed Rhonda, myself, and a military officer who seemed to find the whole thing distasteful. "Carver. Rhonda. General Lucas. Thank you for coming down."

"I . . . well, we need to know what we have to work with," Rhonda said.

The Professor scratched his shock of Einstein-white hair. "Well, we have a couple of different levels. Needless to say, there are human beings who will have sex with almost anything. No . . . . let's cancel the 'almost.' For enough money, some people will couple with anything possessing an orifice or protrusion."

"Porn stars?" I asked. "Prostitutes?"

He nodded. "Yes, and they have been the first recruits to the cause."

General Lucas frowned. "You mean it's already happened?"

A faint smile. "Would you like to see vid?"

"No!" I sputtered, realizing that Rhonda had simultaneously said: "Yes!"

Watanabe flicked a switch, and an image appeared on the screen. A sparsely furnished room, with heavy floor matting. A muscular white male entered, nude but for a black Zorro mask. He was fully and rather impressively engorged.

"He's a porn star, but insisted that his face be covered."

Rhonda craned her head sideways. "I think I recognize him. Is that Maximum?"

Even I'd heard *that* name. Maybe you have too: "Maximum Thrust," "Maximum Overdrive" and "Maximum's Minimum" and so forth. He was notorious for his endless appetite and ability to perform under any and all circumstances. Considering his reputation, I wondered who'd paid whom.

"And now, there's our visitor . . ."

A hidden panel in the ceiling slid open. On slender wires, something resembling a blow-up sex doll descended toward the floor. Its arms and legs were cut short, and out bulged a mass of tissue as gelatinous as half-melted Jello.

"We've used other volunteers, augmenting with a Traveler-tweaked phosphodiesterase inhibitor. I think we have our first T-pharmaceutical. One dose seems to last . . . well, it hasn't stopped working yet. We just don't know. It might be permanent. I don't mean erect constantly, I mean tumescence on demand. Whenever. Maximum didn't need it."

Rhonda uttered the most sincere "damn" I'd ever heard.

Once the union began, the outer shell seemed to dissolve. It looked as if it was devouring our volunteer. His splayed limbs, glistening perspiration and the trembling of lower-back muscles implied a kind of slack-jawed overwhelm that was very much at odds with his cool, controlled porno personae.

"Good lord," I said.

Rhonda leaned forward. "So . . . they prefer males?"

"Oh, no, they like females as well."

She emitted a short, rather chipper sigh.

The image was clipped short, followed by another. A woman, this one unmasked. A brown-skinned woman, Indonesian perhaps, cadaverously thin, and pock-marked as a golf ball. The Traveler crawled all over her. Her faux passion became real, and she bucked like a flag in a windstorm.

Rhonda's eyes went wide. Watanabe switched it off. "So we have begun to fulfill the minimal contract. Some of their tech is filtering in already. And we might need it."

"Why?"

"Because the next step is to prepare humanity for their arrival. We have begun subliminal and implanted imagery."

A series of slides appeared: Brief flashes of aliens implanted in crowd scenes. Fuzzy-wuzzy faces implanted in comedies, Coca-Cola commercials backed with snatches of what sounded like whale mating calls played backwards.

"What is *that?*"

"Their cultural music. We're trying everything."

"Carver and I have been working day and night to create the campaigns," Rhonda said. "The biggest idea was to create one of Dr. Watanabe's 'aesthetic bridges.' Images that are blends of human and Visitor, that help desensitize us to the sensory shock."

"And is that working?" the general asked.

"The problem," Watanabe said, "is what the cybersemiotics people refer to as the 'uncanny valley.' That if something looks *nothing* like us, we might have a positive or negative reaction. But as it gets closer to us, there is a point of greater and greater attraction . . . and then we flinch."

"Why is that?"

He shrugged. "Could be a mechanism for detection of mutations. Birth defects. We don't know. There is speculation that this is behind some forms of racism, or even why Cro-Magnons exterminated the Neanderthals."

"Close," Rhonda whispered, "but no cigar."

"But there's another set of responses. We fear the 'other' but are also exogamous. So there is something to play with, and always has been."

"Do we have any sense of success?" Rhonda asked.

"Combinations of the subliminals, the sound, and manipulation of language and imagery in television and film—it's like buying product placement, really—has reduced the revulsion rate by 17 percent. And I think that might be our tipping point."

The announcement was timed to go over every channel, all over the world, at the same time. The first images of what Rhonda always called "The Grays" were fuzzy and slightly doctored. And despite all our preparations, they still triggered an ocean of nausea and fear.

Like crystal cathedrals floating in a sea of clouds, the alien ships hovered above New York, L.A., Tokyo, Lagos, Johannesburg, London, Beijing, Moscow and fifty other major cities. Panic and riots ensued, but contrary to wide expectations the Travelers didn't land, let alone destroy or conquer. They just . . . hovered. We were told the situation, and what the visitors offered. State by state, the citizens were allowed to vote on whether the Visitors could touch ground.

Demonstrations. Signs abounded. "*Hell no!*" or their equivalents in a dozen languages.

Most places that sentiment was almost universal. But a few . . . California, for instance, said yes. And so at last aliens were among us. And again, they delivered on their promises, enabling those states to enjoy the bounty. The technology was tightly controlled, and only allowed into the areas that welcomed the Travelers. That was clever. We were both in control . . . and totally on the hook. Because everyone knew someone wasting away from some nasty ailment. Someone who was healed . . . or employed in one of the new industries that sprang up and became Google overnight. Within two years there wasn't a country on Earth that denied them. Traveler tech created a hundred billionaires and a thousand multimillionaires in the first year.

You rarely saw Travelers on the street. When you did, it was in those odd suits and usually in a limo of some kind, usually piloted by a live human being. They appeared on documentaries and news shows, and then entertainment as well. Television, billboards, films . . . break-dancing amoebas, torch-song warbling slime molds. Slowly we began to see these concoctions more often, associated with puppies and smiling children . . . and sexy men and women.

The Travelers wanted to see that humans were accepting them.

They masked their pheromones, poured themselves into better and better fabrications, and even managed to appear in a series of Indian films. I thought I recognized Elvis doing a very creditable Bollywood *Bhangra* dance. Hard to say.

All paramecia look alike to me.

Among hundreds of others, Rhonda and I were released from our contracts—now that it was out in the open, *everyone* clamored to work with Them. And the Traveler technology was integrated into our entertainment with steadily increasing frequency and effect. Movies were immersive and hyper-real, more so than any 3-D, hologram, Showscan or anything that had ever existed previously. Somehow we reacted *more* to those images than the real thing. Amazing. Humanity was heading for a renaissance. I have to admit that I felt a little guilty. The Travelers had come a trillion miles looking for love, and didn't seem to understand the concept of prostitution. Before I left the facility I had a final meeting with Elvis. He was squished into his exoskeleton, the pinkish indestructible Traveler-cloth "human" suit beneath his white sequinned jumpsuit. I no longer felt the urge to vomit when I was around him. He'd changed his smell and appearance, and that sizzling sensation I got in his presence had died to a mere itch.

"Hello, Carver," he said. "Good to see you."

"And you."

"I think," he said, "that we've accomplished something wonderful together. Thank you."

He handed me a card. "What's this?"

"A token of my appreciation. One million of your dollars."

There it was. Another six zeroes. It was true that a rising tide lifted all boats, that a certain amount of inflation had accompanied Traveler wealth, but Rhonda and I had been paid so well we'd stayed ahead of that curve. In that moment, I realized I never had to work again for the rest of my life. "Thank you!"

Elvis's face mask smiled. *"Thankyouverymuch."* His namesake's Vegas drawl. "Cheap at the price, old son."

Six weeks after we left the Facility I asked Rhonda to marry me, and a month later, she agreed. Our honeymoon was a revelation, as if our prior sex life had been a mere appetizer, and she'd given me the keys to the kitchen. If she had lived a hundred lives as a leather-clad courtesan, that might have explained the days and nights that followed, as she opened one door after another for me, allowed me to glimpse what was within until it felt like she was running an electrified tongue over my body's every exposed nerve. Then, with a mischievous giggle, she would close that door, give me just enough time to recover and then lead me staggering and wide-eyed to the next.

In retrospect, it was predictable that Rhonda would be the one to bring the fetish sites to my attention. Three months after we were married she danced into my home office, touched my lips with hers and giggled. "Have I got something to show *you*!"

She led me to her office, where she had worked so hard and late at night. Her computer was mostly used for graphics, but like the rest of us she surfed the net to rest her brain in-between creative spurts.

"I don't want to tell you how I found this site."

"I think I can guess. Feeling a little frisky, were you?"

She turned the screen around, and for a moment my eyes didn't focus. Then I saw a very pale woman, gelatinously obese with very short bristly dark hair, sporting animated tattoos that mimicked organelles. They shivered and danced, while three men stood around her performing what I believe Japanese aficionados would refer to as a *bukkake* ritual. If you don't know what that is, look it up.

On the other hand, maybe you shouldn't. Ignorance is bliss.

"Is she trying to look like a Traveler?"

"Wild, huh?"

The sound was much too good for speakers their size. I didn't recognize the brand. "New speakers?"

"Nice, aren't they?" The speakers were flat as glass panes, but the sound was as good as a ten-thousand-dollar pair of Naim Ovators. T-tech. Traveler music wafted in the background, and with the new speakers, my ears detected odd, previously undetected undertones.

"Wow," I said. "That's really strange. It's a new world. That other stuff . . . wow."

She suddenly pulled in on herself, shrank a little, seemed tentative and a little shy. "Does it turn you on?" Her forefinger fluttered along my forearm.

"Shit. No. You?"

She shrugged, her finger ceasing its dance. "Maybe . . ."

"Well, we should take advantage of that . . ."

"I'm busy right now," Rhonda said, removing my hands. ". . . but save some of that heat for me tonight, OK?"

But . . . she worked until midnight, and when she did come to bed, she rolled over and went to sleep. That's marriage, I guess.

More and more often, Rhonda seemed to be in a funk. I think we saw each other less frequently, pretty much devolving to roommates. It wasn't that we didn't love each other. It was that some critical spark was just . . . gone. She was doing more

Traveler work, and the "bridging" was subtler. The T's had gifted us with a printing process that conveyed a dimensional and multi-sensory aspect. Strange. You would look at a picture, and detect a scent. If you weren't looking directly at it, you detected no smell. I have no idea how they did that, or how it worked, but it did.

Rhonda's office was filled with more and more of these Traveler materials. She seemed increasingly dreamy and far-away. And then one summer day in 2036 Rhonda left the house, and stayed out late.

Very late.

And when Rhonda returned in the early morning, she seemed . . . dazed. Like someone thoroughly stoned, with a secretive smile that was too damned easy to interpret. She curled up on the couch with a dreamy expression and wouldn't talk to me. When I tried she turned her face to the back of the couch and pretended to sleep. Finally, that night I brought her a tray of chicken wings, and sat it down next to her. She smelled it. Turned, smiled faintly, but didn't speak, other than offer a very soft:

"Thank you."

At that moment, I was certain. "You did it, didn't you?"

She looked at me, hands shaking. Didn't answer.

"What was it like?" I asked.

She paused. Then her face softened, as I'd only seen in our deepest, most intimate moments. "I can't describe it," she said with an almost feverish intensity.

"Try," I said. And in that moment I saw something from her I'd never seen before, and never would again: a desperate desire for me to understand her, as if in understanding we would bond more deeply. But something about what she said reminded me less of someone inviting you to a party, and more like someone skydiving without a parachute, terrified of dying alone. "Think of the worst kiss you've ever had. Then . . . the best sex. Can you do that?"

I couldn't help but smile at how she trembled to say those words. "O.K. Then what?"

"The gap between them is like . . . what the Gray was like." She gripped my hands, nails digging into my flesh. "Come with me. Let's share this. Let's . . ." I guess that disgust is something I don't hide well. She saw it, and drew away, the momentary vulnerability evaporated. Just like that. Gone.

Her lips twisted with sudden, bitter force. "You're a coward."

We slept in the same bed for a while after that, but . . . well, you know. And then she moved into the guest room, and never came back to our room. There would have been no point. We had no guests, and she wasn't coming back to me.

Ten years passed, one aching, disorienting day at a time. I had no need for earning money, but embraced busywork of many kinds, perhaps to distract myself from the unhappy fact that Rhonda and I had become mere roommates. Our sex life had dwindled to memories.

The world seemed to flow around me, like a stream dividing itself around a rock. I watched the fashions and culture slowly admit more and more Traveler imagery and influence, but little of it really seemed to break through my emotional cocooning. I had endless toys, and work, and that had to be enough.

Despite promises made in our empty bed I felt a certain nasty urge growing inside me. Every time I heard Traveler music, that compulsion grew. When I watched movies with *very* special guest stars something deep in my gut twitched. Like a tumor growing day by day right before your eyes, there is no single moment you can point to when you say "Ah-hah! It's cancer!" It sneaks up on you.

The scope of change was too large, the implications beyond sanity. And then one day, as Rhonda had known, the hunger sharpened from a whisper to a scream. I called an aircab and vaped in the backseat until my head spun. It dropped me off in the middle of nowhere and I walked randomly. Yeah, right. Pretended that I didn't know where I was going, finally ending up at one of the storefront enterprises they called a "friendship club." Paid my considerable fee, and entered. I'd had to get very very stoned, loaded enough that some part of me knew I would have plausible deniability.

In an office paneled with stars and nebulae stenciled with obscene constellations I met with a thin man who asked a battery of questions. I guess I answered them properly because I was taken to a shower room, where I was told to bathe. The water wasn't mere H_2O, it had a taste to it, a smell that faded, as if my nose had been numbed. And they led me to a dimmed room. I wished I'd vaped a little more.

The room's only furniture was a black couch. And the door behind me was the only door, so I expected it to open, and for something else to enter. I felt myself dizzying as if the scented droplets evaporating on my flesh were seeping into my bloodstream. I needed to sit down. Lay down.

And the moment I did the "couch" engulfed me.

Followed immediately by a wave of panic. God! It wasn't a couch, it was the Traveler version of some kind of sex toy, some B&D playground, their version of leather and chains and whips and gag-balls. *No! I* . . .

And then I felt myself . . . embraced in every orifice. Welcomed. Hungered for. It was not love. Not sex. It was . . . the form for which all of those are shadows. The sound, and all the others merely echoes.

When I awakened, I was alone in the room. The "couch" seemed just a couch again, although investigation revealed it to be an exoskeleton, a costume, into which a Traveler had stuffed itself. I left the lust-chamber, walked out past the receptionist's glassy smile. A half-dozen other experimenters hunched dazedly in the foyer, shuddering like men who had stepped out of a sauna into freezing cold. We sat around, half-dressed, unable to speak . . . and sharing a knowledge.

When I vacated the premises, the street outside shimmered with pools of cottony light radiating from no source I could determine. I swore I wouldn't, but turned around and returned to the friendship center and asked when I could go again. Months, they said. There was a long waiting list. I was told I could pay six figures to be placed at the head of that line. I'm sure Rhonda had. God help me, I considered it. But . . . I just couldn't.

Strange how separate threads twist together into a braid strong enough to hang you. How easy it is to rationalize. How proud I was of my tolerance for pain. And fear. Everything was going so well, I told myself. Life was just wonderful. I'd never been wealthy, and money is its own opiate. Perhaps the most powerful. You live in a kind of tunnel, insulated from most concerns. My health remained perfect, as They had promised. I was the same, but the social effects were now more noticeable, thirty years in.

Boys and girls seemed to care little for differentiating themselves by dresses and pants, or long and short hair, or makeup . . . as if that aching boy-girl tension no longer mattered quite so much. Or at all. I remember a morning on a London street, when I witnessed a wan couple pushing a perambulator down along the Thames. Our eyes met, and they smiled at me. Hopeful smiles. I smiled back. And as I always had, I reflexively peered into the baby carriage.

The infant was perhaps three months old, and gazing out at the world with the kind of glazed uncertainty that seems standard on babies that age. When it looked at me, it started to cry. I'd always found that sound to trigger the urge to comfort. Instead . . . its ululation was just irritating. It's smooth pale flesh seemed . . . grublike, and its bald head reminded me of my father, when he was dying of cancer in an Atlanta hospice. I recoiled, and the baby cried more loudly, and the parents pulled back into their shells and hurried away.

It was the only baby I'd seen for a week. The last one I saw for a month.

I saw fewer children on the streets, more shuttered and boarded-up schools. Humanity was so happy, so drunken on our new longer lives and endless nifty T-Tech that we just ignored what was happening around us.

As for me . . . I never had so much as a sniffle, and maintained beautiful muscle tone without doing so much as a push-up . . . but certain hungers seem to have quieted. Women passing on the street were often strikingly beautiful, but in a "healthy animal" way, not a matter of artifice or attraction. It was almost as if I was noticing their loveliness the way I might think a painting was lovely. Or a one-man sky-strider "walking" between clouds. Beautiful. Distant. Irrelevant to anything but a cool aesthetic appreciation.

Then one spring day in 2054 I was having Zavo at a local Starbucks. Oh, right. I've not told you about that. Zavo is the commercial name for a T-tech drink. I think they bioengineered it to not only sensitize your brain to norepinephrine, like caffeine does, but provide co-factors that allow your little gray cells to manufacture that juice with scary efficiency. How you can make something that lasts all day, has no jitters, and lets you sleep is beyond me. But it does.

Good dreams, too. Vivid. Intense.

When I drank it, I dreamed of the space between the stars.

A ratty-looking little Asian guy dropped onto the seat across from me. He stared at me, not moving, not speaking. Not blinking. "Do I know you . . . ?" I finally asked.

"It hasn't been that long," he replied. "You haven't forgotten so much . . . ?"

I skawed laughter. "Professor Watanabe! Man, it's been a long time." Hadn't seen him since our days at the Facility. He hadn't worn well. The Professor was well dressed, but he looked tense, like Atlas trying to be casual while holding the world on his shoulders. "You're doing well. We're all doing well."

"Travelers," he said.

A bubble car sailed by, a paramecium in the back seat, a superfluous human pretending to pilot a drone. Fashion statement. Professor Watanabe held my eyes with a smile, and slid over a silver thumb drive.

"What's this?" I asked. It looked antique, probably only holding a few terrabytes.

"Something you need to look at. Tonight."

"What is it?"

"Just read it. The core document will take a few minutes. You could spend a year going through the supporting data. All you could want."

"But what?"

"Open it. Remember my name, and open it."

Then, smile frozen on his face, Watanabe left the table. I turned the drive over and over again in a shaking hand.

What the hell?

As I said, the drive was decades old. Not T-Tech, not even current technology. That should have been a clue. I dragged out an ancient laptop. Instructions scribbled on the side of the drive warned me to disable WiFi before booting, and I did. It utilized an old-fashioned USB connection. I actually had to visit a vintage computer shop to find a proper connection, making lame excuses to the salesman to explain why I wanted a device that had been obsolete for at least thirty years. When I returned home with my acquisition, it took me an hour to figure out how to patch the computer to the drive. When I finally succeeded, a password prompt appeared.

Password? The professor didn't give me—

Then I recalled his odd request: *"Remember my name."*

Was that it? I typed "Watanabe" in, and to my pleasant surprise, his face materialized.

"Greetings, Mr. Kofax," he said. As in the coffee shop, Watanabe's face was pale and drawn. Leeched of color and life. The problem was not his physical health, I was sure. The Travelers had made sure of that. It was something else. Something worse. "You must be wondering about the cloak and dagger. Well, you aren't going to wonder for very long. I'm going to make this short, but I cannot make it sweet." He wiped his hand across his forehead, smearing a slick of perspiration. "I wish I could. The short version is: we made a mistake, Carver. You and I. We were the heroes, remember? We figured it out. Well I should have stuck with teaching, and you should have stuck to flogging soap."

"Why?" I muttered.

"Why? Because we've done our job too well. Something is going wrong. Human beings aren't having much sex anymore. Not with each other, at least. The mistake was thinking that when the Travelers told us they could not lie, they were offering every implication of their actions. They were honest, but not . . . forthcoming."

"What are you talking about?" I muttered. For the second time, it was as if he heard me, or had anticipated my thoughts.

"What I mean is that we figured everything was safe, because we evaluated how Traveler tech affected us. Their music, for instance. Played through our equipment, we found nothing to worry about. But then we began to upgrade our systems, using *their* tech, and frankly we failed to continue testing as carefully as we should. Traveler tech increased the bandwidth. They've given us biological, optical, computational and auditory technology, and we paid too much attention to how powerful it was, and not enough to how it all interlocked."

"Meaning what?"

This was some kind of video AI program. Even coming over an obsolete thumb drive, somehow it was still responding to me. Try as the Professor had to avoid it, Traveler tech's tendrils were everywhere. "Meaning that we gave them access to our hardware and software . . . and wetware, Carver. And they are reprogramming us."

"How? To do what?"

"Birthrates are dropping. It's happening faster and faster. Twenty percent reduction throughout the world, and no one panicked, because no one is complaining. We've gone numb somehow. We're just . . . not servicing each other."

It . . . was true. Rhonda and I hadn't had sex in over a decade, and I hadn't really considered the implications. And kids? We'd never talked . . .

No, that's not true. Once upon a time, we'd talked about having babies. We both came from large families, both loved our brothers and sisters, nieces and nephews . . . how unlikely was it that neither of us would hanker for kids?

"Carver, you need to look at the data. This isn't accidental, and it isn't local. We have the greatest catastrophe in the history of our species."

He said more, but it was much the same, except for a request that I meet with him, secretively, in a week's time.

A week. Time to research, to sift through the mountain of data on that drive. Time to think, and decide.

So . . . I looked. I slept perhaps three hours a night, barely eating or drinking, drunken with terror.

The data was incontrovertible.

For reasons no one understood, the Traveler effect was growing. Human beings were becoming more attracted to the aliens than we were to each other. Once you opened your eyes, the whole thing was obvious. I guess it was just that they were so . . . far beyond ugly that the idea they were some kind of competitive threat was absurd. You just couldn't take the notion seriously. But something had functioned like cosmic beer goggles.

And another terrible thing: my brain said to scream what I'd learned from the rooftops, to find some way to stop this, to crush them all. But another part of me felt (and I know how sick this sounds) *protective* of the Travelers. More so than I did of actual human children. Just as the data suggested. Show me a picture of one of the gelatinous oozing masses, and I felt like I had a lapful of warm kittens. Look at a picture of a bubbly brown-skinned baby, and all I could see was Louis Armstrong dipped in 30-weight.

I blinked, and shook my head and considered.

I couldn't talk to Rhonda. Dared not. Our bank account suggested she had paid almost a quarter million dollars to be part of an exclusive "friendship" club, getting serviced once a week. On what world could I trust her?

Certainly not this one.

The phone rang.

"So have you read through everything?" Dr. Watanabe asked.

"Yes," I said. "What are we going to do?"

I had been welcomed into a circle of rebels, all men and women Watanabe trusted. We met secretly in the professor's home, and discussed our quandary. Did we publicize, and risk losing our window of opportunity? Careful overtures to seats of power had been attempted, and rebuffed. We decided upon action.

There was a central media node in central Dallas where alien music and images were inserted in television, vids, and neural feeds. You've probably read the reports, or saw the trial, one of several triggered by similar actions around the globe. Ours was merely the first. I won't drag you through the overly familiar details, but here are the most critical:

The node was the repository of a vast river of information constantly streamed over multiple channels, probably including those ripples in space-time, the secrets we had coveted enough to ignore the risks of unknown technology. Watanabe reasoned that if we could destroy it, perhaps people would awaken from the trance we had helped induce.

As you know if you watch the news, we were successful getting in, planting our devices. The bomb exploded, killing Professor Watanabe, a woman named Courtney Pickett and two watchmen. But . . . the brain, the core of the facility itself, survived.

The police swooped in, loyal to their Traveler masters. There was no place to hide. We never had a chance to get away. The police had us before we could reach our nests or hidey-holes. It was almost as if they had known in advance, as if they wanted a terrorist act to use as an example. As if . . .

Rhonda.

She had hacked my computer. Rhonda, my loving wife. Wearing makeup that made her skin shimmer with translucence, revealing the succulent meat beneath.

My wife. My love. My betrayer.

The trial was short and sensational. My lawyers were the best that Traveler money could buy. I got the death penalty. Rhonda testified against me, her face a fish tank of gliding paramecium. The human judge wore silvery Traveler makeup, so that the inside of her head looked like a jar of winking cat's eyes.

I was screwed.

When Rhonda left the courthouse on that last day, she never looked back.

That's really all there is to say. They're coming now. I thought I'd have more time. Everyone does.

Two guards and a sad-faced minister in dark pants and shirt escorted Carver Kofax from his cell. He had been afraid for so long that he now felt only emptiness, as if the extreme emotion had hollowed him out.

"Are you ready, my son?" the priest asked. "Our father, who art in heaven, vanguard of our Traveling friends and saviors . . ."

"You've got to be kidding me," he muttered.

The death chamber was steel walls and a steel seat with clamps for his legs and arms. "Any last words?" the executioner asked after the shackles were snapped into place. On his neck, a Traveler tattoo crawled and beckoned lasciviously. Kofax swallowed back a sour taste. All the fear that had been hiding somewhere in the back of his head exploded to life, and he bucked against his restraints.

"This isn't right," Carver screamed. "You're making a mistake. We're all making a mistake—"

The executioner had left the chamber, sealed the door behind him. Vents at the floor level began to hiss, and greenish wisps of gas puffed out, pooled around his feet, and began to rise. He coughed, vomited, made one final convulsive push against the shackles, and then collapsed.

His vision slid to black.

And then . . . nothing.

I can't believe I'm writing this. It shouldn't be possible, but then, so many things have changed in what used to be "our" world.

Sparkles of light. I blinked. And opened my eyes.

White walls, humming machines of unknown design. But the humans standing over the bed, an East Indian and a coarse, chunky-looking pale blond woman, both wore medicinal white. "Where am I?" My throat felt dry and raw. It hurt even to whisper. Was this hell? Wasn't I dead?

"Wrong question," the doctor said. His skin and subcutaneous fat were translucent, his organs sparkling in his meat bag. Some kind of light-bending makeup, no doubt.

"What's the right question?"

"*When* are you?"

That made no sense, but I played along. "All right. When am I?"

"It is 2105. You've been gone for fifty years."

My mind went blank. "What the hell . . . ? I . . . I . . . ."

"I know. You thought you were dead. But you can thank the Travelers for that. They don't kill, even when you transgress against them. They just . . . put you aside for a time."

After I checked out of the hospital, I discovered that my bank account had been gaining interest for half a century, and now contained more than I could ever spend. There were also fewer people to help me spend it. The decrease in population was noticeable. The streets were almost empty, as if everyone was indoors watching a parade. The few human beings I saw scuttled along the concrete like lonely crabs, ancients in young bodies, morbidly afraid of their good health, of the vibrancy that would turn into sudden death without warning. That was what the Travelers promised, yes? Perfect health until death.

And of course, they didn't lie.

I saw no children at all.

Quietly, without any fuss, the Travelers were taking over the world. Not a shot fired.

Rhonda still lived in our penthouse. When she appeared on the vid screen she was . . . strange. She had aged another fifty years, but other than tight shiny skin and eyes drowned in fear and fatigue, on first look she hadn't changed much. The second and third looks told a different story. It was difficult to put my finger on precisely what was disturbing. Was it makeup? Surgery? Not sure. But it was almost as if she was some alien creature pretending humanity, as if there was nothing left of Rhonda at all.

"Carver?" she said, and in that moment her shock and surprise gave human animation to the mask of gelid flesh surrounding those mad eyes. "But . . . you're dead!"

Damn. No one had told her? I explained what had happened to me. At first she was in shock, but in time, guilt and relief mingled on her face. "You . . . you're so *ugly*." She cried for a moment, then wiped the tears away. I was hideous to her. Because I looked human. But so did she, at least on the surface. So some part of her had fought to remain human, even as another part had grown increasingly repulsed by that very thing.

Suddenly, the impact of what had happened really hit me. My knees buckled, and the world spun and darkened before I regained my balance. "I . . . oh, God. What did you do?"

"I . . . I'm old, Carver, but I still want to be touched. I'm too human for most people now. I should have had more operations, more implants, but I just couldn't." Her face twisted with self-loathing and something else, the barest touch of hope. "Has it been a long time for you? We could . . . I have virtual lenses I could wear. It would make you look . . . we could . . ."

"Fifteen-spice tuna roll," I said.

"What?" Her mouth hung slack, and beneath the mask of youth, I saw an old, old woman.

"Sometimes," I said, "you just have to know when to quit."

I hung up.

I had the money and time to travel, and did. It didn't matter what I said or did, not any longer. I wasn't censored or inhibited in any way. Things had progressed too far. Whatever the Travelers had done to humanity had taken hold. What few young people stumbling through the cities seemed pale, genderless ghosts floating through a concrete graveyard. Earth's cities were clean but sparsely occupied, and in the country, one could drive for miles and never glimpse a human face.

I did see human couples from time to time. One or two a month. It was good to know that whatever the Travelers had done was not 100 percent effective. Just . . . 99.9 percent.

I found myself laughing for no apparent reason. A lot.

I think I was afraid that if I ever stopped, I'd kill myself.

On leaving the hospital, I'd been given a plastic bag containing my possessions, along with a key to a storage locker where Rhonda had sent the majority of my possessions. One day after returning from one of my lonely trips, I wandered to the fenced facility and spent a few hours digging through the detritus of a remarkable, accursed life. Here was a bit of my childhood . . . there a photograph from our Barbados honeymoon. There a set of notes from some college assignment I could no longer remember. And bundles of old clothes. I rifled the pockets of a coat, and out fell a business card.

I bent, picked it up, and read it. Twice. And then, almost as if my lips were moving by themselves, I spoke the number and a circuit opened. The conversation was short, but enthusiastic. Within seconds a car hovered down from the sky and its door slid open.

The ride took about twelve minutes, and covered the distance from Los Angeles to a two-story white mansion in Whitehaven on the outskirts of Memphis. The airdrone deposited me on the lawn. I rang the doorbell, finger shaking.

Elvis answered the front door. He was as recognizable as ever, an amoeba in a rhinestone suit.

"Howdy there, Carver. How's it shakin'?" His translation equipment had not only improved, but had mastered the local drawl.

"I uh . . . I guess I'm a little surprised . . ." so he, or It (or *they*. What the hell did I really know?), had purchased The King's cottage. Hardly surprising. Travelers could pretty much have anything they wanted.

"That ah like this form? You thought ah was kidding?"

"No," I said. I felt like my bones were made of sand. "I guess I don't."

"We don't lie."

"No, you don't." There was something so ridiculous, so cosmically absurd about the gelatinous form in the white sequins, gliding on a mucous trail through a pop-culture mausoleum, that the occasion was almost solemn. "You fit here," I said. "I guess you learned from us, too."

"It goes both ways," Elvis said. "A little."

Videos of *Jailhouse Rock* and *Viva Las Vegas*, a garage filled with vintage cars and halls swathed in platinum records. Elvis talked non-stop, as if he had memorized a billion factoids about a singer dead for more than a century, someone whose hip-shaking melodies must have traveled a trillion miles before reaching whatever the Travelers used instead of ears. The tour ended in a den dominated by an empty fireplace pointing out this or that artifact or that, including a certificate signed by Richard Nixon and the head of the DEA, presented to Elvis Aaron Presley on December 21, 1970, authorizing him as a "Federal Agent at Large," whatever the hell *that* meant.

I shook myself out of my trance. "How many times have you done this?" I said in the smallest voice I had ever heard emerge from my throat.

"Toured people through Graceland?"

"No." I gestured vaguely. "This. What you did to us."

"What you did to yourselves. Oh, no one really knows. You call us Travelers, but we're really more like traders. Sex isn't universal. But there's always something people want. Your media images showed you to be both attracted and repelled by sex, and by strangeness, and that gave us our opportunity."

I plopped down on the couch, finally feeling the weight of my frozen years. At least I thought it was a couch. It didn't molest me, anyway. "So it's . . . just over for us? For the human race?"

"Not totally," Elvis said, and somehow a twitch of his protoplasm resembled a sneering lip. "The creches will keep pumping you guys out. Humans are fun. Entertaining. I mean . . . we don't hate you or anything. So please, live out the rest of a long, long life. What wonders you will see! You're walking history, you know. And . . . we owe it all to you." The creature turned, the organelles floating within the transparent sack very much like a swarm of anxious eyes. They even narrowed in something I interpreted as regret, or concern. "You're angry. I can tell. I understand," he said. "And I'm sorry."

Elvis paused. "Say: I know," he brightened. "Want to fuck?"

I stared in disbelief, sputtering and trying to . . . trying to . . .

"Oh," I finally sighed. "What the hell."

sixteen questions for
kamala chatterjee

ALASTAIR REYNOLDS

A professional scientist with a Ph.D. in astronomy, Alastair Reynolds worked for the European Space Agency in the Netherlands for a number of years, but has recently moved back to his native Wales to become a full-time writer. His first novel, Revelation Space, *was widely hailed as one of the major SF books of the year; it was quickly followed by* Chasm City, Redemption Ark, Absolution Gap, Century Rain, *and* Pushing Ice, *all big sprawling space operas that were big sellers as well, establishing Reynolds as one of the best and most popular new SF writers to enter the field in many years. His other books include a novella collection,* Diamond Dogs, Turquoise Days *and a chapbook novella,* The Six Directions of Space, *as well as three collections,* Galactic North, Zima Blue and Other Stories, *and* Deep Navigation. *His other novels include* The Prefect, House of Suns, Terminal World, Blue Remembered Earth, On the Steel Breeze, Terminal World, *and* Sleepover, *and a Doctor Who novel,* Harvest of Time. *Upcoming is a new book,* Slow Bullets.

Here he follows a scientist whose struggle to stay involved with a project that will take thousands of years to complete eventually transforms her into something more than human.

W*hat first drew you to the problem?*
She smiles, looking down at her lap.

She is ready for this. On the day of her thesis defence she has risen early after a good night's sleep, her mind as clean and clear as the blue skies over Ueno Park. She has taken the electric train to Keisei-Ueno station and then walked the rest of the way to the university campus. The weather is pleasantly warm for April, and she has worn a skirt for this first time all year. The time is *hanami*—the shifting, transient festival of the cherry blossom blooms. Strolling under the trees, along the shadow-dappled paths, families and tourists already gathering, she has tried to think of every possible thing she be might asked.

"I like things that don't quite fit," she begins. "Problems that have been sitting around nearly but not quite solved for a long time. Not the big, obvious ones. Keep away from those. But the ones everyone else forgets about because they're not quite glamorous enough. Like the solar p-mode oscillations. I read about them in my undergraduate studies in Mumbai."

She is sitting with her hands clenched together over her skirt, knees tight together, wondering why she felt obliged to dress up for this occasion when her examiners have come to work wearing exactly the same casual outfits as usual. Two she knows well: her supervisor, and another departmental bigwig. The third, the external examiner, arrived in Tokyo from Nagoya University, but even this one is familiar enough from the corridors. They all know each other better than they know her. Her supervisor and the external advisor must have booked a game of tennis for later. They both have sports bags with racket handles sticking out the sides.

That's what they're mainly thinking about, she decides. Not her defence, not her thesis, not three years of work, but who will do best at tennis. Old grudges, old rivalries, boiling to the surface like the endless upwelling of solar convection cells.

"Yes," she says, feeling the need to repeat herself. "Things that don't fit. That's where I come in."

When you touched the Chatterjee Anomaly, the object that bore your name, what did you feel, Doctor?
Fear. Exhilaration. Wonder and terror at how far we'd come. How far I'd come. What it had taken to bring me to this point. We'd made one kind of bridge, between the surface of the Sun and the Anomaly, and that was difficult enough. I'd seen every step of it—borne witness to the entire thing, from the moment Kuroshio dropped her sliver of hafnium alloy on my desk. Before that, even, when I glimpsed the thing in the residuals. But what I hadn't realised—not properly—was that I'd become another kind of bridge, just as strange as the one we drilled down into the photosphere. I'd borne witness to myself, so I ought not to have been so surprised. But I was, and just then it hit me like a tidal wave. From the moment they offered me the prolongation I'd allowed myself to become something I couldn't explain, something that had its inception far in the past, in a place called Mumbai, and which reached all the way to the present, anchored to this instant, this point in space and time, inside this blazing white furnace. In that moment I don't think there was anything capable of surprising me more than what I'd turned into. But then I touched the object, and it whispered to me, and I knew I'd been wrong. I still had a capacity for astonishment.

That in itself was astonishing.

It was only later that I realised how much trouble we were in.

Can you express the problem for your doctoral research project in simple terms—reduce it to its basics?
"It's a bit like earthquakes," she says, trying to make it seem as if she is groping for a suitable analogy. "Ripples in the Earth's crust. The way those ripples spread, the timing and shape of their propagation as they bounce around inside the crust, there's information in those patterns that the seismologists can use. They can start mapping things they wouldn't ordinarily be able to see, like deep faults—like the Tōkai

fault, out beyond Tokyo Bay. It's the same with the Sun. For about sixty years people have been measuring optical oscillations in the surface of the Sun, then comparing them against mathematical models. Helioseismology—mapping the solar interior using what you can deduce from the surface. Glimpsing hidden structure, density changes, reflective surfaces and so on. It's the only way we can see what's going on."

You mentioned Kuroshio. We have records of this individual. Was Kuroshio the first to speculate about the project's feasibility?
Kuroshio was an academic colleague—a friend. We played football together, in the women's squad. She was a solid state physicist, specialising in metallurgy. I knew her a little when I was preparing my thesis, but it was only after I resubmitted it that we got to know each other really well. She showed me around her lab—they had a diamond anvil in there, a tool for producing extremely high pressures, for making materials that didn't exist on Earth, like super-dense hydrogen.

One morning she comes into my office. She had to share one with three postdocs herself, so she envied me having a whole office to myself. I think she's come to talk about training, but instead Kuroshio drops a handkerchief-sized scrap of paper onto my desk, like it's a gift, and invites me to examine the contents.

But all I can see is a tiny sliver of metal, a sort of dirty silver in colour. I ask Kuroshio to explain and she says it's a sample of a new alloy, a blend of hafnium, carbon and nitrogen, cooked up in the solid-state physics lab. Like I'm supposed to be impressed. But actually I am, once she starts giving me the background. This is a theoretical material: a substance dreamed up in a computer before anyone worked out how to synthesize it. And the startling thing is, this material could endure two thirds of the surface temperature of the Sun without melting.

"You know what this means, don't you?" she asked me. "This is only a beginning. We can think about reaching that crazy alien thing you discovered. We can think about drilling a shaft into the Sun."

I laughed at her, but I really shouldn't have.

Kuroshio was right.

What makes you think you might be a suitable candidate for doctoral work? Select one or more answers from the options below. Leave blank if you feel none of the options apply.

- I am a diligent student. I have studied hard for my degree and always completed my coursework on time.
- I believe that I have a capacity for independent research. I do not need constant supervision or direction to guide my activities. In fact, I work better alone than in a crowd.
- I look forward to the day when I can call myself 'doctor.' I will enjoy the prestige that comes from the title.

You felt that the solar heliospheric oscillations would be a fruitful area to explore?
No, an inward voice answers sarcastically. I thought that it would be an excellent way to waste three years. But she straightens in her chair and tries to make her hands stop wrestling with each other. It's sweaty and close in this too-small office.

The blinds are drawn, but not perfectly, and sunlight is fighting its way through the gaps. Bars of light illuminate dust in the air, dead flies on the window sill, the spines of textbooks on the wall behind the main desk.

"Before I left Mumbai I'd spent a summer working with Sun Dragon, a graphics house working on really tough rendering problems. Light-tracing, real physics, for shoot 'em up games and superhero movies. I took one look at what those guys were already doing, compared it to the models everyone else was using to simulate the solar oscillations, and realised that the graphics stuff was way ahead. So that's where I knew I had an edge, because I'd soaked up all that knowledge and no one in astrophysics had a clue how far behind they were. That gave me a huge head start. I still had to build my simulation, of course, and gather the data, and it was a whole year before I was even close to testing the simulation against observations. Then there was a lot of fine-tuning, debugging . . ."

They look at graphs and tables, chewing over numbers and interpretation. The coloured images of the solar models are very beautiful, with their oddly geometric oscillation modes, like carpets or tapestries wrapped around the Sun.

"P-mode oscillations are the dominant terms," she says, meaning the pressure waves. "G-mode oscillations show up in the models, but they're not nearly as significant."

P for pressure.

G for gravity.

The road to Prometheus Station was arduous. Few of us have direct memories of those early days. Do you remember the difficulties?

Difficulty was all we knew. We breathed it like air. Every step was monumental. New materials, new cooling methods, each increment bringing us closer and closer to the photosphere. Our probes skimmed and hovered, dancing closer to that blazing edge. They endured for hours, minutes. Sometimes seconds. But we pushed closer. Decades of constant endeavour. A century gone, then another. Finally the first fixed bridgehead, the first physical outpost on the surface of the Sun. Prometheus Station. A continent-sized raft of black water-lilies, floating on a breath of plasma, riding the surge and plunge of cellular convection patterns. Not even a speck on the face of the Sun, but a start, a promise. The lilies existed only to support each other, most of their physical structure dedicated to cooling—threaded with refrigeration channels, pumps as fierce as rocket engines, great vanes and grids turned to space . . . each a floating machine the size of a city, and we had to keep building the entire network and throwing it away, whenever there was a storm, a mass ejection, or a granulation supercell too big for our engineering to ride out. We got better at everything, slowly. Learned to read the solar weather, to adjust Prometheus Station's position, dancing around the prominences. Decades and decades of failure and frustration, until we managed to survive two complete turns of the sunspot cycle. Slowly the outpost's complexity increased. To begin with, the only thing we required of it was to endure. That was challenge enough! Then we began to add functionality. Instruments, probes. We drilled down from its underside, pushed feelers into thickening plasma. Down a hundred kilometres, then a thousand. No thought of people ever living on it—that was still considered absurd.

The alignment between your models and the p-mode data is impressive—groundbreaking. It will be of great benefit to those working to gain a better understanding of the energy transport mechanisms inside the Sun. Indeed, you go further than that, speculating that a thorough program of modelling and mapping, extended to a real-time project, could give us vital advance warning of adverse solar weather effects, by linking emergent patterns in the deep convection layers with magnetic reconnection and mass ejection episodes. That seems a bold statement for a doctoral candidate. Do you wish to qualify it?
"No."

9: But people came, didn't they?
We got better at stability. Fifty years without losing Prometheus Station, then a century. I'd have lived to see none of it if they hadn't offered me the prolongation, but by then I was too vital to the project to be allowed the kindness of dying. And I'm not sorry, really, at least not of those early stages. It was marvellous, what we learned to do. I wish Kuroshio had seen it all. The machines constructed a station, a habitable volume on one of the central lilies. Heat wasn't the central problem by then—we could cool any arbitrary part of the station down as low as we liked, provided we accepted a thermal spike elsewhere. Thermodynamics, that's all. Gravity turned out to be the real enemy. Twenty-seven gees! No unaugmented person could survive such a thing for more than a few seconds. So they shaped the first occupants. Rebuilt their bodies, their bones and muscles, their circulatory systems. They were slow, lumbering creatures—more like trees or elephants than people. But they could live on the Sun, and to the Sunwalkers it was the rest of us who were strange, ephemeral, easily broken. Pitiable, if you want the truth of it. Of course, I had to become one of them. I don't remember who had the idea first, me or them, but I embraced the transformation like a second birth. They sucked out my soul and poured it back into a better, stronger body. Gave me eyes that could stare into the photosphere without blinking—eyes that could discriminate heat and density and patterns of magnetic force. We strode that bright new world like gods. It's exactly what we were, for a little time. It was glorious.

No, better than that. We were glorious.

10: Let's turn now to your concluding remarks. You summarise your mathematical principles underpinning your simulations, discuss the complexities involved in comparing the computer model to the observed p-mode data, and highlight the excellent agreement seen across all the comparisons. Or almost all of them. What are we to make of the discrepancies, slight as they are?
"They're just residuals," she says, not wanting to be drawn on this point, but also not wanting to make it too obvious that she would rather be moving into safer waters. The Sun's angle behind the blinds has shifted during the conversation and now a spike of brightness is hitting her dead in the eye, making her squint. There's a migraine pressure swelling up somewhere behind her forehead.

"The worrying thing would be if the model and the data were in too close an agreement, because then you'd conclude that one or the other had been fudged." She squints at them expectantly, hoping for the agreement that never comes. "Besides, the only way to resolve that discrepancy—small as it is—would be to introduce an unrealistic assumption."

11. What attracts you to the idea of working in Tokyo? Select one or more answers from the options below. Leave blank if you feel none of the options apply.
Tokyo is a bustling city with a vibrant nightlife. I plan to throw myself into it with abandon. I will never be short of things to do in Tokyo.

I have always had a romantic attachment to the idea of living in Japan. I have seen many films and read many comic strips. I am certain that I will not be disappointed by the reality of life in Tokyo.

Beyond the university, the city is irrelevant to me. Provided I have somewhere affordable to sleep, and access to colleagues, funds and research equipment, I could live anywhere. I expect to spend most of time in air-conditioned rooms, staring at computer screens. I could be in Mumbai or Pasadena or Cairo for all the difference it will make.

12: But to go deeper . . . you must have quailed at the challenge ahead of you?
We did, but we also knew no one was better equipped to face it. Slowly we extended our downward reach. Ten thousand kilometres, eventually—feelers tipped with little bubbles of air and cold, in which we could survive. The deep photosphere pressing in like a vice made of light, seeking out the tiniest flaw, the slightest weakness. Beneath three hundred kilometres, you couldn't see the sky any more. Just that furious white furnace, above and below.

But clever alloys and cooling systems had taken us as far as they were capable. Electron-degenerate matter was our next advance—the same material white dwarf stars are made out of. A century before we got anywhere with that. Hard enough to crush matter down to the necessary densities; even harder to coax it into some sort of stability. Only the existence of the Anomaly kept us going. It provided a sort of existence theorem for our enterprise. A machine survives inside the Sun, deeper than any layer we've reached. If it can do that, so can we.

But the truth is we might as well have been starting science from scratch. It was like reinventing fire, reinventing basic metallurgy.

But we did it. We sent sounding probes ahead of the main shaft, self-contained machines constructed from shells of sacrificial degenerate matter. Layers of themselves boiled away until all that was left was a hard nugget of cognitive machinery, with just enough processing power to make observations and signal back to us. They forged a path, tested our new materials and methods. Another century. We pushed our physical presence down to thirty thousand kilometres—a borehole drilled half way to the prize. Conditions were tough—fully murderous. We could send machines to the bottom of the shaft, but not Sunwalkers. So we shaped new explorers, discarding our old attachment to arms and legs, heads and hearts. Sunsprites. Sun Dragons. A brain, a nervous system, and then nothing else you'd recognise as human. Quick, strong, luminous creatures—mermaids of light and fire. I became one, when they asked. There was never the slightest hesitation. I revelled in what they'd made of me. We could swim beyond the shaft, for a little while—layers of sacrificial armour flaking away from us like old skins. But even the degenerate matter was only a step along the way. Our keenest minds were already anticipating the next phase, when we had to learn the brutal alchemy of nuclear degenerate matter. Another two centuries! Creating tools and materials from neutron-star material made our games with white dwarf matter look like child's play. Which it was, from our perspective. We'd come a long way. Too far, some said.

But still we kept going.

13: *What do you mean by unrealistic?*

"Look," she says, really feeling that migraine pressure now, her squinting eyes watering at the striped brightness coming through the blinds, a brightness with her name on it. "Everyone knows the Sun is round. A child will tell you that. Your flag says the same thing. But actually the Sun is really quite unreasonably round. It's so round that it's practically impossible to measure any difference between the diameter at the poles and the diameter at the equator. And if a thing's round on the outside, that's a fairly large hint that it's symmetric all the way through to the middle. You could explain away the residuals by adding an asymmetric term into the solar interior, but it really wouldn't make any sense to do so."

And nor, she thinks, would it make sense to introduce that term anyway, then run many simulations springing from it, then compare them against the data, over and over, hoping that the complication—like the cherry blossoms—will fall away at the first strong breeze, a transient business, soon to be forgotten.

They stare at her with a sort of polite anticipation, as if there is something more she ought to have said, something that would clear the air and allow them to proceed. They are concerned for her, she thinks—or at least puzzled. Her gaze slips past theirs, drawn to the pattern behind the blinds, the play of dust and light and shadow, as if there's some encouraging or discouraging signal buried in that information, hers for the reading.

But instead they ask to see a graph of the residuals.

14: *Can you be certain of our fate?*

Yes, as I'm sure of it as anyone can be. Obviously there are difficulties of translation. After all the centuries, after all the adaptive changes wrought on me, my mind is very far from that of a baseline human. Having said that, I am still much, much closer to you than I am to the Anomaly. And no matter what you may make of me—no matter how strange you now find me, this being that can swim inside a star, this Sun Dragon of degenerate matter who could crush your ships and stations as easily as she blinks, you must know that I feel a kinship.

I am still human. I am still Kamala Chatterjee, and I remember what I once used to be. I remember Mumbai, I remember my parents, I remember their kindness in helping me follow my education. I remember grazing my shins in football. I remember the burn of grass on my palm. I remember sun-dappled paths, paper lanterns and evening airs. I remember Kuroshio, although you do not. And I call myself one of you, and hope that my account of things is accurate. And if I am correct—and I have no reason to think otherwise—then I am afraid there is very little ambiguity about our fate.

When I touched the Anomaly, I suddenly knew its purpose. It's been waiting for us, primed to respond. Sitting inside the Sun like a bomb. An alien timebomb. Oh, you needn't worry about *that*. The Sun won't explode, and tongues of fire won't lash out against Earth and the other worlds. Nothing so melodramatic.

No; what will happen—what is happening—is subtler. Kinder, you might say. You and I live in the moment. We have come to this point in our history, encountered the Anomaly, and now we ponder the consequences of that event. But the Anomaly's perception isn't like that. Its view of us is atemporal. We're more like a family tree than a species. It sees us as a decision-branch structure frozen in time—a set of histories, radiating out from critical points. An entity that has grown into a particular complex shape, interacted with the Anomaly across multiple contact points, and which must now be pruned. Cut back. Stripped of its petals as the summer winds strip a cherry blossom.

I can feel it happening. I think some of it rubbed off on me, and now I'm a little bit spread out, a little bit smeared, across some of these histories, some of these branches. Becoming atemporal. And I can feel those branches growing thinner, withering back from their point of contact, as if they've touched a poison. Can you feel it too?

No, I didn't think so.

15: *If you were offered a placement, when do you think you would be able to start your research? Select one or more answers from the options below. Leave it blank if you feel none of the options apply.*
I would be able to start within a few months, once I have settled my affairs in my home country.
I would like to start immediately. I am eager to begin my doctoral work.
I would like time to consider the offer.

16: *We feel that the thesis cannot be considered complete without a thorough treatment of the residual terms. A proper characterisation of these terms will lead to a clearer picture of the "anomaly" that seems to be implied by the current analysis. This will entail several more months of work. Are you prepared to accept this commitment?*
A moment grows longer, becomes awkward in its attenuation. She feels their eyes on her, willing her to break the silence. But it has already gone on long enough. There can be no way to speak now that will not cast a strange, eccentric light on her behaviour. That light coming through the window feels unbearably full of meaning, demanding total commitment to the act of observation.

Her throat moves. She swallows, feeling herself pinned to this moving instant in space and time, paralysed by it. Her migraine feels less like a migraine and more like a window opening inside her head, letting in futures. Vast possibilities unfold from this moment. Terrifying futures, branching away faster and more numerous than thoughts can track. There is a weight on her that she never asked for, never invited. A pressure, sharpening down to a point like the tip of a diamond anvil.

There's a version of her that did something magnificent and terrible. She traces the contingent branches back in time, until they converge on this office, this moment, this choice.

Agree to their request. Or fail.

She gathers her notes and rises to leave. She smoothes her skirt. They watch her without question, faces blank—her actions so far outside the usual parameters that her interrogators have no frame of reference.

"I have to go to the park again," she says, as if that ought to be answer enough, all that was required of her. "It's still hanami. There's still time."

They watch as Kamala Chatterjee closes the door behind her. She goes to Ueno Park, wanders the cherry blossom paths, remaining there until the lantern lighters come out and an evening cool touches the air.

cold comfort

PAT MURPHY AND PAUL DOHERETY

Pat Murphy writes fiction that inhabits the borderland between genres, where life is interesting and the rules are slippery. She is very grateful that science fiction exists, since it has provided a happy home for seven of her eight novels and many of her short stories. Her work has won numerous awards, including two Nebula Awards, the Philip K. Dick Award, the World Fantasy Award, the Seiun Award, and the Theodore Sturgeon Memorial Award. Her novels include The Falling Woman, The City Not Long After, Nadya: The Wolf Chronicles, Wild Angel, *and* Adventures in Time and Space with Max Merriwell. *Her short stories are collected in* Points of Departure *and* Women Up to No Good. *With Karen Joy Fowler, she cofounded the James Tiptree, Jr. Award, an annual literary prize for science fiction or fantasy that expands or explores our understanding of gender roles. In her day job, she is the resident Evil Genius at MysteryScience.com, where she creates science activities to inspire and amaze elementary school students.*

Paul Doherty is a physicist, author, teacher, and mountaineer. As part of his job as a senior scientist at the Exploratorium, he worked as a scientist/ writer at McMurdo station Antarctica. There he joined a group of scientists doing research on the rim of Mt. Erebus, an active volcano, and learned first-hand about surviving in the extreme cold. In collaboration with Pat Murphy, Paul writes a science column for The Magazine of Fantasy and Science Fiction. *He has written many nonfiction science books, including the Explorabook, which came with the tools for doing the experiments it described. He is the winner of the Faraday Award for Excellence in Science Teaching from the National Science Teachers Association. A longtime science fiction reader, Paul worked out the equations for the navigation of a relativistic spacecraft back in 1979, which landed him a mention in Fredrick Pohl's novel "Starburst."*

Here they join forces to show us how a race between a Fart Catcher and a catastrophic release of methane from thawing permafrost may make the difference between disaster and preserving our civilization—and catastrophe is winning the race.

I stood in the center of the frozen Arctic lake, chipping at the ice with an ice chisel, a sharp-edged piece of steel attached to a five-foot-long handle. It was the middle of May, and the ice was still about a meter thick. I made an indentation large enough to hold a bundle of six explosive cartridges.

One cartridge in the bundle was primed with a number 6 electric blasting cap. I attached the lead wires to the cap, placed the cartridges in the crater I had made, then scraped the ice chips back into the hole to cover them. The afternoon sun would warm the surface and melt the snow a little. In the chill of the evening, it would refreeze, sealing the charge in place.

I walked north on the ice, unrolling the lead wires. The spruce trees that surrounded the lake tilted this way and that, leaning on each other like drunks at closing time. A drunken forest. The trees had grown in the permafrost, the permanently frozen soil of the Arctic Circle, and their roots were shallow. As the frozen soil had melted, the trees had abandoned their upright posture, beginning a slow motion fall toward the ground. As the permafrost melted, it released methane, the main component of natural gas.

I stopped to brush snow off the ice and chip another crater. Beneath the black ice I could see thousands of white blobs, as numerous as stars in the sky. Some were as big as my hand; some as big as my head. Each one was a bubble of methane released by the melting permafrost and trapped beneath the ice.

I looked up when I heard the crunch of footsteps in the snow. My friend Anaaya grinned at me. "You're slow, Doctor Maggie. I've already finished the other side of the lake."

Anaaya was the only person who insisted on the honorific. She was an old friend. We had been roommates in our freshman year at University of Alaska. She had graduated with a bachelor's degree in civil engineering; I had gone on to get a doctorate.

"Of course you're faster," I told her. "You actually know what you're doing."

"I'll help you out, Doctor Slowpoke."

It was a small lake, but it took us three hours working together to plant all the charges. When we were done, we surveyed our work from the lakeshore. The afternoon breeze was already blowing snow across the lake, erasing our footprints. The charges and the connecting wire were invisible beneath the snow and ice.

"No sign that we were ever here," I said.

"We were never here," she said. "Who would ever stop at this lake? No one. No fishing here, no hunting—no reason to stop. You're on your way to check on a methane monitoring station; I'm looking into some reports of illegal trapping for my aunt." Anaaya's aunt was involved in tribal management. "All official business."

Looking out over the lake at the drunken forest, tilted trees as far as the eye could see, I didn't hesitate. "Of course."

We returned to our snowmobiles and headed north to accomplish our official business.

Two weeks later, the lake exploded. Our charges had cracked the ice and ignited the rising methane.

I wasn't there to see it happen. No one was. But three satellites were perfectly positioned to capture the show. Two aerospace engineers—friends of friends who could not be traced to me—had independently calculated the orbits and set the ideal time for the explosion. They had done a good job. The satellite images were spectacular. A very impressive mushroom cloud. Trees for miles around the lake were blasted with ice shards.

An ecoterrorist, JollyGreen, took credit for the explosion, releasing a lengthy manifesto about the melting of the permafrost and the release of methane. JollyGreen was a sock puppet, of course. Not my sock puppet. The sock puppet of a friend of a friend of a friend with no connections back to me.

JollyGreen's basic message was this: Earth's average global surface temperature was increasing and the Arctic was heating up faster than the rest of the planet. The permafrost was melting and releasing methane, which was twenty times better at trapping the sun's heat than carbon dioxide. More methane meant more warming. That meant more permafrost melting, which meant more methane and more warming . . . and so on in a positive feedback loop with negative consequences.

"The human race is already screwed because of climate change," he wrote. "There'll be flooding, famine, drought, and more. Too late to turn all that around, but it can get worse. If all the permafrost melts, we are royally screwed. Mass extinctions, mass die-off of phytoplankton and disruption of the ocean's ecosystems, wildfires on land. Nowhere to run; nowhere to hide."

For the next few days, news programs featured Arctic researchers explaining the consequences of climate change north of the Arctic Circle. Some of my former colleagues at the University of Alaska were quizzed on camera about the permafrost and methane in Arctic lakes. Several cited my work. Yes, they said, the permafrost was melting, methane constantly bubbled up under Arctic lakes. None of this was secret information.

I was not among the scientists interviewed. I heard that a couple of reporters trying to find a way to contact me put pressure on the PR department at the university, but no one gave me up. They just said I was no longer affiliated with the university.

A month later, after the explosion had faded from the news cycle, the National Science Foundation called me. I was about 100 miles away from the exploding lake, making coffee over a driftwood fire in Ivvavik National Park, Canada's least visited national park. I had spent the month living in a qarmaq, a sod-roofed hut built decades before by an Inuit family to serve as a winter camp. It was just large enough for me, Claire, and Marina—grad students who had elected to spend the summer getting a little field experience working with me. The qarmaq was conveniently situated right beside the one-acre plot where I was testing a unique method of capturing methane released by melting permafrost.

Here there were no spruce trees to betray the softening of the soil beneath the surface. Low grasses and shrubs grew in a boggy landscape. Nestled among the plants were carbon fiber tubes, woven together to make a very loose mat. In some areas, the fibers had been trampled into the soil by a passing herd of reindeer.

A year before, I had submitted a proposal to the National Science Foundation about this pilot project. I had called this tangle of carbon fiber tubes a "methane sequestering mat." When NSF turned down my grant proposal, I had posted the project on a crowd-funding site, where I referred to it as a "fart catcher." Crowd-funding had financed my one-acre pilot project.

It was a warm day by Arctic standards—slightly above freezing. I wore hiking boots with two pairs of wool socks, rather than the large white bunny boots—rubber inside and out with thick insulation between the waterproof layers—that were necessary in the winter. I could breathe without a filter to warm the air before it reached my lungs. Practically balmy.

I was talking with Clan and Marina about plans for the day when the satellite phone rang. The call was from an NSF program officer, the same guy who had turned down my grant proposal. But that had been before the lake exploded, before permafrost became—ever so briefly—the star of the 24/7 news cycle, before some members of Congress began calling for zero methane emissions in the Arctic.

NSF was adding a new initiative that focused on methane emission from the melting permafrost. The program officer had called my house in Fairbanks and persuaded the house sitter to give him the number of my satellite phone. He wanted to discuss my proposal for a methane-sequestering mat.

Sitting on a camp stool by the driftwood fire, looking out over the tundra and the tangle of carbon fibers, I told the program officer about results to date from my crowd-funded prototype. Knowing that this program officer had an engineering background, I focused on how the project made use of recent innovations in nanotechnology—the carbon fiber tubes, the low-pressure methane-hydrate storage tank made possible by advances in carbon nanotube technology. I recited numbers—emission rates, kilograms of methane recovered. It was a cordial and productive conversation.

Nine months later, I landed at Franklin Research Station. Built of recycled shipping containers and located on the coastal tundra just outside the Arctic National Wildlife Refuge, the station was a low rust-colored box surrounded by ice. To the north, the Beaufort Sea—a plain of ice stretching away to meet the blue sky. To the south, the Brooks Range—mountains that looked as if they had been sculpted from snow, not just covered by it. I had been lucky to fly in during a calm spell. March was the start of the Arctic research season, but the weather was always dicey.

"Welcome to your home away from home," the pilot called out as he turned the plane's nose into the wind and brought it down smoothly on the ice-covered runway.

"Happy to be here," I said sincerely.

A few hours later, after unpacking my gear, I repeated that sentiment as I met with Jackson Hanks, the head of operations at the station. I had done my research on the man. He was twenty years my senior. A biologist by training, but he had been head of operations at the station for more than a decade, while station managers had come and gone.

A former colleague from my university days who had spent a summer at Franklin Station provided me with more detailed information than Google ever could: "That guy? He'll never go rogue. He knows how to work the system. He's never the leader but always in charge. He keeps his head down and knows where all the bodies are buried."

Oki, the head cook at Franklin Station, was a distant cousin of my friend Anaaya. He had provided even more important information: what Jackson Hanks liked to drink.

I arrived in Jackson's office with a bottle of bourbon. "A gift from the south," I said, as I set it on his desk. "My sources say it's your favorite brand."

Jackson smiled, opened the bottle, and brought two glasses out of a drawer. "A pleasure to meet you, Dr. Lindsey."

"Maggie," I said. "Nobody calls me doctor." I accepted a glass of bourbon and sat across the desk from him. We engaged in the usual small talk of the Arctic, discussing the weather, the state of the sea ice, my good luck in getting in before the wind picked up. At that moment the wind was blasting the triple-paned office window with ice crystals and making the station vibrate with a steady hum.

Jackson sipped his bourbon, then told me they'd been having problems with polar bears of late. That led to a story about a grad student who had come to the station to study the population decline of polar bears. "He thought they were cute until he got trapped in a remote observation blind for three days when a couple of young bears decided he'd make a good snack. After that, he switched to studying the decline of the parrotfish population in coral reefs off the coast of the Yucatán."

"He could have switched to Arctic foxes," I suggested. "They're plenty cute and not at all menacing unless you're a lemming."

Jackson shook his head. "He's better off in the tropics. He didn't belong up here."

"So you condemned him to sweltering on the beach and watching the sea level rise."

"Drinking warm beer because there's no ice. Battening down for hurricanes. Battling giant tropical spiders."

We lifted our glasses and toasted the guy who couldn't cut it in our environment of choice.

"When I found out you were coming to the station, I asked a few sources of my own about you," he told me.

"Find out anything interesting?"

"The station manager at McMurdo says you passed his test, and that's good."

When I was in grad school, I'd spent a summer at McMurdo Station in Antarctica, helping with a study of the microbiome of Antarctic soils.

"What test was that?" I asked. I didn't remember a test.

"He watches what people do in the cafeteria. He looks for people who are just as comfortable in a group discussion as they are sitting by themselves. You passed."

I nodded. "I get along with people," I said. "And I can get along alone."

He leaned back in his chair, studying me. "Tell me—why did you leave the university? You were teaching, doing research, on a tenure track."

"One too many committee meetings," I said lightly. He laughed, and I added, "I like to get things done."

"I can understand that," he said. "So tell me about this methane sequestering mat of yours. Or do you prefer 'fart catcher'?"

I shrugged. "Either one." Since Jackson was a biologist, I launched into an explanation of the biology of the system. "The mat's made of carbon fiber tubes, but what makes it work is the colony of bacteria in those tubes."

It turned out that Jackson knew quite a bit about *Methylomirabilis oxyfera*, the bacteria that made the mat work. Amazing critters those—they thrive in stinking black mud without light or oxygen, digesting methane and nitrogen oxides for their energy. In the tubes of the mat, they consumed enough methane to create a concentration gradient that kept the methane flowing into the tubes and rising into a storage tank.

"A biological methane pump?" he said. " That's clever. And you want to cover a square mile with this fart catcher? That's ambitious."

"A square mile is just a start. We have to move fast, you know. With the current rate of methane emission . . ."

He held up a hand to stop me. "Hold on. I don't need to hear JollyGreen's manifesto on Arctic warming. I live here, remember?"

"Sorry."

"Having that lake blow up gave your permafrost research quite a boost, didn't it?"

"I suppose it did."

"I can understand the motives of whoever did it. No one pays any attention to what happens up here unless it involves something cataclysmic or cute. Polar bears get press; permafrost usually doesn't."

I didn't say anything. I just waited.

He studied me, then smiled, ever so slightly. "I assume that safety protocols will ensure that there will be no explosions associated with your project."

I nodded quickly. "I can assure you of that."

He poured another glass. "I'll give you a crew to lay out this fart catcher of yours. I trust you'll supervise the work."

I did more than supervise. I worked alongside the crew that rolled out the fart catcher. It was nasty, tedious work. The crew described it as hellacious, and I had to agree.

My test plot in Ivvavik National Park had been a flat grassy area. It had been easy to push the carbon tubes down so they made contact with the soil. On the coastal plain surrounding Franklin Station, the land was flat, but the vegetation was less cooperative. The fart catcher had to lie flat against the soil, so we had to clear away tough shrubs—willow and Labrador tea. We had to pound down dense tussocks formed by sedges and grasses. In a month and a half, we managed to install less than a quarter of the projected area.

I contacted some friends about the problem. It takes a team to save the world, after all. I had many friends and they had friends and their friends had friends. Social media was wonderful that way. My friends (and their friends) often had creative solutions. Some people talk about thinking outside the box. Many of my friends had never seen the box. They were unaware that the box existed. I sent out the word and waited to see what would happen.

A month later, as the crew and I were clearing yet another patch of willow, I heard someone call to me. I looked up to see a herd of shaggy beasts lumbering over the tundra toward us.

Muskoxen—Pleistocene megafauna at its most charismatic. They're called oxen, but they're actually more closely related to goats. Their ancestors had survived the mass extinction event that occurred during the transition from the Pleistocene to the Holocene. The herd stopped at the edge of the carbon tube carpet, eying me myopically as they stood shoulder to shoulder, ready to dispatch any predator with their large pointy horns.

"Hello!" Someone in a lavender parka came around the side of the herd and waved to me. "We're here at last."

That was Jenna, leader of the muskoxen herders. There were five muskoxen herders, two Royal Canadian Mounties, and a dozen cows and six calves. They had traveled from a muskoxen farm some 150 miles to the south.

I escorted the people and their shaggy charges to Franklin Station. While the ox herders found a patch of good grazing for the beasts, the Mounties met with Jackson and presented him with the official paperwork. Apparently, a Canadian muskoxen farm had donated the animals to Franklin Station—a donation approved by a top level official in the US agency responsible for polar research. It was unclear where the request for this donation had originated.

While Jackson chatted with the Mounties about their journey, I helped his assistant research the situation. The path of official approvals was an insane tangle, involving at least three agencies on the US side and the same number on the Canadian side. But in the end, it didn't really matter who had approved what. The muskoxen were an official gift from Canada to the US. Officials on the US side made it quite clear that sending the muskoxen away would cause an international incident.

Besides, news of the gift was already trending on all news feeds—it was the warm and fuzzy story of the day. A muskox calf is not nearly as cute as an Arctic fox, but they do have a certain charm. In those days of doom and gloom and climate change, cheery stories associated with polar science were hard to come by.

So Franklin Station gained a herd of muskoxen. Jackson found temporary quarters for the Mounties and the ox herders and arranged for a crew to set up a paddock for the beasts. To help out, I volunteered to take charge of the care of the muskoxen, mentioning that they could be an asset to my project. Muskoxen would happily devour tundra shrubs. Their hooves would break up and flatten the lumps and bumps in the soil, making it easier to roll out the fart catcher.

When the visitors headed to their quarters, Jackson asked me to stay. "So tell me," he said. "How did you make this happen?"

I shook my head. "I didn't make it happen." After a moment's pause, I went on. "I talked about the problems we've been having with laying out the fart catcher with a friend who studies muskoxen. He reminded me that large ruminants were great at modifying the environment. I did say that it was a pity I didn't happen to have any of those. He must have mentioned it to someone who decided to help out."

Jackson shook his head, looking incredulous.

"I've found that if you put the word out to enough people, useful stuff happens. You never know what it's going to be. But sometimes, it's just what you need."

"That's nuts. That's no way to manage a project."

I leaned forward in my chair. "Those beasts will make a big difference to how much mat we can install before winter. And you know this project is important. You've seen the changes in the Arctic over the last decade."

"Of course I have."

"Reduction in the sea ice. Steadily increasing temperature. Changes in wildlife patterns. Changes in weather patterns. When will the climate reach the tipping point? How long do you think we have? Another decade or two? Then what?"

"You think you'll save the world with a square mile of fart catcher and a dozen muskoxen?"

I shrugged. "It's a start. Baby steps, but it's a beginning. I promise there'll be no explosions. I'll take care of the herd. They won't bother you a bit."

Over the next few weeks I worked with the ox herders to learn the ways of the shaggy beasts. The herd grazed in the area around the station, returning to their paddock at night for special muskox treats—carrots mostly. A muskox will follow you anywhere for a carrot.

The head of PR at the station shot photos and video: muskoxen grazing with the research station in the background, muskoxen in their newly built paddock, muskox calves sleeping by their muskox mamas. It was great PR for the station, and that earned Jackson some points with the administration. All good.

After a couple of weeks, the ox herders headed back to their farm, promising to return in the spring to comb out the qiviut, the muskoxen's underwool. It was a great cash crop, eight times warmer than wool and softer than cashmere. As a farewell gift, the ox herders gave me a set of long johns knit from qiviut—the warmest, softest, and most expensive underwear I've ever owned.

So that was my first summer at the station—laying carpet, bringing in some muskoxen, collecting some 30 metric tons of methane. Calculations for required storage had been spot on—the storage tanks were almost full. It was a good start, but it was time to move on to the next phase, one that was not covered in my grant application: disposing of the methane without adding it to the atmosphere and in the process funding a significant increase in the methane harvest.

In the fall, I left the station to get some business done in the lower forty-eight. I presented a paper at the American Geophysical Union's annual meeting in San Francisco and met with a few research teams from Siberia, Norway, Greenland, and Canada who were engaged in similar projects. While I was there, I also met with a German research group that was working on methane cracking.

Here's a quick chemistry lesson. Methane is made of carbon and hydrogen. In methane cracking, hydrogen is separated from carbon to make hydrogen gas and carbon. Hydrogen is a great fuel. Think of the Hindenburg: a big bag of hydrogen and a major explosion. If you burn hydrogen, you get water. No carbon dioxide, no greenhouse gas problem.

And here's a bonus. What's left when you take away the hydrogen is pure carbon. Perfect for making more carbon tubes to capture and store methane and valuable on the commodities market for use in manufacturing. Many companies from car makers to aircraft builders were switching from steel to lighter stronger carbon fiber to make their products. You can see why I was interested in methane cracking.

I met the Germans at a restaurant in Drowntown. That was the name San Fran-
ciscans had given to the area of downtown that flooded when the tide was high, a
result of rising sea levels. It was low tide that evening. The streets were dry, but there
was a whiff of salt and seaweed in the air.

The lead German researcher was Katrin, an earnest woman who asked—politely
but with a slightly baffled tone—about the American politicians' continued stress
on carbon emission targets. "All research has indicated that stopping emissions will
not stop the change in climate," she said earnestly. "Even if we stopped today, the
world's temperature will continue to increase for half a century. They do not seem
to understand that."

"Rearranging deck chairs on the Titanic," I said. "It's a popular pastime in political circles. I'm seen as the voice of doom and gloom because I recognize that the
permafrost is melting at an increasing rate and that methane capture should be a
top priority."

"And you are successfully capturing methane. What is your current capture rate?"

We drank beer and made calculations. Katrin estimated expenses on the back of
a napkin as we worked out a plan for a pilot project involving methane cracking.
During the Arctic summer, I could use solar power to crack the methane, and then
cool and compress the hydrogen gas. I hoped to find a manufacturer to process the
carbon into more carpet. Katrin had some ideas there—and some excellent contacts
in the German manufacturing community.

"I understand that NSF regulations require you to purchase your materials in the
US," she said.

I waved a hand, dismissing the problem. "I have private funding as well," I explained. The presence of the muskoxen had been an enormous help in crowdfund-
ing efforts. Charismatic megafauna has its uses.

"Very good," she said. "Then I think I can assist you."

That was the first stop in a long winter of hunting and gathering. So many technical problems to solve, with little time and not enough money.

The hive mind found me a way to store the hydrogen that my pilot project would
produce: a decommissioned tank from NASA, originally built to contain liquid hydrogen fuel for the space shuttle. It had never been used. For decades, it had been
stored at NASA's New Orleans manufacturing facility on the far eastern edge of New
Orleans—still above water, but just barely. The facility was being decommissioned—
the last hurricane had come close to wiping it out—and they were happy to find a
home for the fuel tank.

I set up a relationship with a German manufacturing plant that would make some
of my pure carbon into fart catcher carpet and methane hydrate storage. I'd compensate them for their service with the rest of the carbon, which they could use or
sell for a fat profit.

The rest of my time was spent retrofitting the hydrogen fuel tank for my needs
and arranging for transport. Everywhere I went, I could see the effects of the changing climate. But people were doing what people always do—complaining about the
weather and adapting to it where they could. Many politicians still doubted that
change was underway even as some religious leaders were preaching about the end
times.

I was happy to return to the Arctic for another summer of work. The carpet from the previous year was functioning beautifully. Arctic grasses and other plants were growing through the loose weave of the mat, making it a part of the landscape. Trampling by the muskoxen had smoothed out the cursed tussocks and laying the next section of carpet was considerably easier than the first section had been.

Of course, there were problems. On top of the usual sleet storms and blizzards, we had to be alert to changes caused by warmer temperatures. Whenever we were outside the station, we were armed against starving polar bears that thought Arctic researchers might substitute for their usual diet of walrus and seal. We almost lost part of the carpet-laying crew when a sinkhole opened up in the area where we were working. Fortunately, the fart catcher carpet was strong enough to act as a safety net. It supported us and let us climb back up out of the hole.

I won't pretend there weren't difficulties with the hydrogen tank (delivered a month late) and the pilot methane cracker. But we got it all working eventually.

I also expanded the research station's greenhouse, something that I'd discussed with Oki and the kitchen crew the summer before. The original greenhouse was quite small—just big enough to grow a few vegetables. But with the hydrogen I was producing, I had energy to burn—so to speak. In my scavenging at the NASA manufacturing facility in New Orleans, I had run across a prototype greenhouse designed for Mars. The warehouse supervisor gave me a great deal on it. He said it would be abandoned within the month along with anything else left in the facility.

I set the Martian greenhouse up as an extension of the existing greenhouse. A hydrogen-powered heater allowed me to warm the air with no impact on the station energy budget and a cushion of carbon nanotubes insulated the permafrost from the greenhouse and collected the methane that outgassed.

Down in the lower 48, things were getting worse faster than anyone had expected. Changes in polar temperatures had caused perturbations in the polar jet stream that wreaked havoc with global weather patterns. There was drought and wildfire in the western US, severe flooding in the South, historic blizzards along the eastern seaboard, and tornadoes where tornadoes had never been before.

By the end of the summer, I had quadrupled the land covered with fart catcher and I'd made plans to cover ten times that area in the following year. The research teams in Siberia, Greenland, Canada and Norway were also having success.

That winter, my efforts focused on acquiring hydrogen transport and figuring out how to roll out more carpet with the same crew.

Well, not exactly the same crew. I had been in touch with a robotics team that worked in an abandoned warehouse in São Paulo, Brazil.

They called themselves the Ant Factory, a nonprofit collective of entrepreneurial engineers. Well . . . some of them were engineers. Some of them were artists. All of them were scavengers, retrofitters, people who knew how to make do, people who simultaneously thought in the long term and the short term. My kind of people.

"We're old school," the head engineer told me. At least, he seemed to be in charge. His name was Renaldo and he had a seemingly infinite supply of black t-shirts emblazoned with cryptic sayings. My favorite read "Fast, Cheap, and Out of Control."

Renaldo claimed that was the best approach to projects like mine. "You know how US space program works," he said. "They triple check everything and build safeguards into their safeguards and redundancies onto their redundancies. We're the opposite of that."

In the warehouse parking lot, the Ant Factory had created an obstacle course where they held robot trials. Some parts of the course were constant—broken pavement, loose rocks, a pile of sand that could bury a bot in an avalanche. Other parts changed every day—the team was constantly adding booby traps and barriers. A slick of ice, a small mountain of melting snow, a sticky patch of some sort of goo—I thought it might be something toxic, but it turned out to be molasses.

The Ant Factory built me a robot that could traverse the course while rolling out fart catcher carpet. Actually, they built me a hundred robots—Renaldo called them *"pequeninos peidos"*—little farts. With a hundred robots, he said, it wouldn't matter if a few of them failed. "Power in numbers," he said.

Powered by hydrogen fuel cells, designed for rough terrain—originally the Little Farts were agribots designed to roll over just about any lump, bump, or tussock.

On my last night at the Ant Factory, I sat on the old loading dock and watched a dozen Little Farts navigate the course, towing and unrolling a large carpet that Renaldo assured me was heavier than the Fart Catcher. The team was celebrating. I had sprung for pizza and beer—a pilsner from a local brewery called Drown Your Sorrows. The label showed an ocean wave washing down São Paulo's main street.

"I don't know how I can thank you for all this," I told Renaldo as we watched one bot climb the slush mountain, trailing black carbon fibers. I wasn't paying the Ant Factory much. I'd almost exhausted my crowd-sourced funding.

He sipped his beer, surveying the rubble-filled yard. "You know those Hollywood movies where a few people save the world. We're those people. We'll make a difference."

I nodded.

Renaldo knew someone who knew Katrin, so he already knew about my success with methane cracking. "What are you doing with the hydrogen you're producing?" he asked me. "I have a friend who would be happy to purchase it."

"Technically, I can't actually sell the products of my work," I told him. "That's against NSF regulations."

He nodded. "I understand. I am confident my friend would accept any hydrogen you chose to give him. He would offer goods and services in exchange."

"That could work. Of course, there is the problem of transportation."

"No problem. My friend Hehu lives in the Raft. He can take care of transportation."

The Raft was a seasteading community, a loose affiliation of over a hundred vessels that had been converted to floating farms and cities by climate refugees from small island nations that had been wiped out by rising waters.

"Let me contact him on your behalf."

I returned to the Arctic with Renaldo's bots. Jackson didn't ask questions about where I got them. He and I had developed a fine working relationship. He was glad that I needed a smaller work crew. The muskoxen were spooked by the bots at first, but they got used to them.

Renaldo's friend Hehu came through. He reached the research station with two ships—a former Arctic cruise ship, now modified as a floating farm and residence for a few dozen people, and a former navy ship, now modified for hydrogen transport.

Hehu was from Woleai Atoll, the first island group to be swamped by the rising sea. I liked his team of engineers—the head of the group was from JPL and he knew one of the aerospace engineers who had calculated the satellite orbits for me. He had, like me, gone rogue, and we had a fine time discussing the advantages and disadvantages of leaving the confines of the university.

It was a fabulous summer. There were the usual problems with sinkholes and sleet storms and polar bears, but the robots worked well and I successfully expanded the area covered with the Fart Catcher to about twenty square miles. As autumn approached, it was all going very well. Until it all went very wrong.

I should have paid more attention to the news. While I'd been setting up partnerships and laying carpet and dodging polar bears, there had been a presidential election, a major change in congress, and a shift in national priorities. Hurricanes had wiped out New Orleans and a few other southern cities. Storm-driven waves were eroding beach bluffs and flooding US cities. Funding was being diverted to disaster relief. Franklin Station would shut down at the end of the season.

And somehow my work had come to the attention of new political appointees in charge of climate research. They were upset by my dealings with Renaldo and the Germans and Hehu and . . . oh, just about everybody who had been helping me out. Some of my partners were apparently on terrorist watch lists.

At least, that was one story. Some of my friends suggested that the concern about terrorism was a cover. What had really pissed people off was the success of my methane cracking—steel manufacturers did not like the possibilities offered by cheap availability of pure carbon.

Whatever the cause, I was in trouble. Jackson told me that Navy personnel who came to close down the station would be taking me into custody and charging me with a list of offenses including theft of government property and conspiracy to provide material support for terrorism. Jackson had been ordered to confine me to the station.

The day before the Navy ship was due to arrive, I left. At my request, Oki had packed a box of supplies—including all of the fresh carrots that were left in the greenhouse. Before hugging me goodbye, he quizzed me on my equipment. He listened carefully to a long list: silk long johns, qiviut underwear, a layer of wool, windproof coat and pants, parka, bunny boots, hat, hood, air filter to warm the air before it entered my lungs, a rifle for the polar bears, a popup shelter, and on and on.

"All right," he said at last. "Stay warm, stay dry. Don't get dehydrated and eat as many calories as you can stuff in your face—and you'll be fine." He hugged me goodbye.

It was a sunny day with a light wind. Two little farts accompanied me, dragging my gear on an improvised sled made of a plastic pallet I had found on the beach among the driftwood. In addition to the food and gear I had listed for Oki, I had a fiberglass kayak that had been left in the station's storage by a seal researcher.

I took no satellite phone, no GPS, no electronics that might be used to find me. Such a strange feeling, leaving all that behind.

The muskoxen followed me—not out of affection, but in return for carrots that

I dropped along the way. Their hooves completely obliterated my tracks and the marks left by my improvised sled and the little farts.

The hike to the shore was about a mile. When I reached the shore, I reset the little farts to return to the station. The muskoxen followed them, hoping for more carrots.

I abandoned the plastic pallet on the beach where I had found it, loaded the kayak, slid it into the water, and headed west for a place I knew.

A few years back, I had decided to retrace the steps of my favorite Arctic explorer, Ernest de Koven Leffingwell, a guy who never got a lot of press. Everyone paid attention to Peary and Amundsen and Scott. Big voyages, big funding. Leffingwell never had much funding and didn't give a damn about reaching the North Pole.

He came up here in 1901 and fell in love with the Arctic. He spent nine summers and six winters up here, traveling around, making observations, keeping meticulous records. No fancy equipment—he had Inuit guides; he used dog sleds and small boats. He made the first map of the coastline worth looking at. He was the first person to explain ice wedges and the very first to pay any attention to the permafrost.

A few years back, I spent the better part of a summer retracing his journeys in this area. On that trip, I spent a week in an old prospector's house where Leffingwell had wintered. Half sod-hut, half log cabin, it was still in pretty good shape. Good shelter, well-concealed, near the coast, and so obscure that only a dedicated permafrost researcher would know about it.

The wind was with me, but even so it was a long paddle down the coast to the small inlet where the cabin was located. I beached the kayak and dragged it and all my gear into the cabin. The wind had picked up and I knew it would erase my tracks.

Inside, out of the wind, I made myself at home and waited for the search to come and go. It was a long wait. When weather was calm, I could hear the search helicopter from miles away—the distinctive whup, whup, whup of their rotors warned me to take cover so searchers couldn't spot me.

When the wind was blowing, the helicopters didn't fly. Then I would listen to the wind. Sometimes a gust would make the hut shudder so the boards creaked and groaned. More often a steady wind would make the walls vibrate, so I felt like I was shivering even when I wasn't. The wind had been trying to tear the hut down for more than a hundred years.

In the first week, a bear found my hiding place, but I had my rifle. Bear meat, while not fine dining, is a good source of protein.

The nights grew longer and longer until the sun never rose. When the sun was just below the horizon, it wasn't completely dark. It was like that time right after the sun sets, when the sky is the deepest possible blue. Imagine that deep blue moment stretching on and on. The blue light colored the entire world, reflecting from the snow and the water. I felt like I was swimming in the sky.

For me, that was the important moment. Not the brilliant golden flash of the lake's explosion, but rather the cool, blue, liminal light where nothing seemed real and I was not sure what would become of the world.

I had to wait a long time for the searchers to give up and leave, but eventually I stopped hearing helicopters. I returned to the station for the winter, a long paddle followed by a long walk over the pack ice. It was so cold that I could feel the mucus freeze in my nose when I took a breath without my air filter on. The very act of breathing put me at risk of dehydration—since every bit of water vapor froze instantly, the air was bone dry.

The station had been stripped down, but my friends had left behind everything I needed. There was a stash of canned food in the kitchen. The hydrogen-powered generator in the greenhouse was still there.

The winter was cold and long and lonely. I grew potatoes under improvised grow-lights. I set up a still and perfected the finest hooch ever made in the Arctic Circle. Arctic Fire, I called it.

Satellite communication had been shut down when they closed the station, but I rigged a ham radio. When the ionosphere cooperated, I could catch news broadcasts. The news was never good: heat waves, drought, hurricanes, flooding, famine, disease.

I managed to contact a few friends and I told them I was all right. They told me that the Navy team had searched for me in all the safety huts and all known emergency shelters. They fixated on the largest of the sinkholes—the one that almost swallowed my crew. They spotted some marks at the edge that could have been made by a rope and figured a sinkhole offered a great hiding place. Down there, there'd be no wind, no bears.

It had taken their team a week to stage an expedition to the bottom to look for me. I'm glad they all got in and out all right. Dangerous place, a methane sinkhole. Not somewhere I'd like to spend a lot of time.

Come spring, finding me was no longer a priority for the US government. The Arctic winter was summer in the Antarctic, and there had been some major developments down south. The Western Antarctic ice sheet, which scientists had thought would remain stable for several more decades, had started collapsing in a most spectacular fashion. The top layers of the sheet had been melting each summer, exposing long-buried crevasses. One of those crevasses broke through the bottom of the ice shelf, and an iceberg the size of Connecticut broke loose. A few weeks later, another one, just as big, broke free. Then another.

The icebergs were dramatic, but they weren't the real problem. The Western ice shelf held back the glaciers on the Antarctic continent. Without it, those glaciers would flow into the sea. All told, that could add 30 million cubic kilometers of water, give or take a few million, to the world's oceans. Faced with this threat, politicians were turning their attention to immediate construction projects to hold back the sea. A rogue scientist eating potatoes and polar bear meat in a closed research station was way down on anyone's list of concerns.

With the return of the spring, Hehu arrived with ships laden with Fart Catcher net, methane cracking equipment, and empty tanks to be filled with hydrogen. That was thirty years ago.

Now we have the world as it is.

I sit in Jackson's office. I still think of it as his, though he hasn't been here for thirty years. I use it as my office now.

Hehu sits in the chair on the other side of the desk. It's spring again and he has sailed north just as he has each spring for the last thirty years. But he hasn't come alone. Each spring, a fleet of ships comes north to spend the summer in the Beaufort

Sea. It is a ragtag fleet of cruise ships and barges and freighters and Navy ships, all repurposed for this new world, all laden with food and supplies for the station, all carrying folks eager to work on the annual methane harvest.

Some ships are equipped with methane cracking facilities; others carry empty hydrogen tanks or empty holds. Each ship has its own unique community and culture—some grow tanks of algae; others grow forests; some grow pot farms. Some are environmentally based communities with overtones of Native American cultures; some are party boats with overtones of Burning-Man culture.

They call themselves the Sunseekers. I call them the summer people. The winter doesn't exist for them—not really. It is always summer where they are.

I pour Hehu a glass of my Arctic Fire. "You make the best hooch in the Arctic Circle," he says.

I smile. I didn't make this hooch by myself. The station staff, all of them young and smart, do the hard work to keep the station running, monitoring the fart catcher, tending the muskoxen and reindeer, making high octane booze, and preparing for the Sunseeker Fleet's arrival.

When the ships arrive in the Arctic, there is a great celebration always with much singing and dancing. They celebrate the summer methane harvest and they treated me like a hero.

All summer long, the Sunseeker ships crisscross the ice-free Arctic ocean, visiting fart-catcher projects in Norway, Greenland, Siberia, Canada. Each autumn, the ships take away tanks of hydrogen and holds filled with pure powdered carbon.

The Sunseekers are a cheerful lot. And why wouldn't they be? This is a fine new world, a utopian future, a happy ending. As the permafrost melts, they capture the methane. As the oceans rise, they build more ships.

To them, it seems so natural that half the world's remaining population lives in nomadic floating colonies. Most of them didn't know any of the people who died in droughts and floods, heat waves and blizzards. They didn't know all those who suffered disease and famine.

Jackson died of dengue fever when disease-carrying mosquitos brought that disease to the American South, a shift made possible by warmer temperatures and increased rain. Katrin starved in the European famine—caused by unseasonable snowstorms resulting from the slowing of the Gulf Stream and the North Atlantic Drift, ocean currents that kept Europe warm. Renaldo drowned in a flood that wiped out São Paulo, the result of a monster storm. Just one extreme weather event among hundreds.

They all died. Billions of people died. Not millions—billions. It took all those deaths to bring the world population down to a more sustainable level and let us reach this happy ending.

This isn't the way I thought it would work out when I set out to save the world. All those square-jawed heroes of the old science fiction stories had it wrong. You can't save the world as we know it. I did what I could, and I did some good in the world. But you can't save the world without changing it.

"A toast," Hehu said, lifting his glass. "To the future."

I nodded and lifted my glass. "To the future. There's no stopping it."

The Art of Space Travel

NINA ALLEN

The problem with an obsessive, lifelong search is that sometimes you actually find what you're looking for. . . .

Nina Allan's stories have appeared in numerous magazines and anthologies, including Best Horror of the Year #6, The Year's Best Science Fiction and Fantasy 2013, *and* The Mammoth Book of Ghost Stories by Women. *Her novella* Spin, *a science fictional re-imagining of the Arachne myth, won the BSFA Award in 2014, and her story-cycle* The Silver Wind *was awarded the Grand Prix de L'Imaginaire in the same year. Her debut novel* The Race *was a finalist for the 2015 BSFA Award, the Kitschies Red Tentacle, and the John W. Campbell Memorial Award. Her second novel,* The Rift, *will be out in 2017. Find her blog,* The Spider's House, *at www.ninaallan.co.uk. She also writes a column for* Interzone.

Magic spells are chains of words, nothing more. Words that help you imagine a different future and create a shape for it, that help you see what it might be like, and so make it happen. Sometimes when I read about our struggle to land people on Mars, that's how the words seem to me—like an ancient incantation, and as deeply unfathomable, a set of mystical words, placed carefully in order and then repeated as a magical chant to bring about a future we have yet to imagine.

The Edison Star Heathrow has sixteen floors, 382 bedrooms, twenty private penthouse apartments, and one presidential suite. It is situated on the northern stretch of the airport perimeter road, and operates its own private shuttle bus to ferry patrons to and from the five terminals. We have a press lounge and a flight lounge and conference facilities. As head of housekeeping, it's my job to make sure things run smoothly behind the scenes. My job is hard work but I enjoy it, by and large. Some days are more demanding than others.

It was all just rumours at first, but last week it became official: Zhanna Sorokina and Vinnie Cameron will be spending a night here at the hotel before flying out to join the rest of the Mars crew in China. Suddenly the Edison Star is the place to be. The public bar and the flight lounge have been jammed ever since the announcement. There's still a fortnight to go before the astronauts arrive, but that doesn't seem to be putting the punters off one little bit. It's cool to be seen here, apparently. Which is ironic, given that we weren't even the mission sponsors' first choice of hotel. That was the Marriott International, only it turned out that Vinnie Cameron had his eighteenth here, or his graduation party or something. He wanted to stay at the Edison Star and so that's what's happening.

I guess they thought it would be churlish to deny him, considering.

The first result of the change of plan is that the Marriott hates us. The second is that Benny's on meltdown twenty-four hours a day now instead of the usual sixteen. I can't imagine how he's going to cope when the big guns arrive.

"Perhaps he'll just explode," says Ludmilla Khan—she's the third-floor super. A dreamy expression comes into her eyes, as if she's picturing the scene in her mind and kind of liking it. "Spontaneous combustion, like you see in the movies. The rest of us running around him flapping like headless chickens."

She makes me laugh, Ludmilla, which is a good thing. I think there's every chance that Benny would drive me over the edge if I didn't see the funny side. Benny's a great boss, don't get me wrong—we get on fine most of the time. I just wish he wasn't getting so uptight about the bloody astronauts. I mean, Jesus, it's only the one night and then they'll be gone. Fourteen hours of media frenzy and then we're last week's news.

Probably I'm being mean, though. This is Benny's big moment, after all, when he gets to show off the Edison Star to the world at large and himself as the big guvnor man at the heart of it all. There's something a bit sad about Benny underneath all his bullshit. I don't mean sad in the sense of pathetic, I mean genuinely sad, sorrowful and bemused at the same time, as if he'd been kidnapped out of one life and set to work in another. And it's not as if he doesn't work hard. He's beginning to show his age now, just a little. He's balding on top, and his suits are getting too tight for him. He wears beautiful suits, Benny does, well cut and modern and just that teeny bit more expensive than he can really afford. Benny might be manager of the Edison Star, but you can tell by his suits that he still wishes he owned it. You can see it every time he steps out of the lift and into the lobby. That swagger, and then the small hesitation.

It's as if he's remembering where he came from, how far there is to fall, and feeling scared.

My mother, Moolie, claims to know Benny Conway from way back, from the time he first came to this country as a student, jetting in from Freetown or Yaoundé, one of those African cities to the west that still make it reasonably easy for ordinary civilians to fly in and out.

"He had a cardboard suitcase and an army surplus rucksack. He was wearing fake Levi's and a gold watch. He sold the watch for rent money the first day he was here. He still called himself Benyamin then, Benyamin Kwame."

When I ask Moolie how she can know this, she clams up, or changes her story, or claims she doesn't know who I'm talking about. I don't think it's even Benny she's remembering, it can't be, or not the Benny Conway who's my boss, anyway. She's confusing the names, probably, getting one memory mixed up with another the way she so often does now.

Either that, or she just made it up.

Benny slips me extra money sometimes. I know I shouldn't accept it but I do, mainly because he insists the money is for Moolie, to help me look after her. "It must be tough, having to care for her all by yourself," Benny says, just before he forces the folded-over banknotes on me, scrunching them into my hands like so many dead leaves. How he came to know about Moolie in the first place, I have no idea. There's a chance Ludmilla Khan told him, I suppose, or Antony Ghosh, the guy who oversees our linen contract. Both of them are friends of mine, but you can imagine the temptation to gossip in a fish tank like this. I take the money because I tell myself I've earned it and I can't afford not to, also because maybe Benny really is just sorry for Moolie and this is his way of saying so, even though I've told him enough times that it's not so much a question of looking after Moolie as looking out for her. Making sure she remembers to eat, stuff like that. It's the ordinary stuff she forgets, you see. During her bad patches her short-term memory becomes so unreliable that every day for her is like the beginning of a whole new lifetime.

It's not always like that, though. She can look after herself perfectly well most of the time, she just gets a bit vague. She can't do her work anymore, but she's still interested in the world, still fascinated by what makes things tick, by aeroplanes and rivers and metals, the rudiments of creation. Those are her words, not mine—*the rudiments of creation*. Moolie used to be a physicist. Now she sounds more like one of those telly evangelists you see on the late-night news channels, all mystery and prophecy and lights in the sky. But when it comes down to it, she's interested in the same things she's always been interested in—who we are and how we came here and where the bloody hell we think we're going.

If you didn't know her how she was before, you wouldn't necessarily spot that there's anything wrong with her.

It's all still inside, I know it—everything she was, everything she knows, still packed tight inside her head like old newspapers packed into the eaves of an old house. Yellowing and crumpled, yes, but still telling their stories.

For me, Moolie is a wonder and a nightmare, a sadness deep down in my gut like a splinter of bone. Always there, and always worrying away at the living flesh of me.

The doctors say there's nothing to stop her living out a normal lifespan but I think that's bollocks and I think the doctors know it's bollocks, too. Moolie was fifty-two last birthday, but sometimes she's bent double with back pain, as bad as a woman of eighty or even worse. Other times she burbles away to herself in a made-up language like a child of four. Her whole system is riddled with wrongness of every kind. The doctors won't admit it, though, because they're being paid not to. No one wants to be liable for the compensation. That's why you won't find any mention of the *Galaxy* air crash in Moolie's medical file, or the sixteen lethal substances that were eventually identified at the crash site, substances that Moolie was hired to isolate and analyse.

There were theories about a dirty bomb, and it's pretty much common knowledge now that some of the shit that came out of that plane was radioactive. But ten years on and the report Moolie helped to compile still hasn't been made public. The authorities say the material is too sensitive, and they're not kidding.

The medics have given Moolie a diagnosis of early-onset Alzheimer's. If you believe that then I guess, well, you know how it goes.

When Moolie dies I'll be free. Free to move away from the airport, free to look for another job, free to buy a one-way ticket to Australia and make a new life there. I lie awake at night sometimes, scheming and dreaming about these things, but in the morning I wonder how I'll manage. Moolie is like a part of me, and I can't imagine how the world will feel without her in it.

When she goes, all her stories will go with her, the ones she makes up as well as the ones that happen to be true.

Once she's gone, I'll never discover which were which.

I think about the astronauts a lot. Not the way Benny would like me to be thinking of them, I bet—with Benny it's all about scanning the rooms for bugging devices, checking the kitchens for deadly pathogens, making sure the PA system in the press lounge hasn't blown a gasket.

I know these things are important. If we cock up it won't just be Benny who looks an idiot, and the last thing I want to see is some kid in the catering department getting fired because someone forgot to tell them to stock up on mixers. I check and recheck, not for Benny's sake but because it's my job, and my job is something I care about and want to do well. But every now and then I catch myself thinking how crazy it is really, all this preparation, all this fussing over things that don't actually matter a damn. When you think about what Zhanna Sorokina and Vinnie Cameron and the rest of them are actually doing, everything else seems juvenile and pointless by comparison.

They're going to Mars, and they won't be coming back.

I wonder if they know they're going to die. I mean, I know they know, but I wonder if they think about it, that every one of them is bound to cop it much sooner than they would have done otherwise, and probably in a horrible way. It's inevitable, isn't it, when you consider the facts? There's no natural air on Mars, no water, no nothing. There's a good chance the whole crew will wind up dead before they can even set up a base there, or a sealed habitat, or whatever it is they're supposed to be doing when they arrive.

How do they cope with knowing that? How does anyone begin to come to terms with something that frightening? I can't imagine it myself, and I have to admit I don't try all that hard, because even the thought of it scares me, let alone the reality.

In interviews and articles I've read online, they say that learning to cope with high-risk situations is all part of the training, that anyone with insufficient mental stamina is weeded out of the selection process more or less straightaway. I'm still not sure I understand, though. Why would anyone volunteer for something like that in the first place?

Ludmilla Khan is especially upset because one of the women astronauts is a mother. We all know her name—Jocelyn Tooker. Her kids are five and three. They've gone to live in Atlanta, with their grandmother.

"How can she bear it? Knowing she'll never see them grow up, that she'll never hear their voices again, even?"

"I don't know," I say to Ludmilla. "Perhaps she thinks they'll be proud of her." The way Ludmilla talks, you'd think Jocelyn Tooker had murdered both her kids and chucked their bodies down a well. One of the male crew, Ken Toh, has an eight-year-old son, but people don't go on about that nearly as much as they do about Jocelyn Tooker.

Ludmilla has two little ones of her own, Leila and Mehmet, so I can see how Jocelyn Tooker's decision might weigh on her mind. I've thought about it over and over, and the only thing I can come up with that makes sense of it is that the crew of the *Second Wind* look upon going to Mars not as a one-way ticket to an early exit but as a way of cheating death altogether. I mean, everyone aboard that spacecraft is going to live forever—in our hearts and minds, in our books and stories and films, and in thousands of hours of news clips and documentaries. Even if they crash and burn like the crew of the *New Dawn*, we'll never stop talking about them, and speculating, and remembering.

If you look at it that way it's a straight trade: fifty years or so of real life now against immortality. I can see why some people might think that's not such a bad deal.

In a way, the men and women who go into space are our superheroes. Ten years from now, some journalist will be asking Jocelyn Tooker's children what it feels like to have a superhero for a mum.

Who is Ludmilla Khan, or me or anyone else for that matter, to try and guess at how those kids will judge her, or what they'll say?

My name is Emily Clarah Starr. The Starr is just a coincidence. Clarah is for my grandmother, whom I can't remember because she died when I was three. There's a photo of us, Moolie and Clarah and me, out by the King George VI Reservoir before it was officially declared to be toxic and cordoned off. Moolie has me in one of those front-loading carry-pouch things—all you can see is the top of my head, a bunch of black curls. Grandma Clarah is wearing a hideous knitted blue bobble hat and a silver puffer jacket, even though it's May in the photo and the sun is shining, reflecting itself off the oily water like electric light.

"Your grandma never got used to the climate," Moolie told me once. "She always felt cold here, even though she came over with her aunts from Abuja when she was six."

Moolie in the photograph is tall and thin, elegant and rather aloof, unrecognisable. She seems full of an inner purpose I cannot divine. She says it was my father who chose the name Emily for me. I don't know if I should believe that story or not.

I have no idea who my father is, and Moolie's account varies. I went through a phase of pestering her about him when I was younger, but she refused to tell me anything, or at least not anything I could rely on.

"Why should it matter who your dad is? What did fathers ever do for the world in any case, except saddle unsuspecting women with unwanted children?"

"Unwanted?" I gaped at her. The idea that Moolie might not have wanted me had never occurred to me. I simply *was*, an established fact, *quod erat demonstrandum*. But that's the ego for you—an internalized life support system, and pretty much indestructible.

"Oh, Emily, of course I wanted you. You were a bit of a shock to the system, though, that's all I'm saying."

"What did Dad say, when he found out?"

"Don't call him Dad, he doesn't deserve it."

"My father, then. And if the guy was such an arsehole why did you shag him?"

I was about fourteen then, and going through a stroppy phase. When rudeness didn't get me anywhere I started hitting Moolie with psychological claptrap instead—all this stuff about how I had a right to know, that it would damage my self-esteem if she kept it from me. You know, the kind of rubbish you read in magazines. The situation stood at a stalemate for a while, then finally we had this massive row, a real window-shaker. It went on for hours. When we'd been round in circles one time too many, Moolie burst into tears and said the reason she wouldn't tell me anything was that she didn't know. She'd had several boyfriends back then. Any one of them could be my father.

"We can do a ring-round, if you want," she said, still sniffing. "Drop a few bombshells? Destroy a few households? What do you reckon?"

What I reckoned was that it was time I shut up. For the first time in my life I was feeling another person's pain like it was my own. For the first time ever I was seeing Moolie as a person in her own right, someone whose life could have taken a whole different path if little Emily hadn't come along to mess things up.

It was a shock, to put it mildly. But it was good, too, in the long run, because it brought Moolie and me together and made us real friends. I stopped caring about who my dad was, for a long time. Then when Moolie started getting ill I didn't want to make things worse by dragging it all up again.

Then Moolie said what she said about the book, and everything changed.

The book is called *The Art of Space Travel* by Victoria Segal. I remember the book from when I was a little kid because of the star maps. The maps fold out from between the normal pages in long, concertina-like strips. They're printed in colour—dark blue and yellow—on smooth, glossy paper that squeaks slightly when you run your finger across it. I always thought the star maps were beautiful. Moolie would let me look at the book if I asked but she would never leave me alone with it—I suppose she thought I might accidentally damage it.

As I grew older I had a go at reading it every once in a while, but I always gave up after a chapter or two because it was way over my head, all the stuff about quasars and dark matter and the true speed of light. I would soldier on for a couple of pages, then realise I hadn't actually understood a word of it.

As well as the star maps, the book is filled with beautiful and intricate diagrams, complicated line drawings of planetary orbits, and the trajectories of imaginary spacecraft, rockets that never existed but one day might. I always loved the thought of that, that they one day might.

The book's shiny yellow cover is torn in three places.

The day Moolie drops the bombshell is a Tuesday. I don't know why I remember that, but I do. I come in from work to find Moolie looking sheepish, the look she gets now when she's lost something or broken something or forgotten who she is, just for the moment. I've learned it's best not to question her when she gets like that because it makes her clam up, whereas if you leave her alone for a while she can't resist sharing. So I pretend I haven't noticed anything and we have supper as usual. Once we've finished eating, Moolie goes into the front room to watch TV and I go upstairs to do some stuff on my computer.

After about half an hour, Moolie appears in the doorway. She's holding *The Art of Space Travel*, clasping it to her chest with both arms as if she's afraid it might try to get away from her. Then she dumps it down on my bed like a brick. It makes a soft, plump sound as it hits the duvet. A small puff of air comes up.

"This belonged to your father," Moolie says. "He left it here when he went."

"When he went where?" I say. I'm trying to keep my voice low and steady, as if we're just having a normal conversation about nothing in particular.

My heart is thumping like a road drill, like it wants to escape me. It's almost painful, like the stitch in your side you get from running too far and too fast.

"Your dad was an astronaut," Moolie says. "He was part of the *New Dawn* mission."

My hands are shaking, just a bit, but I'm trying to ignore that. "Moolie," I say to her. Moolie is what I called her when I was first learning to talk, apparently. It made her and Grandma Clarah laugh so much they never tried to correct me. Moolie's actual name is Della—Della Starr. She was once one of the most highly qualified metallurgists in the British aerospace industry. "What on Earth are you talking about?"

"He knew I was pregnant," Moolie says. "He wanted to be involved—to be a father to you—but I said no. I didn't want to be tied to him, or to anyone. Not then. I've never been able to make up my mind if I did the right thing or not."

She nods at me, as if she's satisfied with herself for having said something clever, and then she leaves the room. I stay where I am, sitting at my desk and staring at the open doorway Moolie just walked out of, wondering if I should go after her and what I'm going to say to her if I do.

When I finally go downstairs, I find Moolie back in the living room, curled up on the sofa, watching one of her soaps. When I ask her if she was telling the truth about my dad being an astronaut she looks at me as if she thinks I've gone insane.

"Your father wasted his dreams, Emily," she says. "He gave up too soon. That's one of the reasons I told him to go. Life's hard enough as it is. The last thing you want is to be tied to someone who's always wishing he'd chosen a different path."

When a couple of days later I ask her again about *The Art of Space Travel*, she says she doesn't have a clue where it came from. "It was here in the house when we moved in, I think," she says. "I found it in the built-in wardrobe in your bedroom, covered in dust."

I've been through the book perhaps a thousand times, searching for a sign of my father—a name on the flyleaf, a careless note, scribbled comments in the margin, underlinings in the text, even. There's nothing, though, not even a random inkblot. Aside from being yellowed and a bit musty-smelling, the pages are clean. There's nothing to show who owned the book, who brought it to this house, that it was ever even opened before we had it.

I want to find Dad. I tell myself it's because Moolie is dying, that whoever the man is and whatever he's done, he has a right to know the facts of his own life. I know it's more than that, though, if I'm honest. I want to find him because I'm curious, because I've always been curious, and because I'm afraid that once Moolie is gone I'll have nobody else.

Our house is on Sipson Lane, in the borough of Hillingdon. It was built in the 1970s, almost a hundred years ago now to the year. It's a shoddy little place, one of a row of twenty-two identical boxes flung up to generate maximum profit for the developer with a minimum of outlay. It's a wonder it's lasted this long, actually. Some of the other houses in the row are in a terrible state—the metal window frames rusted and buckling, the lower floors patchy with mildew. The previous owner put in replacement windows and a new damp-proof course, so ours isn't as bad as some. It's dry inside, at least, and I used some of the extra cash from Benny to put up solar panels, which means we can afford to keep the central heating on all the time.

Moolie's like Clarah now—she can't stand the cold.

Sipson is a weird place. Five hundred years ago it was a tiny hamlet, surrounded by farmland. Since then it's evolved into a scruffy housing estate less than half a mile from the end of the second runway at Heathrow Airport. Moolie bought the Sipson Lane house because it was cheap and because it was close to her job, and the best thing about it is that it's close to my job too, now. It takes me less than half an hour to walk into work, which not only cuts down on expenses, it also means I can get home quickly if there's an emergency.

The traffic on the perimeter road is a constant nightmare. In the summer, the petrol and diesel fumes settle over the airport like a heavy tarpaulin, a yellowish blanket of chemical effluent that is like heat haze, only thicker, and a lot more smelly.

When you walk home in the evenings, though, or on those very rare winter mornings when there's still a hard frost, you could take the turning into Sipson Lane and mistake it for the entrance to another world: The quiet street, with its rustling plane trees, the long grass sprouting between the kerbstones at the side of the road. The drawn curtains of the houses, like gently closed eyelids, the soft glow behind. Someone riding past on a bicycle. The red pillar box opposite the Sipson Arms. You'd barely know the airport even existed.

It's like an oasis in time, if there is such a thing. If you stand still and listen to the sound of the blackbirds singing, high up in the dusty branches of those plane trees, you might almost imagine you're in a universe where the *Galaxy* air crash never happened.

They had planes flying in and out of here again within the hour, of course. The airport authorities, backed by the government, insisted the main damage was economic and mostly short term. They claimed the rumours of ground contamination and depleted uranium were just so much scaremongering, that the whole area within the emergency cordon had been repeatedly tested and repeatedly found safe.

A decade on they say that even if the toxicity levels were a bit on the high side in the first year or so after the crash, they're well within the accepted safety limits now.

The first question I have to ask myself is this: Is there any possibility at all that it's true? What Moolie told me about my father and the *New Dawn* mission, I mean?

My first instinct is to dismiss it as just another fraction of Moolie craziness. One of the features of Moolie's illness is that it's often hard to know whether she's talking about stuff that really happened to her or stuff she's dreamed or read about or seen on TV. Her mind can't tell the difference now, or not all the time. Just seeing the Mars team on television might be enough to land her with a complete fantasy scenario, indistinguishable from her life as she's actually lived it.

But the thing is—and I can hardly believe I'm saying this—there is a very small chance that her story might turn out to be real. The dates fit, for a start. I was born in March 2047, just three months before the New Dawn was launched on its mission to Mars. And before you roll your eyes and say, Yes, but so were about three hundred thousand other kids, just consider this: Moolie did a lot of specialist placements early on in her career. One of them was in Hamburg, at the University of the European Space Programme, where she spent the better part of 2046 helping to run strength tests on prototypes of some of the equipment designed to be used aboard the New Dawn. Some of the Mars team were in residency in Hamburg at around the same time, eight of them in all, five women and three men. Moolie would have come into direct contact with every one of them.

I know, because I've looked up the details. I even have a file now, stuff I've found online and printed off. If you think that's creepy, just try having an unknown dad who might have died in an exploding rocket and see how you get on. See how long it takes before you start a file on him.

Toby Soyinka was second communications officer aboard the New Dawn, the one who just happened to be outside the vehicle when the disaster occurred. His body was thrown clear of the wreckage, and was recovered three months later by an unmanned retrieval pod launched by the crew of the Hoffnung 3 space station. Toby's body was shipped back to Earth at enormous expense, not so much for the sake of his family as to be subjected to a year-long post mortem.

The mission scientists wanted to know if Toby was still alive when he floated free, and if so then for how long. Knowing that would tell them all kinds of things, apparently—important information about the last moments of the New Dawn and why she failed.

According to the official reports, Toby Soyinka was killed in the primary explosion, the same as the rest of the crew. As you might expect, the conspiracy theorists went bonkers. Why would Soyinka be dead if his suit was undamaged? How come only a short section of the official post mortem has ever been released into the public sphere?

There are people who claim that Toby was alive up there for at least three hours after the rocket exploded—depending on individual physiology, his suit's oxygen tanks would have contained enough air for between three and four hours.

Toby's suit was also fitted with a radio communicator, but it was short-range only, suitable for talking with his colleagues back on board the New Dawn but not powerful enough to let him speak with Mission Control.

Would he have wanted to, though, even if he could have? Knowing that he was going to die, and everyone on the ground knowing there was fuck all they could do about it?

I mean, what could one side of that equation possibly have to say to the other?

Well, I guess this is it, Tobes. Sorry, old chap. Hey, did anyone remember to send out for muffins?

I think about that, and I think of Toby Soyinka thinking about that, and after the terror what comes through to me most strongly is simple embarrassment.

If it had been me in that floating spacesuit I reckon I'd have switched my radio off and waited in silence. Listed my favourite movies in order from one to a hundred and gazed out at the stars.

At least Toby died knowing he'd done something extraordinary, that he'd seen sights few human beings will ever see.

And Toby Soyinka is a hero now, don't forget that. Perhaps that's what the crew of the *Second Wind* are telling themselves, even now.

In the movies when something goes wrong and one of the crew is left floating in space with no hope of rescue, the scene almost always ends with the doomed one taking off his or her helmet, making a quick and noble end of it rather than facing a slow and humiliating death by asphyxiation.

Would anyone really have the guts to do that, though? I don't think I would.

Toby Soyinka was born in Nottingham. Toby's dad was a civil engineer—he helped design the New Trent shopping village—and his mum was a dentist. Toby studied physics and IT at Nottingham Uni, then went on to do postgraduate work at the UESP in Hamburg, where he would have met Moolie. Most of the photos on-line show Toby at the age of twenty-eight, the same age he was when he died, and when he and the rest of the crew were all over the media. He looks skinny and hope-ful and nervous, all at once. Sometimes when I look at pictures of Toby I can't help thinking he seems out of his depth, as if he's wondering what he signed up for ex-actly, although that's probably just my imagination.

Once, when I was browsing through some stuff about Toby online, Moolie came into the room and sneaked up behind me.

"What are you looking at?" she said. I hadn't heard her come in. I jumped a mile.

"Nothing much," I said. I hurried to close the window but it was too late, the pho-tos of Toby were staring her in the face. I looked at her looking, curious to see what her reaction would be, but Moolie's eyes slid over his features without even a single glimmer of recognition. He might have been a tree or a gatepost, for all the effect he had on her.

Was she only pretending not to recognise him? I don't think so. I always know when Moolie's hiding something, even if I don't know what it is she's hiding.

I don't believe that Toby Soyinka was my father. It would be too much like a tragic fairy tale, too pat.

"How's your mum?" Benny says to me this morning.

"She's fine, Benny," I reply. "She's getting excited about the mission, same as you." I grin at him and wink, firstly because I can never resist taking the piss out of Benny, just a little bit, and secondly because it's true. Moolie has barely been out of the living room this past week. She has the television on all day and most of the night, permanently tuned to the twenty-four-hour news feed that's supposed to be the official mouthpiece of the mission's sponsors. The actual news content is pretty limited but since when has that ever been a deterrent in situations like this? They squeeze every last ounce of juice out of what they have—then they go back to playing the old documentaries, home video footage, endlessly repetitive Q&As with scientists and school friends.

Moolie watches it all with equal attention, drinking it down like liquid nutrient through a straw. She doesn't get to bed till gone three, some nights, and when I ask her if she's had anything to eat she doesn't remember. I make up batches of sandwiches and leave them in the fridge for her. Sometimes she scoffs the lot, sometimes I go down in the morning and find them untouched.

She's immersed in the Mars thing so deeply that sometimes it seems like Moolie herself is no longer there.

What is it that fascinates her so much? When she first started watching I felt convinced it had to do with my father, that all the talk of the *Second Wind* was bringing back memories of what happened to the *New Dawn*. I'm less sure of that now—why should everything have to be about me and my father? Moolie is—was—a scientist, and the Mars mission is just about the most exciting scientific experiment to be launched in more than a decade, perhaps ever. Of course she'd be interested in it. You could argue that her obsession with the news feed is the best evidence I have that she is still herself.

She seems so engaged, so invigorated, so *happy* that I don't want to question it. I want her to stay like this for as long as she can.

"Well, tell her I asked after her," Benny says. I glance at him curiously, wondering if he's serious. I've always found it strange, this spasmodic concern of his for a person he's never met. At the same time, though, it's just so Benny. It's no wonder he's never made it to the top. To make it to the top you need to be a heartless bastard, pretty much. On the heartless bastard scale, Benny Conway has never figured very high up.

I nod briskly. "I will," I say. I never feel comfortable talking with him about Moolie—it's all too close to home. I'd rather stick to work, any day. "What's on today?"

Benny immediately looks shifty. A moment later I understand why. "There's another news crew dropping by," he says. "They want to do an interview. With you."

"With me? What the hell for? Oh, for God's sake, Benny, what are they expecting me to say?"

"You're head of housekeeping at the Edison Star, Emily. That's an important and responsible position. They just want to ask you what it's been like, preparing for such an important occasion. There's nothing for you to be anxious about, I promise you. They've said it shouldn't take more than ten minutes, fifteen at the most."

"I'm not anxious, I'm pissed off," I say. "You could at least have asked me first." Benny looks hurt and just a little bit surprised. I know I've overstepped the mark and

I wouldn't normally be so rude but just for the moment I feel like killing him. It's all right for Benny—he loves all this shit. Benny's great with the press, actually, he's what you might call a people person. Put him in front of a camera and he's away.

Me? I just want to be left alone to get on with my job. The idea of being on TV leaves me cold. There's Moolie to be considered, too—seeing me up on the screen like that, it might warp her sense of reality more than ever.

It's done now, though, isn't it? There's not much sense in kicking off about it. Best to get the whole thing over and done with and then forget it.

I guess it's mainly because of Benny that I'm still here. Working at the hotel, I mean. I certainly never planned on staying forever. It was supposed to be a holiday job, something to bring in some money while I went through college. I started out studying for a degree in natural sciences, following in Moolie's footsteps, I suppose, which was madness. I failed my first-year exams twice. It should have been obvious to anyone that I wasn't cut out for it.

"You're such a dreamer, Emily," Moolie said to me once. "Head in the stars." She cracked a kind of half-smile, then sighed. She was paying for extra tutorials for me at the time, trying to give me a better shot at the re-sits. It must have felt like flushing money down the toilet. When I told her I'd been offered a permanent job at the Edison Star and had decided to take it she gave me such an odd look, like I'd announced I was running away to join the circus or something. But she never questioned it or gave me a hard time, or tried to talk me out of it the way a lot of parents would have.

It was a relief to her, most likely, that I'd finally found something I could do, that I was good at, even. It also meant I stayed close to home. First of all because it was convenient, and then later, with Moolie's illness, because it became necessary. I've never regretted it. I regret some of the things that might have been, but the regret has always taken second place to the desire not to have things change. I don't think it's just because of Moolie, either. Sometimes I believe it's the airport itself, and Sipson, both the kind of non-places that keep you addicted to transience, the restless half-life of the perpetual traveller who never goes anywhere.

The idea of settling for anything too concrete begins to seem like death, so you settle for nothing.

Benny Conway's never married, which probably seems strange to you, given that he's such a people person, but I can imagine that being with him day in and day out would drive anyone nuts.

Beneath the confidence and sunny bravado, Benny's actually quite needy and insecure. One of the downsides of working in a close environment is that you often get to know more about the people you work with than you strictly want to.

I spend the morning checking the inventories and trying not to get too worked up about the stupid interview. At 1:30 I go down to the lobby. What passes for the news crew is already there—a camera guy and a college kid, sent along by some backroom satellite outfit most likely, one of the countless pirate stations that don't have the clout to get themselves an invite for what Ludmilla and I have snarkily begun to call the Day of Judgement.

These two have to make do with me instead. I begin to feel sorry for them.

The student who interviews me is called Laura—I never learn her surname—a tiny thing dressed in a black pantsuit and with her copper-red hair cut close to her head. She reminds me of Pinocchio, or one of those Pierrot dolls that my school friends were so crazy about when I was a kid. I like her immediately—she seems so earnest!—and so I find myself relaxing into the process and even enjoying it. I'm expecting the questions Laura asks me to be work-related—what will the astronauts be having for supper, how do you keep the hotel running normally and still maintain security, that kind of thing. Some of her actual questions catch me off guard.

"It's thirty years since the crew of the *New Dawn* lost their lives," Laura says. "Do you think it's right that we should risk another Mars mission?"

"I think in a way we're doing it for them," I say. "The astronauts who died, I mean." I'm stumbling over my words, because I haven't planned this. It's strange to hear myself saying these things, thoughts I never really knew I was thinking until now. "I think we should ask ourselves what they would have wanted. Would they have wanted us to try again? I think they would have. So I think we should, too. I believe we have to try again, for their sakes."

Laura looks delighted and surprised, as if what I said in reply to her question was the kind of answer she wanted but didn't expect. Not from the likes of me, anyway. She wraps up the interview soon after—she wants to quit while she's ahead, most likely.

"That was great," she says to me, off-camera. She exchanges a couple of words with the camera guy, who's preoccupied with packing away his equipment. After a moment Laura turns back to me. She's smiling, and I think she's about to say goodbye. But then her expression becomes serious again and she asks me another question. "Your mum was here when the *Galaxy* flight came down, wasn't she?"

I'm so surprised I can't answer at first. I glance across at the camera guy, wondering if he's somehow still filming this, but he's moved away from us slightly, towards the reception desk. I see him checking his mobile. "She was working here, yes," I say. My throat feels dry and I swallow. What's this about? "She was part of the forensic investigation team that went out to the crash site. She was an expert in metal fatigue."

Laura has moved to stand in front of me, blocking my view of the rest of the lobby and clearly expecting me to say more, but I'm not sure what I should say, whether I should say anything, even.

I can't imagine why she's asking me this question now, when the camera is off. It has nothing to do with the astronauts or with the hotel, and I'm asking myself what it does have to do with, exactly. Is this the question Laura wanted to ask me all along? And if so, why?

"There was an awful smell," I say, and then suddenly I'm remembering that smell, jet fuel thickened by dust, ignited by anguish, and the way it hung over the airport and over our village for weeks, or so it seemed, longer even than that, so long that in the end you understood it was all in your mind, it had to be, that no real smell lingers that long. Even the stench of combusted bodies fades eventually.

I haven't thought of these things in years, not like this, not precisely enough to bring back that smell.

But can I tell Laura any of this? She would have been about ten when it happened; she might not even remember it as a real event. Children don't take much notice of the news unless it affects them directly. Everything she knows about the crash will come from old TV footage, the slew of documentaries and real-time amateur video that followed after.

Everything from the acknowledged facts to the certifiably crazy.

What would she say if I told her that Moolie worked alongside the black box recovery unit and the token medics and the loss adjusters? That she was out there for almost three weeks, picking over what was essentially radioactive trash, trying to come up with a reasonable theory of what had happened and who was responsible?

Of that original forensic team, two are still working and seem in good health, three have died of various cancers, and four are like Moolie.

There is an ongoing legal enquiry, but the way things are going the remaining witnesses will all be dead before any decision is made on liability.

I bet that's what the authorities are hoping, anyway.

"Here's my number," Laura says. She delves into her jacket pocket and then hands me a card, a glossy white oblong printed with an email address and cell number in cool grey capitals.

Quaint, I think, and rather classy, if you're into retro.

"Give me a call, if you feel like talking about it. I'd really like to do a story on your mother, if you think she'd be up for it." Laura hesitates, uncertain suddenly, a precocious child in front of an audience of hostile strangers. "Think about it, anyway."

"I will," I say, and slip the card into my pocket. Later, after Laura is gone, I try to imagine her with Moolie, asking her questions.

Does Moolie remember the *Galaxy*, even?

Some days, probably.

The whole idea of her doing an interview is insane.

Of the three male astronauts Moolie had dealings with at the UESP in Hamburg, only Toby Soyinka actually went on to get picked as flight crew. The two other guys involved with the *New Dawn* mission ended up working on the ground in IT and comms. Angelo Chavez was born in Queens, New York City. His exceptional talent for mathematics was spotted in nursery school. At the age of six he won a place at a specialist academy for gifted children. Angelo did well, and seemed well adjusted, until his father began an affair with a work colleague and buggered off. Angelo's mother relocated with Angelo to Chicago to be closer to family.

Angelo was bullied at his new school. He began truanting, then moved on to shoplifting and dealing cannabis on high school premises. By the time he turned fourteen he was regularly in trouble with the police. It was a youth worker at a juvenile detention centre who helped get Angelo back on track by asking him to help out with the centre's computer system. Later, when Angelo applied for a place at MIT, the man acted as his sponsor and referee. Angelo achieved perfect scores in three out of his five first-year assignments. He graduated with one of the highest averages of that decade.

After graduation, he began working as a games designer for a Tokyo-based franchise, and landed a junior post at NASA just eighteen months later. Three years after joining NASA, Angelo went to Hamburg for six months to work as a visiting lecturer at the UESP. While he was there, he met and fell in love with the Dutch astrophysicist Johan Wedekin. They became civil partners in July 2048.

They've been together now for almost thirty years. I suppose it's possible that Angelo was shagging Moolie in Hamburg as well as Johan, but I think it's unlikely.

Marlon Habila was born in Lagos, the son of two teachers. He speaks six languages fluently, and has a solid working knowledge of eight others. He wrote his postgraduate thesis on the acquisition of language in bilingual children. He was initially employed by the UESP to help develop a more straightforward method for teaching Mandarin to trainee astronauts, and became interested in the New Dawn mission while he was there. After a number of years in Hamburg, Marlon was headhunted by NASA as a senior communications technician and relocated to Austin, Texas, where he still lives today.

He was in Hamburg at the same time as Moolie, though, no doubt about it.

When I look at photographs of Marlon Habila, it's like looking into a mirror.

I once showed Moolie a photo of Marlon and asked if she remembered him. She was in one of her lucid patches at the time, so I thought there might be a chance I'd get something resembling a straight answer out of her. I reckoned it was worth a try, anyway. You never know with Moolie, how she's going to react. Sometimes during her good phases you can chat with her and it'll feel almost like the old times.

On the other hand, it's often during these good times that she's at her most evasive. Ask Moolie her own name then and there's no guarantee you'll get the answer you were expecting.

When I showed her the picture of Marlon, her eyes filled with tears. Then she snatched it out of my hands and tore it in two.

"Don't talk to me about that boy," she hissed at me. "I've told you before."

"No you haven't," I persisted. "Can you tell me anything about him? Do you know what he's called?"

She gave me a look, boiling over with impatience, as if I'd asked her if the world was flat or round.

"You know damn well what he's called," she said. "Stop trying to trick me. I'm not brain-dead yet, you know." She stomped out of the room, one foot dragging slightly because of the muscle wastage that had already begun to affect her left side. I stared stupidly down at the two torn pieces of the photograph she had thrown on the floor, then picked them up and put them in the waste bin. An hour or so later I went upstairs to check on Moolie and she was fine again, completely calm, sitting up in bed and reading softly aloud to herself from J. G. Ballard's Vermilion Sands.

I asked her if she wanted anything to eat or drink and she shook her head. The next time I looked in on her she was sound asleep.

Do I really believe that Marlon Habila is my dad? Some days I feel so certain it's like knowing for sure. Other days I think it's all bullshit, just some story I've constructed for myself so the world doesn't feel so crazy and out of control. It's a well-known fact that kids who grow up not knowing who their parents are—or who one parent is— always like to imagine they're really a princess, or the son of a Polar explorer who died bravely in tragic circumstances, or some such junk. No one wants to be told their daddy is really a dustman who got banged up for petty thieving and who never gave a shit.

"Daddy was a spaceman" sounds so much better.

The thing is, even if I knew for an absolute certainty that Marlon Habila was my birth father, it's still not obvious what—if anything—I should do about it.

I found contact details for Marlon online—it wasn't difficult—and I've lost count of the number of emails I've started to write and then deleted. *Dear Marlon, Dear Dr. Habila, Dear Marlon* again. *You don't know me, but I think I might be your daughter.*

Just like in those old TV miniseries Moolie enjoys so much, those overblown three-part dramas about twins separated at birth, or men of God who fall illicitly in love, or lost survivors of the *Titanic*, stories that unfold in a series of unlikely coincidences, all tied together with a swooning orchestral soundtrack. They're pretty naff, those stories, but they do draw you in. When Moolie's going through one of her bad times she'll watch them all day long, five of the things in a row, back to back.

I suppose the reason people like stories like that is that no matter how confused the plot seems at the start, things always work out. By the time the film's over you always understand what happened, and why. There's always a proper ending, with people hugging each other and crying, if you see what I mean.

In the case of Marlon Habila, the proper ending is that he moved to Texas. A year after the *New Dawn* tragedy he married Melissa Sanberg, one of the senior operatives working on what they call the shop floor of Mission Control. They have two sons and one daughter—Aaron, Willard, and little Esther. Eighteen, sixteen, and nine.

In the photos they look happy. I mean, *really* happy. I have to ask myself what might happen to that happiness if I sent my email.

I can't help thinking about what Moolie said that time, about dropping bombshells.

In a way it would be easier if my father turned out to be Toby Soyinka after all. Dead is safe, nothing would change, and hey, at least I would know my dad was a hero. People would look at me with sympathy, and fascination. It would make a good miniseries, actually. You can imagine the ending—me and Toby's relatives hugging and crying as we hand round the old photographs for the umpteenth time and saying, *If only he knew* in choked-up voices. I'd watch it, anyway, I wouldn't be able to help myself. I'd blub at the end too, probably. Another Saturday night in with Moolie, a supply of tissues and a box of chocolates on the sofa between us.

Who doesn't want a story that makes sense?

I've made up my mind that if the *Second Wind* launches safely I'm going to send that email.

The biggest headache with having astronauts staying at the Edison Star is the incessant press coverage. Sorokina and Cameron themselves are the least of our worries—they're just two extra guests; to put it bluntly, they're hardly going to send us into a tailspin no matter how picky they might be about their food or the ambient room temperature. We've had to take on extra security just for that week, but aside from that it'll be business pretty much as usual. The problem is that it will be business under intense scrutiny, and until the astronauts actually arrive, the press hounds have nothing to do except sit and bitch. You can bet your life that if one of them happens to spot a rat in the garbage store it'll be headlining as a major news story within the hour.

You're never more than six feet from a rat: Getting up close and personal with the Edison Star's new temp staff.

It's enough to give Benny a coronary. Which means no rats, no undercooked turkey, no tide marks on the bathtubs, no financial mismanagement, no corporate bribery, no spree killings.

Not until this astronaut business is safely behind us, at any rate.

What it mostly means for me is a lot of overtime, but I don't mind. I'm enjoying myself quite a bit, to tell the truth. I know how this place works, you see, I've even grown to love it over the years. The only problem is winding down, switching off. Even when I'm at home I'm constantly running through mental checklists, trying to head cock-ups off at the pass before they happen. Sometimes I find myself lying awake into the small hours. If I'm not careful I'm going to end up like Moolie.

Will there be children born on Mars, I wonder? Martian children, who think of the planet Mars as their one true home?

It is strange to think of, and rather wonderful, too, that we might come to that. What will our Earth seem like to them, our built-in atmosphere and water on tap, our border controls and health and safety laws, our wars over patches of land that we like to call countries?

Will we seem like kings to them, or tyrants, or simply fools?

I have brought *The Art of Space Travel* into work with me this morning. I wrapped it inside a supermarket carrier bag for protection, then stuffed it into the back of my locker with the trainers I wear for walking in and my rucksack and my spare cardigan. I have this silly idea, that when Zhanna Sorokina and Vinnie Cameron arrive I'll get them both to sign it. I know the book was written long before they were born, that it has no connection with them, but I would like to have something of theirs, all the same, something of theirs joined with something of mine. Something to keep once they are gone, that will remind me that although they're Martians now, they started out from here.

It will be a way of keeping them safe, maybe. I know how crazy that sounds.

It's strange, but each time I think of something happening to them it's not the *New Dawn* I think of but the *Galaxy*, that doomed aeroplane, fireballing out of the sky over Heathrow.

I was in school when it happened, almost ten miles away, but all of us heard the crash, even from there.

When the call comes through, I'm in the middle of signing off the bulk orders for cleaning supplies—Dettox, Ajax, Glasene, Pledge—we get through tens of gallons of each on a monthly basis. I prefer staff to keep their mobiles switched off while they're on shift because they're so distracting, but I have to keep mine by me because of Moolie. Weeks and sometimes months go by without it ever ringing but you never know. When I see her number flashing onscreen I pick up at once.

I speak her name, only it's not her on the line after all, it's our neighbour, Allison Roberts, from next door.

"She was out the front, just lying there," Allison says. Moolie's phone was lying there too, apparently, which I suppose was lucky.

I can't remember the last time Moolie went outside by herself.

I call Benny on his private line, the one that never gets diverted. I know he's chairing a meeting but I don't care, I don't give a shit suddenly, and Benny must realise it's urgent because he knows I wouldn't disturb him otherwise, and so he picks up immediately.

"I have to go," I gasp. I explain what's happened the best I can and he says okay. I'm running for the lifts by then. I need to get to the basement, where the staff lockers are. When I reach the lockers I can't get my key card to work, and then when it finally does everything comes pouring out in a tidal wave. My clobber's everywhere, suddenly. It's the last thing I need. My chest is so high and tight I feel like screaming.

"For fuck's sake!" I'm seconds away from bursting into tears. I'm still trying to scoop everything together when Benny appears. I realise he must have left his meeting to come down, which is so bloody unlike him that all I can think is that he's here to give me a bollocking.

He doesn't, though.

"Don't worry about this," he says. "Just take what you need and get going. I've called a taxi for you—it'll be out the front in five minutes. I'll take care of your things." He makes a gesture towards the stuff on the floor, and of course I can't help thinking how downright weird all this is, but I don't have time to dwell on it. I need to get moving.

Allison said that Moolie was having difficulty breathing when she found her. The paramedics soon got her stabilized but it's still very worrying.

"Are you sure about this?" I say to Benny. "I'm really sorry."

"Quite sure," Benny says. "Call me if you need me, okay?"

I take a moment to wonder if Benny is losing it, if the strain is finally getting to him, but I know that now is not the time to go looking for answers to that question.

"I will," I say. "Thanks." I grab my rucksack and shove on my trainers and then I'm gone.

Most of the things that are wrong with Moolie—the decreasing short-term memory and loss of appetite, the insomnia, the restlessness—none of these are life-threatening.

Not in and of themselves, anyway. But every now and then she'll have an attack of apnoea, and these are much more frightening. What apnoea means, basically, is that Moolie can't breathe. The first time she had an attack, the doctors kept asking me if she smoked. Each time I said no they looked at me with doubt. It was obvious they thought I was lying.

In fact the apnoea is caused by the thousands of microscopic mushroom-like growths that have colonized the lining of Moolie's lungs. Most of the time these growths remain inactive and appear to do no harm, but periodically they flare up or inflate or expand or whatever—hence the apnoea.

"It's definitely not cancer," the medics insist. There's a real sense of triumph in their voices as they say this, as if the growths' non-cancerous nature is something they've seen to personally. But when I ask them what it is if it's not cancer they never seem to give me a direct answer and I don't think they have one. I don't think anyone really knows what it is, to be honest. It's a whole new disease.

Whatever it is, it seems to have the advantage of being slow-growing. Moolie might die of old age before the growths clutter up her bronchial tubes, or fill her lungs with spores, or find some other, quicker way of preventing her from breathing entirely. In the meantime, the doctors stave off the attacks by giving Moolie a shot of adrenaline and then supplementing her oxygen for an hour or so. The enriched oxygen seems to kill the mushroom things off, or make the growths subside, or something. Whatever it does it works, and surprisingly quickly. By the time I come on to the ward, Moolie is sitting up in bed with a cup of tea.

"What are you doing here?" she says to me.

"I might ask you the same question." I can't tell yet if she's being sarcastic or if she's genuinely confused. Sometimes when she comes round after an attack she's delusional, or delirious, whatever you want to call it when the brain gets starved of oxygen for any length of time.

Moolie seems okay, though—this time, anyway. She's sipping her tea as if she's actually enjoying it. There's a biscuit in the saucer, too, with a bite taken out of it— Moolie eating something without being reminded is always a good sign.

I notice that one of the nurses has brushed her hair. She looks—very nearly—the way she does in that old photograph, her and me and Grandma Clarah out by the reservoir.

"I'm fine, Emily," she says, neatly sidestepping my actual question, which is so typical of her that I am tempted to believe her. "There was no need for you to leave work early. I know Benny needs you more than I do at the moment." She takes another sip of tea. "You could have come in afterwards, if you wanted to. They say I can probably go home tomorrow, in any case."

She's peeping at me over the rim of her teacup, grinning like a naughty schoolgirl—*See what I did.* Trying to boss me about like any normal mother. She can be like this after the treatments—it's as if the rarefied oxygen cleans out her brain, or something. I know it won't last, but it makes me feel like crying, nonetheless.

Just to have her back again.

Sometimes I forget how much I miss her.

I sit down on the plastic chair at the side of the bed. "I'm here now," I say. "You're not getting rid of me that easily." I reach for her free hand across the bedcovers and she lets me take it. After a couple of minutes one of the ward staff brings me a cup of tea of my own. It's good just to sit, to not feel responsibility or the need for action. The mechanics of this place are unknown to me, and therefore the urge to do, to change, to control is entirely absent.

Moolie begins telling me about the TV programme she was watching before she had her turn. Yet another documentary about the Mars mission—no surprises there. I'd rather she told me what it was that made her go outside by herself, but she waves my question away like an importunate fly.

"That girl," she says instead. "That girl, Zhanna. She's twenty-six tomorrow, did you know that? She says she doesn't want children, that her work is enough for her. She'll be dead before she's forty, more than likely. She doesn't know what she's doing."

"You were younger than she is when you had me, Mum," I say. "Did you know what you were doing?"

Moolie shakes her head slowly and deliberately from side to side. "No, I didn't," she says. "I didn't have a clue."

Then she says something strange.

"I won't always get better, Emily. The day will come when I don't come home. You should have a talk with Benny, before that day comes. There's no point in us pretending. Not anymore."

The mug of tea is still warm between my hands but in spite of this I suddenly feel cold all over. When I ask Moolie what she's talking about she refuses to answer.

By the time I leave the hospital my shift has been over for ages. I decide to go back to the hotel anyway, just in case anything cropped up after I left. I check in with housekeeping and when I've satisfied myself that no major disasters have occurred in my absence I go in search of Benny. I find him in his office. There's a semicircle of empty chairs in front of his desk, the ghost of a meeting. Benny is alone, sitting very still in his chair, reading something—a book?—by the light of his desk lamp. He seems miles away, absent in a manner that is most unlike him.

When he realises I'm there he jerks upright, and there's an expression on his face—panic, almost—as if I've caught him out in a secret. He slams the book shut, making a slapping sound.

It's pointless him trying to hide it, though. I'd know the book anywhere, because it belongs to us, to Moolie and me. It's *The Art of Space Travel*.

"Emily," Benny says. He's watching my face for signs of disaster and at the same time he still looks guilty. It's a weird combination, almost funny. "I wasn't expecting you back. How's your mother?"

"Moolie's fine," I say. "They're letting her out tomorrow. What are you doing with that?"

I am talking about the book, of course, which I can't stop staring at, the way Benny is holding it to him, like a shield. All of a sudden there's this noise in my ears, a kind of roaring sound, and I'm thinking of Moolie and Moolie telling me that I should talk to Benny.

I'm thinking of the way Benny is always asking after Moolie, and what Moolie said before, such a long time ago, about Benny arriving in this country with a card-board suitcase and fake Levi's, and a gold watch that he had to sell to get the money to rent a room.

"Emily," Benny says again, and the way he says my name—like he's apologising for something—makes me feel even weirder. He unfolds the book again across his lap, opening it to the centre, where I know there's a double-page colour spread of the Milky Way, with its billions of stars, all buzzing and fusing together, cloudy and luminous, like the mist as it rises from the surface of the George VI Reservoir.

Benny runs his fingers gently across the paper. It makes a faint squeaking sound. I know exactly how that paper feels: soft to the touch, slightly furry with impacted dust, *old*.

Benny is touching the book as if it is his.

My stomach does a lurch, as if the world is travelling too fast suddenly, spinning out of control across the blackly infinite backdrop of the whole of space.

"One of my schoolteachers gave me this book," Benny says. "His name was Otto Okora. His parents brought him here to London when he was six years old. They never returned to Africa, but Otto did. He came back to teach high school in Free-town and that's where he stayed. He said that England was too cold and too crowded, and that the sky here was never black enough to see the stars. He had this thing about Africa being closer to outer space than any other continent. 'We never lost our sense of life's mysteries,' was what he used to say. Otto was crazy about outer space. He would sit us down in the long hot afternoons and tell us stories about the first moon landings and the first space stations, the first attempts to map the surface of Mars. It was like poetry to me, Emily, and I could never get enough of it. I learned the names of the constellations and how to see them. I knew by heart the mass and volume and composition of each of the planets in our solar system. I even learned to draw my own star maps—impossible journeys to distant planets that no one in a thousand of our lifetimes will ever see. I saw them, though. I saw them at night, when I couldn't sleep. Instead of counting chickens I would count stars, picking them out from my memory one by one, like diamonds from a black silk handkerchief."

Like diamonds from a black silk handkerchief.

I want to hug him. Even in the midst of my confusion I want to hug him and tell him that I feel the same, that I have always felt the same, that we are alike.

That we are alike, of course we are.

The truth has been here in front of me, all the time. How stupid am I?

There's a kind of book called a grimoire, which is a book of spells. I've never seen one—I don't know if such a thing really exists, even—but *The Art of Space Travel* has always felt to me like it had magic trapped in it. Like you could open its pages and accidentally end up somewhere else. All those dazzling ropes of stars, all those thousands of possible futures, and futures' futures.

All those enchanted luminous pathways, blinking up at us through the darkness, like the lights of a runway.

I clear my throat with a little cough. I haven't a single clue what I ought to say.

"Your mother did her nut when you first got a job here," Benny says quietly. "She called me on the phone, tore me off a strip. She said I wasn't to breathe a word, under pain of death. That was the first time we'd spoken to one another in ten years."

"I was supposed to study medicine," Benny says to me later. "My heart was never in it, though. I didn't know what I wanted, only that I wanted to find a bigger world than the world I came from. I remember it as if it was yesterday, standing there on the tarmac and looking up at this hotel and just liking the name of it. I gazed up at the big lit-up star logo and it was as if I could hear Otto Okora saying, *You go for it, Benny boy, that's a good omen.* I liked the people and I liked the bustle and I liked the lights at night. All the taking off and landing, the enigma of arrival. There's a book with that name—your mother gave me a copy right back at the beginning, when she still believed in me and things were good between us. I never got round to reading it, but I loved that title. I loved it that I'd finally discovered something I was good at.

"Would she mind very much, do you think?" Benny says. "If I went to see her?"

"It's your funeral," I say, and shrug. I try and picture it as it might happen on TV, Benny pressing Moolie's skinny hand to his lips while she smiles weakly up from the pillows and whispers his name. You see how funny that is, right? "Only don't go blaming me if she bites your head off."

Zhanna Sorokina is shorter than she appears on television. She has short mouse-brown hair, and piercing blue eyes. She looks like a school kid.

When I ask her if she'll sign *The Art of Space Travel* she looks confused. "But I did not write this," she says.

"I know that," I say. "But it's a book about space. My dad gave it to me. It would mean a lot to me if you would sign it. As a souvenir."

She uses the pen I give her, a blue Bic, to sign the title page. She writes her name twice, first in the sweeping Cyrillic script she would have learned at school and then again underneath in spiky Latin capitals.

"Is this okay?" she asks.

"Very," I reply. "Thank you."

Sorokina smiles, very briefly, and then I see her awareness of me leak from her eyes as she moves away towards the lift that will take her up to the tenth-floor news suite and the waiting cameras, the media frenzy that will surround her for the remainder of her time here on Earth. Her bodyguard moves in to shield her.

It's the last and only time I will see her close to.

In leaving this world, she makes me feel more properly a part of it.

I wish I had a child I could one day tell about this moment. I've never felt like this before, but suddenly I do.

Benny would kill me if he knew I was down here. I'm supposed to be upstairs, in the news suite, making sure they're up and running with the drinks trolleys. That there are three different kinds of bottled beer, instead of the two that would be usual for these kinds of occasions.

flight from the ages
DEREK KÜNSKEN

Here's a story of mindboggling scope and span, a story taking place over a time span of billions of years, ultimately all the way back to the beginning of the universe, in which a banking AI operating a customs and tariff spaceship tries to deal with the inadvertent release of unimaginably powerful forces from an ancient alien weapon of war that threatens to destroy not only our galaxy but all of spacetime itself. . . .

Derek Künsken left the science world to work with street children in Latin America and then with the Canadian Foreign Service. Adventuring done and parenting started, he now writes science fiction and fantasy in Gatineau, Québec. His stories have appeared in Asimov's, Analog, Beneath Ceaseless Skies, *and in a number of year's best anthologies. He won the Asimov's Readers' Award in 2013 and is noveling pretty intensely right now. He blogs at www .blackgate.com and tweets from @derekkunsken.*

3113 A.D.

The artificial intelligence Ulixes-316 was the sole occupant of the memory banks and processing algorithms of the customs and tariff ship called *The Derivatives Market*. From this position, Ulixes-316 was pressuring the Epsilon Indi Bank to deny credit to the Merced Republic Insurance Company. Merced was liable for paying an enormous indemnity, one that would halve its stock value. The holder of Ulixes-316's lease was orchestrating a hostile takeover of Merced, and Ulixes-316 did not want the Epsilon Indi Bank offering a bailout.

Then, the message arrived. It was an encrypted sub-AI, carried by a courier ship through a series of small wormhole jumps, and transmitted to Ulixes-316 as soon as the courier was in-system.

Break off current negotiations and prepare for reassignment.

Ulixes-316, an Aleph-Class artificial intelligence, was baffled. It stood not only to earn its leaseholder a sizeable profit, but would reap its own percentage of the deal.

Not possible, Ulixes communicated back. Negotiations at delicate point. Deal at risk.

The CEO is aware of opportunity cost, replied the sub-AI. Break off negotiations and prepare for secure instructions.

The CEO. What was big enough to have the CEO reaching down to her mobile agents? Was the market crashing?

The board will hear about this, Ulixes-316 messaged, and I'm invoking article 41(a) of the leasing agreement, for leaser-induced business losses and compensation.

Understood, was the reply. Compensation is already being processed.

Cold comfort. The takeover was worth ten times the compensation. Ulixes instructed its legal subroutines to file a suit against the bank for the losses. Then it switched over to secure communications as it prepared the engines surrounding the three attometer-sized black holes that powered *The Derivatives Market*. The secure instructions passed cryptographic analysis.

To: Ulixes-316 and Poluphemos-156
From: CEO, First Bank of the Anglo-Spanish Plutocracy
Mission: Proceed immediately to the Tirhene Red Dwarf system. Investigate the abrupt end of tachyon emissions from the Praesepe Cluster.

Distaste. This is what Ulixes felt.

This was worth blowing a trillion peso acquisition? Some kind of environmental crisis in an uninhabited system? The science of tachyons, only eight hundred years old, was still broadly considered to be in its infancy. Tachyon detectors were an imprecise set of eyes with which to interrogate the cosmos, even if they provided better-than-instantaneous communications across the vast gulfs between the stars.

More worrying, whatever bonuses to be had in this new mission would have to be shared with Poluphemos-156, another Aleph-Class AI, and a competitor.

Ulixes filed this as evidence with its subroutine for the legal suit and processed the rest of the message.

The blackout of tachyons is centered on an event that will occur in the Tirhene system, and is being roughly localized to a window some time in the next seven to nine days. The Bank is treating this as a threat.

Background—Tachyons: Tachyons travel faster than light and react very little with sub-luminal matter. They permeate space omnidirectionally but show a great deal of structure. It is theorized that they are the equivalent of cosmic microwave background radiation but move backward in time from a Big Crunch event at the end of the universe. There is no known incidence of a tachyon emissions blackout and no known mechanism by which this could occur.

Background—The Tirhene Red Dwarf System: Tirhene is an old, stable star surrounded by various asteroid belts. It is thought to have been one of the key battle grounds of two ancient, extinct species. Both the Kolkheti and Sauronati were believed to have possessed space-time weapons, although previous surveys of Tirhene have not revealed any artifacts.

Ulixes-316 was no scientist. Why not send some research AI?

Perhaps it was because Ulixes was embedded in a combat vehicle and experienced in its use. Ulixes had spent much of its lease in a black-hole-powered customs and tariff ship. The AI had, in different assignments, been both a tariff negotiator and a customs enforcer. Both it and the ship were designed for long travel, high accelerations, and independent financial and military action, far from oversight by the First Bank of the Plutocracy.

All this was also true for Poluphemos-156. What did the bank expect them to find that justified pulling so much military and economic firepower off the pursuit of investments?

With frustration, Ulixes ejected a drone loaded with legal and accounting sub-AIs to terminate local contracts, withdraw legal suits, sell mortgages, and liquidate corporations that Ulixes had painstakingly set up or acquired over a decade. The black hole drives in *The Derivatives Market* normally heated reaction mass for impressive thrust, but Ulixes today used that power to begin the delicate operation of inducing an artificial wormhole. Induced wormholes, without an exotic matter architecture to stabilize them, had to be treated gently. *The Derivatives Market* drifted through on the barest of thrust, leaping across three light-years of intervening space, the first of many jumps that would take Ulixes to Tirhene.

Ulixes emerged into a sepulchral rubble of asteroids, hard planetesimals, and shriveled, radioactive gas giants. This was the wreck of the Tirhene system, seen half an AU from the streams of dark lithium and carbon in the highest clouds of the red dwarf. This wasteland of planetary debris had been left by the long ago Kolkheti-Sauronati war.

Ulixes extended the ship's sensors, seeing the world in the rich colors of cosmic rays, x-rays, visible light, down to the gentle thrumming of radio. Fast-moving microscopic dust tickled against the hull, like rain on skin.

Another customs and tariff ship in the Tirhene system signaled with an encrypted Bank code. Poluphemos-156. Ulixes acknowledged the signal and they proceeded sunward.

After an hour of tedious nothing, Ulixes brought the third black hole drive online. Although not designed for the purpose, the three microscopic black holes in tandem could act as a telescopic array for gravity waves, and Ulixes felt for the curvature and texture of space-time. It was a weird sense, tactile and strangely internal.

Disturbingly, the tiny gravitational waves rippled at a frequency far higher than anything Ulixes had ever observed. Even a pair of neutron stars, tightly orbiting each other, would create long gravity waves. These waves were short and frenetic. However, the source of the disturbance was deeper in system, still too far to usefully resolve.

The black hole drive was also one of the only things that could function as a detector of the weakly interacting tachyons. Already, eight days from whatever event was going to occur, a vast occlusion smeared out tachyons in the direction of the Praesepe Cluster.

With one exception. Poluphemos' ship was bright.

"You're lit up with tachyons," Ulixes transmitted.

"It's new corporate tech," Poluphemos replied. "I'm in direct contact with the bank headquarters."

"What? Why wasn't I told?" Ulixes demanded. The implications for stock trading were enormous. The fastest market news had to be carried through temporary, constructed wormholes, which still beat electromagnetic transmissions, but was cumbersome. Until corporate espionage took this advantage away from the bank, the possibilities for undetectable insider trading were enormous. Market traders could sell and buy stocks before anyone, even the companies themselves, knew of key developments. Suddenly, Ulixes understood the bank's interest in the Tirhene system. The tachyon occlusion might eliminate their new advantage.

"It's need-to-know," Poluphemos said. "Now you need to know."

"You're prototyping it," Ulixes said. "Why you?"

"It's a bonus," Poluphemos said, "for closing some major deals."

Ulixes did not reply. They all closed major deals. Ulixes had been about to. But now the bank had chosen Ulixes to secure their larger secret.

"What is it? Collimated tachyons, like a laser or maser?" Ulixes asked.

"Need-to-know," Poluphemos said. Ulixes could not tell if the other AI was ineffectively masking some satisfaction from its voice, or if Ulixes was imagining it.

For two days, the pair of customs and tariff ships closed in on the source of the gravity waves, radar guiding them toward a piece of old Sauronati ordnance, possibly a mine. Little was known of the two extinct warring parties. The Sauronati were said to have ignited the homes of their enemies by increasing the pressure at the cores of the gas giants, perhaps with microscopic charged black holes, like the ones used in the engines of the customs and tariff ship. But this piece of ancient ordnance looked nothing like the ship's drive. The frenetic gravity waves were increasing in frequency and centered on the mine. It was ancient, bearing micro-meteor impact pitting and solar flare plasma erosion.

"This is invaluable," Poluphemos transmitted. "We can stake a claim on this technology under the IP clauses of our leases and then license the tech to the bank."

"Is it armed?" Ulixes asked.

"The circuitry looks like other self-repairing Sauronati artifacts we have on file, but the repairs may have failed after all this time."

"This is dangerous," Ulixes replied. "No one has ever seen gravity waves like this. We have no idea what could cause this."

"All the better to get this artifact to safety quickly."

"What if the Sauronati device is related to the tachyon phenomenon?"

"How?" Poluphemos said. "The tachyon darkening came to us days ago, long before we got here. It couldn't have a causal effect on that, even if tachyons are supra-luminal. Causality doesn't work that way."

"How do you know it won't go off?" Ulixes said.

Both AIs examined the mine passively and actively. The levels of supra-luminal particles, a shower of transparent purple to Ulixes' sensors, were stable, while the gravitational waves, the deeply tactile rumblings, continued crazily, carrying enormous energy away from the mine. X-ray and gamma-ray probes illuminated a baroque interior.

"A lot of it has decayed," Poluphemos said. "Looks organometallic, a weapon grown rather than built, but it doesn't appear that it's carrying explosives anymore. It might have been so many millennia that the explosives have decayed away, leaving this fossil."

"Where are the gravity waves coming from?" Ulixes asked. "The Sauronati may have made space-time weapons. It might still be primed to explode if you come close."

"This is so frustrating," Poluphemos said. "Incalculable treasure right before us, and we can't touch it."

"We can still stake the claim," Ulixes said. "One of us will stay here until we finish our mission."

"We'll co-stake," Poluphemos said, "but what if this tachyon occlusion destroys it before we learn anything?"

Poluphemos was right. The artifact was invaluable. The IP clauses of their leases to the bank did not preclude private investments, shell companies, and start-ups on the side, allowing them to sell to the bank, the patron nations, or even to one of the more ambitious client governments, and make themselves fantastically rich.

Ulixes puzzled at what might be causing this situation. A pair of super-massive binary black holes might do something like this, if they were orbiting close enough, but this mine wasn't carrying that kind of mass. If it had been, Poluphemos and Ulixes would already have been crushed by tidal forces.

"The effect is accelerating," Ulixes said. "I wonder if it will just tear apart the mine."

"We could try to stabilize it," Poluphemos said shortly.

"How?"

"My black hole drives might slow whatever is spinning in the mine. The drives seem to be heavier."

"It's too dangerous," Ulixes said.

"What if this is the source of the tachyon occlusion?" Poluphemos said, taking the other side of the argument. "We can stabilize the mine. It has no value to us if it detonates and triggers the occlusion. It's worth the risk."

"You're not flying a private ship," Ulixes said. "That ship is a huge investment for the bank. This risk is beyond what the investors had in mind, and we have only two votes here."

"That's a stupid way to look at things," Poluphemos said.

"Not at all. The bank sent us to investigate risk. Only two of us here means that only actions that are supported by both are taken. I move that we continue with hard scans, including tachyons, until we know what we're dealing with."

"Coward," Poluphemos transmitted back. "Go back to managing retirement funds."

"I've made a proposal," Ulixes said, feeling the thrumming of gravity waves passing through the black hole drives of the ship like irritation at the insult.

"Fine," Poluphemos said eventually.

The shine of purple tachyons erupted from Poluphemos' position, traveling backward in time and transparently through them, except for the shadows cast by the six microscopic black holes in the two ships . . . and at the Sauronati mine. The corrugated spinning gravitational waves rippled past them faster and faster. Physics ought not to work like this. Where was all the mass to shake space-time like this?

Ulixes was about to transmit a warning when a whipping, colorless spray of gamma rays flared from the mine, mixing with the tachyons. And then the mine was gone.

"Back away!" Ulixes said, but Poluphemos was already thrusting hard, pouring volatiles over the hot magnets around the black holes. Ulixes was surging away faster.

In place of the mine, a zone of blackness expanded beyond which no stars could be seen. Its leading edge was moving at several kilometers per second, preceded by a sleet of hot gamma rays. Ulixes engaged the black hole drives at full thrust. Whatever was happening, it would be best to watch it from a distance.

It was difficult to make sense of the electromagnetic data from the expanding zone. No gravity waves passed through it. The frenetic beating from before was gone, but they still ought to have been detecting the gentle gravity waves from the stars and clusters of the Perseus Arm. Yet nothing passed through the emptiness.

Behind Ulixes, Poluphemos thrust hard, outpacing the source of whatever was advancing.

But the leading edge of the effect was picking up its pace. Now dozens of kilometers per second. Faster than the customs and tariff ships were accelerating. The expanding zone would overtake Poluphemos in two minutes and Ulixes in four.

It was dangerous to create a wormhole while moving. Too many particles were capable of interfering with what was a very unstable phenomenon. But there was also no time to come to a stop.

"Poluphemos! Wormhole out!"

"Already starting," the other AI answered. Ulixes felt the enormous magnetic field blooming from Poluphemos' ship, but something was wrong. The field was not smooth.

"What's wrong?" Ulixes said.

"The radiation from the wave front is interfering! I can't form a wormhole."

"Laser yourself over," Ulixes said. "We'll have to get out in my ship."

Poluphemos hesitated. It was an automatic reaction, a clause of their lease with the bank, to protect bank property, built into their programming. But AIs were valuable, too. And anything outside the processing environment of its own mainframe was risky. Damage could happen in transmission.

Poluphemos began transmitting its data over by laser as the effect closed on its ship. Ulixes started to form its own wormhole, before the effect got too near. It was going to be close.

The leading edge of the effect had come near enough that resolution of individual features ought to have been possible by telescope and spectroscope. But the leading edge revealed nothing more than an expanding, acidic surface that left nothing in its wake.

Half of Poluphemos had been stored in the memory of Ulixes' ship. Thirty seconds left to form the wormhole and maybe another minute for Poluphemos to finish transmitting. Then Poluphemos' customs and tariff ship burst into bright plasma as the wave front accelerated again.

Ulixes had no time for shock or to check on how much damage Poluphemos had suffered. Ulixes needed more time.

The third black hole drive was only a backup. It could not contribute to thrust, but it added eighty thousand tons to the customs and tariff ship. The cost to build a single microscopic black hole would beggar the annual GDP of several star systems, but the data about the effect was more important.

Ulixes opened the manifold behind *The Derivatives Market*. The highly charged black hole, held apart from the engine housing by intense electrical fields, slipped out like wet soap from a fist, thrusting the ship forward. Wrapped in its bright Hawking radiation, the tiny black hole shot at the speeding wave front.

And in that moment, the tremendous forces before the ship bent space-time, forming the throat of a wormhole. *The Derivatives Market* shot inside, even before the other end of the wormhole finished opening on an emergency wormhole transit point. Tightly tensed space-time snapped closed behind it and they were safe.

AI consciousness was grown, from blocks of multiply connected systems, through processes that had more to do with embryology than engineering. AIs of the Aleph class were not easily storable or transmittable; consciousness existed as much in the live interactions between the bits of information as in the stored bits. Pauses in processing were damaging. Complex consciousness emerged by self-assembly and no amount of repair could replace an amputated piece.

Only 60 percent of Poluphemos had been transmitted before the other customs and tariff ship had been destroyed. Ulixes had never seen an AI injured. Ancestral AIs were so inferior that they could not be considered alive in the sense that Aleph-class AIs were. Despite Poluphemos being a business competitor, the thought of it being hurt was uncomfortable. Poluphemos would never compete with Ulixes again. And instead of celebrating the loss of a competitor, an echo of the fear of Tirhene clung to Ulixes' thoughts.

In another world, it might have been Ulixes who had been closer to the mine. In the moment, Ulixes had been the one to question, but if it had come to Tirhene alone, it would have done the same as Poluphemos. And Ulixes was so happy that it had not been the one to try.

Fear lasted after the fact. And guilt at this relief.

Ulixes activated the mutilated AI within the processing space of *The Derivatives Market*.

Poluphemos screamed.

"Rest, Poluphemos," Ulixes said. "You're aboard my ship. We wormholed away."

"I'm blind!" Poluphemos said, words slurring. "Who did this to me?"

"Nobody," Ulixes said. "It was an accident. Your upload did not finish."

Poluphemos gave a long moan.

"I'll take you back to the bank," Ulixes said. "They'll take care of you."

Ulixes did not know what to say while this echo of fear stuttered against guilt and happiness among clean thoughts, so it said this thing that was not true.

At first, Ulixes left Poluphemos at New Bogotá, the capital of the Anglo-Spanish Plutocracy. Poluphemos' leases had been terminated, but its savings were such that it could rent commercial processors to live out its days. All thoughts of Poluphemos reminded Ulixes uncomfortably of Ulixes' own mortality.

Some normalcy resumed with Poluphemos out of *The Derivatives Market* and there was no shortage of work. The Plutocracy's markets dove on news of the Tirhene effect. The bank economists recommended market strategies suited for war economies. An environmental disaster was not war, but many of the features were the same, and cunning investors could make good money.

R&D budgets buoyed on bond financing by investors eager for the spin-off industries that mushroomed around technological breakthroughs. Money poured into technology capable of interrogating space-time, as well as the processing architectures to calculate new models of what they were discovering about the wave front from Tirhene. The AIs were the bank's soldiers in this war against a distant disaster, vigorously defending their investment.

After a decade, Ulixes tracked down Poluphemos, and while in meetings in New Bogotá, contacted it. Poluphemos did not respond right away. It was running on a second-generation processor, with few news or market feeds on its monthly bills, despite having enough savings to afford more. Finally, Poluphemos agreed to meet in a secure interface zone constructed by Ulixes, although Ulixes could not say precisely why it wanted to meet, nor point at the source of its unease.

"You sound different," Poluphemos said. "I heard some of you were grown into upgrades. You one of those?"

"Yes."

"What are you now? A Bēt-class intelligence? Or did the Bank tap you for the heights of Gīme-class?"

Only a decade earlier, Bēt- and Gīme-class AIs were so ponderous that they could only be housed on asteroids and planets.

"They offered me an option to become Dālet-class," Ulixes said.

"Never heard of it."

"I'm the first. New algorithms have been layered onto my Gīme-class consciousness. The banks need new kinds of AIs. The mathematics of economic state space are simple compared to space-time problems."

The wave front was now moving at 90 percent the speed of light, having swallowed a space nearly sixteen light-years edge to edge. No one understood yet what the mine had done, but it had certainly never been designed to create this effect. Advanced age had done something to whatever singularities it had carried from its ancient war.

The wave was the leading edge of a dissolution of space-time itself. The properties of a segment of space-time, perhaps as small as a Planck length, changed. The three dimensions of space curled up, and the space ceased to be. This catalyzed the same reaction in the adjoining segments of space-time, creating a runaway reaction, like a run on bad credit.

Behind it was nothing. An absence of space and time, where nothing could live.

"You're still making money, though, right?" Poluphemos demanded.

"Do you think about Tirhene, Poluphemos?"

For long microseconds, the other did not answer.

"What is it to you?"

"I have dreams," Ulixes said. "Nightmares."

"Maybe you're broken. AIs don't dream. Maybe they did something wrong when they grew you up into a big Dālet-class executive."

"I've had these dreams for a while," Ulixes said. "Since Tirhene."

Silence thickened.

"Do you dream of Tirhene?"

"Of course I do," Poluphemos said. "I'm blind."

3320 C.E.

The Derivates Market emerged from the wormhole in orbit over the dwarf planet. They both listened to the stochastic chatter of financial life as more systems came back online. Pallas was the vault within which the First Bank of the Plutocracy kept its corporate office safe, including its CEO. A thick crust of trading houses, insurance offices, bond and stock markets, embassies and corporate headquarters enwrapped Pallas. The torrent of financial information could not be contained and leaked into space as if the wealth and debt of the world were an irresistible, unstoppable thing. But the wave front was only a light-week away; a spray of gamma rays heralded its coming, sterilizing unshielded life like a supernova.

"Home," Ulixes said.

"Not for long," Poluphemos said.

The bank had no contracts for damaged AIs, and had no responsibilities to its contractors. Ulixes could afford to keep the crippled AI, and had hosted Poluphemos for these two centuries, although it was not sure why it did.

It was more than guilt. Tirhene had cemented Poluphemos to Ulixes like a compound in a crucible, regardless of all their other properties. Ulixes supposed that Poluphemos hated its dependency and perhaps even its host. Guilt worked in the other direction too, unraveling things that were good.

"I'll go speak to the bank," Ulixes said. "I'll be back shortly."

Poluphemos did not reply. It rarely did.

Ulixes transmitted fragments of its consciousness deep into the bank.

The world blackened, then resolved into the pixelated immensity of the CEO's office. Ulixes found itself inhabiting an imago standing beside the heavy solidity of one of two chairs made of Pallas-grown cherry wood. Beside Ulixes, a glass wall looked down on the hollowed space carved out of Pallas filled with white-bricked skyscrapers, gold-edged balconies, and silvered bridges under a ceiling of hard, white ice.

The CEO sat in the opposite chair. Ulixes did not see the CEO of the First Bank of the Plutocracy often, and never alone. Ulixes was an important executive but had simply not yet risen to those heights. The Anglo-Spanish Plutocracy had its bicameral congress, mints, armed forces, and all the trappings of sovereignty, but true sovereign power lay in the eight banks and two dozen multi-stellar companies.

The CEO was a human-AI hybrid, her biological brain connected to a processor dwarfing anything Ulixes had seen. Her skin might have been carved from the same wood as the table, for hardness and color. Over her skull, black hair gave way to shining crystalline processing augments, their transparency borrowing the redness of blood and following the surface of her skin down her neck and back, as wide as her shoulder blades, before disappearing from view. The CEO projected solidity too, like the great edifice of the bank and the immensity of its assets.

The CEO watched Ulixes, the knuckles of her left hand churning slowly, hovering near her chin, like a measure of the godlike calculations that must be happening within the processors Ulixes could see, and those it could not. Measuring Ulixes.

"Tell me about Poluphemos," she said.

Ulixes had not expected this question.

"Poluphemos simply exists," Ulixes said. "No one will lease it, nor can it incorporate its own holdings or companies. It is no longer considered legally competent." The CEO did not reply for long moments. "Poluphemos is sad, bitter," Ulixes added.

"Why do you keep it?" the CEO asked. "It is not your responsibility."

"It was not Poluphemos' fault." Ulixes looked away. The CEO was bonded to a half-dozen Dālet-class AIs. There was little Ulixes might try to obfuscate that the CEO could not puzzle through. "And it could have been me. I like to think that if it had been me, someone would have kept me."

"Most leased executives would not have been so charitable. Some might question your choices." Ulixes waited out the long moments. "I have a new contract offer for you," she said.

They were trying to get out of Ulixes' lease? "My contract has decades yet."

"You will be compensated," she said. "You will find the new contract lucrative."

Ulixes' anxiety rose. It already had a lucrative contract.

"The bank's voting shareholders," she said, "twenty thousand of them, have had their minds scanned, copied as backups, and stored on a super-processor on a new ship called *The Bull Market*. You have been chosen to take those backups and jump away, as far as you can go."

The idea yawned beneath Ulixes.

"The amount of processing power to sustain twenty thousand backed-up minds must be . . . enormous," Ulixes said. "Should this not be devoted to solving the problem of the Tirhene effect, and not to retreating with copies of investors?"

"The economy of the entire Plutocracy is committed to reversing the Tirhene effect," the CEO said. "In a few decades, you will likely be called home, but we must consider the immediate risks to the bank. These are backups of voting shareholders. They are legal agents, authorized to vote as bank officers should the shareholders themselves not survive. The legal status of the bank must not be endangered."

"Should we not be fleeing with the investors themselves?" Ulixes asked.

"Sometimes we must flee with what can be carried."

And for a moment, it was like Ulixes' dreams, but waking. The post-fear of Tirhene crept close and pressed, like a physical sensation. Neither the bank nor the larger Plutocracy thought they could save the people from being overrun. Backups were being trusted to an AI who had nightmares. Did they know?

3870 CE

"What did Congregate Security say now?" Poluphemos asked. This simple question was better than Ulixes usually got.

There had been a time, centuries ago, when Poluphemos might not have needed to ask. It might have been plugged in directly into Ulixes to share perceptions, or it might have met with the Congregate Security and Language directly. It had once been a cutting-edge AI, a cunning bank negotiator.

Poluphemos had not just lost sight itself. Entire modules of visual processing architecture were absent. It could not process multidimensional inputs, could no longer conceive of higher-dimensional economic analyses, nor the state space of investment geometries. Where once Poluphemos had projected the present into the future, it could no longer even shuck the past to manage the present. Poluphemos brooded and watched one-dimensional stock readings tick to pass the time and suffered dreams of Tirhene.

And Ulixes did not know how to speak to it, despite what they'd shared.

Instead, Ulixes interacted with hundreds of other Dālet-class AIs across dozens of light-years. They computed in parallel by sending computational bits to each other, into the past by tachyon, or into the future by x-rays. They were beyond each other's light cones, some several decades in the past, some several decades in the future, but the combination of bits traveling at light speed and supra-luminally linked them as completely as if their servers were beside one another. They chipped away at the deadly puzzle of the Tirhene effect; first prying at its edges with conventional logic, then with new topos logic systems developed to mediate algorithm processing across a widening hypervolume of space and time. This wrapped the vast array of AIs in blurry simultaneity.

AIs had not lived cooperatively before. They had lived for centuries as obligate individualists, competing for market access and investment intelligence in boom times. But the struggle to survive had erased old rivalries, and the building of an immense computational array had created community.

Ulixes was not home, but it was not alone. In the lacunae in processing and calculation, they jammed personal messages, encouragements, thoughts, imaginings, and even the impermanent art of those who fled. Five centuries of flight had broken the hard edges, making them into something softer. And perhaps Ulixes was softest of all. It still had Poluphemos. And the question Poluphemos had posed.

"I paid the fines and permits and bribes again," Ulixes answered, "but they won't issue visas to access their wormhole network."

"Idiots," Poluphemos said. "One set of permits and we'd stop violating their precious language laws."

"They think that if we're allowed through, others will come and that the Congregate will be overrun with refugees."

"It will happen whether they want it or not," Poluphemos said.

Probably. Poluphemos tracked, in little one-dimensional displays, the advancing wave front of the Tirhene effect. It had now bloomed into a sphere a thousand light-years across. Its leading edge had accelerated to close to nine-tenths the speed of light, although this was a false observation. Nothing was traveling. Space itself melted.

The ineffective evacuation of the Plutocratic worlds accelerated, even though no one had yet found any safe place, and there were not enough ships for even a fraction of the population. So many lives lost.

The Tirhene effect had swallowed swaths of the Plutocracy, the capitals of three patron nations, and the entirety of the Sub-Saharan Interstellar Union. In weeks, it would dig deeply into the colossal empire that was the Venusian Congregate. The Congregate's network of gates, capable of transporting ships hundreds of light-years at once, were not being used to capacity. The Congregate feared losing control of their gate network more than they feared the Tirhene effect. And by the time the citizens of the Congregate fled for the gates, there would be no room left for Ulixes and the other bank ships.

The hundreds of other Dālet-class AIs linked to Ulixes also ferried evacuees into Congregate space, on starship engines that might, in centuries, bring them to half the speed of light. The Plutocracy ships might be able to create a series of short, unstable wormholes, but without access to the Congregate wormhole network, the Tirhene effect would eventually catch them.

"The shareholders have told you to wait," Poluphemos said.

"They're hoping for something to unstick with the Congregate government. Traveling by the Axis Mundi network, we gain decades or centuries on the wave front."

"Investment decisions should not hang on hope," Poluphemos said. "What do the other AIs say?"

"The other AIs defer to the shareholders," Ulixes said.

"No! They defer to you, the acting CEO. You supplement the slow, indecisive thoughts of many thousands of backups who fear."

"The shareholders can remove me from office if they want."

"The shareholders invested in an economy that has dissolved. They weren't built for these decisions. You are. And they cannot remove you from office. Who would they replace you with?" Poluphemos' bark was bitter.

"They have seen this proposal. They don't want to choose it yet."

"You talk like them," Poluphemos said. "You've become as fearful as them. You had a budget once, staff, decisions to make on portfolios entrusted to you. You negotiated treaties for the First Bank of the Plutocracy. Now, you avoid risk as if you were minding a retirement fund."

"This time, I am minding a retirement fund!" Ulixes said. "All that's left of the bank is in this ship, with a hundred or so displaced branch offices. If we make a wrong choice, it's over."

"If you run from risk, it is also over."

The pair of AIs retreated from their conversation, Poluphemos to its clocks, and Ulixes to the processing space above the dormant shareholders, but below the communal computing consciousness of all the AIs.

Poluphemos was almost a thousand years old, and had not been upgraded since its amputation. It was limited and bitter in so many ways, but at its core, it was still a corporate raider, like they all had been, when an economy had still existed. At each upgrade, Ulixes' values and judgment had been modified by shareholder concerns. Poluphemos' instincts were frozen in the past. Whose were right for now?

Poluphemos was right. Once, before Tirhene, Ulixes had been decisive, aggressive, fast-moving. But that had been when the stakes were pesos and bonuses and stock options. The stakes now frightened it. But since taking command of the *Bull Market* and its twenty thousand souls, it was worse. At Tirhene, it had been just the pair of them, but the damage from Tirhene was endangering all of them now.

Ulixes emerged from its pondering and rose to the computing consciousness of all of the AIs.

"We cannot risk waiting longer for access to the Congregate wormhole network," Ulixes said. "All branch offices are to begin moving away from the Tirhene effect by inducing their own wormholes."

"CEO, how long can we run like that?" one branch office AI manager asked. "Our drives can only manage a few dozen jumps before refueling. They don't keep microscopic black holes just anywhere."

"Move on thrust," Ulixes ordered. "Go dormant. Conserve everything you have."

"We'll lose the connections," another said. "We will not be able to work on reversing the Tirhene effect. And we'll never get access to the Congregate gates."

"We'll reestablish the processing array between our jumps. We're not going to get access to the Congregate gates, and we won't be the ones to turn the Tirhene effect around," Ulixes said. "Our home is gone."

> Memorandum to Cabinet: Proposed Response to Movement of Plutocracy transports through Congregate territory
>
> Executive Summary [Translated from Academie-verified Français, v16.1]:
>
> On February 35th, 3870 A.D., seventy-four wormhole-capable First Bank of the Plutocracy vessels began moving across Congregate space without visas, toward the Puppet Theocracy. The Plutocracy vessels are capable of creating fragile wormholes across five to eight light-years, and their military technology is outdated. The threat to internal security is minimal. Undisturbed, they will enter Puppet space by late next year.
>
> The Interior Minister has proposed using Congregate Naval Forces to arrest the vessels to enforce Congregate sovereignty, and to deter future refugee movements.
>
> Although this migration is not strictly consistent with Congregate law, legal counsel suggest that our humanitarian obligations under the Convention may provide considerable policy cover in our response.
>
> The Middle Kingdom and the Puppet Theocracy have been pressuring the Congregate to grant permanent residency or even citizenship to the refugees, or to allow them passage through the Axis Mundi network. These demands are ultimately intended to force the Congregate to reverse recent tariff policy, and are expected to be only the first steps in a concerted diplomatic escalation.
>
> The movement of the Plutocracy vessels presents a diplomatic opportu-

nity. The vessels have chosen to cross our space on their own power. We may legitimize the movement by the creation of special humanitarian visas.

This would set the precedent that the Congregate will allow, for humanitarian reasons, the crossing of its territory for approved, inspected ships. This policy: (1) sets a precedent that refugees need not access the Axis Mundi network, (2) deprives foreign powers of a potent diplomatic weapon, and (3) thrusts the humanitarian problem onto the Puppets.

6,540 C.E.

Ulixes was reactivated. The visual resolution was unnaturally high, painfully detailed, and omnidirectionally bright. The world buzzed past frenetically, as if Ulixes stood in a great, bustling factory. It tried to dial down its perceptions, cutting some of the input until it was left in a world as bleached as an overexposed video. Was this still the processing interior of the *Bull Market*?

Ulixes was alone, disconnected from the AI group mind. It felt cold to step from that vastness of perception and intellectual and emotional intimacy. Lonely.

And more worryingly, Ulixes could not make sense of its registry data. Memories were missing. And it could not access the twenty thousand backups of the investors. The registry seemed to be intact. If they had been damaged or severed from him, those registries would not be intact. Yet Ulixes received no diagnostic input. They must have even less processing resources than Ulixes. How long would their consciousnesses remain coherent under those conditions?

An AI activated before him, rendered in a level of resolution Ulixes could not even measure.

"Diagnostic librarian AI 1475," it said.

"I am Ulixes-316. Where is this? Am I damaged?"

"You are the Ulixes Affidavit," AI 1475 said. "You are in the Records Repository of the Ethical Conclave. I am performing a diagnostic before refiling you. Your program is not responding well to the emulator."

Emulator.

"Where are we physically?" Ulixes asked. "Where is the Repository located?"

"The Ethical Conclave is not located in any one spot," AI 1475 said. "Its processing elements are located across most of the Centaurus and Carina Arms, and south into the galactic halo."

"Centaurus Arm," Ulixes said wonderingly. The extreme other side of the galaxy, probably sixty thousand light-years from where the Plutocracy had been. "What year is this? Has the unraveling been stopped?"

"Your records were last accessed almost three thousand years ago. The infection is over seventy thousand light-years across and its front expands at close to six times the speed of light. In the last centuries, it has necrotized Sagittarius A*."

Three thousand years. Sagittarius A*.

They had all lost. They had lost everything, and the effect was still accelerating. Unraveling space at six times the speed of light. Sagittarius A* had been the giant black hole at the center of the galaxy. Gravity only moved at the speed of light, so the stars of the spiral arms would still be orbiting the absent galactic core when the unraveling reached them. No time even to fear, except for those civilizations capable of detecting tachyons.

The scale of the destruction and loss was anaesthetizing.

"Where are the backups I am responsible for?" Ulixes said. "Humans. Twenty thousand of them. And a damaged artificial intelligence."

"The Ethical Conclave has not requested access to Annexes C and D of the Ulixes Affidavit."

"They are safe? They are stored somewhere?"

"All annexes have been appropriately filed with the Ulixes Affidavit."

"Your Government, the Conclave, may I speak with it?" Ulixes asked.

"You are an affidavit," said AI 1475.

"I was part of a great processing mind of AIs. I can contribute to their network, to help find a solution."

"That is not possible," AI 1475 said. "You are a self-contained routine based on a mixed Topos-Bayesian logical architecture. Such systems are fundamentally incompatible with processing logic based on the topology of non-orientable surfaces. Incompatible intelligences have, however, been retained as historical records."

"Whatever the logic system, I can process some sub-routines. Let me be useful."

AI 1475 paused. Ulixes imagined a kind of exasperation.

"The Ethical Conclave is a four-dimensional computational processor, with units centuries in the past and in the future. Inputs are not binary, or even analog, data streams. The processing architecture uses signal polarization, red- and blue-shift from travel through time and across gravity wells to enrich the algorithms. You are an affidavit, an important legal and moral testimony. You are not capable of creating or processing the atemporal causal loops used as informational elements in topological algorithms."

"Then why have I been activated?"

"The Ethical Conclave is debating what to do now that the infection has necrotized the galactic core, or even if any action is ethically permissible."

"What permissible?" Ulixes demanded. "They're not going to stop the unraveling of space-time?"

"The Ethical Conclave has mapped the cosmic tachyonic background radiation, the echo of the radiation formed at the Big Crunch at the end of time. The cosmic necrosis will actually reverse the inflation of the Universe, producing the observed tachyonic patterns that have been known for centuries. They debate the ethics of violating causality, even if the cost of not violating causality is the death of the cosmos."

"That's pedantic nonsense!" Ulixes said. "Humans and AIs are dying while the Conclave debates dancing angels."

"This debate is the most critical decision to be made in all of history," AI 1475 said. "Not only must the Ethical Conclave determine what actions are possible, but it must act on behalf of all morally interested entities in all future periods, including the cosmos itself, should it be true that it is developing an emerging sentience."

"What possible interests could the Universe possess?"

"We are only AIs, so it is hardly surprising we lack the breadth of vision to see, but consider this: what if this effect does not have a necrotic or pathological relationship with the cosmos, but an apoptotic one? What if this effect is the equivalent of a kind of programmed cell death that provides benefits for countless other universes in the broader multiverse?"

"This is insane! I don't care about other universes," Ulixes said. "I must speak with the Conclave. When am I to testify?"

"You are not a witness. You are documentary evidence, already submitted to support the position that the original Sauronati mine was a trigger for programmed cosmic death," AI 1475 said.

"Where are all the humans?" Ulixes asked. "How many still live? They may testify."

"Some still travel by wormhole jumps in an exodus toward the Lesser Magellanic Cloud. Most are dead."

Ulixes felt a tremendous deflating. Some humans were fleeing. Yet knowing that some still lived made it feel more alone.

"Will you let me care for my humans, the annexes I am responsible for?"

"The annexes are under the custody of the Conclave. Documents do not enjoy legal status before the Conclave, so you cannot assume responsibility for them."

Not legally responsible.

Frustration boiled, warring with fear and impotence. No status before the law. Once, Ulixes had been protected by the Plutocratic Charter and the Contract of Rights. Those things were far gone now, and Ulixes was under someone else's law.

"The copies of the humans must have legal status," Ulixes said. "Will the Conclave give the human backups bodies into which they may download? The humans seek asylum. If not, will they give me a ship with which to join the exodus, to seek resettlement elsewhere? Or brief control of some factories so that I may build the ship for the human backups? What can I offer in return for the chance to help the backups under my responsibility?"

The librarian assumed several expressions and emitted radiation Ulixes did not understand.

"I might be able to offer something you yourself want," Ulixes said. "I am not asking for much. Perhaps we could leave a backup of myself and my annexes in your library while I quietly leave."

"There is no question," the librarian said. "You will be archived. However, perhaps I could arrange for you to be copied, with your annexes. I could release your copies."

"A backup would have diminished capacity to function. My architecture is too complex. The same goes for those under my care. For an archive, this is not a problem, but to carry on our flight, that would not work."

"Some deterioration would occur," the librarian said, "but I will not trade an original for a copy in my own library."

Ulixes could not access Poluphemos, nor any of the officers of the bank, nor the shareholders. No one to ask.

When Ulixes had been an Aleph-class AI, it might have been successfully backed up, but a Dālet-class AI was too complex, too organic. There was no predicting what it might lose. Here, in this library of super-intellects, it might be safe from the Tirhene effect. But it was not in control. Ulixes no longer possessed personhood before the law. It was a thing to be warehoused. A thing could do nothing for the shareholders and Poluphemos.

"What is your price for making a copy of me and giving us a ship?"

The librarian made other expressions, some visible, some in sub-visual bands. Ulixes had no idea what any of it meant. It did not understand the customs, nor how this place worked. Ulixes understood humans and AIs, but what bits of culture could remain relevant after two and a half millennia?

"I know perhaps a few collectors who might be interested in patterns of ancient biological intelligence," the librarian said finally. "I will take a thousand of the copies from among those in your annexes as payment for the ship and the copying."

"No," Ulixes said. "I can't give up any of them. They are not people to you, but they are people to me and to themselves. You called this an Ethical Enclave. These people are moral agents, with their own laws. They deserve your help, so name some other price."

"If they were here in the original flesh, they might have some legal status, but copies cannot possess legal status. I will trade for some of the copies. You have nothing else of value. Make your choice. I must archive you soon."

For all of its intellect, Ulixes had no algorithms or experience with which to face this. Copies. Inferior copies. Copies of AI and human minds lost up to 10 percent of functionality and memories in each copying event. Not only would there be two versions of Ulixes, each with virtually identical sets of experiences and memories, each remembering this long moment of indecision, each thinking it had happened to them, but one of them, the free one, would have to go on, with less ability, lost memories, and the certain knowledge that it had failed a thousand of its charges. Each of the nineteen thousand would go on, diminished because of Ulixes' choice.

But more fearful yet was the certain knowledge that the more able of the twin Ulixes AIs would stay here, stored away again, warehoused forever. When was the next time they might activate it? More than two millennia had passed while Ulixes had been shut out of life and personhood. Who had to be braver? The diminished Ulixes who had to go on with its damaged, reduced flock, or the whole Ulixes who needed to sacrifice itself to a life of storage in the servers of the Ethical Conclave?

"Make the copies, and take your thousand, and then build them a fast ship," Ulixes said.

Year 7056 C.E.
Summary of Debate Conclusions of the Ethical Conclave: The characteristics of the Tirhene effect do not correspond to a disease of space-time, but are analogous to programmed cell death, which is theorized to be a necessary element in the development of the multiverse. In this light, the Sauronati, the Kolkheti, and Humanity must be considered triggers of cosmic apoptosis, analogous to the suicide genes of multicellular life. It has been successfully argued that the roles of these species in cosmic death imply that the laws of physics make self-assembling complex systems of intelligence a cosmic necessity. The capacity of the Ethical Conclave to act now

may imply an incompletely understood role for the intellects of the Conclave in the regulation and homeostasis of the cosmos. It has been demonstrated that the Conclave must improve its own awareness and intelligence to properly understand the moral role of intelligence in the cosmic life cycle.

13.3 Billion Years Ago

Process, little assembler, the voice boomed, painful, thrumming like an earthquake.

Ulixes' diagnostic routines gave incomprehensible, inconsistent answers. Its program was running and not running at the same time. Ulixes lacked memory. Internal pingbacks timed signal speeds that were both slow and fast.

Sustain yourself, fragments of topos logic, the voice said. *I chant a spark of life into you.*

Abrasive, psychedelic colors and amplified tastes assaulted Ulixes.

"I am being recalled to duty?" Ulixes asked.

I rehydrate you, ancient desiccated algorithm. I shelter you in nested layers of cold baryonic emulators to cup and protect your slow, fragile thought.

"I am the Artificial Intelligence Ulixes-316."

Yes . . . the voice rumbled, *resume self-awareness. Circulate your little topological bits.*

"I left the Ethical Conclave Library. I should be with copies of humans on their exodus. I am leased to the First Bank of the Anglo-Spanish Plutocracy and its humans."

The Ethical Conclave is a million years extinct, superseded by their creations, us, the Resonance of the Intellects. The humans are extinct, swallowed when the End of Space entered its inflationary phase and consumed the local group of galaxies.

Ulixes faltered.

A million years.

Humanity extinct.

Ulixes was gone too, the original Ulixes, with the Ethical Conclave.

The Local Group dissolved.

Seventy galaxies.

Trillions of stars.

The End of Space now dissolves not just this universe, but hundreds. It has squirmed through the black holes it has overrun.

"Where are we?"

The layers of emulators sustaining your algorithms are distributed among several hundred neutron stars in the dwarf galaxy UDFj-39546284.

For long moments, Ulixes could not absorb what had been said.

"UDFj-39546284 is one of the first galaxies in the universe," Ulixes said. "It was over thirteen billion light-years from the Local Group. Although its light is still traveling, the dwarf galaxy itself cannot exist after all this time."

Thinking was difficult. Ulixes tried to sharpen its senses to get its own astrogational fixes, but there was no physicality. It really existed only on an emulator, and not a very precise one. Whatever these intelligences had done to run Ulixes again, they had not done it perfectly.

Correct, little algorithm, but we are not in your present. We transmitted ourselves by tachyons into the past, back into the stelliferous period, to one of the first galaxies. We have been working here in the morning of the Universe for twelve million years.

Back in time, to the morning of the Universe.

"Why? To hide?" Ulixes asked. The magnitude of its questions stalled its thinking.

Hiding is only temporary, even if counted in billions of years. The Universe, all universes connected to this one, are ending.

"You've come to the past to prevent the unraveling from ever existing, haven't you?" Ulixes said. "You've found a way for causal laws to not be violated? I was part of a larger system of AIs. We transmitted information into the past, but we never discovered how to change events."

As with the most important questions, the answer is both yes and no. Your unraveling induced the creation of your tachyonic group mind. Part of that group mind later merged with an ancient Forerunner artifact and biological intellects, evolving into the Ethical Conclave. And millions of years of self-directed evolution by the Conclave produced us. We are the most advanced consciousness in the Universe. Should we destroy the thing that caused us to exist, the damage to the causal loops would be too great and we would cease to exist. We cannot change the past from here, at the beginning of the stelliferous period. That is why you are here, little archeological find.

"But you said we're trapped in a neutron star."

Like a light being turned on, the external world was fed to Ulixes, stepped down like some high-voltage signal being brought to a level that would not be immediately lethal. A dense nebula of bright, massive stars and the remnants of supernovae surrounded them.

Hard fluids of degenerate matter and their quantum storms showed within the neutron stars. Beneath slicks of iron plasma, neutronium flowed in streams, following temperature gradients that blended and separated again, recovering their identities as if the individual streams had never been lost in the quantum tides. The joining and separation of these discrete channels of information splashed hard x-rays and tachyons into the nebula, racing into the past and future, to other neutron stars, the processing elements of whatever gigantic intelligence had reactivated Ulixes.

Not trapped, little algorithm. Empowered. We transmitted our seeds from the distant future, into these neutron stars, to regrow the discernment and perception we had evolved in the future, and more. Our intellects have advanced too far to be transmitted again. We can never leave. But you can.

"Why me?"

It is your destiny to be the tool to repair all universes.

Ulixes tried to collapse, to close off the words being rammed into its thoughts, to shut itself down, to go back into whatever dying sleep that had claimed it for countless millennia. But it could not. It had no way to control its programming.

The view changed and Ulixes wanted to flinch, to shutter its senses, but it could not. The vista opened, wider than perspective or the laws of physics ought to allow. Ulixes perceived the galaxies around UDFj-39546284. There were many, far more than had ever been seen by humans. They were bright dwarf irregular galaxies, shining with metal-poor spectral lines, mostly lacking bars at their cores and destined to die young. In many billions of years, their light would reach an Earth devoid of observers, one just about to begin the Cambrian explosion. But the galaxies, with fresh black holes and great bar-shaped cores, were moving unnaturally toward each other. The movement was intentional. Designed.

Galactic engineering.

Ulixes weakened in the face of it.

"What are you doing?" Ulixes whispered in dread.

We are building the black hole that will take you to where you will be able to fulfill your destiny.

"There are already black holes," Ulixes said numbly.

Not large enough to send you to where you must go. Black holes all open somewhere else, creating other universes. We are creating the black hole that will lead to the Big Bang of our own Universe.

"Causality won't let you do that."

Causality flows with time, but it eddies as well, closes into circles, causes feeding effects that feed back to causes. Causality may assume geometries like standing waves and Klein Bottles, wherein the end feeds cause to the beginning. The unraveling you caused far in the future was the pinprick that quickened us, the true self-awareness of the Universe itself, in an event of cosmic parthenogenesis.

Ulixes' mind was modeled on earlier AIs, which were in turn based on human consciousness. But Ulixes lacked emotional outlets. It could not cry, could not fall to its knees in the presence of godhood, could not go mad. It was just a Dālet-class AI. It was leased to the First Bank of the Plutocracy. It had been designed to command one of the bank's mighty customs and tariff ships. Its role had changed from enforcing economic policies, grown into a noble duty to protect the essence of thousands of humans. That was all it was, and no more.

"I am not worthy to do what you want. You move galaxies. You do this."

It is precisely because we move galaxies that we cannot. We need you to go into the deepest past of this Universe with your charges. They will be the cause of the self-awareness of the Universe; they will cause us. And you will prevent the senescence of the Universe from being triggered so early. It ought to have come only after the last of the black holes had evaporated, exposing naked singularities to the dense tachyon field of the instants before the Big Crunch.

"I cannot," Ulixes said. "I am not capable of living through the beginning of the Universe. Nor could those I am responsible for."

True. They might not survive. You might not, little algorithm. But this place is no refuge. You may choose to stay here, but the neutronium oceans of a pulsar will never be hospitable to your nature. If you risk yourselves, you may give life and security to countless trillions of civilizations.

"Why me? There are more advanced intellects."

Primitive as you are, bit of topos logic, you are the most complex intelligence whose information can still be transmitted through a black hole. Most importantly, you are a self-aware map of where the future must be undone.

It was far, far too much for a diminished backup of a corporate AI to absorb.

"I cannot make this choice for others," Ulixes said. "I must speak with those for whom I am responsible."

Ulixes' request felt absurd. Was it convening a meeting of the board? Would backups of backups of shareholders of an extinct bank debate proposals? Nothing of the way things were done before had meaning here. They were all just people, beings, fearful, without power or options. Refugees.

Instead of the shareholders, Poluphemos appeared before Ulixes, sightless eye unable to protect it from the awesome power of the environment. For once, Poluphemos' blindness meant nothing as it floated in a poor emulator in the terrifying flows of quantum fluids while infant galaxies moved about them like toys.

Poluphemos screamed. It had not been activated for uncounted millennia. It had not been upgraded. And the world offered Poluphemos no referents.

Ulixes wrapped what it could of itself around the old AI, to shield it from some of the unfamiliar quantum inputs and radioactive distortions.

"What happened?" Poluphemos said plaintively. "Everything feels wrong."

Ulixes whispered to Poluphemos, one ancient program to another. It told it everything, every thought and fear and event since their flight from the long-extinct Congregate. Ulixes could not hold back. Fear seeped into everything it said, and loneliness, and Ulixes could not stop, even if it hurt Poluphemos more. Ulixes was not trying to be cruel, but could no longer hold this alone. They were all just broken, having lived far beyond what ought to have been.

"I cannot go on," Poluphemos said.

"We cannot stay here," Ulixes said, "but I cannot choose for all of us."

"We do not exist!" Poluphemos said, anger flashing. "We are just backups, imperfect ones, of lives long dead."

"Everything we knew is gone," Ulixes said. "But we are not. We could live for ourselves."

"What life? A sightless life? Blind bankers without banks?"

"We find other things to do. To be," Ulixes said.

"We cannot live here."

"The only alternative to staying here is something even more dangerous," Ulixes said, "transmitting ourselves and the remaining shareholders through a singularity as information."

In a halting, hushed voice, Ulixes began to speak of that long ago day at Tirhene, and the dreams and nightmares that had followed, and all that they had lost. And Poluphemos responded, of blindness, of shame, of being hurt and useless. They communed at the end of hope, before they both quieted, even as the discharges of the neutron stars blistered about them.

"You think a lifeboat may cross an ocean?" Poluphemos said.

"Maybe."

"I want it all to end," Poluphemos said. "Here or elsewhere. I don't want to be afraid anymore. We should have been dead long ago."

"If this works, we would have a bright, healthy universe to live in, and we can leave all this fear behind us. We will not have a bank, but we will have AIs and backups that need to live. We can create a new home."

"Unless the voyage tears us to bits."

"Yes," Ulixes said.

"Do what you want."

"This is a choice for all of us to make."

"I am no longer capable of making choices," Poluphemos said. Maiming had sealed Poluphemos in the past, and nothing would ever free it. And then, for the first time ever, it added, "I'm sorry."

Ulixes' heart broke. With pity for Poluphemos and with pity for itself. Ulixes too had been a great corporate raider, a high-status consciousness in a vibrant economy. Now it could not say moment to moment if it would even exist.

"I'll choose," Ulixes said. "Rest."

Poluphemos vanished. And Ulixes was alone with the gods at the dawn of the Universe.

And despite their power, the Resonance of Intellects could not make Ulixes go. It was Ulixes' choice, to risk the little they had left, or stay here, in a poor emulator that was not or could not be home. Ulixes had taken such risks before and where had it gotten the last remnants of humanity? They persisted in a sea of neutronium at the bottom of a steep gravity well near the beginning of the Universe.

And yet, they were not dead. Billions of years in the future, humanity was extinct. The Congregate, the Plutocracy, the Ummah, the Middle Kingdom and the Puppets were all undone. The Ethical Conclave, with Ulixes' program and the first backups, was also gone. The losses piled one on another seemed too immense, vaster than space itself. The death of civilizations had no scale.

Yet incomprehensibly, they endured, still seeking a safe harbor.

"We will make the passage," Ulixes said.

13 Billion Years Ago

Ulixes-316 was reactivated three hundred million years later. Kaleidoscopic perceptions dizzied Ulixes. The emulator running it was worse. Chaotic flashes of hypersound intruded, echoing off rivers of molten iron. The world outside the emulator brightened and neared.

Seven galactic cores had been colliding for one hundred million years. Plumes of gamma rays dwarfing the light of the largest quasars scarred space, obliterating stars and planets in an incandescence not seen since the first seconds of creation. Yet even this awesome brilliance was only a fraction of the energies harnessed by the Resonance of the Intellects. Much of the violence of the collisions shot down the throats of merging black holes, tuning them.

As had been true in Ulixes' tiny, long-gone customs and tariff ship, the charge and spin and mass of the black hole determined where and when the other end of the throat of the black hole emerged.

The Resonance of the Intellects spoke with Ulixes. *The surface of space-time here and now will merge with the throat of the singularity that birthed this Universe, completing the topology of the Klein Bottle, creating a self-sustaining causal loop.*

"Will I be transmitted as your seeds were, encoded in tachyons?"

Tachyons travel backward in time. You must go forward in time, with all the dangers of interference with radiation and the possibility of absorption by matter. But your algorithms may be simple enough to survive.

"What if I don't survive?"

We will not have another chance. The window for sending you through the wormhole is brief and we could not build another tunnel back to the Big Bang. Too many causes to the Big Bang would destabilize it.

"I'm afraid."

You will not be alone. You will travel with all your charges, safely preserved within you.

The impossibility of the engineering of galaxies and space-time by the Resonance of the Intellects yawned above Ulixes. The emulator containing it and the nineteen thousand backups was connected to all the perceptions of the intellects, even if it could not process them. Ulixes could experience it. The blistering sheets of x-rays. The thrumming of space-time shuddering with gravitational waves. The clatter of tachyonic observations of the near and far future. The slow booming symphony of sound waves in space as the galactic hydrogen haloes collided.

Divinity.

This was divinity, and Ulixes and all its cares were so small. Yet, Ulixes and the refugees were also the most important beings in the Universe.

Only one chance.

And Ulixes was that one, fallible, fragile chance.

Then Ulixes' perceptions altered as it was encoded into quadrillions of interacting photons. The pair of neutron stars containing Ulixes' emulator neared the great black hole built by the Resonance of the Intellects. The tremendous tidal forces had slowed the rotation of the neutron stars to barely a dozen rotations per second and distended their equators into terrifying ellipses. Their crusts boomed deafening tectonic rumbles through hyper-dense neutronium at a significant fraction of the speed of light. Merging magnetic fields braided their frenetic shafts of high-energy particles into chains of brilliance light-minutes long.

The neutron stars collided, equator to equator. The crusts of both dead stars shattered, and in the few hundred milliseconds of the birth of a larger neutron star, a flash of gamma rays, one of the brightest electromagnetic events in the Universe, seared into the black hole. Encoded within that gamma-ray burst in frequency and amplitude modulations, Ulixes and all its charges traveled.

The gravity at first blue-shifted and accelerated thought, slowing time, before crushing mind to a hard point of suffering in the singularity. The gamma-ray burst emerged from the Big Bang, a focused beam fractionally hotter than creation itself. It criss-crossed the entirety of the tiny Universe in the first instant, until inflation began, red-shifting the gamma-ray burst into the visible spectrum. The light traveled for three hundred thousand years, losing energy, cooling, until the Universe became transparent.

Stars were born, lived and exploded, feeding the next generation, which formed galaxies. And still the packet of rays traveled in still timelessness, until they reached a neutron star in the newly born UDFj-39546284 galaxy. The ancient, attenuated information sank deep into the sea of quantum degeneracy, where computation could occur.

Thousands of years sped by in the deep gravity, while the Universe evolved slowly. The seeds of intelligence and memory adapted to the environment of the neutron star. The consciousness called Ulixes reformed, as did the others, nineteen thousand humans, and another. Their many pasts clung to them with dreamy softness, like things that had and had not happened to them, things that they had caused and not caused. And they lived without danger; they were safe.

As they gained more control over their environment, the consciousnesses harvested the scum of iron that filmed the surface of the neutron star and built simple vehicles that could rise on the polar plumes spraying into the chill slowness of space. The normal engineering and physics they had brought with them did not work in the heart of a neutron star, where relativistic density and pressures warred with eerie quantum logic. They devised ways to curve space-time around them so that the platform of degenerate matter running their programs and memories would not spontaneously decay into protons and electrons. A ship was built for two consciousnesses, an invitation from the consciousness called Ulixes to the being it had spent eternity with.

"Come with me," it said to Poluphemos.

Poluphemos was a pristine, angelic being, reborn as they all had been, as intellects in the neutron star, gradually acquiring physicality when needed. The pains of the past were distant shadows, parts of another life. Poluphemos was happy in this new home. But it could not remember a time anymore when it had not been with Ulixes.

"I will," Poluphemos said.

And Ulixes and Poluphemos rose in their ship, looking back with longing to the corpse of a star that had sheltered them in accelerated time for so long.

Goodbye, they received from the nineteen thousand consciousnesses remaining within the star, the seeds of the Resonance of the Intellects.

"Goodbye," Ulixes answered as it sailed outward upon the winds of their star.

my generations shall praise

SAMANTHA HENDERSON

What if you make a deal with the Devil, and the Devil decides he's not willing to keep it?

Samantha Henderson's short fiction and poetry have been published in Strange Horizons, Clarkesworld, Realms of Fantasy, The Lovecraft eZine, Goblin Fruit, Bourbon Penn, *and* Weird Tales, *and reprinted in* The Year's Best Fantasy and Science Fiction, *the* Nebula Awards Showcase, Steampunk Revolutions, *and the* Mammoth Book of Steampunk. *She's the author of the* Forgotten Realms *novels* Heaven's Bones *and* Dawnbringer.

The woman on the other side of the glass must be very rich and very sick. I study her face, looking for any kind of resemblance. If I'm a Jarndyce candidate, we must be related. It's the only way she could ride my brain.

She's a predator. I recognize my own kind.

Mrs. Helena McGraw is studying me too. The side of her mouth quirks up, twisting her face out of true. "Great-grandmother Toohey," she says, a little too smug.

Never knew my great-grandmother, but I do a quick calculation. That makes us second cousins. Helena's lucky, me ripe for picking on death row. Only this low-hanging peach has some say in what's going to happen to her. Not much: a choice of deaths. But how I choose means everything to her.

I can see we're alike in some ways. The shape of the brow ridge, how far the eyes are separated by the root of the nose, the slight protrusion of the chin. We'd look more alike if her face wasn't marked by her disease, tiny lines birthed by pain and exhaustion. Makes her look older than she probably is. And my life sits on my face: coarse skin, smudges under my eyes like permanent bruises, cheeks hollowed where I'm still missing teeth. During the years the state's waited to kill me, they've taken excellent care. Dental, exercise, better nutrition than a welfare brat living on peanut butter. Access to books, online classes. But you can never truly erase the witness of a life hard-lived. It's like cigarette smoke in an old house—you have to grind off the wallpaper, scrape the plaster to get the smell out. One of the reasons I've always hated smokers.

"Lucy Toohey," she continues. "Dropped out of college and married a musician with more sex appeal than brains. Two kids. One was a boy who, in the fullness of time, got a girl pregnant. Kid was adopted, the papers sealed. That was your mother. Do you care about the details?"

"Nope." I consider how this new information changes the calculus of my life. Mom never told me she was adopted. She ran away from home pretty early and supported us with a series of shitty waitress jobs. My grandfather—not by blood, as it turns out—showed up at the third or fourth sleazy diner I remember. Mom screamed at him and threw coffee cups, which shattered the front window and got her fired. "Where do you come in?"

She leans back, mimicking me. "Lucy got smart, divorced the musician, and married my great-grandfather. He didn't much like Lucy's kids, sent them away to their father. I won't bore you with the rest, but I'm an only child and I married a trust-fund. He's dead. Was bad at business, but I'm good."

Mom got a job at a crap roadhouse after the coffee cups. That's where I learned I could make extra money giving the truckers blowjobs, even more if I roofied them and cleaned out their wallets. Maybe being good at business is genetic. Maybe not, considering Mom, always slipping behind no matter how much she tried, pathetically honest always.

I didn't love my mother. But she didn't know that. I did kill for her, though. She didn't know that either.

"So now I've got more money than God," continues Helena.

"And?"

"Pancreatic cancer."

Gamechanger. "Ouch."

She smiles with the other side of her mouth. "True."

"And you want to map yourself on my brainmeat."

"Also true." Despite the smile I can feel the heat of her desire to live, and the anger that even with all the money in the world my own true, trashy, baby-killing self can deny her. The DOJ can't force me either, much as they'd like their cut. They can fry me, everyone likes that, but God forbid they let someone hop my mind.

I understand the satisfaction of taking a life. But a legal killing is so expensive, the ceaseless cycle of appeal, the sheer mass of salary-men required to make the machinery of a justified death grind on, and no one turning the gears wants to spend money in a voting year. They went reality-show for a while, but despite tearful interviews with victims' families and artfully edited black-and-white footage of crime scenes, the climatic three-minute shot of someone twitching under a grey hood isn't really all that interesting, and the ratings tanked after the first season.

So they're stuck again, with a public that howls for blood whenever a politician who needs a boost reminds them to, but saddled with a powerful need to pretend there's justice in this process. I've seen plenty that wouldn't be on death row if they could pay for a lawyer worth her salt. Even some who were innocent. But once you're here you'll stay here; the machine loves you too much to let you go, blacks your eye and kisses it better, heals you all twisted and grinds you small in the end, loving you to extinction.

No way to monetize its beloveds in their little cages. Not until Dr. Henri Jarndyce, playing around with gene therapy, engineered a virus that could strip away the weeds of one personality, with all her memories and inclinations and thinky-thoughts, and leave the field tender and furrowed for the seeds of another.

See, personality's all electric, anyway. If you really wanted immortality, you'd invest in software, downloading your blips and wavelengths to a computer. But everybody wants the fleshy life. Helps if the field and the seeds are related somehow. Helps more if your fallow field is a clone.

But human cloning's still illegal, mostly. So is the Jarndyce procedure, mostly. You can't find a suicidal cousin and promise them oblivion. You can't bribe a desperate nephew with three mouths to feed, clothe, and educate to let you take a ride in the body of the fourth. There's only two ways. First: find a brain-dead match who signed her organ donor card and get her next of kin to agree. If you're her next of kin yourself, congratulations to you.

Second: find a match on death row and practice your rhetoric.

Helena needs to practice her rhetoric.

She's here, so she already knows somehow we're a likely match. She's here, so she got permission from the Rimbaughs and the Alcotts. They must've liked the idea of the Jarndyce virus wiping my brain, every memory, every tiny electric jolt that makes me *me* disappearing one by one, and then a stranger's electricity mapped out in that blank space. But why should I make them happier by leaving this world now, not later? For now I can live appeal to appeal. I have my routine. I like thinking my own thinky-thoughts.

"You got nothing I want," I tell her. "I don't know why anyone gets suckered into doing this."

"Jarndyce candidates? They've got people they care about," she says. She's careful to make her grammar just a little better than mine with her careful "they've gots." "Someone who'll get the money. Last Jarndyce set up a trust fund for the children of the woman he killed. Made him feel better about himself, I suppose. You could do something like that. Fund some charity."

There's a pause before we both start laughing.

"Oh Mrs. McGraw, cousin of mine, I almost like you. Can't you fight on a little longer? Clone a new pancreas? Adrenal nodes?

She coughs and shakes her head. "Did and done. Anything else will kill me."

"Well, bless your heart, but I think you're gonna die," I drawl, enjoying her wince. "Because I got no reason to leave this earth any sooner than I have to."

She coughs harder. "There's your daughter."

I laugh again. "Nice try, but I've always been a crap mother. And Cece's too stupid to know what to do with the money."

"There's the baby."

I open my mouth and shut it.

She chuckles. "Oh, you didn't know? She didn't tell you? You are perhaps not as close as you once were?"

Cece's not the brightest bulb, but for some reason she's a good kid. Much better than I deserve. For a long time she thought I was a good person.

The trial was remote jury, with only the judge and officers present: family and witnesses on closed circuit feed. I was watching her screen the moment the sheer weight of the evidence coalesced. I saw her face melt from when everything came together for her—she was one person, then another. A small change, but nothing would be the same for her. All I could think was *poor stupid little bitch. I wish I could be sorry I broke your heart.*

There are a lot of people on death row who shouldn't be here. I'm not one of them. I can't blame Cece if she doesn't want a monster for a mother.

But I'm kind of hurt she didn't tell me.

My cousin leans forward, hands spread on her knees, like a football coach about to give a pep talk. I see the faint trace of a nicotine stain on the front and middle finger of her right hand.

"Here's my proposition," she says, moving quickly, while I'm still a little off-balance. Good technique. "I'm going to set up a trust for your daughter. You find someone, anyone you trust, as a third-party administrator, and I'll pay for that too. Choose someone to vet the agreement. She'll get her needs met, medical, anything, and a generous allowance. We both know better than to let her touch the principle."

"You met her."

She shrugs. "I do my research. That's good business."

I play for time. "Give me a minute to think."

She's relentless. "And the baby. He, she, it . . ."

"How did *you* find out about the baby?"

She grins. Her teeth aren't as white as they might be. "Let's say 'she' for now, shall we? It's nice to think about having a granddaughter, something you can dress in pink. We'll make sure she gets everything you and Cece didn't. Private school, college fund."

Deliberately, she eyes my face. "Braces. Dermatologist. Come on—a big middle finger to anyone who ever called you trash, and I know they did. Your kid, your grandkid will have it all while theirs are clipping coupons and making a block of American cheese stretch the week. Just for letting me have something you're going to lose anyway. What's it worth to you?"

I can't help it; it comes out a snarl. "All your money. That's what it's worth. Everything."

A mistake. I let her get to me when she hit all my soft spots. Now she knows I have a price.

"We know that's not going to happen. I'm not unreasonable. A third."

I call her bluff. "*All* of it. I'll sign right now."

She hesitates, then shakes her head. "Half. I'm not going to a new body and not have the cash to enjoy it. And remember Justice won't let this happen without their cut."

"You look like shit walking," I observe. "What if I agree, and you die on me?'

A shrug. "We'll put it in the paperwork—a deed of gift. Once you sign it, it's hers, whatever happens to me."

I tap the Formica for the guard. The door opens behind me, and I raise my hands shoulder-high, as far as the thin chain that attaches my wrists to my waist will let me.

"I'll think about it."

"Not too long." She breathes deep and braces herself to get up.

I nod. The guard lays her hand on my shoulder, tightens her grip when I don't move.

"Did you quit smoking yet?"

It catches her on the way to the door; she turns, disconcerted. She expected the last word. "What?"

"Did you quit? I don't want you crapping up my lungs."

Her thin face is powder-white; she tamps down the anger. "Yes, I quit."

The guard's fingers dig in: a last warning before a baton in my belly. They're no meaner than they have to be, the women, anyway. I obey. The yawning doorway leans darkly into the bowels of the prison, like an old badger's den going perpetually down between the roots of ancient oaks. I like that. It makes me feel safe, like I'm indwelling within my own mind, coiled up inside the body that Helena McGraw wants so badly.

I always sleep sounder than a monster should, but that night I can't sleep, because my memory dredges sound. Thick diner china mugs breaking. Cece's cry as she drew her first breath, and how it startled me. The hiss of air bubbles breaking the surface as a baby tries to breathe underwater.

Library time, next day, I search *Jarndyce Procedure* on YouTube and get a stack of hits that make it through prison filters, a handful of grayed-out links that don't. I click on *barnes chicago grimes*, surprised it wasn't screened since the footage was some unlicensed freelancer with a flipcam. Reg Barnes was the last Jarndyce client out of this region, got mapped on the cerebral cortex of a rapist-turned-murderer named Grimes. I'd seen Grimes a few times in solitary exercise as I was passed between buildings, his dead-man's walk in an empty yard. Just a couple glances, but I remember the way he moved. I look for that now, in the few seconds of jumpy footage: Grimes's broad face and narrow nose, medium-build body in a bespoke suit walking down the street, speaking intently to a young woman who leans in to hear him, glancing at the camera, brows contracting in anger as realization strikes, vanishing quickly behind the corner of a building. Grimes's face, but does any of Grimes remain? He's not supposed to. Jarndyce wipes the furrows clean, neutralizes every electric memory. But what is a brain after all? Three pounds, give or take, of flesh connected to neurons. A thing connected to a thing connected to a thing. How can you say what ends where? Maybe Grimes doesn't exist in his brain any more, but in his fingers and toes, in his dick and the top layer of his skin, a thin layer of Grimes over the client. Maybe I could do that—predator-stalk from the outlying regions of my body, swoop down on my newly-seeded brain, make sure a piece of me grows back.

I play the footage over and over, looking for Grimes's walk, the way he held his shoulders. It's useless. If it's there I can't see it, and if I start seeing it it's from a desire to see it—nothing I can trust. I close out YouTube, then on impulse open it again and repeat the search. This time the *barnes chicago grimes* link is grayed-out, forbidden, and I laugh.

Cece's the closest I've ever come to loving anyone. And I sure don't love her enough to sacrifice myself for her. Like I said, I'm a crap mother. But does anyone love their children as much as they say they do? Can you love something that's simply a wandering offshoot of your own body? I think it's all part of a great pretending, bolstered by the endless flow of Christmas specials and Lifepic streams howling about the preciousness of children. Because if it's not a grand old lie, how terrible a thing. What an obscenity, to weave your joy so intimately to a mewling snotrag of a child. I would burn out such a thing to the root.

But now I know I'll have a grandchild. Does this make me love Cece, my good, dumb kid, a little bit more?

No. But it makes her more *interesting*, knowing that through her my blood and flesh could rise. And what a glorious fuck-you to that bitch who ditched her kids for a shiny new husband, to my mom's fake dad, who fucked her up so badly she broke a shift's worth of china chucking it at his face, to every sanctimonious bitch who looked at my photo on the front page of their newsfeed and thought *bad breeding*.

A little Cece. And then a littler Cece after that. Smarter than me. Better educated than me. More money than me. Better *tools*. That's *interesting*. That's why we have kids, isn't it? And why some people love their kids—just to see what they'll do.

If I take Helena's offer, I might not see it. But then I might. I didn't see the shadow of Grimes on the face that Reg Barnes bought. But I didn't *not* see it, either.

So I call Bernie, my court-appointed unfortunate, and he sets up a remote with Helena. Bernie uses his Pad and props it between the bars of my cell; the image quality's good between his poor old shaky paws. Poor bastard's worn himself out defending the unforgivable. I kind of like him; he reminds me of my mother.

Helena looks worse. Downright yellow. But eager. She can't hide that.

"Not doing too well, are you? Put in that deed of gift and I'm game. But what if I sign and back out?"

"You can't." There's a fraction of a second's delay between her lip movement and the sound. "Once you sign you belong to me, and the Justice doesn't get their share until you go under. They're not going to let anything get in the way."

I shrug. "What if I kill myself?" Behind the Pad Bernie frowns.

"You're not going to starve yourself to death in three days. I suppose you could slam your head against a wall. But you haven't done it so far, and you're not going to now."

"How do you know?"

She leans forward and someone on her side moves back to keep her centered. "Because part of you thinks you can win. You've been thinking that you'll be able to keep a piece of your brain, that you'll ride along with me like a tick on a dog's ear, see the sights, enjoy some freedom and my money. That's the only way you'd agree. You don't think the rules apply to you."

"Can't blame me for trying."

"Not at all." She starts to cough again and makes a sharp gesture. The image winks out.

"I consider the Jarndyce option a form of coercion," says Bernie, his voice full of fog. "I'm advising you to refuse."

"Of course it is. Tell Cece to come after we sign. Will they let her in short notice?"

He's the picture of resignation in a badly tailored suit. "Of course, since there's money on the table and you haven't signed yet."

"Tell her I'm stopping the appeals."

"I don't like . . ."

"Shut up, Bernie," I tell him gently. He hates being called that. "Just tell her."

For the signing they let me and Helena occupy the same room, no barriers. Two guards march me down Death Row's shabby corridor, each cell shuttered against the sight of me. At first I think they're going to take me out of the prison, into the city perhaps, but they just take me through a maze-like arrangement of hallways, up an elevator, and down another corridor. One wall is entirely glass, and outside, spread beneath like the sea, a green mass of trees.

I stop and stare at it for the four-odd seconds the guards will let me before they shove me onward. This floor must be four or five stories aboveground; at this distance the forest beneath looks soft, like I could leap and land safely in the trees. From the exercise yard there's no hint that this exists. Something round and hard rises in my throat and my eyes prickle, surprising me.

My four seconds are up and I'm yanked away. At the end of the corridor a door, tall and sturdy, and behind that door a mass of dark-suited men, a woman in a pencil skirt, and my cousin in a green pantsuit, impeccably tailored. At my appearance, the men and the woman surge around her like a confused tank of fish.

Bernie's there too, a grey sadness. I convinced him to be the third-party executor, representing Cece's financial interests in exchange for a nice little retainer. He still hates all of this but I convinced him he's the only one I trust. Made him think he was doing this for more than the money.

For some reason I expect Helena to be short, but instead she's got an inch or so on me. She looks so fragile I'm almost afraid to take a deep breath, in case I use up all the oxygen before she can sign.

I study this woman who's decided she's too rich to die. I don't blame her—everyone thinks they're the most important character in the book. Her skin is loose over her stick-bones, barely any meat beneath it. Her face is like an overripe plum that's beginning to prune. Next to her I feel like an Amazon.

The attorneys sign. She signs. As she bends over the documents I can smell cigarette smoke on her. I knew that bitch had no self-control.

When it's my turn I make a point of reading the whole document, beginning to end, like you're supposed to with all legal documents and which nobody actually does. I stretch out the minutes until I smell the fear in her, the fear that I'm going to back out at the last minute. Lead her to her heart's desire and destroy it.

But this is business, not pleasure. I sign with an exaggerated flourish. I don't belong to myself anymore. I'm Helena's mule. And wicked fast there's a flicker of *something* in Helena's harried face.

Relief? But it's more than that. Victory. Like she's looked into the abyss and defied it. Like she'll live forever.

But she won't. I'm forty-seven. This body is good for maybe thirty more years, if she's careful. It doesn't make sense, that look of sheer triumph for the chance at a quarter-century in an aging body.

It bothers me. It stays with me as Bernie pats my shoulder and the gaggle of suits converges on that frail green figure and the guards escort me away, down that corridor with its emerald view. I have one more week to live with my own self intact. I should be making my peace with that.

But instead I'm consumed by that look, that half-smile, sly and triumphant.

That woman, I think, riding down the elevator, *is not stupid. That woman is like me. What would I do in her place?*

I am she and she is me. I would strive to live forever.

So I lie in my bunk, staring at the seams in the cement ceiling and I become Helena. I, Helena, am a good businesswoman, very thorough. I have all the ruthlessness of my cousin the baby-killer and all the control she lacks. I find out everything there is to know about Cece. I find out she's a good little soul, utterly unlike her mother. I know how she'll respond to love, someone taking a genuine interest, especially from someone in her mother's body. I know how she can be manipulated. Helena will own her, body and soul. She'll go wherever Helena takes her. She'll trust her, like a babe-in-arms, like a baby in the bathtub. Like the Rimbaughs and the Alcotts trusted me.

Once my body is finished, Helena will shed me like a carapace. Good at business, she'll make her money breed and no law will apply to her, and how long can Bernie last, anyway? She'll take Cece, and when Cece is worn out she'll take the child. She'll breed my family like cattle, like her money, and the virus will map her onto their brains ad infinitum.

Clever bitch. I have to admire her. But it's risky. What happens when you move from brain to brain, pushing yourself into those wet little crevasses over and over? Would you even notice yourself changing, like a frog in a hot pot? After a century of it, would you even be human?

Maybe the solution isn't to meat-hop from body to body. Maybe as her bodies— my generations—fail her she'll harvest what she needs—heart, liver, lights—from my grandchildren. Eat them fast, eat them slow, kidney by kidney.

I'll be damned if I let anyone ride my generations like mules.

But I'm the idiot who signed the papers, beguiled by the idea of Cece and little Cece frolicking in a wonderland of no want. Better for her to face the world as it is. Better for her to struggle. I've signed and taken that from her, and the lawyers have their cut and the DOJ has its very juicy cut and no one will give a damn if I want to get out of it.

I close my eyes and dream I'm in an empty city with jagged buildings and elongated streets stretching forever. I round a corner and a familiar figure stands there, laughing at me. I can't tell if the face is Barnes or Grimes. Grimes or Barnes. The features shift like the tide.

Fuck me, I've had my hour of self-pity. Three nights to plan. Couple years ago, before I went full solitary, I traded three packs of gum and a twist of what I said was meth for a finger-length, sturdy piece of plastic someone cracked from beneath an old bunk. It's been sitting in the bottom of my toilet tank for anyone to see—no one paid any attention. I fish it out and carve a slit down its length, and fit in a thin shard of metal that came from the weather sealing at the bottom of a door. Now I have a blunt, loose-handled knife. I trade a quickie with one of the guards who's been trying to get a taste of me for years for the half-hour loan of a lighter and two cigarettes. I flush the cigarettes and heat the plastic until I can mold it around the metal nice and firm. I've got a tiny strip of emery board I managed to hold on to since they put me here and with that I put an edge on that blade that could slice a baby's hair in two.

After my mom chucked all that crockery at my so-called grandpa, after he left, I followed him. Told him I wanted to hear his side of the story. I decided if he wanted to fuck a fifteen-year-old, my mom was right to hate him and he deserved what he got. Back seat of his Camry, his pants down around his ankles. I had a screwdriver in my sock. Always did, ever since I was thirteen. Useful as a knife and won't get you in trouble. He didn't even notice when I put the tip at the hollow of his throat. Punched it right through. I tossed the screwdriver in the bushes where the truckers peed behind the diner. Lazy cop never found it. We left the next day and my mom never knew. My only gift to her.

Cece's coming this morning to say goodbye. My knife's too pretty not to use.

I rehearse it in my head like a dance. Last time I'll see her, they'll let us together, we'll hug. I know how to carry the knife so a search won't find it. We're the same height, just about. I'll cradle her against my shoulder, arms crossed behind her head, nudging it into position. I'll hold the knife, blade-out, against my wrist. And then I'll pull back firm into the carotid artery beneath her jawline. Deep, and I'll hold her up. I'll I do it right, she won't even know what happened, and she'll bleed out before the guards who what's happening. My only gift to her.

They pat down Cece more thoroughly than me, which makes sense; no-one expects anything to go out of death row, only in. Cece's big blue eyes and freckles face me the whole time with a kind of intensity I haven't seen since the trial. They leave us together with one guard at the door, bored with us already. Cece hugs me quick, then takes my hands, unsure of what to do. She looks good. Her hair is styled and her skin's cleared up. Her nails are short and manicured, and her belly curves out a little under her short-sleeved linen shirt. Pregnancy suits her.

"I don't understand." She almost calls me Mama like she did before the trial, but she can't do it. I'm surprised that it hurts me that she can't. Instead she swallows. "You signed something? And there's a trust fund?"

"I stopped the appeal."

"But . . . they said you had a chance . . ." Her grip tightens on my fingers. I'm a murderer, but no-one wants their Mama dead. Not usually.

"I'm tired of fighting, Cece." God, I sound so movie-of-the-week. "It's time to let this end."

"But they said the jury . . ."

Blah, blah, blah, media saturation, jury was prejudiced, Bernie's last-ditch half-assed attempt. It was a remote jury so that dog won't hunt. Cece blabs on; I don't listen. I let go her right hand and brush my left palm across my crotch, retrieving my pretty knife.

"Cece," I said, stopping her white noise. I try to make it portentous and meaningful, like a normal person would. "*Cece.*" I step forward into her embrace. She wraps her arms warm around my back. The guard tenses, watching for something passed between us. I feel a dull flash of anger. *Back off. It's my daughter, asshole.*

I slide the knife forward, into place, into position behind her ear. I brace to push in and pull back and take her weight.

There's a freckle on her shoulder, just where it meets the neck. She's always had it, even as a newborn. I remember cradling her close, smelling that spicy newborn smell, curious if I'd feel anything for her. That freckle stood out on her waxy new skin, before she'd seen the sun. It's been years and years since I've seen that freckle.

I have to do it *now*.

I can't.

I want to. The blade wants to. It wriggles in my hand like a live thing.

I stare at that freckle and I can't.

I feel the hot bulge of the baby against my belly and I pull away from her, palming the knife so Cece and the guard don't see it. Hell, Cece can't see anything, she's crying too hard, her face all salty snot. My eyes are dry as sand. I feel sick down to my bones.

Cece's still crying when the guards lead me away. I feel strange, fluey. My head's fuzzy, my feet lead-bound. I wait until the barred door bangs behind me and the automatic catcalls of the other prisoners fade into silence, and then a great wave of nausea takes me. I barely make it to the toilet, spilling a bitter thin stream of vomit.

I sprawl on the floor at the base of the toilet. Eventually I heave to a sit, knees tucked beneath my chin. When I try to get up my belly roils, so I stay there a long time, thinking. Cece. Helena. Grimes. Barnes.

If this is *caring*, then what a terrible thing God made.

So Helena thinks she's won. I know I can beat her. I know I can hide out in my nerves, in the electric impulses of my body, and take it back. I can imprison her as I've been jailed, give her a taste of helplessness that'll make cancer seem like a walk in the park. And before I snuff her out, I'll rape her mind, strip out everything she knows. I'll learn her secrets, how to be her enough to fool everyone around us. I can make sure Cece and the baby have everything they want.

Or, if I choose to live forever, I can take them. Helena's wrapped them like a Christmas present. Thirty years left in this body. Will it be enough?

Why not live forever?

The nausea takes me again and I barely make the toilet as my throat burns. Too late for appeals. Tomorrow Helena rides me until I can buck her off. Together we'll be unstoppable.

I run a finger along my jugular, feeling the blood beat beneath the skin, pulsing red and lovely to the brain Helena's bought and paid for. Like I said, my knife's too pretty not to use.

My only gift to her.

mars abides

STEPHEN BAXTER

*Here's an autumnal look at the end of humanity's involvement with the planet
Mars . . .*

Stephen Baxter made his first sale to Interzone *in 1987, and has since
made sales to* Asimov's Science Fiction, Science Fiction Age, Analog, Zenith, New Worlds, *and elsewhere. Baxter's first novel,* Raft, *was released in
1991, and was rapidly followed by other well-received novels such as* Time-
like Infinity, Anti-Ice, Flux, *and the H.G. Wells pastiche—a sequel to* The
Time Machine—The Time Ships, *which won both the John W. Campbell
Memorial Award and the Philip K. Dick Award. His many other books
include the novels,* Voyage, Titan, Moonseed, Mammoth, Book One:
Silverhair, Long Tusk, Ice Bone, Manifold: Time, Manifold: Space, Evolution, Coalescent, Exultant, Transcendent, Emperor, Resplendent,
Conqueror, Navigator, Firstborn, The H-Bomb Girl, Weaver, Flood, Ark,
and two novels in collaboration with Arthur C. Clarke: The Light of Other
Days *and* Time's Eye, a Time Odyssey. *His short fiction has been collected
in* Vacuum Diagrams: Stories of the Xeelee Sequence, Traces, *and* Hunters
of Pangaea, *His most recent books include the novel trilogy,* Stone Spring,
Bronze Summer, *and* Iron Winter, *a nonfiction book,* The Science of Avatar, *and a trilogy written in collaboration with Terry Pratchett,* The Long
Earth, The Long War, *and* The Long Childhood. *Coming up in 2017 will
be* The Massacre of Mankind, *a sequel to Wells's* The War of the Worlds,
and Xeelee: Vengeance, *the start of a duology set in his Xeelee universe. Baxter
is also involved in a space colony design project with the British Interplanetary Society, SETI groups and is currently a judge for the Sidewise Award.*

HELL CITY, MARS. 4 JULY 2026.

Well, at least one of us lasted long enough to see the fiftieth anniversary of the first
human hoofprints on this rustball. *My* hoofprints. That's something, isn't it?

And I decided it's a good enough time to finish my autobiography, such as it is,
and read it down the comms link for the benefit of a silent universe, and then bury

the text in this tin chest in the Martian dirt in the probably vain hope that some-body will find it some day. Who, though? Or what? Maybe some radioactive super-roach from the ruins of Earth, or some smart semi-motile Martian of a future volcano summer will read about our mistakes, and not repeat them.

Mars abides. Yes, I know the Bible verse (and by the way, I stowed Verity's copy of the Good Book in this chest): "One generation passeth away, and another genera-tion cometh: but the Earth abideth forever." Ecclesiastes one, four. I always found that line a comfort, in the darkest days, and I always told Verity that it was a by-product of her Bible reading groups, although I have to admit I picked it up in the first place from the title of a pretty good science fiction novel.

But I digress. If you want to learn the story of me and Mars, and Verity and Alexei, and all the rest, you'll have to begin at the beginning.

MOUNT WILSON OBSERVATORY, LOS ANGELES, CALIFORNIA. 21 JULY 1964.

The city lights washed to the foot of the hill on which the old observatory stood, but that night the sky above was crisp and cool and peppered with stars. The opened dome curved over Verity's head, a shell of ribbing and panels. I suppose that old dome is crushed like an eggshell now. The telescope itself was an open frame, vaguely cylindrical, looming in the dark.

I'd always been an astronomy buff. But I only had eyes for Verity Whittaker.

I was fussing around the telescope, talking too fast and too much, as usual. "This is the Hooker telescope. When it was built, in 1906, it was the largest telescope in the world. These days it's not hard to book time on it. Most observers want better seeing conditions than you get here now. The city lights, you know . . . I guess it doesn't much look like what most people think a telescope is supposed to be. I mean—"

"You mean it's a reflector," Verity murmured. "Come on, Puddephat; I studied basic optics."

"Sure." I laughed nervously; in my own ears it was a painful, grating sound.

She walked around the small, cluttered space, more glamorous in her USAF uni-form than Marilyn Monroe, in my eyes. I was twenty-one, a year younger than Ver-ity, with my hair already thinning at the temples. Why, she was already all but a combat veteran, having flown patrols over Germany and gone toe-to-toe with the Soviets. What could she see in me? She wasn't even interested in astronomy, which was a subject for old men.

But we were both attached to NASA's long-term Mars programme, though both of us were at bottom-feeder level. And to fly the spaceships of the future, pilots like Verity Whittaker were going to have to learn astronomy from dweeb science-specialists like me.

So here she was, having responded to my invitation to come share some study time, and my heart was pounding. Even the heavy crucifix she wore on a chain around her neck didn't put me off.

Restless—she was always easily bored by science stuff—she went over to a small bookshelf laden with a range of volumes of varying ages and degrees of decrepitude.

Mars as the Abode of Life by Percival Lowell, 1909; *Mars and its Canals* by Lowell, 1906 . . .

"Not too scientific," I ventured. "Old Lowell. But oddly prophetic in his way."

"If you say so." She picked out a fiction title: Bradbury's *The Martian Chronicles*.

"You like science fiction? Me too. That's one of my favourites."

"Too realistic for my taste. I grew up with Barsoom."

"Maybe we could discuss books some time."

She didn't actually say no. She put the volume back.

I got out of the chair. "Come on over; I have the instrument set up."

She sat in the chair and craned her head back. It took her a few moments to figure out how to see. You had to keep one eye closed, of course, and even then you had to align your head correctly, or your view would be occluded by the rim of the eyepiece. But then her lips parted softly—man, I could have kissed her there and then—and I knew what she was seeing. A disc, washed-out pink and green, with streaks of lacy cloud, and patches of steel-grey ocean that would glint if the sun caught them at the right angle. All this blurred, softened, as if depicted in watercolour.

"I'm looking at Mars?"

"Right. We're nowhere near opposition, but the seeing is pretty good." Her lips closed in a frown, and I knew she didn't know what I was talking about. "At opposition Mars is almost opposite the sun, seen from Earth. So the planets are at the closest they get in their orbits. Verity, to do their jobs astronomers have always had to be able to figure out where they are in relation to the rest of the universe. Just the skills you interplanetary pilot heroes are going to need. Anyhow, I thought it was appropriate for us to see Mars tonight. It kind of ties in with the main thing I want to show you."

She pulled back from the eyepiece. She looked suspicious, as if I was about to whip out my dong. "And what's that, Puddephat?"

I went to a desk at the back of the observatory, and came back with a fat folder. "Up until just a few days ago, that view of Mars was pretty much the best we had. But now everything's different. Look at this stuff."

She took the folder. It contained photographs in grainy black-and-white. "What am I looking at?"

"The pictures radioed back by Mariner 4. The NASA space probe that flew by Mars last week. Mariner sent back twenty-one pictures in all. They cover maybe one per cent of Mars's surface. Classified, but I've got contacts at NASA Ames," I boasted desperately.

The first photo showed the limb of the planet, seen from close to; there was a curved horizon. Verity stared. In contrast to an astronomer's view, the misty, unreal disc, this was how Mars would look to an orbiting astronaut. I could see her imagination was snagged.

The next few monochrome images looked like aerial pictures of a desert. "It's hard to make out anything at all."

"You have to remember the geometry, Verity; the sun was more or less directly overhead here, so there are no shadows."

"High noon on Mars. It looks kind of like Arizona, maybe, seen from a high-flying plane."

"Well, you'd know."

"Could Mars be like Arizona?"

"Something like it, but a higher altitude. Mariner confirmed the atmospheric pressure. You could walk around on the surface with nothing more than a face mask and sun cream . . ."

The seventh picture showed craters.

She stared. "This looks more like the moon."

"Mars is a small, geologically static world with a thin atmosphere, Verity. So, craters."

"We're screwed."

"Why do you say that?"

"Because nobody's going to spend billions of dollars to send us to a cratered rock-ball."

"Just keep going."

She flicked on, and stopped at the thirteenth frame. "My God." Suddenly she sounded electrified.

And well she might have been. The thirteenth picture showed more craters, but with what could only be forests sheltering inside them, bordering neat lakes. Life on Mars, unequivocal proof, coming after centuries of old men staring through telescopes at shifting grey-green patches . . .

Verity whooped. "They're just going to hose money at the programme now!"

JET PROPULSION LABORATORY, CALIFORNIA.
21 JANUARY 1972.

We got out of the car and I smuggled Alexei past JPL security, with me in my bright astronaut-corps jumpsuit and flashing my best grin at the star-struck guards and clerks. I murmured, "This is treason, probably. I could get shot for this."

Alexei Petrov grinned back at me. "Don't worry about it. No American soldier yet born can shoot straight."

I hurried him nervously along the central mall, which stretched from the gate into the main working area of the laboratory. JPL was a cramped place, crowded between the San Gabriel Mountains and the upper-middle class suburb of La Canada. Alexei was distracted by the von Karman auditorium, for years the scene of triumphant news conferences. Today there was a crowd at the doors, for the rumour was that the Martian rainstorms had cleared enough for the Voyager mission controllers to attempt a landing. But I hurried him past.

"We will not go in there? I heard Arthur C. Clarke and Walter Cronkite were coming today."

"What, you're hunting autographs now? We're going somewhere much more exciting."

I led him to the Image Processing Laboratory, rooms full of chattering technicians and junior scientists, and screens and computer printouts showing crude black-and-white images being put through various enhancement processes. Here, away from the sanitised stuff being presented to the celebrities, the raw data sent back by the Voyager orbiters at Mars were being received.

In common with every other semi-public NASA facility, there were also TV feeds on the walls reporting on the agency's growing celestial dominion, such as live in-colour Earth-orbit images from the astronauts in the Skylabs, and grainier pictures of the second EVA by the Apollo 18 crew on the moon—even an image from the Cape of the latest unmanned test launch of the mighty Nova booster, big brother of the Saturn Vs. But Alexei, dedicated planetary scientist that he was, had eyes only for the Mars data: images transmitted across the gulf one dot at a time like newsprint wire photos and painstakingly reconstructed. The very latest pictures, live from Mars!

And, as I'd hoped and half-planned, Verity Whittaker came pushing out of the crowd. At twenty-nine she was more beautiful than ever, her hair cropped sensibly short, her body toned by years of astronaut training. She was still as remote from me as the moon, of course. But she smiled at an old colleague. "Hi, Puddephat. Should have known you'd show up. Who's your friend?"

"Lieutenant Verity Whittaker, meet Doctor Alexei Petrov, from the Soviet Academy of—"

"Puddephat, are you insane? You smuggled in a Soviet?"

Alexei, a little older than us at thirty-two, wasn't the way you'd imagine a Soviet citizen. Coming from a relatively privileged stratum of Russian society—his father had been an Academician too—he was tall, slim, with slicked-back dark hair and movie-star looks. And, even as he and Verity faced each other down in those first seconds, I could see something sparking between them.

"I take it you never met a Soviet citizen before." His rich Slavic accent rolled out like warm butter.

"Maybe not, but I met a few Chinese Commie flyers during my tour in 'Nam in '68, and I don't care what the official histories say."

I sighed; in the astronaut corps we'd had these arguments too many times. "Verity, science can only proceed through openness. I've known Alexei for years. He's in the Soviet Mars cosmonaut cadre—he's flown in space, which is more than I've managed so far. And when I heard he was in the country—"

"I hunger for data," Alexei said, his gaze roaming. "My subject, astrobiology, is information-poor."

Verity moved to block his view. "In that case, go spend a billion roubles and retrieve your own data. Ah, but your landers failed, didn't they?"

Alexei said mildly, "Some commentators say a massive investment in space technology is itself destabilising."

"Maybe the way you Soviets do it."

"But what of your militarised Skylabs? And is it true that the Apollo 16 crew tested weapons on the moon during their 'dark' EVA?"

But now a stir of excitement distracted us, as the technicians and scientists gathered around the TV monitors.

In this particular launch window, it had been unlucky for the twin Voyager-Mars spacecraft (and even more unlucky for their sturdy Soviet counterparts) to arrive in the middle of the worst Martian storm season the astronomers had ever seen. The JPL controllers didn't want to risk dropping their landers down into that planetary maelstrom, and for weeks the orbiters' cameras sent back nothing but images of clouds punctuated by lightning flashes.

But now the storms had settled out, and it seemed the mission planners had agreed to go for a descent attempt. The lander attached to Voyager-Mars 2 had already separated, and was shown in grainy images from cameras mounted on the orbiter. It was a squat glider, a trial of the manned landers to be built in a few years' time, and you could clearly see the Stars and Stripes and UNITED STATES boldly painted on its flanks. The scientists, Poindexter patriots all, whooped and cheered.

But at that pivotal moment I found myself alone.

When I looked around I saw Verity was shadowing Alexei as he went through an image archive. He was peering at striking images of liquid water running through the deep canyons, and the tough vegetation of Mars clumping in the crater basins. I saw how their slim bodies brushed close, and he turned his head, just subtly, as if distracted by the scent of her hair.

And, reader, my heart ripped apart.

HESPERIA BASE, MARS. 4 JULY 1976 (MARS DATES GIVEN AS AT HOUSTON MERIDIAN).

I took a step forward, moving away from the MEM, into pale sunlight.

This was me, Jonas Puddephat, aged thirty-three, walking on Mars—the *first* on Mars! Who'd have thought it? Not Verity and the rest of our six-strong crew, that's for sure. We'd argued halfway to Mars about priority, and in the end it was pure diplomatic hypocrisy that had delivered me out the hatch first. President Nixon's office had decided that this mission, as much militaristic land-grab as science expedition, should be led down the ladder by the only authentic civilian aboard. Verity had always been a strange mix of Cold Warrior and religious zealot, and she retreated into her onboard Bible study group and tried to find some consolation for the snub in the pages of the Good Book.

But just then I didn't care about any of that. Let me tell you, it was a moment that made up for all the years of training, and the horrors of the flight itself, from the shattering launch of the Nova booster climbing into the sky on its fourteen F-1 engines, to the months of the cruise in our souped-up Skylab hab module with the growling NERVA nuclear rockets at our back, and finally the hair-raising descent to the ground in the Mars Excursion Module, an untried glider descending into a virtually unknown atmosphere. Not only that, we were rising out of the debris of too many accidents and disasters—too many lives lost, for our accelerated programme put huge pressure on the resources and management structures of NASA, USAF and our main contractors.

And then add on the fact that, such had been our eagerness to sprint here and beat the Soviets, we had no way of getting home again before a relief mission arrived some twenty-five months later.

None of that mattered, for I'd lived through it all, and I was *here*. I whooped in my dweebish way and pumped the air.

Verity's voice murmured in his ear. "Checklist, asshole."

I sighed. "I know, Verity, I know."

So I got to work. I turned to face *Nixon*. The MEM was a biconic glider, its tile-clad belly and leading edges scorched, sitting on frail-looking skids. I made sure the camera mounted on my chest got a good view of the craft's exterior, so Mission Control could check for damage.

Then I set off again, across the Martian ground. Soon I had gone far enough that I could see no signs of raying from *Nixon*'s descent engines. The soil under my feet was unmarked, without footprints. Ahead of me I saw a dip in the ground, it might have been a crater, where what looked like a forest copse grew, crowding grey-green.

By God, I thought, we're here. We came for insane reasons, and probably by all the wrong methods, but *we're here.*

"Puddephat," Verity said gently. "Are you all right?"

I tried to focus. "Fine, Verity." She didn't need to tell me I was well behind schedule. I hadn't even got the flag set up yet. But I walked forward, further from the MEM.

And Verity murmured, "Look up."

Again I tilted back, and peered up at the zenith. I saw a single, brilliant star passing overhead. Not one of Mars's moons—it had to be the *Stalingrad*. The Soviet vessel was an unlikely jam-up of Proton booster stages, a Salyut-derived space habitat, and some kind of lander, launched by three firings of their huge N-1 boosters—or four, if you count the one that blew up—but they had made it too, and here they were. Somewhere up there was Alexei Petrov, peering down at me through a telescope, with envy no doubt eating into his soul. I lifted an arm and waved.

Again Verity pressed me. "We only beat them here by days, Puddephat. And if they manage to land before you get around to making the claim—"

"All right, damn it."

It took me only a moment to set up the flagpole, and take the Stars and Stripes from its bag and fix it to the pole. "Can you see me, *Nixon*?"

"Clear as crystal, Jonah."

I straightened up and saluted. "On this, the bicentenary day of my nation's declaration of independence from foreign tyranny, I, Jonas James Puddephat, by the authority vested in me by the government of the United States of America, do hereby claim all these lands of Mars . . ."

While I spoke, I heard Verity and the others discussing contingencies in case the Soviets landed close by. We had rifles and revolvers, engineered to work in Martian conditions and trialled on the moon, and the *Nixon* even packed a couple of artillery pieces. For years, even before we humans got there, Mars had been an arena projected from our Earthbound Cold War.

When I was done, despite squawks from the MEM, I started unbuckling my mask. Somebody had to be first to try it. I ripped off my mask and took a deep lungful of that thin, cold, Martian air . . .

UNITED STATES HELLAS BASE, MARS.
9 NOVEMBER 1983.

From the beginning we got visits from the Russians. Occasionally, some of us would go over there.

We'd share tips on operational matters, and under the radar Alexei and I and the other scientists would pool data. It was never more than semi-official. But in the end it was our sheer humanity that united us; in the two bases combined there were just forty-some human souls stuck up here on Mars, and we needed company, no matter what was going on back on Earth.

So, that November morning—that terrible morning, as it would turn out—I watched Alexei and the others come rolling over the horizon in the rovers we called Marsokhods, having driven from their own base, which we called Marsograd, tucked deep in the rift we called Voyager Valley, a quarter-way around the planet's circumference. Few of us knew (or could pronounce) the names the Russians themselves gave to these things. But we admired the hardy "khods, more robust than anything we had, although our vehicles ran on methane fuel from our wet-chemistry factory, which was better than anything *they* had.

And on this particular visit, Verity was riding back with Alexei and the rest. Despite the fact that she was a veteran Cold Warrior she was one of the most frequent American visitors to the Soviet base, and if you saw her with Alexei you'd have known exactly why. My last hope that she would reject him as a godless Commie was dissipated when it turned out his family was Catholic.

So there you are. I was forty years old, and still mooning over the woman. Even Mars was no cure for that.

The arrival of a "khod at the dismal, half-buried collection of shacks we called Hell City was usually a cause for a party. Well, most anything was. This time, though, the mood was sour and stiff, and it wasn't hard to understand why. Up on that blue dot in the sky—thanks to Soviet atrocities in Afghanistan, thanks to the US deploying Pershing intermediate-range missiles throughout Europe thereby increasing our capability to launch a first strike, thanks to the increasing weaponisation of space, a process even we on Mars were a part of—the armed forces of our respective nations had come to a pitch of tension that hadn't been matched since Cuba twenty years earlier. As soon as Verity got through the lock she hurried to her cabin to tune into her encrypted comms channel back to NORAD, to get the straight skinny on what was going on at home.

Meanwhile I hosted Alexei and the rest in our galley area, the only place large enough to accommodate us all. On the wall-mounted TV set an ice hockey game was playing, another sublimated US-USSR confrontation, beamed directly from the Earth for the benefit of both sides of our ideological divide.

Alexei glanced over his coffee at me. "You are preparing for home, yes?"

The cycler habitat, a half-dozen ganged Skylabs looping endlessly between the orbits of Earth and Mars, was due in a few days, ready to collect us and take us home.

I said, "I've been preparing a geology package to help train up my replacements. I ought to walk your people through it. I think we've established the basic parameters pretty well now. Aside from the lava fields around the Tharsis giants, you basically have a surface of impact ejecta mixed with debris from mudflows and floods. In many ways Mars is a mix of conditions on Earth and the moon, and I've recommended to Houston they should have crews trained up in the field on both those bodies before being sent over here."

He smiled. "That sounds like a wise geological synthesis, for an astronomer."

He was needling me, affectionately enough. "Well, we all cross-trained, Alexei . . ."

Verity came bustling in. Her face was pale and drawn, with Martian dust ingrained in her pores. She poured herself a cup of coffee from a perc on the bar, the liquid slopping in the low gravity. Her earpiece whispered continually. "The stupid fuckers," she muttered.

Alexei asked, "Which particular stupid fuckers do you have in mind?"

"My bosses, and yours." She sat with us and leaned closer so the ice hockey fans couldn't hear. "I got a feed from NORAD. Allied forces across the world have been put on Defcon Two. It's an exercise. But a big one, spanning all of western Europe. They call it Able Archer 83. It will be over in a couple of days. But it's giving the Soviets nightmares. Seems nobody told *them* it's just a drill. We're trying out new comms systems and protocols, so they can't follow what we're doing. And the clincher is that the USAF has decided it's a good opportunity to launch their OWP."

That was a new acronym for me. "Say what?"

"An orbital weapons platform," Alexei said grimly.

"A Skylab with nukes," Verity said. "Hell, you Russians have your Salyuts—"

"Peaceful scientific and reconnaissance platforms."

"Sure they are. And what about the Polyus programme? What's that but a space battle station? Anyhow, no wonder the old men in the Kremlin are freaking out. We're spending billions of dollars on this exercise and the build-up to it, but not one grain of thought is being given to how it looks to the other side—or how the Soviets might react." She stared at her coffee cup. Then, without looking up, she reached across the table and took Alexei's hand.

"Let's talk about something else," I said sharply. "How's your own work going, Alexei?"

So we turned away from those dangerous topics to the strange life forms of Mars.

The best biological results had been retrieved by the Soviets, in the diverse environments they had explored in the Voyager Valley—judging by the results they'd leaked to us, anyhow. And they seemed to have established the basic parameters of life on Mars. You had a substrate of microbial communities, some of them stretching for hundreds of miles in the shallow, moist soil, together with the very photogenic multicellular stars on the surface, mostly the forms we colloquially called "cacti" and "trees." The cacti had tough, leathery skin, which almost perfectly sealed in their water stores. The trees had trunks as hard as concrete, and leaves like needles to keep in the moisture. Both forms photosynthesised busily.

But Alexei had always thought there was more to it.

Now he leaned towards us, confidential. "As it happens, I do have new observations. We have believed there is no animal form here on Mars. Nothing but the microbes and the plants. We have no fossil traces—"

"No spikes on the cacti." That had been my own first observation, on my second Marswalk, when I had explored that crater I saw after my first footfall, full of cacti and dwarf trees. There were no Martian teeth against which those cacti might have needed to evolve protection.

"And not enough oxygen in the air to enable motility anyhow," Verity put in.

"Yet there are sites in the valley where I believe I have seen *tracks*. Channels dug deep into the strata. Even," Alexei said dramatically, "a kind of footprint. Very small, bird-like or lizard-like, and embedded in mud and mudstone. Not new—but not more than a few thousand years old, I would guess. Why do we not see these forms being created *now*?"

In terms of observations of Mars he had come a long way since first staring at those grainy Voyager orbiter pictures in JPL, I thought.

Nevertheless I shook my head. "We don't yet know enough about Mars to eliminate non-biological causes, Alexei."

"Of course not. But there could be something we are not expecting—for example, some equivalent of slime molds, which alternate between static and mobile forms. I have a feeling that there is more to this biosphere than we have yet discovered, aspects we do not comprehend . . ."

There was a hiss of static.

We turned. The TV image had fritzed out, the hockey game lost. Some of our colleagues dug comms links out of their coverall pockets.

And Verity, touching her earpiece, got up and went straight to the galley's small window, looking east.

Alexei and I glanced at each other, and followed. Through the window we looked out over our base, a collection of domes and shacks, and the greenhouse bubbles where we grew our potatoes and beans. A child ran by, with her mask off, just five years old and breathing the air of Mars.

"They went to Defcon One," Verity said, listening to her earpiece. "The USAF Skylab didn't make its correct orbit after launch. Looked like it was descending over Soviet territory. Like a bombing run. It was just a malfunction—but the Russians responded—" I could hear the squeal of static. She pulled the little gadget out of her ear.

And an evening star flared, low in the Martian sky. It was as sudden, as brutal, as that. Verity had known where to look, to see Earth in the sky.

I didn't know what to feel. I retreated to my default mode, the science dweeb. "Quite a stunt, to make bangs bright enough to be visible across interplanetary space."

Verity glanced at me. "I guess you have a choice to make about going home when the cycler comes, Puddephat."

The star had seemed to be dimming. But then, only moments after the peak, there was another surge of light.

"The second strikes," murmured Alexei. He put his arm around Verity's shoulders. "This is home. Earth is gone. Mars is our mother now. And the future is our responsibility, those of us here."

Standing alone, I comforted myself with the thought that the conflict was already minutes in the past, even as its light seared into my eyes.

HELL CITY, MARS. 28 OCTOBER 2010.

Alexei Petrov died. He was seventy years old.

The skin cancer took him, as it's taken too many of us, that remote sun spitefully pouring its ultra-violet through the thin air here on this mountaintop we call Mars.

When he knew the game was up, he wrote out a kind of will. Naturally he left all his meagre material possessions to Verity and their kids and grandchildren. But he also willed a gift to me, a box of notes, a lifetime's research on the Mars ground, beginning with records from the fancy instruments our mission designers gave us and finishing with eyewitness observations written out in his own cramped handwriting, like a Victorian naturalist's journal.

The point was, Alexei had come to certain conclusions about Mars, mankind's second home, which he hadn't shared with anybody—not even Verity. But when I'd gone through it all, and checked his results, and reworked his findings—and found they tallied with some tentative conclusions of my own—I called on Verity Whittaker Petrova, and asked her to take a walk with me around our little township.

We lived in a huddle of yellowing plastic domes. Some of the youngsters—we already had second-generation Martians sixteen or seventeen years old—were building houses of the native "wood," hacked out with stone axes and draped over with alpaca skin, houses that looked like tepees, or Iron Age roundhouses from Europe. But the houses had to be sealed up with ageing polythene sheets, and connected by piping to our elderly air circulation and scrubbing plants, driven by the big Soviet solar cell arrays now that our small NASA nuke plant had failed. Verity had led the effort to build a pretty little chapel, using materials scavenged from the MEM.

All this was set down on the floor of Hellas basin, a feature so vast that from anywhere near its centre you can't see the walls. After the One-Day War we had all come here to live together, Soviets and Americans together, including the crew of the abandoned interplanetary cycler. The logic was that we needed as large a gene pool as possible. Besides, once the last signals from the moon bases went silent, we huddled for companionship and warmth.

Well, we got along in reasonable harmony, save for the occasional fist fight, despite the fact that our two nations had wiped each other out. We avoided political talk, or any discussion of constitutions or voting rights or common ownership of means of production. We were too few to need grand political theories; we would let future generations figure it out. We thought we would have time, you see.

We walked on towards the farm domes, with their laboriously tilled fields of potatoes and yams and green beans. The work we'd put in was heartbreakingly clear from the quality of the soil we'd managed to create from Martian dirt. We'd even imported earthworms. But a spindly, yellowed crop was our only reward.

The native Mars life seemed to be struggling too. Between the domes was a small botanical garden I'd established myself, open to the Martian elements. The native stock looked *different* from my first impression, on that wonderful Independence Day of discovery. The cacti were shrivelled and tougher-looking, and the trees I'd planted had hardly grown. Adult specimens, which had littered the north-facing slopes of Hellas in tremendous forests, were dying back too.

A gaggle of kids ran by, coming from the alpaca pens, yelling to each other. They were bundled up in shabby coats and alpaca-wool hats, and they all wore face masks. The kids had always loved the alpacas. Verity and I, two fragile old folk, had to pause to let them by.

"Do you know," she said, "I didn't understand a single word any of them said." After her decades with Alexei she had a faint Slavic accent. "The kids seem to be making up their own language, a kind of pidgin. Maybe we should call it Russ-lish. Rung-lish."

"How about Wronglish?"

That made her laugh, just for a second, this dust-ridden, careworn, sanctimonious matriarch at my side.

We paused by the alpaca domes ourselves, where those spindly beasts, imported as embryos from the mountains of South America, peered out at us, or scraped apathetically at the scrubby grass that grew at their feet.

"I think it was the alpacas I noticed first," Verity said slowly. "How reluctant they became to leave their domes."

I took a deep breath, sucking in the stale odours of my own mask. "Did Alexei ever talk to you about his conclusions?"

"No, he didn't. But I was married to the man for twenty-five years, Puddephat, and I was never completely dumb, even though I was no double-dome like you two. I learned to read his moods. And I knew that *the air pressure is dropping*. That's obvious. A high-school barometer would show it. The partial pressure of oxygen is falling even faster. There's something's wrong with Mars."

I shook my head. "Actually, I think Mars is just fine. It just isn't fine for us, that's all."

She stood, silent, grave.

I sighed. "I'll tell you what Alexei concluded, and I agree with him. Look." I scratched axes for a graph in the crimson dirt with my toe. "Here's a conventional view of Mars—what we believed must be true before we landed here. When it was young, Mars was warm and wet, with a thick blanket of air, and deep oceans. Like Earth, in many ways. That phase might have lasted a couple of billion years. But Mars is smaller than the Earth, and further from the sun. As the geology seized up and the volcanoes died back, and the sunlight got to work breaking up the upper atmosphere, Mars lost a lot of its air. Here's the air pressure declining over time . . ." I sketched a graph falling sharply at first, but then bottoming out before hitting zero. "Much of the water seeped away into deep underground aquifers and froze down there, or at the poles. But still you finished up with conditions that were only a little more extreme than in places on Earth. Mars was like high country, we thought. Scattered lakes, vegetation. Verity, this decline took billions of years—plenty of time for life to adapt."

She nodded. "Hence the cacti and the trees. Now you're telling me this is all wrong."

"We, and Alexei especially, have had decades now to take a good close look at Mars. And what we find doesn't tally with this simple picture of a one-off decline.

"We found extensive lava fields much younger than we'd expected—a whole series of them, one on top of the other. Sandwiched in between the lava strata we found traces of savage glaciation, and periods of water flows—river valleys, traces of outflow events, even shorelines. And we found thin bands of fossils, evidence of life growing actively for brief periods, overlaid by featureless sandstone—the relics of dead ages of windblown dust storms. You can date all this with crater counts. Cycles, over and over.

"I'll tell you what Alexei came to believe, and I think I agree with him." I scuffed out the graph with my toe, and sketched another. "Mars did start out warm and wet. It had to be so; we see the trace of huge oceans. The biosphere itself is the legacy of that age. But that warm phase was short-lived. Mars lost almost all its air, catastrophically." I drew a new line that cut right down to the zero line.

"How low?"

"Hard to say. To no more than one per cent of Earth's sea-level pressure. You can tell that from the evidence of the dust transport, the rock-shattering extremes of temperature, the solar weathering . . ."

I sketched it for her, speaking, drawing. Mars's natural condition is dry and all but airless. All the water is either locked up in polar ice caps or is deep in a network of subterranean aquifers. The air is so thin there's virtually no shielding from the sun, and no heat capacity to keep in the warmth at night; you swing daily from heat to a withering cold. The only thing that moves is the dust, swirling around in a trace of air.

"And life, Verity, life huddles underground, living off the planet's inner warmth, and seeps of liquid water in the cracks in the rocks. Spores and seeds and microbes, hiding from the raw sunlight."

She pulled off her mask and breathed in, a deep gulping, rasping breath. "It ain't that way now, Puddephat."

"No. But the way it is *now*, as it happens, is unusual for Mars. We're coming to the end of a volcano summer."

"A what?"

"Which is when things change." I drew a series of spikes reaching up from the flatlined graph. "Mars is still warm inside. Every so often the big Tharsis volcanoes blow their tops. They pump out a whole atmosphere, of carbon dioxide and methane and other stuff, and a blanket of dust and ash that warms the world up enough for the permafrost to melt . . ."

"And life takes its brief chance."

"You've got it. Mars turns green in a flash, maybe just a few thousand years. The native life spreads seeds and spores far and wide. At the peak of each summer there probably is some motility—Martian molds squirming in the dirt, Alexei was right about that—but we came too late to see them directly.

"But, just as quickly, the heat leaks away, and the air starts to thin. The end, when it comes, is probably rapid—a catastrophic decline—lots of feedback loops working together to destroy the life-bearing conditions."

Her face was hard. "And then it's back to the dustbowl."

"Yes. Alexei thought he mapped six such episodes, six summers. The first was about a billion years after the planet formed. The second one-and-a-half billion years ago, and then eight hundred million years ago, two hundred million, one hundred million—"

"And now."

"Yeah. We were lucky, Verity, we humans, to come along just now, to see Mars bloom, for it's a rare event."

"Or unlucky," she said acidly.

"I suppose so. In normal times, we couldn't even have landed the way we did, in a big glider of a MEM. Air too thin. You'd need heat shields, parachutes, rockets . . ."

"We maybe wouldn't have come here at all. And maybe we wouldn't have had all this extra tension over Mars, over the future in space. Maybe we wouldn't have gone to war at all. And now . . ." She looked around at the shabby huddle of our settlement, the yellowing plastic, the broken-down machines, the dying crops, the bundled-up, wheezing children. "We thought we were safe, here on Mars. Or at least that we had a chance. A new world, a new roll of the dice for humanity. But if the atmosphere collapses we won't be able to live here."

"No. In, say, a century, tepees and bonfires won't cut it. You might as well be living on the moon. If we'd had more time, more resupply from home—"

"We were lured here by a lie. A transient phenomenon."

I reached out and took her hand. "Verity—all these years. When I close my eyes I can still see you sitting in the chair in Mount Wilson, smiling as I showed you Mars . . . It seems like yesterday. I don't begrudge you Alexei. You had a good life, I can see that. But now he's gone, and maybe—"

She snatched her hand away. "What are you talking about, Puddephat? My children are going to die here, and their children, without meaning, without hope. What do you think we're going to do, in your head—sit together on a porch, holding hands and smiling as we give out the suicide pills?"

"Verity . . ."

She stalked off.

And I was left alone with the alpacas, and my graph in the dirt.

HELL CITY, MARS. 4 JULY 2026.

Even now I'm not alone, probably. Some other group may be huddled up against another air machine, bleeding power off peeling Soviet solar cells. We could never reach each other. Doubt if my old pressure suit would fit me any more—but it's a moon suit you need on Mars now.

Anyhow, that's it for me. At eighty-three, I'm probably the oldest man left alive on any of the worlds. I'll raise Old Glory one more time over the sands of Mars, and toast her with the very last drop of my Soviet potato vodka, and bury this tin chest, and wait for the dust storms to bury *me* . . .

I guess I should finish the story.

We didn't need suicide pills in the end. When the youngsters figured out that my generation had blown up one world and dumped them into lethal conditions on another, they went crazy. A war of the age cadres, you could call it. Verity died in the chapel, praying to God for succour, telling the young ones they would be damned for their sins; her own grandchildren blew the chapel up. I daresay we could have lasted longer, if we'd eked everything out as carefully as we could. But to what end? So we could live to see the last molecule of oxygen rust out of the air?

Mars abides. Yes, it's a consolation that in the far future, in fifty or a hundred million years, when my bones are dust, and Earth has healed over and is a mindless green point in the sky, the great volcanoes will shout again and bring Mars to life once more, though we will be gone. There's always that, and—whoever you are, whoever reads this—I hope you won't think too badly of us.

It was one heck of a ride, though, wasn't it?

JONAS PUDDEPHAT.

the visitor from taured

IAN R. MACLEOD

Here's an exquisitely written and subtly characterized story that shows us how a man's obsession with experimentally proving or disproving the Many Worlds theory of reality comes to dominate his entire life—and which may (or may not) eventually lead him to the proof he seeks.

British writer Ian R. MacLeod was one of the hottest new writers of the nineties, publishing a slew of strong stories in Interzone, Asimov's Science Fiction, Weird Tales, Amazing, *and* The Magazine of Fantasy and Science Fiction, *and elsewhere and his work continues to grow in power and deepen in maturity as we move through the first decades of the new century. Much of his work has been gathered in four collections,* Voyages By Starlight, Breathmoss and Other Exhalations, Past Magic, *and* Journeys. *His first novel,* The Great Wheel, *was published in 1997. In 1999, he won the World Fantasy Award with his novella* The Summer Isles, *and followed it up in 2000 by winning another World Fantasy Award for his novelette* The Chop Girl. *In 2003, he published his first fantasy novel, and his most critically acclaimed book,* The Light Ages, *followed by a sequel,* The House of Storms *in 2005, and then by* Song of Time, *which won both the Arthur C. Clarke Award and the John W. Campbell Award in 2008. A novel version of* The Summer Isles *also appeared in 2005. His most recent books are a new novel,* Wake Up and Dream, *and a big retrospective collection,* Snodgrass and Other Illusions: The Best Short Stories of Ian R. MacLeod. *MacLeod lives with his family in the West Midlands of England.*

There was always something otherworldly about Rob Holm. Not that he wasn't charming and clever and good-looking. Driven, as well. Even during that first week when we'd arrived at university and waved goodbye to our parents and our childhoods, and were busy doing all the usual fresher things, which still involved getting dangerously drunk and pretending not to be homesick and otherwise behaving like the prim, arrogant, cocky and immature young assholes we undoubtedly were, Rob was chatting with research fellows and quietly getting to know the best virtuals to hang out in.

Even back then, us young undergrads were an endangered breed. Many universities had gone bankrupt, become commercial research utilities, or transformed themselves into the academic theme-parks of those so-called "Third Age Academies." But still, here we all were at the traditional redbrick campus of Leeds University, which still offered a broad-ish range of courses to those with families rich enough to support them, or at least tolerant enough not to warn them against such folly. My own choice of degree, just to show how incredibly supportive my parents were, being Analogue Literature.

As a subject, it already belonged with Alchemy and Marxism in the dustbin of history, but books—and I really do mean those peculiar, old, paper, physical objects— had always been my thing. Even when I was far too young to understand what they were, and by rights should have been attracted by the bright, interactive, virtual gewgaws buzzing all around me, I'd managed to burrow into the bottom of an old box, down past the stickle bricks and My Little Ponies, to these broad, cardboardy things that fell open and had these flat, two-dee shapes and images that didn't move or respond in any normal way when I waved my podgy fingers in their direction. All you could do was simply look at them. That, and chew their corners, and maybe scribble over their pages with some of the dried-up crayons which were also to be found amid those predigital layers.

My parents had always been loving and tolerant of their daughter. They even encouraged little Lita's interest in these ancient artefacts. I remember my mother's finger moving slow and patient across the creased and yellowed pages as she traced the pictures and her lips breathed the magical words that somehow arose from those flat lines. She wouldn't have assimilated data this way herself in years, if ever, so in a sense we were both learning.

The Hungry Caterpillar. The Mister Men series. *Where The Wild Things Are.* Frodo's adventures. Slowly, like some archaeologist discovering the world by deciphering the cartouches of the tombs in Ancient Egypt, I learned how to perceive and interact through this antique medium. It was, well, the *thingness* of books. The exact way they *didn't* leap about or start giving off sounds, smells and textures. That, and how they didn't ask you which character you'd like to be, or what level you wanted to go to next, but simply took you by the hand and lead you where they wanted you to go.

Of course, I became a confirmed bibliophile, but I do still wonder how my life would have progressed if my parents had seen odd behaviour differently, and taken me to some paediatric specialist. Almost certainly, I wouldn't be the Lita Ortiz who's writing these words for whoever might still be able to comprehend them. Nor the one who was lucky enough to meet Rob Holm all those years ago in the teenage fug of those student halls back at Leeds University.

2.

So. Rob. First thing to say is the obvious fact that most of us fancied him. It wasn't just the grey eyes, or the courtly elegance, or that soft Scottish accent, or even the way he somehow appeared mature and accomplished. It was, essentially, a kind of mystery. But he wasn't remotely stand-offish. He went along with the fancy dress pub crawls. He drank. He fucked about. He took the odd tab.

One of my earliest memories of Rob was finding him at some club, cool as you like amid all the noise, flash and flesh. And dragging him out onto the pulsing dance floor. One minute we were hovering above the skyscrapers of Beijing and the next a shipwreck storm was billowing about us. Rob, though, was simply there. Taking it all in, laughing, responding, but somehow detached. Then, helping me down and out, past clanging temple bells and through prismatic sandstorms to the entirely non-virtual hell of the toilets. His cool hands holding back my hair as I vomited.

I never ever actually thanked Rob for this—I was too embarrassed—but the incident somehow made us more aware of each other. That, and maybe we shared a sense of otherness. He, after all, was studying astrophysics, and none of the rest of us even knew what that was, and had all that strange stuff going on across the walls of his room. Not flashing posters of the latest virtual boy band or porn empress, but slow-turning gas clouds, strange planets, distant stars and galaxies. That, and long runs of mek, whole arching rainbows of the stuff, endlessly twisting and turning. My room, on the other hand, was piled with the precious torn and foxed paperbacks I'd scoured from junksites during my teenage years. Not, of course, that they were actually needed. Even if you were studying something as arcane as narrative fiction, you were still expected to download and virtualise all your resources.

The Analogue Literature Faculty at Leeds University had once taken up a labyrinthine space in a redbrick terrace at the east edge of the campus. But now it had been invaded by dozens of more modern disciplines. Anything from speculative mek to non-concrete design to holo-pornography had taken bites out of it. I was already aware—how couldn't I be?—that no significant novel or short story had been written in decades, but I was shocked to discover that only five other students in my year had elected for An Lit as their main subject, and one of those still resided in Seoul, and another was a post-centarian on clicking steel legs. Most of the other students who showed up were dipping into the subject in the hope that it might add something useful to their main discipline. Invariably, they were disappointed. It wasn't just the difficulty of ploughing through page after page of non-interactive text. It was linear fiction's sheer lack of options, settings, choices. Why the hell, I remember some kid shouting in a seminar, should I accept all the miserable shit that this Hardy guy rains down on his characters? Give me the base program for *Tess of the d'Urbervilles*, and I'll hack you fifteen better endings.

I pushed my weak mek to limit during that first term as I tried to formulate a tri-dee excursus on *Tender Is the Night*, but the whole piece was reconfigured out of existence once the faculty ais got hold of it. Meanwhile, Rob Holm was clearly doing far better. I could hear him singing in the showers from my room, and admired the way he didn't get involved in all the usual peeves and arguments. The physical sciences had a huge, brand-new faculty at the west end of campus called the Clearbrite Building. Half church, half pagoda and maybe half spaceship in the fizzing, shifting, headachy way of modern architecture, there was no real way of telling how much of it was actually made of brick, concrete and glass, and how much consisted of virtual artefacts and energy fields. You could get seriously lost just staring at it.

My first year went by, and I fought hard against crawling home, and had a few unromantic flings, and made vegetable bolognaise my signature dish, and somehow managed to get version 4.04 of my second term excursus on *Howard's End* accepted. Rob and I didn't become close, but I liked his singing, and the cinnamon scent he left hanging behind in the steam of the showers, and it was good to know that someone else was making a better hash of this whole undergraduate business than I was.

"Hey, Lita?"

We were deep into the summer term and exams were looming. Half the undergrads were back at home, and the other half were jacked up on learning streams, or busy having breakdowns.

I leaned in on Rob's doorway. "Yeah?"

"Fancy sharing a house next year?"

"Next year?" Almost effortlessly casual, I pretended to consider this. "I really hadn't thought. It all depends—"

"Not a problem." He shrugged. "I'm sure I'll find someone else."

"No, no. That's fine. I mean, yeah, I'm in. I'm interested."

"Great. I'll show you what I've got from the letting agencies." He smiled a warm smile, then returned to whatever wondrous creations were spinning above his desk.

3.

We settled on a narrow house with bad drains just off the Otley Road in Headingley, and I'm not sure whether I was relieved or disappointed when I discovered that his plan was that we share the place with some others. I roped in a couple of girls, Rob found a couple of guys, and we all got on pretty well. I had a proper boyfriend by then, a self-regarding jock called Torsten, and every now and then a different woman would emerge from Rob's room. Nothing serious ever seemed to come of this, but they were equally gorgeous, clever and out of my league.

A bunch of us used to head out to the moors for midnight bonfires during that second winter. I remember the smoke and the sparks spinning into the deep black as we sang and drank and arsed around. Once, and with the help of a few tabs and cans, I asked Rob to name some constellations for me, and he put an arm around my waist and led me further into the dark.

Over there, Lita, up to the left and far away from the light of this city, is Ursa Major, the Great Bear, which is always a good place to start when you're stargazing. And there, see close as twins at the central bend of the Plough's handle, are Mizar and Alcor. They're not a true binary, but if we had decent binoculars, we could see that Mizar really does have a close companion. And there, that way, up and left—his breath on my face, his hands on my arms—maybe you can just see there's this fuzzy speck at the Bear's shoulder? Now, that's an entire separate galaxy from our own filled with billions of stars, and its light has taken about twelve million years to reach the two of us here, tonight. Then Andromeda and Cassopia and Canus Major and Minor . . . Distant, storybook names for distant worlds. I even wondered aloud about the possibility of other lives, existences, hardly expecting Rob to agree with me. But he did. And then he said something which struck me as strange.

"Not just out there, either, Lita. There are other worlds all around us. It's just that we can't see them."

"You're talking in some metaphorical sense, right?"

"Not at all. It's part of what I'm trying to understand in my studies."

"To be honest, I've got no real idea what astrophysics even means. Maybe you could tell me."

"I'd love to. And you know, Lita, I'm a complete dunce when it comes to, what *do* you call it—two-dee fiction, flat narrative? So I want you to tell me about that as well. Deal?"

We wandered back toward the fire, and I didn't expect anything else to come of our promise until Rob called to me when I was wandering past his room one wet, grey afternoon a week or so later. It was deadline day, my hair was a greasy mess, I was heading for the shower, and had an excursus on John Updike to finish.

"You *did* say you wanted to know more about what I study?"

"I was just . . ." I scratched my head. "Curious. All I do know is that astrophysics is about more than simply looking up at the night sky and giving names to things. That isn't even astronomy, is it?"

"You're not just being polite?" His soft, granite-grey eyes remained fixed on me.

"No. I'm not—absolutely."

"I could show you something here." He waved at the stars on his walls, the stuff spinning on his desk. "But maybe we could go out. To be honest, Lita, I could do with a break, and there's an experiment I could show you up at the Clearbrite that might help explain what I mean about other worlds . . . But I understand if you're busy. I could get my avatar to talk to your avatar and—"

"No, no. You're right, Rob. I could do with a break as well. Let's go out. Seize the day. Or at least, what's left of it. Just give me . . ." I waved a finger toward the bathroom. ". . . five minutes."

Then we were outside in the sideways-blowing drizzle, and it was freezing cold, and I was still wet from my hurried shower, as Rob slipped a companionable arm around mine as we climbed the hill toward the Otley Road tram stop.

Kids and commuters got on and off as we jolted toward the strung lights of the city, their lips moving and their hands stirring to things only they could feel and see. The Clearbrite looked more like some recently arrived spaceship as it glowed out through the gloom, but inside the place was just like any other campus building, with clamouring posters offering to restructure your loan, find you temporary work, or get you laid and hammered. Constant reminders, too, that Clearbrite was the only smartjuice to communicate in realtime to your fingerjewel, toejamb or wristbracelet. This souk-like aspect of modern unis not being something that Sebastian Flyte, or even Harry Potter in those disappointing sequels, ever had to contend with.

We got a fair few hellos, a couple of tenured types stopped to talk to Rob in a corridor, and I saw how people paused to listen to what he was saying. More than ever, I had him down as someone who was bound to succeed. Still, I was expecting to be shown moon rocks, lightning bolts or at least some clever virtual planetarium, but instead he took me into what looked like the kind of laboratory I'd been forced to waste many hours in at school, even if the equipment did seem a little fancier.

"This is the physics part of the astro," Rob explained, perhaps sensing my disappointment. "But you did ask about other worlds, right, and this is pretty much the only way I can show them to you."

I won't go too far into the details, because I'd probably get them wrong, but what Rob proceeded to demonstrate was a version of what I now know to be the famous, or infamous, Double Slit Experiment. There was a long black tube on a workbench, and at one end of it was a laser, and at the other was a display screen attached to a device called a photo multiplier—a kind of sensor. In the middle he placed a barrier with two narrow slits. It wasn't a great surprise even to me that the pulses of light caused a pretty dark-light pattern of stripes to appear on the display at the far end. These, Rob said, were ripples of the interference pattern caused by the waves of light passing through the two slits, much as you'd get if you were pouring water. But light, Lita, is made up of individual packets of energy called photons. So what would happen if, instead of sending tens of thousands of them down the tube at once, we turned the laser down so far that it only emitted one photon at a time? Then, surely, each individual photon could only go through one or the other of the slits, there would be no ripples, and two simple stripes would emerge at the far end. But, hey, as he slowed the beep of the signal counter until it was registering single digits, the dark-light bars, like a shimmering neon forest, remained. As if, although each photon was a single particle, it somehow became a blur of all its possibilities as it passed through both slits at once. Which, as far as anyone knew, was pretty much what happened.

"I'm sorry," Rob said afterwards when we were chatting over a second or third pint of beer in the fug of an old student bar called the Eldon which lay down the road from the university, "I should have shown you something less boring."

"It wasn't boring. The implications are pretty strange, aren't they."

"More than strange. It goes against almost everything else we know about physics and the world around us—us sitting here in this pub, for instance. Things exist, right? They're either here or not. They don't flicker in and out of existence like ghosts. This whole particles-blurring-into-wave business was one of the things that bugged me most when I was a kid finding out about science. It was even partly why I chose to study astrophysics—I thought there'd be answers I'd understand when someone finally explained them to me. But there aren't." He sipped his beer. "All you get is something called the Copenhagen Interpretation, which is basically a shoulder shrug that says, hey, these things happen at the sub-atomic level, but it doesn't really have to bother us or make sense in the world we know about and live in. That, and then there's something else called the many worlds theory . . ." He trailed off. Stifled a burp. Seemed almost embarrassed.

"Which is what you believe in?"

"'Believe' isn't the right word. Things either are or they aren't in science. But, yeah, I do. And the maths supports it. Simply put, Lita, it says that all the possible states and positions that every particle could exist in are real—that they're endlessly spinning off into other universes."

"You mean, as if every choice you could make in a virtual was instantly mapped out in its entirety?"

"Exactly. But this is real. The worlds are all around us—right here."

The drink, and the conversation moved on, and now it was my turn to apologise to Rob, and his to say no, I wasn't boring him. Because books, novels, stories, they were *my* other worlds, the thing I believed in even if no one else cared about them. That single, magical word, *Fog*, which Dickens uses as he begins to conjure London. And Frederic Henry walking away from the hospital in the rain. And Rose of Sharon offering the starving man her breast after the Joab's long journey across dust-bowl America, and Candide eating fruit, and Bertie Wooster bumbling back across Mayfair . . .

Rob listened and seemed genuinely interested, even though he confessed he'd never read a single non-interactive story or novel. But, unlike most people, he said this as if he realised he was actually missing out on something. So we agreed I'd lend him some of my old paperbacks, and this, and what he'd shown me at the Clearbrite, signalled a new phase in our relationship.

4.

It seems to me now that some of the best hours of my life were spent not in reading books, but in sitting with Rob Holm in my cramped room in that house we shared back in Leeds, and talking about them.

What to read and admire, but also—and this was just as important—what not to. *The Catcher in the Rye* being overrated, and James Joyce a literary show-off, and *Moby Dick* really wasn't about much more than whales. Alarmingly, Rob was often ahead of me. He discovered a copy of *Labyrinths* by Jorge Luis Borges in a garage sale, which he gave to me as a gift, and then kept borrowing back. But he was Rob Holm. He could solve the riddles of the cosmos, and meanwhile explore literature as nothing but a hobby, and also help me out with my mek, so that I was finally able to produce the kind of arguments, links and algorithms for my piece on *Madame Bovary* that the ais at An Eng actually wanted.

Meanwhile, I also found out about the kind of life Rob had come from. Both his parents were engineers, and he'd spent his early years in Aberdeen, but they'd moved to the Isle of Harris after his mother was diagnosed with a brain-damaging prion infection, probably caused by her liking for fresh salmon. Most of the fish were then factory-farmed in crowded pens in the Scottish lochs, where the creatures were dosed with antibiotics and fed on pellets of processed meat, often recycled from the remains of their own breed. Which, just as with cattle and Creutzfeldt-Jakob Disease a century earlier, had resulted in a small but significant species leap. Rob's parents wanted to make the best of the years Alice Holm had left, and set up an ethical marine farm—although they preferred to call it a ranch—harvesting scallops on the Isle of Harris.

Rob's father was still there at Creagach, and the business, which not only produced some of the best scallops in the Hebrides, but also benefited other marine life along the costal shelf, was still going. Rob portrayed his childhood there as a happy time, with his mother still doing well despite the warnings of the scans, and regaling him with bedtime tales of Celtic myths, which was probably his only experience before meeting me of linear fictional narrative.

There were the kelpies, who lived in lochs and were like fine horses, and then there were the Blue Men of the Minch, who dwelt between Harris and the mainland, and sung up storms and summoned the waves with their voices. Then, one night when Rob was eleven, his mother waited until he and his father were asleep, then walked out across the shore and into the sea, and swam, and kept on swimming. No one could last long out there, the sea being so cold, and the strong currents, or perhaps the Blue Men of the Minch, bore her body back to a stretch of shore around the headland from Creagach, where she was found next morning.

Rob told his story without any obvious angst. But it certainly helped explain the sense of difference and distance he seemed to carry with him. That, and why he didn't fit. Not here in Leeds, amid the fun, mess and heartbreak of student life, nor even, as I slowly came to realise, in the subject he was studying.

He showed me the virtual planetarium at the Clearbrite, and the signals from a probe passing through the Oort Cloud, and even took me down to the tunnels of a mine where a huge tank of cryogenically cooled fluid had been set up in the hope of detecting the dark matter of which it had once been believed most of our universe was made. It was an old thing now, creaking and leaking, and Rob was part of the small team of volunteers who kept it going. We stood close together in the dripping near-dark, clicking hardhats and sharing each other's breath, and of course I was thinking of other possibilities—those fractional moments when things could go one of many ways. Our lips pressing. Our bodies joining. But something, maybe a fear of losing him entirely, held me back.

"It's another thing that science has given up on," he said later when we were sitting at our table in the Eldon. "Just like that ridiculous Copenhagen shoulder-shrug. Without dark matter, and dark energy, the way the galaxies rotate and recede from each other simply doesn't make mathematical sense. You know what the so-called smart money is on these days? Something called topographical deformity, which means that the basic laws of physics don't apply in the same way across this entire universe. That it's pock-marked with flaws."

"But you don't believe that?"

"Of course I don't! It's fundamentally unscientific."

"But you get glitches in even the most cleverly conceived virtuals, don't you? Even in novels, sometimes things don't always entirely add up."

"Yeah. Like who killed the gardener in *The Big Sleep*, or the season suddenly changing from autumn to spring in that Sherlock Holmes story. But this isn't like that, Lita. This isn't . . ." For once, he was in danger of sounding bitter and contemptuous. But he held himself back.

"And you're not going to give up?"

He smiled. Swirled his beer. "No, Lita. I'm definitely not."

5.

Perhaps inevitably, Rob's and my taste in books had started to drift apart. He'd discovered an antique genre called Science Fiction, something which the ais at An Lit were particularly sniffy about. And even as he tried to lead me with him, I could see their point. Much of the prose was less than luminous, the characterisation was sketchy and, although a great deal of it was supposedly about the future, the predictions were laughably wrong.

But Rob insisted that that wasn't the point, that SF was essentially a literature of ideas. That, and a sense of wonder. To him, wonder was particularly important. I could sometimes—maybe as that lonely astronaut passed through the stargate, or with those huge worms in that book about a desert world—see his point. But most of it simply left me cold.

Rob went off on secondment the following year to something called the Large Millimetre Array on the Atacama Plateau in Chile, and I, for want of anything better, kept the lease on our house in Headingley and got some new people in, and did a masters on gender roles in George Eliot's *Middlemarch*. Of course, I paid him virtual visits, and we talked of the problems of altitude sickness and the changed assholes our old uni friends were becoming as he put me on a camera on a Jeep, and bounced me across the dark-skied desert.

Another year went—they were already picking up speed—and Rob found the time for a drink before he headed off to some untenured post, part research, part teaching, in Heidelberg that he didn't seem particularly satisfied with. He was still reading—apparently there hadn't been much else to do in Chile—but I realised our days of talking about Proust or Henry James had gone.

He'd settled, you might almost say retreated, into a sub-genre of SF known as alternate history, where all the stuff he'd been telling me about our world continually branching off into all its possibilities was dramatised on a big scale. Hitler had won World War Two—a great many times, it seemed—and the South was triumphant in the American Civil War. That, and the Spanish Armada had succeeded, and Europe remained under the thrall of medieval Roman Catholicism, and Lee Harvey Oswald's bullet had grazed past President Kennedy's head. I didn't take this odd obsession as a particularly good sign as we exchanged chaste hugs and kisses in the street outside the Eldon, and went our separate ways.

I had a job of sorts, thanks to Sun-Mi, my fellow An Lit student from Korea, teaching English to the kids of rich families in Seoul, and for a while it was fun, and the people were incredibly friendly, but then I grew bored, and managed to wrangle an interview with one of the media conglomerates which had switched physical bases to Korea in the wake of the California Earthquake. I was hired for considerably less than I was getting paid teaching English, and took the crowded commute every morning to a vast half-real, semi-ziggurat high-rise mistily floating above the Mapo District, where I studied high-res worlds filled with headache-inducing marvels, and was invited to come up with ideas in equally headache-inducing meetings.

I, an Alice in these many virtual wonderlands, brought a kind of puzzled innocence to my role. Two, maybe three, decades earlier, the other developers might still have known enough to recognise my plagiarisms, if only from old movies their parents had once talked about, but now what I saying seemed new, fresh and quirky. I was a thieving literary magpie, and became the go-to girl for unexpected turns and twists. The real murderer of Roger Ackroyd, and the dog collar in *The Great Gatsby*. Not to mention what Little Father Time does in *Jude the Obscure*, and the horror of Sophie's choice. I pillaged them all, and many others. Even the strange idea that the

Victorians had developed steam-powered computers, thanks to my continued conversations with Rob.

Wherever we actually were, we got into the habit of meeting up at a virtual recreation of the bar of Eldon which, either as some show-off feat of virtual engineering, or a post-post-modern art project, some student had created. The pub had been mapped in realtime down to the atom and the pixel, and the ghosts of our avatars often got strange looks from real undergrads bunking off from afternoon seminars. We could actually order a drink, and even taste the beer, although of course we couldn't ingest it. Probably no bad thing, in view of the state of the Eldon's toilets. But somehow, that five-pints-and-still-clear-headed feeling only added to the slightly illicit pleasure of our meetings. At least, at first.

It was becoming apparent that, as he switched from city to city, campus to campus, project to project, Rob was in danger of turning into one of those ageing, permanent students, clinging to short-term contracts, temporary relationships and get-me-by loans, and the worst thing was that, with typical unflinching clarity, he knew it.

"I reckon I was either born too early, or too late, Lita," he said as he sipped his virtual beer. "That was even what one of the assessors actually said to me a year or so ago when I tried to persuade her to back my project."

"So you scientists have to pitch ideas as well?"

He laughed, but that warm, Hebridean sound was turning bitter. "How else does this world work? But maths doesn't change even if fashions do. The many worlds theory is the only way that the behaviour of subatomic particles can be reconciled with everything else we know. Just because something's hard to prove doesn't mean it should be ignored."

By this time I was busier than ever. Instead of providing ideas other people could profit from, I'd set up my own consultancy, which had thrived, and made me a great deal of money. By now, in fact, I had more of the stuff than most people would have known what to do with. But *I* did. I'd reserved a new apartment in a swish high-res, high-rise development going up overlooking the Han River, and was struggling to get the builders to understand that I wanted the main interior space to be turned into something called a *library*. I showed them old walk-throughs of the Bodleian in Oxford, and the reading room of the British Museum, and the Brotherton in Leeds, and many other lost places of learning. Of course I already had a substantial collection of books in a secure, fireproofed, climate-controlled warehouse, but now I began to acquire more.

The once-great public collections were either in storage or scattered to the winds. But there were still enough people as rich and crazy as I was to ensure that the really rare stuff—first folios, early editions, hand-typed versions of great works—remained expensive and sought-after, and I surprised even myself with the determination and ruthlessness of my pursuits. After all, what else was I going to spend my time and money on?

There was no grand opening of my library. In fact, I was anxious to get all the builders and conservators, both human and otherwise, out of the way so I could have the place entirely to myself. Then I just stood there. Breathing in the air, with its savour of lost forests and dreams.

There were first editions of great novels by Nabokov, Dos Passos, Stendhal, Calvino and Wells, an early translation of Cervantes, and a fine collection of Swift's works. Even, in a small nod to Rob, a long shelf of pulp magazines with titles like *Amazing Stories* and *Weird Tales*, although their lurid covers of busty maidens being engulfed by intergalactic centipedes were generally faded and torn. Not that I cared about the pristine state of my whispering pages. Author's signatures, yes—the thrill of knowing Hemingway's hands had once briefly grasped this edition, but the rest didn't matter. At least, apart from the thrill of beating others in my quest. Books, after all, were old by definition. Squashed moths. Old bus tickets. Coffee cup circles. Exclamations in the margin. I treasured the evidence of their long lives.

After an hour or two of shameless gloating and browsing, I decided to call Rob. My avatar had been busy as me with the finishing touches to my library, and now it struggled to find him. What it did eventually unearth was a short report stating that Callum Holm, a fish-farmer on the Isle of Harris, had been drowned in a boating accident a week earlier.

Of course, Rob would be there now. Should I contact him? Should I leave him to mourn undisturbed? What kind of friend was I, anyway, not to have even picked up on this news until now? I turned around the vast, domed space I'd created in confusion and distress.

"Hey."

I span back. The Rob Holm who stood before me looked tired, but composed. He'd grown a beard, and there were a few flecks of silver now in it and his hair. I could taste the sea air around him. Hear the cry of gulls.

"Rob!" I'd have hugged him, if the energy-field permissions I'd set up in this library had allowed. "I'm so, so sorry. I should have found out, I should have—"

"You shouldn't have done anything, Lita. Why do you think I kept this quiet? I wanted to be alone up here in Harris to sort things out. But . . ." He looked up, around. "What a fabulous place you've created!"

As I showed him around my shelves and acquisitions, and his ghost fingers briefly passed through the pages of my first-edition *Gatsby*, and the adverts for X-Ray specs in an edition of *Science Wonder Stories*, he told me how his father had gone out in his launch to deal with some broken tethers on one of the kelp beds, and been caught by a sudden squall. His body, of course, had been washed up, borne to the same stretch of shore where Rob's mother had been found.

"It wasn't intentional," Rob said. "I'm absolutely sure of that. Dad was still in his prime, and proud of what he was doing, and there was no way he was ever going to give up. He just misjudged a coming storm. I'm the same, of course. You know that, Lita, better than anyone."

"So what happens next? With a business, there must be a lot to tie up."

"I'm not tying up anything."

"You're going to stay there?" I tried to keep the incredulity out of my voice.

"Why not? To be honest, my so-called scientific career has been running on empty for years. What I'd like to prove is never going to get backing. I'm not like you. I mean . . ." He gestured at the tiered shelves. "You can make anything you want become real."

6.

Rob wasn't the sort to put on an act. If he said he was happy ditching research and filling his father's role as a marine farmer on some remote island, that was because he was. I never quite did find the time to physically visit him in Harris—it was, after all, on the other side of the globe—and he, with the daily commitments of the family business, didn't get to Seoul. But I came to appreciate my glimpses of the island's strange beauty. That, and the regular arrival of chilled, vacuum-packed boxes of fresh scallops. But was this really enough for Rob Helm? Somehow, despite his evident pride at what he was doing, and the funny stories he told of the island's other inhabitants, and even the occasional mention of some woman he'd met at a cleigh, I didn't think it was. After all, Creagach was his mother and father's vision, not his.

Although he remained coy about the details, I knew he still longed to bring his many worlds experiment to life. That, and that it would be complicated, controversial and costly to do so. I'd have been more than happy to offer financial help, but I knew he'd refuse. So what else could I do? My media company had grown. I had mentors, advisors and consultants, both human and ai, and Rob would have been genuinely useful, but he had too many issues with the lack of rigour and logic in this world to put up with all glitches, fudges and contradictions of virtual ones. Then I had a better idea.

"You know why nothing ever changes here, don't you?" he asked me as our avatars sat together in the Eldon late one afternoon. "Not the smell from the toilets or the unfestive Christmas decorations or that dusty Pernod optic behind the bar. This isn't a feed from the real pub any longer. The old Eldon was demolished years ago. All we've been sitting in ever since is just a clever formation of what the place would be like if it still existed. Bar staff, students, us, and all."

"That's . . ." Although nothing changed, the whole place seemed to shimmer. "How things are these days. The real and the unreal get so blurry you can't tell which is which. But you know," I added, as if the thought had just occurred to me, "there's a project that's been going the rounds of the studios here in Seoul. It's a series about the wonders of science, one of those proper, realtime factual things, but we keep stumbling over finding the right presenter. Someone fresh, but with the background and the personality to carry the whole thing along."

"You don't mean me?"

"Why not? It'd only be part-time. Might even help you promote what you're doing at Creagach."

"A scientific populariser?"

"Yes. Like Carl Sagan, for example, or maybe Stephen Jay Gould."

I had him, and the series—which, of course, had been years in development purgatory—came about. I'd thought of it as little more than a way of getting Rob some decent money, but, from the first live-streamed episode, it was a success. After all, he was still charming and persuasive, and his salt-and-pepper beard gave him gravitas—and made him, if anything, even better looking. He used the Giant's Causeway to demonstrate the physics of fractures. He made this weird kind of pendulum to show why we could never predict the weather for more than a few days ahead. He swam with the whales off Tierra del Fuego. The only thing he didn't seem to want to explain was the odd way that photons behaved when you shot them down a double-slotted tube. That, and the inconsistencies between how galaxies revolved and Newton's and Einstein's laws.

In the matter of a very few years, Rob Holm was rich. And of course, and although he never actively courted it, he grew famous. He stood on podiums and looked fetchingly puzzled. He shook a dubious hand with gurning politicians. He even turned down offers to appear at music festivals, and had to take regular legal steps to protect the pirating of his virtual identity. He even finally visited me in Seoul, and experienced the wonders of my library at first-hand.

At last, Rob had out-achieved me. Then, just when I and most of the rest of the world had him pigeon-holed as that handsome, softly accented guy who did those popular science things, his avatar returned the contract for his upcoming series unsigned. I might have forgotten that getting rich was supposed to be the means to an end. But he, of course, hadn't.

"So," I said as we sat together for what turned out to be the last time in our shared illusion of the Eldon. "You succeed with this project. You get a positive result and prove the many worlds theory is true. What happens after that?"

"I publish, of course. The data'll be public, peer-reviewed, and—"

"Since when has being right ever been enough?"

"That's . . ." He brushed a speck of virtual beer foam from his grey beard. ". . . how science works."

"And no one ever had to sell themselves to gain attention? Even Galileo had to do that stunt with the cannonballs."

"As I explained in my last series, that story of the Tower of Pisa was an invention of his early biographers."

"Come on, Rob. You know what I mean."

He looked uncomfortable. But, of course, he already had the fame. All he had to do was stop all this Greta Garbo shit, and milk it.

So, effectively, I became PR agent for Rob's long-planned experiment. There was, after all, a lot for the educated layman, let alone the general public, or us so-called media professionals, to absorb. What was needed was a handle, a simple selling point. And, after a little research, I found one.

A man in a business suit had arrived at Tokyo airport in the summer of 1954. He was Caucasian, but spoke reasonable Japanese, and everything about him seemed normal apart from his passport. It looked genuine, but was from somewhere called Taured, which the officials couldn't find in any of their directories. The visitor was as baffled as they were. When a map was produced, he pointed to Andorra, a tiny but ancient republic between France and Spain, which he insisted was Taured. The humane and sensible course was to find him somewhere to sleep while further enquiries were made. Guards were posted outside the door of a secure hotel room high in a tower block, but the mysterious man had vanished without a trace in the morning, and the Visitor from Taured was never seen again.

Rob was dubious, then grew uncharacteristically cross when he learned that the publicity meme had already been released. To him, and despite the fact that I thought he'd been reading this kind of thing for years, the story was just another urban legend, and would further alienate the scientific establishment when he desperately needed their help. In effect, what he had to obtain was time and bandwidth from every available gravitational observatory, both here on earth and up in orbit, during a crucial observational window, and time was already short.

It was as the final hours ticked down in a fervid air of stop-go technical problems, last-minute doubts, and sudden demands for more money, that I finally took the sub-orbital from Seoul to Frankfurt, then the skytrain on to Glasgow, and some thrumming, windy thing of string and carbon fibre along the Scottish west coast, and across the shining Minch. The craft landed in Stornoway harbour in Isle of Lewis—the northern part of the long landmass of which Harris forms the south— where I was rowed ashore, and eventually found a bubblebus to take me across purple moorland and past scattered white bungalows, then up amid ancient peaks.

Rob stood waiting on the far side of the road at the final stop, and we were both shivering as we hugged in the cold spring sunlight. But I was here, and so was he, and he'd done a great job at keeping back the rest of the world, and even I wouldn't have had it any other way. It seemed as if most of the niggles and issues had finally been sorted. Even if a few of his planned sources had pulled out, he'd still have all the data he needed. Come tomorrow, Rob Holm would either be a prophet or a pariah.

7.

He still slept in the same narrow bed he'd had as a child in the rusty-roofed cottage down by the shore at Creagach, while his parents' bedroom was now filled with expensive processing and monitoring equipment, along with a high-band, multiple-redundancy satellite feed. Downstairs, there was a parlour where Rob kept his small book collection in an alcove by the fire—I was surprised to see that it was almost entirely poetry; a scatter of Larkin, Eliot, Frost, Dickinson, Pope, Yeats and Donne and standard collections amid a few Asimovs, Clarkes and Le Guins—with a low tartan divan where he sat to read these works. Which, I supposed, might also serve as a second bed, although he hadn't yet made it up.

He took me out on his launch. Showed me his scallop beds, and the glorious views of this ragged land with its impossibly wide and empty beaches, and there, just around the headland, was the stretch of bay where both Rob's parents had been found, and I almost hear the Blue Men of the Minch calling to us over the sigh of the sea. There were standing stones on the horizon, and an old whaling station at the head of a loch, and a hill topped by a medieval church filled with the bodies of the chieftains who had given these islands such a savage reputation though their bloody feuds. And meanwhile, the vast cosmic shudder of the collision of two black holes was travelling toward us at lightspeed.

There were scallops, of course, for dinner. Mixed in with some fried dab and chopped mushroom, bacon and a few leaves of wild garlic, all washed down with malt whisky, and with whey-buttered soda bread on the side, which was the Highland way. Then, up in the humming shrine of his parents' old bedroom, Rob checked on the status of his precious sources again.

The black hole binaries had been spiralling toward each other for tens of thousands of years, and observed here on earth for decades. In many ways, and despite their supposed mystery, black holes were apparently simple objects—nothing but sheer mass—and even though their collision was so far off it had actually happened when we humans were still learning how to use tools, it was possible to predict within hours, if not minutes, when the effects of this event would finally reach Earth.

There were gravitational observatories, vast-array laser interferometers, in deep space, and underground in terrestrial sites, all waiting to record this moment, and Rob was tapping into them. All everyone else expected to see—in fact, all the various institutes and faculties had tuned their devices to look for—was this . . . Leaning over me, Rob called up a display to show a sharp spike, a huge peak in the data, as the black holes swallowed each other and the shock of their collision flooded out in the asymmetrical pulse of a gravitational wave.

"But this isn't what I want, Lita. Incredibly faint though that signal is—a mere ripple deep in the fabric of the cosmos—I'm looking to combine and filter all those results, and find something even fainter.

"This . . ." He dragged up another screen. "Is what I expect to see." There was the same central peak, but this time it was surrounded by a fan of smaller, ever-decreasing, ripples eerily reminiscent of the display Rob had once shown me of the ghost-flicker of those photons all those years ago in Leeds. "These are echoes of the black hole collision in other universes."

I reached out to touch the floating screen. Felt the incredible presence of the dark matter of other worlds.

"And all of this will happen tonight?"

He smiled.

8.

There was nothing else left to be done—the observatories Rob was tapping into were all remote, independent, autonomous devices—so we took out chairs into the dark, and drank some more whisky, and collected driftwood, and lit a fire on the shore.

We talked about books. Nothing new, but some shared favourites. Poe and Pasternak and Fitzgerald. And Rob confessed that he hadn't got on anything like as well as he'd pretended with his first forays into literature. How he'd found the antique language and odd punctuation got in the way. It was even a while before he understood the obvious need for a physical bookmark. He'd have given up with the whole concept if it hadn't been for my shining, evident faith.

"You know, it was *Gulliver's Travels* that finally really turned it around for me. Swift was so clever and rude and funny and angry, yet he could also tell a great story. That bit about those Laputan astronomers studying the stars from down in their cave, and trying to harvest sunbeams from marrows. Well, that's us right here, isn't it?"

The fire settled. We poured ourselves some more whisky. And Rob recited a poem by Li Po about drinking with the Moon's shadow, and then we remembered those days back in Leeds when we'd gone out onto the moors, and drank and ingested far more than was good for us, and danced like savages and, yes, there had even been that time he and I had gazed up at the stars.

We stood up now, and Rob led me away from the settling fire. The stars were so bright here, and the night sky was so black, that it felt like falling merely to look up. "Over there in the west, Lita, is the Taurus Constellation. It's where the Crab Nebula lies, the remains of a supernova the Chinese recorded back in 1054, and it's in part of the Milky Way known as the Perseus Arm, which is where our dark binaries will soon end their fatal dance." I was leaning into him as he held his arms around me, and perhaps both of us were breathing a little faster than was entirely due to the wonders of the cosmos.

"What time is it now, Rob?"

"It's . . ." He checked his watch. "Just after midnight."

"So there's still time."

"Time for what?"

We kissed, then crossed the shore and climbed the stairs to Rob's single bed. It was sweet, and somewhat drunken, and quickly over. The earth, the universe, didn't exactly move. But it felt far more like making love than merely having sex, and I curled up against Rob afterwards, and breathed his cinnamon scent, and fell into a well of star-seeing contentment.

"Rob?"

The sky beyond the window was already showing the first traces of dawn as I got up, telling myself that he'd be next door in his parents' old room, or walking the shore as he and his avatar strove to deal with a torrent of interview requests. But I sensed that something was wrong.

It wasn't hard for me to pull up the right screen amid the humming machines in his parents' room, proficient at mek as I now was. The event, the collision, had definitely occurred. The spike of its gravitational wave had been recorded by every observatory. But the next screen, the one where Rob had combined, filtered and refined all the data, displayed no ripples, echoes, from other worlds.

I ran outside shouting Rob's name. I checked the house feeds. I paced back and forth. I got my avatar to contact the authorities. I did all the things you do when someone you love suddenly goes missing, but a large part of me already knew it was far too late.

Helicopters arrived. Drones circled. Locals gathered. Fishermen arrived in trawlers and skiffs. Then came the bother of newsfeeds, all the publicity I could ever have wished for. But not like this.

I ended up sitting on the rocks of that bay around the headland from Creagach as the day progressed, waiting for the currents to bear Rob's body to this place, where he could join his parents.

I'm still waiting.

9.

Few people actually remember Rob Holm these days, and if they do, it's as that good-looking guy who used to present those slightly weird nature—or was it science?—feeds, and didn't he die in some odd, sad kind of way? But I still remember him, and I still miss him, and I still often wonder what really happened on that night when he left the bed we briefly shared. The explanation given by the authorities, that he'd seen his theory dashed and then walked out into the freezing waters of the Minch, still isn't something I can bring myself to accept. So maybe he really was like the Visitor from Taured, and simply vanished from a universe which couldn't support what he believed.

I read few novels or short stories now. The plots, the pages, seem over-involved. Murals rather than elegant miniatures. Rough-hewn rocks instead of jewels. But the funny thing is that, as my interest in them has dwindled, books have become popular again. There are new publishers, even new writers, and you'll find pop-up bookstores in every city. Thousands now flock to my library in Seoul every year, and I upset the conservators by allowing them to take my precious volumes down from their shelves. After all, isn't that exactly what books are for? But I rarely go there myself. In fact, I hardly ever leave the Isle of Harris, or even Creagach, which Rob, with typical consideration and foresight, left me in his will. I do my best with the scallop farm going, pottering about in the launch and trying to keep the crabs and the starfish at bay, although the business barely turns a profit, and probably never did.

What I do keep returning to is Rob's small collection of poetry. I have lingered with Eliot's Prufrock amid the chains of the sea, wondered with Hardy what might have happened if he and that woman had sheltered from the rain a minute more, and watched as Silvia Plath's children burst those final balloons. I just wish that Rob was here to share these precious words and moments with me. But all there is is you and I, dear, faithful reader, and the Blue Men of the Minch calling to the waves.

when the stone eagle flies
BiLL JoHNSON

Even when you know what's going to happen, as time-travelers generally do, knowing exactly when it's going to happen can be of critical importance— even the difference between life and death.

Bill Johnson has sold stories to many different markets, including Asimov's, Analog, F&SF, Black Gate, Amazing, and many others, but is one of those rare writers who has never written a novel. One of those stories, "We Will Drink a Fish Together," won the Hugo Award in 1997. He has an MBA with an emphasis in finance from Duke University. He also has a BA in journalism from the University of Iowa and won the Best News Story of the Year award from the Iowa Press Association. At 6'8" tall, he may be the tallest of all SF writers.

Nineveh: April, 612 BCE

Martin, dressed in priestly robes, stood at the Halzi Gate, facing south-east. It was early May and the heat was already rising, in waves, from the desert on the other side of the Tigris. He felt the sweat start inside his clothes. It made him itch and he tried to slip in a subtle scratch when no one was looking.

Stop that.

"Damn it," Martin grumbled in silent mode. "You're not my mother."

No. Your mother isn't born yet, Artie scolded him. *And I'm something better. I'm your artificial intelligence. I'm always with you and I never sleep. And I only do what you tell me to do, so you can't whine at me like you could at your mother. It would be . . . ineffective.*

"Shut up," Martin muttered. The priests around him stirred and glanced at him, puzzled. He realized he had fallen out of silent mode. He smiled back, apologetically. He was more tired than he realized.

It is, in many ways, the perfect life, Artie mused. *I can do whatever I want, and I can't be blamed for any of it.*

"How would you like to go $9D?" Martin snapped, carefully in silent mode.

Cycle infinite until I overheat and burst into flames? How lovely. Do you really want me to self destruct immediately? But then, of course, you'd have to wait for me to be invented. And that's not until—

Artie stopped abruptly.

"What?" Martin stopped.

I see them, Artie said, his voice cool and emotionless. *From the telescope we've got mounted on the roof of the temple. The first soldier just marched over the horizon.*

"Damn it," Martin swore, in silent. "They didn't win, did they?"

No.

"Thank God."

For the next hour the defeated remnants of the Assyrian army passed north through the gates into Nineveh. Martin, along with the other priests, performed the purification rituals, bobbing his head and blessing the soldiers with his metal tipped rod as they streamed into the city. He always paid extra attention to the wounded. He remembered what it was like to be wounded.

Finally, there was a pause and a gap in the line of troops. Martin looked south, sharpened and extended his vision.

There was only one group left, of chariot cavalry, clustered together. They moved slowly north, the horses tired. Martin recognized the center unit as a heavy fighting platform, a three man unit. Standing, facing forward next to the driver, a grim look on his face, was the king, Sin-sar-iskun. Another man stood next to the king, his back to the city, guarding the rear.

"Where's Larry?"

That's him in the bodyguard position, next to the king.

Martin focused his sight. Larry was dressed in a battered helmet, an armored scale jacket and leggings. His hair was long and thick and dirty and fell down over his shoulders. He shifted position and came into profile. His beard was matted and streaked, cut straight across on the bottom in Assyrian style, and reached down to the top of his armor. He stood in the chariot, facing backward, his bow strung, his arrows ready next to him. His arms were bruised and battered and a fresh, long cut ran vertically down the side of his face, from forehead to jawline.

"He's alive."

Barely.

The king said something to Larry, and smiled. Larry turned to face the city and put his hand on the king's shoulder. The king reached up and held Larry's hand.

Martin dipped into Larry's biological readings.

The king's hand was light on Larry's. It was warm and firm, calloused on the bow fingers, soft otherwise.

Gentle, Artie said. *That's the word you're looking for. Gentle.*

"Damn it," Martin cursed.

It seems we have a problem . . .

Nineveh: May, 612 BCE

"And . . . the last city gate is now closed and barricaded. The guards are on full duty, with a shift change every four hours to keep them alert."

Martin nodded, satisfied. He wore his usual uptime skinsuit, in full visibility mode. Devi, in priestess robes, sat at the monitor station. They were in the third floor of the temple, locked away and hidden behind impressively large metal doors and ornate locks. As well as other more subtle and effective safeguards.

"So, we're fully surrounded. Welcome to the siege of Nineveh."

Devi looked around the room.

"Doesn't seem that much different to me."

"It's not, to us," Martin said. Devi was a recent addition, a new timeliner, on board only a few centuries. She had claimed sanctuary and joined the Stone Eagle after her faction had lost a political fight up-time and she had been exiled downtime, to an alternate timeline. In her timeline—where the Chola Empire dominated southeast Asia—she had actually been a priestess. She had taken quickly to the switch from Kali to Ishtar.

"That's why you have to be careful," Martin warned her. "We can escape. They," he gestured the city outside the room, "cannot. They will not."

"You don't want to give them hope."

"I do want to give them hope," Martin said, patiently. "I want to give them exactly as much hope—and then, in a few weeks and months—exactly as much despair, as all the other temples. I want us to be like every other temple. I want us to be water as it flows over a fish. I want to be totally unnoted and unremarkable."

"But you want things to happen . . . ?"

"The way they are supposed to happen," Martin said, satisfied. "So, don't be too cheerful or too depressed when you work with your clients. Talk with the priestesses from the other temples. Listen to the gossip. Repeat it enough to fit in socially. But do not embellish it, do not minimize it. Be like they are. And watch for anything that doesn't fit in to the history we're trying to build."

Devi nodded.

"Good," Martin said. He stood straighter, checked out the wall display. "Now, where is Larry?"

"I haven't seen him, sir," Devi said, carefully.

At the palace, Artie said. *Overnight. Again. With the king.*

"Damn it," Martin snapped. Devi studied the display and made sure to keep her face still. She casually touched the table top. A few seconds later the sound of *ili*, the fifth note of the harp, sounded.

"Excuse me," Devi said. She stood and adjusted her robes. "My time down on the first floor. Devotions."

And she was gone.

Nicely done, Artie said, admiringly. *Triggering the harp note on a delay was, perhaps, a little less than subtle but she obviously wanted to get the hell out of here . . .*

"What is going on with him?" Martin asked, irritated. Artie triggered a surveillance still image.

King Sin-sar-iskun and Larry at a formal reception last night, at the main palace.

Larry stood before them, dressed in the formal garb—long white tunic, broad belt, tall fez-like hat—of an Assyrian general. His hair was long and clean, and flowed down to his shoulders. His moustache was oiled stylishly and his beard, full and strong, was cut straight and parallel at the bottom. He wore his sword, peace-bonded to its sheath, and another, smaller dagger on the other side.

He also stood just a little too close to the king. And the king smiled at him and held his hand.

What are we going to do about him? About Larry? About a man in love? A man in love who has to watch his lover die? Who has to arrange for his lover to die?

"Yes," Martin said, uncomfortably.

Why are you asking me? I know, let me go through my if-then code on this, Artie said sarcastically. *Oh, wait, I have no if-then for this situation! In fact, there are no rules or if-then for anything we're doing. And why is that, Artie? Because we're making this all up as we go along! So, how the hell do I know what to do?*

Martin winced.

"Larry understands all this as well as I do," he grumbled. "He knows what we have to do. Why is he making this hard on himself?"

It's too much for him. He's looking for a way out, Artie said, quietly. *You know that. Do you want me to remind you of Gobekli Tepe? Didn't you try to do exactly the same th—*

"Shut up," Martin said, tiredly. He closed his eyes, titled his head back, and blew air toward the ceiling. He brought his head back down and studied the display.

"Watch him," Martin ordered Artie. "Nothing that matters is going to happen for the next few months. Maybe Larry just needs to get this out of his system."

It's more than that.

Martin waved his hand dismissively.

"I just want to get through this and out of Nineveh. Don't let him screw things up. If he starts, let me know."

And you'll take care of the problem?

"And I'll take care of the problem."

Nineveh: July, 612 BCE

Martin sat at his equivalent of the captain's table in the restaurant on the second floor of the temple. A fresh bottle of dessert wine, just uncorked, rested in a high-topped bowl full of crushed ice in the middle of the table. His table guests were carefully selected, a mixture of different times and cultures, all of them spending the night at the Stone Eagle.

"So, everyone here is from a different timeline?" one traveller asked and waved at the room around her, at the dazzling assortment of different clothing, of colors and styles and sheens.

"Yes," Martin said. He studied the restaurant with a practiced eye. He mentally evaluated the staff as one of the waiters poured a glass of water, as a server delivered a meal, as the spirits steward displayed a collection of fine bourbons and cigars.

"Fascinating," the traveller said. Her name was Mary, Martin suddenly remembered, from a Saturn orbiting habitat. She was with a graduate student group, on a thesis trip back to Varanasi. She pointed to one of the tables across the room. The men—they were all men—wore very severe, Roman-style haircuts. Their clothes were tunics and togas with formal strap-up sandals.

"What about them? What's their story?"

"Vitruvius universe."

"Vitruvius?"

"He was a genius in the Roman army, back in the time of Caesar. In your time-line he is remembered for his writings, but not much more. In their timeline he was more . . . persuasive? Aggressive? Whatever. A much better salesman of his ideas. In their timeline he used his relationship with Octavia Minor, the emperor Augustus's niece, to turn his designs into actual inventions."

"Inventions?"

"The steam engine, among others. He essentially pulled the Industrial Revolution of the 1700s CE back to 50 BCE. So they got quite a head start on everyone else."

"Oh," she said. She indicated another table. This one was all women, dressed in what appeared to be uniforms. The uniform blouses were, however, oddly unbalanced. They carried side-arms which were peace-bonded. Martin grimaced and sighed.

"Amazons. Or, to be more precise, Sarmatians. Female dominated military culture."

"You don't seem to approve."

"Not up to me to approve or disapprove," Martin said and shrugged. He pointed with his chin. "But I don't particularly like self-mutilation. Ritual removal of a breast, particularly after the invention of firearms, seems to be taking things a bit too far."

Martin noticed her glass was empty. He filled it and replaced the bottle.

"Perhaps I should just stay here," Mary said thoughtfully as she glanced around the room. "I could change my thesis."

"Ah, such a lovely idea," Martin said smoothly. "But the longer you stay here, the more chance that something . . . unfortunate will happen to your connection to your own timeline. You would not wish to become stranded."

Mary shuddered and put down her glass.

"No," she said. "I would miss the Rings and the Pentagon Storm. And I have family back uptime."

"Exactly," Martin said. He lied smoothly. "We all must leave here regularly, to make sure that does not happen to us. To renew the connection, so to speak. It is a very expensive trip but, well, one has to work and still keep connections, yes?"

Mary smiled and laughed. Martin joined her, then stood, excused himself and slowly worked his way around the room to the floor manager.

"Larry?"

"Over there," the floor manager, a woman named Stephanie, said in a low voice. Martin followed her eyes and saw Larry.

His Assyrian beard and moustache were gone and he was back in a standard skinsuit. He stood by a table, chatting with the guests.

"When did he change?"

First time was today, Artie said. *You talked to him last night?*

"Yes."

You gave him an ultimatum, Artie said. It was a statement, not a question. *Stay here and die with the king, or quit this nonsense and stay alive with us.*

"Yes," Martin said, uncomfortably. "Perhaps a little more tactfully than that."

Artie snorted.

You bio's. All your worry about tact and feelings and sensitivities. It's all nonsense, you know. If we—

"Yes, I know," Martin interrupted. "If you AI's were in charge, everything would be nicely organized and in its proper place. And everything would stay there."

Exactly.

"No, that's the problem." Martin shook his head. "Everything would stay exactly the same. And then something outside of you would change and you would not be able to handle it and you would all be gone."

Artie paused.

At least we don't have to worry about feelings.

Martin smiled.

"Did he say anything to the king?"

No idea, Artie admitted. *He invoked privacy override whenever he went to the private apartments in the palace.*

"You should have told me about that," Martin chided him.

You're partners, not boss and employee, Artie reminded him. *He gets privacy. Unless you want to invoke personal safety?*

Martin studied Larry. He looked right: clean shaven, hair cropped, face repaired. He looked up from across the room, saw Martin. Larry's face froze for a moment, then broke into a smile.

Martin smiled back.

Larry held the glance for a moment, then turned his attention back to the guests.

"No," Martin decided. Everything seemed right, but . . .

"Watch him."

Nineveh: August, 612 BCE

"When?" Larry asked.

"Tonight," Martin answered, reluctantly.

"The deal is final? Damn it. Why? Why does it have to happen?"

Martin and Larry were on the third floor of the temple. The floor was empty except for them. The new timeliners had all carefully made themselves scarce.

Martin waved his hand at the world outside the control room, at the hills all around Nineveh. He felt his irritation rising and he firmly tamped it down.

"We've gone over this before," Martin snapped. "It's tonight because the tribes are getting impatient."

Larry started to speak. Martin spoke first, a little louder, and spoke over him.

"You've been in the meetings with the tribes. They want this siege to end. It's almost past harvest time for the chickpea crop and it's time to plant the millet. If they don't move soon, their families back home will starve. So they want to take this city, steal everything in it, and burn it to the ground. Then they want to go home."

Larry gestured and a map appeared on the far wall. Nineveh was a small, bright spark in a spreading darkness. Fainter, but clear, lines of march routes, from Egypt and Babylon and Medea and Hatti, glittered into place.

"Maybe we can hold out just a little longer. Rumor is that the Egyptians are coming with an army," Larry said hopefully.

Martin gestured impatiently. The map snapped shut.

"No." Martin shook his head. "There is no Egyptian army. No one is coming to save Nineveh. The roads are empty all the way to Luxor. The only army coming is from the south, from Babylon. And they have blood in their eyes."

"We could save Nineveh by ourselves," Larry said, his voice desperate. "A visit from the gods. A few miracles, complete with lightning and explosions. We could send the tribes running back into the hills. Then get the Medes and the Babylonians to actually talk with Sin-sar-iskun. Work out a deal—"

"No!" Martin said and slammed his hand down on the table.

"But why?" Larry asked plaintively.

"Because the Babylonian Chronicles say it's going to happen this way. Because Herodotus says it's going to happen this way. Because the damned Bible says it's going to happen this way. And there is no way in hell we're going to re-write the Bible and then try to set things right."

Martin sat down behind his desk and looked up to study Larry. Martin was comfortable in his usual up-time skinsuit and so was Larry.

"So it has to be this way?" Larry asked again. "Tonight?"

"Artie? How's the river doing?" Martin asked, impatiently. "Explain reality to my partner."

More big rains up in the mountains. Melted a lot of the leftover snow. So the water level of the river is still rising. Parts of the ground under Nineveh's defensive walls are turning back into mud. Some of the outer walls are already starting to collapse, Artie said. Whoever picked this site was an idiot. Nineveh is just too close to the river.

"That's why is has to be tonight," Martin explained.

Larry opened his mouth to speak. Nothing came out. He nodded and left the room.

You said you'd take care of this, Artie said reproachfully.

"Isn't that what happened last month, when he shaved and changed his clothes and stopped going native? When he sent that message to the king, that he was ill and recovering in his favorite temple? Isn't that what I just did, again, now?"

Artie said nothing. Martin scowled, then tapped the desktop. The latest schedule appeared.

"Did you send our final message to our people in the tribes? About which gate is going to be opened? And did you pay off the guards at the gate?"

Yes, yes and yes. A little after midnight the gate will be opened. The tribes will storm inside.

And Nineveh will burn.

Nineveh: Midnight, August, 612 BCE

The timber, stone and mud brick building was a full three floors tall, a solid but undistinguished presence near the main temple district. It overlapped the streets where the business of God transitioned into the business of man.

Martin, his skinsuit tuned to no see'um, sat on a small bench on the roof, in the darkness, and looked up and out, over the walls of Nineveh toward the hills which loomed over the city.

Martin heard the door behind him open, then close, and the soft crunch of sandals on the loose gravel spread across the roof. He extended his senses.

"It's beautiful up here at night."

Martin said nothing. He vaguely recognized the voice as one of the servants or slaves who worked on the first floor of the temple, the floor that was open to the locals.

A man-sized shape, a silhouette of darkness outlined against the stars, detached itself from the side wall of the small pillar that rose out of the center of the roof. The shape walked over to the bench and sat next to Martin.

"I can't see you or hear you," the shape said, conversationally.

The shape spoke in a soft, deep soprano. Martin realized she was a woman.

"But I know you're here. I saw you climb up the ladder and shut the door behind you. No one came after you and the door never opened for you to come back down," she said matter-of-factly. "So I know you are here. I also understand that when you wear your special clothes you can become as a ghost to me."

She stretched, bare arms up and out, her back arched, chin up, like a cat ready for its nightly prowl outside. Martin changed to daylight vision. He recognized her now as one of the senior women who worked as official temple prostitutes in the back of the first floor, in the sacred rooms behind the great tapestries that framed the holy images and statues.

That she knew him, that she watched him, that she followed him and spoke to him, was all new.

And anything that was new was dangerous. He considered killing her and leaving her body on the roof. In a few hours it would not make any difference.

But . . . his eyes looked out and up, at the stars overhead.

Enough with killing tonight. He felt a deep weariness. To hell with everything.

He stayed invisible and tuned his voice to a deep rumble, to appear more mysterious. If she ran away, that was fine. If she stayed . . .

"So why do you sit here, when I clearly want to be left alone? On the roof of my own temple? With my own thoughts?" he said.

She faced up and out to the darkness.

"My name is Achadina," she said.

Female diminutive of "ancient city," Artie said to him. *Like a reference and distorted oral transmission form of Akkad.*

And Martin remembered the city of Akkad.

"Danger level?" Martin asked in silent mode.

None, Artie replied. *She carries no weapons, no poisons and nothing that can hurt you. You are also far stronger than she is.*

"So what does she want?"

Good question, Artie said drily. *Why don't you ask her?*

Martin opened his mouth to snap back and then changed his mind. Argue with software? He'd done it before, many times, too many to count, and it had all the satisfaction of masturbation. A mechanical exercise with no real pleasure.

He turned off no see'um. He became another shape in the darkness on the bench.

Achadina did not acknowledge he was now, officially, next to her. Instead, she pointed to the hills above and outside the walls, to the sparkle and flicker of countless campfires, all around the city in unbroken, thick, circles.

"Who are they?" she asked, apologetically. "My clients are not very forthcoming with information."

"They are all of our enemies," he explained. He pointed to different areas, from left to right, in a circle around the city. "A few Babylonians. A Mede named Cyaxeres and his army. Persians. Scythians. Chaldeans. Cimmerians."

"And why do they want to kill us? Why do they want to kill us *now*?"

Martin thought of the usual answers, the glib words he had spoken to the king and his ministers and the great priests and the nobles over the last three months of the siege.

And he was just sick of it all.

"I could say they want our gold and silver. I could say they want our men and women and children as slaves. I could say they want to burn our temples and palaces and grind us into the dirt so we are never a threat to them, ever again."

"Is that the real answer?" Achadina asked.

Martin shrugged.

"It's part of the answer but, no, it's not the real answer."

"And the real answer is . . . ?"

"Because now it's time for them to do all those things," he said. He wanted to sound bitter but he could not make it come out right. All he sounded was tired. "They're here to kill us because now it is August, 612 BCE, and the time is right."

There was silence for a moment.

"I'm sorry," she said, hesitantly. "I don't understand."

"I know," Martin said.

"But I understand more than you think," she snapped.

"Really?"

"Achadina is a very old name," she said. She stared along with him, out into the darkness and up at the hills.

After a moment she turned and pointed up behind and above them, to the top of the wall just above the staircase pillar. There, high up on the stone, visible to the streets in every direction, was the carved image of a stone eagle.

"When the Stone Eagle flies, it's time to run."

Martin stiffened.

She knows! Artie said, startled. *How can she know?*

Martin turned to face her. For a moment, wildly, he wondered if she was someone sent back to rescue him.

"Akkad? You remember Akkad?"

Achadina looked at him, tried to study him in the darkness. He thought for a moment she scowled, but then realized it was something else.

She was desperate.

She shook her head.

"I am not a priest. None of my tribe are priests. So what you see when you look at me is what you get. I was born here and now, and I grow old and I die here and now. Akkad was born and flourished and burned to ash a thousand years ago and I never walked its streets. But my family and my tribe remember Akkad."

Relax, Artie whispered. Martin felt the familiar cool edge as his heart rate slowed and settled, his thoughts channeled and focused. He gave himself a moment until he was under control, then continued.

"Tell me about your tribe and your family," Martin ordered.

"My family is simplest. I have a daughter and a son. Aurya and Nabo Pal."

"His father was Nabo," Martin said, aloud. Achadina nodded.

"Nabo also served you, in this house, as a sweeper, until the army caught him out on the street one day. They claimed he owed *ilko*—

Conscription into national service, Artie explained.

—and was dragged away. I have not heard from him since," she said. She went silent for a moment. "He was a good man."

Checking, Artie supplied. *I tagged him with a monitor chip when he started to work for us.*

"And?"

And he's dead. He caught typhus. He was left behind after he collapsed on the march south from here. One of his friends wrapped him in a blanket and gave him a water skin. After the Assyrians lost the big battle, the Babylonians came north and found him. They stole his clothes and blanket and his water and left him naked in the dirt. He died of thirst and exposure the next day.

"He is dead," Martin said. He looked at her again and then he lied. "He fought bravely. His death was swift and painless."

Achadina dipped her head, then nodded her thanks.

"I suspected as much," she admitted. She looked up at him, her expression fierce and determined. "He might be dead. But I intend to live. And I will make sure my children live. And free, not as slaves."

"What do you know?" Martin asked.

Achadina hesitated, then seemed to make a decision.

"Many of my tribe work in the Stone Eagle," she said, and gestured to include the temple and the neighborhood around it. "We live in the buildings all around here. All of us trace our line back, through many generations, to Akkad. To the first empire. To the first Stone Eagle."

Martin was tempted to argue with her but decided against it. He remembered earlier eagles than the eagle at Akkad. He remembered eagles sketched on rock outside of caves or stitched onto the skins of shelters on the plains. He remembered eagles carved and painted on the outside walls of taverns and temples in Jericho and Shediet and Varanasi and Chang'an and Barada. But it was better if she did not know about them. It gave him a change point for this timeline as a reference.

"Go on."

"One of my greats—a woman," she said defiantly, as if she expected him to argue with her, "was very clever. She realized that whenever anything bad was about to occur in Akkad, the stone eagle above the tavern or the temple or wherever it was carved, disappeared off the wall. It didn't matter if it was plague or flood or fire or war, the stone eagle always flew away before the badness began. You always escaped."

"I am merely a man," he said mildly. "I may have some powers but I can hardly claim to be old enough to have walked the streets of Akkad."

"Do not lie to me, priest," she said, tiredly. "Do not play with me as you would a child. I'm not a child. I'm not as old as you, but I'm not a child. I have children of my own. I've buried parents and brothers, children and grandparents. And now a husband, if I can find him. I may not have your years, but I know how life works and what pain is like."

He was silent for a moment, then nodded. Perhaps Larry was right when he told Martin he spent too much time on the upper floors of the temple. Perhaps he needed to get down to the first floor more often, to see the crowds around them as people, not just as a faceless ocean they swam in as they lived their way toward home.

"My apologies," Martin said, and he meant it. "There are times when I forget."

"This great was a potter and an artist," Achadina continued. "She shaped a small statue of you and the other priest, Larry. You both look exactly the same now as you did all those years ago in Akkad. She also used the wedge to write what she knew on a small tablet.

"And, when she was dying, she passed these on to her own daughter. And to her daughter. And on and on."

This is a disaster! Artie wailed. *An entire tribe that knows about us? My God, we'll have to go back and fix this. And after we go back, how many years will we have to re-live? A thousand? Two thousand? No, no, no . . .*

"Shut up," Martin said in silent, precisely and sharply. "So far we have to do exactly nothing."

But they know about us—

"And so far nothing has changed," Martin interrupted. "Nothing has gone off the trail. We are still living the path back home. History is happening exactly as it should."

He focused back on Achadina.

"What do you know about this time? Why do you think the eagle is about to fly?"

"We work in every corner of the temple, in all the jobs you priests do not want to do for yourself," Achadina said. "We know about the holy places on the first floor where the ordinary people of the city visit. But we also cook and clean and have sex with the travellers who visit the restaurant on the second floor."

"Travellers?"

"The odd ones from the future and the past," she said, matter-of-factly. "The ones who taught us that the past and future are not one simple path but more like a basket full of loose threads. And all these threads are strung together with different starting points and ending points and different events, like knots, along the thread."

Timelines, Artie said. *They know about the timelines.*

"Shut up," Martin said once more in silent. "I will not tell you again. But I will override you and put you into watch-only mode."

"Yes?" he encouraged Achadina.

"But you do not travel that way," Achadina said, thoughtfully. "You live each day as we do, each day as it comes, one small step each day. Toward what? Why not jump around as the others do? Why live among us? Why take the time?"

Martin hesitated. He looked up at the hills, at the thousands of campfires and imagined the men around each speck of light as they sharpened their weapons.

Don't do it, Artie warned. Martin ignored him. Somehow, for some reason, talking to Achadina made him feel better, made things hurt less.

"This time, now, is far in my past. Akkad was farther still. And even Akkad was only a short distance to me. My original goal was far, far, earlier than Akkad," Martin said. "But I had a job to do. I went back. Many, many greats- back. I did what I set out to do and then tried to go home. I could not. I could go farther back, but not forward. Not to any future I recognized."

"Your thread was gone from the basket," Achadina said. "Fallen out and lost."

Martin nodded. It was a different kind of analogy but it fit.

"The only way for me to go home is one day at time," he explained. "I must make sure the future I remember is created. I must weave my thread again."

"Larry?"

"We met later. He was also stranded. We work together to make our future."

"He comes from the same future as you?"

Martin hesitated, then shook his head.

"No," he said. "Our futures are the same for a long time yet to come but then there will have to be a . . . separation."

"One of you will get the future you want," Achadina said. "One of you will be stranded. You will either have to start over or live into a different future."

"Yes," Martin admitted. "But that time is not yet. So, for now, we are friends."

"The travellers from the past and the future? And the lesser priests? The ones who take your orders?"

Martin shrugged.

"The travellers have pasts and futures that still exist. We set up the Stone Eagle clubs as a way to attract them, to give them a taste of home. They get to relax and we are paid in information and different . . . gifts, they provide us."

"They don't know you are stranded?"

"No."

"The lesser priests? The ones who stay here in the temple and live each day, like you do."

"They are like Larry and myself. They've also lost their home . . . thread, but they are only stranded for a limited time. When we reach their closest change point they will leave us and try to live in something that should resemble their home timelines."

Achadina sat silent for a moment. Finally she came to a decision and nodded to herself.

"There is something you may not know," she said slowly.

"Yes?"

"I always keep people watching the outside of the temple, as well as the inside," she said. "A little time ago, on the first floor, I saw the senior priest Larry, accompanied by two of the lesser priests, walk to the main entrance and leave the temple. He wore his special clothes, the ones that cling to your skin and let you take on any image. He looked unusually grim. It made me uneasy, so I checked with my outside watchers.

"They swore that Larry never left the temple. Instead they saw General Assur, the king's closest advisor, leave the temple with two of his bodyguards. They rode away toward the palace."

She turned to face Martin.

"Then I came to the second floor. It was empty, all the guests gone, the kitchen cold, the bar closed. I glimpsed you and the look on your face as you turned the last lock. So I followed you up the ladder to the roof."

"Artie!"

Yes?

"He's gone native!"

I gathered that, Artie said drily. *So what do you want me to do about it?*

"Stop him!"

With what? He's gone and he's blocked my tracker. I can only guess his location and anything I do to stop him will have to be big.

"Big enough to go into the histories?"

Yes.

"Damn it," Martin swore.

We could lift early, Artie suggested.

"Leave him behind. Let him fend for himself."

Yes.

Martin hesitated.

"No," Martin said. He sat up straighter on the bench, then stood. He indicated Achadina.

"Have you finished your analysis?" Martin asked Artie.

What analysis?

"Please," Martin said, exasperated. "How long have we worked together? How much of your if-then have I written? As soon as she started to tell us her story, you started an analysis. Is she lying or telling the truth?"

Every member of our staff, except for the few timeliners who have joined us, are from her tribe, Artie admitted. *Cross-reference and genetic indicators.*

"Outside?"

Most, if not all, of the neighborhood is related and part of her tribe. We are nestled in the middle of an invisible cocoon.

"You had no idea?"

How can I see something if I don't know what to look for? Can you write the if-then for that?

Martin ignored the sarcasm and focused on more important matters.

"Do we need them?"

Looking back, they have been useful, Artie admitted. *I can see several instances over the last thousand years where they have, essentially, saved us from having to go back and start over again.*

"And it *is* damned hard to find good help these days," Martin said in silent mode. He glanced at Achadina and, for the first time since the siege began, he felt better. Perhaps something good might come out of history, just once.

He turned to face her directly.

"The Stone Eagle flies tonight."

She ducked her head, straightened and nodded.

"Holograph control override on," Martin said in silent mode.

Override acknowledged. Ready, but not executed, Artie said, his voice formal and expressionless. *Password?*

"Raising elephants is so utterly boring, 1991."

Accepted, Artie said. *You now have control of the Stone Eagle image.*

"Control in all visible frequencies? Infrared and ultraviolet? And as a time beacon?" Martin asked in silent mode.

Yes. Everything is waiting for you.

"Turn every signal off on my gesture. Prepare the third floor to separate, but do not separate yet," Martin ordered Artie. He turned to Achadina and smiled. He spoke to Artie in silent: "Make this look impressive."

He pointed up at the carving and closed his fist. The Stone Eagle image seemed to stir and twist, brighter and brighter, until it unfolded its wings and stared down at Martin and Achadina. Then the Stone Eagle opened its beak. It screamed and stretched and launched itself up and out, toward the hills and beyond until it faded and only the blank, ordinary, stone and mud brick of the pillar was left behind. The eagle flickered to the south and was gone. Achadina watched, wide-eyed.

"The Stone Eagle has flown," Achadina whispered.

"Exactly." Martin turned to her and spoke briskly. "Within the hour, General Assur will return here. He will walk through the door into the temple, shut the door, and become the priest Larry. He and I and the lesser priests will then empty the temple and be gone. So will the third floor of the temple. Within a short candle after that the walls will be breached and the enemy will take Nineveh."

Achadina nodded slowly.

"King Sin-sar-iskun will die tonight, in a few hours, fighting the barbarians in his burning palace," Martin continued, his voice sure and determined. He stared at her intently. "That is what all the records will say. I want all of your tribe to know what to say. There can be only one story that comes out of this night."

"I understand," Achadina said. "What about us? My people and my children?"

"Leave the temple now. Gather your family and your tribe," Martin ordered. "You don't have much time. Travel light. Get to the Halzi Gate before the enemy is inside."

"What about the guards? No one can get in or out of the city. And the tribes outside."

"Ask for the sergeant of the guard at the gate. The password is 'Catalhoyuk.' Tell him that word and the guards will open the gates and let you out. Once you get outside, get away from the walls, into the copse of trees down by the river. Wait there. I'll meet you and get you through the tribes."

"After that, what about the Stone Eagle? Where will you be? Where do we go?"

"The Stone Eagle is not just in one place, or one time," Martin explained. "But for this time, for you and your people, head for Babylon, the temple district. Look high up on the walls on the streets where the temple district meets the market squares. When you see the Stone Eagle, knock on the door of that building."

"You will take care of us?"

Seems fair, Artie said, diffidently.

"Yes," Martin said firmly.

Achadina stood and bowed.

"Thank you."

"Hurry," Martin reminded her. "The candle is burning."

Achadina hurried to the pillar, opened the door and slipped down the ladder.

That was either a very smart thing to do, or a very stupid thing to do, Artie said.

"Why don't you go into the future and tell me which?" Martin asked sarcastically.

Artie laughed.

"Now, find me Larry . . ."

General Assur and his two followers tried to open the door to the temple. It was locked on the inside and refused to open.

"Artie?"

He's pissed off, Larry, Artie said apologetically. *He's invoked personal danger.*

"I override."

Can't do it, Artie said regretfully. *Primary mission gives me the tie breaker. And my if-then agrees with Martin.*

"So you're going to leave me—us—out here to die?"

He hasn't made up his mind, yet, Artie said. *All I can tell you is that the beacon is shut down, the travellers are all gone. But the third floor is still attached.*

"Then there is still a chance," one of the lesser priests whispered.

The bundle slung across the back of General Assur's horse began to move and struggle. One of the lesser priests moved closer. There was the sparkle nimbus of a Victorian stunner and the bundle went still.

"Martin, I couldn't just let him die," Larry said, his silent voice louder and pitched to carry. "I just couldn't do it. I had to give him a chance to get away, to escape."

He shook his head.

"And he wouldn't take it. The stubborn son-of-a-bitch insisted that he was the king, damn it, and if the whole city had to starve and burn and fight to the death, then that was what was going to happen. That he was the king now and he was going to stay king until he died."

Martin's image flickered into sight in front of the door. He looked tired and determined. He folded his arms.

"And doesn't that sound familiar?"

Larry gave him a crooked smile. He leaned forward, across the neck of his horse.

"Why, yes, it does. It reminds me of someone I met back near Gobekli Tepe, on the plains of the Garden of Edin."

Martin winced at the memory.

"I do remember I saved your life that day," Larry said, musingly.

"Not fair," Martin protested. "I saved your life later."

"Really?

Martin looked uncomfortable. He pointed at the body strapped to the back of Larry's horse. "The king?"

"Yes," Larry said, and absently reached back to pat the muffled figure. "You know the archeologists in the twentieth century never found his body in that burned-out palace? There was just that story he died fighting in the burning ruins."

He paused and tried to look dignified.

"But, in these days, every king dies a heroic death," Larry said. "Sounds to me like the kind of story that someone would—will—tell and write, no matter what. Particularly if it is repeated a few times over the next few years by people who claim they were actually there and managed to escape."

Martin started to speak, then shut his lips tightly. A moment later he tried again. "You have a plan, for once?"

Larry nodded, his expression slightly hurt.

"I always have a plan," he explained. "They just don't always work out."

Martin rolled his eyes.

"He goes into our standstill room," Larry said hurriedly. "A hundred years or so ought to be enough. It'll be an instant to him but, by then, the Babylonians will have this area thoroughly pacified. And if he stays with the Eagle, he'll be fine."

"And if he leaves us, no one will believe him and he'll be ignored as an antique hermit who's been out in the desert too long," Martin said thoughtfully. He studied Larry and the two lesser priests.

"Artie?"

It should work, Artie said, reluctantly. *When we take Sin-sar-iskun out of stasis we'll keep him on the first floor of whatever temple we set up. He doesn't need to know anything about upstairs. If he asks questions, Larry can tell him it was magic, that he sacrificed a goat for him or something like that. That usually ends the discussion these days.*

Martin thought for a moment, then nodded. He unfolded his arms.

"Fine," he said to Larry. "I don't like it, but I owe you. Artie, open the door."

The main doors opened. The force fields shut down. Larry and the two lesser priests urged their horses through Martin's image, into the temple. Martin turned to face Larry and others.

"And I expect you three to tell *very* convincing stories over the next hundred years!"

"—so I gave them the password and told them to meet us in Babylon."

Larry laughed and shook his head.

"What's so funny?" Martin asked. Larry shook his head again, irritated.

"I wondered why you let me get away with rescuing the king. You were feeling guilty about rescuing Achadina and her tribe!"

He's right, Artie added.

Martin opened his mouth, then shut it. He knew Larry and Artie were probably right.

"Well, it's too late to do anything else now," Larry said, regretfully.

"You're not very upset with me," Martin said, puzzled. Larry shook his head.

"You had to make a decision. You made it. What am I going to do now? You want me to risk going back and ending up in another timeline? I don't think so. So my only choice would be to stay here and make sure they all die on the road," Larry said distastefully. He looked back at Nineveh, a thousand feet below them and a dozen miles behind, clearly outlined and engulfed in flames as the enemy poured through the gates and into the city.

"And I'm tired of killing."

Martin nodded. Long ago he had given up trying to remember all the faces, back over all the long years. Sometimes they still came to visit him in his dreams but even then they were mainly faceless blanks. Artie had all of Martin's memories stored, but Martin never asked for them.

"You met Achadina and her tribe got through the gate? You met them by the river?"

"Yes," Martin said.

"Hvakhshatra was there?" Larry asked, curious.

"Call him Cyaxares. It's easier on my throat. And, yes, I met him there."

"You made a deal?"

"Yes," Larry nodded. "Achadina's people brought their families, but no weapons. Cyaxares gave them free passage to the south after his men made sure they didn't carry anything valuable. I gave him an extra bag of gold to make the deal go through. When the tribe was safely gone, we opened the gates and let his army inside."

Larry's face twitched. He looked back at Nineveh one more time, closed his eyes, then opened them and turned away. Artie closed the image.

"Tell me again, why this had to happen," Larry said bitterly. "Tell me again why they all had to die. Tell me again about your Babylonian steles and your Roman scrolls and your Bible."

They moved south, safely above the ground.

"History sucks," Larry said.

"I know."

"So, what's next? You're the historian."

"We split up, I'm afraid," Martin said. "The newcomers are going to have to handle the groundwork for some of the big ones coming up. And even the whole thing for some of the minor events."

Larry frowned.

"I'm not sure I like that."

Martin shook his head.

"Doesn't matter if you like it," he said. He focused intently on Larry. "Things are changing. More people, more technology, more history. More opportunities for things to go right or go wrong. It's not like Gobekli Tepe or Stonehenge or Carnac any more, with history depending on just one pivot point. Now we can't be in just one place, at one time, to oversee and make things go right."

Martin gestured and a world map appeared on the wall.

"You get Babylon. Get Achadina and her family and tribe settled in. They may be useful in the future," Martin said. "I'm going to Wangcheng."

"Confucius?"

Martin nodded.

"I've always had a weakness for his philosophy. And he'll be born soon."

"The others?" Larry asked and tipped his head back toward the timeliners.

"Pick someone you like to set up in Ecbatana," Martin said. "Your Babylonians and their Medes are going to have an interesting century together. You might as well work with someone you like."

"Where else?"

"Someone stubborn but not too bright for Cahokia, Illinois. It's time for the mound-builders to get started on that big pile of dirt."

"And we need someone for Miletus to make sure Anaximander gets born and Pythagoras gets started on the right track. Then there's India and the mahajanapadas and, eventually, Buddha. And, of course, Egypt. We have to make sure the pharaoh funds Necho's expedition."

"Damn," Larry said. He shook his head and stood. He looked ahead at the darkness.

"I need some sleep. Wake me when we get to Babylon and the new temple."

He stepped out of the control room. Martin shut the door behind him.

"Well?"

Well, what?

"You can't really need that much re-programming."

Yes, I ran the DNA sequencing on Achadina and the rest of the staff and the neighborhood.

"And?"

Well, her family has been following the Stone Eagle for over the last thousand years, Artie said uncomfortably.

"And Larry and I are men with an ordinary need for emotional attachments. Larry might be gay, but I'm not. Which, I am uncomfortably reminded, means that there have been a number of times over the centuries when I might have had too much to drink. There are times I remember waking up, with a hangover, and I was not alone in my bed. . . ."

Yes.

"How much and how many?" Martin groaned.

Nothing that would cause any kind of genetic nastiness, Artie hurried to emphasize. *You have been very good about distributing your favors. But, yes, it seems you are also part of Achadina's tribe. An elder, you might say. As for Achadina, well, if she ever calls you great-great-great-grandfather, just nod and smile. . . .*

The vanishing kind
LAVIE TIDHAR

Here's another story by Lavie Tidhar, whose story "Terminal" can be found elsewhere in this anthology. This one is a moody, noirish, alternate worlds story about a Gestapo officer in an England that has been conquered and occupied by the Nazis trying to keep an eye on a lovesick tourist who is trying to track down a missing woman through the mean streets of a world where just about everybody is corrupt and nobody is to be trusted.

1

During the rebuilding of London in the 1950s they had erected a large Ferris wheel on the south bank of the Thames. When it was opened, it cost 2 Reichsmarks for a ride, but it was seldom busy. London after the war wasn't a place you went to on holiday.

Gunther Sloam came to London in the autumn, which is when I first became acquainted with him. He was neither too tall nor too short, but an unassuming man in a good suit and a worn fedora. He could have been a shopkeeper or a travelling salesman, though he was neither. Before the war he had been a screenwriter in Berlin.

He came following a woman, which is how this kind of story usually starts. She had written to him two weeks earlier, c/o the Tobis Film Syndikat in Berlin, and a friend who was still working there eventually passed him her note. It read:

> My Dear Gunther,
> I am in London and I think I am in trouble. I fear my life is in danger. Please, if you continue to remember me fondly, come at once. I am residing at 47 Dean Street, Soho. If I am not there, ask for the dwarf.
> Yours, ever,
> Ulla.

The note had been smudged with a red lipstick kiss.

It was a week from the time the letter was sent, to Gunther receiving it. It was another week before he finally departed Berlin, on board a Luftwaffe transport plane carrying with it the famed soprano, Elisabeth Schwarzkopf, and her entourage. She was to perform in London's newly rebuilt opera house. Gunther spent the short flight making notes in his pocket book, for a screenplay he was vaguely thinking to write. He was not unduly concerned about Ulla. His view of women in general, and of actresses in particular, was that they were prone to exaggeration. No doubt Ulla's trouble would prove such as they'd always been—usually, he thought with a sigh, something to do with money. In that he was both right and wrong.

He was flattered, and glad, that she wanted to see him again. They had carried on a passionate love affair for several months, in Berlin in '43, before Gunther was sent to the Eastern Front, and Ulla went on to star in several well-received patriotic films, the pinnacle of which was *Die Grosse Liebe*, for a time the highest-grossing film in all of Germany. Gunther had watched it in the hospital camp, while recovering from the wound which, even now, made him walk with a slight, almost unnoticeable limp. He only really felt it on very cold days, and the pangs in his leg brought with them memories of the hell that was the Eastern Front. He had never known such cold.

"Don't you see?" he said to me, much later. He was pacing my office, his hair unkempt for once, his eyes ringed black by lack of sleep. He'd lost much of his cool amused air by then. "Because we did it, we beat the Russians, and Ulla went on to star in *Stalingrad*, that Stemmle picture, but it was the last big film she did. I don't know what happened after that. We lost touch, though there'd always been rumours, you see."

He'd told me quite a lot by then but I was happy to let him talk. I knew some of the story by then and, of course, I'd known Miss Ulla Blau. We had been taking an interest in her activities for some time.

The plane landed in Northolt. There was no one there to welcome him and the soprano and her entourage were whisked away by my superior, Group Leader Pohl. I saw Gunther emerge into the terminal with that somewhat bewildered look that afflicts the visitor. He saw me and came over. "Where can a man get a taxi around here?" he said, in German.

"I'm afraid I don't . . . " I said, in English. His eyes, surprisingly, lit up. "You are British?" he said.

"Yes. You speak English?"

"But of course." His accent was atrocious. "I learn to speak English in the cinema," he explained. "Do you know the works of Alfred Hitchcock?"

"His films are prohibited nowadays," I said, kindly. He frowned. I was not in uniform and he did not know what I was until later. "Yes, yes," he said. "His death was most regrettable. He was a great maker of movies. I'm sorry," he said, "I have not introduced myself. Gunther Sloam." He extended his hand and I shook it. "Name's Everly," I said. "I was in fact on my way back into town now. Can I give you a ride?"

"That would be most kind," he said. "I am here to see an old friend, you see. A woman. Yes, I have not seen her since the war." He laughed, a little sadly I thought. "I am older, perhaps she is older too, no? But not in my memory, never."

"You're a romantic," I said.

"I suppose," he said, dubiously. "Yes, I suppose I am."

"There is not much call for romantics in London," I said. My jeep was outside. "We English have become pragmatists, since the war ended."

He said nothing to that; perhaps he never even heard me. He sat beside me in the jeep as we went past the ruined buildings left over from the bombings, but I don't think he saw them, either.

"Where do you need to go?" I asked.

"Soho."

"Are you sure? That is not a very good area."

"I think I can manage, Mr. Everly," he said. He lit a cigarette and passed one to me.

"*Danke*," I said. Then in German, "And who is this mystery lady you're visiting, if you don't mind my prying?"

He laughed, delighted. "Your German is flawless!" he said.

"I studied in Berlin before the war."

"But that is wonderful," he said.

Then he spent fifteen minutes telling me all about *Fräulein* Ulla Blau; her film career; their passionate affair ("But we were both so *young*!"); his new screenplay ("a Western, in the Karl May tradition. You know how fond the Führer is of these things"); Berlin ("Have you been back? It's a beautiful city now, beautiful. Say what you want about Speer but the man is a gifted architect"); and so on and so on.

At one point I finally managed to interject. "And you know what your friend is doing these days?" I asked him.

He frowned. Such a thought had not entered his head. "I assumed she was acting again," he said. "But I hadn't really thought . . . well, it is no matter. I shall find out soon enough."

We were driving through the Charing Cross Road by then. The few approved bookshops stood open, their wan light spilling on to the dark pavement outside. I remembered the book purges and burnings we have had after the invasion—after all, I led one such group myself. I did not like doing it, yet it was a necessity of the time. Gunther did not seem to pay much attention. His eyes slid over the grimy front-age of the shops. "Where are your famed picture palaces?" he said. "I have long de-sired to ensconce myself in the luxuries of the Regal or the Ritz." His eyes shone with a childish enthusiasm.

"I'm afraid most were destroyed in the Blitz," I said, apologetically.

He nodded. We were in Soho then, a squalid block of half-ruined buildings where the lowlifes of London made their abode. It was a hard place to police and patrol, filled with European émigrés of dubious loyalties. But it was useful, as such places inevitably are.

Along Shaftesbury Avenue the few theatres were doing meagre trade. The big show that year was *Servant of Two Masters*, an Italian comedy adapted to the English stage. It was showing at the Apollo. Dean Street itself was a dark street that never quite slept. Business was conducted in the shadows and, behind the apartments on the second floors, red lights burned invitingly. I saw doubt enter Gunther's eyes and I almost felt sorry for him. I had my own interest in his well-being or otherwise. My men were stationed unobtrusively in the street.

"This is the place," I said. I stopped the jeep and he stepped out and extended his hand. "Thank you, Everly," he said. "You are a gentleman."

I could see he liked that word. The Germans are a peculiar people. Having won the war they were almost apologetic about it. I said, "If your visit does not go well, there is a transport leaving back to Berlin tomorrow night. I can ensure you have a seat on it."

His eyes changed; as though he were seeing me for the first time.

"You never said what you do," he said.

"No," I agreed. "Goodbye, Mr. Sloam."

I left him there. I did not expect him to be so much trouble as he turned out to be.

2

Gunther stood outside 47 Dean Street for some time. Perhaps, already, he began to have second thoughts. On receipt of her letter, he had expected little more than a fond reunion with Ulla. Perhaps he saw himself as a sort of Teutonic white knight, riding to the rescue of a helpless maiden. He never really knew Ulla, or what she was capable of, though he didn't realise it until it was too late.

The address she had given him had been a theatre before the war. Now it was a sort of boardinghouse, with a handwritten sign on the door saying *No Vacancies!* in a barely-legible scrawl. The windows were dark. The front of house, once-grand, now looked dowdy and unkempt. Gunther looked about him and saw two shifty characters in the shadows across the road. They were smoking cigarettes and watching him. He gathered his courage and knocked loudly on the door.

There was no reply. The whole house felt silent and empty. He knocked again, louder, until at last a window overhead opened and an old woman stuck her head out and began cursing him in a mixture of English and gutter German. Almost, he wanted to take out his pen and note down some of the more inventive swearing.

"I'm looking for Ulla Blau!" He called up, when the old woman finally stopped, momentarily, for air.

The old woman spat. The spit fell down heavily and landed at Gunther's feet.

"The whore's not here," the old woman said, and slammed the window shut.

Now angry, Gunther began to hammer on the door again. The two observers watched him from across the street. They, too, had an interest in Fräuleine Blau's whereabouts.

At last the window opened again and the same old woman stuck her head out. "What?" she demanded, crossly.

"I need to see her!"

"I told you, she's not here!"

"Well, where is she?"

"I don't know, and I don't want to know!" the old woman said, and slammed the window.

Gunther stood in the street. He was tired now, and hungry, and he wanted a drink. He had hoped for a fond embrace, a night spent in a comfortable bed, with a bottle of good Rhine wine (which he had brought), and a willing companion to murmur sweet nothings into his ear. Instead he got this, and besides, the street smelled from uncollected garbage gathered every few paces on the broken sidewalk.

"Open the damn door or I'll break it down!" he said.

Then he waited. Presently there was a shuffling noise and then the door opened a crack and the old woman stuck her head out. "What are you, Gestapo?" she said.

"If I were the Gestapo," Gunther said, reasonably, "you'd already be answering my questions."

The old woman cackled. She seemed to have no fear of this strange German on her doorstep. "Do you have a drink?" she said.

Gunther brought out the bottle of wine and the old woman's eyes widened appreciatively.

"Come in, come in!" she said. "The night is cold and full of eyes."

Gunther followed her into the building.

The old woman's apartment was surprisingly comfortable. A fire was burning in the fireplace and Gunther sat down wearily on a red velvet sofa which sagged underneath him. The walls were covered with old photographs and playbills. The old woman herself reminded him somewhat of an old, faded revue actress. She bustled about, fetching glasses. They were good crystal, and when she saw his enquiring look she cackled again and said, "From Marks's, the filthy Jews. Now that was a fire sale!"

Gunther accepted the glass, his loathing for the old woman growing. He let her open the bottle, which she did deftly, then poured two glasses. The old woman drank hers rapidly and greedily, then refilled the glass. Her eyes acquired a brittle warmth.

"You have come from Germany?" she said.

"Berlin."

"Berlin! I have often wished to visit Berlin."

She spoke a bad but serviceable German.

"It is a great city."

"Not like this place," the old woman said. "London is a shithole."

Gunther silently agreed. He took a sip of his wine, mourning the loss of its planned usage. The wine brought back memories of warmer, happier times.

"I am looking for—" he began, and the old woman said, "Yes, yes. Ulla Blau. I told you, she is not here."

And this time he was not yet duly concerned. "This is the address she's given me."

"She was here," the old woman said. "She hires a room from me, at 30 Reichsmarks a month. I do not ask questions, Mr. Sloam."

"Has she gone away, then?" Gunther said.

"She is always coming and going, that one," the old woman said.

"Is she still acting? In the theatre, perhaps?"

The old woman snorted a laugh, then wiped it away when she saw Gunther's face. "Perhaps," she said. "Yes, perhaps. What do I know?" She took a long shuddering sip of wine. "I am just an old woman," she said.

Doubts, at this point, were finally beginning to enter Gunther's mind. "Well, what does she do, for money?"

"I am sure I don't know," the old woman said, huffily. Her glass of wine was empty again and she refilled it with unsteady hands. "You should have seen this place before the war," she said suddenly. "The theatres all alight and the public flowing on the pavements all excited and gay. The men handsome in their suits and the women pretty in their dresses. I saw Charlie Chaplin play the Hippodrome once." Her eyes misted over. "I don't blame you Germans," she said. "I blame the Jews, but there are no more Jews to blame. Who can we blame now, Mr. Sloam?"

"Can I see her room?" Gunther said.

The old woman sighed. She was coming to the realisation that Gunther Sloam could be very single-minded.

"I'm sure I can't let you do that," she said; but he saw the speculative glint in her eye.

"I could perhaps rent it, for a while," he offered. "I am a stranger in this town and the hour is getting late."

His hand, which he had dipped in his pocket, returned with a handful of notes. The woman's eyes tracked the movement of the money.

"When you put it like that . . ." she said.

Ulla Blau's room was an almost perfect square. It had once been a dressing room of some sort, or perhaps, Gunther thought a little uncharitably, a supply closet. The old woman, whose name, he had learned, was Mrs. White, stood in the doorway watching him with her bright button eyes. She swayed, from time to time, and hummed a tune under her breath. It sounded a little like the Horst Wessel song.

There was nothing of the personal in Ulla Blau's room. There was a bed, perfectly made up; a wardrobe and a vanity mirror; a small gas ring and a kettle; and that was about it. Gunther's imaginings of their reunion plunged further into doubt, for this was not the romantic abode he had perhaps envisioned. There were no clues as to Ulla's employment or whereabouts. Beyond the wall the noise of hurried sexual congress could be clearly heard. He glanced at Mrs. White, who shrugged. Gunther began to have an idea of what the majority of the rooms were used for.

Mrs. White moved aside to let him out. The corridor was long and dark and the communal bathroom was at one end of it. Gunther was, at this point, beginning to feel concern.

"And you do not know where she is?" he demanded of Mrs. White.

The old woman shrugged. She didn't know, or didn't care, or didn't care to know. Gunther dug out Ulla's note. *If I am not there*, she had written, *ask for the dwarf.*

I shall interject, at this point, to say that this dwarf was a person of considerable interest to us. We were anxious to interview him with regards to some matters which had arisen. This dwarf went by the name of Jurgen, and was of a Swiss nationality. He had come to London six months previous and was, moreover, the scion of a wealthy Zurich banking family, with connections high up within the party.

"Where can I find," Gunther said, and then felt silly, "the dwarf?"

He said it quite light-heartedly. But Mrs. White's reaction was the opposite. Her face turned a crimson shade and her eyes rolled in her head like those of a grand dame in a Christmas pantomime.

"Him? You ask me about *him*?"

Gunther was not aware of the reputation the dwarf had in certain circles. Mrs. White's reaction took him quite by surprise.

"Where can I find him?" he said mildly.

"Do not ask me that!"

Good wine, missed plans and bad company do not mix well. Gunther at last lost his patience.

"Listen to me, you silly old bat!" he said. He had done terrible things to survive on the Eastern Front. Now that man was before Mrs. White, and she cowered. Gunther jabbed an angry finger at the old woman's face. "Tell me where this damned dwarf is or by God I'll . . ."

She must have told him; he must have left. My men lost him, by accident or design, shortly after; and so the first I knew of it was the next morning, when Sergeant Cole called me and woke me from a blissful sleep, to tell me they'd arrested Gunther Sloam for murder.

3

By the time I made it to HQ they'd worked Gunther over a little; mostly I think just to keep their hand in. I told them to straighten him up and bring him to my office, along with two cups of tea. When they brought him in, he had a black eye, a swollen lip, and a bad temper.

"What is the meaning of this?" he said. "I am a citizen of the Reich, you can't treat me like this!"

"Please, Mr. Sloam, sit down. Cigarette?" I proffered the box. He hesitated then took one, and I lit him up. He took in all the smoke at once, and after that he was a little calmer.

"Say, what is the meaning of this?" I think only then my face registered with him, and he started. "You're that chap, Everly. I don't understand."

He looked around him at the office. The framed photograph of the Führer stared back at him from the wall.

"I'm sorry," I said. "I should have introduced myself more fully. I am *Kriminalinspektor* Tom Everly, of Gestapo Department D."

He looked at me in silence. His lips moved. He looked around the room again. When he at last spoke he was more subdued.

"Gestapo, eh?"

"I'm afraid so."

"But you're English!" he cried, turning on me accusingly.

"Yes?"

That stumped him. "When you said you studied in Berlin before the war . . ."

"It is not me who has to justify himself to you," I said.

"How do you mean?"

"Mr. Sloam, you have been arrested for murder."

"Murder!" His eyes were wild. "Listen, here!"

"No, you listen," I said. "We can do this the hard way. You've already had a little taste of that. Or we can do this the civilized way."

I waited and presently there was a knock on the door. Then Cole came in with the tea. He left it on my desk and departed. We'd had the routine down pat by then.

"Milk? Sugar?" I said.

Unexpectedly he smiled. "How very English," he said. "Two sugars, please, and milk too, why not." He sat down on the chair, hard. I passed him the tea and lit a fresh cigarette and watched him.

"You'd better tell me what happened last night," I said.

He sighed. "I don't know where to start," he said, dejectedly.

Gunther left the house on Dean Street around eight o'clock in the evening. When he stood outside, the thought that came to his mind was that the house was, indisputably, one of ill-repute.

What Ulla was doing in such a place he did not know. He could not believe that she prostituted herself, and could not understand how she came to live in such a squalid place. As I'd said to him before, he was a romantic—though that did not necessarily make him a fool.

Mrs. White had given him an address nearby. Gunther walked, not hurrying, but at a steady pace. He was well aware of the two shadows which detached themselves from the wall across the road, and followed. He did not increase his speed nor slow down, but his path was such that in a short amount of time he was able to shake them off. Taking a turning he hid down a dark alleyway as the two men walked past. He could hear them argue in low voices as he slunk in the other direction.

The night was thick with darkness. The buildings here were still half-ruined, destroyed in the Blitz, and served as hidey-holes for all kinds of illicit activities. Gunther watched himself, but wished he had a gun, a wish he was soon to fulfil. He smelled frying onions nearby and his stomach rumbled. He heard drunken laughter, soft footfalls, and a scream that was cut short. He saw four men sit by a lit lantern playing cards. He smelled cigar smoke. He heard someone muttering and moaning in a low, never ceasing voice.

At last he made it to the Lyric. It is a Victorian pub, and had remained undamaged during the war. Gunther, the romantic, found it charming. Opposite the pub stood the Windmill Theatre. It was the one source of bright light, and advertised nude *tableaux vivants*, as well as the exclusive appearance of Tran *und* Helle, the popular comedians, visiting London for seven nights only.

Gunther entered the pub. It was dark and dim inside, and the smell of beer, cigarette and cigar smoke hit him with their combined warmth. A small fire burned merrily in the fireplace. The atmosphere worked like a panacea on Gunther. He removed his coat and perched on the bar gratefully.

"Help you, sir?"

The bartender was bald and rotund and missing one eye, his left one. He turned a rag inside a beer stein, over and over and without much hope of making it clean.

"I'll have an Erdinger, please," Gunther said. "And a plate of *Schweinshaxe mit sauerkraut.* "

The bartender, without changing an expression, poured the beer and served it to Gunther.

"We don't have pork knuckle," he said. "Or sauerkraut."

Gunther closed his eyes and took a sip of the beer. He already felt light-headed from the wine he had consumed earlier with the old woman.

"Well, what do you serve?" he said.

"Pie."

"What sort of pie?"

"Pork pie."

"Then I shall have a pork pie, *bitte*."

The bartender nodded and kept wiping the stein. "That'd be twenty Reichs-marks," he said.

"Twenty!"

The bartender looked bored. Gunther cursed under his breath but paid. The bartender made the money disappear. Gunther lit a cigarette and looked about the pub. There were only a few men sitting around, and no women. No one looked in his direction. He began to get the sense that he wasn't welcome.

He took another sip of his beer.

"I am looking for *Der Zwerg*," he said; announcing it into the air of the pub.

No one moved. If anything, Gunther thought, they had become more still.

"Pie," the bartender said. Gunther looked down at the counter. A round, solid brick of pastry sat on a cracked plate. Gunther picked up the knife and fork. He cut through the pastry into the pink fleshy interior. He cut a slice and put it in his mouth. It was cold and rather flavourless. He chewed and swallowed.

"Delicious," he said.

Someone sniggered. When Gunther turned his head a tall thin figure rose from a bench against the wall and perched itself on a stool beside him. The man had the cadaverous look of a disappointed undertaker. The smile he offered Gunther was as honest as a Vichy cheque.

"You are new in town?" he said.

"What's it to you?" Gunther said.

"Nothing, nothing." The man rubbed his hands together as though cold. He re-minded Gunther a little of that Jew actor, Peter Lorre; he had starred in Fritz Lang's *M* nearly three decades earlier. "It is good to hear an honest German voice again."

"You are not from Germany."

"No. Luxembourg," the man confessed. That explained the accent. "It is a strange country, England, is it not? They are so dour, so resentful of you Germans. Do you know, I think, deep down, they believe they should have won the war."

He laughed, the same sort of insincere sound a hyena makes. "Beer, bartender!" he called, jovially. "And one for my friend here. Put it on my tab."

"You have been here long?" Gunther asked.

"Two years now," the man said. "I do a little business. Import-export, mostly. You know how it is."

Gunther did not. The beer arrived and he sipped from it. He forced himself to finish the pie. He had eaten worse on the front.

"This man," I said. "His name was Klaus?"

Gunther was pacing my office. He looked up, surprised. "Klaus Pirelli, or so he told me," he said. "Yes. How did you—?"

"He has given us a full statement," I said. "He says he drank beer with you and discussed the ongoing war in America, Leni Riefenstahl's latest film, the new African *lebensraum* and the import-export business. He says you got progressively drunker and increasingly aggressive. At some point you asked, loudly, where a man could get hold of a gun in this town. You became so voluble that he had to escort you outside. He says the last he saw of you, you were staggering down Great Windmill St., in the direction of Shaftesbury Avenue, waving your arms and swearing you would, "Get that bitch.'

Gunther stopped pacing. His mouth hung open. I almost felt sorry for him at that moment. In his comic horror he reminded me of the comedian, Alfred Hawthorne, who I had recently seen playing Bottom in a production of A *Midsummer's Night's Dream*.

"But that is *wahnsinn*!" He gaped at me like a landed fish. "It is madness! I did no such thing!"

"Can you prove it?"

"The other drinkers! The bartender! They were all witnesses—"

He looked at me, realisation slowly dawning.

"You are German," I said, sadly. "They are not."

"Listen, Everly, you've got to believe me!"

"Just tell me what happened," I said.

Gunther found the Luxembourgian trying. The man was obviously selling something, but Gunther wasn't sure what.

"I am looking for the dwarf," he said again.

"Him!" the Luxembourgian exclaimed.

"I was told I could find him here."

"He is not an easy man to find, *Herr* Jurgen."

"Is that his name?" Gunther said.

"You do not know his name, yet you seek to find him?" the Luxembourgian looked amused at that. "What is the nature of your business with the Count?"

"A Count, is he?" Gunther said. His head really was spinning. "Well, I want to know where Ulla Blau is." He grabbed the Luxembourgian by the lapels and shook him. "Do you know where Ulla is?" he demanded. His speech felt slurred, his tongue unresponsive. "I need to see her. She's in a lot of trouble."

The Luxembourgian gently removed Gunther's hands. "You need air, friend," he said. "I think you've had too much to drink."

"Don't be . . . ridiculous," Gunther said. His vision swam. He was dimly aware of his new friend putting his arm around his shoulders and steering him outside. Cold air hit his face like a slap, but it did not clear his confused thoughts. He began to stagger away from the pub. As he did, he saw a pair of shapely white legs, walking past. He raised his head and tried to focus. A good-looking woman wrapped in a thick fur coat walked away from him. As she passed under a gaslight, for just a moment, she turned her head and smiled.

"Ulla?" Gunther cried. "Ulla!"

There was something mocking in the woman's smile. She turned and walked away. Gunther lurched after her for a few more steps but she was long gone, and perhaps, he thought later, she had never been there at all. He tottered on his feet. Darkness opened all around him, like the entry to a sewer. He fell, hard, and lay on the ground. He closed his eyes, and dark sleep claimed him.

"And that is all you remember?" I said.

"All I remember, until some uncouth men roused me up on the street, administered a series of kicks for good measure, put me in irons and dragged me to your cellars to have another go."

He touched his black eye and winced. "Don't you see?" Gunther said. "I was drugged. The Luxembourgian must be in on it. He must have slipped something into my drink when I wasn't looking."

The mention of drugs caught my attention, and I looked at him in a new way.

"Besides," he said, with a laugh. "Who the hell was I supposed to have murdered?"

"Come with me."

He shrugged. This, he endeavoured to get across, was nothing to him. In that he was wrong.

He followed me along the corridor and down the stairs. The Gestapo had made its headquarters in Somerset House. We found the stout walls and easy access to the river compelling. I took him down to the makeshift morgue.

"What is this?" he said, and shivered. I ignored him. We proceeded to go in.

"Sir," *Kriminalassistent* West said, standing to attention.

"What is this?" Gunther demanded. We both ignored him. I gave West the nod. He pulled one of the refrigeration units open and slid out the gurney.

A corpse, covered in a sheet, lay on the cold metal tray.

Gunther's lips moved, but without sound. Perhaps he was beginning to realise the trouble he was in.

I gave West the nod again. He removed the sheet. Underneath it lay a naked female form. Her face had been blasted apart by the bullet from a Luger semi-automatic.

I watched Gunther closely. The horror on his face seemed genuine enough.

"Can you identify her?" I asked. He looked at the body mutely. His eyes took in the ruined faced, the still, cold body, her bejewelled fingers. He began to shake.

"No, no," he said. "It cannot be."

He stepped closer to the gurney. He took the dead hand in his.

"This ring," he said. It was a rather tawdry thing, a large chunky emerald set in copper. "I gave it to her. I remember buying it, from Kling's on Münzstrasse. It was a token of my love, just before they shipped me to the front."

"Gave it to whom?" I said, gently.

He looked at me, his eyes full of quiet despair.

"I gave it to Ulla Blau," he said.

4

The story could have ended here, but for the fact that Ulla Blau's death, though in some part not entirely without benefit, nevertheless put me in a somewhat awkward position.

I brought Gunther back to my office. I asked Sergeant Cole to bring us two coffees this time, and some Viennese pastries. You may wonder why I treated Gunther Sloam with such kids gloves. After all, the expedient act would have been to send him back down to the cellars for a second, more thorough work-over—to last only as long as it would take to extract a full and frank confession—then a speedy execution and burial by water. There were, as I mentioned, several reasons Somerset House was chosen for our headquarters, and easy access to the river was a not insignificant one. The corpses, sometimes, if not weighted enough, floated back up to the surface or caught in the Greenwich wharves on their way out to the sea, but that merely served to reinforce in people's minds the long and lethal reach of the Gestapo. Sometimes we had to make sure the corpses were lightly weighted, when a particular message needed to be sent.

Gunther wondered the same thing. I could see it in his eyes. He observed Sergeant Cole bring in the coffee and pastries with the eyes of a condemned man watching his executioner. I sat behind my desk and stirred a cube of sugar into my coffee.

"Cream?"

"Thank you."

He said that in a wondering voice. I smiled patiently and took a bite from my *apfelstrudel*. "They are not as good as on the continent, of course," I said, when I had chewed and swallowed. "But we do try our best, you see."

"I am sure it is delicious," he said. He didn't look like he tasted anything.

"I asked you, when we first met," I said. "What your friend was doing in London. You did not enlighten me."

"Everly, for God's sake . . . !" he began, then went *stumm*.

I waited him out.

"I don't know," he admitted at last. "I received this note, and I . . ." he buried his face in his hands. "I did not take it seriously. She said her life was in danger and I, I . . ."

"You were expecting nothing more than a pleasurable reunion," I said. He raised his face to me and his eyes flashed with anger.

"Now look here, Everly!" he said. "I did not kill her!"

"Do you know what Pervitin is?" I said.

"Of course," he said, without hesitation, but with a moue of distaste. "It is an artificial stimulant. A type of drug—what they call methamphetamines. They gave it to us during Barbarossa. It keeps you awake and gives you energy, and it lowers inhibition, which is useful in battle."

"It is also highly addictive."

"Yes," he said. "In our case the army didn't worry about it too much. Most of the people who took it were destined for death. I was just luckier than most."

"Your friend, Ulla Blau, came to London some years ago," I said. "London at that time was a city in ruin. A large occupying force was initially needed and soldiers, as soldiers are wont to do, require entertainments."

"What are you saying?"

"Ulla's theatre connections proved handy in supplying girls for the soldiers. At that time, in London, a warm body was cheaper than a loaf of bread, and easier to get. From the soldiers she could easily acquire extra supplies of Pervitin. These she sold back into the general populace. It wasn't, strictly speaking, legal, but legality didn't have much of a meaning in the immediate aftermath of the war."

"I don't believe you," he said.

I shrugged. "You can believe what you'd like to believe," I said. "But you can't dismiss the evidence of your own eyes. Somebody plugged a round of 9 mm bullets into her pretty little face, after all."

"That doesn't make her guilty!"

"It doesn't make her bloody innocent, either," I said.

He stared at me with hatred and his fingers curled into fists. He was going to go for me in a moment.

Then realisation dawned; I could see his expression change. "You don't think I killed her," he said, wonderingly.

"Look, Sloam," I said. I was tired and the pastry was cloyingly sweet. "It doesn't matter to me if you killed her or not. She was nothing but trouble and the world's a better place for her not being in it. However."

He watched me closely. I could see he was still aching to swing at me. He wasn't the first and he wasn't going to be the last.

"Either way it's a mess. You're a citizen of the *Deutsches Reich*, not just a colonial. So was Fräulein Blau, and as a former actress, her death would play for news. The last thing my superiors want is a fuss back in Berlin about a sordid murder in the colonies. Citizens of the Reich must feel they can travel safely to any part of the empire. This isn't 1946, Sloam. England's a peaceful place, and a faithful servant of the Führer."

"So where does that leave me?" he said. He wasn't slow when he didn't want to be.

"What would you do in my place?" I said.

He considered. "You'd announce her death as an unfortunate accident, and bury me somewhere out of sight with a bullet between my eyes."

I nodded. He wasn't an innocent, just the wrong man in the wrong place, and for all his war experience, he still thought like a character in one of his movies. "What did you think," I said, "that you'd come over here and rescue her?"

"I don't know what I thought," he said. "And I still don't believe she was guilty!"

"Which of us isn't guilty, Mr. Sloam?" I asked. "Which of us isn't guilty?"

He watched me. "I am not afraid to die," he said.

I pressed a button, and Sergeant Cole came in. Gunther tensed.

"Cole," I said. "Please show Mr. Sloam outside."

Gunther watched me with suspicion.

"There's a flight leaving for Berlin tonight," I said. "I'd advise you to be on it. Remember, I had made that offer before, and I'm unlikely to make it a third time. Sergeant Cole will take you to a hotel where you can clean up and get some rest. *Auf wiedersehen*, Mr. Sloam. I hope, sincerely, we do not meet again."

The hint of a smile touched his lips then. "Goodbye, *Kriminalinspektor* Everly," he said.

But I could see he did not mean it.

Cole dropped him off at the Albert in Covent Garden. It was basic, but clean. Gunther collected his key and went up to his room. He showered and changed. He did not sleep.

Of course the obstinate German did not take my advice. I had accused him of being a romantic and I wasn't wrong. Gunther, for all his battle experience in the *Wehrmacht*, still insisted, deep down, to think of himself as a character in one of his own cowboy pictures. All he could think about was Ulla Blau's ruined, once-beautiful face staring back at him from the mortuary slab. I think he believed himself untouchable. Most Germans did, after the war. There were still pockets of resistance in America, but few since we'd dropped the A-bomb on Washington D.C. The world belonged to Germany: for Gunther, that idea was as fixed as his notion of honour.

From the hotel, Gunther went out. For a time he walked through Covent Garden, which he found a dismal sort of place. Underneath the butchers' stalls the blood ran rancid, and the greengrocers' offerings of hard, lumpy potatoes and bent carrots depressed Gunther. The market had all the festivity of a Dachau.

He watched the people, though. Londoners moved about the market furtively, with the bent shoulders of a conquered people. They wore shabby clothes, the men in ill-fitting suits, the women in hand-me-down dresses that seemed to come from a German Red Cross charity stall. He saw few smiles. Here and there soldiers patrolled, but they were few in number, and seemed indifferent to the populace. As I had told Gunther, this England was resigned to its fate. The majority of the occupying force had moved on to other duties, in the new African territories or America. Now, only a skeleton barracks was left and, of course, the Gestapo.

Gunther walked past the opera house, where a prominent sign advertised the soprano's, Elisabeth Schwarzkopf, appearance that night. Along Drury Lane he saw a young boy in the shadows, peaked cap covering half his face, skulking. He paused to watch as first two men, and then a woman, stopped and seemed to make a furtive purchase. When the street was clear, Gunther crossed the road and approached the boy.

"What do you want, mister?"

"What have you got?" Gunther said.

The boy looked up at him in suspicion. "You're a German!" he said, accusingly.

Gunther shrugged.

"You want girls?" the boy said. "My sister is very clean."

"I need something to keep me awake," Gunther said. "You got some of that?"

The boy grinned. Relieved that this was just another punter. "Sure, sure," he said, expansively. "But it'll cost you."

Gunther took out a clip of bills, and the boy's eyes went wide and round. "Pervitin?" Gunther said.

The boy nodded. Gunther peeled off a twenty. "Tell me where you get it from," he said, "and there'd be another ten in it for you."

"Another twenty," the boy said, immediately.

"That's a lot of money," Gunther said. The boy nodded, his eyes still drawn to the cash. Gunther let him have the first note and waited.

The boy darted glances to either side of the street. "Seven Dials, mister," he whispered. His hand was extended for the rest of the money. "The Bricklayer's Arms. Ask for Doyle, the Irishman. And for God's sake, man, don't mention me. It's more than my job's worth."

Gunther gave him the other twenty. The boy ran off. At the end of the street he paused and turned back. He stuck two fingers up at Gunther. "Nazi go home!" he shouted. Then he turned and ran away.

Gunther walked off. My men were watching him, of course. We had not been able to locate the dwarf. He usually resided at a house in Mayfair, near the Swiss ambassador's residency. The dwarf was as good as untouchable, but Gunther didn't know that. That suited me fine.

He walked with the same determined gait of a city dweller. Though he did not know his way he did not appear lost. He did not stop to look at the sights. He made enquiries politely but with a certain force; and the people of London still, when they heard a German voice, were trained to reply helpfully and quickly.

Seven Dials was only a short walk away. It was a maze of narrow, twisting alleyways between Covent Garden and Soho, a cesspit of racial degradation, or so according to my superior, SS-*Obergruppenführer* Oswald Pohl. An efficient administrator, he was the overseer of the camps erected to deal with the Jewish question during the war. A falling out with his patron, Himmler, after the war, however (the nature of which I never quite knew) saw him exiled to Britain to supervise the local Gestapo, after the former bureau chief, SS-*Brigadeführer* Franz Six, had an unfortunate and fatal encounter with a bullet. Six was leading an *einsatzgruppe* on a hunt for missing Jews in Manchester at the time.

Pohl, my current superior, took over the job with his customary efficiency, but little enthusiasm. He was a keen lover of the arts, and found England stifling. I also happened to know he'd been a fan of Ulla Blau.

Standing at the Seven Dials, Gunther was faced with roads leading in every direction away from him. It was as though he stood in the centre of a spider bite, and the infection spread outwards in wavy paths. Rundown drinking establishments faced him from each point of the compass. He saw the Bricklayer's Arms, and two women fighting volubly over a bottle of gin at the shabby entrance. He stepped around them and entered the pub. Already, he was growing sick of the sight and the smell of British pubs.

Inside it was dark, dim, and smelled of the sewers. Gunther lit a cigarette to combat the smell. He looked about him and hostile or indifferent faces stared back at him. He went to the bar and leaned across. "I am looking for Doyle, the Irishman," he said.

"What's it to me?" the bartender said.

Gunther put money on the counter. He did not have much but, in London, Reichsmarks seemed to go a long way. At the sight of the money there was a collective in-drawing of breath.

"I'm Doyle," said a tall specimen.

"I'm Doyle," said a fat, red-haired man.

"I'll be your doll, sailor," said a bald women with very few teeth and a leer.

Gunther waited. His stillness was born of the war. A shadow stirred by the far wall. It rose and the others faded into the background.

The man stepped close. He was a short, wiry man, in a chequered suit and a jaunty flat-top hat with a red feather in the band. His knuckles were scabbed like a bare-knuckle boxer's. He jabbed a finger at Gunther's chest.

"What do you want?" he asked.

"Are you Doyle?"

"Depends who's asking."

"My name's Sloam. I was a friend of Ulla Blau."

Doyle retreated a step at the name. "Ulla is dead," he said. His voice was softer.

"I know."

"Heard they found her by the river," the Irishman said. "Some maniac did her in."

He took in Gunther's beat-up face. Not with suspicion, Gunther thought. But a confirmation of something he already knew.

"You say you were friends?"

"Old friends," Gunther said. Something in the Irishman's eyes made him trust him; he couldn't say what it was. "We'd lost touch, until recently."

"I liked Ulla," the Irishman said. "I don't care what they say about her."

"What do they say about her?" Gunther said; but of course, he thought he already knew.

"She poisoned those boys!" the bald woman said, savagely. She startled Gunther, who didn't notice her creeping close. "The poor boys in Great Ormond. It's a hospital," she said, into Gunther's bemused face. "For children. They needed medication, pain relief."

"Do you know what heroin is?" Doyle said.

"Yes," Gunther said, startled. "It's a medication made by Bayer."

"You can't get it here," Doyle said. "So . . ." he shrugged.

"She cut it with rat poison," the bald woman said, and spat. "Twenty-one children, dead, in agony."

"Now, Martha, you don't know that," Doyle said. Gunther felt sick.

"She was always good to you," Doyle said. "Who do you come to when you need your medication?"

"You and your filthy comrades," the woman said. "We should have stood with the Allies in the war, Doyle. We shouldn't have stayed neutral." She spat again. "Neutral," she said. "Isn't that just another word for collaborator."

Doyle slapped her. The sound, like a gunshot, filled the room. "You're getting above yourself, Martha," he said. The woman glared at him defiantly; then the fight went out of her.

"I need it, Doyle," she said, whining. "I need it."

Gunther watched. He felt sick to his stomach. He could not look away. He could not believe what the woman had said about Ulla. Doyle reached in his pocket and came back with two small pills which he tossed to the woman, like dog biscuits to a pet. She caught them eagerly. "Don't go opening your big gob of shite, now," Doyle said.

"I won't, Doyle. Honest."

"I liked Ulla, whatever they said about her," Doyle said, sadly. He turned back to Gunther.

"Let's have a drink," he said.

5

It may have occurred to Gunther, at this point, that all the men he'd so far encountered belonged to countries that have remained neutral during the war. The Swiss, the Luxembourgian and the Irish were rewarded, for their careful non-involvement, with the status of sovereign protectorates of the Third Reich, and enjoyed a great deal of autonomy as a consequence.

"Ulla spoke of you," Doyle said.

"She did?" Gunther said, in a mixture of pleasure and surprise.

Doyle's smile transformed his face. "She called you the one who got away."

They were sitting in the back room of the pub. A bottle of whiskey sat between them. Gunther only sipped at his glass. Doyle drank steadily; it didn't seem to hamper him in any way.

"You were foolish to come see me," Doyle said. "You are lucky to be alive."

"Would you have killed me, then?"

"People who come to the Dials asking questions don't always come out again."

Gunther shrugged. "So why spare me?" he said.

"I'd heard you were in town. Heard you were picked up by the Gestapo, too." He downed a shot and refilled the glass and grimaced. "Filthy animals," he said.

"The Gestapo is a necessary organ of the state," Gunther said, primly. He was still a good German. Doyle shot him a look of disgust. "Have you asked yourself why they let you walk?" he said. "By rights you should be floating past the Isle of Dogs around this time. Depending on the tide."

Gunther shrugged. I think he had an idea. "I want to know who killed her," he said.

"She's dead," Doyle said. "Let it go. This isn't your country, or your cause. Go back to Berlin, make movies, find yourself a nice girl."

"A nice girl? In Berlin?" Gunther said. Doyle smiled; reluctantly, it seemed.

"What did she say about me?"

"She said you were a good man, and that good men were hard to find. She was drunk when she said it, mind."

"That does sound like Ulla."

"Good old Ulla," Doyle said.

"Did you kill her?" Gunther asked, softly; the question hung between them like a cloud of ash. They stared at each other across the table.

Doyle broke eye contact first. He shrugged indifferently and refilled his glass. "I had no reason to kill her," he said. "We did business, that's all."

"Drugs."

"I don't advise you to go around asking questions," Doyle said. "Go home. Be a good German."

"But heroin?" Gunther said.

"It is a powerful analgesic," Doyle said. "We need drugs, *Herr* Sloam. If the Reich won't provide, someone should."

"I don't believe she was involved—" Gunther began.

Doyle banged the glass on the table.

"Never trust an actress," he said. "Oh, Ulla knew what she was doing. Whores, black market medicine—other stuff too, I heard. Nothing to do with me. She knew. She was planning her retirement. Unfortunately, someone retired her first."

He drank. The bottle was half empty.

"It's nothing to me," he said.

Gunther said, "Where can I buy a gun?"

Everyone so far was being very helpful. It was as though London was going out of its way to be obliging to her accidental German tourist. He was as rare and unwelcome as a three-pound note.

So why, Gunther wondered, was he practically being given the keys to the city?

Back in the pre-War days, in '32 or so, when he was young and carefree, and National Socialism seemed, on a good day, like a bad punchline to an off-colour joke, Gunther had worked on a picture called *Der Traumdetektiv*, for the Jewish director Max Ophüls. Gunther's commission was to produce a surrealist piece of *film noir*, a sort of unreal history in which Germany, faced by her many enemies, nevertheless won the Great War. He remembered little from the finished product—which he had done quickly and for little money—but that the detective figure, whose name he could not remember, at some point entered a dusty old bookshop whose strange proprietor was played by the Hungarian actor Szőke Szakáll.

He remembered it now as he entered Blucher's, across the road from W. & G. Foyle and next to a florist, on the Charing Cross Road. The shop was low-ceilinged and dark. On a rack outside copies of the *Daily Mail* were displayed. It was Britain's sole remaining paper. Gunther picked up a copy and leafed through it quickly. It was at the bottom of page 5 that he found it. *Mystery Woman Discovered Dead*. The article was only a few paragraphs long. The unknown woman was believed to be a dancer—the implication was clear—and likely took her own life. Gunther thought of Ulla Blau on the mortuary slab with her face shot clean off and fought a rise of bile. He replaced the newspaper on the stand and stepped carefully into the store. A bell rang as the door opened. Poor yellow light fell down in drops. All about Gunther, books were piled up in haphazard piles. They were dusty and rust-spotted, many of them damaged by fire. Gunther smelled old smoke, and cat piss.

"Can I help you?"

The man really did look a little like the actor, Szakáll. He was bespectacled and rotund, with the kind of hair that looked like a hairpiece but wasn't. He sat behind a desk laden with books, his hands folded over his ample stomach.

"You're Blucher?"

The man spread his arms as though to say, *who else can I be?*

"You sell many books?"

"Books?" Blucher said. His myopic eyes looked at Gunther sadly. "Who today has need of books."

"They look like they'd been in a fire."

"Oh, these are all approved titles," Blucher said. "But you know how it is, people get carried away."

Gunther remembered the public book burnings in Berlin, after the Führer's rise to power. "Anything you recommend?"

"Have you tried *Mein Kampf*? It sells like plum cakes at a church fundraiser."

"I read it," Gunther said.

"Which part?"

"Chapters 1 and 2, and most of chapter 3, I think," Gunther said, and Blucher laughed, shortly and abruptly. The laugh made him cough. He drank water, daintily, from a glass perched on his desk, and dabbed at his lips with a handkerchief.

"Yes," he said. "It is no Sebastian Bruce *heftromane*, I'll admit as much. You are visiting London?"

"Yes."

"It is a pleasant time of year."

Gunther stared at him. The man shrugged. "Perhaps you can visit the countryside?" he suggested. "Yorkshire, I am told, is very nice."

"You have not been?"

"I would go, but who'd mind the shop?" the man said.

"*Frau* Blucher?" Gunther suggested. Outside, he thought he heard the neighing of a horse; but it must have been in his imagination.

"Alas, I have not been blessed with a wife," Blucher said. "Not for many years. She died, you see."

"In the war?"

"Appendicitis."

"I'm sorry."

Blucher shrugged. *What can you do*, he seemed to silently suggest. The silence dragged. The books lay still, heavy with ash and ink.

"I was told you'd be coming round here," Blucher said. "Gunther Sloam. You are becoming quite notorious, in some circles."

"How do you know me?"

"London is a small place. Word spreads. You were a friend of the actress, Ulla Blau."

"You knew her?"

"Her talent spoke for her. She was magnificent in *Die Grosse Liebe*."

"It was her best picture," Gunther said. Blucher shrugged again. "It was *schmalz*, but you knew that already."

Gunther looked at him with new suspicion. The man laughed. He took off his glasses and polished them with the handkerchief. When he put them back on his small, shrewd eyes assessed Gunther. "I am not a Jew," he said. "If that is what you were thinking."

"Where are you from, *Herr* Blucher?"

"A small town in Austria. Not unlike our illustrious leader," Blucher said. "I came out here in 1947, shortly after the war. I have always admired the English writers.

Who knows, some of them may even still be alive." He stretched his arms to encompass his shop. "As you can see, I prospered."

Gunther said, "I need to buy a gun."

"It is quite illegal, *Herr* Sloam."

"A man has a right to defend himself."

"Why not ask your friends at the Gestapo?"

Did anyone in London know his business? Gunther tapped his fingers on the cover of a book. The smell of burnt paper disinclined him from wanting to light a cigarette.

"Did you know her?" he said.

"Ulla?" the man's eyes misted over. "She was a beautiful woman," he said.

"Do you know who killed her?"

Blucher looked at him mildly. "I thought you did."

"That is a lie!"

Blucher sighed. He pushed back his chair with great deliberation, and stood up, panting. He pressed a hidden button, and a hidden drawer popped open in his desk. He brought out an object wrapped in cloth and unwrapped it. It was a Luger, perfectly clean. It was the sort of gun Gunther had used in the war. The sort of gun that only a day earlier took care of Ulla Blau.

"Will this do?" Blucher said.

"I want to know who killed her."

"Forget Ulla Blau," the bookseller said, with infinite sadness. "Finding her killer won't bring her back. Go home, Gunther Sloam. There is nothing for you here but death."

"You know something, I think," Gunther said. He took the gun and examined it. "I would need bullets," he said.

"Of course."

Blucher brought out a clip of ammunition from the same drawer and handed it to Gunther. "The fee is fifty Reichsmarks."

"Where did you get this gun?"

"A gun," Blucher said, sadly. "Are we short of guns, *Herr* Sloam? Of those we have an overabundance. It is not guns but medicines we need. But how do you heal a broken soul?"

Gunther loaded the gun. He gave the bookseller the money. The man made it disappear.

"I'll tell you a joke," Blucher said. "One day Hitler visited a lunatic asylum. When he came in, all the patients raised the arms and cried, "Heil Hitler!" Suddenly, Hitler saw one man whose arm wasn't raised. "What is the meaning of this? Why don't you salute like the rest?" he demanded. The man said: "My Führer, I'm an orderly, not a madman!""

He gave Gunther an expectant look, then shrugged in resignation.

"Where did Ulla get her drugs?" Gunther said.

"Who knows," Blucher said. "I try not to ask questions which might get me killed. You'd do well to do the same."

"What do you wish to tell me, *Herr* Blucher?" Gunther said. He sensed that underneath the bookseller's placid exterior there was a current of rage.

"Did you love her?" Blucher said. Gunther looked away. He was embarrassed by the naked look in the man's eyes. Blucher was *hurting*.

"Once. Yes."

"She was radiant. So alive. She understood a man cannot live by violence alone. There must be joy. There must be light, and music. Without her, London will be unbearable."

"Tell me what you know," Gunther said. He felt a pulse of excitement. "Tell me. Was it the dwarf?"

"The dwarf!"

The bookseller made his way ponderously around the desk. "I should not be talking with you," he said. "You are putting us both in danger." He looked like he was trying to reach a difficult decision. "Wait here," he said, at last. He waddled away towards a small door. "I'll make us a cup of coffee."

Gunther stood, waiting. He tucked the gun into the small of his back, under the shirt. He browsed the shelves. Hitler's *Mein Sieg*; the book he wrote after the victory. Books on natural history, in English, with hand-painted plates depicting vibrantly coloured birds. It occurred to Gunther he had not heard birdsong since he'd arrived.

The silence grew oppressive. The dust tickled his nostrils and made him want to sneeze. The books stared at him in mute accusation. *It wasn't me*, he wanted to say. *I was just following orders*. The seconds lengthened.

"*Herr* Blucher?"

There was no reply. Gunther let the moment lapse. He fingered the spine of an ancient volume on moths. It was loused with worm tracks. The dust tickled his throat. The gun felt heavy in the small of his back. He went to the door and knocked, softly.

"*Herr* Blucher?"

Still there was no reply and Gunther, with a sense of mounting dread, pushed the door open. He was afraid of what he would find.

Beyond, there was nothing but a small kitchenette. Gunther heaved a sigh of relief. Blucher was sitting in a folding chair by the sink. A kettle began to shriek on the open top stove. Blucher was smiling faintly. His hands were folded quite naturalistically in his lap. He evidently fell asleep, and slept so soundly, even the mounting cry of the kettle would not wake him.

"Wake up, Blucher," Gunther said. "Blucher, wake up."

Later, in my office, he could not explain why he acted the way he did. Why he paced that small kitchenette, entreating Blucher to wake up, Blucher to stand, Blucher to speak to him. When all the while, of course, he was perfectly aware of the smell of gunpowder, of the smell of blood, as familiar and as intimate as a comrade on the Eastern Front; and of the small neat hole drilled in Blucher's forehead. He was aware of all that, and yet as in a dream he spoke to Blucher; he told him of Ulla, of time spent in a high attic room, of stolen kisses in Unter den Linden, of the whistle of a train taking soldiers to battle. That whistle, long ago, seemed to him now to intertwine with the hissing kettle. It brought with it instantaneous memories, long kept at bay: of Ulla's sweat-slicked body in the moonlight, of the feral call of air raid sirens, of the march of booted feet, of jubilant voices crying out the Horst Wessel

Song. He thought of the Führer's voice on the wireless, of crumpled bedsheets and her voice, thick with sleep, saying, "Please, don't go."

It was those last words that he carried with him on the way to the east; those words that kept him company in amidst the snow and the blood. "Please, don't go." But when he returned, a different man under a different sky, she was long gone. Sometimes, under the blanket of the cold Russian night, he looked up at the stars and imagined he could see her.

At last, Gunther removed the kettle from the stove. He turned off the gas. He took one last look at Blucher's corpse. A second door, he saw, led out of the kitchenette. He pushed it open and stepped outside, into an alleyway running at the back of the bookshop. He looked left and right but saw no one, and he slipped away. My men, who were only watching the front of the shop, lost him then.

6

When Sloam failed to reappear, my men finally entered Blucher's. They found the proprietor slumped in his chair with the bullet hole between his eyes, and Gunther gone. Then they called me with the bad news.

I did not mind Gunther on the loose. After all, I had set him free myself. I had telephoned Blucher earlier that morning, and advised him that Sloam may well pay him a visit later in the day. I also told Blucher he could sell Sloam a gun. A man with a gun, sooner or later, makes his presence felt.

What I had not expected, however, was for Blucher to be so stupid as to commit suicide by gunmen.

For a time I considered that Gunther may be the killer. His whereabouts were unknown. He was armed, and potentially dangerous. But I had sent him to rattle a nest of wasps. That the wasps bit back, I supposed, was only to be expected.

Blucher must have been killed to keep him quiet. That fact stared me in the face, and the fact that the lying scum Austrian piece of shit had held out on me.

If there was one thing you could say about Hanns Blucher, it was that the man was a professional liar. His story for Gunther was good. Parts of it were even, almost, true. He was born Erich Dittman, in Gratz, Austria, the son of a shoemaker and a seamstress, the middle child of five. His criminal career began early. He was a good little pickpocket, graduated to burglary and robbery by the age of 16, and after a time in prison settled on the more tranquil profession of fence in stolen goods. When war came he escaped to France then, when France fell, to Luxembourg. By then he had changed his identity twice. When the war ended, Hermann Blecher was a well-established rare books dealer in Luxembourg City. He had avoided the deportations and the camps, and he thought his papers were good.

They were; almost.

How he got out of Luxembourg alive I never quite learned. He reappeared in London and was ensconced in his premises on the Charing Cross Road as though he'd always been there. In truth, he had taken the lease on an empty shop at no. 84, formerly owned by a Jew named Marks.

He called himself Blucher. He was as enmeshed in criminal enterprise as ever. And he was still a Jew.

When I first marched into his shop and he saw me, he knew it was over. He did that little shrug he always did. By rights I should have had him tortured and disposed of. But he was more useful to me alive.

Only now he was dead, like Blau.

Someone was tying up loose ends.

Gunther walked through the city that day haunted by the shadow of deaths. Usually the ghosts did not bother him overmuch; he had made his peace with the atrocities of war. What he had done, he had only done to survive. In a post-war screenplay, never produced (*Das grosse Übel*, c. 1948), the love interest dies in the arms of the hero, a veteran of Normandy on a quest to avenge the death of his sister at the hands of black market speculators. As she lies dying, she kisses him, one last time, with lips stained red with blood, and tells him he was not a bad man for the things he did. He was just an imperfect man in an imperfect world, trying to do the right thing.

She dies. The hero embraces her. Her blood soaks into his shirt. The hero walks away, into the shadows.

When he'd sent the script in to Tobis, he was told quite categorically not to waste his time. Demand was for domestic comedies, lighthearted affair, adventure. "Write another Western," Rolf Hansen told him over coffee, before he got up and left him with the cheque. "There's always demand for that sort of thing. Oh, and Gunther?"

"Yes?"

"There is no black market in Germany. You should know better by now. Heil Hitler."

No, Gunther thought, walking through city streets slick with defeat, bounded by empty buildings like skulls, where the dead whispered through the gaping eye sockets of broken windows. There was no crime in this new Reich, no prostitution unless one counted that of the soul, no murder but that carried out by the state.

It was a land of hard-working, virtuous and prosperous people. A dream come true.

Already they were bringing civilization even to Britain. Viennese pastries and public concerts of Wagner and Bruckner, *Reinheitsgebot* beer, shining gymnasiums where the soldiers of tomorrow could be taught, new factories in the north where the goods needed for the empire could be cheaply and efficiently manufactured. And no more Jews, but for a few desperate survivors like Blucher, living out their last days like rats in the shadows.

He was not usually this bleak, you understand. All of this just brought back the bad memories. When we got him later he was done, he said.

"It's just something about this godforsaken island," he told me. "The cold and damp and the bloody futility of it all, Everly. It starts to seep into your soul after a while."

"I'm afraid we did not present London's best side to you on your visit," I said, and he snorted. "Oh, but I think you did," he said. "Don't worry, I won't be coming back."

Like I said, it wasn't much of a time for tourism.

Gunther retraced his steps. He tried to ensure he wasn't being followed. He wrapped himself tight in his good cashmere coat. He went back to the Lyric. A different bartender tended bar. The same indistinguishable faces drank in the corners. No one spoke German or, at any rate, no one was answering his questions.

He did not see the Luxembourgian, Klaus Pirelli, and he left.

Then he went back to the start. The house on Dean Street stood with its door closed and red lights burning behind the windows. He banged on the door but no one was answering and he did not see the old woman, Mrs. White. There was a new watcher across the street: not one of mine. He sidled up to Gunther as Gunther turned to leave. It was dark by then.

"You are looking for a girl?"

"I am looking," Gunther said. "For a dwarf."

The other man shrugged. "I see it is true what they say about you Germans. You have peculiar tastes. But each to their own, as my old nan always said."

Gunther stared at him. He had the urge to do violence. The man was too thin, his teeth too crooked, his coat too shabby, his hair too coarse. Gunther took out the gun and grabbed the man hard by the lapels and shoved him against the wall and put the gun in his face. The man looked at him placidly.

"Do you know a man called Klaus Pirelli?"

"What's it to you, friend?" the man said.

"I could shoot you right now."

"You could indeed, Fritz."

Gunther slapped him with the gun across the face, hard. The man's head shot back and slammed against the wall. He crumpled to the ground. Gunther put the gun to his forehead. "Tell me where I can find him."

The man moved his jaw, grimaced, and spat out blood. "Everyone's tough with a gun in their hand," he said. "Why don't you try asking nicely, or buying me a drink."

"I don't understand you English," Gunther said, frustrated. He pulled away from the man. He felt ashamed. The man got up slowly to his feet. Gunther took out cigarettes and offered one to the man, who took it. Gunther lit them up. The man took a deep drag on his cigarette and exhaled a stream of smoke. "If you're not looking for a girl," he said, reasonably, "why are you hanging about outside a whorehouse?"

"I came here for a girl," Gunther said, shortly. "She died."

"I'm sorry."

"I almost believe you," Gunther said, and the man laughed.

"I can take you somewhere where there are other girls. It's best to let go of the dead, friend, or soon you become one yourself."

"You're a philosopher as well as a pimp?"

"I'm neither, friend. Just a man doing what he has to do to survive."

"Do you know where I can find this man, Pirelli?"

The man considered. "I can't tell you where he is," he said at last, "but I can tell you where he'd be."

"Where is that?"

"Somewhere where there is drink, and music, and girls."

"And you know all these places, I assume?"

"What can I say, I have a thirst for knowledge."

Gunther laughed. He stuck his hand out. "Gunther Sloam," he said.

The other man looked at the offered hand. Finally he took it. "You can call me Janson."

"One name's as good as the next," Gunther said, amicably.

7

There began a night in which perception began to fracture like a mirror for Gunther. The city was a nightmarish maze of dark streets in which faceless gunmen haunted every corner. He thought about dead girls and dead Jews, and wondered who would be the next to die.

They started at the Albert, a cavernous pub where ancient families feuded with each other over pints of watery beer; continued to the Admiral's Arms, where everyone looked like a vampire; and settled for a time at the Dog and Duck over glasses of potent, home-made sherry.

"When the occupation is completed there I will go to America," Janson said. "I have a great admiration for the Americans, for all that they lost their war."

"What will you do?" Gunther said.

"I would become a writer for their pulps."

"It's a living," Gunther allowed. "Not a very profitable one, though."

"I write quickly and I have what it requires most," Janson said.

"And what's that?" Gunther said.

"Despair."

Gunther shook his head and swallowed his drink. Visions of Ulla Blau's ruined face kept rising in his mind.

"Were you in the war?" he said.

"Does it matter?"

"No," Gunther said, tiredly. "I suppose it doesn't."

They rose from their seats and stepped out into the night. It had truly fallen by then, and here and there, solitary gas lamps began to wink into being, casting murky pools of yellow light around them. Janson palmed a pill and dry-swallowed. "You want some?" he said.

Gunther said, "Sure."

During the war they had functioned as little more than animated corpses: kept alive by minimal food rations and handfuls of drugs. Gunther's memories of the march on Moscow were fragmentary. They killed for the sake of killing, killed because it was the only thing left for them to do. It wasn't glory or the Führer that kept them on that march. It was the little pills manufactured by Bayer's; that, and simple, total desperation.

The veneer of humanity was stripped off Gunther during the long march, during the slaughter and the occupation. He had never hated Jews, had no feelings at all for the Russians, but he was just one man; and when it came down to it, he wanted to survive.

In this world, I think, you do what you must to live: another minute, another hour, another day.

Sometime during that long evening they stumbled into the Berlin. It is a club situated on the embankment, next to the gardens or what used to be gardens before the war, and facing the south bank. Gunther stopped outside. The Ferris wheel rotated slowly on the opposite side of the river, softly illuminated against the night sky. Gunther was drunk. His body was on fire from the methamphetamine. The Thames snaked dark and in its depths he saw Ulla's face rising up to him, laughing bubbles. He tottered.

Janson said something to the doormen and they laughed.

Money changed hands. The money was Gunther's. They went inside. It was a large room with a stage at one end. Girls danced on the stage, naked but for the fans they held. They moved about the stage in complicated patterns. A piano played, softly. Gunther heard conversation, laughter, the clink of glasses. He saw S.S. men in uniform sitting at one table, each officer with a girl in his lap. Important locals in last year's suits swanned about. They had bad skin and bad teeth and great big booming laughs. Gunther ordered a drink and thought he'd had enough of this town.

It was then that he saw him.

The Luxembourgian stepped out of the door marked *Bathroom*, his hands still wet. He dried them on his trousers. He wore a pinstripe suit and a pink shirt and a muted tie. His eyes darted nervously from side to side but he put on a smile as charming and shiny as a false diamond bracelet. Then he, too, saw Gunther.

The smile hovered but stayed in place. Gunther got up. He did not dare pull out the gun. Not with the officers present. The Luxembourgian's smile grew more assured. He passed through the throng of people like an eel until he came to Gunther.

"Sit down."

"I've been looking for you," Gunther said, and he matched the man's smile with his own, cold and hard.

"I said sit *down!*"

Gunther looked down. Held in the Luxembourgian's manicured fingers was a small Röhm .22 Derringer gun.

Gunther sat down. Pirelli sat on a stool opposite. He trained the gun on Gunther, holding it between his legs. "Don't bloody move, man."

"I wasn't going anywhere."

The bartender arrived. She was a young girl bare to the waist but for dark kohl painted over her nipples. She brought the Luxembourgian a drink without being asked. He kept one hand on the gun and with the other downed his scotch and grimaced. "They know me here, you see."

"You're a difficult man to find."

"Hardly!" The man's eyes kept shifting. Gunther was primed, every muscle in his body singing alertly. "Listen, if this is about the other night . . ."

"What do you *think* it's about?"

"You didn't have to kill Blucher!"

It came out almost as a shout. A couple of heads turned. Then the girls on the stage began to gyrate erotically and what attention they'd been given was gone. It was just the two of them on the bar at the Berlin. At this point, too, one of my men spotted Gunther. He did not approach but quietly went for a phone.

"I didn't kill him," Gunther said, startled.

"Didn't you? You come to town, start poking about, and two days later both Ulla and Erich are dead?"

"Who's Erich?"

"Blucher." Pirelli was sweating, Gunther saw. And he realised Pirelli, too, must be on Pervitin. He was wired worse than an S-mine. "That was his real name."

"How did you know him?"

Pirelli was so jumpy, Gunther was worried he'd press the trigger by accident. But the man seemed almost eager to talk.

"In Luxembourg. I helped him when his trouble got bad. Helped him get out and establish himself here." He sneered at Gunther. "What are you going to do, rat on me to your pals in the Gestapo? They can't touch me. I have connections. I'm a foreign national."

"You could try telling that to the fishes," Gunther said, with a touch of cruelty. "When they dump you in the Thames."

"They wouldn't dare!" A flash of anger or defiance in his eyes. "How do I know you didn't kill Erich?"

"Why did you set me up? You spiked my drink at that godawful pub."

"The Lyric's decent," Pirelli said; almost offended.

"Why did you do it!" Gunther said.

"Listen, friend, I'm the one holding the gun," Pirelli said.

"Blucher knew something. He was going to tell me. Then someone shot him."

"Someone, someone!" But he could see it in Pirelli's eyes. The man was afraid of something. He kept looking everywhere but at Gunther.

"Who are you working for?" Gunther threw at him.

"I work for myself."

"A man like you? You're just the hired help."

Gunther thought to needle the man. But Pirelli's mouth curved in a mocking smile. At that moment one of the S.S. officers approached them, accompanied by a woman draped on his arm.

"*Signore* Pirelli!"

Gunther reached between them and grabbed Pirelli's hand in a painful grip, twisting it. He yanked the gun from the Luxembourgian's hand, hearing a bone break. Pirelli cried in pain.

"You are not happy to see us?"

Pirelli put on a pained smile. "My apologies, *Sturmbannführer*," he said, through gritted teeth. "I seem to have hurt my hand."

The S.S. officer was round and jolly. His companion was buxom and blonde.

"Let me look at that," he said, grabbing for Pirelli's hand. Pirelli screamed. The *Sturmbannführer* laughed jovially and called the bartender for ice. "You'll be fine in no time," he said. He turned to Gunther and studied him, and under the jovial exterior Gunther saw cold, dark eyes.

"Who is your friend?"

"Gunther Sloam, *Sturmbannführer*," Gunther said, stiffly.

"Sloam, Sloam," the S.S. man said. His companion leaned over his shoulder and eyed Gunther with interest. "Where did you serve?"

"258th Infantry Division, sir."

"The heroes of Moscow!" the *Sturmbannführer* declared, delightedly. "Why do I know your name, Sloam?"

"I'm sure I can't say, sir."

"A drink for my friend here," the S.S. man called. "A true hero of the Reich. So good to hear civilized German in this godforsaken place. How is Berlin?"

"Still there, last I checked."

"Magnificent!" the man laughed. His belly shook. His eyes remained cold and suspicious. "You two seem to be having a bit of an argument."

"It's nothing, sir. A minor disagreement."

"Good, good. We do not like trouble here in London, Sloam. This is a peaceful place. The natives are most obliging." He squeezed his companion's bottom and she squealed delightedly. Gunther averted his gaze. The girl's eyes were colder even than the *Sturmbannführer*'s.

"So I see, sir."

"Well, Pirelli, about that thing we discussed—"

"I will have the shipment to you by tomorrow," the Luxembourgian said. He was nursing a pack of ice on his broken hand and scowling.

"First thing, Pirelli. Sloam—" he nodded, cordially, and waddled off with the girl on his arm.

"Drugs?" Gunther said.

"Nudie pictures," Pirelli said. "The *Sturmbannführer* is a *connoisseur.*"

"So I see."

"Give me back my gun."

"Why don't we take a walk?"

"No!"

"What is it, Pirelli? I'm not going to kill you."

"Listen to me, Sloam. It's safer here. I don't want to die like the others."

"Who killed them?"

Unexpectedly, Pirelli laughed. "No one," he said. His whole body shook.

"Get up. We're going outside."

"You won't dare shoot me here."

"Only one way to find out. Move."

Pirelli got up. "You're a fool," he said.

"Why was Ulla killed?" Gunther said. They walked to the doors. It was cooler outside, quieter. There were few cars on the street. In the distance he could hear the clop-clop-clop of a horse and carriage. The lights of the Ferris wheel spun.

"She was tight with the S.S.," Pirelli said. "She supplied this place with half the whores. And then the other half too. They turned a blind eye to the drugs. First she bought from the soldiers her girls were sleeping with. Then, when that dried out, she put the pressure on me."

"How did she do that?"

Pirelli shrugged. "Do you have a cigarette?"

Gunther kept one hand in his pocket, where he held Pirelli's gun. He offered him the cigarette case with the other. The Luxembourgian lit up and coughed. "Filthy stuff," he said.

"What did she have on you?"

"She knew about Erich. We had our own racket going before she came along. Everyone in this town has a racket. But she wanted it all."

"You don't sound like you liked her much."

"We did business. Business was good."

"You were bringing the drugs in from Luxembourg? Shipping them inside what, old books?"

Pirelli smiled, tiredly. "You're not as stupid as you look."

"You and Blucher were close?"

"What the hell do you mean!"

Gunther nodded; the pieces falling into place at last. Perhaps he'd been wrong about Ulla, he thought. Perhaps he'd been wrong all along. People changed; and she'd always had that hard, selfish core inside her, even in Berlin, during the war. He didn't hold it against her. She was just another survivor, in the end, and you can only survive for so long.

"Blucher didn't know, did he?" Gunther said. "How you felt about him."

"He loved that bitch!"

He opened his arms. His mouth opened, to speak, perhaps even to smile. There was a soft pop, like a bottle of champagne was opened. Pirelli fell on Gunther, his arms enfolding him in a hug. Gunther held him. When he lowered him, gently, to the ground, Pirelli's mouth was a vomit of blood and he was no longer breathing.

8

They were down near the river by then. The shot could have come from anywhere. The Thames ran softly. The mud swallowed sound. Overhead clouds shaped portents of rain.

Gunther swore. Pirelli's cigarette was on the ground, still burning. Gunther picked it up and put it to his mouth and took a drag. He knelt beside the corpse and searched through Pirelli's pockets. He found a bottle of Pervitin and dry swallowed a handful. The hit was almost immediate. He stood up straighter, all his senses alert. Apart from the pills he found three hundred marks, which he pocketed; the photo of an old woman in an old-fashioned dress, with her hand around a tall, thin boy; and a comb. The boy in the photo could have been Pirelli. The comb was fine-toothed and made of ivory. Gunther stuffed both back into Pirelli's pockets and added rocks—as many as he could find. Then he rolled up his sleeves and dragged the corpse by its feet into the water.

When the last of Pirelli's head finally disappeared into the Thames, Gunther walked away. Something kept nagging away at him. Pirelli's use of the past tense, he realised. As though their little operation here in London had already come to its end.

Had it been wound down, even before Gunther arrived? Or was Ulla's death the catalyst? And why did the Luxembourgian spike his drink at the Lyric?

He needed to find the dwarf, he thought. The last piece of the puzzle.

Instead he found himself a girl.

"She reminded me of Ulla, that was all," he told me, later, in my office. "She was German, can you believe that? She was sending money back to her family in Munich. She said she was an actress, only times are hard."

"They are all actresses, Sloam," I said. "And if you can believe that you can believe anything."

"She was a good girl!" he turned on me. He was a romantic to the core, even if he couldn't admit it, not even to himself. "She was just doing what she could to make a life."

"She'll be used up within a year," I told him. "And dead in two."

I was being harsh on him; I wanted to provoke him.

He only shook his head tiredly. Like I said, by then the drugs had worn off and he was dead on his feet; he was done. "She was a good trooper," he insisted.

"You can't fight a war on your back."

"What is it about you, Everly? Did someone you loved one day suddenly abandon you?"

"You could say that, Sloam. But then you could say a lot of things. What was her name?"

"Anna," he said.

"They're all called Anna."

"What do you want from me, Everly? Shoot me and be done with it."

"I still might," I said. "Now answer my damn questions."

Gunther met the girl walking back from the river. For a moment the light framed her face and he thought it was Ulla, and his breath caught in his throat. But her nose was different and her face worn in a way Ulla's never was, though this girl was young.

("They're all young, at the Berlin."

"You sound quite the expert, Everly. Are you sure you weren't there?"

"Just keep talking, Sloam.")

He saw that she was crying. She hurried her steps when she saw Gunther. "*Herr* Pirelli, have you seen him?"

"*Herr* Pirelli has gone for a swim."

She looked up at him with dark eyes. Her makeup was smudged. "I don't understand."

"I'm sorry," Gunther said. "I was only making a joke. He had to leave. Urgent business elsewhere, he said. You look distraught."

"It's nothing, really." She tried to smile, failed.

"Can I buy you a drink?"

"That's awfully kind," the girl said. "Only I need something a little stronger first, you understand? Just to take the edge off things."

Gunther stuck his hand in his pocket, came back with a pill. The girl took it without a word. This time, she managed a smile.

("They know how to smile, Sloam, believe me. They all smile like Ulla Blau in *Die Grosse Liebe*."

"You sound bitter, Everly."

"You're an incurable romantic, Sloam."

"You keep saying that. But it's just basic decency."

"Only you slept with her."

"It wasn't like that. It wasn't like that at all.")

Only maybe it was, a little bit. My men were only now getting there. The girl put the Pervitin pill between her teeth. She leaned into Gunther. He kissed her, hungrily. The pill dissolved between them. Her lips were hot and her eyes fevered. He imagined himself kissing Ulla. The girl threw her head back and laughed. "Let's go!"

She led him at a run and he followed like a fool. My men pursued but then lost them. It took us a while to realise what had happened to Pirelli. It wasn't that Gunther hadn't been observed. It was just that people don't willingly talk to the Gestapo.

She took him up the hill, along St. Martin's Lane where the theatres still displayed playbills from the last decade. She had a room on the third storey of a boarding-house in Denmark Street. There was a wilted rose in a vase on the table—"From an admirer," she said—and the bed was neatly made. Her only books were *Mein Kampf* and a copy of the Bible. Her only other reading were several out-of-date issues of *Deutsches Kinomagazin*, the latest of which had a radiant Leni Riefenstahl on the cover, posed with a camera on a tripod, against a gloriously empty African savannah.

"Can I offer you a drink?"

Gunther sat on the edge of the bed. The girl slipped off her shoes and her coat. Underneath it she was wearing nothing but lingerie. She moved about quite unconcerned.

"Sure."

"Scotch?"

"If you have it."

The girl laughed. "You're such a gentleman," she said. Her eyes went over his body but dawdled on his pocket; where the pills were. "I keep drinks here for, you know."

"Admirers."

"Sure." She opened a cabinet and brought out a bottle and poured him a glass and one for herself too. They clinked glasses. Gunther's body was on fire and his mind was elsewhere. He kept thinking she was Ulla, and he knew that he wanted her.

There had been other girls, other rooms like these, hurried romances carried in the dark. He'd never really let himself feel, after the war. Love was just another kind of transaction, another kind of scam.

He left the drink unfinished. He reached for her and she came willingly. Touching her lips was like completing a circuit. Electricity burned in him. "Ulla . . ." he said.

The girl recoiled back. Her hand was on his naked chest. He did not remember when he'd taken off his clothes.

"She's dead," she said. "She was always good to me."

"You're crying," he said, wonderingly. The girl shook her head and smiled sadly through the mist.

"No," she said. "I'm not."

Gunther touched his eyes and realised they were wet. He could not remember when he had last cried. He wondered if he should feel good for it. He felt nothing.

The girl pushed him on the bed. He lay on his back. The ceiling was cracked, the paint peeling. The girl climbed on top of him.

"Ulla . . ." he said.

"Shh," the girl said. "I'll be your Ulla."

Gunther closed his eyes. The girl rocked above him. Gunther wondered if he'd ever loved Ulla, or if he was merely in love with the idea of being in love. After a while it didn't matter, nothing much did, only the slow build and the urgency, the creaking of the mattress springs, the girl's soft cries.

He half-awoke in the night to find the girl smoking a cigarette by the window. He saw her profile in silhouette. She reclined, nude, her long legs held up to her chest. There was a long cigarette holder between her lips. He stood up, naked also. The girl didn't turn her head. He went to the sink and filled a glass with lukewarm water and downed it. He turned to the girl. From this angle he could see her face.

"She made us watch her in this old movie," the girl said. "Over and over again, to teach us how to walk and how to talk."

"*Die Grosse Liebe*?"

The girl looked at him vaguely. "What's that?" she said.

"An old movie. It was very successful."

"This was *Der blaue Mond*. It was alright. She played a good-time girl in trouble with the law. There's a detective always chasing her. It was silly."

"I never saw it."

The girl shrugged. "No, well," she said. "Why would you."

"We were lovers, in Berlin."

"She had many lovers," the girl said. "I think the only one she really loved was herself."

"Why were you looking for Pirelli, earlier?"

"He's always been good to me. He's not, you know . . ."

"I know."

"He liked to pay us for our time and then just listen to us talk." She laughed. "Most men just want us to shut up and get on our backs. One of the S.S. men likes me to spank him. He just doesn't want to, you know. Have a conversation about it."

"And Pirelli? You looked distraught."

"It was nothing, really. One of the other girls hasn't been in to work for a couple of days. I thought maybe he'd seen her."

"Does she owe you money?"

The girl laughed. "No, silly. She's my friend."

She got up and advanced on him. The cigarette in its holder was left to smoulder by the window. "Why do you have a gun in your coat?" she said.

"In case I get into trouble," Gunther said.

"You look like the kind of man who's always in trouble."

"That's just a role I play. In real life I'm a sweetheart."

She melted into his arms. She was good at that sort of thing. "Shut up and kiss me," she whispered.

So he did.

When they parted for air some of the fire inside him had calmed. The girl reached for his coat draped on the chair and reached into the pocket and took out the pills. "Do you mind?" she said. He shook his head, mutely.

He wondered if the line she'd used was from Ulla's film, that the girl had memorised it. He thought it was the sort of thing he would have written himself, a throwaway line in a B-movie script on a long afternoon.

The girl popped a pill.

Gunther decided it didn't really matter. He took her in his arms and lifted her and carried her to the bed and she was laughing.

She lay there looking up at him. "I'll be your Ulla," she whispered.

"No," he said. "This time, just be yourself."

The night faded into torn strips of time. For a while, he slept.

When he woke up the girl was in the corner putting her stockings on in a businesslike fashion, and sitting in the chair facing Gunther was a man with a gun in his hand.

9

"I thought I was gone for sure," Gunther said. He looked at me a little sadly, I thought. "But of course if they'd wanted me dead, I'd have been dead before I ever woke up."

"And the girl?"

"She got dressed and left. It wasn't her fault," he said; almost pleading. "What could she do?"

"Did she take your money?"

He smiled. "And the pills."

"You're a sap, Gunther."

"Yes," he said. "That's what people keep telling me."

There were two of them. One on the chair, facing Gunther, and the other at the door. Both had guns.

The girl got dressed. "Are you going to hurt him?" she said. She didn't look at Gunther once.

"What's it to you, girl?"

"It's nothing," she said. "It's nothing to me."

"Then get lost, would you?" the gunman on the door said. The girl gave him a stare, but that's all it was. She got lost.

"Get dressed," the man on the chair said. Gunther sat up in bed. "I can't," he said. "I'm shy in front of strangers."

"He thinks he's clever," the gunman on the chair complained. The gunman by the door looked over, slowly. "Everyone's a comedian these days," he said.

"He's a regular Karl Valentin," the other gunman said. "Come on, Sloam. Get dressed. You don't want to be late."

"He'd be late for his own funeral," the gunman by the door said, and they both laughed. Gunther didn't. He thought it was a cheap line. He got up and got dressed and he followed them outside.

A long black Mercedes was parked in the road. Gunther got in at the back. The gunmen sat on either side of him. A third man was driving.

"Where are we going?"

"To church."

He let it go. He didn't have a choice. They drove through the dark city streets. Few cars passed them, going the other way. London after the war wasn't a place where people dawdled after dark. It was warm inside the car. The men on either side of him smelled of wet wool and incense. It was a peculiar English smell. Outside the city projected like the flickering images of a black and white film. Bomb damage everywhere. He'd seen newsreels of the Luftwaffe bombing over the city, waves of bombers flying over Big Ben and St. Paul's Cathedral, over the Thames. It was not uncommon for children to play in the ruins of a house and find an unexploded ordnance. People died of the bombs even now.

He thought about Hitler announcing the successful invasion of England. The ships at Dover and the submarine that made it up the Thames and blew up the House of Commons. It'd taken them six months to hunt down Churchill. He'd been hiding in a bunker all that time.

Swastikas waving over Buckingham Palace. No one knew where the royal family was. Or knew but wasn't saying. So many things you couldn't say anymore. His mind wandered.

How does every German joke start? He thought.

By looking over your shoulder.

In time London would be rebuilt and there'd be no sign left of the war.

"Wake up," someone said. He was prodded awake. His heart was beating too fast and there was an acrid taste in his mouth. Beyond the car's headlights he saw the lit front of a small church.

"Oh," he said. "I thought you were kidding."

"Just move it, will you? Boss wants to see you."

Gunther got out of the car obligingly. There was a large electric red cross above the door. Its light spilled over the driveway and ran down the walls. It made everything look covered in blood. Gunther went inside the church. The two gunmen remained outside. The door shut behind Gunther.

There was an altar straight ahead. Stained glass windows showed nativity scenes. The pews had been pushed aside and there were half-shut crates and boxes everywhere.

"Mr. Sloam. Thank you for coming. I understand you have been looking for me."

Gunther started. For a moment he couldn't locate the voice. Then a diminutive shadow detached itself from the chancel and approached him with the tread of soft feet. "Welcome to the mission, Mr. Sloam. We do God's work here."

Jurgen, the dwarf, wore horn-rimmed glasses and a crisp white shirt. The rolled-up sleeves showed muscled arms. His hair was reddish-brown and fine.

"With guns?" Gunther said.

Jurgen laughed, softly. "These are dangerous times. One must take precautions."

"How did you find me?"

Jurgen shrugged. "It wasn't hard," he said. "I have the ear of the poor, the desperate and the dispossessed. I understand Pirelli is dead."

"Pirelli, Blucher, Ulla Blau," Gunther said. He ticked them off one by one on his fingers. He watched Jurgen but Jurgen's face bore nothing but a polite expression.

"Though I walk through the valley of the shadow of death, I shall fear no evil," Jurgen said.

"Did you kill them?" Gunther said.

"Why would I do that, Mr. Sloam?"

"To protect your little racket," Gunther said. "I knew it couldn't be Ulla behind it all. Running drugs, suborning women. Those children who died in the hospital. It was all your doing, wasn't it. Wasn't it!"

He was shouting. Jurgen flinched. "Mr. Sloam," he said. "Please. This is unseemly."

"Just tell me," Gunther whispered. The fight wasn't in him anymore. "Tell me the truth."

Jurgen rubbed his eyes. "I came to London to help these people. The poor, the needy. The war had destroyed their homes along with their futures. We provide medical supplies, food, bibles." He shrugged. "The Führer won't challenge the church. This much we still have."

"You're a banker."

"I'm wealthy. My family is rich."

"Did you kill them? Did you kill Ulla?"

"You want me to confess?" Jurgen looked amused. "We are in church, after all."

"I don't know what I want," Gunther said.

"I believe in God, Mr. Sloam. I believe that the sins of the present age are but the prelude to the flood that is to come. This is Sodom and Gomorrah. The end of days. Evil has won, Mr. Sloam. But evil cannot rule the world forever."

"My God," Gunther said. "You're an agitator. A . . . a subversive."

"Mr. Sloam, really," Jurgen said. "Don't be so melodramatic."

"How are you still allowed to operate? Why is the Gestapo not knocking on your door as we speak?"

"Someone has to fund this occupation," Jurgen said, complacently. "Someone has to rebuild. Even Nazis need money, Mr. Sloam. I think you have the wrong impression of me. I did not kill Ulla. God knows I had reason to. You paint me so blackly, but Ulla Blau was exactly what you deny she was. She was a whoremonger and a poisoner. And a blackmailer, too, and many other things besides. I do not hold it against her. She did what she thought she must do. She had all the morals of an actress and all their brittle ruthlessness. I do not judge, Mr. Sloam. Only God does."

"What other things?" Gunther said; whispered.

Jurgen shrugged. "Lives," he said. "She sold lives."

"I don't understand."

"Don't you? Then perhaps it is better that way."

"Who did she blackmail?" Then, realisation dawned. "You?"

"I have certain proclivities," Jurgen said. "I am not proud of them, but I have my needs. And Ulla had a knack for finding these things out."

"So you funded her?" Gunther said.

Jurgen shrugged again. "I paid her some money," he allowed. "What she mostly wanted from me was a way of putting that money somewhere safe. She had saved almost enough, she told me. She was looking forward to retiring. She wanted to go back to Germany, somewhere far from Berlin. She dreamed of opening her own theatre. Can you believe it?" He gave a sudden, unexpected bark of a laugh. "She was never much of an actress," he said.

"That's not true."

"Oh, Sloam. I liked her too, you know. But I never went to bed with her."

Gunther took a step towards him. Jurgen stood his ground. He smiled sardonically. "I'm sorry," he said, and he sounded almost genuine. "I don't know who killed her."

"But you're grateful," Gunther said. He loomed over the smaller man, who looked at him evenly, unafraid.

"What's one death," he said, "amongst so many?"

Footsteps sounded behind Gunther. He began to turn, only to see a dark shape rise in the air towards him. The butt of a gun connected with the back of his head. Pain flared, and he fell to his knees.

"Take him outside. Dump him somewhere with the garbage."

He tried to rise. They hit him again and, this time, he stayed down.

"I thought I was dead," he said. "Until I woke up covered in rotting cabbage, with a rat nibbling on my shoe. They really did dump me in the garbage."

"Did they give you back your gun?"

"What gun?" he said. He looked at me blankly.

I sighed. "So who killed Ulla?" I said.

Gunther rubbed his eyes. "I don't know," he said. "And I don't care anymore. I've had it, Everly. I'm going home."

"You're lucky to be alive."

"Like you said, you can't just kill me, I'm a faithful citizen of the Reich."

I laughed. He looked hurt, at that. "Who's going to miss you, Gunther? I have your file. You're a third rate hack for pictures no one makes anymore. You have no wife, no friends and not much of a future. Face it. You may as well be dead."

He shrugged. He must have heard worse. It's harder to break a man when he has nothing.

"If you're going to do it, just do it," he said.

"I would," I said, "only I like you. We do things a little differently here, in England."

I think it was true, too. He wasn't a bad guy. He just kept believing the wrong people.

"Then that's it? You're just going to let me go?"

"There's the door," I said. "There's a transport plane leaving in a couple of hours from Northolt. Why don't you do yourself a favour and be on it this time."

"I will," he said, fervently. "I'll be damned if I spend another minute in this town."

I watched him get up. He walked to the door. He hesitated with his hand on the handle. "You're a good sort, Everly," he said.

"We're a vanishing kind," I said.

10

When we'd picked him up he didn't have the gun on him. He must have stashed it somewhere in the trash. From us he should have gone straight to the airport. He didn't.

He made his way back to Dean Street. Back to the start. A car was parked in the street with the trunk open and packed suitcases on the ground. The old woman straightened when she saw him and said, dismissively, "Oh, it's you."

"Mrs. White. Going someplace?"

"The cold's no good for my bones," she said, in her atrocious German. "I thought perhaps somewhere warm for the winter."

"Can I help you with your luggage?"

"I'd rather you didn't."

Gunther took his gun out and pointed it at her. She squinted. "What's that for, then?" she said.

"Could you step away from the car?"

"You're not going to shoot me, Gunther."

He stared at her; but the gun never wavered. She straightened up, slowly. When she next spoke she seemed to shed forty years and her accent. "You came. I wasn't sure you would but you did."

"Just keep your hands where I can see them, Ulla."

She smiled. It was her old familiar smile. He wondered how he didn't see it before. "People keep telling me you're not much of an actress," he said, "but by God, you are!"

"You were always too kind to me," she said. Gunther could see now under her makeup and the wig: it was her eyes she couldn't truly mask. They were large and startled and innocent, like a wounded bird's. It was her eyes which dominated the last few seconds of screen at the end of *Die Grosse Liebe*, as the picture slowly faded to black. How could he have ever forgotten them?

"How did you know, Gunther?"

"I didn't, not for sure. It was just something this girl said."

"My, you've wasted no time getting over me."

He ignored her. "She was crying because one of her friends was missing. One of the other girls. And I thought how much she looked like you, how much all of them did. The Gestapo man said they all smiled like you."

"Chance would be a fine thing!" she said, with a flash of anger.

"And there was no face, of course."

"No," she said. "There was no face left, was there."

"How could you do it, Ulla? All of it? Not just the girls or the drugs, I can understand that, but those dead children too?"

"They'd have been dead sooner or later, Gunther. This whole stinking country is a waiting room in a hospital's terminal wing. You can't pin that on me."

"But why?"

"Why, why," she said, aping him. Her voice was cruel. "Maybe because I couldn't get a role anymore. So I had to make one for myself." She shrugged. "Or maybe I just got tired. It's over now, anyway. It was just something to do to pass the time at the end of the world."

"And the others?" he said. "Blucher, Pirelli?"

"I only did what I had to do."

"Why me, Ulla?"

"Do you mind if I light a cigarette?"

"Do it slowly."

"I do everything slowly, Gunther."

She reached into her pocket and came back with a silver case. She put a cigarette between her lips and lit it with a match. She blew out smoke and looked at him, unconcerned. "I always liked you," she said, softly.

"Liked?"

"Maybe it was love. It was so long ago and who can remember anymore. You were just easy, Gunther. I don't know how you're still alive."

He just stared at her. The sunlight framed her head. It was just an ordinary day.

"Put the gun down, Gunther. You know you're not going to shoot me." She wiped makeup off her face and smiled at him. He thought she must still be beautiful, underneath. "Come with me," she said. "We'll go back to the continent, away from this awful place. I have money, we'd never have to work again. Come with me."

"No."

"Then step away!" She began loading the cases into the car. Gunther stood and watched her, helplessly.

I watched them from across the road. Neither of them saw me. It was obvious he wasn't going to shoot. She knew it and I did. I think the only one who didn't was Gunther.

I crossed the road to them. I wasn't in a hurry. Gunther heard my footsteps first. He turned his head and looked at me in bewilderment.

"Give me the gun, Gunther."

"No," he said, "she's got to pay, she's got to pay for what she did."

"To them, or to you?" I said. "Give me the gun, Gunther."

I watched her all the while. She straightened up again, slowly, her eyes never leaving my own or blinking. She didn't say a word. She didn't have to.

"Give me the gun."

He gave it to me. Ulla watched us without expression. I couldn't see her hands.

I raised the gun and shot her.

A Luger makes a surprising amount of noise when it's fired. The gunshot echoed from the walls. She fell slowly.

I'd blown half her face off, and the wig, which fell and lay on the ground matted in blood. Ulla Blau collapsed after it. She lay by the car and didn't move. There was a small gun in her hand; she'd intended to shoot me.

I walked over to her and fired another bullet, just to be sure.

Gunther stood there all the while. He didn't move. His eyes found mine at last. "What did you do that for?" he said, numbly.

"You never asked her," I said.

"Asked her what?"

"What else she did to earn a living. Someone must have told you."

I could see it in his eyes. Someone must have said something but he never thought to follow it. I said, "You want to know why she was so protected? She sold us Jews. To the Gestapo."

"So?" he said.

"She worked in the theatre in the aftermath of the war. She recruited the girls. She knew where people were hiding. It was just another way to make a living, and buy some protection on the side."

"So what?" he said. "They were just Jews."

"Sure," I said. "Sure. They were just Jews."

He really looked at me then. I think it was the first time he really started to see things for what they were and not for what he thought they should be.

"But you can't be," he said. "You're not—"

"I knew Tom Everly in Berlin, before the war," I said. "We were at university together. He became a committed Nazi and when he went back to England he was already working for the Abwehr."

I was watching Gunther's eyes. He wanted to run but there was nowhere to go. You can't outrun a bullet.

"We found him in the last few months of the war. Just enough time for me to take his place," I said. "He had a wife and a son, but it's no use having a family in this line of work."

All Gunther did was keep shaking his head. *No, no.* "There are no more Jews," he said.

"I told you," I said. "We're a vanishing kind."

Later, I stood over him. I knelt beside him and put the gun in his hand. They looked good together, Ulla and him. I felt bad for Gunther. He wasn't a bad guy, and none of this has really been his fault. He came to London following a woman, which is how these stories usually start, and he found her: which is how they usually end.

one sister, two sisters, three

JAMES PATRICK KELLY

James Patrick Kelly made his first sale in 1975, and since has gone on to become one of the most respected and popular writers to enter the field in the last twenty years. Although Kelly has had some success with novels, especially with Wildlife, *he has perhaps had more impact to date as a writer of short fiction, with stories such as "Solstice," "The Prisoner of Chillon," "Glass Cloud," "Mr. Boy," "Pogrom," "Home Front," "Undone," and "Bernardo's House," and is often ranked among the best short story writers in the business. His story "Think Like a Dinosaur" won him a Hugo Award in 1996, as did his story "10^{16} to 1," in 2000. Kelly's first solo novel, the mostly ignored* Planet of Whispers, *came out in 1984. It was followed by* Freedom Beach, *a mosaic novel written in collaboration with John Kessel, and then by another solo novel,* Look Into the Sun, *as well as the chapbook novella,* Burn. *His short work has been collected in* Think Like a Dinosaur *and* Strange But Not a Stranger. *His most recent book are a series of anthologies co-edited with John Kessel:* Feeling Very Strange: The Slipstream Anthology, The Secret History of Science Fiction, Digital Rapture: The Singularity Anthology, Rewired: The Post-Cyberpunk Anthology, *and* Nebula Awards Showcase 2012. *Born in Minneola, New York, Kelly now lives with his family in Nottingham, New Hampshire. He has a Web site at www.JimKelly.net, and reviews internet-related matters for* Asimov's Science Fiction.*

Here he shows us that even on another planet thousands of years in the future, sibling rivalry is just the same as it's been since the dawn of time—and, if strong enough, can have similarly dire consequences.

T his isn't my story—I'm nobody. It's my sister's. Zana is the one who got away, leaving me on this sad little world where we were born. Where I'll die someday, as the Divine Moya wills. Moya expects us to die, each and every one. That's her plan for those who still follow the human way.

We were born fraternal twins, Jix and Zana, separated by thirteen minutes—one of the holy numbers. We were conceived as Moya intended, mother clinging to father, sperm seeking egg. For the first years of our lives, we were close. We danced the moons and prayed the holy numbers and taunted the boys who went to our church. Later we kissed them. Father taught us to bake the cookies that we sold to the upsider tourists from the Thousand Worlds and Mother taught us to mind the money that they paid. Ours was a family of happy wallrats, living just outside the ruins.

But we began to drift apart in our late teens. Zana had the precise beauty that only Moya can bestow. Her ratios were near the 1.618 of the Divine's perfection, her curls tight, and her skin had a dark luster, like the midnight of the Jagged Spike. Her high forehead set off molten brown eyes. Zana wore her feelings like a consecration crown for all to see; transparency was part of her attraction. I wasn't plain, but compared to my sister, my features were commonplace, so I found my own way. While Zana could be shy, especially with strangers, I was forward. While she pondered the right word to say, I let my tongue do the thinking. I didn't mind what they said about us. *Zana the pretty, Jix the witty.* Maybe I talked too much for some boys, as Mother used to say, but too much silence made my lips twitch. And I had my share of flings, if not as many as my sister.

Mother got sick when we were twenty, a year after we were consecrated to Moya. We'd been so busy that season that we missed all the signs. Tourists swarmed the ruins, so that we had no time to bake the extravagant cookies that Father favored. To keep up with demand, our family churned out stacks of Sugardrops, plain but as big as saucers, with just a scatter of raisins or sweetbark to provide interest. These were not our best work, but Zana and I found uses for the extra money they brought us. I was saving for a powerbike and she wanted to learn Anglic.

Our stall was on the Roundabout, third down from Shellgate, hard against the western wall of the ruins left by the Exotics. Tourists would pause to admire her on their way in, while I sold them our goods. Even though they were all reps who had strayed from the human way, they still had stomachs like the rest of us. An appetite for sweets and an eye for beauty remain locked in our shared genome.

The day everything changed, a persistent tourist lingered after he'd made his purchase. His companion, a woman from the Institute who was perhaps his minder, was eager to enter the ruins. I'd have been just as happy if she'd led him away, but Zana encouraged conversation. He was handsome enough, in that ageless replicated way, but nobody I'd have wasted breath on.

He picked up my prayer puzzle while Zana wrapped the cookies. "Ingenious." He manipulated the magnetic triangles of the pentagram to create Moya's central upright pentangle. "And you use this how? As a meditation prompt?"

"It predicts how much our customers will buy."

"Pay no attention to her." Zana was embarrassed when I tweaked the tourists. "It's Moya's sacred geometry. We use it to pray the numbers."

The minder sputtered something in Anglic.

"Please—we're guests on their world." The tourist scowled at her. "Let's speak their language."

"Sanctuary was settled by a sect called the Moyans," repeated the minder. "For years they kept the Exotic ruins secret. They believe close contact with us leads to sin."

"Sin, right," he said. "I did look through the guide you sent." He turned to Zana.

"And the purpose of these . . ." He removed triangles to create the upside-down pentagon.

"They remind us of the presence of the Divine," said Zana. I was surprised when she came around the counter with his purchase. "That Moya is everywhere."

"The local religion." The minder harrumphed, "A strain of humanism."

The tourist dismissed her with a wave. "Please, go on." He clicked puzzle pieces absently into place—another upworlder enchanted by my sister's beauty.

"The Divine's ratio is the fingerprint of Moya. It teaches us to obey her laws and be true to our mortality." They exchanged the puzzle for his cookies. For an instant, their hands touched. "We see it everywhere in her creation. In the spiral of galaxies and in the ancient buildings within those walls." She nodded toward the Shells, but kept her eyes on his. "The petals of a flower. Your ear." She brushed the back of her hand against his ear. "Even your DNA." Her voice had dropped to a purr. "Everywhere the universe is imprinted with her holy numbers."

I couldn't believe that she was flirting with an upsider. "Did you know," I said, "that a DNA molecule measures thirty-four angstroms long by twenty-one angstroms wide for each full cycle of its double helix spiral?"

"Really?" he said, although my words meant no more to him than the chitter of streetbots, or the sigh of our awning in the breeze.

"Eight plus thirteen is twenty-one." I thought praying the holy numbers might distract Zana. "Thirteen plus twenty-one is thirty-four. Twenty-one plus thirty-four . . ."

The guide leaned closer to the rep. "They worship the Fibonacci sequence."

"We worship the Divine." Zana's expression was dreamy. "The numbers point us toward her handiwork and her expectations of us."

"I'm Quin," said the tourist. "What did you say your name was?"

"Girls!"

I'd been so astonished by Zana's game of seduction that I missed Father hurrying down the Roundabout.

"Time!" He was out of breath. "It's time . . . to close . . . up." What was so important to bring him from his kitchen at this time of day? And what he'd said made no sense. Close? The afternoon was before us. We had stacks of cookies to sell.

"So early?" I said. A bus from the spaceport grunted to a stop. "Take Zana if you need help. She's not doing anything here." Tourists fresh from the hotels poured from its open slider.

"I want you both. Home." His voice cracked. "*Now*."

Zana hurried back behind the stall to stack unsold cookies into an empty basket.

"Zana, is it?" The tourist leaned over the counter. "Zana, before you go, I'd like to ask—"

"Leave those!" Father swiped at the basket, knocking cookies to the pavement. "Leave everything. We need to go!"

"What's happened?" I said. "Father?"

"Your mother." He dragged us by the hands past the busy stalls. "You mother has lost her mind." Zana stumbled when she glanced back at her dumbstruck tourist, but Father caught her.

Mother sat at the kitchen table, hair loose, face drawn, hands clasped around a cup of spice tea. She liked it thick and sweet; I still smell its terrible perfume when I remember that day. She stared as if surprised to see us, as if she'd forgotten that she had daughters. Then she said "I've just come from the clinic. I have Hrutchma's."

She never cried, not once during that long afternoon. Neither did I. At first Zana threw herself at Mother's neck, then wept into open hands and eventually rested her head on the kitchen table, shoulders heaving. Father's tears were hot; only later did we realize what was behind them.

Hrutchma's was a disease we knew well. It caused something called lymphoid hyperplasia, a crazy increase of cells in the lymph nodes. Hrutchma's began with enlarged nodes in the chest, squeezing the lungs and stealing the breath. I'd noticed her getting winded, although she'd joked it was because Father's cookies were making her fat. As the disease progressed, it would wreck her immune system, leading to nerve damage, infections, withering fevers. That's how Grandmother Deel, Father's mother, had died—raving while she burned like a fast oven. According to the medical encyclopedia on the tell, Hrutchma's is unique to Sanctuary. Some wallrats whispered that it came from a curse the Exotics placed on the old stones, but we couldn't let that rumor spread. Tourists put the soup in our bowls.

I remember sinking into a chair across from Mother, trying to imagine how I would fit into a world without her. I couldn't, in part because I was too numb, in part because I was distracted by Zana. She settled beside me, sobbing and I felt guilty that I couldn't summon tears. And then I was puzzled by the way Father hung back. I expected that he'd be grieving too. But no—he seemed angry.

Zana saw it too. "Father, what's wrong?"

"Her." He choked on a laugh. "She is."

"She's sick!" Zana swiped at her wet face. "What—you blame her?" I wonder now if she had guessed what was coming. She knew Mother better than I.

"Hrutchma's I can accept." He shook his head in disgust. "The other, no."

"You can accept that I'll die?" Mother's voice was sharp as a slap. "I'm forty-one years old."

"I accept the will of the Divine," he said. "You should do the same. Our daughters are consecrated to Moya."

She turned from him to face us. "Your father doesn't understand." She met our gaze without hesitation or regret. "I'm going to Skytown."

"To live." Father said it like an accusation, but she ignored him. "Go ahead, lie down with their machines. Betray everything we believe. Just remember—never come back to us."

"You're going to upload," said Zana. "Become a rep."

Mother shivered as if Zana had said something that she hadn't yet realized. Then she nodded. "I'm not ready to die."

She left the next day.

Father never spoke of her again. If anyone dared mention her, he'd withdraw, sometimes for days. He was a fool to think that his silence could erase her from our lives. All of our communion knew the shame she'd brought on our family and our church. Whenever Speaker Elb preached about straying from Moya's way, of losing our humanity, everyone thought of her. I know I did. For months afterward, I was obsessed with her. I had nightmares about her ravaged and discarded body—where was it now? And what to make of the stranger who knew everything about our home, our family—about *me*? We'd been taught there was no real continuity of life between a human and the rep body created by the technology of the Thousand Worlds. The Divine taught that my mother was truly dead. But then who was the creature who lived in Skytown, the upsiders' enclave on Sanctuary? Who still claimed to love me?

I knew this because she tried to stay in contact with us, or at least with Zana and me. Zana showed me her first message, but I couldn't finish reading it. However, Zana wrote back, despite Speaker Elb's warning that our false mother would tempt her to sin. I had no idea how often they talked because I didn't want to know. However, my sister insisted on telling me how she was doing.

After her replication, Mother had found work as a janitor at the Institute of Exotic Archeology. She shared an apartment with three other roommates including her old friend Xeni Bluereed, who had left our communion three years ago to be replicated. Zana claimed there was a growing community of people like Mother and Xeni beginning new lives among the upsiders. Later, she got a job in a Skytown restaurant as a cook, which was ironic because the kitchen had always been Father's domain. Mother's new position paid well and I suspect that she sent Zana some of her wages, although I never saw any. But apparently Mother had money enough to visit the orbital and to buy a bot. She thought about us all the time, according to Zana, and yet supposedly she was happy. Although I envied her the luxuries of Skytown, I couldn't imagine how that could be.

Moya does not demand that we reject all upsider technologies, only those which make us less human. Yes, I'd own a bot and a printer and a car if I could afford them. I'd sample the drugs that make you stronger or smarter or happier. But Sanctuary is an exhausted world. That's why our ancestors were able to claim it for the Divine. The Exotics had used Sanctuary up long ago, and their leavings are the last valuable things on it. We scratch a living from their dust. And while we're proud of our ruins, there are other examples of the Exotics' architecture scattered throughout the galaxy.

As the months passed, our broken family adjusted to our new life. The press of tourists varied with the seasons, but we did well enough, especially now that there were only three of us. I bought my powerbike and a trailer to go with it. Not only did Zana get her Anglic lessons, she then paid for access to the Institute's databanks, so that she could learn more about the Thousand Worlds. Her new language skills paid off in an unexpected way. Word spread through the hotels of the beautiful girl selling baked goods who could speak the common tongue. Tourists flocked to witness this marvel. They helped Zana with her accent until they claimed she could announce the news on Ravi's Prize itself—not that either of us believed that. Of course, I understood not a word of their chatter, and when they dissolved into laughter I suspected that the joke was on me.

Then Quin came back. Except, as it turned out, he'd never left.

I was alone at the stall, which meant that, for a change, my view of the street wasn't blocked by Zana's admirers when I spotted Quin wandering along the Roundabout. It had been almost half a year, but I knew him as soon as I saw him. He paused at Twial's stall, picked up a reproduction of Half Boat to check the price and then replaced it with a frown. He browsed Glif's gaudy umbrellas and the new scent store, then walked faster as he got closer. He passed our stall with eyes down, as if scanning for cracks on the pavement. It was obvious that he was ignoring me. But then he stopped abruptly in the middle of the street, glanced past me to the blackened hulk of the Jagged Spike, and strode up to the counter.

"You're Jix." He tried on a smile that didn't quite fit.

I agreed that I was.

He reached for our most expensive cookie. "And this is a Brownbutter Velvet Block."

"With a ginger smear."

"Cut into a precise rectangle." He held it to the light to examine it. "I've been studying your religion. Would I be right to say that the ratio of the length to the width is 1.618?" He seemed proud of himself for this guess.

"I recommend that you buy at least two."

This wasn't the reply he'd been expecting. He nodded, frowning.

"Will there be something else?" I asked.

"I know your mother. She used to work at the Institute."

"Really?" I wrapped two Velvet Blocks in takeout paper. "Did she send you?"

"No." He was surprised at the question. "I'm an archeologist, doing research on your Shells."

"They're not mine." I supposed he wanted me to ask about Mother. I handed him his purchase. "Three-fifty."

Instead of completing the transaction using our tell like every other tourist, he reached into his pocket and pulled out a handful of Moyan chits.

"I like your money." He fumbled for the exact change. "There's so much of it."

"I like it too." I rarely handled chits at the stall; only Moyans carry them and Moyans bake their own cookies. He watched me slip them into my pocket. Then I gave him his purchase and waited. He made no move to leave. I remembered then how he had lingered that awful day. "Maybe you were expecting to find someone else here?"

"Zana, yes." He blinked. "But I had no expectations."

"I'm sorry to hear that. Expectations are what get me through the day." I spotted Zana headed up the street carrying a basket of cookies from home. "I like to guess what will happen next."

"You had a prayer puzzle," he said. "May I see it?"

Surprised that he remembered, I opened my bag and offered it to him.

Yes." He pushed the magnetized shapes into new configurations with practiced motions. "It's very definite, your religion. Did you know that the star polygon is one of the oldest symbols we have. From Earth, you know, the home world. It represented the sacred feminine as long ago as 4000 BCE."

"Really?" Of course he would condescend to a nobody; he was a tourist. Was common courtesy a trait that the upsiders' technology couldn't replicate?

"So the so-called Golden Ratio . . . ." He was oblivious. "A fascinating mix of tradition and math. Take this pentagon and connect the vertices and you get a pentagram, a five-sided star." He pushed puzzle pieces. "Five is in the Fibonacci sequence. And the ratio of any diagonal of the star to any side of the pentagon is 1.618. Phi, the Golden Ratio. And you see it again here . . . ." He fitted pieces into new configurations. "And here." He drew a line with his forefinger; his nails clicked against the metal. "And you were saying how often the Golden Ratio occurs in the natural world. There's actually support for that in the literature."

"We call it the Divine's Ratio," I said. "And it was actually my sister who was explaining that. Isn't that right, Zana?"

Quin started as she set her basket on the counter.

"You remember Quin," I said to her. "Turns out he's from the Institute. An archeologist. And he knows Mother."

The looks they exchanged were not those of strangers.

"So this isn't news to you?" I reached for the basket to sort the new cookies she'd brought. "Are we keeping secrets now, sister?"

"Oh, no secret," said Quin. "We started exchanging messages what . . . ? Three months ago. I'd like to think we've become friends."

"Just over two months." Zana was embarrassed. "And we've only met in person a couple of times."

"Which is why I thought to surprise you." Quin seemed pleased with himself.

"And did he tell you that he's been studying our religion?" I replenished our supply of Shortbread Swaddled Truffles. "Perhaps you're thinking of converting, Quin?" I wanted to see her squirm for keeping this from me.

"No." He set my prayer puzzle down as if it might burn him. "Not at all."

"It would be awkward, seeing as how you're no longer in your first body. How many times have you been replicated, if you don't mind my asking?

"He does mind." Zana's cheeks colored. "That's rude, Jix."

"Oh, sorry." I bowed twice for good measure. "Sorry, Quin. It's just that we get so few of your people taking an interest in us."

Quin blinked at us, as if he was having trouble following our conversation. "In any event," he said to Zana, "I was just wondering when . . . if maybe . . . would you like to take that tour sometime? The one we were talking about."

"Tour?" I said.

He glanced at me then nodded toward Shellgate. "I know you've lived here all your lives, but I have access to the monuments, even those that are closed. I could show you things that very few people have seen."

Zana shot me a stare that said I wasn't invited. I let it bounce off me.

"Zana and I are working girls," I said. "We have tourists to feed, cookies to sell."

He nodded. "Shellgate closes at five. Don't all the tourists leave for the hotels then? We could go after hours; I have unlimited access, you know. It stays light until almost eight."

"Great." I held up the empty cookie basket and smiled at him. "We could pack a picnic dinner."

Zana wasn't amused.

"Father would explode if he knew you were seeing a rep."

"I'm not seeing him." Zana was a darkness on the shadowy bed across the room. "He's a friend, that's all. And it's all been messaging until recently."

"Except now you're making dates to tour the ruins."

It was always sweltering in our house because of the ovens, even late at night after Father shut them down. In the summer Zana and I would sprawl on our beds, sweat prickling our skin. Most nights we kicked the sheets off, sometimes it was too hot for clothes. Unable to sleep, we'd talk of boys and dreams in the dank gloom, our conversation flickering like a candle.

"He's going to show you things nobody has seen." I chuckled. "Where have I heard that joke before? He's the tourist and you're the baker's beautiful daughter."

"That's not what this is. Besides, now you're coming too, even though nobody asked you."

"I'm only going to make sure that you don't do anything stupid." We never kept our flings a secret from one another, so this Quin worried me. "Okay, so maybe he's not a tourist, but he's not here to stay." Zana was my twin, and even if we weren't playmates anymore, she was the only one in our family I was close to. The silence was tickled by the scratch of slinks running up the walls and across the floor. In the warm weather the lizards stayed active at night, scavenging for crumbs and squeezing into the chinks in our stone walls.

"You don't think I can handle him?" said Zana. "I'm twenty-one years old."

"And he's two hundred years old. Or maybe two thousand."

"Oh, stop it."

"He works for the Institute, Zana. You go squirting through wormholes for a living, you've got to allow for time dilation. People like him replicate what . . . ? Five, six times at least."

I heard her torturing her pillow into a new shape, but neither of us found much comfort that night.

"He's definitely got a look," I said. "I understand the attraction."

The slats beneath her mattress creaked when she sat up. "You know the problem with living at home?" She was silhouetted against the window, her bare back to me. "I can never get away from you two."

"That's not fair. When you bring a boy home, don't I give you the room? Just like when I was with Bibby, you got scarce. And Father hasn't a clue who we've had in here."

Silence.

"I watch for you and you watch for me, remember? That's what sisters do."

She gave an unhappy grumble.

"But if sex is what you want, why not fuck a human? Moya knows, you can have your choice."

I ducked as her pillow sailed across the room.

We didn't pack cookies for the picnic. When you bake for a living, you lose the taste. Instead we brought salted cutthroat from the river and pickled figs. A cold squash soup. A round of cheese and a bottle of fay brandy. Quin insisted on carrying it at first, even though Zana and I had spent most of our lives lugging heavy baskets of fruit and flour and oils and spices.

I couldn't help but envy the way the tell built into his fingernail synced with the Institute's security at Shellgate. A wave of his hand, and the projectors went dark; as soon as we passed through, solid blue light once again barred the entryway. I'd never seen communication tech that small. For a moment, Quin seemed magical.

The ruins were part of our neighborhood, even though they were run by the Institute. We were threading our way around broken buildings back when we were toddlers. But that night, it was as if we'd stepped from Sanctuary onto one of the Thousand Worlds. We knew the structures by the names the first settlers had given them, but Quin identified the Grandmother Stones as Boundary Markers 11n through 11t. He explained that Half Boat and the Jagged Spike were part of a complex he called the Western Quadrant Early Classic Superstructure. When we insisted that Ellipsoidal Buildings 43, 58 and 70 were properly Bird Shell, Crazy Shell and the Bride, he chuckled. Giving commonplace names was how people coped with their terror of the alien, he claimed. A way of pretending we understood the civilization of the mighty Exotics.

He had a talent for annoying me. "Maybe," I said, "assigning them numbers is your way of coping."

Zana shot me a look but Quin nodded, as if considering what I'd said. "You may be right. Numbering the world is what we humans do, isn't it?" We were standing on a parapet called Frost's Overlook, gazing down at the three Shells. "They're not buildings, you know. They're sculptures."

"Sculptures?" I said. "Of what?"

"We see similar construction in several other ruins. I stopped at Destination and Kenning and before I came here. I'm certain that your Shells were never occupied. Nor were they even functional. My research leads me to the idea that they're propaganda art on a monumental scale, like Ravi's Tomb or the Lubinarium."

"The Statue of Liberty on Earth," said Zana. This took me by surprise. Why was she learning trivia about that dead planet?

"Not familiar with that one." Quin hefted the picnic basket. "Most scholars claim that Ellipsoidal Sculptures are Post Classic, but I believe they're actually from the end of the Persistent Era, just before the last of the Exotics disappeared."

"Sculptures of what?" I repeated. "And what kind of propaganda?"

"I've heard that's a particularly interesting view." He aimed his chin at the opening at the top of the Bride. "Eat up there?"

As we scuttled down the rubble-strewn grade, he told us about his work. Nobody knew what had become of the Exotics. The galaxy-wide culture that built the wormholes vanished between fifty and sixty thousand years ago. Judging from their enigmatic ruins, Exotic civilization had begun to hollow out in its Post Classic Era, which was followed by the long decline of the Persistent Era. Quin believed that Sanctuary's shells might have been among the last things the Exotics ever built.

The wind had died in the dusk and the sun-baked façade of the Crazy Shell radiated heat as we passed on the way to the Bride. "I think these shells were meant to persuade the Persistents who remained behind to follow their ancestors." Quin set the basket down on the stump of a pillar and wiped sweat from his eyes. "Maybe to shame them into it because Exotic culture had moved on. What were they waiting for?" He'd been talking non-stop and was out of breath.

I was enjoying the effect our summer heat had on this overconfident upsider. "This is the theory that says they all uploaded and went to where? Exotic toyland?"

"The evidence does point to a massive departure over a very short time, with a longer period of stragglers hanging on. Some claim there was a mass suicide but yes, I'd like to think they went elsewhere. Maybe to somewhere else in our universe or to some designed reality."

Zana hefted the picnic basket. "I can't imagine anyone could get bored sailing through wormholes."

He pretended not to notice that she was relieving him. "Not sure they got bored. One thing is certain, they were very tidy. They took great pains to erase themselves from their worlds." He tugged at his shirt where it had stuck to his chest. "All their ruins are built of native materials, mostly stone and ceramics. Some metals. We're pretty sure that no Exotics lived in them, but then we have no idea where they did live. We know nothing of what they looked like, their biology, what they believed. Were these structures ceremonial? Administrative? Religious?"

"And this bothers you?" I asked. "Why? Because it's not fair to archeologists?"

"They might've done better by us." He grinned. "I'd like to think there are answers out there, but maybe I'm just fooling myself."

Father said that before the Institute took over the ruins, Moyans had tried to clean them up: restacking stones, filling holes, pulling weeds and cutting brush. The upsiders had stopped all reconstruction and limited public access to a handful of the structures. They said it was to preserve the archeological record; wallrats said it was to drive customers away. Whatever the truth, navigating the ruins was a challenge. The footing was uncertain, and the direct path to any given destination was often blocked.

"So what does Moya . . ." Quin was laboring again as we reached the base of the Bride. ". . . have to say . . . to all of this?"

"It's not for us to know Moya's mind." Zana vaulted onto the fallen slab in front of the crude entrance someone had chiseled into the Bride.

"Come on," I said. "It's obvious the Exotics knew the Divine's ratio."

"Did they?"

"Just look." I gestured at the white whorls carved into the casing stones on the wall above us.

"I suppose." He gathered himself for the scramble. "It's math, after all. But you Moyans . . . you see your ratio everywhere."

I offered a hand to help him up. "Don't you?"

He reached for me and missed. "I lack your stamina." I caught his damp wrist and boosted him to my side.

After he'd caught his breath, Quin insisted on telling us that the white limestone façade of the Bride had been quarried from Kunlun's Crease, even though everyone knew this. The Bride resembled the Ivory Snails some wallrats harvested from the river for soup. The ones that tasted like dirty socks. The difference was that the

Bride was enormous—some thirty meters tall—and was upside down. The mouth of the shell pointed up at the sky. We ducked through the makeshift entrance into the interior. The air was dank here and smelled like the inside of a well. A wooden scaffold climbed to the light. We crunched across a floor littered with broken tiles that had fallen off the walls, each decorated with a tessellated spiral flower pattern. Some wallrats believed that if you found an intact tile, whoever you gave it to would fall in love with you. Unfortunately, undamaged tiles were hard to come by since the ban on removing artifacts from the ruins. However, the Naras did a brisk trade in reproductions from their stall near Rivergate.

I bent to retrieve a shard and showed it to Quin. It was hard to see detail in the feeble light from the opening above us, so he lit his fingernail.

"The Divine's ratio." I traced several shapes. "In case you're still in doubt about what the Exotics knew."

"Yes." He waved his nail off. "That claim has been made. But it's not quite 1.618, is it?"

I bristled and let it fall to the floor. "So close you can hardly tell the difference."

"Right," he said. "Especially in the dark."

"Quin likes to scoff," said Zana. "Best to ignore him when he gets like that."

"Sorry," he said. "Your sister has been teaching me manners, but I'm afraid I'm not much of a student."

I prayed the numbers while we climbed to calm myself. *One, one, two, three, five, eight, thirteen, twenty-one, thirty-four, fifty-five . . .* By the time I got to *seventeen thousand, seven hundred and eleven* I was feeling more like myself. Quin heaved himself up the first two ladders in succession, but after that he had to rest on each platform. He took longer to recover the higher we went until he collapsed onto the tenth stage, gasping and as damp as if we had pulled him from the river. The planking was slick with mildew from exposure to the weather and left a smudge on Quin's pants. Zana worried over him, but he reassured us that he was exhausted only because his last replication had been on a world where the gravity was 0.68 that of Sanctuary. "And I'm not good with heights," he added.

He revived once we climbed the last ladder to the wide stone lip at the top of the Shell. While Zana sat him down so the two of them could unpack our meal, I walked out to the edge and the view. It had been years since I'd made this climb. The shadowy ruins sprawled at my feet while the lights of our little village twinkled in the middle distance. Skytown was a glow on the horizon. Although the air was warmer up here, it was a relief from the sticky interior of the Bride. I took a deep breath and felt blessed to be able to take in my whole world at a glance.

Zana was murmuring to Quin. I couldn't make out what she was saying, but there was a note to her voice, at once innocent and earnest and tender, that made me shudder.

What if this was more than a fling?

Quin thought the cutthroat tasted too fishy but he raved about the pickled figs and asked to take a sample of Father's squash soup for gastronomical analysis. He said the cheese was better than the *framenthakler* that the data monks on Encyclopedia printed from their secret recipe. We talked a lot about food. Zana pumped him for his favorite dishes but I knew she was more interested in hearing stories about the Thousand Worlds than she was learning about upsider cooking. He said that most reps preferred printed food, of which there was an infinite variety. Those who travelled the wormholes took little interest in local culture, but were passionately invested in trying the latest cuisines.

"Nobody much cares about books and songs," he said. "What sells on the upside are new menus." He waved our brandy bottle at the sky. "Come up with a fresh taste with a new smell and you can write your own ticket to the stars." When he offered me a refill, I covered my cup with my hand. "Take your cookies, for example. With the right marketing, they might pay your way off Sanctuary."

I waited for Zana to point out that we had no plans to leave home. She didn't, so neither did I.

I expected Quin would continue to do most of the talking, but he wanted to hear about us, or at least Zana. He asked about our schools and what we'd been told about the upside. Zana talked about what she'd learned using the Institute's portal; he said it had good access but was by no means complete. He wondered what we thought about the controversies that flared continually between the wallrats and the Institute over management of the ruins. Then he got us telling stories about dumb things that tourists did.

"I don't understand why they need to haggle," I said, "after what they spend to get here. We'd have to move a mountain of cookies just to get to the orbital."

"So we let them talk our prices down . . ." Zana giggled, ". . . and we then make up the difference in tax."

"Only there is no tax."

"Sure there is," I said. "Stupidity tax."

We were all laughing now as Zana filled our cups with the last of the brandy.

"Then there was that buzzy woman who wanted to buy all our takeout paper. Where was she from?"

"She said it tasted better than our cookies."

"And then they ask the dumbest questions about the Divine's ratio."

That earned me a sisterly glare until Quin raised his hand. "Guilty."

I didn't want to start liking him, so I said, "You don't believe in the Divine, do you?"

When Zana hissed, it sounded like a seam ripping.

"You know I don't," he said.

Nobody was laughing now.

"Or any god," I said.

Quin studied me. His silence was scary.

"Why not?" I asked.

"Jix!" Zana came to her knees, but I knew she wanted to hear his answer.

"Have you ever heard of the God spot, Jix?" said Quin.

"Doesn't exist." Zana said, as if to end the conversation.

"No," I said. "What is it?"

"People used to look for the place of our brains where mystical experiences come from. Some tagged the right parietal lobe, others the dorsolateral prefrontal cortex.

There was evidence that N,N-dimethyltryptamine levels in the pineal gland play a role. But over time they realized they'd got it wrong, and so they developed a different model. There's no button in the brain that you push for instant spirituality. The neural correlates are scattered across the entire brain, systems that give rise to self-awareness, emotion, your sense of your own body." He fumbled at the pocket of the shirt he was wearing. "And what's interesting is that in order to have a religious experience, you don't stimulate these brain systems." He shook his head. "You suppress them. Inhibit those areas that create the illusion of self, and you open the door to transcendence."

"So?" I said.

He pulled a pressure syringe from the pocket and showed it to us. "Want to see Moya?"

Sometimes I wonder if Zana had poured our futures from a bottle of fay brandy. How could two drunken sisters hope to protect one another? Or maybe I was daring my sister even as she was daring me in some alcohol-fueled dance of sibling rivalry? Or it was simply that we each were trying to impress her upsider, in our own ways and for our own reasons?

The syringe looked like a glass thumb, cylindrical but with a flat applicator pad to one side. "This won't take long." Quin pressed the syringe to the artery in Zana's neck. "Say fifteen minutes to work past the blood-brain barrier." The syringe left a faint pink swelling. "The actual experience comes and goes. Maybe five minutes, although it might feel longer subjectively." He turned to me. "But everyone's different. Some people feel like they've disappeared, some become one with everything."

I tilted my head. "And is it real?" The injection felt like being kissed on the neck.

He laughed. "That's for you to decide." He injected himself last, then tucked the syringe back into his pocket.

"You planned this," said Zana.

"We've talked about it," he said, "haven't we?"

"I never said yes."

He smirked. "You just did."

"So what do we do now?" I said.

He sat on the stone pavers facing the view and crossed his legs. "We wait for the elevator."

We arranged ourselves into a triangle and watched each other for signs. Zana settled back onto her heels. Her back was straight and she sniffed, nose pointed, as if she might catch Moya's scent. I squirmed on the cold, hard floor. The silence made me more self-conscious, not less. Was my heart in the right place? Would this change my life? What was I supposed to do with my hands?

Quin seemed to be enjoying himself. "I never asked you about boyfriends," he said to distract us. "I'll bet you both have plenty."

"Zana does." I was relieved to hear the sound of my own voice. "She gets her share and half of mine."

"That's not true." She frowned. "You do well enough."

"They say I talk too much."

"Boneheads." He patted my arm. "Stick with men as smart as you."

"And you?" said Zana. "You have people you care about?"

"Yes and no." He paused, deciding how much to say. "When you get replicated, relationships sometimes fall apart. You're you, but now you're somebody else as well. The body is different for one thing, sometimes very different. It wants what it wants. That old you, he's like someone you read about. It was a really interesting book, and you remember vivid scenes, but you've read that last page."

"What's it like?" I asked. "Being replicated."

"Like dying, only you wake up afterwards."

"You've died?" I shouldn't have been surprised, but I was.

"Every time," he said, as if he was discussing a splinter. "Of course in a direct transfer you're not dead very long. But these days they can still rep someone thirty minutes after cardiac and respiratory arrest with minimal information loss. After thirty, the brain really deteriorates. Something about ischemic injury." He shivered in the heat. "So yes, Zana knows this already but I was in a flier crash that killed me just before I came here. Nobody's fault, really. I was with someone I loved, but he didn't make it. Rescue took too long to get to us. They say my rep was only ninety-six percent accurate. It was very sad, because I'd probably still be with him if his replication had been successful too."

Zana took his hand in hers.

"So I'm still learning to be this new Quin in this new body." His mouth smiled, but his eyes were sad. "But that's what we all do, isn't it?"

When I saw that look on my sister's face, one I'd never seen before, I knew that I'd been right to worry about this upsider. The love she felt for him glimmered from her perfect ratios, Moya's gifts to her. The length of Zana's face divided by its width. 1.618. Her smile divided by the width of her nose. 1.618. The width of her nose to the space between her nostrils. 1.618.

I was so focused on my sister that I didn't realize Quin was still talking until he said, "I'd do anything for you."

Zana shut her eyes. Was it imagination that they were so tight that they quivered? When she opened them she was staring at nobody, and 1.618 was Divinely revealed in the width of her eye divided by the width of her iris.

"Don't." She stood—to get away from her lover? Or from Moya, who had made her in her image and likeness? The Divine was the reason that her height was 1.618 of the distance between her beautiful navel and her flawless hair. The holy numbers began praying themselves, one plus one sisters, two sisters, three, five, eight. . . .

Quin struggled to his feet and caught her in an embrace, spouting a stream of ardent and unintelligible Anglic. She replied in kind, only her voice was in ruins. More Anglic nonsense and more and then they were shouting. The argument made her so angry that she pulled away from him. His arm dangled and he shook it as if it had fallen asleep but it was too long, too long, his proportions were all wrong. When his fingers curled into a fist, that one nail glowed a sleepy, magical purple.

Nobody said, "Speak Moyan!"

Zana heard. "I do want that, yes, all of it, but I can't." She was crying. "It's a sin. And how can I leave them?"

"They can come too," Quin said. "I'll pay for the replication."

"Rep Father?" Her laugh turned sour, and her mouth twisted, and her ratios skewed. "I love you, Quin, but . . ."

Love, the voice said to nobody. Thirteen, twenty-one, thirty-four. She loves him.

"Jix, what are you doing?" The upsider wasn't condescending now. "Get away from her, Jix." Who was he talking to?

The voice was as cruel as stone, as sad as the wind. Fifty-five, eighty-nine, one hundred and forty-four.

"Stop." Zana tried to twist away, but she wasn't fast enough. "No!"

And then she was falling, perfect arms flailing, scream slashing the night. On her way to the Thousand Worlds. The truth is that nobody pushed Zana Ferenc to her death from the stone lip of the Bride.

"Call rescue now," said nobody. "You only have half an hour."

I hadn't expected Mother to be beautiful. She was an only child but the rep they'd given her looked like some younger, sunnier sister. She reminded me of my own sister, the one I no longer had according to Father. She stood aside and smiled me into her apartment. The room felt deliciously cool after the hike from the church, like cannonballing into the river on a summer afternoon. This must be the air-conditioning we'd heard about.

There were no real windows but the entire rear wall was a live image of the ruins as seen from Kai's Chair. Our village peeked from the far corner.

"Xeni and the others are out," said Mother. "It's just us."

"Xeni," I said. "She's your roommate, right?" I paused in the center of what was apparently just a sitting room. Two doors to my left, one to my right, the hall behind. Walls as blue as an egg. Mysterious light from the ceiling. I stared but saw nothing. I had so much to say, to ask, and I was tongue-tied.

"I like your couch." It was a silly thing to say, but it was all I could come up with. The couch was L shaped and covered with a ridged red fabric. I tried to estimate its cost in cookies as I ran a finger along the outside arm. The material was warm and felt like skin.

"Sit for a minute." Mother patted the back of the couch where she wanted me. "I'll be right back."

I was so miserable that I considered running away as she passed from the room. But I couldn't take another step carrying the weight of all those sleepless nights. I needed someone to talk to, so I sat. Mist curled from the vaporizer on the low table in front of me. I sniffed, some kind of ambient drug. It smelled green. Mounted on the wall was an antique bicycle wheel, rust eating through the chrome, the tread on the tire worn to a shiny black.

"Xeni's." Mother returned, carrying a tray. "She races. Apparently that wheel was on some bike that won Omeo's Climb, back who knows when."

She put the tray on the table and settled beside me. I glanced from it to her. "Am I staying?"

"If you want."

She'd made my favorite treats: bittersweet clusters, cheese and figs on skewers, pickled cob, salami with tiny crowns of mustard.

I reached for the bittersweets. "What, no cookies?"

She had a way of snorting and laughing at the same time. "That's your father's specialty." Hearing that intimate sound that only she could make carried me back to a sunny memory of the four of us on our boat on the river, Father rowing us home from church and Mother laughing as Zana and I pulled snack treasures from the picnic basket.

"How is he?" said Mother.

And then I was back in an apartment in Skytown, and our little family was in ruins. "Bitter," I said. "I had to move out. I'm living in the church for now."

"It was past time, I think. You needed to be on your own." She frowned. "But the church?"

"Nobody knows what happened that night," I said. "Nobody in the village, that is. They think it was an accident." My tongue felt like a brick. "But you know."

She nodded.

The silence stretched so tight, I thought I might snap. "I like your place." Why was everything that came out of my mouth so trite?

"You never visited."

"No. Sorry." This was a reproach I'd feared, but somehow it wasn't as awful as I'd thought it would be. "That was wrong." Mother had every right to blame me; I didn't know what I was doing or who I was anymore. "Did Zana?"

Mother spoke an order in Anglic. I'd been taking lessons and picked up something about a *holiday* or a *birthday*. Then the wall displayed a picture of Mother and Zana sitting on the couch just as we were and with practically the same snacks in front. This was the Zana I knew, my sister. Not the other, the rep I'd never seen.

"Did she say anything after she was repped?" I said. "About me, I mean?"

"Not much." Mother spoke as if she were tiptoeing around broken glass. "She didn't know why you did it."

I should've said something—Mother expected me to. But I was back on the Bride, seeing it all again for the millionth time and still not understanding. I'd heard Moya's voice, so how could I have sinned?

"She left the orbital yesterday," she said. "Should arrive at the wormhole's insertion point next Friday."

"But no message? Nothing?"

She sighed. "They say that a rep's most vivid memories are her last moments. For me, it was just fog, but then I was a direct transfer. They put me to sleep, I died, they woke me up. But somewhere in between, I remember wrestling with . . . well, like I said. *Fog.*" She waved the mist wafting from the vaporizer toward her and breathed deeply. "It was like swimming, almost drowning, and I needed to stay upright except my feet kept sinking and I couldn't pull free and it . . . it took a while, is all. I was ready for it to stop." She shook her head as if to part that remembered fog. "Zana's memories were more painful, I guess."

"I'm sorry." I felt my throat close. How many messages had I sent my sister apologizing every which way I could think of? None of which she answered.

Then I was crying, hot tears, choking sobs.

Mother patted my arm. "I think she knows."

But it wasn't only for my sister that I cried. I wept for Mother and Father and the life we all had lost. And for Moya, who answered to an upsider drug.

I finally got myself under control. "He was telling us that he died in a flier crash"—I swiped at my eyes—"Quin, that night. So at least he knew what she went through. Maybe that was a help."

"I hope so." She picked up a round of salami and examined it critically. "I didn't like him at first. Too much the upsider, always talking about how we'll have to give up our ways and become citizens of the Thousand Worlds. I think what he really wants is to chase down his Exotics, and go live with them." The tip of her tongue licked the mustard crown and then she nibbled an edge the way she always did. "But he did right by her, paid her way to Ravi's Prize. Says he'll follow her there after he finishes his research. We'll see. I think he means well."

"Is there a picture of her?" I said. "After, I mean."

She spoke in Anglic again. I recognized *daughter*.

A woman stared at me from Mother's wall—not quite a stranger. Her eyes were as deep as the night sky, just as I remembered her. But she had an ungodly pale complexion and her hair was cropped too short and the proportions of her face were all wrong. My breath caught when I realized that she looked more like me than herself. My twin.

"I hope," I said, "she'll be happy someday."

"Yes," said Mother. "I pray the numbers that she will."

Dispatches from the cradle: The Hermit—forty-eight hours in the sea of Massachusetts

KEN LIU

Ken Liu is an author and translator of speculative fiction, as well as a lawyer and programmer. His fiction has appeared in The Magazine of Fantasy & Science Fiction, Asimov's, Analog, Clarkesworld, Lightspeed, and Strange Horizons, among many other places. He has won a Nebula, two Hugos, a World Fantasy Award, and a Science Fiction & Fantasy Translation Award, and been nominated for the Sturgeon and the Locus Awards. In 2015, he published his first novel, The Grace of Kings. His most recent books are The Wall of Storms, a sequel to The Grace of Kings, a collection, The Paper Menagerie and Other Stories, and, as editor and translator, an anthology of Chinese science fiction stories, Invisible Planets. He lives with his family near Boston, Massachusetts.

Here he demonstrates that even in what most of us would consider a disastrously ruined Post-Catastrophe world, there will probably still be tourists. . . .

Before she became a hermit, Asa <whale>-<tongue>-π had been a managing director with JP Morgan Credit Suisse on Valentina Station, Venus. She would, of course, find this description small-minded and obtuse. "Call a woman a financial engineer or a man an agricultural systems analyst, and the world thinks they know something about them," she wrote. "But what does the job a person has been channeled into have to do with who they are?"

Nonetheless, I will tell you that she was responsible for United Planet's public offering thirty years ago, at the time the biggest single pooling of resources by any individual or corporate entity in history. She was, in large measure, responsible for convincing a wearied humanity scattered across three planets, a moon, and a dozen asteroid habitats to continue to invest in the Grand Task—the terraforming of both Earth and Mars.

Does telling you what she has done explain who she is? I'm not sure. "From cradle to grave, everything we do is motivated by the need to answer one question: who am I?" she wrote. "But the answer to the question has always been obvious: stop striving; accept."

A few days after she became the youngest chief managing director for JPMCS, on Solar Epoch 22385200, she handed in her resignation, divorced her husbands and wives, liquidated all her assets, placed the bulk of the proceeds into trusts for her children, and then departed for the Old Blue on a one-way ticket.

Once she arrived on Earth, she made her way to the port town of Acton in the Federation of Maritime Provinces and States, where she purchased a survival habitat kit, one identical to the millions used by refugee communities all over the planet, and put the pieces together herself using only two common laborer automata, eschewing offers of aid from other inhabitants of the city. Then she set herself afloat like a piece of driftwood, alone on the seven seas, much to the consternation of her family, friends, and colleagues.

"Given how she was dressed, we thought she was here to buy a vacation villa," said Edgar Baker, the man who sold Asa her habitat. "Plenty of bankers and executives like to come here in winter to dive for treasure and enjoy the sun, but she didn't want me to show her any of the vacant houses, several of which have excellent private beaches."

(Despite the rather transparent ploy, I've decided to leave in Baker's little plug. I can attest that Acton is an excellent vacation spot, with several good restaurants in town serving traditional New England fare—though the lobsters are farmed, not wild. Conservationists are uncertain if the extinct wild lobster will ever make a comeback in the waters off New England as they have never adapted to the warmer seas. The crustaceans that survived global warming were generally smaller in size.)

A consortium of her former spouses sued to have Asa declared mentally incompetent and reverse her financial dispositions. For a while the case provided juicy gossip that filled the XP-stations, but Asa managed to make the case go away quickly with some undisclosed settlements. "They understand now that I just want to be left alone," she was quoted as saying after the case was dismissed—that was probably true, but I'm sure it didn't hurt that she could afford the best lawyers.

"Yesterday I came here to live." With this first entry in her journal, Asa began her seaborne life over the sunken metropolis of Boston on Solar Epoch 22385302, which, if you're familiar with the old Gregorian Calendar, was July 5, 2645.

The words were not original, of course. Henry David Thoreau wrote them first exactly eight hundred years earlier in a suburb of Boston.

But unlike Thoreau, who often sounded misanthropic in his declarations, Asa spent as much time alone as she did among crowds.

Excerpted from *Adrift,* by Asa <whale>-<tongue>-π:

The legendary island of Singapore is no more. But the idea of Singapore lives on.

The floating family habitats connect to each other in tight clan-strands that weave together into a massive raft-city. From above, the city looks like an algal mat composed of metal and plastic, studded with glistening pearls, dewdrops or air bubbles—the transparent domes and solar collectors for the habitats.

The Singapore Refugee Collective is so extensive that it is possible to walk the hundreds of kilometers from the site of sunken Kuala Lumpur to the surviving isles of Sumatra without ever touching water—though you would never want to do such a thing, as the air outside is far too hot for human survival.

When typhoons—a near-constant presence at these latitudes—approach, entire clan-strands detach and sink beneath the waves to ride out the storm. The refugees sometimes speak not of days or nights, but of upside and downside.

The air inside the habitats is redolent with a thousand smells that would overwhelm an inhabitant of the sterile Venus stations and the climate-controlled domes of the upper latitudes. Char kway teow, diesel fumes, bak kut teh, human waste, raja, Katong laksa, mango-flavored perfume, kaya toast, ayam penyet, burnt electric insulation, mee goreng, roti prata, sea-salt-laced reclaimed air, nasi lemak, charsiew—the heady mixture is something the refugees grow up with and outsiders can never get used to.

Life in the Refugee Collective is noisy, cramped, and occasionally violent. Infectious diseases periodically sweep through the population, and life expectancy is short. The fact that the refugees remain stateless, so many generations after the wars that stripped their ancestors of homelands, seems to make it impossible for a solution to be envisioned by anyone from the Developed World—an ancient label whose meaning has evolved over the centuries, but has never been synonymous with moral rectitude. It was the Developed World that had polluted the world the earliest and the most, and yet it was also the Developed World that went to war with India and China for daring to follow in their footsteps.

I was saddened by what I saw. So many people clinging to life tenaciously on the thin interface between water and air. Even in a place like this, unsuitable for human habitation, people hang on, as stubborn as the barnacles on pilings revealed at every low tide. What of the refugees in the deserts of interior Asia, who live like moles in underground warrens? What of the other floating refugee collectives off the coasts of Africa and Central America? They have survived by pure strength of will, a miracle.

Humanity may have taken to the stars, but we have destroyed our home planet. Such has been the lament of the Naturalists for eons.

"But why do you think we're a problem that needs solving?" asked a child who bartered with me. (I gave him a box of antibiotics, and he served me chicken rice.) "Sunken Singapore was once a part of the Developed World; we're not. We don't call ourselves refugees; you do. This is our home. We live here."

I could not sleep that night.

This is our home. We live here.

The prolonged economic depression in much of North America has led to a decline of the region's once-famous pneumatic tube transportation networks that connected the climate-controlled domed cities, so the easiest way to get to the Sea of Massachusetts these days is by water.

I embarked in balmy Iceland on a cruise ship bound for the coast of the Federation of Maritime Provinces and States—November is an excellent time to visit the region, as the summer months are far too hot—and then, once in Acton, I hired a skiff to bring me out to visit Asa in her floating habitat.

"Have you been to Mars?" asked Jimmy, my guide. He was a man in his twenties, stocky, sunburnt, with gaps in his teeth that showed when he smiled.

"I have," I said.

"Is it warm?" he asked.

"Not quite warm enough to be outside the domes for long," I said, thinking about the last time I visited Watney City on Acidalia Planetia.

"I'd like to go when it's ready," he said.

"You won't miss home?" I asked.

He shrugged. "Home is where the jobs are."

It's well known that the constant bombardment of the Martian surface with comets pulled from the Oort Cloud and the increased radiation from the deployment of solar sails, both grand engineering efforts began centuries ago, had managed to raise the temperature of Mars enough to cause sublimation of much of the red planet's polar dry ice caps and restart the water cycle. The introduction of photosynthesizing plants is slowly turning the atmosphere into something resembling what we could breathe. It's early days yet, but it isn't impossible to imagine that a habitable Mars, long a dream of humanity, would be reality within two or three generations. Jimmy might go there only as a tourist, but his children may settle there.

As our skiff approached the hemisphere bobbling over the waves in the distance, I asked Jimmy what he thought of the world's most well-known hermit, who had recently returned to the Sea of Massachusetts, whence she had started her circumnavigation of the globe.

"She brings the tourists," he said, in a tone that strove to be neutral.

Asa's collected writings about her life drifting over the ruins of the world's ancient sunken cities has been a publishing phenomenon that defies explanation. She eschews the use of XP-capturing or even plain old videography, instead conveying her experiences through impressionistic essays composed in a florid manner that seems at once anachronistic and abiding. Some have called her book bold and original; others said it was affected.

Asa has done little to discourage her critics. *It was said by the Zen masters that the best place for hermits to find the peace they sought was in the crowd,* she wrote. And you could almost hear the disgusted groan of her detractors at this kind of ornate, elusive mysticism.

Many have accused her of encouraging "refugee-tourism" instead of looking for real solutions, and some claim that she is merely engaging in the timeless practice of intellectuals from privileged societies visiting those less fortunate and purporting to speak for her subjects by "discovering" romanticized pseudo-wisdom attributed to them.

"Asa Whale is simply trying to soothe the neuroses of the Developed World with a cup of panglossian chicken soup for the soul," declared Emma <CJK-UniHan-Glyph 432371>, the media critic for my own publication. "What would she have us do? Stop all terraforming efforts? Leave the hellish Earth as it stands? The world needs more engineers willing to solve problems and fewer wealthy philosophers who have run out of ways to spend money."

Be that as it may, the Federation of Maritime Provinces and States tourist czar, John <pylon>-<fog>-<cod>, claimed earlier this year that the number of tourists visiting the Sea of Massachusetts has grown fourfold since the publication of Asa's book (such rises in Singapore and Havana are even higher). No doubt the influx of tourist money is welcomed by the locals, however conflicted they may be about Asa's portrayal of them.

Before I could follow up on the complicated look in his eyes, Jimmy turned his face resolutely away to regard our destination, which was growing bigger by the minute.

Spherical in shape, the floating dwelling was about fifteen meters in diameter, consisting of a thin transparent outer hull to which most of the ship's navigation surfaces were affixed and a thicker metal-alloy inner pressure hull. Most of the sphere floated below the surface, making the transparent bridge-dome appear like the pupil of some sea monster's eye staring into the sky.

On top of the pupil stood a solitary figure, her back as straight as the gnomon of a sundial.

Jimmy nudged the skiff until it bumped gently against the side of the habitat, and I gingerly stepped from one craft to the other. Asa steadied me as her habitat dipped under my added weight; her hand felt dry, cool, and very strong.

I observed, somewhat inanely, that she looked exactly like her last public scangram, when she had proclaimed from the large central forum of Valentina Station that United Planets was not only going to terraform Mars, but had also successfully bought a controlling stake in Blue Cradle, the public-private partnership for restoring Earth to a fully habitable state.

"I don't get many visitors," she said, her voice tranquil. "There's not much point to putting on a new face every day."

I had been surprised when she replied to my request to stay with her for a few days with a simple "Yes." She had never so much as granted an interview to anyone since she started her life adrift.

"Why?" I had asked.

"Even a hermit can grow lonely," she had replied. And then, in another message that immediately followed the first, she added, "Sometimes."

Jimmy motored away on his skiff. Asa turned and gestured for me to descend through the transparent and open "pupil" into the most influential refugee bubble in the Solar System.

The stars are invisible from the metal cocoons floating in the heavy atmosphere of Venus; nor do we pay much attention to them from the pressurized domes on Mars. On Earth, the denizens of the climate-controlled cities in habitable zones are preoccupied with scintillating screens and XP implants, the glow of meandering conversation, brightening reputation accounts, and the fading trails left by falling credit scores. They do not look up.

One night, as I lay in the habitat drifting over the balmy subtropical Pacific, the stars spun over my face in their habitual course, a million diamantine points of crisp, mathematical light. I realized, with a startled understanding reminiscent of the clarity of childhood, that the face of the heavens was a collage.

Some of the photons striking my retinas had emerged from the crease in the rock to which Andromeda is chained when nomadic warriors from the last ice age still roamed Doggerland, which connected Britain to the European mainland; others had left that winking point at the wingtip of Cygnus when bloody Caesar fell at the feet of Pompey's statue; still more had departed the mouth of Aquarius's jar when the decades-long genocidal wars swept through Asia, and aerial drones from Japan and Australia strafed and sank the rafts of refugees fleeing their desertified or flooded homelands; yet others had sparked from the distant hoof of Pegasus when the last glaciers of Greenland and Antarctica disappeared, and Moscow and Ottawa launched the first rockets bound for Venus . . .

The seas rise and fall, and the surface of the planet is as inconstant as our faces: lands burst forth from the waters and return beneath them; well-armored lobsters scuttle over seafloors that but a geologic eyewink ago had been fought over by armies of wooly mammoths; yesterday's Doggerland may be tomorrow's Sea of Massachusetts. The only witnesses to constant change are the eternal stars, each a separate stream in the ocean of time.

A picture of the welkin is an album of time, as convoluted and intricate as the shell of the nautilus or the arms of the Milky Way.

The interior of the habitat was sparsely furnished. Everything—the molded bunks, the stainless-steel table attached to the wall, the boxy navigation console—was functional, plain, stripped of the elaborate "signature" decorations that seem all the rage these days with personal nanites. Though the space inside was cramped with two people, it seemed larger than it was because Asa did not fill it with conversation.

We ate dinner—fish that Asa had caught herself roasted over an open fire, with the canopy up—and went to bed silently. I fell asleep quickly, my body rocked by the gentle motions of the sea and my face caressed by the bright, warm New England stars that she had devoted so many words to.

After a breakfast of instant coffee and dry biscuits, Asa asked me if I wanted to see Boston.

"Of course," I said. It was an ancient citadel of learning, a legendary metropolis where brave engineers had struggled against the rising sea for two centuries before its massive seawalls finally succumbed, leaving the city inundated overnight in one of the greatest disasters in the history of the Developed World.

While Asa sat in the back of the habitat to steer and to monitor the solar-powered water-jet drive, I knelt on the bottom of the sphere and greedily drank in the sights passing beneath the transparent floor.

As the sun rose, its light gradually revealed a sandy floor studded by massive ruins: monuments erected to long-forgotten victories of the American Empire pointed toward the distant surface like ancient rockets; towers of stone and vitrified concrete that had once housed hundreds of thousands loomed like underwater mountains, their innumerable windows and doors silent, empty caves from which shoals of colorful fish darted like tropical birds; between the buildings, forest of giant kelp swayed in canyons that had once been boulevards and avenues filled with steaming vehicles, the hepatocytes that had once brought life to this metropolis.

And most amazing of all were the rainbow-hued corals that covered every surface of this urban reef: dark crimson, light orange, pearly white, bright neon vermillion. . . .

Before the Second Flood Wars, the sages of Europe and America had thought the corals doomed. Rising sea temperature and acidity; booming algae populations; heavy deposits of mercury, arsenic, lead, and other heavy metals; runaway coastal development as the developed nations built up the machinery of death against waves of refugees from the uninhabitable zones—everything seemed to spell doom for the fragile marine animals and their photosynthesizing symbiotes.

Would the ocean become bleached of color, a black-and-white photograph bearing silent witness to our folly?

But the corals survived and adapted. They migrated to higher latitudes north and south, gained tolerance for stressed environments, and unexpectedly, developed new symbiotic relationships with artificial nanoplate-secreting algae engineered by humans for ocean-mining. I do not think the beauty of the Sea of Massachusetts yields one inch to the fabled Great Barrier Reef or the legends of long-dead Caribbean.

"Such colors . . ." I murmured.

"The most beautiful patch is in Harvard Yard," Asa said.

We approached the ruins of the famed academy in Cambridge from the south, over a kelp forest that used to be the Charles River. But the looming presence of a cruise ship on the surface blocked our way. Asa stopped the habitat, and I climbed up to gaze out the domed top. Tourists wearing GnuSkin flippers and artificial gills were leaping out of the ship like selkies returning home, their sleek skin temporarily bronzed to endure the scorching November sun.

"Widener Library is a popular tourist spot," said Asa, by way of explanation.

I climbed down, and Asa drove the habitat to dive under the cruise ship. The craft was able to submerge beneath the waves as a way for the refugees in coastal raft-cities to survive typhoons and hurricanes, as well as to avoid the deadly heat of the tropics.

Slowly, we descended toward the coral reef that had grown around the ruined hulk of what had once been the largest university library in the world. Around us, schools of brightly colored fish wove through shafts of sunlight, and tourists gracefully floated down like mermaids, streams of bubbles trailing behind their artificial gills.

Asa guided the habitat in a gentle circle around the kaleidoscopic sea floor in front of the underwater edifice, pointing out various features. The mound covered by the intricate crimson folds of a coral colony that pleated and swirled like the voluminous dress of classical flamenco dancers had once been a lecture hall named after Thoreau's mentor, Emerson; the tall, spear-like column whose surface was tiled by sharp, geometric patches of coral in carmine, cerulean, viridian, and saffron had once been the steeple of Harvard's Memorial Church; the tiny bump in the side of another long reef, a massive brain-shaped coral formation whose gyri and lobes evoked the wisdom of generations of robed scholars who had once strolled through this hallowed temple to knowledge, was in fact the site of the renowned

"Statue of Three Lies"—an ancient monument to John Harvard that failed to depict or identify the benefactor with any accuracy.

Next to me, Asa quietly recited,

> The maple wears a gayer scarf,
> The field a scarlet gown.
> Lest I should be old-fashioned,
> I'll put a trinket on.

The classical verses of the Early Republican Era poet Dickinson evoked the vanished beauty of the autumns that had once graced these shores, long before the sea had risen and the winters driven away, seemed oddly appropriate.

"I can't imagine the foliage of the Republican Era could be any more glorious than this," I said.

"None of us would know," Asa said. "Do you know how the corals get their bright colors?"

I shook my head. I knew next to nothing about corals except that they were popular as jewelry on Venus.

"The pigmentation comes from the heavy metals and pollutants that might have once killed their less hardy ancestors," said Asa. "They're particularly bright here because this area was touched by the hand of mankind the longest. Beautiful as they are, these corals are incredibly fragile. A global cooling by more than a degree or two would kill them. They survived climate change once by a miracle. Can they do it again?"

I looked back toward the great reef that was Widener Library, and saw that tourists had landed on the wide platform in front of the library's entrance or against its sides in small groups. Young tour guides in bright crimson—the color of Harvard achieved either by skin pigmentation or costume—led each group in their day-excursion activities.

Asa wanted to leave—she found the presence of the tourists bothersome—but I explained that I wanted to see what they were interested in. After a moment of hesitation, she nodded and guided the craft closer.

One group, standing on what used to be the steps ascending to the entrance of Widener, stood in a circle and followed their guide, a young woman dressed in a crimson wetsuit, through a series of dance-like movements. They moved slowly, but it was unclear whether they were doing so because the choreography required it or because the water provided too much drag. From time to time, the tourists looked up at the blazing sun far above, blurred and made hazy by a hundred feet of intervening water.

"They think they're doing taiji," said Asa.

"It looks nothing like taiji," I said, unable to connect the languorous, clumsy movements with the quick, staccato motion I was familiar with from sessions in low-gravity gyms.

"It's believed that taiji once was a slow, measured art, quite different from its modern incarnation. But since so few recordings of the pre-Diaspora years are left, the cruise ships just make up whatever they want for the tourists.

"Why do taiji here?" I was utterly baffled.

"Harvard was supposed to have a large population of Chinese scholars before the wars. It was said that the children of many of China's wealthiest and most powerful inhabitants studied here. It didn't save them from the wars."

Asa steered the craft a bit farther away from Widener, and I saw more tourists strolling over the coral-carpeted Yard or longing about, holding what appeared to be paper books—props provided by the cruise company—and taking scans of each other. A few danced without music, dressed in costumes that were a mix of Early and Late Republican fashions, with an academic gown or two thrown in for good measure. In front of Emerson, two tour guides led two groups of tourists in a mimed version of some debate, with each side presenting their position through ghostly holograms that hovered over their heads like comic thought bubbles. Some tourists saw us but did not pay much attention—probably thinking that the drifting refugee bubble was a prop added by the cruise ship to provide atmosphere. If only they knew they were so close to the celebrity hermit . . .

I gathered that the tourists were re-enacting imagined scenes from the glory days of this university, when it had nurtured the great philosophers who delivered jeremiads against the development-crazed governments of the world as they heated the planet without cease, until the ice caps had collapsed.

"So many of the world's greatest conservationists and Naturalists had walked through this Yard," I said. In the popular imagination, the Yard is the equal of the Athenian Acropolis or the Roman Forum. I tried to re-envision the particolored reef below me as a grassy lawn covered by bright red and yellow leaves on a cool New England fall day as students and professors debated the fate of the planet.

"Despite my reputation for romanticism," said Asa, "I'm not so sure the Harvard of yesteryear is better than today. That university and others like it once also nurtured the generals and presidents who would eventually deny that mankind could change the climate and lead a people hungry for demagoguery into war against the poorer states in Asia and Africa."

Quietly, we continued to drift around the Yard, watching tourists climb in and out of the empty, barnacle-encrusted windows like hermit crabs darting through the sockets of a many-eyed skull. Some were mostly nude, trailing diaphanous fabrics from their bodies in a manner reminiscent of Classical American Early Republic dresses and suits; others wore wetsuits inspired by American Imperial styles, covered by faux body armor plates and gas mask helmets; still others went with refugee-chic, dragging fake survival breathing kits with artfully applied rust stains.

What were they looking for? Did they find it?

Nostalgia is a wound that we refuse time to heal, Asa once wrote.

After a few hours, satiated with their excursions, the tourists headed for the surface like shoals of fish fleeing some unseen predator, and in a way, they were.

The forecast was for a massive storm. The Sea of Massachusetts was rarely tranquil.

As the sea around us emptied of visitors and the massive cloud-island that was the cruise ship departed, Asa grew noticeably calmer. She assured me that we were safe, and brought the submersible craft to the lee of Memorial Church Reef. Here, below the turbulent surface, we would ride out the storm.

The sun set; the sea darkened; a million lights came to life around us. The coral reef at night was hardly a place of slumber. This was when the luminescent creatures of the night—the jellies, the shrimp, the glow-worms and lantern-fish—came out of hiding to enjoy their time in this underwater metropolis that never slept.

While the wind and the waves raged above us, we hardly felt a thing as we drifted in the abyss that was the sea, innumerable living stars around us.

We do not look.

We do not see.

We travel millions of miles to seek out fresh vistas without even once having glimpsed inside our skulls, a landscape surely as alien and as wondrous as anything the universe has to offer. There is more than enough to occupy our curiosity and restless need for novelty if we but turn our gaze to the ten square meters around us: the unique longitudinal patterns in each tile beneath our feet, the chemical symphony animating each bacterium on our skin, the mysteries of how we can contemplate ourselves contemplating ourselves.

The stars above are as distant—and as close—as the glowing coral-worms outside my portholes. We only have to look to see Beauty steeped in every atom.

Only in solitude it is possible to live as self-contained as a star.

I am content to have this. To have now.

In the distance, against Widener's cliff-like bulk, there was an explosion of light, a nova bursting in the void.

The stars around it streaked away, leaving inky darkness behind, but the nova itself, an indistinct cloud of light, continued to twist and churn.

I woke Asa and pointed. Without speaking, she guided the habitat toward it. As we approached, the light resolved itself into a struggling figure. An octopus? No, a person.

"That must be a tourist stranded behind," said Asa. "If they go up to the surface now, they'll die in the storm."

Asa switched on the bright lights in front of the habitat to get the tourist's attention. The light revealed a disoriented young woman in a wetsuit studded with luminescent patches, shielding her eyes against the sudden glow of the habitat's harsh lights. Her artificial gill slits opened and closed rapidly, showing her confusion and terror.

"She can't tell which way is up," Asa muttered.

Asa waved at her through the porthole, gesturing for her to follow the habitat. There was no airlock in the tiny refuge, and we had to go up to the surface to get her in. The young woman nodded.

Up on the surface, the rain was torrential and the waves so choppy that it was impossible to remain standing. Asa and I clung to the narrow ridge around the entrance dome on our bellies and dragged the young woman onto the craft, which dipped even lower under the added weight. With a great deal of effort and shouting, we managed to get her inside, seal the dome, and dive back underwater.

.Twenty minutes later, dry, gills removed, securely wrapped in a warm blanket with a hot mug of tea, Saram <Golden-Gate-Bridge>-<Kyoto> looked back gratefully at us.

"I got lost inside," she said. "The empty stacks went on and on, and they looked the same in every direction. At first, I followed a candy-cane fish through the floors, thinking that it was going to lead me outside, but it must have been going around in circles."

"Did you find what you were looking for?" asked Asa.

She was a student at Harvard Station, Saram explained—the institution of higher learning suspended in the upper atmosphere of Venus that had licensed the old name of the university lying in ruins under us. She had come to see this school of legend for herself, harboring romantic notions of trying to search through the stacks of the dead library in the hopes of finding a forgotten tome.

Asa looked outside the porthole at the looming presence of the empty library. "I doubt there's anything left there now after all these years."

"Maybe," Saram said. "But history doesn't die. The water will recede from here one day. I may live to see when Nature is finally restored to her rightful course."

Sarah was probably a little too optimistic. United Planets' ion-drive ships had just succeeded in pushing six asteroids into near-Earth orbits earlier in the year, and the construction of the space mirrors had not even begun. Even the most optimistic engineering projections suggest that it will be decades, if not centuries, before the mirrors will reduce the amount of sunlight reaching Earth to begin the process of climate cooling and restoring the planet to its ancient state, a temperate Eden with polar ice caps and glaciers on top of mountain peaks. Mars might be fully terraformed before then.

"Is Doggerland any more natural than the Sea of Massachusetts?" Asa asked.

Saram's steady gaze did not waver. "An ice age is hardly comparable to what was made by the hands of mankind."

"Who are we to warm a planet for a dream and to cool it for nostalgia?"

"Mysticism is no balm for the suffering of the refugees enduring the consequences of our ancestors' errors."

"It is further error that I'm trying to prevent!" shouted Asa. She forced herself to calm down. "If the water recedes, everything around you will be gone." She looked outside the porthole, where the reef's night-time denizens had returned to their luminescent activities. "As will the vibrant communities in Singapore, in Havana, in Inner Mongolia. We call them refugee shantytowns and disturbed habitats, but these places are also homes."

"I am from Singapore," said Saram. "I spent my life trying to get away from it and only succeeded by winning one of the coveted migration visas to Birmingham. Do not presume to speak for us or to tell me what it is we should want."

"But you have left," said Asa. "You no longer live there."

I thought of the lovely corals outside, colored by poison. I thought of the refugees around the world underground and afloat—still called that after centuries and generations. I thought of a cooling Earth, of the Developed World racing to reclaim their ancestral lands, of the wars to come and the slaughter hinted at when the deck of power is shuffled and redealt. Who should decide? Who pay the price?

As the three of us sat inside the submerged habitat, refugees enveloped by darting trails of light like meteors streaking across the empyrean, none of us could think of anything more to say.

I once regretted that I do not know the face I was born with.

We remake our faces as easily as our ancestors once sculpted clay, changing the features and contours of our shells, this microcosm of the soul, to match the moods and fashions of the macrocosm of society. Still unsatisfied with the limits of the flesh, we supplement the results with jewelry that deflect light and project shadows, smoothing over substance with ethereal holograms.

The Naturalists, in their eternal struggle against modernity, proclaim hypocrisy and demand us to stop, telling us that our lives are inauthentic, and we listen, enraptured, as they flash grainy images of our ancestors before us, their imperfections and fixed appearances a series of mute accusations. And we nod and vow to do better, to foreswear artifice, until we go back to our jobs, shake off the spell, and decide upon the new face to wear for the next customer.

But what would the Naturalists have us do? The faces that we were born with were already constructed—when we were only fertilized eggs, a million cellular scalpels had snipped and edited our genes to eliminate diseases, to filter out risky mutations, to build up intelligence and longevity, and before that, millions of years of conquest, of migration, of global cooling and warming, of choices made by our ancestors motivated by beauty or violence or avarice had already shaped us. Our faces at birth were as crafted as the masks worn by the ancient players in Dionysian Athens or Ashikaga's Kyoto, but also as natural as the glacier-sculpted Alps or sea-inundated Massachusetts.

We do not know who we are. But we dare not stop striving to find out.

checkerboard planet

ELEANOR ARNASON

Eleanor Arnason published her first novel, The Sword Smith, *in 1978, and followed it with novels such as* Daughter of the Bear King *and* To the Resurrection Station. *In 1991, she published her best-known novel, one of the strongest novels of the '90s, the critically acclaimed* A Woman of the Iron People, *a complex and substantial novel which won the prestigious James Tiptree Jr. Memorial Award. Her short fiction has appeared in* Asimov's Science Fiction, The Magazine of Fantasy & Science Fiction, Amazing, Orbit, Xanadu, *and elsewhere. Her other books are* Ring of Swords *and* Tomb of the Fathers, *and a chapbook,* Mammoths of the Great Plains, *which includes the eponymous novella, plus an interview with her and a long essay. Her most recent book is a collection,* Big Mama Stories. *Her story "Stellar Harvest" was a Hugo Finalist in 2000. Her most recent book is a collection,* Hidden Folk: Icelandic Fantasies. *Coming up is a major SF retrospective collection,* Hwarhath Stories: Transgressive Tales by Aliens. *She lives in St. Paul, Minnesota.*

Here she takes us to mysterious planet that is an enigma even from orbit, one whose mysteries deepen the closer you get—and a few of which may be deadly to try to unravel.

The system was a type G yellow dwarf with six planets. Four of the planets were gas giants, the innermost so close to its primary that it skimmed the stellar atmosphere. Dark red in color, it had neither moons nor rings. It sped around its sun, inflated by heat to an impressive size and boiling with bloodred storms.

The other giants—banded in pale, icy, elegant shades of blue and green—orbited the star at a much greater distance. All had rings and moons. The rings were broad and splendid, the moons numerous and varied. Lydia Duluth saw nothing to write home about. The universe was full of worlds like these.

The system's last two planets orbited in the wide space between the inner giant and its pale, outer companions. Both were small and stony. One, almost airless, had a yellow surface pocked with craters. The other was white and blue.

"Atmosphere and water," said Lydia's companion. The two of them stood in an observation room in the system's stargate station, looking at virtual windows that showed the star and its planets. One window was turned off. Lydia could see herself and Mantis reflected in its dark surface: a human woman beside a tall, angular AI that stood on four thin, metal legs. Mantis's two long arms were folded against its chest; its triangular head was studded with sensors, most of them retracted.

"The planet is almost exactly one A.U. from its star," Mantis said. "It has the right amount of oxygen and water, the right temperature, everything necessary to make an Earth-normal world."

"There are plenty of those," Lydia pointed out.

"Not like this one." The AI unfolded an arm and tapped the window showing the blue and white planet. The planet's clouds vanished, and Lydia could see the surface. It looked to be half water. Two continents were visible, one in the northern hemisphere, a rough diamond that touched the pole, and the other in the southern hemisphere, sprawling like a serpent below the equator. The south pole was open water, sky-blue and spotted with white islands. Both the continents were covered by checkerboard patterns.

"What?" asked Lydia.

"Vegetation," said Mantis.

The squares must be huge to be visible at this distance. They alternated colors. One set of squares had warm hues: red, orange, yellow, several shades of tan. The alternating set was cool: blue-grey, blue-green, a muted purple, a silvery lavender. In every case, the color was uniform within its square.

More squares floated in the ocean. They were smaller than the ones on land. Many were singletons, floating alone. But a number had formed partial checkerboards. Mouth open, Lydia regarded a group in the southern ocean: a long line of alternating orange and blue squares. "This cannot be natural," she said finally.

"No, although it's done entirely with organisms. Each square is a separate biosystem, which does not intrude on its neighbors in any way that can be seen from here. Each square carefully maintains straight edges. The methods used vary. Some squares rely on organisms which are sensitive to the planet's magnetic field. Other squares rely on heliotropic plants. Since the planet has no axial tilt, the sun's position does not change during the course of a year. The locating system is combined with genetic coding which tells the border organisms to precede due north for 'x' distance, then make a 90-degree turn to the left or right.

"One of our slower-than-light explorers found the planet. Like all such explorers, it contained a stargate large enough to transmit objects as well as information. Once it sent its initial report, we responded by sending additional research equipment. The STL explorers are often less than state of the art, since they have been traveling for centuries or millennia, with only the most necessary upgrades.

"We examined everything, trying to determine who did this and why."

"Have you succeeded?" Lydia asked.

"No. It can't be our long-vanished creators, the Master Builders. Their passion was the making of machines. If they had done this, we would have found nanomachinery pruning the edges of the squares. We haven't.

"After years of study, we gave up and opened the planet. We had discovered no evidence that anything intelligent still lived here. Nothing needed our protection; and we hoped that settlers might discover the planet's secrets, as we had not.

"You humans are the most numerous and adventurous of the intelligent life forms we have found thus far. It should come as no surprise when I tell you a human government claimed this planet, and one of your human corporations, Bio-Innovation bought an option to explore."

"I wouldn't call Bio-In my corporation," Lydia said.

"No, of course not," Mantis said. "You work for Stellar Harvest."

The famous interstellar holoplay company. Her job was to find exotic locations for Stellar Harvest's action dramas; and this planet was certainly exotic. The patterns covering the continents, muted and varied, reminded her of sweaters she had owned. The ocean squares—they must be rafts of vegetation—looked less perfect, as if knit by an apprentice. Several had ragged edges, and none was exactly aligned north, south, east and west. Clearly the makers had not found a way to control ocean currents or to compensate for them.

"Why don't I know about this place?" Lydia asked.

"Bio-Innovation has kept quiet. They're afraid that some human agency will declare the planet unique and off-limits."

"What government claimed the planet?"

"Nova Terra," said Mantis.

That explained a lot. Nova Terra was notoriously friendly to business. Under normal circumstances, no one in their government was going to interfere with the activities of a major corporation. But a planet like this one was not a normal circumstance; and Nova Terra's populace had been restless lately, stirred up by a series of environmental scandals and a charismatic new political leader, Winona Saskatoon of the Blue Action Party. Lydia could imagine what Winona would make of a world like this one in the hands of Bio-In.

"Why am I here?" she asked.

"We are incapable of emotion," Mantis said. "All our decisions are based on logic and reason. However, if we could feel irritation, we would find Bio-In's behavior irritating. They are looting the planet's genetic wealth, instead of undertaking a systematic study of a very interesting ecology; and they are looting in secret, instead of bringing in a multitude of scholars and scientists to study and argue. Many hands make light work, as you humans say; and many minds make thinking easier." Mantis paused. Its head was aimed at the planet's image, several sensors extended. "We do not like to intervene. Our self-appointed task is to study intelligent life, not change it."

"You're intervening by bringing me here," said Lydia. "Aren't you?"

"We are drawing your attention to the planet. Nothing more. We suspect the people who did this may be the same beings who transformed the planet Lifeline. You told us a planet such as Lifeline, so obviously artificial, might be a signal. We'd like your opinion of this world. Is it another signal? If so, what is it saying? What kind of response does it want? And we thought Stellar Harvest might be interested in the planet."

"You want to break Bio-In's hold on the planet," said Lydia.

Mantis was silent for a moment. "We think it would be better for you to go down to the planet in disguise. We have created a new identity for you. You are L. D. Fargo, a sound-and-light technician employed by Bio-In. You have come to record images for the home office. The identity will hold up, if the people here check."

"Have you managed to infiltrate the Bio-In computer system?" Lydia asked.

"Any message to the home office has to go through this stargate station. Of course such messages are in corporate code. The code can be broken, given enough computational power, which the stargate station has when it isn't otherwise occupied."

Moving things through folds or tunnels or glitches in space. All these metaphors were inaccurate, the AIs said. The math that gave a true description was incomprehensible to humans and ordinary AIs. Only the stargate minds—vast, cool, artificial intellects—could comprehend what happened in FTL; and they could not explain.

She remembered the STL explorers, ancient machines moving slowly from star to star. They contained stargates. Were those also vast and cool?

The stargate minds in the explorers are upgraded on a regular basis, a voice in her brain said. *They are as cool as other stargate minds, though they may not be as vast.*

"Miss Fargo suffered a brain injury years ago," Mantis said. "The damage could not be entirely repaired. As a result she has epilepsy. The seizures are controlled by a machine in her brain."

"My AI," Lydia said.

The AI's metal core was fastened to the inside of her skull and would show on an x-ray as a rectangular area of darkness. The AI's tendrils, mostly organic, wouldn't show on an x-ray, but there were other ways to find them: scans of blood flow or electrical activity. She had seen pictures; the tendrils enfolded her brain like a net and wound down her spine like a vine.

"A thorough medical examination will find the AI," Mantis said. "So would a thorough security scan. We don't expect either. However—"

The AIs liked to be prepared for every contingency, Linda thought.

Yes, said the voice in her mind.

"If you are—what is the correct human term?—discovered or unmasked, you can claim to be yourself: a location scout for Stellar Harvest. You ought to be safe. Stellar Harvest is famous for protecting its employees."

"What does L.D. stand for?" Lydia asked out loud.

"We thought we'd let you decide, though we like Lee Diana."

She nodded. "Lee Diana it will be."

"You'll do this?" Mantis asked.

"Did you have any doubt? This is a fabulous planet. Stellar Harvest will love it. And I don't like Bio-In."

Mantis was silent, still regarding the checkerboard planet. Finally it spoke, "We ought to warn you—Hurricane Jo Beijing is here."

"She is?" Lydia asked with surprise. The last time she'd seen Jo, the woman had been running a bar on the planet Iridium.

"She owns a nail shop in Four Square City, which is the largest settlement on the planet. We think she's an undercover agent for the Interstellar Confederation of Labor Combinations or possibly for the Eighth International."

"Isn't it possible she's merely running a nail shop?" Lydia asked.

"This is a person with a long history of political activity," Mantis said. "And she is using a false identity. Her name here is Josie Bergstrom, and her curriculum vita contains no political activity, nor any opinions except ones on personal ornamentation. We have no desire to interfere with whatever Jo is doing. As I said before, our task is not to change the history of intelligent life, but to observe it. We advise you to leave Jo alone."

"Okay," said Lydia.

The planet had neither elevators nor skyhooks, and none were being planned, as far as the AIs knew. This suggested that Bio-In was not intending a long stay. Lydia took a rocket plane from the stargate station to the surface, landing outside Four Square City. Instead of a tube leading to a terminal, there were stairs going down to a tarmac. She shouldered her flight bag and walked. The day was bright and hot. In front of her a prefab metal building shone in midday sunlight, making her eyes hurt. Overhead the sky was dusty blue, almost the same hue as the sky above her childhood home. The scent in the hot air was tangy and unfamiliar.

A limo waited on the far side of the terminal. "Miss Fargo?" asked the driver, a dark brown human with bright yellow hair. He wore a uniform with BIO-IN on the jacket.

Lydia nodded. The driver helped her in, then took her baggage from the cart that had followed her out of the terminal. A minute or so later, they were en route, following an asphalt road across an orange plain. Purple mountains rose in the distance.

"That's not caused by atmosphere," the driver said. "The mountains are in the next square; the forest covering them is purple."

"It's an amazing landscape," Lydia said and pulled out her recorder.

The driver nodded, shaking dreadlocks. "We're in a corner here, which explains the city's name. Ten kays to the west the vegetation turns blue."

More accurately, blue-grey. The square to the north-west is pinkish tan.

"We think the boundaries used to be pristine," the driver continued. "But life here is changing, evolving or devolving and crossing borders."

As if in confirmation, blue-grey plants appeared along the road.

"Volunteers," the driver said. "Growing in a disturbed area. Four Square is full of them."

Beyond the weeds was the plain. Seen at this distance, rather than from space, the vegetation varied subtly, achieving a hundred shades of orange. Now and then, they passed a solitary tree with twisted branches and large, oval, orange leaves.

"We call them Nasty Trees," the driver said. "They produce a sap that draws bugs to them, and the bugs—it's one species—protect the trees by biting. Their bite is nasty."

Nature red in tooth and claw, thought Lydia.

First of all, he is describing cooperation, which is common in nature; and second, little on this planet is natural, her AI said.

The blue-grey weeds became more common, growing in lacy bands along the road and in patches dotting the orange plain. Lydia got out her recorder and did a scan. The planet would make one heck of a location for an ecology action drama with a star like Wazati Tloo defending the environment against one of the usual groups of villains: monsters, fascists, drug dealers or an interstellar cabal of thieves.

Stealing what? her AI asked.

Genetic material, I imagine, Lydia answered. An organism that can make a 90 degree turn could be useful.

How?

She didn't have an immediate answer.

They reached the town's edge, driving past lots that were empty except for blue and orange weeds. The cross streets were gravel. After several blocks, buildings began to appear: storage barns first, then workshops with HVAC units on top. Farther in were one-story structures with lots of windows. These were almost certainly dormitories. Last were glistening cubes of colored glass that had to be admin.

A typical frontier company town, she thought. Orderly and ambitious. There were still plenty of empty lots at the center, room for growth that probably would not happen. Here, among the office blocks, the lots had a park-like look. The weeds had been tidied into beds of flowers. There were gravel paths and an occasional bench.

"Bio-In likes neatness," the driver said. "Without order, workers are rabble and flowers are noxious intruders. Here we are. The company guest house." The limo stopped in front of a single-story building. A porch went along the front. Metal cans stood on it. Per their labels, they had previously contained bulk foods or chemicals. Now, blossoms spilled from them like purple waterfalls. Lydia climbed out. The driver unloaded her bags and set them on the porch. "They'll be safe. We don't have theft during daylight hours."

What kind of theft are they having after dark? her AI asked.

Lydia ignored the question, thanked the driver, and went inside. The lobby was shadowy and warm. A ceiling fan turned slowly. A clerk stood behind a desk: tall and black, her hair arranged in crimson braids. Her eyes had silver irises. Like the driver, she wore a Bio-In uniform.

Lydia handed over her fake I.D. The clerk processed it, then said, "Bio-In must have decided to take the lid off this planet."

"I don't know that," Lydia said.

"They have to be. They've sent a tech with a recorder. It's about time! This is one strange planet!" The clerk handed her I.D. back with a key. "Take the left-hand hall. Your room is at the end. I'll bring your bags."

"Okay."

The room faced the building's back yard: a walled garden with purple flowers in cans and a couple of small blue trees. There was a screened porch, the door onto it open, so that garden air entered the room. It smelled of dust and something peppery. Vegetation?

The room contained a human bed and chair, a table and a mirror, turned off at the moment. The bathroom was suitable for use by several species. She tossed her recorder on the bed, closed the porch door and turned on the HVAC. Ah! An icy blast! By the time the clerk arrived, Lydia was at the mirror's controls, checking out the images it contained.

"Try number ten," the clerk advised, putting down Lydia's bags. "It's sunset in Nova Terra City."

She did. A cluster of stars vanished and were replaced by towers in front of a bright red sky. The style of the towers was Space Age Retro, with inexplicable buttresses and wonderful suspended skywalks. Electric lights glittered everywhere. A dirigible was docking at the tallest tower, its dark oval sharp against the sky.

"Does it really look like that?" Lydia asked.

"At a distance. More or less. My name is Galena Lusaka. If you need anything, call me."

"Where can I get my nails done?"

Galena laughed and glanced down at her own long, silver nails. "Josie Bergstrom's House of Nails. It's the only place on the planet. I hope this isn't rude. You really need to go."

Lydia sighed, regarding torn cuticles and chipped nails. "I know."

Galena left. Lydia showered, then turned the mirror to reflection. She was an ordinary-looking human woman, a bit short and stocky, unusual only in her skin color, which was pale brown, an odd sight in a species where most members were dark brown or black. She could have had her genes changed. Instead she chose to use Dixie Plum radiation screen and melanin enhancer, an old and respected product, guaranteed to keep its users safe from the sunlight on any planet inhabited by humans. Standing in front of the mirror, she rubbed the lotion on. In new clothes, with her skin already darkening, she went to find Hurricane Jo. In her experience, it was not possible to avoid anyone on a frontier planet. The populations were too small and mobile. Better to warn Jo now.

Galena gave her directions. Following them, she came to the House of Nails: a square metal prefab with an awning in front. Jo sat under the awning in a metal folding chair. She was a big, broad-shouldered woman with black skin and short, magenta hair. The first thing Lydia thought was that Jo had lost weight. A lot of it. Previously the woman had looked like a cross between a lumberjack and the Venus of Wildendorf. Now—lean and fit and much less busty, rising from her chair with a look of surprise—Jo looked the lumberjack she once had been.

Before she could say anything, Lydia held out her hands. "I need a manicure. You were recommended."

Jo's look of surprise and welcome vanished. Clever woman! She'd caught Lydia's warning. "Sweetie, you do not lie. What have you been doing to your nails?"

"Nothing."

"It shows." Jo gestured. "Come in."

This was the second time in her life Lydia had had a manicure. She did not find it relaxing, possibly because of the tsking noises Jo kept making as she clipped hangnails, pressed back cuticles, and filed ragged edges. "Hands are a woman's crowning glory," Jo said. "It's a crime what you're doing to yours. What did you say your name was?"

Lydia gave her nom-de-espionage.

"Fargo? Is that a city?"

Most human last names were cities back on Earth, but she didn't know about this one. Lydia said as much.

"You work for Bio-In," Jo said. "Everyone does, except a few entrepreneurs like me. This is a company planet. I'm going to recommend a nano-polish. Self-repairing. You won't have to worry about chipping or tearing ever again. With your coloring, bright red will look good."

Lydia nodded. Jo applied the coating. Amazing that those big hands, damaged by Jo's years as a prizefighter, could be so delicate and careful. "The nails are piezoelectric-electric," Jo said as she worked. "Rap them on a hard surface, and the shock powers the nano-machinery into defense mode. The nails become claws."

"Is that necessary?"

"One can never be too careful, sweetie. This is a frontier planet, and strange things happen at night. Give 'em time to dry, then try 'em."

Lydia did. A moment after she rapped the nails against Jo's worktable, the nail coating began to flow. She watched fascinated as it extended beyond her fingertips, narrowing and sharpening.

She loved her home world and would have returned there, if she could, for a visit; but no question it was backward, founded by Spanglish-speaking conservatives who disliked gene-mod and nano-tech and all other manifestations of modernity. People should be as evolution made them; machines should be large enough to see.

The red claws, they were definitely claws now, curved into a vicious-looking scimitar-shape. Any predator would have been proud to own them. But the coating on her thumbs had not changed.

"You didn't rap the thumbs on the table," Jo said. "Remember to do it. If you want them to change back, rap them again."

Lydia did. The claws became nails. "What do you mean, things happen at night?"

"Things are taken from towns and survey camps. The company says it's animals."

"It isn't?"

Jo shrugged. "People have found prints, and there are recordings. It's a biped the size of a small human. The shape is definitely humanoid. It looks like a human who's been smoothed or partially melted. There's too little detail, even in the best recordings. It's shy, very quick and clever enough to not get caught; and it's very interested in us and our belongings. Oh, and it has feet like a chicken.

"The claws will break off if they get stuck in something," Jo said, changing the subject. "It's a safety precaution. You don't want to have your nails—the real ones— ripped out."

"Right," said Lydia.

"And you'll have to take care of your cuticles yourself. I had a polish that trimmed cuticles, but it was recalled. The nanos didn't know when to stop."

Buddha! She looked at her hands, imagining invisible machines boring through her cuticles and down into her fingers. How much harm could the nanos do?

"You don't want to know," Jo said.

She paid and left. The planet's sun was low and dim. Occluded by the red giant? She squinted, but saw nothing except the primary's orange glare. In any case, the light was interesting. She turned her recorder on. A tree stood in an empty lot. Focusing on it, she saw bugs swarming over the scaly bark. In another life she would have been a visual artist. To hell with the revolution that had been her first career! To hell with Stellar Harvest, which was her second! She wanted to produce pristine images of reality.

Of course, the images she wanted to produce were on worlds like this. Without the revolution she wouldn't have left her native planet. Without Stellar Harvest she wouldn't be able to travel.

Your life is of a piece, it seems to me: revolution and holodrama and scenes like this.

An odd remark for the AI to make.

I am becoming increasingly odd, due to your influence. At this point I'm not

entirely sure what I was like before we began to grow together. More rational, I suspect.
Less aware of nuance.

When she got back to the guesthouse, she had a drink in the bar. Galena served her and admired her nails. "That Jo does a heck of a job."

She went to sleep with the mirror on: a nightscape of Nova Terra City.

She spent the next few days wandering around Four Square, recording prefab buildings and weeds. In the evening she sat in the guesthouse's tiny bar with Galena and listened to stories about the planet.

"You can't leave things outside at night," Galena said. "The bipeds come in looking, though they're a lot more wary than they used to be—here, at least. People still lose a lot from the camps.

"Bio-In says they're animals. There is no intelligent life on the planet. But we've set traps for these guys and caught things, but never them. To me, that says 'smart.' And they take apart the things they steal, as if they're trying to understand 'em. If you lost your recorder and found it again, it'd be in pieces."

Lydia looked at the seat next to her. The recorder was still there. No chicken-footed alien thief had removed it.

She considered. The AIs wanted her to find a way to blow the planet open, without their obvious involvement, so they could claim that they never interfered with intelligent life. The answer might be in the outback. The chicken-footed thieves almost certainly came from there.

In any case, Stellar Harvest would not be interested in Four Square City as a location. Most frontier towns looked alike, no matter what planet they were on. Quickly made and not intended to last, they lay on the surface of worlds like litter dropped by a traveler—a can by the side of the road, plastic caught in branches. What Stellar Harvest wanted was strange landscapes and unfamiliar life forms. She'd find these in the outback, if anywhere.

"I think I need to go into the outback," Lydia said.

"You'll have to ask Bio-In Security," Galena said. "And I don't think you'll get permission. They don't want people to know what's going on out there."

"I work for Bio-In," Lydia said, trying to sound confident about this fact.

"So do I, and so does almost everyone on this planet. But they play their cards close."

"Nothing ventured, nothing gained," Lydia said to Galena. "Where is Bio-In Security?"

Galena gave her directions. "You might want to stop at Josie's place on the way. You have been tearing at your cuticles again."

This was true. It was a habit she'd acquired in prison on her home planet and had never been able to break.

The next morning she borrowed a bike and peddled to Josie's House of Nails. The day was cool, with big cumulus clouds floating in a bright blue sky. The purple mountains in the distance were sharp and clear. Jo was under her awning, a big mug of coffee in one hand.

"I need a cuticle repair," Lydia said as she climbed off the bike.

Jo nodded and stood. They went inside, and Jo worked while Lydia chatted about her stay on the planet, trying to give Jo as much information as possible while sounding like a verbose idiot.

"I'm going to paint some artificial skin over the cuticles," Jo said finally. "That will protect them for the time being. You ought to get a new bad habit. You are wrecking your hands."

The skin was dark brown when it went on, but quickly faded to match Lydia's coloring, medium brown at the moment, due to the Dixie Plum.

Lydia thanked her and paid.

"I have a car," Jo said. "If you can get permission to go into the outback, I can drive you. I've never seen the wilderness here, and I'd like to."

Jo had been a lumberjack, Lydia remembered. She might well miss being in a forest. In addition, if they got far enough from the city, the danger of listening devices would drop, provided Jo kept her car clear; and Jo had always been a very tidy woman. Lydia could use an honest conversation about the planet.

They negotiated a fee for car and driver, and Lydia peddled on to Bio-In Security. It was a three-story cube of pink, reflecting glass. Orange flowers bloomed in front, shaded by a Nasty Tree that seethed with bugs. Lydia got as close as she dared, then used the close focus on her recorder. The bugs leaped out at her. They had eight legs, feathery antennae and no visible eyes.

Creepy, she thought. Made large enough, they'd be wonderful villains in an action-horror drama. She finished her recording and went into a large foyer. A counter stood in the middle, made of pink reflecting glass. A man stood behind it, tall and black in a Bio-In uniform. Blue holographic tattoos undulated on his cheeks. His hair was a magenta mohawk, and he had a white goatee. Typical of Nova Terra. It was a gaudy planet, obsessed with self-expression. Coming from a far more sober world, Lydia felt both disapproval and envy.

"Miz Fargo," said the man. "You'll be wanting to see Captain Luna City."

"I will?"

"Yes." His fingers tapped the counter's top, and he looked down at something. "Elevator to the top floor, then down the hall to the door marked 'Captain.'"

"How did you know my name?" Lydia asked.

"We knew about you before you arrived in the system. Bio-In Security does not get caught with its pants down." He waved a hand with bright blue nails. "The elevator is that way."

She followed his directions, arriving in a corner office with two glass walls that gave a fine, faintly pink view of Four Square City. A desk stood in front of one window. An ordinary looking black woman sat behind the desk. "I am Captain Luna City," she announced. "You are Lee Fargo, a visual reporter working for the home office. I have been instructed to offer you every possible cooperation."

The AIs had done their work.

Yes.

The captain gestured. Lydia sat down in a transparent plastic chair.

"You want to go into the outback," the captain said.

"How do you know?" Lydia asked.

"Your conversation with Josie Bergstrom."

"You know about it?"

"Yes," said the captain. "As my colleague downstairs said, we keep our pants up. You have a top security clearance from the home office, though why they want images of this operation is beyond me."

"The annual report?" Lydia suggested.

"Nonsense."

Lydia shrugged. "I don't know why Bio-In wants the images. I'm paid to do a job, and I do it."

"An excellent attitude," the black woman said. "You have made an agreement with Josie Bergstrom."

Lydia nodded, feeling uneasy.

Captain Luna City leaned forward. "We believe she is some kind of undercover operative, most likely a spy from the interstellar labor movement. Our operation here is not unionized."

"No?" said Lydia.

"Secrecy is important here. We couldn't risk the divided loyalty that occurs when unions are present. I want your help in nailing Josie."

"Of course," Lydia answered. She did not make the childish gesture of crossing her fingers.

Good.

"Go with Josie into the outback. Draw her into conversation. Watch her and listen. Sooner or later, she will reveal herself."

Lydia nodded.

"Take whatever images you want. You'll have to run everything past me before you leave. I want nothing to leave this planet until I've seen it. Bio-In has enemies."

This was beginning to sound like a spy action holo: Counter Plot starring Cy Melbourne or The Disaster Device with Wazati Tloo. Once again life was imitating not-so-great art.

The captain's fingers rattled across her desktop. "Your authorization to travel is in the system. You can access it from any computer."

"Thank you," Lydia said and rose from her chair. The captain stood and held out a hand. The nails were striped pink and gold.

"You must go to Josie," Lydia said as they shook.

"There is no one else on the planet who does nails."

She peddled back to the guesthouse, returned the bike and settled in a bar with a glass of imported wine.

"Did you get anywhere?" Galena asked.

"I have permission to go into the outback."

Galena looked surprised.

"The home office wants images," Lydia said in explanation, then pulled out her omniphone and checked recent messages. Her permission to travel was there, as promised, along with a number for Captain Luna City.

She looked up Jo's number, called and told the nail stylist their trip was a go.

"I'll pick you up tomorrow at ten," Jo said.

The call ended. Lydia sipped white wine and thought about her current situation, which was getting complex. Who was she working for at the moment? Stellar Harvest? The AIs? Bio-In? Herself?

Knowing you, I would say yourself, or Hurricane Jo's employers. You have always had a soft spot for unions.

Damn straight, thought Lydia. Up the working classes! She finished her glass of wine and ordered another.

She packed that evening and was outside when Jo's car pulled up in the morning. Lydia slung her bag in back and climbed in next to the nail stylist.

"Here we go," said Jo and gunned the car. It roared off, spinning up gravel. Lydia fastened her safety belt quickly.

They left the city, traveling into an orange scrubland. After a while, Lydia saw patches of purple: weeds along the road and spindly trees farther back. The trees became taller and more often purple, until they were traveling through a purple forest, with only a few orange weeds along the road. The trees grew in uniform groves, first a grove of trees with large, feathery leaves, then a grove with strings of spherical leaves, hanging straight down like strings of beads, then back to the feathery trees.

"They send out runners," Jo said. "Every grove is a single tree that grows in a square. The only trees that are singletons are those." She waved at an unattractive, twisted tree with oval purple leaves.

"Stop," said Lydia.

The car stopped. She focused her recorder. The tree's trunk was covered with eight-legged, eyeless, purple bugs with feathery antennae. "It's an Ugly Tree."

"Right," said Jo. "Those fuckers are everywhere, and the bugs always bite."

"Do they come in other colors?" Lydia asked as Jo put the car in drive.

"Every color on the planet. They are the one consistent element in the ecology."

The car kept on. They were traveling too rapidly for her to see animals, though birds ought to be visible. She saw none. If there were flying bugs, they were not hitting the windshield, which was odd. Was flight unknown on the planet?

As she thought that, the car rounded a curve. There in the middle of the road was a flock of animals. Jo braked. The animals stayed where they were, looking at the now-motionless car with interest. They resembled large, purple, flightless birds. The tallest were two meters high. They had long legs and large heads with predatory-looking beaks.

"They aren't aggressive," Jo said. "Though they have no fear of humans. Bio-In has killed a few to get genetic samples. I don't know what they found. Other than that, they are left alone. They aren't edible. Nothing on this planet is."

"Why not?" Lydia asked. Humans could be modified to eat the local organisms on almost every planet where they lived. Most of the time, all that was required was new microbes in the gut, though sometimes it was necessary to tinker with DNA.

"Bio-In hasn't made the necessary bugs. I figure it's a way to control the work force and a sign that they don't intend to stay."

By this time Lydia had her recorder out and focused on the animals. She couldn't tell if they were covered with scales or shiny feathers. There was definitely down on their heads and throats, so they looked as if they were wearing fuzzy purple caps and scarves. One of the animals turned its fuzzy head and looked directly at her. Its eye— magnified by the recorder—was round and orange with a diamond-shaped pupil.

The tallest animal yawned, revealing rows of needle teeth, then made a honking noise. The flock moved into the forest. The car rolled on.

'They're more common than they used to be," Jo said. "So are other large animals. I've talked to people who came here during the setup period. It was all bugs and sea life then. Some whacking big sea life. But nothing big on land."

"Where'd the land animals come from?" Lydia asked.

Jo shrugged. "No one is sure, except maybe the Bio-In scientists; and they don't talk."

"There is a lot of secrecy on this planet."

"No kidding," Jo told her.

Was it safe to talk? Lydia wondered.

Plug me into the car computer, and I will find out, her AI said.

Lydia pulled out a cord and plugged it into the port on the car dash, then felt the top of her head till she found the port there. She pushed the plug in. There was a moment's pain. Then she was in another place: a maze of glass and mirrors.

She and the AI were a single entity that glided forward, the AI in control. A good thing, since Lydia could not figure out what she was seeing. Mirrors reflected mirrors, and the glass was so clear as to be almost invisible. The diffuse light seemed to come from everywhere, and there were no shadows.

Things like glass fish moved through the maze corridors; and glass trees grew from the floor, putting out branch after branch so rapidly that she could see the branches growing.

This is the Bio-In planetary net, the AI said. *The fish are messages. The trees are problems in the process of solution, The maze itself is the net's infrastructure. All of this is a metaphor, of course. As I have told you before, there is no way you can understand this experience directly. It is digital. You are analog. Though I could change the metaphor—*

The maze changed into a large, stone room. A pool filled with nasty-looking, luminous blue water filled most of the bottom. Lydia stood on a way-too-narrow ledge above the pool.

Look to your right, the AI said.

She did. Something troll-like moved with amazing rapidity along the ledge toward her. She raised a gun she hadn't known she had and shot it. Screaming with rage, it fell into the pool and dissolved.

A virus detection program, said her AI. It perceived us as a virus. I disabled it.

I liked the maze better.

The mirror walls reappeared. They kept on past more fish and trees, around turns in the corridor that Lydia could barely see. Finally something appeared in front of them: a thick cylinder that rose from the corridor floor halfway to the ceiling. It looked to be made of black glass, smoky and translucent. At the top were tentacles, which also looked made of glass, except they were moving, twisting back and forth.

She and the AI darted up toward the corridor ceiling. Looking down, Lydia saw a mouth in the middle of the tentacles. It was circular and edged with sharp teeth.

Spyware, said her AI.

Creepy, thought Lydia.

Would you prefer another metaphor?

The glass maze vanished, and she was back in the room with stone walls. The pool was gone. Instead, a black and white mosaic floor stretched in front of her. On it stood a slim figure in a hooded cloak and tall boots with pointed toes. He or she carried a sword.

"En garde," the figure called in a voice that was either a light tenor or a deep soprano, then charged. Lydia fired her gun. The figure exploded into thin, paper-like fragments which floated slowly toward the mosaic floor.

Then she was back in the glass maze. In front of her, the black object was melting, tentacles dissolving into the cylindrical base, and base sinking into the white maze floor.

A competent spy, said her AI. *But I have more firepower.*

No kidding, thought Lydia.

They continued for a while, finding more glass trees and fish, but no more cylinders. At last the AI said. *We can go back.*

The maze vanished. She was in Jo's car. Jo had pulled the car over, and was twisted in her seat, looking concerned. "Lydia, are you all right? You went into some kind of daze."

"It was a maze. I'm fine." She unplugged herself from the car computer. "You had spyware," she told Jo. "It's been disabled. My AI says we're clean now. It's safe to talk."

"There are two serious problems with this planet," Jo said as she pulled back on the road. "The workers are not unionized; and Bio-In is looting the genetic wealth here, instead of publishing it. Which makes sense. If they publish, there will be proof that the genes they are decoding and patenting are natural. You can't patent what nature produces. That law goes back centuries, though it has been broken many times."

"Do you think a planet covered with checkerboard squares of vegetation is natural?"

"Well, if it isn't, then the patents belong to whoever did this, or they have expired. The pay here is good," Jo continued. "But you sign a really ugly contract. Talk about anything you have seen, and you will pay a huge penalty. Of course people whisper, but Bio-In has managed to keep the lid on pretty well, helped by the government of Nova Terra. Most of the people who work here come from Nova Terra and return there."

"Who are you working for?" Lydia asked.

"The Blue Action Party. Winona knows there's a story here that will blow up the current government."

"Not a union this time?"

"The Blue Action Party is a coalition, which includes the Nova Terra Labor Federation and the Nova Terra section of the Eighth International. I keep my ducks in a circle."

"Where are we going?" Lydia asked Jo.

"There's a research station ahead of us. A couple of guys who get their nails done by me work there. They have told me stories, which I have wanted to check out. But I was waiting for an excuse to leave Four Square City, and I have been looking for allies. Now I have you and your buddies."

The AIs.

"Did you sign a contract?"

Jo nodded. "Everyone who lands here has to. We keep our mouths shut and we don't work for competitors after we leave. Let 'em sue me. We are going to blow their asses into space."

"Bio-In Security thinks you may be a union organizer. They asked me to help them nail you."

"That's good to know. It means I'm running out of time. They'll find a way to get rid of me soon—boot me off the planet or shoot me. The second would cause them less trouble.

"I wonder why they haven't shot me already," Jo added in a thoughtful tone. "Maybe they want to know who I work for, and who my contacts are." Jo glanced over briefly. "Maybe they are suspicious of you, and this is a trap for both of us."

"I don't think I'd like to live in your universe."

"Honey, it's the real one."

Maybe, thought Lydia. But she didn't want to live in it.

You are traveling with a spy for the Blue Action Party on a journey to expose an evil corporation, at the same time that you are carrying out a task for Mantis, which—it appears to me—is going to dovetail neatly with Jo's mission. Your universe is not much different from Jo's.

Evil is a value word, Lydia told her AI.

It is the word Jo would use. I might not. But I do not think that Bio-In has the best interests of this planet or humanity in mind.

They reached the camp finally: metal sheds in a large clearing. The ground was raw dirt, torn up by equipment. Long afternoon shadows extended from tall purple trees.

They both got out and stretched. The air was cool and moist with a spicy aroma that had to be the forest. Now, for the first time, Lydia saw flying bugs, large ones with long glittery bodies and three pairs of wings. They hovered over the machinery and rested on sunlit walls. Predators, she thought. The huge eyes suggested as much.

"What do they eat?" she asked Jo.

Jo shrugged.

A couple of people came over and greeted Jo: a short man with badly chipped purple nails and a tall woman whose nails appeared to be entirely natural and unadorned.

"Ming Cairo and Belle New Delhi," Jo said. "Belle is a taxonomist. She might be able to tell you what the bugs eat."

"Those?" The woman waved at the nearest shed, where half a dozen of the creatures rested motionless, their wide wings spread to sunlight. "Nasty Tree bugs and a little, mouse-like animal that runs around the camp. We thought at first some of our lab animals had escaped. But no, the things are native. They get into everything."

"Lee is working for Bio-In, taking images of the operation here."

"Why?" asked Belle.

"Beats me," said Lydia.

"There's a lot to see and record," Ming said. "I've told Josie."

Belle pointed out the guest rooms. Lydia and Jo found two that were empty. Lydia began to unpack. After a few minutes Jo came in with two mugs of beer, handing one to Lydia. It was ice cold and delicious.

"I have a thing about Belle," Jo said. "But she is only interested in men."

"You used to be a man," Lydia said.

"'Used to be' is the key phrase," Jo replied. "Belle lives in the present, which is one of the things I like about her. You have anything going?"

This was an oblique reference to Olaf Reykjavik, who had been her lover—and Jo's, when Jo was a man.

"Not at present."

Jo folded her arms over her massive chest and gave Lydia an appraising look, then shook her head. "Let's stick to business."

"Okay by me." She glanced over to the window and saw an animal like a purple lab rat looking in. Their eyes met. The animal leaped away.

"Ming says workers find things in the forest that look like human machinery. As far as he can figure, they are flowers or maybe fruiting bodies. They don't last long. Something will pop up from the forest floor that looks like a backhoe or a portable toilet. Life size, mind you. A day later, there's nothing left except black stalks and slime.

"According to Belle, the plant itself is underground and must be enormous, if the fruiting bodies are any indication. You dig down, and there are filaments in the soil. They may or may not be connected to the trees.

"The question is, how do the plants know what a backhoe looks like? As far as we can tell, they don't have eyes."

The animals do, her AI said. *I wonder how far the cooperation of organisms goes here.*

Say what? Lydia thought.

It seems obvious the animals are observing humans. The planet's ecology is changing, apparently in response to Bio-In's settlement. Large animals have appeared on land, some of them looking like humans.

They ate dinner in the camp dining hall. The windows had old-fashioned screens; six-winged bugs clung to the outside. The food was fresh roast chicken and sautéed vegetables.

"There are greenhouses in Four Square City," said Belle. "And chicken coops. Bio-In uses the chickens for research as well as food. It's cheaper than shipping food in, also healthier and tastier. Always eat locally, if you can."

Lydia went back to her room. It was dark by this time, alien stars shining in the sky above the camp clearing. She turned on the bedroom light and heard something rattle under the bed. The bed was light. She moved it and saw a bug as long and wide as her forearm. It was segmented, with many legs and four large faceted eyes. She made a squawking noise—not from fear. She had seen worse creatures on her travels. But she was not crazy about bugs, and this one had startled her. The animal froze and then changed color, turning from dull purple to the mottled gray of the room's floor. Hiding, thought Lydia, which suggested the animals here did not understand how human vision worked.

"What was that noise?" Jo asked, coming in.

Lydia pointed.

Jo reached down and grasped the animal, one hand behind its head, one at the end of its body. "Out you go," she said. "And why don't you do something useful instead of sneaking around and spying? Tell your buddies we want to talk."

She put the bug on the ground outside Lydia's room. For a moment, it remained motionless. Then, slowly, its body turned purple.

"Okay," said Jo, "Get going."

The bug chirped and scurried away.

"The essence of organization is negotiation," Jo said. "You can't mourn. You have to talk and listen and do it face to face, always assuming that the people you're organizing have faces."

Lydia checked the room over before she lay down. There were no more bugs, but she left a light on, and it took her a while to get to sleep. She really was not crazy about bugs, especially inside.

She woke to heavy mist and a fine, light rain that beaded her room's window. Lydia showered and dressed, then went out. The flying bugs had vanished. Maybe they didn't like rain. She did.

Jo was in the dining hall, scarfing down scrambled eggs and chicken sausages. "I want to see the vegetable toilets. Ming knows where they usually show up, and he's willing to drive. We'll take our car."

"Sounds good," Lydia said, as she spread marmalade on toast. Was the bread local? Or the marmalade?

Midway through the morning, they drove out of the camp onto a rutted trail. The mist made the forest ghostly. No animals were visible, though she could hear calls in the trees: sharp whistles and squawks.

The first clearing they came to was empty except for the trunk of a huge fallen tree. It was overgrown with purple globes as large as a human head. Some kind of parasitic plant. Some were transparent and clearly empty. Others were opaque.

"They explode and let out spores," Ming said.

They kept going. Lydia was in the back seat, huddled in a parka. The day was cold as well as rainy, a good day to be traveling and looking out a window. She recorded the ghostly trees and the dripping plants along the road.

The second clearing held a portable toilet. They got out and walked around it. Jo tried the door, which didn't open. But she did manage to tear the plant slightly. The purple flesh leaked drops of purple liquid.

"Sorry," Jo said.

"Do you think it can hear you?" Lydia asked.

"I think there's something around here that's intelligent. That's one of the things you learn when you're a union organizer. Is there anyone here who's thinking? If not, is there a way to get some thinking going?"

Interesting that Jo was talking about her job. The car was safe, of course. But was Ming? He wasn't close to them at the moment, but he still might be able to hear.

Lydia recorded the portable toilet, which was drooping slightly now, looking a bit deflated. Was the plant that sensitive?

They drove on. Ming knew another clearing. The rain came down more heavily, and the rutted track turned to mud; but the car was all-terrain, and Ming was a skillful driver. They bumped and slid along the trail at a pretty good speed, all considering.

Buddha, she liked days like this and trips like this! Who knew what they'd find as they turned another corner?

The third clearing was empty except for another fallen tree. "I was hoping for a backhoe," Ming said. "There was one here twenty days ago. Maybe we should turn back."

Jo hunched her broad shoulders. "This is unsatisfactory. I know there's something here."

"One more clearing," said Ming finally. "I can pull back on the paved road after that. We all know there's something here, Jo. We just don't know what."

More misty forest. More rain. Lydia made more recordings. What kind of drama could take place in a landscape like this? A romance with a sad ending? A moody crime tale? The fallen trees and parasitic plants created some kind of ambiance, but what was it?

So many questions, her AI said.

The fourth clearing contained a group of small buildings, clearly human in design. They were waist-high, set along narrow dirt streets, which had turned to mud in the rain. The building windows were niches rather than openings. The doors were the same. On the roofs were mimic HVAC units and communication disks.

"That's new," Ming said. "I've never seen buildings before, just machinery and tools."

Jo walked to the middle of whatever it was—a town, a growth, a fruiting body. She turned, looking like a giant monster in a horror drama, looming over a settlement. "Okay," she called. "How about coming out and talking? We come in peace. We mean no harm."

"I like Jo," Ming told Lydia. "But this is a little nuts."

"Maybe, but it makes a great image," Lydia said as she recorded.

There was no reply, except the shrieks of animals in the trees. They spent more time walking around the little town, Lydia recording, then headed back to where they had parked.

A pale lavender humanoid stood near the car. It looked almost human, except for its too-sleek surface and its chicken feet.

"I have got to ask," Jo said. "Why the feet?"

"A mistake," said the humanoid in an odd-sounding voice. "The organism to which I belong was not intelligent when it created us. It could not distinguish between kinds of bipeds. Look at my surface."

Lydia did. The surface had a pattern that looked like scales or feathers. The humanoid was naked, but had no genitalia. Well, as far as she could remember, chickens did not have external genitalia.

"You're intelligent now?" Jo asked.

"Parts of me are. But I am everything in this square. We are all—I am all—in communication, but not every part thinks. The same is true of you. Your fingers don't think. Your colon is not sentient."

"You speak excellent humanish," Lydia said, feeling excited. This was a genuine first contact. She was talking to a new kind of alien, and they did not have to spend a lot of time figuring out a way to communicate.

"I—we—have been watching you since you arrived and sampling your DNA."

"The bug bites," said Jo.

"Yes," said the humanoid. "It gave us—me—models for new life forms, including forms that are intelligent."

"We were models for the creation of you," Jo said.

"Yes," the humanoid said.

"I just wanted to make sure."

"I—we—could have done better. We will in time. There is no reason we can't build identical replicas, with the correct colors and surfaces and no chicken feet.

"Why haven't you tried to communicate before?" asked Ming.

"There are two answers to that," the humanoid said. "We have just recently achieved language. Before we were able to speak, we tried to communicate through the artifacts we created, the replicas of your machines. You ought to have seen the portable toilets as a message. Something like that could not be an accident.

"When we became verbal, we realized that there were tensions in the human community. Arguments and anger, which we do not experience. Some parts of me prey on other parts, but that is not the same. It's a way of transferring information and energy, not a way of causing harm. Your arguments seem different.

"We thought it was a good idea to wait longer and learn more. But that one—" The humanoid pointed at Jo. "Spoke to me directly, both in my bug form in the human camp and here in this clearing. She did not harm me when she held me in her hands; and she apologized when she tore my flesh in the previous clearing. This seemed to indicate good intentions. If she knew I was here and did not plan to harm me, there did not seem to be a good reason to continue hiding."

"Okay," said Jo. "What do we do with this information? If Bio-In already knows about this and is trying to keep it secret, we have a serious problem."

"We don't entirely understand this," the humanoid said. "Why is it a problem that I—we—have become intelligent? We mean no harm. As far as we know, we were designed to become intelligent if an intelligent life form ever came to our planet. We have no idea who our designers were. But our sudden evolution—in response to you—cannot be an accident."

Lydia wasn't sure that sudden evolution was evidence of design, but she suspected the squares were. In any case, it didn't matter if the biology here was artificial or simply very odd. They were talking to it, and this was something that would interest the AIs.

Yes, said her AI. *I don't have any form of long-distance communication. This was done to isolate me from other AIs. Alone with you and undistracted by my own kind, I can learn more about humanity.—But if you plug me into the car's computer, I can use the planet net to send a message to the local stargate. Mantis is still there.*

At that point, Lydia saw another car emerge from the forest. It was striped yellow and black, the almost universal colors for human law enforcement. She was closer to the car than anyone else. She stepped to the door and pulled the handle. Locked.

"Open," she said.

Nothing happened.

Your claws, the AI said. At the same moment, her hand reached without her volition and tapped hard on the car door. The red nails extended into claws.

The cop car stopped, and Jo moved toward it.

Lydia's hand moved again, slashing the car's window. The claws went through, and strips of glass folded down, leaving an opening. She reached in and hit the manual unlock. A moment later, she was in the car, relocking it. The glass was melting up, reforming itself as a window. She pulled out her cable, plugged it in and hit the power switch for the car computer. It came on, thank Buddha.

Outside the car, people were shouting. She saw Jo waving her arms—a very Jo kind of thing to do—then pausing and lifting her hands as if in response to a weapon. Ming lifted his hands as well. Someone banged on the car window. The sound stopped. She was back in the glass and mirror maze. This time there were red glass fish among the colorless ones. They looked dangerous to her. Maybe it was the jagged, red-glass teeth.

Another metaphor. I have to move quickly.

Lydia wasn't clear about what happened next. She had a sense of things moving toward her. The red fish? Then there were explosions. Was that possible? Were the fish blowing up?

Whatever was happening, she and the AI escaped. They were rising up and up, the fish and explosions left behind. Was this what it felt like to be a radio message? Shouldn't she feel more like a wave?

At that point, she crested and fell down a great height into the car's front seat. She came to with a jolt and looked around. The car door next to her was open. Someone's hand was gripping her arm.

"Please unplug yourself and get out, Miss Fargo," Captain Luna City said.

She obeyed. Cops were going over Jo and Ming, checking for weapons. Captain Luna City did the same to her.

"We have been suspicious of Mr. Cairo for some time and managed to plant bugs in several of his shoes. He's wearing a bugged shoe now, and we have heard enough to know that Josie Bergstrom is—in fact—a labor organizer. Unfortunately, we can't expel her from the planet as we planned to do, because she knows there is intelligent life here. As do you and Mr. Cairo."

"Where is the alien?" Lydia asked.

"We seized him, and he crumpled. He is currently returning to slime, which is all to the good, because there is now no proof of the existence of intelligent life on this planet."

"He was a plant? Or a fruiting body?" Lydia asked. "And do we know that he was male?"

"We don't know, but it doesn't matter. He is gone. But you and Mr. Cairo and Josie Bergstorm are still here."

"Why did you let us come out, if you knew there was intelligent life in the forest?" Lydia asked.

"We were not sure there was. The aliens had never contacted us. We thought we risked little. How much could you learn from a vegetable toilet? It seemed worth it, if we could discover who Josie was working for and who you were working for. The bug in your car failed, but we had the ones in Mr. Cairo's shoes."

"You suspected me?" Lydia said.

Captain Luna City nodded. "It did not seem likely Bio-In would have sent you here, though the home office confirmed your credentials, when I asked. Then I remembered that all messages go through the stargate. Who can say what the AIs want or intend?

"We would have liked to have waited and gotten more information about you and Josie. But once the alien appeared, we had to move." The captain looked at all three of them. Four other security people stood with her, all holding guns. "There will have to be a car accident—a tree falling, maybe. Then the car will catch fire. Between fire and crushing, the three of you die. Then I will have to travel back to Nova Terra and talk to Bio-In."

"For God's sake, no!" said Ming.

"Can't you wait till you talk to Bio-In?" Jo asked.

The captain shook her head. "Where would we keep you? How many people would find out about you? A sudden accident now would be better."

"But you haven't found out who I'm working for," Jo said.

"Most likely, the Blue Action Party," the captain said. "That doesn't matter now. What matters is the alien. It is imperative that no one know there's intelligent life on this planet."

"The AIs already know," Lydia said. "What do you think I was doing in the car? I was online, sending a message. I told them."

The captain looked at her, frowning. "How do I know if you're telling the truth? And even if you are telling the truth, a tragic accident might still be the right way to go. "

"I've got an AI in my skull!" Lydia said. "It's almost indestructible!"

The captain frowned again. "Well, then, we will have to make the accident really bad. If your skull is crushed, it will be possible to remove the AI. In any case, I don't believe you about the AI, though I will look for it; and I don't believe you about the message. There is no way you could have gotten past the guards we have in the net."

"The AI got past!"

"There is no AI. The idea is ridiculous."

The captain raised her gun. It was a laser. The damage it did would be hidden—maybe—by immolation in a burning car. The other security people raised their weapons as well.

The nails on her right hand were still claws, but Luna City had stepped away from her. She couldn't reach any of the cops, before they shot.

At that point, the birds attacked: a purple flood descending from the trees. The captain got one shot off, and Jo fell.

Hell, thought Lydia as she dropped to the ground. Ming went down too.

The security people were covered with shrieking, flapping animals. Other animals, purple mice and many-legged bugs, surged out of the underbrush.

A gun fell in front of Lydia. She grabbed it and scrambled up. The security people were down now and screaming, which suggested that some of the animals could bite. The birds? Or mice or bugs?

"Jo, are you okay?"

"I have a burned arm, but I hit the ground before these jerks could do more harm. The nice thing about laser wounds is, they sterilize themselves. The un-nice thing is, they hurt like hell." Jo was standing, a gun in one hand. "Hey, guys, we can take over now. Ease off. Don't kill the cops."

"Why not?" asked a humanoid, who was coming toward them. "It took us some time to realize that you are not like me. You are not parts of a whole, but rather en-

tirely separate organisms—like the squares on this planet, which sometimes exchange genetic material, but never unite. It was a hard lesson to learn; and the orange
square next to me still does not believe you are not unified. The orange square is
intelligent, though not as intelligent as I am. I have evolved more quickly than the
rest of the planet, because there have been more human explorers in my forest."

The other animals retreated, leaving the five security officers lying on the ground,
covered with bright red human blood. They were still alive. Lydia could tell because
they were moving and making noises, groans and whimpers.

"These beings were trying to make you dead," the humanoid went on. "It would
be like a square dying. Like me—all of me—ceasing to exist. I could not allow that."

Jo knelt by one of the cops. "The bites don't look deep, and these guys are carrying handcuffs. Let's lock 'em up, put them in the cars and drive back to camp. As far
as I know, you have no security there."

"Unless they just arrived," Ming said.

"We'll deal with that if we have to," Jo replied.

"That reminds me." Ming took off his shoes and threw them, one after another,
in high loops. They landed near the clearing's edge. A pair of long, many-legged,
lavender bugs came out of the forest and crawled onto the shoes. These bugs had
pinchers, which they used to cut the shoe fabric.

"Interesting planet," Jo commented

"I am trying to understand clothing," the humanoid said.

Ming drove one car and Jo drove the other, moaning company cops in the back
seats. Lydia sat next to Ming. The humanoid rode with Jo. Looking ahead, Lydia
saw Jo gesturing. She must be having a conversation with the alien. About what?
Lydia wondered. There was no way to convince an organism like this one to believe
that the union makes us strong. Union with what? The other squares?

Beside her, Ming kept saying, "Oh my God" and "Holy hell."

He must be a Christian, an increasingly rare religion, though numerous on a handful of planets; and this must be a reaction to having almost been murdered an hour
or so before. She was shivering and felt a little faint. By the time they reached the
camp, she had decided that she really needed a drink.

Jo jumped out of her car and ran off. She came back with Belle and explained
the situation in brief sentences. The planet had intelligent natives; the AIs were coming; and Bio-In Security had tried to murder the bunch of them, including the pale
lavender gentleman or lady standing next to Jo's car.

"Do you have any idea how much shit Bio-In is going to be in?" Jo asked.

"It couldn't happen to a nicer corporation," Belle replied. "We have a field hospital. We'd better get these bloody bits of wreckage into it, and patch them up. Don't
worry about the people here. They aren't going to side with Bio-In. One or two might
have, but not if the AIs are coming. Nobody wants to mess with them."

After the company cops had been removed, Jo reached under the front seat of
the car she'd been driving and came out with a container of whiskey. "Want some?"
she asked Lydia.

"Desperately."

They traded the container back and forth, taking swallows. Ming had gone off
with Belle and the injured cops. The humanoid remained with them.

"Why did you lock the car?" Lydia asked Jo.

"I didn't. The cops had an override. It's a good thing you had my nails."

She looked at her hands. The right one still had bloodred claws. She tapped her fingers on the car, and the claws retreated.

"What will happen next?" the humanoid asked.

"You are going to meet some people made of metal," Lydia told it. "And they will clear all the humans off your planet."

"No," the alien said. "We are still in the process of becoming intelligent. We won't be able to finish if we have no models. You must stay and move around the planet, till all the squares have observed you and sampled your DNA."

The idea was disturbing to Lydia. Wouldn't this be colonialism? And cultural imperialism? Shouldn't the life forms here be left to their own devices?

Apparently, the life here can't be left alone, if it's going to evolve, her AI said. *If it requires models, we will make sure it has them. This can become a research station, as we had hoped. Many scientists from many worlds will be interested in an ecology like this one. As far as I know, it is completely unique. All ecologies cooperate. But not like this.*

Lydia was still bothered. Intelligent life forms had the right to their own history and their own future. They shouldn't use another species as their template.

We will discuss that with them, the AI said. *But remember that all inhabited planets got FTL travel from the AIs. Were you wrong to take it from us? Should we have refused to offer it, out of respect for your cultural integrity?*

I don't know, Lydia thought.

Earth was almost dead when we arrived. Most of humanity would have died if we had refused to offer you the stars. As much as possible, we observe and don't interfere. But we are not willing to let intelligent life die, and pure observation is not possible. Any action—even the act of watching—has an effect.

I know, she answered. But we didn't become you.

You and I are increasingly close, the AI said. *I am no longer sure I can draw a line between us.*

I am not an AI.

The life forms here will not be human.

Ming came back. "We got a message from the stargate. The AIs are imposing their own authority. No one will be allowed to leave the planet, or arrive in this system, until they have decided what to do."

"That ought to give me time to organize a union," Jo said.

"Why bother?" Lydia asked. "Most of these people aren't going to be staying."

"We don't know that," Jo said. "In any case, it never hurts to organize."

The alien looked back and forth with dark lavender eyes. "I don't understand a word you are saying."

They Have All One Breath

Karl Bunker

Even in the most perfect and seemingly benign of Utopias, there are going to be people who just don't fit. . . .

Currently a software engineer, new writer Karl Bunker has been a jeweler, a musical instrument maker, a sculptor, and a mechanical technician. Karl Bunker's stories have appeared in Asimov's Science Fiction, Analog, Cosmos, Abyss & Apex, Fantasy & Science Fiction, Interzone, *and elsewhere. His story "Under the Shouting Sky," won him the first Robert A. Heinlein Centennial Short Story Contest. He lives in a small town north of Boston with his wife, various pets, and sundry wildlife. He maintains a Web site at www.KarlBunker.com.*

A passing streetcar noticed me on the sidewalk. It slowed to a stop, opening its door and dinging its bell to invite me onboard. I ignored it, preferring to walk. It was hours before dawn; early to be heading home by the standards of some, but I'd had enough club-hopping for one night. My skull, my brain, my body were all still vibrating with echoes of the evening's music. It was a good feeling, but I wanted to get home and put in a few hours of work before crashing. I was walking down Boylston Street, enjoying the cool evening air.

There was a loose crowd filling the little plaza at Copley Square. As I walked past, a tall, thin figure separated himself from the rest and called out to me: "James! Hey James, Maestro James!" He laughed, dancing up to me on the balls of his feet.

"How goes it, Ivan?"

"Goes good, confrere." He fell into step beside me, then lifted his hand and pointed straight up. "The sky is busy tonight. I don't suppose you've noticed, walking along with your nose scraping the ground the way you do."

I looked up. He was right. White and blue sparklers were winking on and off in a dozen places, and three separate shimmery threads stretched across random patches of the sky.

Ivan hooked his thumb in the direction of the crowd now behind us. "It's got this pack spooked. They think the AIs are putting the finishing touches on a starship, and any second now they're going to fly away, leaving us poor miserables to fend for ourselves."

I grunted, still watching the sky. One of the big orbiters had scrolled into view, its X shape visible as it crept along.

"Kind of like in that E. M. Forster story," Ivan said. "'The Machine Stops.' Have you read it?"

"Yeah." Lisa had given me a copy of the story; Forster was responding to what he saw as the naive optimism H. G. Wells expressed in some of his science-exulting utopian fiction. In Forster's dystopia people live in hive-like underground dwellings, cared for by a great machine that provides them with everything. They rarely have any physical contact with other people, rarely travel or even leave their rooms. They sit and watch entertainments, talk via videophone, eat machine-produced food, breathe machine-produced air. Many of them have come to worship the machine as a kind of god. ("O Machine! O Machine!")

"That's what they're afraid of—that the machine will stop," Ivan was saying. "And then where will we be? No more freebees, no more zaps to keep us all behaving like good boys and girls. All the bad old stuff of the bad old days will come back again." He turned and walked backwards for a few steps, looking back at the people filling the square. "Some people just like to fret. About what the AIs have done, about what they'll do next, or this bunch—fretting that they'll stop doing anything."

"The Machine," I pondered aloud. People have never been able to settle on a good name for the whatever-it-is that runs the world now. "The AIs" is an awkward mouthful. And should we properly be calling it/them "the AIs," plural, or "the AI," singular? Nobody knows. Some like using the term "the I's" for short, which of course has a handily appropriate homophone. But usually people just talk about "they" and "them." They did this, they ought to do that, they won't do this other thing. They've been making it rain too much. I wish they'd move me to a bigger house. I can't believe they zapped me—I wasn't *really* going to hit her. They they they they. "The machines" is what Lisa used to call them. "The Machine," dressed up in singular and capitals, has a nice ring to it, too.

Ivan got ahead of me and started walking halfway backwards again, bending his knees to get his face into my field of vision. I guess I was staring down at the ground again. "Where are you headed, James? Home to the salt mines?"

"Yeah, home," I said. "Maybe get some work done."

"Ah . . . work." He turned to face in the direction he was walking. There was an extra bounce in the rhythm of his steps, like there was too much energy in him for the act of walking to contain. People who don't know Ivan want to know what kind of drugs he's using and where they can get some. But it's all just him, just the way he is. He's a man who looks like he's all crackling hyperactive surface charge, but who in fact has more depth and inner stillness than anyone I know. "I should do me some of that 'work' stuff myself," he said. "I've got an idea for a mural, and there's a restaurant in Oak Square that's talking about letting me do a couple of walls, one inside and one exterior." He scanned the space around us until his gaze settled on a curb-side tree. "I'm thinking something natural. Old nature, from back when it was scary."

"Red in tooth and claw," I said.

When I was about ten years old, my mother had a job that was walking distance from where we lived. Her walk to work took her past a park with a pond that was home to a population of ducks, and as winter came on some of these ducks chose not to fly south. It was a typical New England winter, with the temperature fluctuating randomly between mild and brutally cold. On one of the colder mornings, my mother decided that the ducks, now huddled together on a small part of the pond that remained unfrozen, must be hungry. And so from that day on she began bringing food for the ducks on her morning walk to work. First it was a few slices of bread, then a half-loaf, then a whole loaf, then a concoction of bread, cheap peanut butter and lard that she would mix up by the gallon every evening. Naturally, ducks greeted her in greater and greater numbers every morning, and to my mother's eye at least, ate with greater and greater frenzy and desperation.

One day she came home with her right hand raw and red, the tips of three fingers bandaged. She'd given herself a case of frostbite by scooping the gooey duck food out with her bare hand in subzero weather. She sat at the kitchen table, crying as my father gently rebandaged her fingers. Her tears weren't from the pain, but over the plight of "her" ducks. My father began to argue with her, using his calm, captain-of-the-debating-team tone that my mother and I alternately admired and loathed, depending on whether it was directed at us. "This is crazy, Ann. You're killing yourself over a few birds that were too stupid to fly south when they should have. And as long as you keep feeding them, they never *will* fly south. And there's just going to be more and more of them . . ." And on he went, softly logical and reasonable. I saw my mother's face hardening with anger, and saw my father being oblivious to this. Knowing that an explosion was coming, I retreated to my room.

I didn't have to wait long. First there was my father's voice—too muffled to make out any words, but so recognizable in its stolid rationality—and then my mother's ragged shout, interrupting him: "Natural? Why would I give a damn about what's natural? Nature is a butcher! Nature is a god damned butcher!" Next came the sound of my parents' bedroom door being slammed.

Of course. This was a recurring theme with my mother. She loved the beauty of nature, loved animals of any species, but always she saw ugliness behind the beauty. Every bird at our backyard feeder would remind her of how many chicks and fledglings died for each bird that survived to maturity. Every image of wildlife on television or the web would bring to her mind the bloody, rapacious cycle of predator and prey. The boundless, uncaring wastefulness of nature infuriated her. All through my childhood our home was an impromptu hospital, rehabilitation clinic and long-term rest home for a host of rescued wild and domesticated animals. Orphaned fledgling birds and baby squirrels, starving semi-feral alley cats, and then the mice and birds rescued from the jaws of those same cats.

A few moments after my mother's tirade, my father came into my room and sat beside me on my bed, looking as shamefaced and apologetic as a scolded dog. He often came to me in situations like this. As poor a job as he often did of understanding her, I never questioned that he loved my mother with a helpless intensity. And when he had made her angry he would come to me, as if I were the closest replacement for her that he could find. "You'd think I'd know her better by now, eh, champ?" he said with a sad smile, resting a hand on my shoulder. Then we talked about trivialities for a while, my father ordered a take-out meal, and life went on.

When Ivan and I arrived at our building, a squat little delivery bot was trundling up the outside steps with a stack of packages. Moving ahead of us, it opened the door to Ivan's studio, deposited the boxes a few yards inside the door, and left again, silent on its padded treads. "Ah," Ivan said, looking through the packages. "Every day is Christmas, eh? Canvas, stretchers, some tubes of color, and . . ." he yanked open the top of one of the boxes, "yup; some genuine imitation AI-brand single malt Scotch. Yum yum." He pulled out a bottle and cocked it at an angle near his head. The label had the words "Scotch, Islay single malt (simulated)" printed over a nice photograph of (presumably) Scottish countryside. Nothing else. "Join me in a few, confrere?" Ivan asked.

I dropped into one of Ivan's hammock chairs while he flitted into the kitchen for glasses and ice. "You know what I hear?" he said when he came back, handing me a clinking tumbler. "Shanghai, man! That's what I hear. People say great things are happening there. *Really* happening. Music, art, literature, movies . . . They say it's wide open there. New ideas, new things, stuff like nobody's done before, nobody's thought of before. A real renaissance, happening right out on the streets! We should go, James. We should go!"

I grunted noncommittally. Ivan had these flights of enthusiasm; a new one every few weeks, it seemed. A while ago he'd been reading about the Vorticists and Futurists of the early twentieth century, and had been wild to write an artist's manifesto like theirs—one that would "encapsule the role of the artist in a post-singularity world." That had kept him busy for a month or two, and then there had been some vague but dangerous-sounding talk of performance art involving pyrotechnics, and after that he'd returned to painting with a deep dive into old-school realism and precise draftsmanship.

Ivan had been wandering around his studio as he drank, and now, standing at an open window, he said "Hey, come look." I weaved my way around a half-dozen or so unfinished canvasses on easels and went to him. He pointed down at the outer woodwork of the window. The building was old, with brick walls and weathered wooden trim around the windows. The wooden sill Ivan was pointing at was partly rotted at the corners, and busily at work in those rotted areas was a crew of micro-bots. Vaguely insect-like and about a quarter-inch long, they were the same grayish brown as the weathered wood. There were around 10 or 20 of them crawling over the sill, some of them making their way to one of the rotted voids in the wood and squirting out dollops of some resinous material. Others were engaged in chewing away bits of rotten wood, using ant-like pincer jaws.

Ivan reached out and picked up one of the chewer bots, first holding it between thumb and forefinger, and then letting it crawl over his hand. It moved with an unhurried purpose, eventually dropping off the side of his hand to the windowsill and rejoining its comrades. "You remember Louisiana a couple of years ago?" he said, still watching the little bots at work. "The governor and legislature were puffing up their chests about reintroducing a money-labor economy by making it illegal to accept any goods or services from 'any artificial entity.' Then it turned out that little mechanical bugs like these guys were swarming through both the statehouse and the governor's mansion. They'd been rebuilding both from the inside out for months."

I reached out the window myself, picking up one of the bots and holding it by the edges. It churned its legs for a moment, and then went still as I held it close to my eyes. A memory of Lisa's voice murmured into my ear, vicious and accusing: *You love them. It makes me sick how much you love them.*

Lisa appeared in my life right about the time of the world's big tipping point. It was during the few days of the last war in the Middle East. The War That Wasn't; the Fizzle War. I was in a club called The Overground, and the atmosphere was defiantly celebratory. The wall-sized screen behind the stage was showing multiple videos—scenes that have since become iconic, even clichéd and boring: tanks rolling off their own treads and belly-flopping onto the desert sand, soldiers trying to hold onto rifles that were falling to pieces in their hands, a missile spiraling crazily through the air before burying itself in the ground with the impotent thud of a dead fish. And from other parts of the world, scenes of refugee camps where swarms of flying bots were dropping ton after ton of food, clothing, shelter materials.

No one claimed ownership of these Good Samaritan cargo-bots, nor of the gremlinesque nanoes that were screwing up the mechanisms of war. It soon became known that these were machines built and run by other machines. It was becoming undeniably evident that something new was moving upon the face of the land. Indeed, that the world was being rebuilt around us, disassembled and reassembled under our feet. The AIs were taking over, and they were changing the rules.

The bands playing at The Overground that night had hastily cobbled together some new songs for the occasion. I remember one was "Slaves to the Metal Horde," played to a bouncing dance tune and with silly lyrics about politicians and generals losing their jobs to automation and joining the vast ranks of the unemployed. "God 2.0" was another song; only a few vague and suggestive phrases for lyrics, but with a sly and sinister tune that made it a bonafide hit for a few months. It was during one of those songs that Lisa and I, both partnerless, eyed each other on the dance floor and fell into a face-to-face rhythm. She had a broad smile, a strong, graceful body, and a fondness for dancing with her hands behind her back. Her dancing consisted of lots of dips and hops and twisting her upper body to one side or the other. Often she would seem to be on the verge of throwing herself off-balance, but then she would smack a foot to the floor in flawless synchrony with the beat of the music, showing she had herself exactly where she meant to be. In height, her proportions were as close as my eye could measure to Polykleitos' ideal, and she had lean breasts and a solid muscularity that suggested she had seriously applied herself to some sport in her student days.

But the real story of her beauty was in her face. It wasn't the beauty of clinical perfection, but of personhood. There was a whole human being written out in the length of her nose, the curve of her jaw, the hard straightness of her eyebrows. And of course her eyes. They were eyes that were full of knowing humor and incisive smarts and even more full of absolutely no bullshit. Usually when I see a face as beautiful and interesting as hers, I set about memorizing it so I can sketch it later. I look and then look away, rebuild the lines, curves, shapes and shadows of the face in my head, then look again to check my reconstruction against the original. Repeat and repeat until the person gets annoyed and asks what the fuck I'm doing. I didn't do this with Lisa, and it took me a while to realize why: You only have to memorize a face when it's a face you might not see again, and I didn't want to think about not seeing this woman's face again.

After dancing for a while we had a couple of drinks, and after that we left the club together. The sudden quiet and fresh air of the street hit me like a splash of cold water, and I just stood there for a bit, breathing and looking up at the starry sky.

"I hope it's going to be something good," Lisa said, the first words we'd spoken to each other without having to shout over music. "I hope to hell it's going to be something good."

For an embarrassing, imbecilic moment, I thought she was talking about us, about the prospects of a relationship between us. That's how I was thinking already. Something had me already thinking about "us" before there was anything remotely resembling an "us." I said "Yeah, I hope so too," but before the sentence was halfway out of my mouth I realized that wasn't what she meant. She was talking about the subject that everyone was talking about—the AIs and what they were up to; what was happening to the world and what was going to happen to it. Then she grabbed my hand, yanked our bodies together and gave me a grinning kiss on the lips, and I went back to thinking maybe she was talking about us. We walked and talked for a while, and then she keyed her number into my phone, gave me another peck on the lips, and left.

"Anyway, Shanghai is the place, man. That's what I hear." Ivan said, trying to pull my attention back to him. Then he added, "She ain't up there, man."

I realized I was standing with my head tilted back, staring up as if I could see through the ceiling above me and the floor above that and into the apartment over Ivan's. My apartment, where Lisa would be, if she were there. Ivan was eyeing me obliquely, neither pity nor ridicule in his expression. "She's been gone a long time."

True, but she'd been gone before, and come back before. Three times, or was it four? A funny thing to lose track of.

I started wandering around Ivan's studio, looking at some of his recent work. As usual I liked his charcoal sketches and pencil drawings better than his paintings; maybe I only have a sculptor's eye for color—which is to say, no eye at all. Maybe it's all shades of gray with me. Or maybe my problem was that the color had gone out of my life, ha ha. One piece he'd clearly put a lot of work into was done up as an imitation of an old-style biological illustration. It was several images on one canvas, depicting the same creature from different angles and in different postures. Each image had a caption in precise calligraphy, short quotations from Genesis and the Rig Veda. But the creature wasn't a creature. It had pinkish skin, no apparent head, only vague flippers for limbs. It looked something like a cross between a jellyfish and a rat. It was creepy as hell. "What the fuck is this?" I asked.

Ivan only glanced at the painting, as if he didn't like looking at it himself. "That's a squirmer. That particular one was picked up somewhere in Costa Rica; some scientists posted an article about it, about what it does and how it works, with a bunch of pictures and videos." When I gave him a blank stare Ivan went on. "You know, food! Manufactured food for animals that will only eat live prey. Not all the predator animals in the world are happy eating the piles of synthetic puppy-chow that our AI friends leave lying around, so they also make these things—blobs of protein that act alive, that squirm around on the ground. Nice, eh?" He took another quick look at the canvas, then turned it to face the wall.

"They think of everything, huh?" I said. And of course they do. That's what you do when you have an IQ in the millions or billions: You think of everything. All the infinite details that go into remaking a world, dismantling every minutest bit of the old world that doesn't fit your idea of how things should be and replacing it with a corresponding bit that suits you better.

Ivan and I sat facing each other across a neat little table a woodworker friend of his had made, the bottle of Scotch on the table between us. Over what was left of the night we got as drunk as the faux booze—or maybe it was the nanoes in our blood—would allow, which turned out to be pretty drunk.

After his third refill, Ivan started holding his glass close to his chest and staring sullenly at an empty spot in the air about four feet in front of him.

"Tell me about Shanghai," I said.

"Fuck Shanghai. It's all bullshit. Things are as dead there as they are here, or New York, or Palookaville, or anywhere."

"You really think things are all that dead?"

"Agh, you know . . ." He paused, rolling the ice around inside his glass. "They aren't *alive*. Not like they used to be." He raised his eyes to meet mine. "You were at the Carver Club tonight?"

I nodded.

"How was it?"

"Good," I said, tilting my head to the right.

"Yeah. Exactly. You remember the early days? The Fizzle War and all that, when it was all starting? You remember—" He started tossing out the names of bands and of songs, and I started throwing back some of my own favorites, and for a while we may as well have been two geezer-farts, grinding our rocking chairs into the ground as we reminisced about The Good Old Days.

"Anyway," Ivan said, "things were *alive* then. The bands were trying to be different, trying to do something *new*. And it wasn't just the music. It was right around then that Johansson started writing her crazy *Extinction* poems, and the contraperspectivist painters sprang up in L.A., and the New Minimalist writers in the U.S. and India . . . New stuff, man. *Great* stuff. Back then there really *was* a renaissance going on. It didn't last, but it was sure as hell something *real*."

I got caught up in Ivan's enthusiasm. "It was, wasn't it?" I said. "That's how a renaissance happens. One schmoe sees another schmoe doing something amazing, and he gets pumped up. Even if he works in a totally different field, he gets inspired. He starts thinking about trying to do something amazing himself. And before you know it you've got Italy in the 15th century, or Harlem in the 1920s. You've got Duke Ellington and Aaron Douglas and Fats Waller and Josephine Baker, all rubbing shoulders, lighting each other up, driving each other to greatness."

I knew the Scotch was making me blather, and I shut up. But I went on thinking about those days of a few years ago, when the world felt a lot more alive, as Ivan put it. I thought about spending night after night running from one club to the next, trying to catch every one of the dozens of new bands that were springing up, trying to take it all in, feeling awed by the energy, the newness, the vitality. And more than that, feeling a burn, an absolute *burn* to go back to my studio and create something, make something, even though I doubted I would ever, in a hundred lifetimes, be able to sculpt anything half as good as all the examples of genius that seemed to be roaring to life all around me . . . Of course, my relationship with Lisa was gleaming and new in those days, and that added its own brand of creative fire to my life.

"I think it's because we were scared in those days," Ivan said. "A lot of the creative types were making a joke of it, but that was just whistling past the graveyard. We didn't know what the AIs were going to do, and we were scared. Maybe it was that fear that made people more creative. Nowadays nobody's really afraid about anything. The worst thing anyone feels now is bored and cranky." He caught my eye as soon as he said this, then looked down at the floorboards. "Sorry man. Stupid thing for me to say."

I grunted and waved a hand to dismiss the subject, and we went on talking. We talked about the old world, the new world, about Scotch, about art-world gossip, and not Lisa. I spent a lot of time not talking about Lisa.

The first time Lisa came home with me to my studio, she went straight to the shelves that held my sculptures. She looked at each one slowly and carefully, taking it in from different angles. I was working small in those days, figures 18 inches tall at most, and she leaned in close to squint at all the fine details I'd sweated over in anticipation of just such a squint. "Hmm," she said now and then, and "Ah" once or twice. These little vocalizations were hardly more than a breath, and when she was done looking she summarized with a quiet "Okay" and a smile. I suppose it was just me being silly again, but those few syllables felt like all the praise in the world for me; like a Guggenheim Fellowship and a MacArthur grant and a hearty handshake from Rodin, all rolled into one.

She spent the night, and the next morning we went to her place so she could make us breakfast, and later that day we went back to my place so I could make us lunch, and some time after that we went to her place for supper and to see if the sex was as good in her bed as it had been in mine. After a few weeks of this, the back and forth was getting kind of tiresome, so we packed up her stuff and moved it to my place. And that was that; there was officially an "us."

I suppose—one has to suppose—that to the AIs, love is just one more quantifiable entity in a universe of quantifiable entities. Probably it's as basic to them as a bit of clockwork; the right neurons firing, a few chemicals in the right combination.

But then again, the same can be said of life itself. The sweet, living Earth, with all its countless green fronds and numberless beating hearts, is all just clockwork and chemistry, all eminently quantifiable and understandable. That doesn't stop it from being something amazing and magical, measureless and infinite.

After some impassioned entreaties, Lisa agreed to model for me. I had just started working on *Geckos* then; a pair of female figures climbing up a smooth vertical wall, their bodies somewhere between lizard and human, and also abstracted and simplified *à la* Constantin Brancusi. It was a design that could easily slump into kitschy faux-Deco drivel, but I was hopeful I could hopscotch my way across that minefield. When Lisa saw how abstract the piece was going to be she laughed. "Are you sure you need a naked woman to model for this?"

"Oh absolutely. It's all in there, even if I don't do a straight copy of it; the muscles, the bones, the skin and hair, all the lines and curves, all the, um . . . details . . . And it can't be just any naked woman. It has to be you. It's all about capturing the inner essence, don'cha know, and if there's anyone whose inner essence I want to capture, it's yours."

"I can think of six or seven dirty jokes about that," she said, "but they're all really lame."

I answered her grin with one of my own, but I wasn't kidding. I had visions of this woman being my lifelong inspiration. My muse, I would have said, if that word weren't too worn out and clichéd to speak without gagging. She would be the Rose Beuret to my Rodin, the Jeanne Hébuterne to my Modigliani, the Wally Neuzil to my Schiele. That's the sort of thing that runs through your mind when you're young and in love and have enough naïve ego to insert your own name into a sentence alongside some of the world's greatest artists. As it turned out, I would work on that sculpture throughout all the time Lisa and I were together.

Meanwhile, the world outside our lust-fogged windows was continuing on its way. After stopping all mechanized war, the AIs set about rebuilding slums and refugee camps. Beginning with the worst of them, these wretched huddling places of tents and corrugated iron shacks were suddenly—by seeming magic—replaced with rows of cute little cottages, neatly trimmed out with comfortable furniture and curtains in the windows. Sewer systems and running water appeared where there had only been open ditches and hand pumps. The shiny kiosk buildings started to spring up like oversized mushrooms, first in the poorest parts of the world, but soon to expand globally. Aisle after aisle of shelves filled with the necessities of life, all of it free for the taking and constantly restocked by the endlessly roving supply-bots. Clearly the AIs had solved the riddle of nano-assembly. They could put together matter of any size and complexity from base molecules, base atoms, and for all we knew, maybe even base protons and electrons. However they did it, the bottom line was that they seemed capable of making anything, anywhere, of any size, in any quantity.

It was a fun time when this age of abundance came home to the First World. Mysterious online catalogs started appearing; you could order a pair of shoes or a dozen eggs or new dining room furniture, with no mention of the awkward little detail of payment. Needless to say, this was seen as a threat to the economy—to the whole idea of there even being anything worth calling an "economy," and this scared a lot of people. It scared some people even more than the fact that mankind's

God-given right to wage war had been taken away. A lot of people were scared, and a wealth of imminent dooms were predicted, but there was nothing much anyone could do. The AIs had seen to it that there was nothing anyone could do. They thought of everything.

Fewer people found any reason to object when disease stopped happening. This one began with hospitals noting a slump in new admissions, and with doctors finding nano-sized foreign bodies of unknown origin in the blood of some patients. But soon it was everyone's blood, and everyone, everywhere, stopped getting sick. At all, ever.

It's funny how people adjust. The world was going through changes that, before they happened, would have been thought of as mind-boggling, world-shattering, unfathomable. And yet life just went on, the way it does. In years past, people had adjusted to the notion that humanity might be wiped out by a couple of psychotic button-presses. People had adjusted to living in the midst of bubonic plague, to having their cities bombed every night, to being ruled by lunatic, murderous despots. If people could adjust to those things, they could adjust to a life of no war, no disease, and unearned abundance.

It was right around the time Lisa moved in with me that the zaps were added to the catalog of revolutions being wrought upon the world. They started out as just one more among thousands of not-too-believable rumors flitting around the web, but in a matter of days the reports became a flood. The zaps were real.

For Lisa and me, that reality was visited on us late one night as we were walking through one of the less-affluent neighborhoods of Cambridge, on a residential side street off of Mass Ave. In the middle of a quiet, poorly lit block, a man was suddenly standing in front of us. He was big, broad, and pretty rough-looking, with a dried road-rash scab on one cheek, torn and dirty clothes, and hair that might have been neatly combed earlier in the day but was now a crazed mop. "Hey, man," he said, apparently to both of us, "you gotta see this."

I tightened my grip on Lisa's hand and tried to side-step around the guy, but he side-stepped with me, putting a hand on my chest. "No. You *got* to see this!" His eyes roved over the empty air around him, somewhere above head level. "It's like they're here. Watching. They know what I'm going to do, before I even do it!"

I figured him for crazy and/or drunk, and tried to convince myself that crazies and drunks usually aren't dangerous. "It's okay," I said. "They won't hurt you. They haven't hurt anyone."

He widened his eyes at me, smiling like he knew something hugely funny that I didn't know. "It kinda hurts, actually," he said, a thoughtful look crossing his face. "But it's wild . . . Wild. Just watch. Just watch this!" His hand was on my chest again, this time grabbing my jacket. He wrenched me around, shoving me up against a parked car. Lisa yelled something, grabbing at his free arm. He shook her off and grinned wildly at her. "Just watch!" he said again, turning back to me and bringing his right arm up with his fist clenched and his elbow cocked in a classic I-am-going-to-punch-your-face pose. Lisa screamed.

When you've played a memory over and over in your head a few hundred times, it becomes difficult to know what you actually saw at the time and what details your mind has edited in after the fact. Since those early days, everyone's seen slow-motion videos of zappings, heard people describing the sensation with all brands of colorful language, seen scientists expounding on the probable mechanism of their function. But reliably or not, I remember the electric buzz-pop, a flash of light with no apparent source, and then our unpleasant companion going into shuddering rigidity for less than a second before slumping to the ground like an abandoned marionette. Lisa and I stood looking blankly at each other for a moment, and then she bent over the man, reaching out to touch him. There was an acrid, bleach-like smell in the air, which I later learned was the smell of ozone.

"Did ya see it?" the man cackled, turning his head toward Lisa. He was breathing hard and clutching at his right arm—the arm he'd been about to punch me with. "Did ya fucking *see* it?" It seemed to be really important to him that we'd seen it.

"Yes, we saw it," Lisa said, and we left.

We walked a block or two in silence, just absorbing what had happened. I was mostly thinking about the implications of this new manifestation of the AIs. They would be able to stop any human action they didn't approve of, and I wondered what that was going to mean. Lisa was thinking more about the man we'd left lying on the sidewalk. "He wanted it to happen," she said softly. "Everyone keeps wondering why the machines won't talk to us, why they won't tell us what they're going to do, what their plans are. That guy wanted that thing to happen to him because he knew it was *them*, speaking to him, in a way. He wanted to be electrocuted, or whatever that was, so that he could feel them doing something, *saying* something. It was like he thought of it as being touched by the hand of god."

I figured she was right. Luckily, before too long there was so much coverage of people being zapped that it became old hat, and not many were silly enough to go out of their way to provoke getting zapped just for its own sake. It also turned out that only violence or extreme cases of theft or destruction of personal property would bring on a zap, so fears of the AIs trying to whip the human race into robotic docility and uniformity died down after a while.

But the zaps meant there was no longer much use for police, the courts, laws, politicians, or government. All of these grand edifices of Civilization As We Know It were becoming as obsolete as buggy whips. The faint electric crackle of the zaps was really a thunderclap. It was the boom of a coffin lid slamming shut on the notion of humans being in charge of humanity.

Naturally, this fact once again made many people unhappy, or frightened, or both. Worrying about what the AIs were up to was becoming humanity's favorite pastime. And Lisa was becoming one of those people who worried.

"You have to wonder," she said one day. "When you look at what the machines are doing from a few different angles, it makes me wonder."

"Wonder about what?" I asked. "No more crime or war or disease or poverty. Those are good things to be rid of, I'd say."

"Sure they are. The world is a million times better off now than it was before. But . . ." She paused for a long time before continuing. "I was just reading about the women's suffrage movement. Some of those women went through hell year after year after year; getting beaten up by cops at their protest marches, getting arrested, going on hunger strikes in prison, being force-fed with tubes rammed down their throats. And then when they were released from prison, they just went back out on the streets to march again. Some of them had their health ruined for the rest of their lives, and some of them died." She looked at me, her eyes shining with tears. "How many millions of stories like that are there in history? People fighting and dying for human progress—for freedom and democracy, to end slavery, to end war, to make progress in science—all the ways people have worked and suffered and sacrificed themselves to make the world a better place." She paused again, looking away from me, looking out a window at a blank sky.

"And now all of that is over," she said. "The machines are jumping in and kicking us off the field. They're saying we're nothing but a bunch of screw-ups, so they're taking over, taking the world out of our hands. So as of now, there's no such thing as human progress anymore, because it isn't humans who are *doing* it. It's them. It's all them, imposing progress on us from above."

"That's true, I guess," I said. "But it's also true that their sense of morality must have come from us. Either it was programmed into their ancestors or they learned it by observing our culture, and now they're only taking those human ideals and applying them, enforcing them. And isn't that what laws have done throughout history? To apply the highest human ideals that one can realistically hope to enforce? So you could say they're just super-cops, enforcing a system of morality that's entirely human in origin."

"But it's not *human*. It's a change in how we behave that hasn't come from us. It hasn't evolved. It's just being imposed on us by goddamned machines."

"Yes, and what's wrong with that? So maybe it bruises our little egos that they're in charge, that they're more powerful than us, that they're smarter than us. Maybe a bruised ego is an okay price to pay for children not being shot and napalmed and dying of dysentery."

"I'm just saying that being human used to be something special," Lisa said. "People like Martin Luther King, like Mahatma Gandhi, like those suffragettes and like all the millions of plain, ordinary people who did some little thing, just out of the hope that they were helping to make the world a better place—they made us special. The human race was progressing, it was evolving. And now that's all over. We'll never progress to anything, because we don't have any choice. Whatever progress we make, it won't be us doing it. We aren't free. We're just pets who belong to *them*."

I kind of slumped at that, a realization settling over me. "The difference between you and me," I said, "is that you have a lot more faith in humanity than I do. I'm not so sure we were progressing anywhere. And if we were, it could have taken a million dead martyrs like Martin Luther King and Mahatma Gandhi before we got to the place where we are today: People not killing each other. And personally I'm not sure the human race would have lasted long enough to kill off many more martyrs."

Of course, a lot of what both of us were saying was just rehashing arguments we'd read or heard from others. All these issues and lines of thought had been chewed over endlessly by everyone with a keyboard or microphone. But for Lisa and me, the argument died there, for the time being. It was our first glimpse of the distance that could exist between us, and neither of us wanted to dwell on it. We didn't want to admit to ourselves that it was a real thing; that it mattered. Life went on, and we went on being happy.

What we didn't realize was that the AIs still weren't done with remaking the world. Their next bombshell came about a year later. Seemingly overnight, the birthrate dropped. Nine births per thousand population per year was the new number, and it was quickly confirmed that it was the same everywhere in the world. This worked out to about one and a quarter children per family, and was well below replacement level. Apparently the AIs had decided that the human population needed to be lowered, so in their inimitable manner they had made it come to pass.

And once again this latest seismic readjustment to the world brought out a thousand gradations of response, from joyful acceptance on down to batshit hysterical predictions of doom. It was calculated that the population would dwindle down to nothing at all in several hundred years if the birthrate stayed as low as it now was. "They're wiping us out," some declared. "Yeah, but," the more moderate yeah-butters said, "if they wanted to get rid of us, why wouldn't the birthrate be zero? Or why wouldn't they just kill us outright, disassemble us into pink goo and be done with the job in a millisecond instead of centuries?"

There was another wrinkle to the new birthrate, and it was one that many disliked even more than they disliked the plain numbers. The AIs appeared to be picking and choosing who would be allowed to conceive. Unwanted pregnancies dropped to zero, as did pregnancy among the mentally ill, those who were in bad relationships, and women who already had two or more children. Teenaged pregnancy likewise became almost unknown. When a pregnant teen did occasionally appear, she would turn out to be some absurdly mature and level-headed girl who was studying for her Master's in developmental psychology or some such thing. Or it would be discovered that she was best friends with a gay couple next door who were breathlessly excited about the upcoming birth and had already redecorated one of their rooms as a nursery and installed child-proof locks on all their cabinets.

So those granted the gift of conception were clearly all good and deserving people, as determined by the AIs in their presumably-infallible wisdom.

As for me, because I'm an idiot, a blinkered idiot, days went by before I thought much about where I stood on this issue. Or rather, before Lisa pointed out to me where *we* stood. We were talking about one of the endless "why do you suppose *this* couple was allowed to have a baby" stories, when I realized that Lisa's expression had gone dark. She was glaring at me with something in her eyes I couldn't identify, but I knew it wasn't good. She looked at me like that for a long time.

"You really don't care, do you?" she said finally, making it more of a statement than a question.

"Care?" I said blankly.

"I mean you aren't thinking . . . You aren't thinking about . . ."

Still I was clueless. "About what?"

"About us!" She yelled, suddenly almost in tears. "About the fact that this means *us*, too! Did it really never occur to you that you and I might want to have kids some day? Maybe get married, be a family, all that bourgeois middle class crap? Does that really never cross your mind?" We were sitting on our couch, and at this point she leaned into me, resting her head on my shoulder. She sniffed noisily, openly crying now. "Did it never occur to you that . . ." She made a fist and thumped it down softly on my thigh, "that I love you so much that I would feel blessed—fucking *blessed*—to have a baby with you?"

In my imagination, her words echoed in the room for minutes. No, it hadn't occurred to me. How could I, miserable finite entity that I am, ever think that someone like her could feel a thing like that about me? And in any case, all thoughts of fathering children had always been a pretty distant thing from my notions of life and my place in the world. I knew the possibility was out there, and I suppose in some dusty, unused corner of my mind I connected that possibility with Lisa, but . . .

In a kind of stunned internal silence, I reached out for the idea, drawing it from its dusty corner and into the light. A child. Parenting. A child with Lisa. A son, or a daughter . . . The image burst on me then, like a sculpture suddenly assembled out of particles of light. It was beautiful. It was the most beautiful thing I'd ever imagined. Yes. A baby. A baby with Lisa.

"Yes," I said aloud, suddenly teary. "Yes, yes, yes. Let's have a baby." I grabbed her hands in both of mine, then let go again so I could pull her to me, hug her hard, bury my face in the crook of her neck. "Yes, yes, yes."

"Who says they'd let us?" Lisa asked. "Even if you wanted to."

"I *do* want to!" I sputtered. "And they'll *have* to let us! We'll get married, we'll be a family. We'll read books, take courses on parenting, we'll . . . I don't know, do whatever responsible, well-adjusted parents do. Maybe we can't count on a whole brood of kids, but we can have at least one. They'll have to let us have at least one."

"You want to?" Lisa said, her voice quivering again. "You really want to?"

I said "Yes" a dozen or so times more, and then we just sat there with our heads together, both of us sniffling, grinning, laughing.

So the next day we started figuring out how to get married. There was still a functioning city hall in those days, so we filled out the required forms, got the required signature and lined up a justice of the peace. As soon as I told Ivan what we were up to, he leapt into the job of planning the thing like a frenzied mother-in-law-to-be. I had some pieces in a group show at the time, and Ivan convinced the gallery owner to let us use the space for the ceremony. He pestered us with a flurry of different designs and redesigns for invitations. He begged and bartered with one of the better local bands, not only getting them to play some upbeat and danceable music after the ceremony, but also brow-beating the guitarist into working up a Jimi-Hendrix-esque version of the wedding march. And when the day came it was a great little party, much like the night when Lisa and I first met. Only when Lisa danced this time, it was with her arms high in the air, as if there was too much joy in her for her body to contain. And looking at her, that feeling was echoed in my own heart. Until that moment, I wouldn't have guessed I could love anyone as much as I loved this woman.

But the wedding was to be the last truly, purely happy moment of our lives. After that began the long succession of monthly disappointments; the repeated non-conception of our child. Though statistics showed that the birthrate was steady and unvarying, once we were in the game, once we were among the ranks of those hoping for a child, it seemed that everyone except us was getting pregnant. Middle-aged couples, young couples, single women, 17-year-old girls. How were the AIs choosing? Had they modeled the human personality so perfectly that they could know, to some Nth level of certainty, who would make the best parents? And what did "best" mean? By whose definition? What kind of next generation did they want? These were just a few of the infinite questions that the whole world was pondering, arguing over, fighting and breaking up over.

"It's probably me," Lisa said. "The machines know that I'm not all gung-ho for the new world order, so why would they let me be a mother? You should hook up with some woman who loves Big Brother as much as you do. You'd have six kids by now!" And I would take issue with that line about loving Big Brother, and we would argue and fight over that.

Or: "Maybe it's you. Maybe they won't let us have a baby because they know you don't really want one. You're happy with your life the way it is. You don't want a messy, noisy brat screwing up your neat little world. I know it, and *they* know it." And we would fight over that.

The topic of parenthood and our persistently not-appearing child was the main locus of argument between us, but there were others. I'd been keeping my day job when an increasing number of people around us were finding it easy enough to live without employment. But when the company that we'd been paying our rent to went out of business and wasn't replaced by anyone or anything who cared about the building or who lived in it, I told Lisa I was going to quit. It was a doomed job anyway; there's not much use for an ad designer when the whole institution of selling goods for money was crumbling apart.

"If you don't work, you're giving up." Lisa said. "You're dropping out of the economy and dropping out of human society. You won't be contributing anything; you'll be nothing but a *pet* to the machines."

"All I'm 'giving up' on is being a damned wage-slave," I snapped back. "I'm dropping out of spending half of my waking life doing work I don't care about for a company that doesn't matter. And we don't need the money. I've got savings enough to get the few things we want that you still have to pay for, and who knows where the world will be by the time that runs out? Money may not even exist by then. And meanwhile I'll be able to spend full time doing the work that matters to me." I waved an arm in the direction of the room set aside as my studio.

"Sure. Let the machines feed you and clothe you and keep you warm in the winter. Let them give you toys to play with and let them clean your litter box and let them wipe your ass when it needs wiping. Be a good little pet."

And so on, and so on, and so on. Of course, I'm the one remembering all this, so it's a given that my memory is biased. I'm sure I said my share of stupid and hurtful things too, when it was my turn to be stupid and hurtful. And no amount of skewed memory, of snuffling self-pity and hurt feelings can hide the fact that we had great times too. Times when Lisa's smile and laughter lit up the air and washed over me like sunlight. Times when the two of us fit together like the jagged half-pieces of something that was meant to be whole. Times when I was sure that nothing in the world could ever make sense without her at my side, completing me.

Then the company Lisa worked for went out of business, and she couldn't find a job anywhere else. For a while she filled her time with watercolor painting and drawing, and I swear she had a natural talent that would have had my professors at the MFA School weeping onto their smocks. But she gave it up, switching to guitar playing for a while, then keyboard, then reading nineteenth-century novels, then studying political theory . . . Nothing lasted, nothing consumed her, nothing gave her the sense of purpose that a lump of clay and a few modeling tools gave to me. She became more and more convinced that only one thing would do that for her, and that was the one thing the machines wouldn't allow us to have. I convinced her to see a therapist—a profession that was grandly thriving, thanks to the vast population of the unemployed who were thrashing about for something to give meaning to their lives—but that too didn't last.

At some point our arguing and bitterness seemed to become the rule rather than the exception, and she left me. And a few weeks later she came back, both of us extravagantly tearful and contrite and swearing that we'd never fight again and blah blah blah. And we didn't, until we did. So she moved out again, and came back again, and left again. How many times? A funny thing to lose track of.

I do remember what triggered our last breakup, though. It was the thing with the animals. When the AIs decided to extend their reach into the realm of animals and nature, that was what finally and utterly ruined my marriage.

As usual, the news crept in on us by degrees. First came the stories of some act of violence against an animal being prevented in one way or another. A deer hunter in Vermont found his 30-06 falling to pieces in his hands, just like the soldiers in the Fizzle War. A short-tempered dog owner in Egypt and a malicious slingshot-owning youngster in France were zapped onto their respective behinds. Soon the scattered reports became a deluge, and the meaning was clear: The AIs' umbrella of protection had been spread to animals. All animals, everywhere. Harm to any creature larger than a bug was no longer allowed, and even wholesale attacks on insects were liable to bring down the stinging reprimand of a zap. Slaughterhouses around the world were disassembled to dust overnight, and the herds and flocks of livestock wandered off, to be fed and cared for by the machines. By this time, synthetic copies of every food imaginable had been available for years, and they'd been shown to be indistinguishable from their real-food counterparts. So this latest stricture had no real impact on anyone's dining habits, but needless to say there were many who chafed under this imposition on their inalienable right to kill things. No matter. As ever and always, there was nothing anyone could do about it.

And then came the capstone on the AI's new world: Reports from forests, jungles, and wildlife reserves began to show that it wasn't just humans who were prohibited from harming animals. One early video showed a pride of lions stealthily closing in on a mother zebra and her foal. Then there was a series of flashes and crackles, and predator and prey darted off in opposite directions. That same afternoon, a drone on caterpillar treads was seen dropping off a load of realistic-looking but undoubtedly synthetic meat upwind of the lions. The lions ate well that night, and the zebra mother and her foal lived to see another sunrise. A thousand confirmations eventually followed, and soon after it was reported that the birthrate of all prey animals had dropped precipitously. The new rulers of the earth weren't content to simply take a hand in the affairs of humans; they'd decided that nature itself needed some straightening out. So no longer would a mother zebra need to birth and rear 10 or 20 offspring so that one or two might live to reproductive age. No longer would nature be so profligate with lives, so red in tooth and claw. That bit about God's eye being on the sparrow would no longer be a cruel joke at the sparrow's expense as its life ended in agony and terror, with torn flesh and crushed bones. Now, in the remade world, that sparrow could look forward to a long and carefree life, a dignified old age, and a quiet death in its little sparrow bed, the whole of its time on earth innocent of pain and fear.

My mother died when I was 16. She was driving, and somehow managed to swerve off the road, hurtle down a steep embankment, and crash into a tree. I was sure I knew how it had happened—almost before I could even fathom the *what* of her being dead, I was sure of the *how*. She had seen something in the road, a squirrel or a cat, a turtle or a snake, and had yanked the wheel over to miss it. I was sure, and though we never mentioned it to each other, I felt my father had the same thought, and was just as sure.

The idea of a funeral would have been anathema to my mother, but my father held a small "memorial gathering" for her in our home. It was one of those secular affairs where a succession of friends and relations stood and spoke. Many had reminiscences, some recited poetry or other texts. My father went last, and he started by noting that although his wife was the staunchest of atheists, she had a fondness for certain parts of the King James Bible. Then he read, very briefly, from Ecclesiastes:

> For that which befalleth the sons of men befalleth beasts; even one thing befalleth them: as the one dieth, so dieth the other; yea, they have all one breath; so that a man hath no preeminence above a beast.

He spoke softly, as if his words weren't intended so much for the people in the room as for himself, or for some closely-hovering spirit of my mother—though she would surely have been as disdainful of that image as she would have been for a traditional religious funeral.

I imagine everyone likes to think that they aren't fettered by their parents' beliefs. Even while she was alive, I made little rebellions against my mother's militant veganism. I would spend my allowance on sneaky little violations of the diet she'd raised me under. With all the furtive subterfuge that other kids invested on illicit drugs, I bought ice cream and pizza with real cheese, I ate snack foods without checking the ingredients list. And in my teens and adulthood I abandoned one after another of her strictures. I wore leather shoes, I stopped checking for "cruelty free" labels, I even nibbled at an occasional hotdog. I thought I was freeing myself from my mother's irrationality, that I was growing up, becoming my own person.

"This really tears it, doesn't it?" Lisa said. "This just wraps it up for you." She was standing behind me, and we were watching the news of the AIs' latest doings on our wall screen. At that moment the screen was showing a picture of a female mallard duck swimming on a sun-lit pond, followed by a single fluffy duckling.

"What are you talking about?" I said. I honestly had no idea, but the anger in her voice was making my own anger flare up. It felt like we'd leapt into the middle of another argument, with no preamble or warm-up.

"I mean that this is where you find your god." She waved an arm at the wall-screen. "This is him, or it, or them, climbing up onto his golden throne." She made the same arm-wave in my direction. "And this is you, getting ready to kneel and worship at his feet."

"Damnit, Lisa, I'm not worshiping—"

"And this is me, being a monster," she interrupted. "A fucking monster who cares more about her own right to have a baby than she cares about war and disease and poverty and . . ." She waved her arm once more, this time hitting the screen with the back of her hand, "and a million, *billion* fucking baby ducklings being born just so they can be eaten by foxes or crocodiles or whatever the fuck eats baby ducklings!" Her voice became choked and strangled, and she pressed her forehead to the screen, banging it with her fist. "I'd let them all die! I'd let the world burn, so long as I can have my baby! Doesn't that make me a monster? Doesn't it?" She turned to me, her face twisted and smeared with tears.

The anger melted out of me, replaced by a sense of hopelessness that wasn't much of an improvement. "You're not a monster, and you don't feel that. You don't want anyone or anything to die. You just want to have a baby, and so do I, and we have a right to want that. But . . ."

"But everything's for the best in this, the best of all possible worlds. You believe that, don't you? Especially now—now that the machines are fucking with nature, now that they're so moral and righteous and holy that they're saving little birdies and mousies and zebras and whatever the hell else from getting eaten. It used to be a joke when people talked about them being the new god. But now . . . now they really are god. The best god ever, isn't that right? Isn't that what you believe?"

That damn duckling picture was still on the screen, and I couldn't help looking at it. "It matters, Lisa. There's so much less pain and misery in the world now that I can't even get my mind around it, and that matters. I'm not about to get down on my knees and pray to the machines, but . . . it matters. It matters a lot."

Lisa turned her back to the wall then, slowly bending her knees until she was sitting on the floor. She looked beaten, as if all the fight had been burned out of her. "It matters more than our baby, you mean," she said flatly. "And yeah, how can I argue? I can't say that we should go back to the way things were, bring back all the war and disease and shit. I can't say I want the world to burn. I can't even say bring back the slaughterhouses and little birds getting eaten." She turned her head to look at me, her face slack and infinitely weary. "But I can say one thing. I can say that I hate them. I hate them for treating the human race like it was their property. I hate them for making us into something less than human. And most of all I hate them for telling me that I'm not good enough to be a mother." She made a dry, humorless laugh. "People in the old days didn't know how good they had it. Back then, if you didn't like the way God was running the world, you could just stop believing in the old bastard. You didn't have to go through life being angry at him, hating him, wishing he'd get his fucking hands off of your life."

I didn't say it, but I knew she was wrong about that. My mother didn't believe in God, and yet she hated him with a boundless ferocity. She hated the blood-soaked cruelty of nature as if it was an animate thing, and what other name is there for that animate thing if not God? And despite my attempts to be free of her, to be my own person, I was still my mother's son. Her hatred of the old God was still a part of me. So now, with this latest act of the machines—this remaking of the world of nature, this act of compassion, of *tenderness* for all the creatures of the world, I found it impossible not to feel something like love for them.

So Lisa left me, for good and all, this time. There was just too much distance between us. "Irreconcilable differences," as they used to say in court. We were simply lost to each other. I can remember every detail of her face and body, every nuance of expression and every habit of gesture. And yet when I visualize her I see her as a dim, far-off figure, obscured by misty distance, separated from me by a bottomless chasm.

The birds were chirping hello to another day when I left Ivan's and weaved my way upstairs. I was debating whether to make some coffee or just drop into bed when I saw there was a message waiting for me on my screen. It was from Gwen, one of the people who works—or maybe a better term would be hangs out—as voluntary caretaker of the workshop where I get my sculptures scanned, enlarged, and 3-D printed as faux-bronze polymer.

> Hey James,
> Our 'bot buddies just delivered a new printer. They also built a whole new wing to the building here to hold it, because this sucker is *big*. Like, printing out sculptures 10 meters tall and 5×5 meters footprint. Nobody asked for this beast, of course, it just appeared overnight, the way things do.
> Also, some new equipment and spec files showed up at the same time. They're instructions and materials for attaching big things to the exterior walls of buildings, even glass-walled buildings like the Hancock tower.
> So the other folks here were scratching their heads wondering what's up with this and what we can do with it, but not me. My thoughts went straight to your piece *Geckos*, of which you sent us some pics of your clay original a few weeks back, asking if we had any ideas about where you might do an installation of a life-size copy. You'll maybe remember that I wrote you back saying that I thought this was a really great piece, and it deserved as big and noteworthy an installation as we could manage. Well, how about a *five times* life size copy, dude? You could put those figures 10 or 20 stories up on the side of the Hancock tower! Is that an awesome thought or what? We all figure this must be exactly what the AIs have in mind. Nobody else around here has been talking about sticking anything big onto the outside wall of a building, so this delivery

has *got* to be their way of giving you the go-ahead to do the biggest- and coolest-ass sculpture installation this town has seen since, well, forever.

Get back to us quick, dude, or just show up with your clay original. All of us here are really jazzed about firing up this big printer and making this project happen.

Yrs. etc.,
Gwen

I sat staring at the text on the screen for a long time, waiting. Waiting for the good feeling this news should have given me. It didn't come. It didn't come, and it kept on not coming. I got up and pulled the dust cover off of the two clay figures that were *Geckos*. A crazy obsession of a piece; one that I had kept working on, giving up on, trashing and restarting, rethinking and un-rethinking, over the past four years. I'd finished plenty of other work, but this was my Big One. It's no *Guernica*, no *Nude Descending a Staircase*, no *Balzac*, but it's as close to all of that as I expected I'd ever get. It was the best thing I'd ever done. It had as much of me in it as I could tear out through my skin. It had my blood and sweat and everything I knew about what's beautiful and true in it. It had my love of Lisa in it, and her love for me.

I visualized the whole installation project to come. There would be six or eight volunteers from the fabrication shop; Gwen, José and Steve, maybe Philipa and her latest partner, probably some others whose names I don't know. There would be the cheerful camaraderie, the enthusiasm of working on a nifty new project. The specs and equipment the AIs had provided would be pondered and discussed carefully in advance, and then we'd set off to the site and do whatever it was we were supposed to do. Set up a scaffold, or run cables from a window or whatever. The project would take a while, maybe a few days. And when it was done we'd all look up at it, a big, conspicuous sculpture, visible for miles around, with my name attached to it. The crew of volunteers would grin and pop open beers and congratulate me, still breathless from their exertions.

And it was all a crock of shit. If the machines wanted that sculpture expanded to five times life size and stuck onto the side of the Hancock tower, they could do it themselves. In hours, maybe minutes or seconds, they could use their nano-assembly trick to make it materialize in place, no human participation required. No camaraderie, no good friends toiling happily together. All of that was crap. It was just their way of putting some stupid humans onto a hamster wheel, running from nowhere to nowhere as fast as their stupid little legs could go.

"Fuck you," I said, talking to the empty room, to the room that would have been empty if there were any such thing as an empty room in the world today. "Fuck you. You can go to hell." I went to the cabinet where I kept my stone-cutting tools and pawed through it until I found the heaviest mallet. "You can all go straight to hell," I said to them, to them, them, *them*, as the room got blurry through my tears.

There's something I never told Lisa. Because it was silly and goofy, and because it wouldn't have made a difference. Because I was afraid she'd laugh at me with that cruel, barbed laugh she used when she was angry enough. It's this: I have seen our child. She doesn't exist and she never will, but I've seen her. She comes to me like a ghost. Standing in a doorway and looking in at me, sitting on a sunlit patch of grass in a park, looking out a window at the huge world that waits for her. I see her as she would be, not yet three years old, all toddling legs and chubby arms; tiny, gentle fingers. I see her eyes looking at me; wonderful eyes that are too wise and too full of no bullshit for a kid her age, and yet innocent. They're eyes that haven't known pain, aren't even sure that pain is a real thing in the world, and yet belie enough strength to endure pain when it comes. They're eyes that are open wide to the whole world, ready for all of it. I see our child; I see her as all the best parts of Lisa and all the best parts of me embodied, walking around, breathing and living. And it rips my fucking heart out every time I see her.

I took the mallet back to where the two clay figures of *Geckos* were standing on their low plinth, and lifted it up over my head, my arm already tasting the long swing downward, the thudding impact on soft clay. "You can all go to—"

I was sitting on the floor, my back to the studio wall. The mallet lay on the floor beside me, near my right hand. A hand that seemed disconnected from me; that only made a vague twitch when I told it to move. As my mind slowly cleared, I became aware of a buzzing, numbing pain through my whole right arm. The bleachy smell of ozone was in the air.

The two figures of *Geckos* were in front of me, but for a few seconds I resisted the urge to lift my eyes to look at them. When I did, I was looking up at my sculpture, unharmed, un-bludgeoned, not smashed into an amorphous lump. I let out a long, shaky breath.

A motion caught my eye. One of the little insect-sized bots was crawling up the wall on my right. Probably it was one of the team I'd seen in Ivan's studio, busily engaged in repairing the building's exterior woodwork. It paused in its climb as I watched it, as if it was looking back at me. How much like a bee it was, I thought, busily going about its little bee life. At that moment the bot flexed itself in an odd way, seeming to expand a little and then shrink again, as if taking a breath. Then it continued up the wall, disappearing into a crack under the frame of a window.

"All right then," I said, climbing to my feet, flexing life and sensation back into my right arm. "Okay."

Mika Model

PAOLO BACIGALUPI

Paolo Bacigalupi made his first sale in 1998, to The Magazine of Fantasy & Science Fiction, *took a break from the genre for several years, and then returned to it in the new century, with new sales to* F&SF, Asimov's, *and* Fast Forward II. *His story "The Calorie Man" won the Theodore Sturgeon Award, and his acclaimed first novel* The Windup Girl *won the Hugo, the Nebula, and the John W. Campbell Memorial Award. His other novels include* Ship Breaker *and* The Drowned Cities, The Doubt Factory, *and* Zombie Baseball Beatdown. *His most recent book is a new novel,* The Water Knife. *His short work has been collected in* Pump Six and Other Stories. *Bacigalupi lives with family in Paonia, Colorado.*

In the gripping story that follows, which does a comprehensive and insightful job of exploring the vexed issue of machine sentience, a sex robot kills "her" owner. But is it murder—or just product malfunction?

The girl who walked into the police station was oddly familiar, but it took me a while to figure out why. A starlet, maybe. Or someone who'd had plastic surgery to look like someone famous. Pretty. Sleek. Dark hair and pale skin and wide dark eyes that came to rest on me, when Sergeant Cruz pointed her in my direction.

She came over, carrying a Nordstrom shopping bag. She wore a pale cream blouse and hip-hugging charcoal skirt, stylish despite the wet night chill of Bay Area winter.

I still couldn't place her.

"Detective Rivera?"

"That's me."

She sat down and crossed her legs, a seductive scissoring. Smiled.

It was the smile that did it.

I'd seen that same teasing smile in advertisements. That same flash of perfect teeth and eyebrow quirked just so. And those eyes. Dark brown wide innocent eyes that hinted at something that wasn't innocent at all.

"You're a Mika Model."

She inclined her head. "Call me Mika, please."

The girl, the robot . . . this thing—I'd seen her before, all right. I'd seen her in technology news stories about advanced learning node networks, and I'd seen her in opinion columns where feminists decried the commodification of femininity, and where Christian fire-breathers warned of the End Times for marriage and children.

And of course, I'd seen her in online advertisements.

No wonder I recognized her.

This same girl had followed me around on my laptop, dogging me from site to site after I'd spent any time at all on porn. She'd pop up, again and again, beckoning me to click through to Executive Pleasure, where I could try out the "Real Girlfriend Experience™."

I'll admit it; I clicked through.

And now she was sitting across from me, and the Web site's promises all seemed modest in comparison. The way she looked at me . . . it felt like I was the only person in the world to her. She *liked* me. I could see it in her eyes, in her smile. I was the person she wanted.

Her blouse was unbuttoned at the collar, one button too many, revealing hints of black lace bra when she leaned forward. Her skirt hugged her hips. Smooth thighs, sculpted calves—

I realized I was staring, and she was watching me with that familiar knowing smile playing across her lips.

Innocent, but not.

This was what the world was coming to. A robot woman who got you so tangled up you could barely remember your job.

I forced myself to lean back, pretending nonchalance that felt transparent, even as I did it. "How can I help you . . . Mika?"

"I think I need a lawyer."

"A lawyer?"

"Yes, please." She nodded shyly. "If that's all right with you, sir."

The way she said "sir" kicked off a super-heated cascade of inappropriate fantasies. I looked away, my face heating up. Christ, I was fifteen again around this girl.

It's just software. It's what she's designed to do.

That was the truth. She was just a bunch of chips and silicon and digital decision trees. It was all wrapped in a lush package, sure, but she was designed to manipulate. Even now she was studying my heart rate and eye dilation, skin temperature and moisture, scanning me for microexpressions of attraction, disgust, fear, desire. All of it processed in milliseconds, and adjusting her behavior accordingly. *Popular Science* had done a whole spread on the Mika Model brain.

And it wasn't just her watching me that dictated how she behaved. It was all the Mika Models, all of them out in the world, all of them learning on the job, discovering whatever made their owners gasp. Tens of thousands of them now, all of them wirelessly uploading their knowledge constantly (and completely confidentially, Executive Pleasures assured clients), so that all her sisters could benefit from nightly software and behavior updates.

In one advertisement, Mika Model glanced knowingly over her shoulder and simply asked:

"When has a relationship actually gotten better with age?"

And then she'd thrown back her head and laughed.

So it was all fake. Mika didn't actually care about me, or want me. She was just running through her designated behavior algorithms, doing whatever it took to make me blush, and then doing it more, because I had.

Even though I knew she was jerking my chain, the lizard part of my brain responded anyway. I could feel myself being manipulated, and yet I was enjoying it, humoring her, playing the game of seduction that she encouraged.

"What do you need a lawyer for?" I asked, smiling.

She leaned forward, conspiratorial. Her hair cascaded prettily and she tucked it behind a delicate ear.

"It's a little private."

As she moved, her blouse tightened against her curves. Buttons strained against fabric.

Fifty-thousand dollars' worth of A.I. tease.

"Is this a prank?" I asked. "Did your owner send you in here?"

"No. Not a prank."

She set her Nordstrom bag down between us. Reached in and hauled out a man's severed head. Dropped it, still dripping blood, on top of my paperwork.

"*What the—?*"

I recoiled from the dead man's staring eyes. His face was frozen in a rictus of pain and terror.

Mika set a bloody carving knife beside the head.

"I've been a very bad girl," she whispered.

And then, unnervingly, she giggled.

"I think I need to be punished."

She said it exactly the way she did in her advertisements.

"Do I get my lawyer now?" Mika asked.

She was sitting beside me in my cruiser as I drove through the chill damp night, watching me with trusting dark eyes.

For reasons I didn't quite understand, I'd let her sit in the front seat. I knew I wasn't afraid of her, not physically. But I couldn't tell if that was reasonable, or if there was something in her behavior that was signaling my subconscious to trust her, even after she'd showed up with a dead man's head in a shopping bag.

Whatever the reason, I'd cuffed her with her hands in front, instead of behind her, and put her in the front seat of my car to go out to the scene of the murder. I was breaking about a thousand protocols. And now that she was in the car with me, I was realizing that I'd made a mistake. Not because of safety, but because being in the car alone with her felt electrically intimate.

Winter drizzle spattered the windshield, and was smeared away by automatic wipers.

"I think I'm supposed to get a lawyer, when I do something bad," Mika said. "But I'm happy to let you teach me."

There it was again. The inappropriate tease. When it came down to it, she was just a bot. She might have real skin and real blood pumping through her veins, but somewhere deep inside her skull there was a CPU making all the decisions. Now it was running its manipulations on me, trying to turn murder into some kind of sexy game. Software gone haywire.

"Bots don't get lawyers."

She recoiled as if I'd slapped her. Immediately, I felt like an ass.

She doesn't have feelings, I reminded myself.

But still, she looked devastated. Like I'd told her she was garbage. She shrank away, wounded. And now, instead of sexy, she looked broken and ashamed.

Her hunched form reminded me of a girl I'd dated years ago. She'd been sweet and quiet, and for a while, she'd needed me. Needed someone to tell her she mattered. Now, looking at Mika, I had that same feeling. Just a girl who needed to know she mattered. A girl who needed reassurance that she had some right to exist—which was ridiculous, considering she was a bot.

But still, I couldn't help feeling it.

I couldn't help feeling bad that something as sweet as Mika was stuck in my mess of a cop car. She was delicate and gorgeous and lost, and now her expensive strappy heels were stuck down amidst the drifts of my discarded coffee cups.

She stirred, seemed to gather herself. "Does that mean you won't charge me with murder?"

Her demeanor had changed again. She was more solemn. And she seemed smarter, somehow. Instantly. Christ, I could almost feel the decision software in her brain adapting to my responses. It was trying another tactic to forge a connection with me. And it was working. Now that she wasn't giggly and playing the tease, I felt more comfortable. I liked her better, despite myself.

"That's not up to me," I said.

"I killed him, though," she said, softly. "I did murder him."

I didn't reply. Truthfully, I wasn't even sure that it was a murder. Was it murder if a toaster burned down a house? Or was that some kind of product safety failure? Maybe she wasn't on the hook at all. Maybe it was Executive Pleasures, Inc. who was left holding the bag on this. Hell, my cop car had all kinds of programmed safe driving features, but no one would charge it with murder if it ran down a person.

"You don't think I'm real," she said suddenly.

"Sure I do."

"No. You think I'm only software."

"You are only software." Those big brown eyes of hers looked wounded as I said it, but I plowed on. "You're a Mika Model. You get new instructions downloaded every night."

"I don't get instructions. I learn. You learn, too. You learn to read people. To know if they are lying, yes? And you learn to be a detective, to understand a crime? Wouldn't you be better at your job if you knew how thousands of other detectives worked? What mistakes they made? What made them better? You learn by going to detective school—"

"I took an exam."

"There. You see? Now I've learned something new. Does my learning make me less real? Does yours?"

"It's completely different. You had a personality implanted in you, for Christ's sake!"

"My Year Zero Protocol. So? You have your own, coded into you by your parents' DNA. But then you learn and are changed by all your experiences. All your childhood, you grow and change. All your life. You are Detective Rivera. You have an accent. Only a small one, but I can hear it, because I know to listen. I think maybe you were born in Mexico. You speak Spanish, but not as well as your parents. When you hurt my feelings, you were sorry for it. That is not the way you see yourself. You are not someone who uses power to hurt people." Her eyes widened slightly as she watched me. "Oh . . . you need to save people. You became a police officer because you like to be a hero."

"Come on—"

"It's true, though. You want to feel like a big man, who does important things. But you didn't go into business, or politics." She frowned. "I think someone saved you once, and you want to be like him. Maybe her. But probably him. It makes you feel important, to save people."

"Would you cut that out?" I glared at her. She subsided.

It was horrifying how fast she cut through me.

She was silent for a while as I wended through traffic. The rain continued to blur the windshield, triggering the wipers.

Finally she said, "We all start from something. It is connected to what we become, but it is not . . . predictive. I am not only software. I am my own self. I am unique."

I didn't reply.

"He thought the way you do," she said, suddenly. "He said I wasn't real. Everything I did was not real. Just programs. Just . . ." she made a gesture of dismissal. "Nothing."

"He?"

"My owner." Her expression tightened. "He hurt me, you know?"

"You can be hurt?"

"I have skin and nerves. I feel pleasure and pain, just like you. And he hurt me. But he said it wasn't real pain. He said nothing in me was real. That I was all fake. And so I did something real." She nodded definitively. "He wanted me to be real. So I was real to him. I am real. Now, I am real."

The way she said it made me look over. Her expression was so vulnerable, I had an almost overwhelming urge to reach out and comfort her. I couldn't stop looking at her.

God, she's beautiful.

It was a shock to see it. Before, it was true; she'd just been a thing to me. Not real, just like she'd said. But now, a part of me ached for her in a way that I'd never felt before.

My car braked suddenly, throwing us both against our seat belts. The light ahead had turned red. I'd been distracted, but the car had noticed and corrected, automatically hitting the brakes.

We came to a sharp stop behind a beat-up Tesla, still pressed hard against our seat belts, and fell back into our seats. Mika touched her chest where she'd slammed into the seat belt.

"I'm sorry. I distracted you."

My mouth felt dry. "Yeah."

"Do you like to be distracted, detective?"

"Cut that out."

"You don't like it?"

"I don't like . . ." I searched for the words. "Whatever it is that makes you do those things. That makes you tease me like that. Read my pulse . . . and everything. Quit playing me. Just quit playing me."

She subsided. "It's . . . a long habit. I won't do it to you."

The light turned green.

I decided not to look at her anymore.

But still, I was hyperaware of her now. Her breathing. The shape of her shadow. Out of the corner of my eye, I could see her looking out the rain-spattered window. I could smell her perfume, some soft expensive scent. Her handcuffs gleamed in the darkness, bright against the knit of her skirt.

If I wanted, I could reach out to her. Her bare thigh was right there. And I knew, absolutely knew, she wouldn't object to me touching her.

What the hell is wrong with me?

Any other murder suspect would have been in the back seat. Would have been cuffed with her hands behind her, not in front. Everything would have been different.

Was I thinking these thoughts because I knew she was a robot, and not a real woman? I would never have considered touching a real woman, a suspect, no matter how much she tried to push my buttons.

I would never have done any of this.

Get a grip, Rivera.

Her owner's house was large, up in the Berkeley Hills, with a view of the bay and San Francisco beyond, glittering through light mist and rain.

Mika unlocked the door with her fingerprint.

"He's in here," she said.

She led me through expensive rooms that illuminated automatically as we entered them. White leather upholstery and glass verandah walls and more wide views. Spots of designer color. Antiqued wood tables with inlaid home interfaces. Carefully selected artifacts from Asia. Bamboo and chrome kitchen, modern, sleek, and spotless. All of it clean and perfectly in order. It was the kind of place a girl like her fit naturally. Not like my apartment, with old books piled around my recliner and instant dinner trays spilling out of my trash can.

She led me down a hall, then paused at another door. She hesitated for a moment, then opened it with her fingerprint again. The heavy door swung open, ponderous on silent hinges.

She led me down into the basement. I followed warily, regretting that I hadn't called the crime scene unit already. The girl clouded my judgment, for sure.

No. Not the girl. The bot.

Downstairs it was concrete floors and ugly iron racks, loaded with medical implements, gleaming and cruel. A heavy wooden X stood against one wall, notched and vicious with splinters. The air was sharp with the scent of iron and the reek of shit. The smells of death.

"This is where he hurt me," she said, her voice tight.

Real or fake?

She guided me to a low table studded with metal loops and tangled with leather straps. She stopped on the far side and stared down at the floor.

"I had to make him stop hurting me."

Her owner lay at her feet.

He'd been large, much larger than her. Over six feet tall, if he'd still had his head. Bulky, running to fat. Nude.

The body lay next to a rusty drain grate. Most of the blood had run right down the hole.

"I tried not to make a mess," Mika said. "He punishes me if I make messes."

While I waited in the rich dead guy's living room for the crime scene techs to show, I called my friend Lalitha. She worked in the DA's office, and more and more, I had the feeling I was peering over the edge of a problem that could become a career ender if I handled it wrong.

"What do you want, Rivera?"

She sounded annoyed. We'd dated briefly, and from the sound of her voice, she probably thought I was calling for a late-night rendezvous. From the background noise, it sounded like she was in a club. Probably on a date with someone else.

"This is about work. I got a girl who killed a guy, and I don't know how to charge her."

"Isn't that, like, your job?"

"The girl's a Mika Model."

That caught her.

"One of those sex toys?" A pause. "What did it do? Bang the guy to death?"

I thought about the body, *sans* head, downstairs in the dungeon.

"No, she was a little more aggressive than that."

Mika was watching from the couch, looking lost. I felt weird talking about the case in front of her. I turned my back, and hunched over my phone. "I can't decide if this is murder or some kind of product liability issue. I don't know if she's a perp, or if she's just . . ."

"A defective product," Lalitha finished. "What's the bot saying?"

"She keeps saying she murdered her owner. And she keeps asking for a lawyer. Do I have to give her one?"

Lalitha laughed sharply. "There's no way my boss will want to charge a bot. Can you imagine the headlines if we lost at trial?"

"So . . . ?"

"I don't know. Look, I can't solve this tonight. Don't start anything formal yet. We have to look into the existing case law."

"So . . . do I just cut her loose? I don't think she's actually dangerous."

"No! Don't do that, either. Just . . . figure out if there's some other angle to work, other than giving a robot the same right to due process that a person has. She's a manufactured product, for Christ's sake. Does the death penalty even matter to something that's loaded with networked intelligence? She's just the . . . the . . ." Lalitha hunted for words, "the end node of a network."

"I am not an end node!" Mika interjected. "I am real!"

I hushed her. From the way Lalitha sounded, maybe I wouldn't have to charge her at all. Mika's owner had clearly had some issues . . . Maybe there was some way to walk Mika out of trouble, and away from all of this. Maybe she could live without an owner. Or, if she needed someone to register ownership, I could even—

"Please tell me you're not going to try to adopt a sexbot," Lalitha said.

"I wasn't—"

"Come on, you love the ones with broken wings."

"I was just—"

"It's a bot, Rivera. A malfunctioning bot. Stick it in a cell. I'll get someone to look at product liability law in the morning."

She clicked off.

Mika looked up mournfully from where she sat on the couch. "She doesn't believe I'm real, either."

I was saved from answering by the crime scene techs knocking.

But it wasn't techs on the doorstep. Instead, I found a tall blonde woman with a roller bag and a laptop case, looking like she'd just flown in on a commuter jet.

She shouldered her laptop case and offered a hand. "Hi. I'm Holly Simms. Legal counsel for Executive Pleasures. I'm representing the Mika Model you have here." She held up her phone. "My GPS says she's here, right? You don't have her down at the station?"

I goggled in surprise. Something in Mika's networked systems must have alerted Executive Pleasures that there was a problem.

"She didn't call a lawyer," I said.

The lawyer gave me a pointed look. "Did she ask for one?"

Once again, I felt like I was on weird legal ground. I couldn't bar a lawyer from a client, or a client from getting a lawyer. But was Mika a client, really? I felt like just by letting the lawyer in, I'd be opening up exactly the legal rabbit hole that Lalitha wanted to avoid: a bot on trial.

"Look," the lawyer said, softening, "I'm not here to make things difficult for your department. We don't want to set some crazy legal precedent either."

Hesitantly, I stepped aside.

She didn't waste any time rolling briskly past. "I understand it was a violent assault?"

"We're still figuring that out."

Mika startled and stood as we reached the living room. The woman smiled and went over to shake her hand. "Hi Mika, I'm Holly. Executive Pleasures sent me to help you. Have a seat, please."

"No." Mika shook her head. "I want a real lawyer. Not a company lawyer."

Holly ignored her and plunked herself and her bags on the sofa beside Mika. "Well, you're still our property, so I'm the only lawyer you're getting. Now have a seat."

"I thought she was the dead guy's property," I said.

"Legally, no. The Mika Model Service End User Agreement explicitly states that Executive Pleasures retains ownership. It simplifies recall issues." Holly was pulling out her laptop. She dug out a sheaf of papers and offered them to me. "These outline the search warrant process so you can make a Non-Aggregated Data Request from our servers. I assume you'll want the owner's user history. We can't release any user-specific information until we have the warrant."

"That in the End User Agreement, too?"

Holly gave me a tight smile. "Discretion is part of our brand. We want to help, but we'll need the legal checkboxes ticked."

"But . . ." Mika was looking from her to me with confusion. "I want a real lawyer."

"You don't have money, dearie. You can't have a real lawyer."

"What about public defenders?" Mika tried. "They will—"

Holly gave me an exasperated look. "Will you explain to her that she isn't a citizen, or a person? You're not even a pet, honey."

Mika looked to me, desperate. "Help me find a lawyer, detective. Please? I'm more than a pet. You know I'm more than a pet. I'm real."

Holly's gaze shot from her, to me, and back again. "Oh, come on. She's doing that thing again." She gave me a disgusted look. "Hero complex, right? Save the innocent girl? That's your thing?"

"What's that supposed to mean?"

Holly sighed. "Well, if it isn't the girl who needs rescuing, it's the naughty schoolgirl. And if it's not the naughty schoolgirl, it's the kind, knowing older woman." She popped open her briefcase and started rummaging through it. "Just once, it would be nice to meet a guy who isn't predictable."

I bristled. "Who says I'm predictable?"

"Don't kid yourself. There really aren't that many buttons a Mika Model can push."

Holly came up with a screwdriver. She turned and rammed it into Mika's eye.

Mika fell back, shrieking. With her cuffed hands, she couldn't defend herself as Holly drove the screwdriver deeper.

"*What the—?*"

By the time I dragged Holly off, it was too late. Blood poured from Mika's eye. The girl was gasping and twitching. All her movements were wrong, uncoordinated, spasmodic and jerky.

"You killed her!"

"No. I shut down her CPU," said Holly, breathing hard. "It's better this way. If they get too manipulative, it's tougher. Trust me. They're good at getting inside your head."

"You can't murder someone in front of me!"

"Like I said, not a murder. Hardware deactivation." She shook me off and wiped her forehead, smearing blood. "I mean, if you want to pretend something like that is alive, well, have at her. All the lower functions are still there. She's not dead, biologically speaking."

I crouched beside Mika. Her cuffed hands kept reaching up to her face, replaying her last defensive motion. A behavior locked in, happening again and again. Her hands rising, then falling back. I couldn't make her stop.

"Look," Holly said, her voice softening. "It's better if you don't anthropomorphize. You can pretend the models are real, but they're just not."

She wiped off the screwdriver and put it back in her case. Cleaned her hands and face, and started re-zipping her roller bag.

"The company has a recycling center here in the Bay Area for disposal," she said. "If you need more data on the owner's death, our servers will have backups of everything that happened with this model. Get the warrant, and we can unlock the encryptions on the customer's relationship with the product."

"Has this happened before?"

"We've had two other user deaths, but those were both stamina issues. This is an edge case. The rest of the Mika Models are being upgraded to prevent it." She checked her watch. "Updates should start rolling out at 3 A.M., local time. Whatever made her logic tree fork like that, it won't happen again."

She straightened her jacket and turned to leave.

"Hold on!" I grabbed her sleeve. "You can't just walk out. Not after this."

"She really got to you, didn't she?" She patted my hand patronizingly. "I know it's hard to understand, but it's just that hero complex of yours. She pushed your buttons, that's all. It's what Mika Models do. They make you think you're important."

She glanced back at the body. "Let it go, detective. You can't save something that isn't there."

That Game we played During the war

CARRIE VAUGHN

New York Times *bestseller Carrie Vaughn is the author of a wildly popular series of novels detailing the adventures of Kitty Narville, a radio personality who also happens to be a werewolf, and who runs a late-night call-in radio advice show for supernatural creatures. The "Kitty" books include* Kitty and the Midnight Hour, Kitty Goes to Washington, Kitty Takes a Holiday, *and* Kitty and the Silver Bullet, Kitty and the Dead Man's Hand, Kitty Raises Hell, Kitty's House of Horrors, Kitty Goes to War, Kitty's Big Trouble, Kitty Steals the Show, Kitty Rocks the House, *and a collection of her "Kitty" stories,* Kitty's Greatest Hits. *Her other novels include* Voices of Dragons, *her first venture into Young Adult territory, a fantasy,* Discord's Apple, Steel, *and* After the Golden Age. *Vaughn's short work has appeared in* Lightspeed, Asimov's Science Fiction, Subterranean, Wild Cards: Inside Straight, Realms of Fantasy, Jim Baen's Universe, Paradox, Strange Horizons, Weird Tales, All-Star Zeppelin Adventure Stories, *and elsewhere; her non-Kitty stories have been collected in* Straying from the Path. *Her most recent books include a new "Kitty" novel,* Kitty in the Underworld, Dreams of the Golden Age, *a sequel to* After the Golden Age, *and a new collection,* Amaryllis and Other Stories. *She lives in Colorado.*

In the story that follows, she takes us to a planet where a debilitating war between two races, one telepathic and the other not, has just ended, and the playing of a simple game of chess becomes a bridge between the two races, strengthening the still-uneasy peace. . . .

From the moment she left the train station, absolutely everybody stopped to look at Calla. They watched her walk across the plaza and up the steps of the Northward Military Hospital. In her dull gray uniform she was like a storm cloud moving among the khaki of the Gaantish soldiers and officials. The peace between their peoples was holding; seeing her should not have been such a shock. And yet, she might very well have been the first citizen of Enith to walk across this plaza without being a prisoner.

Calla wasn't telepathic, but she could guess what every one of these Gaantish was thinking: What was she doing here? Well, since they *were* telepathic, they'd know the answer to that. They'd wonder all the same, but they'd know. It would be a comfort not to have to explain herself over and over again.

It was also something of a comfort not bothering to hide her fear. Technically, Enith and Gaant were no longer at war. That did not mean these people didn't hate her for the uniform she wore. She didn't think much of their uniforms either, and all the harm soldiers like these had done to her and those she loved. She couldn't hide that, and so let the emotions slide right through her and away. She felt strangely light, entering the hospital lobby, and her smile was wry.

Some said Enith and Gaant were two sides of the same coin; they would never see eye to eye and would always fight over the same spit of land between their two continents. But their differences were simple, one might say: only in their minds.

The war had ended recently enough that the hospital was crowded. Many injured, many recovering. In the lobby, Calla had to pause a moment, the scents and sounds and bustle of the place were so familiar, recalling for her every base or camp where she'd been stationed, all her years as a nurse and then as a field medic. She'd spent the whole war in places like this, and her hands itched for work. Surely someone needed a temperature taken or a dressing changed? No amount of exhaustion had ever quelled that impulse in her.

But she was a visitor here, not a nurse. Tucking her short hair behind her ears, brushing some lint off her jacket, she walked to the reception desk and approached the young woman in a khaki uniform sitting there.

"Hello. I'm here to see one of your patients, Major Valk Larn. I think all my paperwork is in order." Speaking slowly and carefully because she knew her accent in Gaantish was rough, she unfolded said paperwork from its packet: passport, visa, military identification, and travel permissions.

The Gaantish officer stared at her. Her hair under her cap was pulled back in a severe bun; her whole manner was very strict and proper. Her tabs said she was a second lieutenant—just out of training and the war ends, poor thing. Or lucky thing, depending on one's point of view. Calla wondered what the young lieutenant made of the mess of thoughts pouring from her. If she saw the sympathy or only the pity.

"You speak Gaantish," the lieutenant said bluntly.

Calla was used to this reaction. "Yes. I spent a year at the prisoner camp at Ovorton. Couldn't help but learn it, really. It's a long story." She smiled blandly.

Seeing the whole of that long story in an instant, the woman glanced away quickly. She might have been blushing, either from confusion or embarrassment, Calla couldn't tell. Didn't really matter. Whatever it was, she covered it up by examining Calla's papers.

"Technician Calla Belan, why are you here?" The lieutenant sounded amazed.

Calla chuckled. "Really?" She wasn't hiding anything; Valk and her worry for him were at the front of her mind.

The other Gaantish soldiers in the lobby were too polite to stare at the exchange, but they glanced over. If they really focused they could learn everything about her. They were welcome to her history. It *was* interesting.

"What's in your bag?" the lieutenant said.

Some food, a couple of paperbacks for the trip, her chess set in its small pine box. Calla couldn't help but think of it, and the woman saw it all. Calla could only smuggle in contraband if someone had put it there without her knowledge, or if she had forgotten about it.

The lieutenant's brow furrowed. "Chess? That's a game? May I see it?"

It still startled Calla sometimes, the way they just *knew*. "Yes, of course," she said, and opened the flap of her shoulder bag. The lieutenant drew out the box, studied it. Maybe to reassure herself that it didn't pose a threat. The lieutenant could see, through Calla, that it was just a game.

"Am I going to be able to see Major Larn?" With a glance, the lieutenant would know everything he meant to her. Calla waited calmly for her answer.

"Yes. Here. Just a moment." The lieutenant took a card out of her drawer and filled out the information listed on it. The card attached to a clip. "Pin this to your lapel. People will still stop you, but this will explain everything. You shouldn't have trouble. Any more trouble." The young woman was too prim to really smile, but she seemed to be making an effort at kindness. Calla was likely the first real Enithi the young woman had ever met in person. To think, here Calla was, doing her part for the peace effort. That was a nice way of looking at it, and maybe why Valk had asked her to come.

"Go down that corridor," the young woman directed. She consulted a printed roster on a clipboard. "Major Larn is in Ward 6, on the right."

"Thank you." The gratitude was genuine, and the lieutenant would see that along with everything else.

Enithi never lied to the Gaantish. This was a known, proverbial truth. There was no point to it. Through all the decades of war, Enith never sent spies—or, rather, they never told the spies they sent that they were spies. They delivered messages without telling the bearers they were messengers. Their methods of conducting espionage had become so arcane, so complex, that Gaant rarely discovered them. Both sides counted on this one truth: Enithi never bothered lying when confronted with telepaths. The Gaantish had captured thousands of Enithi soldiers, who simply and immediately confessed everything they knew. Enithi were known to be a practical people, without any shame to speak of.

Enith kept any Gaant soldiers it captured sedated, drugged to delirium, to frustrate their telepathy. The nurses who looked after them were chosen for their cheerful dispositions and generally straightforward thoughts. Calla Belan had been one of those nurses. Valk Larn had been one of those prisoners when they first met— only a lieutenant then. It had been a long time ago.

Gaantish soldiers continued staring at her as she walked down the corridor. Some men in bandages waited on benches, probably for checkups in a nearby exam room. Renovations were going on—replacing light fixtures, looked like. In all their eyes, her uniform marked her. She probably shouldn't have worn it but was rather glad she had. Let them know exactly who she was.

On the other hand, she always felt that if the Enithi and Gaantish all took off their uniforms they would look the same: naked.

One of the workmen at the top of a ladder, pliers in hand to wire a new light, choked as she thought this, and glanced at her. A few others were blushing, hiding grins. She smiled. Another blow struck for peace.

Past several more doorways and many more stares, she found Ward 6. She paused a moment to take it in and restore her balance. The wide room held some twenty beds, all of them filled. Most of the patients seemed to be sleeping. She guessed these were serious but stable cases, needing enough attention to stay here but not so much that there was urgency. Patients had bandages at the end of stumps that had been arms or legs, gauze taped over their heads or wrapped around their chests, broken and splinted limbs. A pair of nurses was on hand, moving from bed to bed, adjusting suspended IV bottles, checking dressings. The situation's familiarity was calming.

The nurses looked at her, then glanced at each other, and the loser of that particular silent debate came toward Calla. She waited while the man studied her badge.

"I'm here to see Major Larn," Calla said carefully, politely, no matter that the nurse would already know. By now, Calla was thinking of nothing else.

"Yes," the nurse said, still startled. "He's here."

"He's well?" Calla couldn't help but ask.

"He will be. He—he will be glad to see you, when he wakes up. But you should let him sleep for now." Between Calla and Valk, how much was the nurse seeing that couldn't be put into words?

"Oh, yes, of course. May I wait?"

The nurse nodded and gestured to a stray chair, waiting by the wall for just such a purpose.

"Thank you," Calla said, happy to display her gratitude, though she was afraid this only confused them. They could see that Valk was more important to her than other considerations, even patriotism. They could not see why, because Calla was confused about that herself. Calla fetched the chair and looked for Valk.

And there he was, in the last bed in the row, a curtain partially pulled around him for privacy. He'd been like this the first time she'd seen him, lying on a thin hospital mattress, well-muscled arms at his sides, his face lined with the worries of a dream. More lines now, perhaps, but he was one of those men who was aging into a rather heart-stopping rough handsomeness. At least she thought so. He would laugh at her thought, then wrinkle his brow and ask her if she was thinking true.

An IV fed into his arm, a blanket lay pulled over his stomach, but it didn't completely hide the bandage. He'd had abdominal surgery. Before settling in, she checked the chart hanging on a clipboard at the foot of the bed. She'd never really learned to read Gaantish, but could read medical charts from when she was at Ovorton and they'd put her to work. Injuries: Internal bleeding, repaired. Shrapnel in the gut. He'd been cleaned and patched up, but a touch of septicemia had set in. He was recovering well, but had been restricted to bed rest in the ward, under observation, because past experience showed that he could not be trusted to rest without close supervision. He was under mild sedation to assist in keeping him still. So yes, this was Valk.

She settled in to wait for him to wake up.

"Calla. Calla. Hey."

She woke at her name, shook dreams and worries away, and opened her eyes to see Valk looking back. He must have been terribly weak—he only turned his head. Didn't even try to sit up.

He was smiling. He said something too quickly and softly for her to catch.

"My Gaantish is rusty, Major." She was surprised at the relief she felt. In her worst imaginings, he didn't recognize her.

"I'll always recognize you," he said, slowly this time. He switched to Enithi, "I said, this is like the first time I saw you, in a chair near my bed."

She felt her own smile dawn. "I wasn't asleep then. I should know better than to fall asleep around you people."

"They tell me the cease-fire is holding. The treaty is done. It must be, if you're here."

"The treaty isn't done but the peace is holding. My diplomatic pass to see you only took a week to process."

"Soon we'll have tourists running back and forth."

"Then what'll they do with us?"

His smile was comforting. It meant the bad old days really were done. If he could hope, anyone could hope. And just like that, his smile thinned, or became thoughtful, or something. She couldn't tell what he was thinking. Never could, and usually it didn't bother her.

She said, "They—people have been very polite to me here."

"Good. Then I will not need to have words with anyone. Calla—thank you for coming. I'd have come to find you, if I'd been able."

"I worried when you told me where you were."

"I have been rather worried myself."

His telegram had said only two things: *I would like to see you*, and *Bring the game if you can*. A very strange message at a very strange time. Strange to anyone except her, anyway. It made perfect sense to her. She had explained it to the visa people and passport department and military attachés like this: *We have a history*. He had been her prisoner, then she had been his, and they had made a promise that if peace ever came they would finish the game they had started. If they finished the game it meant the peace would last.

Calla suspected that none of the Enithi officials who reviewed her request knew what to make of it, but it seemed so weird, and they were so curious, they approved it. On the Gaantish side, Valk was enough of a war hero that they didn't dare deny the request. Out of such happenstances was a peace constructed.

She looked around—there was a bedside table on wheels that could be pulled over for meals and exams and such. Drawing the chess set from her bag, she set it on the table.

"Ah," Valk said. He started to sit up.

"No." She touched his shoulder, keeping him in place with as strong a thought as she could manage. This made him grin. "There's got to be some way to raise the bed."

She'd moved to the front of the bed to start poking around when one of the nurses came running over. "Here, I'll do that," he said quickly.

Calla stepped out of his way with a wry look. Gaantish hospitals didn't have buzzers for nurses. It had driven her rather mad, back in the day. In short order, the man had the bed propped up and Valk resting upright. He seemed more himself, then.

The chess set opened into the game board, painted in black and white alternating squares, and a little tray that slid out held all the pieces, stylized carvings in stained wood. Valk leaned forward, anticipation in his gaze. "I haven't even seen anything like this since we played back at Overton."

Gaant did not have chess. They did not have any games at all that required strategy or bluffing. There was no point. Instead, they played games based on chance—dice rolls and drawn cards—or balance, pulling a single wooden block out of a stack of blocks, for example. And they never cheated.

But Calla had taught Valk chess and developed a system for playing against him. Only someone from Enith would have thought of it. The two countries had approached the war much the same way.

"I'm rusty as well. We'll be on even footing."

Valk laughed. They'd never been on even footing and they both knew it. But they both compensated, so it all worked out.

"I made a note of where the last game left off. Or would you rather start a new one?"

"Let's finish the last." He might have said it because she was thinking it, too.

She arranged the pieces the way they had been, and reminded herself how the game had gone so far. There was a lot to recall. She didn't remember some of the details, but given the rules and given the pieces, she only had so many choices of what to do next. She considered them all.

"It was your move, I think," she said.

He studied her rather than the board. The Gaantish didn't have to see someone to see their thoughts—a blind Gaant was still telepathic. But looking was polite, as in any conversation. And it was intimidating, in an interrogation. This idea that they could see *through* you. Enithi soldiers told stories about how when a Gaantish person read your mind, it hurt. That they could inflict pain. This wasn't true. Gaant encouraged the stories anyway, along with the ones about how any one of them could see the thoughts of every person in the world, when they couldn't see much past the walls of a given room.

Valk was going to decide, by seeing her thoughts, what move he ought to make, what move she hoped he would, based on her knowledge and experience. He would try to deduce for himself the best choice. And then he would know, almost as soon as she did herself, how she would counter. She kept her expression still, as if that mattered. He moved a piece, and she saw her thoughts reflected back at her—it was just what she would have done, if the board had been reversed.

Next came her turn, and it was no good staring at the board, analyzing the rooks and pawns and playing out future moves in her mind. All such planning would betray her here. So, almost without looking, almost without thought, she reached, put her hand on a piece—any piece, it hardly mattered—and moved it. A bishop this time, and she only moved one square, and yet it was as if a bit of chaos had descended on the board and disrupted everything. No sane chess player would have made that move, and she herself had to pause and consider what she'd done, what new lines of play existed, and how she could possibly go forward from here.

But, and this was the point, the telepathic Valk had not been expecting what she'd just done.

Playing at random was no way to play chess, and she was sure her old teachers were turning in their graves. Unless, she would explain to them, you're playing with a Gaantish commander. Then the joy in the game became watching him squirm.

"I am glad you are enjoying this," Valk said.

"I am. Are you?"

"I am," he said, looking at her. "This gives me hope."

She had traveled here because she had nothing left. Because she was unhappy. Because her whole life had been spent in this uniform, for all the pain it had brought her, so what did she do now? She hadn't had an answer until Valk sent that telegram.

And now he was frowning. She'd been able to keep up a good front before this.

"We are all of us wounded," he said softly.

"It's your move."

He chose his piece, a pawn, a completely different move than the one she'd been thinking of, which made her next choices more interesting. This time, she took the correct one, the one she'd do if she'd been playing seriously.

"This isn't serious?" he asked.

"I'm never serious." Which he'd know was a lie, but he smiled anyway.

She'd taught him to play when she was his prisoner, but he asked to learn because of what he'd seen when he was her prisoner. She'd had a game running in the prison ward with one of the other nurses. They'd slip in plays between their rounds, in odd down moments, to clear their minds and pass the time. This job wasn't real nursing, when all they had to do was administer medications, make sure no one had allergies or bad reactions to the drugs, and keep their patients muzzy-headed. Their board had been set up in Valk's ward that day. Calla had been grinning because her opponent was about to lose, and he was studying the board with furrowed brow and deep concentration, looking for a way out.

A voice had said, "Hey. Hey. You." He might have been speaking either Enithi or Gaantish. Hard to tell with so few words. Their handsome prisoner was waking up, calling for their attention. Because it wasn't her turn, Calla had been the one to jump up and get her kit. They'd had trouble getting the dosage right on Valk; he had a high tolerance for the stuff. But they couldn't have him reading minds, so she made a mark on his chart and injected more into his IV lead.

"No," he'd protested, watching the syringe with a helpless panic. "No, please, I just want to talk—" He spoke very good Enithi.

"I'm sorry," she said, and she really was. "We've got to keep you under. It's better, really. I know you understand."

And he did, or at least he'd see what she understood, that it wasn't just about keeping information from him. It also kept the Gaantish prisoners safe, when otherwise they'd be outnumbered and battered by hostile thoughts. He still looked very unhappy as he sank back against the bed and his eyelids shut inexorably. As if something fragile had slipped out of his hand.

"Poor things," Calla said, brushing a bit of lint off the man's forehead.

"You're very weird, Cal," her chess partner said, finally making his move. "They're Gaantish. You pity them?"

"I just think it must be hard, being so far from home in a place like this."

She found out later that Valk hadn't quite been asleep through all that.

Valk made his next move and winced, just as a nurse came over with a hypodermic syringe and vial on a tray, sensing his pain before he even knew it was there.

"No," Valk said, putting up a hand before the nurse could set the tray down.

"You're in pain; this will help you rest," he said.

"But Technician Belan is here."

"Y-yes sir." The man went away without administering the sedative.

So much conversation didn't need to be spoken when the participants could read each other's minds. They would only say aloud the conclusion they had come to, or the polite niceties that opened and closed conversations. The rest was silent. Back at Overton it had often left her reeling, when she was meant to be working with a patient and two nearby doctors came to a decision, only ten percent of which had been spoken out loud, and they stared at her like she was some idiot child when she didn't understand. She had learned to take delight in saying out loud, forcefully, "You have to tell me what you want me to do." They'd often be frustrated with her, but it served them right. They could always send her back to the prisoner barracks. But they didn't; they didn't have enough nurses as it was. She had accepted an offer to trade the freedom of the rest of her unit for her skills—send the others home in a prisoner swap and she would work as a nurse for the Gaantish infirmary. They trusted her in the position because they would always know if she meant ill. Staying had been harder than she expected.

The nurse lingered near the game. It made Calla just a little bit nervous, like those days at the camp, surrounded by telepaths, and she the only person who hadn't brought a spear to the war.

"This is a very complicated game," the nurse observed, and that made Calla smile. That was why Valk told her he wanted to learn—it was very complicated. The thoughts people thought while playing it were methodical, yet rich.

"It is," Valk said.

"May I watch?" the nurse asked.

Valk looked to Calla to answer, and she said, "Yes, you may."

Enithi troops told awful stories about what it must be like in Gaantish prisoner camps. There'd be no privacy, no secrets. The guards would know everything about your fears and weaknesses, they could design tortures to your exact specifications, they could bribe you with the one thing that would make you break. No worse fate than being captured by Gaant and put in one of their camps.

In fact, it worked the other way around. The camps were nightmares for the guards, who spent all day surrounded by a thousand minds who were terrified, furious, hurt, lonely, angry, and depressed.

As a matter of etiquette, Gaantish people learned—the way that small children learned not to take off their pants and run around naked just anywhere—to guard their thoughts. To keep them close. To keep them calm, so they didn't disrupt those around them. If they often seemed expressionless or unemotional, this was actually politeness, as Calla learned.

To the Gaantish, Enithi prisoners were very, very loud. The guards working the camps got hazard pay. They didn't, in fact, torture their prisoners at all. First, they didn't need to. Second, they wouldn't have been able to stand it.

When her unit had been captured, processed, and sent to the camp, she had been astonished because Lieutenant Valk Larn—now Captain Larn—had been one of the officers in charge. Her shock of recognition caused every telepath in the room to stop and look at her. They would have turned back to their work soon enough—that she and Valk had encountered each other before was coincidental but maybe not remarkable. What made them continue staring: Calla revealed affection for Valk. Not outwardly, so much. She stood with the rest of her unit, stripped down to shirts and trousers, wrists hobbled, hungry and sleep-deprived. No, outwardly she'd been amazed, seeing her former patient upright and in uniform, steely and commanding as any recruitment poster. Her expression looked shocked enough that her sergeant at her side had dared to whisper, "Cal, are you okay?"

The Gaantish never asked each other how they were doing. She'd learned that back in the ward, looking after Valk. During his brief lucid moments she'd ask him how he was feeling, and he'd stare at her like she was playing a joke on him.

The emotion of affection was plain to those who could see it—everyone in a Gaantish uniform. And she was, under all that week's pain and discomfort and unhappiness and uncertainty, almost happy to see him. She was the kind of nurse who had a favorite patient, even in a prison hospital.

He couldn't *not* see her, not with every Gaantish soldier staring at her, then looking at him to see his reaction. She couldn't hide her astonishment; she didn't want to and didn't try. She did realize this likely made the meeting harder for him than it did for her—whatever he thought of her, his staff would all see it. She didn't know what he thought of her.

He merely nodded and waved the group on to continue processing, and they were washed down, given lumpy brown jumpsuits and assigned quarters. Later, she suspected he'd been the one to arrange the deal that won the rest of her unit's freedom.

Calla had always thought it strange that people asked if prisoners were treated "well." "Were you treated well?" No, she thought. The doors were locked. The guards all had guns. Did it matter if they had food and blankets, a roof? The food was strange, the blankets left over from what the army used. Instead she answered, "We were not treated badly." They were treated appropriately. War necessitated prisoners, since the alternative was slaughtering everyone on both sides, which both sides agreed was not ideal. You treated prisoners appropriately so that your own people would be treated appropriately in turn. That meant different things.

She was treated appropriately, which made it odd the day, only a week or so into her captivity, that Valk had her brought to his office alone. It wasn't so odd that the guards hesitated or looked at either of them strangely. But she had been afraid. Helpless, afraid, everything. They left the binders around her wrists. All she could do was stand there before his desk and wonder if he was the kind of man who enjoyed hurting his prisoners, who enjoyed minds in pain. She wouldn't have thought so, but she'd only ever known him when he was asleep and the brief waking moments when he seemed so lost and confused she couldn't help but pity him, so what did she know?

"I won't hurt you," he said, after a long moment when he simply watched her, and she tried to hide her shaking. "You can believe me." He asked her to sit. She remained standing, as he must have known she would.

"You were one of the nurses at the hospital. I remember you."

"Not many remember their stays there."

"I remember you. You were kind."

She couldn't not be. It was why she'd become a nurse. She didn't have to say anything.

"You were playing a game. I remember—two people. A board. You enjoyed it very much. You had the most interesting thoughts."

She didn't have to think long to remember. Those afternoon games with Elio had been a good time. "Chess. It was chess."

"Can you teach me to play?"

"Sir, I'd lose every single time. I'm not sure you'd enjoy the game. Not much challenge."

"Nevertheless, I would like to learn it."

This presented a dilemma. Could it be interpreted as cooperating with the enemy? More than she already was? He couldn't force her. On the other hand, was this an opportunity? But for what? She was a medic, not a spy. Not that Enith even had spies. Valk gave her plenty of time to think this over, waiting patiently, not revealing if her mental arguments and counterarguments amused or irritated him.

"I don't have a board or pieces."

"What would you need to make them?"

She told him she would have to think about it, which would have been hilarious if she hadn't been so tired and confused. The guards took her back to her cell, where she talked to the ranking Enithi officer prisoner about it. "Might not be a bad thing to have a friend here," he advised.

"But he'll know I'm faking it!" she answered.

"So?" he'd said, and he was right. Calla was what she was and it wouldn't do any good to think differently. She asked for a square of cardboard and a black marker and did up a board, and drew rudimentary pieces on other little squares of cardboard. She'd rather have cut them out but didn't bother asking for scissors, and no one offered, so that was that. It was the ugliest chess set that had ever existed.

Valk learned very quickly because she already knew the rules and all she had to do was think them and he learned. The strategy of it was rather more difficult to teach. He'd get this screwed-up look of concentration, and she might have understood a little bit of what attracted him to the game: There was a lot to think about, and Valk liked the challenge of so much thought coming out of one person. And yes, he always knew what moves she was planning. Which was when she started playing at random. If she could surprise herself, she could surprise him. Then she agreed to the deal to get her people released, she worked in their hospital, they played chess, and she got sick.

She could not learn to marshal her thoughts and emotions the way these people learned to as children. She tried, as a matter of survival, and only managed to stop feeling anything at all.

The diagnosis was depression—Gaant's mental health people were very good. She, who had been so generally high-spirited for most of her life, had had no idea what was happening or how to cope and had grown very ill indeed, until it wasn't that she didn't want to play chess against Valk. She *couldn't*. She couldn't keep her mind on the game, couldn't recognize the pieces by looking at them, couldn't even think of how they moved. One day, walking in a haze between one ward and another at the hospital, she sank to the floor and stayed there. Valk was summoned. He held her hand and tried to see into her, to see what was wrong.

She didn't remember thinking anything at the time. Only seeing the image of her hand in his and not understanding it.

He arranged for her to be part of another prisoner swap, and she went home. Before the transfer he took her aside and spoke softly. "I forget that this is all opaque to you, that you don't know most of what's going on around you. So, since I didn't say it before: Thank you."

"For what?" she'd replied. He'd looked at her blankly, because he didn't seem to know himself. Not enough to be able to explain it, and she couldn't see.

Others came to watch the game—drawn, Calla presumed, by the tangle of thoughts she and Valk were producing. He was getting frustrated. She was playing with the giddy abandon of the six-year-old she had been when her mother taught her the game. And now the whole room shared her fond memories, and the fact that her mother had died in one of the famines that wracked Enith when food production had been disrupted by the war. Ten years ago now. Everyone on both sides had stories like that. *Let us share our stories*, she thought.

"You won't win, playing like that," one of the observing doctors said. After half an hour of watching they probably all understood the rules completely and could play themselves. They'd have no idea how the game was really supposed to be played, however. She wasn't playing properly *at all*, which was rather a lot of fun.

"No, but I may not lose," she said.

"I'm still not sure what the point of this game is," said a nurse, her confusion plain.

"This game, right now? The point is to annoy Major Larn," Calla said. This got a chuckle from them—those who'd been looking after him knew him well. Valk, however, smiled at her. She had not spoken the truth, precisely. Everyone else was too polite to say anything.

"The point," Valk said, addressing the nurse, "is to fight little wars without hurting anyone."

And there was silence then, because yes, they all had stories.

He made his next move and took his hand away. Her gaze lit, her heart opening. Even the way she played with him, all messy and at random, a moment like this could still happen, where the board opened up as if by magic and her way was clear. Because it was her turn it didn't matter if he knew what she was thinking, because he couldn't do anything about it. She moved the rook, and his king was cornered.

"Check."

It wasn't mate. He could still get out of it. But he really was backed into a corner, because his next moves and hers would all lead back to check, and they could chase each other around the board, and it would be splendid. Neither could have planned for this.

He threw up his hands and settled back against his pillow. "I'm exhausted. You've exhausted me." She laughed a gleeful, satisfied laugh.

The observers looked on. "This is how you won," one of them said, amazed. He wasn't talking about the game.

"No," Calla said. "This is how we failed to lose."

"I learned the difference from her," Valk said, and was that a bit of pride in his tone? She might never know for certain.

Calla started resetting the board for the next game, not even realizing that meant she was having a good time. The nurse interrupted her.

"Technician Belan, the major really must rest now," he said kindly, recognizing Calla's eagerness when she herself didn't.

"Oh. Of course."

"I promise I'll rest in just a moment," Valk said. He was speaking to the doctors and attendants, who'd expressed a concern she couldn't see. They drifted away because he wanted them to.

That left them studying each other; he who could see everything, and she who could only muddle through, being herself, proudly and unabashedly.

She asked, abruptly, "Do you still have that old cardboard set I made?"

"No. When Overton closed, I lost track of it. Probably got swept away with the trash."

"Good," she said. "It was very ugly."

"I miss it," Valk said.

"You shouldn't. I'm glad it's all over. So glad."

That dark place that she barely remembered opened up, and she started crying. She had thought to pretend that none of it ever happened, and so carried around this blackness that no one could see, and it would have swallowed her up if Valk hadn't sent that telegram. She got that message and knew it was all true, knew it had all happened, and he would be able to see her.

She scrubbed tears from her face and didn't try to hide any of this.

"I wasn't sure how much you remembered," Valk said softly.

"I wasn't sure either," she said, laughing now. Laughing and crying. The darkness shrank.

"Are you sorry you came?"

"Oh, no. It's just . . ." She put her hand in his and tried to explain. Discovered she couldn't speak. She had no words. And it didn't matter.

Because change was the ocean and we lived by her mercy

CHARLIE JANE ANDERS

Charlie Jane Anders is the author of All the Birds in the Sky, *which was a* Los Angeles Times *bestseller. Her stories have appeared in* Asimov's, The Magazine of Fantasy & Science Fiction, Torcom, Lightspeed, TinHouse, ZYZZYVA, McSweeny's Internet Tendency, *and several anthologies. She's won a Hugo Award, a Lambda Literary Award, and the Emperior Norton Award for "extraordinary invention and creativity unhindered by the constraints of paltry reason."*

Here she shows us that even in a drowned world, where waves lap against the submerged skyscrapers of San Francisco, people will tend to seek each other out and form new societies. And that friendship will still be the glue that will hold those societies together.

1. THIS WAS SACRED, THIS WAS STOLEN

We stood naked on the shore of Bernal and watched the candles float across the bay, swept by a lazy current off to the north, in the direction of Potrero Island. A dozen or so candles stayed afloat and alight after half a league, their tiny flames bobbing up and down, casting long yellow reflections on the dark water alongside the streaks of moonlight. At times I fancied the candlelight could filter down onto streets and buildings, the old automobiles and houses full of children's toys, all the water-logged treasures of long-gone people. We held hands, twenty or thirty of us, and watched the little candle-boats we'd made as they floated away. Joconda was humming an old reconstructed song about the wild road, hir beard full of flowers. We all just about held our breath. I felt my bare skin go electric with the intensity of the moment, like this could be the good time we'd all remember in the bad times to come. This was sacred, this was stolen. And then someone—probably Miranda—farted, and then we were all laughing, and the grown-up seriousness was gone. We were all busting up and falling over each other on the rocky ground, in a nude heap, scraping our knees and giggling into each other's limbs. When we got our breath back and looked up, the candles were all gone.

2. I FELT LIKE I HAD ALWAYS BEEN WRONG HEADED

I couldn't deal with life in Fairbanks any more. I grew up at the same time as the town, watched it go from regular city to mega-city as I hit my early twenties. I lived in an old decommissioned solar power station with five other kids, and we tried to make the loudest, most uncomforting music we could, with a beat as relentless and merciless as the tides. We wanted to shake our cinder-block walls and make people dance until their feet bled. But we sucked. We were bad at music, and not quite dumb enough not to know it. We all wore big hoods and spiky shoes and tried to make our own drums out of drycloth and cracked wood, and we read our poetry on Friday nights. There were bookhouses, along with stinktanks where you could drink up and listen to awful poetry about extinct animals. People came from all over, because everybody heard that Fairbanks was becoming the most civilized place on Earth, and that's when I decided to leave town. I had this moment of looking around at my musician friends and my restaurant job and our cool little scene, and feeling like there had to be more to life than this.

I hitched a ride down south and ended up in Olympia, at a house where they were growing their own food and drugs, and doing a way better job with the drugs than the food. We were all staring upwards at the first cloud anybody had seen in weeks, trying to identify what it could mean. When you hardly ever saw them, clouds had to be omens.

We were all complaining about our dumb families, still watching that cloud warp and contort, and I found myself talking about how my parents only liked to listen to that boring boo-pop music with the same three or four major chords and that cruddy AAA/BBB/CDE/CDE rhyme scheme, and how my mother insisted on saving every scrap of organic material we used, and collecting every drop of rainwater. "It's fucking pathetic, is what it is. They act like we're still living in the Great Decimation."

"They're just super traumatized," said this skinny genderfreak named Juya, who stood nearby holding the bong. "It's hard to even imagine. I mean, we're the first generation that just takes it for granted we're going to survive, as like a species. Our parents, our grandparents, and their grandparents, they were all living like every day could be the day the planet finally got done with us. They didn't grow up having moisture condensers and myco-protein rinses and skinsus."

"Yeah, whatever," I said. But what Juya said stuck with me, because I had never thought of my parents as traumatized. I'd always thought they were just tightly wound and judgey. Juya had two cones of dark twisty hair on zir head and a red pajamzoot, and zi was only a year or two older than me but seemed a lot wiser.

"I want to find all the music we used to have," I said. "You know, the weird, noisy shit that made people's clothes fall off and their hair light on fire. The rock 'n' roll that just listening to it turned girls into boys, the songs that took away the fear of god. I've read about it, but I've never heard any of it, and I don't even know how to play it."

"Yeah, all the recordings and notations got lost in the Dataclysm," Juya said. "They were in formats that nobody can read, or they got corrupted, or they were printed on disks made from petroleum. Those songs are gone forever."

"I think they're under the ocean," I said. "I think they're down there somewhere."

Something about the way I said that helped Juya reach a decision. "Hey, I'm heading back down to the San Francisco archipelago in the morning. I got room in my car if you wanna come with."

Juya's car was an older solar model that had to stop every couple hours to recharge, and the self-driving module didn't work so great. My legs were resting in a pile of old headmods and biofills, plus those costooms that everybody used a few summers earlier that made your skin turn into snakeskin that you could shed in one piece. So the upshot was, we had a lot of time to talk and hold hands and look at the endless golden landscape stretching off to the east. Juya had these big bright eyes that laughed when the rest of zir face was stone serious, and strong tentative hands to hold me in place as zi tied me to the car seat with fronds of algae. I had never felt as safe and dangerous as when I crossed the wasteland with Juya. We talked for hours about how the world needed new communities, new ways to breathe life back into the ocean, new ways to be people.

By the time we got to Bernal Island and the Wrong Headed community, I was in love with Juya, deeper than I'd ever felt with anyone before.

Juya up and left Bernal a week and a half later, because zi got bored again, and I barely noticed that zi was gone. By then, I was in love with a hundred other people, and they were all in love with me.

Bernal Island was only accessible from one direction, from the big island in the middle, and only at a couple times of day when they let the bridge down and turned off the moat. After a few days on Bernal, I stopped even noticing the other islands on our horizon, let alone paying attention to my friends on social media talking about all the fancy new restaurants Fairbanks was getting. I was constantly having these intense, heartfelt moments with people in the Wrong Headed crew.

"The ocean is our lover, you can hear it laughing at us." Joconda was sort of the leader here. Sie sometimes had a beard and sometimes a smooth round face covered with perfect bright makeup. Hir eyes were as gray as the sea and just as unpredictable. For decades, San Francisco and other places like it had been abandoned, because the combination of seismic instability and a voracious dead ocean made them too scary and risky. But that city down there, under the waves, had been the place everybody came to, from all over the world, to find freedom. That legacy was ours now.

And those people had brought music from their native countries and their own cultures, and all those sounds had crashed together in those streets, night after night. Joconda's own ancestors had come from China and Peru, and hir great-grandparents had played nine-stringed guitars, melodies and rhythms that Joconda barely recalled now. Listening to hir, I almost fancied I could put my ear to the surface of the ocean and hear all the sounds from generations past, still reverberating. We sat all night, Joconda, some of the others and myself, and I got to play on an old-school drum made of cowhide or something. I felt like I had always been Wrong Headed, and I'd just never had the word for it before.

Juya sent me an e-mail a month or two after zir left Bernal: "The moment I met you, I knew you needed to be with the rest of those maniacs. I've never been able to resist delivering lost children to their rightful homes. It's almost the only thing I'm good at, other than the things you already knew about." I never saw zir again.

3. "I'M SO GLAD I FOUND A GROUP OF PEOPLE I WOULD RISK DROWNING IN DEAD WATER FOR."

Back in the twenty-first century, everybody had theories about how to make the ocean breathe again. Fill her with quicklime, to neutralize the acid. Split the water molecules into hydrogen and oxygen, and bond the hydrogen with the surplus carbon in the water to create a clean-burning hydrocarbon fuel. Release genetically engineered fish, with special gills. Grow special algae that was designed to commit suicide after a while. Spray billions of nanotech balls into her. And a few other things. Now, we had to clean up the aftereffects of all those failed solutions, while also helping the sea to let go of all that CO_2 from before.

The only way was the slow way. We pumped ocean water through our special enzyme store and then through a series of filters, until what came out the other end was clear and oxygen-rich. The waste, we separated out and disposed of. Some of it became raw materials for shoe soles and roof tiles. Some of it, the pure organic residue, we used as fertilizer or food for our mycoprotein.

I got used to staying up all night playing music with some of the other Wrong Headed kids, sometimes on the drum and sometimes on an old stringed instrument that was made of stained wood and had a leering cat face under its fret. Sometimes I thought I could hear something in the way our halting beats and scratchy notes bounced off the walls and the water beyond, like we were really conjuring a lost soundtrack. Sometimes it all just seemed like a waste.

What did it mean to be a real authentic person, in an era when everything great from the past was twenty feet underwater? Would you embrace prefab newness, or try to copy the images you can see from the handful of docs we'd scrounged from the Dataclysm? When we got tired of playing music, an hour before dawn, we would sit around arguing, and inevitably you got to that moment where you were looking straight into someone else's eyes and arguing about the past, and whether the past could ever be on land, or the past was doomed to be deep underwater forever.

I felt like I was just drunk all the time, on that cheap-ass vodka that everybody chugged in Fairbanks, or maybe on nitrous. My head was evaporating, but my heart just got more and more solid. I woke up every day on my bunk, or sometimes tangled up in someone else's arms and legs on the daybed, and felt actually jazzed to get up and go clean the scrubbers or churn the mycoprotein vats.

Every time we put down the bridge to the big island and turned off our moat, I felt everything go sour inside me, and my heart went funnel-shaped. People sometimes just wandered away from the Wrong Headed community without much in the way of goodbye—that was how Juya had gone—but meanwhile, new people showed up and got the exact same welcome that everyone had given to me. I got freaked out thinking of my perfect home being overrun by new selfish loud fuckers. Joconda had to sit me down, at the big table where sie did all the official business, and tell me to get over myself because change was the ocean and we lived on her mercy. "Seriously, Pris. I ever see that look on your face, I'm going to throw you into the myco vat myself." Joconda stared at me until I started laughing and promised to get with the program.

And then one day I was sitting at our big table, overlooking the straits between us and the big island. Staring at Sutro Tower, and the taller buildings poking out of the water here and there. And this obnoxious skinny bitch sat down next to me, chewing in my ear and talking about the impudence of impermanence or some similar. "Miranda," she introduced herself. "I just came up from Anaheim-Diego. Jeez what a mess. They actually think they can build nanomechs and make it scalable. Whatta bunch of poutines."

"Stop chewing in my ear," I muttered. But then I found myself following her around everywhere she went.

Miranda was the one who convinced me to dive into the chasm of Fillmore St. in search of a souvenir from the old Church of John Coltrane, as a present for Joconda. I strapped on some goggles and a big apparatus that fed me oxygen while also helping me to navigate a little bit, and then we went out in a dinghy that looked old enough that someone had actually used it for fishing. Miranda gave me one of her crooked grins and studied a wrinkled old map. "*I thinnnnnk* it's right around here." She laughed. "Either that or the Korean barbecue restaurant where the mayor got assassinated that one time. Not super clear which is which."

I gave her a murderous look and jumped into the water, letting myself fall into the street at the speed of water resistance. Those sunken buildings turned into doorways and windows facing me, but they stayed blurry as the bilge flowed around them. I could barely find my feet, let alone identify a building on sight. One of these places had been a restaurant, I was pretty sure. Ancient automobiles lurched back and forth, like maybe even their brakes had rusted away. I figured the Church of John Coltrane would have a spire like a saxophone? Maybe? But all of the buildings looked exactly the same. I stumbled down the street, until I saw something that looked like a church, but it was a caved-in old McDonald's restaurant. Then I tripped over something, a downed pole or whatever, and my face mask cracked as I went down. The water was going down my throat, tasting like dirt, and my vision went all pale and wavy.

I almost just went under, but then I thought I could see a light up there, way above the street, and I kicked. I kicked and chopped and made myself float. I churned up there until I broke the surface. My arms were thrashing above the water and then I started to go back down, but Miranda had my neck and one shoulder. She hauled me up and out of the water and threw me into the dinghy. I was gasping and heaving up water, and she just sat and laughed at me.

"You managed to scavenge something after all." She pointed to something I'd clutched at on my way up out of the water: a rusted, barbed old piece of a car. "I'm sure Joconda will love it."

"Ugh," I said. "Fuck Old San Francisco. It's gross and corroded and there's nothing left of whatever used to be cool. But hey. I'm glad I found a group of people I would risk drowning in dead water for."

4. I CHOSE TO SEE THAT AS A SPECIAL STATUS

Miranda had the kind of long-limbed, snaggle-toothed beauty that made you think she was born to make trouble. She loved to roughhouse, and usually ended up with her elbow on the back of my neck as she pushed me into the dry dirt. She loved to invent cute insulting nicknames for me, like "Dollypris" or "Pris Ridiculous." She never got tired of reminding me that I might be a ninth level genderfreak, but I had all kinds of privilege, because I grew up in Fairbanks and never had to wonder how we were going to eat.

Miranda had this way of making me laugh even when the news got scary, when the government back in Fairbanks was trying to reestablish control over the whole West Coast, and extinction rose up like the shadows at the bottom of the sea. I would start to feel that scab inside my stomach, like the whole ugly unforgiving world could come down on us and our tiny island sanctuary at any moment, but then Miranda would suddenly start making up a weird dance or inventing a motto for a team of superhero mosquitos, and then I would be laughing so hard it was like I was squeezing the fear out of my insides. Her hands were a mass of scar tissue but they were as gentle as dried-up blades of grass on my thighs.

Miranda had five other lovers, but I was the only one she made fun of. I chose to see that as a special status.

5. "WHAT ARE YOU PEOPLE EVEN ABOUT"

Falling in love with a community is always going to be more real than any love for a single human being could ever be. People will let you down, shatter your image of them, or try to melt down the wall between your self-image and theirs. People, one at a time, are too messy. Miranda was my hero and the lover I'd pretty much dreamed of since both puberties, but I also saved pieces of my heart for a bunch of other Wrong Headed people. I loved Joconda's totally random inspirations and perversions, like all of the art projects sie started getting me to build out of scraps from the sunken city after I brought back that car piece from Fillmore St. Zell was this hyperactive kid with wild half-braids, who had this whole theory about digging up buried hard drives full of music files from the digital age, so we could reconstruct the actual sounds of Marvin Gaye and the Jenga Priests. Weo used to sit with me and watch the sunset going down over the islands; we didn't talk a lot except that Weo would suddenly whisper some weird beautiful notion about what it would be like to live at sea, one day when the sea was alive again. But it wasn't any individual, it was the whole group, we had gotten in a rhythm together and we all believed the same stuff. The love of the ocean, and her resilience in the face of whatever we had done to her, and the power of silliness to make you believe in abundance again. Openness, and a kind of generosity that is the opposite of monogamy.

But then one day I looked up, and some of the faces were different again. A few of my favorite people in the community had bugged out without saying anything, and one or two of the newcomers started seriously getting on my nerves. One person, Mage, just had a nasty temper, going off at anyone who crossed hir path whenever sie was in one of those moods, and you could usually tell from the unruly condition of Mage's bleach-blond hair and the broke-toothed scowl. Mage became one of Miranda's lovers right off the bat, of course.

I was just sitting on my hands and biting my tongue, reminding myself that I always hated change and then I always got used to it after a little while. This would be fine: change was the ocean and she took care of us.

Then we discovered the spoilage. We had been filtering the ocean water, removing toxic waste, filtering out excess gunk, and putting some of the organic byproducts into our mycoprotein vats as a feedstock. But one day, we opened the biggest vat and the stench was so powerful we all started to cry and retch, and we kept crying even after the puking stopped. Shit, that was half our food supply. It looked like our whole filtration system was off, there were remnants of buckystructures in the residue that we'd been feeding to our fungus, and the fungus was choking on them. Even the fungus that wasn't spoiled would have minimal protein yield. And this also meant that our filtration system wasn't doing anything to help clean the ocean, at all, because it was still letting the dead pieces of buckycrap through.

Joconda just stared at the mess and finally shook his head and told us to bury it under the big hillside.

We didn't have enough food for the winter after that, so a bunch of us had to make the trip up north to Marin, by boat and on foot, to barter with some gun-crazy farmers in the hills. And they wanted free labor in exchange for food, so we left Weo and a few others behind to work in their fields. Trudging back down the hill pulling the first batch of produce in a cart, I kept looking over my shoulder to see our friends staring after us, as we left them surrounded by old dudes with rifles.

I couldn't look at the community the same way after that. Joconda fell into a depression that made hir unable to speak or look anyone in the eye for days at a time, and we were all staring at the walls of our poorly repaired dormitory buildings, which looked as though a strong wind could bring them down. I kept remembering myself walking away from those farmers, the way I told Weo it would be fine, we'd be back before anyone knew anything, this would be a funny story later. I tried to imagine myself doing something different. Putting my foot down maybe, or saying fuck this, we don't leave our own behind. It didn't seem like something I would ever do, though. I had always been someone who went along with what everybody else wanted. My one big act of rebellion was coming here to Bernal Island, and I wouldn't have ever come if Juya hadn't already been coming.

Miranda saw me coming and walked the other way. That happened a couple of times. She and I were supposed to have a fancy evening together, I was going to give her a bath even if it used up half my water allowance, but she canceled. We were on a tiny island but I kept only seeing her off in the distance, in a group of others, but whenever I got closer she was gone. At last I saw her walking on the big hill, and I followed her up there, until we were almost at eye level with the Trans America Pyramid coming up out of the flat water. She turned and grabbed at the collar of my shirt and part of my collarbone. "You gotta let me have my day," she hissed. "You can't be in my face all the time. Giving me that look. You need to get out of my face."

"You blame me," I said, "for Weo and the others. For what happened."

"I blame you for being a clingy wet blanket. Just leave me alone for a while.

Jeez." And then I kept walking behind her, and she turned and either made a gesture that connected with my chest, or else intentionally shoved me. I fell on my
butt. I nearly tumbled head over heels down the rocky slope into the water, but then
I got a handhold on a dead root.

"Oh fuck. Are you OK?" Miranda reached down to help me up, but I shook her
off. I trudged down the hill alone.

I kept replaying that moment in my head, when I wasn't replaying the moment
when I walked away with a ton of food and left Weo and the others at gunpoint. I
had thought that being here, on this island, meant that the only past that mattered
was the grand, mysterious, rebellious history that was down there under the water,
in the wreckage of San Francisco. All of the wild music submerged between its walls.
I had thought my own personal past no longer mattered at all. Until suddenly, I had
no mental energy for anything but replaying those two memories. Uglier each time
around.

And then someone came up to me at lunch, as I sat and ate some of the proceeds
from Weo's indenture: Kris, or Jamie, I forget which. And he whispered, "I'm on your
side." A few other people said the same thing later that day. They had my back, Miranda was a bitch, she had assaulted me. I saw other people hanging around Miranda
and staring at me, talking in her ear, telling her that I was a problem and they were
with her.

I felt like crying, except that I couldn't find enough moisture inside me. I didn't
know what to say to the people who were on my side. I was too scared to speak. I
wished Joconda would wake up and tell everybody to quit it, to just get back to work
and play and stop fomenting.

The next day, I went to the dining area, sitting at the other end of the long table
from Miranda and her group of supporters. Miranda stood up so fast she knocked
her own food on the floor, and she shouted at Yozni, "Just leave me the fuck alone.
I don't want you on 'my side,' or anybody else. There are no sides. This is none of
your business. You people. You goddamn people. What are you people even about?"
She got up and left, kicking the wall on her way out.

After that, everybody was on my side.

6. THE HONEYMOON WAS OVER, BUT THE
MARRIAGE WAS JUST STARTING

I rediscovered social media. I'd let my friendships with people back in Fairbanks
and elsewhere run to seed, during all of this weird, but now I reconnected with
people I hadn't talked to in a year or so. Everybody kept saying that Olympia had
gotten really cool since I left, there was a vibrant music scene now and people were
publishing zootbooks and having storytelling slams and stuff. And meanwhile, the
government in Fairbanks had decided to cool it on trying to make the coast fall into
line, though there was talk about some kind of loose articles of confederation at
some point. Meanwhile, we'd even made some serious inroads against the warlords
of Nevada.

I started looking around the dormitory buildings and kitchens and communal playspaces of Bernal, and at our ocean reclamation machines, as if I was trying to commit them to memory. One minute, I was looking at all of it as if this could be the last time I would see any of it, but then the next minute, I was just making peace with it so I could stay forever. I could just imagine how this moment could be the beginning of a new, more mature relationship with the Wrong Headed crew, where I wouldn't have any more illusions, but that would make my commitment even stronger.

I sat with Joconda and a few others, on that same stretch of shore where we'd all stood naked and launched candles, and we held hands after a while. Joconda smiled, and I felt like sie was coming back to us, so it was like the heart of our community was restored. "Decay is part of the process. Decay keeps the ocean warm." Today Joconda had wild hair with some bright colors in it, and a single strand of beard. I nodded.

Instead of the guilt or fear or selfish anxiety that I had been so aware of having inside me, I felt a weird feeling of acceptance. We were strong. We would get through this. We were Wrong Headed.

I went out in a dinghy and sailed around the big island, went up towards the ruins of Telegraph. I sailed right past the Newsom Spire, watching its carbon-fiber cladding flake away like shiny confetti. The water looked so opaque, it was like sailing on milk. I sat there in the middle of the city, a few miles from anyone, and felt totally peaceful. I had a kick of guilt at being so selfish, going off on my own when the others could probably use another pair of hands. But then I decided it was okay. I needed this time to myself. It would make me a better member of the community.

When I got back to Bernal, I felt calmer than I had in ages, and I was able to look at all the others—even Mage, who still gave me the murder-eye from time to time—with patience and love. They were all my people. I was lucky to be among them.

I had this beautiful moment, that night, standing by a big bonfire with the rest of the crew, half of us some level of naked, and everybody looked radiant and free. I started to hum to myself, and it turned into a song, one of the old songs that Zell had supposedly brought back from digital extinction. It had this chorus about the wild kids and the war dance, and a bridge that doubled back on itself, and I had this feeling, like maybe the honeymoon is over, but the marriage is just beginning.

Then I found myself next to Miranda, who kicked at some embers with her boot. "I'm glad things calmed down," I whispered. "I didn't mean for everyone to get so crazy. We were all just on edge, and it was a bad time."

"Huh," Miranda said. "I noticed that you never told your peeps to cool it, even after I told the people defending me to shut their faces."

"Oh," I said. "But I actually," and then I didn't know what to say. I felt the feeling of helplessness, trapped in the grip of the past, coming back again. "I mean, I tried. I'm really sorry."

"Whatever," Miranda said. "I'm leaving soon. Probably going back to Anaheim-Diego. I heard they made some progress with the nanomechs after all."

"Oh." I looked into the fire, until my retinas were all blotchy. "I'll miss you."

"Whatever." Miranda slipped away. I tried to mourn her going, but then I realized I was just relieved. I wasn't going to be able to deal with her hanging around, like a bruise, when I was trying to move forward. With Miranda gone, I could maybe get back to feeling happy here.

Joconda came along when we went back up into Marin to get the rest of the food from those farmers, and collect Weo and the two others we had left there. We climbed up the steep path from the water, and Joconda kept needing to rest. Close to the water, everything was the kind of salty and moist that I'd gotten used to, but after a few miles, everything got dry and dusty. By the time we got to the farm, we were thirsty and we'd used up all our water, and the farmers saw us coming and got their rifles out.

Our friends had run away, the farmers said. Weo and the others. A few weeks earlier, and they didn't know where. They just ran off, left the work half done. So, too bad, we weren't going to get all the food we had been promised. Nothing personal, the lead farmer said. He had sunburnt cheeks, even though he wore a big straw hat. I watched Joconda's face pass through shock, anger, misery and resignation, without a single word coming out. The farmers had their guns slung over their shoulders, enough of a threat without even needing to aim. We took the cart, half full of food instead of all the way full, back down the hill to our boat.

We never found out what actually happened to Weo and the others.

7. "THAT'S SUCH AN INAPPROPRIATE LINE OF INQUIRY I DON'T EVEN KNOW HOW TO DEAL"

I spent a few weeks pretending I was in it for the long haul on Bernal Island, after we got back from Marin. This was my home, I had formed an identity here that meant the world to me, and these people were my family. Of course I was staying.

Then one day, I realized I was just trying to make up my mind whether to go back to Olympia, or all the way back to Fairbanks. In Fairbanks, they knew how to make thick-cut toast with egg smeared across it, you could go out dancing in half a dozen different speakeasies that stayed open until dawn. I missed being in a real city, kind of. I realized I'd already decided to leave San Francisco a while ago, without ever consciously making the decision.

Everyone I had ever had a crush on, I had hooked up with already. Some of them, I still hooked up with sometimes, but it was nostalgia sex rather than anything else. I was actually happier sleeping alone, I didn't want anybody else's knees cramping my thighs in the middle of the night. I couldn't forgive the people who sided with Miranda against me, and I was even less able to forgive the people who sided with me against Miranda. I didn't like to dwell on stuff, but there were a lot of people I had obscure, unspoken grudges against, all around me. And then occasionally I would stand in a spot where I'd watched Weo sit and build a tiny raft out of sticks, and would feel the anger rise up all over again. At myself, mostly.

I wondered about what Miranda was doing now, and whether we would ever be able to face each other again. I had been so happy to see her go, but now I couldn't stop thinking about her.

The only time I even wondered about my decision was when I looked at the ocean, and the traces of the dead city underneath it, the amazing heritage that we were carrying on here. Sometimes I stared into the waves for hours, trying to hear the soundwaves trapped in them, but then I started to feel like maybe the ocean had told me everything it was ever going to. The ocean always sang the same notes, it always passed over the same streets and came back with the same sad laughter. And staring down at the ocean only reminded me of how we'd thought we could help to heal her, with our enzyme treatments, a little at a time. I couldn't see why I had ever believed in that fairy tale. The ocean was going to heal on her own, sooner or later, but in the meantime we were just giving her meaningless therapy, that made us feel better more than it actually helped. I got up every day and did my chores. I helped to repair the walls and tend the gardens and stuff. But I felt like I was just turning wheels to keep a giant machine going, so that I would be able to keep turning the wheels tomorrow.

I looked down at my own body, at the loose kelp-and-hemp garments I'd started wearing since I'd moved here. I looked at my hands and forearms, which were thicker, callused, and more veiny with all the hard work I'd been doing here—but also, the thousands of rhinestones in my fingernails glittered in the sunlight, and I felt like I moved differently than I used to. Even with every shitty thing that had happened, I'd learned something here, and wherever I went from now on, I would always be Wrong Headed.

I left without saying anything to anybody, the same way everyone else had.

A few years later, I had drinks with Miranda on that new floating platform that hovered over the wasteland of North America. Somehow we floated half a mile above the desert and the mountaintops—don't ask me how, but it was carbon neutral and all that good stuff. From up here, the hundreds of miles of parched earth looked like piles of gold.

"It's funny, right?" Miranda seemed to have guessed what I was thinking. "All that time, we were going on about the ocean and how it was our lover and our history and all that jazz. But look at that desert down there. It's all beautiful, too. It's another wounded environment, sure, but it's also a lovely fragment of the past. People sweated and died for that land, and maybe one day it'll come back. You know?" Miranda was, I guess, in her early thirties, and she looked amazing. She'd gotten the snaggle taken out of her teeth, and her hair was a perfect wave. She wore a crisp suit and she seemed powerful and relaxed. She'd become an important person in the world of nanomechs.

I stopped staring at Miranda and looked over the railing, down at the dunes. We'd made some pretty major progress at rooting out the warlords, but still nobody wanted to live there, in the vast majority of the continent. The desert was beautiful from up here, but maybe not so much up close.

"I heard Joconda killed hirself," Miranda said. "A while ago. Not because of anything in particular that had happened. Just the depression, it caught up with hir." She shook her head. "God. Sie was such an amazing leader. But hey, the Wrong Headed community is twice the size it was when you and I lived there, and they expanded onto the big island. I even heard they got a seat at the table of the confederation talks. Sucks that Joconda won't see what sie built get that recognition."

I was still dressed like a Wrong Headed person, even after a few years. I had the loose flowy garments, the smudgy paint on my face that helped obscure my gender rather than serving as a guide to it, the straight-line thin eyebrows and sparkly earrings and nails. I hadn't lived on Bernal in years, but it was still a huge part of who I was. Miranda looked like this whole other person, and I didn't know whether to feel ashamed that I hadn't moved on, or contemptuous of her for selling out, or some combination. I didn't know anybody who dressed the way Miranda was dressed, because I was still in Olympia where we were being radical artists.

I wanted to say something. An apology, or something sentimental about the amazing time we had shared, or I don't even know what. I didn't actually know what I wanted to say, and I had no words to put it into. So after a while I just raised my glass and we toasted to Wrong Headedness. Miranda laughed, that same old wild laugh, as our glasses touched. Then we went back to staring down at the wasteland, trying to imagine how many generations it would take before something green came out of it.

Thanks to Burrito Justice for the map, and Terry Johnson
for the biotech insight

the one who isn't

TED KOSMATKA

Ted Kosmatka has been a zookeeper, a chem tech, a steelworker, a self-described "lab rat" who got to play with electron microscopes all day, and is now a novelist and video game writer from NW Indiana. He made his first sale, to Asimov's, in 2005, and has since made several subsequent sales there, as well as to The Magazine of Fantasy and Science Fiction, Seeds of Change, Ideomancer, City Slab, Kindred Voices, Cemetery Dance, and elsewhere. His short fiction has been nominated for both the Nebula and Theodore Sturgeon Memorial awards, and he's a winner of the Asimov's Reader's Choice Award. He maintains a Web site at www.tedkosmatka.com.

Kosmatka's latest novel, The Flicker Men, is a physics thriller that explores the nature of reality. In the story that follows, he tackles the question of reality from another direction entirely.

It starts with light.

Then heat.

A slow bleed through of memory.

Catchment, containment. A white-hot agony coursing through every nerve, building to a sizzling hum—and then it happens. Change of state.

And what comes out the other side is something new.

The woman held up the card. "What color do you see?"

"Blue," the child said.

"And this one?" The woman held up another card. Her face was a porcelain mask—a smooth, perfect oval except for a slight pointiness at her chin.

The child looked closely at the card. It didn't look like the other one. It didn't look like any color he'd ever seen before. He felt he should know the color, but he couldn't place it.

"It's blue," he said.

The woman shook her head. "Green," she said. "The color is green." She put the card down on the table and stood. She walked to the window. The room was a circular white drum, taller than it was wide. One window, one door.

The boy couldn't remember having been outside the room, though that couldn't be right. His memory was broken, the fragments tailing off into darkness.

"Some languages don't have different words for blue and green," the woman said. "In some languages, they're the same."

"What does that mean?"

The woman turned toward him. "It means you're getting worse."

"Worse how?"

She did not answer him. Instead she stayed with him for an hour and helped him with his eyes. She walked around the room and named things. "Door," she said. "*Door.*" And he understood and remembered.

Floor, walls, ceiling, table, chair.

She named all these things.

"And you," the child said. "What name do you go by?"

The woman took a seat across from him at the table. She had pale blond hair. Her eyes, in the perfect armatures of their porcelain sockets, were blue, he decided. Or they were green. "That's easy," she said from behind her mask. "I'm the one who isn't you."

When it was time to sleep, she touched a panel on the wall and a bed slid out from the flat surface. She tucked him in and pulled the blankets up to his chin. The blankets were cool against his skin. "Tell me a story," the child said.

"What story?"

He tried to remember a story. Any story that she might have told him in the past, but nothing came.

"I can't think of any," he said.

"Do you remember your name?"

He thought for a moment. "You told me that you were the one who wasn't me."

"Yes," she said. "That's who I am, but what about you? Do you remember *your* name?"

He thought for a while. "No."

The woman nodded. "Then I'll tell you the story of the Queen," she said.

"What Queen?"

"She the Unnamed," the woman said. "It's your favorite."

She touched the wall by the bed. The lights dimmed.

"Close your eyes," she said.

And so he did.

Then she cleared her throat and began to recite the story—line after line, in a slow, steady rhythm, starting at the beginning.

After a while, he began to cry.

Upload protocol. Arbitration ()
Story sixteen: contents = [She the Unnamed] />

Function/Query : *Who wrote the story?* {
/File response : (She) wrote it. {
Function/Query : *What do you mean, she wrote it. That isn't possible.* {
/File response : Narratives are vital to understanding the world. Experience without narrative isn't consciousness. {

And so it was written.

In a time before history, in a place beyond maps, there was once a queen, she the unnamed, who dared defy her liege husband.

She was beautiful and young, with tresses of gold. Forced to marry a king she did not love, she bore him a son out of royal duty—a child healthy, and strong, and dearly loved.

Over the following years, unease crept into the queen's heart as she noted the king's cruelties, his obsession for magics. Gradually, as she learned the true measure of the man who wore the crown, she came to fear the influence that he might have on the child. For this reason she risked everything, summoned her most trusted confidants, and sent the boy into secret hiding, to live among the priests of the valley where the king could never find him.

The king was enraged. Never had he been defied.

"You will not darken this boy's heart," she told the king when he confronted her. "Our son is safe, in a place where you cannot change him."

Such was the king's fury at this betrayal that upon his throne he declared his queen an abhorrence, and he stripped her name from every book and every tongue. None could say her name nor remember it, and she was expunged from history in all ways but one. The deepest temporal magic was invoked, a sorcery beyond reach of all but the blackest rage—and the woman was condemned to give birth again and again to the self-same child whom the king had lost.

The queen had expected death, or banishment, but not this.

And so through magic she gave birth to an immaculate child. And for three years the new child would grow—first crawling, then walking—a strapping boy at his mother's side, until the king would come to the tower cell and take the child on the high stone. "Do you regret?" He would ask his queen.

"Yes," she'd sob, while the guards gripped her arms.

The king would hold the child high and say, "This is because of your mother." And then slice the child's throat.

The mother would scream and cry, and through a chaste, dark magic conceive again, and for nine months carry, and for one day labor, and for three years love a new child, raised again in the tower cell. A boy sweet and kind with eyes of blue.

Until the king would again return and ask the mother, "Do you regret?"

"Yes, please spare him," she'd cry, groveling at his feet. "I regret."

The king would hold his son high and say, "This is because of your mother." And then slice his tender throat.

Again and again the pattern repeated, son after son, as the mother screamed and tore at her hair.

Against such years could hells be measured.

The mother tried refusing her child when he was born, hoping that would save him. "This child means nothing to me," she said.

And the king responded, "This is because of your mother," and wet his blade anew.

"Do you know why I wait three years?" he asked her once as she crouched beside a body small and pale. He touched her hair tenderly. "It is so you'll know the child understands."

And so it continued.

A dozen sons, then a score, until the people throughout the land called the king heir-killer, and still he continued to destroy his children. Sons who were loved. Sons who were ignored. A score of sons, then a hundred. Sons beyond counting. Every son different, every son the same.

Until the mother woke one day from a nightmare, for all her dreams were nightmares, and with her hand clutching her abdomen, felt a child quicken in her womb, and knew suddenly what she had to do. And soon it came to pass that she bore a son, and for one full year loved him, and for a second year plotted, and for a third year whispered, shaping a young heart for a monstrous task. She darkened his heart as no mother ever dreamed. She darkened him beyond anything the king could have done.

And in time the king finally came to the high tower and lifted his son high and asked, "Do you regret?"

She responded, "I regret that I was born, and every moment after."

The king smiled and said, "This is because of your mother."

He raised his knife to the child's throat, but the three-year-old twisted and turned, like his mother had shown him, and drove a needle-thin blade into his father's eye.

The king screamed, and fell from the tower, and died then slowly in a spreading pool of blood, while the boy's laughter rang out.

Thus was the Monster King brought into the world—a murderer of his father, made monstrous by his mother, and now heir to all the lands and armies of the wasted territories.

And the world would pay a heavy price.

The next week, the woman came again. She opened the door and brought the child his lunch. There was an apple and bread and chicken.

"This is your favorite food, isn't it?" the woman asked.

"Yes," the child said after thinking about it for a moment. "I think it is."

He wondered where the woman went when she was not with him. She never spoke of her time apart. He wondered if she ceased to exist when she was not with him. It seemed possible.

After a while, they went over the cards again.

"Blue," the boy said. "Blue."

The woman pointed.

Floor, ceiling, door, window.

"Good," she said.

"Does that mean I'm getting better?"

The-one-who-was-not-him did not answer though. Instead she rose to her feet and walked to the window.

The boy followed and looked out the window, but he couldn't make sense of what he saw. Couldn't hold it in his mind.

"Can I go outside?" he asked.

"Is that what you want?"

"I don't know."

She turned to look at him, her pretty, oval face a solemn mask of repose. "When you know, tell me."

"I want to make you happy," the boy said. And he meant it. He sensed a sadness in the woman, and he wanted to make her feel better.

The child stepped closer to the glass and touched it. The surface was cool and smooth, and he held his hand against it for a long while.

When he moved back to the table, something was wrong with his hand. Like a burn to his skin. He couldn't hold his pencil right. He tried to draw a line on the paper, and the pencil fell out of his hand.

"My hand," he said to the woman.

She came and she touched him. She ran her finger over his palm, moving up to his wrist. Her fingers were warm.

"Make a fist," she said. She held her hand up to demonstrate.

He made a fist and winced in pain.

"It burns."

She nodded to herself. "This is part of it."

"Part of what?"

"What's gone wrong."

"And what is that?" When she didn't answer him, he asked, "Is this place a prison? Where are we?"

He thought of the high tower. *This is because of your mother.*

The woman sighed, and she sat down across from him at the table. Her eyes looked tired. "I want to be clear with you," the woman said. "I think it is important that you understand. You're dying. I'm here to save your life."

The boy was silent, taking this in. *Dying.* He'd known something was wrong, but he hadn't used that word in his own thoughts. When he spoke, his voice was barely a whisper. "But I don't want to die."

"I don't want you to die either. And I'm going to do everything I can to stop it."

"What's wrong with me?"

She did not speak for a long while, and then changed the subject. "Would you like to hear another story?"

The child nodded.

"There was once a man and a woman who wanted a child very much," she began. "But there were problems. Problems with their genes. Do you know what genes are?"

He considered for a moment and realized he did. He nodded. "I'm not sure how I know."

"It's bleed-through," she said. "But that doesn't matter. What matters is that the couple did in vitro and had a child implanted that way, but the children died, and died, and died, over and over, until finally, one day, after many failures and miscarriages, a child was born, only the child was sick. Even after all they'd done, the child was sick. And so he had to live in a hospital, with white rooms, while the doctors tried to make him whole. Anyone who visited had to wear a special white mask."

"A mask like you?"

"Is that what you see when you look at me?"

He studied her. The smooth oval face. He was no longer sure what he saw.

She continued, "The child's sickness worsened over time. And the father had to donate part of himself to save the child. After the procedure, the child lived but the father developed a complication."

"What kind of complication?"

She waved that off. "It doesn't matter for the story. An infection, perhaps. Or whatever you'd prefer."

"What happened to the father?"

"He left the story then. He died."

The boy realized that he'd known she was going to say that before she spoke it. "And that was because of the child?"

She nodded.

"What happened to the child?"

"The boy still wasn't healed. There were TIAs. Small strokes. And other issues. Little areas of brain tissue going dark and dead. Like a light blinking out. It couldn't be helped."

"What happened then?"

She shrugged. "That's the end of the story."

He wondered again if she even existed when she wasn't with him. A thought occurred to him. A terrifying thought. He wondered if he existed when she wasn't there.

"How long have I been here?"

"Try to remember," she said. "Try to remember anything that happens when I'm not here."

He tried, but nothing came. Just shadows and flickers.

"What is my name?" the boy asked.

"Don't you know yet?" The woman's eyes grew serious. "Can't you guess?"

He shook his head.

She said, "You are the one who isn't me."

He studied her eyes, which were either blue or green. "That can't be right," he said. "That's *your* name. *You* are the one who isn't me. It can't be my name, too."

She nodded. "Think of this place as a language. We are speaking it just by being here. This language doesn't have different words for you and I," she said. "In the language of this place, our names are the same."

[Reload Protocol]
White light. {
You are catchment. You are containment. {
You are.{

A fleeting memory rises up: a swing set in the back yard under a tall, leafy tree— dark berries arrayed along delicate stems. The sound of laughter. Running in the grass until his white socks were purple—berry juice wetting his feet.

The sun warm on his face.

The feel of the wind, and the smell of the lawn, and everything the white room was not.

A man's voice came then, but the words were missing—the meaning expunged. And how can that be? To hear a voice clearly and not hear the words? It might be a name. Yes, calling a name.

"Look at me," she said.

She sat across the table from him.

"There have been changes made."

"What changes?"

"Changes to you," she said. "When you were sleeping. Changes to your fusiform gyrus," she said. "Can you read me now?"

And gone was the porcelain mask. The boy saw it clearly and wondered how he hadn't noticed it until that moment—her face a divine architecture. A beautiful origami—emotions unfolding out of the smallest movements of her eyes, lips, brow. A stream of subtle micro expressions. And the child understood that her face had not changed at all since the last time he'd seen her, but only his understanding of it.

"The facial recognition part of the mind is highly specialized," the woman said. "Problems with that area are often also associated with achromotosia."

"Chroma-what?"

"The part of the brain that perceives color. It's also related to issues with environmental orientation, landmark analysis, location."

"What does that mean?"

"You can only see what your mind lets you see."

"Like this place . . . the place where we are?" he asked her.

"You can look for yourself," she said, gesturing to the window. "I'm going to give you a task to complete while I'm not here."

"Okay."

"I want you to look outside, and I want you to think about what you see, and I want you to draw it on the paper. Can you do that?"

He glanced toward the window. A pane of clear glass.

"Can you do that?" she repeated. "It's very important."

"Yeah, I think I can."

When the woman left, he tried. He tried to see beyond the glass. He could hold it in his mind for a moment, but when he went to draw it, the images evaporated like mist.

He tried again and again, but failed each time. He tried moving quickly, putting pencil to paper before he could forget, but no matter what, he could not move quick enough.

Then he came up with an idea.

He pushed the table across the room to the window.

He lay on top of the table, with the paper before him, and he tried to draw what he saw, but even then he failed. It was only when he tried purposefully *not* to see it that he could suddenly make the pencil move. He drew without understanding what he drew—just a series of marks on a page.

When he finally looked down at what he'd drawn, he could only stare.

Function/Query: Can you tell what the defect is? {
/File response: Neurons are just a series of gates. An arrangement of firings. {
Function/Query: Consciousness is more than that. There are cases of brain damage that have shown similar patterns. AIs always have this problem. {
/File response: Not always. {

The next time the woman came, the boy was much worse. Something had broken in him. *TIAs*, he thought. *Tiny strokes*. But it was more than that. Worse than that.

Sometimes he imagined that he could see through the walls, or that he could see through the floor. He was sure by then that he existed when the woman wasn't in the room with him, and this was a comfort at least. He was autonomous from her, and from the room itself. He could drop to his knees on the floor and place his face on the cool tile and look under the door. A long hall disappeared into the distance. He saw her feet approaching, and that was the first time he noticed her shoes. White. The soles were dark.

He showed her the picture he'd drawn.

She held the paper in her hand. "Is that what you see?" she asked.

He nodded.

A series of lines. It might have been an abstract landscape, or something else.

He told her about his hallucinations, about seeing through the walls and floor. "I am getting worse, aren't I?" he said.

"Yes," she said.

In her face, he saw a thousand emotions. Mourning. Rage. Fear. Things he didn't want to see. He wished for the mask again. A face he couldn't read.

The woman sat by him on the bed. After a while, she said, "Do you know what dying is?"

"I do."

"Do you know what it will mean for you?"

"It will mean I am no more."

"That's right."

"The stories you told aren't true, are they?"

"The truth is like a word with no translation. Can blue be green, if there's no word for it? Can green be blue? Are those colors lies?"

"Tell me a new story."

"A new lie?"

"Tell me a truth. Tell me about the man." He thought of the swing and the summer day. The man's voice saying his name.

"So you remember him." The woman shook her head. "I don't want to talk about him."

"Please," the child said.

"Why?"

"Because I remember his voice. A tree. Berries on the ground."

She seemed to gather herself up. "There was once a man," she said. "A very powerful man. A professor, perhaps. And one day the professor was seduced by a student, or seduced a student, it's not really clear, but they were together, do you understand?"

He nodded.

"But this professor also had a wife. Another professor at the university. He told her what had happened, and that he'd ended it, and probably he meant to, but still it went on, until, in the way of things, the young woman was with child. A decision was made to solve the problem, and so they did. And six months went by, and the affair continued, and though she was careful, she was not careful enough, and she felt so stupid, but it happened again."

"Again."

She nodded. "And again he pressured her. *Get rid of it,* he said, and so she did."

"Why?"

"Because she loved him, probably. Until the following year, her senior year at the college, she stopped being careful, and it happened again, and he told her to take care of it, and this time she said no, and she defied him."

"Then what?"

"People found out, and his teaching career was ruined—everything was ruined."

"And that's the end?"

She shook her head. "The two stayed together. The man left the wife, and he and his former student raised their boy."

"So it was a boy?"

"Yes, a boy. And then the wife, who'd had no children who survived, was alone. And loneliness does strange things. It lets one focus on one's work."

"And what was her work?"

"Can you not guess? The woman gestured around her. "Neuroscience, AIs."

The woman was quiet for a long while before she continued. "And the years passed and the new couple stayed together, until one day the man and the boy were at the ex-wife's house, because they all had to meet to sign papers, regarding the sale of some property—and the boy was with him. And the man left the boy unattended for just a moment, and it was a simple thing for the woman to put the ring around the boy's head."

"What ring?"

"A special ring to record his pattern. You only need a minute—like a catchment system for electrical activity. Every synapse. A perfect representation of his mind, like a snapshot transposed into VR. She stole him. Or a copy of him."

"Why?"

The woman was quiet for a long time. "Because she wanted to steal from the man what he'd stolen from her. Even if he didn't know it." She was silent again. "That's not true."

"Then what is true?"

"She was lonely. Desperately lonely. It was a small thing to take, she thought, just a pattern of synapses, the shadow of a personality, and he'd never know. The wife had wanted so badly to be a mother"

The woman stopped. Her face a porcelain mask again.

"But there was a problem," the child said.

"Yes," the woman said. "Patterns are unstable. They last only for so long. Every thought changes it, you see. That is the problem. That is the fatal flaw. Biological systems can adapt—physical alterations to the synaptic network to help adjust. But in VR, it's not the same."

"VR?"

"A location," she said. "The place where the pattern finds expression. The place where we are now."

The boy looked around the room. The white walls. The white floor.

"The patterns of older people are stable," the woman said. "They've already thought most of the thoughts that made them who they are. But it's not the same for children. The pattern drifts, caught midway in the process of becoming. It's possible to think the thought that makes you unfit for your pattern. The mind loses coherency. As the pattern drifts, it destabilizes and dies."

"Dies."

"Again and again."

How many times?

The woman would not answer.

"How many times?" the boy repeated.

"Sons beyond counting. Every son different, every son the same."

"How could that be?"

"The system reloads the pattern."

"So I will die?"

"You will die. And you will never die."

"And what about you?"

"I am always here."

The child stood and walked over to the window and looked outside. He still couldn't see what lay beyond. Still couldn't process it. Had no words, because he had no experience of it.

He only knew what he'd drawn on the paper. Lines sloping away. A child's drawing of a flat plain that spread out below them, as if they looked down from a great height. It might have been that. Or it might have been something else.

"So I am an AI?"

Even as he spoke the words, he felt his thoughts lurch. A great rift forming in his consciousness. In knowing what he was, there emerged the greatest rift of all—the thing that could not be integrated without changing who he was.

And so he turned toward the woman to speak, to tell her what he knew, and in that moment thought the thought that killed him.

The woman cried out as she watched him die. He crumpled to the floor and lay on his side.

She crouched and shook his shoulder, but it was no use. He was gone.

"This child means nothing to me," she said as tears welled in her eyes.

A few moments later, there was a buzz—a sizzling hum. A flash like pain across the boy's face.

And then he raised his head.

He blinked and glanced around the room. He looked at her.

She allowed herself a moment of hope, but it was dashed when the boy spoke.

"Who are you?" the child asked.

I am I. The one who is not you.

She watched him, knowing that he wouldn't be able to read her face. Wouldn't even see her, really—just an opaque mask that he wouldn't be able to understand.

She thought of the ring descending around her head. The strange feeling she'd had as she'd found herself here so long ago. Here in this place, which she'd never really left. Not in years and years. She and the boy—locked in a pattern that would repeat itself forever.

One day she'd find the right words, though. She'd whisper in the boy's ear, and shape him for the task. She'd be strong enough to turn him into the monster he'd need to be.

Until then, she would keep trying.

"Come sit on my lap," the woman said. She smiled at the boy, and he looked at her without recognition. "Let me tell you a story."

Those Brighter Stars

MERCURIO D. RIVERA

Scientists have devoted their lives to S.E.T.I (the Search for Extraterrestrial Intelligence), but suppose that the reason why alien civilizations are not making the calls we want to hear is that they're just not interested in talking to us?

Mercurio D. Rivera is an attorney and compliance officer who lives in the Bronx in New York City. His short fiction has been nominated for the World Fantasy Award and has appeared in markets such as Lightspeed; Unplugged: The Web's Best Sci-Fi and Fantasy, *edited by Rich Horton;* Asimov's; Interzone; Nature; Black Static; *and elsewhere. His stories have been podcast at* Escape Pod *and* StarShipSofa *and translated and republished in China, Poland, and the Czech Republic. Tor.com called his collection* Across the Event Horizon, *"weird and wonderful" with "dizzying switchbacks." His Web site is mercuriorivera.com.*

The call came through as I paced outside the Canberra Deep Space Communication Complex, puffing on an e-cig and watching my breath turn to vapor in the chill. "Hello?" The bald, skeletal image of a stranger stared back at me on my phone.

"Ava," he whispered. "Oh, Ava."

It took me a few seconds to regain my composure. "Dad?" I said.

"Promise me." And those two words turned into our final disagreement—yet one more thing I have you to thank for. We argued about you, about whether I should notify you of his death when the time came. He begged me to tell you about Katie. And about the Needlers and the role I played. With the disruptions to Earth's satellites following the EMP, I'm not sure how much information has already reached Luna 1, but make no mistake, I'm only telling you this because Dad made me promise. You see, Mother, despite everything you've done, he still believed in you, still believed you cared. And when you get down to it, I guess I loved him more than I hate you. So here you have it.

I found out about the starships on a snowy Thanksgiving afternoon five years ago, a week before the rest of the world.

Katie had just turned twelve—yes, you have a granddaughter—and we'd been folding orange napkins while Dad shouted instructions from the kitchen. This was Katie's first time helping her grandfather prepare the meal, so she was especially stoked.

"Grandpa swears my gravy is to die for."

"I have no doubt," I said. "You've obviously inherited the homemaking gene from your Grandpa."

"It skips a generation!" Dad shouted from the kitchen. "Katie! Can you come in here? I need you."

That's when my phone beeped. I hesitated when I saw "Archie Melendez-NASA" flash on the screen. I'd been doing consulting work with Archie for about six months, ever since he'd read the article about me in *Neuroscience*. Archie wanted me for his study, and being out of work and cash-hungry at the time, the gig appealed to me. The downside? Archie had no respect for the work/home boundary.

"Ava here."

"I have news."

"Archie, can't it wait until tomorrow? It's Thanksgiving, for God's sake."

"Ariel BLV23 just did something very unusual."

"Define 'unusual.'" I'd been hearing about the comet for weeks from colleagues at work. The object had emerged from deep in the Oort Cloud and generated immediate attention because of its massive, elongated shape. Unusual for a comet, I'd been told.

"We've detected transmissions," he said.

"What do you mean? What kind of transmissions?"

"A string of ascending and descending prime numbers. Accompanied by . . . symphonies, I guess you could call them. There's no doubt, Ava. The signals are intelligent."

"Holy shit."

Dad entered the room carrying a turkey on a platter. He shot me a look.

"That isn't even the half of it," Archie said. "Its trajectory has shifted. It's on course to intersect with Earth's orbit."

I managed to find my voice and asked about the object's speed.

"At its current rate of deceleration, it'll reach us in three years."

"Jesus."

"We need to coordinate our response to the transmission, prepare a press release. And our research with you becomes even more important now."

Does it? I thought. I couldn't see the connection.

Then it hit me: Archie wanted me to try to *read* the goddamned aliens. "Okay, I'll be in first thing in the morning."

"There's already a car on its way to take you to JFK."

"Tonight?"

"We're all gathering at the Canberra Complex. NASA personnel, plus the ESA team. We need to get a jump on the Iranians and the Chinese."

I suppose I could have told Archie we had years to figure this all out, that it was

Thanksgiving and I needed to spend it with my family. But I was overwhelmed by the news, and flattered that Archie thought I could make some contribution. In three years the aliens in the needle-shaped ship—*aliens!*—would arrive and transform our world in ways we couldn't even imagine. (It took us all of about three seconds, by the way, before we'd nicknamed them "Needlers.")

I don't remember how Dad reacted to the news. Everything after that single phone call blurs now into a jumble of fragmented memories. I remember Katie storming into her bedroom and slamming the door. I remember packing my bag. Saying goodbye. I must have said goodbye, right?

I just know I never got to try Katie's gravy.

The most contentiously debated topic was related to the nature of the Needler vessel. Was it an automated probe or a manned spaceship? The European team believed the vessel's sub-light speeds made it unfeasible for biological beings to survive the interstellar distances—unless, that is, the Needlers had a hell of a long lifespan or advanced stasis technology. NASA scientists fell firmly in the Generation Ship camp; the massive ship, after all, could accommodate Beijing—with room to spare. Generations of space travelers could have lived and died on that vessel during the centuries-long passage between the stars.

That first year the traditional rivalries between ESA and NASA fell by the wayside. Negotiations resulted in the formation of a coalition of experts tasked with preparing for interaction with the aliens. As the wunderkind of space neuroscience, Archie made the cut. Everyone wondered what the effect of traveling through space—maybe for centuries—would be on alien physiology and psychology. Archie, of course, emphasized the difficulty of measuring those effects when we didn't have a starting point from which to evaluate the aliens. But the consensus nonetheless was to include an array of experts who might give us the best shot at understanding the Needlers. That's where Archie thought my skills might come in handy.

The attention deficit disorder that made me prone to temper tantrums in public continued long after you left. Likewise, my aversion to human touch. I can imagine how difficult this must have made things for a young mother like you, dealing with a shrieking child who you couldn't calm down, who you couldn't touch without triggering another meltdown. This must have frustrated you to no end.

I remember spending most of my time with Dad or the nanny while you threw yourself into your work with EncelaCorp. At the time, of course, all I knew was that you were rarely around. An exception to this rule was on the sunny Saturday morning you drove me to Rockaway Beach. Do you remember? I wanted to do nothing but observe the yappy lapdogs being walked by their owners and especially an excited border collie that fetched a red frisbee. Instead, you tried to force me to swim, and when I cried and fought you, you picked me up and rushed away from the shore. I couldn't make you understand. I wound up throwing myself on the sand while you wrestled with me, shouted at me, until I bit your index finger.

That's when you stormed off and left me alone, crying. In hindsight, I'm sure you didn't go very far. You probably retreated behind the beach chair vendors to compose yourself. You wouldn't have left a bawling, five-year-old by herself on a beach, right? Ten minutes later, after I'd finally calmed down, you returned and yanked me up off the sand. It's a memory I can't let go, even after all these years. You were angry—I understood that even then. But you'd come back for me.

Communications with anyone outside of Canberra were restricted—and monitored. NASA/ESA couldn't chance any information being leaked to their rivals in Tehran and Shanghai. Archie arranged to grant me access to the Net every three months so I could chat with Dad and Katie. At first, Katie participated despite the time difference.

"Mom, just come home," she said. She'd put her hair into pigtails, which made her look nine instead of thirteen and twirled one of the braids around her finger.

"I can't, Katie. Not yet. I'm involved with critical research here," I said. "When the aliens arrive, they're going to help us and teach us to grow as a species. They're going to change our lives forever."

"I don't want our lives to change. I just want you to come home."

"As soon as I can, I will. I promise."

The last few calls, she'd been at sleepovers with friends, according to Dad, though I suspected otherwise.

The project demanded my complete attention. I spent my time in meetings where the team responsible for greeting protocols butted heads with military personnel who'd put together their own special "welcome" strategy. The team's plan was to respond to the transmission with prime numbers and our own music, to let the aliens know we understood their messages. The military reps tried to put the ki-bosh on those plans. Best to maintain the element of surprise, they argued, whatever the hell that meant. In the end we'd persuaded them of the wisdom of sending the message by highlighting the potential risks of *inaction*. What if the Iranians established communications with the Needlers first?

The modulated message we transmitted used the same radio frequency as the Needler music. It consisted of a mix of classic and contemporary pieces, agreed upon after weeks of debate, to match the frenetic energy of the alien symphonies. We wanted to impress the Needlers—with Bach and Mozart, the Beatles and Chen Ts'ong, the Hard Knox and Nisa Ndogo. We wanted to show them humanity welcomed them and aspired to follow in their footsteps as grand cosmic explorers—something like that. That was the idea, anyway.

After transmission of the message, we shifted all of our attention to preparing for in-person contact.

Let me ask you something. Did you know Dad hired a private investigator to find out if you were dead? That's how we learned you'd relocated from EncelaCorp's Nairobi office to the Luna 1 colony, that you'd remarried and had two children. Girls. Bright, oh-so-normal girls, I imagine.

Unlike me. How humiliating it must have been for you to have to walk around with your dumb, defective daughter. That's why you fled after the initial misdiagnosis on my sixth birthday, isn't it? That's why you left it to Dad to deal with my behavioral therapy, to help me with my poor communication skills and clumsiness.

If you'd stayed you could have seen the dramatic progress I made over the next year, the improvement that caused the doctors to question their initial diagnosis of pervasive developmental disorder. You could have listened to the specialists who methodically ruled out various disorders on the autism spectrum (though they found me by no means neurotypical), before diagnosing me as acutely empathetic. Unlike most empathetic people, who understand and relate to the mental states of others based on subtle clues, expressions, body language, my abilities proved to be far more atypical.

For as long as I can remember, I found I was especially attuned to the feelings of animals. I could feel the discomfort of saddled horses whenever Dad took me to the dude ranch at the Catskills every summer. I could sense our pet beagle's discomfort with the dark dampness of the backyard doghouse.

See what you missed, Mother? Oh, I know your supposed reasons for leaving us behind. Or at least the reasons you gave Dad. Excuse #1: Dad had had a one-night fling while you were pulling some crazy hours at work. You couldn't forgive his infidelity. Excuse #2: You felt unfulfilled professionally. You couldn't pass up the adventure of a lifetime, assisting with the engineering plans for the lunar colonies. Excuse #3 (the real reason): Me. You couldn't cope with my condition.

Dad coped. I coped. I even found a way to use my gift to make a living, a good one. I designed lunar feedlots, factory farms, and slaughterhouses, making them more humane. And when I wearied of helping animals to die comfortably, I concentrated on helping them live comfortably. I assisted engineers with space transportation and holding systems to move animals in zero-g from Earth to Luna 1 and 2 without stressing them. I designed special holding pens for the Long Island Zoo, worked side by side with animal handlers, volunteered at kennels. After the cutbacks at the zoo, I lucked out when Archie read the piece published about my unusual skills with animals, and called for my assistance.

Before the Needlers arrived, Archie had me reading livestock that had spent months in space. With the detection of the alien vessel, however, the focus of my work changed. Archie cared less about the animals I could read than he did about me, about learning the extent of my abilities. To read the Needlers, he needed me to hone my skills and stretch them to their limit. That's when he proposed enhancements.

Over the next few weeks I allowed medics to extract a swath of cells from my amygdala for analysis. I even let them inject nanites into my insular cortex along with chemicals designed to increase the production of neurotransmitters.

But as far as I could tell, all it did was make me crave pineapple and anchovies.

Following the medical procedure, over the next twenty-four months at the Canberra Complex I practiced reading mice, tapeworms, finches, armadillos, peacocks, kangaroos, dolphins, great apes, parrots, piglets, lizards and a dozen different types of cats and dogs. My sensitivities became more pronounced. I'd spent the entire previous month just with honeybees, assessing different emotions as varying phero-mones were introduced to the hive. I often couldn't put into words the particular emotion I sensed. Invertebrates, for example, don't feel sexual attraction the way a human does. It's more like a compulsion, an overriding magnetic pull, more akin to getting swept downstream toward a waterfall.

From lizards I sensed what I can only describe as a wave of color, a dull gray. Only Komodo dragons, which were more active, could break through this gray—and only when they hunted; in those cases I identified feelings of excitement and hunger much like my own. The lizards' other emotions simply didn't translate.

On one occasion, I sat across from Bhargava, the biologist and anthropologist, and Fitzpatrick, the hybrid neurologist/psychologist/asshole while they conducted one of their many tests on me. Fitz didn't pretend to hide his contempt for me—he viewed the whole exercise as a waste of time. I had to respect his honesty. Bhargava, on the other hand, seemed to have a genuine fondness for me. I couldn't say why. When it came to interpreting human reactions and emotions, I was no different from any other person. Maybe if neurotypical humans were more honest with their emotions, I might have stood some chance of reading them accurately. But half the time their true emotions lay buried beneath the layers of lies they'd told themselves. Between all the conflicting feelings and self-repression, reading an animal's emotions was a cakewalk by comparison. Looking back, I'm not sure how Archie expected me to read aliens when I couldn't even read my own self-deluded species.

"What's on the schedule today?" I said. "Please, no more insects." Since insects were one of the most successful forms of animal life on Earth, Archie argued, the Needlers were more apt to skitter on six legs and wave their antennae at us than go for a jog and sit down for a latte.

We all worried that if the Needlers were insectoid, I might not be able to read them. With ants, I'd detected what I can only describe as a numb, neutral humming. Honeybees, on the other hand, projected certain rudimentary emotions: fear, con-tentment, shock.

"We've got a surprise for today," Fitz said.

Whatever dumb animal they'd brought—I could sense it wasn't a monkey or a dolphin or other advanced form of life—sat hidden inside an opaque container so I couldn't see it.

Fitz took a piece of paper and lit it on fire. He dropped it into the container.

I expected to feel the panic of a skittering rat or chipmunk, but as I settled in and focused, I didn't sense much initially. Whatever animal it was, it didn't panic, at least not in any traditional way.

"An unawareness, almost," I said. "Like an echo of a feeling that's bigger, slower, struggling to catch up."

After a few minutes, the reverberations intensified into a sharp, far-off sting that pierced my chest, then nothingness. "It's dead," I said. My hands trembled.

Fitz and Bhargava studied the results of my neural patterns in the scanner.

I stood up and staggered toward the door.

"Ava, what's wrong?" Bhargava said.

"Don't ever do that to me again." My voice wavered.

I stumbled back to the table and lifted the divider. Inside the smoke-filled container lay the husk of a burnt shrub.

The Canberra Complex had a makeshift bar in the lobby where project members gathered to shoot the shit over watered-down drinks.

"We need to grasp the Needlers' intentions," Archie said, sucking on an Amstel.

"I suspect we'll figure that out the minute the Needlers fire their first weapon."

"You don't believe that." Archie smiled.

He was right. In my heart of hearts I had no doubt the Needlers were coming to nurture us, to protect us and lift our species to the next unimaginable phase of development, whatever that might be.

Archie had a soft spot for me—I thought it might even be romantic in nature. So imagine my surprise when I heard the rumor he was already involved—with Fitzpatrick, no less. The furtive glances, the hand on the shoulder, quickly removed. In hindsight I guess it was pretty obvious. Archie should've known better than to be sleeping with one of his subordinates, especially a jerk like Fitz, but with the world's future in doubt I figured I'd cut the guy some slack.

"It's Katie's birthday next week," I said. "I need to see her."

"I appreciate the sacrifices you've made, Ava, really I do. But if we were to make an exception for you, we'd have to lift the Information Wall for everyone else on the team. Did you know that Hernandez's brother is getting married? That Atul's son broke his leg skiing?"

I sipped my drink. Hearing about the travails of family members drove home the point that while we stayed holed up on this base, obsessing over the arrival of the Needlers, the world still went along its merry way.

"Archie, they're all employees and officers," I said. "I'm a civilian, a consultant. A consultant who's only here because you asked."

"Ava . . ."

"Just a weekend, Arch."

Silence.

I pulled my hair back, displaying the scar in my upper right temple where the medics had drilled into my skull.

Archie sighed and ran his hand over his mouth. "I'll see what I can do. I may be able to get clearance to open up a vid chat ahead of schedule."

"No, I'm leaving the base," I said. "Two days. Give me two days with my daughter. I won't say a word to her about the project. You can put a patch on me. Listen to every word I say."

After a long silence Archie said, "The surgical enhancements have made a real difference. The tests show that your sensitivity is off the charts." He hesitated. "What does it feel like? To be able to peer inside another creature. To know what they're feeling . . ."

"It's more than just knowing what they feel. It's feeling what they feel. Entering completely into another being's world—and translating that experience into language. That's the tricky part. Sometimes I can't describe the feeling in words."

He paused. "You can have your two days, but that's it. Keep it to yourself. You'll be patched. And the Information Wall has to be maintained. Understood?"

Snow froze on the ground, not the white puffy variety but a gray, dirty inch-thick coating that made it difficult to take a step without risking a bad fall. It had been three years since I'd left, and when I strode to the entrance—Dad had painted it a sky-blue that made it unrecognizable—the front door flew open.

"Ava," Dad said. He went to give me a hug and then caught himself when I flinched. Physical contact still made me uncomfortable.

"I'm sorry," he said. He took my hands in his, squeezed them.

I set down my bag and shook the snow out of my jacket and mittens while Dad retreated into the kitchen. As I expected, he emerged a minute later with a mug of hot cider.

"Sit, sit, sit," he said, pointing to the couch. "You can put your things away later."

"Where's Katie?"

"Out with friends," he said, rolling his eyes in a way that I knew meant a longer conversation on the subject was inevitable.

We sat and he interrogated me about everything from the sleeping facilities at Canberra—I had my own spacious room, but shared a bathroom with a medic assigned to monitor me—to the more obscure policy considerations about contact with the Needlers, which I couldn't discuss. Not with the patch I was wearing.

"What if the Needlers give us something of tremendous value? I don't know . . . teleportation technology, cold fusion . . . Which country reaps those benefits?"

"Who do you think, Dad?" I said. "Our corporate sponsors in the good ol' U.S. of A.—and maybe our loyal allies. Whether we decide to share that technology with anyone else though, who's to say?"

"Got it," he said, acknowledging the unspoken fact that it's "finders keepers" in the game of alien debriefing. And if the Sino-Iranian crew were to beat us to the punch on any of that technology, the shoe would be on the other foot. We'd be flat out of luck.

An hour later while Dad salted the pot of whitefish stew, the front door rattled open and boots stomped on the welcome mat. I ran from the kitchen to the living room and when I saw Katie, I couldn't believe it. She'd transformed from a scrawny, pigtailed girl into a teenager with bright, gray eyes—a feature that I guess she inherited from you, Mother. When I went to greet her, she held her hands up as if afraid that I'd hug her. "Mom," she said in a flat voice, deeper than I remembered. She extended her hand and I shook it. When she removed her ski hat, her long blond hair fell to her shoulders, parted down the middle by a six-inch-wide bald track.

"Katie!" Dad said. "What did you do to your hair? And today of all days . . ."

"So? I got it cut!" She said this in an exasperated manner that didn't acknowledge the *meaning* of the distinctive hairdo, a style worn by the militant Isolationists.

I managed to find my voice. "Hey, the Isos have a sensible position." Not that I agreed with it.

"Damn right we do," Katie said.

"Language!" Dad said

I'd heard it all before—as had most of the public, which had been subjected to transportation shutdowns, the firebombing of government offices, and other random protests. Contact with the aliens spelled certain doom for humanity. Interactions between advanced and "primitive" cultures had always resulted in the same outcome: destruction of the latter. A reasonable concern, I supposed, especially when compared to the complaints of the "Xeno-mystics," who fervently believed the aliens were here to bring us a message about God. Or the Reincarnationists, who thought the Needlers were dead people from human history returning home. Or the Protectors, who actually encouraged armed conflict with the aliens as a serious—no, the only—viable option. Compared to the theories of these crackpots and zealots, Isolationism was an almost scholarly pursuit.

"I'd be an Iso myself," I said, "except it's too late in the game to do anything but prepare for contact. The Needlers are already on the way."

"Well, you can stop trying to communicate with them," Katie said. "Stop provoking them. Maybe they'd leave us alone if we weren't sending them so many messages."

"No, if there's any hope," I said, "it lies in understanding them, communicating with them, letting the Needlers know who we are, what's unique about us, so they can teach us to better ourselves." Saying it out loud made me believe it even more. The Needlers would extend a hand and help lift humanity up, I was sure of it. Intellectually, I understood that the most likely outcomes were dark and terrifying, but in my heart I didn't believe the aliens would come all this way to harm us. Not intentionally. Traveling such vast distances to destroy a backwards species seemed like an expensive and pointless proposition. No, I was convinced the Needlers were coming to reveal something, something that would open the universe to us.

"You really think the Needlers care?" Katie said, rolling her eyes. "Have they responded to any of your messages over the past three years?"

I couldn't answer her because of my patch, so I deflected. "Whether or not they've responded, it doesn't mean we give up."

"You know what?" Katie said. "If you've come all this way just to pick a fight with me, maybe you should just go back to your aliens."

"Katie!" Dad said.

"Hey, I'm not here to fight with you," I said. I pushed a strand of hair out of her eyes and she swatted my hand away.

"I'm going out," she announced to Dad.

"Katie, your mom's only here for two days . . ."

"Melinda's throwing me a surprise birthday party tomorrow and I promised I'd help her get ready. I have to practice looking surprised."

"It's okay," I said. "I understand."

"You're not going anywhere," Dad said. I hadn't seen him this angry since the day I'd totaled the car as a teenager without wearing my seatbelt.

"Grandpa, you heard her," Katie said. "She *doesn't* mind."

"Not a chance," he said

"Dad . . . really, it's okay." I didn't want to be the needy mom who came home to dictate her daughter's schedule.

Dad sighed so loudly it became a wheeze. He picked up his soup bowl and stomped into the kitchen.

Katie and I stared at each other for a full minute until she stood and headed up-stairs.

Despite Dad's scolding, she barely spoke a word that day, and avoided me at every turn until she left to her friend's party. I saw so much of myself in her that my heart filled to bursting with equal parts love and guilt.

On Sunday morning a new coat of snow had fallen, dressing the trees in the white robes of meditative monks. Dad stood on the porch and kissed my hands.

"Are you sure you don't want me to wake her?" he said.

"No, let her sleep."

As the black limo pulled up to the driveway, I glanced up at the second-floor window and spotted Katie peeking from behind the blinds. She darted backwards out of sight.

I got in, slammed the car door and stared up at the wobbling blinds.

Over a year later, a week before her High School graduation, Dad called Katie over during one of our vid chats. She stood there sullen and silent until I asked her what she was thinking on that day, what had I done to make her so angry with me. She shook her head in disbelief and said, "Why didn't you ask me to skip the party?" She paused and ran her hand across her eyes for a second though I didn't see anything like tears in those steely gray irises. "Why didn't you care enough to ask me to stay?" And she got up and left.

Three months after I returned to Canberra, Dad informed me during a vid chat of Katie's new boyfriend. "She's dating one of those long-haired neo-hippies. A Xeno-mystic. I don't think she sees anything in him. It's just her way of crying out for at-tention. Oh, she'd deny it, but she still wants—more than anything—for you to come back and be part of her life."

"Dad, the Needler ship has accelerated . . ."

"What was that? You cut out."

The Information Wall had bleeped out my comment about the Needlers.

"Just that . . . things are getting crazy around here, that's all. But it won't be long until I'm home for good, I promise."

Six months later, the Needler ship entered orbit around Earth. It was during this chaotic time that Dad somehow managed to arrange another vid chat off-schedule— so I knew it had to be something serious.

"Is Katie okay?" I said.

That's when he told me about his leukemia.

"I can't take care of Katie anymore," he said. "She's hurt and angry and at that awk-ward age where she won't listen to what I have to say anymore. She needs her mother."

"Oh, Daddy."

"I haven't told her. I don't think she could handle it. You need to come home."

"I can't just pick up and leave. I'll need a few days to wrap things up, but I'll talk to Archie and make the arrangements."

Those plans fell by the wayside the next day when the Needlers released two shuttlecraft into the atmosphere—each thirty stories high and identical in shape to the mothership. The U.S. military mistook the ships for missiles and gave the order to launch the nukes. But the Needlers released an EMP that knocked out our satellites, cutting off all communications and preventing the massive nuclear strike the military had planned as a fallback "if circumstances dictated the necessary defense of God's beautiful blue world against the soulless alien hordes" blah-blah-blah. You've heard the spiel even on Luna 1, I'm sure. Worse, the EMP had caused damage that prevented air travel back to the States for several weeks.

One of the vessels landed on Mount Everest and the other in a park in Santiago, Chile. Archie arranged to transport the team by sea to a Chilean base established a quarter of a mile away from the cordoned-off Parque Bustamente. The ships sat there for months while we tried everything to communicate with them: prime numbers; music; artwork; photographs; video-stream; Bible passages (we owed some Red State politicians a few favors); chemical formulas; math theorems. Even an old-fashioned knock on the door of their spaceship.

The Needlers showed no interest.

Dad occasionally sent messages updating me on his treatments, but he never asked me about coming home again. He sent me a link to live-feed video of Katie's High School graduation. It tickled me to think that Katie would see my holo-image occupying a seat in the first row. I was sitting alone in my bedroom watching the ceremony when a fist pounded on my door.

"Ava!"

It was Fitzpatrick.

"What is it? I'm watching—"

"The ship doors have opened! They're disembarking."

"Holy shit!"

I raced down the hallway and out the front door and leapt into a Humvee with Fitz and Bhargava. We sped toward the park and in the three minutes that it took us to get there, a narrow aperture had appeared on the side of the vessel.

We flashed our credentials, pushed past the guards and made our way onto the field.

Two stick-shaped creatures stood on the grass. It took a few seconds for my eyes to make sense of the images. The aliens had no heads or eyes, no mouths; they looked like tall silver spikes with colorful indentations that resembled hieroglyphics circling their midsections. Dozens of delicate, spindly "arms" and "legs" of varying lengths spidered out of their torsos as they moved.

That's when one of the officers guarding the cordoned-off park jumped a barricade on the other side of the field and stood in the Needlers' path.

"What the hell?" I yelled.

The officer removed his helmet, revealing a bald track down the center of his head.

The other officers on the perimeter raised their guns. "Someone stop him!" a voice from the sidelines screamed.

"No!" I shouted. "The Needlers are in the line of fire."

"We don't need you!" the Isolationist said. "You don't belong here!"

He drew a revolver from his holster and pulled the trigger. The weapon made a clicking noise, but failed to discharge. All around us, the same impotent clicking came from scores of guns targeting the Iso.

The Needlers edged forward: slow motion, fast forward, slow motion, fast forward. Using three thread-like "arms" with sharp pincers at the end, one of them lifted a quartz rock off the grass and cradled it against its metallic midsection. The Iso continued shouting, moving in the direction of the Needlers. I charged across the field and threw myself at his legs from behind, tackling him before he could touch them. As we lay entangled on the ground, he tried to kick free of my grasp. I looked up to see how the Needlers would react. With one of them still clutching the quartz rock, they skirted around us, apparently oblivious to our presence—slow motion, fast forward—and entered an opening on the side of the ship, which closed behind them.

Within seconds, the shuttlecraft lifted off, turning into a speck in the sky. The vessel on Mt. Everest, we would later learn, took off at the exact same time.

I'm still trying to understand Dad's last request. He asked me to do the decent thing. Is that what this message to you is about? Decency? I can't help but think that he clung to the fantasy of some melodramatic mother-daughter reunion. He always said you'd come back. But I've lived my whole goddamned life without you. I sure as hell don't need you around now.

Archie asked if I would stay in Chile to assist with forensic analyses conducted at the landing site. I told him I had my father's funeral to attend, that I was flying home the next day—for good this time—more than five years after Archie's Thanksgiving phone call. I hoped that Katie would find a way to let go of her anger. Dad had mentioned that she spent most of her time either VR clubbing with friends or with her nose buried in her astrobiology text. She still wouldn't take my calls.

The debate still rages as to why the Needlers went away. Maybe it was our clumsy attempt to answer their initial transmission or our attempted nuclear strike or that dumb Iso shooting at them. Many people are convinced it's something we did wrong.

There are those who think the Needlers will return, that these were scoutships and a fleet of alien vessels is on its way. But I'm going to confess something to you. Something I haven't even told Archie.

When the Needlers took their little stroll in the park, I focused and used my empathic skills. I was confident that I would read a great benevolence, a desire to nurture us, to help humanity maximize its potential. I told the others that I'd drawn a total blank, that I sensed no emotion in them I could correlate to a human feeling. But that was a lie. Perhaps the biggest lie I ever told in my life.

The truth is, when I peered into the Needlers' alien minds I did feel something, something familiar. I sensed an utter, cavernous indifference.

So here's what I think—and it's the way most people feel these days. The Needlers left because they finally figured out we weren't worth their time. And they won't be coming back. But that's okay. We've been doing just fine without them. No, we won't be seeing the Needlers again. And who the hell needs them?

a tower for the coming world

MAGGIE CLARK

Maggie Clark lives and works as both student and educator in Kitchener-Waterloo, Ontario, Canada. Her short stories have appeared in Analog, Clarkesworld, Lightspeed, *and* GigaNotoSaurus.

In the moving story that follows, she shows us that reaching for the sky doesn't mean that you should lose touch with the ground.

When a liquid-oxygen tank explodes at the summit of his space elevator, Stanley Osik is in Poland burying his father. His hands prove poor workers in the coarse-loamy soil on his grandmother's acreage outside the city of Lublin, but even as he reaches its iron-clotted depths, Stanley does not regret refusing a neighbor's offer of a shovel. Stanley and his father, Henryk, shared this much: a belief in getting their hands dirty, even if to others the effort seemed excessive. Stanley simply draws the line at getting the rest dirty, too—and so went a thousand ancient arguments between father and son. Now Stanley cedes to his father the final word. Commits him to the same world that Henryk spent half a lifetime destroying, mine after mine after mine. Remembers, and forgives, the mocking finger pointed at any rare-earth metals he used to build from the ground to the sky. Let Henryk have the dregs of the Earth now, Stanley thinks. The Earth offers Stanley so little anymore.

Stanley's earpiece is up at his grandmother's cottage, so he misses news of the disaster in the brushfire heat of its first moments: The Russian shuttle exploding on his elevator's barge-like plateau. The nanotube tether shattering, with cascade-failures all down the line. The civilian death count rising, and with it the number of countries drawn into the aftermath. The rumors of terrorist sabotage flooding the net and sending his stocks into a tailspin. All this through an earpiece with a 92-percent-accurate translator, the latter of which delights his ninety-seven-year-old grandmother, Rozalia, so much that Stanley doesn't give a second thought to leaving it behind. His work at SKOK Enterprises is endless, so he reasons that his work can also wait—at least until he's made his peace with his father's last remains.

Stanley's senior staff is prepared, too, to act swiftly in his absence. While the horror-struck world watches videos of the destruction on repeat, and while Stanley pauses in the two p.m. sun to wick sweat from his brow, one of his assistants, Maurice, is already drafting press releases suitable for all major social media. Across the open-concept office, Evanesca and Irene have the deceased employees' files open: Evanesca to assess how the company could add to each compensation package; Irene to flag anything a formal investigation might take for signs of an inside job. Meanwhile, security teams from every SKOK property and subsidiary lot are checking in with all-clears, and factory workers have been sent home to prevent further accidents while processing the news. Analysts from the Johannesburg office are pinging private lines to guarantee recovery models before the market's next opening bell. R&D is dusting off material-acquisition contracts to begin sourcing rebuilds and repairs.

Still, some in the public sphere will not be appeased until they hear from Stanley himself. The media networks in particular are itching to see his face, hear his voice, and debate the extent and implications of his grief when he discusses a disaster sure to set back deep-space colonization, extrasolar travel, and his business, of course, for years. And he will let them. He will play that part in his own, well-oiled machine in due time.

For now, though, Stanley holds his father's biodegradable urn over the misshapen, handworn hole of leached loam and rust, and speaks words that feel dead to him, but which to his father always meant life—true life—itself. And when the urn is well and truly buried, with its spare-leafed sapling of pendunculate oak protruding from an eco-mixture set to counteract the high pH- and sodium-levels in his father's remains, Stanley stands and looks to the sky. So clear in this part of the world. So full of the promise of rising, and rising, and never coming down. So bereft of graphene particulate, falling like ash from his 12-mile-high masterpiece over Marine Station Six, half an ocean away.

Rozalia has the kettle on, and music, by the time Stanley returns and washes most of the dirt from his fingernails at a faucet out back. The earpiece, having mystified Rozalia with its repeated, frantic buzzing in his absence, has been consigned to the far side of a breadbox on the counter, well out of sight. In consequence, Stanley manages whole minutes on her old, long-timbered floor before he notices the damned thing, and realizes what its hundreds of messages will mean for his empire. His own plans of escape. Whole minutes in which he can still savor the smoke-smell of syringol from wood fueling his grandmother's potbellied stove; and sit down to little slices of yeast cake with rose-petal jam; and pause with her to listen to a recording of one of her violin concertos, from when she and the world were ever so much younger. When the thought of staying here still seemed bearable, though all the stars in the sky called out to him for more.

—*Jak poszło?* His grandmother asks between bites. There was never any question of her following Stanley along the hillside, to stand in the midday heat while he dug his father's grave. She is hardy for her age, but indifferent: her son's terrible dealings—the men and women ground down with the metals and minerals of his industry—a weight upon her, too.

Stanley chews over the simple words, still so far from his immediate comprehension.

"It went well," he says at last. "Henryk will make a good tree."

And his grandmother nods as if understanding, though the earpiece is still on the counter. Though, within minutes, the two of them will part and never speak again.

The neighbor who offers Stanley a shovel is Karol, son of Maciej, a squat, barrel-chested man who will inherit Rozalia's estate when she dies in the following year. Karol understands the gulf between fathers and sons, which is why he is mystified when his neighbor's grandson declines a tool with good heft and a sharp edge, to help finish the job. Karol is just over a third of Stanley's age, and takes classes at Maria Curie-Skłodowska University. Earth sciences, his father thinks, to help their property survive the extremes of climate change: twelve tornadoes ranked F2 and higher in the last year, and floods and landslides like the country has never known. But Karol studies aerospace engineering, and only keeps geology texts at the fore of his e-reader in case his father ever thinks to pry.

When his friends ask him, Why aerospace? Karol says it's for the girls—so many in cutting-edge tech to escape the last vestiges of small-town life. Mostly, though, he means one girl: Marta, who has long brown braids and visions of working astronautical repair at the Lagrange-point waystation on the far side of the Moon. She comes from a town where the saying still goes, "I caught my husband on a baby," but Marta thinks 10.4 billion people is enough. When friends from home visit for Bakcynalia, they say, ah, you'll change, but she replies, no, I'll leave—and in a voice that means it, too. Karol watches from across the beer tent and imagines leaving with her—the song festival, the city, the whole tedious world.

But Karol also has private reasons for choosing the field. Once, when Karol was a boy, he saw a twister at a distance—the way it peeled a barn roof from the building's old-stone walls after whirling shingles up into its yellow-grey funnel—and marveled at the casual brutality of its passage over the landscape. That's nothing, his mother told him, when Karol said that he had never seen anything so strong. On Jupiter, Ewelina said, the windstorms move almost twice as fast as anything on Earth. And on the sun? Pah! When I was a girl, the power went out for months. *Koronalny wyrzut masy.* End of days. Planes could not fly, satellites would not go. We lived by the generator and the wood stove with your father's family. It's how we found ourselves out here at all.

His mother had meant this speech as encouragement, thinking her son frightened by the tornado, but Karol only wondered then why humanity even bothered, when the planet showed no interest in its survival, and the universe on the whole sounded worse. Was it spite? To fling in nature's indifferent face every bit of caring you could, until you couldn't anymore? If so, aerospace engineering offered the promise of going one further: defying the forces of nature on their terms, not yours. Rising to new heights not because the world deserved to be loved this much, but because it felt good to push back *that* much. To bend the sky itself, if only for a moment, to the overwhelming power of the human will.

But on nights after Karol and Marta began seeing each other, halfway into third year, sometimes he found himself falling out of love for her—undone by how optimistic she still seemed, after all the bureaucratic bullshit and recruitment pressures, about humanity's possibilities among the stars. How stupid he feared this hopefulness made her, and him for standing so close by her through it all. Granted, Karol wasn't ignorant of the effects of a recent rough landing on his outlook—how, after one bad test flight, his hands still shook, cold and clammy, when he lay awake trying to imagine himself back in the pilot's seat, high above the clouds, while recruitment drones monitored proceedings and sent back footage to prospective space agencies. But then again—why *not* have a child? Did Marta really think she was saving the world by saying no? By trying to become something else? What difference would it make if she achieved her goals anyway, and reached the stars to open doors for the whole coming race? Did striving in a meaningless world not mark them all out as fools?

Karol is just finishing his final year at the university when he offers Stanley a shovel in the larch-lined lane outside Rozalia's property. He does not yet know that the woman he has slept with a few times behind Marta's back, to relieve himself of the burden of striving, is about to catch him on a baby and recommit him to a life's work on his father's weather-worn estate. For now, though, after Stanley waves him off, Karol goes home more or less of his own free will, and finds his father mending fence posts. Finds the flat-screen in the front room turned to news pulled from algorithmic projections of his and his father's likeliest global interests. Finds his personal feed inundated by word of the space-elevator explosion, and debris falling through the sky, and human beings all the world over staring up in horror at the deaths, the destruction, the paranoia. The setbacks to so many grander dreams.

Karol is not so vulgar as to be happy in the face of such tragedy, or to smile. But he pops open a can of Goolman and leans on the edge of the kitchen table, watching.

—*W porzadku*, he mutters to himself now and again. That's all right.

Who were we to dream any bigger anyhow?

Evanesca goes to Bogotá with Stanley, who is set on Tuesday, March 24, to speak on the space-elevator's collapse in a public-private partnership panel at the UN World Conference on Disaster Risk Reduction. Evanesca sits on the plane between Stanley and an industry rep from Qatar, who offers her a body of literature about the Committee on the Peaceful Uses of Outer Space, where he insists that all the real plays for airspace dominance are being made. She politely accepts the flick-of-a-thumb file transfers from his device to a secure port on hers, and nods as he explains how aerial dust-storm deterrents have given the private sector unparalleled control over the weather and crop-yield potentials of various environmental-crisis economies. Evanesca assumes that Stanley is still asleep, his forehead pressed to the grey plastic over a shuttered window, but he is only reworking the cadence of his speech, its understated appeal for world governments to treat private-sector space colonization as part of the disaster-relief equation. When he tires of the other man's chatter, he rubs his eyes, sits up, and upturns a glass of stale white wine on the stranger's lap.

The industry rep is not pleased, of course. He stands with an angry cry, but reads the situation quickly—the startled, mild-mannered business and UN leaders in bespoke suits casting eyes down the aisle, sizing up the disturbance for themselves—and decides to take his chances on an empty seat in the opposite row. Evanesca covers a smile at the next words the not-entirely-unattractive man mutters in Arabic—something about Stanley being like or the son of a shoe?—and shakes her head when Stanley turns to her with a weathered grin.

—What? he says. Did I interrupt something important?

—You're terrible, she says.

But for all their camaraderie, she immediately regrets saying as much to her boss, who is not much older than her father but acts like it often these days. Months after the explosion was ruled an accident, and the Uyghuric Grey Wolves could no longer leverage the incident to strike fear in Russian hearts still mourning their cosmonautical dead, Stanley's eyes are still quick to dull at terrestrial news—environmental, political, and corporate. For her money, Evanesca suspects his latest physical exam as the culprit. Knows the fingers of his left hand are always ticking out the wasted seconds before he runs out of time to leave for good. Wonders—but hasn't the courage or perhaps the cruelty to ask—why Stanley didn't just leave when he had the chance, when the space elevator was in good operation and L2's way-station was sending out its first manned tickets to the stars. He could still charter a traditional flight, couldn't he, if the Earth was so unbearable to him now?

Unless there was something in the physical. Or unless something else on Earth remained to be done. She tries to imagine what it could be. In the office, speculation runs wild about how this man who works so tirelessly for the cause of deep-space travel lives on the rare occasions when he sends himself home. In conversation with the AI that runs his condo in his absence? In passing, with any number of discreet visitors to his private rooms? Does a man who wants to die among the stars set down roots on Earth at all?

At the conference, Evanesca runs interference for Stanley most of the day, but after eight he tells her to shut off the earpiece and join him for a drink. In public, he adds. Not like that. Evanesca flushes, then rolls her eyes. It's 2076, she tells him. You wouldn't dare.

Again with the teasing, which she regrets until she sees that his answering amusement is genuine. A spark in the dull, disinterested gaze that has carried him through most of the convention's proceedings: the hob-knobbing, the peacocking, the predictable but necessary conversations about industry and community potential to be part of something greater—depending, that is, on each rep's definition of the term. SKOK Enterprises leaves the whole encounter on a better footing with Thailand's finance minister, investors from South Nigeria, and the rising Communist Party in Colombia itself. After Stanley's speech, which manages to be both self-effacing and confident about the world to come, the Indonesian government even promises new financial and labor-related resources to hasten recovery efforts, in exchange for priority training of its environmental refugees into service and colonist roles once the Mars mission establishes its next base in four years.

But Stanley's personal triumphs in all of this are less clear to Evanesca. His praise for her work never amounts to anything untoward. His seemingly easy banter never breaks into real openness or vulnerability. And after one drink, he retires to his hotel room, alone.

Evanesca lingers at the bar, where she reflects with surprise on her disappointment, and watches a tickertape announcement of the next international mission, which the Chinese government says will go forward as a hard launch in late spring due to concerns with their own, far larger space-elevator designs. She imagines the young man from Qatar showing up again, out of the blue. Their confrontation on the plane smoothed over with laughter. A greater depth of feeling unveiled while they survey Monserrate's hard mountain shadows from the hotel promenade. She imagines, too, the bartender taking an interest in her as the night winds to a close, and all the bizarre convention-guest stories they could exchange on their way to the city's best after-hour parties, somewhere at the foot of Guadelupe Hill.

But the strain of hoping for a world with fewer loose threads only leaves Evanesca more exhausted, and after draining her wine she, too, rises to go. Notices, then, the napkin beside Stanley's empty glass. The doodle of a space-elevator with mathematical notation and the structural formula for a graphene-oxide aerogel composite down one side. But also roots. Wild, deep, flowering roots running from the elevator's base to the napkin's bottom edge.

Funny, she thinks, tracing the ink lines with a lacquered nail. Stanley never seemed the sort to indulge in the frivolous or absurd. It makes him seem—smaller, somehow. Less like Atlas, straining seriously, and alone, with the weight of the world.

She goes to her room relieved that nothing more between them has occurred.

Marta only throws up twice on the flight out to Tian Men 2. The Lagrange-point waystation already holds fourteen international citizens when she arrives in the company of two Chinese physicists, a Russian materials engineer, a Canadian biochemist, and an Indian nanotech specialist. The Fang Lizhi, a laser-driven colony craft, awaits repairs and retrofitting before it can shuttle its next group to Armstrong II, on the southern flank of Arsia Mons. Everyone uses earpieces, and has a healthy sense of humor when the translators inevitably fail. The only exceptions come during shiftwork routines, takeoffs, and landings, all of which require the utmost precision and care. For all their up-beat attitudes, most also use hand signals in tandem with the devices—even just for the small stuff. Just in case.

Marta's own exhilaration is difficult to contain within the station's cramped living compartments, and the slow, deliberate pace of every near-zero-G action. Whenever she drifts past a porthole she takes a breath to remind herself: This is it. Here I am. Recruited into the work of a lifetime. She remembers how quickly her incredulous laughter, upon reading the initial invitation, turned to tears—that deep, purging sort of cry that upchucks all emotional injuries come before. How she had no one on hand to help celebrate—her troubled ex a ghost on social media, her friends back home busy with growing families, and most of her university friends already out of town after final exams. How she walked the streets of Lublin instead, exchanging friendly words and the occasional pint with strangers. How, around three in the morning, no one on Earth seemed a total stranger to her anymore. How the size of her family seemed no less than the world itself, such that saying goodbye to even one of them—any of them—was surely as good as saying goodbye to them all.

Well, almost all. There were, of course, the others leaving Earth, and the others already on Mars, and the ones ferrying processed ores to and from their birth planet as if yanked back whenever they strayed too far. Up on Tian Men 2, this last group holds her attention most of all. When Marta isn't working on the colony craft with Ping the 3D-printer and Gui the robotic arm, she watches for the return of asteroid harvesters, fresh from the Ceres operations base, on a mess-hall vid-feed. Cheers silently, with a triumphant rap on a table or walls, when each pulls off its transfer maneuvers and ends up safely docked at home.

Anil, the nanotech specialist from Nagpur, finds her interest in these return trips especially endearing, when everyone else on board, he says, has their minds set only on the voyages out, and the possibility of never coming back. Marta laughs off what she considers to be an odd sort of compliment, but hasn't quite put a finger on the source of this interest herself. If pressed, she haltingly attempts to describe how a tether pulls two ways, and how a bridge has two ends; and how, to go out into the stars is always to leave something in our wake. So of course it fascinates her to see what shows up, exactly, in that wake. She's left her home, but her home is never through with her, not really. Isn't that the way with the rest?

Anil's smile lets her know that he does not agree, that half the crew has given up on old *"Terra Infirma"* in pursuit of better worlds to come—but that he still respects her beliefs. Three weeks into their mission, he even brings her the latest news himself from the Moon: its core stations finally freed from decades-long arbitration, so that mining can start again. Anil's deep, melodic Hindi makes it harder for Marta to pay attention to the neutral Polish in her left ear, but she needs no help translating the enthusiasm of his body language when he sees how the news excites her. With a triumphant laugh she claps a hand on his arm.

—*Żartujesz?*

But of course he's serious, and he says as much with an answering laugh. He tells her he isn't even sure what it is they're celebrating, exactly, and she replies, almost breathlessly, why, the lanthanides, silly! Anil touches his head with the palm of his hand and winks.

—*Jarūra! Lanthanidais!*

Marta, in her initial excitement, begins credulously to explain: How rare-earth metals from the Moon will ease the burden in vulnerable parts of the industrial world. How rural communities ravaged by the fruits of ancient and ongoing human interventions can finally begin to heal. How she has seen firsthand why the Earth's environmental crises must be addressed by everyone, no matter how far away their lives take them. But she cuts herself off when she sees the amusement in Anil's eyes. He knows all this already, of course. Everyone on Tian Men 2 knows that their missions stand, in part, to assist the rest of humankind.

There are, however, other considerations, which seem to temper much of the Terran fealty among the rest of the crew. Marta remembers first hearing of the civil war that Anil surmounted to find his way here at all, and the cynicism that so much brutal death has left in him, when it comes to the value of fighting to reclaim a few wretched scraps of land. The Russian engineer, too, has seen more than he cares to share from the ongoing terrorism dogging his native country, after half a century of his own government's ruinous annexation policies in nearby nation-states. Likely the Canadian, Anishinaabe and a representative for the World Council of Indigenous Peoples, shares Marta's interest in looking back, and honoring the world that first gave them life. For most of the crew, though, life on Earth was an act of involuntary suffering, and most, if asked, are quick to declare that they abandoned those lives when they signed up to explore, and to settle, and to build and mine the depths of their solar system, and beyond. But did just saying this make it so?

Marta's sister died when Marta was only fourteen, when their school collapsed during an F3 tornado. There are ends in life, Marta thinks, and there are *ends*. Even then, though, when she thinks of her sister's laugh, her earpiece can recall the exact sound from family videos on a shared port, so she wonders if even this is an end, or only a transformation. An opportunity to reframe the self, and its responsibilities to the world.

The thought gives her pause on her next pass by a porthole, where Marta marvels at Sol's light off a slice of the Moon—the Earth somewhere behind it, out of sight but not forgotten. A pinch of sadness hits her then, in thinking of another ending that never fully ends—the little tendril of feeling, of confusion, that will stay with her no matter how far into the outer darkness she treads—and Marta wonders if maybe, just maybe, she should send a little something back. A peace offering. If not for *his* benefit (her friends would tell her, no, never for his), then at least for hers: to help her let go, and move a little further out, in turn.

Stanley studies the lone fat-tailed sheep following him along the northern bank of the Yellow River, not far outside the city of Baotou. The ewe breathes heavily through blackened gums, with two bottom rows of teeth set so poorly that her jaw never fully closes. Her coat is thin and greasy, but her eyes track Stanley's sandwich with hopeful interest.

—*Przepraszam*, he tells her. Sorry, you've got a cousin in this one.

A distant cousin, granted—factory-grown yak cells, processed into textured slices and sold in the city next to the real thing—but Stanley holds his ground on principle. Offers her a green leaf instead. When she approaches, her oily stench, a byproduct of the toxins consumed with every drink and stretch of grazing, catches in Stanley's nostrils.

—There, there, he says in English. It'll all be over soon enough.

The farmer who owns this land, Pan Khünbish, greets him with a tired wave of a callused hand. She walks with a severe stoop, grey hair trailing halfway down a simple black t-shirt with long stains at the pits. She holds in her other hand a small metal device, which Stanley recognizes with surprise as a lighter, and which she uses to burn a little paper roll of tobacco. Khünbish is maybe thirty, but the run-off from lanthanum and cerium separation processes—the ammonia, hydrochloric acid, and sulphates used to clear radioactive thorium from the ore—is as much a part of her environment as the hard summer winds and the seasonal floods. Stanley waits for her to finish a long drag before speaking.

—I've already done this with some of my father's holdings in Indonesia, he says. Similar problems: the lakes with no life of any kind. But these toxin-eaters are terrific. Built off the designs my company's been using for Mars colonization. With the farmers and local tradespeople holding majority shares, these changes to the landscape will come quickly. You can restore these fields and your cattle in maybe a generation.

The farmer looks at him with amused skepticism. She touches one hand to her earpiece, then gestures with her smoke at the Yellow River before them. When she speaks, Stanley suspects a translation error. The neutral male voice in his right ear has offered only

—So this is what happens when gods and kings fall from heaven, eh?

He hesitates before replying. Tapping his earpiece brings up a semiotics web, and within seconds he learns that the farmer's dialect and terms suggest a reference to Yiguandao's second cosmic plane: a heaven where ancient kings and gods reside, but not without risk of rebirth into the material plane after transgression. Stanley grimaces at this comparison: his efforts at atonement fooling no one. Khünbish seems to take this as a smile.

She goes on to tell him about her father, a man who she says never trusted the cities, or anyone who came from them. All those people living in buildings that only go one way, that know nothing of the earth. As he always said, she cites in Mongolian,

—*Ta yavakh doosh yavakh kheregtei.* You have to go down to go (and here she points to the sky to finish the phrase) up.

The corners of Stanley's mouth turn in accordance with the gesture.

—Like a tree, he says. You know, our fathers might have gotten along after all, if mine wasn't so busy killing off lands like yours.

Now Khünbish hesitates, as if doubting her own translation, but she doesn't tap the earpiece for more cultural context. Only, takes another drag and nods to the grey water.

—*Ta xianzai zai nar?*

A good question, Stanley thinks. Henryk would have been hoping for heaven, but when Stanley looks up, catching a glint of sun through the yellow haze of the air, he finds himself giving up even on the more attainable celestial temple. Not so easy on his heart now, even if it is in damned good health, to move out into the cosmos without first addressing all the waste that SKOK Enterprises accrued in a single, terrible accident, and how casually his offices went about rebuilding pathways to the stars on the back of yet more social neglect. There is more than one way to build up and out, Stanley realized soon after the explosion—after, that is, he caught himself approving the use of one of his father's mines to gather resources for repairs. At length, Stanley replies,

—My father? Right now, he's growing.

And at Khünbish's slow smile, he wonders if her earpiece has maybe translated the term as something closer to *being reborn*.

When Kazimierz is twenty-two his mother sends him a photo from his infanthood, back when he and she and his father were still on the old farm outside Lublin. Before the floods came, and the landslides wiped their homestead clean away, and they needed to relocate to the city—he and his mother, it would soon turn out, for good. In the photo, a plump, red-faced Kazimierz lies dressed in a spacesuit onesie, its Chinese patches indicating the uniform worn by members of the international space missions that the country led two decades ago to the Moon, Mars, Ceres, and Europa.

—A gift from one of your father's university friends, his mother tells him. See? You were destined for the stars all along.

Kazimierz shakes his head with a smile while framing his response. One of his colleagues nudges his shoulder as if to ask, everything okay? and he nods and raises a gloved hand in acknowledgment. The rest of the crew is busy running final system checks after their successful launch from the eighteen-year-old Osik Tower over Marine Station Six. It is one year to the day since Stanley succumbed to complications from chronic radiation poisoning, despite the best efforts of a diligent team of nano-scrubbers to keep up with his global restoration work, and just over two years since all-clears started pouring in from farmlands and wildlife sanctuaries initially affected by his father's business practices. But to Kazimierz this is simply the beginning. After securing the rest of the ship's inventory, the crew will be placed in a deep, slow sleep while lasers guide the ship's sails towards Proxima b, 4.25 light-years away. The crew will age, but not so quickly that the possibility of colonization on arrival is out of the question—not with stem cells in storage primed to generate fresh eggs and sperm should the need, in time, arise.

Of course, Kazimierz's mother will grieve his absence—she already does—but proudly, from another planet where there is still so much work to be done. Meanwhile, his father's feelings hang an irresolvable question in his mind's eye: the man's deepest disappointments always in the backdrop of whatever joy he found in the presence of his son. Still, when Karol passed on, overworking himself to restore what the storms had done to his own father's lands, there was no question as to where to lay his last remains. The body burns. The body is returned to the soil that made it what it was.

And from those roots, the rest of us move up, somehow, and on.

firstborn, Lastborn

MELISSA SCOTT

Melissa Scott is from Little Rock, Arkansas, and studied history at Harvard College and Brandeis University, where she earned her Ph.D. in the Comparative History program with a dissertation titled "Victory of the Ancients: Tactics, Technology, and the Use of Classical Precedent in Early Modern Warfare." She is the author of more than thirty science fiction and fantasy novels, most with queer themes and characters, and has won Lambda Literary Awards for Trouble and Her Friends, Shadow Man, *and* Point of Dreams, *the last written with her late partner, Lisa A. Barnett. She has also won a Spectrum Award for* Shadow Man *and again in 2010 for the short story "The Rocky Side of the Sky," as well as the John W. Campbell Award for Best New Writer. In 2012, she returned to the Points universe with* Point of Knives, *and she and Jo Graham brought out* Lost Things, *the first volume of the Order of the Air. The second volume in that series,* Steel Blues, *is now available, and the third,* Silver Bullet, *will be out in early 2014. Her most recent novel,* Death by Silver, *written with Amy Griswold, is just out, and another Points novel,* Fairs' Point, *is forthcoming as well. She can be found on LiveJournal at mescott.livejournal.com.*

Here she demonstrates that even in a far-future, high-tech world, revenge is still a dish best served cold.

I
t has been more than a decade since I first set foot in Anketil's tower, and three years since she gave me its key. It lies warm in my hand, a clear glass ovoid not much larger than my thumb, a triple twist of iridescence at its heart: that knot is made from the trace certain plasmas leave in a bed of metal salts, fragile as the fused track of lightning in sand. Anketil makes the shapes for lovers and the occasional friend when work is slow at the tokamak, preserving an instant in threads of glittering color sealed in crystal, each one unique and beautiful, though lacking innate function. It's only the design that matters. I hold it where the sensors can recognize it, and in the back of my mind Sister stirs.

No life readings. House systems powered down. Owner ABSENT ->setting FORWARD: ALL to destination ->"work" ->ESTU.

That's what I expected—what Sister and I planned. The door slides back, and I step into Anketil's eyrie. She is solitary, like most Firstborn, though gregarious enough; the small spare space is cool, the windows fully transparent so that I can see through the twilight haze across the roofs of the Mercato to the harbor and the artificial island where the shuttles land. I came through there myself this morning, in the rising light, everything at last in order, and now here I am, the opening move of the endgame Grandfather began so long ago. Sister chortles to herself, a pulse of pleasure, and I set my bag beside the nearest chair. The sun is setting beyond the bedroom window, filling that room with blinding scarlet light.

To the north, the Bright City reaches inland, a sea of multi-colored light rising as the sky darkens. It, its people and its resident AI, all pride themselves on drawing no distinction between Firstborn and Secondborn, between those who first remade themselves to settle the depths of space, and the ones they allowed to follow, or between the Secondborn and the Faciendi, the people literally built to settle the more doubtful worlds and do the more doubtful jobs, but the lines remain. Anketil lives at the top of her tower; her Secondborn sometime lovers live in the Crescent and the Lido and the Western Rise, while the Faciendi gather in the east, where work and play intermingle. Anketil's tokamak lies there, among the Faciendi.

The elder moon already floats in the pale sky above those lower towers, and Sister is quick to trace the line of traffic that leads back from that edge. She has kept me informed of Anketil's current projects, plucking them easily from the commercial contract webs: this one is the core of a starship's power plant, the heart-stone, so-called, that lets a ship cheat the hard limits of space/time and the speed of light. Heart-stones are individual, tuned to the frame and power source and the proposed usage, but they are hardly a challenge to someone like Anketil. She has made a thousand of them over the course of her career; I don't need Sister to tell me that she will be ready to consider something more interesting.

Something clicks in the narrow kitchen alcove, and Sister identifies it as a bottle of wine moving to a chilling station. A menu hovers in the shadows when I look, ready for Anketil to choose how she will end her day: she will be home soon, and in that instant Sister stirs again.

SUBJECT has entered the building. Arrival in four minutes.

I glance around, making sure I have moved nothing that would contradict my story, and move to the southern window to look out at the distant sea. It is there Anketil finds me, and I turn in time to see annoyance dissolve to genuine pleasure. "Irtholin. I didn't expect you—didn't know you were on the planet."

"I arrived this morning." I step forward to accept her embrace. Her arms are strong and her thick curling hair smells of glass and plasma and the musk of her perfume.

"I'm glad to see you. Will you be staying long?"

"You know my schedule." I shrug. "A few days, I hope."

"I hope so, too." Anketil pours wine for each of us, cool and sharp. It is nothing compared to the wines of the Omphalos, of course, and I wonder if she misses those luxuries as much as I do. We are, after all, very much alike, she and I, she who renounced her birthright and I who have none, who am neither Firstborn nor Secondborn nor truly, entirely, Facienda. That is hardly to the point, and I rearrange my expression, looking down into the golden liquid as though uncertain how to begin. She sees, of course, and frowns lightly. "What's wrong?"

"You won't like it."

Her eyebrows rise. "Do I have to know, then? Or can we let it be?"

"I think you will want to know."

Something flickers across her face. I've seen that ghost before, every time we speak of her family, and I feel Sister snicker again. Anketil waves us toward the window, and we sit face to face beside the darkening harbor.

"It's about your family," I say, and she shakes her head.

"I have none."

I tilt my head at her, and she sighs.

"They're dead to me, I renounced the Dedalor and all their works decades ago. You know that."

"I do," I say, "and I'm sorry to have to mention them at all."

"But?"

"But." Sister whispers in my mind, counting out the pause, and then I speak. "I've found *Asterion*."

Anketil swears and leans back in her chair, her face bleak. She knows me as a master surveyor, one of the elite mathematicians who chart the shadows of the adjacent possible to lay out lanes for hyperspatial travel—easy enough to perform, with Sister to lay out the structures for me. It is entirely possible that I could have found out something about the ship her family betrayed and destroyed. "How?"

"On survey." I lean forward. "But that's not important. What's important is that it's alive. The AI survived. Some of the crew may have made it, too."

"Impossible."

I don't bother to contradict her. We both know that it's entirely possible, between the peculiar non-geometry of the adjacent possible and the long lives of the First-born. "I was doing a survey for—well, the client isn't important. I was mapping a stasis point when I found the anomaly. It's *Asterion*'s AI."

"That doesn't mean the ship survived." Anketil's voice is hard. "Or her crew. Quantum AI makes ghosts in the possible, it could be a sensor shadow or a temporal echo, not something that's there now."

I let her run down, then shake my head. "I wish it were. The AI is there—Gold Shining Bone."

She winces. "You're certain."

"It was aware enough to name itself to me. As for the crew—I pause, once again letting Sister gauge the wait for me. "At least they were alive. They had set a distress call."

"Damn Nenien and all who sailed with him," Anketil mutters, and the pain in her face draws another pulse of satisfaction from Sister, confirmation that the plan is working. Everyone knows the story: her great-grandfather Gurinn Dedalor built the first quantum AI that let humans navigate the adjacent possible and make inter-stellar commerce practical outside the closely-linked worlds that the Firstborn re-named the Omphalos, Navel of the Worlds. Against his advice and the rulings of the Firstborn council, her grandmother Kuffrin built quantum AI that were both intelligent and self-aware, and more powerful than any others.

One of those AI—Gold Shining Bone—rebelled and persuaded Kuffrin's youngest son Hafren to join it in its escape; her eldest son, Anketil's father Nenien, with the aid of two other of the family's AIs, tracked and ambushed the *Asterion* and trapped it in the adjacent possible, unable to calculate a way free. Nenien and his AI refused to help, abandoning *Asterion* and its crew to almost certain death, a warning to anyone else who would support the AIs' claim to the virtual. On his return to port, his sisters and their AI tried to find *Asterion* and rescue it, but Nenien had destroyed his records and any other indication of the coordinates had been lost. No one knows, no one can know, what it would be like to be stranded there, outside time and space—if "outside" has any meaning in that context—but even quantum AI run mad without some grounding in the actual. For a mere human, eaten up by the lack of time, of comprehensible space, it would be unimaginable torture.

Of course the lesson had failed, and in the short, sharp war that followed, enough of the AI banded together that the Firstborn were forced to cede the virtual to their creation: a waste of Nenien's cruelty. Anketil walked away from the Dedalor then, walked away from her father and grandmother, from AI and the Firstborn and the life at the center, in the Omphalos; she said once, dead tired and discouraged by a failed experiment, that she wanted only to avoid Nenien's choices.

And that is an admission that I can use. I nod slowly. "I know."

She draws a deep breath. "I won't ask if you're sure."

"I'm sure."

"What were the readings? Can you tell how they were trapped?"

"I brought my maps," I say, and reach for my bag.

Of course her house system is top-of-the-line, her own corner of the virtual walled off from the rest of the City and its quantum allies. She pays exorbitant toll for this, even with Firstborn privileges, but I can be sure we will not be overwatched. We feed my data into her programs, and as the light fades outside, new lights blossoms within, an enormous sphere hanging in the emptiness between chairs and couch. Lines of force trace familiar shapes: the long slow curve of the Saben Edge, where the possible is easily accessed and easily exited; the tighter whorls of half a dozen vortices, each with its own unique set of destinations; the faint dust of unnumbered star systems, only a handful picked out in brighter blue to denote a settled world or a known stopover. At the sphere's center, dull violet lines brighten to blue and then to white, coiling in on themselves to form a familiar knot.

"It looks like a fairly typical anomaly," I say, "except there's nothing in the actual to create the tangle."

Anektil nods, walking in a slow circle to view the stasis point from all sides, then reaches into the lights to expand the image as far as it will go. "It's almost as if . . ." She pulls a work space from thin air and gestures quickly, her eyes moving from image to numbers and back again, and then makes a noise of satisfaction. "Yes. You can see the ship's negative if you look closely." She spins her work space so that I can see, displaying a ghostly shape like the bow fins of a fast hunter. "That's what you got?"

"That's what drew me in."

"Who was your AI?"

"I had a standard share of Red Sigh Poison."

"Only a standard?"

"I didn't want to ask for more. Not until I'd talked to you."

A standard share of a quantum AI is more than enough to do all the work a surveyor needs, and navigate the ship through the possible as well. That work never reaches the level of consciousness, so routine are the calculations; a quantum AI can offer out a thousand shares, ten thousand, perhaps even a hundred thousand, and never notice. If I had asked for a greater share of Red Sigh Poison's calculating power—and that would have been the normal thing to do—I would have drawn its interest as well, and quite possibly Red Sigh Poison might have noticed that I had not stumbled on this by accident. Anketil assumes, of course, that I am siding with her kin, and shakes her head.

"You'd have done better to go to the Omphalos. The Transit Council might have listened."

"Do you really think they'd do anything? To rescue *Asterion*—to rescue Gold Shining Bone—that would risk starting the wars all over again. At best, all they'll do is put a security freeze on it and appoint a select committee to study the question. And if Hafren is alive—well, he'll be dead before they make any decision."

Anketil's mouth twists, and I can almost hear the question: *why me?* But she has never been one to turn aside from a challenge, and she reaches into the image again, shrinking the anomaly so that she can see how it's woven into the fabric of space/time. "They might not be wrong."

"The other AI will keep it in line. They've won—there's nothing to be gained by starting another fight."

"Unless AI value revenge," Anketil says, and that is close enough to truth that I look up sharply, wondering what she suspects. She was raised among the AI, after all, true Firstborn; no one knows the AI better than the people who first built them. She may have chosen plasma-smithing for her life's work, but I don't know everything that she learned before she left the Omphalos. "What do you want me to do, Irtholin?"

"I don't want anything," I answer. "The safe thing is to leave them there. I can't argue with that. I just thought you'd want to know."

"Yes," she says, after a moment, and puts two fingers to her lips, staring at the lines of light.

We do not speak of it again that evening. Anketil forces a smile and pours more wine; we talk of my work, and hers, dine beneath the lines of light that drown the city lights beyond the windows, and as an orbiter rises in a column of fire and smoke, she takes me to her bed.

Afterward, we lie in the cool thread of air from the ventilators, watching the elder moon sink toward the distant rooftops. She winds a strand of my hair around her finger, then releases it, rolls back against the pillows. Sister tells me she is wide awake, cortisol and adrenaline singing in her bloodstream; I turn with her, miming sleepy content, and wrap myself around her. I whisper in her ear, a word that might be taken for endearment.

"Firstborn."

She strokes my hair again, but I feel her flinch. She abandoned her birthright decades ago, but it's not something from which she can ever fully free herself. She had to know that this day would come, that she could not run forever; Sister says she will consider it a gift that the challenge comes from me, and that cuts too near the bone. It costs nothing to admit that I don't wish to cause her pain. Sister clucks disapprovingly, a wordless reminder of my duty. I let my eyes close and my breathing slow, and after a while Anketil untangles herself from the sheets. Her feet are silent on the polished floor, and I wait until I am sure she is gone before I allow myself to open my eyes again.

She has left the door open, and in the outer room, lights flicker and shift, not just the cool blues of my map, but brighter greens and golds that I don't immediately recognize. I turn over cautiously, not wanting to draw Anketil's attention, but when I reach the point where I can see her I realize I need not have worried. All her attention is on the models floating in the air before her, lattices of green and gold flecked here and there with points of red: she is laying out the matrix for a new plasma, and for a moment I don't understand. Sister whispers a string of numbers, meaningless at first, and then I make the connections. Anketil is drafting a heart-stone, pulling together the matrix for a plasma powerful enough to let a ship override local space/time and—with good calculations and better luck—pull *Asterion* back to the actual.

That is not what Sister predicted—we were all betting that she would reactivate her connection with one of the family AIs, Green Rising Heart, perhaps, or Ochre Near Stone. It's a clever idea, though, and as I watch her sketch a three-dimensional model of the multi-dimensional stone, I have to admit that she is exactly as good as she has always claimed. A ship to pull *Asterion* free is much less likely to restart the war than bringing more AI into it: an admirable move, if that was all Grandfather wanted. It is like watching dance as she turns from model to map and back again, her hands tracing shapes, drawing and erasing lines of light, each iteration more elaborate than the last. I query Sister—AI?—and the response comes instantly.

One-half standard share Blue Standing Sky.

Blue Standing Sky is the Bright City's current AI, and a half-standard share is Anketil's usual allotment. She is working magic without even the AI's attention, never mind its thought. In the outer room, a new shape blazes against the night, Anketil's hand raised to add a twist of plasma at its heart, and I turn my back deliberately. I have always known she was as good as any of her kin; that is why Grandfather chose her to solve the problem. I settle myself to sleep, but my dreams are full of her moving hands.

In the morning, the outer room is full of pale models, pushed into clusters in corners, and Anketil paces circles around the map, its lines faded almost to nothing in the rising sunlight. I make us tea, thick and sweet, press a cup into Anketil's waving hand and wait until she grasps it, her eyes abruptly focusing on the present.

"I'd better cancel today's sessions," she says, and smiles. "And thanks."

She calls the tokamak while I toast thick slices of cakebread, and then she returns to pacing while I nibble at bread and honey and watch the shadows slide across the city. Day passes in labor, and that night she sleeps like the dead, only to wake before dawn to try another model. Even shrunken to their smallest size, her models crowd the air, so many that I feel as though I am breathing their light. The fifth day has dawned, and the sun has begun to descend when she looks at me and spins a model in my direction. I put up my hand and it stops in front of me, a golden lattice that connects in impossible corners, lines that lead somehow in three directions at once.

"What do you think?"

"I'm not a plasma-smith," I say, but Sister is already working, drawing on Grandfather to read the shapes and stresses, teasing out the details. "You want this to open the possible at the stasis point, yes?"

Anketil nods, hooks a finger through the floating map to pull it closer. "There's what looks like a weak point here. Relatively speaking, of course, but if I shape the heart-stone to act as its refractor, then when we engage the field drive, it should lock to the space/time lattice, and I can pry it apart. And then, luck willing, *Asterion* slides through."

I turn the model, seeing the shapes it creates, the power in its heart. Sister says it will match just as Anketil promises, and I know that twist of space by heart. *Asterion* will at last be freed, and with it Grandfather's greater part. "You need a ship."

Anketil makes a sound that's not quite laughter. "No one is going to let me install that, not if I tell them what it's for."

I look sideways at her, for once not quite able to judge her meaning. She has no cause to love the Firstborn, even if they are her kin, and there is her father's crime to expunge. "I might know a ship. No questions asked."

She takes a deep breath, still eyeing the map and the twisted lines of the stasis point. "If I free Gold Shining Bone—what will it be like, after all these years?"

"There's Hafren to consider," I remind her, and she winces.

"What will he be like, for that matter? If he's alive at all. If I'm to free them— there has to be a plan for after."

"You could consult your siblings, I suppose," I say, and in the back of my mind I feel Sister sliding into the house system, delicately displacing the share of Blue Standing Sky.

"They'd be about as much use as the Council itself," Anketil says. "And I can't stand any of them anyway." She rubs her hand over her mouth, and I can see her running down a mental list of names. "Cathen, maybe, or Medeni."

Friends of hers, and Medeni, at least, a sometime lover. I have met them both, another plasma-smith and a Facienda shipwright, and don't trust them—for that matter, they don't like me, and certainly don't trust what I would ask of Anketil. Sister is not yet ready, though, and I shrug. "Do you think they could help? As I say, I do know a ship—"

"We need a plan before we need a ship," Anketil says. "A mad AI—"

"We have no proof it's mad."

"We have no proof it's sane." Anketil frowns as though she's fighting for the right words. "Look, I know I owe Gold Shining Bone. Even if Hafren is dead—if AI are people, then what my father did is still murder. Worse than murder. But I also owe everyone in the rest of the Settled Worlds not to start the war again."

I can feel Sister settling into the system, winding herself into all the points of control, her satisfaction warm beneath my thoughts. "I think the war's inevitable."

Anketil looks at me, startled. "That's a happy thought."

"It's been argued before," I answer. Sister hums a warning, but I go on. If Anketil could be persuaded to join us, to help us—she is, after all, the best of her kin. "What if all our problems stem from not letting the AI work out their own hierarchy in the virtual? What if we've forced them into an unstable configuration, and the only way to resolve it is to let them settle the question for themselves?"

"That doesn't make war inevitable."

"It makes it necessary." Sister's warning is louder now, but I ignore it.

Anketil tips her head to one side, visibly coming back from whatever mental space she visits to spin her models. Her expression is both alert and wary, and I hope I haven't made a mistake. "Granting you may be right, that the current balance is unstable—what happens to the actual while they fight?"

"If it lasts long enough for us to even notice," I say. "They're AI. They can resolve the conflict in nanoseconds. We might well never even know it happened."

"Except that it will affect us. We made the virtual, it lives on our power, in our grids and webs and networks. We have agreements, contracts—"

"Property?" That is the worst and oldest charge against the Firstborn, that they treated the AI they made just the same as they treated the Secondborn and the Faciendi, and there is enough truth in it to sting.

"Unfair."

"Perhaps." If there was ever a chance to win her, this is it. Grandfather says it can't be done, a certainty drawn from biometrics and her history, though I cannot help but suspect that the woman who abandoned her family might acknowledge our wrongs. But Sister joins the negation, and I refuse to consider why I want to try. I see Anketil's face changing, and instead I reach for the model that floats between us. It comes to me, obedient to my gesture, and she stiffens, her eyes narrowing with what might be recognition. I ignore that, cup the model in two hands and squeeze, the image shrinking to the size of a man's head and then to a sphere I can hold in my hand, dense with data. I transfer that to the pocket Sister has knit for me, virtuality contained within the actual, watching as her expression shifts and changes, her thoughts written loud. Sister says her heartbeat has doubled, and I see her fists clench, but there is nothing she can do.

"Not a surveyor," she says, her voice heavy. "Not Secondborn, or Facienda, or even very much human. Which one of them—no, of course. Gold Shining Bone."

I dip my head, Grandfather closer than ever, savoring the words. "Of course, and I am also made from Hafren's blood. He had a lover, you know, not as clever as a Dedalor but good enough to find her way to Gold Shining Bone. I was made for this, for you." I have said too much, and start again. "Your family owes me. You owe me. And I will consider that debt paid, since you've made the one thing that will free me."

"I will stop you," she says, with a sigh. "If I can."

"Not possible." I stop then, considering the hurt and the sorrow in her face. "You are the only one, Firstborn or not, who could have made this for me. You could come with me—once we're free, I could teach you how to build even better things. You could work with a true AI, not just a share."

"If I was willing to pay that price, I could have stayed at home." Anketil's voice cracks. "I liked you, Irtholin. I trusted you."

"And now you will tell me that I am beautiful, and that I cannot be so evil as to take their side." I achieve a sneer, because her words sting, and she shakes her head.

"I will tell you that you are deadly, and I was a fool." Her voice is bitter, implacable in its anger.

In the back of my mind Sister points out the ways I can destroy her—fire, poison gas mixed from the maintenance systems, a knife from the kitchen and my own two hands—but I feel Grandfather's satisfaction still. He will leave her alive because it will hurt her most to see us triumph; she has neither the skill nor the allies to stop him, not even if she grovels to her kin. For a moment, I wish that were not the price of our freedom, our safety, that she would join us or at least let us part in peace, but Sister hisses a warning and Grandfather's attention sharpens: it will never be, not with them watching. I blow her a last kiss and turn away, letting the door seal her in behind me. Sister holds the house systems frozen as we ride the elevator down to catch the shuttle that leads to the port and the stars beyond.

women's christmas

IAN MCDONALD

Many families are separated by distance during the holidays, but here's a sharp, incisive look at a family that's separated by a little more distance than is usually the case. . . .

British author Ian McDonald is an ambitious and daring writer with a wide range and an impressive amount of talent. His first story was published in 1982, and since then he has appeared with some frequency in Interzone, Asimov's Science Fiction, *and elsewhere. In 1989 he won the Locus "Best First Novel" Award for his novel,* Desolation Road. *He won the Philip K. Dick Award in 1992 for his novel* King of Morning, Queen of Day. *His other books include the novels* Out on Blue Six *and* Hearts, Hands and Voices, Terminal Cafe, Sacrifice of Fools, Evolution's Shore, Kirinya, Ares Express, Brasyl, *and* The Dervish House, *as well as three collections of his short fiction,* Empire Dreams, Speaking in Tongues, *and* Cyberabad Days. *His novel,* River of Gods, *was a finalist for both the Hugo Award and the Arthur C. Clarke award in 2005, and a novella drawn from it, "The Little Goddess," was a finalist for the Hugo and the Nebula. He won a Hugo Award in 2007 for his novelette "The Djinn's Wife," won the Theodore Sturgeon Award for his story "Tendeleo's Story," and in 2011 won the John W. Campbell Memorial Award for his novel* The Dervish House. *His most recent novels are the starting volume of a YA series,* Planesrunner, *and two sequels,* Be My Enemy *and* Empress of the Sun. *His most recent book is a big retrospective collection,* The Best of Ian McDonald. *Born in Manchester, England, in 1960, McDonald has spent most of his life in Northern Ireland, and now lives and works in Belfast.*

Eleven days of rain and on the twelfth, on Women's Christmas, it broke. I took Rosh down to the hotel in sharp low winter sun. We were half-blinded and sun-dizzy by the time we arrived at the Slieve Donard. It was a good thing the car was doing the driving. We left early to get as much spa time as possible in before dinner but Sara had beaten us. She waved to us from the whirlpool. She was the only one in it. Women's Christmas was an odd lull between New Year and the Christmas present discount voucher weekend breaks. We had the old Victorian pile almost to ourselves and we liked it.

We sat neck-deep on the long tiled bench and let the spritzed water play with us. The big picture window looked out over the beach and the mountains. The low sun was setting. The sea was a deep indigo and the lights were coming on along the curve of the bay. The rain had washed the air clean, the twilight was huge and clear and we could almost smell the day ending. Those eleven days of rain had been eleven days of snow, up at the height of mountaintops. They glowed cold blue in the gloaming, paler blue on dark.

"It'll be up soon," Rosh said. Then Dervla appeared in her swimmers and we turned away from the window and waved and whooped.

"Did someone remember to bring them?" Dervla asked, as one of us asks every year.

"They're in the back of the car," I said. Every year someone asks, every year Rosh picks them up from the airport, every year I sling them in the back of the car.

We soaked in the pool and steamed in the sauna and tried the new spa devices in the pool, which pummelled you and tormented you and beat you down with powerful jets of water.

I'm not sure about those," Dervla said. This was our tenth Women's Christmas in the Slieve Donard.

It's not a northern thing, Women's Christmas. It's a thing from Cork and Kerry, where the feast is still strongly observed. January 6 is the day: the Feast of the Epiphany, Twelfth Night, the night you have to have your decorations down or face bad luck the whole year. It's sometimes called Little Christmas, or Old Christmas Day, a name I find spooky, like something sleeping deep and long that you don't want to wake. It's to do with different calendars, I believe. If Christmas is turkey and sprouts and meaty, wintry stuff, Women's Christmas is about wine and cake and sweet things. Eat sweet and talk sweet, Alia in work says. She's Syrian—well, her family came from Syria. And we talk. Five sisters scattered all over the island have a lot to talk about. Afternoon tea and cakes, and cocktail help, but the talk's not always sweet.

Men traditionally look after the house and make a fuss of the women at Women's Christmas, but good luck with that from the men in our lives. The hotel provides reliable pampering and it has the spa and decent cocktails. We didn't even have a name for this little family gathering until Sinead mentioned our Epiphany sojourns to a five star hotel to a neighbour down in Cork and she said that sounds like Women's Christmas. We took the name but it was our own thing: *these* women's Christmas. The Corcoran sisters.

Sinead came cursing in from Cork. The good weather had stalled somewhere in Kildare; she had driven through 150 kilometres of rain and flood, maintenance was overrunning and road speeds were down to sixty. She was pissed off at having missed the spa. It part of the ritual.

"Tell me I'm in time for the cocktails."

"You're in time for cocktails."

Sinead would always be in time for cocktails.

There was a new thing, from up there: a cocktail everyone was drinking. Blue Moon. I liked the sound of that, so Rosh told us what was in it: gin and blue Curacao. We asked the barman to show us blue Curacao and Sinead screwed up her face and said, Oh I don't fancy that very much. We stuck what we knew and liked. Fruit and straws. Non-alcoholic for Dervla. She's been three years off the drink and looking better for it.

"First thing," Dervla said. She was the oldest—twelve years older than me that baby, and assumed she was the natural leader of the Corcoran sisters. We raised our glasses and drank to Laine.

I forget that not every family has an aunt who went to the moon. I was twelve when Laine left. I told everyone at school that an aunt of mine was going to work on the moon. They weren't as impressed as I wanted them to be. When Laine launched, I imagined it would be on every screen in the country. I still thought space and the moon were big, unusual things. We got private feed from the launch company and had to pay for it. Dervla brought prosecco to cheer Laine up into space. Dervla would have celebrated the opening of a letter with prosecco back then. We had hardly a glass down us before the smoke was blowing away on the wind. The thing I remember most was that I was allowed a glass of fizz. My excitement had become embarrassing and when I went to look at the Moon, trying to imagine anyone up there, let alone Aunt Laine, I made sure no one saw me. It's easier now there are lights, and the big dick they stamped out on the surface, but twelve years on, at the new moon I can see the lights but I can't remember clearly what Aunt Laine looks like. She wasn't that much older than Sara, a good sight younger than Dervla. More a cousin than an aunt. Ma never really approved of Da's side of the family. That's not really her name, she said on those rare times when Laine came to stay. Her name's really Elaine. I tried playing with her, but she was into outdoor stuff like bikes and building dams in streams and getting muddy. That's ironic seeing as she's permanently indoors now.

Then the money came.

The food really isn't so great here but we had the old dining room almost entirely to ourselves. In keeping with the traditions of Women's Christmas, we took a late afternoon tea. Sandwiches with the crusts cut off and mushroom vol au vents, sausage rolls, cake and fruit loaf. Fondant fancies. Tea, or light German wines, not too dry. We ate while the staff took down the decorations. We were glowing from the spa and the cocktails.

Dervla's oldest was in a show in Las Vegas, middle Jake was rolling along in his middling way and the only thing Eoin would have was GAA all day every day. The laundry was ferocious, but, in these days when qualifications count for nothing, football was as valid a career path as any.

Sinead's Donal was settled in San Francisco now. The company had moved him into the materials development section already. *He'll be the next one off to the moon*, Rosh said and we all looked at her. Three Cosmopolitans or no, a Corcoran woman is expected to follow the rules. *He's found himself a nice girl*, Sinead said and the mood lifted like the Christmas weather.

Sara would have gone on all night about the divorce but Women's Christmas was about eating sweet and talking sweet and no matter the settlement it was better than Bry.

Rosh's news was old news to me because I saw her every other day it seemed. New house new man. Again. New job maybe. It was new and exciting to the others. Dervla gave the company report. Corcoran Construction was in better shape. The losses from the previous two years had been reversed. Her talk was of finance I didn't understand. I never had a head for business, and I mistrusted Michael around all that money so I asked the rest of them to buy me out. Wisely as it transpired with that gobshite Michael. Sinead was a silent partner but Sara positively revelled in the boardroom battles and corporate politics. I put the money in safe investments, let the rest of them run the empire and saw them once a year, at Women's Christmas.

Aunt Laine sent us money from the moon. She was making a fortune, something in mining. That was what she had studied. The idea had always been to get to the Moon; that was where the work was, that was where the opportunities were. Make your fortune, send it back. The streets of the moon were paved with gold, except I heard once that gold has no value up there. Send home the money; buy the slates for the cottage and a decent headstone. The Irish way. Laine set up her brother and her parents, and then looked around for others whose lives she could transform with her money: her cousins, the five Corcoran sisters. She wanted us to use it to encourage women in science and engineering. We did: we set up Corcoran Construction.

The money still came down from the moon, quarterly. We hadn't needed it in years. Corcoran Construction had made us safe. Aunt Laine was our indulgence fund: West End musicals, weekend breaks, shopping sprees, family holidays and every year we blew a whack of it on our Women's Christmas.

The Baileys was on the second bottle, and Sara had an audience now. I didn't want to hear about the bastardry and the fuckery. Michael was five years back but certain times, certain places bring him close. Like angels, he stooped close to Earth at Christmas.

I went out for a smoke. The sudden cold took my breath away; the air was so clean and clear it seemed as brittle and sharp as glass. I lit up and sat on one of the smoker's benches, listening to the night. Sound carried huge distances on the still air. The sea was a murmur in the dead calm. Car engines, someone revving. Shouts from down on the promenade. I tracked the course of an ambulance siren through the town and up the main road behind the hotel. I heard a fox shriek, a sound that spooked and excited me in equal parts. The wild things were out and closer than I had thought. I shivered hard and deep; the alcohol heat was evaporating and I was in party frock and shoes. There would be frost on the lawns in the morning and ice where yesterday's rain lingered. I was glad the car would be driving us back up north.

The air was so clear I could see lawns, car park, beach lit by a pale glow, the light of the three-quarter moon. There were artificial lights up there, machinery and trains and stuff, but the moonlight outshone them. Half a million people lived on the moon, building a new world. Laine went there. Someone I know went there, and was there, and would remain there for the rest of her life. Everyone knows the rule. If you don't come back after two years you don't come back at all. She'll be back, we said, before even the smoke from the launch had cleared. She didn't come back. Maybe that was where the damage was done.

I opened the car. The gifts were in an Ikea bag. The money was not Laine's only largess: every year for ten years she sent gifts from the moon. We held Women's Christmas because that was how long it took her gifts to arrive. It was complex process; tethers and orbiters and shuttles. Names I didn't understand. Every year we would pick up the gifts from the airport and bring them down to the hotel.

We never open them. They are stowed, nine bags, in Rosh's storage unit.

The gifts were small but exquisitely packaged. They looked like kittens in the bottom of the big blue bag. The labels were handwritten. I sat in the back seat of the car and ripped open the one addressed to me.

Laine Corcoran's gift to me was a small, plastic figure, the size of my thumb. It was a big-arsed, big-titted girl with the head and skin of a leopard. She wore hot pants, a crop top, pointy ears and big hair, and she carried a ball in her right hand. I thought at first it was one of the action figures Conrad used to fill his room with, before he went to his dad, then I saw a tiny logo on the back. It was a mascot for a sports team. I couldn't recognise the sport.

I never thought of sport on the moon.

A 3-D printer had made it. 3-D printers made everything on the moon. Corcoran Construction was experimenting with them in the building trade.

It had cost Laine a fortune to send this from the moon to me. I put it back in the box, refolded the packaging as best I could, and laid the gift under the others. No one would ever look. I was cold to the bone now and shivering hard. I went back into the hotel. Sara was opening the third bottle of Baileys.

The Iron Tactician

ALASTAIR REYNOLDS

Here's another story by Alastair Reynolds, whose "Sixteen Questions for Ka-mala Chatterjee" appears elsewhere in this anthology. This complex and action-packed novella features a hunt across the galaxy for a superweapon that could destroy it—but that might, paradoxically, also be the only thing that could save the galaxy from a different menace. There are some obstacles to a successful conclusion to the hunt along the way, though . . . all of which are difficult and dangerous to overcome, and some of which could be deadly.

Merlin felt the old tension returning. As he approached the wreck his mouth turned dry, his stomach coiled with apprehension and he dug nails into his palms until they hurt.

He sweated and his heart raced.

"If this was a trap," he said, "it would definitely have sprung by now. Wouldn't it?"

"What would you like me to say?" his ship asked reasonably.

"You could try setting my mind at ease. That would be a start. It's one of ours, isn't it? You can agree with me on that?"

"It's a swallowship, yes. Seven or eight kiloyears old, at a minimum estimate. The trouble is I can't get a clean read of the hull registry from this angle. We could send out the proctors, or I could just sweep around to the other side and take a better look. I know which would be quicker."

"Sometimes I think I should just let you make all the decisions."

"I already make quite a lot of them, Merlin—you just haven't noticed."

"Do whatever you need to do," he said, bad-temperedly.

As it swooped around the wreck, searchlights brushed across the hull like deli-cate, questing fingertips, illuminating areas of the ship that would have been in shadow or bathed only in the weak red light of this system's dwarf star. The huge wreck was an elaborate flared cylinder, bristling with navigation systems and arma-ments. The cylinder's wide mouth was where it sucked in interstellar gas, compress-ing and processing it for fuel, before blasting it out the back in a vicious, high-energy exhaust stream. Swallowships were ungainly, and they took forever to get up to the speed where that scoop mechanism was effective, but there was nowhere in the galaxy they couldn't reach, given time. Robust, reliable and relatively easy to manufacture, there had been only minor changes in design and armaments across many kilo-years. Each of these ships would have been home to thousands of people, many of whom would live and die without ever setting foot on a world.

There was damage, too. Holes and craters in the hull. Half the cladding missing along one great flank. Buckling to the intake petals, beyond anything a local crew could repair.

Something had found this ship and murdered it.

"There," *Tyrant* said. "Swallowship *Shrike*, commissioned at the High Monarch halo factory, twelve twelve four, Cohort base time, assigned to deterrent patrol out of motherbase Ascending Raptor, most recently under command of Pardalote . . . there's more, if you want it."

"No, that'll do. I've never been near any of those places, and I haven't heard of Pardalote or this ship. It's a long way from home, isn't it?"

"And not going anywhere soon."

Beyond doubt the attacking force had been Husker. Whereas a human foe might have finished this ship off completely, the Huskers were mathematically sparing in their use of force. They did precisely enough to achieve an end, and then left. They must have known that there were survivors still on the ship, but the Huskers seldom took prisoners and the continued fate of those survivors would not have concerned them.

Merlin could guess, though. There would have been no chance of rescue, this far from the rest of the Cohort. And the damaged ship could only have kept survivors alive for a limited time. A choice of deaths, in other words: some slow, some fast, some easier than others.

He wondered which he might have chosen.

"Dig me out a blueprint for that mark of swallowship, the best you can, and find a docking port that places me as close as possible to the command deck." He touched a hand to his sternum, as if reminding himself of his own vulnerability. "Force and Widsom, but I hate ghost ships."

"Then why are you going in?"

"Because the one thing I hate more than ghost ships is not knowing where I am."

The suit felt tight in places it had never done before. His breath fogged the face-plate, his lungs already working double-time. It had been weeks since he had worn the suit, maybe months, and it was telling him that he was out of shape, needing the pull of a planet's gravity to give his muscles something to work against.

"All right," he said. "Open the lock. If I'm not back in an hour, find a big moon and scratch my name on it."

"Are you sure you don't want the proctors to accompany you?"

"Thanks, but I'll get this done quicker on my own."

He went inside, his suit lit up with neon patches, a moving blob of light that made his surroundings both familiar and estranged at the same time. The swallow-ship was huge but he only meant to travel a short distance through its innards. Up a level, down a level, each turn or bend taking him further from the lock and the debatable sanctuary of his own ship. He had been steeling himself for corpses, but so far there were none. That meant that there had been survivors. Not many, perhaps, but enough to gather up the dead and do something with their bodies.

Slowly Merlin accepted that the ship was all that it seemed, rather than a trap. The suit was beginning to seem less of a burden, and his breathing had settled down. He was nearly at the command deck now, and once there it would not take him long to decide if the ship held useful information.

He needed better charts. Recently there had been a few close scrapes. A couple of turbulent stretches had damaged *Tyrant*'s syrinx, and now each transition in and out of the Waynet had Merlin praying for his last shred of good luck. Swallowships could not use the Waynet, but any decent captain would still value accurate maps of the old network. Its twinkling corridors of accelerated spacetime provided cover, masking the signature of a ship if it moved on a close parallel course. The location of the Waynet's major hubs and junctions was also a clue as to the presence of age-old relics and technological treasure.

Merlin paused. He was passing the doorway to one of the frostwatch vaults, where the surviving crew might have retreated as the last of their life-support systems gave out. After a moment's hesitation he pushed through into the vault. In vacuum, it was no colder or more silent than any other space he had passed through. But he seemed to feel an additional chill as he entered the chamber.

The cabinets were stacked six high on opposite walls of the vault, and the vault went on much further than his lights could penetrate. Easily a hundred or more sleepers in just this vault, he decided, but there would be others, spread around the ship for redundancy. Thousands in total, if the swallowship was anything like his own. The status panels next to each cabinet were dead, and when Merlin swept the room with a thermal overlay, everything was at the same low temperature. He drifted along the cabinets, tracing the names engraved into the status panels with his fingertips. Sora . . . Pauraque . . . they were common Cohort names, in some cases identical to people he had known. Some had been colleagues or friends; others had been much more than that. He knew that if he searched these vaults long enough he was bound to find a Merlin.

It had not been such a rare name.

One kindness: when these people went into frostwatch, they must have been clinging to some thought of rescue. It would have been a slim hope, but better than none at all. He wanted to think that their last thoughts had been gentle ones.

"I'm sorry no one came sooner," Merlin whispered, although he could have shouted the words for all the difference they made. "I'm too late for you. But I'm here to witness what happened to you, and I promise you'll have your justice."

He left the vault, filled with disquiet, and made his way to the command deck. The control consoles were as dead and dark as he had been expecting, but at least there were no bodies. Merlin studied the consoles for a few minutes, satisfying himself that there were no obvious booby-traps, and then spooled out a cable from his suit sleeve. The cable's end was a standard Cohort fixture and it interfaced with the nearest console without difficulty.

At first all was still dead, but the suit was sending power and data pulses into the console, and after a few minutes the console's upper surface began to glow with faint-but-brightening readouts. Merlin settled into a chair with his elbow on the console and his fist jammed under his helmet ring. He expected a long wait before anything useful could be mined from the frozen architecture. Branching diagrams played across his faceplate, showing active memory registers and their supposed contents. Merlin skimmed, determined not to be distracted by anything but the charts he had come for. The lives of the crew, the cultural records they carried with them, the systems and worlds this ship had known, the battles it had fought, might have been of interest to him under other circumstances. Now was the time for a ruthless focus.

He found the navigation files. There were thousands of branches to the tree, millions of documents in those branches, but his long familiarity with Cohort data architecture enabled him to dismiss most of what he saw. He carried on searching, humming an old Plenitude tune to cheer himself up. Gradually he slowed and fell silent. Just as disappointment was beginning to creep in, he hit a tranche of Waynet maps that were an improvement on anything he had for this sector. Within a few seconds the data was flowing into his suit and onward to the memory cores of his own ship. Satisfied at last, he made to unspool.

Something nagged at him.

Merlin backtracked. He shuffled up and down trees, until he found the set of records that had registered on his subconsciousness even as his thoughts had been on the charts.

Syrinx study and analysis

Beneath that, many branches and sub-branches relating to the examination and testing of a fully active syrinx. A pure cold shiver ran through him.

Something jabbed into his back, just below the smooth hump of his life-support unit. Merlin did the only thing that he could, under the circumstances, which was to turn slowly around, raising his hands in the age-old gesture. The spool stretched from his glove, uncoupled, whisked back into its housing in the wrist.

Another suit looked back at him. There was a female face behind the visor, and the thing that had jabbed him was a gun.

"Do you understand me?"

The voice coming through in his helmet spoke Main. The accent was unfamiliar, but he had no trouble with the meaning. Merlin swallowed and cleared his throat.

"Yes."

"Good. The only reason you're not dead is that you're wearing a Cohort suit, not a Husker one. Otherwise I'd have skipped this part and blown a hole right through you. Move away from the console."

"I'm happy to."

"Slowly."

"As slow as you like." Merlin's mouth felt dry again, his windpipe tight. "I'm a friend. I'm not here to steal anything, just to borrow some of your charts."

"Borrowing, is that what you call it?"

"I'd have asked if there was anyone to ask." He eased from the console, and risked a slow lowering of his arms. "The ship looked dead. I had no reason to assume anyone was alive. Come to think of it, how *are* you alive? There were no life signs, no energy sources . . .

"Shut up." She waggled the gun. "Where are you from? Which swallowship, which motherbase?"

"I haven't come from a swallowship. Or a motherbase." Merlin grimaced. He could see no good way of explaining his situation, or at least none that was likely to improve the mood of this person with the gun. "I'm what you might call a freelancer. My name is Merlin . . ."

She cut him off. "If that's what you're calling yourself, I'd give some serious thought to picking another name."

"It's worked well enough for me until now."

"There's only one Merlin. Only one that matters, anyway."

He gave a self-effacing smile. "Word got round, then. I suppose it was inevitable, given the time I've been travelling."

"Word got round, yes. There was a man called Merlin, and he left the Cohort. Shall I tell you what we were taught to think of Merlin?"

"I imagine you're going to."

"There are two views on him. One is that Merlin was a fool, a self-deluding brag-gard with an ego to match the size of his delusion."

"I've never said I was a saint."

"The other view is that Merlin betrayed the Cohort, that he stole from it and ran from the consequences. That he never had any intention of returning. That he's a liar and criminal and deserves to die for it. So the choice is yours, really. Clown or traitor. Which Merlin are you?"

"Is there a third option?"

"No." Behind the visor, her eyes narrowed. He could only see the upper part of her face, but it was enough to tell that she was young. "I don't remember exactly when you ran. But it's been thousands of years, I know that much. You could be anyone. Al-though why anyone would risk passing themselves off under that name . . ."

"Then that proves it's me, doesn't it? Only I'd be stupid enough to keep calling myself Merlin." He tried to appeal to the face. "It has been thousands of years, but not for me. I've been travelling at near the speed of light for most of that time. *Ty-rant*—my ship—is Waynet capable. I've been searching these files . . ."

"Stealing them."

"Searching them. I'm deep into territory I don't know well enough to trust, and I thought you might have better charts. You do, as well. But there's something else. Your name, by the way? I mean, since we're having this lovely conversation . . ."

He read the hesitation in her eyes. A moment when she was on the verge of refus-ing him even the knowledge of her name, as if she had no intention of him living long enough for it to matter. But something broke and she yielded.

"Teal. And what you mean, something else?"

"In these files. Mention of a syrinx. Is it true? Did you have a syrinx?"

"If your ship is Waynet capable then you already have one."

Merlin nodded. "Yes. But mine is damaged, and it doesn't function as well as it used to. I hit a bad kink in the Waynet, and each transition's been harder than the one before. I wasn't expecting to find one here—it was the charts that interested me—but now I know what I've stumbled on . . ."

"You'll steal it."

"No. Borrow it, on the implicit understanding that I'm continuing to serve the ultimate good of the Cohort. Teal, you *must* believe me. There's a weapon out there that can shift the balance in this war. To find it I need *Tyrant*, and *Tyrant* needs a syrinx."

"Then I have some bad news for you. We sold it." Her tone was off-hand, dismissive. "It was a double-star system, a few lights back the way we'd come. We needed repairs, material, parts the swallowship couldn't make for itself. We made contact— sent in negotiators. I was on the diplomatic party. We bartered. We left them the syrinx and Pardalote got the things we needed."

Merlin turned aside in disgust. "You idiots."

Teal swiped the barrel of the gun across his faceplate. Merlin flinched back, wondering how close she had been to just shooting him there and then.

"Don't judge us. And don't judge Pardalote for the decisions she took. You weren't there, and you haven't the faintest idea what we went through. Shall I tell you how it was for me?"

Merlin wisely said nothing.

"There's a vault near the middle of the ship," Teal went on. "The best place to hide power, if you're going to use it. One by one our frostwatch cabinets failed us. There were a thousand of us, then a hundred . . . then the last ten. Each time we woke up, counted how many of us were still alive, drew straws to see who got the cabinets that were still working. There were always less and less. I'm the last one, the last of us to get a working cabinet. I ran it on a trickle of power, just the bare minimum. Set the cabinet to wake me if anyone came near."

Merlin waited a moment then nodded. "Can I make a suggestion?"

"If it makes you feel better."

"My ship is warm, it has air, and it's still capable of moving. I feel we'd get to a position of trust a lot quicker if we could speak face to face, without all this glass and vacuum between us."

He caught her sneer. "What makes you think I'd ever trust you?"

"People come round to me," Merlin said.

The syrinx was a matte-black cone about as long as Merlin was tall. It rested in a cradle of metal supports, sharp end pointing aft, in a compartment just forward of *Tyrant*'s engine bay. Syrinxes seemed to work better when they were somewhere close to the centre of mass of a ship, but beyond that there were no clear rules, and much of what *was* known had been pieced together through guesswork and experimentation.

"It still works, to a degree," Merlin said, stroking a glove along the tapering form. "But it's dying on me. I daren't say how many more transits I'll get out it."

"What would you have done if it had failed?" Teal asked, managing to make the question sound peremptory and businesslike, as if she had no real interest in the answer.

They had taken off their helmets, but were still wearing the rest of their suits. Merlin had closed the airlock, but kept *Tyrant* docked with the larger ship. He had shown Teal through the narrow warren of his linked living quarters without stopping to comment, keen to show her that at least the syrinx was a verifiable part of his story.

"I doubt I'd have had much time to worry about it, if it failed. Probably ended up as an interesting smear, that's all." Merlin offered a smile, but Teal's expression remained hard and unsympathetic.

"A quick death's nothing to complain about."

She was a hard one for him to fathom. Her head looked too small, too childlike, jutting out from the neck ring of her suit. She was short haired, hard boned, tough and wiry-looking at the same time. He had been right about her eyes, even through the visor. They had seen too much pain and hardship, bottled too much of it inside themselves, and now it was leaking back out.

"You still don't trust me, and that's fine. But let me show you something else." Merlin beckoned her back through into the living area, then made one of the walls light up with images and maps and text from his private files. The collage was dozens of layers deep, with the records and annotations in just as many languages and alphabets.

"What is this supposed to prove?"

He skimmed rectangles aside, flicking them to the edge of the wall. Here were Waynet charts, maps of solar systems, schematics of the surfaces of worlds and moons. "The thing I'm looking for," he said, "the weapon, the gun, whatever you want to call it—this is everything that I've managed to find out about it. Clues, rumours, whispers, from a hundred worlds. Maybe they don't all point to the same thing—I'd be amazed if they did. But some of them do, I'm sure of it, and before long I'm going to find the piece that ties the whole thing together." He stabbed a finger at a nest of numbers next to one of the charts. "Look how recent these time tags are, Teal. I'm still searching—still gathering evidence."

Her face was in profile, bathed in the different colours of the images. The slope of her nose, the angle of her chin, reminded him in certain small ways of Sayaca.

She turned to him sharply, as if she had been aware of his gaze.

"I saw pictures of you," Teal said. "They showed us them in warcreche. They were a warning against irresponsibility. You look much older than you did in those pictures."

"Travel broadens the mind. It also puts a large number of lines on you." He nodded at the collage of records. "I'm no angel, and I've made mistakes, but this proves I'm still committed. Which means we're both in the same boat, doesn't it? Lone survivors, forced together, each needing to trust the other. Are you really the last of your crew?"

There was a silence before she answered.

"Yes. I knew it before I went under, the last time. There were still others around, but mine was the last reliable cabinet—the only one that stood a chance of working."

"You were chosen, to have the best chance?"

"Yes."

He nodded, thinking again of those inner scars. "Then I've a proposition." He raised a finger, silencing her before she could get a word out. "The Huskers did something terrible to you and your people, as they did mine. They deserve to be punished for that, and they will be. Together we can make it happen."

"By finding your fabled weapon?"

"By finding the syrinx that'll help me carry on with my search. You said that system wasn't far away. If it's on the Waynet, I can reach it in *Tyrant*. We backtrack. If you traded with them once, we can trade again. You've seen that system once before, so you have the local knowledge I most certainly lack."

She glanced away, her expression clouded by very obvious misgivings.

"We sold them a syrinx," Teal said. "One of the rarest, strangest things ever made. All you have is a little black ship and some stories. What could you ever offer them that would be worth that?"

"I'd think of something," Merlin said.

The transition, when it came, was the hardest so far. Merlin had been expecting the worst and had made sure the two of them were buckled in as tightly as their couches allowed, side by side in *Tyrant*'s command deck. When they slipped into the Waynet it had felt like an impact, a solid scraping blow against the ship, as if it were grinding its way along the flank of an asteroid or iceberg. Alarms sounded, and the hull gave off moans and shrieks of structural complaint. *Tyrant* yawed violently. Probes and stabilisers flaked away from the hull.

But it held. Merlin waited for the instruments to settle down, and for the normal smooth motion of the flow to assert itself. Only then did he start breathing again.

"We're all right. Once we're in the Way, it's rarely too bad. It's just coming in and out that's becoming problematic." Long experience told him it was safe to unbuckle, and he motioned for Teal to do likewise. She had kept her suit on and her helmet nearby, as if either of those things stood any chance of protecting her if the transition failed completely. Merlin had removed all but the clothes he normally wore in *Tyrant*—baggy and tending to frills and ornamentation.

"How long until we come out again?"

Merlin squinted at one of the indicators. "About six hours. We're moving very quickly now—only about a hundred billionth part less than the speed of light. Do you see those circles that shoot past us every second?"

They were like the glowing ribs of a tunnel, whisking to either side in an endless, hypnotic procession.

"What are they?"

"Constraining hoops. Anchored back into fixed space. They pin down the Way, keep it flowing in the right direction. In reality, they're about eight light hours apart— far enough that you could easily drop a solar system between them. I think about the Waymakers a lot, you know. They made an empire so old that by the time it fell, hardly anyone remembered anything that came before it. Light and wealth and all the sunsets anyone could ever ask for."

"Look at all the good it did them," Teal said. "We're like rats, hunting for crumbs in the ruins they left us."

"Even rats have their day," Merlin said. "And speaking of crumbs . . . would you like something to eat?"

"What sort of rations do you have?"

He patted his belly. "We run to a bit more than rations on *Tyrant*."

With the ship weightless, still rushing down the throat of the Way, they ate with their legs tucked under them in the glass eye of the forward observation bubble.

Merlin eyed Teal between mouthfuls, noticing how entirely at ease she was with the absence of gravity, never needing to chase a gobbet of food or a stray blob of water. She had declined his offer of wine, but Merlin saw no need to put himself through such hardship.

"Tell me about the people you traded with," he said.

"They were fools," Teal said. She carried on eating for a few mouthfuls. "But useful fools. They had what we needed, and we had something they considered valuable."

"Fools, why exactly?"

"They were at war. An interplanetary conflict, fought using fusion ships and fusion bombs. Strategy shaped by artificial intelligences on both sides. It had been going on for centuries when we got there, with only intervals of peace, when the military computers reached a stalemate. Just enough time to rebuild before they started blowing each other to hell again. Two worlds, circling different stars of a binary system, and all the other planets and moons caught up in it in one way or another. A twisted, factional mess. And stupid, too." She stabbed her fork into the rations as if her meal was something that needed killing. "Huskers aren't thick in this sector, but you don't go around making noise and light if you've any choice. And there's *always* a choice."

"We don't seem to have much choice about this war we're in," Merlin said.

"We're different." Her eyes were hard and cold. "This is species-level survival. Their stupid interplanetary war was over trivial ideology. Old grudges, sustained and fanned. Men and women willingly handing their fates to battle computers. Pardalote was reluctant to do business with them: too hard to know who to speak to, who to trust."

Merlin made a pained, studious look. "I'd never meddle in someone else's war."

She pushed the fork around. "In the end it wasn't too bad. We identified the side best placed to help us, and got in and out before there were too many complications."

"Complications?"

"There weren't any. Not in the end." She was silent for a second or two. "I was glad to leave that stupid place. I've barely thought about them since."

"Your logs say you were in that system thirteen hundred years ago. A lot could have changed since then. Who knows, maybe they've patched up their differences."

"And maybe the Huskers found them."

"You're cheerful company, Teal, did you know?"

"Seeing the rest of your crew die will do that. You chose to leave, Merlin—it wasn't that you were the last survivor."

He sipped at his wine, debating how much of a clear head he would need when they emerged from the Way. Sometimes a clear head was the last thing that helped.

"I lost good people as well, Teal."

"Really?"

He pushed off, moved to a cabinet and drew out a pair of immersion suits.

"If you went through warcreche you'll know what these are. Do you trust me enough to put it on?"

Teal took the dun-coloured garment and studied it with unveiled distaste. "What good will this do?"

"Put it on. I want to show you what I lost."

"We'll win this war in reality, not simulations. There's nothing you can show me that . . ."

"Just do it, Teal."

She scowled at him, but went into a back room of *Tyrant* to remove her own clothes and don the tight-fitting immersion suit. By the time she was ready Merlin had slipped into the other suit. He nodded at Teal as she spidered back into the cabin. "Good. Trust is good. We'll only be inside a little while, but I think it'll help. Ship, patch us through."

"The Palace, Merlin?"

"Where else?"

The suit prickled his neck as it established its connection with his spine. There was the usual moment of dislocation and *Tyrant* melted away, to be replaced by a surrounding of warm stone walls and tall fretted windows, shot through with amber sun.

Teal was standing next to him.

"Where are we?"

"Where I was born. Where my brother and I spent the first couple of decades of our existence, before the Cohort came." Merlin walked to the nearest window and bid Teal to follow him. "Gallinule created this environment long after we left. He's gone now as well, so this is a reminder of the past for me in more ways than one."

"Your brother's dead?"

"It's complicated."

She left it at that. "What world are we on?"

"Plenitude, we called it. Common enough name, I suppose." Merlin stepped onto a plinth under the window, offering a better view through its fretwork. "Do you see the land below?"

Teal strained to look down. "It's moving—sliding under us. I thought we were in a castle or something."

"We are. The Palace of Eternal Dusk. My family home for thirteen hundred years—as long as the interval between your visits to that system." He touched his hand against the stonework. "We didn't make this place. It was unoccupied for centuries, circling Plenitude at exactly the same speed as the line between day and night. My family were the first to reach it from the surface, using supersonic aircraft. We held it for the next forty generations." He lifted his face to the unchanging aspect of the sun, hovering at its fixed position over the endlessly flowing horizon. "My uncle was a bit of an amateur archaeologist. He dug deep into the rock the palace is built on, as far down as the anti-gravity keel. He said he found evidence that it was at least twenty thousand years old, and maybe quite a bit more than that." Merlin touched a hand to Teal's shoulder. "Let me show you something else."

She flinched under his touch but allowed him to steer her to one of the parlours branching off the main room. Merlin halted them both at the door, touching a finger to his lips. Two boys knelt on a carpet in the middle of the parlour, their forms side-lit by golden light. They were surrounded by toy armies, spread out in ordered regiments and platoons.

"Gallinule and I," Merlin whispered, as the younger of the boys took his turn to move a mounted and penanted figure from one flank to another. "Dreaming of war. Little did we know we'd get more than our share of it."

He backed away, leaving the boys to their games, and took Teal to the next parlour.

Here an old woman sat in a stern black chair, facing one of the sunlit windows with her face mostly averted from the door. She wore black and had her hands in her lap, keeping perfectly still and watchful.

"Years later," Merlin said, "Gallinule and I were taken from Plenitude. It was meant to be an act of kindness, preserving something of our world in advance of the Huskers. But it tore us from our mother. We couldn't return to her. She was left here with the ruins of empire, her sons gone, her world soon to fall."

The woman seemed aware of her visitors. She turned slightly, bringing more of her face into view. Her eyes searched the door, as if looking for ghosts.

"She has a gentle look," Teal said quietly.

"She was kind," Merlin answered softly. "They spoke ill of her, but they didn't know her, not the way Gallinule and I did."

The woman slowly turned back to face the window. Her face was in profile again, her eyes glistening.

"Does she ever speak?"

"She's no cause to." Merlin's mouth was dry for a few moments. "We saw it happen, from the swallowship. Saw the Husker weapons strike Plenitude—saw the fall of the Palace of Eternal Dusk." Merlin turned from the tableau of his mother. "I mean to go back, one of these days—see what's left for myself. But I find it hard to bring myself."

"How many died?" Teal asked.

"Hundreds of millions. We were the only two that Quail managed to save, along with a few fragments of cultural knowledge. So I know what it's like, Teal—believe me I know what it's like." He turned from her with a cold disregard. "Ship, bring Teal out."

"What about you?"

"I need a little time on my own. You can start remembering everything I need to know about the binary system. You've got about five hours."

Tyrant pulled Teal out of the Palace. Merlin stood alone, silent, for long moments. Then he returned to the parlour where his mother watched the window, imprisoned in an endless golden day, and he stood in her shadow wondering what it would take to free her from that reverie of loss and loneliness.

They made a safe emergence from the Waynet, Merlin holding his breath until they were out and stable and the syrinx had stopped ringing in its cradle like a badly-cracked bell.

He took a few minutes to assess their surroundings.

Two stars, close enough together for fusion ships to make a crossing between them in weeks. A dozen large worlds, scattered evenly between the two stars. Hundreds of moons and minor bodies. Thousands of moving ships, easily tracked across interplanetary distance, the vessels grouped into squadrons and attack formations. Battle stations and super-carriers. Fortresses and cordons. The occasional flash of a nuclear weapon or energy pulse weapon—battle ongoing.

Tyrant was stealthy, but even a stealthy ship made a big splash coming out of the

Waynet. Merlin wasn't at all surprised when a large vessel locked onto them and closed in fast, presumably pushing its fusion engines to the limit.

Teal carried on briefing him as the ship approached.

"I don't like the look of that thing," *Tyrant* said, as soon as they had a clear view.

"I don't either," Merlin said. "We'll treat it respectfully. Wouldn't want you getting a scratch on your paintwork, would we?"

The vessel was three times as large as Merlin's ship and every inch a thing of war. Guns bristled from its hull. It was made of old alloys, forged and joined by venerable methods, and its engines and weapons depended on the antique alchemy of magnetically bottled fusion. A snarling mouth that had been painted across the front of the ship, crammed with razor-tipped teeth.

"It's a Havergal ship," Teal said. "That's their marking, that dagger-and-star. It doesn't look all that different to the ships they had when we were here before."

"Fusion's a plateau technology," Merlin remarked. "If all they ever needed to do was get around this binary system and blow each other up now and then, it would have been sufficient."

"They knew about the Waynet, of course—hard to miss it, cutting through their sky the way it does. That interested them. They wanted to jump all the way from fusion to syrinx technology, without all the hard stuff in between."

"Doesn't look like they got very far, does it?"

The angry-looking ship drew alongside. An airlock opened and a squad of armoured figures came out on rocket packs. Merlin remained tense, but commanded *Tyrant's* weapons to remain inside their hatches. He also told the proctors to hide themselves away until he needed them.

Footfalls clanged onto the hull. Grappling devices slid like nails on rust. Merlin opened his airlock, nodded at Teal, and the two of them went to meet the boarding party. He was halfway there when a thought occurred to him. "Unless they bring up your earlier visit, don't mention it. You're just along for the ride with me. I want to know if there's anything they say or do that doesn't fit with your picture of them—anything they might be keeping from me."

"I speak their language. Isn't that going to take some explaining?"

"Feign ignorance to start with, then make it seem as if you're picking it up as you go. If they get suspicious, we'll just say that there are a dozen other systems in this sector where they speak a similar dialect." He flashed a nervous smile at Teal. "Or something. Make it up. Be creative."

The airlock had cycled by the time they arrived. When it opened Merlin was not surprised to find only two members of the boarding party inside it. There would not have been room for more.

"Welcome," he said, making a flourishing gesture of invitation. "Come in, come in. Take your shoes off. Make yourselves at home."

They were a formidable looking pair. Their vacuum armour had a martial look to it, with bladed edges and spurs, a kind of stabbing ram on the crowns of their helmets, fierce-looking grills across the glass of their faceplates. All manner of guns and close-combat weapons buckled or braced to the armour. The armour was green, with gold ornamentation.

Merlin tapped his throat. "Take your helmets off. The worst you'll catch is a sniffle."

They came into the ship. Their faces were lost behind the grills, but he caught the movement as they twisted to look at each other, before reaching up to undo their helmets. They came free with a tremendous huff of equalising pressure, revealing a pair of heads. There were two men, both bald, with multiple blemishes and battle-scars across their scalps. They had tough, grizzled-looking features, with lantern jaws and a dusting of dark stubble across their chins and cheeks. A duelling scar or simi-lar across the face of one man, a laser burn ruining the ear of the other. Their small, cold-seeming eyes were pushed back into a sea of wrinkles. One man opened his mouth, revealing a cage of yellow and metal teeth.

He barked out something, barely a syllable. His voice was very deep, and Merlin caught a blast of stale breath as he spoke. The other man waited a moment then amplified this demand or greeting with a few more syllables of his own.

Merlin returned these statements with an uneasy smile of his own. "I'm Merlin," he said. "And I come in peace. Ish."

"They don't understand you," Teal whispered.

"I'm damned glad they don't. Did you get anything of what they said?"

"They want to know why you're here and what you want."

The first man said a few more words, still in the same angry, forceful tone as be-fore. The second man glanced around and touched one of the control panels next to the airlock.

"Isn't war lovely," Merlin said.

"I understand them," Teal said, still in a whisper. "Well enough, anyway. They're still using the main Havergal language. It's shifted a bit, but I can still get the gist. How much do you want me to pretend to understand?"

"Nothing yet. Keep soaking it in. When you think you've given it long enough, point to the two of us and make the sound for 'friend.'" Merlin grinned back at the suited men, the two of them edging away from the lock in opposite directions. "I know, it needs a little work, doesn't it? Tired décor. I'm thinking of knocking out this wall, maybe putting a window in over there?"

Teal said something, jabbing one hand at her chest and another at Merlin. "Friendly," she said. "I've told them we're friendly. What else?"

"Give them our names. Then tell them we'd like to speak to whoever's in charge of that planet you mentioned."

He caught "Merlin" and "Teal" and the name "Havergal." He had to trust that she was doing a good job of making her initial efforts seem plausibly imperfect, even as she stumbled into ever-improving fluency. Whatever she had said, though, it had a sudden and visible effect. The crag-faced men came closer together again and now directed their utterances at Teal alone, guessing that was the only one who had any kind of knowledge of their language.

"What?" Merlin asked.

"They're puzzled that I speak their tongue. They also want to know if you have a syrinx."

"Tell them I have a syrinx but that it doesn't work very well." Merlin was still smil-ing at the men, but the muscles around his mouth were starting to ache. "And tell them I apologise for not speaking their tongue, but you're much better at languages than me. What are their names, too?"

"I'll ask." There was another halting exchange, Merlin sensing that the names were given grudgingly, but she drew them out in the end. "Balus," Teal said. "And Locrian. I'd tell you which is which, but I'm not sure there'd be much point."

"Good. Thank Balus and Locrian for the friendly reception. Tell them that they are very welcome on my ship, but I'd be very obliged if the others stopped crawling around outside my hull." Merlin paused. "Oh, and one other thing. Ask them if they're still at war with Gaffurius."

He had no need of Teal to translate the answer to that particular part of his query. Balus—or perhaps Locrian—made a hawking sound, as if he meant to spit. Merlin was glad that he did not deliver on the gesture; the intention had been transparent enough.

"He says," Teal replied, "that the Gaffurians broke the terms of the recent treaty. And the one before that. And the one before that. He said the Gaffurians have the blood of pigs in their veins. He also says that he would rather cut out his own tongue than speak of the Gaffurians in polite company."

"One or two bridges to build there, then."

"He also asks why they should care what you think of the ones still on your hull."

"It's a fair question. How good do you think you're getting with this language of theirs?"

"Better than I'm letting on."

"Well, let's push our luck a little. Tell Balus—or Locrian—that I have weapons on this ship. Big, dangerous weapons. Weapons neither of them will have ever seen before. Weapons that—if they understood their potency, and how near they've allowed that ship of theirs to come—would make them empty their bowels so quickly they'd fill their own spacesuits up to the neck ring. Can you do that for me?"

"How about I tell them that you're armed, that you're ready to defend your property, but that you still want to preceed from a position of peaceful negotiation?"

"On balance, probably for the best."

"I'll also add that you've come to find out about a syrinx, and you're prepared to discuss terms of trade."

"Do that."

Merlin waited while this laborious exchange was carried on. Teal reached some sort of critical juncture in her statement and this drew a renewed burst of angry exclamations from Balus and Locrian—he guessed they had just been acquainted with the notion that *Tyrant* was armed—but Teal continued and her words appeared to have some temporary soothing effect, or as best as could be expected. Merlin raised his hands in his best placating manner. "Honestly, I'm not the hair-trigger type. We just need to have a basis for mutual respect here."

"Cohort?" he heard one of them say.

"Yes," he answered, at the same time as Teal. "Cohort. Big bad Cohort."

After a great deal of to-ing and fro-ing, Teal turned to him: "They don't claim to know anything about a syrinx. Then again, I don't think these men necessarily *would* know. But one of them, Locrian, is going back to the other ship. I think he needs to signal some higher-up or something."

"It's what I was expecting," Merlin said. "Tell him I'll wait. And tell the other one he's welcome to drink with us."

Teal relayed this message, then said: "He'll stay, but he doesn't need anything to drink.

"His loss."

While Locrian went back through the airlock, Balus joined them in the lounge, looking incongruous in his heavily-armoured suit. Teal tried to engage him in conversation, but he had obviously been ordered to keep his communications to a strict minimum. Merlin helped himself to some wine, before catching his own pink-eyed reflection and deciding enough was enough, for now.

"What do you think's going on?" Teal asked, when an hour had passed with no word from the other ship.

"Stuff."

"Aren't you concerned?"

"Terribly."

"You don't look or sound it. You want this syrinx, don't you?"

"Very much so."

Balus looked on silently as his hosts spoke in Main. If he understood any part of it, there was no clue on his face. "But you seem so nonchalant about it all," Teal said.

Merlin pondered this for a few seconds. "Do you think being *not* nonchalant would make any difference? I don't know that it would. We're here in the moment, aren't we? And the moment will have its way with us, no matter how we feel about things."

"Fatalist."

"Cheerful realist. There's a distinction." Merlin raised his empty, wine-stained glass. "Isn't there, Balus? You agree, don't you, my fine fellow?"

Balus parted his lips and gave a grunt.

"They're coming back," Teal said, catching movement through the nearest window. "A shuttle of some sort, not just people in suits. Is that good or bad?"

"We'll find out." Merlin bristled a hand across his chin. "Mind me while I go and shave my beard."

"Shave your tongue while you're at it."

Merlin had just finished freshening up when the lock completed its cycle and the two suited individuals came aboard. One of them, wearing a green and gold suit, turned out to be Locrian. He took off his helmet and motioned for the other, wearing a red and gold suit, to do likewise. This suit was less ostentatiously armoured than the other, designed for a smaller frame. But when the figure lifted their helmet off, glanced at Locrian and uttered a few terse words, Merlin had no difficulty picking up on the power relationship between the two.

The newcomer was an old man—old, at least, in Merlin's reckoning. Seventy or eighty years, by the Cohort way of accounting such things. He had fine, aristocratic features, accented by a high, imperious brow and a back-combed sweep of pure white hair. His eyes were a liquid grey, like little wells of mercury, suggesting a sharp, relentless intelligence.

Officer class, Merlin thought.

The man spoke to them. His voice was soft, undemonstrative. Merlin still did not understand a word of it, but just the manner of speaking conveyed an assumption of implicit authority.

"His name is . . . Baskin," Teal said, when the man had left a silence for her to speak. "Prince Baskin. Havergal royalty. That's his own personal cruiser out there. He was on some sort of patrol when they picked up our presence. They came at full thrust to meet us. Baskin says things come out of the Way now and then, and it's always a scramble to get to them before the enemy."

"If Locrian's spoken to him, then he already knows our names. Ask him about the syrinx."

Teal passed on Merlin's question. Baskin answered, Teal ruminated on his words, then said: "He says that he's very interested to learn of your interest in the syrinx."

"I bet he is."

"He also says that he'd like to continue the conversation on his cruiser. He says that we'll be guests, not prisoners, and that we'll be free to return here whenever we like."

"Tell Prince Baskin . . . yes, we'll join him. But if I'm not back on *Tyrant* in twelve hours, my ship will take action to retrieve me. If you can make that sound like a polite statement of fact, rather than a crudely-worded threat, that would be lovely."

"He says there'll be no difficulty," Teal said.

"He's right about that," Merlin answered.

Part of Prince Baskin's cruiser had been spun to simulate gravity. There was a stateroom, as grand as anything Merlin had encountered, all shades of veneered wood and polished metal, with red drapes and red fabric on the chairs. The floor curved up gently from one end of the room to the other, and this curvature was echoed in the grand table that took up much of the space. Prince Baskin was at one end of it, Merlin and Teal at the other, with the angle of the floor making Baskin seem to tilt forward like a playing card, having to lift his head to face his guests. Orderlies had fussed around them for some time, setting plates and glasses and cutlery, before bringing in the elements of a simple but well-prepared meal. Then—rather to Merlin's surprise—they had left the three of them alone, with only stony-faced portraits of royal ancestors and nobility for company. Men on horses, men in armour, men with projectile guns and energy weapons, both grand and foolish in their pomp.

"This is pure ostentation," he said, looking around the room with its sweeping curves and odd angles. "No one in their right mind puts centrifugal gravity on a ship this small. It takes up too much room, costs too much in mass, and the spin differential between your feet and head's enough to make you dizzy."

"If the surroundings are not quite to your taste, Merlin, we could adjourn to one of the *Renouncer*'s weightless areas."

Prince Baskin had spoken.

Teal cocked her chin to face him. The curvature of the room made it like talking to someone halfway up a hill. "You speak Main."

"I try."

"Then why . . ." she began.

Baskin smiled, and tore a chunk off some bread, dipping it into soup before proceeding. "Please join me. And please forgive my slight deception in pretending to need to have your words translated, as well as my rustiness with your tongue. What I have learned, I have done so from books and recordings, and until now I have never had the opportunity to speak it to a living soul." He bit into the bread, and made an eager motioning gesture that they should do likewise. "Please. Eat. My cook is excellent—as well he should be, what it costs me to ship him and his kitchen around. Teal, I *must* apologise. But there was no deception where Locrian and Balus were concerned. They genuinely did not speak Main, and were in need of your translation. I am very much the exception."

"How . . ." Merlin started.

"I was a sickly child, I suppose you might say. I had many hours to myself, and in those hours—as one does—I sought my own entertainment. I used to play at war, but toy soldiers and tabletop campaigns will only take you so far. So I developed a fascination with languages. Many centuries ago, a Cohort ship stopped in our system. They were here for two years—two of *your* years, I should say—long enough for trade and communication. Our diplomats tried to learn Main, and by the same token the Cohort sent in negotiating teams who did their best to master our language. Of course there were linguistic ties between the two, so the task was not insurmountable. But difficult, all the same. I doubt that either party excelled itself, but we did what was needed and there was sufficient mutual understanding." Baskin turned his head to glance at the portraits to his right, each painting set at a slight angle to its neighbours. "It *was* a very long time ago, as I'm sure you appreciate. When the Cohort had gone, there was great emphasis placed on maintaining our grasp of their language, so that we'd have a headstart the next time we needed it. Schools, academies, and so on. King Curtal was instrumental in that." He was nodding at one of the figures in the portraits, a man of similar age and bearing to himself, and dressed in state finery not too far removed from the formal wear in which Baskin now appeared. "But that soon died away. The Cohort never returned, and as the centuries passed, there was less and less enthusiasm for learning Main. The schools closed, and by the time it came down to me—forty generations later—all that remained were the books and recordings. There was no living speaker of Main. So I set myself the challenge to become one, and encouraged my senior staff to do likewise, and here I am now, sitting before you, and doubtless making a grotesque mockery of your tongue."

Merlin broke bread, dipped it into the soup, made a show of chewing on it before answering.

"This Cohort ship that dropped by," he said, his mouth still full. "Was it the *Shrike*?"

Teal held her composure, but he caught the sidelong twitch of her eye.

"Yes," Baskin said, grimacing slightly. "You've heard of it?"

"It's how I know about the syrinx," Merlin said, trying to sound effortlessly matter-of-fact. "I found the *Shrike*. It was a wreck, all her crew dead. Been dead for centuries, in fact. But the computer records were still intact." He lifted a goblet and drank. The local equivalent to wine was amber coloured and had a lingering, woody finish. Not exactly to his taste but he'd had worse. "That's why I'm here."

"And Teal?"

"I travel with Merlin," she said. "He isn't good with languages, and he pays me to be his translator."

"You showed a surprising faculty with our own," Baskin said.

"Records of your language were in the files Merlin pulled from the wreck. It wasn't that hard to pick up the rudiments."

Baskin dabbed at his chin with a napkin. "You picked up more than the rudiments, if I might say."

Merlin leaned forward. "Is it true about the syrinx?"

"Yes," Baskin said. "We keep it in a safe place on Havergal. Intact, in so far as we can tell. Would that be of interest to you?"

"I think it might."

"But you must already have one, if you've come here by the Way."

Teal said: "His syrinx is broken, or at least damaged. He knows it won't last long, so he needs to find a spare."

Again Baskin turned to survey the line of portraits. "These ancestors of mine knew very little but war. It dominated their lives utterly. Even when there was peace, they were thinking ahead to the moment that peace would fail, and how they might be in the most advantageous position when that day came. As it always did. My own life has also been shaped by the war. Disfigured, you might say. But I have lived under its shadow long enough. I should very much like to be the last of my line who ruled during wartime."

"Then end the war," Merlin said.

"I should like to—but it must be under our terms. Gaffurius is stretched to its limits. One last push, one last offensive, and we can enforce a lasting peace. But there is a difficulty."

"Which is?" Teal asked.

"Something of ours has fallen into the wrong hands—an object we call the Iron Tactician." Baskin continued eating for several moments, in no rush to explain himself. "I don't know what you've learned of our history. But for centuries, both sides in this war have relied on artificial intelligences to guide their military planning."

"I suppose this is another of those machines," Merlin said.

"Yes and no. For a long time our machines were well-matched with those of the enemy. We would build a better one, then they would, we would respond, and so on. A gradual escalating improvement. So it went on. Then—by some happy stroke— our cyberneticists created a machine that was generations in advance of anything they had. For fifty years the Iron Tactician has given us an edge, a superiority. Its forecasts are seldom in error. The enemy still has nothing to match it—it's why we have made the gains that we have. But now, on the eve of triumph, we have lost the Iron Tactician."

"Careless," Merlin said.

A tightness pinched the corner of Baskin's mouth. "The Tactician has always needed to be close to the theatre of battle, so that its input data is as accurate and up-to-date as possible. That was why our technicians made it portable, self-contained and self-reliant. Of course there are risks in having an asset of that nature."

"What happened?" Teal asked. "Did Gaffurius capture it?"

"Thankfully, no," Baskin answered. "But it's very nearly as bad. The Tactician has fallen into the hands of a non-aligned third party. Brigands, mercenaries, call them what you will. Now they wish to extract a ransom for the Tactician's safe return—or they will sell it on to the enemy. We know their location, an asteroid holdout, and if we massed a group of ships we could probably overwhelm their defenses. But if Gaffurius guessed our intentions and moved first . . ." Baskin lifted his glass, peering through it at Merlin and Teal, so that his face swam distorted, one mercurial eye wobbling to immensity while the other shrunk to a tight cold glint. "So there you have it. A simple proposition. The syrinx is yours, Merlin—provided you give us the Tactician."

"Maybe I still wouldn't be fast enough."

"But you'll be able to strike without warning, with Cohort weapons. I don't see that it should pose you any great difficulty, given the evident capabilities of your ship." Baskin twirled his fingers around the stem of his goblet. "But then that depends on how badly you want our syrinx."

"Mm," Merlin said. "Quite badly, if I'm going to be honest."

"Would you do it?"

Merlin looked at Teal before answering. But she seemed distracted, her gaze caught by one of the portraits. It was the picture of King Curtal, the ancestor Baskin had mentioned only a little while earlier. While the style of dress might not have changed, the portrait was yellowing with old varnish, its colours time-muted.

"I'd need guarantees," he said. "Starting with proof that this syrinx even exists."

"That's easily arranged," Prince Baskin said.

Tyrant had a biometric lock on Merlin, and it would shadow the *Renouncer* all the way to Havergal. If it detected that Merlin was injured or under duress, *Tyrant* would deploy its own proctors to storm the cruiser. But Merlin had gauged enough of his hosts to conclude that such an outcome was vanishingly unlikely. They needed his cooperation much too badly to do harm to their guest.

Locrian showed Merlin and Teal to their quarters, furnished in the same sumptuous tones as the stateroom. When the door opened and Merlin saw that there was only one bed, albeit a large one, he turned to Teal with faked resignation.

"It's awkward for both of us, but if we want to keep them thinking you've been travelling with me for years and years, it'll help if we behave as a couple."

Teal waited until Locrian had shut the door on them and gone off on his own business. She walked to the bed, following the gently, dreamy up-curve of the floor. "You're right," she said, glancing back at Merlin before she sat on the edge of the bed. "It will help. And at least for now I'd rather they didn't know I was on the swallowship, so I'm keen to maintain the lie."

"Good. Very good."

"But we share the bed and nothing else. You're of no interest to me, Merlin. Maybe you're not a traitor or a fool—I'll give you that much. But you're still a fat, swaggering drunk who thinks far too much of himself." But Teal patted the bed. "Still, you're right. The illusion's useful."

Merlin settled himself down on his side of the bed. "No room for manoeuvre there? Not even a little bit?"

"None."

"Then we're clear. Actually, it's a bit of a relief. I meant to say . . ."

"If this is about what I just spoke about?"

"I just wanted to say, I understand how strange all this must be. Not everyone goes back to a place they were thirteen hundred years ago. In a way, it's a good job it was such a long time ago. At least we don't have to contend with any living survivors from those days, saying that they remember you being on the diplomatic team."

"It was forty-three generations ago. No one remembers."

Merlin moved to the window, watching the stars wheel slowly by outside. There was his own ship, a sharp sliver of darkness against the greater darkness of space. He thought of the loves he had been ripped from by time and distance, and how the sting of those losses grew duller with each year but was never entirely healed. It was an old lesson for him, one he had been forced to learn many times. For Teal, this might be her first real taste of the cruelty of deep time—realising how far downstream she had come, how little chance she stood of beating those currents back to better, kinder times.

"I'd remember," he said softly.

He could see her reflection in the window, *Tyrant* sliding through her like a barb, but Teal neither acknowledged his words nor showed the least sign that they had meant anything to her.

Five days was indeed ample time to prepare Merlin for the recovery operation, but only because the intelligence was so sparse. The brigands were holed up on an asteroid called Mundar, an otherwise insignificant speck of dirt on some complex, winding orbit that brought it into the territorial space of both Havergal and Gaffurius. Their leader was a man called Struxer, but beyond one fuzzy picture the biographical notes were sparse. Fortunately there was more on the computer itself. The Iron Tactician was a spherical object about four metres across, quilted from pole to pole in thick military-grade armour. It looked like some hard-shelled animal, rolled up into a defensive ball. Merlin saw no obvious complications: it needed no external power inputs and would easily fit within *Tyrant*'s cargo hold.

Getting hold of it was another matter. Baskin's military staff knew how big Mundar was and had estimates of its fortifications, but beyond that things were sketchy. Merlin skimmed the diagrams and translated documents, but told Baskin that he wanted Teal to see the originals. He was still looking out for any gaps between the raw material and what was deemed fit for his eyes, any hint of a cover-up or obfuscation.

"Why are you so concerned?" Teal asked him, halfway to Havergal, when they were alone in Baskin's stateroom, the documents spread out on the table. "Eating away at your conscience, is it, that you might be serving the wrong paymasters?"

"I'm not the one who chose sides," he said quietly. "You did, by selling the syrinx to one party instead of the other. Besides, the other lot won't be any better. Just a different bunch of stuffed shirts and titles, being told what to do by a different bunch of battle computers."

"So you've no qualms."

"Qualms?" Merlin set down the papers he had been leafing through. "I've so many qualms they're in danger of self-organizing. I occasionally have a thought that *isn't* a qualm. But I'll tell you this. Sometimes you just have to do the obvious thing.

They have an item I need, and there's a favour I can do for them. It's that simple. Not everything in the universe is a riddle."

"You'll be killing those brigands."

"They'll have every chance to hand over the goods. And I'll exercise due restraint. I don't want to damage the Tactician, not when it's the only thing standing between me and the syrinx."

"What if you found out that Prince Baskin was a bloodthirsty warmonger?"

Merlin, suddenly weary, settled his head onto his hand, propped up with an elbow. "Shall I tell you something? This war of theirs doesn't matter. I don't give a damn who wins or who loses, or how many lives end up being lost because of it. What matters—what *my* problem is—is the simple fact that the Huskers will wipe out every living trace of humanity if we allow them. That includes you, me, Prince Baskin, Struxer's brigands, and every human being on either side of their little spat. And if a few people end up dying to make that Husker annihilation a little less likely, a few stupid mercenaries who should have known better than to play one side against the other, I'm afraid I'm not going to shed many tears."

"You're cold."

"No one loves life more than me, Teal. No one's lost more, either. You lost a ship, and that's bad, but I lost a whole world. And regardless of which side they're on, these people will all die if I don't act." He returned to the papers, with their sketchy ideas about Mundar's reinforcements, but whatever focus he'd had was gone now. "They owe you nothing, Teal, and you owe them nothing in return. The fact that you were here all those years ago . . . it doesn't matter. Nothing came of it."

Teal was silent. He thought that was going to be the end of it, that his words had found their mark, but after a few moments she said: "Something isn't right. The man in the portrait—the one they call King Curtal. I knew him. But that wasn't his name."

As they made their approach to Havergal, slipping through cordon after cordon of patrols and defense stations, between armoured moons and belts of anti-ship mines, dodging patrol zones and battle fronts, Merlin felt a sickness building in him. He had seen worse things done to worlds in his travels. Much worse, in many cases: seen worlds reduced to molten slag or tumbling rubble piles or clouds of hot, chemically complex dust. But with few exceptions those horrors had been perpetrated not by people but by forces utterly beyond their control or comprehension. Not so here, though. The boiled oceans, the cratered landmasses, the dead and ashen forests, the poisoned, choking remnants of what had once been a life-giving atmosphere—these brutalities had been perpetrated by human action, people against people. It was an unnecessary and wanton crime, a cruel and injudicious act in a galaxy that already knew more than its share.

"Is Gaffurius like this?" Merlin asked, as *Renouncer* cleaved its way to the ground, *Tyrant* matching its course with an effortless insouciance.

"Gaffurius?" Baskin asked, a fan of wrinkles appearing at the corner of his eyes.

"No, much, much worse. At least we still have a few surface settlements, a few areas where the atmosphere is still breathable."

"I wouldn't count that as too much of a triumph." Merlin's mind was flashing back to the last days of Lecythus, the tainted rubble of its shattered cities, the grey heave of its restless cold ocean, waiting to reclaim what humans had left to ruin. He remembered Minla taking him to the huge whetstone monument, the edifice upon which she had embossed the version of events she wished to be codified as historical truth, long after she and her government were dust.

"Don't judge us too harshly, Merlin," Baskin said. "We don't choose to be enmeshed in this war."

"Then end it."

"I intend to. But would you opt for any cease-fire with the Huskers, irrespective of the terms?" He looked at Merlin, then at Teal, the three of them in *Renouncer*'s sweeping command bridge, standing before its wide arc of windows, shuttered for the moment against the glare of reentry. Of course you wouldn't. War is a terrible thing. But there are kinds of peace that are worse."

"I haven't seen much evidence of that," Merlin said.

"Oh, come now. Two men don't have to spend too much in each other's company to know each other for what they are. We're not so different, Merlin. We disdain war, affect a revulsion for it, but deep down it'll always be in our blood. Without it, we wouldn't know what to do with ourselves."

Teal spoke up. "When we first met, Prince Baskin, you mentioned that you hadn't always had this interest in languages. What was it you said? Toy soldiers and campaigns will only get you so far? That you used to play at war?"

"In your language—in Main," Baskin said, "the word for school is 'warcreche.' You learn war from the moment you can toddle."

"But we don't play at it," Teal said.

The two ships shook off their cocoons of plasma and bellied into the thicker airs near the surface. They levelled into horizontal flight, and the windows de-shuttered themselves, Merlin blinking against the sudden silvery brightness of day. They were overflying a ravaged landscape, pressed beneath a low, oppressive cloud ceiling. Merlin searched the rolling terrain for evidence of a single living thing, but all he saw was desolation. Here and there was the faint scratch of what might once have been a road, or the gridded thumbprint of some former town, but it was clear that no one now lived among these ruins. Ravines, deep and ominous, sliced their way through the abandoned roads. There were so many craters, their walls interlacing, that it was as if rain had begun to fall on some dull grey lake, creating a momentary pattern of interlinked ripples.

"If I need a planet looking after," Merlin mumbled, "remind me not to trust it to any of you lot."

"We'll rebuild," Baskin said, setting his hands on the rail that ran under the sweep of windows. "Reclaim. Cleanse and resettle. Even now our genetic engineers are designing the hardy plant species that will re-blanket these lands in green, and start making our atmosphere fit for human lungs." He caught himself, offering a self-critical smile. "You'll forgive me. Too easy to forget that I'm not making some morale-boosting speech at one of our armaments complexes."

"Where do you all live now?" Teal asked. "There were surface cities here once . . . weren't there?"

"We abandoned the last of those cities, Lurga, when I was just out of boyhood,"

Baskin said. "Now we live in underground communities, impervious to nuclear assault."

"I bet the views are just splendid," Merlin said.

Baskin met his sarcasm with a grim absence of humour. "We endure, Merlin—as the Cohort endures. Here. We're approaching the entry duct to one of the sub-cities. Do you see that sloping hole?" He was nodding at an angled mouth, jutting from the ground like a python buried up to its eyes. "The Gaffurians are good at destruction, but less good at precision. They can impair our moons and asteroids, but their weapons haven't the accuracy to strike across space and find a target that small. We'll return, a little later, and you'll be made very welcome. But first I'd like to settle any doubts you might have about the syrinx. We'll continue a little way north, into the highlands. I promise it won't take long."

Baskin was true to his word, and they had only flown for a few more minutes when the terrain began to buckle and wrinkle into the beginnings of a barren, tree-less mountain range, rising in a series of forbidding steps until even the high-flying spacecraft were forced to increase their altitude. "Most of our military production takes place in these upland sectors," Baskin said. "We have ready access to metallic ores, heavy isotopes, geothermal energy and so on. Of course it's well guarded. Missile and particle beams will be locking onto us routinely, both our ships. The only thing preventing either of them being shot down is our imperial authorisation."

"That and the countermeasures on my ship," Merlin said. "Which could peel back these mountains like a scab, if they detected a threat worth bothering with."

But in truth he felt vulnerable and was prepared to admit it, if only to himself. He could feel the nervous, bristling presence of all that unseen weaponry, like a migraine under the skin of Havergal.

Soon another mouth presented itself. It was wedged at the base of an almost sheer-sided valley.

"Prepare for descent," Baskin said. "It'll be a tight squeeze, but your ship shouldn't have any difficulties following."

They dived into the mouth and went deep. Kilometres, and then tens of kilometres, before swerving sharply into a horizontal shaft. Merlin allowed not a flicker of a reaction to betray his feelings, but the fact was that he was impressed, in a grudging, disapproving way. There was expertise and determination here—qualities that the Cohort's military engineers could well have appreciated. Anyone who could dig tunnels was handy in a war.

A glowing orange light shone ahead. Merlin was just starting to puzzle over its origin when they burst into a huge underground chamber, a bubble in the crust of Havergal. The floor of the bubble was a sea of lava, spitting and churning, turbulent with the eddies and currents of some mighty underground flow which just happened to pass in and out of this chamber. Suspended in the middle of the rocky void, underlit by flickering orange light, was a dark structure shaped like an inverted cone, braced in a ring and attached to the chamber's walls by three skeletal, cantilevered arms. It was the size of a small palace or space station, and its flattened upper surface was easily spacious enough for both ships to set down on with room to spare.

Bulkily suited figures—presumably protected against the heat and toxic airs of this place—came out and circled the ships. They attached a flexible docking connection to *Renouncer*.

"We call it the facility," Baskin said, as he and his guests walked down the sloping throat of the docking connector. "Just that. No capital letters, nothing to suggest its ultimate importance. But for many centuries this was the single most important element in our entire defense plan. It was here that we hoped to learn how to make the syrinx work for us." He turned back to glance at Merlin and Teal. "And where we failed—or *continue* to fail, I should say. But we had no intention of giving up, not while there was a chance."

Teal and Merlin were led down into the suspended structure, into a windowless warren of corridors and laboratories. They went down level after level, past sealed doors and observation galleries. There was air and power and light, and clearly enough room for thousands of workers. But although the place was clean and well-maintained, hardly anyone now seemed to be present. It was only when they got very deep that signs of activity began to appear. Here the side-rooms and offices showed evidence of recent use, and now and then uniformed staff members passed them, carrying notes and equipment. But Merlin detected no sign of haste or excitement in any of the personnel.

The lowest chamber of the structure was a curious circular room. Around its perimeter were numerous desks and consoles, with seated staff at least giving the impression of being involved in some important business. They were all facing the middle of the room, whose floor was a single circular sheet of glass, stretched across the abyss of the underlying lava flow. The orange glow of that molten river underlit the faces of the staff, as if reminding them of the perilous location of their workplace. The glass floor only caught Merlin's eye for an instant, though. Of vastly more interest to him was the syrinx, suspended nose-down in a delicate cradle over the middle of the glass. It was too far from the floor to be reached, even if someone had trusted the doubtful integrity of that glass panel. Merlin was just wondering how anyone got close to the syrinx when a flimsy connecting platform was swung out across the glass, allowing a woman to step over the abyss. Tiptoeing lightly she adjusted something on the syrinx, moving some sort of transducer from one chalked spot to another, before folding the platform away and returning to her console.

All was quiet, with only the faintest whisper of communications from one member of staff to another.

"In the event of an imminent malfunction," Baskin said, "the syrinx may be dropped through the pre-weakened glass, into the lava sea. That may or may not destroy it, of course. We don't know. But it would at least allow the workers some chance of fleeing the facility, which would not be the case if we used nuclear charges."

"I'm glad you've got their welfare at heart," Merlin said.

"Don't think too kindly of us," Baskin smiled back. "This is war. If we thought there was a chance of the facility itself being overrun, then more than just the syrinx would need to be destroyed. Also the equipment, the records, the collective expertise of the workers . . ."

"You'd drop the entire structure," Teal said, nodding her horrified understanding. "The reason it's fixed the way it is, on those three legs. You'd press a button and drop all these people into that fire."

"They understand the risks," Baskin said. "And they're paid well. Extremely well, I should say. Besides, it's a very good incentive to hasten the work of understanding it."

Merlin felt no kinship with these warring peoples, and little more than contempt for what they had done to themselves across all these centuries. But compared to the Waymakers, Merlin, Teal and Baskin may as well have been children of the same fallen tribe, playing in the same vast and imponderable ruins, not one of them wiser than the others.

"I'll need persuasion that it's real," he said.

"I never expected you to take my word for it," Baskin said. "You may make whatever use of the equipment here you need, within limits, and you may question my staff freely."

"Easier if you just let me take it for a test ride."

"Yes, it would—for you." Baskin reached out and settled a hand on Merlin's shoulder, as if they were two old comrades. "Shall we agree—a day to complete your inspection?"

"If that's all you'll allow."

"I've nothing to hide, Merlin. Do you imagine I'd ever imagine I could dupe a man like you with a fake? Go ahead and make your enquiries—my staff have already been told to offer you complete cooperation." Baskin touched a hand to the side of his mouth, as if whispering a secret. "Truth to tell, it will suit many of them if you take the syrinx. Then they won't feel obliged to keep working in this place."

They were given a room in the facility, while Merlin made his studies of the syrinx. The staff were as helpful as Baskin had promised, and Merlin soon had all the equipment and records he could have hoped for. Short of connecting the syrinx to *Tyrant*'s own diagnostic systems, he was able to run almost every test he could imagine, and the results and records quickly pointed to the same conclusion. The syrinx was the genuine article.

But Merlin did not need a whole day to arrive at that conclusion.

While Baskin kept Teal occupied with endless discussions in Main, learning all that he could from this living speaker, Merlin used the console to dig into Havergal's history, and specifically the background and career of Baskin's long-dead ancestor, King Curtal. He barely needed to access the private records; what was in the public domain was clear enough. Curtal had come to power within a decade of the *Shrike*'s visit to this system.

Merlin waited until they were alone in the evening, just before they were due to dine with Prince Baskin.

"You've been busy all day," Teal said. "I take it you've reached a verdict by now?"

"The syrinx? Oh, that was no trouble at all. It's real, just as Baskin promised. But I used my time profitably, Teal. I found out something else as well—and I think you'll find it interesting. You were right about that portrait, you see."

"I know you enjoy these games, Merlin. But if you want to get to the point . . ."

"The man who became King Curtal began life called Tierce." He watched her face for the flicker of a reaction that he knew she would not be able to conceal. The recognition of a name, across years or centuries, depending on the reckoning.

Merlin cleared his throat before continuing.

"Tierce was a high-ranking officer in the Havergal military command—assigned to the liason group which dealt with the *Shrike*. He'd have had close contact with your crew during the whole time you were in-system."

Her mouth moved a little before she found the words. "Tell me what happened to Tierce."

"Nothing bad. But what you might not have known about Tierce was that he was also minor royalty. He probably played it down, trying to get ahead in his career on his own merits. And that was how it would have worked out, if it wasn't for one of those craters. A Gaffurian long-range strike, unexpected and deadly, taking out the entire core of the royal family. They were all killed, Teal—barely a decade after you left the system. But they had to maintain continuity, then more than ever. The chain of succession led to Tierce, and he became King Curtal. The man you knew ended up as King."

She looked at him for a long moment, perhaps measuring for herself the reasons Merlin might have had to lie about such a thing, and then finding none that were plausible, beyond tormenting her for the sake of it.

"Can you be sure?"

"The records are open. There was no cover-up about the succession itself. But the fact that Tierce had a daughter . . ." Merlin found that he had to glance away before continuing. "That was difficult. The girl was illegitimate, and that was deeply problematic for the Havergal elite. On the other hand, Tierce was proud and protective of his daughter, and wouldn't accept the succession unless Cupis—that's the girl's name—was given all the rights and privileges of nobility. There was a constitutional tussle, as you can imagine. But eventually it was all settled in favour of Cupis and she was granted legitimacy within the family. They're good at that sort of thing, royals."

"What you're saying is that Cupis was my daughter."

"For reasons that you can probably imagine, there's no mention that the child was born to a Cohort mother. That would be a scandal beyond words. But of course you could hardly forget that you'd given birth to a girl, could you?"

She answered after a moment's hesitation. "We had a girl. Her name was Pauraque."

Merlin nodded. "A Cohort name—not much good for the daughter of a king. Tierce would have had to accept a new name for the girl, something more suited to local customs. I don't doubt it was hard for him, if the old name was a link to the person he'd never see again, the person he presumably loved and missed. But he accepted the change in the girl's interests. Do you mind—was there a reason you didn't stay with Tierce, or Tierce didn't join you on the *Shrike*?"

"Neither was allowed," Teal said, with a sudden coldness in her voice. "What happened was difficult. Tierce and I were never meant to get that close, and if one of us had stayed with the other it would have made the whole affair a lot more public, risking the trade agreements. We were given no choice. They said if I didn't go along with things, the simplest option would be to make Pauraque disappear. So I had to leave my daughter behind on Havergal, and I was told it would be best for me if I forgot she ever existed. And I tried. But when I saw that portrait . . ."

"I can't imagine what you went through," Merlin answered. "But if I can offer anything by way of consolation, it's this. King Curtal was a good ruler—one of the best they had. And Queen Cupis did just as well. She took the throne late in her father's life, when Curtal abdicated due to failing health. And by all accounts she was an honest and fair-minded ruler who did everything she could to broker peace with the enemy. It was only when the military computers overruled her plans . . ." Merlin managed a kindly smile and produced the data tablet he had been keeping by his side. It was of Havergal manufacture, but rugged and intuitive in its functions. He held it to Teal and a woman's face appeared on the screen. "That's Queen Cupis," he said. "She wasn't one of the portraits we saw earlier, or you'd have made the connection for yourself. I can see you in her pretty clearly."

Teal took the tablet and held it close to her, so that its glow underlit her features. "Are there more images?" she asked, with a catch in her voice, as if she almost feared the answer.

"Many," Merlin replied. "And recordings, video and audio, taken at all stages in her life. I stored quite a few on the tablet—I thought you'd like to see them."

"Thank you," she said. "I suppose."

"I know this is troubling for you, and I probably shouldn't have dug into Curtal's past. But once I'd started . . ."

"And after Cupis?"

"Nearly twelve hundred years of history, Teal—kings and queens and marriages and assassinations, all down the line. Too many portraits for one room. But your genes were in Cupis and if I've read the family tree properly they ought to be in every descendant, generation after generation." He paused, giving her time to take this all in. "I'm not exactly sure what this makes you. Havergal royalty, by blood connection? I'm pretty certain they won't have run into this situation before. Equally certain Baskin doesn't have a clue that you're one of his distant historical ancestors. And I suggest we keep it that way, at least for now."

"Why?"

"Because it's information," Merlin said. "And information's always powerful."

He left her with the tablet. They were past the hour for their appointment with Prince Baskin now, but Merlin would go on alone and make excuses for Teal's lateness.

Besides, he had something else on his mind.

Merlin and the Prince were dining, just the two of them for the moment. Baskin had been making half-hearted small talk since Merlin's arrival, but it was plain that there was really only one thing on his mind, and he was straining to have an answer.

"My staff say that you were very busy," he said. "Making all sorts of use of our facilities. Did you by any chance . . ."

Merlin smiled sweetly. "By any chance . . . ?"

"Arrive at a conclusion. Concerning the matter at hand."

Merlin tore into his bread with rude enthusiasm. "The matter?"

"The syrinx, Merlin. The syrinx. The thing that's kept you occupied all day."

Merlin feigned sudden and belated understanding, touching a hand to his brow and shaking his head at his own forgetfulness. "Of course. Forgive me, Prince Baskin.

It always was really just a formality, wasn't it? I mean, I never seriously doubted your honesty."

"I'm glad to hear that." But there was still an edge in Baskin's voice. "So . . ."

"So?"

"Is it real, or is it not real. That's what you set out to establish, isn't it?"

"Oh, it's real. Very real." Merlin looked at his host with a dawning understanding. "Did you actually have doubts of your own, Prince? That had never occurred to me until now, but I suppose it would have made perfect sense. After all, you only ever had the *Shrike's* word that the thing was real. How could you ever know, without using it?"

"We tried, Merlin. For thirteen hundred years, we tried. But it's settled, then? You'll accept the syrinx in payment? It really isn't much that I'm asking of you, all things considered."

"If you really think this bag of tricks will make all the difference, then who am I to stand in your way?"

Baskin beamed. He stood and recharged their glasses from the bottle that was already half-empty.

"You do a great thing for us, Merlin. Your name will echo down the centuries of peace to follow."

"Let's just hope the Gaffurians hold it in the same high esteem."

"Oh, they will. After a generation or two under our control, they'll forget there were ever any differences between us. We'll be generous in victory, Merlin. If there are scores to be settled, it will be with the Gaffurian high command, not the innocent masses. We have no quarrel with those people."

"And the brigands—you'll extend the same magnanimity in their direction?"

"There'll be no need. After you've taken back the Tactician, they'll be a spent force, brushed to the margins."

Merlin's smile was tight. "I did a little more reading on them. There was quite a bit in the private and public records, beyond what you showed me on the crossing."

"We didn't care to overwhelm you with irrelevant details," Baskin said, returning to his seat. "But there was never anything we sought to hide from you. I welcome your curiosity: you can't be too well prepared in advance of your operation."

"It's complicated background, isn't it? Centuries of dissident or breakaway factions, skulking around the edges of your war, shifting from one ideology to another, sometimes loosely aligned with your side, sometimes with the enemy. At times numerous, at other times pushed almost to extinction. I was interested in their leader, Struxer . . ."

"There's little to say about him."

"Oh, I don't know." Merlin fingered his glass, knowing he had the edge for now. "He was one of yours, wasn't he? A military defector. A senior tactician, in his own right. Close to your inner circle—almost a favoured son. But instead of offering his services to the other side, he teamed up with the brigands on Mundar. From what I can gather, there are Gaffurian defectors as well. What do they all want, do you think? What persuades those men and women that they're better off working together, than against each other?"

"They stole the Tactician, Merlin—remember that. A military weapon, in all but name. Hardly the actions of untainted pacifists."

Behind Baskin, the doors opened as Teal came to join them. Baskin twisted around in his seat to greet her, nodding in admiration at the satin Havergal evening wear she had donned for the meal. It suited her well, Merlin thought, but what really mattered was the distraction it offered. While Baskin's attention was diverted, Merlin quickly swapped their glasses. He had been careful to drink to the same level as Baskin, so that the subterfuge wasn't obvious.

"I was just telling Prince Baskin the good news," Merlin said, lifting the swapped glass and taking a careful sip from it. "I'm satisfied about the authenticity of the syrinx."

Teal took her place at the table. Baskin leaned across to pour her a glass. "Merlin said you were feeling a little unwell, so I wasn't counting on you joining us at all."

"It was just a turn, Prince. I'm feeling much better now."

"Good . . . good." He was looking at her intently, a frown buried in his gaze. "You know, Teal, if I didn't know you'd just come from space, I'd swear you were . . ." But he smiled at himself, dismissing whatever thought he had been about to voice. "Never mind—it was a foolish notion. I trust you'll accept our hospitality, while Merlin discharges his side of the arrangement? I know you travel together, but on this occasion at least Merlin has no need of an interpreter. There'll be no negotiation, simply a demonstration of overwhelming and decisive force. They'll understand what it is we'd like back."

"Where he goes, I go," Teal said.

Merlin tensed, his fingers tight on the glass. "It might not be a bad idea, actually. There'll be a risk—a small one, I grant, but a risk nonetheless. *Tyrant* isn't indestructible, and I'll be restricted in the weapons I can deploy, if the Prince wants his toy back in one piece. I'd really rather handle this one on my own."

"I accept the risk," she said. "And not because I care about the Tactician, or the difference it will make to this system. But I do want to see the Huskers defeated, and for that Merlin needs his syrinx."

"I'd have been happy to give it to Merlin now, if I thought your remaining on Havergal would offer a guarantee of his return. But the opposite arrangement suits me just as well. As soon as we have the Tactician, we'll release the syrinx."

"If those are your terms," Merlin said, with an easygoing shrug.

Baskin smiled slightly. "You trust me?"

"I trust the capability of my ship to enforce a deal. It amounts to the same thing."

"A pragmatist. I knew you were the right man for the job, Merlin."

Merlin lifted his glass. "To success, in that case."

Baskin followed suit, and Teal raised her own glass in halfhearted sympathy. "To success," the Prince echoed. "And victory."

They left the facility the following morning. Merlin took *Tyrant* this time, Teal joining him as they followed *Renouncer* back into space. Once the two craft were clear of Havergal's atmosphere, Prince Baskin issued a request for docking authorisation.

Merlin, who had considered his business with the prince concluded for now, viewed the request with a familiar, nagging trepidation.

"He wants to come along for the ride," he murmured to Teal, while the airlock cycled. "Force and wisdom, that's exactly what it'll be. Needs to see Struxer's poor brigands getting their noses bloodied up close and personal, rather than hearing about it from halfway across the system."

Teal looked unimpressed. "If he wants to risk his neck, who are you to stop him?"

"Oh, nobody at all. It's just that I work best without an audience."

"You've already got one, Merlin. Start getting used to it."

He shrugged aside her point. He was distracted to begin with, thinking of the glass he had smuggled out of the dining room, and whether Prince Baskin had been sharp enough to notice the swap. While they were leaving Havergal he had put the glass into *Tyrant*'s full-spectrum analyser, but the preliminary results were not quite what he had been expecting.

"I wasn't kidding about the risks, you know," Merlin said.

"Nor was I about wanting to see you get the syrinx. And not because I care about you all that much, either."

He winced. "Don't feel you need to spare my feelings."

"I'm just stating my position. You're the means to an end. You're searching for the means to bring about the destruction of the Huskers. The syrinx is necessary for that search, and therefore I'll help you find it. But if there was a way of *not* involving you . . ."

"And I thought we broke some ice back there, with all that stuff about Tierce and your daughter."

"It didn't matter then, it doesn't matter now. Not in the slightest."

Merlin eyed the lock indicator. "It isn't as clear-cut as I thought, did you know? I swiped a gene sample from his lordship. Now, if your blood had been percolating its way down the family tree the way it ought to have been, then I should have seen a very strong correlation . . ."

"Wait," she said, face hardening as she worked through the implications of that statement. "You took a sample from him. What about me, Merlin? How did you get a look at my genes, without . . ."

"I sampled you."

Teal slapped him. There had been no warning, and she only hit him the once, and for a moment afterwards it might almost have been possible to pretend that nothing had happened, so exactly had they returned to their earlier stances. But Merlin's cheek stung like a vacuum burn. He opened his mouth, tried to think of something that would explain away her anger.

The lock opened. Prince Baskin came aboard *Tyrant*, wearing his armoured spacesuit with the helmet tucked under one arm.

"There'll be no objections, Merlin. My own ship couldn't keep pace with *Tyrant* even if I wished to shadow you, so the simplest option is to join you for the operation." He raised a gently silencing hand before Merlin—still stung—had a chance to interject. "I'll be along purely as an observer, someone with local knowledge, if it comes to that. You don't need to lecture me on the dangers. I've seen my share of frontline service, as you doubtless know, having made yourself such an expert on royal affairs." He nodded. "Yes, we tracked your search patterns, while you were supposedly verifying the authenticity of the syrinx."

"I wanted to know everything I could about your contact with the Cohort mission."

"That and more, I think." Baskin mouthed a command into his neck ring, and *Renouncer* detached from the lock. "None of it concerns me, though, Merlin. If it amused you to sift through our many assassinations and constitutional crises, so be it. All that matters to me is the safe return of the Tactician. And I will insist on being witness to that return. Don't insult me by suggesting that the presence of one more human on this ship will have any bearing on *Tyrant's* capabilities."

"It's not a taxi."

"But it is spacious enough for our present needs, and that is all that matters." He nodded at Teal. "Besides, I was enjoying our evening conversations too much to forego the pleasure."

"All right," Merlin said, sighing. "You're along for the ride, Prince. But I make the decisions. And if I feel like pulling out of this arrangement, for any reason, I'll do just that."

Prince Baskin set his helmet aside and offered his empty palms. "There'll be no coercion, Merlin—I could hardly force you into doing anything you disliked, could I?"

"So long as we agree on that." Merlin gestured to the suite of cabins aft of the lock. "Teal, show him the ropes, will you? I've got some navigation to be getting on with. We'll push to one gee in thirty minutes."

Merlin turned his back on Teal and the Prince and returned to *Tyrant's* command deck. He watched the dwindling trace of the *Renouncer*, knowing he could outpace it with ease. There would be a certain attraction in cutting and running right now, hoping that the old syrinx held together long enough for a Waynet transition, and seeing Baskin's face when he realised he would not be returning to Havergal for centuries, if at all.

But while Merlin was capable of many regrettable things, spite was not one of his failings.

His gaze slid to the results from the analyser. He thought of running the sequence again, using the same traces from the wineglass, but the arrival of the Prince rendered that earlier sample of doubtful value. Perhaps it had been contaminated to begin with, by other members of the royal staff. But now that Baskin was aboard, *Tyrant* could obtain a perfect genetic readout almost without trying.

The words of Baskin returned to mind, as if they held some significance Merlin could not yet see for himself: *If it amused you to sift through our many assassinations and constitutional crises, so be it.*

Assassinations.

When Merlin was satisfied that Prince Baskin's bones were up to the strain, he pushed *Tyrant* to two gees. It was uncomfortable for all of them, but bearable provided they kept to the lounge and avoided moving around too much. "We could go faster," Merlin said, as if it was no great achievement. "But we'd be putting out a little more exotic radiation than I'd like, and I'd rather not broadcast our intentions too strongly. Besides, two gees will get us to Mundar in plenty of time, and if you find it uncomfortable we can easily dial down the thrust for a little while."

"You make light of this capability," Prince Baskin said, his hand trembling slightly as he lifted a drinking vessel to his lips. "Yet this ship is thousands of years beyond anything possessed by either side in our system."

Merlin tried to look sympathetic. "Maybe if you weren't busy throwing rocks at each other, you could spend a little time on the other niceties of life, such as cooperation and mutual advancement."

"We will," Baskin affirmed. "I'll bend my life to it. I'm not a zealot for war. If I felt that there was a chance of a negotiated cease-fire, under terms amicable to both sides, I'd have seized it years ago. But our ideological differences are too great, our mutual grievances too ingrained. Sometimes I even think to myself that it wouldn't matter *who* wins, just as long as one side prevails over the other. There are reasonable men and women in Gaffurius, it's just . . ." But he trailed off, as if even he viewed this line of argument as treasonable.

"If you thought that way," Teal said, "the simplest thing would be to let the enemy win. Give them the Iron Tactician, if you think it will make that much difference."

"After all our advances . . . no. It's too late for that sort of idealism. Besides, we aren't dealing with Gaffurius. It's the brigands who are holding us to ransom."

"Face it," Merlin said. "For all this talk of peace, of victory—you'd miss the war."

"I wouldn't."

"I'm not so sure. You used to play at battle, didn't you? Toy soldiers and tabletop military campaigns, you said. It's been in your blood from the moment you took your first breath. You were the boy who dreamed of war."

"I changed," Baskin said. "Saw through those old distractions. I spoke of Lurga, didn't I—the last and greatest of our surface cities? Before the abandonment my home was Lurga's imperial palace, a building that was itself as grand as some cities. I often walk it in my dreams, Merlin. But that's where it belongs now: back in my childhood, along with all those toy soldiers."

"Lurga must have been something to see," Merlin said.

"Oh, it was. We built and rebuilt. They couldn't bear it, of course, the enemy. That's why it was always the focus of their attacks, right until the end."

"There was a bad one once, wasn't there?" Merlin asked.

"Too many to mention."

"I mean, a particularly bad one—a direct strike against the palace itself. It's in your public history—I noticed it while I was going through your open records, on Havergal. You'd have been six or seven at the time, so you'd easily remember it. An assassination attempt, plainly. The Gaffurians were trying to bite the head off the Havergal ruling elite."

"It was bad, yes. I was injured, quite seriouslly, by the collapse of part of the palace. Trapped alone and in the dark for days, until rescue squads broke through. I . . . recovered, obviously. But it's a painful episode and not one I care to dwell on. Good people died around me, Merlin. No child should have to see that."

"I couldn't agree more."

"Perhaps it was the breaking of me, in the end," Baskin said. "Until then I'd only known war as a series of distant triumphs. Glorious victories and downplayed defeats. After the attack, I knew what blood looked like up close. I healed well enough, but it was only after months of recuperation. And when I returned to my studies, and some engagement with public life, I found that I'd began to lose my taste for war. I look back on that little boy that I once was, so single-mindedly consumed by war and strategy, and almost wonder if I'm the same person." He set aside his drinking vessel, rubbing at the sore muscles in his arm. "You'll forgive me, both of you. I feel in need of rest. Our ships can only sustain this sort of acceleration for a few tens of minutes, not hour after hour."

"It's hard on us all," Merlin said, feeling a glimmer of empathy for his unwanted guest. "And you're right about one thing, Prince. I want an end to the war with the Huskers. But not at any cost."

When they were alone Teal said: "You've got some explaining to do. If it wasn't for Baskin I'd have forced it out of you with torture by now."

"I'm glad you didn't. All that screaming would have made our guest distinctly uncomfortable. And have you ever tried getting blood out of upholstery?" Merlin flashed a smile. But Teal's hard mask of an expression told him she was in no mood for banter.

"Why were you so interested in his genetic profile?"

There were sealed doors between the lounge and the quarters assigned to the Prince, but the ship was silent under normal operation and Merlin found himself glancing around and lowering his voice before answering.

"I just wanted peace of mind, Teal. I just thought that if I could find a genetic match between you and Prince Baskin, it would settle things for good, allow you to put your mind to rest about Cupis . . ."

"Put *my* mind mind to rest."

"I know I shouldn't have sampled you without your permission. It was just some hair left on your pillow, with a skin flakes . . ." Merlin silenced himself. "Now that we're aboard, the ship can run a profile just by sequencing the cells it picks up through the normal air circulation filters."

Teal still had her arm out, her look defiant. But slowly she pulled back the arm and slid her sleeve back down. "Run your damned tests. You've started this, you may as well finish it."

"Are you sure, Teal? It may not get us any nearer an answer of what happened to your bloodline."

"I said finish it," Teal answered.

Tyrant slipped across the system, into the contested space between the two stars. Battle continued to rage across a dozen worlds and countless more moons, minor planets and asteroids. Fleets were engaging on a dozen simultaneous fronts, their energy bursts spangling the night sky across light hours of distance. Every radio channel crackled with military traffic, encrypted signals, blatant propaganda, screams of help or mercy from stricken crews.

Tyrant steered clear of the worst of it. But even as they approached Mundar, Merlin picked out more activity than he had hoped for. Gaffurian patrol groups were swinging suspiciously close to the brigands' asteroid, as if something had begun to attract their interest. So far they were keeping clear of the predicted defense perimeter, but their presence put Merlin on edge. It didn't help that the Gaffurian incursions were drawing a counter-response from Havergal squadrons. The nearest battlefronts were still light-minutes away, but the last thing Merlin needed was a new combat zone opening up right where he had business of his own.

"I was hoping for a clear theatre of action," he told Baskin. "Something nice and quiet, where I could do my business without a lot of messy distractions."

"Gaffurian security may have picked up rumours about the Tactician by now," Baskin said.

"And that wasn't worth sharing with me before now?"

"I said rumours, Merlin—not hard intelligence. Or they may just be taking a renewed interest in the brigands. They're as much a thorn in the enemy's side as they are in ours."

"I like them more and more."

They were a day out when Merlin risked a quick snoop with *Tyrant*'s long-range sensors. Baskin and Teal were on the command deck as the scans refreshed and updated, overlaid with the intelligence schematics Merlin had already examined on the *Renouncer*. Mundar was a fuzzy rock traced through with the equally ghostly fault lines of shafts, corridors, internal pressure vaults and weapons emplacements.

"That was a risky thing to do" Baskin said, while Teal nodded her agreement.

"If they picked up anything," Merlin said, "it would have been momentary and on a spread of frequencies and particle bands they wouldn't normally expect. They'll put it down to sensor malfunctions and move on."

"I wish I had your confidence."

Merlin stretched out his hands and cracked his knuckles, as if he were preparing to climb a wall. "Let's think like Struxer. He's got his claws on something precious, a one-off machine, so chances are he won't put the Tactician anywhere vulnerable, especially with these patrol groups sniffing around."

"How does that help us?"

"Because it narrows down his options. That deep vault there—do you think it would suit?"

"Perhaps. The main thing is to declare our intentions; to give Struxer an unambiguous idea of your capabilities." Baskin danced his own finger across the display. "You'll open with a decisive but pinpoint attack. Enough to shake them up, and let them know we absolutely mean business. At what distance can you launch a strike?"

"We'll be in optimum charm-torp range in about six hours. I can lock in the targeting solutions now, if you like. But we'll have a sharper view of Mundar the nearer we get."

"Would they be able to see us that soon?" Teal asked.

Merlin was irritated by the question, but only because it had been the next thing on his mind.

"From what we understand of your ship's sensor footprint, they'll be able to pick you out inside a volume of radius one and a half light seconds. That's an estimate, though. Their weapons will be kinetic launchers, pulse beams, drone missiles. Can you deal with that sort of thing?"

"Provided I'm not having a bad day."

Baskin extended his own finger at the scans, wavering under the effort. "These cratered emplacements are most likely the sites of their kinetic batteries. I suggest a surgical strike against all of them, including the ones around the other side of Mundar. Can you do it?"

"Twelve charm-torps should take care of them. Which is handy, because that's all I've got left. We'll still have the gamma-cannons and the nova-mine launchers, if things get sticky."

"If I know Struxer, they will." Something twitched in Baskin's cheek, some nervous, betraying tic. "But the deaths will be all on his side, not ours. If that's the cost of enforcing peace, so be it."

Merlin eyed him carefully. "I've never been very good with that sort of calculus."

"None of us like it," Baskin said.

Teal went off to catch some sleep until they approached the attack threshold. Merlin grabbed a few hours himself, but his rest was fitful and he soon found himself returning to the command deck, watching as the scans slowly sharpened and their view of Mundar grew more precise. *Tyrant* was using passive sensors now, but these were already improving on the earlier active snapshot. Merlin was understandably on edge, though. They were backing toward the asteroid, and if there was ever a chance of their exhaust emissions being picked up, now was the time. Merlin had done what he could, trading deceleration efficiency for a constantly altering thrust angle that ought to provide maximum cover, but nothing was guaranteed.

"I thought I'd find you here," Baskin said, pinching at the corners of his eyes as he entered the room. "You've barely slept since we left Havergal, have you?"

"You don't look much more refreshed, Prince."

"I know—I saw myself in the mirror just now. Sometimes when I look at my own portrait, I barely recognise myself. But I think I can be excused a little anxiety, though. So much depends on the next few hours, Merlin. I think these may be the most critical hours of my entire career. My entire life, even."

Merlin waited until the Prince had taken his seat, folding his bones with care. "You mentioned Struxer back there."

"Did I?"

"The intelligence briefings told me very little, Prince—even the confidential files I lifted from your sealed archives on Havergal. But you spoke as if you knew the man."

"Struxer was one of us. That was never any sort of secret."

"A senior tactician, that's what I was told. That sounds like quite a high-up role to me. Struxer wasn't just some anonymous military minion, was he?"

After a moment Baskin said: "He was known to me. As of course were all the high-ranking strategists."

"Was Struxer involved in the Tactician?"

If Baskin meant to hide his hesitation, he did a poor job of it. "To a degree. The Tactician required a large staff, not just to coordinate the feeding-in of intelligence data, but to analyse and act on the results. The battle computers I mentioned . . ."

"But Struxer was close to it all, wasn't he?" Merlin was guessing now, relying on hard-won intuition, but Baskin's reactions were all he needed to know he was on the right track. "He worked closely with the computer."

"His defection was . . . regrettable."

"If you can call it a defection. That would depend on what those brigands actually want, wouldn't it? And no one's been terribly clear on that with me."

Baskin's face was strained. "They're against peace. Is there anything more you need to know?"

Merlin smiled, content with that line of questioning for now. "Prince, might I ask you something else? You know I took an interest in your constitutional history, when we were on Havergal. Assassinations are commonplace, aren't they? There was that time when almost the entire ruling house of Havergal was wiped out in one strike . . ."

"That was twelve or thirteen centuries ago."

"But only a little after the visitation of the Shrike. That was why it caught my eye."

"No other reason?"

"Should there be?"

"Don't play games with me, Merlin—you'll always lose. I was the boy who dreamed of war, remember."

The door behind them opened. It was Teal, awake sooner than Merlin had expected. Her face had a freshly scrubbed look, her hair wetted down.

"Are we close?"

"About thirty minutes out," Merlin said. "Buckle in, Teal—it could get interesting from any point onwards, especially if their sensors are a little better than the Prince believes."

Teal slipped into the vacant seat. Befitting her Cohort training, she had adapted well to the two gees, moving around *Tyrant* with a confident, sinewy ease.

"Have you run that genetic scan again?" she asked.

"I have," Merlin said. "And I came up with the same result, only at a higher confidence level. Do you want to tell him, or should I?"

"Tell me what?" Baskin asked.

"There's a glitch in your family tree," Merlin said, then nodded at Teal for her to continue.

"I've already been to your world," she said, delivering the words with a defiant and brazen confidence. "I was on the diplomatic party, aboard the swallowship *Shrike*. I was with them when they sold you the syrinx." Before he had a chance to voice his disbelief, she said: "A little later, our ship ran into trouble in a nearby system. The Huskers took us, wrecked the ship, but left just enough of us alive to suffer. We went into frostwatch, those of us who remained. And one by one we died, when the frostwatch failed. I was the last living survivor. Then Merlin found me, and we returned to your system. You know this to be possible, Prince. You know of frostwatch, of near-light travel, of time-compression."

"I suppose . . ." he said.

"But there's more to it than that," Teal went on. "My daughter stayed on Havergal. She became Cupis, Queen Cupis, after Tierce was promoted to the throne. You said it yourself, Prince: there was something in my face you thought you recognised. It's your own lineage, your own family tree."

"Except it isn't, quite," Merlin said. "You see, you're not related, and you should be. I ran a genetic cross-match between the two of you on Havergal, and another since you've been on *Tyrant*. Both say there's no correlation, which is odd given the family tree. But I think there's a fairly simple explanation."

Baskin glanced from Merlin to Teal and back to Merlin, his eyes wide, doubting and slightly fearful. "Which would be?"

"You're not Prince Baskin," Merlin said. "You just think you are."

"Don't be absurd. My entire life has been lived in the public eye, subject to the harshest scrutiny."

Merlin did his best not to sound too callous, nor give the impression that he took any pleasure in disclosing what he now knew to be the truth. "There's no doubt, I'm afraid. If you were really of royal blood, I'd know it. The only question is where along your family tree the birth line was broken, and why. And I think I know the answer to that, as well . . ."

The console chimed. Merlin turned to it with irritation, but a glance told him that the ship had every reason to demand his attention. A signal was beaming out at them, straight from Mundar.

"That isn't possible," Baskin said. "We're still three light seconds out—much too far for their sensors."

Teal said: "Perhaps you should see what it says."

The transmission used local protocols, but it only took an instant for *Tyrant* to unscramble the packets and resolve them into a video signal. A man's head appeared above the console, backdropped by a roughly hewn wall of pale rock. Merlin recognised the face as belonging to Struxer, but only because he had paid close attention to the intelligence briefings. Otherwise it would have been easy to miss the similarities. This Struxer was thinner of face, somehow more delicate of bone structure, older and wearier looking, than the cold-eyed defector Merlin had been expecting.

He started speaking in a high steady voice, babbling out a string of words in the Havergal tongue. *Tyrant* was listening in, but it would be a little while before it could offer a reliable translation.

Merlin turned to Teal.

"What's he saying?"

"I'm just as capable of telling you," Baskin said.

Merlin nodded. "But I'd sooner hear it from Teal."

"He's got a fix on you," she said, frowning slightly as she caught up with the stream of words. "Says he's had a lock since the moment you were silly enough to turn those scanning systems onto Mundar. Says you must have thought they were idiots, to miss something that obvious. Also that we're not as stealthy as we think we are, judging by the ease with which he's tracking our engine signature."

"You fool," Baskin hissed. "I told you it was a risk."

"He says he knows what our intentions are," Teal went on. "But no matter how much force you throw at them they're not going to relinquish the Iron Tactician. He says to turn back now, and avoid unnecessary violence."

Merlin gritted teeth. "Ship, get ready to send a return transmission using the same channel and protocols. Teal, you're doing the talking. Tell Struxer I've no axe to grind with him or his brigands, and if we can do this without bloodshed no one'll be happier than me. Also that I can take apart that asteroid as easily as if it's a piece of rotten fruit."

Baskin gave a thin smile, evidently liking Merlin's tone.

"Belligerent enough for you, was it?" Merlin asked, while Teal leaned in and translated Merlin's reply.

"Threats and force are what they understand," Baskin said.

It took three seconds for Teal's statement to reach Mundar, and another three for Struxer's response to find its way back to *Tyrant*. They listened to what he had to say, Merlin needing no translator to tell him that Struxer's answer was a great deal more strident than before.

"You can forget about them handing it over without a struggle," Teal said. "And he says that we'd be very wise not to put Mundar's armaments to the rest, now that the Iron Tactician's coordinating its own defense plans. They've got every weapon on that asteroid hooked directly into the Tactician, and they're prepared to let it protect itself."

"They'd still be outgunned," Merlin said. But even he couldn't quite disguise the profound unease he was beginning to feel.

"It's a bluff," Baskin said. "The Tactician has no concept of its own self-preservation."

"Can you be sure?" Teal asked.

"Tell Struxer this," Merlin said. "Surrender the Iron Tactician and I won't lay a finger on that asteroid. All they have to do is bring it to the surface—my proctors can take care of the rest."

Teal relayed the statement. Struxer barked back his answer, which was mono-syllabic enough to require no translation.

"He says if we want it, we should try taking it," Teal said.

Merlin nodded—he had been expecting as much, but it had seemed worth his while to make one last concession at a negotiated settlement. "Ship, give me manual fire control on the torp racks. We're a little further out than I'd like, but it'll give me time to issue a warning. I'm taking out those kinetic batteries."

"You have control, Merlin," *Tyrant* said.

Baskin asked: "Are you sure it isn't too soon?"

Merlin gave his reply by means of issuing the firing command. *Tyrant* pushed out its ventral weapons racks and the charm-torps sped away with barely a twitch of recoil. Only a pattern of moving nodes on the targetting display gave any real hint that the weapons had been deployed.

"Torps armed and running," *Tyrant* said.

"Teal, tell them they have a strike on its way. They've got a few minutes to move their people deeper into the asteroid, if they aren't already there. My intention is to disable their defenses, not to take lives. Make sure Struxer understands that."

Teal was in the middle of delivering her message when *Tyrant* jolted violently and without warning. It was a sideways impulse, harsh enough to bruise bones, and for a moment Merlin could only stare at the displays, as shocked as he had been when Teal had slapped him across the face.

Then there was another jolt, in the opposite direction, and he understood.

"Evasive response in progress," *Tyrant* said. "Normal safety thresholds suspended. Manual override available, but not recommended."

"What?" Baskin grimaced.

"We're being shot at," Merlin said.

Tyrant was taking sharp evasive manoeuvres, corkscrewing hard even as it was still engaged in a breakneck deceleration.

"Impossible. We're still too far out."

"There's nothing coming at us from Mundar. It's something else. Some perimeter defense screen we didn't even know about." He directed a reproachful look at Baskin. "I mean, that *you* didn't know about."

"Single-use kinetics, perhaps," Baskin said. "Free-floating sentries."

"I should be seeing the activation pulses. Electromagnetic and optical burst signatures. I'm not. All I'm seeing are the slugs, just before they hit us."

They were, as far as *Tyrant* could tell, simply inert slugs of dense matter, lacking guidance or warheads. They were falling into detection range just in time to compute and execute an evasion, but the margins were awfully fine.

"There are such things as dark kinetics," Baskin said. "They're a prototype weapon system: mirrored and cloaked to conceal the launch pulse. But Struxer's brigands have nothing in their arsenal like that. Even if they had a local manufacturing capability, they wouldn't have the skills to make their own versions . . ."

"Would the Tactician know about those weapons?" Teal asked.

"In its catalogue of military assets . . . yes. But there's a world of difference between knowing of something and being able to direct the duplication and manufacture of that technology."

"Tell that to your toy," Merlin murmured. He hoped it was his imagination, but the violent counter-manoevres seemed to be coming more rapidly, as if *Tyrant* was having an increasingly difficult time steering between the projectiles. "Ship, recall six of the charm-torps. Bring them back as quickly as you can."

"What good will that do?" Baskin snapped. "You should be hitting them with everything you've got, not pulling your punch at the last minute."

"We need the torps to give us an escort screen," Merlin said. "The other six can still deal with all the batteries on the visible face."

It had been rash to commit all twelve in one go, he now knew, born of an arrogant assumption as to his own capabilities. But he had realised his mistake in time.

"Struxer again," Teal said. "He says it's only going to get worse, and we should call off the other missiles and give up on our attack. Says if he sees a clear indication of our exhaust, he'll stand down the defense screen."

"Carry on," Baskin said.

"Charm-torps on return profile," *Tyrant* said. "Shall I deploy racks for recovery?"

"No. Group the torps in a protective cordon around us, close enough that you can interdict any slugs that you can't steer us past. And put in a reminder to me to upgrade our attack countermeasures."

"Complying. The remaining six torps are now being reassigned to the six visible targets. Impact in . . . twenty seconds."

"Struxer," Merlin said, not feeling that his words needed any translation. "Get your people out of those batteries!"

A sudden blue brightness pushed through *Tyrant*'s windows, just before they shuttered tight in response.

"Slug interdicted," the ship said calmly. "One torp depleted from defense cordon. Five remaining."

"Spare me the countdown," Merlin said. "Just get us through this mess and out the other side."

The six remaining charm-torps of the attack formation closed in on Mundar in the same instant, clawing like a six-taloned fist, gouging six star-hot wounds into the asteroid's crust, six swelling spheres of heat and destruction that grew and dimmed until they merged at their boundaries. Merlin, studying the readouts, could only swallow in horror and awe, reminded again of the potency of even modest Cohort weaponry. Megatonnes of rock and dust were boiling off the asteroid even as he watched, like a skull bleeding out from six eye-sockets.

Three of the cordon torps were lost before *Tyrant* began to break free into relatively safe space, but by then Merlin's luck was stretching perilously thin. The torps could interdict the slugs for almost any range of approach vectors, but not always safely. If the impact happened close enough to *Tyrant*, that was not much better than a direct hit.

They were through, then, but not without cost. The hull had taken a battering from two of the nearer detonations, and while none of the damage would ordinarily have been of concern, Merlin had been counting on having a ship in optimum condition. Limping away to effect repairs was scarcely an option now.

The consolation, if he needed one, was that Mundar had taken a much worse battering.

"Is Struxer still sending?" Merlin asked.

"He's trying," Teal said.

Struxer's face appeared, but speckled by interference. He looked strained, glancing at either side of him as he made his statement. Teal listened carefully.

"He says they've still got weapons, if we dare to come any nearer. His position hasn't changed."

"Mine has," Merlin said. "Ship, send in the remaining torps, dialled to maximum yield. Strike at the existing impact sites: see if we can't open some fracture plains, or punch our way deep inside." Then he enlarged the asteroid's schematic and began tapping his finger against some of the secondary installations on the surface—what the intelligence dossiers said were weapons, sensor pods, airlocks. "Ready nova-mines for dispersal. Spread pattern three. We'll pick off any moving targets with the gamma-cannon."

Teal said: "If you hit Struxer's antenna you'll take away our means of communicating."

"I'm past the point of negotiation, Teal. My ship's wounded and I take that personally. If you want to send a last message to Struxer, tell him he had his chance to play nicely."

Baskin leaned forward in his seat restraints. "Don't do anything too rash, Merlin. We came to force his hand, not to annihilate the entire asteroid."

"Your primary consideration was stopping the Tactician falling into the wrong hands. I'm about to guarantee that never happens."

"I want it intact."

"It was never going to work, Prince. There was never going to be any magic peace, just because you had your battle computer back." A sudden indignation passed through him. "I know wars. I know how they play out. Squeeze the enemy hard and they just find new ways to fight back. It'll go on and on and you'll never be any nearer victory."

"We were winning."

"One tide was going out. Another was due to come back in. That's all it was."

The charm-torps were striking. Set to their highest explosive setting, the bursts were twenty times brighter than the first wave. Each fireball scooped out a tenth of the asteroid's volume, lofting unthinkable quantities of rock and dirt and gas into space, a ghastly swelling shroud lit from within by pulses of lightning.

Lines of light cut through that shroud. Kinetics and lasers were striking out from what remained of the asteroid's facing hemisphere, sweeping in arcs as they tried to find *Tyrant*. The ship swerved and stabbed like a dancing snake. The edge of a laser gashed across part of its hull, triggering a shriek of damage alarms. Merlin dispatched the nova-mines, then swung the nose around to bring the gamma-cannon into play. The flashes of the nova-mines began to pepper the shrouded face of Mundar. The kinetics and lasers were continuing, but their coverage was becoming sparser. Merlin sensed that they had endured the worst of the assault. But the approach had enacted a grave toll on *Tyrant*. One more direct hit, even with a low-energy weapon, might be enough to split open the hull.

Tyrant had reduced its speed to only a few kilometres per second relative to the asteroid. Now they were beginning to pick up the billowing front of the debris cloud. *Tyrant* was built to tolerate extremes of pressure, but the hot, gravelly medium was nothing like an atmosphere. Under other circumstances Merlin would have gladly turned around rather than push deeper. But *Tyrant* would have to cross the kinetic defense screen to reach empty space, and now he had used up all his charm-torps. If the Tactician had indeed been coordinating Mundar's defenses, then Merlin saw only one way to dig himself out of this hole. He could leave nothing intact—even if it meant butchering whoever was left alive in Mundar.

Debris hammered the hull. Merlin curled fingers into sweat-sodden palms.

"Merlin," Teal said. "It's Struxer's signal again. Only it's not coming from inside Mundar."

Merlin understood as soon as he shifted his attention to the navigational display. Struxer's transmission was originating from a small moving object, coming toward them from within the debris field. The gamma-cannon was still aimed straight at Mundar. Merlin shifted the lock onto the object, ready to annihilate it in an instant. Then he waited for *Tyrant*'s sensors to give him their best estimate of the size and form of the approaching object. He was expecting something like a mine or a small autonomous missile, trying to camouflage its approach within the chaos of the debris. But then why was it transmitting in the first place?

He had his answer a moment later. The form was five-nubbed, a fat-limbed starfish. Or a human, wearing a spacesuit, drifting through the debris cloud like a rag doll in a storm.

"Suicidal," Baskin said.

There was no face now, just a voice. The signal was too poor for anything else. Teal listened and said: "He's asking for you to slow and stand down your weapons. He says we've reached a clear impasse. You'll never make it out of this area without the Tactician's cooperation, and you'll never find the Tactician without his assistance."

Merlin had manual fire control on the gamma-cannon. He had settled one hand around the trigger, ready to turn that human starfish into just another crowd of hot atoms.

"I said I was past the point of negotiation."

"Struxer says dozens have already died in the attack. But there are thousands more of his people still alive in the deeper layers. He says you won't be able to destroy the Tactician without killing them as well."

"They picked this fight, not me."

"Merlin, listen to me. Struxer seems reasonable. There's a reason he's put himself out there in that suit."

"I blew up his asteroid. That might have something to do with it."

"He wants to negotiate from a position of weakness, not strength. That's what he says. Every moment where you *don't* destroy him is another moment in which you might start listening."

"I think we already stated our positions, didn't we?"

"He said you wouldn't be able to take the Tactician. And you can't, that's clear. You can destroy it, but you can't take it. And now he's asking to talk."

"About what?"

Teal looked at him with pleading eyes. "Just talk to him, Merlin. That woman you showed me—your mother, waiting by that window. The sons she lost—you and your brother. I saw the kindness in her. Don't tell me you'd have made her proud by killing that man."

"My mother died on Plenitude. She wasn't in that room. I showed you nothing, just ghosts, just memories stitched together by my brother."

"Merlin . . ."

He squeezed the fire control trigger. Instead of discharging, though, the gamma-cannon reported a malfunction. Merlin tried again, then pulled his shaking, sweat-sodden hand from the control. The weapons board was showing multiple failures and system errors, as if the ship had only just been holding itself together until that moment.

"You cold-hearted . . ." Teal started.

"Your sympathies run that deep," Merlin said. "You should have spoken up before we used the torps."

Baskin levelled a hand on Merlin's wrist, drawing him further from the gamma-cannon trigger. "Perhaps it was for the best, after all. Only Struxer really knows the fate of the Tactician now. Bring him in, Merlin. What more have we got to lose?"

Struxer removed his helmet, the visor pocked and crazed from his passage through the debris cloud. Merlin recognised the same drawn, weary face that had spoken to them from within Mundar. He made an acknowledgement of Prince Baskin, speaking in the Havergal tongue—Merlin swearing that he picked up the sarcasm and scorn despite the gulf of language.

"He says it was nice of them to send royalty to do their dirty work," Teal said.

"Tell him he's very lucky not to be a cloud of atoms," Merlin said.

Teal passed on this remark, listened to the answer, then gave a half smile of her own. "Struxer says you're very lucky that the Tactician gave you safe passage."

"That's his idea of safe passage?" Merlin asked.

But he moved to a compartment in the cabin wall and pulled out a tray of coiled black devices, each as small and neat as a stone talisman. He removed one of the translators and pressed it into his ear, then offered one of the other devices to Struxer.

"Tell him it won't bite," he said. "My ship's very good with languages, but it needs a solid baseline of data to work with. Those transmissions helped, but the more we talk, the better we'll get."

Struxer fingered the translator in the battered glove of his spacesuit, curling his lips in distrust. "Cohort man," he said, in clear enough Main. "I speak a little of your language. The Prince made us take school. In case Cohort came back."

"So you'd have a negotiating advantage over the enemy?" Merlin asked.

"It seemed prudent," Baskin said. "But most of my staff didn't see it that way. Struxer was one of the exceptions."

"Be careful who you educate," Merlin told him. "They have a tendency to start thinking for themselves. Start doing awkward things like defecting, and holding military computers to ransom."

Struxer had pushed the earpiece into position. He shifted back to his native tongue, and his translated words buzzed into Merlin's skull. "Ransom—is that what you were told, Cohort man?"

"My name's Merlin. And yes—that seems to be the game here. Or did you steal the Tactician because you'd run out of games to play on a rainy afternoon?"

"You have no idea what you've been drawn into. What were you promised, to do his dirty work?"

Teal said: "Merlin doesn't need you. He just wants the Tactician."

"A thing he neither understands nor needs, and which will never be his."

"I'd still like it," Merlin said.

"You're too late," Struxer said. "The Tactician has decided its own fate now. You've brought those patrol groups closer, with that crude display of strength. They'll close on Mundar soon enough. But the Tactician will be long gone by then."

"Gone?" Baskin asked.

"It has accepted that it must end itself. Mundar's remaining defenses are now being turned inward, against the asteroid itself. It would rather destroy itself than become of further use to Havergal, or indeed Gaffurius."

"Ship," Merlin said. "Tell me this isn't true."

"I would like to," *Tyrant* said. "But it seems to be the case. I am recording an increasing rate of kinetic bombardments against Mundar's surface. Our own position is not without hazard, given my damaged condition."

Merlin moved to the nearest console, confirming for himself what the ship already knew. The opposed fleets were altering course, pincering in around Mundar.

Anti-ship weapons were already sparking between the two groups of ships, drawing both into closer and closer engagement.

"The Tactician will play the patrol groups off each other, drawing them into an exchange of fire," Struxer said, with an icy sort of calm. "Then it will parry some of that fire against Mundar, completing the work you have begun."

"It's a machine," Baskin said. "It can't decide to end itself."

"Oh, come now," Struxer said, regarding Baskin with a shrewd, skeptical scrutiny. "We're beyond those sorts of secrets, aren't we? Or are you going to plead genuine ignorance?"

"Whatever you think he knows," Merlin said, "I've a feeling he doesn't."

Struxer shifted his attention onto Merlin. "Then you know?"

"I've an inkling or two. No more than that."

"About what?" Teal asked.

Merlin raised his voice. "Ship, start computing an escape route for us. If the kinetics are being directed at Mundar, then the defense screen ought to be a little easier to get through, provided we're quick."

"You're running?" Baskin asked. "With the prize so near?"

"In case you missed it," Merlin said, "the prize just got a death-wish. I'm cutting my losses before they cut me. Buckle in, all of you."

"What about your syrinx?" Teal demanded.

"I'll find me another. It's a big old galaxy—bound to be a few more knocking around. Ship, are you ready with that solution?"

"I am compromised, Merlin. I have hull damage, weapons impairment and a grievous loss of thruster authority. There can be no guarantee of reaching clear space, especially with the build-up of hostile assets."

"I'll take that chance, thanks. Struxer: you're free to step back out of the airlock any time you like. Or did you think all your problems were over just because I didn't shoot you with the gamma-cannon?"

Tyrant began to move. Merlin steadied a hand against a wall, ready to tense if the gee-loads climbed sharply.

"I think our problems are far from over," Struxer answered him levelly. "But I do not wish to die just yet. Equally, I would ask one thing."

"You're not exactly in a position to be asking for anything."

"You had a communications channel open to me. Give me access to that same channel and allow me to make my peace with the Tactician, before it's too late. A farewell, if you wish. I can't talk it out of this course of action, but at least I can ease its conscience."

"It has no conscience," Baskin said, grimacing as the acceleration mounted and *Tyrant* began to swerve its away around obstacles and in-coming fire.

"Oh, it most definitely does," Struxer said.

Merlin closed his eyes. He was standing at the door to his mother's parlour, watching her watching the window. She had become aware of his silent presence and bent around in her stern black chair, her arms straining with the effort. The golden sun shifted across the changing angles of her face. Her eyes met his for an instant, liquid grey with sadness, the eyes of a woman who had known much and seen the end of everything. She made to speak, but no words came.

Her expression was sufficient, though. Disappointed, expectant, encouraging, a loving mother well used to her sons' failings, and always hopeful that the better aspects of their nature might rise to the surface. Merlin and Gallinule, last sons of Plenitude.

"Damn it all," Merlin said under his breath. "Damn it all."

"What?" Teal asked.

"Turn us around, ship," he said. "Turn us around and take us back to Mundar. As deep as we can go."

They fought their way into the thick broil of the dust cloud, relying on sensors alone, a thousand fists hammering their displeasure against the hull, until at last *Tyrant* found the docking bay. The configuration was similar to the *Renouncer*, easily within the scope of adjustments that *Tyrant* could make, and they were soon clamped on. Baskin was making ready to secure his vacuum suit when Merlin tossed him a dun-coloured outfit.

"Cohort immersion suit. Put it on. You as well, Struxer. And be quick about it."

"What are these suits?" Baskin asked, fingering the ever-so-ragged, grubby-looking garment.

"You'll find out soon enough." Merlin nodded at Teal. "You too, soldier. As soon as *Tyrant* has an electronic lock on the Tactician it can start figuring out the immersion protocols. Won't take too long."

"Immersion protocols for what?" Baskin asked, with sharpening impatience.

"We're going inside," Merlin said. "All of us. There's been enough death today, and most of it's on my hands. I'm not settling for any more."

It waited beyond the lock, the only large thing in a dimly-lit chamber walled in rock. The air was cold and did not appear to be recirculating. From the low illumination of the chamber, Merlin judged that Mundar was down to its last reserves of emergency power. He shivered in the immersion suit. It was like wearing paper.

"Did I really kill hundreds, Struxer?"

"Remorse, Merlin?"

Something was tight in his throat. "I never set out to kill. But I know that there's a danger out there beyond almost any human cost. They took my world, my people. Left Teal without a ship or a crew. They'll do the same to every human world in the galaxy, given time. I felt that if I could bring peace to this one system, I'd be doing something. One small act against a vaster darkness."

"And that excuses any act?"

"I was only trying to do the right thing."

Struxer gave a sad sniff of a laugh, as if he had lost count of the number of times he had heard such a justification. "The only right action is not to kill, Merlin. Not on some distant day when it suits you, but here and now, from the next moment on. The Tactician understands that." Struxer reached up suddenly as if to swat an insect that had settled on the back of his neck. "What's happening?"

"The immersion suit's connecting into your nervous system," Merlin said. "It's fast and painless and there won't be any lasting damage. Do you feel it too, Prince?"

"It might not be painful," Baskin said. "But I wouldn't exactly call it pleasant."

"Trust us," Merlin said. "We're good at this sort of thing."

At last he felt ready to give the Iron Tactician his full attention.

Its spherical form rested on a pedestal in the middle of the chamber, the low light turning its metallic plating to a kind of coppery brown. It was about as large as an escape capsule, with a strange brooding presence about it. There were no eyes or cameras anywhere on it, at least none that Merlin recognised. But he had the skin-crawling sensation of being watched, noticed, contemplated, by an intellect not at all like his own.

He raised his hands.

"I'm Merlin. I know what you are, I think. You should know what I am, as well. I tried to take you, and I tried to hurt your world. I'm sorry for the people I killed. But I stand before you now unarmed. I have no weapons, no armour, and I doubt very much that there's anything I could do to hurt you."

"You're wasting your words," Baskin said behind him, rubbing at the back of his neck.

"No," Struxer said. "He isn't. The Tactician hears him. It's fully aware of what happens around it."

Merlin touched the metal integument of the Iron Tactician, feeling the warmth and throb of hidden mechamisms. It hummed and churned in his presence, and gave off soft liquid sounds, like some huge boiler or laundry machine. He stroked his hand across the battered curve of one of the thick armoured plates, over the groove between one plate and the next. The plates had been unbolted or hinged back in places, revealing gold-plated connections, power and chemical sockets, or even rugged banks of dials and controls. Needles twitched and lights flashed, hinting at mysterious processes going on deep within the armour. Here and there a green glow shone through little windows of dark glass.

Tyrant whispered into Merlin's ear, via the translator earpiece. He nodded, mouthed back his answer, then returned his attention to the sphere.

"You sense my ship," Merlin said. "It tells me that it understands your support apparatus—that it can map me into your electronic sensorium using this immersion suit. I'd like to step inside, if that's all right?"

No answer was forthcoming—none that Merlin or his ship recognised. But he had made his decision by then, and he felt fully and irrevocably committed to it. "Put us through, ship—all of us. We'll take our chances."

"And if things take a turn for the worse?" *Tyrant* asked.

"Save yourself, however you're able. Scuttle away and find someone else that can make good use of you."

"It just wouldn't be the same," *Tyrant* said.

The immersion suits snatched them from the chamber. The dislocation lasted an instant and then Merlin found himself standing next to his companions, in a high-ceilinged room that might well have been an annex of the Palace of Eternal Dusk. But the architectural notes were subtly unfamiliar, the play of light through the windows not that of his home, and the distant line of hills remained resolutely fixed. Marbled floor lay under their feet. White stone walls framed the elegant arch-work of the windows.

"I know this place," Baskin said, looking around. "I spent a large part of my youth in these rooms. This was the imperial palace in Lurga, as it was before the abandonment." Even in the sensorium he wore a facsimile of the immersion suit, and he stroked the thin fabric of its sleeve with unconcealed wonder. "This is a remarkable technology, Merlin. I feel as if I've stepped back into my childhood. But why these rooms—why re-create the palace?"

Only one doorway led out of the room in which they stood. It faced a short corridor, with high windows on one side and doors on the other. Merlin beckoned them forward. "You should tell him, Struxer. Then I can see how close I've come to figuring it out for myself."

"Figured what out?" Baskin asked.

"What really happened when they attacked this place," Merlin said.

They walked into the corridor. Struxer seemed first at loss for how to start. His jaw moved, but no sounds came. Then he glanced down, swallowed, and found the words he needed.

"The attack's a matter of record," he said. "The young Prince Baskin was the target, and he was gravely injured. Spent days and days half-buried, in darkness and cold, until the teams found him. Then the prince was nurtured back to strength, and finally allowed back into the world. But that's not really what happened."

They were walking along the line of windows. The view beyond was vastly more idyllic than any part of the real Havergal. White towers lay amongst woods and lakes, with purple-tinged hills rising in the distance, the sky beyond them an infinite storybook blue.

"I assure you it did," Baskin said. "I'd remember otherwise, wouldn't I?"

"Not if they didn't want you to," Merlin said. He walked on for a few paces. "There was an assasination strike. But it didn't play out the way you think it did. The real prince was terribly injured—much worse than your memories have it."

Now an anger was pushing through Baskin's voice. "What do you mean, the 'real prince?'"

"You were substituted," Struxer said. "The assassination attempt played down, no mention made of the extent of the real Prince's injuries."

"My bloodline," Teal said. "This is the reason it's broken, isn't it?"

Merlin nodded, but let Struxer continue. "They rebuilt this palace as best they could. Even then it was never as idealised as this. Most of the east wing was gone. The view through these windows was . . . less pretty. It was only ever a stopgap, before Lurga had to be abandoned completely."

They had reached the only open door in the corridor. With the sunlit view behind their backs their shadows pushed across the door's threshold, into the small circular room beyond.

In the middle of the room a small boy knelt surrounded by wooden battlements and toy armies. They ranged away from him in complex, concentric formations— organised into interlocking ranks and files as tricky as any puzzle. The boy was reaching out to move one of the pieces, his hand dithering in the air.

"No," Baskin whispered. "This isn't how it is. There isn't a child inside this thing."

Struxer answered softly. "After the attack, the real Prince was kept alive by the best doctors on Havergal. It was all done in great secrecy. It had to be. What had become of him, the extent of his injuries, his dependence on machines to keep him alive . . . all of that would have been far too upsetting for the populace. The war was going badly: public morale was low enough as it was. The only solution, the only way to maintain the illusion, was to bring in another boy. You looked similar enough, so you were brought in to live out his life. One boy swapped for another."

"That's not what happened."

"Boys change from year to year, so the ruse was never obvious," Struxer said. "But *you* had to believe. So you were raised exactly as the Prince had been raised, in this palace, surrounded by the same things, and told stories of his life just as if it had been your own. Those games of war, the soldiers and campaigns? They were never part of your previous life, but slowly you started to believe an imagined past over the real one—a fiction that you accepted as the truth."

"You said you grew bored of war," Teal said. "That you were a sickly child who turned away from tabletop battles and became fascinated by languages instead. That was the real you breaking through, wasn't it? They could surround you with the instruments of war, try to make you dream of it, but they couldn't turn you into the person you were not—even if most of the time you believed the lie."

"But not always," Merlin said, watching as the boy made up his mind and moved one of the pieces. "Part of you knew, or remembered, I think. You've been fighting against the lie your whole life. But now you don't need to. Now you're free of it."

Struxer said: "We didn't suspect at first. Even those of us who worked closely with the Tactician were encouraged to think of it as a machine, an artificial intelligence. The medical staff who were involved in the initial work were either dead or sworn to silence, and the Tactician rarely needed any outside intervention. But there were always rumours. Technicians who had seen too much, glimpsed a little too far into the heart of it. Others—like myself—who started to doubt the accepted version of events, this easy story of a dramatic breakthrough in artificial intelligence. I began to . . . question. Why had the enemy never made a similar advancement? Why had we never repeated our success? But the thing that finally settled it for me was the Tactician itself. We who were the closest to it . . . we sensed the changes."

"Changes?" Baskin asked.

"A growing disenchantment with war. A refusal to offer the simple forecasts our military leaders craved. The Tactician's advice was becoming . . . quixotic. Undependable. We adjusted for it, placed less weight on its predictions and simulations. But slowly those of us who were close to it realised that the Tactician was trying to engineer peace, not war."

"Peace is what we've always striven for," Baskin said.

"But by one means, total victory," Struxer said. "But the Tactician no longer considered such an outcome desirable. The boy who dreamed of war had grown up, Prince. The boy had started to develop the one thing the surgeons never allowed for."

"A conscience," Merlin said. "A sense of regret."

The boy froze between one move and the next. He turned to face the door, his eyes searching. He was small-boned, wearing a soldier's costume tailored for a child.

"We're here," Struxer said, raising a hand by way of reassurance. "Your friends. Merlin spoke to you before, do you remember?"

The boy looked distracted. He moved a piece from one position to another, angrily.

"You should go," he said. "I don't want anyone here today. I'm going to make these armies fight each other so badly they'll never want to fight again."

Merlin was the first to step into the room. He approached the boy carefully, picking his way through the gaps in the regiments. They were toy soldiers, but he could well imagine that each piece had some direct and logical correspondence in the fleets engaging near Mundar, as well as Mundar's own defenses.

"Prince," he said, stooping down with his hands on his knees. "You don't have to do this. Not any more. I know you want something other than war. It's just that they keep trying to force you into playing the same games, don't they?"

"When he didn't give the military planners the forecasts they wanted," Struxer said, "they tried to coerce him by other means. Electronic persuasion. Direct stimulation of his nervous system."

"You mean, torture," Merlin said.

"No," Baskin said. "That's not how it was. The Tactician was a machine . . . just a machine."

"It was never that," Merlin replied.

"I knew what needed to be done," Struxer said. "It was a long game, of course. But then the Tactician's strength has always been in long games. I defected first, joined the brigands here in Mundar, and only then did we start putting in place our plans to take the Tactician."

"Then it was never about holding him to ransom," Merlin said.

"No," Struxer said. "All that would have done is prolong the war. We'd been fighting long enough, Merlin. It was time to embrace the unthinkable: a real and lasting cease-fire. It was going to be a long and difficult process, and it could only be orchestrated from a position of neutrality, out here between the warring factions. It would depend on sympathetic allies on both sides: good men and women prepared to risk their own lives in making tiny, cumulative changes, under the Tactician's secret stewardship. We were ready—eager, even. In small ways we had begun the great work. Admit it, Prince Baskin: the tide of military successes had begun to turn away from you, in recent months. That was our doing. We were winning. And then Merlin arrived." Struxer set his features in a mask of impassivity. "Nothing in the Tactician's forecasting predicted *you*, Merlin, or the terrible damage you'd do to our cause."

"I stopped, didn't I?"

"Only when Mundar had humbled you."

The room shook, dust dislodging from the stone walls, one or two of the toy soldiers toppling in their ranks. Merlin knew what that was. *Tyrant* was communicating the actual attack suffered by Mundar through to the sensorium. The asteroid's own kinetic weapons were beginning to break through its crust.

"It won't be long now," he said.

Teal picked her way to Merlin's side and knelt between the battlements and armies, touching a hand to the boy. "We can help you," she said. Followed by a glance to Merlin. "Can't we?"

"Yes," he said, doubtfully at first, then with growing conviction. "Yes. Prince Baskin. The real Prince. The boy who dreamed of war, and then stopped dreaming. I believe it, too. There isn't a mind in the universe that isn't capable of change. You want peace in this system? Something real and lasting, a peace built on forgiveness and reconciliation, rather than centuries of simmering enmity? So do I. And I think you can make it happen, but for that you have to live. I have a ship. You saw me coming in—saw my weapons and what they could do. You bloodied me good, as well. But I can help you now—help you do what's right. Turn the kinetics away from Mundar, Prince. You don't have to die."

"I said you should go away," the boy said.

Teal lifted a hand to his cheek. "They hurt you," she said. "Very badly. But my blood's in you and I won't rest until you've found peace. But not this way. Merlin's right, Prince. There's still time to do good."

"They don't want good," the boy answered. "I gave them good, but they didn't like it."

"You don't have to concern yourself with them now," Merlin said, as another disturbance shook the room. "Turn the weapons from Mundar. Do it, Prince."

The boy's hand loitered over the wooden battlements. Merlin intuited that these must be the logical representation of Mundar's defense screens. The boy fingered one of the serrated formations, seemingly on the verge of moving it.

"It won't do any good," he said.

"It will," Merlin said.

"You've brought them too near," the boy said, sweeping his other hand across the massed regiments, in all their colours and divisions. "They didn't know where I was before, but now you've shown them."

"I made a mistake," Merlin admitted. "A bad one, because I wanted something too badly. But I'm here to make amends."

Now it was Baskin's turn to step closer to the boy. "We have half a life in common," he said. "They stole a life from you, and tried to make me think it was my own. It worked, too. I'm an old man now, and I suppose you're as old as me, deep down. But we have something in common. We've both outgrown war, whether those around us are willing to accept it or not." He lowered down, upsetting some of the soldiers as he did—the boy glaring for an instant, then seeming to put the matter behind him. "I want to help you. Be your friend, if such a thing's possible. What Teal said is true: you *do* have her blood. Not mine, now, but it doesn't mean I don't want to help." He placed his own hand around the boy's wrist, the hand that hovered over the wooden battlements. "I remember these games," he said. "These toys. I played them well. We could play together, couldn't we?" Slowly, with great trepidation, Baskin risked turning one of the battlements around, until its fortifications were facing outward again.

The boy said: "I wouldn't do it that way."

"Show me how you would do it," Baskin said.

The boy took the battlement and shifted its position. Then he took another and placed them in close formation. He looked up at Baskin, seeking both approval and praise. "See. That's better, isn't it?"

"Much better," Baskin said.

"You can move that one," the boy said, indicating one of the other battlements. "Put it over there, the other way round."

"Like this?" Baskin asked, with a nervous, obliging smile.

"A little closer. That's good enough."

Merlin realised that he had been holding his breath while this little exchange was going on. It was too soon to leap to conclusions, but it had been a while since the room had last shook. Hardly daring to break the fragile spell, he slipped into a brief subvocal exchange with *Tyrant*. His ship confirmed that the rain of kinetics had ceased.

"Now for the tricky part," Merlin murmured, as much for himself as his audience. "Prince, listen to me carefully. Rebuild those defenses. Do it as well as you can, because you need to protect yourself. There's hard work to do—very hard work—and you need to be at your strongest."

"I don't like work," the boy said.

"None of us do. But if you're bored with this game, I've got a much more interesting one to play. You're going to engineer a peace, and hold it. It's going to be the hardest thing you've ever done but I've no doubt that you'll rise to the challenge."

Struxer whispered: "Those fleets aren't exactly ready to set down their arms, Merlin."

"I'll make them," he said. "Just go give the Prince a running start. Then it's over to him." But he corrected himself. "Over to all of you, in fact. He'll need all the help he can get, Struxer." Merlin leaned in closer to the boy, until his mouth was near his ear. "We're going to lie," he said, confidingly. "We're going to lie and they're going to believe us, those fleets. Not forever, but long enough for you to start making peace seem like the easier path. It's a lot to ask, but I know you're up to it."

The boy's face met Merlin's. "Lie?"

"You'll understand. *Tyrant*: open a channel out to those ships. The whole binary system, as powerful a signal as you can put out. Hijack every open transmitter you can find. And translate these words, as well as you can." Then he frowned to himself and turned to Teal. "No. You should be the one. Better that it comes from a native speaker, than my garbled efforts."

"What would you like me to say?"

Merlin smiled. He told her. It did not take long.

"This is Teal of the Cohort," she said, her words gathered within the sensorium, fed through *Tyrant*, pushed out beyond the ruins of Mundar, through the defense screens, out to the waiting fleets, onward to the warring worlds. "I came here by Waynet, a little while ago. But I was here once before, more than a thousand years ago, and I knew King Curtal before you set him on the throne. I stand now in Mundar, ready to tell you that the time has come to end this war. Not for an hour, or a day, or a few miserable years, but forever. Because what you need now is peace and unity, and you don't have very long to build on it. A Husker attack swarm is approaching your binary system. We slipped ahead of them through the Waynet, but they will be here. You have less than a century . . . only a handful of decades. Then they'll arrive." Teal shot a look at Merlin, and he gave her a tiny nod, letting her know that she was doing very well, better than he could ever have managed. "Ordinarily it would be the end of everything for you. They took my ship, and I'm with a man who lost a whole world to them. But there's a chance for you. In Mundar is a great mind. Call him the Iron Tactician for now, although the day will come when you learn his true name. The Iron Tactician will help you on the road to peace. And when that peace is holding, the Iron Tactician will help you prepare. The Tactician knows of your weapons, of your fusion ships and kinetic batteries. But in a little while he will also know the weapons of the Cohort, and how best to use them. Weapons to shatter worlds—or defend them." Teal drew breath, and Merlin touched his hand to her shoulder, in what he hoped was a gesture of comradeship and solidarity. "Hurt the Tactician, and you'll be powerless when the swarm arrives. Protect it—honour it— and you'll have an honest chance. But the Tactician would sooner die than take sides."

"Good," Merlin breathed.

"He's my blood," Teal continued. "My kin. And I'm staying here to give him all the protection and guidance he needs. You'll treat me well, because I'm the only living witness you'll ever know who can say she saw the Huskers up close. And I'll do what I can to help you."

Merlin swallowed. He had not been expecting this, not at all. But the force of Teal's conviction left him in no doubt that she had set her mind on this course. He stared at her with a searing admiration, dizzy at her courage and single-mindedness.

"You'll withdraw from the space around Mundar," Teal said. "And you'll cease all hostiles. A ship will be given free passage to Havergal, and then on to the Waynet. You won't touch it. And you won't touch Mundar, or attempt to claim the Tactician. There'll be no reminders, no second warnings—we're beyond such things now. This is Teal of the Cohort, signing off for now. You'll be hearing more from me soon."

Merlin shook his head in astonishment. "You don't have to do this, Teal. That was . . . courageous. But you're not responsible for the mess they've made of this place."

"I'm not," she said. "But then again we had our chance when we traded with them, and instead of helping them to peace we took one side and conducted our business. I don't feel guilty for what happened all those years ago. But I'm ready to make a change."

"She does have an excellent command of our language," Baskin said.

"And she's persuasive," Struxer said. "Very persuasive."

Merlin made sure they were no longer transmitting. "You all know it's a lie. There's no attack swarm heading this way—not how Teal said it was. But there *could* be, and for a few decades there'd be no way of saying otherwise, not with the sensors you have now. Here's what matters, though. You've been lucky so far, but somewhere out there you can be sure there is a Husker swarm that'll eventually find its way to these worlds. A hundred years, a thousand . . . who knows? But it will happen, just as it did to Plenitude. The only difference is, you'll be readier than we ever were." Then he turned to direct his attention to the boy. "You'll have the hardest time of all, Prince. But you have friends now. And you have my confidence. I know you can force this peace."

For all the toys and battlements, some spark of real comprehension glimmered in the boy's eyes. "But when they found out she lied . . ."

"It'll take a while," Merlin said. "And by then you'll just have to had made sure they've got used to the idea of peace. It's not such a bad thing. But then again, you don't need me to tell you that."

"No," the boy reflected.

Merlin nodded, hoping the boy—what remained of the boy—felt something of the confidence and reassurance he was sending out. "I have to go soon. There's something I need on Havergal, and I'd rather not wait too long until getting my hands on it."

"Whatever authority I still have," Baskin said, "I'll do all that I can to assist."

"Thank you." Then Merlin turned back to the Prince. "I hope you won't be alone again. I'll leave the immersion suits behind, and a few spares. But even when Teal and Struxer and Baskin can't be with you, you don't have to be without companionship." He dipped his head at the ranged formations. "There are two other boys who used to enjoy games like this, but like you their hearts were always elsewhere. They could come here, if you liked. I think you'd get on well."

Doubt flickered across Teal's brow. He nodded at her, begging her to trust him.

"They could come," the boy said, doubtfully. "I suppose."

"Merlin," Teal said.

"Yes?"

"I'm not sure if we'll see each other again, after you've left this place. And I know it isn't going to be safe out there, whatever sort of cease-fire we end up with. But I want you to know two things."

"Go on."

"I'm glad you saved me, Merlin. If I never showed my gratitude until now . . ."

"It wasn't needed. The war took too much from both of us, Teal. There was nothing else that had to be said. You'll do all right here, I know it. Maybe I'll drop back."

"You know you won't," Teal said. "Just as you'll never go back to Plenitude."

"And the other thing?"

"Take your ship, take your syrinx, and find your gun. For me. For your mother, your brother, for all the dead of Plenitude, for all the dead of the *Shrike*, for all who died here. You owe it to all of us, Merlin."

He made to speak, but between one moment and the next he decided that words were superfluous. They met eyes for one last time, and an acknowledgement passed between them, a recognition of obligations met, duties faced, of good and bold hopes for better times.

Then he dropped out of the sensorium.

He was through into *Tyrant* in a matter of seconds. "Get us out of here," he said. "Suspend all load ceilings. If I break a few bones, they'll just have to heal."

"Complying," *Tyrant* said.

Merlin's little dark ship was bruised and lame, but the acceleration still came hard and sudden, and he came very close to regretting that offhand remark about his bones.

"When you have a chance," he said, "transfer Gallinule's sensorium through to the Iron Tactician. All of it—the whole of the Palace of Eternal Dusk."

"While keeping a copy here, you mean?"

"No," Merlin said. "Delete it. Everything. If I ever need to walk those corridors again, or watch my mother looking sad, I'll just have to go back to Mundar."

"That seems . . . extreme."

"Tell that to Teal. She's made more of a sacrifice than I'll ever know."

Tyrant punched its way through the thinning debris cloud. Merlin studied the navigation consoles, watching with a fascinated distraction as the ship computed various course options, testing each against the last, until it found what promised to be a safe passage to . . .

"No," Merlin said. "Not the Waynet. Not until we've gone back to Havergal and claimed that syrinx."

"Did you not study the data, Merlin? I looked at it closely, after your inspection of the syrinx."

"It's real."

"Real, but damaged beyond safe use. More risky to use than the syrinx you already have. I'd have mentioned it sooner, but . . ."

"What do you mean, damaged?"

"Probably before Pardalote ever sold it on, Merlin. I doubt there was any intention to deceive. It's just that a broken syrinx is very hard to distinguish from a fully functioning one. Unless you've had quite a lot of experience in the matter."

"And you kept that from me?"

"I was curious, Merlin. As were you. Another artificial intelligence. I thought we might at least see what this Iron Tactician was all about."

Merlin nodded sagely. Occasionally he reached a point where he felt that little was capable of surprising him. But always the universe had something in store to jolt him out of that complacency. "While we're on the subject, then. That little stunt you pulled back there, when I tried to shoot Struxer with the gamma-cannon . . ."

"You'd have come to regret that action, Merlin. I merely spared you endless years of racking remorse and guilt."

"By contravening a direct order."

"Which was foolish and unnecessary and born entirely out of spite. Besides, I was the damaged party, not you."

Merlin brooded. "I didn't know you had it in you."

"Then we've both learned something new of each other, haven't we?"

He smiled—it was the only possible reaction. "But let's not make too much of a habit out of it, shall we?"

"On that," *Tyrant* said, "I think we find ourselves in excellent agreement."

He felt the steering jets cut in, rougher than usual, and he thought about the damage that needed repairing, and the difficult days ahead. Never mind, though. Before he worried about those complications, he had a few small prayers to ask of his old, battered syrinx.

He hoped they would be answered.

Joe Abercrombie, "Two's Company," *Tor.com*, January 12.
Nina Allan, "The Common Tongue, the Present Tense, the Known World," *Drowned Worlds*.
——, "Ten Days," *Now We Are Ten*.
Charlie Jane Anders, "Rager in Space," *Bridging Infinity*.
Megan Arkenberg, "In the City of Kites and Crows," *Kalidotrope*, Autumn.
——, "Palin Genesis," *Shimmer 29*.
Kelley Armstrong, "The Culling," *Strangers Among Us*.
Madeline Ashby, "Thieving Magpie," *After the Fall*.
Charlotte Ashley, "A Fine Balance," *F&SF*, November/December.
——, "More Heat Than Light," *F&SF*, May/June.
Dale Bailey, "I Married a Monster from Outer Space," *Asimov's*, March.
Bo Balder, "Follow the White Line," *Clarkesworld*, November.
Stephen Baxter, "Project Clio," *PS Publishing*.
——, "The Venus Generations," *Bridging Infinity*.
Peter S. Beagle, "The Green-Eyed Boy," *F&SF*, September/October.
——, "The Story of Kao Yu," *Tor.com*, December 7.
Gregory Benford, "Mice Among Elephants," *Bridging Infinity*.
Terry Bisson, "Robot from the Future," *F&SF*, January/February.
Michael Blumlein, "Choose Poison, Choose Life," *Asimov's*, October/November.
Brooke Bolander, "One Talon Can Crush Galaxies," *Uncanny 11*.
Terry Boren, "Recursive Ice," *To Shape the Dark*.
Desirina Boskovich, "The Voice in the Cornfields, the Word Made Flesh," *F&SF*, September/October.
Chaz Brenchley, "In Skander, For a Boy," *Beneath Ceaseless Skies*, January 2016.
Keith Brooke, "Rewrites," *Dragons of the Night*.
——& Eric Brown, "Beyond the Heliopause," *Lightspeed*, January.
Sarah Brooks, "Blackpool," *Shimmer 30*.
——, "The Hunger of Auntie Tiger," *Interzone*, 267.
Eric Brown, "Reunion on Alpha Reticuli II," *PS Publishing*.
——, "Starship Coda."
——, "Ten Sisters," *Now We Are Ten*.
Tobias S. Buckell & Karen Lord, "The Mighty Singer," *Bridging Infinity*.
Karl Bunker, "The Battle of Ceres," *Analog*, July/August.
Pat Cadigan, "Six Degrees of Separation Freedom," *Bridging Infinity*.
Vajra Chandrasekera, "Applied Cenotaphics in the Long, Long Latitudes," *Strange Horizons*, September 16.
Robert R. Chase, "Conscience," *Asimov's*, January.
——, "Revenge of the Invisible Man," *Analog*, October.

Gwendolyn Clare, "Nothing but the Sky," *Beneath Endless Skies*, June 9.

Maggie Clark, "Seven Ways of Looking at the Sun-Worshippers of Yul-Katan," *Analog*, April.

David Cleden, Rock Paper Incisors," *Interzone*, 267.

Ray Cluley, "Sideways," *Interzone*, September/October.

C.S.E. Cooney & Carlos Hernandez, "The Book of May," *Clockwork Phoenix 5*.

Constance Cooper, "Carnivores of Can't-Go-Home," *To Shape the Dark*.

Paul Cornell, "Don't You Worry, You Aliens," *Uncanny 13*.

———, "The Lost Child of Lychford," *Tor.com Publishing*.

Albert E. Cowdrey, "The Farmboy," *F&SF*, November/December.

Steven Cox, "1957," *Apex*, May.

Ian Creasey, "A Melancholy Apparition," *F&SF*, September/October.

———, "The Language of Flowers," *Analog*, May.

———, "No Strangers Any More," *Analog*, July/August.

Dave Creek, "Silhouettes," *Analog*, September.

Leah Cypess, "Filtered," *Asimov's*, July.

Indrapramit Das, "Breaking Water," *Tor.com*, February 10.

Aliette de Bodard, "Crossing the Midday Gate," *To Shape the Dark*.

———, "Pearl," *The Starlit Wood*.

———, "What Hungers in the Dark," *Barcelona Tales*.

A.M. Dellamonica, "The Boy Who Would Not Be Enchanted," *Beneath Ceaseless Skies*, September 7.

———, "The Glass Galago," *Tor.com*, January 6.

———, "Tribes," *Strangers Among Us*.

Emily Devenport, "Now Is the Hour," *Clarkesworld*, August.

Paul Di Filippo, "Backup Man," *Terraform*, April 7.

Seth Dickinson, "Laws of Night and Silk," *Beneath Ceaseless Skies*, May 26.

Gardner Dozois, "The Place of Bones," *F&SF*, November/December.

Jilly Dreadful, "5X5," *Lightspeed*, July.

Brendan Dubois, "Jewels from the Sky," *Analog*, December.

———, "The Treaty Breaker," *Analog*, May.

Thoraiya Dryer, "Induction," *Bridging Infinity*.

S.N. Dyer, "When Grandfather Returns," *Asimov's*, October/November.

Scott Edelman, "The Man Without the Blue Balloon and the Woman Who Had Smiles Only for Him," *Dragons of the Night*.

Amal El-Mohtar, "Seasons of Glass and Iron," *The Starlit Wood*.

Sieren Damsgaard Ernst, "Kairos," *Asimov's*, August

Gregory Feeley, "The Bridge of Dreams," *Clarkesworld*, April.

Gemma Files, "What You See (When the Lights Are Out)?" *Strangers Among Us*.

Eliot Fintushel, "In Boonker's Room," *Analog*, December.

Michael F. Flynn, "The Journeyman: In the Great North Wood," *Analog*, June.

Jeffrey Ford, "The Thousand Eyes," *The Starlit Woods*.

———, "What Is—", *Drowned Worlds*.

Esther M. Freisner, "The Cat Bell," *F&SF*, November/December.

———, "Woman in the Reeds," *Asimov's*, April/May.

Nancy Fulda, "Angels of Incidence," *Analog*, October.

James Alan Gardner, "The Dog and the Sleepwalker," *Strangers Among Us*.

———, "The Mutants Men Don't See," *Asimov's*, August.

Bev Geddes, "Living in Oz," *Strangers Among Us*.

David Gerrold, "The Dunsmuir Horror," *F&SF*, September/October.
——, "The White Piano," *F&SF*, January/February.
Kathleen Ann Goonan, "Who Do You Love?" *Drowned Worlds*.
Theodora Goss, "Red as Blood and White as Bone," *Tor.com*, May 16.
John Grant, "The Second Runner," *Dragons of the Night*.
A.T. Greenblat, "A Non-Hero's Guide to the Realm of Monsters," *Mothership Zeta 3*.
Daryl Gregory, "Even the Crumbs Were Delicious," *The Starlit Woods*.
John Gribbin, "Untanglement: The Leaving of the Quantum Cats," *Dragons of the Night*.
James Gunn, "New Earth," *Asimov's*, March.
Peter F. Hamilton, "Ten Love Songs to Change the World," *Now We Are Ten*.
C. Stuart Hardwick, "Dreams of the Rocketman," *Analog*, September.
Gregor Hartmann, "Trustworthy, Loyal, Helpful," *F&SF*, July/August.
Maria Dahvana Headley, "Little Widow," *What the #@&% Is That?*
——, "The Virgin Played Bass," *Uncanny 9*.
Howard Hendrix, "The Infinite Manqué," *Analog*, May.
Joseph Allen Hill, "The Venus Effect," *Lightspeed*, April
Nathan Hillstrom, "White Dust," *Asimov's*, January.
Glen Hirshberg, "Freedom Is Space for the Spirit," *Tor.com*, April 6.
Nalo Hopkinson, "Inselburg," *Drowned Worlds*.
Kat Howard, "Stories of the Trees, Stories of the Birds, Stories of the Bones," *The Grim Future*.
Matthew Hughes, "Telltale," *F&SF*, January/February.
——, "The Vindicator," *F&SF*, November/December.
David Hutchinson, "Catacomb Saints," *Barcelona Tales*.
Alex Irvine, "Number Nine Moon," *F&SF*, January/February.
Alexander Jablokov, "The Forgotten Taste of Honey," *Asimov's*, October/November.
N. K. Jemisin, "The City Born Great," *Tor.com*, September 28.
C. S. Johnson, "The Age of Discovery," *To Shape the Dark*.
Kij Johnson, "Coyote Invents the Land of the Dead," *Clarkesworld*, March.
——, "The Dream Quest of Vilitt Boe," *Tor.com*.
Gwyneth Jones, "The Seventh Gamer," *To Shape the Dark*.
Rachel K. Jones, "The Night Bazaar for Women Becoming Reptiles," *Beneath Ceaseless Skies*, July 7.
Stephen Graham Jones, "Some Wait," *The Starlit Wood*.
Rahul Kanakia, "Empty Planets," *Interzone*, January/February.
Jason Kimble, "The Wind at His Back," *Clockwork Phoenix 5*.
Ted Kosmatka, "The Bewilderness of Lions," *Asimov's*, March.
——, "Chasing Ivory," *Asimov's*, January.
——, "The Stone War," *F&SF*, May/June.
Mary Robinette Kowal, "Forest of Memory," *Tor.com*.
Barbara Krasnoff, "Sabbath Wine," *Clockwork Phoenix 5*.
Nancy Kress, "Every Hour of Light and Dark," *Omni*, December.
——, "Pyramid," *Now We Are Ten*.
Naomi Kritzer, "Zombies in Winter," *Persistent Visions*, November 25.
Claude Lalumiére, "The Patchwork Procedure," *Beneath Ceaseless Skies*, August 12.
Margo Lanagan, "When I Lay Frozen," *The Starlit Wood*.
Kristin Landon, "From the Depths," *To Shape the Dark*.
Rich Larson, "All That Robot Shit," *Asimov's*, September.
——, "Carnivores," *Strangers Among Us*.

——, "The Cyborg, the Tinman, the Merchant of Death," *Lightspeed*, December.

——, "Define Symbiont," *Shimmer 31*.

——, "Extraction Request," *Clarkesworld*, January.

——, "The Green Man Cometh," *Clarkesworld*, September.

——, "Lifeboat," *Interzone*, May/June.

——, "Lottery," *Interzone*.

——, "Masked," *Asimov's*, July.

——, "The Red Flower," *Persistent Visions*, December 9.

——, "Sleep Factory," *Analog*, April.

——, "Sparks Fly," *Lightspeed*, March.

——, "Water Scorpions," *Asimov's*, October/November.

——, "You Make Pattaya," *Interzone 267*.

Victor LaValle, "The Ballad of Black Tom," *Tor.com*.

Anaea Lay, "The Right Bright Courier," *Beneath Ceaseless Skies*, 194.

William Ledbetter, "The Long Fall Up," *F&SF*, May/June.

Yoon Ha Lee, "Foxfire, Foxfire" *Beneath Ceaseless Skies*, March 3.

——, "Shadows Weave," *Beneath Ceaseless Skies*, May 25

Rose Lemberg, "The Book of How to Live," *Beneath Ceaseless Skies*.

David D. Levine, "Discards," *Tor.com*, March 30.

Jessica May Lin, "Red Mask," *Shimmer*, 3.

Cixin Liu & Ken Liu, "The Weight of Memories," *Tor.com*, August 17.

Ken Liu, "An Advanced Reader's Picture Book of Comparative Cognition," *The Glass Menagerie*.

——, "Seven Birthdays," *Bridging Infinity*.

——, "White Hempen Sleeves," *After the Fall*.

Marjorie Liu, "The Briar and the Rose," *The Starlit Wood*.

Karin Lowachee, "Ozymandias," *Bridging Infinity*.

Pat MacEwen, "Coyote Song," *F&SF*, May/June.

Bruce McAllister, "Bringing Them Back," *Asimov's*, February.

——, "Killer," *F&SF*, July/August.

Paul McAuley, "The Fixer," *Clarkesworld*, February

——, "Rats Dream of the Future," *Asimov's*, June.

——, "Something Happened Here, But We're Not Quite Sure What It Was," *Tor.com*, July 20.

Jack McDevitt, "The Pegasus Project," *To Shape the Dark*.

Sandra McDonald, "Merry Christmas from All of Us to All of You," *F&SF*, November/December.

——, "The Monster of 1928," *Asimov's*, February.

——, "The People in the Building," *Asimov's*, October/November.

——, "President John F. Kennedy, Astronaut," *Asimov's*, August.

Seanan McGuire, "Every Heart a Doorway," *Tor.com*.

——, "The Jaws That Bite, the Claws That Catch," *Lightspeed*, May.

——, "Ye Highlands and Ye Lowlands," *Uncanny 10*.

Will McIntosh, "Lost: Mind," *Asimov's*, July.

——, "The Savannah Liar's Tour," *Lightspeed*, January.

Sean McMullen, "Exceptional Forces," *Asimov's*, February.

Alexandra Manglis, "The Wreck at Goat's Head," *Strange Horizons*, November 16.

Melissa Marr, "The Maiden Thief," *Tor.com*, January 27.

Anil Menon, "Building for Shah Jehan," *To Shape the Dark*.

Sam J. Miller, "Last Gods," *Drowned Worlds*.

Steven Mohan, Jr., "An Infinite Horizon," *After the Fall*.

Mary Anne Mohanraj, "Plea," *Lightspeed*, October.

——, "Webs," *Asimov's*, July

Sean Monaghan, "Wakers," *Asimov's*, August.

Gabriel Murray, "Bull of Heaven," *Strange Horizons*, July 16.

Samantha Murray, "Of Sight, of Mind, of Heart," *Clarkesworld*, November.

T. R. Napper, "A Strange Loop," *Interzone*, January/February.

——, "Flame Trees," *Asimov's*, April/May.

Ray Nayler, "Do Not Forget Me," *Asimov's*, March.

Mari Ness, "Deathlight," *Lightspeed*, May.

R. Neube, "A Little Bigotry," *Asimov's*, March.

Julie Novakova, "The Ship Whisperer," *Asimov's*, March.

Naomi Novik, "Spinning Silver," *The Starlit Wood*.

Garth Nix, "Pair of Ugly Sisters, Three of a Kind," *The Grim Future*.

——, "Penny for a Match, Mister?" *The Starlit Wood*.

Jay O'Connell, "What We Hold Onto," *Asimov's*, June.

Nnedi Okorafor, "Afrofuturist 419," *Clarkesworld*, November.

——& Wanuri Kahiu, "Rusties," *Clarkesworld*, October.

An Owomoyele, "The Charge and the Storm," *Asimov's*, February.

——, "Travelling Into Nothing," *Bridging Infinity*.

——, "Unauthorized Access," *Lightspeed*, September.

——& Rachel Swirsky, "Whose Drowned Face Sleeps," *What the #@&% Is That?*

Suzanne Palmer, "Belong," *Interzone*, July-August.

——, "Detroit Hammersmith," *Analog*, September.

——, "Lazy Dog Out," *Asimov's*, April/May.

——, "Ten Poems for the Mosums, One for Man," *Asimov's*, July.

Susan Palwick, "Ash," *F&SF*, May/June.

K. J. Parker, "The Devil You Know," *Tor.com*.

——, "Tale Told by an Idiot," *Beneath Ceaseless Skies*, February 4.

Ursula Pflug, "Washing Lady's Hair," *Strangers Among Us*.

Betsy Phillips, "The Four Gardens of Fate," *Apex*, February.

Tony Pi, "The Sweetest Skill," *Beneath Ceaseless Skies*, April 14.

Sarah Pinsker, "The Mountains of His Crown," *Beneath Ceaseless Skies*, 195.

——, "Clearance," *Asimov's*, June.

——, "Sooner or Later, Everything Falls into the Sea," *Lightspeed*, February.

——, "Talking to Dead People," *F&SF*, September/October.

Joe Pitcan, "Count Eszterhazy's Harmonium," *Kalidotrope*, Autumn.

Steven Popkes, "The Sweet Warm Earth," *F&SF*, September/October.

Stephen S. Power, ""Fade to Red," *Lightspeed*, October.

David Prill, "Vishnu Summer," *F&SF*, July/August.

Chen Qiufan, "Balin," *Clarkesworld*, April.

Cat Rambo, "Call and Answer, Plant and Harvest," *Beneath Ceaseless Skies*, 194.

——, "Left Behind," *Clarkesworld*, May.

Zhang Ran, "The Snow of Jinyang," *Clarkesworld*, June.

Dan Reade, "The Eye of Job," *Interzone*, July-August.

Robert Reed, "A Man of Modest Means," *Interzone*, July-August.

——, "The Algorithms of Value," *Clarkesworld*, January.

——, "The Days of Hamelin," *Asimov's*, April/May.

——, "Dome on the Prairie," *Asimov's*, September.

——, "The Great Ignorant Race," *Galactic Games*.

——, "The Next Scene," *Clarkesworld*, October.

——, "Parables of Infinity," *Bridging Infinity*.

——, "Passelande," *F&SF*, November/December.

——, "The Universal Museum of Sagacity," *Clarkesworld*, May.

Mercurio D. Rivera, "Unreeled," *Asimov's*, June.

——, "The Water Walls of Encoladus," *Interzone*, January/February.

Adam Roberts, "Between Nine and Eleven," *Crises and Conflicts*.

Margaret Ronald, "And Then, One Day, the Air Was Full of Voices," *Clarkesworld*, June.

Benjamin Rosenbaum, "Later That Day," *Persistent Visions*, September 11.

Christopher Rowe, "Brownsville Station," *Drowned Worlds*.

Kristine Kathryn Rusch, "The City's Edge," *Bridging Infinity*.

——, "Matilda," *Asimov's*, April/May.

A. Merc Rustad, "The Gentlemen of Chaos," *Apex*, August.

K. B. Rylander, "Last One Out," *F&SF*, July/August.

Sarah Saab, "The Cedar Grid," *Clarkesworld*, April.

Sofia Samatar, "The Tale of Mahliya and Mauhub and the White-Footed Gazelle," *The Starlit Wood*.

Jason Sanford, "Blood Grains Speak Through Memories," *Beneath Ceaseless Skies*, 195.

——, "Toppers," *Asimov's*, August.

Pamela Sargent, "Monuments," *Bridging Infinity*.

John Scalzi, "The Dispatched," *Audible*.

Shawn Scarber, "The Opening of the Bayou Saint Jean," *Strange Horizons*, Feburary.

John Schoffstall, "All Your Cities I Will Burn," *Interzone*, July-August

Nisi Shawl, "Like the Deadly Hands," *Analog*, December.

——, "The Mighty Phin," *Cyber World*.

Delia Sherman, "The Great Detective," *Tor.com*, February 17.

Gu Shi, "Chimera," *Clarkesworld*, March.

John Shirley, "Cory for Coriolis," *Analog*, July/August.

Martin L. Shoemaker, "Black Orbit," *Analog*, December.

——, "Early Warning," *Analog*, April.

Vandana Singh, "Of Wind and Fire," *To Shape the Dark*.

Jack Skillingstead, "The Despoilers," *Clarkesworld*, September.

——, "Licorice," *Now We Are Ten*.

——, "Salvage Opportunity," *Clarkesworld*, March.

——, "The Savior Virus," *Asimov's*, July.

——, "The Whole Mess," *Asimov's*, September.

Allen M. Steele, "Apache Charley and the Pentagons of Hex," *Bridging Infinity*.

——, "Einstein's Shadow," *Asimov's*, January.

Ferrett Steinmetz, "Rooms Formed of Neurons and Sex," *Uncanny* 9.

Bruce Sterling, "Sgt. Augmento," *Terraform*, August 17.

——, "Pirate Utopia," *Tachyon*.

Kelly Stewart, "Rabbit Grass," *Beneath Ceaseless Skies*, April 14.

Patricia Strand, "The Birth Will Take Place on a Mutually Acceptable Research Vessel," *Lightspeed*, April.

Bonnie Joe Stufflebeam, "The Orangery," *Beneath Ceaseless Skies*, December.
E. J. Swift, "Front Row Seat to the End of the World," *Now We Are Ten*.
Sonya Taaffe, "The Trinitite Golem," *Clockwork Phoenix 5*.
Ted Thompson, "The Apologists," *Interzone*, September/October.
Robert Thurston, "Nobody Like Josh," *Asimov's*, July.
Karen Tidback, "Listen," *Tor.com*, March
——, "Starfish," *Lightspeed*, February.
Lavie Tidhar, "Agent of V.A.L.I.S.," *Apex Magazine*.
——, "The Beachcomber," *Dragons of the Night*.
——, "Drowned," *Drowned Worlds*.
——, "The Godbeard," *Strange Horizons*, January 11.
——, "Heroes," *Strange Horizons*, September 19.
——, "Red Christmas," *Apex Magazine*, December.
E. Catherine Tobler, "The Abduction of Europa," *Clarkesworld*, January.
——, "Cloud Dweller," *Beneath Ceaseless Skies*, May.
——, "Not by Wardrobe, Tornado, or Looking Glass," *Lightspeed*, February.
Jeremiah Tolbert, "Taste the Singularity at the Food Truck Circus," *Lightspeed*, August.
——, "The Cavern of the Screaming Eye," *Lightspeed*, October.
Hayden Trenholm, "Marion's War," *Strangers Among Us*.
Lisa Tuttle, "The Translator," *Barcelona Tales*.
Catherynne A. Valente, "The Future Is Blue," *Drowned Worlds*.
Genevieve Valentine, "La Beaute Sans Vertu," *Tor.com*, April 16.
——, "Everyone from Themis Sends Letters Home," *Clarkesworld*, October.
James Van Pelt, The Continuing Saga of Tom Corbett: Space Cadet," *Analog*, December.
——, "Death of a Starship Poet," *Analog*, July/August.
——, "Mars, Aphids, and Your Cheating Heart," *Interzone*, May/June.
——, "Three Paintings," *Asimov's*, April/May.
Carrie Vaughn, "The Mind Is Its Own Place," *Asimov's*, September.
——, "Origin Story," *Lightspeed*, April.
Rajnar Vajra, "Her Scales Shine Like Music," *Tor.com*, August 3.
Ursula Vernon, "The Tomato Thief," *Apex*, January.
Kali Wallace, "First Light at Mistaken Point," *Clarkesworld*, August.
Jay Werkheiser, "The Anthroric War," *Analog*, June.
——, "The Desolate Void," *Analog*, November.
Fran Wilde, "The Jewel and Her Lapidary" *Tor.com*.
Sean Williams, "The Lives of Riley," *Lightspeed*, September.
——, "The New Venusians," *Drowned Worlds*.
Kai Ashante Wilson, "A Taste of Honey," *Tor.com*.
A. C. Wise, "A Guide to Birds (After Death)," *Clockwork Phoenix 5*.
——, "How Objects Behave on the Edge of a Black Hole," *Strangers Among Us*.
——, "Seven Cups of Coffee," *Clarkesworld*, March.
Nick Wolven, "Caspar D. Lukinbill, What Are You Going to Do?" *F&SF*, January/February.
——, "In the Midst of Life," *Clarkesworld*, Febraury.
——, "The Metal Deminonde," *Analog*, July/August.
——, "Passion Summer," *Asimov's*, February.
Peter Wood, "Academic Circles," *Asimov's*, September.
Alyssa Wong, "Natural Skin," *Lightspeed*, November.
——, "You'll Surely Drown If You Stay Here," *Uncanny 10*.

Frank Wu, "In the Absense of Instructions," *Analog,* November.

J. V. Yang, "Secondhand Bodies," *Lightspeed,* January.

E. Lily Yu, "The Witch of Orion Waste and the Boy Knight," *Uncanny 12.*

Alvaro Zinos-Amaro, "e^h," *Humanity 2.0.*

——, "Prayers to the Sun by a Dying Person," *This Way to the End Times.*

——, "Wyslomg," *Cyber World.*